15

ANNA KARENINA

'William Faulkner, it's said, was once asked to name the three best novels ever. He replied: "*Anna Karenina, Anna Karenina, Anna Karenina.*" If you don't recall why, rush to buy a fine new translation by Richard Pevear and Larissa Volokhonsky'
Boyd Tonkin, *Independent*

'If there's such a thing as a definitive translation, this might be it' Jean Dubail, *Cleveland Plain Dealer*

'All happy families will receive a copy of this new translation this Christmas; each unhappy family will want one' Eric Griffiths, *Evening Standard*

'The newest English-language translation by Richard Pevear and Larissa Volokhonsky is a significant achievement . . . They have applied their hands-off, no-nonsense idea of translation . . . the shining result is that Tolstoy's book reads as if it could have been written yesterday' Ingrid Lunden, *San Francisco Chronicle*

'Tolstoy's greatness lies in not turning the story into sentimental tragedy . . . His world is huge and vast, filled with complex family lives and great social events. His characters are well-rounded presences. They have complete passions: a desire for love, but also an inner moral depth' Malcolm Bradbury, *Mail on Sunday*

'It's so fantastic that it can be read over and over again . . . I don't know any other writer who is so adept at peopling their pages' Maggie O'Farrell, *Daily Mail*, Desert Island Books

ABOUT THE AUTHOR AND TRANSLATORS

COUNT LEO TOLSTOY was born in 1828 at Yasnaya Polyana, in the Tula province, and educated privately. He studied Oriental languages and law at the University of Kazan, then led a life of pleasure until 1851 when he joined an artillery regiment in the Caucasus. He took part in the Crimean War and after the defence of Sebastopol he wrote *The Sebastopol Sketches* (1855–6), which established his reputation. After a period in St Petersburg and abroad, where he studied educational methods for use in his school for peasant children in Yasnaya Polyana, he married Sofya Andreyevna Behrs in 1862. The next fifteen years was a period of great happiness; they had thirteen children, and Tolstoy managed his vast estates in the Volga Steppes, continued his educational projects, cared for his peasants and wrote *War and Peace* (1869) and *Anna Karenina* (1877). *A Confession* (1879–82) marked a spiritual crisis in his life; he became an extreme moralist and in a series of pamphlets after 1880 expressed his rejection of state and church, indictment of the weaknesses of the flesh and denunciation of private property. His teaching earned him numerous followers at home and abroad, but also much opposition, and in 1901 he was excommunicated by the Russian Holy Synod. He died in 1910, in the course of a dramatic flight from home, at the small railway station of Astapovo.

RICHARD PEVEAR and LARISSA VOLOKHONSKY have translated Bulgakov's *The Master and Margarita* for Penguin Classics, and produced acclaimed translations of Tolstoy, Dostoyevsky and Gogol. Their translation of *The Brothers Karamazov* won the 1991 PEN Book of the Month Club Translation Prize.

JOHN BAYLEY (CBE 1999) was Warton Professor of English Literature, Oxford University, from 1974–92. Among his many books are *The Characters of Love: A Study in the Literature of Personality*; *Tolstoy and the Novel*; *Pushkin: A Comparative Commentary*; *Shakespeare and Tragedy*; *Iris: A Memoir of Iris Murdoch*; *Iris and the Friends: A Year of Memories*; and a detailed study of A. E. Housman's poems. *Alice* (1994), *The Queer Captain* (1995) and *George's Lair* (1996) are his trilogy of novels. For Penguin Classics he has introduced Pushkin's *Tales of Belkin and Other Prose Writings* and *Eugene Onegin* and edited Henry James's *The Wings of the Dove*.

LEO TOLSTOY

Anna Karenina

A NOVEL IN EIGHT PARTS

Translated by RICHARD PEVEAR
and LARISSA VOLOKHONSKY
With a Preface by JOHN BAYLEY

PENGUIN BOOKS

PENGUIN BOOKS

Published by the Penguin Group
Penguin Books Ltd, 80 Strand, London WC2R ORL, England
Penguin Group (USA) Inc., 375 Hudson Street, New York, New York 10014, USA
Penguin Group (Canada), 90 Eglinton Avenue East, Suite 700, Toronto, Ontario, Canada M4P 2Y3
(a division of Pearson Penguin Canada Inc.)
Penguin Ireland, 25 St Stephen's Green, Dublin 2, Ireland (a division of Penguin Books Ltd)
Penguin Group (Australia), 250 Camberwell Road, Camberwell, Victoria 3124, Australia
(a division of Pearson Australia Group Pty Ltd)
Penguin Books India Pvt Ltd, 11 Community Centre, Panchsheel Park, New Delhi – 110 017, India
Penguin Group (NZ), cnr Airborne and Rosedale Roads, Albany, Auckland 1310,
New Zealand (a division of Pearson New Zealand Ltd)
Penguin Books (South Africa) (Pty) Ltd, 24 Sturdee Avenue,
Rosebank, Johannesburg 2196, South Africa

Penguin Books Ltd, Registered Offices: 80 Strand, London WC2R ORL, England

www.penguin.com

First published in Russian, 1873–7
This edition first published by Allen Lane The Penguin Press 2000
Published in Penguin Classics 2001
Reprinted with new Preface 2003
This anniversary edition published 2006

038

Printed and bound in Great Britain by Clays Ltd, Elcograf S.p.A.

ISBN-13: 978–0–140–44917–4

www.greenpenguin.co.uk

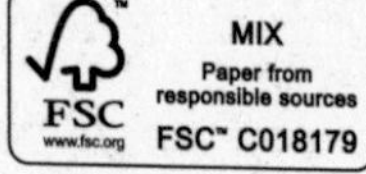

Penguin Books is committed to a sustainable future for our business, our readers and our planet. This book is made from Forest Stewardship Council™ certified paper.

Contents

Preface

Devoted readers of Tolstoy, and there are a great many of them, would find it hard to say which of his two great novels is their particular favourite. They are very different from each other, although neither could have been written by anyone else. Tolstoy himself always claimed that *War and Peace* was not a novel at all, 'as the West understands the term', but a form unique to himself, and only possible in Russia; whereas *Anna Karenina* he described to a friend as 'this novel, the first I have attempted . . .' Later in his long life he claimed that neither had any value, because all that mattered was God and the Truth, and the search to find them. But there is some irony in the fact that Tolstoy's later parables and polemical works are not much read today, whereas his two great novels – if for convenience we can agree to call them that – remain as popular as ever.

Tolstoy began to write *Anna Karenina* between four and five years after the completion and publication of *War and Peace*, and he began it, as he claimed, partly as a result of an accident. A woman threw herself under a train near his country estate of Yasnaya Polyana, and Tolstoy was involved in the subsequent inquiry. Jealousy and an unhappy love affair were involved, and led Tolstoy to reflect very seriously on the role of love and marriage in society. Then one evening he happened to be reading to his children a story by Pushkin, and was filled with admiration at the terseness and simplicity of its opening. 'That is how one should write', he exclaimed, and the famous beginning of *Anna Karenina* may well have been suggested by that moment.

'All happy families are alike; each unhappy family is unhappy in its own way.' A wonderful opening it is; and it has never been better translated than by Richard Pevear and Larissa Volokhonsky in this edition. At one stroke, and in a single sentence, we are brought into the heart and soul of the story: family life and the lives led by the separate members of families. Everyone in the novel knows all about the others; many are related. It is of importance, for example, that Dolly's feckless and charming husband, Stiva Oblonsky, is also Anna's brother. What is acceptable, or at least excusable, in his behaviour is culpable and ultimately fatal in hers. And in revealing this, as it were, Tolstoy and his novel are far from endorsing what used to be called the 'double standard' of sexual morality. When D. H. Lawrence said that Anna and Vronsky should have defied and banished the world by going away together, he was thinking of himself and his own wife Frieda, with whom he ran away and afterwards married, and he was missing the point. The point that the novel makes is that Anna and Vronsky *think* they can escape from society, but find they cannot. Without the freedom of the society they are accustomed to, their passion eventually becomes its own prison. Their world is too much a part of them: they need it too much; and the attempt to do without it in the end destroys them both.

However much Tolstoy himself may have tried later in life to escape from that world and to live in a more spiritual dimension, as he felt he saw the peasants doing, he himself knew society, the society described in *Anna Karenina*, through and through. And, with whatever apparent unwillingness, he always remained fascinated by it. Late in his life he would still ask his grown-up daughters who was doing what in Moscow and St Petersburg, and what the women were wearing at the balls. The idea of a novel about the *grande monde* had long haunted him, and he told his wife of the notion of writing about a married lady of that world who would ruin herself. He felt that as soon as he had 'got hold' of such a character the other persons in the story would also 'become real'.

That is certainly what happened. All the characters in *Anna Karenina* are intensely real; and that includes the peasants mowing the field, the servants at the Moscow club where Stiva and Levin have lunch together, even the horses in the great steeplechase, where Vronsky makes a fatal error in going over a jump, and his mount, poor Frou-Frou, breaks her back. Such events are too much alive to be symbolic, and yet the symbolism of disaster is there and very much a part of the novel's rich and complex background.

Some critics and readers have felt that the seeming division of the novel almost into two different worlds – that of Levin (and later Kitty) in the country, and Anna and her friends in town – weakens and distracts us from the main theme. And yet this division is more apparent than real. They all know each other; they all live in the same world with the rest of the Russian upper class; and at the same time the inner mental life and struggle of Levin, which reflects Tolstoy's own state of mind at the time he was writing, parallels the emotional drama which engulfs Anna herself.

Is this drama now out of date? Would Anna today get a divorce, receive custody of her son, marry Vronsky and live happily ever after? Tolstoy did not think so; and the power of the novel, its truth to life and to human character, ultimately persuades the reader not to think so either. Tragedies like that of Anna Karenina do not depend on social change and enlightened social arrangements. Tolstoy's grip on the story, and his own remarkable identification with Anna and her situation – he too was beginning to be a self-appointed exile from the Russian society he still loved, in the teeth of his own growing spiritual convictions – ensure that the drama of the novel touches everyone in it, and that includes ourselves as readers.

And yet there is so much vitality there too, and richness, and gaiety. Anna has as much a power of happiness and life in her as of passion and affliction. How different she is, for instance, from Flaubert's Madame Bovary! There is so much humour in the great novel too, as there is in the personality of Anna herself. One of its most moving moments comes near the end of the novel, when Anna is driving to the railway station and to her death under the train. She sees outside a shop on the street a hairdresser's name which strikes her as comical, and she thinks she will tell Vronsky – it will amuse him too. But then she remembers she won't be seeing Vronsky any more. It is a poignant moment. Quite unexpectedly Tolstoy makes us feel that if anything could have saved Anna it would have been her own sense of the comedy and absurdity of life, and the simple wish to share a joke with her lover. Tolstoy understood the comedy as well as he understood the sadness of things, and his great novels are full of both.

John Bayley

Introduction

> We make out of the quarrel with others, rhetoric,
> but of the quarrel with ourselves, poetry.
>
> – W. B. Yeats

I

'I am writing a novel,' Tolstoy informed his friend the critic Nikolai Strakhov on 11 May 1873, referring to the book that was to become *Anna Karenina*. 'I've been at it for more than a month now and the main lines are traced out. This novel is truly a novel, the first in my life . . .'

Tolstoy was then forty-five. He had been writing and publishing for over twenty years. Along with some remarkable shorter pieces – 'The Snowstorm', 'Two Hussars', 'Three Deaths', 'The Wood Felling', 'Sebastopol Stories', 'Family Happiness' – he had produced longer works which he himself referred to as novels. For instance, it was as 'the first part of a novel' that Tolstoy sent the manuscript of *Childhood*, the opening section of the trilogy *Childhood, Boyhood and Youth*, to Nikolai Nekrasov, editor of *The Contemporary*, in 1852. Ten years later, apologizing to the editor Mikhail Katkov for his delay in producing the book he had promised him in return for a loan of a thousand roubles, he wrote: 'I've only just settled down to the novel I sold you the rights to, I couldn't get to it earlier.' This was *The Cossacks*, begun in 1857, worked on intermittently, and finished 'with sweat and blood' in 1862. In 1864, again writing to Katkov, Tolstoy mentioned that he was 'in the process of finishing the first part of [his] novel on the period of the wars of Alexander and Napoleon', known then as *The Year 1805* but soon to be renamed *War and Peace*. Why, then, did he call *Anna Karenina* his first novel?

It is true that the early trilogy and *The Cossacks* are semi-fictionalized autobiography and in retrospect Tolstoy may have decided they could not properly be considered novels. But what of *War and Peace*? Isn't it the quintessential novel, the greatest of the species? Not according to its author. In a statement published after the appearance of the first three volumes, he declared enigmatically: 'What is *War and Peace*? It is not a novel, still less is it a poem, and even less a historical chronicle. *War and Peace* is what the author wished and was able to express in the form in which it is expressed.' For Tolstoy, a 'true novel' was evidently something more specific than a fictitious prose narrative of considerable length.

In fact, none of the great Russian prose writers of the nineteenth century, with the possible exception of Turgenev, was on easy terms with the novel as a genre. Gogol called *Dead Souls*, his only novel-length work, a poem. To define this unusual 'poem' he invented the notion of a hybrid genre, midway between epic and novel, to which he gave the name 'minor epic'. He found the novel too static a form, confined to a conventional reality, involving a set of characters who all had to be introduced at the start and all had to have some relation to the hero's fate, and whose possible interactions were too limited for his inventive gifts. It was the form for portraying ordinary domestic life, and Gogol had no interest in ordinary domestic life. Dostoevsky, who also referred to his work as 'poetry', transformed the novel into another sort of hybrid – the 'novel-tragedy' of some critics, the 'polyphonic novel' of others. Nikolai Leskov, an artist almost equal in stature to Dostoevsky and Tolstoy, though less known outside Russia, made masterful use of the forms of the chronicle, the legend, the tale, the saint's life, even the local anecdote and the newspaper article, but lost all his gifts when he turned to the novel. As for Chekhov, though he tried several times to write one, the novel was simply alien to his genius.

When Tolstoy called *Anna Karenina* his first novel, he was conceiving the form in the same restricted sense that Gogol found so uncongenial. He was deliberately embracing the conventional limits of the genre. This was to be a novel *in excelsis*, portraying a small group of main characters (in the final version there are seven, all related by birth or marriage), set in the present and dealing with the personal side of upper-class family and social life. Indeed, *Anna Karenina* introduces us to the most ordinary Russian aristocrats of the 1870s, concerned with the most ordinary issues of the day, behaving in the most ordinary ways, experiencing the most ordinary joys and sorrows. The one character who might seem out of the ordinary – Konstantin Levin – is also most ordinary, as Dostoevsky pointed out in his *Diary of a Writer* (February 1877, II, 2): 'But of Levins there are a great many in Russia, almost as many as Oblonskys.' The author's task was to manoeuvre us, for some seven or eight hundred pages, through and among these ordinary people and their doings. It was not that Tolstoy was so charmed by ordinary life. In 1883, six years after finishing *Anna Karenina*, he would begin the second chapter of a famous novella with the words: 'Ivan Ilyich's life was most ordinary, and therefore most terrible.' As with the novella, so with the novel: the polemic of *Anna Karenina* rests on the ordinariness of its characters.

Anna Karenina is polemical, first of all, in its genre. To publish such a book in the 1870s was an act of defiance, and Tolstoy meant it as one. By then the family novel was hopelessly out of fashion. The satirist Saltykov-Shchedrin noted at the time that the family, 'that warm and cosy element . . . which once gave the novel its content, has vanished from sight . . . The novel of contemporary man finds its resolution in the street, on the public way, anywhere but in the home.' The radical intelligentsia had been attacking the 'institution' of the family for more than a decade. Newspapers, pamphlets, ideological novel-tracts like N. G. Chernyshevsky's *What Is to Be Done?*, advocated sexual freedom, communal living and the communal raising of children. Questions of women's education, women's enfranchisement, the role of women in public life, were hotly debated in the press. On all these matters Tolstoy held rather conservative views. For him, marriage and childrearing were a woman's essential tasks, and family happiness was the highest human ideal. As Nabokov observed in his lecture notes on *Anna Karenina*, 'Tolstoy considers that two married people with children are tied together by divine law forever.' An intentional anachronism, his novel was meant as a challenge, both artistic and ideological, to the ideas of the Russian nihilists.

There was always a provocative side to Tolstoy's genius, and it was most often what spurred him to write. *Anna Karenina* is a tissue of polemics on all the questions then being discussed in aristocratic salons and the newspapers, with Konstantin Levin acting as spokesman for his creator. There are arguments with the aristocracy as well as with the nihilists on the 'woman question'; with the conservative Slavophiles as well as with the radical populists on the question of 'going to the people' and the exact geographical location of the Russian soul; with both landowners and peasants on questions of farm management; with advocates of old and new forms of political representation – local councils, provincial elections among the nobility – and of such judicial institutions as open courts and rural justices of the peace; with new ideas about the education of children and of peasants; with the new movements in art and music; with such recent fashions among the aristocracy as spiritualism, table-turning, pietism and non-Church mysticism, but also with the 'official' Church, its teachings and practices; with corrupt and ineffective bureaucrats, lawyers, capitalists foreign and domestic; with proponents of the 'Eastern question' and supporters of the volunteers who went to aid the Serbs and Montenegrins in their war with the Turks (Tolstoy's handling of this last issue was so hot that his publisher refused to print the final part of the novel, and Tolstoy had to bring it out in a separate edition at his own expense).

There is, in other words, no neutral ground in Tolstoy's novel. His writing is 'characterized by a sharp internal dialogism', as Mikhail Bakhtin has noted, meaning that Tolstoy is conscious at every moment not only of what he is presenting but of his own attitude towards it, and of other possible attitudes both among his characters and in his readers' minds. He is constantly engaged in an internal dispute with the world he is describing and with the reader for whom he is describing it. 'These two lines of dialogization (having in most cases polemical overtones) are tightly interwoven in his style,' as Bakhtin says, 'even in the most "lyrical" expressions and the most "epic" descriptions.'* The implicit conflict of attitudes gives Tolstoy's writing its immediate grip on our attention. It does not allow us to remain detached. But, paradoxically, it also does not allow Tolstoy the artist to be dominated by Tolstoy the provocateur. His own conflicting judgements leave room for his characters to surprise him, lending them a sense of unresolved, uncalculated possibility. Pushkin, speaking of the heroine of his *Evgeny Onegin*, once said to Princess Meshchersky, 'Imagine what happened to my Tatiana? She up and rejected Onegin . . . I never expected it of her!' Tolstoy loved to quote this anecdote, which he had heard from the princess herself.

* See 'Translators' Note' below.

II

Tolstoy was mistaken when he told Strakhov that the main lines of *Anna Karenina* were already traced out. In an earlier letter, dated 25 March 1873 but never sent, he spoke even more optimistically about finishing the book quickly. The letter is interesting for its description of what started him writing. For more than a year he had been gathering materials – 'invoking the spirits of the time', as he put it – for a book set in the early eighteenth century, the age of Peter the Great. That spring his wife had taken a collection of Pushkin's prose down from the shelf, thinking that their son Sergei might be old enough to read it. Tolstoy says:

> The other day, after my work, I picked up this volume of Pushkin and as always (for the seventh time, I think) read it from cover to cover, unable to tear myself away, as if I were reading it for the first time. More than that, it was as if it dispelled all my doubts. Never have I admired Pushkin so much, nor anyone else for that matter. 'The Shot', 'Egyptian Nights', *The Captain's Daughter*!!! There was also the fragment, 'The guests arrived at the summer house'. Despite myself, not knowing where or what it would lead to, I imagined characters and events, which I developed, then naturally modified, and suddenly it all came together so well, so solidly, that it turned into a novel, the first draft of which was soon finished – a very lively, very engaging, complete novel, which I'm quite pleased with and which will be ready in fifteen days, if God grants me life. It has nothing to do with what I've been plugging away at for this whole year.

As it happened, the novel took him not fifteen days but four more years of work, during which much that had come together so suddenly through the agency of 'the divine Pushkin' was altered or rejected and much more was added that had not occurred to him in that first moment of inspiration.

The earliest mention of the subject of *Anna Karenina* comes to us not from Tolstoy but from his wife, Sophia Andreevna, who noted in her journal on 23 February 1870 that her husband said he had 'envisioned the type of a married woman of high society who ruins herself. He said his task was to portray this woman not as guilty but as only deserving of pity, and that once this type of woman appeared to him, all the characters and male types he had pictured earlier found their place and grouped themselves around her. "Now it's all clear," he told me.' Tolstoy did not remain faithful to this first glimpse of the guiltless adultress when he began writing the novel three years later, but she re-emerged in the course of his work and finally overcame the severe moral judgement he tried to bring against her.

The fate of Tolstoy's heroine was suggested to him by a real incident that occurred in January 1872, a few miles from his estate. A young woman, Anna Stepanovna Pirogov, the mistress of a neighbouring landowner and friend of the Tolstoys, threw herself under a goods train after her lover abandoned her. Tolstoy went to view the mangled body in the station house. It made an indelible impression on him.

Thus, well before inspiration struck him in the spring of 1873, Tolstoy had in mind the general 'type' of his Anna and her terrible end. When he did begin writing, however, despite his admiration for Pushkin's artless immediacy ('The guests arrived at the summer house'), he began with his ideas. And the main idea, the one he struggled with most bitterly and never could resolve, was that Anna's suicide was the punishment for her adultery. It was from this struggle with himself that he made the poetry of his heroine.

In the first versions, Anna (variously called Tatiana, Anastasia, and Nana) is a rather fat and vulgar married woman, who shocks the guests at a party by her shameless conduct with a handsome young officer. She laughs and talks loudly, moves gracelessly, gestures improperly, is all but ugly – 'a low forehead, small eyes, thick lips and a nose of a disgraceful shape . . .' Her husband (surnamed Stavrovich – from the Greek *stavros*, 'cross' – then Pushkin, and finally Karenin) is intelligent, gentle, humble, a true Christian, who will eventually surrender his wife to his rival, Gagin, the future Vronsky. In these sketches Tolstoy emphasized the rival's handsomeness, youth and charm; at one point he even made him something of a poet. The focus of these primitive versions was entirely on the triangle of wife, husband and lover, the structure of the classic novel of adultery. Tolstoy planned until very late in his work to have the husband grant a divorce and the wife marry her lover. In the end, the renegades were to be rejected by society and find a welcome only among the nihilists. The whole other side of the novel, the story of Levin and Kitty, was absent from the early variants; there were no Shcherbatskys, the Oblonsky family barely appeared, and Levin, called Ordyntsev and then Lenin, was a minor character.

In the early versions, Tolstoy clearly sympathized with the saintly husband and despised the adulterous wife. As he worked on the novel, however, he gradually enlarged the figure of Anna morally and diminished the figure of the husband; the sinner grew in beauty and spontaneity, while the saint turned more and more hypocritical. The young officer also lost his youthful bloom and poetic sensibility, to become, in Nabokov's description, 'a blunt fellow with a mediocre mind'. But the most radical changes were the introduction of the Shcherbatskys – Kitty and her sister Dolly, married to Anna's brother, Stiva Oblonsky – and the promotion of Levin to the role of co-protagonist. These additions enriched the thematic possibilities of the novel enormously, allowing for the contrasts of city and country life and all the variations on love and family happiness played out among Stiva and Dolly, Anna and Karenin, Kitty and Vronsky, Anna and Vronsky, Kitty and Levin. The seven main characters create a dynamic imbalance, with one character always on the outside, moving between couples, uniting or dividing them, and shifting the scene of the action as they move – from Petersburg to Moscow, from Russia to Germany, from the capitals to the provinces. At some point each of the seven plays this role of shuttle. The novel they weave together goes far beyond the tale of adultery that Tolstoy began writing in the spring of 1873.

III

'Levin is you, Lyova, minus the talent,' Sophia Andreevna said to her husband after reading the first part of *Anna Karenina*. (And she added, 'Levin is an impossible man!') Indeed, though Tolstoy often lent features of his own character to his protagonists, Levin is his most complete self-portrait. He has the same social position as his creator, the same 'wild' nature, the same ideas and opinions, the same passion for hunting, the same almost physical love of the Russian peasant. He shares Tolstoy's favourite method of criticism by feigned incomprehension, applied here to such matters as government bureaucracy, the provincial elections, and the latest fashions in music (the fullest development of this method is found in Tolstoy's *What Is Art?*, published in 1898, particularly in his deadpan treatment of Wagner's operas). Levin's estate reproduces Tolstoy's Yasnaya Polyana, and his marriage to Kitty duplicates Tolstoy's marriage to Sophia Andreevna in the minutest details – his unusual way of proposing, his turning over of his diaries, his compunction about confessing before the ceremony, his visit to the Shcherbatskys on the day of the wedding, even the forgotten shirt. The death of Levin's brother Nikolai is drawn from the death of Tolstoy's own brother Nikolai, also from consumption. In fact, most of the major characters in the novel and many of the minor ones, including the servants, had their counterparts in Tolstoy's life. The only notable exceptions, interestingly enough, are Anna and Vronsky.

Levin also goes through the same religious crisis that Tolstoy went through while he was writing the novel, and reaches the same precarious conversion at the end. The following passages suggest how closely Tolstoy modelled Levin's spiritual struggle on his own. The first is from Part Eight of *Anna Karenina*:

> 'Without knowing what I am and why I'm here, it is impossible for me to live. And I cannot know that, therefore I cannot live,' Levin would say to himself . . .
>
> It was necessary to be delivered from this power. And deliverance was within everyone's reach. It was necessary to stop this dependence on evil. And there was one means – death.
>
> And, happy in his family life, a healthy man, Levin was several times so close to suicide that he hid a rope lest he hang himself with it, and was afraid to go about with a rifle lest he shoot himself.

The second is from his *Confession*, begun in 1879, just a year after the definitive version of *Anna Karenina* was published. In it Tolstoy gives a forthright account of his own agonized search for some meaning in life:

> Though happy and in good health, I became persuaded that it was impossible for me to live much longer . . . And, though happy, I kept away from the least bit of rope, so as not to hang myself from the beam between the wardrobes in my bedroom, where I found myself alone each day while I dressed, and I stopped going hunting with my rifle, so as not to yield to this too-easy way of delivering myself from existence.

Anna Karenina was written at the most important turning-point in Tolstoy's life. Up to then the artist in him had balanced the moralist; after *Anna* the moralist dominated the artist.

How difficult it was for Tolstoy to keep that balance we can see from his work on the portrayal of Anna. The enigma of Anna is at the heart of the novel. In the earlier drafts she was quite fully explained. Tolstoy described her past, how she came to marry, at the age of eighteen, a man who was twelve years her senior, mistaking her wish to shine in society for love, how she discovered her full femininity only at the age of thirty. He stated explicitly that 'the devil had taken possession of her soul', that she had known these 'diabolical impulses' before, and so on. Of this abundance of commentary only a few traces remain in the final portrait of Anna. As Tolstoy worked, he removed virtually all the details of her past, all explanations, all discussion of her motives, replacing them by hints, suggestions, half-tones, blurred outlines. There is a glimpse of Anna's dark side at the ball in Part One, where she takes Vronsky away from Kitty, but it seems to surprise Anna as much as anyone. There are moments when she does seem 'possessed' by some alien power, but they are only touched on in passing. Tolstoy became more and more reluctant to analyse his heroine, with the result that, in the final version, her inner changes seem to come without preparation and often leave us wondering. The final portrait of Anna has about it a 'vivid insubstantiality', in John Bayley's fine phrase, which we do not find anywhere else in Tolstoy. He lost sight of her, in a sense, as he drew closer to her and finally became one with her. The stream of consciousness in which he narrates Anna's last hours gives us what are surely the most remarkable pages in the novel, and some of the most remarkable ever written.

A friend of Tolstoy's, the editor and educator S. A. Rachinsky, complained to him that *Anna Karenina* had no architecture, that the two 'themes' developed side by side in it, magnificently, but with no connection. His criticism prompted an interesting reply from Tolstoy, in a letter dated 27 January 1878:

> Your judgement of *Anna Karenina* seems wrong to me. On the contrary, I am proud of my architecture. But my vaults have been assembled in such a way that the keystone cannot be seen. Most of my effort has gone into that. The cohesion of the structure does not lie in the plot or in the relations (the meetings) of the characters, it is an internal cohesion . . . look well and you will find it.

In a letter to Strakhov some two years earlier he had already raised the question of this hidden cohesion:

> In everything or almost everything I have written, I have been moved by the need to bring together ideas that are closely knit, in order to express myself, but each idea, expressed separately in words, loses its meaning, is enormously impoverished when removed from the network around it. This network itself is not made up of ideas (or so I think), but of something else, and it is absolutely

impossible to express the substance of this network directly in words: it can be done only indirectly, by using words to describe characters, acts, situations.

This is perhaps Tolstoy's most perfect definition of his artistic practice.

Among the many thematic links between the two 'sides' of the novel, the most obvious is the contrast of the happy marriage of Levin and Kitty with the tragic relations of Anna and Vronsky. More hidden is the connection between Anna and Levin, who meet only once. Under the moral problem of adultery, which was Tolstoy's starting point, lies the 'problem' that obsessed Tolstoy most of all – death. Death and Anna enter the novel together; death is present at her first meeting with Vronsky; death is also present in their first embrace and in their mysteriously shared dream; death haunts their entire brief life together. But for Levin, too, death comes to darken the happiest moments of his life. It gives a stark title to the only chapter with a title in the whole novel – chapter XX of Part Five, describing the last agony of Levin's brother Nikolai. Anna surrenders to death; Levin struggles with it and wins, momentarily. But even in his victory, surrounded by his family, his estate, his peasants, he is as alone as Anna in her last moments. Metaphysical solitude is the hidden connection between them, and is what connects them both to their author.

Richard Pevear

TRANSLATORS' NOTE

Tolstoy's narrative voice poses a particular challenge to the translator. To apply general notions of natural, idiomatic English and good prose style to Tolstoy's writing is to risk blunting the sharpness of its internal dialogization. The narrator's personal attitudes often intrude on the objectivity of his discourse. Sometimes the intrusion is as slight as a single word, a sudden shift of tone, as, for instance, when he adds to the list of those enjoying themselves at the skating rink the 'old people who skated for hygienic [*gigienicheskiy*] purposes'. It is the word 'hygienic' that Tolstoy scorns, as much as the practice – one of the 'new' terms made current by the popularization of medical science in the later nineteenth century. At other times the intrusion is not so slight. An example is the description of the merchant Ryabinin's carriage standing in front of Levin's house: 'A little gig was already standing by the porch, tightly bound in iron and leather, with a sleek horse tightly harnessed in broad tugs. In the little gig, tightly filled with blood and tightly girdled, sat Ryabinin's clerk, who was also his driver.' Tolstoy clearly despises the merchant, and therefore his carriage and driver, as much as Levin does. There is also the narrator's undercutting of Kitty's admiration for the very spiritual Mme Stahl: '"And here's Mme Stahl," said Kitty, pointing to a bath-chair in which something lay, dressed in something grey and blue, propped on pillows under an umbrella.' Or the description of Karenin's meeting with his new lady-friend: 'Catching sight of the yellow shoulders rising from the corset of Countess Lydia Ivanovna . . . Alexei Alexandrovich smiled, revealing his unfading white teeth, and went up to her.' That 'unfading' (as in 'unfading glory'), worthy of Gogol or Dostoevsky, comes unexpectedly from Count Tolstoy. There are other times when his artistic purpose is less clear: for instance, in the scene at the railway station early in the novel, when the watchman is killed: '. . . several men with frightened faces suddenly ran past. The stationmaster, in a peaked cap of an extraordinary colour, also ran past. Evidently something extraordinary had happened.' Vladimir Nabokov says of this passage: 'There is of course no actual connection between the two [uses of 'extraordinary'], but the repetition is characteristic of Tolstoy's style with its rejection of false elegancies and its readiness to admit any robust awkwardness if that is the shortest way to sense.' In previous English translations such passages have generally been toned down if not eliminated. We have preferred to keep them as evidence of the freedom Tolstoy allowed himself in Russian.

Further Reading

Bakhtin, Mikhail, *The Dialogic Imagination*, ed. Michael Holquist, trans. Caryl Emerson and Michael Holquist (University of Texas Press, Austin, 1981)

Bayley, John, *Tolstoy and the Novel* (Chatto and Windus, London, 1966)

Berlin, Isaiah, *The Hedgehog and the Fox: An Essay on Tolstoy's View of History* (Simon and Schuster, New York, 1966; Weidenfeld and Nicolson, London, 1967)

Eikhenbaum, Boris, *Tolstoi in the Seventies*, trans. Albert Kaspin (Ardis, Ann Arbor, 1982)

Evans, Mary, *Anna Karenina* (Routledge, London and New York, 1989)

Leavis, F. R., *Anna Karenina and Other Essays* (Chatto and Windus, London, 1967)

Mandelker, Amy, *Framing 'Anna Karenina': Tolstoy, the Woman Question, and the Victorian Novel* (Ohio State University Press, Columbus, 1993)

Nabokov, Vladimir, *Lectures on Russian Literature* (Weidenfeld and Nicolson, London and Harcourt Brace Jovanovich, New York, 1981)

Orwin, Donna Tussing, *Tolstoy's Art and Thought, 1847–1880* (Princeton University Press, Princeton, 1993)

Sémon, Marie, *Les Femmes dans l'oeuvre de Léon Tolstoï* (Institut d'Études Slaves, Paris, 1984)

Thorlby, Anthony, *Leo Tolstoy, 'Anna Karenina'* (Cambridge University Press, Cambridge and New York, 1987)

Tolstoy, Leo, *Correspondence*, 2 vols., selected, ed. and trans. by R. F. Christian (Athlone Press, London and Scribner, New York, 1978)

—*Diaries*, ed. and trans. by R. F. Christian (Athlone Press, London and Scribner, New York, 1985)

Tolstoy, Sophia A., *The Diaries of Sophia Tolstoy*, ed. O. A. Golinenko, trans. Cathy Porter (Random House, New York, 1985)

Wasiolek, Edward, *Critical Essays on Tolstoy* (G. K. Hall, Boston, 1986)

—*Tolstoy's Major Fiction* (University of Chicago Press, Chicago, 1978)

List of Principal Characters

Guide to pronunciation stresses, with diminutives and variants. Russian names are made up of first name, patronymic (from the father's first name), and family name. Formal address requires the use of the first name and patronymic. Among family and intimate friends, a diminutive of the first name is normally used, such as Tanya for Tatiana or Kostya for Konstantin, never coupled with the patronymic. Some of Tolstoy's aristocrats have adopted the fashion of using English or Russified English diminutives – Dolly, Kitty, Betsy, Stiva. With the exception of Karenina, we use only the masculine form of family names.

Oblónsky, Prince Stepán Arkádyich (Stiva)
Princess Dárya Alexándrovna (Dolly, Dásha, Dáshenka, Dóllenka), *his wife, oldest of the three Shcherbatsky sisters*

Shcherbátsky, Prince Alexander Dmítrievich *or* Alexandre (*French*)
Princess ('the old princess', no first name or patronymic given), *his wife*
Princess Ekaterína Alexándrovna (Katerína, Kitty, Kátia, Kátenka), *their third daughter*

Karénina, Anna Arkádyevna, *née* Princess Oblonsky, *Stepan Arkadyich's sister*
Karénin, Alexéi Alexándrovich, *her husband*
Sergéi Alexéich (Seryózha, Kútik), *their son*

Vrónsky, Count Alexéi Kiríllovich (Alyósha)
Countess (no first name and patronymic given), *his mother*

Alexander Kiríllovich, *his brother*
Várya (diminutive of Varvára), *née* Princess Chirkóv, *wife of Alexander Vronsky*

Lévin, Konstantín Dmítrich (Kóstya)
Nikolái Dmítrich (Nikólenka), *his brother*

Kóznyshev, Sergéi Ivánovich, *half-brother of Konstantin and Nikolai Levin*

Lvov, Princess Natálya Alexándrovna (Natalie), *née* Shcherbatsky, *sister of Dolly and Kitty*
Arsény (no patronym given), *her husband*

Tverskóy, Princess Elizavéta Fyódorovna (Betsy), *Vronsky's first cousin*

Márya Nikoláevna (Masha, no family name given), *companion of Nikolai Levin*

Agáfya Mikháilovna (no family name given), *Levin's former nurse, now his housekeeper*

Countess Lydia Ivánovna (no family name given), *friend of Karenin*

Sviyázhsky, Nikolái Ivánovich, *friend of Levin, marshal of nobility in Súrov district*

Katavásov, Fyódor Vassílyevich, *friend of Levin*

Varvára Andréevna (Várenka, no family name given), *friend of Kitty*

Veslóvsky, Vásenka (or Váska, diminutives of Vassíly, no patronymic given), *friend of Oblonsky*

Yáshvin, Captain or Prince (no name or patronymic given), *friend of Vronsky*

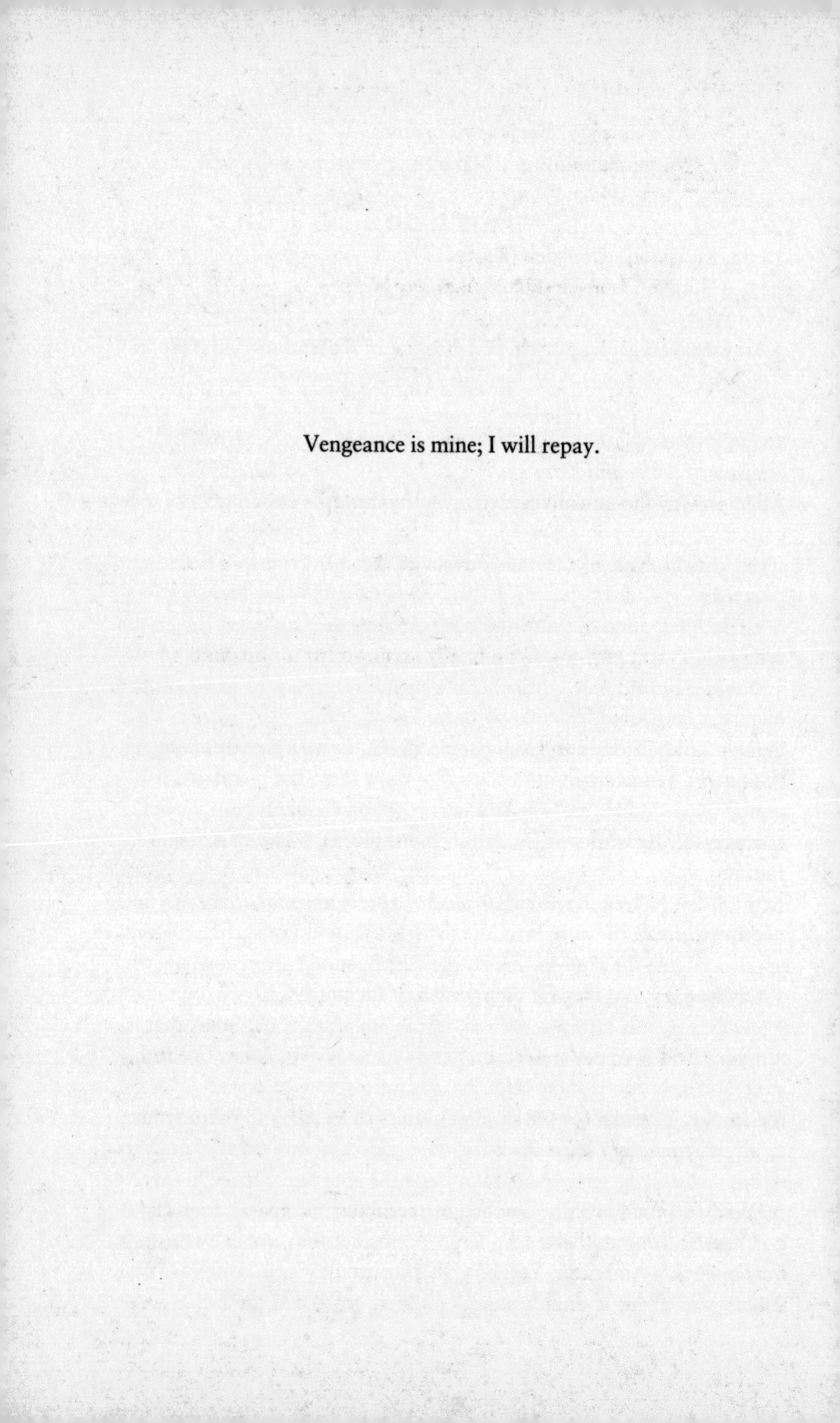

Vengeance is mine; I will repay.

Part One

I

All happy families are alike; each unhappy family is unhappy in its own way.

All was confusion in the Oblonskys' house. The wife had found out that the husband was having an affair with their former French governess, and had announced to the husband that she could not live in the same house with him. This situation had continued for three days now, and was painfully felt by the couple themselves, as well as by all the members of the family and household. They felt that there was no sense in their living together and that people who meet accidentally at any inn have more connection with each other than they, the members of the family and household of the Oblonskys. The wife would not leave her rooms, the husband was away for the third day. The children were running all over the house as if lost; the English governess quarrelled with the housekeeper and wrote a note to a friend, asking her to find her a new place; the cook had already left the premises the day before, at dinner-time; the kitchen-maid and coachman had given notice.

On the third day after the quarrel, Prince Stepan Arkadyich Oblonsky – Stiva, as he was called in society – woke up at his usual hour, that is, at eight o'clock in the morning, not in his wife's bedroom but in his study, on a morocco sofa. He rolled his full, well-tended body over on the springs of the sofa, as if wishing to fall asleep again for a long time, tightly hugged the pillow from the other side and pressed his cheek to it; but suddenly he gave a start, sat up on the sofa and opened his eyes.

'Yes, yes, how did it go?' he thought, recalling his dream. 'How did it go? Yes! Alabin was giving a dinner in Darmstadt – no, not in Darmstadt but something American. Yes, but this Darmstadt was in America. Yes, Alabin was giving a dinner on glass tables, yes – and the tables were singing *Il mio tesoro*,[1] only it wasn't *Il mio tesoro* but something better, and there were some little carafes, which were also women,' he recalled.

Stepan Arkadyich's eyes glittered merrily, and he fell to thinking with a smile. 'Yes, it was nice, very nice. There were many other excellent things there, but one can't say it in words, or even put it into waking thoughts.' And, noticing a strip of light that had broken through the side of one of the heavy blinds, he cheerfully dropped his feet from the sofa, felt for the slippers trimmed with gold morocco that his wife had embroidered for him (a present for last year's birthday), and, following a nine-year-old habit, without getting up, reached his hand out to the place where his dressing gown hung in the bedroom. And here he suddenly remembered how and why he was sleeping not in his wife's bedroom but in his study: the smile vanished from his face, and he knitted his brows.

'Oh, oh, oh! Ohh! . . .' he moaned, remembering all that had taken place. And in his imagination he again pictured all the details of his quarrel with his wife, all the hopelessness of his position and, most painful of all, his own guilt.

'No, she won't forgive me and can't forgive me! And the most terrible thing is that I'm the guilty one in it all – guilty, and yet not guilty. That's the whole drama,' he thought. 'Oh, oh, oh!' he murmured with despair, recalling what were for him the most painful impressions of this quarrel.

Worst of all had been that first moment when, coming back from the theatre, cheerful and content, holding a huge pear for his wife, he had not found her in the drawing room; to his surprise, he had not found her in the study either, and had finally seen her in the bedroom with the unfortunate, all-revealing note in her hand.

She – this eternally preoccupied and bustling and, as he thought, none-too-bright Dolly – was sitting motionless, the note in her hand, looking at him with an expression of horror, despair and wrath.

'What is this? this?' she asked, pointing to the note.

And, in recalling it, as often happens, Stepan Arkadyich was tormented not so much by the event itself as by the way he had responded to these words from his wife.

What had happened to him at that moment was what happens to people when they are unexpectedly caught in something very shameful. He had not managed to prepare his face for the position he found himself in with regard to his wife now that his guilt had been revealed. Instead of being offended, of denying, justifying, asking forgiveness, even remaining indifferent – any of which would have been better than what he did! – his face quite involuntarily ('reflexes of the brain', thought Stepan Arkadyich, who liked physiology)[2] smiled all at once its habitual, kind and therefore stupid smile.

That stupid smile he could not forgive himself. Seeing that smile, Dolly had winced as if from physical pain, burst with her typical vehemence into a torrent of cruel words, and rushed from the room. Since then she had refused to see her husband.

'That stupid smile is to blame for it all,' thought Stepan Arkadyich.

'But what to do, then? What to do?' he kept saying despairingly to himself, and could find no answer.

II

Stepan Arkadyich was a truthful man concerning his own self. He could not deceive himself into believing that he repented of his behaviour. He could not now be repentant that he, a thirty-four-year-old, handsome, amorous man, did not feel amorous with his wife, the mother of five living and two dead children, who was only a year younger than he. He repented only that he had not managed to conceal things better from her. But he felt all the gravity of his situation, and pitied his wife, his children and himself. Perhaps he would have managed to hide his sins better from his wife had he anticipated that the news would have such an effect on her. He had never thought the question over clearly, but vaguely imagined that his wife had long suspected him of being unfaithful to her and was looking the other way. It even seemed to him that she, a worn-out, aged, no longer beautiful woman, not remarkable for anything, simple, merely a kind mother of a family, ought in all fairness to be indulgent. It turned out to be quite the opposite.

'Ah, terrible! Ay, ay, ay! terrible!' Stepan Arkadyich repeated to himself and could come up with nothing. 'And how nice it all was before that, what a nice life we had! She was content, happy with the children, I didn't hinder her in anything, left her to fuss over them and the household however she liked. True, it's not nice that *she* used to be a governess in our house. Not nice! There's something trivial, banal, in courting one's own governess. But what a governess!' (He vividly recalled Mlle Roland's dark, roguish eyes and her smile.) 'But while she was in our house, I never allowed myself anything. And the worst of it is that she's already . . . It all had to happen at once! Ay, ay, ay! But what to do, what to do?'

There was no answer, except the general answer life gives to all the most complex and insoluble questions. That answer is: one must live for the needs of the day, in other words, become oblivious. To become oblivious in dreams was impossible now, at least till night-time; it was impossible to return to that music sung by carafe-women; and so one had to become oblivious in the dream of life.

'We'll see later on,' Stepan Arkadyich said to himself and, getting up, he put on his grey dressing gown with the light-blue silk lining, threw the tasselled cord into a knot, and, drawing a goodly amount of air into the broad box of his chest, went up to the window with the customary brisk step of his splayed feet, which so easily carried his full body, raised the blind and rang loudly. In response to the bell his old friend, the valet Matvei, came at once, bringing clothes, boots, and a telegram. Behind Matvei came the barber with the shaving things.

'Any papers from the office?' Stepan Arkadyich asked, taking the telegram and sitting down in front of the mirror.

'On the table,' Matvei replied, glancing inquiringly, with sympathy, at his master, and, after waiting a little, he added with a sly smile: 'Someone came from the owner of the livery stable.'

Stepan Arkadyich said nothing in reply and only glanced at Matvei in the mirror; from their eyes, which met in the mirror, one could see how well they understood each other. Stepan Arkadyich's eyes seemed to ask: 'Why are you saying that? as if you didn't know?'

Matvei put his hands in his jacket pockets, thrust one foot out and looked at his master silently, good-naturedly, with a slight smile.

'I told them to come next Sunday and till then not to trouble you or themselves needlessly.' He uttered an obviously prepared phrase.

Stepan Arkadyich understood that Matvei wanted to joke and attract attention to himself. Tearing open the telegram, he read it, guessing at the right sense of the words, which were garbled as usual, and his face brightened.

'Matvei, my sister Anna Arkadyevna is coming tomorrow,' he said, stopping for a moment the glossy, plump little hand of the barber, who was clearing a pink path between his long, curly side-whiskers.

'Thank God,' said Matvei, showing by this answer that he understood the significance of this arrival in the same way as his master, that is, that Anna Arkadyevna, Stepan Arkadyich's beloved sister, might contribute to the reconciliation of husband and wife.

'Alone or with her spouse?' asked Matvei.

Stepan Arkadyich, unable to speak because the barber was occupied with his upper lip, raised one finger. Matvei nodded in the mirror.

'Alone. Shall I prepare the rooms upstairs?'

'Tell Darya Alexandrovna, wherever she decides.'

'Darya Alexandrovna?' Matvei repeated, as if in doubt.

'Yes, tell her. And here, take the telegram, let me know what she says.'

'Testing her out,' Matvei understood, but he said only: 'Very well, sir.'

Stepan Arkadyich was already washed and combed and was about to start dressing, when Matvei, stepping slowly over the soft rug in his creaking boots, telegram in hand, came back into the room. The barber was no longer there.

'Darya Alexandrovna told me to inform you that she is leaving. Let him do as he – that is, you – pleases,' he said, laughing with his eyes only, and, putting his hands in his pockets and cocking his head to one side, he looked fixedly at his master.

Stepan Arkadyich said nothing. Then a kind and somewhat pathetic smile appeared on his handsome face.

'Eh? Matvei?' he said, shaking his head.

'Never mind, sir, it'll shape up,' said Matvei.

'Shape up?'

'That's right, sir.'

'You think so? Who's there?' Stepan Arkadyich asked, hearing the rustle of a woman's dress outside the door.

'It's me, sir,' said a firm and pleasant female voice, and through the door peeked the stern, pock-marked face of Matryona Filimonovna, the nanny.

'What is it, Matryosha?' Stepan Arkadyich asked, going out of the door to her.

Although Stepan Arkadyich was roundly guilty before his wife and felt it himself, almost everyone in the house, even the nanny, Darya Alexandrovna's chief friend, was on his side.

'Well, what is it?' he said dejectedly.

'You should go to her, sir, apologize again. Maybe God will help.

She's suffering very much, it's a pity to see, and everything in the house has gone topsy-turvy. The children should be pitied. Apologize, sir. No help for it! After the dance, you must pay the . . .'

'But she won't receive me . . .'

'Still, you do your part. God is merciful, pray to God, sir, pray to God.'

'Well, all right, go now,' said Stepan Arkadyich, suddenly blushing. 'Let's get me dressed.' He turned to Matvei and resolutely threw off his dressing gown.

Matvei was already holding the shirt like a horse collar, blowing away something invisible, and with obvious pleasure he clothed the pampered body of his master in it.

III

After dressing, Stepan Arkadyich sprayed himself with scent, adjusted the cuffs of his shirt, put cigarettes, wallet, matches, a watch with a double chain and seals into his pockets with an accustomed gesture, and, having shaken out his handkerchief, feeling himself clean, fragrant, healthy, and physically cheerful despite his misfortune, went out, springing lightly at each step, to the dining room, where coffee was already waiting for him, and, next to the coffee, letters and papers from the office.

He sat down and read the letters. One was very unpleasant – from a merchant who was buying a wood on his wife's estate. This wood had to be sold; but now, before his reconciliation with his wife, it was out of the question. The most unpleasant thing here was that it mixed financial interests into the impending matter of their reconciliation. And the thought that he might be guided by those interests, that he might seek a reconciliation with his wife in order to sell the wood, was offensive to him.

Having finished the letters, Stepan Arkadyich drew the office papers to him, quickly leafed through two files, made a few marks with a big pencil, then pushed the files away and started on his coffee. Over coffee he unfolded the still damp morning newspaper and began to read it.

Stepan Arkadyich subscribed to and read a liberal newspaper,[3] not an extreme one, but one with the tendency to which the majority held. And though neither science, nor art, nor politics itself interested him, he firmly held the same views on all these subjects as the majority and his newspaper did, and changed them only when the majority did, or, rather, he did not change them, but they themselves changed imperceptibly in him.

Stepan Arkadyich chose neither his tendency nor his views, but these tendencies and views came to him themselves, just as he did not choose the shape of a hat or a frock coat, but bought those that were in fashion. And for him, who lived in a certain circle, and who required some mental activity such as usually develops with maturity, having views was as necessary as having a hat. If there was a reason why he preferred the liberal tendency to the conservative one (also held to by many in his circle), it was not because he found the liberal tendency more sensible, but because it more closely suited his manner of life. The liberal party said that everything was bad in Russia, and indeed Stepan Arkadyich had many debts and decidedly too little money. The liberal party said that marriage was an obsolete institution and was in need of reform, and indeed family life gave Stepan Arkadyich little pleasure and forced him to lie and pretend, which was so contrary to his nature. The liberal party said, or, rather, implied, that religion was just a bridle for the barbarous part of the population, and indeed Stepan Arkadyich could not even stand through a short prayer service without aching feet and could not grasp the point of all these fearsome and high-flown words about the other world, when life in this one could be so merry. At the same time, Stepan Arkadyich, who liked a merry joke, sometimes took pleasure in startling some simple soul by saying that if you want to pride yourself on your lineage, why stop at Rurik[4] and renounce your first progenitor – the ape? And so the liberal tendency became a habit with Stepan Arkadyich, and he liked his newspaper, as he liked a cigar after dinner, for the slight haze it produced in his head. He read the leading article, which explained that in our time it was quite needless to raise the cry that radicalism was threatening to swallow up all the conservative elements, and that it was the government's duty to take measures to crush the hydra of revolution; that, on the contrary, 'in our opinion, the danger lies not in the imaginary hydra of revolution, but in a stubborn traditionalism that impedes progress', and so on. He also read yet another article, a financial one, in which mention was made of Bentham and Mill[5] and fine barbs were shot at the ministry. With his peculiar quickness of perception he understood the meaning of each barb: by whom, and against whom, and on what occasion it had been aimed, and this, as always, gave him a certain pleasure. But today this pleasure was poisoned by the recollection of Matryona Filimonovna's advice, and of the unhappy situation at home. He also read about Count Beust,[6] who was rumoured to have gone to Wiesbaden, and about the end of grey hair, and about the sale of a light carriage, and a young person's offer of her services; but this information did not, as formerly, give him a quiet, ironic pleasure.

Having finished the newspaper, a second cup of coffee, and a kalatch[7] with butter, he got up, brushed the crumbs from his waistcoat and, expanding his broad chest, smiled joyfully, not because there was anything especially pleasant in his heart – the smile was evoked by good digestion.

But this joyful smile at once reminded him of everything, and he turned pensive.

Two children's voices (Stepan Arkadyich recognized the voices of Grisha, the youngest boy, and Tanya, the eldest girl) were heard outside the door. They were pulling something and tipped it over.

'I told you not to put passengers on the roof,' the girl shouted in English. 'Now pick it up!'

'All is confusion,' thought Stepan Arkadyich. 'Now the children are running around on their own.' And, going to the door, he called them. They abandoned the box that stood for a train and came to their father.

The girl, her father's favourite, ran in boldly, embraced him, and hung laughing on his neck, delighting, as always, in the familiar smell of scent coming from his side-whiskers. Kissing him finally on the face, which was red from bending down and radiant with tenderness, the girl unclasped her hands and was going to run out again, but her father held her back.

'How's mama?' he asked, his hand stroking his daughter's smooth, tender neck. 'Good morning,' he said, smiling to the boy who greeted him.

He was aware that he loved the boy less, and always tried to be fair; but the boy felt it and did not respond with a smile to the cold smile of his father.

'Mama? Mama's up,' the girl replied.

Stepan Arkadyich sighed. 'That means again she didn't sleep all night,' he thought.

'And is she cheerful?'

The girl knew that there had been a quarrel between her father and mother, and that her mother could not be cheerful, and that her father ought to know it, and that he was shamming when he asked about it so lightly. And she blushed for him. He understood it at once and also blushed.

'I don't know,' she said. 'She told us not to study, but to go for a walk to grandma's with Miss Hull.'

'Well, go then, my Tanchurochka. Ah, yes, wait,' he said, still holding her back and stroking her tender little hand.

He took a box of sweets from the mantelpiece, where he had put it yesterday, and gave her two, picking her favourites, a chocolate and a cream.

'For Grisha?' the girl said, pointing to the chocolate.

'Yes, yes.' And stroking her little shoulder once more, he kissed her on the nape of the neck and let her go.

'The carriage is ready,' said Matvei. 'And there's a woman with a petition to see you,' he added.

'Has she been here long?' asked Stepan Arkadyich.

'Half an hour or so.'

'How often must I tell you to let me know at once!'

'I had to give you time for your coffee at least,' Matvei said in that friendly-rude tone at which it was impossible to be angry.

'Well, quickly send her in,' said Oblonsky, wincing with vexation.

The woman, Mrs Kalinin, a staff captain's wife, was petitioning for something impossible and senseless; but Stepan Arkadyich, as was his custom, sat her down, heard her out attentively without interrupting, and gave her detailed advice on whom to address and how, and even wrote, briskly and fluently, in his large, sprawling, handsome and clear handwriting, a little note to the person who could be of help to her. Having dismissed the captain's wife, Stepan Arkadyich picked up his hat and paused, wondering whether he had forgotten anything. It turned out that he had forgotten nothing, except what he had wanted to forget – his wife.

'Ah, yes!' He hung his head, and his handsome face assumed a wistful expression. 'Shall I go or not?' he said to himself. And his inner voice told him that he should not go, that there could be nothing here but falseness, that to rectify, to repair, their relations was impossible, because it was impossible to make her attractive and arousing of love again or to make him an old man incapable of love. Nothing could come of it now but falseness and deceit, and falseness and deceit were contrary to his nature.

'But at some point I'll have to; it can't remain like this,' he said, trying to pluck up his courage. He squared his shoulders, took out a cigarette, lit it, took two puffs, threw it into the mother-of-pearl ashtray, walked with quick steps across the gloomy drawing room and opened the other door, to his wife's bedroom.

IV

Darya Alexandrovna, wearing a dressing-jacket, the skimpy braids of her once thick and beautiful hair pinned at the back of her head, her face pinched and thin, her big, frightened eyes protruding on account of that thinness, was standing before an open chiffonier, taking something out of it. Various articles lay scattered about the room. Hearing her husband's footsteps, she stopped, looked at the door and vainly tried to give her face a stern and contemptuous expression. She felt that she was afraid of him and of the impending meeting. She had just been trying to do something she had already tried to do ten times in those three days: to choose some of her own and the children's things to take to her mother's – and again she could not make up her mind to do it; but now, as each time before, she told herself that things could not remain like this, that she had to do something, to punish, to shame him, to take revenge on him for at least a small part of the hurt he had done her. She still kept saying she would leave him, yet she felt it was impossible, because she could not get out of the habit of considering him her husband and of loving him. Besides, she felt that if she could barely manage to take care of her five children here in her own house, it would be still worse there where she was taking them all. As it was, during those three days the youngest had fallen ill because he had been fed bad broth, and the rest had gone with almost no dinner yesterday. She felt it was impossible to leave; but, deceiving herself, she still kept choosing things and pretending she was going to leave.

Seeing her husband, she thrust her hands into a drawer of the chiffonier as if hunting for something, and turned to look at him only when he came up quite close to her. But her face, to which she had wanted to give a stern and resolute expression, showed bewilderment and suffering.

'Dolly!' he said in a soft, timid voice. He drew his head down between his shoulders, wishing to look pitiful and submissive, but all the same he radiated freshness and health.

She gave his figure radiating freshness and health a quick glance up and down. 'Yes, he's happy and content!' she thought, 'while I . . . ? And this repulsive kindness everyone loves and praises him for – I hate this kindness of his.' She pressed her lips together; the cheek muscle on the right side of her pale, nervous face began to twitch.

'What do you want?' she said in a quick, throaty voice, not her own.

'Dolly,' he repeated with a tremor in his voice, 'Anna is coming today!'

'So, what is that to me? I can't receive her!' she cried.

'But anyhow, Dolly, we must . . .'

'Go away, go away, go away,' she cried out, not looking at him, as if the cry had been caused by physical pain.

Stepan Arkadyich could be calm when he thought about his wife, could hope that everything would *shape up*, as Matvei put it, and could calmly read the newspaper and drink his coffee; but when he saw her worn, suffering face, and heard the sound of that resigned and despairing voice, his breath failed him, something rose in his throat and his eyes glistened with tears.

'My God, what have I done! Dolly! For God's sake! . . . If . . .' He could not go on, sobs caught in his throat.

She slammed the chiffonier shut and looked at him.

'Dolly, what can I say? . . . Only – forgive me, forgive me . . . Think back, can't nine years of life atone for a moment, a moment . . .'

She lowered her eyes and listened, waiting for what he would say, as if begging him to dissuade her somehow.

'A moment of infatuation . . .' he brought out and wanted to go on, but at this phrase she pressed her lips again, as if from physical pain, and again the cheek muscle on the right side of her face began to twitch.

'Go away, go away from here!' she cried still more shrilly. 'And don't talk to me about your infatuations and your abominations!'

She wanted to leave but swayed and took hold of the back of a chair to support herself. His face widened, his lips swelled, his eyes filled with tears.

'Dolly!' he said, sobbing now. 'For God's sake, think of the children, they're not guilty. I'm guilty, so punish me, tell me to atone for it. However I can, I'm ready for anything! I'm guilty, there are no words to say how guilty I am! But, Dolly, forgive me!'

She sat down. He could hear her loud, heavy breathing and felt inexpressibly sorry for her. She tried several times to speak, but could not. He waited.

'You think of the children when it comes to playing with them, Stiva, but I always think of them, and I know that they're lost now.' She uttered one of the phrases she had obviously been repeating to herself during those three days.

She had said 'Stiva' to him. He glanced at her gratefully and made a movement to take her hand, but she withdrew from him with loathing.

'I think of the children and so I'll do anything in the world to save them; but I don't know how I can best save them: by taking them away from their father, or by leaving them with a depraved father – yes, depraved . . . Well, tell me, after . . . what's happened, is it possible for us to live together? Is it possible? Tell me, is it possible?' she repeated, raising her voice. 'After my husband, the father of my children, has had a love affair with his children's governess . . .'

'But what to do? What to do?' he said in a pitiful voice, not knowing what he was saying, and hanging his head lower and lower.

'You are vile, you are loathsome to me!' she cried, growing more and more excited. 'Your tears are just water! You never loved me; there's no heart, no nobility in you! You're disgusting, vile, a stranger, yes, a total stranger to me!' With pain and spite she uttered this word so terrible for her – 'stranger'.

He looked at her, and the spite that showed on her face frightened and astonished him. He did not understand that his pity for her exasperated her. In him she saw pity for herself, but no love. 'No, she hates me. She won't forgive me,' he thought.

'This is terrible! Terrible!' he said.

Just then a child, who had probably fallen down, started crying in the other room. Darya Alexandrovna listened and her face suddenly softened.

It clearly took her a few seconds to pull herself together, as if she did not know where she was or what to do, then she got up quickly and went to the door.

'But she does love my child,' he thought, noticing the change in her face at the child's cry, '*my* child – so how can she hate me?'

'One word more, Dolly,' he said, going after her.

'If you come after me, I'll call the servants, the children! Let everybody know you're a scoundrel! I'm leaving today, and you can live here with your mistress!'

And she went out, slamming the door.

Stepan Arkadyich sighed, wiped his face and with quiet steps started out of the room. 'Matvei says it will shape up – but how? I don't see even a possibility. Ah, ah, how terrible! And what trivial shouting,' he said to himself, remembering her cry and the words 'scoundrel' and 'mistress'. 'And the maids may have heard! Terribly trivial, terribly!' Stepan Arkadyich stood alone for a few seconds, wiped his eyes, sighed, and, squaring his shoulders, walked out of the room.

It was Friday and the German clockmaker was winding the clock in the dining room. Stepan Arkadyich remembered his joke about this punctilious, bald-headed man, that the German 'had been wound up for life himself, so as to keep winding clocks' – and smiled. Stepan Arkadyich loved a good joke. 'But maybe it will shape up! A nice little phrase: *shape up*,' he thought. 'It bears repeating.'

'Matvei!' he called. 'You and Marya arrange things for Anna Arkadyevna there in the sitting room,' he said to Matvei as he came in.

'Very good, sir!'

Stepan Arkadyich put on his fur coat and went out to the porch.

'You won't be dining at home?' Matvei asked, seeing him off.

'That depends. And here's something for expenses,' he said, giving him ten roubles from his wallet. 'Will that be enough?'

'Enough or not, it'll have to do,' Matvei said, shutting the carriage door and stepping back on to the porch.

Meanwhile Darya Alexandrovna, having quieted the child and understanding from the sound of the carriage that he had left, went back to the bedroom. This was her only refuge from household cares, which surrounded her the moment she stepped out. Even now, during the short time she had gone to the children's room, the English governess and Matryona Filimonovna had managed to ask her several questions that could not be put off and that she alone could answer: what should the children wear for their walk? should they have milk? should not another cook be sent for?

'Ah, let me be, let me be!' she said, and, returning to the bedroom, she again sat down in the same place where she had talked with her husband, clasped her wasted hands with the rings slipping off her bony fingers, and began turning the whole conversation over in her mind. 'He left! But how has he ended it *with her*?' she thought. 'Can it be he still sees her? Why didn't I ask him? No, no, we can't come together again. Even if we stay in the same house – we're strangers. Forever strangers!' She repeated again with special emphasis this word that was so terrible for her. 'And how I loved him, my God, how I loved him! . . . How I loved him! And don't I love him now? Don't I love him more than before? The most terrible thing is . . .' she began, but did not finish her thought, because Matryona Filimonovna stuck her head in at the door.

'Maybe we ought to send for my brother,' she said. 'He can at least make dinner. Otherwise the children won't eat before six o'clock, like yesterday.'

'Well, all right, I'll come and give orders at once. Have you sent for fresh milk?'

And Darya Alexandrovna plunged into her daily cares and drowned her grief in them for a time.

V

Stepan Arkadyich had had an easy time at school, thanks to his natural abilities, but he was lazy and mischievous and therefore came out among the last. Yet, despite his dissipated life, none-too-high rank and none-too-ripe age, he occupied a distinguished and well-paid post as head of one of the Moscow offices. This post he had obtained through Alexei Alexandrovich Karenin, his sister Anna's husband, who occupied one of the most important positions in the ministry to which the office belonged; but if Karenin had not appointed his brother-in-law to it, then Stiva Oblonsky would have obtained the post through a hundred other persons – brothers, sisters, relations, cousins, uncles, aunts – or another like it, with a salary of some six thousand, which he needed, because his affairs, despite his wife's ample fortune, were in disarray.

Half Moscow and Petersburg were relatives or friends of Stepan Arkadyich. He had been born into the milieu of those who were or had become the mighty of this world. One-third of the state dignitaries, the elders, were his father's friends and had known him in petticoats; another third were on familiar terms with him, and the final third were good acquaintances; consequently, the distributors of earthly blessings, in the form of positions, leases, concessions and the like, were all friends of his and could not pass over one of their own; and Oblonsky did not have to try especially hard to obtain a profitable post; all he had to do was not refuse, not envy, not quarrel, not get offended, which, owing to his natural kindness, he never did anyway. It would have seemed laughable to him if he had been told that he would not get a post with the salary he needed, the more so as he did not demand anything excessive; he only wanted what his peers were getting, and he could fill that sort of position no worse than anyone else.

Stepan Arkadyich was not only liked by all who knew him for his kind, cheerful temper and unquestionable honesty, but there was in him, in his handsome, bright appearance, shining eyes, black brows and hair, the whiteness and ruddiness of his face, something that physically made an amiable and cheerful impression on the people he met. 'Aha! Stiva! Oblonsky! Here he is!' they would almost always say with a joyful smile on meeting him. And if it sometimes happened that talking with him produced no especially joyful effect, a day or two later they would all rejoice again in the same way when they met him.

Serving for the third year as head of one of the Moscow offices, Stepan Arkadyich had acquired the respect as well as the affection of his colleagues, subordinates, superiors, and all who had dealings with him. The main qualities that had earned him this universal respect in the service were, first, an extreme indulgence towards people, based on his awareness of his own shortcomings; second, a perfect liberalism, not the sort he read about in the newspapers, but the sort he had in his blood, which made him treat all people, whatever their rank or status, in a perfectly equal and identical way; and, third – most important – a perfect indifference to the business he was occupied with, owing to which he never got carried away and never made mistakes.

Arriving at his place of work, Stepan Arkadyich, accompanied by the respectful doorman, went with a portfolio into his small private office, put on his uniform, and entered the main office. The scriveners and clerks all rose, bowing cheerfully and respectfully. Stepan Arkadyich, hastily as always, went to his place, exchanged handshakes with the members and sat down. He joked and talked exactly as much as was proper and then got down to work. No one knew more surely than Stepan Arkadyich how to find the limits of freedom, simplicity and officialness necessary for getting work done in a pleasant way. The secretary, cheerful and respectful as was everyone in Stepan Arkadyich's presence, approached with some papers and said in that familiarly liberal tone which had been introduced by Stepan Arkadyich:

'We did after all obtain information from the Penza provincial office. Here, if you please . . .'

'So you finally got it?' said Stepan Arkadyich, marking the page with his finger. 'Well, gentlemen . . .' And the work began.

'If they only knew,' he thought, inclining his head gravely as he listened to the report, 'what a guilty boy their chairman was half an hour ago!' And his eyes were laughing as the report was read. The work had to go on without interruption till two o'clock, and then there would be a break for lunch.

It was not yet two when the big glass door of the office suddenly opened and someone came in. All the members, from under the imperial portrait and behind the zertsalo,[8] turned towards the door, glad of the diversion; but the porter at once banished the intruder and closed the glass door behind him.

When the case had been read, Stepan Arkadyich stood up, stretched, and, giving the liberalism of the time its due, took out a cigarette while still in the room, then went into his private office. His two comrades, the veteran Nikitin and the kammerjunker[9] Grinevich, followed him out.

'We'll have time to finish after lunch,' said Stepan Arkadyich.

'That we will!' said Nikitin.

'And he must be a regular crook, this Fomin,' Grinevich said of one of the people involved in the case they were considering.

Stepan Arkadyich winced at Grinevich's words, thereby letting it be felt that it was inappropriate to form a premature judgement, and did not reply to him.

'Who was it that came in?' he asked the porter.

'Some man, your excellency, slipped in the moment I turned my back. He asked for you. I said when the members leave, then . . .'

'Where is he?'

'Went out to the front hall most likely, and before that he kept pacing around here. That's the one,' the porter said, pointing to a strongly built, broad-shouldered man with a curly beard, who, without taking off his lamb-skin hat, was quickly and lightly running up the worn steps of the stone stairway. One skinny clerk going down with a portfolio paused, looked disapprovingly at the running man's feet, and then glanced questioningly at Oblonsky.

Stepan Arkadyich stood at the top of the stairs. His face, beaming good-naturedly from behind the embroidered uniform collar, beamed still more when he recognized the man who was running up.

'So it's he! Levin, at last!' he said with a friendly, mocking smile, looking Levin over as he approached. 'How is it you don't scorn to come looking for me in this *den*?' said Stepan Arkadyich, not satisfied with a handshake, but kissing his friend. 'Been here long?'

'I just arrived, and wanted very much to see you,' Levin replied, looking around bashfully and at the same time crossly and uneasily.

'Well, let's go to my office,' said Stepan Arkadyich, knowing his friend's proud and irascible shyness; and, taking him by the arm, he drew him along, as if guiding him through dangers.

Stepan Arkadyich was on familiar terms with almost all his acquaintances: with old men of sixty and with boys of twenty, with actors, ministers, merchants and imperial adjutants, so that a great many of those who were his intimates occupied opposite ends of the social ladder and would have been very surprised to learn they had something in common through Oblonsky. He was on familiar terms with everyone with whom he drank champagne, and he drank champagne with everyone; therefore when, in the presence of his subordinates, he met his 'disreputable familiars', as he jokingly called many of his friends, he was able, with his peculiar tact, to lessen the unpleasantness of the impression for his subordinates. Levin was not a disreputable familiar, but Oblonsky sensed that Levin was thinking he might not want to show his closeness to him in front of his staff, and therefore hastened to take him to his office.

Levin was almost the same age as Oblonsky and was his familiar not only in the champagne line. Levin had been the comrade and friend of his early youth. They loved each other, in spite of the difference in their characters and tastes, as friends love each other who become close in early youth. But in spite of that, as often happens between people who have chosen different ways, each of them, while rationally justifying the other's activity, despised it in his heart. To each of them it seemed that the life he led was the only real life, and the one his friend led was a mere illusion. Oblonsky could not repress a slightly mocking smile at the sight of Levin. So many times he had seen him come to Moscow from the country, where he did something or other, though Stepan Arkadyich could never understand precisely what, nor did it interest him. Levin always came to Moscow agitated, hurried, a little uneasy, and annoyed at this uneasiness, and most often with a completely new, unexpected view of things. Stepan Arkadyich laughed at this and loved it. In just the same way, at heart Levin despised both his friend's city style of life and his job, which he regarded as trifling, and he laughed at it all. But the difference was that Oblonsky, while doing as everyone else did, laughed confidently and good-naturedly, whereas Levin laughed unconfidently and sometimes crossly.

'We've long been expecting you,' said Stepan Arkadyich, going into his office and releasing Levin's arm, as if to show that the dangers were past. 'I'm very, very glad to see you,' he went on. 'Well, how are you doing? When did you arrive?'

Levin was silent, glancing at the unfamiliar faces of Oblonsky's two colleagues and especially at the elegant Grinevich's hands, with such long white fingers, such long yellow nails curving at the tips, and such huge glittering cuff links on his sleeves, that these hands clearly absorbed all his attention and did not allow him any freedom of thought. Oblonsky noticed it at once and smiled.

'Ah, yes, let me introduce you,' he said. 'My colleagues: Filipp Ivanych Nikitin, Mikhail Stanislavich Grinevich,' and turning to Levin: 'A zemstvo activist,[10] a new zemstvo man, a gymnast, lifts a hundred and fifty pounds with one hand, a cattle-breeder and hunter, and my friend, Konstantin Dmitrich Levin, the brother of Sergei Ivanych Koznyshev.'

'Very pleased,' said the little old man.

'I have the honour of knowing your brother, Sergei Ivanych,' said Grinevich, proffering his slender hand with its long nails.

Levin frowned, shook the hand coldly, and turned at once to Oblonsky. Though he had great respect for his maternal half-brother, a writer known to all Russia, nevertheless he could not stand being addressed as the brother of the famous Koznyshev rather than as Konstantin Levin.

'No, I'm no longer a zemstvo activist. I've quarrelled with them all and no longer go to the meetings,' he said, addressing Oblonsky.

'That was quick!' Oblonsky said with a smile. 'But how? why?'

'A long story. I'll tell you some day,' said Levin, but he began telling it at once. 'Well, to make it short, I became convinced that there is not and cannot be any zemstvo activity.' He spoke as if someone had just offended him. 'On the one hand, it's just a plaything, they play at parliament, and I'm neither young enough nor old enough to amuse myself with playthings. And on the other . . .' (he faltered) 'hand, it's a way for the district coterie to make a little money. Before there were custodies, courts, but now it's the zemstvo . . . not in the form of bribes, but in the form of unearned salaries.' He spoke as hotly as if someone there had argued against his opinion.[11]

'Oho! I see you're in a new phase again, a conservative one,' said Stepan Arkadyich. 'However, of that later.'

'Yes, later. But I had to see you,' Levin said, looking with hatred at Grinevich's hand.

Stepan Arkadyich smiled almost imperceptibly.

'Didn't you say you'd never put on European clothes again?' he said, looking over his new clothes, obviously from a French tailor. 'So! I see – a new phase.'

Levin suddenly blushed, but not as grown-up people blush – slightly, unaware of it themselves – but as boys do, feeling that their bashfulness makes them ridiculous, becoming ashamed as a result, and blushing even more, almost to the point of tears. And it was so strange to see that intelligent, manly face in such a childish state that Oblonsky stopped looking at him.

'So where shall we see each other? I need very, very much to have a talk with you,' said Levin.

Oblonsky appeared to reflect.

'I'll tell you what: let's go to Gourin's for lunch and talk there. I'm free until three.'

'No,' Levin replied after a moment's thought, 'I still have to go somewhere.'

'Well, all right, then let's dine together.'

'Dine? But I have nothing special to say or ask, just a couple of words, and we can have a chat later.'

'Then tell me the couple of words now, and we can discuss things over dinner.'

'The couple of words are these . . .' said Levin. 'Anyway, it's nothing special.'

His face suddenly acquired an angry expression, which came from the effort to overcome his bashfulness.

'What are the Shcherbatskys doing? The same as ever?' he said.

Stepan Arkadyich, who had known for a long time that Levin was in love with his sister-in-law Kitty, smiled almost imperceptibly and his eyes shone merrily.

'A couple of words, you said, but I can't answer in a couple of words, because . . . Excuse me a moment . . .'

The secretary came in with familiar deference and a certain modest awareness, common to all secretaries, of his superiority to his chief in the knowledge of business, approached Oblonsky with some papers and, in the guise of a question, began explaining some difficulty. Stepan Arkadyich, without listening to the end, placed his hand benignly on the secretary's sleeve.

'No, just do as I told you,' he said, softening the remark with a smile, and after briefly explaining the matter as he understood it, he pushed the papers aside, saying: 'Do it that way, please, Zakhar Nikitich.'

The abashed secretary withdrew. Levin, who during this conference with the secretary had recovered completely from his embarrassment, stood with both elbows resting on the chair back, a look of mocking attention on his face.

'I don't understand, I don't understand,' he said.

'What don't you understand?' said Oblonsky, with the same cheerful smile, taking out a cigarette. He expected some strange escapade from Levin.

'I don't understand what you do,' Levin said with a shrug. 'How can you do it seriously?'

'Why not?'

'Why, because there's nothing to do.'

'That's what you think, but we're buried in work.'

'Paperwork. Ah, well, you do have a gift for that,' Levin added.

'That is, you think I'm lacking in something?'

'Maybe so,' said Levin. 'But all the same I admire your grandeur and am proud that my friend is such a great man. However, you didn't answer my question,' he added, with a desperate effort to look straight into Oblonsky's eyes.

'Well, all right, all right. Wait a while, and you'll come round to the same thing. It's all right so long as you've got eight thousand acres in the Karazin district, and those muscles, and the freshness of a twelve-year-old girl – but you'll join us some day. Yes, as for what you asked about: nothing's changed, but it's too bad you haven't been there for so long.'

'Why?' Levin asked timorously.

'No, nothing,' Oblonsky replied. 'We'll talk. But why in fact did you come?'

'Oh, we'll talk about that later as well,' Levin said, again blushing to the ears.

'Well, all right. Understood,' said Stepan Arkadyich. 'You see, I'd invite you to our place, but my wife is not quite well. You know what: if you want to see them, they'll certainly be in the Zoological Garden today from four to five. Kitty goes skating there. Go there yourself, and I'll join you, and we'll dine together somewhere.'

'Excellent. See you later, then.'

'Watch out, I know you, don't forget or suddenly leave for the country!' Stepan Arkadyich called out with a laugh.

'Certainly not.'

And, remembering only at the door that he had forgotten to take leave of Oblonsky's colleagues, Levin walked out of the office.

'Must be a very energetic gentleman,' said Grinevich, after Levin left.

'Yes, old man,' Stepan Arkadyich said, nodding, 'there's a lucky one! Eight thousand acres in the Karazin district, everything to look forward to, and so much freshness! Not like our sort.'

'What do you have to complain about, Stepan Arkadyich?'

'Oh, it's bad, awful,' Stepan Arkadyich said with a heavy sigh.

VI

When Oblonsky had asked Levin why in fact he had come, Levin had blushed and became angry with himself for blushing, because he could not answer: 'I've come to propose to your sister-in-law,' though he had come only for that.

The houses of Levin and Shcherbatsky were old noble Moscow houses and had always been in close and friendly relations with each other. This connection had strengthened still more during Levin's student days. He had prepared for and entered the university together with the young prince Shcherbatsky, brother of Dolly and Kitty. In those days Levin had frequented the Shcherbatskys' house and had fallen in love with the family. Strange as it might seem, Konstantin Levin was in love precisely with the house, the family, especially the female side of it. He did not remember his own mother, and his only sister was older than he, so that in the Shcherbatskys' house he saw for the first time the milieu of an old, noble, educated and honourable family, of which he had been deprived by the death of his father and mother. All the members of this family, especially the female side, seemed to him covered by some mysterious poetic veil, and he not only saw no defects in them, but surmised, behind the cover of this poetic veil, the loftiest feelings and every possible perfection. Why these three young ladies had to speak French and English on alternate days; why at certain hours they took turns playing the piano, the sounds of which were heard in their brother's rooms upstairs, where the students worked; why all these teachers of French literature, music, drawing and dancing came there; why at certain hours all three young ladies, with Mlle Linon, went in a carriage to Tverskoy

Boulevard in their fur-lined satin coats – Dolly in a long one, Natalie in a three-quarter one, and Kitty in a quite short one, so that her shapely legs in tight-fitting red stockings were in full view; why they had to stroll along Tverskoy Boulevard accompanied by a footman with a gold cockade on his hat – all this and much more that went on in their mysterious world he did not understand; but he knew that everything that went on there was beautiful, and he was in love precisely with the mysteriousness of it all.

During his student days he nearly fell in love with the eldest one, Dolly, but she was soon married to Oblonsky. Then he began falling in love with the second one. It was as if he felt that he had to fall in love with one of the sisters, only he could not make out which one. But Natalie, too, as soon as she appeared in society, married the diplomat Lvov. Kitty was still a child when Levin left the university. The young Shcherbatsky, having gone into the navy, was drowned in the Baltic Sea, and Levin's contacts with the Shcherbatskys, despite his friendship with Oblonsky, became less frequent. But when, after a year in the country, Levin came to Moscow at the beginning of that winter and saw the Shcherbatskys, he realized which of the three he had really been destined to fall in love with.

Nothing could seem simpler than for him, a man of good stock, rich rather than poor, thirty-two years old, to propose to the young princess Shcherbatsky; in all likelihood he would be acknowledged at once as a good match. But Levin was in love, and therefore it seemed to him that Kitty was so perfect in all respects, a being so far above everything earthly, while he was such a base earthly being, that it was even unthinkable for others or for Kitty herself to acknowledge him as worthy of her.

After spending two months in Moscow, as if in a daze, seeing Kitty almost every day in society, which he began to frequent in order to meet her, Levin suddenly decided that it could not be and left for the country.

Levin's conviction that it could not be rested on the idea that in the eyes of her relatives he was an unprofitable, unworthy match for the charming Kitty, and that Kitty could not love him. In their eyes, though he was now thirty-two, he did not have any regular, defined activity or position in society, whereas among his comrades one was already a colonel and imperial aide-de-camp, one a professor, one the director of a bank and a railway or the chief of an office like Oblonsky, while he (he knew very well what he must seem like to others) was a landowner, occupied with breeding cows, shooting snipe, and building things, that is, a giftless fellow who amounted to nothing and was doing, in society's view, the very thing that good-for-nothing people do.

Nor could the mysterious and charming Kitty love such an unattractive man as he considered himself to be, and above all such a simple man, not distinguished in any way. Besides that, his former relations with Kitty – the relations of an adult to a child, because of his friendship with her brother – seemed to him another new obstacle to love. An unattractive, kindly man like himself might, he supposed, be loved as a friend, but to be loved with the love he himself felt for Kitty, one had to be a handsome – and above all a special – man.

He had heard that women often love unattractive, simple people, but he did not believe it, because he judged by himself, and he could only love beautiful, mysterious and special women.

Yet, after spending two months alone in the country, he became convinced that this was not one of those loves he had experienced in his early youth; that this feeling would not leave him a moment's peace; that he could not live without resolving the question whether she would or would not be his wife; and that his despair came only from his imagination – he had no proof that he would be refused. And now he had come to Moscow with the firm determination to propose and to marry if he was accepted. Or . . . but he could not think what would become of him if he were refused.

VII

Arriving in Moscow on the morning train, Levin had gone to stay with his older half-brother Koznyshev and, after changing, entered his study, intending to tell him at once what he had come for and to ask his advice; but his brother was not alone. With him was a well-known professor of philosophy, who had actually come from Kharkov to resolve a misunderstanding that had arisen between them on a rather important philosophical question. The professor was engaged in heated polemics with the materialists. Sergei Koznyshev had followed these polemics with interest and, after reading the professor's last article, had written him a letter with his objections; he had reproached the professor with making rather large concessions to the materialists. And the professor had come at once to talk it over. The discussion was about a fashionable question: is there a borderline between psychological and physiological phenomena in human activity, and where does it lie?[12]

Sergei Ivanovich met his brother with the benignly cool smile he gave to everyone and, after introducing him to the professor, went on with the conversation.

The small, yellow-skinned man in spectacles, with a narrow brow, turned away from the conversation for a moment to greet Levin and, paying no further attention to him, went on talking. Levin sat down to wait until the professor left, but soon became interested in the subject of the conversation.

Levin had come across the articles they were discussing in magazines, and had read them, being interested in them as a development of the bases of natural science, familiar to him from his studies at the university, but he had never brought together these scientific conclusions about the animal origin of man,[13] about reflexes, biology and sociology, with those questions about the meaning of life and death which lately had been coming more and more often to his mind.

Listening to his brother's conversation with the professor, he noticed that they connected the scientific questions with the inner, spiritual ones, several times almost touched upon them, but that each time they came close to what seemed to him the most important thing, they hastily retreated and again dug deeper into the realm of fine distinctions, reservations, quotations, allusions, references to authorities, and he had difficulty understanding what they were talking about.

'I cannot allow,' Sergei Ivanovich said with his usual clarity and precision of expression and elegance of diction, 'I can by no means agree with Keiss that my whole notion of the external world stems from sense impressions. The fundamental concept of *being* itself is not received through the senses, for there exists no special organ for conveying that concept.'

'Yes, but they – Wurst and Knaust and Pripasov –[14] will reply to you that your consciousness of being comes from the totality of your sense impressions, that this consciousness of being is the result of sensations. Wurst even says directly that where there are no sensations, there is no concept of being.'

'I would say the reverse,' Sergei Ivanovich began . . .

But here again it seemed to Levin that, having approached the most important thing, they were once more moving away, and he decided to put a question to the professor.

'Therefore, if my senses are destroyed, if my body dies, there can be no further existence?' he asked.

The professor, vexed and as if mentally pained by the interruption, turned to the strange questioner, who looked more like a barge-hauler than a philosopher, then shifted his gaze to Sergei Ivanovich as if to ask: what can one say to that? But Sergei Ivanovich, who spoke with far less strain and one-sidedness than the professor, and in whose head there still remained room enough both for responding to the professor and for understanding the simple and natural point of view from which the question had been put, smiled and said:

'That question we still have no right to answer . . .'

'We have no data,' the professor confirmed and went on with his arguments. 'No,' he said, 'I will point out that if, as Pripasov states directly, sensation does have its basis in impression, we must distinguish strictly between these two concepts.'

Levin listened no more and waited until the professor left.

VIII

When the professor had gone, Sergei Ivanovich turned to his brother.

'Very glad you've come. Staying long? How's the farming?'

Levin knew that his older brother had little interest in farming and that he asked about it only as a concession to him, and therefore he answered only about the sales of wheat and about money.

Levin wanted to tell his brother of his intention to marry and to ask his advice; he was even firmly resolved on it. But when he saw his brother, listened to his conversation with the professor, and then heard the inadvertently patronizing tone with which his brother asked him about farm matters (their mother's estate had not been divided, and Levin was in charge of both parts), for some reason he felt unable to begin talking with his brother about his decision to marry. He felt that his brother would not look upon it as he would have wished.

'Well, how are things with your zemstvo?' asked Sergei Ivanovich, who was very interested in the zemstvo and ascribed great significance to it.

'I don't really know . . .'

'How's that? Aren't you a member of the board?'

'No, I'm no longer a member. I resigned,' replied Konstantin Levin, 'and I don't go to the meetings any more.'

'Too bad!' said Sergei Ivanovich, frowning.

Levin, to vindicate himself, began to describe what went on at the meetings in his district.

'But it's always like that!' Sergei Ivanovich interrupted. 'We Russians are always like that. Maybe it's a good feature of ours – the ability to see our own failings – but we overdo it, we take comfort in irony, which always comes readily to our tongues. I'll tell you only that if they gave some other European nation the same rights as in our zemstvo institutions – the Germans or the English would have worked their way to freedom with them, while we just laugh.'

'But what to do?' Levin said guiltily. 'This was my last attempt. And I put my whole soul into it. I can't. I'm incapable.'

'Not incapable,' said Sergei Ivanovich, 'but you don't have the right view of the matter.'

'Maybe,' Levin replied glumly.

'You know, brother Nikolai is here again.'

Brother Nikolai was Konstantin Levin's older brother and Sergei Ivanovich's half-brother, a ruined man, who had squandered the greater part of his fortune, moved in very strange and bad society, and had quarrelled with his brothers.

'What did you say?' Levin cried out with horror. 'How do you know?'

'Prokofy saw him in the street.'

'Here in Moscow? Where is he? Do you know?' Levin got up from his chair, as though he were about to leave at once.

'I'm sorry I told you,' said Sergei Ivanovich, shaking his head at his brother's agitation. 'I sent to find out where he's living, and returned him his promissory note to Trubin, which I paid. Here's how he answered me.'

And Sergei Ivanovich handed his brother a note from under a paperweight.

Levin read what was written in that strange, so familiar handwriting: 'I humbly beg you to leave me alone. That is the one thing I ask of my gentle little brothers. Nikolai Levin.'

Levin read it and, not raising his head, stood before Sergei Ivanovich with the note in his hand.

His soul was struggling between the desire to forget just then about his unfortunate brother, and the consciousness that to do so would be wrong.

'He obviously wants to insult me,' Sergei Ivanovich went on, 'but insult me he cannot, and I wish with all my heart that I could help him, yet I know it's impossible.'

'Yes, yes,' Levin repeated. 'I understand and appreciate your attitude towards him; but I will go and see him.'

'Go if you like, but I don't advise it,' said Sergei Ivanovich. 'That is, as far as I'm concerned, I'm not afraid of it, he won't make us quarrel with each other; but for your own sake, I advise you not to go. You can't help. However, do as you please.'

'Maybe I can't help, but I feel, especially at this moment – though that's another matter – I feel I can't be at peace.'

'Well, that I don't understand,' said Sergei Ivanovich. 'I understand only one thing,' he added, 'that it's a lesson in humility. I've begun to take a different and more lenient view of what's known as baseness since brother Nikolai became what he is . . . You know what he's done . . .'

'Ah, it's terrible, terrible!' Levin repeated.

Having obtained his brother's address from Sergei Ivanovich's footman, Levin wanted to go to him at once, but, on reflection, decided to postpone his visit till evening. First of all, to be at peace with himself, he had to resolve the matter that had brought him to Moscow. From his brother's Levin went to Oblonsky's office and, learning about the Shcherbatskys, went where he was told he could find Kitty.

IX

At four o'clock, feeling his heart pounding, Levin got out of a cab at the Zoological Garden and walked down the path towards the sledging hills and the skating rink, knowing for certain that he would find her there, because he had seen the Shcherbatskys' carriage at the entrance.

It was a clear frosty day. At the entrance stood rows of carriages, sleighs, cabbies, mounted police. Proper folk, their hats gleaming in the sun, swarmed by the gate and along the cleared paths, among little Russian cottages with fretwork eaves and ridges; the old curly-headed birches in the garden, all their branches hung with snow, seemed to be decked out in new festive garments.

He walked down the path towards the skating rink and said to himself: 'Mustn't be excited, must keep calm. What are you doing? What's the matter with you? Quiet, stupid!' He spoke to his heart. And the more he tried to calm himself, the more breathless he became. An acquaintance went by and called out to him, but Levin did not even recognize who it was. He came to the hills, where there was a clanking of chains towing sledges up and down, the clatter of descending sledges and the sound of merry voices. He walked on a few more steps, and before him opened the skating rink, and at once, among all the skaters, he recognized her.

He knew she was there by the joy and fear that overwhelmed his heart. She stood at the other end of the rink, talking to a lady. There seemed to be nothing very special in her dress, nor in her pose; but for Levin she was as easy to recognize in that crowd as a rose among nettles. Everything was lit up by her. She was the smile that brightened everything around. 'Can I really step down there on the ice and go over to her?' he thought. The place where she stood seemed to him unapproachably holy, and there was a moment when he almost went away – he was so filled with awe. Making an effort, he reasoned that all sorts of people were walking near her and that he might have come to skate there himself. He stepped down, trying not to look long at her, as if she were the sun, yet he saw her, like the sun, even without looking.

On that day of the week and at that hour of the day, people of the same circle, all acquaintances, gathered on the ice. Here there were expert skaters who showed off their art, and learners leaning on chairs,[15] moving timidly and clumsily, and young boys, and old people who skated for hygienic purposes. To Levin they all seemed chosen and lucky because they were there, close to her. It seemed that with perfect equanimity the skaters went ahead, came abreast of her, even talked to her, and enjoyed themselves quite independently of her, taking advantage of the excellent ice and good weather.

Nikolai Shcherbatsky, Kitty's cousin, in a short jacket and narrow trousers, was sitting on a bench with his skates on. Seeing Levin, he called out to him:

'Ah, the foremost Russian skater! Been here long? The ice is excellent, put your skates on!'

'I don't have any skates,' Levin replied, surprised at this boldness and casualness in her presence and not losing sight of her for a moment, though he was not looking at her. He felt the sun approach him. She was turning a corner, her slender feet at a blunt angle in their high boots, and with evident timidity was skating towards him. Desperately swinging his arms and crouching low, a boy in Russian dress was overtaking her. She skated not quite steadily; taking her hands out of a small muff hanging from a cord, she held them ready and, looking at Levin, whom she had recognized, smiled at him and at her own fear. When she finished the turn, she pushed herself off with a springy little foot and glided right up to Shcherbatsky. Holding on to him and smiling, she nodded to Levin. She was more beautiful than he had imagined her.

When he thought of her, he could vividly picture all of her to himself, especially the loveliness of that small fair head, with its expression of a child's brightness and kindness, set so easily on her shapely girlish shoulders. In this childlike expression of her face combined with the slender beauty of her figure lay her special loveliness, which he remembered well; but what was always striking in her, like something unexpected, was the look in her eyes – meek, calm and truthful – and especially her smile, which always transported Levin into a magic world where he felt softened and moved to tenderness, as he could remember himself being on rare days in his early childhood.

'Have you been here long?' she said, giving him her hand. 'Thank you,' she added, as he picked up the handkerchief that had fallen out of her muff.

'I? Not long, I came yesterday . . . today, I mean,' replied Levin, not quite understanding her question in his excitement. 'I was going to call on you,' he said and, remembering at once with what intention he was looking for her, he became embarrassed and blushed. 'I didn't know you skated, and skated so well.'

She looked at him attentively, as if wishing to understand the reason for his embarrassment.

'Your praise is to be valued. There's a tradition here of you being an excellent skater,' she said, flicking off with her small, black-gloved hand the needles of hoar-frost that had fallen on her muff.

'Yes, I used to be a passionate skater; I wanted to achieve perfection.'

'It seems you do everything passionately,' she said, smiling. 'I do so want to see you skate. Put on some skates and let's skate together.'

'Skate together! Can it be possible?' thought Levin, looking at her.

'I'll put them on at once,' he said.

And he went to put on some skates.

'You haven't been here for a long time, sir,' said the skating attendant as he supported his foot, tightening the screw on the heel. 'There have been no experts among the gentlemen since you left. Will that be all right?' he asked, tightening the strap.

'All right, all right, hurry up, please,' Levin replied, barely repressing the smile of happiness that involuntarily appeared on his face. 'Yes,' he thought, 'this is life, this is happiness! "Together", she said, "let's skate together". Shall I tell her now? But that's why I'm afraid to tell her, because I'm happy now, happy at least in hopes . . . And then? . . . But I must! I must! Away, weakness!'

Levin stood up, took his coat off and, taking a run on the rough ice near the shed, raced out on to the smooth ice and glided effortlessly, speeding up, slowing down, and directing his course as if by will alone. He approached her timidly, but again her smile set him at ease.

She gave him her hand, and they set off together, increasing their speed, and the faster they went, the tighter she held on to his arm.

'With you I'd learn quicker; for some reason I have confidence in you,' she said to him.

'And I have confidence in myself when you lean on my arm,' he said, but at once felt afraid of what he had said and blushed. Indeed, as soon as he uttered those words, her face lost all its gentleness, as if the sun had suddenly gone behind a cloud, and Levin recognized the familiar play of her face that indicated the effort of thought: a little wrinkle swelled on her smooth forehead.

'Has anything unpleasant happened to you? Though I have no right to ask,' he said quickly.

'Why? . . . No, nothing unpleasant has happened,' she answered coldly and added at once: 'Have you seen Mlle Linon?'

'Not yet.'

'Go over to her, she likes you so much.'

'What's this? I've upset her. Lord help me!' thought Levin, and he raced over to the old Frenchwoman with grey curls, who was sitting on a bench. Smiling and showing her false teeth, she greeted him like an old friend.

'So, we're getting bigger,' she said to him, glancing in Kitty's direction, 'and older. *Tiny bear* has grown up!' the Frenchwoman went on, laughing, and she reminded him of his joke about the three girls, whom he used to call the three bears from the English tale. 'Remember how you used to say it?'

He decidedly did not remember, but for ten years she had been laughing over this joke and enjoying it.

'Well, go, go and skate. Our Kitty's become a good skater, hasn't she?'

When Levin again raced up to Kitty, her face was no longer stern, the look in her eyes was as truthful and gentle as ever, but it seemed to Levin that her gentleness had a special, deliberately calm tone. And he felt sad. After talking about her old governess and her quirks, she asked him about his life.

'Is it really not boring for you in the country during the winter?' she said.

'No, it's not boring, I'm very busy,' he said, sensing that she was subjecting him to her calm tone, which he would be unable to get out of, just as had happened at the beginning of winter.

'Have you come for long?' Kitty asked him.

'I don't know,' he replied, not thinking of what he was saying. It occurred to him that if he yielded again to this tone of calm friendship, he would again leave without having decided anything, and he decided to rebel.

'Why don't you know?'

'I don't know. That depends on you,' he said and at once was horrified at his words.

She did not hear his words, or did not wish to hear, but seemed to stumble, tapped her foot twice, and hurriedly skated away from him. She skated over to Mlle Linon, said something to her, and went to the shed where the ladies took off their skates.

'My God, what have I done! Lord God! Help me, teach me,' Levin said, praying, and at the same time, feeling a need for strong movement, he speeded up, cutting outer and inner circles.

Just then one of the young men, the best of the new skaters, with skates on and a cigarette in his mouth, came out of the coffee room and, taking a short run, went down the steps on his skates, clattering and jumping. He flew down and, not even changing the free position of his arms, glided away over the ice.

'Ah, that's a new stunt!' said Levin, and immediately ran up to try it.

'Don't hurt yourself, it takes practice!' Nikolai Shcherbatsky called out to him.

Levin got up on the landing, took as much of a run as he could, and raced down, balancing himself with his arms in this unpractised movement. On the last step he caught on something, but, barely touching the ice with his hand, he made a strong movement, righted himself, and, laughing, skated on.

'A nice man, a dear man,' Kitty thought just then, coming out of the shed with Mlle Linon and looking at him with a smile of gentle tenderness, as at a beloved brother. 'And can it be I'm to blame, can it be I did something bad? Coquettishness, they say. I know it's not him I love; but even so, it's fun to be with him, and he's so nice. Only why did he say that? . . .' she thought.

When he saw Kitty leaving and her mother meeting her on the steps, Levin, flushed after such quick movement, stopped and considered. He took off his skates and caught up with the mother and daughter at the exit from the garden.

'Very glad to see you,' said the princess. 'We receive on Thursdays, as usual.'

'Today, then?'

'We shall be very glad to see you,' the princess said drily.

This dryness upset Kitty, and she could not hold back the wish to smooth over her mother's coldness. She turned her head and said with a smile:

'See you soon.'

At that moment Stepan Arkadyich, his hat cocked, his face and eyes shining, came into the garden with a merrily triumphant look. But, coming up to his mother-in-law, he answered her questions about Dolly's health with a mournful, guilty face. Having spoken softly and glumly with her, he straightened up and took Levin's arm.

'Well, then, shall we go?' he asked. 'I kept thinking about you, and I'm very, very glad you've come,' he said, looking into his eyes with a significant air.

'Let's go, let's go,' replied the happy Levin, still hearing the sound of the voice saying 'See you soon' and picturing the smile with which it had been said.

'To the Anglia or the Hermitage?'

'It makes no difference to me.'

'To the Anglia, then,' said Stepan Arkadyich, choosing the Anglia because he owed more in the Anglia than in the Hermitage. He therefore considered it not nice to avoid that hotel. 'Do you have a cab? Excellent, because I dismissed my carriage.'

The friends were silent all the way. Levin thought about the meaning of that change in Kitty's face, and first assured himself that there was hope, then fell into despair and saw clearly that his hope was mad, and yet he felt himself quite a different man, not like the one he had been before her smile and the words: 'See you soon'.

Stepan Arkadyich devised the dinner menu on the way.

'You do like turbot?' he said to Levin, as they drove up.

'What?' asked Levin. 'Turbot? Yes, I'm *terribly* fond of turbot.'

X

As Levin entered the hotel with Oblonsky, he could not help noticing a certain special expression, as if of restrained radiance, on the face and in the whole figure of Stepan Arkadyich. Oblonsky took off his coat and with his hat cocked passed into the restaurant, giving orders to the Tartars[16] in tailcoats who clung to him, napkins over their arms. Bowing right and left to the joyful greetings of acquaintances who turned up there, as everywhere, he went to the bar, followed his glass of vodka with a bit of fish, and said something to the painted Frenchwoman in ribbons, lace and ringlets who was sitting at the counter, so that even this Frenchwoman burst into genuine laughter. Levin did not drink vodka, if only because this Frenchwoman, who seemed to consist entirely of other people's hair, *poudre de riz* and *vinaigre de toilette*,* was offensive to him. He hastened to step away from her as from a dirty spot. His whole soul was overflowing with the remembrance of Kitty, and in his eyes shone a smile of triumph and happiness.

'This way, your highness, if you please, you will not be disturbed here, your highness,' said a particularly clinging, blanched old Tartar with broad hips over which the tails of his coat parted. 'Your hat please, your highness,' he said to Levin, courting the guest as a token of respect for Stepan Arkadyich.

Instantly spreading a fresh tablecloth on a round table, already covered with a tablecloth, under a bronze lamp-bracket, he drew out the velvet chairs and stood before Stepan Arkadyich, napkin and menu in hand, awaiting orders.

* Rice powder *and* cosmetic vinegar.

'If you prefer, your highness, a private room will presently be vacated: Prince Golitsyn and a lady. Fresh oysters have come in.'

'Ah, oysters!'

Stepan Arkadyich fell to thinking.

'Shouldn't we change our plan, Levin?' he said, his finger pausing on the menu. And his face showed serious perplexity. 'Are they good oysters? Mind yourself!'

'Flensburg, your highness, we have no Ostend oysters.'

'Flensburg, yes, but are they fresh?'

'Came in yesterday, sir.'

'In that case, shouldn't we begin with oysters, and then change the whole plan? Eh?'

'It makes no difference to me. I like shchi and kasha best,[17] but they won't have that here.'

'*Kasha à la Russe*, if you please?' the Tartar said, bending over Levin like a nanny over a child.

'No, joking aside, whatever you choose will be fine. I did some skating and I'm hungry. And don't think,' he added, noticing the displeased expression on Oblonsky's face, 'that I won't appreciate your choice. I'll enjoy a good meal.'

'To be sure! Say what you like, it is one of life's enjoyments,' said Stepan Arkadyich. 'Well, then, my good man, bring us two – no, make it three dozen oysters, vegetable soup . . .'

'*Printanière*,' the Tartar picked up. But Stepan Arkadyich evidently did not want to give him the pleasure of naming the dishes in French.

'Vegetable soup, you know? Then turbot with thick sauce, then . . . roast beef – but mind it's good. And why not capon – well, and some stewed fruit.'

The Tartar, remembering Stepan Arkadyich's manner of not naming dishes from the French menu, did not repeat after him, but gave himself the pleasure of repeating the entire order from the menu: '*Soupe printanière, turbot sauce Beaumarchais, poularde à l'estragon, macédoine de fruits* . . .' and at once, as if on springs, laid aside one bound menu, picked up another, the wine list, and offered it to Stepan Arkadyich.

'What shall we drink?'

'I'll have whatever you like, only not much, some champagne,' said Levin.

'What? To begin with? Though why not, in fact? Do you like the one with the white seal?'

'*Cachet blanc*,' the Tartar picked up.

'Well, so bring us that with the oysters, and then we'll see.'

'Right, sir. What table wine would you prefer?'

'Bring us the Nuits. No, better still the classic Chablis.'

'Right, sir. Would you prefer *your* cheese?'

'Yes, the Parmesan. Unless you'd prefer something else?'

'No, it makes no difference to me,' said Levin, unable to repress a smile.

And the Tartar, his tails flying over his broad hips, ran off and five minutes later rushed in again with a plate of opened oysters in their pearly shells and a bottle between his fingers.

Stepan Arkadyich crumpled the starched napkin, tucked it into his waistcoat, and, resting his arms comfortably, applied himself to the oysters.

'Not bad,' he said, peeling the sloshy oysters from their pearly shells with a little silver fork and swallowing them one after another. 'Not bad,' he repeated, raising his moist and shining eyes now to Levin, now to the Tartar.

Levin ate the oysters, though white bread and cheese would have been more to his liking. But he admired Oblonsky. Even the Tartar, drawing the cork and pouring the sparkling wine into shallow thin glasses, then straightening his white tie, kept glancing with a noticeable smile of pleasure at Stepan Arkadyich.

'You don't care much for oysters?' said Stepan Arkadyich, drinking off his glass. 'Or else you're preoccupied? Eh?'

He wanted Levin to be cheerful. Yet it was not that Levin was not cheerful: he felt constrained. With what he had in his soul, it was eerie and awkward for him to be in a tavern, next to private rooms where one dined in the company of ladies, amidst this hustle and bustle. These surroundings of bronze, mirrors, gas-lights, Tartars – it was all offensive to him. He was afraid to soil what was overflowing in his soul.

'Me? Yes, I'm preoccupied. But, besides, I feel constrained by all this,' he said. 'You can't imagine how wild all this is for a countryman like me – or take the nails of that gentleman I saw in your office . . .'

'Yes, I could see poor Grinevich's nails interested you greatly,' Stepan Arkadyich said, laughing.

'I can't help it,' replied Levin. 'Try getting inside me, look at it from a countryman's point of view. In the country we try to keep our hands in a condition that makes them convenient to work with; for that we cut our nails and sometimes roll up our sleeves. While here people purposely let their nails grow as long as they can, and stick on saucers instead of cuff-links, so that it would be impossible for them to do anything with their hands.'

Stepan Arkadyich smiled gaily.

'Yes, it's a sign that he has no need of crude labour. His mind works . . .'

'Maybe. But all the same it seems wild to me, just as it seems wild to me that while we countrymen try to eat our fill quickly, so that we can get on with what we have to do, you and I are trying our best not to get full for as long as possible, and for that we eat oysters . . .'

'Well, of course,' Stepan Arkadyich picked up. 'But that's the aim of civilization: to make everything an enjoyment.'

'Well, if that's its aim, I'd rather be wild.'

'You're wild as it is. All you Levins are wild.'[18]

Levin sighed. He remembered his brother Nikolai, and felt ashamed and pained. He frowned, but Oblonsky began talking about a subject that distracted him at once.

'So you're going to see our people tonight – the Shcherbatskys, I mean?' he said, pushing aside the empty scabrous shells and drawing the cheese towards him, his eyes shining significantly.

'Yes, I'll certainly go,' replied Levin. 'Though it seemed to me the princess invited me reluctantly.'

'Come, now! What nonsense! That's her manner . . . Well, my good man, serve the soup! . . . That's her manner, the *grande dame*,' said Stepan Arkadyich. 'I'll come, too, only I have to go to a choir rehearsal at Countess Banin's first. Well, what are you if not wild? How else explain the way you suddenly disappeared from Moscow? The Shcherbatskys kept asking me about you, as if I should know. I know only one thing: you always do what nobody else does.'

'Yes,' Levin said slowly and with agitation. 'You're right, I am wild. Only my wildness isn't in my leaving, but in my coming now. I've come now . . .'

'Oh, what a lucky man you are!' Stepan Arkadyich picked up, looking into Levin's eyes.

'Why?'

'Bold steeds I can tell by their something-or-other thighs, and young men in love by the look in their eyes,'[19] declaimed Stepan Arkadyich. 'You've got everything before you.'

'And with you it's already behind?'

'No, not behind, but you have the future and I the present – a bit of this, a bit of that.'

'And?'

'Not so good. Well, but I don't want to talk about myself, and besides it's impossible to explain everything,' said Stepan Arkadyich. 'So what have you come to Moscow for? . . . Hey, clear away!' he called to the Tartar.

'Can't you guess?' replied Levin, gazing steadily at Stepan Arkadyich, his eyes lit from within.

'I can, but I can't be the first to speak of it. By that alone you can see whether I've guessed right or not,' said Stepan Arkadyich, glancing at Levin with a subtle smile.

'Well, what do you say?' Levin said in a trembling voice and feeling all the muscles in his face trembling. 'How do you look at it?'

Stepan Arkadyich slowly drank his glass of Chablis, not taking his eyes off Levin.

'I?' said Stepan Arkadyich. 'I'd like nothing better than that – nothing. It's the best thing that could happen.'

'But you're not mistaken? You do know what we're talking about?' Levin said, fastening his eyes on his interlocutor. 'You think it's possible?'

'I think it's possible. Why should it be impossible?'

'No, you really think it's possible? No, tell me all you think! Well, and what if . . . what if I should be refused? . . . And I'm even certain . . .'

'Why do you think so?' Stepan Arkadyich said, smiling at his friend's excitement.

'It sometimes seems so to me. But that would be terrible both for me and for her.'

'Well, in any case, for a girl there's nothing terrible in it. Every girl is proud of being proposed to.'

'Yes, every girl, but not she.'

Stepan Arkadyich smiled. He knew so well this feeling of Levin's, knew that for him all the girls in the world were divided into two sorts: one sort was all the girls in the world except her, and these girls had all human weaknesses and were very ordinary girls; the other sort was her alone, with no weaknesses and higher than everything human.

'Wait, have some sauce,' he said, stopping Levin's hand, which was pushing the sauce away.

Levin obediently took some sauce, but would not let Stepan Arkadyich eat.

'No, wait, wait!' he said. 'Understand that for me it's a question of life and death. I've never talked about it with anyone. And I can't talk about it with anyone but you. Look, here we are, strangers in everything: different tastes, views, everything; but I know that you love me and understand me, and for that I love you terribly. So, for God's sake, be completely open.'

'I'm telling you what I think,' Stepan Arkadyich said, smiling. 'But I'll tell you more: my wife is a most remarkable woman . . .' Stepan Arkadyich sighed, remembering his relations with his wife, and after a moment's silence went on: 'She has a gift of foresight. She can see through people; but, more than that, she knows what's going to happen, especially along marital lines. She predicted, for instance, that Shakhovskoy would marry Brenteln. No one wanted to believe it, but it turned out to be so. And she's on your side.'

'Meaning what?'

'Meaning not just that she loves you – she says Kitty will certainly be your wife.'

At these words Levin's face suddenly lit up with a smile, of the sort that is close to tears of tenderness.

'She says that!' Levin cried. 'I always said she was a delight, your wife. Well, enough, enough talking about it,' he said, getting up from his seat.

'All right, only do sit down, the soup's coming.'

But Levin could not sit down. He paced the little cell of a room twice with his firm strides, blinked his eyes to keep the tears from showing, and only then sat down at the table again.

'Understand,' he said, 'that it isn't love. I've been in love, but this is not the same. This is not my feeling, but some external force taking possession of me. I left because I decided it could not be, you understand, like a happiness that doesn't exist on earth; but I have struggled with myself and I see that without it there is no life. And I must resolve . . .'

'Then why did you go away?'

'Ah, wait! Ah, so many thoughts! I have so much to ask! Listen. You can't imagine what you've done for me by what you've said. I'm so happy that I've even become mean; I've forgotten everything . . . I found out today that my brother Nikolai . . . you know, he's here . . . I forgot about him, too. It seems to me that he's happy, too. It's like madness. But there's one terrible thing . . . You're married, you know this feeling . . . The terrible thing is that we older men, who already have a past . . . not of love, but of sins . . . suddenly become close with a pure, innocent being; it's disgusting, and so you can't help feeling yourself unworthy.'

'Well, you don't have so many sins.'

'Ah, even so,' said Levin, 'even so, "with disgust reading over my life, I tremble and curse, and bitterly complain . . ."[20] Yes.'

'No help for it, that's how the world is made,' said Stepan Arkadyich.

'There's one consolation, as in that prayer I've always loved, that I may be forgiven not according to my deserts, but out of mercy. That's also the only way she can forgive me.'

XI

Levin finished his glass, and they were silent for a while.

'There's one more thing I must tell you. Do you know Vronsky?' Stepan Arkadyich asked Levin.

'No, I don't. Why do you ask?'

'Bring us another,' Stepan Arkadyich addressed the Tartar, who was filling their glasses and fussing around them precisely when he was not needed.

'Why should I know Vronsky?'

'You should know Vronsky because he's one of your rivals.'

'What is this Vronsky?' said Levin, and his face, from that expression of childlike rapture which Oblonsky had just been admiring, suddenly turned spiteful and unpleasant.

'Vronsky is one of the sons of Count Kirill Ivanovich Vronsky and one of the finest examples of the gilded youth of Petersburg. I got to know him in Tver, when I was in government service there and he came for the conscription. Terribly rich, handsome, big connections, an imperial aide-de-camp, and with all that – a very sweet, nice fellow. And more than just a nice fellow. As I've come to know him here, he's both cultivated and very intelligent. He's a man who will go far.'

Levin frowned and kept silent.

'Well, sir, he appeared here soon after you left and, as I understand, is head over heels in love with Kitty, and, you understand, her mother . . .'

'Excuse me, but I understand nothing,' said Levin, scowling gloomily. And he at once remembered his brother Nikolai and how mean he was to have forgotten about him.

'Wait, wait,' said Stepan Arkadyich, smiling and touching his hand. 'I've told you what I know, and I repeat that in this subtle and delicate matter, as far as I can surmise, the chances seem to be on your side.'

Levin leaned back in his chair, his face was pale.

'But I'd advise you to resolve the matter as soon as possible,' Oblonsky went on, filling Levin's glass.

'No thanks, I can't drink any more,' said Levin, pushing his glass away. 'I'll get drunk . . . Well, how are things with you?' he went on, obviously wishing to change the subject.

'One word more: in any event, I advise you to resolve the question quickly. I don't advise you to speak of it tonight,' said Stepan Arkadyich. 'Go tomorrow morning, classically, make a proposal, and God bless you . . .'

'Haven't you always wanted to come for some hunting with me? So, come in the spring,' said Levin.

He now repented with all his heart that he had begun this conversation with Stepan Arkadyich. His *special* feeling had been defiled by talk of rivalry with some Petersburg officer, by Stepan Arkadyich's suppositions and advice.

Stepan Arkadyich smiled. He understood what was going on in Levin's heart.

'I'll come sometime,' he said. 'Yes, brother, women – that's the pivot on which everything turns. And with me, too, things are bad, very bad. And all from women. Tell me frankly,' he went on, taking out a cigar and keeping one hand on his glass, 'give me your advice.'

'But what about?'

'Here's what. Suppose you're married, you love your wife, but you become infatuated with another woman . . .'

'Excuse me, but I decidedly do not understand how I . . . just as I don't understand how I could pass by a bakery, as full as I am now, and steal a sweet roll.'

Stepan Arkadyich's eyes shone more than usual.

'Why not? Sometimes a sweet roll is so fragrant that you can't help yourself.

'Himmlisch ist's, wenn ich bezwungen
Meine irdische Begier;
Aber doch wenn's nicht gelungen,
Hatt' ich auch recht hübsch Plaisir!'[21]

As he said this, Stepan Arkadyich smiled subtly. Levin also could not help smiling.

'No, joking aside,' Oblonsky went on. 'Understand, there's this woman, a dear, meek, loving being, poor, lonely, and who has sacrificed everything. Now, when the deed is already done – understand – how can I abandon her? Suppose we part, so as not to destroy my family; but how can I not pity her, not provide for her, not try to soften it?'

'Well, you must excuse me. You know, for me all women are divided into two sorts . . . that is, no . . . rather: there are women and there are . . . I've never seen and never will see any lovely fallen creatures,[22] and ones like that painted Frenchwoman at the counter, with all those ringlets – they're vermin for me, and all the fallen ones are the same.'

'And the one in the Gospels?'

'Oh, stop it! Christ would never have said those words, if he'd known how they would be misused.[23] Those are the only words people remember from all the Gospels. However, I'm not saying what I think but what I feel. I have a loathing for fallen women. You're afraid of spiders and I of those vermin. You surely have never studied spiders and don't know their ways: it's the same with me.'

'It's fine for you to talk like that; it's the same as that Dickensian gentleman who threw all difficult questions over his right shoulder with his left hand.[24] But the denial of a fact is not an answer. What's to be done, tell me, what's to be done? The wife is getting old, and you're full of life. Before you have time to turn round, you already feel that you can't love your wife as a lover, however much you may respect her. And here suddenly love comes along, and you're lost, lost!' Stepan Arkadyich said with glum despair.

Levin grinned.

'Yes, lost,' Oblonsky went on. 'But what to do?'

'Don't steal sweet rolls.'

Stepan Arkadyich laughed.

'Oh, you moralist! But understand, there are two women: one insists only on her rights, and these rights are your love, which you cannot give her; and the other sacrifices everything for you and demands nothing. What are you to do? How act? There's a terrible drama here.'

'If you want my opinion concerning that, I'll tell you that I don't think there is a drama here. And here's why. To my mind, love . . . the two loves that Plato, remember, defines in his *Symposium*,[25] these two loves serve as a touchstone for people. Some people understand only the one, others the other. And those who understand only non-platonic love shouldn't talk about drama. In such love there can be no drama. "Thank you kindly for the pleasure, with my respects" – there's the whole drama. And for platonic love there can be no drama, because in such love everything is clear and pure, because . . .'

Just then Levin remembered his own sins and the inner struggle he had gone through. And he added unexpectedly:

'However, it's possible you're right. Very possible . . . But I don't know, I really don't know.'

'So you see,' said Stepan Arkadyich, 'you're a very wholesome man. That is your virtue and your defect. You have a wholesome character, and you want all of life to be made up of wholesome phenomena, but that doesn't happen. So you despise the activity of public service because you want things always to correspond to their aim, and that doesn't happen. You also want the activity of the individual man always to have an aim, that love and family life always be one. And that doesn't happen. All the variety, all the charm, all the beauty of life are made up of light and shade.'

Levin sighed and gave no answer. He was thinking of his own things and not listening to Oblonsky.

And suddenly they both felt that, though they were friends, though they had dined together and drunk wine that should have brought them still closer, each was thinking only of his own things, and they had nothing to do with each other. Oblonsky had experienced more than once this extreme estrangement instead of closeness that may come after dinner, and knew what had to be done on such occasions.

'The bill!' he shouted and went to a neighbouring room, where he at once met an aide-de-camp of his acquaintance and got into conversation with him about some actress and the man who kept her. And at once, in his conversation with the aide-de-camp, Oblonsky felt relieved and rested after talking with Levin, who always caused him too much mental and spiritual strain.

When the Tartar came with a bill for twenty-six roubles and change, plus something for a tip, Levin, who at another time, as a countryman, would have been horrified at his share of fourteen roubles, now took no notice, paid and went home, in order to change and go to the Shcherbatskys', where his fate was to be decided.

XII

Princess Kitty Shcherbatsky was eighteen years old. She had come out for the first time this season. Her success in society was greater than that of her two older sisters and greater than the old princess had even expected. Not only were all the young men who danced at the Moscow balls in love with Kitty, but already in this first season two serious suitors had presented themselves: Levin and, immediately after his departure, Count Vronsky.

Levin's appearance at the beginning of winter, his frequent visits and obvious love for Kitty, gave rise to the first serious conversations between Kitty's parents about her future and to disputes between the prince and the princess. The prince was on Levin's side, said he could wish nothing better for Kitty. The princess, however, with that way women have of sidestepping the question, said that Kitty was too young, that Levin had in no way shown that his intentions were serious, that Kitty had no attachment to him, and other arguments; but what she did not say was that she expected a better match for her daughter, that she found Levin unsympathetic, and that she did not understand him. When Levin suddenly left, the princess was glad and said triumphantly to her husband: 'You see, I was right.' And when Vronsky appeared, she was gladder still, being confirmed in her opinion that Kitty was to make not merely a good but a brilliant match.

For the mother there could be no comparison between Vronsky and Levin. The mother disliked in Levin his strange and sharp judgements, his awkwardness in society (caused, as she supposed, by his pride), and his, in her opinion, wild sort of life in the country, busy with cattle and muzhiks; she also very much disliked that he, being in love with her daughter, had visited their house for a month and a half as if waiting for something, spying out, as if he were afraid it would be too great an honour if he should propose, and not understanding that if he visited a house where there was a marriageable daughter, he ought to explain himself. And suddenly, without explanation, he had left. 'It's a good thing he's so unattractive that Kitty didn't fall in love with him,' thought the mother.

Vronsky satisfied all the mother's desires. Very rich, intelligent, wellborn, a brilliant military-courtly career, and a charming man. One could wish for nothing better.

At the balls Vronsky openly courted Kitty, danced with her and visited the house, which meant there could be no doubt of the seriousness of his intentions. But, in spite of that, the mother spent the entire winter in terrible worry and agitation.

The old princess herself had married thirty years ago, with her aunt as matchmaker. The fiancé, of whom everything was known beforehand, came, saw the bride, and was seen himself; the matchmaking aunt found out and conveyed the impression made on both sides; the impression was good; then on the appointed day the expected proposal was made to her parents and accepted. Everything happened very easily and simply. At least it seemed so to the princess. But with her own daughters she had experienced how this seemingly ordinary thing – giving away her daughters in marriage – was neither easy nor simple. So many fears had been lived through, so many thoughts thought, so much money spent, so many confrontations with her husband when the older two, Darya and Natalya, were being married! Now, as the youngest one was brought out, she lived through the same fears, the same doubts, and had still greater quarrels with her husband than over the older ones. The old prince, like all fathers, was especially scrupulous about the honour and purity of his daughters; he was unreasonably jealous over them, and especially over Kitty, who was his favourite, and at every step made scenes with his wife for compromising their daughter. The princess had already grown used to it with the first two daughters, but now she felt that the prince's scrupulousness had more grounds. She saw that much had changed lately in the ways of society, that the duties of a mother had become even more difficult. She saw that girls of Kitty's age formed some sort of groups, attended some sort of courses,[26] freely associated with men, drove around by themselves, many no longer curtsied, and, worse still, they were all firmly convinced that choosing a husband was their own and not their parents' business. 'Nowadays girls are not given in marriage as they used to be,' all these young girls, and even all the old people, thought and said. But how a girl was to be given in marriage nowadays the princess could not find out from anyone. The French custom – for the parents to decide the children's fate – was not accepted, and was even condemned. The English custom – giving the girl complete freedom – was also not accepted and was impossible in Russian society.

The Russian custom of matchmaking was regarded as something outrageous and was laughed at by everyone, the princess included. But how a girl was to get married or be given in marriage, no one knew. Everyone with whom the princess happened to discuss it told her one and the same thing: 'Good gracious, in our day it's time to abandon this antiquity. It's young people who get married, not their parents; that means the young people should be left to arrange it as they can.' It was fine for those who had no daughters to talk that way; but the princess understood that in making friends her daughter might fall in love, and fall in love with someone who would not want to marry or who was not right as a husband. And however much the princess was assured that in our time young people themselves must settle their fate, she was unable to believe it, as she would have been unable to believe that in anyone's time the best toys for five-year-old children would be loaded pistols. And therefore the princess worried more about Kitty than she had about her older daughters.

Now her fear was that Vronsky would not limit himself to merely courting her daughter. She saw that Kitty was already in love with him, but she comforted herself with thinking that he was an honest man and therefore would not do such a thing. But along with that she knew how easy it was, with the present-day freedom of behaviour, to turn a girl's head and, generally, how lightly men looked upon this fault. The week before, Kitty had repeated to her mother her conversation with Vronsky during the mazurka. This conversation had partly set the princess at ease; but she could not be completely at ease. Vronsky had told Kitty that he and his brother were both so used to obeying their mother in all things that they would never dare undertake anything important without consulting her. 'And now I'm waiting, as for a special happiness, for my mother's arrival from Petersburg,' he had said.

Kitty had repeated it without giving any significance to these words. But her mother understood it differently. She knew that the old woman was expected any day, knew that she would be glad of her son's choice, and found it strange that he would not propose for fear of offending his mother; yet she so much wanted the marriage itself and, most of all, a rest from her anxieties, that she believed it. Painful as it was for the princess to see the unhappiness of her eldest daughter, Dolly, who was preparing to leave her husband, her worry over the deciding of her youngest daughter's fate consumed all her feelings. Levin's appearance that same day had added to her trouble. She was afraid that her daughter, who, as it seemed to her, had some feeling for Levin, might refuse

Vronsky out of unnecessary honesty, and generally that Levin's arrival might confuse and delay matters so near conclusion.

'What about him, did he arrive long ago?' the princess said of Levin as they returned home.

'Today, *maman*.'

'I only want to say . . .' the princess began, and by her seriously animated face Kitty could guess what the talk would be about.

'Mama,' she said, flushing and quickly turning to her, 'please, please, don't say anything about it. I know, I know it all.'

She wished for the same thing her mother did, but the motives for her mother's wish offended her.

'I only want to say that, having given hopes to one . . .'

'Mama, darling, for God's sake, don't speak. It's so awful to speak of it.'

'I won't, I won't,' her mother said, seeing the tears in her daughter's eyes, 'but one thing, my dearest: you promised me you wouldn't have any secrets from me. You won't?'

'Never, mama, none,' Kitty answered, blushing and looking straight into her mother's face. 'But I have nothing to tell now. I . . . I . . . even if I wanted to, I don't know what to say or how . . . I don't know . . .'

'No, she can't tell a lie with such eyes,' her mother thought, smiling at her excitement and happiness. The princess was smiling at how immense and significant everything now happening in her soul must seem to the poor dear.

XIII

Between dinner and the beginning of the evening, Kitty experienced a feeling similar to that of a young man before battle. Her heart was beating hard, and she could not fix her thoughts on anything.

She felt that this evening, when the two of them would meet for the first time, must be decisive in her fate. And she constantly pictured them to herself, first each of them separately, then the two together. When she thought about the past, she paused with pleasure, with tenderness, over memories of her relations with Levin. Memories of childhood and memories of Levin's friendship with her dead brother lent her relations with him a special poetic charm. His love for her, which she was certain of, was flattering and joyful for her. And it was easy for her to recall Levin. But in her recollections of Vronsky there was an admixture of something awkward, though he was in the highest degree a calm and worldly man. It was as if there were some falseness – not in him, he was very simple and nice – but in herself, while with Levin she felt completely simple and clear. But on the other hand, the moment she thought of a future with Vronsky, the most brilliantly happy prospects rose before her, while with Levin the future seemed cloudy.

Going upstairs to dress for the evening and glancing in the mirror, she noticed with joy that she was having one of her good days and was in full possession of all her powers, which she so needed for what lay ahead of her: she felt in herself an external calm and a free grace of movement.

At half-past seven, just as she came down to the drawing room, the footman announced: 'Konstantin Dmitrich Levin.' The princess was still in her room, and the prince also did not emerge. 'That's it,' thought Kitty, and the blood rushed to her heart. Glancing in the mirror, she was horrified at her paleness.

Now she knew for certain that he had come earlier in order to find her alone and to propose. And only here did the whole matter present itself to her for the first time with quite a different, new side. Only here did she realize that the question concerned not just herself – with whom would she be happy and whom she loved – but that at this very minute she must hurt a man she loved. And hurt him cruelly . . . Why? Because he, the dear man, loved her, was in love with her. But, no help for it, it must be so, it had to be so.

'My God, can it be that I must tell him myself?' she thought. 'Well, what shall I tell him? Can I possibly tell him I don't love him? It wouldn't be true. What shall I tell him, then? That I love another man? No, that's impossible. I'll go away, just go away.'

She was already close to the door when she heard his steps. 'No, it's dishonest! What am I afraid of? I haven't done anything wrong. What will be, will be! I'll tell the truth. I can't feel awkward with him. Here he is,' she said to herself, seeing his whole strong and timid figure, with his shining eyes directed at her. She looked straight into his face, as if begging him for mercy, and gave him her hand.

'I've come at the wrong time, it seems – too early,' he said, glancing around the empty drawing room. When he saw that his expectations had been fulfilled, that nothing prevented him from speaking out, his face darkened.

'Oh, no,' said Kitty, and she sat down at the table.

'But this is just what I wanted, to find you alone,' he began, not sitting down and not looking at her, so as not to lose courage.

'Mama will come out presently. Yesterday she got very tired. Yesterday . . .'

She spoke, not knowing what her lips were saying, and not taking her pleading and caressing eyes off him.

He glanced at her; she blushed and fell silent.

'I told you I didn't know whether I had come for long . . . that it depended on you . . .'

She hung her head lower and lower, not knowing how she would reply to what was coming.

'That it depended on you,' he repeated. 'I wanted to say . . . I wanted to say . . . I came for this . . . that . . . to be my wife!' he said, hardly aware of what he was saying; but, feeling that the most dreadful part had been said, he stopped and looked at her.

She was breathing heavily, not looking at him. She was in ecstasy. Her soul overflowed with happiness. She had never imagined that the voicing of his love would make such a strong impression on her. But this lasted only a moment. She remembered Vronsky. Raising her light, truthful eyes to Levin and seeing his desperate face, she hastily replied:

'It cannot be . . . forgive me . . .'

How close she had been to him just a minute ago, how important for his life! And now how alien and distant from him she had become!

'It couldn't have been otherwise,' he said, not looking at her.

He bowed and was about to leave.

XIV

But just then the princess came out. Horror showed on her face when she saw them alone and looking upset. Levin bowed to her and said nothing. Kitty was silent, not raising her eyes. 'Thank God, she's refused him,' thought the mother, and her face brightened with the usual smile with which she met her guests on Thursdays. She sat down and began asking Levin about his life in the country. He sat down again, awaiting the arrival of other guests so that he could leave inconspicuously.

Five minutes later Kitty's friend, Countess Nordston, who had been married the previous winter, came in.

She was a dry, yellow woman, sickly and nervous, with black shining eyes. She loved Kitty, and her love expressed itself, as a married woman's love for young girls always does, in her wish to get Kitty married according to her own ideal of happiness, and therefore she wished her to marry Vronsky. Levin, whom she had met often in their house at the beginning of winter, she had always found disagreeable. Her constant and favourite occupation when she met him consisted in making fun of him.

'I love it when he looks down at me from the height of his grandeur: either he breaks off his clever conversation with me because I'm stupid, or he condescends to me. Condescends! I just love it! I'm very glad he can't stand me,' she said of him.

She was right, because Levin indeed could not stand her and had contempt for what she took pride in and counted as a merit – her nervousness, her refined contempt and disregard for all that was coarse and common.

Between Countess Nordston and Levin there had been established those relations, not infrequent in society, in which two persons, while ostensibly remaining on friendly terms, are contemptuous of each other to such a degree that they cannot even treat each other seriously and cannot even insult one another.

Countess Nordston fell upon Levin at once.

'Ah! Konstantin Dmitrich! You've come back to our depraved Babylon,' she said, giving him her tiny yellow hand and recalling the words he had spoken once at the beginning of winter, that Moscow was Babylon. 'Has Babylon become better, or have you become worse?' she added, glancing at Kitty with a mocking smile.

'I'm very flattered, Countess, that you remember my words so well,' answered Levin, who had managed to recover and by force of habit entered at once into his banteringly hostile attitude towards Countess Nordston. 'They must have had a very strong effect on you.'

'Oh, surely! I write it all down. Well, Kitty, so you went skating again?'

And she began talking with Kitty. Awkward as it was for Levin to leave now, it was still easier for him to commit that awkwardness than to stay all evening and see Kitty, who glanced at him now and then yet avoided his eyes. He was about to get up, but the princess, noticing that he was silent, addressed him: 'Have you come to Moscow for long? Though it seems you're involved with the zemstvo and cannot be long away.'

'No, Princess, I'm no longer involved with the zemstvo,' he said. 'I've come for a few days.'

'Something peculiar has happened to him,' thought Countess Nordston, studying his stern, serious face, 'something keeps him from getting into his tirades. But I'll draw him out. I'm terribly fond of making a fool of him in front of Kitty, and so I will.'

'Konstantin Dmitrich,' she said to him, 'explain to me, please, what it means – you know all about this – that on our Kaluga estate the muzhiks and their women drank up all they had and now don't pay us anything? What does it mean? You praise muzhiks all the time.'

Just then another lady came in, and Levin rose.

'Excuse me, Countess, but I really know nothing about it and can tell you nothing,' he said, and turned to look at the military man who came in after the lady.

'That must be Vronsky,' thought Levin and, to make sure of it, he glanced at Kitty. She had already had time to glance at Vronsky and now looked at Levin. And by that one glance of her involuntarily brightened eyes Levin understood that she loved this man, understood it as surely as if she had told it to him in words. But what sort of man was he?

Now – for good or ill – Levin could not help staying: he had to find out what sort of man it was that she loved.

There are people who, on meeting a successful rival in whatever it may be, are ready at once to turn their eyes from everything good in him and to see only the bad; then there are people who, on the contrary, want most of all to find the qualities in this successful rival that enabled him to defeat them, and with aching hearts seek only the good. Levin was one of those people. But it was not hard for him to find what was good and attractive in Vronsky. It struck his eyes at once. Vronsky was a sturdily built, dark-haired man of medium height, with a good-naturedly handsome, extremely calm and firm face. In his face and figure, from his closely cropped dark hair and freshly shaven chin to his wide-cut, brand-new uniform, everything was simple and at the same time elegant. Making way for the lady who was entering, Vronsky went up to the princess and then to Kitty.

As he went up to her, his beautiful eyes began to glitter with a special tenderness, and with a barely noticeable happy and modestly triumphant smile (as it seemed to Levin), bending over her respectfully and carefully, he gave her his small but broad hand.

After greeting and saying a few words to everyone, he sat down, without a glance at Levin, who did not take his eyes off him.

'Allow me to introduce you,' said the princess, indicating Levin. 'Konstantin Dmitrich Levin. Count Alexei Kirillovich Vronsky.'

Vronsky rose and, looking amiably into Levin's eyes, shook hands with him.

'I believe I was to have dined with you this winter,' he said, smiling his simple and frank smile, 'but you unexpectedly left for the country.'

'Konstantin Dmitrich despises and hates the city and us city-dwellers,' said Countess Nordston.

'My words must have a strong effect on you, since you remember them so well,' said Levin and, realizing that he had already said that earlier, he turned red.

Vronsky looked at Levin and Countess Nordston and smiled.

'And do you live in the country all year round?' he asked. 'I suppose the winters are boring?'

'No, not if you're busy and are not bored with your own self,' Levin replied curtly.

'I like the country,' said Vronsky, noticing Levin's tone and pretending he had not noticed it.

'But I do hope, Count, that you would not agree to live in the country all year round,' said Countess Nordston.

'I don't know, I've never tried it. I once experienced a strange feeling,' he went on. 'Nowhere have I ever missed the country, the Russian country, with its bast shoes and muzhiks, so much as when I spent a winter with my mother in Nice. Nice is boring in itself, you know. Naples and Sorrento are also good only for a short time. And it is there that one remembers Russia especially vividly, and precisely the country. It's as if they . . .'

He spoke, addressing both Kitty and Levin and shifting his calm and amiable glance from one to the other – saying, evidently, whatever came into his head.

Noticing that Countess Nordston wanted to say something, he stopped without finishing what he had begun and listened attentively to her.

The conversation never flagged for a minute, so that the old princess, who, in case a topic was lacking, always kept two heavy cannon in reserve – classical versus modern education, and general military conscription – did not have to move them up, and Countess Nordston had no chance to tease Levin.

Levin wanted but was unable to enter into the general conversation; saying 'Go now' to himself every minute, he did not leave, but kept waiting for something.

The conversation moved on to table-turning and spirits,[27] and Countess Nordston, who believed in spiritualism, began telling about the wonders she had seen.

'Ah, Countess, you must take me, for God's sake, take me to them! I've never seen anything extraordinary, though I keep looking everywhere,' Vronsky said, smiling.

'Very well, next Saturday,' Countess Nordston replied. 'But you, Konstantin Dmitrich, do you believe in it?' she asked Levin.

'Why do you ask me? You know what I'm going to say.'

'But I want to hear your opinion.'

'My opinion,' answered Levin, 'is simply that these turning tables prove that our so-called educated society is no higher than the muzhiks. They believe in the evil eye, and wicked spells, and love potions, while we . . .'

'So, then, you don't believe in it?'

'I cannot believe, Countess.'

'But if I saw it myself?'

'Peasant women also tell of seeing household goblins themselves.'

'So you think I'm not telling the truth?'

And she laughed mirthlessly.

'No, Masha, Konstantin Dmitrich says he cannot believe in it,' said Kitty, blushing for Levin, and Levin understood it and, still more annoyed, was about to reply, but Vronsky, with his frank, cheerful smile, at once came to the rescue of the conversation, which was threatening to turn unpleasant.

'You don't admit any possibility at all?' he asked. 'Why not? We admit the existence of electricity, which we know nothing about; why can't there be a new force, still unknown to us, which . . .'

'When electricity was found,' Levin quickly interrupted, 'it was merely the discovery of a phenomenon, and it was not known where it came from or what it could do, and centuries passed before people thought of using it. The spiritualists, on the contrary, began by saying that tables write to them and spirits come to them, and only afterwards started saying it was an unknown force.'

Vronsky listened attentively to Levin, as he always listened, evidently interested in his words.

'Yes, but the spiritualists say: now we don't know what this force is, but the force exists, and these are the conditions under which it acts. Let the scientists find out what constitutes this force. No, I don't see why it can't be a new force, if it . . .'

'Because,' Levin interrupted again, 'with electricity, each time you rub resin against wool, a certain phenomenon manifests itself, while here it's not each time, and therefore it's not a natural phenomenon.'

Probably feeling that the conversation was acquiring too serious a character for a drawing room, Vronsky did not object, but, trying to change the subject, smiled cheerfully and turned to the ladies.

'Let's try it now, Countess,' he began. But Levin wanted to finish saying what he thought.

'I think,' he continued, 'that this attempt by the spiritualists to explain their wonders by some new force is a most unfortunate one. They speak directly about spiritual force and want to subject it to material experiment.'

They were all waiting for him to finish, and he felt it.

'And I think that you'd make an excellent medium,' said Countess Nordston, 'there's something ecstatic in you.'

Levin opened his mouth, wanted to say something, turned red, and said nothing.

'Let's try the tables now, Princess, if you please,' said Vronsky. 'With your permission, Madame?' He turned to the old princess.

And Vronsky stood up, his eyes searching for a table.

Kitty got up from her little table and, as she passed by, her eyes met Levin's. She pitied him with all her heart, the more so as she was the cause of his unhappiness. 'If I can be forgiven, forgive me,' her eyes said, 'I'm so happy.'

'I hate everybody, including you and myself,' his eyes answered, and he picked up his hat. But he was not fated to leave yet. They were just settling around the little table, and Levin was on the point of leaving, when the old prince came in and, after greeting the ladies, turned to him.

'Ah!' he began joyfully. 'Been here long? And I didn't know you were here. Very glad to see you, sir.'

The old prince sometimes addressed Levin formally, sometimes informally. He embraced Levin, talking to him and not noticing Vronsky, who rose and waited calmly for the prince to turn to him.

Kitty sensed that, after what had happened, her father's cordiality would be oppressive for Levin. She also saw how coldly her father finally responded to Vronsky's bow and how Vronsky looked at her father with friendly perplexity, trying but failing to understand how and why it was possible to have an unfriendly attitude towards him, and she blushed.

'Prince, give us Konstantin Dmitrich,' said Countess Nordston. 'We want to make an experiment.'

'What experiment? Table-turning? Well, excuse me, ladies and gentlemen, but I think it's more fun to play the ring game,' said the old prince, looking at Vronsky and guessing that he had started it. 'The ring game still has some sense to it.'

Vronsky gave the prince a surprised look with his firm eyes and, smiling slightly, immediately began talking with Countess Nordston about a big ball that was to take place in a week.

'I hope you'll be there?' he turned to Kitty.

As soon as the old prince turned away from him, Levin went out unobserved, and the last impression he took away with him from that evening was the smiling, happy face of Kitty answering Vronsky's question about the ball.

XV

When the evening was over, Kitty told her mother about her conversation with Levin, and, despite all the pity she felt for Levin, she was glad at the thought that she had been *proposed to*. She had no doubt that she had acted rightly. But when she went to bed, she could not fall asleep for a long time. One impression pursued her relentlessly. It was Levin's face with its scowling eyebrows and his kind eyes looking out from under them with gloomy sullenness, as he stood listening to her father and glancing at her and Vronsky. And she felt such pity for him that tears came to her eyes. But she immediately thought of the one she had exchanged him for. She vividly recalled that manly, firm face, the noble calm and the kindness towards all that shone in him; she recalled the love for her of the one she loved, and again she felt joy in her soul, and with a smile of happiness she lay back on the pillow. 'It's a pity, a pity, but what to do? It's not my fault,' she kept saying to herself; yet her inner voice was saying something else. Whether she repented of having led Levin on, or of having rejected him, she did not know. But her happiness was poisoned by doubts. 'Lord have mercy, Lord have mercy, Lord have mercy!' she kept saying to herself till she fell asleep.

Just then, downstairs in the prince's small study, one of those so often repeated scenes was taking place between the parents over their favourite daughter.

'What? Here's what!' the prince shouted, waving his arms and at once closing his squirrel-skin dressing gown. 'That you have no pride, no dignity, that you disgrace and ruin your daughter with this mean, foolish matchmaking!'

'But, please, for the love of God, Prince, what have I done?' the princess said, almost in tears.

Happy and pleased after talking with her daughter, she had come to say good night to the prince as usual, and though she had not intended to tell him about Levin's proposal and Kitty's refusal, she had hinted to her husband that she thought the matter with Vronsky quite concluded, that it would be decided as soon as his mother came. And here, at these words, the prince had suddenly flared up and begun shouting unseemly things.

'What have you done? Here's what: in the first place, you lure a suitor, and all Moscow is going to be talking, and with reason. If you give soirées, invite everybody, and not some chosen little suitors. Invite all those *twits*' (so the prince called the young men of Moscow), 'invite a pianist and let them dance, but not like tonight – suitors and matchmaking. It's loathsome, loathsome to look at, and you've succeeded, you've turned the silly girl's head. Levin is a thousand times the better man. And this little fop from Petersburg – they're made by machine, they're all the same sort, and all trash. Even if he was a prince of the blood, my daughter doesn't need anybody!'

'But what have I done?'

'Here's what . . .' the prince cried out wrathfully.

'I know that if we listen to you,' the princess interrupted, 'we'll never get our daughter married. In that case, we'll have to move to the country.'

'Better to move.'

'Wait. Am I pursuing anyone? Not at all. But a young man, and a very nice one, has fallen in love, and it seems that she . . .'

'Yes, to you it seems! And what if she really falls in love, and he has as much thought of marrying as I do? . . . Oh! I can't stand the sight of it! . . . "Ah, spiritualism, ah, Nice, ah, the next ball . . ." ' And the prince, imagining he was imitating his wife, curtsied at each word. 'And what if we arrange for Katenka's unhappiness, what if she really takes it into her head . . .'

'But why do you think that?'

'I don't think, I know. It's we who have eyes for that, not women. I see a man who has serious intentions, that's Levin; and I see a popinjay like this whippersnapper, who is only amusing himself.'

'Well, once you've taken it into your head . . .'

'And you'll remember, but it will be too late, just as with Dashenka.'

'Well, all right, all right, let's not talk about it.' The princess stopped him, remembering about the unfortunate Dolly.

'Excellent. Good-bye.'

And having crossed each other and kissed each other, yet sensing that each remained of the same opinion, the spouses parted.

The princess was firmly convinced at first that that evening had decided Kitty's fate and there could be no doubt of Vronsky's intentions; but her husband's words troubled her. And, returning to her room, in terror before the unknown future, just like Kitty, she repeated several times in her heart: 'Lord have mercy, Lord have mercy, Lord have mercy!'

XVI

Vronsky had never known family life. His mother in her youth had been a brilliant society woman who, during her marriage and especially after it, had had many love affairs, known to all the world. He barely remembered his father and had been brought up in the Corps of Pages.[28]

Leaving school as a very young and brilliant officer, he immediately fell in with the ways of rich Petersburg military men. Although he occasionally went into Petersburg society, all his amorous interests lay outside it.

In Moscow, after the luxurious and coarse life of Petersburg, he had experienced for the first time the charm of intimacy with a sweet, innocent society girl who had fallen in love with him. It did not even occur to him that there could be anything bad in his relations with Kitty. At balls he danced mostly with her; he visited their house. He said to her the things that are usually said in society, all sorts of nonsense, but nonsense which he unwittingly endowed with a special meaning for her. Though he said nothing to her that he could not have said before everybody, he felt that she was growing increasingly dependent on him, and the more he felt it, the more pleasant it was for him, and his feeling for her grew more tender. He did not know that his behaviour towards Kitty had a specific name, that it was the luring of a young lady without the intention of marriage, and that this luring was one of the bad actions common among brilliant young men such as himself. It seemed to him that he was the first to discover this pleasure, and he enjoyed his discovery.

If he could have heard what her parents said that evening, if he could have taken the family's point of view and learned that Kitty would be unhappy if he did not marry her, he would have been very surprised and would not have believed it. He could not have believed that something which gave such great and good pleasure to him, and above all to her, could be bad. Still less could he have believed that he was obliged to marry her.

Marriage had never presented itself as a possibility to him. He not only did not like family life, but pictured the family, and especially a husband, according to the general view of the bachelor world in which he lived, as something alien, hostile and, above all, ridiculous. But though Vronsky had no suspicion of what the parents said, he felt as he left the Shcherbatskys' that evening that the secret spiritual bond existing between him and Kitty had established itself so firmly that something had to be done. But what could and should be done, he was unable to imagine.

'The charm of it is,' he thought, going home from the Shcherbatskys' and bringing with him, as always, a pleasant feeling of purity and freshness, partly because he had not smoked all evening, and together with it a new feeling of tenderness at her love for him, 'the charm of it is that nothing was said either by me or by her, yet we understood each other so well in that invisible conversation of eyes and intonations, that tonight she told me more clearly than ever that she loves me. And so sweetly, simply and, above all, trustfully! I feel better and purer myself. I feel that I have a heart and that there is much good in me. Those sweet, loving eyes! When she said: "and very much" . . .

'Well, what then? Well, then nothing. It's good for me, and it's good for her.' And he began thinking about where to finish the evening.

He checked in his imagination the places he might go to. 'The club? A game of bezique,[29] champagne with Ignatov? No, not there. The Château des Fleurs?[30] I'll find Oblonsky there, French songs, the cancan. No, I'm sick of it. That's precisely what I love the Shcherbatskys' for, that I become better there myself. I'll go home.' He went straight to his rooms at the Dussot, ordered supper served, after which he got undressed and, the moment his head touched the pillow, fell into a sound and peaceful sleep, as always.

XVII

The next day at eleven o'clock in the morning Vronsky drove to the Petersburg railway station to meet his mother, and the first person he ran into on the steps of the main stairway was Oblonsky, who was expecting his sister on the same train.

'Ah! Your highness!' cried Oblonsky. 'Here for someone?'

'My mother,' Vronsky replied, shaking his hand and smiling, as did everyone who met Oblonsky, and they went up the stairway together. 'She arrives today from Petersburg.'

'And I waited for you till two o'clock. Where did you go from the Shcherbatskys'?'

'Home,' replied Vronsky. 'I confess, I felt so pleasant last night after the Shcherbatskys' that I didn't want to go anywhere.'

'Bold steeds I can tell by their something-or-other thighs, and young men in love by the look in their eyes,' declaimed Stepan Arkadyich, exactly as he had done to Levin.

Vronsky smiled with a look that said he did not deny it, but at once changed the subject.

'And whom are you meeting?' he asked.

'I? A pretty woman,' said Oblonsky.

'Really!'

'*Honi soit qui mal y pense!*[31] My sister Anna.'

'Ah, you mean Karenina?' said Vronsky.

'I suppose you know her?'

'I think I do. Or else, no . . . I really can't remember,' Vronsky replied absentmindedly, vaguely picturing to himself at the name Karenina something standoffish and dull.

'But surely you know Alexei Alexandrovich, my famous brother-in-law. The whole world knows him.'

'That is, I know him by sight and by reputation. I know he's intelligent, educated, something to do with religion . . . But you know, it's not in my . . . *not in my line*,' Vronsky added in English.

'Yes, he's a very remarkable man – a bit conservative, but a nice man,' observed Stepan Arkadyich, 'a nice man.'

'Well, so much the better for him,' said Vronsky, smiling. 'Ah, you're here.' He turned to his mother's tall old footman, who was standing by the door. 'Come inside.'

Vronsky had recently felt himself attached to Stepan Arkadyich, apart from his general agreeableness for everyone, by the fact that in his imagination he was connected with Kitty.

'Well, then, shall we have a dinner for the *diva* on Sunday?' he said to him, smiling and taking his arm.

'Absolutely. I'll take up a collection. Ah, did you meet my friend Levin last night?' asked Stepan Arkadyich.

'Of course. But he left very early.'

'He's a nice fellow,' Oblonsky went on. 'Isn't he?'

'I don't know why it is,' answered Vronsky, 'but all Muscovites, naturally excluding those I'm talking with,' he added jokingly, 'have something edgy about them. They keep rearing up for some reason, getting angry, as if they want to make you feel something . . .'

'There is that, it's true, there is . . .' Stepan Arkadyich said, laughing merrily.

'Soon now?' Vronsky asked an attendant.

'The train's pulling in,' the attendant answered.

The approach of the train was made more and more evident by the preparatory movements in the station, the running of attendants, the appearance of gendarmes and porters, and the arrival of those coming to meet the train. Through the frosty steam, workers in sheepskin jackets and soft felt boots could be seen crossing the curved tracks. The whistle of the engine could be heard down the line, and the movement of something heavy.

'No,' said Stepan Arkadyich, who wanted very much to tell Vronsky about Levin's intentions regarding Kitty. 'No, you're wrong in your appraisal of my Levin. He's a very nervous man and can be unpleasant, true, but sometimes he can be very nice. He has such an honest, truthful nature, and a heart of gold. But last night there were special reasons,' Stepan Arkadyich went on with a meaningful smile, forgetting completely the sincere sympathy he had felt for his friend yesterday and now feeling the same way for Vronsky. 'Yes, there was a reason why he might have been either especially happy, or especially unhappy.'

Vronsky stopped and asked directly:

'Meaning what? Or did he propose to your *belle-soeur** last night? . . .'

'Maybe,' said Stepan Arkadyich. 'It seemed to me there was something of the sort yesterday. Yes, if he left early and was also out of sorts, then that's it . . . He's been in love for so long, and I'm very sorry for him.'

'Really! . . . I think, however, that she can count on a better match,' said Vronsky, and, squaring his shoulders, he resumed his pacing. 'However, I don't know him,' he added. 'Yes, it's a painful situation! That's why most of us prefer the company of Claras. There failure only proves that you didn't have enough money, while here – your dignity is at stake. Anyhow, the train's come.'

Indeed, the engine was already whistling in the distance. A few minutes later the platform began to tremble, and, puffing steam that was beaten down by the frost, the engine rolled past, with the coupling rod of the middle wheel slowly and rhythmically turning and straightening, and a muffled-up, frost-grizzled engineer bowing; and, after the tender, slowing down and shaking the platform still more, the luggage van began to pass, with a squealing dog in it; finally came the passenger carriages, shuddering to a stop.

A dashing conductor jumped off, blowing his whistle, and after him the impatient passengers began to step down one by one: an officer of the guards, keeping himself straight and looking sternly around; a fidgety little merchant with a bag, smiling merrily; a muzhik with a sack over his shoulder.

Vronsky, standing beside Oblonsky, looked over the carriages and the people getting off and forgot his mother entirely. What he had just learned about Kitty had made him excited and happy. His chest involuntarily swelled and his eyes shone. He felt himself the victor.

'Countess Vronsky is in this compartment,' said the dashing conductor, coming up to Vronsky.

The conductor's words woke him up and forced him to remember his

* Sister-in-law.

mother and the forthcoming meeting with her. In his soul he did not respect her and, without being aware of it, did not love her, though by the notions of the circle in which he lived, by his upbringing, he could not imagine to himself any other relation to his mother than one obedient and deferential in the highest degree, and the more outwardly obedient and deferential he was, the less he respected and loved her in his soul.

XVIII

Vronsky followed the conductor to the carriage and at the door to the compartment stopped to allow a lady to leave. With the habitual flair of a worldly man, Vronsky determined from one glance at this lady's appearance that she belonged to high society. He excused himself and was about to enter the carriage, but felt a need to glance at her once more – not because she was very beautiful, not because of the elegance and modest grace that could be seen in her whole figure, but because there was something especially gentle and tender in the expression of her sweet-looking face as she stepped past him. As he looked back, she also turned her head. Her shining grey eyes, which seemed dark because of their thick lashes, rested amiably and attentively on his face, as if she recognized him, and at once wandered over the approaching crowd as though looking for someone. In that brief glance Vronsky had time to notice the restrained animation that played over her face and fluttered between her shining eyes and the barely noticeable smile that curved her red lips. It was as if a surplus of something so overflowed her being that it expressed itself beyond her will, now in the brightness of her glance, now in her smile. She deliberately extinguished the light in her eyes, but it shone against her will in a barely noticeable smile.

Vronsky entered the carriage. His mother, a dry old woman with dark eyes and curled hair, narrowed her eyes, peering at her son, and smiled slightly with her thin lips. Getting up from the seat and handing the maid her little bag, she offered her small, dry hand to her son and, raising his head from her hand, kissed him on the face.

'You got my telegram? Are you well? Thank God.'

'Did you have a good trip?' her son asked, sitting down beside her and involuntarily listening to a woman's voice outside the door. He knew it was the voice of the lady he had met at the entrance.

'I still don't agree with you,' the lady's voice said.

'A Petersburg point of view, madam.'

'Not Petersburg, merely a woman's,' she answered.

'Well, allow me to kiss your hand.'

'Good-bye, Ivan Petrovich. Do see if my brother is here, and send him to me,' the lady said just by the door, and entered the compartment again.

'Have you found your brother?' asked Countess Vronsky, addressing the lady.

Vronsky remembered now that this was Mme Karenina.

'Your brother is here,' he said, getting up. 'Excuse me, I didn't recognize you, and then our acquaintance was so brief,' Vronsky said, bowing, 'that you surely don't remember me.'

'Oh, no, I would have recognized you, because your mother and I seem to have spent the whole trip talking only of you,' she said, finally allowing her animation, which was begging to be let out, to show itself in a smile. 'And my brother still isn't here.'

'Call him, Alyosha,' said the old countess.

Vronsky went out on the platform and shouted:

'Oblonsky! This way!'

Mme Karenina did not wait for her brother, but, on seeing him, got out of the carriage with a light, resolute step. And as soon as her brother came up to her, she threw her left arm around his neck in a movement that surprised Vronsky by its resoluteness and grace, quickly drew him to her, and gave him a hearty kiss. Vronsky, not taking his eyes away, looked at her and smiled, himself not knowing at what. But remembering that his mother was waiting for him, he again got into the carriage.

'Very sweet, isn't she?' the countess said of Mme Karenina. 'Her husband put her with me, and I was very glad. We talked all the way. Well, and they say that you . . . *vous filez le parfait amour. Tant mieux, mon cher, tant mieux.*'*

'I don't know what you're hinting at, *maman*,' her son replied coolly. 'Let's go, then, *maman*.'

Mme Karenina came back into the carriage to take leave of the countess.

'Well, Countess, so you've met your son and I my brother,' she said gaily. 'And all my stories are exhausted; there was nothing more to tell.'

* You are living love's perfect dream. So much the better, my dear, so much the better.

'Ah, no, my dear,' said the countess, taking her hand, 'I could go around the world with you and not be bored. You're one of those sweet women with whom it's pleasant both to talk and to be silent. And please don't keep thinking about your son: it's impossible for you never to be separated.'

Mme Karenina stood motionless, holding herself very straight, and her eyes were smiling.

'Anna Arkadyevna,' the countess said, explaining to her son, 'has a little boy of about eight, I think, and has never been separated from him, and she keeps suffering about having left him.'

'Yes, the countess and I spent the whole time talking – I about my son, she about hers,' said Mme Karenina, and again a smile lit up her face, a tender smile addressed to him.

'You were probably very bored by it,' he said, catching at once, in mid-air, this ball of coquetry that she had thrown to him. But she evidently did not want to continue the conversation in that tone and turned to the old countess:

'Thank you very much. I didn't even notice how I spent the day yesterday. Good-bye, Countess.'

'Good-bye, my friend,' the countess replied. 'Let me kiss your pretty little face. I'll tell you simply, directly, like an old woman, that I've come to love you.'

Trite as the phrase was, Mme Karenina evidently believed it with all her heart and was glad. She blushed, bent forward slightly, offering her face to the countess's lips, straightened up again, and with the same smile wavering between her lips and eyes, gave her hand to Vronsky. He pressed the small hand offered him and was glad, as of something special, of her strong and boldly energetic handshake. She went out with a quick step, which carried her rather full body with such strange lightness.

'Very sweet,' said the old woman.

Her son was thinking the same. He followed her with his eyes until her graceful figure disappeared, and the smile stayed on his face. Through the window he saw her go up to her brother, put her hand on his arm, and begin animatedly telling him something that obviously had nothing to do with him, Vronsky, and he found that vexing.

'Well, so, *maman*, are you quite well?' he repeated, turning to his mother.

'Everything's fine, excellent. Alexandre was very sweet. And Marie has become very pretty. She's very interesting.'

Again she began to talk about what interested her most – her grandson's baptism, for which she had gone to Petersburg – and about the special favour the emperor had shown her older son.

'And here's Lavrenty!' said Vronsky, looking out the window. 'We can go now, if you like.'

The old butler, who had come with the countess, entered the carriage to announce that everything was ready, and the countess got up to leave.

'Let's go, there are fewer people now,' said Vronsky.

The maid took the bag and the lapdog, the butler and a porter the other bags. Vronsky gave his mother his arm; but as they were getting out of the carriage, several men with frightened faces suddenly ran past. The stationmaster, in a peaked cap of an extraordinary colour, also ran past.

Evidently something extraordinary had happened. People who had left the train were running back.

'What? . . . What? . . . Where? . . . Threw himself! . . . run over! . . .' could be heard among those passing by.

Stepan Arkadyich, with his sister on his arm, their faces also frightened, came back and stood by the door of the carriage, out of the crowd's way.

The ladies got into the carriage, while Vronsky and Stepan Arkadyich went after the people to find out the details of the accident.

A watchman, either drunk or too bundled up because of the freezing cold, had not heard a train being shunted and had been run over.

Even before Vronsky and Oblonsky came back, the ladies had learned these details from the butler.

Oblonsky and Vronsky had both seen the mangled corpse. Oblonsky was obviously suffering. He winced and seemed ready to cry.

'Ah, how terrible! Ah, Anna, if you'd seen it! Ah, how terrible!' he kept saying.

Vronsky was silent, and his handsome face was serious but perfectly calm.

'Ah, if you'd seen it, Countess,' said Stepan Arkadyich. 'And his wife is here . . . It was terrible to see her . . . She threw herself on the body. They say he was the sole provider for a huge family.[32] It's terrible!'

'Can nothing be done for her?' Mme Karenina said in an agitated whisper.

Vronsky glanced at her and at once left the carriage.

'I'll be right back, *maman*,' he added, turning at the door.

When he came back a few minutes later, Stepan Arkadyich was already talking with the countess about a new soprano, while the countess kept glancing impatiently at the door, waiting for her son.

'Let's go now,' said Vronsky, entering.

They went out together. Vronsky walked ahead with his mother. Behind came Mme Karenina with her brother. At the exit, the stationmaster overtook Vronsky and came up to him.

'You gave my assistant two hundred roubles. Would you be so kind as to designate whom they are meant for?'

'For the widow,' Vronsky said, shrugging his shoulders. 'I don't see any need to ask.'

'You gave it?' Oblonsky cried behind him and, pressing his sister's hand, added: 'Very nice, very nice! Isn't he a fine fellow? My respects, Countess.'

And he and his sister stopped, looking around for her maid.

When they came out, the Vronskys' carriage had already driven off. The people coming out were still talking about what had happened.

'What a terrible death!' said some gentleman passing by. 'Cut in two pieces, they say.'

'On the contrary, I think it's the easiest, it's instantaneous,' observed another.

'How is it they don't take measures?' said a third.

Mme Karenina got into the carriage, and Stepan Arkadyich saw with surprise that her lips were trembling and she could hardly keep back her tears.

'What is it, Anna?' he asked, when they had driven several hundred yards.

'A bad omen,' she said.

'What nonsense!' said Stepan Arkadyich. 'You've come, that's the main thing. You can't imagine what hopes I have in you.'

'Have you known Vronsky for long?' she asked.

'Yes. You know, we hope he's going to marry Kitty.'

'Oh?' Anna said softly. 'Well, now let's talk about you,' she added, tossing her head as if she wanted physically to drive away something superfluous that was bothering her. 'Let's talk about your affairs. I got your letter and here I am.'

'Yes, you're my only hope,' said Stepan Arkadyich.

'Well, tell me everything.'

And Stepan Arkadyich started telling.

Driving up to the house, Oblonsky helped his sister out, sighed, pressed her hand, and went to his office.

XIX

When Anna came in, Dolly was sitting in the small drawing room with a plump, tow-headed boy who already resembled his father, listening as he recited a French lesson. The boy was reading, his hand twisting and trying to tear off the barely attached button of his jacket. His mother took his hand away several times, but the plump little hand would take hold of the button again. His mother tore the button off and put it in her pocket.

'Keep your hands still, Grisha,' she said, and went back to knitting a blanket, her handwork from long ago, which she always took up in difficult moments; she was now knitting nervously, flicking the stitches over with her finger and counting them. Though yesterday she had sent word to her husband that she did not care whether his sister came or not, she had everything ready for her arrival and was excitedly awaiting her.

Dolly was crushed by her grief and totally consumed by it. Nevertheless she remembered that Anna, her sister-in-law, was the wife of one of the most important people in Petersburg and a Petersburg *grande dame*. And owing to this circumstance, she did not act on what she had said to her husband, that is, did not forget that Anna was coming. 'After all, she's not guilty of anything,' thought Dolly. 'I know nothing but the very best about her, and with regard to myself, I've seen only kindness and friendship from her.' True, as far as she could remember her impression of the Karenins' house in Petersburg, she had not liked it; there was something false in the whole shape of their family life. 'But why shouldn't I receive her? As long as she doesn't try to console me!' thought Dolly. 'All these consolations and exhortations and Christian forgivenesses – I've already thought of it all a thousand times, and it's no good.'

All those days Dolly was alone with her children. She did not want to talk about her grief, and with this grief in her soul she could not talk about irrelevancies. She knew that one way or another she would tell Anna everything, and her joy at the thought of how she would tell her everything alternated with anger at the need to speak about her humiliation with her, his sister, and to hear ready-made phrases of exhortation and consolation from her.

As often happens, she kept looking at her watch, expecting her every minute, and missed precisely the one when her guest arrived, so that she did not even hear the bell.

Hearing the rustle of a dress and light footsteps already at the door, she turned, and her careworn face involuntarily expressed not joy but surprise. She stood up and embraced her sister-in-law.

'What, here already?' she said, kissing her.

'Dolly, I'm so glad to see you!'

'I'm glad, too,' said Dolly, smiling weakly and trying to make out from the expression on Anna's face whether she knew or not. 'She must know,' she thought, noticing the commiseration on Anna's face. 'Well, come along, I'll take you to your room,' she continued, trying to put off the moment of talking as long as possible.

'This is Grisha? My God, how he's grown!' said Anna and, having kissed him, without taking her eyes off Dolly, she stopped and blushed. 'No, please, let's not go anywhere.'

She took off her scarf and hat and, catching a strand of her dark, curly hair in it, shook her head, trying to disentangle it.

'And you are radiant with happiness and health,' said Dolly, almost with envy.

'I? . . . Yes,' said Anna. 'My God, Tanya! The same age as my Seryozha,' she added, turning to the girl who came running in. She took her in her arms and kissed her. 'A lovely girl, lovely! Show them all to me.'

She called them all by name, remembering not only the names, but the years, months, characters, illnesses of all the children, and Dolly could not help appreciating it.

'Well, let's go to them then,' she said. 'A pity Vasya's asleep.'

After looking at the children, they sat down, alone now, to have coffee in the drawing room. Anna reached for the tray, then pushed it aside.

'Dolly,' she said, 'he told me.'

Dolly looked coldly at Anna. She expected falsely compassionate phrases now, but Anna said nothing of the sort.

'Dolly, dear!' she said, 'I don't want either to defend him or to console you – that is impossible. But, darling, I simply feel sorry for you, sorry with all my heart!'

Tears suddenly showed behind the thick lashes of her bright eyes. She moved closer to her sister-in-law and took her hand in her own energetic little hand. Dolly did not draw back, but the dry expression on her face did not change. She said:

'It's impossible to console me. Everything is lost after what's happened, everything is gone!'

And as soon as she had said it, the expression on her face suddenly softened. Anna raised Dolly's dry, thin hand, kissed it and said: 'But, Dolly, what's to be done, what's to be done? What's the best way to act in this terrible situation? – that's what we must think about.'

'Everything's over, that's all,' said Dolly. 'And the worst of it, you understand, is that I can't leave him. There are the children, I'm tied. And I can't live with him, it pains me to see him.'

'Dolly, darling, he told me, but I want to hear it from you, tell me everything.'

Dolly gave her a questioning look.

Unfeigned concern and love could be seen on Anna's face.

'Very well,' she said suddenly. 'But I'll tell it from the beginning. You know how I got married. With *maman*'s upbringing, I was not only innocent, I was stupid. I didn't know anything. They say, I know, that husbands tell their wives their former life, but Stiva . . .' – she corrected herself – 'Stepan Arkadyich told me nothing. You won't believe it, but until now I thought I was the only woman he had known. I lived like that for eight years. You must understand that I not only didn't suspect his unfaithfulness, I considered it impossible, and here, imagine, with such notions, suddenly to learn the whole horror, the whole vileness . . . You must understand me. To be fully certain of my own happiness, and suddenly . . .' Dolly went on, repressing her sobs, 'and to get a letter . . . his letter to his mistress, to my governess. No, it's too terrible!' She hastily took out a handkerchief and covered her face with it. 'I could even understand if it was a passion,' she went on after a pause, 'but to deceive me deliberately, cunningly . . . and with whom? . . . To go on being my husband together with her . . . it's terrible! You can't understand . . .'

'Oh, no, I do understand! I understand, dear Dolly, I understand,' said Anna, pressing her hand.

'And do you think he understands all the horror of my position?' Dolly went on. 'Not a bit! He's happy and content.'

'Oh, no!' Anna quickly interrupted. 'He's pitiful, he's overcome with remorse . . .'

'Is he capable of remorse?' Dolly interrupted, peering intently into her sister-in-law's face.

'Yes, I know him. I couldn't look at him without pity. We both know him. He's kind, but he's proud, and now he's so humiliated. What moved me most of all . . .' (and here Anna guessed what might move Dolly most of all) 'there are two things tormenting him: that he's ashamed before the children, and that, loving you as he does . . . yes, yes, loving you more than anything in the world,' she hastily interrupted Dolly, who was about to object, 'he has hurt you, crushed you. "No, no, she won't forgive me," he keeps saying.'

Dolly pensively stared past her sister-in-law, listening to her words.

'Yes, I understand that his position is terrible; it's worse for the guilty than for the innocent,' she said, 'if he feels guilty for the whole misfortune. But how can I forgive him, how can I be his wife again after her? For me to live with him now would be torture, precisely because I loved him as I did, because I love my past love for him . . .'

And sobs interrupted her words.

But as if on purpose, each time she softened, she again began to speak of what irritated her.

'You see, she's young, she's beautiful,' she went on. 'Do you understand, Anna, who took my youth and beauty from me? He and his children. I've done my service for him, and that service took my all, and now, naturally, he finds a fresh, vulgar creature more agreeable. They've surely talked about me between them, or, worse still, passed me over in silence – you understand?' Again her eyes lit up with hatred. 'And after that he's going to tell me . . . Am I supposed to believe him? Never. No, it's the end of everything, everything that made for comfort, a reward for toil, suffering . . . Would you believe it? I've just been teaching Grisha: before it used to be a joy, now it's a torment. Why do I strain and toil? Why have children? The terrible thing is that my soul suddenly turned over, and instead of love, of tenderness, I feel only spite towards him, yes, spite. I could kill him and . . .'

'Darling Dolly, I understand, but don't torment yourself. You're so offended, so agitated, that you see many things wrongly.'

Dolly quieted down, and for a minute or two they were silent.

'What's to be done, think, Anna, help me. I've thought it all over and don't see anything.'

Anna could not think of anything, but her heart responded directly to every word, to every expression on her sister-in-law's face.

'I'll say one thing,' Anna began. 'I'm his sister, I know his character, this ability to forget everything, everything' (she made a gesture in front of her face), 'this ability for total infatuation, but also for total remorse. He can't believe, he can't understand now, how he could have done what he did.'

'No, he understands, he understood!' Dolly interrupted. 'But I ... you're forgetting me ... is it any easier for me?'

'Wait. When he was telling me about it, I confess, I still didn't understand all the horror of your position. I saw only him and that the family was upset; I felt sorry for him, but, talking with you, as a woman I see something else; I see your sufferings, and I can't tell you how sorry I am for you! But, Dolly, darling, though I fully understand your sufferings, there's one thing I don't know: I don't know ... I don't know how much love for him there still is in your soul. Only you know whether it's enough to be able to forgive. If it is, then forgive him!'

'No,' Dolly began; but Anna interrupted her, kissing her hand once more.

'I know more of the world than you do,' she said. 'I know how people like Stiva look at it. You say he talked with *her* about you. That never happened. These people may be unfaithful, but their hearth and wife are sacred to them. Somehow for them these women remain despised and don't interfere with the family. Between them and the family they draw some sort of line that can't be crossed. I don't understand it, but it's so.'

'Yes, but he kissed her ...'

'Dolly, wait, darling. I saw Stiva when he was in love with you. I remember the time when he would come to me and weep, talking about you, and what loftiness and poetry you were for him, and I know that the longer he lived with you, the loftier you became for him. We used to laugh at him, because he added "Dolly is a remarkable woman" to every word. You are and always have been a divinity for him, and this infatuation is not from his soul ...'

'But if this infatuation repeats itself?'

'It can't, as I understand it ...'

'Yes, but would you forgive?'

'I don't know, I can't judge ... No, I can,' said Anna, after some reflection; and having mentally grasped the situation and weighed it on her inner balance, she added: 'No, I can, I can. Yes, I would forgive. I wouldn't be the same, no, but I would forgive, and forgive in such a way as if it hadn't happened, hadn't happened at all.'

'Well, naturally,' Dolly quickly interrupted, as if she were saying something she had thought more than once, 'otherwise it wouldn't be forgiveness. If you forgive, it's completely, completely. Well, come along, I'll take you to your room,' she said, getting up, and on the way Dolly embraced Anna. 'My dear, I'm so glad you've come. I feel better, so much better.'

XX

That whole day Anna spent at home, that is, at the Oblonskys', and did not receive anyone, though some of her acquaintances, having learned of her arrival, called that same day. Anna spent the morning with Dolly and the children. She only sent a little note to her brother, telling him to be sure to dine at home. 'Come, God is merciful,' she wrote.

Oblonsky dined at home; the conversation was general, and his wife spoke to him, addressing him familiarly, something she had not done recently. There remained the same estrangement in the relations between husband and wife, but there was no longer any talk of separation, and Stepan Arkadyich could see the possibility of discussion and reconciliation.

Just after dinner Kitty arrived. She knew Anna Arkadyevna, but only slightly, and she now came to her sister's not without fear of how she would be received by this Petersburg society lady whom everyone praised so much. But Anna Arkadyevna liked her, she saw that at once. Anna obviously admired her beauty and youth, and before Kitty could recover she felt that she was not only under her influence but in love with her, as young girls are capable of being in love with older married ladies. Anna did not look like a society lady or the mother of an eight-year-old son, but in the litheness of her movements, the freshness and settled animation of her face, which broke through now as a smile, now as a glance, would have looked more like a twenty-year-old girl had it not been for the serious, sometimes sad expression of her eyes, which struck Kitty and drew her to Anna. Kitty felt that Anna was perfectly simple and kept nothing hidden, but that there was in her some other, higher world of interests, inaccessible to her, complex and poetic.

After dinner, when Dolly went to her room, Anna quickly got up and went over to her brother, who was lighting a cigar.

'Stiva,' she said to him, winking merrily, making a cross over him, and indicating the door with her eyes. 'Go, and God help you.'

He understood her, abandoned his cigar and disappeared through the door.

When Stepan Arkadyich had gone, she returned to the sofa, where she sat surrounded with children. Whether because the children had seen that their mother loved this aunt, or because they themselves felt a special charm in her, the elder two, and after them the young ones, as often happens with children, had clung to the new aunt even before dinner and would not leave her side. Something like a game was set up among them, which consisted in sitting as close as possible to her, touching her, holding her small hand, kissing her, playing with her ring or at least touching the flounce of her dress.

'Well, well, the way we sat earlier,' said Anna Arkadyevna, sitting back down in her place.

And again Grisha put his head under her arm and leaned it against her dress and beamed with pride and happiness.

'So, now, when is the ball?' she turned to Kitty.

'Next week, and a wonderful ball. One of those balls that are always merry.'

'And are there such balls, where it's always merry?' Anna said with tender mockery.

'Strange, but there are. At the Bobrishchevs' it's always merry, and also at the Nikitins', but at the Mezhkovs' it's always boring. Haven't you noticed?'

'No, dear heart, for me there are no longer any balls that are merry,' said Anna, and Kitty saw in her eyes that special world that was not open to her. 'For me there are those that are less difficult and boring . . .'

'How can *you* be bored at a ball?'

'Why can't *I* be bored at a ball?' asked Anna.

Kitty noticed that Anna knew the answer that would follow.

'Because you're always the best of all.'

Anna was capable of blushing. She blushed and said:

'First of all, I never am, and second, if it were so, what do I need it for?'

'Will you go to this ball?' asked Kitty.

'I suppose it will be impossible not to go. Take it,' she said to Tanya, who was pulling the easily slipped-off ring from her white, tapering finger.

'I'll be very glad if you go. I'd like so much to see you at a ball.'

'At least, if I do go, I'll be comforted at the thought that it will give you pleasure . . . Grisha, don't fuss with it, please, it's all dishevelled as it is,' she said, straightening a stray lock of hair Grisha was playing with.

'I imagine you in lilac at the ball.'

'Why must it be lilac?' Anna asked, smiling. 'Well, children, off you go, off you go. Do you hear? Miss Hull is calling you for tea,' she said, tearing the children from her and sending them to the dining room.

'And I know why you're inviting me to the ball. You expect a lot from this ball, and you want everyone to be there, you want everyone to take part.'

'Yes. How do you know?'

'Oh! how good to be your age,' Anna went on. 'I remember and know that blue mist, the same as in the mountains in Switzerland. The mist that envelops everything during the blissful time when childhood is just coming to an end, and the path away from that vast, cheerful and happy circle grows narrower and narrower, and you feel cheerful and eerie entering that suite of rooms, though it seems bright and beautiful . . . Who hasn't gone through that?'

Kitty silently smiled. 'But how did she go through it? I'd so love to know her whole romance!' thought Kitty, recalling the unpoetical appearance of Alexei Alexandrovich, her husband.

'There's something I know. Stiva told me, and I congratulate you, I like him very much,' Anna went on. 'I met Vronsky at the railway station.'

'Ah, he was there?' Kitty asked, blushing. 'But what did Stiva tell you?'

'Stiva gave it all away. And I'd be very glad. I travelled with Vronsky's mother yesterday,' she went on, 'and his mother didn't stop talking to me about him; he's her favourite; I know how partial mothers can be, but . . .'

'But what did his mother tell you?'

'Oh, a lot! I know he's her favourite, but even so one can tell he's chivalrous . . . Well, for instance, she told me he wanted to give the whole fortune to his brother, that while still a child he did something extraordinary, rescued a woman from the water. In short, a hero,' Anna said, smiling and remembering the two hundred roubles he gave at the station.

But she did not mention the two hundred roubles. For some reason it was unpleasant for her to remember it. She felt there was something in it that concerned her, and of a sort that should not have been.

'She insisted that I call on her,' Anna went on, 'and I'll be glad to see the old lady and will call on her tomorrow. However, thank God Stiva has spent a long time in Dolly's boudoir,' Anna added, changing the subject and getting up, displeased at something, as it seemed to Kitty.

'No, me first! no, me!' the children shouted, having finished their tea and rushing out to Aunt Anna.

'All together!' said Anna and, laughing, she ran to meet them, and embraced and brought down the whole heap of swarming, rapturously squealing children.

XXI

For the grown-ups' tea Dolly came from her room. Stepan Arkadyich did not come out. He must have left his wife's room through the back door.

'I'm afraid you'll be cold upstairs,' Dolly remarked, addressing Anna. 'I'd like to move you down, and we'll be nearer each other.'

'Oh, now, please don't worry about me,' Anna replied, peering into Dolly's eyes and trying to make out whether or not there had been a reconciliation.

'There's more light here,' her sister-in-law replied.

'I tell you, I sleep always and everywhere like a dormouse.'

'What's this about?' asked Stepan Arkadyich, coming out of his study and addressing his wife.

By his tone Kitty and Anna both understood at once that a reconciliation had taken place.

'I want to move Anna down here, but the curtains must be changed. No one else knows how to do it, I must do it myself,' Dolly replied, turning to him.

'God knows, are they completely reconciled?' thought Anna, hearing her cold and calm tone.

'Oh, enough, Dolly, you keep making difficulties,' said her husband. 'Well, I'll do it, if you like . . .'

'Yes,' thought Anna, 'they must be reconciled.'

'I know how you'll do it,' Dolly answered, 'you'll tell Matvei to do something impossible, then you'll leave, and he'll get it all wrong' – and a habitual mocking smile wrinkled Dolly's lips as she said it.

'Complete, complete reconciliation, complete,' thought Anna, 'thank God!' and rejoicing that she had been the cause of it, she went over to Dolly and kissed her.

'Not at all, why do you despise me and Matvei so?' Stepan Arkadyich said, smiling barely perceptibly and turning to his wife.

All evening, as usual, Dolly was slightly mocking towards her husband, and Stepan Arkadyich was content and cheerful, but just enough so as not to suggest that, having been forgiven, he had forgotten his guilt.

At half-past nine an especially joyful and pleasant family conversation around the evening tea table at the Oblonskys' was disrupted by an apparently very simple event, but this simple event for some reason seemed strange to everyone. As they talked about mutual Petersburg acquaintances, Anna quickly stood up.

'I have her in my album,' she said, 'and, incidentally, I'll show you my Seryozha,' she added with the smile of a proud mother.

Towards ten o'clock when she usually said good night to her son, and often put him to bed herself before going to a ball, she felt sad to be so far away from him; and whatever they talked about, she kept returning in thought to her curly-headed Seryozha. She wanted to look at his picture and talk about him. Taking advantage of the first pretext, she got up and, with her light, resolute step, went to fetch the album. The stairs that led up to her room began on the landing of the big, heated front stairway.

Just as she was leaving the drawing room, there was a ring at the door.

'Who could that be?' said Dolly.

'It's too early for me and too late for anyone else,' observed Kitty.

'Probably someone with papers,' Stepan Arkadyich put in, and, as Anna was crossing the landing, a servant came running up the stairs to announce the visitor, while the visitor himself stood by the lamp. Anna, looking down, at once recognized Vronsky, and a strange feeling of pleasure suddenly stirred in her heart, together with a fear of something. He stood without removing his coat, and was taking something from his pocket. Just as she reached the centre of the landing, he raised his eyes, saw her, and something ashamed and frightened appeared in his expression. Inclining her head slightly, she went on, and behind her heard the loud voice of Stepan Arkadyich inviting him to come in, and the soft, gentle and calm voice of Vronsky declining.

When Anna came back with the album, he was no longer there, and Stepan Arkadyich was saying that he had dropped in to find out about a dinner they were giving the next day for a visiting celebrity.

'And he wouldn't come in for anything. He's somehow strange,' Stepan Arkadyich added.

Kitty blushed. She thought that she alone understood why he had called by and why he had not come in. 'He was at our house,' she thought, 'didn't find me, and thought I was here; but he didn't come in because he thought it was late, and Anna's here.'

They all exchanged glances without saying anything and began looking through Anna's album.

There was nothing either extraordinary or strange in a man calling at his friend's house at half-past nine to find out the details of a dinner that was being planned and not coming in; but they all thought it strange. To Anna especially it seemed strange and not right.

XXII

The ball had only just begun when Kitty and her mother went up the big, light-flooded stairway, set with flowers and lackeys in powder and red livery. From the inner rooms drifted a steady rustle of movement, as in a beehive, and while they were adjusting their hair and dresses in front of a mirror between potted trees on the landing, the cautiously distinct sounds of the orchestra's violins came from the ballroom, beginning the first waltz. A little old man in civilian dress, who had been straightening his grey side-whiskers at another mirror and who exuded a smell of scent, bumped into them by the stairway and stepped aside, obviously admiring Kitty, whom he did not know. A beardless young man, one of those young men of society whom the old prince Shcherbatsky called *twits*, wearing an extremely low-cut waistcoat, straightening his white tie as he went, bowed to them and, after running past, came back to invite Kitty to a quadrille. The first quadrille had already been given to Vronsky; she had to give this young man the second. A military man, buttoning his glove, stepped aside at the doorway and, stroking his moustache, admired the pink Kitty.

Though Kitty's toilette, coiffure and all the preparations for the ball had cost her a good deal of trouble and planning, she was now entering the ballroom, in her intricate tulle gown over a pink underskirt, as freely and simply as if all these rosettes and laces, and all the details of her toilette, had not cost her and her household a moment's attention, as if she had been born in this tulle and lace, with this tall coiffure, topped by a rose with two leaves.

When the old princess, at the entrance to the ballroom, wanted to straighten the twisted end of her ribbon sash, Kitty drew back slightly. She felt that everything on her must of itself be good and graceful, and there was no need to straighten anything.

Kitty was having one of her happy days. Her dress was not tight anywhere, the lace bertha stayed in place, the rosettes did not get crumpled or come off; the pink shoes with high, curved heels did not pinch, but delighted her little feet. The thick braids of blond hair held to her little head like her own. All three buttons on her long gloves, which fitted but did not change the shape of her arms, fastened without coming off. The black velvet ribbon of her locket encircled her neck with particular tenderness. This velvet ribbon was enchanting, and at home, as she looked at her neck in the mirror, she felt it could almost speak. All the rest might be doubted, but the ribbon was enchanting. Kitty also smiled here at the ball as she glanced at it in the mirror. In her bare shoulders and arms she felt a cold, marble-like quality that she especially liked. Her eyes shone, and her red lips could not help smiling from the sense of her own attractiveness. She had no sooner entered the ballroom and reached the gauzy, ribbony, lacy, colourful crowd of ladies waiting to be invited to dance (Kitty never stayed long in that crowd), than she was invited for a waltz, and invited by the best partner, the foremost partner of the ball hierarchy, the celebrated *dirigeur** of balls, the master of ceremonies, a trim, handsome, married man, Yegorushka Korsunsky. Having only just abandoned Countess Banin, with whom he had danced the first round of the waltz, and surveying his domain, that is, the few couples who had started dancing, he saw Kitty come in, hastened to her with that special loose amble proper only to the *dirigeurs* of balls, bowed and, without even asking her consent, held out his arm to put it around her slender waist. She turned, looking for someone to hold her fan, and the hostess, smiling, took it.

* Director or conductor.

'How nice that you came on time,' he said to her, putting his arm around her waist. 'What is this fashion for being late!'

Bending her left arm, she placed her hand on his shoulder, and her small feet in their pink shoes began to move quickly, lightly and rhythmically across the slippery parquet in time with the music.

'It's restful waltzing with you,' he said to her, falling in with the first, not yet quick, steps of the waltz. 'Lovely, such lightness, *précision*.' He said to her what he said to almost all his good acquaintances.

She smiled at his compliment and went on examining the ballroom over his shoulder. She was not a new debutante, for whom all the faces at a ball blend into one magical impression; nor was she a girl dragged to every ball, for whom all the faces are so familiar that it is boring; she was in between the two – she was excited, but at the same time self-possessed enough to be able to watch. In the left-hand corner of the room she saw grouped the flower of society. There was the impossibly bared, beautiful Lydie, Korsunsky's wife, there was the hostess, there gleamed the bald head of Krivin, always to be found with the flower of society. Young men, not daring to approach, gazed in that direction; and there her eyes picked out Stiva and then noticed the lovely figure and head of Anna, who was in a black velvet dress. And there *he* was. Kitty had not seen him since the evening she refused Levin. With her far-sighted eyes she recognized him at once, and even noticed that he was looking at her.

'What now, another turn? You're not tired?' said Korsunsky, slightly out of breath.

'No, thank you.'

'Where shall I take you?'

'Mme Karenina is here, I think . . . take me to her.'

'Wherever you choose.'

And Korsunsky waltzed on, measuring his step, straight towards the crowd in the left-hand corner of the ballroom, repeating: '*Pardon, mesdames, pardon, pardon, mesdames*,' and, manoeuvring through that sea of lace, tulle and ribbons without snagging one little feather, he twirled his partner so sharply that her slender, lace-stockinged legs were revealed, and her train swept up fan-like, covering Krivin's knees. Korsunsky bowed, straightened his broad shirtfront, and offered her his arm to take her to Anna Arkadyevna. Kitty, all flushed, removed her train from Krivin's knees and, slightly dizzy, looked around, searching for Anna. Anna was not in lilac, as Kitty had absolutely wanted, but in a low-cut black velvet dress, which revealed her full shoulders and bosom, as if shaped from old ivory, and her rounded arms with their very small, slender hands. The dress was all trimmed with Venetian guipure lace. On her head, in her black hair, her own without admixture, was a small garland of pansies, and there was another on her black ribbon sash among the white lace. Her coiffure was inconspicuous. Conspicuous were only those wilful little ringlets of curly hair that adorned her, always coming out on her nape and temples. Around her firm, shapely neck was a string of pearls.

Kitty had seen Anna every day, was in love with her, and had imagined her inevitably in lilac. But now, seeing her in black, she felt that she had never understood all her loveliness. She saw her now in a completely new and, for her, unexpected way. Now she understood that Anna could not have been in lilac, that her loveliness consisted precisely in always standing out from what she wore, that what she wore was never seen on her. And the black dress with luxurious lace was not seen on her; it was just a frame, and only she was seen – simple, natural, graceful, and at the same time gay and animated.

She stood, as always, holding herself extremely erect, and, when Kitty approached this group, was talking with the host, her head turned slightly towards him.

'No, I won't cast a stone,'[33] she replied to something, 'though I don't understand it,' she went on, shrugging her shoulders, and with a tender, protective smile turned at once to Kitty. After a fleeting feminine glance over her dress, she made a barely noticeable but, for Kitty, understandable movement of her head, approving of her dress and beauty. 'You even come into the ballroom dancing,' she added.

'This is one of my most faithful helpers,' said Korsunsky, bowing to Anna Arkadyevna, whom he had not yet seen. 'The princess helps to make a ball gay and beautiful. Anna Arkadyevna, a turn of the waltz?' he said, inclining.

'So you're acquainted?' asked the host.

'With whom are we not acquainted? My wife and I are like white wolves, everybody knows us,' replied Korsunsky. 'A turn of the waltz, Anna Arkadyevna?'

'I don't dance when I can help it,' she said.

'But tonight you can't,' replied Korsunsky.

Just then Vronsky approached.

'Well, if I can't help dancing tonight, let's go then,' she said, ignoring

Vronsky's bow, and she quickly raised her hand to Korsunsky's shoulder.

'Why is she displeased with him?' thought Kitty, noticing that Anna had deliberately not responded to Vronsky's bow. Vronsky approached Kitty, reminding her about the first quadrille and regretting that until then he had not had the pleasure of seeing her. While she listened to him, Kitty gazed admiringly at Anna waltzing. She expected him to invite her for a waltz, but he did not, and she glanced at him in surprise. He blushed and hastened to invite her to waltz, but he had only just put his arm around her slender waist and taken the first step when the music suddenly stopped. Kitty looked into his face, which was such a short distance from hers, and long afterwards, for several years, that look, so full of love, which she gave him then, and to which he did not respond, cut her heart with tormenting shame.

'*Pardon, pardon!* A waltz, a waltz!' Korsunsky cried out from the other side of the ballroom and, snatching up the first girl he met, began to dance.

XXIII

Vronsky and Kitty took several turns of the waltz. After the waltz, Kitty went over to her mother and had barely managed to say a few words to Countess Nordston when Vronsky came to fetch her for the first quadrille. Nothing important was said during the quadrille, there were snatches of conversation, now about the Korsunskys, husband and wife, whom he described very amusingly as sweet forty-year-old children, now about a future public theatre,[34] and only once did the conversation touch her to the quick, when he asked her whether Levin was there and added that he liked him very much. But Kitty expected no more from the quadrille. She waited with fainting heart for the mazurka. She thought that during the mazurka everything would be decided. That he had not invited her for the mazurka during the quadrille did not trouble her. She was sure that she would dance the mazurka with him, as at previous balls, and declined five other invitations, saying she was already engaged. The whole ball up to the final quadrille was for Kitty a magic dream of joyful colours, sounds and movements. She left off dancing only when she felt too tired and asked for a rest. But, dancing the final quadrille with one of those boring young men whom it was impossible to refuse, she found herself vis-à-vis Vronsky and Anna. She had not come close to Anna since her arrival, and here suddenly saw her again in a completely new and unexpected way. She saw in her a streak of the elation of success, which she knew so well herself. She could see that Anna was drunk with the wine of the rapture she inspired. She knew that feeling, knew the signs of it, and she saw them in Anna – saw the tremulous, flashing light in her eyes, the smile of happiness and excitement that involuntarily curved her lips, and the precise gracefulness, assurance and lightness of her movements.

'Who is it?' she asked herself. 'All or one?' And, not helping the suffering young man she was dancing with to carry on the conversation, the thread of which he had lost and was unable to pick up, and outwardly obeying the merrily loud commands called out by Korsunsky, who sent everybody now into the *grand rond*, now into the *chaine*, she watched, and her heart was wrung more and more. 'No, it's not the admiration of the crowd she's drunk with, but the rapture of one man. And that one? can it be him?' Each time he spoke with Anna, her eyes flashed with a joyful light and a smile of happiness curved her red lips. She seemed to be struggling with herself to keep these signs of joy from showing, yet they appeared on her face of themselves. 'But what about him?' Kitty looked at him and was horrified. What portrayed itself so clearly to Kitty in the mirror of Anna's face, she also saw in him. Where was his quiet, firm manner and carefree, calm expression? No, now each time he addressed Anna, he bowed his head slightly, as if wishing to fall down before her, and in his glance there were only obedience and fear. 'I do not want to offend you,' his glance seemed to say each time, 'I want to save myself but do not know how.' There was an expression on his face that she had never seen before.

They talked about mutual acquaintances, carrying on the most insignificant conversation, but it seemed to Kitty that every word they spoke decided their fate and hers. And the strange thing was that, though they indeed talked about how ridiculous Ivan Ivanovich was with his French, and how the Yeletsky girl might have found a better match, these words all had a special significance for them, and they felt it just as Kitty did. The whole ball, the whole world, everything was covered with mist in Kitty's soul. Only the strict school of upbringing she had gone through supported her and made her do what was demanded of her – that is, dance, answer questions, talk, even smile. But before the start of the mazurka, when the chairs were already being put in place and some couples moved from the smaller rooms to the ballroom, Kitty was overcome by a moment of despair and horror. She had refused five partners and now would not dance the mazurka. There was even no hope that she would be asked, precisely because she had had too great a success in society, and it would not have entered anyone's head that she had not been invited before then. She should have told her mother she was sick and gone home, but she did not have the strength for it. She felt destroyed.

She went to the far corner of a small drawing room and sank into an armchair. Her airy skirt rose like a cloud around her slender body; one bared, thin, delicate girlish hand sank strengthlessly into the folds of her pink tunic; in the other she held her fan and waved it before her flushed face with quick, short movements. But though she had the look of a butterfly that clings momentarily to a blade of grass and is about to flutter up, unfolding its iridescent wings, a terrible despair pained her heart.

'But perhaps I'm mistaken, perhaps it's not so?'

And she again recalled all that she had seen.

'Kitty, what on earth is this?' said Countess Nordston, approaching her inaudibly across the carpet. 'I don't understand this.'

Kitty's lower lip trembled; she quickly got up.

'Kitty, you're not dancing the mazurka?'

'No, no,' said Kitty, in a voice trembling with tears.

'He invited her for the mazurka right in front of me,' said Countess Nordston, knowing that Kitty would understand whom she meant. 'She said, "Aren't you dancing with Princess Shcherbatsky?"'

'Oh, it makes no difference to me!' replied Kitty.

No one except herself understood her situation, no one knew that a few days before she had refused a man whom she perhaps loved, and had refused him because she trusted another.

Countess Nordston found Korsunsky, with whom she was to dance the mazurka, and told him to invite Kitty.

Kitty danced in the first pair, and, fortunately for her, had no need to talk, because Korsunsky kept rushing about his domain giving orders. Vronsky and Anna sat almost opposite to her. She saw them with her far-sighted eyes, she also saw them close to when they met while dancing, and the more she saw them, the more convinced she was that her misfortune was an accomplished fact. She saw that they felt themselves alone in this crowded ballroom. And on Vronsky's face, always so firm and independent, she saw that expression of lostness and obedience that had so struck her, like the expression of an intelligent dog when it feels guilty.

Anna smiled, and her smile passed over to him. She lapsed into thought, and he too would turn serious. Some supernatural force drew Kitty's eyes to Anna's face. She was enchanting in her simple black dress, enchanting were her full arms with the bracelets on them, enchanting her firm neck with its string of pearls, enchanting her curly hair in disarray, enchanting the graceful, light movements of her small feet and hands, enchanting that beautiful face in its animation; but there was something terrible and cruel in her enchantment.

Kitty admired her even more than before, and suffered more and more. She felt crushed, and her face showed it. When Vronsky saw her, meeting her during the mazurka, he did not recognize her at first – she was so changed.

'A wonderful ball!' he said to her, so as to say something.

'Yes,' she replied.

In the middle of the mazurka, repeating a complicated figure just invented by Korsunsky, Anna came out to the middle of the circle, took two partners and called another lady and Kitty to her. Kitty looked fearfully at her as she walked up. Anna, her eyes narrowed, looked at her and smiled, pressing her hand. But noticing that Kitty's face responded to her smile only with an expression of despair and surprise, she turned away from her and began talking gaily with the other lady.

'Yes, there's something alien, demonic and enchanting in her,' Kitty said to herself.

Anna did not want to stay for supper, but the host began to insist.

'Come, Anna Arkadyevna,' said Korsunsky, tucking her bare arm under the sleeve of his tailcoat. 'What an idea I have for a cotillion! *Un bijou!*'*

And he moved on a little, trying to draw her with him. The host smiled approvingly.

'No, I won't stay,' Anna replied, smiling; but despite her smile, both Korsunsky and the host understood by the resolute tone of her reply that she would not stay.

'No, as it is I've danced more in Moscow at your one ball than all winter in Petersburg,' Anna said, glancing at Vronsky, who was standing near her. 'I must rest before the trip.'

* A jewel!

'So you're set on going tomorrow?' asked Vronsky.

'Yes, I think so,' replied Anna, as if surprised at the boldness of his question; but the irrepressible tremulous light in her eyes and smile burned him as she said it.

Anna Arkadyevna did not stay for supper but left.

XXIV

'Yes, there's something disgusting and repulsive in me,' thought Levin, having left the Shcherbatskys and making his way on foot to his brother's. 'And I don't fit in with other people. It's pride, they say. No, there's no pride in me either. If there were any pride in me, I wouldn't have put myself in such a position.' And he pictured Vronsky to himself, happy, kind, intelligent and calm, who certainly had never been in such a terrible position as he had been in that evening. 'Yes, she was bound to choose him. It had to be so, and I have nothing and no one to complain about. I myself am to blame. What right did I have to think she would want to join her life with mine? Who am I? And what am I? A worthless man, of no use to anyone or for anything.' And he remembered his brother Nikolai and paused joyfully at this remembrance. 'Isn't he right that everything in the world is bad and vile? And our judgement of brother Nikolai has hardly been fair. Of course, from Prokofy's point of view, who saw him drunk and in a ragged fur coat, he's a despicable man; but I know him otherwise. I know his soul, and I know that we resemble each other. And instead of going to look for him, I went to dinner and then came here.' Levin went up to the street-lamp, read his brother's address, which he had in his wallet, and hailed a cab. On the long way to his brother's, Levin vividly recalled all the events he knew from the life of his brother Nikolai. He remembered how his brother, while at the university and for a year after the university, despite the mockery of his friends, had lived like a monk, strictly observing all the rituals of religion, services, fasts, and avoiding all pleasures, especially women; and then it was as if something broke loose in him, he began keeping company with the most vile people and gave himself up to the most licentious debauchery. Then he remembered the episode with a boy his brother had brought from the country in order to educate him, and to whom he gave such a beating in a fit of anger that proceedings were started against him for the inflicting of bodily harm. Then he remembered the episode with a card-sharper to whom his brother had lost money, had given a promissory note, and whom he had then lodged a complaint against, claiming that the man had cheated him. (It was this money that Sergei Ivanych had paid.) He also remembered how he had spent a night in the police station for disorderly conduct. He remembered a shameful lawsuit he had started against his brother Sergei Ivanych, whom he accused of not having paid him his share of their mother's fortune; and the last case, when he went to serve in the western territory and there stood trial for giving his superior a beating . . . All this was terribly vile, but for Levin it seemed by no means as vile as it might have seemed to those who did not know Nikolai Levin, did not know his whole story, did not know his heart.

Levin recalled how, during Nikolai's period of piety, fasts, monks, church services, when he had sought help from religion as a bridle for his passionate nature, not only had no one supported him, but everyone, including Levin himself, had laughed at him. They had teased him, calling him 'Noah' and 'the monk'; and when he broke loose, no one helped him, but they all turned away with horror and loathing.

Levin felt that in his soul, in the very bottom of his soul, his brother Nikolai, despite the ugliness of his life, was not more in the wrong than those who despised him. He was not to blame for having been born with an irrepressible character and a mind somehow constrained. But he had always wanted to be good. 'I'll tell him everything, I'll make him tell everything, and I'll show him that I love him and therefore understand him,' Levin decided to himself as he drove up, past ten o'clock, to the hotel indicated as the address.

'Upstairs, numbers twelve and thirteen,' the doorman replied to Levin's inquiry.

'Is he at home?'

'Must be.'

The door of No. 12 was half open, and through it, in a strip of light, came thick smoke from bad and weak tobacco and the sound of an unfamiliar voice. But Levin knew at once that his brother was there; he heard his little cough.

As he walked in, the unfamiliar voice was saying:

'It all depends on how reasonably and conscientiously the affair is conducted.'

Konstantin Levin looked through the door and saw that the speaker was a young man with an enormous shock of hair, wearing a quilted jacket, and that a young, slightly pockmarked woman in a woollen dress without cuffs or collar[35] was sitting on the sofa. His brother could not be seen. Konstantin's heart was painfully wrung at the thought of his brother living among such alien people. No one heard him, and Konstantin, taking off his galoshes, was listening to what the gentleman in the quilted jacket was saying. He spoke about some sort of enterprise.

'Well, devil take the privileged classes,' his brother's voice spoke, coughing. 'Masha! Get us something for supper and serve some wine, if there's any left, or else send for some.'

The woman got up, stepped out from behind the partition, and saw Konstantin.

'Some gentleman's here, Nikolai Dmitrich,'[36] she said.

'Who does he want?' Nikolai Levin's voice said crossly.

'It's me,' replied Konstantin Levin, stepping into the light.

'*Me* who?' Nikolai's voice repeated still more crossly. He could be heard quickly getting up, snagging on something, and then Levin saw before him in the doorway the figure of his brother, so familiar and yet so striking in its wildness and sickliness, huge, thin, stoop-shouldered, with big, frightened eyes.

He was still thinner than three years ago when Konstantin Levin had last seen him. He was wearing a short frock coat. His arms and broad bones seemed still more huge. His hair had become thinner, the same straight moustache hung over his lips, the same eyes gazed strangely and naïvely at the man coming in.

'Ah, Kostya!' he said suddenly, recognizing his brother, and his eyes lit up with joy. But in the same second he glanced at the young man and made the convulsive movement with his head and neck that Konstantin knew so well, as if his tie were too tight on him; and a quite different, wild, suffering and cruel expression settled on his emaciated face.

'I wrote to both you and Sergei Ivanych that I don't know and don't wish to know you. What do you, what do the two of you want?'

He was quite different from the way Konstantin had imagined him. The most difficult and worst part of his character, that which made communication with him so hard, had been forgotten by Konstantin Levin when he thought about him; and now, when he saw his face, and especially that convulsive turning of the head, he remembered it all.

'I don't want anything from you,' he replied timidly. 'I simply came to see you.'

Nikolai was apparently softened by his brother's timidity. He twitched his lips.

'Ah, just like that?' he said. 'Well, come in, sit down. Want some supper? Masha, bring three portions. No, wait. Do you know who this is?' he said to his brother, pointing to the gentleman in the sleeveless jacket. 'This is Mr Kritsky, my friend from way back in Kiev, a very remarkable man. He's being sought by the police, of course, because he's not a scoundrel.'

And he looked round, as was his habit, at everyone in the room. Seeing the woman standing in the doorway make a movement as if to go, he shouted to her: 'Wait, I said.' And with that clumsiness in conversation that Konstantin knew so well, he again looked around at everybody and began telling his brother Kritsky's story: how he had been expelled from the university for starting Sunday schools[37] and a society to aid poor students, how he had then become a teacher in a people's school, how he had been expelled from there as well, and how later he had been taken to court for something.

'You were at Kiev University?' Konstantin Levin said to Kritsky, in order to break the awkward silence that ensued.

'Yes, Kiev,' Kritsky began crossly, scowling.

'And this woman,' Nikolai Levin interrupted him, pointing to her, 'is my life's companion, Marya Nikolaevna. I took her from a house' – and his neck twitched as he said it. 'But I love her and respect her, and I ask everyone who wants to know me,' he added, raising his voice and frowning, 'to love and respect her. She's the same as my wife, the same. So there, you know who you're dealing with. And if you think you're lowering yourself, here's your hat and there's the door.'

And again his eyes passed questioningly over them all.

'Why should I be lowering myself? I don't understand.'

'Then tell them to serve supper, Masha: three portions, some vodka and wine . . . No, wait . . . No, never mind . . . Go.'

XXV

'So you see,' Nikolai Levin went on with effort, wrinkling his brow and twitching. It was obviously hard for him to think what to say and do. 'You see . . .' He pointed at some small iron bars tied with string in the corner of the room. 'See that? That's the beginning of a new business we're undertaking. This business is a manufacturing association . . .'

Konstantin was almost not listening. He peered into his brother's sickly, consumptive face, felt more and more sorry for him, and was unable to make himself listen to what his brother was telling him about the association. He could see that this association was only an anchor saving him from despising himself. Nikolai Levin went on speaking:

'You know that capital oppresses the worker – the workers in our country, the muzhiks, bear all the burden of labour, and their position is such that, however much they work, they can never get out of their brutish situation. All the profits earned by their work, with which they might improve their situation, give themselves some leisure and, consequently, education, all surplus earnings are taken from them by the capitalists. And society has developed so that the more they work, the more gain there will be for the merchants and landowners, and they will always remain working brutes. And this order must be changed,' he concluded and looked inquiringly at his brother.

'Yes, of course,' said Konstantin, studying the red patches that had appeared below his brother's prominent cheekbones.

'And so we're organizing a metal-working association, in which all production and profit and, above all, the tools of production, will be common property.'

'Where will the association be located?' asked Konstantin Levin.

'In the village of Vozdryoma, Kazan province.'

'Why in a village? I think there's enough to do in the villages without that. Why have a metal-working association in a village?'

'Because the muzhiks are just as much slaves now as they were before, and that's why you and Sergei Ivanych don't like it that we want to bring them out of this slavery,' Nikolai Levin said, annoyed by the objection.

Konstantin Levin sighed, at the same time looking around the dismal and dirty room. This sigh seemed to annoy Nikolai still more.

'I know the aristocratic views you and Sergei Ivanych have. I know that he employs all his mental powers to justify the existing evil.'

'No, why do you talk about Sergei Ivanych?' said Levin, smiling.

'Sergei Ivanych? Here's why!' Nikolai Levin cried out suddenly at the name of Sergei Ivanych. 'Here's why . . . But what's there to talk about? Nothing but . . . Why did you come to see me? You despise all this, and that's wonderful, so go, go with God!' he shouted, getting up from his chair. 'Go, go!'

'I don't despise it in the least,' Konstantin Levin said timidly. 'I'm not even arguing.'

Just then Marya Nikolaevna came back. Nikolai Levin gave her an angry glance. She quickly went over to him and whispered something.

'I'm not well, I've become irritable,' Nikolai Levin said, calming down and breathing heavily, 'and then you tell me about Sergei Ivanych and his article. It's such nonsense, such lies, such self-deception. What can a man write about justice if he knows nothing of it? Have you read his article?' he asked Kritsky, sitting down at the table again and pushing aside some half-filled cigarettes so as to clear a space.

'No, I haven't,' Kritsky said glumly, obviously unwilling to enter the conversation.

'Why not?' Nikolai Levin now turned to Kritsky with irritation.

'Because I don't find it necessary to waste time on it.'

'Excuse me, but how do you know you'd be wasting your time? The article is inaccessible to many – that is, it's above them. But with me it's a different matter, I can see through his thought, and I know why it's weak.'

Everyone fell silent. Kritsky slowly got up and took his hat.

'You won't have supper? Well, good-bye. Come tomorrow with a metal-worker.'

As soon as Kritsky left, Nikolai Levin smiled and winked.

'He's also in a bad way,' he said. 'I do see . . .'

But just then Kritsky called him from the door.

'What does he want now?' he said and went out to him in the corridor. Left alone with Marya Nikolaevna, Levin turned to her.

'Have you been with my brother long?' he asked her.

'It's the second year now. His health's gone really bad. He drinks a lot,' she said.

'Drinks, meaning what?'

'He drinks vodka, and it's bad for him.'

'Really a lot?' Levin whispered.

'Yes,' she said, glancing timidly at the doorway, in which Nikolai Levin appeared.

'What were you talking about?' he said, frowning, his frightened eyes shifting from one to the other. 'What was it?'

'Nothing,' Konstantin replied, embarrassed.

'If you don't want to say, then don't. Only there's no need for you to talk with her. She's a slut and you're a gentleman,' he said, his neck twitching. 'I see you've understood and appraised everything, and look upon my errors with regret,' he began again, raising his voice.

'Nikolai Dmitrich, Nikolai Dmitrich,' Marya Nikolaevna whispered, going up to him.

'Well, all right, all right! . . . And what about supper? Ah, here it is,' he said, seeing a lackey with a tray. 'Here, put it here,' he said angrily, and at once took the vodka, poured a glass and drank it greedily. 'Want a drink?' he asked his brother, cheering up at once. 'Well, enough about Sergei Ivanych. Anyhow, I'm glad to see you. Say what you like, we're not strangers. Well, have a drink. Tell me, what are you up to?' he went on, greedily chewing a piece of bread and pouring another glass. 'How's your life going?'

'I live alone in the country, as I did before, busy with farming,' Konstantin replied, looking with horror at the greediness with which his brother ate and drank, and trying not to let it show.

'Why don't you get married?'

'Haven't had a chance,' Konstantin replied, blushing.

'Why not? For me – it's all over! I've spoiled my life. I've said and still say that if I'd been given my share when I needed it, my whole life would be different.'

Konstantin Dmitrich hastened to redirect the conversation.

'You know, your Vanyushka works in my office in Pokrovskoe?' he said.

Nikolai twitched his neck and fell to thinking.

'So, tell me, how are things in Pokrovskoe? Is the house still standing, and the birches, and our schoolroom? And Filipp, the gardener, is he still alive? How I remember the gazebo and the bench! Watch out you don't change anything in the house, but get married quickly and arrange it again just as it used to be. I'll come to visit you then, if you have a nice wife.'

'Come to visit me now,' said Levin. 'We'll settle in so nicely!'

'I'd come if I knew I wouldn't find Sergei Ivanych there.'

'You won't find him there. I live quite independently from him.'

'Yes, but, say what you like, you've got to choose between me and him,' he said, looking timidly into his brother's eyes. This timidity touched Konstantin.

'If you want my full confession in that regard, I'll tell you that in your quarrel with Sergei Ivanych I don't take either side. You're both wrong. You are wrong more externally, and he more internally.'

'Ah, ah! You've grasped that, you've grasped that?' Nikolai cried joyfully.

'But, if you wish to know, I personally value my friendship with you more, because . . .'

'Why, why?'

Konstantin could not say that he valued it more because Nikolai was unhappy and in need of friendship. But Nikolai understood that he wanted to say precisely that and, frowning, resorted to his vodka again.

'Enough, Nikolai Dmitrich!' said Marya Nikolaevna, reaching out with her plump, bare arm for the decanter.

'Let go! Don't interfere! I'll beat you!' he cried.

Marya Nikolaevna smiled her meek and kindly smile, which also infected Nikolai, and took away the vodka.

'You think she doesn't understand anything?' Nikolai said. 'She understands everything better than any of us. There's something sweet and good in her, isn't there?'

'You've never been to Moscow before, miss?' Konstantin said to her, so as to say something.

'Don't call her "miss". She's afraid of it. No one, except the justice of the peace, when she stood trial for wanting to leave the house of depravity, no one ever called her "miss". My God, what is all this nonsense in the world!' he suddenly cried out. 'These new institutions, these justices of the peace, the zemstvo – what is this outrage!'

And he started telling about his encounters with the new institutions.

Konstantin Levin listened to him, and that denial of sense in all social institutions, which he shared with him and had often expressed aloud, now seemed disagreeable to him coming from his brother's mouth.

'We'll understand it all in the other world,' he said jokingly.

'In the other world? Ah, I don't like that other world! No, I don't,' he said, resting his frightened, wild eyes on his brother's face. 'And it might seem good to leave all this vileness and confusion, other people's and one's own, but I'm afraid of death, terribly afraid of death.' He shuddered. 'Do drink something. Want champagne? Or else let's go somewhere. Let's go to the gypsies! You know, I've come to have a great love of gypsies and Russian songs.'

His tongue began to get confused, and he jumped from one subject to another. Konstantin, with Masha's help, persuaded him not to go anywhere and put him to bed completely drunk.

Masha promised to write to Konstantin in case of need and to persuade Nikolai Levin to go and live with him.

XXVI

In the morning Konstantin Levin left Moscow and towards evening he arrived at home. On the way in the train he talked with his neighbours about politics, about the new railways, and, just as in Moscow, he was overcome by the confusion of his notions, by dissatisfaction with himself and shame at something; but when he got off at his station, recognized the one-eyed coachman, Ignat, with his caftan collar turned up, when he saw his rug sleigh[38] in the dim light coming from the station windows, his horses with their bound tails, their harness with its rings and tassels, when the coachman Ignat, while they were still getting in, told him the village news, about the contractor's visit, and about Pava having calved – he felt the confusion gradually clearing up and the shame and dissatisfaction with himself going away. He felt it just at the sight of Ignat and the horses; but when he put on the sheepskin coat brought for him, got into the sleigh, wrapped himself up and drove off, thinking over the orders he had to give about the estate and glancing at the outrunner, a former Don saddle horse, over-ridden but a spirited animal, he began to understand what had happened to him quite differently. He felt he was himself and did not want to be otherwise. He only wanted to be better than he had been before. First, he decided from that day on not to hope any more for the extraordinary happiness that marriage was to have given him, and as a consequence not to neglect the present so much. Second, he would never again allow himself to be carried away by a vile passion, the memory of which had so tormented him as he was about to propose. Then, remembering his brother Nikolai, he decided that he would never again allow himself to forget him, would watch over him and never let him out of his sight, so as to be ready to help when things went badly for him. And that would be soon, he felt. Then, too, his brother's talk about communism, which he had taken so lightly at the time, now made him ponder. He regarded the reforming of economic conditions as nonsense, but he had always felt the injustice of his abundance as compared with the poverty of the people, and he now decided that, in order to feel himself fully in the right, though he had worked hard before and lived without luxury, he would now work still harder and allow himself still less luxury. And all this seemed so easy to do that he spent the whole way in the most pleasant dreams. With a cheerful feeling of hope for a new, better life, he drove up to his house between eight and nine in the evening.

Light fell on to the snow-covered yard in front of the house from the windows of the room of Agafya Mikhailovna, his old nurse, who filled the role of housekeeper for him. She was not yet asleep. Kuzma, whom she woke up, ran out sleepy and barefoot on to the porch. The pointer bitch Laska also ran out, almost knocking Kuzma off his feet, and rubbed herself against Levin's knees, stood on her hind legs and wanted but did not dare to put her front paws on his chest.

'You've come back so soon, dear,' said Agafya Mikhailovna.

'I missed it, Agafya Mikhailovna. There's no place like home,' he replied and went to his study.

The study was slowly lit up by the candle that was brought. Familiar details emerged: deer's antlers, shelves of books, the back of the stove with a vent that had long been in need of repair, his father's sofa, the big desk, an open book on the desk, a broken ashtray, a notebook with his handwriting. When he saw it all, he was overcome by a momentary doubt of the possibility of setting up that new life he had dreamed of on the way. All these traces of his life seemed to seize hold of him and say to him: 'No, you won't escape us and be different, you'll be the same as you were: with doubts, an eternal dissatisfaction with yourself, vain attempts to improve, and failures, and an eternal expectation of the happiness that has eluded you and is not possible for you.'

But that was how his things talked, while another voice in his soul said that he must not submit to his past and that it was possible to do anything with oneself. And, listening to this voice, he went to the corner where he had two thirty-six-pound dumb-bells and began lifting them, trying to cheer himself up with exercise. There was a creak of steps outside the door. He hastily set down the dumb-bells.

The steward came in and told him that everything, thank God, was well, but informed him that the buckwheat had got slightly burnt in the new kiln. This news vexed Levin. The new kiln had been built and partly designed by him. The steward had always been against this kiln and now with concealed triumph announced that the buckwheat had got burnt. Levin, however, was firmly convinced that if it had got burnt, it was only because the measures he had ordered a hundred times had not been taken. He became annoyed and reprimanded the steward. But there had been one important and joyful event: Pava, his best and most valuable cow, bought at a cattle show, had calved.

'Kuzma, give me my sheepskin coat. And you have them bring a lantern,' he said to the steward. 'I'll go and take a look.'

The shed for the valuable cows was just behind the house. Crossing the yard past a snowdrift by the lilac bush, he approached the shed. There was a smell of warm, dungy steam as the frozen door opened, and the cows, surprised by the unaccustomed light of the lantern, stirred on the fresh straw. The smooth, broad, black-and-white back of a Frisian cow flashed. Berkut, the bull, lay with his ring in his nose and made as if to get up, but changed his mind and only puffed a couple of times as they passed by. The red beauty, Pava, enormous as a hippopotamus, her hindquarters turned, screened the calf from the entering men and sniffed at it.

Levin entered the stall, looked Pava over, and lifted the spotted red calf on its long, tottering legs. The alarmed Pava began to low, but calmed down when Levin pushed the calf towards her, and with a heavy sigh started licking it with her rough tongue. The calf, searching, nudged its mother in the groin and wagged its little tail.

'Give me some light, Fyodor, bring the lantern here,' said Levin, looking the calf over. 'Just like her mother! Though the coat is the father's. Very fine. Long and deep-flanked. Fine, isn't she, Vassily Fyodorovich?' he asked the steward, completely reconciled with him about the buckwheat, under the influence of his joy over the calf.

'What bad could she take after? And the contractor Semyon came the day after you left. You'll have to settle the contract with him, Konstantin Dmitrich,' said the steward. 'I told you before about the machine.'

This one question led Levin into all the details of running the estate, which was big and complex. From the cowshed he went straight to the office and, after talking with the steward and the contractor Semyon, returned home and went straight upstairs to the drawing room.

XXVII

The house was big, old, and Levin, though he lived alone, heated and occupied all of it. He knew that this was foolish, knew that it was even wrong and contrary to his new plans, but this house was a whole world for Levin. It was the world in which his father and mother had lived and died. They had lived a life which for Levin seemed the ideal of all perfection and which he dreamed of renewing with his wife, with his family.

Levin barely remembered his mother. His notion of her was a sacred memory, and his future wife would have to be, in his imagination, the repetition of that lovely, sacred ideal of a woman which his mother was for him.

He was not only unable to picture to himself the love of a woman without marriage, but he first pictured the family to himself and only then the woman who would give him that family. His notion of marriage was therefore not like the notion of the majority of his acquaintances, for whom it was one of the many general concerns of life; for Levin it was the chief concern of life, on which all happiness depended. And now he had to renounce it!

When he went into the small drawing room where he always had tea, and settled into his armchair with a book, and Agafya Mikhailovna brought his tea and, with her usual 'I'll sit down, too, dear,' took a chair by the window, he felt that, strange as it was, he had not parted with his dreams and could not live without them. With her or with someone else, but they would come true. He read the book, thought about what he had read, paused to listen to Agafya Mikhailovna, who chattered tirelessly; and along with that various pictures of farm work and future family life arose disconnectedly in his imagination. He felt that something in the depths of his soul was being established, adjusted and settled.

He listened to Agafya Mikhailovna's talk of how Prokhor had forgotten God and, with the money Levin had given him to buy a horse, was drinking incessantly and had beaten his wife almost to death; he listened, read the book and remembered the whole course of his thoughts evoked by the reading. This was a book by Tyndall[39] on heat. He remembered his disapproval of Tyndall for his self-satisfaction over the cleverness of his experiments and for his lack of a philosophical outlook. And suddenly a joyful thought would surface: 'In two years I'll have two Frisian cows in my herd, Pava herself may still be alive, twelve young daughters from Berkut, plus these three to show off – wonderful!' He picked up his book again.

'Well, all right, electricity and heat are the same: but is it possible to solve a problem by substituting one quantity for another in an equation? No. Well, what then? The connection between all the forces of nature is felt instinctively as it is . . . It'll be especially nice when Pava's daughter is already a spotted red cow, and the whole herd, with these three thrown in . . . Splendid! To go out with my wife and guests to meet the herd . . . My wife will say: "Kostya and I tended this calf like a child." "How can it interest you so?" a guest will say. "Everything that interests him interests me." But who is she?' And he remembered what had happened in Moscow . . . 'Well, what to do? . . . I'm not to blame. But now everything will take a new course. It's nonsense that life won't allow it, that the past won't allow it. I must fight to live a better life, much better . . .' He raised his head and pondered. Old Laska, who had not yet quite digested the joy of his arrival and had gone to run around the yard and bark, came back wagging her tail, bringing with her the smell of outdoors, went over to him and thrust her head under his hand, making pitiful little whines and demanding to be patted.

'She all but speaks,' said Agafya Mikhailovna. 'Just a dog . . . But she understands that her master's come back and is feeling sad.'

'Why sad?'

'Don't I see it, dear? I ought to know my gentry by now. I grew up among gentry from early on. Never mind, dear. As long as you've got your health and a clear conscience.'

Levin looked at her intently, surprised that she understood his thoughts.

'Well, should I bring more tea?' she said, and, taking the cup, she went out.

Laska kept thrusting her head under his hand. He patted her, and she curled up just at his feet, placing her head on a stretched-out hind leg. And as a sign that all was well and good now, she opened her mouth slightly, smacked her sticky lips, and, settling them better around her old teeth, lapsed into blissful peace. Levin watched these last movements attentively.

'I'm just the same!' he said to himself, 'just the same! Never mind . . . All is well.'

XXVIII

Early on the morning after the ball, Anna Arkadyevna sent her husband a telegram about her departure from Moscow that same day.

'No, I must, I must go.' She explained the change of her intentions to her sister-in-law in such a tone as if she had remembered countless things she had to do. 'No, I'd better go today!'

Stepan Arkadyich did not dine at home, but promised to come at seven o'clock to see his sister off.

Kitty also did not come, sending a note that she had a headache. Dolly and Anna dined alone with the children and the English governess. Because children are either inconstant or else very sensitive and could feel that Anna was different that day from when they had come to love her so, that she was no longer concerned with them – in any case they suddenly stopped playing with their aunt and loving her, and were quite unconcerned about her leaving. All morning Anna was busy with the preparations for the departure. She wrote notes to Moscow acquaintances, jotted down her accounts, and packed. Generally, it seemed to Dolly that she was not in calm spirits, but in that state of anxiety Dolly knew so well in herself, which comes not without reason and most often covers up displeasure with oneself. After dinner Anna went to her room to dress and Dolly followed her.

'You're so strange today!' Dolly said to her.

'I? You think so? I'm not strange, I'm bad. It happens with me. I keep wanting to weep. It's very stupid, but it passes,' Anna said quickly and bent her reddened face to the tiny bag into which she was packing a nightcap and some cambric handkerchiefs. Her eyes had a peculiar shine and kept filling with tears. 'I was so reluctant to leave Petersburg, and now – to leave here.'

'You came here and did a good deed,' said Dolly, studying her intently.

Anna looked at her with eyes wet with tears.

'Don't say that, Dolly. I didn't do anything and couldn't do anything. I often wonder why people have all decided to spoil me. What have I done, and what could I have done? You found enough love in your heart to forgive . . .'

'Without you, God knows what would have happened! You're so lucky, Anna!' said Dolly. 'Everything in your soul is clear and good.'

'Each of us has his skeletons in his soul, as the English say.'

'What skeletons do you have? Everything's so clear with you.'

'There are some,' Anna said suddenly and, unexpectedly after her tears, a sly, humorous smile puckered her lips.

'Well, then they're funny, your skeletons, and not gloomy,' Dolly said, smiling.

'No, they're gloomy. Do you know why I'm going today and not tomorrow? It's a confession that has been weighing on me, and I want to make it to you,' Anna said, resolutely sitting back in the armchair and looking straight into Dolly's eyes.

And, to her surprise, Dolly saw Anna blush to the ears, to the curly black ringlets on her neck.

'Yes,' Anna went on. 'Do you know why Kitty didn't come for dinner? She's jealous of me. I spoiled . . . I was the reason that this ball was a torment for her and not a joy. But really, really, I'm not to blame, or only a little,' she said, drawing out the word 'little' in a thin voice.

'Ah, how like Stiva you said that!' Dolly laughed.

Anna became offended.

'Oh, no, no! I'm not like Stiva,' she said, frowning. 'I'm telling you this because I don't allow myself to doubt myself even for a moment.'

But the moment she uttered these words, she felt that they were wrong; she not only doubted herself, but felt excitement at the thought of Vronsky, and was leaving sooner than she had wanted only so as not to meet him any more.

'Yes, Stiva told me you danced the mazurka with him, and he . . .'

'You can't imagine how funny it came out. I had only just thought of matchmaking them, and suddenly it was something quite different. Perhaps against my own will I . . .'

She blushed and stopped.

'Oh, they feel it at once!' said Dolly.

'But I'd be desperate if there were anything serious here on his part,' Anna interrupted her. 'And I'm sure it will all be forgotten, and Kitty will stop hating me.'

'Anyhow, Anna, to tell you the truth, I don't much want this marriage for Kitty. It's better that it come to nothing, if he, Vronsky, could fall in love with you in one day.'

'Ah, my God, that would be so stupid!' said Anna, and again a deep blush of pleasure came to her face when she heard the thought that preoccupied her put into words. 'And so I'm leaving, having made an enemy of Kitty, whom I came to love so. Ah, she's such a dear! But you'll set things right, Dolly? Yes?'

Dolly could hardly repress a smile. She loved Anna, but she enjoyed seeing that she, too, had weaknesses.

'An enemy? That can't be.'

'I so wish you would all love me as I love you. And now I've come to love you still more,' she said with tears in her eyes. 'Ah, how stupid I am today!'

She dabbed her face with her handkerchief and began to dress.

Late, just before her departure, Stepan Arkadyich arrived, with a red and merry face, smelling of wine and cigars.

Anna's emotion communicated itself to Dolly, and as she embraced her sister-in-law for the last time, she whispered:

'Remember this, Anna: I will never forget what you did for me. And remember that I've loved and will always love you as my best friend!'

'I don't understand why,' said Anna, kissing her and hiding her tears.

'You've understood and understand me. Good-bye, my lovely!'

XXIX

'Well, it's all over, and thank God!' was the first thought that came to Anna Arkadyevna when she had said good-bye for the last time to her brother, who stood blocking the way into the carriage until the third bell. She sat down in her plush seat beside Annushka and looked around in the semi-darkness of the sleeping car.[40] 'Thank God, tomorrow I'll see Seryozha and Alexei Alexandrovich, and my good and usual life will go on as before.'

Still in the same preoccupied mood that she had been in all day, Anna settled herself with pleasure and precision for the journey; with her small, deft hands she unclasped her little red bag, took out a small pillow, put it on her knees, reclasped the bag, and, after neatly covering her legs, calmly leaned back. An ailing lady was already preparing to sleep. Two other ladies tried to address Anna, and a fat old woman, while covering her legs, made some observations about the heating. Anna said a few words in reply to the ladies, but, foreseeing no interesting conversation, asked Annushka to bring out a little lamp, attached it to the armrest of her seat, and took a paper-knife and an English novel from her handbag. At first she was unable to read. To begin with she was bothered by the bustle and movement; then, when the train started moving, she could not help listening to the noises; then the snow that beat against the left-hand window and stuck to the glass, and the sight of a conductor passing by, all bundled up and covered with snow on one side, and the talk about the terrible blizzard outside, distracted her attention. Further on it was all the same; the same jolting and knocking, the same snow on the window, the same quick transitions from steaming heat to cold and back to heat, the same flashing of the same faces in the semi-darkness, and the same voices, and Anna began to read and understand what she was reading. Annushka was already dozing, holding the little red bag on her knees with her broad hands in their gloves, one of which was torn. Anna Arkadyevna read and understood, but it was unpleasant for her to read, that is, to follow the reflection of other people's lives. She wanted too much to live herself. When she read about the heroine of the novel taking care of a sick man, she wanted to walk with inaudible steps round the sick man's room; when she read about a Member of Parliament making a speech, she wanted to make that speech; when she read about how Lady Mary rode to hounds, teasing her sister-in-law and surprising everyone with her courage, she wanted to do it herself. But there was nothing to do, and so, fingering the smooth knife with her small hands, she forced herself to read.

The hero of the novel was already beginning to achieve his English happiness, a baronetcy and an estate, and Anna wished to go with him to this estate, when suddenly she felt that he must be ashamed and that she was ashamed of the same thing. But what was he ashamed of? 'What am I ashamed of?' she asked herself in offended astonishment. She put down the book and leaned back in the seat, clutching the paper-knife tightly in both hands. There was nothing shameful. She went through all her Moscow memories. They were all good, pleasant. She remembered the ball, remembered Vronsky and his enamoured, obedient face, remembered all her relations with him: nothing was shameful. But just there, at that very place in her memories, the feeling of shame became more intense, as if precisely then, when she remembered Vronsky, some inner voice were telling her: 'Warm, very warm, hot!' 'Well, what then?' she said resolutely to herself, shifting her position in the seat. 'What does it mean? Am I afraid to look at it directly? Well, what of it? Can it be that there exist or ever could exist any other relations between me and this boy-officer than those that exist with any acquaintance?' She smiled scornfully and again picked up the book, but now was decidedly unable to understand what she was reading. She passed the paper-knife over the glass, then put its smooth and cold surface to her cheek and nearly laughed aloud from the joy that suddenly came over her for no reason. She felt her nerves tighten more and more, like strings on winding pegs. She felt her eyes open wider and wider, her fingers and toes move nervously; something inside her stopped her breath, and all images and sounds in that wavering semi-darkness impressed themselves on her with extraordinary vividness. She kept having moments of doubt whether the carriage was moving forwards or backwards, or standing still. Was that Annushka beside her, or some stranger? 'What is that on the armrest – a fur coat or some animal? And what am I? Myself or someone else?' It was frightening to surrender herself to this oblivion. But something was drawing her in, and she was able, at will, to surrender to it or hold back from it. She stood up in order to come to her senses, threw the rug aside, and removed the pelerine from her warm dress. For a moment she recovered and realized that the skinny muzhik coming in, wearing a long nankeen coat with a missing button, was the stoker, that he was looking at the thermometer, that wind and snow had burst in with him through the doorway; but then everything became confused again ... This muzhik with the long waist began to gnaw at something on the wall; the old woman began to stretch her legs out the whole length of the carriage and filled it with a black cloud; then something screeched and banged terribly, as if someone was being torn to pieces; then a red fire blinded her eyes, and then everything was hidden by a wall. Anna felt as if she was falling through the floor. But all this was not frightening but exhilarating. The voice of a bundled-up and snow-covered man shouted something into her ear. She stood up and came to her senses, realizing that they had arrived at a station and the man was the conductor. She asked Annushka to hand her the pelerine and a shawl, put them on and went to the door.

'Are you going out?' asked Annushka.

'Yes, I need a breath of air. It's very hot in here.'

And she opened the door. Blizzard and wind came tearing to meet her and vied with her for the door. This, too, she found exhilarating. She opened the door and went out. The wind, as if only waiting for her, whistled joyfully and wanted to pick her up and carry her off, but she grasped the cold post firmly and, holding her dress down, stepped on to the platform and into the lee of the carriage. The wind was strong on the steps, but on the platform beside the train it was quiet. With pleasure she drew in deep breaths of the snowy, frosty air and, standing by the carriage, looked around the platform and the lit-up station.

XXX

The terrible snowstorm tore and whistled between the wheels of the carriages, over the posts and around the corner of the station. Carriages, posts, people, everything visible was covered with snow on one side and getting covered more and more. The storm would subside for a moment, but then return again in such gusts that it seemed impossible to withstand it. Meanwhile, people were running, exchanging merry talk, creaking over the planks of the platform, and ceaselessly opening and closing the big doors. The huddled shadow of a man slipped under her feet, and there was the noise of a hammer striking iron. 'Give me the telegram!' a gruff voice came from across the stormy darkness. 'This way, please!' 'Number twenty-eight!' various other voices shouted, and bundled-up, snow-covered people ran by. Two gentlemen with the fire of cigarettes in their mouths walked past her. She breathed in once more, to get her fill of air, and had already taken her hand from her muff to grasp the post and go into the carriage, when near her another man, in a military greatcoat, screened her from the wavering light of the lantern. She turned and in the same moment recognized the face of Vronsky. Putting his hand to his visor, he bowed to her and asked if she needed anything, if he might be of service to her. She peered at him for quite a long time without answering and, though he was standing in the shadow, she could see, or thought she could see, the expression of his face and eyes. It was again that expression of respectful admiration which had so affected her yesterday. More than once she had told herself during those recent days and again just now that for her Vronsky was one among hundreds of eternally identical young men to be met everywhere, that she would never allow herself even to think of him; but now, in the first moment of meeting him, she was overcome by a feeling of joyful pride. She had no need to ask why he was there. She knew it as certainly as if he had told her that he was there in order to be where she was.

'I didn't know you were going. Why are you going?' she said, letting fall the hand that was already holding the post. And irrepressible joy and animation shone on her face.

'Why am I going?' he repeated, looking straight into her eyes. 'You know I am going in order to be where you are,' he said, 'I cannot do otherwise.'

And just then, as if overcoming an obstacle, the wind dumped snow from the roof of the carriage, blew some torn-off sheet of iron about, and from ahead a low train whistle howled mournfully and drearily. All the terror of the blizzard seemed still more beautiful to her now. He had said the very thing that her soul desired but that her reason feared. She made no reply, and he saw a struggle in her face.

'Forgive me if what I have said is unpleasant for you,' he said submissively.

He spoke courteously, respectfully, but so firmly and stubbornly that for a long time she was unable to make any reply.

'What you're saying is bad, and I beg you, if you are a good man, to forget it, as I will forget it,' she said at last.

'Not one of your words, not one of your movements will I ever forget, and I cannot . . .'

'Enough, enough!' she cried out, trying in vain to give a stern expression to her face, into which he peered greedily. And, placing her hand on the cold post, she went up the steps and quickly entered the vestibule of the carriage. But in this little vestibule she stopped, pondering in her imagination what had just happened. Though she could remember neither his words nor her own, she sensed that this momentary conversation had brought them terribly close, and this made her both frightened and happy. She stood for a few seconds, went into the carriage, and took her seat. The magical, strained condition that had tormented her at the beginning not only renewed itself, but grew stronger and reached a point where she feared that something wound too tight in her might snap at any moment. She did not sleep all night. But in that strain and those reveries that filled her imagination there was nothing unpleasant or gloomy; on the contrary, there was something joyful, burning, and exciting. Towards morning Anna dozed off in her seat, and when she woke up it was already white, bright, and the train was pulling into Petersburg. At once thoughts of her home, her husband, her son, and the cares of the coming day and those to follow surrounded her.

In Petersburg, as soon as the train stopped and she got off, the first face that caught her attention was that of her husband. 'Ah, my God!

what's happened with his ears?' she thought, looking at his cold and imposing figure and especially struck now by the cartilage of his ears propping up the brim of his round hat. Seeing her, he came to meet her, composing his lips into his habitual mocking smile and looking straight at her with his big weary eyes. Some unpleasant feeling gnawed at her heart as she met his unwavering and weary gaze, as if she had expected him to look different. She was especially struck by the feeling of dissatisfaction with herself that she experienced on meeting him. This was an old, familiar feeling, similar to that state of pretence she experienced in her relations with her husband; but previously she had not noticed it, while now she was clearly and painfully aware of it.

'Yes, as you see, your tender husband, tender as in the second year of marriage, is burning with desire to see you,' he said in his slow, high voice and in the tone he almost always used with her, a tone in mockery of someone who might actually mean what he said.

'Is Seryozha well?' she asked.

'Is that all the reward I get for my ardour?' he said. 'He's well, he's well . . .'

XXXI

Vronsky did not even try to fall asleep all that night. He sat in his seat, now staring straight ahead of him, now looking over the people going in and out, and if he had struck and troubled strangers before by his air of imperturbable calm, he now seemed still more proud and self-sufficient. He looked at people as if they were things. A nervous young man across from him, who served on the circuit court, came to hate him for that look. The young man lit a cigarette from his, tried talking to him, and even jostled him, to let him feel that he was not a thing but a human being, but Vronsky went on looking at him as at a lamppost, and the young man grimaced, feeling that he was losing his self-possession under the pressure of this non-recognition of himself as a human being and was unable to fall asleep because of it.

Vronsky did not see anything or anybody. He felt himself a king, not because he thought he had made an impression on Anna – he did not believe that yet – but because the impression she had made on him gave him happiness and pride.

What would come of it all, he did not know and did not even consider. He felt that all his hitherto dissipated and dispersed forces were gathered and directed with terrible energy towards one blissful goal. And he was happy in that. He knew only that he had told her the truth, that he was going where she was, that the whole happiness of life, the sole meaning of life, he now found in seeing and hearing her. And when he got off the train at Bologoye for a drink of seltzer water, and saw Anna, his first words involuntarily told her just what he thought. And he was glad he had said it to her, that she now knew it and was thinking about it. He did not sleep all night. Returning to his carriage, he kept running through all the attitudes in which he had seen her, all her words, and in his imagination floated pictures of the possible future, making his heart stand still.

When he got off the train in Petersburg he felt animated and fresh after his sleepless night, as after a cold bath. He stopped by his carriage, waiting for her to get out. 'One more time,' he said to himself, smiling involuntarily, 'I'll see her walk, her face; she'll say something, turn her head, look, perhaps smile.' But even before seeing her, he saw her husband, whom the stationmaster was courteously conducting through the crowd. 'Ah, yes, the husband!' Only now did Vronsky understand clearly for the first time that the husband was a person connected with her. He knew she had a husband, but had not believed in his existence and fully believed in it only when he saw him, with his head, his shoulders, his legs in black trousers; and especially when he saw this husband calmly take her arm with a proprietary air.

Seeing Alexei Alexandrovich with his fresh Petersburg face[41], his sternly self-confident figure, his round hat and slightly curved back, he believed in him and experienced an unpleasant feeling, like that of a man suffering from thirst who comes to a spring and finds in it a dog, a sheep or a pig who has both drunk and muddied the water. The gait of Alexei Alexandrovich, swinging his whole pelvis and his blunt feet, was especially offensive to Vronsky. Only for himself did he acknowledge the unquestionable right to love her. But she was still the same, and her appearance still affected him in the same way, physically reviving, arousing his soul, and filling it with happiness. He told his German footman, who came running from second class, to take his things and go, and he himself went up to her. He saw the first meeting of husband and wife and, with the keen-sightedness of a man in love, noticed signs of the slight constraint with which she talked to her husband. 'No, she does not and cannot love him,' he decided to himself.

As he came up to Anna Arkadyevna from behind, he noticed with joy that she, sensing his approach, looked around and, recognizing him, turned back to her husband.

'Did you have a good night?' he said, bowing to her and her husband together, and giving Alexei Alexandrovich a chance to take this bow to his own account and recognize him or not, as he wished.

'Very good, thank you,' she replied.

Her face seemed tired, and there was none of that play of animation in it which begged to come out now in her smile, now in her eyes; yet for a moment, as she glanced at him, something flashed in her eyes and, although this fire went out at once, he was happy in that moment. She looked at her husband to see whether he knew Vronsky. Alexei Alexandrovich was looking at Vronsky with displeasure, absently trying to recall who he was. Vronsky's calm and self-confidence here clashed like steel against stone with the cold self-confidence of Alexei Alexandrovich.

'Count Vronsky,' said Anna.

'Ah! We're acquainted, I believe,' Alexei Alexandrovich said with indifference, offering his hand. 'You went with the mother and came back with the son,' he said, articulating distinctly, as if counting out each word. 'You must be returning from leave?' he said and, without waiting for an answer, addressed his wife in his bantering tone: 'So, were there many tears shed in Moscow over the parting?'

By addressing his wife in this way, he made it clear to Vronsky that he wished to be left alone, and, turning to him, he touched his hat; but Vronsky addressed Anna Arkadyevna:

'I hope to have the honour of calling on you,' he said.

Alexei Alexandrovich looked at Vronsky with his weary eyes.

'I'd be delighted,' he said coldly, 'we receive on Mondays.' Then, having dismissed Vronsky altogether, he said to his wife: 'And how good it is that I had precisely half an hour to meet you and that I have been able to show you my tenderness,' continuing in the same bantering tone.

'You emphasize your tenderness far too much for me to value it greatly,' she said in the same bantering tone, involuntarily listening to the sound of Vronsky's footsteps behind them. 'But what do I care?' she thought and began asking her husband how Seryozha had spent the time without her.

'Oh, wonderfully! Mariette says he was very nice and . . . I must upset you . . . didn't miss you, unlike your husband. But *merci* once again, my dear, for the gift of one day. Our dear samovar will be delighted.' (He called the celebrated Countess Lydia Ivanovna 'samovar', because she was always getting excited and heated up about things.) 'She's been asking about you. And you know, if I may be so bold as to advise you, you might just go to see her today. She takes everything to heart so. Now, besides all her other troubles, she's concerned with reconciling the Oblonskys.'

Countess Lydia Ivanovna was her husband's friend and the centre of one of the circles of Petersburg society with which Anna was most closely connected through her husband.

'I did write to her.'

'But she needs everything in detail. Go, if you're not tired, my dear. Well, Kondraty will take you in the carriage, and I'm off to the committee. I won't be alone at dinner any more,' Alexei Alexandrovich went on, no longer in a bantering tone. 'You wouldn't believe how I've got used to . . .'

And, pressing her hand for a long time, with a special smile, he helped her into the carriage.

XXXII

The first person to meet Anna at home was her son. He came running down the stairs to her, despite the cries of the governess, and with desperate rapture shouted: 'Mama, mama!' Rushing to her, he hung on her neck.

'I told you it was mama!' he cried to the governess. 'I knew it!'

And the son, just like the husband, produced in Anna a feeling akin to disappointment. She had imagined him better than he was in reality. She had to descend into reality to enjoy him as he was. But he was charming even as he was, with his blond curls, blue eyes and full, shapely legs in tight-fitting stockings. Anna experienced almost a physical pleasure in the feeling of his closeness and caress, and a moral ease when she met his simple-hearted, trusting and loving eyes and heard his naïve questions. She took out the presents that Dolly's children had sent and told her son about the girl Tanya in Moscow and how this Tanya knew how to read and even taught the other children.

'And am I worse than she is?' asked Seryozha.

'For me you're the best in the world.'

'I know that,' said Seryozha, smiling.

Before Anna had time to have coffee, Countess Lydia Ivanovna was announced. Countess Lydia Ivanovna was a tall, stout woman with an unhealthy yellow complexion and beautiful, pensive dark eyes. Anna loved her, but today she saw her as if for the first time with all her shortcomings.

'Well, my friend, did you bear the olive branch?' Countess Lydia Ivanovna asked as soon as she came into the room.

'Yes, it's all over, but it was not as important as we thought,' Anna replied. 'Generally, my *belle-soeur* is too headstrong.'

But Countess Lydia Ivanovna, who was interested in everything that did not concern her, had the habit of never listening to what interested her. She interrupted Anna:

'Yes, there is much woe and wickedness in the world – but I'm so exhausted today.'

'What's wrong?' asked Anna, trying to repress a smile.

'I'm beginning to weary of breaking lances for the truth in vain, and sometimes I go quite to pieces. The business with the little sisters' (this was a philanthropic, religious and patriotic institution) 'would have gone splendidly, but it's impossible to do anything with these gentlemen,' Countess Lydia Ivanovna added in mock submission to her fate. 'They seized on the idea, distorted it, and now discuss it in such a petty, worthless fashion. Two or three people, your husband among them, understand the full significance of this business, but the others only demean it. Yesterday Pravdin wrote to me . . .'

Pravdin was a well-known Pan-Slavist[42] who lived abroad. Countess Lydia Ivanovna proceeded to recount the contents of his letter.

Then she told of further troubles and schemes against the cause of Church unity and left hurriedly, because that afternoon she still had to attend a meeting of some society and then of the Slavic committee.

'All this was there before; but why didn't I notice it before?' Anna said to herself. 'Or is she very irritated today? In fact, it's ridiculous: her goal is virtue, she's a Christian, yet she's angry all the time, and they're all her enemies, and they're all enemies on account of Christianity and virtue.'

After Countess Lydia Ivanovna had left, an acquaintance came, the wife of a director, and told her all the news about town. At three o'clock she also left, promising to come for dinner. Alexei Alexandrovich was at the ministry. Finding herself alone, Anna spent the time before dinner sitting with her son while he ate (he dined separately), putting her things in order and reading and answering the notes and letters that had accumulated on her desk.

Her agitation and the sense of groundless shame she had experienced during the journey disappeared completely. In the accustomed conditions of her life she again felt herself firm and irreproachable.

She recalled with astonishment her state yesterday. 'What happened? Nothing. Vronsky said a foolish thing, which it was easy to put an end to, and I replied as I ought to have done. To speak of it with my husband is unnecessary and impossible. To speak of it – would mean giving importance to something that has none.' She recalled how she had told him of a near declaration that one of her husband's young subordinates had made to her in Petersburg, and how Alexei Alexandrovich had replied that, living in society, any woman may be subject to such things, but that he fully trusted her tact and would never allow either himself or her to be demeaned by jealousy. 'So there's no reason to tell him? Yes, thank God, and there's nothing to tell,' she said to herself.

XXXIII

Alexei Alexandrovich returned from the ministry at four o'clock, but, as often happened, had no time to go to her room. He proceeded to his study to receive the waiting petitioners and sign some papers brought by the office manager. At dinner (three or four people always dined with the Karenins) there were Alexei Alexandrovich's elderly female cousin, the department director and his wife and a young man recommended to Alexei Alexandrovich at work. Anna came out to the drawing room to entertain them. At exactly five o'clock, before the Peter-the-Great bronze clock struck for the fifth time, Alexei Alexandrovich came out in a white tie and a tailcoat with two stars, because he had to leave right after dinner. Every minute of Alexei Alexandrovich's life was occupied and scheduled. And in order to have time to do what he had to do each day, he held to the strictest punctuality. 'Without haste and without rest' was his motto. He entered the room, bowed to everyone, and hastily sat down, smiling at his wife.

'Yes, my solitude is ended. You wouldn't believe how awkward' (he emphasized the word *awkward*) 'it is to dine alone.'

Over dinner he talked with his wife about Moscow affairs, asked with a mocking smile about Stepan Arkadyich; but the conversation was mainly general, about Petersburg administrative and social affairs. After dinner he spent half an hour with his guests and, again pressing his wife's hand with a smile, left and went to the Council. This time Anna went neither to see Princess Betsy Tverskoy, who, on learning of her return, had invited her for the evening, nor to the theatre, where she had a box for that night. She did not go mainly because the dress she had counted on was not ready. Having turned to her toilette after her guests' departure, Anna was very annoyed. Before leaving for Moscow, she, who was generally an expert at dressing not very expensively, had given her dressmaker three dresses to be altered. The dresses needed to be altered so that they could not be recognized, and they were to have been ready three days ago. It turned out that two of the dresses were not ready at all, and the third had not been altered in the way Anna wanted. The dressmaker came and explained that it was better as she had done it, and Anna got so upset that afterwards she was ashamed to remember it. To calm herself completely, she went to the nursery and spent the whole evening with her son, put him to bed herself, made a cross over him and covered him with a blanket. She was glad that she had not gone anywhere and had spent the evening so well. She felt light and calm. She saw clearly that everything that had seemed so important to her on the train was merely one of the ordinary, insignificant episodes of social life, and there was nothing to be ashamed of before others or herself. Anna sat by the fireplace with her English novel and waited for her husband. At exactly half-past nine the bell rang, and he came into the room.

'It's you at last!' she said, giving him her hand.

He kissed her hand and sat down beside her.

'Generally, I see your trip was a success,' he said to her.

'Yes, very,' she replied, and started telling him everything from the beginning: her journey with Mme Vronsky, her arrival, the accident at the railway station. Then she told of the pity she had felt, first for her brother, then for Dolly.

'I don't suppose one can possibly excuse such a man, though he is your brother,' Alexei Alexandrovich said sternly.

Anna smiled. She understood that he had said it precisely to show that considerations of kinship could not keep him from expressing his sincere opinion. She knew this feature in her husband and liked it.

'I'm glad it all ended satisfactorily and that you've come back,' he continued. 'Well, what are they saying there about the new statute I passed in the Council?'

Anna had heard nothing about this statute, and felt ashamed that she could so easily forget something so important for him.

'Here, on the contrary, it caused a good deal of stir,' he said with a self-satisfied smile.

She could see that Alexei Alexandrovich wanted to tell her something that pleased him about this matter, and by her questions she led him to telling it. With the same self-satisfied smile, he told her about an ovation he had received as a result of the passing of this statute.

'I was very, very glad. This proves that a reasonable and firm view of the matter is finally being established among us.'

Having finished his bread and a second glass of tea with cream, Alexei Alexandrovich got up and went to his study.

'And you didn't go out anywhere – it must have been boring for you?' he said.

'Oh, no!' she replied, getting up after him and accompanying him across the drawing room to his study. 'What are you reading now?' she asked.

'I'm now reading the Duc de Lille, *Poésie des enfers*,'[43] he replied. 'A very remarkable book.'

Anna smiled, as one smiles at the weaknesses of people one loves, and, putting her arm under his, accompanied him to the door of the study. She knew his habit, which had become a necessity, of reading in the evenings. She knew that in spite of the responsibilities of service which consumed almost all his time, he considered it his duty to follow everything remarkable that appeared in the intellectual sphere. She also knew that he was indeed interested in books on politics, philosophy, theology, that art was completely foreign to his nature, but that, in spite of that, or rather because of it, Alexei Alexandrovich did not miss anything that caused a stir in that area, and considered it his duty to read everything. She knew that in the areas of politics, philosophy and theology, Alexei Alexandrovich doubted or searched; but in questions of art and poetry, and especially music, of which he lacked all understanding, he had the most definite and firm opinions. He liked to talk about Shakespeare, Raphael, Beethoven, about the significance of the new schools in poetry and music, which with him were all sorted out in a very clear order.

'Well, God bless you,' she said at the door of the study, where a shaded candle and a carafe of water had already been prepared for him beside the armchair. 'And I'll write to Moscow.'

He pressed her hand and again kissed it.

'All the same, he's a good man, truthful, kind and remarkable in his sphere,' Anna said to herself, going back to her room, as if defending him before someone who was accusing him and saying that it was impossible to love him. 'But why do his ears stick out so oddly? Did he have his hair cut?'

Exactly at midnight, when Anna was still sitting at her desk finishing a letter to Dolly, she heard the measured steps of slippered feet, and Alexei Alexandrovich, washed and combed, a book under his arm, came up to her.

'It's time, it's time,' he said with a special smile, and went into the bedroom.

'And what right did he have to look at him like that?' thought Anna, recalling how Vronsky had looked at Alexei Alexandrovich.

She undressed and went to the bedroom, but not only was that animation which had simply burst from her eyes and smile when she was in Moscow gone from her face: on the contrary, the fire now seemed extinguished in her or hidden somewhere far away.

XXXIV

On his departure from Petersburg, Vronsky had left his big apartment on Morskaya to his friend and favourite comrade Petritsky.

Petritsky was a young lieutenant, of no especially high nobility, not only not rich but in debt all around, always drunk towards evening, and often ending up in the guard house for various funny and dirty episodes, but loved by both his comrades and his superiors. Driving up to his apartment from the railway station towards noon, Vronsky saw a familiar hired carriage by the entrance. In response to his ring, he heard men's laughter from behind the door, a woman's voice prattling in French and Petritsky's shout: 'If it's one of those villains, don't let him in!' Vronsky told the orderly not to announce him and quietly went into the front room. Baroness Shilton, Petritsky's lady-friend, her lilac satin dress and rosy fair face shining, and her canary-like Parisian talk filling the whole room, was sitting at a round table making coffee. Petritsky in a civilian overcoat and the cavalry captain Kamerovsky in full uniform, probably just off duty, were sitting on either side of her.

'Bravo! Vronsky!' cried Petritsky, jumping up noisily from his chair. 'The host himself! Coffee for him, Baroness, from the new coffeepot. We weren't expecting you! I hope you're pleased with the new ornament of your study,' he said, pointing to the baroness. 'You're acquainted?'

'What else!' said Vronsky, smiling gaily and pressing the baroness's little hand. 'We're old friends!'

'You're back from a trip,' said the baroness, 'so I'll run off. Oh, I'll leave this very minute if I'm in the way.'

'You're at home right where you are, Baroness,' said Vronsky. 'Good day, Kamerovsky,' he added, coldly shaking Kamerovsky's hand.

'See, and you never know how to say such pretty things.' The baroness turned to Petritsky.

'No? Why not? I'll do no worse after dinner.'

'After dinner there's no virtue in it! Well, then I'll give you some coffee, go wash and tidy yourself up,' said the baroness, sitting down again and carefully turning a screw in the new coffeepot. 'Pass me the coffee, Pierre.' She turned to Petritsky, whom she called Pierre after his last name, not concealing her relations with him. 'I'll add some more.'

'You'll spoil it.'

'No, I won't! Well, and your wife?' the baroness said suddenly, interrupting Vronsky's conversation with his comrade. 'We've got you married here. Did you bring your wife?'

'No, Baroness. I was born a gypsy and I'll die a gypsy.'

'So much the better, so much the better. Give me your hand.'

And the baroness, without letting go of Vronsky's hand, began telling him her latest plans for her life, interspersing it with jokes, and asking for his advice.

'He keeps refusing to grant me a divorce! Well, what am I to do?' ('He' was her husband.) 'I want to start proceedings. How would you advise me? Kamerovsky, keep an eye on the coffee, it's boiling over – you can see I'm busy! I want proceedings, because I need my fortune. Do you understand this stupidity – that I'm supposedly unfaithful to him,' she said with scorn, 'and so he wants to have use of my estate?'

Vronsky listened with pleasure to this merry prattle of a pretty woman, agreed with her, gave half-jocular advice, and generally adopted his habitual tone in dealing with women of her kind. In his Petersburg world, all people were divided into two completely opposite sorts. One was the inferior sort: the banal, stupid and, above all, ridiculous people who believed that one husband should live with one wife, whom he has married in church, that a girl should be innocent, a woman modest, a man manly, temperate and firm, that one should raise children, earn one's bread, pay one's debts, and other such stupidities. This was an old-fashioned and ridiculous sort of people. But there was another sort of people, the real ones, to which they all belonged, and for whom one had, above all, to be elegant, handsome, magnanimous, bold, gay, to give oneself to every passion without blushing and laugh at everything else.

Vronsky was stunned only for the first moment, after the impressions of a completely different world that he had brought from Moscow; but at once, as if putting his feet into old slippers, he stepped back into his former gay and pleasant world.

The coffee never got made, but splashed on everything and boiled over and produced precisely what was needed – that is, gave an excuse for noise and laughter, spilling on the expensive carpet and the baroness's dress.

'Well, good-bye now, or else you'll never get washed, and I'll have on my conscience the worst crime of a decent person – uncleanliness. So your advice is a knife at his throat?'

'Absolutely, and with your little hand close to his lips. He'll kiss your hand, and all will end well,' Vronsky replied.

'Tonight, then, at the French Theatre!' And she disappeared, her dress rustling.

Kamerovsky also stood up, and Vronsky, not waiting for him to leave, gave him his hand and went to his dressing room. While he washed, Petritsky described his own situation in a few strokes, to the extent that it had changed since Vronsky's departure. Of money there was none. His father said he would not give him any, nor pay his debts. One tailor wanted to have him locked up, and the other was also threatening to have him locked up without fail. The commander of the regiment announced that if these scandals did not stop, he would have to resign. He was fed up with the baroness, especially since she kept wanting to give him money; but there was one, he would show her to Vronsky, a wonder, a delight, in the severe Levantine style, the 'slave-girl Rebecca genre,[44] you know'. He had also quarrelled yesterday with Berkoshev, who wanted to send his seconds, but surely nothing would come of that. Generally, everything was excellent and extremely jolly. And, not letting his friend go deeper into the details of his situation, Petritsky started telling him all the interesting news. Listening to his so-familiar stories, in the so-familiar surroundings of his apartment of three years, Vronsky experienced the pleasant feeling of returning to his accustomed and carefree Petersburg life.

'It can't be!' he cried, releasing the pedal of the washstand from which water poured over his robust red neck. 'It can't be!' he cried at the news that Laura was now with Mileev and had dropped Fertinhoff. 'And he's still just as stupid and content? Well, and what about Buzulukov?'

'Ah, there was a story with Buzulukov – lovely!' cried Petritsky. 'He has this passion for balls, and he never misses a single court ball. So he went to a big ball in a new helmet. Have you seen the new helmets? Very good, much lighter. There he stands . . . No, listen.'

'I am listening,' Vronsky replied, rubbing himself with a Turkish towel.

'The grand duchess passes by with some ambassador, and, as luck would have it, they begin talking about the new helmets. So the grand duchess wants to show him a new helmet . . . They see our dear fellow standing there.' (Petritsky showed how he was standing there with his helmet.) 'The grand duchess tells him to hand her the helmet – he won't do it. What's the matter? They wink at him, nod, frown. Hand it over. He won't. He freezes. Can you imagine? . . . Then that one . . . what's his name . . . wants to take the helmet from him . . . he won't let go! . . . He tears it away, hands it to the grand duchess. "Here's the new helmet," says the grand duchess. She turns it over and, can you imagine, out of it – bang! – falls a pear and some sweets – two pounds of sweets! . . . He had it all stashed away, the dear fellow!'

Vronsky rocked with laughter. And for a long time afterwards, talking about other things, he would go off into his robust laughter, exposing a solid row of strong teeth, when he remembered about the helmet.

Having learned all the news, Vronsky, with the help of his footman, put on his uniform and went to report. After reporting, he intended to call on his brother, then on Betsy, and then to pay several visits, so that he could begin to appear in the society where he might meet Anna. As always in Petersburg, he left home not to return till late at night.

Part Two

I

At the end of winter a consultation took place in the Shcherbatsky home, which was to decide on the state of Kitty's health and what must be undertaken to restore her failing strength. She was ill, and as spring approached her health was growing worse. The family doctor gave her cod-liver oil, then iron, then common caustic, but as neither the one nor the other nor the third was of any help, and as he advised going abroad for the spring, a famous doctor was called in. The famous doctor, not yet old and quite a handsome man, asked to examine the patient. With particular pleasure, it seemed, he insisted that maidenly modesty was merely a relic of barbarism and that nothing was more natural than for a not-yet-old man to palpate a naked young girl. He found it natural because he did it every day and never, as it seemed to him, felt or thought anything bad, and therefore he regarded modesty in a girl not only as a relic of barbarism but also as an affront to himself.

They had to submit, because, though all doctors studied in the same school, from the same books, and knew the same science, and though some said that this famous doctor was a bad doctor, in the princess's home and in her circle it was for some reason acknowledged that he alone knew something special and he alone could save Kitty. After a careful examination and sounding of the patient, who was bewildered and stunned with shame, the famous doctor, having diligently washed his hands, was standing in the drawing room and talking with the prince. The prince frowned and kept coughing as he listened to the doctor. He, as a man who had seen life and was neither stupid nor sick, did not believe in medicine, and in his soul he was angry at this whole comedy, the more so in that he was almost the only one who fully understood the cause of Kitty's illness. 'What a gabbler,' he thought, mentally applying this barnyard term to the famous doctor and listening to his chatter about the symptoms of his daughter's illness. The doctor meanwhile found it hard to keep from expressing his contempt for the old gentleman and descending to the low level of his understanding. He understood that there was no point in talking with the old man, and that the head of this house was the mother. It was before her that he intended to strew his pearls. Just then the princess came into the drawing room with the family doctor. The prince stepped aside, trying not to show how ridiculous this whole comedy was to him. The princess was bewildered and did not know what to do. She felt herself guilty before Kitty.

'Well, doctor, decide our fate,' she said. 'Tell me everything.' ('Is there any hope?' she wanted to say, but her lips trembled and she could not get the question out.) 'Well, what is it, doctor? . . .'

'I will presently confer with my colleague, Princess, and then I will have the honour of reporting my opinion to you.'

'So we should leave you?'

'As you please.'

The princess sighed and went out.

When the doctors were left alone, the family physician timidly began to present his opinion, according to which there was the start of a tubercular condition, but . . . and so forth. The famous doctor listened to him and in the middle of his speech looked at his large gold watch.

'Indeed,' he said. 'But . . .'

The family physician fell respectfully silent in the middle of his speech.

'As you know, we cannot diagnose the start of a tubercular condition. Nothing is definite until cavities appear. But we can suspect. And there are indications: poor appetite, nervous excitation and so on. The question stands thus: given the suspicion of a tubercular condition, what must be done to maintain the appetite?'

'But, you know, there are always some hidden moral and spiritual causes,' the family doctor allowed himself to put in with a subtle smile.

'Yes, that goes without saying,' the famous doctor replied, glancing at his watch again. 'Excuse me, has the Yauza bridge been put up, or must one still go round?' he asked. 'Ah, put up! Well, then I can make it in twenty minutes. So, as we were saying, the question is put thus: to maintain the appetite and repair the nerves. The one is connected with the other, we must work on both sides of the circle.'

'And a trip abroad?' asked the family doctor.

'I am an enemy of trips abroad. And kindly note: if there is the start of a tubercular condition, which is something we cannot know, then a trip abroad will not help. What's needed is a remedy that will maintain the appetite without being harmful.'

And the famous doctor presented his plan of treatment by Soden waters, the main aim in the prescription of which evidently being that they could do no harm.

The family doctor listened attentively and respectfully.

'But in favour of a trip abroad I would point to the change of habits, the removal from conditions evoking memories. Then, too, the mother wants it,' he said.

'Ah! Well, in that case let them go; only, those German charlatans will do harm . . . They must listen to . . . Well, then let them go.'

He glanced at his watch again.

'Oh! it's time,' and he went to the door.

The famous doctor announced to the princess (a sense of propriety prompted it) that he must see the patient again.

'What! Another examination!' the mother exclaimed with horror.

'Oh, no, just a few details, Princess.'

'If you please.'

And the mother, accompanied by the doctor, went to Kitty in the drawing room. Emaciated and red-cheeked, with a special glitter in her eyes as a result of the shame she had endured, Kitty was standing in the middle of the room. When the doctor entered she blushed and her eyes filled with tears. Her whole illness and treatment seemed to her such a stupid, even ridiculous thing! Her treatment seemed to her as ridiculous as putting together the pieces of a broken vase. Her heart was broken. And what did they want to do, treat her with pills and powders? But she could not insult her mother, especially since her mother considered herself to blame.

'Kindly sit down, miss,' said the famous doctor.

He sat down facing her with a smile, felt her pulse, and again began asking tiresome questions. She kept answering him, but suddenly got angry and stood up.

'Forgive me, doctor, but this really will not lead anywhere. You ask me the same thing three times over.'

The famous doctor was not offended.

'Morbid irritation,' he said to the old princess when Kitty had gone. 'Anyhow, I was finished . . .'

And to the princess, as to an exceptionally intelligent woman, the doctor scientifically defined her daughter's condition and concluded with instructions on how to drink those waters of which there was no need. At the question of going abroad, the doctor lapsed into deep thought, as if solving a difficult problem. The solution was finally presented: go, and do not believe the charlatans, but refer to him in all things.

It was as if something cheerful happened after the doctor's departure. The mother cheered up as she came back to her daughter, and Kitty pretended to cheer up. She often, almost always, had to pretend now.

'I'm really well, *maman*. But if you want to go, let's go!' she said, and, trying to show interest in the forthcoming trip, she began talking about the preparations for their departure.

II

After the doctor left, Dolly arrived. She knew there was to be a consultation that day, and though she had only recently got up from a confinement (she had given birth to a girl at the end of winter), though she had many griefs and cares of her own, she left her nursing baby and a daughter who had fallen ill, and called to learn Kitty's fate, which was being decided just then.

'Well, so?' she said, coming into the drawing room and not taking off her hat. 'You're all cheerful. Must be good news?'

They tried to tell her what the doctor had told them, but it turned out that though the doctor had spoken very well and at length, it was quite impossible to repeat what he had said. The only interesting thing was that it had been decided to go abroad.

Dolly sighed involuntarily. Her best friend, her sister, was leaving. And there was no cheer in her own life. Her relations with Stepan Arkadyich after the reconciliation had become humiliating. The welding, done by Anna, had not proved strong, and the family accord had broken again at the same place. There was nothing definite, but Stepan Arkadyich was almost never at home, there was also almost never any money in the house, and Dolly was constantly tormented by suspicions of his unfaithfulness, which this time she tried to drive away, fearing the already familiar pain of jealousy. The first outburst of jealousy, once lived through, could not come again, and even the discovery of unfaithfulness could not affect her as it had the first time. Such a discovery would now only deprive her of her family habits, and she allowed herself to be deceived, despising him and most of all herself for this weakness. On top of that, the cares of a large family constantly tormented her: either the nursing of the baby did not go well, or the nanny left, or, as now, one of the children fell ill.

'And how are all yours?' her mother asked.

'Ah, *maman*, you have enough grief of your own. Lily has fallen ill, and I'm afraid it's scarlet fever. I came now just to find out the news, and then, God forbid, if it is scarlet fever, I'll stay put and not go anywhere.'

The old prince also came out of his study after the doctor's departure, and having offered Dolly his cheek and said a word to her, turned to his wife:

'What's the decision, are you going? Well, and what do you intend to do with me?'

'I think you should stay, Alexander,' said his wife.

'As you wish.'

'*Maman*, why shouldn't papa come with us?' said Kitty. 'It will be more cheerful for him and for us.'

The old prince stood up and stroked Kitty's hair with his hand. She raised her face and, smiling forcedly, looked at him. It always seemed to her that he understood her better than anyone else in the family, though he spoke little with her. As the youngest, she was her father's favourite, and it seemed to her that his love for her gave him insight. When her glance now met his kindly blue eyes gazing intently at her, it seemed to her that he saw right through her and understood all the bad that was going on inside her. Blushing, she leaned towards him, expecting a kiss, but he only patted her hair and said:

'These stupid chignons! You can't even get to your real daughter, but only caress the hair of dead wenches. Well, Dolinka,' he turned to his eldest daughter, 'what's your trump up to?'

'Nothing, papa,' answered Dolly, understanding that he meant her husband. 'He goes out all the time, I almost never see him,' she could not help adding with a mocking smile.

'So he hasn't gone to the country yet to sell the wood?'

'No, he keeps getting ready to.'

'Really!' said the prince. 'And I, too, must get myself ready? I'm listening, ma'am,' he turned to his wife as he sat down. 'And as for you, Katia,' he added to his youngest daughter, 'sometime or other, you'll have to wake up one fine morning and say to yourself: "Why, I'm perfectly well and cheerful, and I'm going to go with papa again for an early morning walk in the frost." Eh?'

What her father said seemed so simple, yet Kitty became confused and bewildered at these words, like a caught criminal. 'Yes, he knows everything, understands everything, and with these words he's telling me that, though I'm ashamed, I must get over my shame.' She could not pluck up her spirits enough to make any reply. She tried to begin, but suddenly burst into tears and rushed from the room.

'You and your jokes!' The princess flew at her husband. 'You always . . .' she began her reproachful speech.

The prince listened for quite a long time to her rebukes and kept silent, but his face frowned more and more.

'She's so pitiful, the poor dear, so pitiful, and you don't feel how any hint at the cause of it hurts her. Ah, to be so mistaken about other people!' said the princess, and by the change in her tone Dolly and the prince realized that she was speaking of Vronsky. 'I don't understand why there are no laws against such vile, ignoble people.'

'Ah, I can't listen!' the prince said gloomily, getting up from his armchair and making as if to leave, but stopping in the doorway. 'There are laws, dearest, and since you're calling me out on it, I'll tell you who is to blame for it all: you, you and you alone. There are and always have been laws against such young devils! Yes, ma'am, and if it hadn't been for what should never have been, I, old as I am, would have challenged him to a duel, that fop. Yes, so treat her now, bring in your charlatans.'

The prince seemed to have much more to say, but as soon as the princess heard his tone, she humbled herself and repented, as always with serious questions.

'*Alexandre, Alexandre*,' she whispered, moving closer, and burst into tears.

As soon as she began to cry, the prince also subsided. He went over to her.

'Well, there, there! It's hard for you, too, I know. What can we do? It's no great calamity. God is merciful . . . give thanks . . .' he said, no longer knowing what he was saying, in response to the princess's wet kiss, which he felt on his hand, and he left the room.

When Kitty left the room in tears, Dolly, with her motherly, family habit of mind, saw at once that there was woman's work to be done, and she prepared to do it. She took off her hat and, morally rolling up her sleeves, prepared for action. During her mother's attack on her father, she tried to restrain her mother as far as daughterly respect permitted. During the prince's outburst, she kept silent; she felt shame for her mother and tenderness towards her father for the instant return of his kindness; but when her father went out, she got ready to do the main thing necessary – to go to Kitty and comfort her.

'I've long been meaning to tell you, *maman*: do you know that Levin was going to propose to Kitty when he was here the last time? He told Stiva so.'

'Well, what of it? I don't understand . . .'

'Maybe Kitty refused him? . . . She didn't tell you?'

'No, she told me nothing either about the one or about the other. She's too proud. But I know it's all because of that . . .'

'Yes, just imagine if she refused Levin – and she wouldn't have refused him if it hadn't been for the other one, I know . . . And then that one deceived her so terribly.'

It was too awful for the princess to think of how guilty she was before her daughter, and she became angry.

'Ah, I understand nothing any more! Nowadays they all want to live by their own reason, they tell their mothers nothing, and then look . . .'

'I'll go to her, *maman*.'

'Go. Am I forbidding you?' said the mother.

III

Entering Kitty's small boudoir, a pretty little pink room, with *vieux saxe** dolls as young, pink and gay as Kitty had been just two months earlier, Dolly remembered with what gaiety and love they had decorated this little room together last year. Her heart went cold when she saw Kitty sitting on the low chair nearest the door, staring fixedly at a corner of the rug. Kitty glanced at her sister, and her cold, somewhat severe expression did not change.

'I'll leave now and stay put at home, and you won't be allowed to

* Old Saxony porcelain.

visit me,' said Darya Alexandrovna, sitting down next to her. 'I'd like to talk with you.'

'About what?' Kitty asked quickly, raising her eyes in fear.

'What else if not your grief?'

'I have no grief.'

'Come now, Kitty. Can you really think I don't know? I know everything. And believe me, it's nothing . . . We've all gone through it.'

Kitty was silent, and her face had a stern expression.

'He's not worth your suffering over him,' Darya Alexandrovna went on, going straight to the point.

'Yes, because he scorned me,' Kitty said in a quavering voice. 'Don't talk about it! Please don't!'

'Why, who told you that? No one said that. I'm sure he was in love with you, and is still in love, but . . .'

'Ah, these condolences are the most terrible thing of all for me!' Kitty cried out, suddenly getting angry. She turned on her chair, blushed, and quickly moved her fingers, clutching the belt buckle she was holding now with one hand, now with the other. Dolly knew this way her sister had of grasping something with her hands when she was in a temper; she knew that Kitty was capable of forgetting herself in such a moment and saying a lot of unnecessary and unpleasant things, and Dolly wanted to calm her down. But it was already too late.

'What, what is it you want to make me feel, what?' Kitty was talking quickly. 'That I was in love with a man who cared nothing for me, and that I'm dying of love for him? And I'm told this by my sister, who thinks that . . . that . . . that she's commiserating! . . . I don't want these pityings and pretences!'

'Kitty, you're unfair.'

'Why do you torment me?'

'On the contrary, I . . . I see that you're upset . . .'

But, in her temper, Kitty did not hear her.

'I have nothing to be distressed or comforted about. I'm proud enough never to allow myself to love a man who does not love me.'

'But I'm not saying . . . One thing – tell me the truth,' Darya Alexandrovna said, taking her hand, 'tell me, did Levin speak to you? . . .'

The mention of Levin seemed to take away the last of Kitty's self-possession; she jumped up from the chair, flinging the buckle to the floor and, with quick gestures of her hands, began to speak:

'Why bring Levin into it, too? I don't understand, why do you need to torment me? I said and I repeat that I'm proud and would never, *never* do what you're doing – go back to a man who has betrayed you, who has fallen in love with another woman. I don't understand, I don't understand that! You may, but I can't!'

And, having said these words, she glanced at her sister and, seeing that Dolly kept silent, her head bowed sadly, Kitty, instead of leaving the room as she had intended, sat down by the door and, covering her face with a handkerchief, bowed her head.

The silence lasted for some two minutes. Dolly was thinking about herself. Her humiliation, which she always felt, echoed especially painfully in her when her sister reminded her of it. She had not expected such cruelty from her sister and was angry with her. But suddenly she heard the rustling of a dress, along with the sound of suppressed sobs bursting out, and someone's arms encircled her neck from below. Kitty was kneeling before her.

'Dolinka, I'm so, so unhappy!' she whispered guiltily.

And she hid her sweet, tear-bathed face in Darya Alexandrovna's skirts.

As if tears were the necessary lubricant without which the machine of mutual communication could not work successfully, the two sisters, after these tears, started talking, not about what preoccupied them, but about unrelated things, and yet they understood each other. Kitty understood that her poor sister had been struck to the depths of her heart by the words she had spoken in passion about her husband's unfaithfulness and her humiliation, but that she forgave her. Dolly, for her part, understood everything she had wanted to know; she was satisfied that her guesses were right, that Kitty's grief, her incurable grief, was precisely that Levin had made a proposal and that she had refused him, while Vronsky had deceived her, and that she was ready to love Levin and hate Vronsky. Kitty did not say a word about it; she spoke only of her state of mind.

'I have no grief,' she said, once she had calmed down, 'but can you understand that everything has become vile, disgusting, coarse to me, and my own self first of all? You can't imagine what vile thoughts I have about everything.'

'Why, what kind of vile thoughts could you have?' Dolly asked, smiling.

'The most, most vile and coarse – I can't tell you. It's not anguish, or boredom, it's much worse. As if all that was good in me got hidden, and only what's most vile was left. Well, how can I tell you?' she went on, seeing the perplexity in her sister's eyes. 'Papa started saying to me just now . . . it seems to me all he thinks is that I've got to get married. Mama takes me to a ball: it seems to me she only takes me in order to get me married quickly and be rid of me. I know it's not true, but I can't drive these thoughts away. The so-called suitors I can't even look at. It seems as if they're taking my measurements. Before it was simply a pleasure for me to go somewhere in a ball gown, I admired myself; now I feel ashamed, awkward. Well, what do you want! The doctor . . . Well . . .'

Kitty faltered; she wanted to go on to say that ever since this change had taken place in her, Stepan Arkadyich had become unbearably disagreeable to her, and that she could not see him without picturing the most coarse and ugly things.

'Well, yes, I picture things in the most coarse, vile way,' she went on. 'It's my illness. Maybe it will pass . . .'

'But don't think . . .'

'I can't help it. I feel good only with children, only in your house.'

'It's too bad you can't visit me.'

'No, I will come. I've had scarlet fever, and I'll persuade *maman*.'

Kitty got her way and moved to her sister's, and there spent the whole time of the scarlet fever, which did come, taking care of the children. The two sisters nursed all six children back to health, but Kitty's condition did not improve, and during the Great Lent[1] the Shcherbatskys went abroad.

IV

There is essentially one highest circle in Petersburg; they all know each other, and even call on each other. But this big circle has its subdivisions. Anna Arkadyevna Karenina had friends and close connections in three different circles. One was her husband's official service circle, consisting of his colleagues and subordinates, who, in social condition, were connected or divided in the most varied and whimsical way. It was hard now for Anna to remember the sense of almost pious respect she had first felt for all these people. Now she knew them all as people know each other in a provincial town; knew who had which habits and weaknesses, whose shoe pinched on which foot; knew their relations to one another and to the main centre; knew who sided with whom, and how, and in what; and who agreed or disagreed with whom, and about what; but this circle of governmental, male interests never could interest her, despite Countess Lydia Ivanovna's promptings, and she avoided it.

Another circle close to Anna was the one through which Alexei Alexandrovich had made his career. The centre of this circle was Countess Lydia Ivanovna. It was a circle of elderly, unattractive, virtuous and pious women and of intelligent, educated and ambitious men. One of the intelligent men who belonged to this circle called it 'the conscience of Petersburg society'. Alexei Alexandrovich valued this circle highly, and at the beginning of her Petersburg life, Anna, who was so good at getting along with everyone, also found friends for herself in it. But now, on her return from Moscow, this circle became unbearable to her. It seemed to her that both she and all the others were pretending, and she felt so bored and awkward in this company that she called on Countess Lydia Ivanovna as seldom as possible.

The third circle, finally, in which she had connections, was society proper – the society of balls, dinners, splendid gowns, a *monde* that held on with one hand to the court, so as not to descend to the *demi-monde*, which the members of this circle thought they despised, but with which they shared not only similar but the same tastes. Her connection with this circle was maintained through Princess Betsy Tverskoy, her cousin's wife, who had an income of a hundred and twenty thousand and who, since Anna's appearance in society, had especially liked her, courted her, and drawn her into her circle, laughing at the circle to which Countess Lydia Ivanovna belonged.

'When I'm old and ugly, I'll become like that,' said Betsy, 'but for you, for a young, pretty woman, it's too early for that almshouse.'

At first Anna had avoided this society of Princess Tverskoy's as much as she could, because it called for expenses beyond her means, and also because at heart she preferred the other; but after her visit to Moscow it turned the other way round. She avoided her virtuous friends and went into the great world. There she met Vronsky and experienced an exciting joy at these meetings. She met Vronsky especially often at Betsy's, whose maiden name was Vronsky and who was his cousin. Vronsky went wherever he might meet Anna, and spoke to her whenever he could about his love. She never gave him any cause, but each time she met him, her soul lit up with the same feeling of animation that had come over her that day on the train when she had seen him for the first time.

She felt joy shining in her eyes when she saw him and puckered her lips into a smile, and she was unable to extinguish the expression of that joy.

At first Anna sincerely believed that she was displeased with him for allowing himself to pursue her; but soon after her return from Moscow, having gone to a soirée where she thought she would meet him, and finding that he was not there, she clearly understood from the sadness which came over her that she was deceiving herself, that his pursuit not only was not unpleasant for her but constituted the entire interest of her life.

The famous singer was singing for the second time, and all the great world was in the theatre.[2] Seeing his cousin from his seat in the front row, Vronsky went to her box without waiting for the interval.

'Why didn't you come for dinner?' she said to him. 'I'm amazed at the clairvoyance of people in love,' she added with a smile and so that he alone could hear: '*She wasn't there*. But drop in after the opera.'

Vronsky gave her a questioning glance. She lowered her head. He smiled in thanks and sat down next to her.

'And how I remember your mockery!' continued Princess Betsy, who found special pleasure in following the success of this passion. 'Where has it all gone! You're caught, my dear.'

'My only wish is to be caught,' Vronsky replied with his calm, good-natured smile. 'If I have any complaint, it is at not being caught enough, if the truth be told. I'm beginning to lose hope.'

'What hope can you have?' said Betsy, getting offended for her friend. '*Entendons nous* . . .'* But there was a twinkle in her eye which said that she understood very well, and exactly as he did, what hope he might have.

'None,' said Vronsky, laughing and showing a solid row of teeth. 'Excuse me,' he added, taking the opera-glasses from her hand and beginning to scan the facing row of boxes over her bared shoulder. 'I'm afraid I'm becoming ridiculous.'

He knew very well that in the eyes of Betsy and all society people he ran no risk of being ridiculous. He knew very well that for those people the role of the unhappy lover of a young girl, or of a free woman generally, might be ridiculous; but the role of a man who attached himself to a married woman and devoted his life to involving her in adultery at all costs, had something beautiful and grand about it and

* Let's understand each other . . .

could never be ridiculous, and therefore, with a proud and gay smile playing under his moustache, he lowered the opera-glasses and looked at his cousin.

'And why didn't you come to dinner?' she added, looking at him with admiration.

'That I must tell you about. I was busy, and with what? I'll lay you a hundred, a thousand to one . . . you'll never guess. I was trying to make peace between a husband and his wife's offender. Yes, really!'

'And what, did you succeed?'

'Nearly.'

'You must tell me about it,' she said, getting up. 'Come during the next interval.'

'Impossible. I'm going to the French Theatre.'

'From Nilsson?' said Betsy in horror, though she would never have been able to tell Nilsson from any chorus girl.

'No help for it. I have an appointment there, all to do with this peacemaking business.'

'Blessed are the peacemakers, for they shall be saved,'[3] said Betsy, remembering hearing something of the sort from someone. 'Sit down, then, and tell me about it.'

And she sat down again.

V

'This is a bit indiscreet, but so charming that I want terribly to tell it,' said Vronsky, looking at her with laughing eyes. 'I won't mention names.'

'But I'll guess them – so much the better.'

'Listen, then. Two gay young men are out driving . . .'[4]

'Officers from your regiment, naturally.'

'I'm not saying officers, simply two young men after lunch . . .'

'Translate: slightly drunk.'

'Maybe so. They're going to their friend's for dinner, in the gayest spirits. They see a pretty young woman overtake them in a cab, look back and, so at least it seems to them, nod to them and laugh. Naturally, they go after her. They drive at full speed. To their surprise, the beauty stops at the entrance to the same house they're going to. The beauty runs upstairs. They see only red lips under a short veil and beautiful little feet.'

'You're telling it with such feeling that I suppose you were one of the two yourself.'

'And what did you say to me just now? Well, the young men go to their friend, he's having a farewell dinner. Here they do indeed drink, maybe too much, as is usual at farewell dinners. And over dinner they ask who lives upstairs in that house. Nobody knows, and only the host's footman, to their question whether any *mamzelles* live upstairs, answers that there are lots of them there. After dinner the young men go to the host's study and write a letter to the unknown woman. They write a passionate letter, a declaration, and take the letter upstairs themselves, to explain in case the letter isn't quite clear.'

'Why do you tell me such vile things? Well?'

'They ring. A maid comes out. They hand her the letter and assure the maid that they're both so much in love that they're going to die right there on the doorstep. The maid, quite perplexed, conveys the message. Suddenly there appears a gentleman with sausage-shaped side-whiskers, red as a lobster, who announces to them that no one lives in the house except his wife, and throws them both out.'

'And how do you know his side-whiskers are sausage-shaped, as you say?'

'Just listen. Today I went to try and make peace between them.'

'Well, and what then?'

'Here's the most interesting part. It turned out that they're a happy titular councillor and councilloress.[5] The titular councillor lodges a complaint, and I act as the make-peace – and what a one! I assure you, Talleyrand[6] has nothing on me.'

'So what's the difficulty?'

'Listen now . . . We apologized properly: "We are in despair, we beg you to forgive us this unfortunate misunderstanding." The titular councillor with the little sausages begins to soften, but he also wants to express his feelings, and as soon as he starts expressing them, he starts getting excited and saying rude things, and I again have to employ all my diplomatic talents. "I agree that they did not behave nicely, but I beg you to consider the misunderstanding and their youth; then, too, the young men had just had lunch. You understand. They repent with all their soul, they beg to be forgiven their fault." The titular councillor softens again: "I agree, Count, and I'm ready to forgive them, but you understand that my wife, my wife, an honourable woman, has been subjected to the pursuit, rudeness and brazenness of some boys, scound . . ." And, remember, one of the boys is right there, and I'm supposed to make peace between them. Again I use diplomacy, and again, as soon as the whole affair is about to be concluded, my titular councillor gets excited, turns red, the little sausages bristle, and again I dissolve into diplomatic subtleties.'

'Ah, this I must tell you!' Betsy, laughing, addressed a lady who was entering her box. 'He's made me laugh so!'

'Well, *bonne chance*,'* she added, giving Vronsky a free finger of the hand holding her fan, and lowering the slightly ridden-up bodice of her dress with a movement of her shoulders, so as to be well and properly naked when she stepped out to the foot of the stage under the gaslights and under everyone's eyes.

Vronsky went to the French Theatre, where he indeed had to see the regimental commander, who never missed a single performance at the French Theatre, in order to talk over his peacemaking, which had already occupied and amused him for three days. Petritsky, whom he liked, was involved in this affair, as was another nice fellow, recently joined up, an excellent comrade, the young prince Kedrov. And, above all, the interests of the regiment were involved.

Both were in Vronsky's squadron. An official, the titular councillor Wenden, had come to the regimental commander with a complaint about his officers, who had insulted his wife. His young wife, so Wenden recounted (he had been married half a year), had gone to church with her mother and, suddenly feeling unwell owing to a certain condition, had been unable to continue standing[7] and had gone home in the first cab that came along. Here the officers had chased after her, she had become frightened and, feeling still more sick, had run up the stairs to her home. Wenden himself, having returned from work, had heard the bell and some voices, had gone to the door and, seeing drunken officers with a letter, had shoved them out. He had demanded severe punishment.

'No, say what you like,' the regimental commander had said to Vronsky, whom he had invited to his place, 'Petritsky is becoming impossible. Not a week passes without some story. This official won't let the affair drop, he'll go further.'

* Good luck.

Vronsky had seen all the unseemliness of the affair, and that a duel was not possible here, that everything must be done to mollify this titular councillor and hush the affair up. The regimental commander had summoned Vronsky precisely because he knew him to be a noble and intelligent man and, above all, a man who cherished the honour of the regiment. They had talked it over and decided that Petritsky and Kedrov would have to go to this titular councillor with Vronsky and apologize. The regimental commander and Vronsky had both realized that Vronsky's name and his imperial aide-de-camp's monogram ought to contribute greatly to the mollifying of the titular councillor. And, indeed, these two means had proved partly effective; but the result of the reconciliation remained doubtful, as Vronsky had told Betsy.

Arriving at the French Theatre, Vronsky withdrew to the foyer with the regimental commander and told him of his success, or unsuccess. Having thought everything over, the regimental commander decided to let the affair go without consequences, but then, just for the pleasure of it, began asking Vronsky about the details of his meeting, and for a long time could not stop laughing as he listened to Vronsky telling how the subsiding titular councillor would suddenly flare up again, as he remembered the details of the affair, and how Vronsky, manoeuvring at the last half word of the reconciliation, had retreated, pushing Petritsky in front of him.

'A nasty story, but killingly funny. Kedrov really cannot fight with this gentleman! So he got terribly worked up?' he asked again, laughing. 'And isn't Claire something tonight? A wonder!' he said about the new French actress. 'Watch all you like, she's new each day. Only the French can do that.'

VI

Princess Betsy left the theatre without waiting for the end of the last act. She had just time to go to her dressing room, sprinkle powder on her long, pale face and wipe it off, put her hair to rights and order tea served in the big drawing room, when carriages began driving up one after the other to her huge house on Bolshaya Morskaya. The guests stepped out on to the wide porch, and the corpulent doorkeeper, who used to read newspapers in the morning behind the glass door for the edification of passers-by, noiselessly opened this huge door, allowing people to pass.

Almost at one and the same time the hostess, with freshened hair and freshened face, came through one door and the guests came through another into the big drawing room with its dark walls, plush carpets and brightly lit table shining under the candlelight with the whiteness of the tablecloth, the silver of the samovar, and the translucent porcelain of the tea service.

The hostess sat by the samovar and took off her gloves. Moving chairs with the help of unobtrusive servants, the company settled down, dividing itself into two parts – one by the samovar with the hostess, the other at the opposite end of the drawing room, round the ambassador's wife, a beautiful woman in black velvet and with sharp black eyebrows. The conversation in both centres, as always in the first minutes, vacillated, interrupted by meetings, greetings, offers of tea, as if seeking what to settle on.

'She's remarkably good as an actress; one can see that she's studied Kaulbach,'[8] said a diplomat in the ambassador's wife's circle, 'did you notice how she fell . . .'

'Ah, please, let's not talk about Nilsson! It's impossible to say anything new about her,' said a fat, red-faced, fair-haired woman with no eyebrows and no chignon, in an old silk dress. This was Princess Miagky, well known for her simplicity and rudeness of manner, and nicknamed the *enfant terrible*. Princess Miagky was sitting between the two circles, listening, and participating now in one, now in the other. 'Today three people have said this same phrase to me about Kaulbach, as if they'd agreed on it. And the phrase – I don't know why they like it so much.'

The conversation was interrupted by this remark, and they had to invent a new topic.

'Tell us something amusing but not wicked,' said the ambassador's wife, a great expert at graceful conversation, called 'small talk' in English, turning to the diplomat, who also had no idea how to begin now.

'They say that's very difficult, that only wicked things are funny,' he began with a smile. 'But I'll try. Give me a topic. The whole point lies in the topic. Once the topic is given, it's easy to embroider on it. I often think that the famous talkers of the last century would now find it difficult to talk intelligently. Everything intelligent is so boring . . .'

'That was said long ago,' the ambassador's wife interrupted him, laughing.

The conversation had begun nicely, but precisely because it was much too nice, it stopped again. They had to resort to that sure, never failing remedy – malicious gossip.

'Don't you find something Louis Quinze in Tushkevich?' he said, indicating with his eyes a handsome, fair-haired young man standing by the table.

'Oh, yes! He's in the same style as this drawing room, which is why he frequents it so much.'

This conversation sustained itself because they spoke in allusions precisely about something that could not be talked about in that drawing room – that is, the relations between Tushkevich and the hostess.

Meanwhile, by the samovar and the hostess, the conversation, after vacillating for some time among three inevitable topics: the latest social news, the theatre, and the judging of one's neighbour, also settled as it struck on this last topic – that is, malicious gossip.

'Have you heard, that Maltishchev woman, too – not the daughter, but the mother – is making herself a *diable rose*[9] costume.'

'It can't be! No, that's lovely!'

'I'm amazed, with her intelligence – for she's not stupid – how can she not see how ridiculous she is?'

Each had something demeaning and derisive to say about the unfortunate Mme Maltishchev, and the conversation began to crackle merrily, like a blazing bonfire.

The princess Betsy's husband, a fat good-natured man, a passionate collector of etchings, learning that his wife had guests, stopped in the drawing room before going to his club. He approached Princess Miagky inaudibly over the soft carpet.

'How did you like Nilsson?' he said.

'Ah, how can you sneak up like that! You frightened me so,' she replied. 'Please don't talk to me about opera, you understand nothing about music. Better if I descend to your level and talk about your majolica and etchings. Well, what treasure have you bought recently at the flea market?'

'Want me to show you? But you know nothing about it.'

'Show me. I've learned from those – what's their name . . . the bankers . . . they have excellent etchings. They showed them to us.'

'So you visited the Schützburgs?' the hostess asked from her samovar.

'We did, *ma chère*. They invited my husband and me for dinner, and I was told that the sauce at that dinner cost a thousand roubles,' Princess

Miagky said loudly, sensing that everyone was listening to her, 'and it was a most vile sauce – something green. I had to invite them back, and I made a sauce for eighty-five kopecks, and everybody liked it. I can't make thousand-rouble sauces.'

'She's one of a kind!' said the ambassador's wife.

'Amazing!' someone said.

The effect produced by Princess Miagky's talk was always the same, and the secret of it consisted in her saying simple things that made sense, even if, as now, they were not quite appropriate. In the society in which she lived, such words produced the impression of a most witty joke. Princess Miagky could not understand why it worked that way, but she knew that it did work, and she took advantage of it.

Since everyone listened to Princess Miagky while she talked and the conversation around the ambassador's wife ceased, the hostess wanted to unite the company into one, and she addressed the ambassador's wife:

'You definitely don't want tea? You should move over here with us.'

'No, we are quite all right here,' the ambassador's wife replied with a smile and continued the conversation they had begun.

It was a very pleasant conversation. They were denouncing the Karenins, wife and husband.

'Anna's changed very much since her trip to Moscow. There's something strange about her,' said a friend of hers.

'The main change is that she's brought a shadow with her – Alexei Vronsky,' said the ambassador's wife.

'What of it? Grimm has a fable – a man without a shadow, a man deprived of a shadow.[10] And it's his punishment for something. I could never understand where the punishment lay. But it must be unpleasant for a woman to be without a shadow.'

'Yes, but women with a shadow generally end badly,' said Anna's friend.

'Button your lip,' Princess Miagky suddenly said, hearing these words. 'Karenina is a wonderful woman. Her husband I don't like, but I like her very much.'

'Why don't you like the husband? He's such a remarkable man,' said the ambassador's wife. 'My husband says there are few such statesmen in Europe.'

'And my husband says the same thing to me, but I don't believe it,' said Princess Miagky. 'If our husbands didn't say it, we'd see what's there, and Alexei Alexandrovich, in my opinion, is simply stupid. I say it in a whisper . . . Doesn't that make everything clear? Before, when I was told to find him intelligent, I kept searching and found myself stupid for not seeing his intelligence; but as soon as I say "He's stupid" in a whisper – everything becomes so clear, doesn't it?'

'How wicked you are today!'

'Not in the least. I have no other way out. One of us is stupid. Well, and you know one can never say that about oneself.'

'No one is pleased with his fortune, but everyone is pleased with his wit,' said the diplomat, quoting some French verse.[11]

'That's it exactly.' Princess Miagky turned to him hastily. 'But the thing is that I won't let you have Anna. She's so dear, so sweet. What can she do if they're all in love with her and follow her like shadows?'

'But I never thought of judging her.' Anna's friend tried to excuse herself.

'If no one follows us like a shadow, it doesn't prove that we have the right to judge.'

And having dealt properly with Anna's friend, Princess Miagky stood up and, together with the ambassador's wife, joined the table where a conversation was going on about the king of Prussia.

'Who were you maligning there?' asked Betsy.

'The Karenins. The princess gave a characterization of Alexei Alexandrovich,' the ambassador's wife replied with a smile, sitting down at the table.

'A pity we didn't hear it,' said the hostess, glancing at the door. 'Ah, here you are at last!' She addressed Vronsky with a smile as he came in.

Vronsky was not only acquainted with all those he met there but saw them every day, and therefore he entered with that calm manner with which one enters a room full of people one has only just left.

'Where am I coming from?' he replied to the ambassador's wife's question. 'No help for it, I must confess. From the *Bouffe*.[12] It seems the hundredth time and always a new pleasure. Lovely! I know it's shameful, but at the opera I fall asleep, and at the *Bouffe* I stay till the last moment and enjoy it. Tonight . . .'

He named a French actress and wanted to tell some story about her; but the ambassador's wife interrupted him in mock alarm:

'Please, don't talk about that horror.'

'Well, I won't then, the more so as everybody knows about these horrors.'

'And everybody would have gone there, if it was as accepted as the opera,' put in Princess Miagky.

VII

Steps were heard at the door, and Princess Betsy, knowing that it was Anna, glanced at Vronsky. He was looking at the door, and his face had a strange new expression. He was looking joyfully, intently, and at the same time timidly at the entering woman and slowly getting up from his seat. Anna was entering the drawing room. Holding herself extremely straight as always, with her quick, firm and light step, which distinguished her from other society women, and not changing the direction of her gaze, she took the few steps that separated her from the hostess, pressed her hand, smiled, and with that smile turned round to Vronsky. Vronsky made a low bow and moved a chair for her.

She responded only with an inclination of the head, then blushed and frowned. But at once, while quickly nodding to acquaintances and pressing the proffered hands, she addressed the hostess:

'I was at Countess Lydia's and intended to come earlier, but had to stay. Sir John was there. He's very interesting.'

'Ah, it's that missionary?'

'Yes, he was telling very interesting things about Indian life.'

The conversation, disrupted by her arrival, began to waver again like a lamp flame being blown out.

'Sir John! Yes, Sir John. I've seen him. He speaks well. The Vlasyev girl is completely in love with him.'

'And is it true that her younger sister is marrying Topov?'

'Yes, they say it's quite decided.'

'I'm surprised at the parents. They say it's a marriage of passion.'

'Of passion? What antediluvian thoughts you have! Who talks about passions these days?' said the ambassador's wife.

'What's to be done? This stupid old fashion hasn't gone out of use,' said Vronsky.

'So much the worse for those who cling to it. The only happy marriages I know are arranged ones.'

'Yes, but how often the happiness of an arranged marriage scatters like dust, precisely because of the appearance of that very passion which was not acknowledged,' said Vronsky.

'But by arranged marriages we mean those in which both have already had their wild times. It's like scarlet fever, one has to go through it.'

'Then we should find some artificial inoculation against love, as with smallpox.'

'When I was young, I was in love with a beadle,' said Princess Miagky. 'I don't know whether that helped me or not.'

'No, joking aside, I think that in order to know love one must make a mistake and then correct it,' said Princess Betsy.

'Even after marriage,' the ambassador's wife said jokingly.

'It's never too late to repent.' The diplomat uttered an English proverb.

'Precisely,' Betsy picked up, 'one must make a mistake and then correct oneself. What do you think?' She turned to Anna, who with a firm, barely noticeable smile on her lips was silently listening to this conversation.

'I think,' said Anna, toying with the glove she had taken off, 'I think . . . if there are as many minds as there are men, then there are as many kinds of love as there are hearts.'

Vronsky was looking at Anna and waiting with a sinking heart for what she would say. He exhaled as if after danger when she spoke these words.

Anna suddenly turned to him:

'And I have received a letter from Moscow. They write that Kitty Shcherbatsky is very ill.'

'Really?' said Vronsky, frowning.

Anna looked at him sternly.

'That doesn't interest you?'

'On the contrary, very much. What exactly do they write, if I may ask?' he said.

Anna rose and went over to Betsy.

'Give me a cup of tea,' she said, stopping behind her chair.

While Princess Betsy poured her tea, Vronsky came over to Anna.

'What do they write to you?' he repeated.

'I often think that men don't understand what is noble and what is ignoble, though they always talk about it,' Anna said without answering him. 'I've long wanted to tell you,' she added and, moving a few steps away, sat down by a corner table with albums on it.

'I don't quite understand the meaning of your words,' he said, handing her the cup.

She glanced at the sofa beside her, and he sat down at once.

'Yes, I've wanted to tell you,' she said without looking at him. 'You acted badly – very, very badly.'

'Don't I know that I acted badly? But who was the cause of my acting so?'

'Why do you say that to me?' she said, glancing sternly at him.

'You know why,' he replied boldly and joyfully, meeting her eyes and continuing to look.

It was not he but she who became embarrassed.

'That proves only that you have no heart,' she said. But her eyes said that she knew he did have a heart, and because of it she was afraid of him.

'What you were just talking about was a mistake, and not love.'

'Remember, I forbade you to utter that word, that vile word,' Anna said with a shudder; but she felt at once that by this one word 'forbade' she showed that she acknowledged having certain rights over him and was thereby encouraging him to speak of love. 'I've long wanted to tell you that,' she went on, looking resolutely into his eyes, and all aflame with the blush that burned her face, 'and tonight I came on purpose, knowing that I would meet you. I came to tell you that this must end. I have never blushed before anyone, but you make me feel guilty of something.'

He looked at her, struck by the new, spiritual beauty of her face.

'What do you want of me?' he said simply and seriously.

'I want you to go to Moscow and ask Kitty's forgiveness,' she said, and a little light flickered in her eyes.

'You don't want that,' he said.

He saw that she was saying what she forced herself to say, and not what she wanted.

'If you love me as you say you do,' she whispered, 'make it so that I am at peace.'

His face lit up.

'Don't you know that you are my whole life? But I know no peace and cannot give you any. All of myself, my love . . . yes. I cannot think of you and myself separately. You and I are one for me. And I do not see any possibility of peace ahead either for me or for you. I see the possibility of despair, of unhappiness . . . or I see the possibility of happiness, such happiness! . . . Isn't it possible?' he added with his lips only; but she heard him.

She strained all the forces of her mind to say what she ought to say;

but instead she rested her eyes on him, filled with love, and made no answer.

'There it is!' he thought with rapture. 'When I was already in despair, and when it seemed there would be no end – there it is! She loves me. She's confessed it.'

'Then do this for me, never say these words to me, and let us be good friends,' she said in words; but her eyes were saying something quite different.

'We won't be friends, you know that yourself. And whether we will be the happiest or the unhappiest of people – is in your power.'

She wanted to say something, but he interrupted her.

'I beg for only one thing, I beg for the right to hope, to be tormented, as I am now; but if that, too, is impossible, order me to disappear, and I will disappear. You will not see me, if my presence is painful for you.'

'I don't want to drive you away.'

'Just don't change anything. Leave everything as it is,' he said in a trembling voice. 'Here is your husband.'

Indeed just then Alexei Alexandrovich, with his calm, clumsy gait, was entering the drawing room.

Having glanced at his wife and Vronsky, he went over to the hostess, sat down to his cup of tea, and began speaking in his unhurried, always audible voice, in his usual jocular tone, making fun of somebody.

'Your Rambouillet is in full muster,' he said, glancing around the whole company, 'graces and muses.'[13]

But Princess Betsy could not bear this tone of his, which she called by the English word 'sneering', and, being an intelligent hostess, at once led him into a serious conversation on universal military conscription.[14] Alexei Alexandrovich at once got carried away with the conversation and began, earnestly now, to defend the new decree against Princess Betsy, who attacked it.

Vronsky and Anna went on sitting by the little table.

'This is becoming indecent,' one lady whispered, indicating with her eyes Vronsky, Anna and her husband.

'What did I tell you?' Anna's friend replied.

And not these ladies alone, but almost everyone in the drawing room, even Princess Miagky and Betsy herself, glanced several times at the two who had withdrawn from the general circle, as if it disturbed them. Alexei Alexandrovich was the only one who never once looked in their direction and was not distracted from the interest of the conversation that had started.

Noticing the unpleasant impression produced on everyone, Princess Betsy slipped some other person into her place to listen to Alexei Alexandrovich, and went over to Anna.

'I'm always surprised at the clarity and precision of your husband's expressions,' she said. 'The most transcendental notions become accessible to me when he speaks.'

'Oh, yes!' said Anna, radiant with a smile of happiness and not understanding a word of what Betsy was saying to her. She went over to the big table and took part in the general conversation.

Alexei Alexandrovich, after staying for half an hour, went up to his wife and suggested they go home together; but she, without looking at him, replied that she would stay for supper. Alexei Alexandrovich made his bows and left.

The Karenin coachman, a fat old Tartar in a glossy leather coat, had difficulty holding back the chilled grey on the left, who kept rearing up by the entrance. The footman stood holding the carriage door open. The doorkeeper stood holding the front door. Anna Arkadyevna, with her small, quick hand, was freeing the lace of her sleeve, which had caught on the hooks of her fur coat, and, head lowered, listened with delight to what Vronsky was saying as he saw her off.

'You've said nothing; let's suppose I also demand nothing,' he said, 'but you know it's not friendship I need, for me there is only one possible happiness in life, this word you dislike so . . . yes, love . . .'

'Love . . .' she repeated slowly with her inner voice, and suddenly, just as she freed the lace, added: 'That's why I don't like this word, because it means too much for me, far more than you can understand,' and she looked him in the face: 'Good-bye!'

She gave him her hand, and with a quick, resilient step walked past the doorkeeper and disappeared into the carriage.

Her look, the touch of her hand, burned him through. He kissed his palm in the place where she had touched him, and went home, happy in the awareness that he had come closer to attaining his goal in that one evening than he had in the past two months.

VIII

Alexei Alexandrovich found nothing peculiar or improper in the fact that his wife was sitting at a separate table with Vronsky and having an animated conversation about something; but he noticed that to the others in the drawing room it seemed something peculiar and improper, and therefore he, too, found it improper. He decided that he ought to say so to his wife.

On returning home, Alexei Alexandrovich went to his study, as he usually did, sat in his armchair, opened a book about the papacy at a place marked by a paper-knife, and read till one o'clock, as usual; only from time to time he rubbed his high forehead and tossed his head, as if chasing something away. At the usual hour, he rose and prepared for bed. Anna Arkadyevna was not home yet. Book under his arm, he went upstairs; but this evening, instead of the usual thoughts and considerations about official matters, his mind was full of his wife and something unpleasant that had happened with her. Contrary to his habit, he did not get into bed, but, clasping his hands behind his back, began pacing up and down the rooms. He could not lie down, feeling that he had first to think over this newly arisen circumstance.

When Alexei Alexandrovich had decided to himself that he ought to have a talk with his wife, it had seemed an easy and simple thing to him; but now, as he began to think over this newly arisen circumstance, it seemed to him very complicated and difficult.

Alexei Alexandrovich was not a jealous man. Jealousy, in his opinion, was insulting to a wife, and a man ought to have trust in his wife. Why he ought to have trust – that is, complete assurance that his young wife would always love him – he never asked himself; but he felt no distrust, because he had trust and told himself that he had to have it. But now, though his conviction that jealousy was a shameful feeling and that one ought to have trust was not destroyed, he felt that he stood face to face with something illogical and senseless, and he did not know what to do. Alexei Alexandrovich stood face to face with life, confronting the possibility of his wife loving someone else besides him, and it was this that seemed so senseless and incomprehensible to him, because it was life itself. All his life Alexei Alexandrovich had lived and worked in spheres of service that dealt with reflections of life. And each time he had encountered life itself, he had drawn back from it. Now he experienced a feeling similar to what a man would feel who was calmly walking across a bridge over an abyss and suddenly saw that the bridge had been taken down and below him was the bottomless deep. This bottomless deep was life itself, the bridge the artificial life that Alexei Alexandrovich had lived. For the first time questions came to him about the possibility of his wife falling in love with someone, and he was horrified at them.

Without undressing, he paced with his even step up and down the resounding parquet floor of the dining room lit by a single lamp, over the carpet in the dark drawing room, where light was reflected only from the large, recently painted portrait of himself that hung over the sofa, and through her boudoir, where two candles burned, lighting the portraits of her relations and lady-friends, and the beautiful knick-knacks on her desk, long intimately familiar to him. Passing through her room he reached the door of the bedroom and turned back again.

At each section of his walk, and most often on the parquet of the lamp-lit dining room, he stopped and said to himself: 'Yes, it is necessary to resolve this and stop it, to express my view of it and my resolution.' And he turned back. 'But express what? What resolution?' he said to himself in the drawing room, and found no answer. 'But, finally,' he asked himself before turning into the boudoir, 'what has happened? Nothing. She talked with him for a long time. What of it? A woman can talk with all sorts of men in society. And besides, to be jealous means to humiliate both myself and her,' he told himself, going into her boudoir; but this reasoning, which used to have such weight for him, now weighed nothing and meant nothing. And from the bedroom door he turned back to the main room; but as soon as he entered the dark drawing room again, some voice said to him that this was not so, that if others had noticed it, it meant there was something. And again he said to himself in the dining room: 'Yes, it is necessary to resolve this and stop it and to express my view . . .' And again in the drawing room, before turning back, he asked himself: resolve it how? And then asked himself, what had happened? And answered: nothing, and remembered that jealousy was a feeling humiliating for a wife, but again in the drawing room he was convinced that something had happened. His thoughts, like his body, completed a full circle without encountering anything new. He noticed it, rubbed his forehead, and sat down in her boudoir.

Here, looking at her desk with the malachite blotter and an unfinished letter lying on it, his thoughts suddenly changed. He began thinking about her, about what she thought and felt. For the first time he vividly pictured to himself her personal life, her thoughts, her wishes, and the thought that she could and should have her own particular life seemed so frightening to him that he hastened to drive it away. It was that bottomless deep into which it was frightening to look. To put himself in thought and feeling into another being was a mental act alien to Alexei Alexandrovich. He regarded this mental act as harmful and dangerous fantasizing.

'And most terrible of all,' he thought, 'is that precisely now, when my work is coming to a conclusion' (he was thinking of the project he was putting through), 'when I need all my calm and all my inner forces, this senseless anxiety falls upon me. But what am I to do? I'm not one of those people who suffer troubles and anxieties and have no strength to look them in the face.'

'I must think it over, resolve it and cast it aside,' he said aloud.

'Questions about her feelings, about what has been or might be going on in her soul, are none of my business; they are the business of her conscience and belong to religion,' he said to himself, feeling relieved at the awareness that he had found the legitimate category to which the arisen circumstance belonged.

'And so,' Alexei Alexandrovich said to himself, 'questions of her feelings and so on are questions of her conscience, which can be no business of mine. My duty is then clearly defined. As head of the family, I am the person whose duty it is to guide her and am therefore in part the person responsible: I must point out the danger I see, caution her, and even use authority. I must speak out to her.'

And in Alexei Alexandrovich's head everything he would presently say to his wife took clear shape. Thinking over what he would say, he regretted that he had to put his time and mental powers to such inconspicuous domestic use; but, in spite of that, the form and sequence of the imminent speech took shape in his head clearly and distinctly, like a report. 'I must say and speak out the following: first, an explanation of the meaning of public opinion and propriety; second, a religious explanation of the meaning of marriage; third, if necessary, an indication of the possible unhappiness for our son; fourth, an indication of her own unhappiness.' And, interlacing his fingers, palms down, Alexei Alexandrovich stretched so that the joints cracked.

This gesture, a bad habit – joining his hands and cracking his fingers – always calmed him down and brought him to precision, which he had such need of now. There was the sound of a carriage driving up by the entrance. Alexei Alexandrovich stopped in the middle of the drawing room.

A woman's footsteps came up the stairs. Alexei Alexandrovich, prepared for his speech, stood pressing his crossed fingers, seeing whether there might be another crack somewhere. One joint cracked.

By the sound of light footsteps on the stairs he could already sense her approach and, though he was pleased with his speech, he felt afraid of the imminent talk . . .

IX

Anna was walking with her head bowed, playing with the tassels of her hood. Her face glowed with a bright glow; but this glow was not happy – it was like the terrible glow of a fire on a dark night. Seeing her husband, Anna raised her head and, as if waking up, smiled.

'You're not in bed? What a wonder!' she said, threw off her hood and, without stopping, went on into her dressing room. 'It's late, Alexei Alexandrovich,' she said from behind the door.

'Anna, I must have a talk with you.'

'With me?' she said in surprise, stepping out from behind the door and looking at him.

'Yes.'

'What's the matter? What is it about?' she asked, sitting down. 'Well, let's have a talk, if it's so necessary. But it would be better to go to sleep.'

Anna said whatever came to her tongue, and was surprised, listening to herself, at her ability to lie. How simple, how natural her words were, and how it looked as if she simply wanted to sleep! She felt herself clothed in an impenetrable armour of lies. She felt that some invisible force was helping her and supporting her.

'Anna, I must warn you,' he said.

'Warn me?' she said. 'About what?'

She looked at him so simply, so gaily, that no one who did not know her as her husband did could have noticed anything unnatural either in the sound or in the meaning of her words. But for him who knew her, who knew that when he went to bed five minutes late, she noticed it and asked the reason, who knew that she told him at once her every joy, happiness, or grief – for him it meant a great deal to see now that she did not want to notice his state or say a word about herself. He saw that the depth of her soul, formerly always open to him, was now closed to him. Moreover, by her tone he could tell that she was not embarrassed by it, but was as if saying directly to him: yes, it's closed, and so it ought to be and will be in the future. He now felt the way a man would feel coming home and finding his house locked up. 'But perhaps the key will still be found,' thought Alexei Alexandrovich.

'I want to warn you,' he said in a low voice, 'that by indiscretion and light-mindedness you may give society occasion to talk about you. Your much too animated conversation tonight with Count Vronsky' (he articulated this name firmly and with calm measuredness) 'attracted attention.'

He spoke and looked at her laughing eyes, now frightening to him in their impenetrability, and as he spoke he felt all the uselessness and idleness of his words.

'You're always like that,' she replied, as if she had not understood him at all and had deliberately grasped only the last thing he had said. 'First you're displeased when I'm bored, then you're displeased when I'm merry. I wasn't bored. Does that offend you?'

Alexei Alexandrovich gave a start and bent his hands in order to crack them.

'Ah, please don't crack them, I dislike it so,' she said.

'Anna, is this you?' Alexei Alexandrovich said in a low voice, making an effort and restraining the movement of his hands.

'But what is all this?' she said with sincere and comical surprise. 'What do you want from me?'

Alexei Alexandrovich paused and rubbed his forehead and eyes with his hand. He saw that instead of what he had wanted to do, that is, warn his wife about a mistake in the eyes of society, he was involuntarily worrying about something that concerned her conscience and was struggling with some wall that he had imagined.

'Here is what I intend to say,' he went on coldly and calmly, 'and I ask you to listen to me. As you know, I look upon jealousy as an insulting and humiliating feeling, and I would never allow myself to be guided by it. But there are certain laws of propriety against which one cannot trespass with impunity. I did not notice it this evening, but judging by the impression made upon the company, everyone noticed that you behaved and bore yourself not quite as one might wish.'

'I really don't understand,' said Anna, shrugging her shoulders. 'He doesn't care,' she thought. 'But society noticed and that troubles him.'

'You're unwell, Alexei Alexandrovich,' she added, stood up, and was about to go out of the door, but he moved forward as if wishing to stop her.

His face was ugly and sullen, as Anna had never seen it before. She stopped and, leaning her head back to one side, with her quick hand began taking out her hairpins.

'Well, sir, I'm listening for what comes next,' she said calmly and mockingly. 'And even listening with interest, because I wish to understand what it's all about.'

She spoke and was surprised by the naturally calm, sure tone with which she spoke and her choice of words.

'I have no right to enter into all the details of your feelings, and generally I consider it useless and even harmful,' Alexei Alexandrovich began. 'Rummaging in our souls, we often dig up something that ought to have lain there unnoticed. Your feelings are a matter for your conscience; but it is my duty to you, to myself, and to God, to point out your duties to you. Our lives are bound together, and bound not by men but by God. Only a crime can break this bond, and a crime of that sort draws down a heavy punishment.'

'I don't understand a thing. Ah, my God, and unfortunately I'm sleepy!' she said, quickly running her hand over her hair, searching for any remaining hairpins.

'Anna, for God's sake, don't talk like that,' he said meekly. 'Perhaps I am mistaken, but believe me, what I am saying I say as much for myself as for you. I am your husband and I love you.'

For a moment her face fell and the mocking spark in her eye went out; but the word 'love' again made her indignant. She thought: 'Love? But can he love? If he hadn't heard there was such a thing as love, he would never have used the word. He doesn't even know what love is.'

'Alexei Alexandrovich, really, I don't understand,' she said. 'Explain what it is you find . . .'

'Please allow me to finish. I love you. But I am not speaking of myself. The main persons here are our son and yourself. It may well be, I repeat, that my words will seem completely unnecessary and inappropriate to you; it may be that they are caused by an error on my part. In that case I beg you to pardon me. But if you yourself feel that there are even the slightest grounds, I beg you to think and, if your heart speaks, to tell me . . .'

Alexei Alexandrovich, not noticing it himself, was saying something quite other than what he had prepared.

'There's nothing for me to tell. And . . .' she suddenly said quickly, with a barely restrained smile, 'really, it's time for bed.'

Alexei Alexandrovich sighed and, saying no more, went into the bedroom.

When she came into the bedroom, he was already lying down. His lips were sternly compressed, and his eyes were not looking at her. Anna got into her own bed and waited every minute for him to begin talking to her again. She feared that he would, and at the same time she wanted it. But he was silent. For a long time she waited motionless and then forgot about him. She was thinking about another man, she could see him, and felt how at this thought her heart filled with excitement and criminal joy. Suddenly she heard a steady, peaceful nasal whistling. At first, Alexei Alexandrovich seemed startled by this whistling and stopped; but after two breaths the whistling began again with a new, peaceful steadiness.

'It's late now, late, late,' she whispered with a smile. She lay for a long time motionless, her eyes open, and it seemed to her that she herself could see them shining in the darkness.

X

From that evening a new life began for Alexei Alexandrovich and his wife. Nothing special happened. Anna went into society as always, visited Princess Betsy especially often, and met Vronsky everywhere. Alexei Alexandrovich saw it but could do nothing. To all his attempts at drawing her into an explanation she opposed the impenetrable wall of some cheerful perplexity. Outwardly things were the same, but inwardly their relations had changed completely. Alexei Alexandrovich, such a strong man in affairs of state, here felt himself powerless. Like a bull, head lowered obediently, he waited for the axe that he felt was raised over him. Each time he began thinking about it, he felt that he had to try once more, that by kindness, tenderness and persuasion there was still a hope of saving her, of making her come to her senses, and he tried each day to talk with her. But each time he started talking with her, he felt that the spirit of evil and deceit that possessed her also took possession of him, and he said something to her that was not right at all and not in the tone in which he had wanted to speak. He talked with her involuntarily in his habitual tone, which was a mockery of those who would talk that way seriously. And in that tone it was impossible to say what needed to be said to her.

. . . .

. . . .

XI

That which for almost a year had constituted the one exclusive desire of Vronsky's life, replacing all former desires; that which for Anna had been an impossible, horrible, but all the more enchanting dream of happiness – this desire had been satisfied. Pale, his lower jaw trembling, he stood over her and pleaded with her to be calm, himself not knowing why or how.

'Anna! Anna!' he kept saying in a trembling voice. 'Anna, for God's sake! . . .'

But the louder he spoke, the lower she bent her once proud, gay, but now shame-stricken head, and she became all limp, falling from the divan where she had been sitting to the floor at his feet; she would have fallen on the carpet if he had not held her.

'My God! Forgive me!' she said, sobbing, pressing his hands to her breast.

She felt herself so criminal and guilty that the only thing left for her was to humble herself and beg forgiveness; but as she had no one else in her life now except him, it was also to him that she addressed her plea for forgiveness. Looking at him, she physically felt her humiliation and could say nothing more. And he felt what a murderer must feel when he looks at the body he has deprived of life. This body deprived of life was their love, the first period of their love. There was something horrible and loathsome in his recollections of what had been paid for with this terrible price of shame. Shame at her spiritual nakedness weighed on her and communicated itself to him. But, despite all the murderer's horror before the murdered body, he had to cut this body into pieces and hide it, he had to make use of what the murderer had gained by his murder.

And as the murderer falls upon this body with animosity, as if with passion, drags it off and cuts it up, so he covered her face and shoulders with kisses. She held his hand and did not move. Yes, these kisses were what had been bought by this shame. Yes, and this one hand, which will always be mine, is the hand of my accomplice. She raised this hand and kissed it. He knelt down and tried to look at her face; but she hid it and said nothing. Finally, as if forcing herself, she sat up and pushed him away. Her face was still as beautiful, but the more pitiful for that.

'Everything is finished,' she said. 'I have nothing but you. Remember that.'

'How can I not remember what is my very life? For one minute of this happiness . . .'

'What happiness?' she said with loathing and horror, and her horror involuntarily communicated itself to him. 'For God's sake, not a word, not a word more.'

She quickly stood up and moved away from him.

'Not a word more,' she repeated, and with an expression of cold despair on her face, which he found strange, she left him. She felt that at that moment she could not put into words her feeling of shame, joy, and horror before this entry into a new life, and she did not want to speak of it, to trivialize this feeling with imprecise words. But later, too, the next day and the day after that, she not only found no words in which she could express all the complexity of these feelings, but was unable even to find thoughts in which she could reflect with herself on all that was in her soul.

She kept telling herself: 'No, I can't think about it now; later, when I'm more calm.' But this calm for reflection never came; each time the thought occurred to her of what she had done, of what would become of her and what she ought to do, horror came over her, and she drove these thoughts away.

'Later, later,' she kept saying, 'when I'm more calm.'

But in sleep, when she had no power over her thoughts, her situation presented itself to her in all its ugly nakedness. One dream visited her almost every night. She dreamed that they were both her husbands, that they both lavished their caresses on her. Alexei Alexandrovich wept, kissing her hands and saying: 'It's so good now!' And Alexei Vronsky was right there, and he, too, was her husband. And, marvelling that it had once seemed impossible to her, she laughingly explained to them that this was much simpler and that now they were both content and happy. But this dream weighed on her like a nightmare, and she would wake up in horror.

XII

In the first period after his return from Moscow, when he still gave a start and blushed each time he remembered the disgrace of the refusal, Levin said to himself: 'I blushed and shuddered in the same way, thinking all was lost, when I got the lowest grade in physics and had to repeat my second year; I thought myself lost in the same way after I bungled my sister's affair, which had been entrusted to me. And what happened? Now that years have passed, I remember it and wonder how it could have upset me. It will be the same with this grief. Time will pass, and I'll grow indifferent to it.'

But three months passed and he did not grow indifferent to it, and it was as painful for him to remember it as in the first days. He could not be at peace, because he, who had dreamed of family life for so long, who felt himself so ripe for it, was still not married and was further than ever from marriage. He himself felt painfully, as all those around him also felt, that at his age it was not good for a man to be alone. He remembered how, before his departure for Moscow, he had said once to his cow-man Nikolai, a naïve muzhik with whom he liked to talk: 'Well, Nikolai, I mean to get married!' – and Nikolai had quickly replied, as if to something of which there could be no doubt: 'It's high time you did, Konstantin Dmitrich.' But marriage was now further from him than ever. The place was taken, and when in imagination he put some of the girls he knew into that place, he felt it was completely impossible. Besides, the memory of the refusal and of the role he had played then tormented him with shame. However often he said to himself that he was in no way to blame, this memory, on a par with other shameful memories of the same sort, made him start and blush. In his past, as in any man's past, there were actions he recognized as bad, for which his conscience ought to have tormented him; yet the memory of the bad actions tormented him far less than these insignificant but shameful memories. These wounds never healed. And alongside these memories there now stood the refusal and the pitiful position in which he must have appeared to others that evening. But time and work did their part. Painful memories were screened from him more and more by the inconspicuous but significant events of country life. With every week he remembered Kitty less often. He impatiently awaited the news that she was already married or would be married any day, hoping that this news, like the pulling of a tooth, would cure him completely.

Meanwhile spring had come, beautiful, harmonious, without spring's anticipations and deceptions, one of those rare springs that bring joy to plants, animals and people alike. This beautiful spring aroused Levin still more and strengthened him in the intention to renounce all former things, in order to arrange his solitary life firmly and independently. Though many of those plans with which he had returned to the country had not been carried out, he had observed the main thing – purity of life. He did not experience the shame that usually tormented him after a fall and was able to look people boldly in the eye. Already in February he had received a letter from Marya Nikolaevna saying that his brother Nikolai's health had worsened but that he did not want to be treated, and as a result of this letter Levin had gone to see his brother in Moscow and had succeeded in persuading him to consult a doctor and go to a watering-place abroad. He had succeeded so well in persuading his brother and in lending him money for the trip without vexing him, that in this respect he was pleased with himself. Apart from managing the estate, which required special attention in the spring, apart from reading, Levin had also begun that winter to write a work on farming, the basis of which was that the character of the worker had to be taken as an absolute given in farming, like climate and soil, and that, consequently, all propositions in the science of farming ought to be deduced not from the givens of soil and climate alone, but also from the known, immutable character of the worker. So that, in spite of his solitude, or else owing to it, his life was extremely full, and only once in a while did he feel an unsatisfied desire to tell the thoughts that wandered through his head to someone besides Agafya Mikhailovna, though with her, too, he often happened to discuss physics, the theory of farming, and especially philosophy. Philosophy was Agafya Mikhailovna's favourite subject.

Spring was a long time unfolding. During the last weeks of Lent the weather was clear and frosty. In the daytime it thawed in the sun, but at night it went down to seven below;[15] there was such a crust that carts could go over it where there was no road. There was still snow at Easter. Then suddenly, on Easter Monday, a warm wind began to blow, dark clouds gathered, and for three days and three nights warm, heavy rain poured down. On Thursday the wind dropped, and a thick grey mist gathered, as if concealing the mysteries of the changes taking place in nature. Under the mist waters flowed, ice blocks cracked and moved off, the muddy, foaming streams ran quicker, and on the eve of Krasnaya Gorka[16] the mist scattered, the dark clouds broke up into fleecy white ones, the sky cleared, and real spring unfolded. In the morning the bright sun rose and quickly ate up the thin ice covering the water, and the warm air was all atremble, filled with the vapours of the reviving earth. The old grass and the sprouting needles of new grass greened, the buds on the guelder-rose, the currants and the sticky, spiritous birches swelled, and on the willow, all sprinkled with golden catkins, the flitting, newly hatched bee buzzed. Invisible larks poured trills over the velvety green fields and the ice-covered stubble, the peewit wept over the hollows and marshes still filled with brown water; high up the cranes and geese flew with their spring honking. Cattle, patchy, moulted in all but a few places, lowed in the meadows, bow-legged lambs played around their bleating, shedding mothers, fleet-footed children ran over the drying paths covered with the prints of bare feet, the merry voices of women with their linen chattered by the pond, and from the yards came the knock of the peasants' axes, repairing ploughs and harrows.[17] The real spring had come.

XIII

Levin put on big boots and, for the first time, a cloth jacket instead of his fur coat, and went about the farm, striding across streams that dazzled the eyes with their shining in the sun, stepping now on ice, now in sticky mud.

Spring is the time of plans and projects. And, going out to the yard, Levin, like a tree in spring, not yet knowing where and how its young shoots and branches, still confined in swollen buds, will grow, did not himself know very well which parts of his beloved estate he would occupy himself with now, but felt that he was filled with the very best plans and projects. First of all he went to see the cattle. The cows had been let out into the pen and, their new coats shining, warmed by the sun, they lowed, asking to go to pasture. Having admired the cows, familiar to him down to the smallest details, Levin ordered them driven to pasture and the calves let out into the pen. The cowherd ran merrily to get ready for the pasture. The dairymaids, hitching up their skirts, their bare, white, as yet untanned legs splashing in the mud, ran with switches after the calves and drove them, lowing and crazed with spring joy, into the yard.

After admiring that year's young, which were exceptionally good – the early calves were as big as a peasant's cow, Pava's three-month-old daughter was the size of a yearling – Levin gave orders for a trough to be brought out and hay to be put in the racks. But it turned out that the racks, made in the autumn and left for winter in the unused pen, were broken. He sent for the carpenter, who by his order ought to have been working on the thresher. But it turned out that the carpenter was repairing the harrows, which ought to have been repaired before Lent.[18] That was extremely vexing to Levin. What vexed him was the repetition of this eternal slovenliness of farm work, which he had fought against with all his strength for so many years. The racks, as he learned, not needed in winter, had been taken to the work horses' stable and there had got broken, since they had been lightly made, for calves. Besides that, it also turned out that the harrows and all the agricultural tools, which he had ordered to be looked over and repaired back in the winter, and for which purpose three carpenters had been hired, were still not repaired, and the harrows were being repaired when it was already time for the harrowing. Levin sent for the steward, but at once went himself to look for him. The steward, radiant as everything else that day, was coming from the threshing floor in his fleece-trimmed coat, snapping a straw in his hands.

'Why is the carpenter not at the thresher?'

'I meant to tell you yesterday: the harrows need repair. It's time for ploughing.'

'And what about last winter?'

'And what do you want with the carpenter, sir?'

'Where are the racks for the calves' yard?'

'I ordered them to be put in place. What can you do with these folk?' said the steward, waving his arm.

'Not with these people, but with this steward!' said Levin, flaring up. 'What on earth do I keep you for!' he shouted. But remembering that this was not going to help, he stopped in mid-speech and merely sighed. 'Well, can we start sowing?' he asked after a pause.

'Beyond Turkino we can, tomorrow or the day after.'

'And the clover?'

'I sent Vassily and Mishka, they're sowing it. Only I don't know if they'll get through: it's soggy.'

'How many acres?'

'Sixteen.'

'Why not the whole of it?' shouted Levin.

That clover was being sown on only sixteen and not fifty acres was still more vexing. Planting clover, both in theory and in his own experience, was only successful if it was done as early as possible, almost over the snow. And Levin could never get that done.

'No people. What can you do with these folk? Three didn't show up. And now Semyon . . .'

'Well, you could have let the straw wait.'

'That's what I did.'

'Where are the people?'

'Five are making compote' (he meant compost). 'Four are shovelling oats – lest they go bad, Konstantin Dmitrich.'

Levin knew very well that 'lest they go bad' meant that the English seed oats were already spoiled – again what he had ordered had not been done.

'But I told you back in Lent – the vent pipes!' he shouted.

'Don't worry, we'll get everything done on time.'

Levin waved his hand angrily, went to the barns to have a look at the oats, and returned to the stables. The oats were not spoiled yet. But the workers were transferring them with shovels, whereas they should simply have been dumped directly on the barn floor, and, after giving orders about that and taking two workers from there to plant clover, Levin's vexation with the steward subsided. Besides, the day was so fine that it was impossible to be angry.

'Ignat!' he cried to the coachman, who had rolled up his sleeves and was washing the carriage by the well. 'Saddle me up . . .'

'Which do you want, sir?'

'Well, take Kolpik.'

'Right, sir.'

While the horse was being saddled, Levin again called over the steward, who was hanging around in view, to make it up with him, and began telling him about the impending spring work and his plans for the estate.

The carting of manure had to begin earlier, so that everything would be finished before the early mowing. The far field had to be ploughed continually, so as to keep it fallow. The hay was to be got in not on half shares with the peasants but by hired workers.

The steward listened attentively and obviously made an effort to approve of the master's suggestions; but all the same he had that hopeless and glum look, so familiar to Levin and always so irritating to him. This look said: 'That's all very well, but it's as God grants.'

Nothing so upset Levin as this tone. But it was a tone common to all stewards, as many of them as he had employed. They all had the same attitude towards his proposals, and therefore he now no longer got angry, but became upset and felt himself still more roused to fight this somehow elemental force for which he could find no other name than 'as God grants', and which was constantly opposed to him.

'If we manage, Konstantin Dmitrich,' said the steward.

'Why shouldn't you?'

'We need to hire more workers, another fifteen men or so. But they don't come. There were some today, but they asked seventy roubles each for the summer.'

Levin kept silent. Again this force opposed him. He knew that, hard as they tried, they had never been able to hire more than forty workers, thirty-seven, thirty-eight, at the real price; they might get forty, but not more. Yet he could not help fighting even so.

'Send to Sury, to Chefirovka, if they don't come. We must look.'

'So I will,' Vassily Fyodorovich said glumly. 'And the horses have also gone weak.'

'We'll buy more. Oh, I know,' he added, laughing, 'you'd have it all smaller and poorer, but this year I won't let you do it your way. I'll do everything myself.'

'You don't seem to sleep much as it is. More fun for us, under the master's eye . . .'

'So they're sowing clover beyond Birch Dale? I'll go and have a look,' he said, mounting the small, light bay Kolpik, brought by the coachman.

'You won't get across the brook, Konstantin Dmitrich,' cried the coachman.

'Well, through the woods then.'

And at the brisk amble of the good, too-long-inactive little horse, who snorted over the puddles and tugged at the reins, Levin rode across the mud of the yard, out of the gate and into the fields.

If Levin felt happy in the cattle- and farm-yards, he felt still happier in the fields. Swaying rhythmically to the amble of his good little mount, drinking in the warm yet fresh smell of the snow and the air as he went through the forest over the granular, subsiding snow that still remained here and there with tracks spreading in it, he rejoiced at each of his trees with moss reviving on its bark and buds swelling. When he rode out of the forest, green wheat spread before him in a smooth, velvety carpet over a huge space, with not a single bare or marshy patch, and only spotted here and there in the hollows with the remains of the melting snow. Nor was he angered by the sight of a peasant horse and colt trampling his green wheat (he told a muzhik he met to drive them away), nor by the mocking and stupid reply of the muzhik Ipat, whom he met and asked: 'Well, Ipat, time for sowing?' 'Have to plough first, Konstantin Dmitrich,' replied Ipat. The further he rode, the happier he felt, and plans for the estate, one better than another, arose in his mind: to plant willows along the meridional lines of all the fields, so that the snow would not stay too long under them; to divide them into six fertilized fields and three set aside for grass; to build a cattle-yard at the far end of the field and dig a pond; to set up movable pens for the cattle so as to manure the fields. And then he would have eight hundred acres of wheat, two hundred and fifty of potatoes, and four hundred of clover, and not a single acre exhausted.

In such dreams, turning the horse carefully along the borders, so as not to trample his green wheat, he rode up to the workers who were sowing clover. The cart with the seed stood not at the edge but in the field, and the winter wheat was all dug up by the wheels and the horse. The two workers were sitting on a balk, probably taking turns smoking a pipe. The soil in the cart, with which the seed was mixed, had not been rubbed fine, but was caked or frozen in lumps. Seeing the master, the worker Vassily went to the cart, while Mishka started sowing. This was not good, but Levin seldom got angry with hired workers. When Vassily came up, Levin told him to take the horse to the edge.

'Never mind, sir, it'll grow back,' Vassily replied.

'No discussion, please,' said Levin, 'just do as you've been told.'

'Right, sir,' said Vassily, and he took hold of the horse's head. 'And the sowing is first rate, Konstantin Dmitrich,' he said, fawning. 'Only the walking's pretty terrible! You drag ten pounds on each shoe.'

'And why hasn't the soil been sifted?' Levin asked.

'We break it up with our hands,' Vassily answered, taking some seed and rubbing the lump between his hands.

It was not Vassily's fault that they had given him unsifted soil, but it was vexing all the same.

Having already experienced more than once the usefulness of the remedy he knew for stifling his vexation and turning all that seemed bad back to good, Levin employed it here as well. He looked at how Mishka strode along, lugging huge lumps of earth stuck to each foot, got off his horse, took the seed basket from Vassily, and went to sow.

'Where did you stop?'

Vassily pointed to a mark with his foot, and Levin went, as well as he could, scattering the seeds mixed with soil. It was hard walking, as through a swamp, and having gone one row, Levin became sweaty, stopped and handed the seed basket back.

'Well, master, mind you don't scold me for this row come summer,' said Vassily.

'What for?' Levin said gaily, already feeling the effectiveness of the remedy.

'You'll see come summer. It'll be different. You just take a look where I sowed last spring. So neat! You know, Konstantin Dmitrich, it seems I try and do it as I would for my own father. I don't like doing bad work myself and I tell others the same. If the master's pleased, so are we. Look there now,' Vassily said, pointing to the field, 'it brings joy to your heart.'

'It's a fine spring, Vassily.'

'Such a spring as the old folk don't remember. I went home, and our old man there has also sowed two acres of wheat. He says you can't tell it from rye.'

'How long have you been sowing wheat?'

'Why, it's you that taught us two years ago. And you gave me two bushels. We sold a quarter of it and sowed the rest.'

'Well, make sure you rub out these lumps,' said Levin, going towards his horse, 'and keep an eye on Mishka. If it comes up well, you'll get fifty kopecks per acre.'

'Thank you kindly. Seems we're right pleased with you anyway.'

Levin mounted his horse and rode to the field where last year's clover was and to the one that had been ploughed for the spring wheat.

The clover sprouting among the stubble was wonderful. It was all revived already and steadily greening among the broken stalks of last year's wheat. The horse sank fetlock-deep, and each of his hoofs made a sucking sound as it was pulled from the half-thawed ground. It was quite impossible to go across the ploughed field: it held only where there was ice, but in the thawed furrows the leg sank over the fetlocks. The ploughing was excellent; in two days they could harrow and begin sowing. Everything was beautiful, everything was cheerful. Levin rode back across the brook, hoping the water had subsided. And indeed he did get across and frightened two ducks. 'There must also be woodcock,' he thought, and just at the turning to his house he met a forester, who confirmed his guess about woodcock.

Levin went home at a trot, so as to arrive in time to have dinner and prepare a gun for the evening.

XIV

Approaching his house in the cheerfullest spirits, Levin heard a bell from the direction of the main entrance.

'Yes, it's from the railway station,' he thought, 'exactly the time of the Moscow train . . . Who could it be? What if it's my brother Nikolai? He did say, "Maybe I'll go to a watering-place, or maybe I'll come to you."' He found it frightening and unpleasant in the first moment that the presence of his brother might spoil this happy spring mood of his. Then he became ashamed of this feeling, and at once opened, as it were, his inner embrace and with tender joy now expected and wished it to be his brother. He urged the horse on and, passing the acacia tree, saw the hired troika driving up from the railway station with a gentleman in a fur coat. It was not his brother. 'Ah, if only it's someone pleasant that I can talk with,' he thought.

'Ah!' Levin cried joyfully, raising both arms high. 'What a delightful guest! Oh, I'm so glad it's you!' he called out, recognizing Stepan Arkadyich.

'I'll find out for certain whether she's married or when she's going to be,' he thought.

And on that beautiful spring day he felt that the memory of her was not painful for him at all.

'What, you didn't expect me?' said Stepan Arkadyich, getting out of the sledge with flecks of mud on the bridge of his nose, his cheek and his eyebrow, but radiating health and good cheer. 'I've come – one – to see you,' he said, embracing and kissing him, 'and – two – to do some fowling, and – three – to sell a wood in Yergushovo.'

'Splendid! And what a spring, eh? How did you make it by sledge?'

'It's even worse by cart, Konstantin Dmitrich,' replied the coachman, whom he knew.

'Well, I'm very, very glad you've come,' Levin said with a sincere and childishly joyful smile.

Levin led his guest to the visitors' bedroom, where Stepan Arkadyich's belongings were also brought – a bag, a gun in a case, a pouch for cigars – and, leaving him to wash and change, went meanwhile to the office to give orders about the ploughing and the clover. Agafya Mikhailovna, always very concerned for the honour of the house, met him in the front hall with questions about dinner.

'Do as you like, only be quick,' he said and went to the steward.

When he returned, Stepan Arkadyich, washed, combed, with a radiant smile, was coming out of his door, and together they went upstairs.

'Well, how glad I am that I got to you! Now I'll understand what these mysteries are that you perform here. No, really, I envy you. What a house, how nice it all is! Bright, cheerful!' Stepan Arkadyich said, forgetting that it was not always spring and a clear day like that day. 'And your nanny's such a dear! A pretty maid in a little apron would be preferable, but with your monasticism and strict style – it's quite all right.'

Stepan Arkadyich brought much interesting news, and one piece of news especially interesting for Levin – that his brother Sergei Ivanovich was going to come to him in the country for the summer.

Stepan Arkadyich did not say a single word about Kitty or generally about the Shcherbatskys; he only gave him greetings from his wife. Levin was grateful to him for his delicacy, and was very glad of his guest. As always during his time of solitude, he had accumulated a mass of thoughts and feelings that he could not share with anyone around him, and now he poured into Stepan Arkadyich his poetic joy of spring, his failures and plans for the estate, his thoughts and observations about the books he was reading, and in particular the idea of his own book, which was based, though he did not notice it, on a critique of all the old books on farming. Stepan Arkadyich, always nice, understanding everything from a hint, was especially nice during this visit, and Levin also noticed in him a new trait of respect and a kind of tenderness towards himself, which he found flattering.

The efforts of Agafya Mikhailovna and the cook to make an especially good dinner had as their only result that the two hungry friends, sitting down to the hors d'oeuvres, ate their fill of bread and butter, polotok and pickled mushrooms, and that Levin ordered the soup served without the pirozhki with which the cook had wanted especially to surprise the guest. But Stepan Arkadyich, though accustomed to different dinners, found everything excellent: the herb liqueur, the bread and butter, and especially the polotok, the mushrooms, the nettle soup,[19] the chicken with white sauce, and the white Crimean wine – everything was excellent and wonderful.

'Splendid, splendid,' he said, lighting up a fat cigarette after the roast. 'Here it's just as if, after the noise and vibration of a steamer, I've landed on a quiet shore. So you say that the element of the worker himself must be studied and serve as a guide in the choice of farming methods. I'm not an initiate, but it seems to me that the theory and its application will influence the worker himself.'

'Yes, but wait: I'm not talking about political economy, I'm talking about scientific farming. It must be like a natural science, observing given phenomena, and the worker with his economic, ethnographic . . .'

Just then Agafya Mikhailovna came in with the preserves.[20]

'Well, Agafya Mikhailovna,' Stepan Arkadyich said to her, kissing the tips of his plump fingers, 'what polotok you have, what herb liqueur! . . . But say, Kostya, isn't it time?' he added.

Levin looked out of the window at the sun setting beyond the bare treetops of the forest.

'It's time, it's time,' he said. 'Kuzma, harness the trap!' And he ran downstairs.

Stepan Arkadyich, having come down, carefully removed the canvas cover from the varnished box himself and, opening it, began to assemble his expensive, new-fashioned gun. Kuzma, already scenting a big tip for vodka, would not leave Stepan Arkadyich and helped him on with his stockings and boots, which Stepan Arkadyich willingly allowed him to do.

'Kostya, tell them that if the merchant Ryabinin comes – I told him to come today – they should receive him and have him wait . . .'

'Are you selling the wood to Ryabinin?'

'Yes. Do you know him?'

'That I do. I've dealt with him "positively and finally".'

Stepan Arkadyich laughed. 'Positively and finally' were the merchant's favourite words.

'Yes, he has a funny way of talking. She knows where her master's going!' he added, patting Laska, who was fidgeting around Levin with little squeals, licking now his hand, now his boots and gun.

The trap was already standing by the porch when they came out.

'I told them to harness up, though it's not far – or shall we go on foot?'

'No, better to drive,' said Stepan Arkadyich, going up to the trap. He got in, wrapped his legs in a tiger rug and lit a cigar. 'How is it you don't smoke! A cigar – it's not so much a pleasure as the crown and hallmark of pleasure. This is the life! How good! This is how I'd like to live!'

'Who's stopping you?' said Levin, smiling.

'No, you're a lucky man. You have everything you love. You love horses – you have them; dogs – you have them; hunting – you have it; farming – you have it.'

'Maybe it's because I rejoice over what I have and don't grieve over what I don't have,' said Levin, remembering Kitty.

Stepan Arkadyich understood, looked at him, but said nothing.

Levin was grateful to Oblonsky for noticing, with his usual tact, that he was afraid of talking about the Shcherbatskys and saying nothing about them; but now Levin wanted to find out about what tormented him so and did not dare to begin.

'Well, and how are things with you?' Levin said, thinking how wrong it was on his part to think only of himself.

Stepan Arkadyich's eyes twinkled merrily.

'You don't accept that one can like sweet rolls when one has a daily ration of bread – in your opinion, it's a crime. But I don't accept life without love,' he said, understanding Levin's question in his own way. 'No help for it, that's how I'm made. And really, it brings so little harm to anyone, and so much pleasure for oneself . . .'

'What, is there something new?' asked Levin.

'There is, brother! Look, you know there's this type of Ossianic[21] women . . . women you see in your dreams . . . But these women exist in reality . . . and these women are terrible. Woman, you see, it's such a subject that, however much you study her, there'll always be something new.'

'Better not to study then.'

'No. Some mathematician said that the pleasure lies not in discovering the truth, but in searching for it.'

Levin listened silently and, despite all his efforts, was simply unable to get inside his friend's soul and understand his feelings or the charms of studying such women.

XV

The shooting place was not far away, across a stream in a small aspen grove. Nearing the wood, Levin got out and led Oblonsky to the corner of a mossy and marshy clearing that was already free of snow. He himself went back to a double birch at the other end and, leaning his gun against the fork of a dry lower branch, took off his caftan, tightened his belt, and made sure he had freedom to move his arms.

The old, grey-haired Laska, who had followed behind him, carefully sat down facing him and pricked up her ears. The sun was setting behind the large forest, and in its light the little birches scattered among the aspens were distinctly outlined with their hanging branches and buds swollen to bursting.

From a thicket in which there was still snow came the barely audible sound of water trickling in narrow, meandering streams. Small birds chirped and occasionally flew from tree to tree.

In intervals of complete silence one could hear the rustling of last year's leaves, stirred by the thawing ground and the growing grass.

'Imagine! You can hear and see the grass grow!' Levin said to himself, noticing the movement of a wet, slate-coloured aspen leaf beside a spear of young grass. He stood, listened, and looked down at the wet, mossy ground, at the attentive Laska, then at the sea of bare treetops of the forest spreading before him at the foot of the hill and the fading sky streaked with white clouds. A hawk, unhurriedly flapping its wings, flew high over the distant forest; another flew the same way in the same direction and disappeared. The birds chirped more loudly and busily in the thicket. An owl hooted not far away, and Laska gave a start, took several cautious steps and, cocking her head, began to listen. From across the stream came the call of a cuckoo. It cuckooed twice in its usual call, then wheezed, hurried and became confused.

'Imagine! a cuckoo already!' said Stepan Arkadyich, coming out from behind a bush.

'Yes, I can hear,' Levin replied, reluctantly breaking the silence of the forest with his voice, which he found disagreeable. 'It won't be long now.'

Stepan Arkadych's figure stepped back behind the bush, and Levin saw only the bright flame of a match, replaced at once by the red glow of a cigarette and blue smoke.

'Chik! chik!' clicked the hammers of Stepan Arkadyich's gun.

'And what's that cry?' asked Oblonsky, drawing Levin's attention to a drawn-out yelping, as of a frolicking colt whinnying in a high voice.

'Ah, don't you know? It's a male hare. Enough talk! Listen, they're coming!' Levin almost cried out, cocking his gun.

They heard a high, distant whistling, and two seconds later, in the usual rhythm so well known to hunters, a second, a third, and after the third whistle came a chirring.

Levin cast a glance right, left, and there before him in the dull blue sky, over the merging, tender sprouts of the aspen tops, a flying bird appeared. It flew straight towards him: the close, chirring sounds, like the measured ripping of taut fabric, were just above his ears; the bird's long beak and neck could already be seen, and just as Levin aimed, red lightning flashed from behind the bush where Oblonsky stood; the bird dropped like an arrow and again soared up. Lightning flashed again and a clap was heard; fluttering its wings as if trying to stay in the air, the bird paused, hung there for a moment, then plopped heavily to the marshy ground.

'Could we have missed?' cried Stepan Arkadyich, who was unable to see on account of the smoke.

'Here it is!' said Levin, pointing at Laska, who, with one ear raised and the tip of her fluffy tail wagging on high, stepping slowly as if she wished to prolong the pleasure, and almost smiling, brought the dead bird to her master. 'Well, I'm glad you got it,' said Levin, at the same time already feeling envious that it was not he who had succeeded in shooting this woodcock.

'A rotten miss with the right barrel,' Stepan Arkadyich replied, loading the gun. 'Shh . . . here they come.'

Indeed, they heard a quick succession of piercing whistles. Two woodcock, playing and chasing each other and only whistling, not chirring, came flying right over the hunters' heads. Four shots rang out and, like swallows, the woodcock made a quick swerve and vanished from sight.

The fowling was splendid. Stepan Arkadyich shot another two birds, and Levin two, one of which could not be found. It was getting dark. Bright, silvery Venus, low in the west, was already shining with her tender gleam behind the birches, and high in the east the sombre Arcturus already played its red fires. Overhead Levin kept finding and losing the stars of the Great Bear. The woodcock had stopped flying; but Levin decided to wait longer, until Venus, which he could see under a birch branch, rose above it and the stars of the Great Bear showed clearly. Venus had already risen above the branch, the chariot of the Great Bear with its shaft was already quite visible in the dark blue sky, but he still waited.

'Isn't it time?' said Stepan Arkadyich.

It was quiet in the forest and not a single bird moved.

'Let's stay longer.'

'As you wish.'

They were now standing about fifteen paces apart.

'Stiva!' Levin said suddenly and unexpectedly. 'Why don't you tell me whether your sister-in-law got married or when she's going to?'

Levin felt himself so firm and calm that he thought no answer could stir him. But he never expected what Stepan Arkadyich replied.

'She wasn't and isn't thinking of getting married, but she's very ill, and the doctors have sent her abroad. They even fear for her life.'

'What's that!' cried Levin. 'Very ill? What's wrong with her? How did she . . .'

While they were saying this, Laska, her ears pricked up, kept glancing at the sky and then reproachfully at them.

'Found a fine time to talk!' she thought. 'And there's one coming . . . There it is, all right. They'll miss it . . .' thought Laska.

But just then both men heard the piercing whistle, which seemed to lash at their ears, and they suddenly seized their guns and lightning flashed twice and two claps rang out simultaneously. The high-flying woodcock instantly folded its wings and fell into the thicket, bending the slender shoots.

'That's excellent! We shared one!' Levin cried out and ran into the thicket with Laska to look for the woodcock. 'Ah, yes, what was that unpleasant thing?' he recollected. 'Yes, Kitty's sick . . . Nothing to be done, very sorry,' he thought.

'Ah, she's found it! Good girl,' he said, taking the warm bird out of Laska's mouth and putting it into the nearly full game bag. 'I've found it, Stiva!' he cried.

XVI

On the way home, Levin asked for all the details of Kitty's illness and the Shcherbatskys' plans, and though he would have been ashamed to admit it, what he learned was pleasing to him. Pleasing because there was still hope, and all the more pleasing because she, who had made him suffer so much, was suffering herself. But when Stepan Arkadyich began to speak of the causes of Kitty's illness and mentioned Vronsky's name, Levin interrupted him:

'I have no right to know family details and, to tell the truth, I'm also not interested.'

Stepan Arkadyich smiled barely perceptibly, catching one of those instantaneous changes so familiar to him in Levin's face, which became as gloomy as it had been cheerful a moment before.

'You've already quite settled with Ryabinin about the wood?' asked Levin.

'Yes, I have. An excellent price, thirty-eight thousand. Eight down and the rest over six years. I was busy with it for a long time. No one offered more.'

'That means you gave your wood away,' Levin said gloomily.

'Why is that?' Stepan Arkadyich asked with a good-natured smile, knowing that Levin would now find everything bad.

'Because that wood is worth at least two hundred roubles an acre,' Levin replied.

'Ah, these country squires!' Stepan Arkadyich said jokingly. 'This tone of scorn for us city people! . . . Yet when it comes to business, we always do better. Believe me, I worked it all out,' he said, 'and the wood has been sold very profitably – I'm even afraid he'll go back on it. You see, it's mostly second growth,' said Stepan Arkadyich, wishing with the words 'second growth' to convince Levin completely of the unfairness of his doubts, 'fit only for stove wood. It won't stand you more than ten cord per acre, and he's giving me seventy-five roubles.'

Levin smiled scornfully. 'I know that manner,' he thought, 'not just his but all city people's, who come to the country twice in ten years, pick up two or three country words and use them rightly or wrongly, in the firm conviction that they know everything. "Second growth, stand you ten cord". He says the words but doesn't understand a thing himself.'

'I wouldn't teach you about what you write there in your office,' he said, 'and if necessary, I'd ask you. But you are so certain you understand this whole business of selling the wood. It's hard. Did you count the trees?'

'How can I count the trees?' Stepan Arkadyich said with a laugh, still wishing to get his friend out of his bad mood. ' "To count the sands, the planets' rays, a lofty mind well may . . ." '[22]

'Well, yes, and Ryabinin's lofty mind can. And no merchant will buy without counting, unless it's given away to him, as you're doing. I know your wood. I go hunting there every year, and your wood is worth two hundred roubles an acre outright, and he's giving you seventy-five in instalments. That means you've made him a gift of thirty thousand.'

'Come, don't get so carried away,' Stepan Arkadyich said pitifully. 'Why didn't anyone make an offer?'

'Because he's in with the other merchants; he paid them off. I've dealt with them all, I know them. They're not merchants, they're speculators. He wouldn't touch a deal where he'd make ten or fifteen per cent, he waits till he gets a rouble for twenty kopecks.'

'Come, now! You're out of sorts.'

'Not in the least,' Levin said gloomily, as they drove up to the house.

A little gig was already standing by the porch, tightly bound in iron and leather, with a sleek horse tightly harnessed in broad tugs. In the little gig, tightly filled with blood and tightly girdled, sat Ryabinin's clerk, who was also his driver. Ryabinin himself was in the house and met the friends in the front room. He was a tall, lean, middle-aged man, with a moustache, a jutting, clean-shaven chin and protruding, dull eyes. He was dressed in a long-skirted dark-blue frock coat with buttons below his rear and high boots wrinkled at the ankles and straight on the calves, over which he wore big galoshes. He wiped his face in a circular motion with a handkerchief and, straightening his frock coat, which sat well enough to begin with, greeted the entering men with a smile, holding his hand out to Stepan Arkadyich, as if trying to catch something.

'So you've come.' Stepan Arkadyich gave him his hand. 'Splendid.'

'I dared not disobey your highness's commands, though the road's much too bad. I positively walked all the way, but I got here in time. My respects, Konstantin Dmitrich.' He turned to Levin, trying to catch his hand as well. But Levin, frowning, pretended not to notice and began taking out the woodcock. 'Had a good time hunting? What bird might that be?' Ryabinin added, looking with scorn at the woodcock. 'Must have taste to it.' And he shook his head disapprovingly, as if doubting very much that the hide was worth the tanning.

'Want to go to my study?' Levin, frowning gloomily, said to Stepan Arkadyich in French. 'Go to my study, you can talk there.'

'That we can, or wherever you like, sir,' Ryabinin said with scornful dignity, as if wishing to make it felt that others might have difficulties in dealing with people, but for him there could never be any difficulties in anything.

Going into the study, Ryabinin looked around by habit, as if searching for an icon,[23] but when he found one, he did not cross himself. He looked over the bookcases and shelves and, with the same doubt as about the woodcock, smiled scornfully and shook his head disapprovingly, refusing to admit that this hide could be worth the tanning.

'Well, have you brought the money?' Oblonsky asked. 'Sit down.'

'The money won't hold us up. I've come to see you, to have a talk.'

'A talk about what? Do sit down.'

'That I will,' said Ryabinin, sitting down and leaning his elbow on the back of the chair in a most painful way for himself. 'You must come down a little, Prince. It's sinful otherwise. And the money's all ready, to the last kopeck. Money won't ever hold things up.'

Levin, who meanwhile had put his gun away in a cupboard, was going out of the door, but hearing the merchant's words, he stopped.

'You got the wood for nothing as it is,' he said. 'He was too late coming here, otherwise I'd have set the price.'

Ryabinin rose and with a smile silently looked up at Levin from below.

'Konstantin Dmitrich is ver-ry stingy,' he said with a smile, turning to Stepan Arkadyich, 'there's finally no dealing with him. I wanted to buy wheat, offered good money.'

'Why should I give you what's mine for nothing? I didn't steal it or find it lying around.'

'Good gracious, nowadays stealing's positively impossible. Everything nowadays is finally in the open courts, everything's noble today; there's no more of that stealing. We talked honest. He asked too much for the wood, it doesn't tally. I beg you to come down at least a little.'

'But have you concluded the deal or not? If you have, there's no point in bargaining. If you haven't,' said Levin, 'I'll buy the wood myself.'

The smile suddenly vanished from Ryabinin's face. A hawk-like, predatory and hard expression settled on it. With quick, bony fingers he undid his frock coat, revealing a shirt not tucked in, a brass-buttoned waistcoat and a watch chain, and quickly took out a fat old pocket-book.

'If you please, the wood is mine,' he said, quickly crossing himself and holding out his hand. 'Take the money, the wood is mine. That's how Ryabinin buys, without counting pennies,' he went on, frowning and brandishing the pocket-book.

'I wouldn't be in a hurry if I were you,' said Levin.

'Gracious,' Oblonsky said in surprise, 'I've given him my word.'

Levin left the room, slamming the door. Ryabinin, looking at the door, shook his head with a smile.

'It's all on account of youth, nothing but childishness finally. I'm buying it, trust my honour, just for the glory alone, meaning that it was Ryabinin and nobody else who bought a grove from Oblonsky. And God grant it tallies up. Trust in God. If you please, sir. Write me out a receipt . . .'

An hour later the merchant, neatly closing his robe and fastening the hooks of his frock coat, the receipt in his pocket, got into his tightly bound little gig and drove home.

'Ah, these gentlemen!' he said to his clerk, 'all the same subject.'

'That's so,' the clerk replied, handing him the reins and fastening the leather apron. 'So it's congratulations, Mikhail Ignatyich?'

'Well, well . . .'

XVII

Stepan Arkadyich came upstairs, his pocket bulging with the bank notes that the merchant had given him for three months ahead. The business with the wood was concluded, the money was in his pocket, the fowling had been splendid, and Stepan Arkadyich was in the merriest spirits, and therefore he especially wanted to dispel the bad mood that had come over Levin. He wanted to end the day over supper as pleasantly as it had begun.

Indeed, Levin was out of sorts and, in spite of all his desire to be gentle and amiable with his dear guest, he could not master himself. The intoxication of the news that Kitty was not married had begun to affect him.

Kitty was unmarried and ill, ill from love for a man who had scorned her. This insult seemed to fall upon him. Vronsky had scorned her, and she had scorned him, Levin. Consequently, Vronsky had the right to despise Levin and was therefore his enemy. But Levin did not think all that. He vaguely felt that there was something insulting to him in it, and now was not angry at what had upset him but was finding fault with everything he came across. The stupid sale of the wood, the swindle Oblonsky had fallen for, which had taken place in his house, annoyed him.

'Well, so it's concluded?' he said, meeting Stepan Arkadyich upstairs. 'Want to have supper?'

'Yes, I won't refuse. What an appetite I have in the country, it's a wonder! Why didn't you offer Ryabinin a bite to eat?'

'Ah, devil take him!'

'How you treat him, though!' said Oblonsky. 'You didn't shake hands with him. Why not shake hands with him?'

'Because I don't shake hands with my footman, and my footman is a hundred times better.'

'What a reactionary you are, though! What about the merging of the classes?' said Oblonsky.

'Whoever likes merging is welcome to it. I find it disgusting.'

'I see, you're decidedly a reactionary.'

'Really, I've never thought about what I am. I'm Konstantin Levin, nothing more.'

'And a Konstantin Levin who is badly out of sorts,' said Stepan Arkadyich, smiling.

'Yes, I'm out of sorts, and do you know why? Because of – forgive me – your stupid sale . . .'

Stepan Arkadyich winced good-naturedly, like a man hurt and upset without cause.

'Well, come now!' he said. 'When did it ever happen that somebody sold something without being told right after the sale: "It was worth a lot more"? But while it's for sale, no one offers . . . No, I see you have a bone to pick with this unfortunate Ryabinin.'

'Maybe I do. And do you know why? You'll say again that I'm a reactionary, or some other dreadful word like that; but all the same it's vexing and upsetting for me to see on all sides this impoverishment of the nobility, to which I belong and, despite the merging of the classes, am glad to belong. And impoverishment not owing to luxury – that would be nothing. To live with largesse is a nobleman's business, which only noblemen know how to do. Now muzhiks are buying up the land around us. That doesn't upset me – the squire does nothing, the muzhik works and pushes out the idle man. It ought to be so. And I'm very glad for the muzhik. But it upsets me to see this impoverishment as a result of – I don't know what to call it – innocence. Here a Polish tenant buys a beautiful estate at half price from a lady who lives in Nice. Here land worth ten roubles an acre is leased to a merchant for one. Here you gave that cheat a gift of thirty thousand for no reason at all.'

'What, then? Count every tree?'

'Certainly count them. You didn't count them, but Ryabinin did. Ryabinin's children will have the means to live and be educated, and yours may not!'

'Well, excuse me, but there's something petty in this counting. We have our occupations, they have theirs, and they need profits. Well, anyhow, the deal's concluded, and there's an end to it. And here are the fried eggs, my favourite way of doing them. And Agafya Mikhailovna will give us that wonderful herb liqueur . . .'

Stepan Arkadyich sat down at the table and began joking with Agafya Mikhailovna, assuring her that he had not eaten such a dinner or supper for a long time.

'You praise it at least,' said Agafya Mikhailovna, 'but Konstantin Dmitrich, whatever you serve him, even a crust of bread, he just eats it and walks out.'

Hard as Levin tried to master himself, he was gloomy and silent. He had to ask Stepan Arkadyich one question, but he could not resolve to ask it and could not find either the form or the moment. Stepan Arkadyich had already gone to his room downstairs, undressed, washed again, put on his goffered nightshirt and got into bed, but Levin still lingered in his room, talking about various trifles, and could not bring himself to ask what he wanted to ask.

'How amazingly they make soap,' he said, examining and unwrapping a fragrant cake of soap that Agafya Mikhailovna had put out for the guest but that Oblonsky had not used. 'Just look, it's a work of art.'

'Yes, all sorts of improvements have been made in everything,' said Stepan Arkadyich, with a moist and blissful yawn. 'The theatres, for instance, and these amusement . . . a-a-ah!' he yawned. 'Electric light everywhere . . . a-a-ah!'[24]

'Yes, electric light,' said Levin. 'Yes. Well, and where is Vronsky now?' he said, suddenly putting down the soap.

'Vronsky?' asked Stepan Arkadyich, suppressing a yawn. 'He's in

Petersburg. He left soon after you did and hasn't come to Moscow once since then. And you know, Kostya, I'll tell you the truth,' he continued, leaning his elbow on the table and resting on his hand his handsome, ruddy face, from which two unctuous, kindly and sleepy eyes shone like stars. 'It was your own fault. You got frightened by your rival. And as I told you then, I don't know which side had the greater chances. Why didn't you just push right through? I told you then that . . .' He yawned with his jaws only, not opening his mouth.

'Does he know I proposed, or doesn't he?' thought Levin, looking at him. 'Yes, there's something sly and diplomatic in his face,' and, feeling himself blushing, he silently looked straight into Stepan Arkadyich's eyes.

'If there was anything on her part then, it's that she was carried away by externals,' Oblonsky continued. 'That perfect aristocratism, you know, and the future position in society affected not her but her mother.'

Levin frowned. The offence of the refusal he had gone through burned his heart like a fresh, just-received wound. He was at home, and at home even the walls help.

'Wait, wait,' he began, interrupting Oblonsky. 'Aristocratism, you say. But allow me to ask, what makes up this aristocratism of Vronsky or whoever else it may be – such aristocratism that I can be scorned? You consider Vronsky an aristocrat, but I don't. A man whose father crept out of nothing by wiliness, whose mother, God knows who she didn't have liaisons with . . . No, excuse me, but I consider myself an aristocrat and people like myself, who can point to three or four honest generations in their families' past, who had a high degree of education (talent and intelligence are another thing), and who never lowered themselves before anyone, never depended on anyone, as my father lived, and my grandfather. And I know many like that. You find it mean that I count the trees in the forest, while you give away thirty thousand to Ryabinin; but you'll have rent coming in and I don't know what else, while I won't, and so I value what I've inherited and worked for . . . We're the aristocrats, and not someone who can only exist on hand-outs from the mighty of this world and can be bought for twenty kopecks.'

'But who are you attacking? I agree with you,' Stepan Arkadyich said sincerely and cheerfully, though he felt that Levin included him among those who could be bought for twenty kopecks. He sincerely liked Levin's animation. 'Who are you attacking? Though much of what you say about Vronsky is untrue, that's not what I'm talking about. I'll tell you straight out, if I were you I'd go with me to Moscow and . . .'

'No, I don't know whether you're aware of it or not, and it makes no difference to me, but I'll tell you – I made a proposal and received a refusal, and for me Katerina Alexandrovna is now a painful and humiliating memory.'

'Why? That's nonsense!'

'Let's not talk about it. Forgive me, please, if I was rude to you,' said Levin. Now, having said everything, he became again the way he had been in the morning. 'You're not angry with me, Stiva? Please don't be angry,' he said and, smiling, took him by the hand.

'No, not in the least, and there's no reason. I'm glad we've had a talk. And you know, morning shooting can be good. Why don't we go? I won't even sleep, I'll go straight from shooting to the station.'

'Splendid.'

XVIII

Though the whole of Vronsky's inner life was filled with his passion, his external life rolled inalterably and irresistibly along the former, habitual rails of social and regimental connections and interests. Regimental interests occupied an important place in Vronsky's life, because he loved his regiment and still more because he was loved in the regiment. They not only loved him, they also respected him and were proud of him, proud that this enormously wealthy man, with an excellent education and abilities, with an open path to every sort of success, ambition and vanity, disdained it all and of all interests in life took closest to heart the interests of his regiment and his comrades. Vronsky was aware of their view of him and, besides the fact that he liked that life, also felt it his duty to maintain the established view of himself.

It goes without saying that he never spoke with any of his comrades about his love, did not let it slip even during the wildest drinking parties (however, he never got so drunk as to lose control of himself), and stopped the mouths of those of his light-minded comrades who tried to hint at his liaison. But, in spite of that, his love was known to the whole town – everyone had guessed more or less correctly about his relations with Mme Karenina – and the majority of the young men envied him precisely for what was most difficult in his love, for Karenin's high position and the resulting conspicuousness of this liaison in society.

The majority of young women, envious of Anna and long since weary of her being called *righteous*, were glad of what they surmised and only waited for the turnabout of public opinion to be confirmed before they fell upon her with the full weight of their scorn. They were already preparing the lumps of mud they would fling at her when the time came. The majority of older and more highly placed people were displeased by this impending social scandal.

Vronsky's mother, on learning of his liaison, was pleased at first – both because nothing, to her mind, gave the ultimate finish to a brilliant young man like a liaison in high society, and because Anna, whom she had liked so much, who had talked so much about her son, was after all just like all other beautiful and decent women, to Countess Vronsky's mind. But recently she had learned that her son had refused a post offered to him and important for his career, only in order to stay in the regiment and be able to see Anna, had learned that highly placed people were displeased with him for that, and had changed her opinion. Nor did she like it that, judging by all she had learned of this liaison, it was not a brilliant, graceful society liaison, of which she would have approved, but some sort of desperate Wertherian[25] passion, as she had been told, which might draw him into foolishness. She had not seen him since the time of his unexpected departure from Moscow, and demanded through his older brother that he come to see her.

The elder brother was also displeased with the younger. He did not care what sort of love it was, great or small, passionate or unpassionate, depraved or not depraved (he himself, though he had children, kept a dancer, and was therefore indulgent about such things); but he knew that this love displeased those whose good pleasure was necessary, and he therefore disapproved of his brother's behaviour.

Besides the service and society, Vronsky had one more occupation – horses, of which he was a passionate fancier.

That year an officers' steeplechase was planned. Vronsky signed up for the race, bought an English thoroughbred mare and, in spite of his love, was passionately, though restrainedly, carried away with the forthcoming races . . .

These two passions did not interfere with each other. On the contrary, he needed an occupation and an enthusiasm not dependent on his love, in which he could refresh himself and rest from impressions that excited him too much.

XIX

On the day of the Krasnoe Selo[26] races, Vronsky came earlier than usual to eat his beefsteak in the common room of the regimental mess. He did not need to maintain himself too strictly, because his weight was exactly the regulation hundred and sixty pounds; but he also had not to gain any weight, and so he avoided starches and sweets. He was sitting in a jacket unbuttoned over a white waistcoat, both elbows leaning on the table, and, while awaiting the beefsteak he had ordered, was looking into a French novel that lay open on his plate. He looked into the book only to avoid having to talk with the officers going in and out while he was thinking.

He was thinking that Anna had promised to arrange to meet him that day after the races. But he had not seen her for three days, and, since her husband had returned from abroad, he did not know whether it was possible that day or not, and did not know how to find it out. The last time he had seen her was at his cousin Betsy's country house. To the Karenins' country house he went as seldom as possible. Now he wanted to go there and was pondering the question of how to do it.

'Of course, I can say that Betsy sent me to ask if she was coming to the races. Of course I'll go,' he decided to himself, raising his head from the book. And, as he vividly pictured to himself the happiness of seeing her, his face lit up.

'Send to my place and tell them to harness the carriage quickly,' he said to the servant who brought him the beefsteak on a hot silver dish, and, drawing the dish towards him, he began to eat.

From the next room came talk and laughter and the click of billiard balls. At the entrance two officers appeared: one young, with a weak, thin face, who had come to the regiment from the Corps of Pages not long ago; the other a plump old officer with a bracelet on his wrist and puffy little eyes.

Vronsky glanced at them, frowned and, as if not noticing them, looked sideways at the book and began to eat and read at the same time.

'Fortifying yourself before work?' said the plump officer, sitting down near him.

'As you see,' said Vronsky, frowning and wiping his mouth without looking at him.

'Not afraid of gaining weight?' the first said, offering the young officer a chair.

'What?' Vronsky said angrily, making a grimace of disgust and showing his solid row of teeth.

'Not afraid of gaining weight?'

'Sherry, boy!' Vronsky said without replying, and, moving the book to the other side, he went on reading.

The plump officer took the wine list and turned to the young officer.

'You choose what we'll drink,' he said, handing him the list and looking at him.

'Maybe Rhine wine,' the young officer said, timidly casting a sidelong glance at Vronsky and trying to grasp his barely grown moustache in his fingers. Seeing that Vronsky did not turn, the young officer stood up.

'Let's go to the billiard room,' he said.

The plump officer obediently stood up, and they went to the door.

Just then the tall and well-built cavalry captain Yashvin came into the room and, giving the two officers a scornful toss of the head, went over to Vronsky.

'Ah, here he is!' he cried, slapping him hard on the epaulette with his big hand. Vronsky turned angrily, but his face at once lit up with his own special, calm and firm gentleness.

'That's wise, Alyosha,' the captain said in a loud baritone. 'Eat now and drink a little glass.'

'I don't want to eat.'

'There go the inseparables,' Yashvin added, looking mockingly at the two officers who at that moment were leaving the room. And he sat down beside Vronsky, his thighs and shins, much too long for the height of the chairs, bending at a sharp angle in their tight breeches. 'Why didn't you come to the Krasnoe Theatre last night? Numerova wasn't bad at all. Where were you?'

'I stayed late at the Tverskoys',' replied Vronsky.

'Ah!' responded Yashvin.

Yashvin, a gambler, a carouser, a man not merely without any principles, but with immoral principles – Yashvin was Vronsky's best friend in the regiment. Vronsky loved him for his extraordinary physical strength, which the man usually showed by his ability to drink like a fish, go without sleep and yet remain the same, and for his great force of character, which he showed in his relations with his superiors and comrades, making himself feared and respected, and at cards, where he staked tens of thousands and, despite the wine he drank, was always so subtle and steady that he was regarded as the foremost player in the

English Club. Vronsky loved and respected him especially because he felt that Yashvin loved him not for his name or wealth but for himself. And of all people it was with him alone that Vronsky would have liked to talk about his love. He felt that Yashvin alone, though he seemed to scorn all feelings, could understand that strong passion which now filled his whole life. Besides, he was sure that Yashvin took no pleasure in gossip and scandal, but understood his feeling in the right way – that is, knew and believed that this love was not a joke, not an amusement, but something more serious and important.

Vronsky did not speak to him of his love, but he knew that he knew everything and understood everything in the right way, and he was pleased to see it in his eyes.

'Ah, yes!' he said in response to Vronsky's having been at the Tverskoys', and, flashing his black eyes, he took hold of the left side of his moustache and began twirling it into his mouth – a bad habit of his.

'Well, and what happened last night? Did you win?' asked Vronsky.

'Eight thousand. But three are no good, it's unlikely he'll pay.'

'Well, then you can lose on me,' said Vronsky, laughing. (Yashvin had bet a large sum on Vronsky.)

'There's no way I can lose.'

'Makhotin's the only danger.'

And the conversation turned to the expectations of the day's race, which was all Vronsky was able to think about.

'Let's go, I'm finished,' said Vronsky and, getting up, he went to the door. Yashvin also got up, straightening his enormous legs and long back.

'It's too early for me to dine, but I could use a drink. I'll come at once. Hey, wine!' he cried in his deep voice, famous for commanding, which made the windowpanes tremble. 'No, never mind,' he shouted again at once. 'Since you're going home, I'll come with you.'

And he went with Vronsky.

XX

Vronsky stood in the spacious and clean Finnish cottage, which was divided in two. Petritsky shared quarters with him in camp as well. Petritsky was asleep when Vronsky and Yashvin entered the cottage.

'Get up, you've slept enough,' said Yashvin, going behind the partition and giving the dishevelled Petritsky, whose nose was buried in the pillow, a shove on the shoulder.

Petritsky suddenly jumped to his knees and looked around.

'Your brother was here,' he said to Vronsky. 'Woke me up, devil take him, said he'd come back.' And, drawing up his blanket, he threw himself back on to the pillow. 'Leave me alone, Yashvin,' he said, angry at Yashvin, who was pulling the blanket off him. 'Leave me alone!' He turned over and opened his eyes. 'You'd better tell me what to drink – there's such a vile taste in my mouth that . . .'

'Vodka's best of all,' boomed Yashvin. 'Tereshchenko! Vodka for the master, and pickles,' he shouted, obviously fond of hearing his own voice.

'Vodka, you think? Eh?' Petritsky asked, wincing and rubbing his eyes. 'And will you drink? Together, that's how to drink! Vronsky, will you drink?' Petritsky said, getting up and wrapping himself under the arms in a tiger rug.

He went through the door in the partition, raised his arms and sang in French: '"There was a king in Thu-u-ule."[27] Vronsky, will you drink?'

'Get out,' said Vronsky, who was putting on the jacket his footman held for him.

'Where are you off to?' Yashvin asked him. 'Here's the troika,' he added, seeing the carriage pull up.

'To the stables, and I also have to see Bryansky about the horses,' said Vronsky.

Vronsky had indeed promised to go to Bryansky's, nearly seven miles from Peterhof,[28] and bring him money for the horses; he hoped he would have time to get there as well. But his comrades understood at once that he was not going only there.

Petritsky, continuing to sing, winked and puffed his lips, as if to say: 'We know which Bryansky that is.'

'See that you're not late!' Yashvin merely said and, to change the subject, asked, 'So my roan serves you well?' looking out of the window at the shaft horse he had sold him.

'Wait,' Petritsky shouted to Vronsky, who was already going out. 'Your brother left a letter for you and a note. Hold on, where are they?'

Vronsky stopped.

'Well, where are they?'

'Where are they? That's the question!' Petritsky said solemnly, gesturing upwards from his nose with his index finger.

'Speak up, this is stupid!' Vronsky said, smiling.

'I haven't made a fire. They must be here somewhere.'

'Well, enough babbling! Where's the letter?'

'No, really, I forget. Or did I dream it? Hold on, hold on! What's the use of getting angry? If you'd drunk four bottles each, like I did last night, you'd forget where you flopped down. Hold on, I'll remember in a second!'

Petritsky went behind the partition and lay down on his bed.

'Wait! I was lying like this, he was standing like that. Yes, yes, yes, yes . . . Here it is!' And Petritsky pulled the letter from under the mattress, where he had hidden it.

Vronsky took the letter and his brother's note. It was just what he expected – a letter from his mother with reproaches for not coming, and a note from his brother saying that they had to have a talk. Vronsky knew it was about the same thing. 'What business is it of theirs!' he thought and, crumpling the letters, tucked them between the buttons of his frock coat, to read attentively on his way. In the front hall of the cottage he met two officers: one theirs, and the other from another regiment.

Vronsky's quarters were always a den for all the officers.

'Where are you off to?'

'I must go to Peterhof.'

'And has the horse come from Tsarskoe?'

'She has, but I haven't seen her yet.'

'They say Makhotin's Gladiator has gone lame.'

'Nonsense! Only how are you going to race in this mud?' said the other.

'Here come my saviours!' cried Petritsky, seeing the men come in. His orderly was standing in front of him holding a tray with vodka and pickles. 'Yashvin here tells me to drink so as to refresh myself.'

'Well, you really gave it to us last evening,' said one of the newcomers. 'Wouldn't let us sleep all night.'

'No, but how we finished!' Petritsky went on. 'Volkov got up on the roof and said he was feeling sad. I said: "Give us music, a funeral march!" He fell asleep on the roof to the funeral march.'

'Drink, drink the vodka without fail, and then seltzer water with a lot of lemon,' Yashvin said, standing over Petritsky like a mother making a child take its medicine, 'and after that a bit of champagne – say, one little bottle.'

'Now that's clever. Wait, Vronsky, let's have a drink.'

'No, good-bye, gentlemen, today I don't drink.'

'Why, so as not to gain weight? Well, then we'll drink alone. Bring on the seltzer water and lemon.'

'Vronsky!' someone shouted when he was already in the front hall.

'What?'

'You should get your hair cut, it's too heavy, especially on the bald spot.'

Vronsky was indeed beginning to lose his hair prematurely on top. He laughed merrily, showing his solid row of teeth, pulled his peaked cap over his bald spot, went out and got into the carriage.

'To the stable!' he said and took out the letters to read them, then changed his mind, so as not to get distracted before examining the horse. 'Later! . . .'

XXI

The temporary stable, a shed of wooden planks, had been built just next to the racetrack, and his horse was supposed to have been brought there yesterday. He had not seen her yet. For the last two days he had not ridden her himself, but had entrusted her to the trainer, and had no idea what condition his horse had arrived in or was in now. As soon as he got out of the carriage, his groom, known as 'boy', having recognized his carriage from a distance, called the trainer. The dry Englishman in high boots and a short jacket, with only a tuft of beard left under his chin, came out to meet him with the awkward gait of a jockey, spreading his elbows wide and swaying.

'Well, how's Frou-Frou?' Vronsky asked in English.

'All right, sir,' the Englishman's voice said somewhere inside his throat. 'Better not go in,' he added, raising his hat. 'I've put a muzzle on her, and the horse is agitated. Better not go in, it upsets the horse.'

'No, I'd rather go in. I want to have a look at her.'

'Come along,' the frowning Englishman said, as before, without opening his mouth and, swinging his elbows, he went ahead with his loose gait.

They entered the little yard in front of the shed. The dashing, smartly dressed lad on duty, in a clean jacket, with a broom in his hand, met them as they came in and followed after them. In the shed five horses stood in stalls, and Vronsky knew that his main rival, Makhotin's sixteen-hand chestnut, Gladiator, was to have been brought that day and should be standing there. Even more than his own horse, Vronsky wanted to have a look at Gladiator, whom he had never seen; but Vronsky knew that by the rules of horse-fanciers' etiquette, he not only should not see him, but could not even decently ask questions about him. As he went down the corridor, the lad opened the door to the second stall on the left, and Vronsky saw a big chestnut horse with white legs. He knew it was Gladiator, but, with the feeling of a man turning away from a temptingly open letter, he turned away and went to Frou-Frou's stall.

'Here's the horse that belongs to Mak . . . Mak . . . I never can say the name,' the Englishman said over his shoulder, pointing with his dirty-nailed thumb to Gladiator's stall.

'Makhotin? Yes, that's my one serious rival,' said Vronsky.

'If you were riding him,' said the Englishman, 'I'd place my bet on you.'

'He's stronger, Frou-Frou's more high-strung,' said Vronsky, smiling at the compliment to his riding.

'In a steeplechase everything depends on riding and pluck,' said the Englishman.

Vronsky not only felt that he had enough 'pluck' – that is, energy and boldness – but, what was much more important, he was firmly convinced that no one in the world could have more of this 'pluck' than he had.

'And you're sure there was no need for a longer work-out?'

'No need,' the Englishman replied. 'Please don't talk loudly. The horse is excited,' he added, nodding towards the closed stall they were standing in front of, from which they heard a stirring of hoofs on straw.

He opened the door, and Vronsky went into the stall, faintly lit by one little window. In the stall stood a dark bay horse, shifting her feet on the fresh straw. Looking around the half-lit stall, Vronsky again inadvertently took in at a glance all the qualities of his beloved horse. Frou-Frou was of average height and not irreproachable. She was narrow-boned all over; though her breast-bone protruded sharply, her chest was narrow. Her rump drooped slightly, and her front legs, and more especially her hind legs, were noticeably bowed inwards. The muscles of her hind and front legs were not particularly big; on the other hand, the horse was of unusually wide girth, which was especially striking now, with her trained shape and lean belly. Her leg bones below the knee seemed no thicker than a finger, seen from the front, but were unusually wide seen from the side. Except for her ribs, she looked as if she was all squeezed from the sides and drawn out in depth. But she possessed in the highest degree a quality that made one forget all shortcomings; this quality was *blood*, that blood which *tells*, as the English say. Her muscles, standing out sharply under the web of veins stretched through the thin, mobile and satin-smooth skin, seemed strong as bones. Her lean head, with prominent, shining, merry eyes, widened at the nose into flared nostrils with bloodshot inner membranes. In her whole figure and especially in her head there was a distinctly energetic and at the same time tender expression. She was one of those animals who, it seems, do not talk only because the mechanism of their mouths does not permit it.

To Vronsky at least it seemed that she understood everything he was feeling now as he looked at her.

As soon as he came in, she drew a deep breath and, rolling back her prominent eye so that the white was shot with blood, looked at the people coming in from the opposite side, tossing her muzzle and shifting lithely from one foot to the other.

'Well, there you see how excited she is,' said the Englishman.

'Oh, you sweetheart!' said Vronsky, approaching the horse and coaxing her.

But the closer he came, the more excited she grew. Only when he came to her head did she suddenly quiet down, her muscles quivering under her thin, tender skin. Vronsky stroked her firm neck, straightened a strand of her mane that had fallen on the wrong side of her sharp withers, and put his face to her nostrils, taut and thin as a bat's wing. She noisily breathed in and out with her strained nostrils, gave a start, lay her sharp ear back, and stretched out her firm black lip to Vronsky, as if she wanted to nibble his sleeve. Then, remembering the muzzle, she tossed it and again began shifting from one sculpted leg to the other.

'Calm down, sweetheart, calm down!' he said, patting her on the rump again; and with a joyful awareness that the horse was in the best condition, he left the stall.

The horse's excitement had communicated itself to Vronsky; he felt the blood rushing to his heart and, like the horse, he wanted to move, to bite; it was both terrifying and joyful.

'Well, I'm relying on you,' he said to the Englishman, 'six-thirty, at the appointed place.'

'Everything's in order,' the Englishman said. 'And where are you going, my lord?' he asked, unexpectedly using this title 'my lord', which he hardly ever used.

Vronsky raised his head in surprise and looked as he knew how to look, not into the Englishman's eyes but at his forehead, surprised by the boldness of the question. But, realizing that the Englishman, in putting this question, was looking at him as a jockey, not as an employer, he answered him:

'I must go to Briansky's, I'll be back in an hour.'

'How many times have I been asked that question today!' he said to himself and blushed, something that rarely happened to him. The Englishman looked at him intently and, as if he knew where he was going, added:

'The first thing is to be calm before you ride. Don't be out of sorts or upset by anything.'

'All right,' Vronsky, smiling, replied in English and, jumping into his carriage, gave orders to drive to Peterhof.

He had driven only a few paces when the storm clouds that had been threatening rain since morning drew over and there was a downpour.

'That's bad!' Vronsky thought, putting the top up. 'It was muddy to begin with, but now it will turn into a real swamp.' Sitting in the solitude of the closed carriage, he took out his mother's letter and his brother's note and read them.

Yes, it was all the same thing over and over. His mother, his brother, everybody found it necessary to interfere in the affairs of his heart. This interference aroused his spite – a feeling he rarely experienced. 'What business is it of theirs? Why does everybody consider it his duty to take care of me? And why do they pester me? Because they see that this is something they can't understand. If it was an ordinary, banal, society liaison, they'd leave me in peace. They feel that this is something else, that this is not a game, this woman is dearer to me than life. That's what they don't understand, and it vexes them. Whatever our fate is or will be, we have made it, and we don't complain about it,' he said, uniting himself and Anna in the word 'we'. 'No, they have to teach us how to live. They've got no idea what happiness is, they don't know that without this love there is no happiness or unhappiness for us – there is no life,' he thought.

He was angry with everybody for their interference precisely because in his soul he felt that they, all of them, were right. He felt that the love which joined him to Anna was not a momentary passion that would go away, as society liaisons do, leaving no traces in the life of either one of them except some pleasant or unpleasant memories. He felt all the painfulness of his position and of hers, how difficult it was, exposed as they were to the eyes of all society, to conceal their love, to lie and deceive; and to lie, and deceive, and scheme, and constantly think of others, while the passion that joined them was so strong that they both forgot everything but their love.

He vividly remembered all those oft-repeated occasions of the necessity for lying and deceit, which were so contrary to his nature; he remembered especially vividly the feeling of shame he had noticed in her more than once at this necessity for deceit and lying. And he experienced a strange feeling that had sometimes come over him since his liaison with Anna. This was a feeling of loathing for something – whether for Alexei Alexandrovich, or for himself, or for the whole world, he did not quite know. But he always drove this strange feeling away. And now, rousing himself, he continued his train of thought.

'Yes, she was unhappy before, but proud and calm; and now she cannot be calm and dignified, though she doesn't show it. Yes, this must be ended,' he decided to himself.

And for the first time the clear thought occurred to him that it was necessary to stop this lie, and the sooner the better. 'To drop everything, both of us, and hide ourselves away somewhere with our love,' he said to himself.

XXII

The downpour did not last long, and when Vronsky drove up at the full trot of his shaft horse, pulling along the outrunners who rode over the mud with free reins, the sun was already peeking out again, the roofs of the country houses and the old lindens in the gardens on both sides of the main street shone with a wet glitter, and water dripped merrily from the branches and ran off the roofs. He no longer thought of how the downpour would ruin the racetrack, but now rejoiced that, owing to this rain, he would be sure to find her at home and alone, because he knew that Alexei Alexandrovich, who had recently returned from taking the waters, had not yet moved from Petersburg.

Hoping to find her alone, Vronsky got out before crossing the bridge, as he always did in order to attract less attention, and continued on foot. He did not go to the porch from the street but went into the courtyard.

'Has the master come?' he asked the gardener.

'No, sir. The mistress is at home. Use the porch if you please; there are people there, they'll open the door,' replied the gardener.

'No, I'll go through the garden.'

Having made sure that she was alone and wishing to take her unawares, because he had not promised to come that day and she probably did not think that he would come before the race, he walked towards the terrace that looked out on the garden, holding his sword and stepping carefully over the sand of the flower-lined path. Vronsky now forgot everything he had thought on the way about the difficulty and painfulness of his position. He thought of only one thing, that he was about to see her, not just in imagination, but alive, all of her, as she was in reality. He was already going up the low steps of the terrace, placing his whole foot on each step to avoid making noise, when he suddenly remembered something that he always forgot and that constituted the most painful side of his relations with her – her son, with his questioning and, as it seemed to him, hostile look.

This boy was a more frequent hindrance to their relations than anyone else. When he was there, not only would neither Vronsky nor Anna allow themselves to speak of something they could not repeat in front of everyone, but they would not allow themselves to say even in hints anything that the boy would not understand. They did not arrange it that way, but it got established by itself. They would have considered it insulting to themselves to deceive this child. In his presence they spoke to each other as acquaintances. But in spite of this precaution, Vronsky often saw the attentive and perplexed look of the child directed at him, and the strange timidity, the unevenness – now affectionate, now cold and shy – in the boy's attitude towards him. As if the child felt that between this man and his mother there was some important relation the meaning of which he could not understand.

Indeed, the boy did feel that he could not understand this relation, and he tried but was unable to make out what feeling he ought to have for this man. With a child's sensitivity to any show of feelings, he saw clearly that his father, his governess, his nanny – all of them not only disliked Vronsky, but looked at him with disgust and fear, though they never said anything about him, while his mother looked at him as at a best friend.

'What does it mean? Who is he? How should I love him? If I don't understand, I'm to blame, or else I'm stupid, or a bad boy,' the child thought; and this led to his probing, questioning, partly inimical expression, and to his timidity and unevenness, which so embarrassed Vronsky. The child's presence always and inevitably provoked in Vronsky that strange feeling of groundless loathing he had been experiencing lately. It provoked in Vronsky and Anna a feeling like that of a mariner who can see by his compass that the direction in which he is swiftly moving diverges widely from his proper course, but that he is powerless to stop the movement which every moment takes him further and further from the right direction, and that to admit the deviation to himself is the same as admitting disaster.

This child with his naïve outlook on life was the compass which showed them the degree of their departure from what they knew but did not want to know.

This time Seryozha was not at home, and she was quite alone, sitting on the terrace, waiting for the return of her son, who had gone for a walk and had been caught in the rain. She had sent a man and a maid to look for him and sat waiting. Wearing a white dress with wide embroidery, she was sitting in a corner of the terrace behind some flowers and did not hear him. Her dark, curly head bowed, she leaned her forehead to the cold watering can that stood on the parapet, and her two beautiful hands with their so-familiar rings held the watering can in place. The beauty of her whole figure, her head, neck, and arms, struck Vronsky each time as something unexpected. He stood gazing at her in admiration. But as soon as he wanted to take a step to approach her, she felt his approach, pushed the watering can away, and turned her flushed face to him.

'What's the matter? You're unwell?' he said in French, going up to her. He wanted to run to her, but remembering that other people might be there, he glanced back at the balcony door and blushed as he did each time he felt he had to be afraid and look around.

'No, I'm well,' she said, getting up and firmly pressing the hand he held out. 'I didn't expect . . . you.'

'My God, what cold hands!' he said.

'You frightened me,' she said. 'I'm alone and waiting for Seryozha. He went for a walk, they'll come from that way.'

But, despite all her efforts to be calm, her lips were trembling.

'Forgive me for coming, but I couldn't let the day pass without seeing you,' he went on in French, as he always did, avoiding the impossible coldness of formal Russian and the danger of the informal.

'What is there to forgive? I'm so glad!'

'But you're unwell or upset,' he went on, without letting go of her hand and bending over her. 'What were you thinking about?'

'Always the same thing,' she said with a smile.

She was telling the truth. Whenever, at whatever moment, she might be asked what she was thinking about, she could answer without mistake: about the same thing, about her happiness and her unhappiness. Precisely now, when he found her, she had been thinking about why it was all so easy for others – Betsy, for instance (she knew of her liaison with Tushkevich, concealed from society) – while for her it was so painful? That day, owing to certain considerations, this thought was particularly painful for her. She asked him about the races. He answered her and, seeing that she was excited, tried to divert her by describing in the simplest tone the details of the preparation for the races.

'Shall I tell him or not?' she thought, looking into his calm, tender eyes. 'He's so happy, so taken up with his races, that he won't understand it as he should, won't understand all the significance of this event for us.'

'But you haven't told me what you were thinking about when I came,' he said, interrupting his account. 'Please tell me!'

She did not answer and, bowing her head slightly, looked at him questioningly from under her brows, her eyes shining behind their long lashes. Her hand, playing with a plucked leaf, was trembling. He saw it, and his face showed that obedience, that slavish devotion, which touched her so.

'I see that something has happened. Can I be calm for a moment, knowing you have a grief that I don't share? Tell me, for God's sake!' he repeated pleadingly.

'No, I will never forgive him if he doesn't understand all the significance of it. Better not to tell. Why test him?' she thought, gazing at him in the same way and feeling that her hand holding the leaf was trembling more and more.

'For God's sake!' he repeated, taking her hand.

'Shall I tell you?'

'Yes, yes, yes . . .'

'I'm pregnant,' she said softly and slowly.

The leaf in her hand trembled still more violently, but she did not take her eyes off him, wanting to see how he would take it. He paled, was about to say something, but stopped, let go of her hand and hung his head. 'Yes, he understands all the significance of this event,' she thought, and gratefully pressed his hand.

But she was mistaken in thinking that he understood the significance of the news as she, a woman, understood it. At this news he felt with tenfold force an attack of that strange feeling of loathing for someone that had been coming over him; but along with that he understood that the crisis he desired had now come, that it was no longer possible to conceal it from her husband and in one way or another this unnatural situation had to be broken up quickly. Besides that, her excitement communicated itself physically to him. He gave her a tender, obedient look, kissed her hand, rose and silently paced the terrace.

'Yes,' he said, resolutely going up to her. 'Neither of us has looked on our relation as a game, and now our fate is decided. It's necessary to end,' he said, looking around, 'the lie we live in.'

'End it? But end it how, Alexei?' she said softly. She was calm now, and her face shone with a tender smile.

'Leave your husband and unite our lives.'

'They're already united,' she replied, barely audibly.

'Yes, but completely, completely.'

'But how, Alexei, teach me how?' she said with sad mockery at the hopelessness of her situation. 'Is there a way out of such a situation? Am I not my husband's wife?'

'There's a way out of every situation. A decision has to be made,' he said. 'Anything's better than the situation you are living in. I can see how you suffer over everything, over society, and your son, and your husband.'

'Ah, only not my husband,' she said with a simple smile. 'I don't know him, I don't think about him. He doesn't exist.'

'You're not speaking sincerely. I know you. You suffer over him, too.'

'But he doesn't even know,' she said, and bright colour suddenly began to rise in her face; her cheeks, forehead, and neck turned red, and tears of shame welled up in her eyes. 'And let's not talk about him.'

XXIII

Vronsky had already tried several times, though not as resolutely as now, to bring her to a discussion of her situation, and each time had run into that superficiality and lightness of judgement with which she now responded to his challenge. It was as if there were something in it that she could not or would not grasp, as if the moment she began talking about it, she, the real Anna, withdrew somewhere into herself and another woman stepped forward, strange and alien to him, whom he did not love but feared, and who rebuffed him. But today he ventured to say everything.

'Whether he knows or not,' Vronsky said in his usual firm and calm tone, 'whether he knows or not is not our affair. We can't . . . you can't go on like this, especially now.'

'What's to be done, then, in your opinion?' she asked, with the same light mockery. She, who had so feared he might take her pregnancy lightly, was now vexed that he had drawn from it the necessity for doing something.

'Tell him everything and leave him.'

'Very well, suppose I do that,' she said. 'Do you know what will come of it? I'll tell you everything beforehand.' And a wicked light lit up in her eyes, which a moment before had been tender. ' "Ah, madam, so you love another man and have entered into a criminal liaison with him?" ' (Impersonating her husband, she stressed the word 'criminal', just as Alexei Alexandrovich would have done.) ' "I warned you about the consequences in their religious, civil and familial aspects. You did not listen to me. Now I cannot lend my name to disgrace . . ." ' – 'nor my son's,' she was going to say, but she could not joke about her son – ' "lend my name to disgrace," and more of the same,' she added. 'Generally, he will say in his statesmanly manner, and with clarity and precision, that he cannot release me but will take what measures are in his power to prevent a scandal. And he will do, calmly and accurately, what he says. That's what will happen. He's not a man, he's a machine, and a wicked machine when he gets angry,' she added, recalling Alexei Alexandrovich in all the details of his figure, manner of speaking and character, holding him guilty for everything bad she could find in him and forgiving him nothing, on account of the terrible fault for which she stood guilty before him.

'But, Anna,' Vronsky said in a soft, persuasive voice, trying to calm her down, 'all the same it's necessary to tell him, and then be guided by what he does.'

'What, run away?'

'Why not run away? I see no possibility of this continuing. And not on my account – I see you're suffering.'

'Yes, run away, and I'll become your mistress?' she said spitefully.

'Anna!' he said, with reproachful tenderness.

'Yes,' she went on, 'I'll become your mistress and ruin . . . everything.'

Again she was going to say 'my son', but could not utter the word.

Vronsky could not understand how she, with her strong, honest nature, could endure this situation of deceit and not wish to get out of it; but he did not suspect that the main reason for it was that word 'son' which she could not utter. When she thought of her son and his future attitude towards the mother who had abandoned his father, she felt so frightened at what she had done that she did not reason, but, like a woman, tried only to calm herself with false reasonings and words, so that everything would remain as before and she could forget the terrible question of what would happen with her son.[29]

'I beg you, I implore you,' she said suddenly in a completely different, sincere and tender tone, taking his hand, 'never speak to me of that!'

'But, Anna . . .'

'Never. Leave it to me. I know all the meanness, all the horror of my situation; but it's not as easy to resolve as you think. Leave it to me and listen to me. Never speak of that to me. Do you promise me? . . . No, no, promise! . . .'

'I promise everything, but I can't be at peace, especially after what you've said. I can't be at peace when you are not at peace . . .'

'I?' she repeated. 'Yes, I'm tormented sometimes; but it will go away if you never speak to me of that. It's only when you speak of it that it torments me.'

'I don't understand,' he said.

'I know,' she interrupted him, 'how hard it is for your honest nature to lie, and I'm sorry for you. I often think how you ruined your life for me.'

'I was thinking the same thing just now,' he said. 'How could you have sacrificed everything for me? I can't forgive myself that you are unhappy.'

'I'm unhappy?' she said, coming close to him and looking at him with a rapturous smile of love. 'I'm like a starving man who has been given food. Maybe he's cold, and his clothes are torn, and he's ashamed, but he's not unhappy. I'm unhappy? No, this is my happiness . . .'

She heard the voice of her returning son and, casting a quick glance around the terrace, rose impetuously. Her eyes lit up with a fire familiar to him, she raised her beautiful, ring-covered hands with a quick gesture, took his head, gave him a long look and, bringing her face closer, quickly kissed his mouth and both eyes with her open, smiling lips and pushed him away. She wanted to go, but he held her back.

'When?' he said in a whisper, looking at her rapturously.

'Tonight, at one,' she whispered and, after a deep sigh, walked with her light, quick step to meet her son.

The rain had caught Seryozha in the big garden, and he and the nanny had sat it out in the gazebo.

'Well, good-bye,' she said to Vronsky. 'We must be going to the races soon now. Betsy has promised to come for me.'

Vronsky looked at his watch and left hastily.

XXIV

When Vronsky looked at his watch on the Karenins' balcony, he was so agitated and preoccupied by his thoughts that he saw the hands on the face, but could not grasp what time it was. He went out to the road and walked to his carriage, stepping carefully through the mud. He was so full of his feeling for Anna that he did not even think what time it was and whether he could still manage to get to Briansky's. He was left, as often happens, with only the external faculty of memory, which indicated what was to be done after what. He came up to his coachman, who had dozed off on the box in the already slanting shade of a thick linden, admired the iridescent columns of flies hovering over the sweaty horses and, waking the coachman, told him to go to Briansky's. Only after driving some four miles did he recover sufficiently to look at his watch and grasp that it was half-past five and he was late.

There were to be several races that day: a convoys' race, then the officers' mile-and-a-half, the three-mile, and the race in which he would ride. He could make it to his race, but if he went to Briansky's, he would come barely in time and when the whole court was there. That was not good. But he had given Briansky his word that he would come and therefore decided to keep going, telling the coachman not to spare the troika.

He arrived at Briansky's, spent five minutes with him, and galloped back. This quick drive calmed him down. All the difficulty of his relations with Anna, all the uncertainty remaining after their conversation, left his head; with excitement and delight he now thought of the races, of how he would arrive in time after all, and every now and then the expectation of the happiness of that night's meeting flashed like a bright light in his imagination.

The feeling of the coming races took hold of him more and more the further he drove into their atmosphere, overtaking the carriages of those driving to the course from their country houses or Petersburg.

There was no one at his quarters by then: they had all gone to the races, and his footman was waiting for him at the gate. While he was changing, the footman told him that the second race had already started, that many gentlemen had come asking for him, and the boy had come running twice from the stable.

After changing unhurriedly (he never hurried or lost his self-control), Vronsky gave orders to drive to the sheds. From the sheds he could see a perfect sea of carriages, pedestrians, soldiers surrounding the racetrack and pavilions seething with people. The second race was probably under way, because he heard the bell just as he entered the shed. As he neared the stables, he met Makhotin's white-legged chestnut Gladiator, being led to the racetrack in an orange and blue horse-cloth, his ears, as if trimmed with blue, looking enormous.

'Where's Cord?' he asked the stableman.

'In the stables, saddling up.'

The stall was open, and Frou-Frou was already saddled. They were about to bring her out.

'Am I late?'

'All right, all right! Everything's in order, everything's in order,' said the Englishman, 'don't get excited.'

Vronsky cast a glance once more over the exquisite, beloved forms of the horse, whose whole body was trembling, and tearing himself with difficulty from this sight, walked out of the shed. He drove up to the pavilions at the best time for not attracting anyone's attention. The mile-and-a-half race was just ending, and all eyes were turned to the horse-guard in the lead and the life-hussar behind him, urging their horses on with their last strength and nearing the post. Everyone was crowding towards the post from inside and outside the ring, and a group of soldiers and officers of the horse-guards shouted loudly with joy at the anticipated triumph of their officer and comrade. Vronsky slipped inconspicuously into the midst of the crowd almost at the moment when the bell ending the race rang out, and the tall, mud-spattered horse-guard, who came in first, lowering himself into the saddle, began to ease up on the reins of his grey, sweat-darkened, heavily breathing stallion.

The stallion, digging his feet in with an effort, slackened the quick pace of his big body, and the horse-guard officer, like a man awakening from a deep sleep, looked around and smiled with difficulty. A crowd of friends and strangers surrounded him.

Vronsky deliberately avoided that select high-society crowd which moved and talked with restrained freedom in front of the pavilions. He could see that Anna was there, and Betsy, and his brother's wife, but he purposely did not approach them, so as not to become diverted. But the acquaintances he met constantly stopped him, telling details of the earlier races and asking why he was late.

Just as all the participants were summoned to the pavilion to receive their prizes and everyone turned there, Vronsky's older brother, Alexander, a colonel with aiguillettes, of medium height, as stocky as Alexei but more handsome and ruddy, with a red nose and a drunken, open face, came up to him.

'Did you get my note?' he said. 'You're impossible to find.'

Alexander Vronsky, despite the dissolute and, in particular, drunken life he was known for, was a perfect courtier.

Now, talking with his brother about something very disagreeable for him, and knowing that the eyes of many might be directed at them, he had a smiling look, as if he were joking about some unimportant matter.

'I did, and I really don't understand what *you* are worried about,' said Alexei.

'I'm worried about this – that it was just observed to me that you were not here and that on Monday you were seen in Peterhof.'

'There are matters that may be discussed only by those directly involved, and the matter you are worried about is such a . . .'

'Yes, but then don't stay in the service, don't . . .'

'I ask you not to interfere, that's all.'

Alexei Vronsky's frowning face paled and his jutting lower jaw twitched, something that seldom happened to him. Being a man with a very kind heart, he seldom got angry, but when he did, and when his chin twitched, he could be dangerous, as his brother knew. Alexander Vronsky smiled gaily.

'I only wanted to give you mother's letter. Answer her and don't get upset before the race. *Bonne chance!*' he added, smiling, and walked away from him.

But just then another friendly greeting stopped Vronsky.

'You don't want to know your friends! Good afternoon, *mon cher*!' said Stepan Arkadyich, and here, amidst this Petersburg brilliance, his ruddy face and glossy, brushed-up side-whiskers shone no less than in Moscow. 'I arrived yesterday, and I'm very glad I'll see your triumph. When shall we meet?'

'Come to the officers' mess tomorrow,' Vronsky said and, pressing his sleeve apologetically, walked to the middle of the racetrack, where the horses were already being brought for the big steeplechase.

Sweating horses, exhausted from racing, were led home accompanied by grooms, and new ones appeared one after the other for the forthcoming race – fresh, for the most part English, horses, in hoods, their bellies tightly girt, looking like strange, huge birds. On the right the lean beauty Frou-Frou was brought in, stepping on her supple and rather long pasterns as if on springs. Not far from her the cloth was being taken off the big-eared Gladiator. Vronsky's attention was inadvertently drawn to the stallion's large, exquisite, perfectly regular forms, with wonderful hindquarters and unusually short pasterns, sitting just over the hoof. He wanted to go to his horse but again was stopped by an acquaintance.

'Ah, there's Karenin,' the acquaintance with whom he was talking said to him. 'Looking for his wife, and she's in the central pavilion. You haven't seen her?'

'No, I haven't,' Vronsky replied and, not even glancing at the pavilion in which he had been told Anna was, he went over to his horse.

Vronsky had just managed to inspect the saddle, about which he had to give some instructions, when the participants were summoned to the pavilion to draw numbers and start. With serious, stern faces, many of them pale, seventeen officers gathered at the pavilion and each took a number. Vronsky got number seven. The call came: 'Mount!'

Feeling that he and the other riders were the centre towards which all eyes were turned, Vronsky, in a state of tension, which usually made him slow and calm of movement, approached his horse. In honour of the races, Cord had put on his gala outfit: a black, high-buttoned frock coat, a stiffly starched collar propping up his cheeks, a black Derby hat and top-boots. He was calm and imposing, as always, and held the horse himself by both sides of the bridle, standing in front of her. Frou-Frou continued to tremble as in a fever. Her fire-filled eye looked askance at the approaching Vronsky. Vronsky slipped a finger under the girth. The horse looked still more askance, bared her teeth, and flattened one ear. The Englishman puckered his lips, wishing to show a smile at his saddling being checked.

'Mount up, you'll be less excited.'

Vronsky gave his rivals a last look. He knew that during the race he would no longer see them. Two were already riding ahead to the starting place. Galtsyn, one of the dangerous rivals and Vronsky's friend, was fussing around a bay stallion that would not let him mount. A little life-hussar in tight breeches rode by at a gallop, hunched on the croup like a cat, trying to imitate the English. Prince Kuzovlev sat pale on his thoroughbred mare from Grabov's stud, while an Englishman led her by the bridle. Vronsky and all his comrades knew Kuzovlev and his peculiarity of 'weak' nerves and terrible vanity. They knew that he was afraid of everything, afraid of riding an army horse; but now, precisely because it was scary, because people broke their necks, and because by each obstacle there was a doctor, an ambulance wagon with a cross sewn on it and a sister of mercy, he had decided to ride. Their eyes met, and Vronsky winked at him gently and approvingly. There was only one man he did not see – his chief rival, Makhotin on Gladiator.

'Don't rush,' Cord said to Vronsky, 'and remember one thing: don't hold her back at the obstacles and don't send her over, let her choose as she likes.'

'Very well, very well,' said Vronsky, taking the reins.

'Lead the race, if you can; but don't despair till the last moment, even if you're behind.'

Before the horse had time to move, Vronsky, with a supple and strong movement, stood in the serrated steel stirrup and lightly, firmly placed his compact body on the creaking leather saddle. Putting his right foot into the stirrup, he evened up the double reins between his fingers with an accustomed gesture, and Cord loosed his grip. As if not knowing which foot to put first, Frou-Frou, pulling at the reins with her long neck, started off as if on springs, rocking her rider on her supple back.

Cord, increasing his pace, walked after them. The excited horse, trying to trick her rider, pulled the reins now to one side, now to the other, and Vronsky tried in vain to calm her with his voice and hand.

They were already nearing the dammed-up stream, heading for the place where they were to start. Many of the riders were in front of him, many behind, when Vronsky suddenly heard the sound of galloping in the mud of the road behind him and was overtaken by Makhotin on his white-legged, big-eared Gladiator. Makhotin smiled, showing his long teeth, but Vronsky gave him an angry look. He generally did not like him and now considered him his most dangerous rival, and he was vexed that the man had ridden past, alarming his horse. Frou-Frou kicked up her left leg in a gallop, made two leaps and, angered by the tight reins, went into a jolting trot, bouncing her rider up and down. Cord also frowned and almost ambled after Vronsky.

XXV

In all there were seventeen officers riding in the race. It was to take place on the big three-mile, elliptical course in front of the pavilion. Nine obstacles had been set up on this course: a stream, a five-foot-high solid barrier right in front of the pavilion, a dry ditch, a water ditch, a slope, an Irish bank (one of the most difficult obstacles), consisting of a raised bank stuck with brush, beyond which, invisible to the horse, was another ditch, so that the horse had to clear both obstacles or get badly hurt; then two more water ditches and a dry one – and the finishing line was in front of the pavilion. But the start of the race was not on the course, but some two hundred yards to the side of it, and within that stretch was the first obstacle – a dammed-up stream seven feet wide, which the riders at their discretion could either jump or wade across.

Three times the riders lined up, but each time someone's horse broke rank, and they had to start over again. The expert starter, Colonel Sestrin, was beginning to get angry when, finally, at the fourth try, he shouted: 'Go!' – and the riders took off.

All eyes, all binoculars were turned to the bright-coloured little group of riders as they lined up.

'They're off and running!' came from all sides, after the expectant hush.

In groups and singly, people on foot began rushing from place to place in order to see better. In the very first moment, the compact group of riders stretched out and could be seen in twos and threes, one after another, nearing the stream. For the spectators it looked as if they were all riding together; but for the riders there were seconds of difference that were of great significance to them.

Excited and much too high-strung, Frou-Frou lost the first moment, and several horses took off ahead of her, but before reaching the stream, Vronsky, holding the horse back with all his strength as she moved into her stride, easily overtook three of them and ahead of him there remained only Makhotin's chestnut Gladiator, whose rump bobbed steadily and easily just in front of Vronsky, and ahead of them all the lovely Diana, carrying Kuzovlev, more dead than alive.

For the first few minutes Vronsky was not yet master either of himself or of his horse. Up to the first obstacle, the stream, he was unable to guide his horse's movements.

Gladiator and Diana came to it together and almost at one and the same moment: one-two, they rose above the river and flew across to the other side; effortlessly, as if flying, Frou-Frou soared after them, but just as Vronsky felt himself in the air, he suddenly saw, almost under his horse's feet, Kuzovlev floundering with Diana on the other side of the stream (Kuzovlev had let go of the reins after the leap, and the horse, along with him, had gone flying head over heels). These details Vronsky learned afterwards; now all he saw was that Diana's leg or head might be right on the spot where Frou-Frou had to land. But Frou-Frou, like a falling cat, strained her legs and back during the leap and, missing the horse, raced on.

'Oh, you sweetheart!' thought Vronsky.

After the stream, Vronsky fully mastered the horse and began holding her back, intending to go over the big barrier behind Makhotin and then, in the next unobstructed stretch of some five hundred yards, to try to get ahead of him.

The big barrier stood right in front of the tsar's pavilion. The emperor, and the entire court, and throngs of people – all were looking at them, at him and at Makhotin, who kept one length ahead of him, as they approached the devil (as the solid barrier was called). Vronsky felt those eyes directed at him from all sides, but he saw nothing except the ears and neck of his horse, the earth racing towards him, and Gladiator's croup and white legs beating out a quick rhythm ahead of him and maintaining the same distance. Gladiator rose, not knocking against anything, swung his short tail and disappeared from Vronsky's sight.

'Bravo!' said some single voice.

That instant, just in front of him, the boards of the barrier flashed before Vronsky's eyes. Without the least change of movement the horse soared under him; the boards vanished, and he only heard something knock behind him. Excited by Gladiator going ahead of her, the horse had risen too early before the barrier and knocked against it with a back hoof. But her pace did not change, and Vronsky, receiving a lump of mud in the face, realized that he was again the same distance from Gladiator. In front of him he again saw his croup, his short tail, and again the same swiftly moving white legs not getting any further away.

That same instant, as Vronsky was thinking that they now had to get ahead of Makhotin, Frou-Frou herself, already knowing his thought, speeded up noticeably without any urging and started to approach Makhotin from the most advantageous side – the side of the rope. Makhotin would not let her have the rope. Vronsky had just thought that they could also get round him on the outside, when Frou-Frou switched step and started to go ahead precisely that way. Frou-Frou's shoulder, already beginning to darken with sweat, drew even with Gladiator's croup. They took several strides together. But, before the obstacle they were approaching, Vronsky, to avoid making the larger circle, began working the reins and, on the slope itself, quickly got ahead of Makhotin. He saw his mud-spattered face flash by. It even seemed to him that he smiled. Vronsky got ahead of Makhotin, but he could feel him right behind him and constantly heard just at his back the steady tread and the short, still quite fresh breathing of Gladiator's nostrils.

The next two obstacles, a ditch and a barrier, were passed easily, but Vronsky began to hear Gladiator's tread and snort coming closer. He urged his horse on and felt with joy that she easily increased her pace, and the sound of Gladiator's hoofs began to be heard again from the former distance.

Vronsky was leading the race – the very thing he had wanted and that Cord had advised him to do – and was now certain of success. His excitement, his joy and tenderness for Frou-Frou kept increasing. He would have liked to look back but did not dare to, and tried to calm himself down and not urge his horse on, so as to save a reserve in her equal to what he felt was still left in Gladiator. There remained one obstacle, the most difficult; if he got over it ahead of the others, he would come in first. He was riding towards the Irish bank. Together with Frou-Frou he could already see this bank in the distance, and the two together, he and his horse, had a moment's doubt. He noticed some indecision in the horse's ears and raised his whip, but felt at once that his doubt was groundless: the horse knew what was needed. She increased her speed and measuredly, exactly as he had supposed, soared up, pushing off from the ground and giving herself to the force of inertia, which carried her far beyond the ditch; and in the same rhythm, effortlessly, in the same step, Frou-Frou continued the race.

'Bravo, Vronsky!' He heard the voices of a group of people – his regiment and friends, he knew – who were standing by that obstacle; he could not mistake Yashvin's voice, though he did not see him.

'Oh, my lovely!' he thought of Frou-Frou, listening to what was happening behind him. 'He cleared it!' he thought, hearing Gladiator's hoofbeats behind him. There remained one little ditch of water five feet wide. Vronsky was not even looking at it, but, wishing to come in a long first, began working the reins in a circle, raising and lowering the horse's head in rhythm with her pace. He felt that the horse was drawing on her last reserve; not only were her neck and shoulders wet, but sweat broke out in drops on her withers, her head, her pointed ears, and her breathing was sharp and short. But he knew that this reserve was more than enough for the remaining five hundred yards. Only because he felt himself closer to the earth, and from the special softness of her movement, could Vronsky tell how much the horse had increased her speed. She flew over the ditch as if without noticing it; she flew over it like a bird; but just then Vronsky felt to his horror that, having failed to keep up with the horse's movement, he, not knowing how himself, had made a wrong, an unforgivable movement as he lowered himself into the saddle. His position suddenly changed, and he knew that something terrible had happened. He was not yet aware of what it was, when the white legs of the chestnut stallion flashed just beside him and Makhotin went by at a fast clip. Vronsky was touching the ground with one foot, and his horse was toppling over on that foot. He barely managed to free the foot before she fell on her side, breathing heavily and making vain attempts to rise with her slender, sweaty neck, fluttering on the ground at his feet like a wounded bird. The awkward movement Vronsky had made had broken her back. But he understood that much later. Now he saw only that Makhotin was quickly drawing away, while he, swaying, stood alone on the muddy, unmoving ground, and before him, gasping heavily, lay Frou-Frou, her head turned to him, looking at him with her lovely eye. Still not understanding what had happened, Vronsky pulled the horse by the reins. She again thrashed all over like a fish, creaking the wings of the saddle, freed her front legs, but, unable to lift her hindquarters, immediately staggered and fell on her side again. His face disfigured by passion, pale, his lower jaw trembling, Vronsky kicked her in the stomach with his heel and again started pulling at the reins. She did not move but, burying her nose in the ground, merely looked at her master with her speaking eye.

'A-a-ah!' groaned Vronsky, clutching his head. 'A-a-ah, what have I done!' he cried. 'The race is lost! And it's my own fault – shameful, unforgivable! And this poor, dear, destroyed horse! A-a-ah, what have I done!'

People – the doctor and his assistant, officers from his regiment – came running towards him. To his dismay, he felt that he was whole and unhurt. The horse had broken her back and they decided to shoot her. Vronsky was unable to answer questions, unable to talk to anyone. He turned and, without picking up the cap that had fallen from his head, left the racetrack, not knowing himself where he was going. He felt miserable. For the first time in his life he had experienced a heavy misfortune, a misfortune that was irremediable and for which he himself was to blame.

Yashvin overtook him with the cap, brought him home, and a half hour later Vronsky came to his senses. But the memory of this race remained in his soul for a long time as the most heavy and painful memory of his life.

XXVI

Externally Alexei Alexandrovich's relations with his wife remained the same as before. The only difference was that he was even busier than before. As in previous years, with the coming of spring he went to a spa abroad to restore his health, upset each year by his strenuous winter labours. Returning in July, as usual, he at once sat down with increased energy to his customary work. And as usual, his wife moved to their country house while he stayed in Petersburg.

Since the time of that conversation after the evening at Princess

Tverskoy's, he had never spoken to Anna of his suspicions and jealousy, and his usual mocking tone could not have been better for his present relations with his wife. He was somewhat colder towards her. It was merely as if he were slightly displeased with her for that first night's conversation, which she had fended off. There was a tinge of vexation in his relations with her, nothing more. 'You did not wish to have a talk with me,' he seemed to be saying, mentally addressing her. 'So much the worse for you. Now you'll ask me, and *I* won't talk. So much the worse for you,' he said mentally, like a man who, after a vain attempt to put out a fire, gets angry at his vain efforts and says: 'Serves you right! So for that you can just burn down!'

He who was so intelligent and subtle in official business, did not understand all the madness of such an attitude towards his wife. He did not understand it, because it was too dreadful for him to recognize his real position, and in his soul he closed, locked and sealed the drawer in which he kept his feelings for his family – that is, his wife and son. He who had been an attentive father had become especially cold towards his son since the end of that winter, and took the same bantering attitude towards him as towards his wife. 'Ah! young man!' was the way he addressed him.

Alexei Alexandrovich thought and said that he had never had so much official business in any other year as he had that year; but he did not realize that he had invented things for himself to do that year, that this was one way of not opening the drawer where his feelings for his wife and family and his thoughts about them lay, becoming more dreadful the longer they lay there. If anyone had had the right to ask Alexei Alexandrovich what he thought about his wife's behaviour, the mild, placid Alexei Alexandrovich would have made no reply, but would have become very angry with the man who had asked him about it. And that was why there was something proud and stern in the expression of Alexei Alexandrovich's face when he was asked about his wife's health. He did not want to think anything about his wife's behaviour and feelings, and in fact did not think anything about them.

Alexei Alexandrovich's permanent country house was in Peterhof, and Countess Lydia Ivanovna usually spent the summers there, too, in the neighbourhood and in constant contact with Anna. This year Countess Lydia Ivanovna refused to live in Peterhof, never once visited Anna Arkadyevna, and hinted to Alexei Alexandrovich at the awkwardness of Anna's closeness to Betsy and Vronsky. Alexei Alexandrovich sternly interrupted her, expressing the thought that his wife was above suspicion, and after that he began to avoid Countess Lydia Ivanovna. He did not want to see, and did not see, that in society many were already looking askance at his wife; he did not want to understand, and did not understand, why his wife insisted especially on moving to Tsarskoe, where Betsy lived, which was not far from the camp of Vronsky's regiment. He did not allow himself to think of it, and did not think of it; but, nevertheless, in the depths of his soul, without ever saying it to himself and having not only no proofs of it but even no suspicions, he knew without doubt that he was a deceived husband, and it made him deeply unhappy.

How many times during his eight years of happy life with his wife, looking at other people's unfaithful wives and deceived husbands, had Alexei Alexandrovich said to himself: 'How can one let it come to that? How can one not undo this ugly situation?' But now, when the disaster had fallen on his head, he not only did not think of how to undo the situation, but did want to know about it at all – did not want to know precisely because it was too terrible, too unnatural.

Since his return from abroad, Alexei Alexandrovich had been to the country house twice. Once he had dinner, the other time he spent the evening with guests, but neither time did he spend the night, as he had usually done in previous years.

The day of the races was a very busy day for Alexei Alexandrovich; but, having made a schedule for himself that morning, he decided that immediately after an early dinner he would go to see his wife at their country house and from there to the races, which the whole court would attend and which he, too, had to attend. He would visit his wife, because he had decided to see her once a week for propriety's sake. Besides, according to the established rule, that day being the fifteenth, he had to give her money for her expenses.

With his customary control over his mind, having pondered all this about his wife, he did not allow his thoughts to go further into what concerned her.

That morning Alexei Alexandrovich was very busy. The day before, Countess Lydia Ivanovna had sent him a booklet by a famous traveller to China, then in Petersburg, with a letter asking him to receive the traveller himself – a very interesting and necessary man in many regards. Alexei Alexandrovich had not finished the booklet the night before and so he finished it in the morning. Then petitioners came, reports began, receptions, appointments, dismissals, distributions of awards, pensions, salaries, correspondence – all that everyday business, as Alexei Alexandrovich called it, which took up so much time. Then there were personal matters – visits from his doctor and his office manager. The office manager did not take much time. He merely handed Alexei Alexandrovich the money he needed and gave a brief report on the state of his affairs, which was not entirely good, because it so happened that, having gone out frequently that year, they had spent more and there was a deficit. But the doctor, a famous Petersburg doctor who was on friendly terms with Alexei Alexandrovich, took much time. Alexei Alexandrovich did not expect him that day and was surprised by his arrival and still more by the fact that the doctor questioned him very attentively about his condition, sounded his chest, tapped and palpated his liver. Alexei Alexandrovich did not know that his friend Lydia Ivanovna, noticing that his health was not good that year, had asked the doctor to go and examine the patient. 'Do it for me,' she had said to him.

'I shall do it for Russia, Countess,' the doctor had replied.

'A priceless man!' Countess Lydia Ivanovna had said.

The doctor remained very displeased with Alexei Alexandrovich. He found his liver considerably enlarged, his appetite insufficient, and the waters of no effect. He prescribed as much physical movement and as little mental strain as possible, and above all no sort of distress – that is, the very thing which for Alexei Alexandrovich was as impossible as not to breathe; and he went off, leaving Alexei Alexandrovich with the unpleasant awareness that something was wrong with him and that it could not be put right.

On the porch, as he was leaving, the doctor ran into Slyudin, Alexei Alexandrovich's office manager, whom he knew well. They had been at the university together and, though they saw each other rarely, respected each other and were good friends, and therefore the doctor would not have given anyone so frank an opinion of the patient as he gave to Slyudin.

'I'm so glad you visited him,' said Slyudin. 'He's unwell, and I think . . . Well, what is it?'

'Here's what,' said the doctor, waving over Slyudin's head for his coachman to drive up. 'Here's what,' he said, taking a finger of his kid glove in his white hands and stretching it. 'If a string isn't tight and you try to break it, it's very hard to do. But tighten it to the utmost and put just the weight of your finger on it, and it will break. And he, with his assiduousness, his conscientiousness about his work, is tightened to the utmost degree; and there is an external pressure and a heavy one,' the doctor concluded, raising his eyebrows significantly. 'Will you be at the races?' he added, going down to the waiting carriage. 'Yes, yes, naturally, it takes a lot of time,' the doctor replied to some remark of Slyudin's that he had not quite heard.

After the doctor, who had taken so much time, came the famous traveller, and Alexei Alexandrovich, using the just-read booklet and his previous knowledge of the subject, struck the traveller with the depth of his grasp and the breadth of his enlightened outlook.

Along with the traveller, the arrival of a provincial marshal[30] was announced, who had come to Petersburg and with whom he had to talk. After his departure, he needed to finish the everyday work with his office manager and also go to see a very significant person on some serious and important business. Alexei Alexandrovich just managed to get back by five o'clock, his dinner-time, and, having dined with his office manager, invited him to come along to his country house and the races.

Without realizing it, Alexei Alexandrovich now sought occasions for having a third person present at his meetings with his wife.

XXVII

Anna was standing in front of the mirror upstairs, pinning the last bow to her dress with Annushka's help, when she heard the sound of wheels crunching gravel at the entrance.

'It's too early for Betsy,' she thought and, looking out the window, saw the carriage with Alexei Alexandrovich's black hat and so-familiar ears sticking out of it. 'That's untimely. Does he mean to spend the night?' she thought, and all that might come of it seemed to her so terrible and frightening that, without a moment's thought, she went out to meet them with a gay and radiant face and, feeling in herself the presence of the already familiar spirit of lying and deceit, at once surrendered to it and began talking without knowing herself what she was going to say.

'Ah, how nice!' she said, giving her hand to her husband and greeting Slyudin with a smile as a member of the household. 'You'll spend the night, I hope?' were the first words that the spirit of deceit prompted her to say. 'And now we can go together. Only it's a pity I promised Betsy. She's coming for me.'

Alexei Alexandrovich winced at the name of Betsy.

'Oh, I wouldn't separate the inseparables,' he said in his usual jocular tone. 'I'll go with Mikhail Vassilyevich. And the doctors tell me to walk. I'll stroll on the way and imagine I'm back at the spa.'

'There's no hurry,' said Anna. 'Would you like tea?'

She rang.

'Serve tea, and tell Seryozha that Alexei Alexandrovich has come. Well, how is your health? Mikhail Vassilyevich, you've never been here; look how nice it is on my balcony,' she said, addressing first one, then the other.

She spoke very simply and naturally, but too much and too quickly. She felt it herself, the more so as, in the curious glance that Mikhail Vassilyevich gave her, she noticed that he seemed to be observing her.

Mikhail Vassilyevich at once went out on the terrace.

She sat down by her husband.

'You don't look quite well,' she said.

'Yes,' he said, 'the doctor came today and took an hour of my time. I have the feeling that one of my friends sent him: my health is so precious . . .'

'No, but what did he say?'

She asked him about his health and work, persuading him to rest and move out to stay with her.

She said all this gaily, quickly, and with a special brightness in her eyes, but Alexei Alexandrovich now ascribed no significance to this tone. He heard only her words and gave them only that direct meaning which they had. And he answered her simply, though jocularly. There was nothing special in their conversation, but afterwards Anna could never recall that whole little scene without a tormenting sense of shame.

Seryozha came in, preceded by the governess. If Alexei Alexandrovich had allowed himself to observe, he would have noticed the timid, perplexed look with which Seryozha glanced first at his father, then at his mother. But he did not want to see anything, and did not see anything.

'Ah, the young man! He's grown up. Really, he's becoming quite a man. Hello, young man.'

And he gave the frightened Seryozha his hand.

Seryozha had been timid towards his father even before, but now, since Alexei Alexandrovich had started calling him young man and since the riddle about whether Vronsky was friend or foe had entered his head, he shrank from his father. As if asking for protection, he looked at his mother. He felt good only with her. Alexei Alexandrovich, talking meanwhile with the governess, held his son by the shoulder, and Seryozha felt so painfully awkward that Anna saw he was about to cry.

Anna, who had blushed the moment her son came in, noticing that Seryozha felt awkward, quickly jumped up, removed Alexei Alexandrovich's hand from the boy's shoulder, kissed him, took him out to the terrace and came back at once.

'Anyhow, it's already time,' she said, glancing at her watch, 'why doesn't Betsy come! . . .'

'Yes,' said Alexei Alexandrovich and, rising, he interlaced his fingers and cracked them. 'I also came to bring you money, since nightingales aren't fed on fables,' he said. 'You need it, I suppose.'

'No, I don't . . . yes, I do,' she said, not looking at him and blushing to the roots of her hair. 'I suppose you'll stop here after the races.'

'Oh, yes!' answered Alexei Alexandrovich. 'And here comes the pearl of Peterhof, Princess Tverskoy,' he added, glancing out of the window at the English equipage driving up, the horses in blinkers and the tiny body of the carriage extremely high-sprung. 'What elegance! Lovely! Well, then we'll be going as well.'

Princess Tverskoy did not get out of the carriage, only her footman, in gaiters, cape and a little black hat, jumped down at the entrance.

'I'm off, good-bye!' said Anna and, having kissed her son, she went up to Alexei Alexandrovich and offered him her hand. 'It was very nice of you to come.'

Alexei Alexandrovich kissed her hand.

'Well, good-bye then. You'll come for tea, that's splendid!' she said and walked out, radiant and gay. But as soon as she no longer saw him, she felt the place on her hand that his lips had touched and shuddered with revulsion.

XXVIII

When Alexei Alexandrovich appeared at the races, Anna was already sitting in the pavilion beside Betsy, in that pavilion in which all of high society was gathered. She saw her husband from a distance. Two men, husband and lover, were the two centres of life for her, and she felt their nearness without the aid of external senses. She felt her husband's approach from a distance and involuntarily watched him in the undulating crowd through which he moved. She saw how he came to the pavilion, now condescendingly responding to obsequious bows, now amicably, distractedly greeting his equals, now diligently awaiting a glance from the mighty of the world and raising his big, round hat that pressed down the tops of his ears. She knew all his ways and they were all disgusting to her. 'Nothing but ambition, nothing but the wish to succeed – that's all there is in his soul,' she thought, 'and lofty considerations, the love of learning, religion, are all just means to success.'

From his glances towards the ladies' pavilion (he looked straight at his wife, but did not recognize her in that sea of muslin, ribbons, feathers, parasols and flowers), she realized that he was searching for her; but she deliberately ignored him.

'Alexei Alexandrovich!' Princess Betsy called to him. 'You probably don't see your wife: here she is!'

He smiled his cold smile.

'There's so much splendour here, one's eyes are dazzled,' he said and went into the pavilion. He smiled to his wife as a husband ought to smile, meeting her after having just seen her, and greeted the princess and other acquaintances, giving each what was due – that is, joking with the ladies and exchanging greetings with the men. Down beside the pavilion stood an adjutant-general whom Alexei Alexandrovich respected, a man known for his intelligence and cultivation. Alexei Alexandrovich began talking with him.

There was a break between races, and therefore nothing hindered the conversation. The adjutant-general condemned races. Alexei Alexandrovich objected, defending them. Anna listened to his high, even voice, not missing a word, and each of his words seemed false to her and grated painfully on her ear.

When the three-mile steeplechase began, she leaned forward and, not taking her eyes off Vronsky, watched him going up to his horse and mounting her, and at the same time listened to her husband's disgusting, incessant voice. She was tormented by her fear for Vronsky, but tormented still more by the sound of her husband's high and, as it seemed to her, incessant voice, with its familiar intonations.

'I'm a bad woman, I'm a ruined woman,' she thought, 'but I don't like to lie, I can't bear lying, and lying is food for *him*' (her husband).

'He knows everything, he sees everything; what does he feel, then, if he can talk so calmly? If he were to kill me, if he were to kill Vronsky, I would respect him. But no, he needs only lies and propriety,' Anna said to herself, not thinking of precisely what she wanted from her husband or how she wanted to see him. Nor did she understand that Alexei Alexandrovich's particular loquacity that day, which so annoyed her, was only the expression of his inner anxiety and uneasiness. As a child who has hurt himself jumps about in order to move his muscles and stifle the pain, so for Alexei Alexandrovich mental movement was necessary in order to stifle those thoughts about his wife, which in her presence and that of Vronsky, and with his name constantly being repeated, clamoured for his attention. And as it is natural for a child to jump, so it was natural for him to speak well and intelligently. He said:

'The danger in military and cavalry races is a necessary condition of the race. If England in her military history can point to the most brilliant cavalry exploits, it is only thanks to the fact that historically she has developed this strength in animals and people. Sport, in my opinion, has great importance, and, as usual, we see only what is most superficial.'

'Not so superficial,' Princess Tverskoy said. 'They say one officer has broken two ribs.'

Alexei Alexandrovich smiled his smile which only revealed his teeth, but said nothing more.

'Let's suppose, Princess, that it is not superficial,' he said, 'but internal. But that is not the point,' and he again turned to the general, with whom he was speaking seriously. 'Don't forget that racing is for military men, who have chosen that activity, and you must agree that every vocation has its reverse side of the coin. It's a military man's duty. The ugly sport of fist fighting or of the Spanish toreadors is a sign of barbarism. But a specialized sport is a sign of development.'

'No, I won't come next time; it upsets me too much,' said Princess Betsy. 'Isn't that so, Anna?'

'It's upsetting, but you can't tear yourself away,' said another lady. 'If I'd been a Roman, I wouldn't have missed a single circus.'

Anna said nothing and looked at one spot without taking her binoculars away.

Just then a tall general passed through the pavilion. Interrupting his speech, Alexei Alexandrovich rose hastily, but with dignity, and bowed low to the passing military man.

'You're not racing?' joked the officer.

'Mine is a harder race,' Alexei Alexandrovich replied respectfully.

And though the reply did not mean anything, the officer pretended that he had heard a clever phrase from a clever man and had perfectly understood *la pointe de la sauce*.*

'There are two sides,' Alexei Alexandrovich went on again, sitting down, 'the performers and the spectators; and the love of such spectacles is the surest sign of low development in the spectators, I agree, but . . .'

'A bet, Princess!' the voice of Stepan Arkadyich came from below, addressing Betsy. 'Who are you backing?'

'Anna and I are for Prince Kuzovlev,' replied Betsy.

'I'm for Vronsky. A pair of gloves.'

'You're on!'

'It's so beautiful, isn't it?'

Alexei Alexandrovich paused while the people around him talked, but at once began again.

'I agree, but manly games . . .' he tried to go on.

But at that moment the riders were given the start, and all conversation ceased. Alexei Alexandrovich also fell silent, and everyone rose and turned towards the stream. Alexei Alexandrovich was not interested in the race and therefore did not watch the riders, but began absent-mindedly surveying the spectators with his weary eyes. His gaze rested on Anna.

Her face was pale and stern. She obviously saw nothing and no one except one man. Her hand convulsively clutched her fan, and she held her breath. He looked at her and hastily turned away, scrutinizing other faces.

'Yes, that lady and the others are also very upset,' Alexei Alexandrovich said to himself. He wanted not to look at her, but his glance was involuntarily drawn to her. He peered into that face again, trying not to read what was so clearly written on it, and against his will read on it with horror what he did not want to know.

The first fall – Kuzovlev's at the stream – upset everyone, but Alexei Alexandrovich saw clearly on Anna's pale, triumphant face that the one she was watching had not fallen. When, after Makhotin and Vronsky cleared the big barrier, the very next officer fell on his head and knocked himself out, and a rustle of horror passed through all the public, Alexei Alexandrovich saw that Anna did not even notice it and hardly under-

* The savour of the sauce.

stood what the people around her were talking about. But he peered at her more and more often and with greater persistence. Anna, all absorbed in watching the racing Vronsky, could feel the gaze of her husband's cold eyes fixed on her from the side.

She turned for an instant, looked at him questioningly, and with a slight frown turned away again.

'Ah, I don't care,' she all but said to him, and never once glanced at him after that.

The race was unlucky: out of seventeen men more than half fell and were injured. Towards the end of the race everyone was in agitation, which was increased still more by the fact that the emperor was displeased.

XXIX

Everyone loudly expressed his disapproval, everyone repeated the phrase someone had uttered: 'We only lack circuses with lions,' and horror was felt by all, so that when Vronsky fell and Anna gasped loudly, there was nothing extraordinary in it. But after that a change came over Anna's face which was positively improper. She was completely at a loss. She started thrashing about like a trapped bird, now wanting to get up and go somewhere, now turning to Betsy.

'Let's go, let's go,' she kept saying.

But Betsy did not hear her. She was bending forward to talk to a general who had come up to her.

Alexei Alexandrovich approached Anna and courteously offered her his arm.

'Let us go, if you wish,' he said in French; but Anna was listening to what the general was saying and ignored her husband.

'He also broke his leg, they say,' the general said. 'It's quite unheard-of.'

Anna, without answering her husband, raised her binoculars and looked at the place where Vronsky had fallen; but it was so far away, and there were so many people crowding there, that it was impossible to make anything out. She lowered the binoculars and made as if to leave; but just then an officer galloped up and reported something to the emperor. Anna leaned forward, listening.

'Stiva! Stiva!' she called out to her brother.

But her brother did not hear her. She again made as if to leave.

'I once again offer you my arm, if you want to go,' said Alexei Alexandrovich, touching her arm.

She recoiled from him in revulsion and, without looking at his face, replied:

'No, no, let me be, I'll stay.'

She saw now that an officer was running across the track towards the pavilion from the place where Vronsky had fallen. Betsy was waving a handkerchief to him.

The officer brought the news that the rider was unhurt, but the horse had broken her back.

Hearing that, Anna quickly sat down and covered her face with her fan. Alexei Alexandrovich could see that she was weeping and was unable to hold back not only her tears but the sobs that heaved her bosom. Alexei Alexandrovich shielded her, giving her time to recover.

'For the third time I offer you my arm,' he said after a short while, addressing her. Anna looked at him and did not know what to say. Princess Betsy came to her aid.

'No, Alexei Alexandrovich, I brought Anna here and promised to take her back,' Betsy interfered.

'Excuse me, Princess,' he said, smiling courteously but looking her firmly in the eye, 'but I see that Anna is not quite well, and I wish her to leave with me.'

Anna glanced fearfully at him, obediently stood up and placed her hand on her husband's arm.

'I'll send to him to find out and get word to you,' Betsy whispered to her.

On the way out of the pavilion, Alexei Alexandrovich, as always, talked with people he met, and Anna also had, as always, to respond and talk; but she was not herself and walked at her husband's side as if in a dream.

'Hurt or not? Is it true? Will he come or not? Will I see him tonight?' she thought.

She silently got into Alexei Alexandrovich's carriage, and they silently drove away from the crowd of vehicles. Despite all he had seen, Alexei Alexandrovich still did not allow himself to think of his wife's real situation. He saw only the external signs. He saw that she had behaved improperly and considered it his duty to tell her so. Yet it was very hard for him not to say more, but to say just that. He opened his mouth in order to tell her how improperly she had behaved, but involuntarily said something quite different.

'How inclined we all are, though, to these cruel spectacles,' he said. 'I observe . . .'

'What? I don't understand,' Anna said contemptuously.

He was offended and at once began saying what he had wanted to.

'I must tell you,' he said.

'Here it comes – the talk,' she thought and became frightened.

'I must tell you that you behaved improperly today,' he said to her in French.

'In what way did I behave improperly?' she said loudly, quickly turning her head to him and looking straight into his eyes, now not at all with the former deceptive gaiety, but with a determined look, behind which she barely concealed the fear she felt.

'Do not forget,' he said to her, pointing to the open window facing the coachman.

He got up and raised the window.

'What did you find improper?' she repeated.

'The despair you were unable to conceal when one of the riders fell.'

He waited for her to protest; but she was silent, looking straight ahead of her.

'I have asked you before to conduct yourself in society so that wicked tongues can say nothing against you. There was a time when I spoke of our inner relations; now I am not speaking of them. Now I am speaking of our external relations. You conducted yourself improperly, and I do not wish it to be repeated.'

She did not hear half of his words, she felt afraid of him and was wondering whether it was true that Vronsky had not been hurt. Was it of him they had said that he was well, but the horse had broken its back? She only smiled with false mockery when he finished and made no reply, because she had not heard what he said. Alexei Alexandrovich had begun speaking boldly, but when he understood clearly what he was speaking about, the fear that she experienced communicated itself to him. He saw this smile and a strange delusion came over him.

'She's smiling at my suspicions. Yes, she will presently tell me what she said to me the other time: that there are no grounds for my suspicions, that they are ridiculous.'

Now, when the disclosure of everything was hanging over him, he wished for nothing so much as that she would mockingly answer him, just as before, that his suspicions were ridiculous and had no grounds. So dreadful was what he knew, that he was now ready to believe anything. But the expression of her face, frightened and gloomy, did not promise even deceit.

'Perhaps I am mistaken,' he said. 'In that case I beg your pardon.'

'No, you are not mistaken,' she said slowly, looking desperately into his cold face. 'You are not mistaken. I was and could not help being in despair. I listen to you and think about him. I love him, I am his mistress, I cannot stand you, I'm afraid of you, I hate you . . . Do what you like with me.'

And, throwing herself back into the corner of the carriage, she began to sob, covering her face with her hands. Alexei Alexandrovich did not stir or change the straight direction of his gaze. But his entire face suddenly acquired the solemn immobility of a dead man, and that expression did not change during the whole drive to their country house. As they approached the house, he turned his head to her with the same expression.

'So be it! But I demand that the outward conventions of propriety be observed until' – his voice trembled – 'until I take measures to secure my honour and inform you of them.'

He got out first and helped her out. In the presence of the servants he silently pressed her hand, got into the carriage and drove off to Petersburg.

After he left, a footman came from Princess Betsy and brought Anna a note:

'I sent to Alexei to find out about him, and he wrote me that he is safe and sound, but in despair.'

'So *he* will come!' she thought. 'How well I did to tell him everything.'

She looked at her watch. There were still three hours to go, and the memory of the details of their last meeting fired her blood.

'My God, what light! It's frightening, but I love seeing his face and love this fantastic light . . . My husband! Ah, yes . . . Well, thank God it's all over with him.'

XXX

As in all places where people gather, so in the small German watering-place to which the Shcherbatskys came there occurred the usual crystallization, as it were, of society, designating for each of its members a definite and invariable place. As definitely and invariably as a particle of water acquires the specific form of a snowflake in freezing, so each new person arriving at the spa was put at once into the place appropriate for him.

Fürst Shcherbatsky *sammt Gemahlin und Tochter*,* by the quarters they occupied, by name, and by the acquaintances they found, crystallized at once into their definite and allotted place.

At the spa that year there was a real German *Fürstin*† owing to whom the crystallization of society took place still more energetically. The princess was absolutely set on introducing her daughter to the *Fürstin* and performed this ritual the very next day. Kitty made a low and graceful curtsy in her *very simple* – that is, very smart – summer dress, ordered from Paris. The *Fürstin* said: 'I hope the roses will soon return to this pretty little face' – and at once certain paths of life were firmly established for the Shcherbatskys, from which it was no longer possible to stray. The Shcherbatskys became acquainted with the family of an English lady, and with a German countess and her son, wounded in the last war, and with a Swedish scholar, and with M. Canut and his sister. But the main company of the Shcherbatskys involuntarily constituted itself of the Moscow lady Marya Evgenyevna Rtishchev, her daughter, whom Kitty found disagreeable because, like Kitty, she had become ill from love, and a Moscow colonel whom Kitty had seen and known since childhood in a uniform and epaulettes and who was extraordinarily ridiculous here, with his little eyes and open neck in a brightly coloured tie, and tedious because there was no getting rid of him. When all this became firmly established, Kitty began to be bored, the more so as the prince left for Karlsbad and she stayed alone with her mother. She was not interested in those she knew, feeling that nothing new would come from them. Her main heartfelt interest at the spa now consisted in her observations and surmises about those she did not know. By virtue of

* Prince Shcherbatsky with wife and daughter.

† Princess.

her character, Kitty always assumed the most beautiful things about people, especially those she did not know. And now, making guesses about who was who, what relations they were in, and what sort of people they were, Kitty imagined to herself the most amazing and beautiful characters and found confirmation in her observations.

Among these people she was especially taken by a Russian girl who had come to the spa with an ailing Russian lady, Mme Stahl, as everyone called her. Mme Stahl belonged to high society, but was so ill that she was unable to walk, and only on rare good days appeared at the springs in a bath-chair. But, less from illness than from pride, as the princess explained, Mme Stahl was not acquainted with any of the Russians. The Russian girl looked after Mme Stahl and, besides that, as Kitty noticed, made friends with all the gravely ill, of whom there were many at the spa, and looked after them in the most natural way. This Russian girl, from Kitty's observation, was not related to Mme Stahl and at the same time was not a hired helper. Mme Stahl called her Varenka, and the others 'Mlle Varenka'. Not only was Kitty interested in observing the relations of this girl with Mme Stahl and other persons unknown to her, but, as often happens, she felt an inexplicable sympathy for this Mlle Varenka and sensed, when their eyes met, that she, too, was liked.

This Mlle Varenka was not really past her first youth, but was, as it were, a being without youth: she might have been nineteen, she might have been thirty. If one studied her features, she was more beautiful than plain, despite her sickly complexion. She would also have been of good build, if it had not been for the excessive leanness of her body and a head much too large for her medium height; but she must not have been attractive to men. She was like a beautiful flower which, while still full of petals, is scentless and no longer blooming. Besides that, she also could not be attractive to men because she lacked what Kitty had in over-abundance – the restrained fire of life and an awareness of her attractiveness.

She always seemed to be busy doing something that could not be doubted, and therefore it seemed she could not be interested in anything outside it. By this contrast with herself she especially attracted Kitty. Kitty felt that in her, in her way of life, she would find a model for what she now sought so tormentingly: interests in life, virtues in life, outside the social relations of a girl with men, which Kitty found repulsive, picturing them now as a disgraceful exhibition of wares awaiting their buyers. The more Kitty observed her unknown friend, the more convinced she was that this girl was that same perfect being she pictured to herself, and the more she wished to make her acquaintance.

The two girls met several times a day and at each meeting Kitty's eyes said: 'Who are you? What are you? Are you truly the lovely being I imagine you to be? But for God's sake don't think,' her eyes added, 'that I would allow myself to force an acquaintance. I simply admire you and love you.' 'I love you, too, and you are very, very sweet. And I would love you still more if I had time,' the unknown girl's eyes answered. And indeed Kitty saw that she was always busy: she would take the children of a Russian family home from the springs, or bring a rug for an ailing woman and wrap her up, or try to divert some irritated patient, or choose and buy pastries for someone's coffee.

Soon after the Shcherbatskys' arrival, two more people appeared at the morning session, attracting general and unfriendly attention. These were a very tall, stoop-shouldered man with enormous hands, in an old coat that was too short for him, with dark, naïve and at the same time frightening eyes, and a nice-looking, slightly pockmarked woman, very poorly and tastelessly dressed. Having recognized these people as Russians, Kitty had already begun putting together in her imagination a beautiful and moving romance about them. But the princess, learning from the *Kurliste** that they were Nikolai Levin and Marya Nikolaevna, explained to Kitty what a bad man this Levin was, and all her dreams about these two persons vanished. Not so much because of what her mother told her as because this was Konstantin's brother, these persons suddenly became highly disagreeable to her. This Levin, by his habit of twitching his head, now provoked in her an irrepressible feeling of disgust.

It seemed to her that his big, frightening eyes, which followed her persistently, expressed a feeling of hatred and mockery, and she tried to avoid meeting him.

* Patients' list.

XXXI

It was a nasty day, rain fell all morning, and patients with umbrellas crowded into the gallery.

Kitty was walking with her mother and the Moscow colonel, who gaily showed off his little European frock coat, bought ready-to-wear in Frankfurt. They were walking along one side of the gallery, trying to avoid Levin, who was walking along the other side. Varenka, in her dark dress and a black hat with the brim turned down, was walking with a blind Frenchwoman the whole length of the gallery, and each time she met Kitty, they exchanged friendly looks.

'Mama, may I speak to her?' said Kitty, who was watching her unknown friend and noticed that she was approaching the springs and that they might come together there.

'If you want to so much, I'll find out about her first and approach her myself,' her mother replied. 'What do you find so special about her? A lady's companion, she must be. If you wish, I'll make the acquaintance of Mme Stahl. I knew her *belle-soeur*,' the princess added, raising her head proudly.

Kitty knew that the princess was offended that Mme Stahl seemed to avoid making her acquaintance. She did not insist.

'A wonder, such a dear!' she said, looking at Varenka, just as she was handing a glass to the Frenchwoman. 'Look, it's all so simple and sweet.'

'I find these *engouements** of yours so funny,' said the princess. 'No, better let's go back,' she added, noticing Levin coming their way with his lady and a German doctor, to whom he was saying something loudly and crossly.

They were turning to go back when they suddenly heard not loud talking now, but shouting. Levin had stopped and was shouting, and the doctor, too, was excited. A crowd was gathering around them. The princess and Kitty hastily withdrew, and the colonel joined the crowd to find out what was the matter.

A few minutes later, the colonel caught up with them.

'What was it?' asked the princess.

'Shame and disgrace!' replied the colonel. 'There is only one thing to

* Infatuations.

fear – meeting Russians abroad. That tall gentleman quarrelled with the doctor, said impertinent things to him for not treating him correctly, and even raised his stick. It's simply a disgrace!'

'Ah, how unpleasant!' said the princess. 'Well, how did it end?'

'Thank heavens, that girl intervened . . . the one in the mushroom hat. A Russian, it seems,' said the colonel.

'Mlle Varenka?' Kitty asked joyfully.

'Yes, yes. She found the way more quickly than anyone: she took the gentleman by the arm and led him away.'

'See, mama,' Kitty said to her mother, 'and you're surprised that I admire her.'

The next day, observing her unknown friend, Kitty noticed that Mlle Varenka already had the same sort of relations with Levin and his woman as with her other *protégés*. She went up to them, talked, served as interpreter for the woman, who could not speak any foreign languages.

Kitty started pleading still more with her mother to allow her to make Varenka's acquaintance. And, disagreeable though it was for the princess to take, as it were, the first step towards becoming acquainted with Mme Stahl, who permitted herself to be proud of something, she made inquiries about Varenka and, learning details about her allowing her to conclude that there was nothing bad, though also little good, in this acquaintance, first approached Varenka herself and became acquainted with her.

Choosing a moment when her daughter had gone to the springs and Varenka had stopped in front of the bakery, the princess approached her.

'Allow me to make your acquaintance,' she said with her dignified smile. 'My daughter is in love with you,' she said. 'Perhaps you do not know me. I am . . .'

'It's more than reciprocated, Princess,' Varenka replied hastily.

'What a good deed you did yesterday for our pathetic compatriot!' said the princess.

Varenka blushed.

'I don't remember. I don't think I did anything,' she said.

'Why, you saved this Levin from unpleasantness.'

'Yes, *sa compagne** called me, and I did my best to calm him down:

* His companion.

he's very ill and was displeased with the doctor. And I'm used to looking after these patients.'

'Yes, I've heard that you live in Menton with Mme Stahl – your aunt, I believe. I knew her *belle-soeur*.'

'No, she's not my aunt. I call her *maman*, but I'm not related to her; I was brought up by her,' Varenka replied, blushing again.

This was said so simply, so sweet was the truthful and open expression of her face, that the princess understood why her Kitty loved Varenka.

'Well, what about this Levin?' asked the princess.

'He's leaving,' replied Varenka.

At that moment, beaming with joy that her mother had made the acquaintance of her unknown friend, Kitty came from the springs.

'So, Kitty, your great desire to make the acquaintance of Mlle . . .'

'Varenka,' prompted Varenka, smiling, 'that's what everyone calls me.'

Kitty blushed with joy and for a long time silently pressed her new friend's hand, which did not respond to this pressing but lay motionless in her hand. But though her hand did not respond, the face of Mlle Varenka lit up with a quiet, joyful, though also somewhat sad smile, revealing big but beautiful teeth.

'I've long wanted this myself,' she said.

'But you're so busy . . .'

'Ah, on the contrary, I'm not busy at all,' replied Varenka, but that same minute she had to leave her new acquaintances because two little Russian girls, daughters of one of the patients, came running to her.

'Varenka, mama's calling!' they shouted.

And Varenka went after them.

XXXII

The details that the princess had learned about Varenka's past and her relations with Mme Stahl, and about Mme Stahl herself, were the following.

Mme Stahl, of whom some said that she had tormented her husband, and others that he had tormented her with his immoral behaviour, had always been a sickly and rapturous woman. She gave birth to her first child when she was already divorced from her husband. The child died at once, and Mme Stahl's family, knowing her susceptibility and fearing the news might kill her, replaced the baby, taking the daughter of a court cook born the same night and in the same house in Petersburg. This was Varenka. Mme Stahl learned later that Varenka was not her daughter, but continued to bring her up, the more so as Varenka soon afterwards had no family left.

Mme Stahl had lived abroad in the south for a period of more than ten years, never getting out of bed. Some said that she had made a social position for herself as a virtuous, highly religious woman, while others said that she was at heart that same highly moral being she made herself out to be, living only for the good of others. No one knew what religion she adhered to – Catholic, Orthodox or Protestant – but one thing was certain: she was in friendly relations with the highest persons of all Churches and confessions.

Varenka lived permanently abroad with her, and all who knew Mme Stahl, knew and loved Mlle Varenka, as everyone called her.

Having learned all these details, the princess found nothing reprehensible in her daughter making friends with Varenka, especially since Varenka had the very best manners and upbringing: she spoke excellent French and English and, above all, conveyed regrets from Mme Stahl that, owing to her illness, she was deprived of the pleasure of making the princess's acquaintance.

Once she had made Varenka's acquaintance, Kitty became more and more charmed by her friend and found new virtues in her every day.

The princess, on hearing that Varenka sang well, invited her to come to them in the evening to sing.

'Kitty plays, and we have a piano, not a good one, true, but you will give us great pleasure,' the princess said with her false smile, which was now especially unpleasant for Kitty because she noticed that Varenka did not want to sing. But Varenka nevertheless came in the evening and brought with her a book of music. The princess invited Marya Evgenyevna with her daughter and the colonel.

Varenka seemed perfectly indifferent to the fact that there were people there whom she did not know, and went to the piano at once. She could not accompany herself, but vocally she could sight-read music wonderfully. Kitty, who played well, accompanied her.

'You have extraordinary talent,' the princess said to Varenka, after she had sung the first piece beautifully.

Marya Evgenyevna and her daughter thanked and praised her.

'Look,' said the colonel, glancing out the window, 'what an audience has gathered to listen to you.' Indeed, a rather big crowd had gathered by the windows.

'I'm very glad that it gives you pleasure,' Varenka replied simply.

Kitty looked at her friend with pride. She admired her art, and her voice, and her face, but most of all she admired her manner, the fact that Varenka evidently did not think much of her singing and was perfectly indifferent to praise; she seemed to ask only: must I sing more, or is that enough?

'If it were me,' Kitty thought to herself, 'how proud I'd be! How I'd rejoice, looking at this crowd by the windows! And she is perfectly indifferent. She is moved only by the wish not to say no and to do something nice for *maman*. What is it in her? What gives her this strength to disregard everything, to be so calmly independent? How I wish I knew and could learn it from her,' Kitty thought, studying that calm face. The princess asked Varenka to sing more, and Varenka sang another piece as smoothly, distinctly and well, standing straight by the piano and beating the rhythm on it with her thin, brown hand.

The next piece in the book was an Italian song. Kitty played the prelude, which she liked very much, and turned to Varenka.

'Let's skip this one,' Varenka said, blushing.

Kitty rested her timorous and questioning eyes on Varenka's face.

'Well, another then,' she said hastily, turning the pages, understanding immediately that something was associated with that piece.

'No,' replied Varenka, putting her hand on the score and smiling, 'no, let's sing it.' And she sang as calmly, coolly and well as before.

When she had finished, everyone thanked her again and went to have tea. Kitty and Varenka went out to the little garden near the house.

'Am I right that you have some memory associated with that song?' Kitty said. 'Don't tell me,' she added hastily, 'just say – am I right?'

'No, why not? I'll tell you,' Varenka said simply and, without waiting for a response, went on: 'Yes, there is a memory, and it was painful once. I was in love with a man, and I used to sing that piece for him.'

Kitty, her big eyes wide open, gazed silently and tenderly at Varenka.

'I loved him and he loved me; but his mother didn't want it, and he married someone else. He lives not far from us now, and I sometimes meet him. You didn't think that I, too, could have a love story?' she said, and in her beautiful face there barely glimmered that fire which, Kitty felt, had once lit up her whole being.

'Of course I did! If I were a man, I wouldn't be able to love anyone after knowing you. I just don't understand how he could forget you to please his mother and make you unhappy. He had no heart.'

'Oh, no, he's a very good man, and I'm not unhappy; on the contrary, I'm very happy. Well, so we won't sing any more today?' she added, heading for the house.

'How good, how good you are!' Kitty cried and, stopping her, she kissed her. 'If only I could be a little bit like you!'

'Why do you need to be like anyone? You're good as you are,' said Varenka, smiling her meek and weary smile.

'No, I'm not good at all. Well, tell me . . . Wait, let's sit down,' said Kitty, seating her on the bench again next to herself. 'Tell me, isn't it insulting to think that a man scorned your love, that he didn't want . . . ?'

'But he didn't scorn it. I believe he loved me, but he was an obedient son . . .'

'Yes, but if it wasn't by his mother's will, but he himself simply . . .' Kitty said, feeling that she had given away her secret and that her face, burning with a blush of shame, had already betrayed her.

'Then he would have acted badly, and I would not feel sorry about him,' Varenka replied, obviously understanding that it was now a matter not of her but of Kitty.

'But the insult?' said Kitty. 'It's impossible to forget an insult, impossible,' she said, remembering how she had looked at him at the last ball when the music stopped.

'Where is the insult? Did you do anything bad?'

'Worse than bad – shameful.'

Varenka shook her head and placed her hand on Kitty's hand.

'But why shameful?' she said. 'You couldn't have told a man who is indifferent to you that you loved him?'

'Of course not, I never said a single word, but he knew. No, no, there are looks, there are ways. If I live to be a hundred, I won't forget it.'

'So what then? I don't understand. The point is whether you love him now or not,' said Varenka, calling everything by its name.

'I hate him; I can't forgive myself.'

'So what then?'

'The shame, the insult.'

'Ah, if everybody was as sensitive as you are!' said Varenka. 'There's no girl who hasn't gone through that. And it's all so unimportant.'

'Then what is important?' asked Kitty, peering into her face with curious amazement.

'Ah, many things are important,' Varenka said, smiling.

'But what?'

'Ah, many things are more important,' Varenka replied, not knowing what to say. But at that moment the princess's voice came from the window:

'Kitty, it's chilly! Either take your shawl or come inside.'

'True, it's time!' said Varenka, getting up. 'I still have to stop and see Mme Berthe. She asked me to.'

Kitty held her by the hand and with passionate curiosity and entreaty her eyes asked: 'What is it, what is this most important thing that gives such tranquillity? You know, tell me!' But Varenka did not even understand what Kitty's eyes were asking her. All she remembered was that she still had to stop and see Mme Berthe and be in time for tea with *maman* at twelve. She went in, collected her music and, having said good-bye to everyone, was about to leave.

'Allow me to accompany you,' said the colonel.

'Yes, how can you go alone now that it's night?' the princess agreed. 'I'll send Parasha at least.'

Kitty saw that Varenka could hardly keep back a smile at the suggestion that she needed to be accompanied.

'No, I always go alone and nothing ever happens to me,' she said, taking her hat. And, kissing Kitty once more and never saying what was important, at a brisk pace, with the music under her arm, she vanished into the semi-darkness of the summer night, taking with her the secret of what was important and what gave her that enviable tranquillity and dignity.

XXXIII

Kitty made the acquaintance of Mme Stahl as well, and this acquaintance, together with her friendship for Varenka, not only had great influence on her, but comforted her in her grief. The comfort lay in the fact that, thanks to this acquaintance, a completely new world was opened to her which had nothing in common with her past: a lofty, beautiful world, from the height of which she could calmly look over that past. It was revealed to her that, besides the instinctive life to which Kitty had given herself till then, there was a spiritual life. This life was revealed by religion, but a religion that had nothing in common with the one Kitty had known from childhood and which found expression in the liturgy and vigils at the Widows' Home,[31] where one could meet acquaintances, and in learning Slavonic[32] texts by heart with a priest; it was a lofty, mysterious religion, bound up with a series of beautiful thoughts and feelings which one could not only believe in because one was told to, but could also love.

Kitty did not learn all this from words. Mme Stahl spoke with Kitty as with a dear child, whom one looks upon fondly as a memory of one's youth, and she only once mentioned that in all human griefs consolation is given by faith and love alone and that no griefs are too negligible for Christ's compassion for us, and at once turned the conversation to something else. Yet in her every movement, in every word, in every heavenly glance, as Kitty put it, especially in the whole story of her life, which she knew from Varenka, in everything, Kitty learned 'what was important', which till then she had not known.

But however lofty Mme Stahl's character was, however touching her whole story, however lofty and tender her speech, Kitty inadvertently noticed features in her that she found troubling. She noticed that, when asking about her family, Mme Stahl smiled contemptuously, which was contrary to Christian kindness. She also noticed that when she found a Catholic priest with her, Mme Stahl carefully kept her face in the shadow of a lampshade and smiled peculiarly. However negligible these two observations were, they troubled her, and she doubted Mme Stahl. But Varenka, lonely, without family, without friends, with her sad disappointment, desiring nothing, regretting nothing, was that very perfection of which Kitty only allowed herself to dream. From Varenka she understood that you had only to forget yourself and love others and you would be calm, happy and beautiful. And that was how Kitty wanted to be. Now that she had clearly understood what was *most important*, Kitty did not content herself with admiring it, but at once, with all her soul, gave herself to this new life that had opened to her. From Varenka's stories about what Mme Stahl and the others she mentioned did, Kitty made herself a plan for her future life. Just like Mme Stahl's niece, Aline, of whom Varenka had told her so much, wherever she lived she would seek out the unfortunate people, help them as much as possible, distribute the Gospel, read the Gospel to the sick, the criminal, the dying. The thought of reading the Gospel to criminals, as Aline did, especially attracted Kitty. But these were all secret thoughts which Kitty did not speak about either to her mother or to Varenka.

Even now, however, in anticipation of the time for fulfilling her plans on a large scale, Kitty easily found occasion, in imitation of Varenka, for applying her new rules at the spa, where there were so many sick and unfortunate people.

At first the princess noticed only that Kitty was under the strong influence of her *engouement*, as she called it, for Mme Stahl and especially for Varenka. She saw that Kitty not only imitated Varenka in her activity, but involuntarily imitated her way of walking, speaking and blinking her eyes. But then the princess noticed that, independently of this fascination, a serious inner turnabout was taking place in her daughter.

The princess saw that in the evenings Kitty read the French Gospel that Mme Stahl had given her, something she had not done before; that she avoided society acquaintances and made friends with the sick people who were under Varenka's patronage, especially with the poor family of the sick painter Petrov. Kitty was obviously proud that she was fulfilling the duties of a sister of mercy in this family. That was all good, and the princess had nothing against it, the more so as Petrov's wife was a perfectly decent woman and the *Fürstin*, noticing Kitty's activity, praised her, calling her a ministering angel. All this would have been very good, had it not been for its excessiveness. But the princess saw that her daughter was running to extremes, which she proceeded to tell her.

'*Il ne faut jamais rien outrer*,'* she told her.

But her daughter said nothing in reply; she only thought in her heart that one could not speak of excessiveness in matters of Christianity. What excessiveness could there be in following a teaching that tells you to turn the other cheek when you have been struck, and to give away your shirt when your caftan is taken?[33] But the princess did not like this excessiveness, and still less did she like it that, as she felt, Kitty did not want to open her soul to her entirely. In fact, Kitty kept her new views and feelings hidden from her mother. She kept them hidden, not because she did not respect or love her mother, but because she was her mother. She would sooner have revealed them to anyone than to her mother.

* One must do nothing in excess.

'It's some while since Anna Pavlovna has visited us,' the princess said once of Petrov's wife. 'I invited her. But she seemed somehow displeased.'

'No, I didn't notice, *maman*,' Kitty said, flushing.

'Have you visited them recently?'

'We're going for an outing in the mountains tomorrow,' Kitty replied.

'Well, go then,' the princess replied, looking into her daughter's embarrassed face and trying to guess the cause of her embarrassment.

That same day Varenka came for dinner and told them that Anna Pavlovna had changed her mind about going to the mountains tomorrow. And the princess noticed that Kitty blushed again.

'Kitty, have you had any unpleasantness with the Petrovs?' the princess said when they were alone. 'Why has she stopped sending the children and coming to see us?'

Kitty replied that there had been nothing between them, and that she decidedly did not understand why Anna Pavlovna seemed displeased with her. Kitty's reply was perfectly truthful. She did not know the reason for Anna Pavlovna's change towards her, but she guessed it. Her guess was something she could not tell her mother any more than she could tell it to herself. It was one of those things that one knows but cannot even tell oneself – so dreadful and shameful it would be to be mistaken.

Again and again she went over her whole relationship with this family in her memory. She remembered the naïve joy that had shown on Anna Pavlovna's round, good-natured face when they met; remembered their secret discussions about the sick man, conspiracies for distracting him from his work, which was forbidden him, and taking him for a walk; the attachment of the younger boy, who called her 'my Kitty' and refused to go to bed without her. How good it had all been! Then she remembered the thin, thin figure of Petrov, with his long neck, in his brown frock coat – his scant, wavy hair, his inquisitive blue eyes, which Kitty had found so frightening at first, and his painful attempts to look cheerful and animated in her presence. She remembered her own efforts at first to overcome the revulsion she felt for him, as for all the consumptives, and her attempts to think of something to say to him. She remembered the timid, tender gaze with which he had looked at her, and the strange feeling of compassion and awkwardness, and then the consciousness of her own virtue which she had experienced at that. How good it had all been! But all that was in the beginning. And now, a few days ago, everything had suddenly gone bad. Anna Pavlovna met Kitty with a false amiability and constantly watched her and her husband.

Could it be that his touching joy at her coming was the cause of Anna Pavlovna's chilliness?

'Yes,' she remembered, 'there had been something unnatural in Anna Pavlovna, and quite unlike her kindness, when she had said crossly two days ago: "Here, he's been waiting for you, didn't want to have coffee without you, though he got terribly weak."

'Yes, maybe it was unpleasant for her when I gave him the rug. It's all so simple, but he took it so awkwardly, thanked me so profusely, that I, too, felt awkward. And then the portrait of me that he painted so well. And above all – that embarrassed and tender look! Yes, yes, it's so!' Kitty repeated to herself in horror. 'No, it cannot, it must not be! He's so pathetic!' she said to herself after that.

This doubt poisoned the charm of her new life.

XXXIV

Before the end of the course of waters, Prince Shcherbatsky, who had gone on from Karlsbad to Baden and Kissingen to visit Russian acquaintances and pick up some Russian spirit, as he said, returned to his family.

The prince and the princess held completely opposite views on life abroad. The princess found everything wonderful and, despite her firm position in Russian society, made efforts abroad to resemble a European lady – which she was not, being a typical Russian lady – and therefore had to pretend, which was somewhat awkward for her. The prince, on the contrary, found everything abroad vile and European life a burden, kept to his Russian habits and deliberately tried to show himself as less of a European than he really was.

The prince came back thinner, with bags of skin hanging under his eyes, but in the most cheerful state of mind. His cheerful disposition was strengthened when he saw Kitty completely recovered. The news of Kitty's friendship with Mme Stahl and Varenka, and the observations conveyed to him by the princess about some change that had taken place in Kitty, troubled the prince and provoked in him the usual feeling of jealousy towards everything that interested his daughter to the exclusion of himself, and a fear lest his daughter escape from his influence into some spheres inaccessible to him. But this unpleasant news was drowned in the sea of good-natured cheerfulness that was always in him and that had been especially strengthened by the waters of Karlsbad.

The day after his arrival the prince, in his long coat, with his Russian wrinkles and bloated cheeks propped up by a starched collar, in the most cheerful state of mind, went to the springs with his daughter.

It was a wonderful morning; the tidy, cheerful houses with their little gardens, the sight of the red-faced, red-armed, beer-filled, cheerfully working German maids and the bright sun gladdened the heart; but the closer they came to the springs, the more often they met sick people, and their appearance seemed all the more doleful amidst the ordinary conditions of comfortable German life. Kitty was no longer struck by this contrast. The bright sun, the cheerful glittering of the greenery, the sounds of music, were for her the natural frame for all these familiar faces and the changes for worse or better that she followed; but for the prince the light and glitter of the June morning, the sounds of the orchestra playing a popular, cheerful waltz, and especially the sight of the stalwart serving-women, seemed something indecent and monstrous in combination with these glumly moving dead people gathered from every corner of Europe.

Despite the feeling of pride and the return of youth that he experienced when his beloved daughter walked arm in arm with him, he now felt awkward and ashamed, as it were, for his strong stride, for his big, fat-enveloped limbs. He almost had the feeling of a man undressed in public.

'Introduce me, introduce me to your new friends,' he said to his daughter, pressing her arm with his elbow. 'I've even come to like this vile Soden of yours for having straightened you out so well. Only it's a sad, sad place. Who's this?'

Kitty named for him the acquaintances and non-acquaintances they met. Just at the entrance to the garden they met the blind Mme Berthe with her guide, and the prince rejoiced at the old Frenchwoman's tender expression when she heard Kitty's voice. She at once began talking to him with a French excess of amiability, praising him for having such a wonderful daughter, and praising Kitty to the skies, calling her a treasure, a pearl and a ministering angel.

'Well, then she's the second angel,' the prince said, smiling. 'She calls Mlle Varenka angel number one.'

'Oh! Mlle Varenka – there is a real angel, *allez*,'* Mme Berthe agreed.

In the gallery they met Varenka herself. She walked hurriedly towards them, carrying an elegant red handbag.

'See, papa has arrived!' Kitty said to her.

As simply and naturally as she did everything, Varenka made a movement between a bow and a curtsy, and at once began talking with the prince as she talked with everyone, simply and without constraint.

'Certainly, I know you, know you very well,' the prince said with a smile, from which Kitty joyfully learned that her father liked her friend. 'Where are you off to in such a hurry?'

'*Maman* is here,' she said, turning to Kitty. 'She didn't sleep all night, and the doctor advised her to go out. I'm bringing her some handwork.'

'So that's angel number one!' said the prince, when Varenka had gone.

Kitty saw that he wanted to make fun of Varenka, but that he simply could not do it, because he liked her.

'Well, now we'll be seeing all your friends,' he added, 'including Mme Stahl, if she deigns to recognize me.'

'Did you know her before, papa?' Kitty asked in fear, noticing a flicker of mockery lighting up in the prince's eyes at the mention of Mme Stahl.

'I knew her husband, and her a little, back before she signed up with the Pietists.'[34]

'What is a Pietist, papa?' asked Kitty, already frightened by the fact that what she valued so highly in Mme Stahl had a name.

'I don't quite know myself. I only know that she thanks God for everything, for every misfortune – and for the fact that her husband died, she also thanks God. Well, and that's rather funny, because they had a bad life together. Who is that? What a pitiful face!' he said, noticing a sick man, not very tall, sitting on a bench in a brown coat and white trousers that fell into strange folds on the fleshless bones of his legs.

This gentleman raised his straw hat over his scant, wavy hair, revealing a high forehead with an unhealthy red mark from the hat.

'That's the painter Petrov,' Kitty replied, blushing. 'And that's his wife,' she added, pointing to Anna Pavlovna, who, as if on purpose, went after a child who had run down the path just as they were approaching.

* Come now.

'How pitiful, and what a nice face he has!' said the prince. 'Why didn't you go over? He wanted to say something to you.'

'Well, let's go then,' Kitty said, turning resolutely. 'How are you today?' she asked Petrov.

Petrov stood up, leaning on his stick, and looked timidly at the prince.

'This is my daughter,' said the prince. 'Allow me to introduce myself.'

The painter bowed and smiled, revealing his strangely gleaming white teeth.

'We were expecting you yesterday, Princess,' he said to Kitty.

He staggered as he said it, then repeated the movement, trying to make it appear that he had done it on purpose.

'I wanted to come, but Varenka told me Anna Pavlovna sent word that you weren't going.'

'How's that? Not going?' said Petrov, blushing and seeking his wife with his eyes. 'Annetta, Annetta!' he said loudly, and on his thin, white neck the thick tendons strained like ropes.

Anna Pavlovna came over.

'How is it you sent word to the princess that we weren't going?' he whispered to her vexedly, having lost his voice.

'Good morning, Princess!' Anna Pavlovna said with a false smile, so unlike her former manner. 'How nice to make your acquaintance.' She turned to the prince. 'You've long been expected, Prince.'

'How is it you sent word to the princess that we weren't going?' the painter rasped in a still angrier whisper, obviously vexed still more that his voice had failed him and he could not give his speech the expression he wanted.

'Ah, my God! I thought we weren't going,' his wife answered irritably.

'How so, when . . .' He started coughing and waved his hand.

The prince tipped his hat and walked on with his daughter.

'Ahh,' he sighed deeply, 'how unfortunate!'

'Yes, papa,' Kitty replied. 'You should know that they have three children, no servants, and almost no means. He gets something from the Academy,' she told him animatedly, trying to stifle the agitation that arose in her owing to the odd change in Anna Pavlovna's manner towards her.

'And here's Mme Stahl,' said Kitty, pointing to a bath-chair in which something lay, dressed in something grey and blue, propped on pillows under an umbrella.

This was Mme Stahl. Behind her stood the stalwart, sullen German hired-man who wheeled her around. Beside her stood a blond Swedish count whom Kitty knew by name. Several sick people lingered about the bath-chair, gazing at this lady as at something extraordinary.

The prince went up to her. And Kitty noticed at once the disturbing flicker of mockery in his eyes. He went up to Mme Stahl and addressed her extremely courteously and pleasantly, in that excellent French which so few speak nowadays.

'I do not know whether you remember me, but I must remind you of myself in order to thank you for your kindness to my daughter,' he said to her, removing his hat and not putting it back on.

'Prince Alexander Shcherbatsky,' said Mme Stahl, raising to him her heavenly eyes, in which Kitty noticed displeasure. 'I'm delighted. I've come to love your daughter so.'

'You are still unwell?'

'I'm used to it by now,' said Mme Stahl, and she introduced the prince and the Swedish count to each other.

'You've changed very little,' the prince said to her. 'I have not had the honour of seeing you for some ten or eleven years.'

'Yes, God gives the cross and the strength to bear it. I often wonder why this life drags on so . . . From the other side!' she said irritably to Varenka, who had wrapped the rug round her legs in the wrong way.

'So as to do good, most likely,' the prince said, laughing with his eyes.

'That is not for us to judge,' said Mme Stahl, noticing the nuance in the prince's expression. 'So you'll send me that book, my gentle Count? I'll be much obliged.' She turned to the young Swede.

'Ah!' cried the prince, seeing the Moscow colonel standing near by, and, with a bow to Mme Stahl, he walked on with his daughter and the Moscow colonel, who joined them.

'There's our aristocracy, Prince!' said the Moscow colonel, wishing to be sarcastic, as he had a grudge against Mme Stahl for not being acquainted with him.

'The same as ever,' replied the prince.

'You knew her before her illness, Prince, that is, before she took to her bed?'

'Yes. She took to it in my time.'

'They say she hasn't got up for ten years.'

'She doesn't get up because she's stubby-legged. She has a very bad figure . . .'

'Papa, it can't be!' cried Kitty.

'Wicked tongues say so, my little friend. And your Varenka does catch it too,' he added. 'Ah, these ailing ladies!'

'Oh, no, papa!' Kitty protested hotly. 'Varenka adores her. And besides, she does so much good! Ask anybody you like! Everybody knows her and Aline Stahl.'

'Maybe,' he said, pressing her arm with his elbow. 'But it's better to do it so that, if you ask, nobody knows.'

Kitty fell silent, not because she had nothing to say, but because she did not want to disclose her secret thoughts even to her father. Strangely, however, despite having prepared herself not to submit to her father's opinion, not to let him into her sanctuary, she felt that the divine image of Mme Stahl that she had carried in her soul for a whole month had vanished irretrievably, as the figure made by a flung-off dress vanishes once you see how the dress is lying. There remained only a stubby-legged woman who stayed lying down because of her bad figure and tormented the docile Varenka for not tucking in her rug properly. And by no effort of imagination could she bring back the former Mme Stahl.

XXXV

The prince imparted his cheerful state of mind to his household, to his acquaintances, and even to the German landlord with whom the Shcherbatskys were staying.

Having come back from the springs with Kitty, the prince, who had invited the colonel, Marya Evgenyevna and Varenka for coffee, ordered a table and chairs to be taken out to the garden under the chestnut tree and had lunch served there. The landlord and servants revived under the influence of his cheerfulness. They knew his generosity, and a half hour later the sick doctor from Hamburg who lived upstairs was looking enviously out the window at this cheerful and healthy Russian company gathered under the chestnut tree. In the shade of the trembling circles of leaves, by the table covered with a white cloth and set with coffeepots, bread, butter, cheese and cold game, sat the princess in a fichu with lilac ribbons, handing out cups and tartines. At the other end sat the prince, eating heartily and talking loudly and cheerily. The prince laid his purchases out beside him – carved boxes, knick-knacks, paper-knives of all kinds, which he had bought in quantity at each watering-place and gave to everybody, including the maid Lischen and the landlord, with whom he joked in his comically bad German, assuring him that it was not the waters that had cured Kitty but his excellent food, especially the prune soup. The princess chuckled at her husband's Russian habits, but was more lively and cheerful than she had been during her entire stay at the spa. The colonel smiled, as always, at the prince's jokes; but with regard to Europe, which he had studied attentively, as he thought, he was on the princess's side. The good-natured Marya Evgenyevna rocked with laughter at everything amusing that the prince said, and Varenka – something Kitty had not seen before – melted into weak but infectious laughter, provoked in her by the prince's witticisms.

All this cheered Kitty up, yet she could not help being preoccupied. She could not solve the problem her father had unwittingly posed for her by his merry view of her friends and the life she had come to like so much. To this problem was added the change in her relations with the Petrovs, which had shown itself so obviously and unpleasantly today. Everyone was merry, but Kitty was unable to be merry, and this pained her still more. She had the same feeling as in childhood, when she was punished by being locked in her room and heard her sisters' merry laughter.

'Well, what did you buy such a mountain of things for?' said the princess, smiling and handing her husband a cup of coffee.

'You go for a walk, and you come to a shop, and they beg you to buy something: "*Erlaucht, Excellenz, Durchlaucht.*"* Well, by the time they get to "*Durchlaucht*" I can't hold out: there go ten thalers.'

'It's only out of boredom,' said the princess.

'Certainly it's out of boredom. Such boredom, my dear, that you don't know what to do with yourself.'

'How can you be bored, Prince? There's so much that's interesting in Germany now,' said Marya Evgenyevna.

'But I know all the interesting things: I know prune soup, I know pea sausages. I know it all.'

'No, like it or not, Prince, their institutions are interesting,' said the colonel.

'What's so interesting? They're all pleased as Punch: they've beaten everybody.[35] Well, but what's there for me to be pleased about? I didn't beat anybody, I just have to take my boots off myself and put them outside the door myself. In the morning I get up, dress myself at once,

* Your grace, your excellency, your highness.

go downstairs and drink vile tea. Home is quite another thing! You wake up without hurrying, get angry at something, grumble a little, come properly to your senses, think things over, don't have to hurry.'

'But time is money, you're forgetting that,' said the colonel.

'Which time! There are times when you'd give a whole month away for fifty kopecks, and others when you wouldn't give up half an hour for any price. Right, Katenka? Why are you so dull?'

'I'm all right.'

'Where are you going? Stay longer,' he said to Varenka.

'I must go home,' said Varenka, getting up and again dissolving in laughter.

Having recovered, she said good-bye and went into the house to get her hat. Kitty followed her. Even Varenka looked different to her now. She was not worse, but she was different from what she had formerly imagined her to be.

'Ah, I haven't laughed like that for a long time!' said Varenka, collecting her parasol and bag. 'He's so nice, your father!'

Kitty was silent.

'When shall we see each other?' asked Varenka.

'*Maman* wanted to call on the Petrovs. You won't be there?' Kitty said, testing Varenka.

'I will,' replied Varenka. 'They're leaving, so I promised to come and help them pack.'

'Well, I'll come, too.'

'No, why should you?'

'Why not? why not? why not?' Kitty said, opening her eyes wide and taking hold of Varenka's parasol to keep her from leaving. 'No, wait, why not?'

'It's just that your father has come, and, then, they're embarrassed with you.'

'No, tell me, why don't you want me to visit the Petrovs often? You don't want it, do you? Why?'

'I didn't say that,' Varenka said calmly.

'No, please tell me!'

'Tell you everything?' asked Varenka.

'Everything, everything!' Kitty repeated.

'There's nothing special, only that Mikhail Alexeevich' – that was the painter's name – 'wanted to leave sooner, and now he doesn't want to leave at all,' Varenka said, smiling.

'Well? Well?' Kitty urged, giving Varenka a dark look.

'Well, and for some reason Anna Pavlovna said he didn't want to leave because you are here. Of course, it was inappropriate, but because of it, because of you, there was a quarrel. And you know how irritable these sick people are.'

Kitty, frowning still more, kept silent, and Varenka alone talked, trying to soothe and calm her and seeing the explosion coming – whether of tears or of words, she did not know.

'So it's better if you don't go . . . And you understand, you won't be offended . . .'

'It serves me right, it serves me right!' Kitty began quickly, snatching the parasol out of Varenka's hands and looking past her friend's eyes.

Varenka wanted to smile, seeing her friend's childish anger, but she was afraid of insulting her.

'How does it serve you right? I don't understand,' she said.

'It serves me right because it was all pretence, because it was all contrived and not from the heart. What did I have to do with some stranger? And it turned out that I caused a quarrel and that I did what nobody asked me to do. Because it was all pretence! pretence! pretence! . . .'

'But what was the purpose of pretending?' Varenka said softly.

'Oh, how vile and stupid! There was no need at all . . . It was all pretence! . . .' she said, opening and closing the parasol.

'But for what purpose?'

'So as to seem better to people, to myself, to God – to deceive everyone. No, I won't fall into that any more! Be bad, but at least don't be a liar, a deceiver!'

'But who is a deceiver?' Varenka said reproachfully. 'You talk as if . . .'

But Kitty was having her fit of temper. She did not let her finish.

'I'm not talking about you, not about you at all. You are perfection. Yes, yes, I know you're perfection; but what's there to do if I'm bad? This wouldn't have happened if I weren't bad. So let me be as I am, but I won't pretend. What do I care about Anna Pavlovna! Let them live as they please, and me as I please. I can't be different . . . And all this is not it, not it! . . .'

'What is not it?' Varenka said in perplexity.

'It's all not it. I can only live by my heart, and you live by rules. I loved you simply, but you probably only so as to save me, to teach me!'

'You're unfair,' said Varenka.

'But I'm not talking about others, I'm talking about myself.'

'Kitty!' came her mother's voice. 'Come here, show Papa your corals.'

Kitty, with a proud look, not having made peace with her friend, took the little box of corals from the table and went to her mother.

'What's the matter? Why are you so red?' her mother and father said in one voice.

'Nothing,' she replied. 'I'll come straight back.' And she ran inside again.

'She's still here!' she thought. 'What shall I tell her? My God, what have I done, what have I said! Why did I offend her? What am I to do? What shall I tell her?' thought Kitty, and she stopped by the door.

Varenka, her hat on and the parasol in her hands, was sitting at the table, examining the spring that Kitty had broken. She raised her head.

'Varenka, forgive me, forgive me!' Kitty whispered, coming up to her. 'I didn't know what I was saying. I . . .'

'I really didn't mean to upset you,' Varenka said, smiling.

Peace was made. But with the arrival of her father that whole world in which Kitty had been living changed for her. She did not renounce all that she had learned, but she understood that she had deceived herself in thinking that she could be what she wished to be. It was as if she came to her senses; she felt all the difficulty of keeping herself, without pretence and boastfulness, on that level to which she had wished to rise; besides, she felt all the weight of that world of grief, sickness and dying people in which she had been living; the efforts she had made to force herself to love it seemed tormenting to her, and she wished all the sooner to go to the fresh air, to Russia, to Yergushovo, where, as she learned from a letter, her sister Dolly had already moved with the children.

But her love for Varenka did not weaken. As she was saying good-bye, Kitty begged her to come and see them in Russia.

'I'll come when you get married,' said Varenka.

'I'll never get married.'

'Well, then I'll never come.'

'Well, then I'll get married only for that. Watch out, now, remember your promise!' said Kitty.

The doctor's predictions came true. Kitty returned home to Russia cured. She was not as carefree and gay as before, but she was at peace. Her Moscow griefs became memories.

Part Three

I

Sergei Ivanovich Koznyshev wanted to rest from intellectual work and, instead of going abroad, as usual, went at the end of May to stay with his brother in the country. He was convinced that country life was the best life. He had now come to enjoy that life at his brother's. Konstantin Levin was very glad, the more so as he no longer expected his brother Nikolai that summer. But, despite his love and respect for Sergei Ivanovich, Konstantin Levin felt awkward in the country with his brother. It was awkward and even unpleasant for him to see his brother's attitude towards the country. For Konstantin Levin the country was the place of life, that is, of joy, suffering, labour; for Sergei Ivanovich the country was, on the one hand, a rest from work and, on the other, an effective antidote to corruption, which he took with pleasure and an awareness of its effectiveness. For Konstantin Levin the country was good in that it presented a field for labour that was unquestionably useful; for Sergei Ivanovich the country was especially good because there one could and should do nothing. Besides that, Sergei Ivanovich's attitude towards the peasantry also made Levin cringe slightly. Sergei Ivanovich said that he loved and knew the peasantry and often conversed with muzhiks, something he was good at doing, without pretence or affectation, and from each such conversation he deduced general data in favour of the peasantry and as proof that he knew them. Konstantin Levin did not like such an attitude towards the peasantry. For Konstantin the peasantry was simply the chief partner in the common labour, and, despite all his respect and a sort of blood-love for the muzhiks that he had probably sucked in, as he himself said, with the milk of his peasant nurse, he, as partner with them in the common cause, while sometimes admiring the strength, meekness and fairness of these people, very often, when the common cause demanded other qualities, became furious with them for their carelessness, slovenliness, drunkenness and lying. If Konstantin Levin had been asked whether he loved the peasantry, he would have been quite at a loss to answer. He loved and did not love the peasantry, as he did people in general. Of course, being a good man, he tended to love people more than not to love them, and therefore the peasantry as well. But it was impossible for him to love or not love the peasantry as something special, because not only did he live with them, not only were all his interests bound up with theirs, but he considered himself part of the peasantry, did not see any special qualities or shortcomings in himself or in them, and could not contrast himself to them. Besides that, though he had lived for a long time in the closest relations with the muzhiks as a master and a mediator, and above all as an adviser (the muzhiks trusted him and came from twenty-five miles away for his advice), he had no definite opinion of the peasantry and would have had the same difficulty replying to the question whether he knew the peasantry as to the question whether he loved the peasantry. To say that he knew them would be the same for him as to say that he knew people. He constantly observed and came to know all sorts of people, muzhik-people among them, whom he considered good and interesting people, and continually noticed new traits in them, changed his previous opinions and formed new ones. Sergei Ivanovich did the contrary. Just as he loved and praised country life in contrast to the life he did not love, so he loved the peasantry in contrast to the class of people he did not love, and so he knew the peasantry as something in contrast to people in general. In his methodical mind certain forms of peasant life acquired a clear shape, deduced in part from peasant life itself, but mainly from this contrast. He never changed his opinion about the peasantry or his sympathetic attitude towards them.

In the disagreements that occurred between the brothers during their discussions of the peasantry, Sergei Ivanovich always defeated his brother, precisely because Sergei Ivanovich had definite notions about the peasantry, their character, properties and tastes; whereas Konstantin Levin had no definite and unchanging notions, so that in these arguments Konstantin was always caught contradicting himself.

For Sergei Ivanovich his younger brother was a nice fellow with a heart *well placed* (as he put it in French), but with a mind which, though rather quick, was subject to momentary impressions and therefore filled with contradictions. With the condescension of an older brother, he occasionally explained the meaning of things to him, but could find no pleasure in arguing with him, because he beat him too easily.

Konstantin Levin regarded his brother as a man of great intelligence and education, noble in the highest sense of the word, and endowed with the ability to act for the common good. But, in the depths of his soul, the older he became and the more closely he got to know his brother, the more often it occurred to him that this ability to act for the common good, of which he felt himself completely deprived, was perhaps not a virtue but, on the contrary, a lack of something – not a lack of good, honest and noble desires and tastes, but a lack of life force, of what is known as heart, of that yearning which makes a man choose one out of all the countless paths in life presented to him and desire that one alone. The more he knew his brother, the more he noticed that Sergei Ivanovich and many other workers for the common good had not been brought to this love of the common good by the heart, but had reasoned in their minds that it was good to be concerned with it and were concerned with it only because of that. And Levin was confirmed in this surmise by observing that his brother took questions about the common good and the immortality of the soul no closer to heart than those about a game of chess or the clever construction of a new machine.

Besides that, Konstantin Levin also felt awkward in the country with his brother because in the country, especially during the summer, he was constantly busy with the farming, and the long summer day was not long enough for him to do everything he had to do, while Sergei Ivanovich rested. But though he rested now, that is, did not work on his book, he was so used to intellectual activity that he liked to utter in beautifully concise form the thoughts that occurred to him and liked it when there was someone there to listen to him. His most usual and natural listener was his brother. And therefore, despite the friendly simplicity of their relations, Konstantin felt awkward leaving him alone. Sergei Ivanovich liked to stretch out on the grass in the sun and lie there like that, baking and lazily chatting.

'You wouldn't believe,' he said to his brother, 'how I love this rustic idleness. There's not a thought in my head, you could play ninepins in it.'

But Konstantin Levin was bored sitting and listening to him, especially since he knew that, without him, they were carting dung to the fields that were not yet crossploughed, and would heap it up any old way if he was not watching; and they would not screw the shares to the ploughs, but would take them off and then say that iron ploughs were a worthless invention, nothing like the good old wooden plough, and so on.

'Enough walking about in the heat for you,' Sergei Ivanovich would say to him.

'No, I'll just run over to the office for a minute,' Levin would say, and dash off to the fields.

II

In the first days of June it so happened that the nurse and housekeeper Agafya Mikhailovna, while carrying a jar of freshly pickled mushrooms to the cellar, slipped, fell, and dislocated her wrist. The district doctor came, a talkative young man who had just finished his studies. He examined the wrist, said it was not dislocated, applied compresses and, having stayed for dinner, obviously enjoyed conversing with the famous Sergei Ivanovich Koznyshev, and to show his enlightened view of things, told him all the local gossip, complaining about the bad state of zemstvo affairs. Sergei Ivanovich listened attentively, asked questions and, excited to have a new listener, talked a lot and produced several apt and weighty observations, respectfully appreciated by the young doctor, and recovered the animated state of mind, so familiar to his brother, to which he was usually brought by a brilliant and lively conversation. After the doctor's departure, Sergei Ivanovich expressed a wish to go to the river with a fishing rod. He liked fishing and seemed to take pride in being able to like such a stupid occupation.

Konstantin Levin, who had to go to the ploughing and the meadows, volunteered to take his brother in the cabriolet.

It was that time of year, the turning point of summer, when the harvest of the current year is assured, when concerns about the sowing for the year to come begin and the mowing is at hand, when the rye has all come into ear and its grey-green, unswollen, still light ears sway in the wind, when green oats, with clumps of yellow grass scattered among them, thrust themselves unevenly amidst the late-sown crops, when the early buckwheat is already bushing out, covering the ground, when the fallow fields are half ploughed, leaving the cattle paths beaten down hard as stone, which the plough could not break up; when crusted-over heaps of dung give off their smell at dawn and sunset together with the honeyed grasses, and in the bottoms, awaiting the scythe, the intact meadows stand in an unbroken sea, with blackening piles of weeded sorrel stalks here and there.

It was that time when a short break comes in the farm work, before the beginning of the harvest, annually repeated and annually calling on all the strength of the peasantry. The crops were excellent, and clear, hot summer days set in, with short, dewy nights.

The brothers had to pass through a wood in order to reach the meadows. Sergei Ivanovich kept admiring the beauty of the wood overgrown with leaves, pointing out to his brother now an old linden, dark on its shady side, rippling with yellow stipules and ready to flower, now the brilliant emerald of that year's young shoots on the trees. Konstantin Levin did not like talking or hearing about the beauty of nature. For him words took away the beauty of what he saw. He agreed with his brother, but involuntarily began thinking of other things. When they reached the other side of the wood, all his attention was absorbed by the sight of a fallow field on a hillock, in some places yellow with grass, in others trodden down and cut criss-cross or dotted with heaps, or even ploughed under. A file of carts moved across the field. Levin counted the carts and was pleased that they were bringing out all that was necessary, and at the sight of the meadows his thoughts turned to the mowing. He always experienced something that especially touched him to the quick during the haymaking. Driving up to the meadow, Levin stopped the horse.

The morning dew lingered below in the thick undergrowth of the grass, and Sergei Ivanovich, to avoid getting his feet wet, asked to be taken across the meadow in the cabriolet, to that willow bush where the perch took the bait so well. Sorry as Konstantin Levin was to crush his grass, he drove into the meadow. The tall grass softly twined around the wheels and the horse's legs, leaving its seeds on the wet spokes and hubs.

His brother sat down under the bush, sorting his fishing rods, while Levin led the horse away, tied it up, and went into the enormous grey-green sea of the meadow, unstirred by the wind. The silky grass with its ripening seeds reached his waist in the places flooded in spring.

Cutting across the meadow, Konstantin Levin came out on the road and met an old man with a swollen eye, carrying a hive of bees.

'Did you catch it, Fomich?' he asked.

'Catch it, Konstantin Dmitrich! I'll be happy to keep the one I have. It's the second time a swarm got away . . . Thanks be, the boys rode after it.

Yours are ploughing. They unhitched a horse and rode after it . . .'

'Well, what do you say, Fomich – shall we mow or wait?'

'There, now! We'd say wait till St Peter's.[1] But you always mow earlier. Why not? The grass is fine, thank God. The cattle will have plenty.'

'And the weather, what do you think?'

'That's God's doing. Maybe the weather'll hold.'

Levin went back to his brother. He had caught nothing, but Sergei Ivanovich was not bored and seemed in the most cheerful spirits. Levin saw that he had been stirred by the conversation with the doctor and wanted to talk. Levin, on the contrary, wanted to get home quickly, to arrange for mowers to be called in by tomorrow and resolve the doubt concerning the mowing, which greatly preoccupied him.

'Let's go then,' he said.

'What's the hurry? Let's sit here. How soaked you are, though! I'm not catching anything, but it's nice here. Any hunting is good in that you have to do with nature. This steely water is so lovely!' he said. 'Those meadows along the bank,' he went on, 'always remind me of a riddle – do you know it? The grass says to the water: we'll sway and sway.'

'I don't know that riddle,' Levin replied glumly.

III

'You know, I've been thinking about you,' said Sergei Ivanovich. 'What's happening in your district is unheard-of, from what this doctor tells me – he's quite an intelligent fellow. I've said to you before and I'll say it again: it's not good that you don't go to the meetings and have generally withdrawn from zemstvo affairs. Of course, if decent people start withdrawing, God knows how things will go. We pay money, it goes to pay salaries, and there are no schools, no medical aid, no midwives, no dispensaries, nothing.'

'But I tried,' Levin answered softly and reluctantly, 'I just can't! There's no help for it!'

'Why can't you? I confess, I don't understand. Indifference, inability, I don't accept; can it be simple laziness?'

'Neither the one, nor the other, nor the third. I tried and I see that I can't do anything,' said Levin.

He hardly entered into what his brother was saying. Peering across the river at the ploughed field, he made out something black, but could not tell whether it was a horse or the mounted steward.

'Why can't you do anything? You made an attempt, it didn't succeed as you wanted, and you gave up. Where's your self-esteem?'

'Self-esteem,' said Levin, cut to the quick by his brother's words, 'is something I do not understand. If I had been told at the university that others understood integral calculus and I did not – there you have self-esteem. But here one should first be convinced that one needs to have a certain ability in these matters and, chiefly, that they are all very important.'

'And what, then? Aren't they important?' said Sergei Ivanovich, also cut to the quick that his brother should find what interested him unimportant, and especially that he was obviously hardly listening to him.

'It doesn't seem important to me, I'm not taken with it, what do you want? . . .' answered Levin, having made out that what he saw was the steward, and that the steward had probably allowed the muzhiks to quit ploughing. They were turning their ploughs over. 'Can it be they're already done ploughing?' he thought.

'But listen,' the elder brother said, his handsome, intelligent face scowling, 'there are limits to everything. It's all very well to be an eccentric and to be sincere and to dislike falseness – I know all that; but what you're saying either has no meaning or has a very bad meaning. When you find it unimportant that the peasantry, whom you love, as you assure me . . .'

'I never assured him,' thought Konstantin Levin.

'. . . dies without help? Crude midwives kill off babies, and the peasantry rot in ignorance and remain in the power of every scrivener, and you are given the means to help them, but you don't help them, because in your opinion it's not important.'

And Sergei Ivanovich confronted him with a dilemma:

'Either you're so undeveloped that you cannot see all that you could do, or you cannot give up your peace, your vanity, whatever, in order to do it.'

Konstantin Levin felt that it only remained for him to submit or to confess to a lack of love for the common cause. And this offended and upset him.

'Both the one and the other,' he said resolutely. 'I don't see how it's possible . . .'

'What? Impossible to give medical help, if money is placed in the right way?'

'Impossible, it seems to me . . . In our district, with its three thousand square miles, with our slush, blizzards, seasonal field work, I see no possibility of providing medical help everywhere. Besides, I generally don't believe in medicine.'

'Well, excuse me, but that's not fair . . . I can give you a thousand examples . . . Well, and schools?'

'Why schools?'

'What are you saying? Can there be any doubt of the usefulness of education? If it's good for you, it's good for everyone.'

Konstantin Levin felt himself morally driven into a corner and therefore got excited and involuntarily let out the main reason for his indifference to the common cause.

'Maybe all that is good, but why should I worry about setting up medical centres that I'll never use and schools that I won't send my children to, that the peasants don't want to send their children to either, and that I have no firm belief that they ought to send them to?' he said.

Sergei Ivanovich was momentarily surprised by this unexpected view of things, but he at once devised a new plan of attack.

He paused, raised one rod, dropped the line in again, and turned to his brother with a smile.

'Well, excuse me . . . First, there's a need for medical centres. Here we just summoned the district doctor for Agafya Mikhailovna.'

'Well, I think her arm will stay crooked.'

'That's still a question . . . And then, a literate muzhik or worker is more needful and valuable to you.'

'No, ask anybody you like,' Konstantin Levin replied resolutely, 'a literate peasant is much worse as a worker. And the roads can't be repaired, and bridges are no sooner put up than they steal them.'

'However,' said the frowning Sergei Ivanovich, who did not like contradictions, especially the sort that kept jumping from one thing to another and introduced new arguments without any connection, so that it was impossible to know which to answer, 'however, that's not the point. Excuse me. Do you acknowledge that education is good for the peasantry?'

'I do,' Levin said inadvertently, and immediately thought that he had not said what he thought. He sensed that, once he acknowledged that, it would be proved to him that he was speaking rubbish that did not make any sense. How it would be proved to him he did not know, but he knew that it would doubtless be proved to him logically, and he waited for this proof.

The argument turned out to be much simpler than he expected.

'If you acknowledge it as a good,' said Sergei Ivanovich, 'then, being an honest man, you can't help liking and sympathizing with such a cause and therefore working for it.'

'But I have not yet acknowledged it as a good,' said Konstantin Levin, blushing.

'How's that? You just said . . .'

'That is, I do not acknowledge it either as good or as possible.'

'You can't know that without having tried.'

'Well, suppose,' said Levin, though he did not suppose it at all, 'suppose it's so; but all the same I don't see why I should worry about it.'

'How do you mean?'

'No, since we're talking, explain it to me from a philosophical point of view,' said Levin.

'I don't understand what philosophy has got to do with it,' said Sergei Ivanovich, in such a tone, it seemed to Levin, as if he did not recognize his brother's right to discuss philosophy. And that vexed Levin.

'It's got this to do with it!' he began hotly. 'I think that the motive force of all our actions is, after all, personal happiness. In our present-day zemstvo institutions I, as a nobleman, see nothing that contributes to my well-being. The roads are no better and cannot be better; my horses carry me over the bad ones as well. I have no need of doctors and centres, I have no need of any justice of the peace – I've never turned to one and never will. Schools I not only do not need but also find harmful, as I told you. For me the zemstvo institutions are simply an obligation to pay six kopecks an acre, go to town, sleep with bedbugs, and listen to all sorts of nonsense and vileness, and personal interest does not move me to do that.'

'Excuse me,' Sergei Ivanovich interrupted with a smile, 'but personal interest did not move us to work for the emancipation of the serfs, and yet we did.'

'No!' Konstantin interrupted, growing more heated. 'The emancipation of the serfs was a different matter. There was a personal interest. We wanted to throw off the yoke that oppressed us and all good people. But to be a council member,[2] arguing about how many privy cleaners are needed and how the sewer pipes should be installed in a town I don't live in; to be a juror and judge a muzhik who has stolen a ham, and listen for six hours to defence lawyers and prosecutors pouring out all sorts of drivel, and hear the foreman of the jury ask my old Alyoshka-the-fool: "Mister defendant, do you acknowledge the fact of the stolen ham?" "Wha?"'

Konstantin Levin was already side-tracked, impersonating the foreman of the jury and Alyoshka-the-fool; it seemed to him that it was all to the point.

But Sergei Ivanovich shrugged his shoulders.

'Well, what do you mean to say?'

'I only mean to say that I will always defend with all my might those rights that I . . . that touch on my interests. When the gendarmes searched us as students and read our letters, I was ready to defend those rights with all my might, to defend my rights to education, to freedom. I understand military service, which touches the future of my children, my brothers and myself. I'm ready to discuss anything that concerns me. But to decide how to dispose of forty thousand in zemstvo funds, or to judge Alyoshka-the-fool – that I do not understand and cannot do.'

Konstantin Levin spoke as if his words had burst their dam. Sergei Ivanovich smiled.

'And if you were brought to trial tomorrow, do you mean you'd rather be tried by the old criminal courts?'[3]

'I won't be brought to trial. I'm not going to kill anybody, and I have no need of all that. Really!' he went on, again skipping to something completely inappropriate, 'our zemstvo institutions and all that – it's like the birches we stick up on the day of the Trinity,[4] so that it looks like the forest that grew up by itself in Europe, and I can't put my heart into watering and believing in those birches!'

Sergei Ivanovich merely shrugged his shoulders, expressing by this gesture his surprise at the appearance out of nowhere of these birches in their discussion, though he immediately understood what his brother meant to say by it.

'Excuse me, but one cannot argue that way,' he observed.

But Konstantin Levin wanted to vindicate himself in this shortcoming which he knew he had, in his indifference to the common good, and he went on.

'I think,' said Konstantin, 'that no activity can be solid unless it's based on personal interest. That is a general truth, a philosophical one,' he said, resolutely repeating the word 'philosophical', as if wishing to show that he, too, had the right, like anyone else, to speak of philosophy.

Sergei Ivanovich smiled once more. 'And he, too, has some sort of philosophy of his own to serve his inclinations,' he thought.

'Well, you should leave philosophy alone,' he said. 'The chief task of philosophy in all ages has consisted precisely in finding the connection that necessarily exists between personal and common interests. But that is not the point, the point is that I must correct your comparison. The birches are not stuck in, they are planted or seeded, and they ought to be carefully tended. Only those nations have a future, only those nations can be called historical, that have a sense of what is important and significant in their institutions, and value them.'

And Sergei Ivanovich transferred the question to the philosophical-historical realm, inaccessible to Konstantin Levin, and showed him all the incorrectness of his view.

'As regards your not liking it, forgive me, but that is our Russian laziness and grand manner, and I'm sure that with you it's a temporary error and will pass.'

Konstantin was silent. He felt himself roundly beaten, but together with that he felt that his brother had not understood what he had wanted to say. Only he did not know why he had not understood: whether it was because he had not been able to say clearly what he meant, or because his brother had been unwilling or unable to understand him. But he did not go deeper into these thoughts and, without objecting to his brother, began thinking about a completely different matter, a personal one for him.

Sergei Ivanovich reeled in the last line, Konstantin untied the horse, and they drove off.

IV

The personal matter that had occupied Levin during his conversation with his brother was the following: once last year, coming to the mowing and getting angry with the steward, Levin had used his remedy for calming down – he had taken a scythe from a muzhik and begun mowing.

He had liked the work so much that he had taken to mowing several more times; he had mowed the whole meadow in front of the house, and since the spring of that year he had made a plan for himself – to spend whole days mowing with the muzhiks. Since his brother's arrival, he had been pondering: to mow or not? He was ashamed to leave his brother alone for whole days, and he feared that his brother would laugh at him for it. But having walked through the meadow, recalling his impressions of mowing, he was now almost decided that he would mow. And after the vexing conversation with his brother, he again recalled this intention.

'I need physical movement, otherwise my character definitely deteriorates,' he thought, and he decided to mow no matter how awkward it was in front of his brother and the peasants.

In the evening Konstantin Levin went to the office, gave orders about the work, and sent to the villages to summon mowers for tomorrow to mow the Viburnum Meadow, the biggest and best.

'And please send my scythe to Titus to be sharpened and brought along tomorrow – perhaps I'll do some mowing myself,' he said, trying not to be embarrassed.

The steward smiled and said:

'Yes, sir.'

That evening over tea Levin told his brother as well.

'The weather seems to have settled,' he said. 'Tomorrow I'll start mowing.'

'I like that work very much,' said Sergei Ivanovich.

'I like it terribly. I've mowed with the muzhiks occasionally, and tomorrow I intend to mow the whole day.'

Sergei Ivanovich raised his head and looked at his brother with curiosity.

'How do you mean? On a par with the muzhiks, the whole day?'

'Yes, it's very satisfying,' said Levin.

'It's wonderful as physical exercise, only you'll hardly be able to hold out,' Sergei Ivanovich said without any mockery.

'I've tried it. It's hard at first, but then you get into the rhythm. I don't think I'll lag behind . . .'

'Really! But tell me, how do the muzhiks look at it? They must be chuckling over the master's whimsies.'

'No, I don't think so; but it's such cheerful and at the same time such hard work, that one has no time to think.'

'But how are you going to have dinner with them? It's a bit awkward to send Lafite[5] and roast turkey to you out there.'

'No, I'll just come home when they take their break.'

The next morning Konstantin Levin got up earlier than usual, but tasks on the estate detained him and when he came to the mowing, the mowers had already started the second swath.

From the top of the hill there opened out before him, at its foot, the shady, already mowed part of the meadow, with greying rows and black heaps of caftans, which the mowers had taken off where they started their first swath.

As he rode nearer, the muzhiks came into his view, following each other in a strung out line and swinging their scythes variedly, some in caftans, some just in shirts. He counted forty-two men.

They moved slowly along the uneven lower edge of the meadow, where the old dam was. Levin recognized some of his people. There was old Yermil in a very long white shirt, bent over and swinging his scythe; there was the young lad Vaska, Levin's former coachman, taking each swath at one swing. There was also Titus, Levin's tutor in mowing, a small, skinny muzhik. He walked straight ahead without bending, as if playing with his scythe, cutting down his wide swath.

Levin got off his horse, tethered it by the road, and met Titus, who took a second scythe from a bush and handed it over.

'It's ready, master; like a razor, mows by itself,' said Titus, doffing his hat with a smile and handing him the scythe.

Levin took the scythe and began to get the feel of it. Their swaths finished, the sweaty and cheerful mowers came out on the road one after another, chuckling and greeting the master. They all gazed at him, but nobody said anything until a tall old man with a wrinkled, beardless face, in a sheepskin coat, came out on the road and addressed him.

'Watch out, master, once you start there's no stopping!' he said, and Levin heard repressed laughter among the mowers.

'I'll try to keep up,' he said, taking a stand behind Titus and waiting for the moment to start.

'Watch out now,' the old man repeated.

Titus cleared his place and Levin followed him. The grass near the road was low, and Levin, who had done no mowing for a long time and was embarrassed by the looks directed at him, mowed poorly for the first few minutes, though he swung strongly. Voices were heard behind him:

'It's not hafted right, the handle's too long, see how he has to bend,' one voice said.

'Bear down on the heel,' said another.

'Never mind, he'll get himself set right,' the old man went on. 'See, there he goes . . . The swath's too wide, you'll get tired . . . He's the owner, never fear, he's doing his best! And look at the hired men! Our kind would get it in the neck for that.'

The grass became softer, and Levin, listening but not answering, and trying to mow the best he could, followed after Titus. They went some hundred steps. Titus kept on without stopping, without showing the slightest fatigue, but Levin was already beginning to fear that he would not hold out, he was so tired.

He felt he was swinging with his last strength and decided to ask Titus to stop. But just then Titus himself stopped and, bending down, took some grass, wiped the blade and began to whet it. Levin straightened up and, taking a deep breath, looked back. Behind him came a muzhik, and evidently he was also tired because he stopped at once, before reaching Levin, and began to whet. Titus whetted his and Levin's scythes, and they went on.

The second time it was all the same. Titus moved on swing after swing, without pausing and without tiring. Levin followed him, trying not to lag behind, and finding it harder and harder: there came a moment when he felt he had no strength left, but just then Titus stopped and whetted his scythe.

So they finished the first swath. And this long swath seemed especially hard to Levin; but then, when the swath was finished and Titus, shouldering his scythe, went back with slow steps over his own heel-prints in the mowing, and Levin went back the same way over his own mowing, though sweat streamed down his face and dripped from his nose, and his back was all wet as if soaked with water, he felt very good. He rejoiced especially knowing now that he would hold out.

His satisfaction was poisoned only by the fact that his swath did not look good. 'I'll swing less with my arm, more with my whole body,' he thought, comparing Titus's swath, straight as an arrow, with his own rambling and unevenly laid swath.

Titus had taken the first swath very quickly, as Levin had noticed, probably wanting to test his master, and the swath happened to be a long one. The following swaths were easier, but even so Levin had to strain all his strength not to lag behind the muzhiks.

He thought of nothing, desired nothing, except not to lag behind and to do the best job he could. He heard only the clang of scythes and ahead of him saw Titus's erect figure moving on, the curved semicircle of the mowed space, grass and flower-heads bending down slowly and wavily about the blade of his scythe, and ahead of him the end of the swath, where rest would come.

Not understanding what it was or where it came from, in the midst of his work he suddenly felt a pleasant sensation of coolness on his hot, sweaty shoulders. He glanced at the sky while his blade was being whetted. A low, heavy cloud had come over it, and big drops of rain were falling. Some muzhiks went for their caftans and put them on; others, just like Levin, merely shrugged their shoulders joyfully under the pleasant freshness.

They finished another swath and another. They went through long swaths, short swaths, with bad grass, with good grass. Levin lost all awareness of time and had no idea whether it was late or early. A change now began to take place in his work which gave him enormous pleasure. In the midst of his work moments came to him when he forgot what he was doing and began to feel light, and in those moments his swath came out as even and good as Titus's. But as soon as he remembered what he was doing and started trying to do better, he at once felt how hard the work was and the swath came out badly.

Having finished one more swath, he wanted to walk back again, but Titus stopped, went over to the old man and quietly said something to him. They both looked at the sun. 'What are they talking about? Why doesn't he go back down the swath?' thought Levin, to whom it did not occur that the muzhiks had been mowing without a break for no less than four hours and it was time for them to have breakfast.

'Breakfast, master,' the old man said.

'Already? Well, let's have breakfast then.'

Levin handed the scythe back to Titus and, together with the muzhiks, who were going to their caftans to fetch bread, walked to his horse over the swaths of the long mowed space lightly sprinkled with rain. Only now did he realize that his guess about the weather had been wrong and that the rain was wetting his hay.

'The hay will be spoiled,' he said.

'Never mind, master, mow when it rains, rake when it shines!' said the old man.

Levin untethered the horse and went home to have coffee.

Sergei Ivanovich had just risen. After having coffee, Levin went back to the mowing, before Sergei Ivanovich had time to get dressed and come out to the dining room.

V

After breakfast Levin landed not in his former place in the line, but between an old joker who invited him to be his neighbour and a young muzhik married only since autumn, for whom it was his first summer of mowing.

The old man, holding himself erect, went ahead, moving his turned-out feet steadily and widely, and in a precise and steady movement that apparently cost him no more effort than swinging his arms while walking, as if in play, laid down a tall, uniform swath. Just as though it were not him but the sharp scythe alone that swished through the succulent grass.

Behind Levin came young Mishka. His fair young face, with a wisp of fresh grass bound round his hair, worked all over with the effort; but as soon as anyone looked at him, he smiled. He clearly would sooner have died than admit it was hard for him.

Levin went between them. In this hottest time the mowing did not seem so hard to him. The sweat that drenched him cooled him off, and the sun, burning on his back, head and arm with its sleeve rolled to the elbow, gave him firmness and perseverance in his work; more and more often those moments of unconsciousness came, when it was possible for him not to think of what he was doing. The scythe cut by itself. These were happy moments. More joyful still were the moments when, coming to the river, where the swaths ended, the old man would wipe his scythe with thick, wet grass, rinse its steel in the cool water, dip his whetstone box and offer it to Levin.

'Have a sip of my kvass![6] Good, eh?' he said with a wink.

And, indeed, Levin had never before drunk such a drink as this warm water with green floating in it and tasting of the rusty tin box. And right after that came a blissfully slow walk with scythe in hand, during which he could wipe off the streaming sweat, fill his lungs with air, look at the whole stretched-out line of mowers and at what was going on around him in the woods and fields.

The longer Levin mowed, the more often he felt those moments of oblivion during which it was no longer his arms that swung the scythe, but the scythe itself that lent motion to his whole body, full of life and conscious of itself, and, as if by magic, without a thought of it, the work got rightly and neatly done on its own. These were the most blissful moments.

It was hard only when he had to stop this by now unconscious movement and think, when he had to mow around a tussock or an unweeded clump of sorrel. The old man did it easily. The tussock would come, he would change movement and, using the heel or tip of the scythe, cut around it on both sides with short strokes. And as he did so, he studied and observed what opened up before him; now he picked off a corn-flag, ate it or offered it to Levin, now flung aside a branch with the tip of his scythe, or examined a quail's nest from which the female had flown up right under the scythe, or caught a snake that had got in his way and, picking it up with the scythe as with a fork, showed it to Levin and tossed it aside.

For Levin and the young lad behind him these changes of movement were difficult. Both of them, having got into one strenuous rhythm, were caught up in the passion of work and were unable to change it and at the same time observe what was in front of them.

Levin did not notice how the time passed. If he had been asked how long he had been mowing, he would have said half an hour – yet it was nearly dinner-time. Walking back down the swath, the old man drew Levin's attention to the girls and boys, barely visible, coming towards the mowers from different directions, through the tall grass and along the road, their little arms weighed down with bundles of bread and jugs of kvass stoppered with rags.

'See the midges come crawling!' he said, pointing to them, and he looked at the sun from under his hand.

They finished two more swaths and the old man stopped.

'Well, master, it's dinner-time!' he said resolutely. And, having reached the river, the mowers set out across the swaths towards their caftans, near which the children who had brought their dinners sat waiting for them. The muzhiks gathered together – those from far away under their carts, those from near by under a willow bush on which they heaped some grass.

Levin sat down with them; he did not want to leave.

Any constraint before the master had long since vanished. The muzhiks were preparing to have dinner. Some were washing, the young fellows were bathing in the river, others were preparing a place to rest, untying sacks of bread and unstopping jugs of kvass. The old man crumbled some bread into a bowl, kneaded it with a spoon handle, poured in some water from his whetstone box, cut more bread, sprinkled it with salt, and turned eastward to pray.

'Here, master, try a bit of my mash,' he said, squatting down in front of the bowl.

The mash tasted so good that Levin changed his mind about going home for dinner. He ate with the old man and got to talking with him about his domestic affairs, taking a lively interest in them, and told him about all his own affairs and all circumstances that might interest the old man. He felt closer to him than to his brother, and involuntarily smiled from the tenderness that he felt for this man. When the old man stood up again, prayed, and lay down right there under the bush, putting some grass under his head, Levin did the same and, despite the flies and bugs, clinging, persistent in the sunlight, tickling his sweaty face and body, he fell asleep at once and awoke only when the sun had passed over to the other side of the bush and begun to reach him. The old man had long been awake and sat whetting the young fellows' scythes.

Levin looked around him and did not recognize the place, everything was so changed. An enormous expanse of the meadow had been mowed, and its already fragrant swaths shone with a special new shine in the slanting rays of the evening sun. The mowed-around bushes by the river, the river itself, invisible before but now shining like steel in its curves, the peasants stirring and getting up, the steep wall of grass at the unmowed side of the meadow, and the hawks wheeling above the bared meadow – all this was completely new. Coming to his senses, Levin began to calculate how much had been mowed and how much more could be done that day.

They had done an extraordinary amount of work for forty-two men. The whole of the big meadow, which in the time of the corvée[7] used to be mowed in two days by thirty scythes, was already mowed. Only some corners with short swaths remained unmowed. But Levin wanted to get as much mowed as possible that day and was vexed with the sun for going down so quickly. He felt no fatigue at all; he only wanted to work more and more quickly and get as much done as possible.

'What do you think, can we still mow Mashka's Knoll?' he said to the old man.

'As God wills, the sun's not high. Or might there be some vodka for the lads?'

At break time, when they sat down again and the smokers lit up, the old man announced to the lads that if they 'mow Mashka's Knoll – there'll be vodka in it'.

'See if we can't! Go to it, Titus! We'll clear it in a wink! You can eat tonight. Go to it!' came the cries, and, finishing their bread, the mowers went to it.

'Well, lads, keep the pace!' said Titus, and he went ahead almost at a trot.

'Get a move on!' said the old man, hustling after him and catching up easily. 'I'll cut you down! Watch out!'

And it was as if young and old vied with each other in the mowing. But no matter how they hurried, they did not ruin the grass, and the swaths were laid as cleanly and neatly. A little patch left in a corner was cleared in five minutes. The last mowers were coming to the end of their rows when the ones in front threw their caftans over their shoulders and went across the road to Mashka's Knoll.

The sun was already low over the trees when, with whetstone boxes clanking, they entered the wooded gully of Mashka's Knoll. The grass was waist-high in the middle of the hollow, tender and soft, broad-bladed, speckled with cow-wheat here and there under the trees.

After a brief discussion – to move lengthwise or crosswise – Prokhor Yermilin, also a famous mower, a huge, swarthy man, went to the front. He finished the first swath, went back and moved over, and everybody started falling into line after him, going downhill through the hollow and up to the very edge of the wood. The sun sank behind the wood. The dew was already falling, and only those mowing on the hill were in the sun, while below, where mist was rising, and on the other side, they walked in the fresh, dewy shade. The work was in full swing.

Sliced down with a succulent sound and smelling of spice, the grass lay in high swaths. Crowding on all sides in the short swaths, their whetstone boxes clanking, to the noise of scythes clashing, of a whetstone swishing along a sharpening blade, and of merry shouts, the mowers urged each other on.

Levin went as before between the young lad and the old man. The old man, who had put on his sheepskin jacket, was just as gay, jocular and free in his movements as ever. In the wood they were constantly happening upon boletus mushrooms, sodden in the succulent grass, which their scythes cut down. But the old man, each time he met a mushroom, bent down, picked it up, and put it into his jacket. 'Another treat for my old woman,' he would mutter.

Easy as it was to mow the wet and tender grass, it was hard going up and down the steep slopes of the gully. But the old man was not hindered by that. Swinging his scythe in the same way, with the small, firm steps of his feet shod in big bast shoes, he slowly climbed up the steep slope, and, despite the trembling of his whole body and of his trousers hanging lower than his shirt, he did not miss a single blade of grass or a single mushroom on his way and joked with the muzhiks and Levin just as before. Levin came after him and often thought that he would surely fall, going up such a steep slope with a scythe, where it was hard to climb even without a scythe; but he climbed it and did what was needed. He felt that some external force moved him.

VI

Mashka's Knoll was mowed. They finished the last swaths, put on their caftans and cheerfully went home. Levin got on his horse and, regretfully taking leave of the muzhiks, rode homewards. He looked back from the hill; the men could not be seen in the mist rising from below; he could only hear merry, coarse voices, loud laughter, and the sound of clashing scythes.

Sergei Ivanovich had long ago finished dinner and was drinking water with lemon and ice in his room, looking through some newspapers and magazines that had just come in the post, when Levin, with his tangled hair sticking to his sweaty brow and his dark, drenched back and chest, burst into his room talking cheerfully.

'And we did the whole meadow! Ah, how good, it's remarkable! And how have you been?' said Levin, completely forgetting yesterday's unpleasant conversation.

'Heavens, what a sight!' said Sergei Ivanovich, glancing round at his brother with displeasure in the first moment. 'The door, shut the door!' he cried out. 'You must have let in a good dozen.'

Sergei Ivanovich could not bear flies. He opened the window in his room only at night and kept the doors carefully shut.

'By God, not a one. And if I did, I'll catch it. You wouldn't believe what a pleasure it was! How did your day go?'

'Very well. But did you really mow for the whole day? I suppose you're hungry as a wolf. Kuzma has everything ready for you.'

'No, I don't even want to eat. I ate there. But I will go and wash.'

'Well, go, go, and I'll join you presently,' said Sergei Ivanovich, shaking his head as he looked at his brother. 'Go, go quickly,' he added with a smile and, gathering up his books, he got ready to go. He suddenly felt cheerful himself and did not want to part from his brother. 'Well, and where were you when it rained?'

'What rain? It barely sprinkled. I'll come presently, then. You had a nice day, then? Well, that's excellent.' And Levin went to get dressed.

Five minutes later the brothers came together in the dining room. Though it seemed to Levin that he did not want to eat, and he sat down to dinner only so as not to offend Kuzma, once he started eating, the dinner seemed remarkably tasty to him. Smiling, Sergei Ivanovich looked at him.

'Ah, yes, there's a letter for you,' he said. 'Kuzma, bring it from downstairs, please. And see that you close the door.'

The letter was from Oblonsky. Levin read it aloud. Oblonsky was writing from Petersburg: 'I received a letter from Dolly, she's in Yergushovo, and nothing's going right for her. Go and see her, please, help her with your advice, you know everything. She'll be so glad to see you. She's quite alone, poor thing. My mother-in-law and the others are all still abroad.'

'That's excellent! I'll certainly go and see them,' said Levin. 'Or else let's go together. She's such a nice woman. Isn't it so?'

'Are they near by?'

'Some twenty miles. Maybe twenty-five. But the road is excellent. An excellent trip.'

'Delighted,' said Sergei Ivanovich, still smiling.

The sight of his younger brother had immediately disposed him to cheerfulness.

'Well, you've got quite an appetite!' he said, looking at his red-brown sunburnt face and neck bent over the plate.

'Excellent! You wouldn't believe what a good regimen it is against all sorts of foolishness. I want to enrich medical science with a new term: *Arbeitskur*.'*

'Well, it seems you've no need for that.'

'No, but for various nervous patients.'

'Yes, it ought to be tried. And I did want to come to the mowing to have a look at you, but the heat was so unbearable that I got no further than the wood. I sat a little, then walked through the wood to the village, met your nurse there and sounded her out about the muzhiks' view of

* Work-cure.

you. As I understand, they don't approve of it. She said: "It's not the master's work." Generally it seems to me that in the peasants' understanding there is a very firmly defined requirement for certain, as they put it, "master's" activities. And they don't allow gentlemen to go outside the limits defined by their understanding.'

'Maybe. But I've never experienced such a pleasure in my life. And there's no harm in it. Isn't that so?' Levin replied. 'What can I do if they don't like it? Nothing, I suppose. Eh?'

'I can see,' Sergei Ivanovich continued, 'that you're generally pleased with your day.'

'Very pleased. We mowed the whole meadow. And what an old man I made friends with there! Such a delightful man, you'd never imagine it!'

'Well, so you're pleased with your day. And so am I. First, I solved two chess problems, one of them a very nice one – it opens with a pawn. I'll show you. And then I was thinking about our conversation yesterday.'

'What? Our conversation yesterday?' said Levin, blissfully narrowing his eyes and puffing after he finished dinner, quite unable to recall what this yesterday's conversation had been.

'I find that you're partly right. Our disagreement consists in this, that you take personal interest as the motive force, while I maintain that every man of a certain degree of education ought to be interested in the common good. You may be right that materially interested activity would be desirable. Generally, your nature is much too *primesautière*,* as the French say; you want either passionate, energetic activity or nothing.'

Levin listened to his brother, understood decidedly nothing and did not want to understand. He was afraid only that his brother might ask him a question which would make it clear that he had heard nothing.

'So there, my good friend,' said Sergei Ivanovich, touching his shoulder.

'Yes, of course. Anyhow, I don't insist,' Levin replied with a childish, guilty smile. 'What was it I was arguing about?' he thought. 'Of course, I'm right, and he's right, and everything's splendid. Only I have to go to the office and give orders.' He stood up, stretching himself and smiling.

Sergei Ivanovich also smiled.

* Impulsive.

'You want to have a stroll, let's go together,' he said, not wanting to part from his brother, who simply exuded freshness and briskness. 'Let's go, and call in at the office if you need to.'

'Good heavens!' cried Levin, so loudly that he frightened Sergei Ivanovich.

'What? What's the matter?'

'How is Agafya Mikhailovna's arm?' said Levin, slapping his forehead. 'I forgot all about it.'

'Much better.'

'Well, I'll run over to see her all the same. I'll be back before you can put your hat on.'

And with a rattle-like clatter of his heels, he ran down the stairs.

VII

While Stepan Arkadyich, having taken almost all the money there was in the house, went to Petersburg to fulfil the most natural and necessary duty, known to all who serve in the government though incomprehensible to those who do not, and without which it is impossible to serve – that of reminding the ministry of himself – and, in going about the fulfilment of this duty, spent his time merrily and pleasantly at the races and in summer houses, Dolly moved with the children to their country estate in order to reduce expenses as much as possible. She moved to her dowry estate, Yergushovo, the same one where the wood had been sold in spring and which was about thirty-five miles from Levin's Pokrovskoe.

In Yergushovo the big, old house had been torn down long ago, and the prince had refurbished and enlarged the wing. Some twenty years ago, when Dolly was still a child, the wing had been roomy and comfortable, though it stood, as all wings do, sideways to the front drive and the south. But this wing was now old and decayed. When Stepan Arkadyich had gone to sell the wood in the spring, Dolly had asked him to look it over and order the necessary repairs. Stepan Arkadyich, who, like all guilty husbands, was very solicitous of his wife's comfort, looked the house over himself and gave orders about everything he thought necessary. To his mind, there was a need to re-upholster all the furniture with cretonne, to hang curtains, to clean up the garden, make a little bridge by the pond and plant flowers; but he forgot many other necessary things, the lack of which later tormented Darya Alexandrovna.

Hard as Stepan Arkadyich tried to be a solicitous father and husband, he never could remember that he had a wife and children. He had a bachelor's tastes, and they alone guided him. On returning to Moscow, he proudly announced to his wife that everything was ready, that the house would be a little joy, and that he strongly advised her to go. For Stepan Arkadyich his wife's departure to the country was very agreeable in all respects: good for the children, less expensive, and freer for him. And Darya Alexandrovna considered a move to the country for the summer necessary for the children, especially for the little girl, who could not get over her scarlet fever, and also as a way of being rid of petty humiliations, paltry debts to the woodmonger, the fishmonger, the shoemaker, which tormented her. On top of that, the departure also pleased her because she dreamed of enticing her sister Kitty, who was to return from abroad in midsummer and for whom bathing had been prescribed, to join her there. Kitty had written to her from the spa that nothing could be more to her liking than to spend the summer with Dolly in Yergushovo, so filled with childhood memories for them both.

At first country life was very difficult for Dolly. She had lived in the country in childhood, and had been left with the impression that the country was salvation from all city troubles, that life there, though not elegant (Dolly was easily reconciled to that), was cheap and comfortable: everything was there, everything was cheap, everything could be had, and it was good for the children. But now, coming to the country as mistress, she saw that it was not at all what she had thought.

The day after their arrival there was torrential rain, and during the night there were leaks in the corridor and the children's room, so that the beds had to be moved to the living room. There was no cook in the household; of the nine cows, according to the dairymaid, some were with calf, some had dropped their first calf, some were too old, some were hard-uddered; there was not enough butter and milk even for the children. There were no eggs. No chicken could be found; they had to roast and boil old, purple, sinewy roosters. No woman could be found to wash the floors – everyone was in the potato fields. To go for a drive was impossible, because one of the horses was restive and pulled at the shaft. There was nowhere to bathe – the entire river bank was trampled by cattle and open to the road; it was even impossible to go for a walk, because cattle got into the garden through the broken fence, and there was one terrible bull who bellowed and therefore probably would also charge. There were no proper wardrobes. Such as there were would not close, or else opened whenever someone passed by. No pots or crocks; no tub for laundry, not even an ironing board in the maids' quarters.

At first, instead of peace and quiet, finding herself in what, for her, were terrible calamities, Darya Alexandrovna was in despair: she bustled about with all her strength, felt the hopelessness of her situation and constantly kept back the tears that welled up in her eyes. The manager, a former cavalry sergeant whom Stepan Arkadyich liked and had promoted from hall porter for his handsome and respectful appearance, took no share in Darya Alexandrovna's calamities, said respectfully: 'Impossible, ma'am, such nasty folk,' and did nothing to help.

The situation seemed hopeless. But there was in the Oblonsky house, as in all family houses, one inconspicuous but most important and useful person – Matryona Filimonovna. She calmed her mistress, assured her that everything would *shape up* (it was her phrase, and it was from her that Matvei had taken it), and, without haste or excitement, went into action herself.

She immediately got in with the steward's wife and on the first day had tea with her and the steward under the acacias and discussed everything. Soon there was a Matryona Filimonovna club established under the acacias, and here, through this club, which consisted of the steward's wife, the village headman and the clerk, the difficulties of life began gradually to be put right, and within a week everything indeed *shaped up*. The roof was repaired, a cook was found (a female crony of the headman's), chickens were bought, the cows began to produce milk, the garden was fenced with pickets, the carpenter made a washboard, the wardrobes were furnished with hooks and no longer opened at will, an ironing board, wrapped in military flannel, lay between a chair arm and a chest of drawers, and the maids' quarters began to smell of hot irons.

'Well, there! And you kept despairing,' said Matryona Filimonovna, pointing to the ironing board.

They even constructed a bathing house out of straw mats. Lily started bathing, and Darya Alexandrovna's expectations of a comfortable, if not calm, country life at least came partly true. With six children Darya Alexandrovna could not be calm. One got sick, another might get sick, a third lacked something, a fourth showed signs of bad character, and so on, and so on. Rarely, rarely would there be short periods of calm. But these troubles and anxieties were for Darya Alexandrovna the only possible happiness. Had it not been for them, she would have remained alone with her thoughts of her husband, who did not love her. But besides that, however painful the mother's fear of illnesses, the illnesses themselves, and the distress at seeing signs of bad inclinations in her children, the children themselves repaid her griefs with small joys. These joys were so small that they could not be seen, like gold in the sand, and in her bad moments she saw only griefs, only sand; but there were also good moments, when she saw only joys, only gold.

Now, in her country solitude, she was more aware of these joys. Often, looking at them, she made every possible effort to convince herself that she was mistaken, that as a mother she was partial to her children; all the same, she could not but tell herself that she had lovely children, all six of them, each in a different way, but such as rarely happens – and she was happy in them and proud of them.

VIII

At the end of May, when everything was already more or less settled, she received her husband's reply to her complaints about country inconveniences. He wrote to her, asking forgiveness for not having thought of everything, and promised to come at the first opportunity. The opportunity did not present itself, and until the beginning of June Darya Alexandrovna lived alone in the country.

On Sunday during St Peter's, Darya Alexandrovna went to the liturgy and had all her children take communion. In her intimate, philosophical conversations with her sister, mother and friends, she very often surprised them with her freethinking in regard to religion. She had her own strange religion of metempsychosis, in which she firmly believed, caring little for the dogmas of the Church. But in the family she strictly fulfilled all the requirements of the Church – not only to set an example, but with all her heart – and the fact that the children had not received communion for more than a year[8] troubled her greatly. And so, with Matryona Filimonovna's full approval and sympathy, she decided to do it now, in the summer.

Darya Alexandrovna thought about how to dress the children several days ahead of time. Dresses were made, altered and washed, seams and ruffles were let out, buttons were sewn on and ribbons prepared. Only

Tanya's dress, which the governess had undertaken to make, considerably soured Darya Alexandrovna's disposition. The governess, as she made the alterations, had taken tucks in the wrong places, cut the arm-holes too big, and all but ruined the dress. Tanya's shoulders were so tight it was painful to see. Matryona Filimonovna thought of putting in gussets and making a little pelerine. That improved things, but there was nearly a quarrel with the governess. In the morning, however, everything was settled, and by nine o'clock – the priest had been asked to wait till then with the liturgy – the dressed-up children, radiant with joy, stood before the carriage at the porch waiting for their mother.

In place of the restive Raven, through Matryona Filimonovna's patronage, the steward's Brownie was harnessed to the carriage, and Darya Alexandrovna, delayed by the cares of her toilette, came out in a white muslin dress to get in.

Darya Alexandrovna had done her hair and dressed with care and excitement. Once she used to dress for herself, to be beautiful and admired; then, the older she became, the more unpleasant it was for her to dress; she saw that she had lost her good looks. But now she again dressed with pleasure and excitement. Now she dressed not for herself, not for her own beauty, but so that, being the mother of these lovely things, she would not spoil the general impression. And taking a last look in the mirror, she remained satisfied with herself. She was pretty. Not as pretty as she had once wanted to be at a ball, but pretty enough for the purpose she now had in mind.

There was no one in the church except some muzhiks, the caretakers and their women. But Darya Alexandrovna saw, or it seemed to her that she saw, the admiration aroused by her children and herself. The children were not only beautiful in their fine clothes, but were also sweet in behaving so well. True, Alyosha did not want to stand quite properly; he kept turning and wanted to see his jacket from behind; but all the same he was remarkably sweet. Tanya stood like a big girl and looked after the little ones. But the smallest, Lily, was lovely with her naïve surprise at everything, and it was hard not to smile when, after taking communion, she said in English: 'Please, some more.'

Returning home, the children felt that something solemn had taken place and were very quiet.

Everything went well at home, too; but at lunch Grisha started whistling and, what was worst of all, did not obey the governess and had to go without cake. Darya Alexandrovna, had she been there, would not have let it go as far as punishment on such a day, but she had to uphold the governess's orders, and she confirmed her decision that Grisha would not have any cake.

Grisha wept, saying that Nikolenka had also whistled but was not being punished, and that he was weeping not because of the cake – it made no difference to him – but because he had been unfairly dealt with. This was much too sad, and Darya Alexandrovna decided to talk with the governess and get her to forgive him. But, passing through the drawing room, she saw a scene that filled her heart with such joy that tears came to her eyes, and she herself forgave the culprit.

The punished boy was sitting at the corner window in the drawing room; next to him stood Tanya with a plate. Under the pretext of wishing to feed her dolls, she had asked the governess's permission to take her portion of cake to the nursery and had brought it to her brother instead. Continuing to weep about the unfairness of the punishment he was suffering, he ate the cake she had brought, saying between sobs: 'You eat it, too, we'll eat it together . . . together.'

Tanya was affected first by pity for Grisha, then by the consciousness of her virtuous deed, and there were tears in her eyes, too; but she did not refuse and was eating her share.

Seeing their mother, they were frightened, but peering into her face, they understood that they were doing a good thing, laughed and, their mouths full of cake, began wiping their smiling lips with their hands, smearing tears and jam all over their beaming faces.

'Goodness! Your new white dress! Tanya! Grisha!' the mother said, trying to save the dress, but with tears in her eyes, smiling a blissful, rapturous smile.

The new clothes were taken off, the girls were told to put on blouses and the boys old jackets, and the order was given to harness up the break – again, to the steward's chagrin, with Brownie as the shaft-horse – to go gathering mushrooms and then to the bathing house. A sound of rapturous squealing arose in the nursery and never stopped till they left for the bathing house.

They gathered a whole basket of mushrooms, even Lily found a birch boletus. Before, it used to be Miss Hull who would find one and show her, but now she herself found a big, squishy boletus, and there was a general cry of delight: 'Lily found a squishy one!'

Then they drove to the river, left the horses under the birches and went to the bathing house. The coachman, Terenty, having tethered the horses to a tree, where they stood swishing away gadflies, lay down in the shade of the birches, flattening out the grass, and smoked tobacco, while from the bathing house there came to him the ceaseless merry squealing of the children.

Though it was a chore to look after all the children and stop their pranks, though it was hard to remember and not mix up all those stockings, drawers, shoes from different feet, and to untie, unbutton and retie so many tapes and buttons, Darya Alexandrovna, who had always loved bathing herself, and considered it good for the children, enjoyed nothing so much as this bathing with them all. To touch all those plump little legs, pulling stockings on them, to take in her arms and dip those naked little bodies and hear joyful or frightened shrieks; to see the breathless faces of those splashing little cherubs, with their wide, frightened and merry eyes, was a great pleasure for her.

When half the children were clothed again, some dressed-up peasant women, who had gone gathering angelica and milkwort, approached the bathing house and stopped timidly. Matryona Filimonovna called to one of them to give her a towel and a shirt that had dropped into the water so that she could wring them out, and Darya Alexandrovna struck up a conversation with the women. The women laughed behind their hands at first, but then became bolder and began to talk, winning Darya Alexandrovna over at once by the sincere admiration they showed for her children.

'See what a beauty, white as sugar,' said one, admiring Tanechka and wagging her head. 'But thin . . .'

'Yes, she was ill.'

'You see, he must have been bathing, too,' another said about the baby.

'No, he's only three months old,' Darya Alexandrovna replied proudly.

'Just look at that!'

'And do you have children?'

'I've had four, there's two left, a boy and a girl. I weaned her before this past Lent.'

'And how old is she?'

'Over a year.'

'Why did you nurse her so long?'

'That's how we do it: three fasts . . .'[9]

And the conversation came to what interested Darya Alexandrovna most: how was the birth? what illnesses have they had? where is the husband? does he visit often?[10]

Darya Alexandrovna did not want to part from the women, so interesting was it for her to talk with them, so completely identical were their interests. What pleased Darya Alexandrovna most was that she could see clearly that all these women particularly admired how many children she had and how good they were. The women made Darya Alexandrovna laugh and offended the governess, who was the cause of this – for her incomprehensible – laughter. One of the young women was watching the governess, who got dressed last of all, and as she put on her third petticoat, could not help observing: 'See, she wraps and wraps and can't get done wrapping!' – and they all burst into laughter.

IX

Surrounded by all her bathed, wet-headed children, Darya Alexandrovna, a kerchief on her head, was driving up to her house when the coachman said:

'Some gentleman's coming, looks like the one from Pokrovskoe.'

Darya Alexandrovna peered ahead and rejoiced, seeing the familiar figure of Levin in a grey hat and grey coat coming to meet them. She was always glad to see him, but she was especially glad now that he would see her in all her glory. No one could understand her grandeur better than Levin.

Seeing her, he found himself before one of the pictures of his imaginary future family life.

'You're just like a mother hen, Darya Alexandrovna.'

'Ah, I'm so glad!' she said, giving him her hand.

'Glad, but you didn't even let me know. My brother's staying with me. I got a note from Stiva saying that you were here.'

'From Stiva?' Darya Alexandrovna asked in surprise.

'Yes. He wrote that you'd moved, and he thought you might allow me to help you in some way,' Levin said and, having said it, suddenly became embarrassed, fell silent and went on walking beside the break, plucking linden shoots and biting them in two. He was embarrassed by the realization that it might be unpleasant for Darya Alexandrovna to be helped by an outsider in something that should have been done by her husband. Darya Alexandrovna indeed disliked this way Stepan Arkadyich had of foisting his family affairs on others. And she knew at once that Levin understood it. It was for this subtle understanding, for this delicacy, that Darya Alexandrovna loved him.

'I understood, of course,' said Levin, 'that it only meant you wanted to see me, and I'm very glad of it. Of course, I can imagine that you, the mistress of a town house, may find it wild here, and if there's any need, I'm entirely at your service.'

'Oh, no!' said Dolly. 'At first it was uncomfortable, but now everything's settled beautifully, thanks to my old nanny,' she said, pointing to Matryona Filimonovna, who, realizing that they were talking about her, smiled gaily and amiably to Levin. She knew him, knew that he was a good match for the young lady, and wished things would work out.

'Get in, please, we'll squeeze over,' she said to him.

'No, I'll walk. Children, who wants to race the horses with me?'

The children scarcely knew Levin, did not remember when they had last seen him, but did not show that strange feeling of shyness and aversion towards him that children so often feel for shamming adults, for which they are so often painfully punished. Shamming in anything at all can deceive the most intelligent, perceptive person; but the most limited child will recognize it and feel aversion, no matter how artfully it is concealed. Whatever Levin's shortcomings were, there was no hint of sham in him, and therefore the children showed him the same friendliness they found in their mother's face. At his invitation the two older ones at once jumped down and ran with him as simply as they would have run with the nanny, with Miss Hull, or with their mother. Lily also started asking to go with him, and her mother handed her down to him; he put her on his shoulders and ran with her.

'Don't be afraid, don't be afraid, Darya Alexandrovna!' he said, smiling gaily to the mother. 'There's no chance I'll hurt her or drop her.'

And seeing his deft, strong, cautiously mindful and all-too-tense movements, the mother calmed down and smiled gaily and approvingly as she watched him.

Here, in the country, with the children and Darya Alexandrovna, who was so sympathetic to him, Levin got into that childishly merry state of mind that often came over him, and which Darya Alexandrovna especially loved in him. He ran with the children, taught them gymnastics, made Miss Hull laugh with his bad English, and told Darya Alexandrovna about his occupations in the country.

After dinner, sitting alone with him on the balcony, Darya Alexandrovna began talking about Kitty.

'Do you know, Kitty's coming here and will spend the summer with me.'

'Really?' he said, flushing; and to change the subject, said at once: 'Shall I send you two cows then? If you want to keep accounts, then you can pay me five roubles a month, if you're not ashamed.'

'No, thank you. We're all settled.'

'Well, then I'll have a look at your cows and, with your permission, give orders on how to feed them. The whole thing is in the feeding.'

And Levin, only to divert the conversation, explained to Darya Alexandrovna the theory of dairy farming, the essence of which was that a cow is merely a machine for processing feed into milk, and so on.

He was saying that while passionately wishing to hear the details about Kitty and at the same time fearing it. He was afraid that the peace he had attained with such difficulty might be disturbed.

'Yes, but anyhow all that has to be looked after, and who will do it?' Darya Alexandrovna replied reluctantly.

She had now set up her housekeeping so well through Matryona Filimonovna that she did not want to change anything in it; nor did she trust Levin's knowledge of agriculture. The argument that a cow is a machine for producing milk was suspect to her. It seemed to her that such arguments could only hinder things. To her it all seemed much simpler: as Matryona Filimonovna explained, they had only to give Spotty and Whiterump more to eat and drink, and keep the cook from taking the kitchen scraps to the washerwoman's cow. That was clear. And all this talk about starchy and grassy feeds was dubious and vague. Above all she wanted to talk about Kitty.

X

'Kitty writes to me that she wishes for nothing so much as solitude and quiet,' Dolly said after the ensuing pause.

'And has her health improved?' Levin asked anxiously.

'Thank God, she's quite recovered. I never believed she had anything wrong with her lungs.'

'Ah, I'm very glad!' said Levin, and it seemed to Dolly that there was something touching and helpless in his face as he said it and silently looked at her.

'Listen, Konstantin Dmitrich,' said Darya Alexandrovna, smiling her kind and slightly mocking smile, 'why are you angry with Kitty?'

'I? I'm not angry,' said Levin.

'No, you are angry. Why didn't you come either to see us or to see them when you were in Moscow?'

'Darya Alexandrovna,' he said, blushing to the roots of his hair, 'I'm even astonished that you, with all your kindness, don't feel it. Aren't you simply sorry for me, since you know . . .'

'What do I know?'

'You know that I proposed and was refused,' said Levin, and all the tenderness he had felt for Kitty a moment before was replaced in his soul by a feeling of anger at the insult.

'Why do you think I know?'

'Because everybody knows.'

'There you're mistaken; I didn't know, though I guessed.'

'Ah! Well, now you know.'

'I knew only that there was something, but Kitty never told me what it was. I could see that there was something that tormented her terribly, and she asked me never to speak of it. And if she didn't tell me, she didn't tell anybody. But what happened between you? Tell me.'

'I've told you what happened.'

'When was it?'

'When I last visited you.'

'And, you know, I shall tell you,' said Darya Alexandrovna, 'that I'm terribly, terribly sorry for her. You only suffer from pride . . .'

'Maybe,' said Levin, 'but . . .'

She interrupted him:

'But for her, poor thing, I'm terribly, terribly sorry. Now I understand everything.'

'Well, Darya Alexandrovna, you will excuse me,' he said, getting up. 'Goodbye! Goodbye, Darya Alexandrovna.'

'No, wait,' she said, holding him by the sleeve. 'Wait, sit down.'

'Please, please, let's not talk about it,' he said, sitting down and at the same time feeling a hope he had thought buried rising and stirring in his heart.

'If I didn't love you,' said Darya Alexandrovna, and tears welled up in her eyes, 'if I didn't know you as I do . . .'

The feeling that had seemed dead revived more and more, rising and taking possession of Levin's heart.

'Yes, I understand everything now,' Darya Alexandrovna went on. 'You can't understand it. For you men, who are free and can choose, it's always clear whom you love. But a young girl in a state of expectation, with that feminine, maidenly modesty, a girl who sees you men from afar, who takes everything on trust – a girl may and does sometimes feel that she doesn't know who she loves or what to say.'

'Yes, if her heart doesn't speak . . .'

'No, her heart speaks, but consider: you men have your eye on a girl, you visit the house, you make friends, you watch, you wait to see if you're going to find what you love, and then, once you're convinced of your love, you propose . . .'

'Well, it's not quite like that.'

'Never mind, you propose when your love has ripened or when the scale tips towards one of your two choices. But a girl isn't asked. She's expected to choose for herself, but she can't choose and only answers yes or no.'

'Yes,' thought Levin, 'a choice between me and Vronsky,' and the dead man reviving in his heart died again and only weighed his heart down painfully.

'Darya Alexandrovna,' he said, 'one chooses a dress that way, or I don't know what purchase, but not love. The choice has been made and so much the better . . . And there can be no repetition.'

'Ah, pride, pride!' said Darya Alexandrovna, as if despising him for the meanness of this feeling compared with that other feeling which only women know. 'At the time you proposed to Kitty, she was precisely in a position where she could not give an answer. She hesitated. Hesitated between you and Vronsky. Him she saw every day, you she had not seen for a long time. Suppose she had been older – for me, for example, there could have been no hesitation in her place. I always found him disgusting, and so he was in the end.'

Levin remembered Kitty's answer. She had said: 'No, it cannot be . . .'

'Darya Alexandrovna,' he said drily, 'I appreciate your confidence in me, but I think you're mistaken. I may be right or wrong, but this pride that you so despise makes any thought of Katerina Alexandrovna impossible for me – you understand, completely impossible.'

'I'll say only one more thing. You understand that I'm speaking of a sister whom I love like my own children. I'm not saying that she loves you, but I only want to say that her refusal at that moment proves nothing.'

'I don't know!' said Levin, jumping up. 'If you realized what pain you're causing me! It's the same as if your child were dead, and you were told he would have been like this and that, and he might have lived, and you would have rejoiced over him. And he's dead, dead, dead . . .'

'How funny you are,' Darya Alexandrovna said with a sad smile, despite Levin's agitation. 'Yes, I understand it all now,' she went on pensively. 'So, you won't come to see us when Kitty's here?'

'No, I won't. Naturally, I'm not going to avoid Katerina Alexandrovna but, wherever possible, I'll try to spare her the unpleasantness of my presence.'

'You're very, very funny,' Darya Alexandrovna repeated, studying his face tenderly. 'Well, all right, it will be as if we never spoke of it. What is it, Tanya?' she said in French to the girl who had just come in.

'Where's my shovel, mama?'

'I am speaking French, and you should do the same.'

The girl wanted to do the same, but forgot what a shovel is called in French; her mother told her and then proceeded to tell her in French where to find the shovel. And Levin found this disagreeable.

Now everything in Darya Alexandrovna's house and in her children seemed less nice to him than before.

'And why does she speak French with the children?' he thought. 'How unnatural and false it is! And the children can feel it. Teaching French and unteaching sincerity,' he thought to himself, not knowing that Darya Alexandrovna had already thought it all over twenty times and, to the detriment of sincerity, had found it necessary to teach her children in this way.

'But where are you going? Stay a little.'

Levin stayed till tea, but all his merriment had vanished and he felt awkward.

After tea he went to the front hall to order the horses to be readied and, on returning, found Darya Alexandrovna looking agitated and upset, with tears in her eyes. While Levin was out of the room, an event had occurred which had suddenly destroyed for Darya Alexandrovna all that day's happiness and pride in her children. Grisha and Tanya had fought over a ball. Darya Alexandrovna, hearing shouts in the nursery, had run there and found a terrible sight. Tanya was holding Grisha by the hair, while he, his face disfigured by anger, was hitting her with his fists wherever he could reach. Something snapped in Darya Alexandrovna's heart when she saw this. It was as if darkness came over her life: she understood that her children, of whom she was so proud, were not only most ordinary, but even bad, poorly brought up children, wicked children, with coarse, beastly inclinations.

She could neither speak nor think of anything else and could not help telling Levin of her unhappiness.

Levin saw that she was unhappy and tried to comfort her, saying that this did not prove anything bad, that all children fought; but, as he said it, Levin thought in his heart: 'No, I will not be affected and speak French with my children, but my children will not be like that: one need only not harm, not disfigure children, and they will be lovely. Yes, my children will not be like that.'

He said goodbye and left, and she did not try to keep him.

XI

In the middle of July the headman of his sister's village, fifteen miles from Pokrovskoe, came to Levin with a report on the course of affairs and the mowing. The main income from his sister's estate came from the water meadows. In former years the hay had been taken by the muzhiks at eight roubles per acre. When Levin took over the management, he examined the meadows, discovered that they were worth more, and set a price of ten roubles per acre. The muzhiks would not pay that price and, as Levin suspected, drove away other buyers. Then Levin went there in person and arranged for the meadows to be reaped partly by hired help, partly on shares. His muzhiks resisted this innovation in every possible way, but the thing went ahead, and in the first year the income from the meadows nearly doubled. Two years ago and last year the muzhiks had kept up the same resistance, and the reaping had been done in the same way. This year the muzhiks had cut all the hay for a share of one-third, and now the headman had come to announce that the mowing was done and that, fearing rain, he had sent for the clerk and in his presence had already divided the hay, piling up eleven stacks as the master's share. From his vague answers to the question of how much hay there had been in the main meadow, from the headman's haste in dividing the hay without asking permission, from the muzhik's whole tone, Levin realized that there was something shady in this distribution of the hay and decided to go himself to verify the matter.

Arriving at the village at dinner-time and leaving his horse with an old friend, the husband of his brother's wet nurse, Levin went to see the old man in the apiary, wishing to learn the details of the hay harvest. A garrulous, fine-looking old man, Parmenych received Levin joyfully, showed him what he was doing, told him all the details about his bees and about that year's hiving; but to Levin's questions about the mowing he spoke uncertainly and unwillingly. That further confirmed Levin in his surmises. He went to the field and examined the stacks. The stacks could not have contained fifty cartloads each, and, to catch the muzhiks, Levin at once gave orders to send for the carts used in transporting hay, to load one stack and transport it to the barn. There turned out to be only thirty-two cartloads in the stack. Despite the headman's assurances about the fluffiness of the hay and its settling in the stacks, and his swearing that everything had been done in an honest-to-God way, Levin insisted on his point that the hay had been divided without his order, and that he therefore did not accept this hay as fifty cartloads to a stack. After lengthy arguments, the decision was that the muzhiks would take those eleven stacks, counting them as fifty cartloads each, towards their share, and apportion the master's share again. These negotiations and the distribution of the stacks went on till the afternoon break. When the last of the hay had been distributed, Levin, entrusting the clerk with supervising the rest, seated himself on a haystack marked with a willow branch and admired the meadow teeming with peasants.

In front of him, where the river bent around a little bog, a motley line of women moved with a merry chatter of ringing voices, and the scattered hay quickly stretched out in grey, meandering ridges over the pale green new growth. Behind the women came muzhiks with forks, and the ridges grew into broad, tall, fluffy haystacks. To the left, carts rattled over the already reaped meadow, and the haystacks, lifted in huge forkfuls, vanished one after another, replaced by heavy cartloads of fragrant hay overhanging the horses' croups.

'Fine weather for it! What hay we'll have!' said the old man, sitting down beside Levin. 'It's tea, not hay! They pick it up like ducklings after grain!' he added, pointing to the stacks being forked. 'A good half's been carted off since dinner.'

'The last one, is it?' he shouted to a young fellow who was driving by, standing in front of the cart-box and waving the ends of the hempen reins.

'The last one, pa!' the young fellow shouted, holding the horse back, and, smiling, he turned round to the gay, red-cheeked woman, also smiling, who was sitting in the cart-box, and drove on.

'Who's that? Your son?' asked Levin.

'My youngest,' said the old man with a tender smile.

'A fine young fellow!'

'Not bad.'

'Already married?'

'Yes, two years ago St Philip's.'[11]

'And what about children?'

'Children, hah! For a whole year he understood nothing, and was bashful besides,' the old man replied. 'Ah, what hay! Just like tea!' he repeated, wishing to change the subject.

Levin looked more attentively at Ivan Parmenov and his wife. They were loading a haystack not far from him. Ivan Parmenov stood on the cart, receiving, spreading and stamping down the enormous loads of hay that his young beauty of a wife deftly heaved up to him, first in armfuls and then on the fork. The young woman worked easily, cheerfully and skilfully. The thick, packed-down hay would not go right on the fork. She first loosened it up, stuck the fork in, then leaned the whole weight of her body on it with a supple and quick movement and, straightening up at once, curving her back tightly girded with a red sash, her full breasts showing under the white smock, deftly shifted her grip on the fork and heaved the load high up on to the cart. Ivan, obviously trying to spare her every moment of extra work, hastily picked up the load pitched to him in his wide-open arms and spread it on the cart. After pitching him the last of the hay on a rake, the woman shook off the hay dust that had got on her neck, straightened the red kerchief that had gone askew on her white, untanned forehead, and went under the cart to tie down the load. Ivan showed her how to loop it under the axle-tree and burst into loud laughter at something she said. Strong, young, recently awakened love showed in the expression on both their faces.

XII

The load was tied down. Ivan jumped off and led the fine, well-fed horse by the bridle. The woman threw the rake up on to the load and went with brisk steps, swinging her arms, to join the women gathered in a circle. Ivan drove out to the road and joined the line of other carts. The women, with rakes on their shoulders, bright colours flashing, chattering in ringing, merry voices, walked behind the carts. One coarse, wild female voice struck up a song and sang till the refrain, and then, all at once, with one accord, the same song was taken up from the beginning by some fifty different coarse, high, healthy voices.

The singing women approached Levin, and it seemed to him that a thundercloud of merriment was coming upon him. The cloud came over him and enveloped him; and the haystack on which he lay, and all the other haystacks and carts, and the whole meadow with the distant fields all started moving and heaving to the rhythm of this wild, rollicking song with its shouts, whistles and whoops. Levin was envious of this healthy merriment; he would have liked to take part in expressing this joy of life. But he could do nothing and had to lie there and look and listen. When the peasants and their song had vanished from his sight and hearing, a heavy feeling of anguish at his loneliness, his bodily idleness, his hostility to this world, came over him.

Some of those same muzhiks who had argued most of all with him over the hay, whom he had offended or who had wanted to cheat him, those same muzhiks greeted him cheerfully and obviously did not and could not have any malice towards him, nor any repentance or even memory of having wanted to cheat him. It was all drowned in the sea of cheerful common labour. God had given the day, God had given the strength. Both day and strength had been devoted to labour and in that lay the reward. And whom was this labour for? What would its fruits be? These considerations were irrelevant and insignificant.

Levin had often admired this life, had often experienced a feeling of envy for the people who lived this life, but that day for the first time, especially under the impression of what he had seen in the relations of Ivan Parmenov and his young wife, the thought came clearly to Levin that it was up to him to change that so burdensome, idle, artificial and individual life he lived into this laborious, pure and common, lovely life.

The old man who had been sitting with him had long since gone home;

the peasants had all dispersed. Those who lived near by had gone home, those from far away had gathered to have supper and spend the night in the meadow. Levin, unnoticed by the peasants, went on lying on the haystack, watching, listening and thinking. The peasants who were staying overnight in the meadow spent almost the whole short summer night without sleeping. First there was general, merry talk and loud laughter over supper, then again songs and laughter.

The long, laborious day had left no other trace in them than merriment. Before dawn everything quieted down. Only the night sounds of the never silent frogs in the swamp and the horses snorting in the morning mist rising over the meadow could be heard. Coming to his senses, Levin got down off the haystack, looked at the stars and realized that night was over.

'Well, what am I to do then? How am I to do it?' he said to himself, trying to put into words all that he had thought and felt during that short night. All those thoughts and feelings were divided into three separate lines of argument. One was to renounce his old life, his useless knowledge, his utterly needless education. This renunciation gave him pleasure and was easy and simple for him. Other thoughts and notions concerned the life he wished to live now. The simplicity, the purity, the legitimacy of this life he felt clearly, and he was convinced that he would find in it that satisfaction, repose and dignity, the absence of which he felt so painfully. But the third line of argument turned around the question of how to make this transition from the old life to the new. And here nothing clear presented itself to him. 'To have a wife? To have work and the necessity to work? To leave Pokrovskoe? To buy land? To join a community? To marry a peasant woman? How am I to do it?' he asked himself again, and found no answer. 'However, I didn't sleep all night and can't give myself a clear accounting,' he told himself. 'I'll clear it up later. One thing is sure, that this night has decided my fate. All my former dreams about family life are nonsense, not the right thing,' he said to himself. 'All this is much simpler and better . . .

'How beautiful!' he thought, looking at the strange mother-of-pearl shell of white, fleecy clouds that stopped right over his head in the middle of the sky. 'How lovely everything is on this lovely night! And when did that shell have time to form? A moment ago I looked at the sky, and there was nothing there – only two white strips. Yes, and in that same imperceptible way my views of life have also changed!'

He left the meadow and walked down the main road to the village. A slight breeze sprang up, and it turned grey, gloomy. The bleak moment came that usually precedes dawn, the full victory of light over darkness.

Hunched up with cold, Levin walked quickly, his eyes on the ground. 'What's that? Someone's coming,' he thought, hearing bells, and he raised his head. Forty paces away from him, on the grassy main road down which he was walking, a coach-and-four with leather trunks on its roof came driving towards him. The shaft-horses pressed towards the shafts, away from the ruts, but the adroit driver, sitting sideways on the box, guided the shafts along the ruts, so that the wheels ran over the smooth ground.

That was the only thing Levin noticed and, without thinking who it might be, he glanced absentmindedly into the coach.

Inside the coach an old lady dozed in the corner and a young girl, apparently just awakened, sat by the window, holding the ribbons of her white bonnet with both hands. Bright and thoughtful, all filled with a graceful and complex inner life to which Levin was a stranger, she looked through him at the glowing sunrise.

At the very instant when this vision was about to vanish, the truthful eyes looked at him. She recognized him, and astonished joy lit up her face.

He could not have been mistaken. There were no other eyes in the world like those. There was no other being in the world capable of concentrating for him all the light and meaning of life. It was she. It was Kitty. He realized that she was driving to Yergushovo from the railway station. And all that had troubled Levin during that sleepless night, all the decisions he had taken, all of it suddenly vanished. He recalled with disgust his dreams of marrying a peasant woman. There, in that carriage quickly moving away and bearing to the other side of the road, was the only possibility of resolving the riddle of his life that had been weighing on him so painfully of late.

She did not look out again. The noise of the springs could no longer be heard; the bells were barely audible. The barking of dogs indicated that the coach had entered the village – and around there remained the empty fields, the village ahead, and he himself, solitary and a stranger to everything, walking alone down the deserted main road.

He looked at the sky, hoping to find there the shell he had admired, which had embodied for him the whole train of thoughts and feelings of the past night. There was no longer anything resembling a shell in the sky. There, in the inaccessible heights, a mysterious change had already been accomplished. No trace of the shell was left, but spread over half the sky was a smooth carpet of ever diminishing fleecy clouds. The sky had turned blue and radiant, and with the same tenderness, yet also with the same inaccessibility, it returned his questioning look.

'No,' he said to himself, 'however good that life of simplicity and labour may be, I cannot go back to it. I love *her*.'

XIII

No one except the people closest to Alexei Alexandrovich knew that this ostensibly most cold and reasonable man had one weakness that contradicted the general cast of his character. Alexei Alexandrovich was unable to hear and see the tears of a child or a woman with indifference. The sight of tears perplexed him and made him lose all ability to reason. His office manager and his secretary knew it and warned lady petitioners that they should not weep, if they did not want to ruin their chances. 'He'll get angry and won't listen to you,' they said. And, indeed, in such cases the inner disturbance produced in Alexei Alexandrovich by tears expressed itself in quick anger. 'I can do nothing, nothing. Kindly get out!' he usually shouted.

When, on the way home from the race, Anna told him about her relations with Vronsky and immediately after that covered her face with her hands and wept, Alexei Alexandrovich, despite the anger aroused in him against her, felt at the same time the surge of that inner disturbance which tears always produced in him. Aware of it and aware that an expression of his feelings at that moment would be unsuitable to the situation, he tried to suppress in himself any manifestation of life, and therefore did not move and did not look at her. From this came that strange expression of deadness on his face, which so struck Anna.

When they drove up to their house, he helped her out of the carriage and, making an inner effort, took leave of her with his usual courtesy, uttering words that did not oblige him to anything; he said that he would tell her his decision tomorrow.

His wife's words, confirming his worst doubts, produced a cruel pain in Alexei Alexandrovich's heart. This pain was further intensified by a strange feeling of physical pity for her, produced in him by her tears. But, left alone in the carriage, Alexei Alexandrovich, to his own surprise and joy, felt complete deliverance both from this pity and from the doubt and suffering of jealousy that had lately tormented him.

He felt like a man who has had a long-aching tooth pulled out. After the terrible pain and the sensation of something huge, bigger than his head, being drawn from his jaw, the patient, still not believing his good fortune, suddenly feels that what had poisoned his life and absorbed all his attention for so long exists no more, and that he can again live, think and be interested in something other than his tooth. This was the feeling Alexei Alexandrovich experienced. The pain had been strange and terrible, but now it was gone; he felt that he could again live and think about something other than his wife.

'No honour, no heart, no religion – a depraved woman! I always knew it, and always saw it, though I tried to deceive myself out of pity for her,' he said to himself. And indeed it seemed to him that he had always seen it; he recalled details of their past life which before had not seemed to him to be anything bad – now these details showed clearly that she had always been depraved. 'I made a mistake in binding my life to hers, but there is nothing bad in this mistake, and therefore I cannot be unhappy. I am not the guilty one,' he said to himself, 'she is. But I have nothing to do with her. For me she doesn't exist . . .'

All that was going to befall her and their son, towards whom his feeling had changed just as it had towards her, ceased to concern him. The only thing that concerned him now was the question of how to shake off in the best, most decent, most convenient for him, and therefore most just way, the mud she had spattered on him in her fall, and to continue on his path of active, honest and useful life.

'I cannot be unhappy because a despicable woman has committed a crime; I must only find the best way out of the painful situation she has put me in. And I will find it,' he said to himself, frowning more and more. 'I am not the first, nor am I the last.' And, to say nothing of historical examples, beginning with Menelaus, refreshed in everyone's memory by *La Belle Hélène*,[12] a whole series of cases of contemporary unfaithfulness of wives to husbands in high society emerged in Alexei Alexandrovich's imagination. 'Daryalov, Poltavsky, Prince Karibanov, Count Paskudin, Dram . . . Yes, Dram, too . . . such an honest, efficient man . . . Semyonov, Chagin, Sigonin,' recalled Alexei Alexandrovich. 'Granted, some unreasonable *ridicule* falls on these people, but I never saw anything but misfortune in it, and I always sympathized with them,' he said to himself, though it was not true; he had never sympathized with misfortunes of that sort, but had valued himself the higher, the more frequent were the examples of women being unfaithful to their husbands. 'It is a misfortune that may befall anybody. And this misfortune has befallen me. The only thing is how best to endure this situation.' And he began going through the details of the modes of action chosen by others who had found themselves in the same position.

'Daryalov fought a duel . . .'

In his youth Karenin's thoughts had been especially drawn to duelling, precisely because he was physically a timid man and knew it very well. Alexei Alexandrovich could not think without horror of a pistol pointed at him, and had never in his life used any weapon. In his youth this horror had made him think often about duelling and measure himself against a situation in which he would have to put his life in danger. Having achieved success and a firm position in life, he had long forgotten this feeling; yet the habit of the feeling claimed its own, and the fear of cowardliness proved so strong in him even now that Alexei Alexandrovich pondered and mentally fondled the question of a duel for a long time from all sides, though he knew beforehand that he would not fight under any circumstances.

'No doubt our society is still so savage (a far cry from England) that a great many' – and among the many were those whose opinion Alexei Alexandrovich especially valued – 'would look favourably upon a duel. But what result would be achieved? Suppose I challenge him,' Alexei Alexandrovich went on to himself and, vividly imagining the night he would spend after the challenge and the pistol pointed at him, he shuddered and realized that he would never do it. 'Suppose I challenge him to a duel. Suppose they teach me how,' he went on thinking. 'They place me, I pull the trigger,' he said to himself, shutting his eyes, 'and it turns out that I've killed him.' Alexei Alexandrovich shook his head to drive these foolish thoughts away. 'What is the sense of killing a man in order to define one's attitude towards a criminal wife and a son? I'll have to decide what I am to do with her just the same. But what is still more likely and what would undoubtedly happen, is that I would be killed or wounded. I, the innocent one, the victim, would be killed or wounded. Still more senseless. But not only that: a challenge to a duel would be a dishonest act on my part. Do I not know beforehand that my friends would never allow me to go as far as a duel, would not allow the life of a statesman, needed by Russia, to be put in danger? What would it mean? It would mean that I, knowing beforehand that the thing would never go as far as danger, merely wanted to give myself a certain false glitter by this challenge. It is dishonest, it is false, it is deceiving others and myself. A duel is unthinkable, and no one expects it of me. My goal consists in safeguarding my reputation, which I need for the unimpeded continuation of my activity.' His official activity, of great importance in his eyes even before, now presented itself as especially important.

Having considered and rejected a duel, Alexei Alexandrovich turned to divorce – another way out chosen by some of the husbands he remembered. Going through all the cases of divorce he could remember (there were a great many in the highest society, which he knew so well), he did not find a single one in which the purpose of the divorce was the same as the one he had in mind. In all these cases the husband had yielded up or sold the unfaithful wife, and the very side which, being guilty, had no right to remarry, had entered into fictional, quasi-legitimate relations with a new consort. And in his own case Alexei Alexandrovich saw that to obtain a legal divorce – that is, one in which the guilty wife would simply be rejected – was impossible. He saw that the complex conditions of life in which he found himself did not allow for the possibility of the coarse proofs the law demanded to establish the wife's criminality; he saw that there was a certain refinement of that life which also did not allow for the use of such proofs, if there were any, that the use of these proofs would harm him more than it would her in the eyes of society.

An attempt at divorce could only lead to a scandalous court trial, which would be a godsend for his enemies, for the slandering and humiliation of his high position in society. Nor could the chief goal – to define the situation with the least disturbance – be achieved through divorce. Besides that, divorce, or even an attempt at divorce, implied that the wife had broken relations with her husband and joined with her lover. And in Alexei Alexandrovich's soul, despite what now seemed to him an utter, contemptuous indifference to his wife, there remained one feeling with regard to her – an unwillingness that she be united with Vronsky unhindered, that her crime be profitable for her. This one thought so vexed him that, merely imagining it, he groaned with inner pain, got up, changed his position in the carriage and, frowning, spent a long time after that wrapping his chilled and bony legs in a fluffy rug.

'Apart from formal divorce, it would also be possible to do what Karibanov, Paskudin, and the good Dram did – that is, to separate from my wife,' he went on thinking once he had calmed down. But that measure presented the same inconvenience of disgrace as did divorce, and above all, just like formal divorce, it would throw his wife into Vronsky's arms. 'No, this is impossible, impossible!' he spoke aloud, beginning to fuss with his rug again. 'I cannot be unhappy, but neither should she and he be happy.'

The feeling of jealousy that had tormented him while he did not know, had gone away the moment his tooth was painfully pulled out by his wife's words. But that feeling had been replaced by another: the wish not only that she not triumph, but that she be paid back for her crime. He did not acknowledge this feeling, but in the depths of his soul he wished her to suffer for disturbing his peace and honour. And again going over the conditions of a duel, a divorce, a separation and again rejecting them, Alexei Alexandrovich became convinced that there was only one solution: to keep her with him, concealing what had happened from society, and taking all possible measures to stop their affair and above all – something he did not admit to himself – to punish her. 'I must announce my decision, that, having thought over the painful situation in which she has put the family, any other solution would be worse for both sides than the external status quo, which I agree to observe, but on the strict condition that she carry out my will, that is, cease all relations with her lover.' In confirmation of this decision, once it was finally taken, another important consideration occurred to Alexei Alexandrovich. 'Only with such a decision am I also acting in conformity with religion,' he said to himself, 'only with this decision am I not rejecting a criminal wife, but giving her an opportunity to reform and even – hard though it may be for me – devoting part of my strength to reforming and saving her.' Though Alexei Alexandrovich knew that he could not have any moral influence on his wife, that nothing would come of this attempt at reformation except lies; though, while living through these difficult moments, he never once thought of seeking guidance from religion – now that his decision coincided, as it seemed to him, with the requirements of religion, this religious sanction of his decision gave him full satisfaction and a measure of peace. It gladdened him to think that, even in so important a matter of life as this, no one would be able to say that he had not acted in accordance with the rules of that religion whose banner he had always held high, amidst the general coolness and indifference. In thinking over the further details, Alexei Alexandrovich did not see why his relations with his wife might not even remain almost the same as before. Doubtless he would never be able to give her back his respect; but there were not and could not be any reasons for him to upset his life and to suffer as a result of her being a bad and unfaithful wife. 'Yes, time will pass, all-amending time, and the former relations will be restored,' Alexei Alexandrovich said to himself, 'that is, restored far enough so that I will not feel as if the whole course of my life has been upset. She should be unhappy, but I am not guilty and therefore cannot be unhappy.'

XIV

Approaching Petersburg, Alexei Alexandrovich was not only fully set on this decision, but had also composed in his head the letter he would write to his wife. Going into the hall porter's lodge, he glanced at the letters and papers sent from the ministry and ordered them to be brought to him in the study.

'Unharness and admit no one,' he said to the porter's question, emphasizing the words 'admit no one' with a certain pleasure, which in him was a sign of good spirits.

In his study Alexei Alexandrovich paced up and down a couple of times, stopped by the enormous desk, on which six candles had been lit beforehand by the valet, cracked his fingers and sat down, sorting out his writing accessories. Placing his elbows on the desk, he inclined his head to one side, thought for a moment, and began to write, not stopping for a second. He wrote without addressing her and in French, using the plural pronoun 'you', which does not have that character of coldness which it has in Russian.

In our last conversation I expressed my intention to inform you of my decision with regard to the subject of that conversation. Having thought it all over attentively, I am now writing with the purpose of fulfilling that promise. My decision is the following: whatever your actions may have been, I do not consider myself justified in breaking the bonds by which a higher power has united us. A family may not be destroyed by the caprice, arbitrariness or even crime of one of the spouses, and our life must go on as before. That is necessary for me, for you, for our son. I am fully convinced that you have repented and do repent for being the occasion of this present letter and that you will assist me in eradicating the cause of our discord and in forgetting the past. Otherwise you yourself can imagine what awaits you and your son. All this I hope to discuss in more detail in a personal meeting. Since the summer season is coming to an end, I would ask you to move back to Petersburg as soon as possible, not later than Tuesday. All necessary arrangements for your move will be made. I beg you to note that I ascribe particular importance to the fulfilment of my request.

A. Karenin

PS Enclosed is the money you may need for your expenses.

He read the letter over and remained pleased with it, especially with having remembered to enclose money; there was not a cruel word, not a reproach, but no lenience either. Above all, there was a golden bridge for return. Having folded the letter, smoothed it with a massive ivory paper-knife, and put money in the envelope, with the pleasure always aroused in him by the handling of his well-arranged writing accessories, he rang.

'Give this to the courier, to be delivered tomorrow to Anna Arkadyevna at the country house,' he said and stood up.

'Yes, your excellency. Will you take tea in the study?'

Alexei Alexandrovich ordered tea to be served in the study and, toying with the massive paper-knife, went to the armchair by which a lamp had been prepared, with a French book he had begun reading on the Eugubine Tables.[13] Above the armchair, in a gilt frame, hung an oval portrait of Anna, beautifully executed by a famous painter. Alexei Alexandrovich looked at it. The impenetrable eyes looked at him insolently and mockingly, as on that last evening of their talk. The sight of the black lace on her head, her black hair and the beautiful white hand with its fourth finger covered with rings, splendidly executed by the painter, impressed him as unbearably insolent and defiant. After looking at the portrait for about a minute, Alexei Alexandrovich gave such a start that his lips trembled and produced a 'brr', and he turned away. Hastily sitting down in the armchair, he opened the book. He tried to read, but simply could not restore in himself the quite lively interest he had formerly taken in the Eugubine Tables. He was looking at the book and thinking about other things. He was thinking not about his wife but about a certain complication that had recently emerged in his state activity, which at that time constituted the main interest of his work. He felt that he was now penetrating this complication more deeply than ever, and that in his head there was hatching – he could say it without self-delusion – a capital idea, which would disentangle this whole affair, raise him in his official career, do harm to his enemies, and thus be of the greatest use to the state. As soon as the servant set down the tea and left the room, Alexei Alexandrovich got up and went to his desk. Moving the portfolio of current cases into the middle, with a barely noticeable smile of self-satisfaction he took a pencil from the stand and immersed himself in reading a complex case he had sent for, having to do with the forthcoming complication. The complication was the following. Alexei Alexandrovich's particularity as a statesman, that characteristic feature proper to him alone (every rising official has such a feature), which, together with his persistent ambition, reserve, honesty and self-assurance, had made his career, consisted in his scorn for paper bureaucracy, in a reducing of correspondence, in taking as direct a relation to living matters as possible, and in economy. It so happened that in the famous commission of June 2nd, a case had been brought up about the irrigation of the fields in Zaraysk province,[14] which belonged to Alexei Alexandrovich's ministry and presented a glaring example of unproductive expenditure and a paper attitude towards things. He knew that this was correct. The case of irrigating the fields in Zaraysk province had been started by the predecessor of his predecessor. And indeed, a good deal of money had been and was still being spent on this case, altogether unproductively, and it was obvious that the whole case could lead nowhere. Alexei Alexandrovich, on taking over the post, understood this at once and wanted to get his hands on the case; but in the beginning, when he still felt himself not quite secure, he realized that this would be unwise, as it touched on too many interests; later, occupied with other cases, he simply forgot it. Like other cases, it went on by itself, by the force of inertia. (Many people lived off this case, in particular one very moral and musical family: all the daughters played stringed instruments. Alexei Alexandrovich knew this family and had given away the bride at the oldest daughter's wedding.) To bring up the case was, in his opinion, unfair on the part of a hostile ministry, because in every ministry there were even worse cases which, according to a certain official decency, no one brought up. Now, since the gauntlet had been thrown down before him, he boldly picked it up and demanded that a special commission be appointed to study and inspect the work of the commission on the irrigation of the fields in Zaraysk province; but in return he would give those gentlemen no quarter. He also demanded that a special commission be appointed in the case of the settling of racial minorities.[15] The case of the settling of racial minorities had been brought up accidentally in the committee of June 2nd, and had been vigorously supported by Alexei Alexandrovich as brooking no delay owing to the lamentable situation of the minorities. In the committee this matter had served as a pretext for wrangling among several ministries. The ministry hostile to Alexei Alexandrovich had argued that the situation of the minorities was quite prosperous and the proposed reorganization might ruin their prosperity; and if there was anything wrong, it came from the failure of Alexei Alexandrovich's ministry to carry out the measures prescribed by law. Now Alexei Alexandrovich intended to demand: first, that a new commission be set up which would be charged with investigating the conditions of the minorities on the spot; second, if it should turn out that the situation of the minorities was indeed as it appeared from official data available in the hands of the committee, another new expert commission should be appointed to investigate the causes of the dismal situation of the minorities from the (a) political, (b) administrative, (c) economic, (d) ethnographic, (e) material and (f) religious points of view; third, the hostile ministry should be required to supply information about the measures taken by that ministry over the last decade to prevent those unfavourable conditions in which the minorities now found themselves; fourth, and finally, the ministry should be required to explain why, as could be seen from the information in files No. 17015 and 18308, of 5 December 1863 and 7 June 1864, it had acted in a sense directly contrary to the meaning of the fundamental and organic law, Vol. ——, art. 18 and note to art. 36. A flush of animation covered Alexei Alexandrovich's face as he quickly noted down these thoughts for himself. Having covered a sheet of paper with writing, he got up, rang and sent a little note to his office manager about providing him with the necessary references. Getting up and pacing the room, he again glanced at the portrait, frowned and smiled contemptuously. After reading a bit more in the book on the Eugubine Tables and reviving his interest in them, Alexei Alexandrovich went to bed at eleven o'clock, and when, lying in bed, he recalled the incident with his wife, it no longer presented itself to him in the same gloomy light.

XV

Though Anna had stubbornly and bitterly persisted in contradicting Vronsky when he told her that her situation was impossible and tried to persuade her to reveal everything to her husband, in the depths of her soul she considered her situation false, dishonest, and wished with all her soul to change it. Coming home from the races with her husband, in a moment of agitation she had told him everything; despite the pain she had felt in doing so, she was glad of it. After her husband left, she told herself that she was glad, that now everything would be definite and at least there would be no falsehood and deceit. It seemed unquestionable to her that now her situation would be defined for ever. It might be bad, this new situation, but it would be definite, there would be no vagueness or falsehood in it. The pain she had caused herself and her husband by uttering those words would be recompensed by the fact that everything would be defined, she thought. That same evening she saw Vronsky but did not tell him about what had happened between her and her husband, though to clarify the situation she ought to have told him.

When she woke up the next morning, the first thing that came to her was the words she had spoken to her husband, and they seemed so terrible to her now that she could not understand how she could have resolved to utter those strange, coarse words, and could not imagine what would come of it. But the words had been spoken, and Alexei Alexandrovich had left without saying anything. 'I saw Vronsky and didn't tell him. Even at the very moment he was leaving, I wanted to call him back and tell him, but I changed my mind, because it was strange that I hadn't told him at the very first moment. Why didn't I tell him, if I wanted to?' And in answer to this question, a hot flush of shame poured over her face. She understood what had kept her from doing it; she understood that she was ashamed. Her situation, which had seemed clarified last night, now suddenly appeared to her not only not clarified, but hopeless. She became terrified of the disgrace which she had not even thought of before. When she merely thought of what her husband was going to do, the most terrible notions came to her. It occurred to her that the accountant would now come to turn her out of the house, that her disgrace would be announced to the whole world. She asked herself where she would go when she was turned out of the house, and could find no answer.

When she thought of Vronsky, she imagined that he did not love her, that he was already beginning to be burdened by her, that she could not offer herself to him, and she felt hostile to him because of it. It seemed to her that the words she had spoken to her husband, and which she kept repeating in her imagination, had been spoken to everyone and that everyone had heard them. She could not bring herself to look into the eyes of those she lived with. She could not bring herself to call her maid and still less to go downstairs to see her son and the governess.

The maid, who had been listening by the door for a long time, came into the room on her own. Anna looked questioningly into her eyes and blushed timorously. The maid apologized for coming in and said she thought she had heard the bell. She brought a dress and a note. The note was from Betsy. Betsy reminded her that she had Liza Merkalov and Baroness Stolz, with their admirers, Kaluzhsky and old Stremov, coming that morning for a croquet party. 'Do come just to see it, as a study in manners. I'll expect you,' she ended.

Anna read the note and sighed deeply.

'Nothing, I need nothing,' she said to Annushka, who kept rearranging the flacons and brushes on the dressing table. 'Go, I'll get dressed now and come out. There's nothing I need.'

Annushka left, but Anna did not begin to dress; she went on sitting in the same position, her head and arms hanging down, and every once in a while her whole body shuddered, as if wishing to make some gesture, to say something, and then became still again. She kept repeating: 'My God! My God!' But neither the 'my' nor the 'God' had any meaning for her. Though she had never doubted the religion in which she had been brought up, the thought of seeking help from religion in her situation was as foreign to her as seeking help from Alexei Alexandrovich. She knew beforehand that the help of religion was possible only on condition of renouncing all that made up the whole meaning of life for her. Not only was it painful for her, but she was beginning to feel fear before the new, never experienced state of her soul. She felt that everything was beginning to go double in her soul, as an object sometimes goes double in tired eyes. Sometimes she did not know what she feared, what she desired: whether she feared or desired what had been or what would be, and precisely what she desired, she did not know.

'Ah, what am I doing!' she said to herself, suddenly feeling pain in both sides of her head. When she came to herself, she saw that she was clutching the hair on her temples and squeezing them with both hands. She jumped up and began pacing.

'Coffee's ready, and Mamzelle and Seryozha are waiting,' said Annushka, coming back again and finding Anna in the same position.

'Seryozha? What about Seryozha?' Anna asked, suddenly becoming animated, remembering her son's existence for the first time that whole morning.

'He's been naughty, it seems,' Annushka answered, smiling.

'What has he done?'

'You had some peaches on the table in the corner room, and it seems he ate one on the sly.'

The reminder of her son suddenly brought Anna out of that state of hopelessness which she had been in. She remembered the partly sincere, though much exaggerated, role of the mother who lives for her son, which she had taken upon herself in recent years, and felt with joy that, in the circumstances she was in, she had her domain, independent of her relations with her husband and Vronsky. That domain was her son. Whatever position she was in, she could not abandon her son. Let her husband disgrace her and turn her out, let Vronsky grow cool towards her and continue to lead his independent life (again she thought of him with bitterness and reproach), she could not desert her son. She had a goal in life. And she had to act, to act in order to safeguard that position with her son, so that he would not be taken from her. She even had to act soon, as soon as possible, while he had not yet been taken from her. She had to take her son and leave. Here was the one thing she now had to do. She needed to be calm and to get out of this painful situation. The thought of a matter directly connected with her son, of leaving with him at once for somewhere, gave her that calm.

She dressed quickly, went downstairs, and with a resolute stride entered the drawing room where, as usual, coffee and Seryozha with the governess were waiting for her. Seryozha, all in white, stood by the table under the mirror and, his back and head bowed, with an expression of strained attention which she knew in him and in which he resembled his father, was doing something with the flowers he had brought.

The governess had an especially severe look. Seryozha cried out shrilly, as he often did: 'Ah, mama!' and stopped, undecided whether to go and greet his mother, abandoning the flowers, or to finish the garland and go to her with the flowers.

The governess, having greeted her, began to tell her at length and with qualifications about Seryozha's trespass, but Anna was not listening to her; she was thinking whether she would take her along or not. 'No, I won't,' she decided. 'I'll go alone with my son.'

'Yes, that's very bad,' said Anna and, taking her son by the shoulder, she looked at him not with a severe but with a timid gaze, which embarrassed and delighted the boy, and kissed him. 'Leave him with me,' she said to the astonished governess and, not letting go of her son's hand, sat down at the table where the coffee was waiting.

'Mama! I . . . I . . . didn't . . .' he said, trying to guess from her expression how he would be punished for the peach.

'Seryozha,' she said, as soon as the governess left the room, 'that's bad, but you won't do it again? . . . Do you love me?'

She felt tears coming to her eyes. 'How can I help loving him?' she said to herself, peering into his frightened and at the same time joyful eyes. 'And can it be that he will join with his father to punish me? Won't he pity me?' The tears ran down her cheeks and, to hide them, she got up impulsively and all but ran out to the terrace.

After the thunderstorms of the past few days, cold, clear weather had set in. The bright sun shone through the washed leaves, but there was a chill in the air.

She shivered both from the cold and from the inner horror that seized her with new force in the fresh air.

'Go, go to Mariette,' she said to Seryozha, who came out after her, and she began pacing the straw matting of the terrace. 'Can it be that they won't forgive me, won't understand that all this could not be otherwise?' she said to herself.

She stopped and looked at the tops of the aspens swaying in the wind, their washed leaves glistening brightly in the cold sun, and she understood that they would not forgive, that everything and everyone would be merciless to her now, like this sky, like this greenery. And again she felt things beginning to go double in her soul. 'I mustn't, I mustn't think,' she said to herself. 'I must get ready to go. Where? When? Whom shall I take with me? Yes, to Moscow, on the evening train. Annushka and Seryozha, and only the most necessary things. But first I must write to them both.' She quickly went into the house, to her boudoir, sat down at the desk and wrote to her husband:

After what has happened, I can no longer remain in your house. I am leaving and taking our son with me. I do not know the laws and therefore do not know which of the parents keeps the son; but I am taking him with me, because I cannot live without him. Be magnanimous, leave him with me.

Up to that point she wrote quickly and naturally, but the appeal to his magnanimity, which she did not recognize in him, and the necessity of concluding the letter with something touching, stopped her.

'I cannot speak of my guilt and my repentance, because . . .'

Again she stopped, finding no coherence in her thoughts. 'No,' she said to herself, 'nothing's needed,' and, tearing up the letter, she rewrote it, removing the mention of magnanimity, and sealed it.

The other letter had to be written to Vronsky. 'I have told my husband,' she wrote, and sat for a long time, unable to write more. It was so coarse, so unfeminine. 'And then, what can I write to him?' she said to herself. Again a flush of shame covered her face. She remembered his calm, and a feeling of vexation with him made her tear the sheet with the written phrase into little shreds. 'Nothing's necessary,' she said to herself. She folded the blotting pad, went upstairs, told the governess and the servants that she was going to Moscow that day, and immediately started packing her things.

XVI

In all the rooms of the country house caretakers, gardeners and footmen went about, carrying things out. Wardrobes and chests of drawers were opened; twice they ran to the shop for more string; newspapers lay about on the floor. Two trunks, several bags, and some tied-up rugs were taken out to the front hall. Her carriage and two hired cabs stood by the porch. Anna, having forgotten her inner anxiety in the work of packing, was standing at the table in her boudoir packing her travelling bag when Annushka drew her attention to the noise of a carriage driving up. Anna looked out the window and saw Alexei Alexandrovich's courier on the porch, ringing at the front door.

'Go and find out what it is,' she said, and with a calm readiness for anything, her hands folded on her knees, she sat in the armchair. A footman brought a fat envelope with Alexei Alexandrovich's handwriting on it.

'The courier has been ordered to bring a reply,' he said.

'Very well,' she said, and as soon as the man went out, she tore open the letter with trembling fingers. A wad of unfolded bank notes in a sealed wrapper fell out of it. She freed the letter and began reading from the end. 'I have made the preparations for the move, I ascribe importance to the fulfilment of my request,' she read. She skipped further back, read everything and once again read through the whole letter from the beginning. When she finished, she felt that she was cold and that a terrible disaster, such as she had never expected, had fallen upon her.

She had repented in the morning of what she had told her husband and had wished for only one thing, that those words might be as if unspoken. And here was a letter recognizing the words as unspoken and granting her what she had wished. But now this letter was more terrible for her than anything she could have imagined.

'He's right! He's right!' she said. 'Of course, he's always right, he's a Christian, he's magnanimous! Yes, the mean, vile man! And I'm the only one who understands or ever will understand it; and I can't explain it. They say he's a religious, moral, honest, intelligent man; but they don't see what I've seen. They don't know how he has been stifling my life for eight years, stifling everything that was alive in me, that he never once even thought that I was a living woman who needed love. They don't know how he insulted me at every step and remained pleased with himself. Didn't I try as hard as I could to find a justification for my life? Didn't I try to love him, and to love my son when it was no longer possible to love my husband? But the time has come, I've realized that I can no longer deceive myself, that I am alive, that I am not to blame if God has made me so that I must love and live. And what now? If he killed me, if he killed him, I could bear it all, I could forgive it all, but no, he . . .

'How did I not guess what he would do? He'll do what's proper to his mean character. He'll remain right, and as for me, the ruined one, he will make my ruin still worse, still meaner . . .

'"You yourself can imagine what awaits you and your son",' she recalled the words of the letter. 'That's a threat that he'll take my son away, and according to their stupid law he can probably do it. But don't I know why he says it? He doesn't believe in my love for my son either, or else he despises (how he always did snigger at it), he despises this feeling of mine, but he knows that I won't abandon my son, I cannot abandon my son, that without my son there can be no life for me even with the one I love, but that if I abandon my son and run away from him, I'll be acting like the most disgraceful, vile woman – he knows that and knows I wouldn't be able to do it.

'"Our life must go on as before",' she recalled another phrase from the letter. 'That life was a torment even before, it has been terrible recently. What will it be now? And he knows it all, he knows that I cannot repent that I breathe, that I love; he knows that, except for lies and deceit, there will be nothing in it; yet he must go on tormenting me. I know him, I know that he swims and delights in lies like a fish in water. But no, I won't give him that delight, I'll tear apart this web of lies he wants to wrap around me, come what may. Anything is better than lies and deceit!

'But how? My God! My God! Was any woman ever as unhappy as I am? . . .

'No, I'll tear it, I'll tear it apart!' she cried out, jumping up and forcing back her tears. And she went to the desk in order to write him another letter. But in the depths of her soul she already sensed that she would be unable to tear anything apart, unable to get out of her former situation, however false and dishonest it was.

She sat down at the desk but, instead of writing, she folded her arms on it, put her head on them, and wept, sobbing and heaving her whole breast, the way children weep. She wept that her dream of clarifying, of defining her situation was destroyed for ever. She knew beforehand that everything would stay as it had been, and would even be far worse than it had been. She felt that the position she enjoyed in society, which had seemed so insignificant to her in the morning, was precious to her, and that she would not be able to exchange it for the shameful position of a woman who has abandoned her husband and son and joined her lover; that, try as she might, she could not be stronger than she was. She would never experience the freedom of love, but would forever remain a criminal wife, under threat of exposure every moment, deceiving her husband for the sake of a disgraceful affair with another, an independent man, with whom she could not live a life as one. She knew that this was how it would be, and at the same time it was so terrible that she could not even imagine how it would end. And she wept without restraint, as punished children weep.

The sound of the footman's steps brought her back to herself and, hiding her face from him, she pretended to be writing.

'The courier is asking for the reply,' the footman reported.

'Reply? Yes,' said Anna, 'have him wait. I'll ring.'

'What can I write?' she thought. 'What can I decide alone? What do I know? What do I want? What do I love?' Again she felt that things had begun to go double in her soul. She became frightened at this feeling and seized on the first pretext for action that came to her, to distract her from thoughts of herself. 'I must see Alexei' (so she called Vronsky in her mind), 'he alone can tell me what I must do. I'll go to Betsy: maybe I'll see him there,' she said to herself, completely forgetting that just yesterday, when she had told him that she would not go to Princess Tverskoy's, he had said that in that case he would not go either. She went to the table, wrote to her husband: 'I have received your letter. A.' – rang and handed it to the footman.

'We're not going,' she said to Annushka as she came in.

'Not going at all?'

'No, don't unpack until tomorrow, and hold the carriage. I'm going to see the princess.'

'What dress shall I prepare?'

XVII

The company at the croquet party to which Princess Tverskoy had invited Anna was to consist of two ladies with their admirers. These two ladies were the chief representatives of a select new Petersburg circle which, in imitation of an imitation of something, was called *Les sept merveilles du monde.** [16] These ladies belonged to a high circle, true, but one totally hostile to the one frequented by Anna. Besides, old Stremov, one of the influential people of Petersburg, the admirer of Liza Merkalov, was Alexei Alexandrovich's enemy in the service. Because of all these considerations, Anna had not wished to go, and it was to this refusal that the hints in Princess Tverskoy's note had referred. But now, in hopes of seeing Vronsky, she wanted to go.

Anna arrived at Princess Tverskoy's earlier than the other guests.

Just as she came in, Vronsky's footman, resembling a kammerjunker with his brushed-up side-whiskers, also came in. He stopped by the door and, taking off his cap, allowed her to pass. Anna recognized him and only then remembered Vronsky's saying the day before that he would not come. Probably he had sent a note to that effect.

As she was taking off her coat in the front hall, she heard the footman, even pronouncing his *r*s like a kammerjunker, say: 'From the count to the princess,' and hand over a note.

* The seven wonders of the world.

She would have liked to ask where his master was. She would have liked to go home and send him a letter that he should come to her, or to go to him herself. But neither the one, nor the other, nor the third was possible: the bells announcing her arrival were already ringing ahead of her, and Princess Tverskoy's footman was already standing sideways in the opened door, waiting for her to pass into the inner rooms.

'The princess is in the garden, you will be announced presently. Would you care to go to the garden?' another footman in another room asked.

The situation of indecision, of uncertainty, was the same as at home; still worse, because it was impossible to do anything, impossible to see Vronsky, and she had to stay here in an alien society so contrary to her mood; but she was wearing a costume that she knew became her; she was not alone, around her were the customary festive surroundings of idleness, and that made it easier for her than at home. She did not need to invent something to do; everything was being done by itself. Meeting Betsy coming towards her in a white gown that struck her with its elegance, Anna smiled at her as always. Princess Tverskoy was walking with Tushkevich and a young lady relation who, to the great delight of her provincial parents, was spending the summer with the famous princess.

Probably there was something special in Anna, because Betsy noticed it at once.

'I slept badly,' Anna replied, studying the footman who was coming towards them and, she supposed, bringing Vronsky's note.

'I'm so glad you've come,' said Betsy. 'I'm tired and just wanted to have a cup of tea before they arrive. Why don't you and Masha,' she turned to Tushkevich, 'go and try the croquet ground where it's been cut? You and I will have time for a heart-to-heart talk over tea – we'll have a cosy chat, won't we?' she added in English, turning to Anna with a smile and pressing her hand, which was holding a parasol.

'The more so as I can't stay with you long, I must go to see old Vrede. I promised her ages ago,' said Anna, for whom lying, foreign to her nature, had not only become simple and natural in society, but even gave her pleasure.

Why she had said something that she had not thought of a second before, she would have been quite unable to explain. She had said it only with the idea that, since Vronsky was not coming, she had to secure some freedom for herself and try to see him somehow. But why precisely she had mentioned the old lady-in-waiting Vrede, whom she had to visit no more than many others, she would not have known how to explain, and yet, as it turned out later, had she been inventing the cleverest way of seeing Vronsky, she could have found nothing better.

'No, I won't let you go for anything,' replied Betsy, peering attentively into Anna's face. 'Really, if I didn't love you, I'd be offended. As if you're afraid my company might compromise you. Please bring us tea in the small drawing room,' she said, narrowing her eyes as she always did when addressing a footman. She took a note from him and read it. 'Alexei has made us a false leap,' she said in French.* 'He writes that he can't come,' she added in such a natural, simple tone as if it never could have entered her head that Vronsky was anything more to Anna than a croquet partner.

Anna knew that Betsy knew everything, but, listening to the way she talked about Vronsky, she always had a momentary conviction that she knew nothing.

'Ah!' Anna said indifferently, as if it was of little interest to her, and went on with a smile: 'How could your company compromise anyone?' This playing with words, this concealment of the secret, held great charm for Anna, as for all women. It was not the need for concealment, not the purpose of the concealment, but the very process of concealment that fascinated her. 'I cannot be more Catholic than the pope,' she said. 'Stremov and Liza Merkalov are the cream of the cream of society. They are also received everywhere, and *I*,' she especially emphasized the *I*, 'have never been strict and intolerant. I simply have no time.'

'Perhaps you don't want to run into Stremov? Let him and Alexei Alexandrovich be at loggerheads on some committee, that's no concern of ours. But in society he's the most amiable man I know and a passionate croquet player. You'll see. And despite his ridiculous position as Liza's aged wooer, you must see how he gets himself out of it! He's very sweet. You don't know Sappho Stolz? This is a new, a quite new, tone.'

While Betsy was saying all this, Anna sensed from her cheerful, intelligent look that she partly understood her position and was up to something. They were in the small drawing room.

'Anyhow, I must write to Alexei,' and Betsy sat down at the table, wrote a few lines and put them in an envelope. 'I'm writing that he should come for dinner. I have one lady for dinner who is left without a

* I.e. '*nous a fait un faux bond*', i.e. 'has let us down'.

man. See if it sounds convincing. Excuse me, I'll leave you for a moment. Seal it, please, and send it off,' she said from the door, 'I must make some arrangements.'

Without a moment's thought, Anna sat down at the table with Betsy's letter and, without reading it, added at the bottom: 'I must see you. Come to Vrede's garden. I'll be there at six o'clock.' She sealed it, and Betsy, having returned, sent the letter off in her presence.

Over tea, which was brought to them on a tray-table in the cool small drawing room, the two women indeed engaged in a 'cosy chat', as Princess Tverskoy had promised, until the guests arrived. They discussed the people who were expected, and the conversation came to rest on Liza Merkalov.

'She's very sweet and I've always found her sympathetic,' Anna said.

'You ought to love her. She raves about you. Yesterday she came up to me after the race and was in despair at not finding you. She says you're a real heroine from a novel and that if she were a man she would have committed a thousand follies for you. Stremov tells her she commits them anyway.'

'But tell me, please, I never could understand,' Anna said after some silence and in a tone which showed clearly that she was not putting an idle question, but that what she was asking was more important for her than it ought to be. 'Tell me, please, what is her relation to Prince Kaluzhsky, the so-called Mishka? I've seldom met them. What is it?'

Betsy smiled with her eyes and looked attentively at Anna.

'It's the new way,' she said. 'They've all chosen this way. They've thrown their bonnets over the mills.* But there are different ways of throwing them over.'

'Yes, but what is her relation to Kaluzhsky?'

Betsy unexpectedly laughed, gaily and irrepressibly, something that rarely happened with her.

'You're encroaching on Princess Miagky's province. It's the question of a terrible child.'† And Betsy obviously tried to restrain herself but failed and burst into the infectious laughter of people who laugh rarely. 'You'll have to ask them,' she said through tears of laughter.

'No, you're laughing,' said Anna, also involuntarily infected with

* Tolstoy literally translates the French saying: *jeter son bonnet par-dessus les moulins*, meaning to throw caution to the winds.

† Literal translation of the French *enfant terrible*.

laughter, 'but I never could understand it. I don't understand the husband's role in it.'

'The husband? Liza Merkalov's husband carries rugs around for her and is always ready to be of service. And what else there is in fact, nobody wants to know. You see, in good society one doesn't speak or even think of certain details of the toilette. It's the same here.'

'Will you be at Rolandaki's fête?' Anna asked, to change the subject.

'I don't think so,' Betsy replied and began carefully filling the small, translucent cups with fragrant tea. Moving a cup towards Anna, she took out a slender cigarette, put it into a silver holder, and lit it.

'So you see, I'm in a fortunate position,' she began, no longer laughing, as she picked up her cup. 'I understand you and I understand Liza. Liza is one of those naïve natures, like children, who don't understand what's good and what's bad. At least she didn't understand it when she was very young. And now she knows that this non-understanding becomes her. Now she may purposely not understand,' Betsy spoke with a subtle smile, 'but all the same it becomes her. You see, one and the same thing can be looked at tragically and be made into a torment, or can be looked at simply and even gaily. Perhaps you're inclined to look at things too tragically.'

'How I wish I knew others as I know myself,' Anna said seriously and pensively. 'Am I worse than others or better? Worse, I think.'

'Terrible child, terrible child!' Betsy repeated. 'But here they are.'

XVIII

Footsteps were heard and a man's voice, then a woman's voice and laughter, and the expected guests came in: Sappho Stolz and a young man radiant with a superabundance of health, the so-called Vaska. It was evident that he prospered on a diet of rare beef, truffles and Burgundy. Vaska bowed to the ladies and glanced at them, but only for a second. He came into the drawing room after Sappho, and followed her across the room as if tied to her, not taking his shining eyes off her, as if he wanted to eat her up. Sappho Stolz was a dark-eyed blonde. She walked with brisk little steps in her high-heeled shoes and gave the ladies a firm, mannish handshake.

Anna had not met this new celebrity before and was struck by her beauty, by how extremely far her costume went, and by the boldness of her manners. On her head, hair of a delicately golden colour, her own and other women's, was done up into such an edifice of a coiffure that her head equalled in size her shapely, well-rounded and much-exposed bust. Her forward movement was so impetuous that at every step the forms of her knees and thighs were outlined under her dress, and the question involuntarily arose as to where, at the back of this built-up, heaving mountain, her real, small and shapely body actually ended, so bare above and so concealed behind and below.

Betsy hastened to introduce her to Anna.

'Can you imagine, we nearly ran over two soldiers,' she began telling them at once, winking, smiling, and thrusting her train back in place, having first swept it too far to one side. 'I was driving with Vaska ... Ah, yes, you're not acquainted.' And, giving his family name, she introduced the young man and, blushing, laughed loudly at her mistake, that is, at having called him Vaska to a stranger.

Vaska bowed to Anna once again, but said nothing to her. He turned to Sappho:

'You've lost the bet. We came first. Pay up,' he said, smiling.

Sappho laughed still more gaily.

'But not now,' she said.

'Never mind, I'll get it later.'

'All right, all right. Ah, yes!' she suddenly turned to the hostess, 'a fine one I am ... I quite forgot ... I've brought you a guest. Here he is.'

The unexpected young guest whom Sappho had brought and forgotten was, however, such an important guest that, despite his youth, both ladies rose to meet him.[17]

This was Sappho's new admirer. He now hung on her heels, just as Vaska did.

Soon Prince Kaluzhsky arrived, and Liza Merkalov with Stremov. Liza Merkalov was a slender brunette with a lazy, Levantine type of face and lovely – unfathomable, as everyone said – eyes. The character of her dark costume (Anna noticed and appreciated it at once) was perfectly suited to her beauty. She was as soft and loose as Sappho was tough and collected.

But to Anna's taste Liza was far more attractive. Betsy had said of her to Anna that she had adopted the tone of an ingenuous child, but when Anna saw her, she felt it was not true. She was indeed an ingenuous, spoiled, but sweet and mild woman. True, her tone was the same as Sappho's; just as with Sappho, two admirers followed after her as if sewn to her, devouring her with their eyes, one young, the other an old man; but there was something in her that was higher than her surroundings – there was the brilliance of a diamond of the first water amidst glass. This brilliance shone from her lovely, indeed unfathomable, eyes. The weary and at the same time passionate gaze of those dark-ringed eyes was striking in its perfect sincerity. Looking into those eyes, everyone thought he knew her thoroughly and, knowing, could not but love her. When she saw Anna, her face suddenly lit up with a joyful smile.

'Ah, how glad I am to see you!' she said, going up to her. 'Yesterday at the races I was just about to go to you, but you left. I wanted so much to see you precisely yesterday. Wasn't it terrible?' she said, looking at Anna with those eyes that seemed to reveal her entire soul.

'Yes, I never expected it would be so upsetting,' said Anna, blushing.

The company rose just then to go to the garden.

'I won't go,' said Liza, smiling and sitting down beside Anna. 'You won't go either? Who wants to play croquet!'

'No, I like it,' said Anna.

'But how do you manage not to be bored? One looks at you and feels gay. You live, but I'm bored.'

'Bored? You're the gayest company in Petersburg,' said Anna.

'Maybe those who aren't in our company are more bored; but for us, for me certainly, it's not gay, it's terribly, terribly boring.'

Sappho, lighting a cigarette, went to the garden with the two young men. Betsy and Stremov stayed at tea.

'Boring?' said Betsy. 'Sappho says they had a very gay time with you yesterday.'

'Ah, it was excruciating!' said Liza Merkalov. 'We all went to my house after the races. And it was all the same people, all the same! All one and the same thing. We spent the whole evening lolling on the sofa. What's gay about that? No, how do you manage not to be bored?' She again turned to Anna. 'One looks at you and sees – here is a woman who can be happy or unhappy, but not bored. Tell me, how do you do it?'

'I don't do anything,' said Anna, blushing at these importunate questions.

'That's the best way,' Stremov mixed in the conversation.

Stremov was a man of about fifty, half grey, still fresh, very ugly, but with an expressive and intelligent face. Liza Merkalov was his wife's niece, and he spent all his free time with her. Meeting Anna Karenina, he, who was Alexei Alexandrovich's enemy in the service, being an intelligent man of the world, tried to be especially amiable to her, his enemy's wife.

'Don't do anything,' he repeated with a subtle smile, 'that's the best way. I've long been telling you,' he turned to Liza Merkalov, 'that to keep things from being boring, you mustn't think they'll be boring. Just as you mustn't be afraid you won't fall asleep if you fear insomnia. And Anna Arkadyevna is telling you the same thing.'

'I'd be very glad if I had said that, because it's not only intelligent, but also true,' Anna said, smiling.

'No, tell me, why is it impossible to fall asleep and impossible not to be bored?'

'To fall asleep you must work, and to be gay you also must work.'

'But why should I work, if nobody needs my work? And I cannot and do not want to pretend on purpose.'

'You're incorrigible,' said Stremov without looking at her, and again he turned to Anna.

As he met Anna rarely, he could say nothing but banalities, but he uttered these banalities about when she was moving back to Petersburg, about how Countess Lydia Ivanovna loved her, with an expression which showed that he wished with all his heart to be agreeable to her and show his respect and even more.

Tushkevich came in, announcing that the whole company was waiting for the croquet players.

'No, please don't leave,' begged Liza Merkalov, learning that Anna was leaving. Stremov joined her.

'It's too great a contrast,' he said, 'to go to old Vrede after this company. And besides you'll give her an occasion for malicious gossip, while here you'll call up only other, very good, feelings, the opposite of malicious gossip.'

Anna reflected hesitantly for a moment. The flattering talk of this intelligent man, the naïve, childlike sympathy that Liza Merkalov showed for her, and this whole accustomed social situation was so easy, while what awaited her was so difficult, that for a moment she was undecided whether she might not stay, whether she might not put off the painful moment of explanation a little longer. But, remembering what awaited her at home alone if she took no decision, remembering that gesture, which was terrible for her even in remembrance, when she had clutched her hair with both hands, she said good-bye and left.

XIX

Vronsky, despite his seemingly frivolous social life, was a man who hated disorder. While young, still in the corps, he had experienced the humiliation of refusal when, having got entangled, he had asked for a loan, and since then he had never put himself into such a position.

To keep his affairs in order at all times, he would go into seclusion more or less frequently, some five times a year, depending on the circumstances, and clear up all his affairs. He called it squaring accounts or *faire la lessive*.*

Waking up late the day after the races, Vronsky put on his uniform jacket without shaving or bathing and, laying out money, bills and letters on the table, set to work. When Petritsky, who knew that in such situations he was usually cross, woke up and saw his friend at the writing desk, he quietly got dressed and went out without bothering him.

Every man, knowing to the smallest detail all the complexity of the conditions surrounding him, involuntarily assumes that the complexity of these conditions and the difficulty of comprehending them are only his personal, accidental peculiarity, and never thinks that others are surrounded by the same complexity as he is. So it seemed to Vronsky. And he thought, not without inner pride and not groundlessly, that anyone else would long ago have become entangled and been forced to act badly if he had found himself in such difficult circumstances. Yet he felt that to avoid getting entangled he had to do the accounts and clear up his situation there and then.

The first thing Vronsky attacked, being the easiest, was money matters. Having written out in his small handwriting on a sheet of notepaper everything he owed, he added it all up and discovered that he owed seventeen thousand and some hundreds, which he dismissed for the sake of clarity. Then he counted up his cash and bank book and discovered that he had one thousand eight hundred left, with no prospect of getting

* Doing the laundry.

more before the New Year. Rereading the list of his debts, Vronsky wrote it out again, dividing it into three categories. To the first category belonged debts that had to be paid at once, or in any case for which he had to have ready cash, to be paid on demand without a moment's delay. These debts came to about four thousand: one thousand five hundred for the horse, and two thousand five hundred as security for his young comrade Venevsky, who in his presence had lost that amount to a card-sharper. Vronsky had wanted to pay the money right then (he had had it on him), but Venevsky and Yashvin had insisted that they would pay it, not Vronsky, who had not even been playing. That was all very fine, but Vronsky knew that in this dirty business, which he had taken part in if only by giving verbal security for Venevsky, he had to have the two thousand five hundred ready to fling at the swindler and have no further discussions with him. And so, for this first and most important category, he had to have four thousand. In the second category, of eight thousand, there were less important debts. These were mostly debts to the racing stables, to the oats and hay supplier, to the Englishman, the saddler and so on. Of these debts he had to pay off some two thousand in order to be perfectly at ease. The last category of debts – to shops, hotels, the tailor – were of the sort not worth thinking about. Therefore he needed at least six thousand, and had only one thousand eight hundred for current expenses. For a man with an income of a hundred thousand, as everyone evaluated Vronsky's fortune, such debts, it would seem, could not be burdensome; but the thing was that he was far from having a hundred thousand. His father's enormous fortune, which alone had brought an annual income of two hundred thousand, had not been divided between the two brothers. At the time when the older brother, having a heap of debts, married Princess Varya Chirkov, the daughter of a Decembrist,[18] with no fortune at all, Alexei had given up to his older brother all the income from his father's estates, reserving for himself only twenty-five thousand a year. Alexei had told his brother then that this money would suffice him until he married, which most likely would never happen. And his brother, commander of one of the most expensive regiments[19] and recently married, could not but accept the gift. On top of the reserved twenty-five thousand, his mother, who had her own fortune, gave Alexei some twenty thousand more, and Alexei spent it all. Lately, having quarrelled with him over his liaison and his leaving Moscow, she had stopped sending him the money. As a result, Vronsky, who was used to living on forty-five thousand a year and that year had received only twenty-five, now found himself in difficulties. He could not ask his mother for money in order to get out of these difficulties. Her latest letter, received the day before, had especially vexed him, as there were hints in it that she was ready to help him towards success in society and in the service, but not for a life that scandalized all good society. His mother's wish to buy him had insulted him to the depths of his soul and cooled him still more towards her. But he could not renounce the generous words he had spoken, though he now felt, vaguely foreseeing some eventualities of his affair with Anna, that those generous words had been spoken light-mindedly, and that, unmarried, he might need the whole hundred thousand of income. But to renounce them was impossible. He had only to recall his brother's wife, recall how that dear, sweet Varya reminded him at every chance that she remembered his generosity and appreciated it, to understand the impossibility of taking back what had been given. It was as impossible as stealing, lying, or striking a woman. One thing could and had to be done, which Vronsky resolved upon without a moment's hesitation: to borrow ten thousand from a moneylender, which would be easy enough, to cut down his expenses in general, and to sell his racehorses. Having decided on that, he straight away wrote a note to Rolandaki, who had sent to him more than once with an offer to buy his horses. Then he sent for the Englishman and for the moneylender, and divided the money he had available into payments. After finishing these matters, he wrote a cold and sharp response to his mother's letter. Then, taking three of Anna's notes from his wallet, he reread them, burned them, and, recalling his talk with her the evening before, fell to thinking.

XX

Vronsky's life was especially fortunate in that he had a code of rules which unquestionably defined everything that ought and ought not to be done. The code embraced a very small circle of conditions, but the rules were unquestionable and, never going outside that circle, Vronsky never hesitated a moment in doing what ought be done. These rules determined unquestionably that a card-sharper must be paid but a tailor need not be, that one should not lie to men but may lie to women, that it is wrong to deceive anyone but one may deceive a husband, that it is wrong to pardon insults but one may give insults, and so on. These rules might not all be very reasonable or very nice, but they were unquestionable, and in fulfilling them Vronsky felt at ease and could hold his head high. Only most recently, in regard to his relations with Anna, had he begun to feel that his code of rules did not fully define all circumstances, and to envisage future difficulties and doubts in which he could no longer find a guiding thread.

His present relations with Anna and her husband were simple and clear. They were clearly and precisely defined in the code of rules by which he was guided.

She was a respectable woman who had given him her love, and he loved her; therefore she was a woman worthy of equal and even greater respect than a lawful wife. He would have let his hand be cut off sooner than allow himself a word or a hint that might insult her or fail to show her that respect which a woman may simply count on.

His relations with society were also clear. Everyone might know or suspect it, but no one should dare to talk. Otherwise he was prepared to silence the talkers and make them respect the non-existent honour of the woman he loved.

His relations with the husband were clearest of all. From the moment of Anna's love for him, he had considered his own right to her unassailable. The husband was merely a superfluous and interfering person. No doubt his position was pathetic, but what could be done? One thing the husband had the right to do was ask for satisfaction, weapon in hand, and for that Vronsky had been prepared from the first moment.

But recently there had appeared new, inner relations between himself and her that frightened Vronsky with their indefiniteness. Just yesterday she had announced to him that she was pregnant. And he felt that this news and what she expected of him called for something not wholly defined by the code of rules that guided him in his life. He had indeed been caught unawares, and in the first moment, when she had announced her condition to him, his heart had prompted him to demand that she leave her husband. He had said it, but now, thinking it over, he saw clearly that it would be better to do without that; and yet, in saying so to himself, he was afraid – might it not be a bad thing?

'If I said she must leave her husband, it means to unite with me. Am I ready for that? How can I take her away now, when I have no money? Suppose I could arrange it . . . But how can I take her away when I'm in the service? If I say it, then I have to be ready for it, that is, to have money and resign from the service.'

And he fell to thinking. The question of resigning or not resigning led him to another secret interest, known only to himself, all but the chief, though hidden, interest of his whole life.

Ambition was the old dream of his childhood and youth, a dream which he did not confess even to himself, but which was so strong that even now this passion struggled with his love. His first steps in the world and in the service had been successful, but two years ago he had made a blunder. Wishing to show his independence and move ahead, he had refused a post offered to him, hoping that his refusal would endow him with greater value; but it turned out that he had been too bold, and he was passed over. Having willy-nilly created a position for himself as an independent man, he bore with it, behaving quite subtly and intelligently, as if he was not angry with anyone, did not consider himself offended by anyone and wished only to be left in peace, because he liked it that way. But in fact, a year ago, when he went to Moscow, he ceased to like it. He sensed that this independent position of a man who could do anything but wanted nothing was beginning to wear thin, that many were beginning to think he could do nothing but be an honest and good fellow. His liaison with Anna, which had made so much noise and attracted general attention, had lent him new brilliance and pacified for a time the worm of ambition that gnawed at him, but a week ago this worm had awakened with renewed force. His childhood comrade, of the same circle, the same wealth, and a comrade in the corps, Serpukhovskoy, who had graduated in the same year, had been his rival in class, in gymnastics, in pranks, and in ambitious dreams, had come back from Central Asia the other day,[20] having received two promotions there and a decoration rarely given to such young generals.

As soon as he arrived in Petersburg, he began to be talked about as a new rising star of the first magnitude. Of the same age as Vronsky and his classmate, he was a general and expected an appointment that might influence the course of state affairs, while Vronsky, though independent and brilliant and loved by a charming woman, was none the less only a cavalry captain, who was left to be as independent as he liked. 'Naturally, I do not and cannot envy Serpukhovskoy, but his rise shows me that, if one bides one's time, the career of a man like me can be made very quickly. Three years ago he was in the same position I am in now. If I resign, I'll be burning my boats. By remaining in the service, I won't lose anything. She said herself that she didn't want to change her situation. And, with her love, I cannot envy Serpukhovskoy.' Twirling his moustache in a slow movement, he got up from the table and walked around the room. His eyes shone especially brightly, and he felt that firm, calm and joyful state of mind which always came over him after clarifying his situation. As after previous squarings of accounts, everything was clean and clear. He shaved, washed, took a cold bath and went out.

XXI

'I was coming to get you. Your laundry took a long time today,' said Petritsky. 'Well, are you done?'

'Done,' replied Vronsky, smiling with his eyes alone and twirling the tips of his moustache carefully as if, after the order he had brought to his affairs, any too bold and quick movement might destroy it.

'Afterwards it's always as if you just got out of the bath,' said Petritsky. 'I'm coming from Gritska' (as they called the regimental commander). 'You're expected.'

Vronsky gazed at his comrade without replying, thinking of something else.

'Ah, is that music at his place?' he said, catching the familiar sounds of tubas playing polkas and waltzes. 'What's the celebration?'

'Serpukhovskoy's arrived.'

'Ahh,' said Vronsky, 'and I didn't know!'

The smile in his eyes shone still brighter.

Having once decided to himself that he was happy in his love and was sacrificing his ambition to it, or at least having taken this role upon himself, Vronsky could no longer feel either envy for Serpukhovskoy, or vexation with him for not visiting him first on coming to the regiment. Serpukhovskoy was a good friend, and he was pleased that he had come.

'Ah, I'm very glad.'

Regimental commander Diomin occupied a large landowner's house. The whole party was on the spacious lower balcony. In the yard, the first thing that struck Vronsky's eyes was the singers in uniform blouses standing by a barrel of vodka, and the robust, jovial figure of the regimental commander surrounded by officers; coming out on the top step of the balcony, loudly out-shouting the band, which was playing an Offenbach quadrille, he was giving orders and waving to some soldiers standing to one side. A bunch of soldiers, a sergeant-major and several non-commissioned officers, approached the balcony together with Vronsky. Going back to the table, the regimental commander again came to the porch with a glass in his hand and proposed a toast: 'To the health of our former comrade and brave general, Prince Serpukhovskoy. Hurrah!'

After the regimental commander, Serpukhovskoy also came out, smiling, a glass in his hand.

'You keep getting younger, Bondarenko.' He addressed the dashing, red-cheeked sergeant-major, now serving his second term, who was standing right in front of him.

Vronsky had not seen Serpukhovskoy for three years. He looked more manly, having let his side-whiskers grow, but he was still as trim, striking not so much by his good looks as by the delicacy and nobility of his face and build. One change that Vronsky noticed in him was the quiet, steady glow that settles on the faces of those who are successful and are certain that their success is recognized by everyone. Vronsky knew that glow and noticed it at once in Serpukhovskoy.

Going down the stairs, Serpukhovskoy saw Vronsky. A smile of joy lit up his face. He tossed his head and raised his glass, greeting Vronsky and showing by this gesture that he could not help going first to the sergeant-major who, drawing himself up, had already puckered his lips for a kiss.

'Well, here he is!' cried the regimental commander. 'And Yashvin told me you were in one of your dark moods.'

Serpukhovskoy kissed the dashing sergeant-major on his moist and fresh lips and, wiping his mouth with a handkerchief, went up to Vronsky.

'Well, I'm so glad!' he said, pressing his hand and leading him aside.

'Take care of him!' the regimental commander cried to Yashvin, pointing at Vronsky, and went down to the soldiers.

'Why weren't you at the races yesterday? I thought I'd see you there,' said Vronsky, looking Serpukhovskoy over.

'I came, but late. Sorry,' he added and turned to his adjutant. 'Please tell them this is to be handed out from me, however much it comes to per man.'

And he hastily took three hundred-rouble notes from his wallet and blushed.

'Vronsky! Want anything to eat or drink?' asked Yashvin. 'Hey, bring the count something to eat! And here's a drink for you.'

The carousing at the regimental commander's went on for a long time. They drank a lot. They swung and tossed Serpukhovskoy. Then they swung the regimental commander. Then in front of the singers the regimental commander himself danced with Petritsky. Then the regimental commander, grown somewhat slack now, sat down on a bench in the yard and began proving to Yashvin Russia's advantages over Prussia, especially in cavalry attack, and the carousing subsided for a moment. Serpukhovskoy went inside to the dressing room, to wash his hands, and found Vronsky there; Vronsky was dousing himself with water. Taking off his jacket, he put his hairy red neck under the stream from the tap and rubbed it and his head with his hands. When he had finished washing, Vronsky sat down with Serpukhovskoy. The two men sat on a little sofa, and a conversation began between them that was very interesting for them both.

'I knew everything about you through my wife,' said Serpukhovskoy. 'I'm glad you saw her often.'

'She's friends with Varya, and they're the only women in Petersburg I enjoy seeing,' Vronsky replied with a smile. He smiled because he foresaw the subject the conversation would turn to, and it was pleasing to him.

'The only ones?' Serpukhovskoy repeated, smiling.

'Yes, and I knew about you, but not only through your wife,' said Vronsky, forbidding the allusion with a stern look. 'I was very glad of your success, but not surprised in the least. I expected still more.'

Serpukhovskoy smiled. He was obviously pleased by this opinion of him, and found it unnecessary to conceal it.

'I, on the contrary, will sincerely admit that I expected less. But I'm glad, very glad. I'm ambitious, that's my weakness, and I admit it.'

'You might not admit it if you weren't successful,' said Vronsky.

'I don't think so,' said Serpukhovskoy, smiling again. 'I won't say life wouldn't be worth living without it, but it would be boring. Of course, I may be wrong, but it seems to me that I have some ability for the sphere of action I've chosen, and that power, whatever it might be, if I should get it, would be better in my hands than in the hands of many men I know,' he said, with a glowing awareness of success. 'And therefore, the closer I come to it, the more pleased I am.'

'That may be so for you, but not for everyone. I thought the same thing, but now I live and find that it's not worth living just for that,' said Vronsky.

'There it is! There it is!' Serpukhovskoy said, laughing. 'I began by saying that I'd heard about you, about your refusal . . . Naturally, I approved of you. But there's a right and wrong way for everything. And I think that the action was good, but you didn't do it as you should have.'

'What's done is done, and you know I never renounce what I've done. And then, too, I'm quite fine.'

'Quite fine – for the time being. But you won't remain satisfied with that. It's not your brother I'm talking to. He's a sweet child, just like our host – there he goes!' he added, hearing a shout of 'Hurrah!' 'And he has his fun. But for you that's not enough.'

'I'm not saying I'm satisfied.'

'It isn't just that. People like you are needed.'

'By whom?'

'By whom? By society. Russia needs people, needs a party, otherwise everything goes and will go to the dogs.'

'Meaning what? Bertenev's party against the Russian communists?'[21]

'No,' said Serpukhovskoy, wincing with vexation at being suspected of such stupidity. '*Tout ça est une blague.** It always has been and always will be. There aren't any communists. But people given to intrigue always have to invent some harmful, dangerous party. It's an old trick. No, what's needed is a party of independent people like you and me.'

'But why?' Vronsky named several people in power. 'Why aren't they independent people?'

'Only because they don't have or weren't born with an independent fortune, didn't have a name, weren't born as near to the sun as we were. They can be bought either by money or by favours. And in order to hold out they have to invent a trend. And they put forth some idea, some trend which they don't believe in themselves, and which does harm; and this whole trend is only a means of having a government house and a salary of so much. *Cela n'est pas plus fin que ça*,† when you look into their cards. Maybe I'm worse or stupider than they are, though I don't see why I should be worse. But you and I certainly have the one important advantage that we're harder to buy. And such people are needed now more than ever.'

* That is all a joke.

† It's no more subtle than that.

Vronsky listened attentively, but was taken up not so much with the actual content of his words as with Serpukhovskoy's attitude towards things, how he already thought of struggling with the ruling powers and already had his sympathies and antipathies in this world, while for him there was nothing in the service but the interests of his squadron. Vronsky also realized how strong Serpukhovskoy could be in his unquestionable ability to reflect, to comprehend things, in his intelligence and gift for words, which occurred so rarely in the milieu in which he lived. And, much as it shamed him, he was envious.

'All the same I lack the one chief thing for that,' he replied, 'I lack the desire for power. I had it, but it went away.'

'Excuse me, but that's not true,' Serpukhovskoy said, smiling.

'No, it's true, it's true! . . . now,' Vronsky added, to be sincere.

'Yes, it's true *now*, that's another matter; but this *now* is not for ever.'

'Maybe not,' replied Vronsky.

'You say *maybe not*,' Serpukhovskoy went on, as if guessing his thoughts, 'and I tell you *certainly not*. And that's why I wanted to see you. You acted as you had to. I understand that, but you should not *persevere*. I'm only asking you for *carte blanche*. I'm not patronizing you . . . Though why shouldn't I patronize you? You've patronized me so many times! I hope our friendship stands above that. Yes,' he said, smiling at him tenderly, like a woman. 'Give me *carte blanche*, leave the regiment, and I'll draw you in imperceptibly.'

'But do understand, I don't need anything,' said Vronsky, 'except that everything be the same as it has been.'

Serpukhovskoy got up and stood facing him.

'You say everything should be as it has been. I understand what that means. But listen. We're the same age. You may have known a greater number of women than I have,' Serpukhovskoy's smile and gestures told Vronsky that he need not be afraid, that he would touch the sore spot gently and carefully. 'But I'm married, and believe me, knowing the one wife you love (as someone wrote), you know all women better than if you'd known thousands of them.'

'We're coming!' Vronsky shouted to the officer who looked into the room to summon them to the regimental commander.

Now Vronsky wanted to listen to the end and learn what Serpukhovskoy was going to tell him.

'And here is my opinion for you. Women are the main stumbling block in a man's activity. It's hard to love a woman and do anything.

For this there exists one means of loving conveniently, without hindrance – that is marriage. How can I tell you, how can I tell you what I'm thinking,' said Serpukhovskoy, who liked comparisons, 'wait, wait! Yes, it's as if you're carrying a *fardeau** and doing something with your hands is only possible if the *fardeau* is tied to your back – and that is marriage. And I felt it once I got married. I suddenly had my hands free. But dragging this *fardeau* around without marriage – that will make your hands so full that you won't be able to do anything. Look at Mazankov, at Krupov. They ruined their careers on account of women.'

'What sort of women!' said Vronsky, recalling the Frenchwoman and the actress with whom the two men mentioned had had affairs.

'So much the worse. The firmer a woman's position in society, the worse it is. It's the same as not only dragging the *fardeau* around in your arms, but tearing it away from someone else.'

'You've never loved,' Vronsky said softly, gazing before him and thinking of Anna.

'Maybe not. But remember what I've told you. And also: women are all more material than men. We make something enormous out of love, and they're always *terre-à-terre*.'[†]

'Right away, right away!' he said to a footman who came in. But the footman had not come to call them again, as he thought. The footman brought a note for Vronsky.

'A man brought it from Princess Tverskoy.'

Vronsky unsealed the letter and flushed.

'I have a headache, I'm going home,' he said to Serpukhovskoy.

'Good-bye, then. Do you give me *carte blanche*?'

'We'll talk later, I'll look you up in Petersburg.'

XXII

It was past five o'clock, and therefore, so as not to be late and at the same time not to take his own horses, which everyone knew, Vronsky took Yashvin's hired cab and ordered the driver to go as fast as he could.

* Burden.

† Down to earth.

The old four-seater coach was roomy. He sat in the corner, stretched his legs out on the front seat and fell to thinking.

The vague awareness of the clarity his affairs had been brought to, the vague recollection of the friendship and flattery of Serpukhovskoy, who considered him a necessary man, and, above all, the anticipation of the meeting – all united into one general, joyful feeling of life. This feeling was so strong that he smiled involuntarily. He put his feet down, placed one leg across the knee of the other and, taking it in his hand, felt the resilient calf, hurt the day before in his fall, and, leaning back, took several deep breaths.

'Good, very good!' he said to himself. Before, too, he had often experienced the joyful awareness of his body, but never had he so loved himself, his own body, as now. He enjoyed feeling that slight pain in his strong leg, enjoyed feeling the movement of his chest muscles as he breathed. That same clear and cold August day which had had such a hopeless effect on Anna, to him seemed stirringly invigorating and refreshed his face and neck that tingled from the dousing. The smell of brilliantine on his moustache seemed especially enjoyable to him in that fresh air. Everything he saw through the coach window, everything in that cold, clean air, in that pale light of sunset, was as fresh, cheerful and strong as himself: the rooftops glistening in the rays of the sinking sun, the sharp outlines of fences and the corners of buildings, the figures of the rare passers-by and the carriages they met, the motionless green of the trees and grass, the fields with regularly incised rows of potatoes, the slanting shadows cast by the houses, trees, and bushes and the rows of potatoes themselves. Everything was as beautiful as a pretty landscape just finished and coated with varnish.

'Faster, faster!' he said to the cabby. Leaning out the window, he took a three-rouble bill from his pocket and handed it to the driver as he turned. The cabby's hand felt for something by the lantern, the whip whistled, and the carriage rolled quickly along the smooth road.

'I need nothing, nothing but this happiness,' he thought, gazing at the ivory knob of the bell between the windows and imagining Anna as he had seen her the last time. 'And the further it goes, the more I love her. Here's the garden of Vrede's government country house. Where is she? Where? How? Why did she arrange the meeting here and write it in Betsy's letter?' he wondered only now; but there was no more time for thinking. He stopped the coach before it reached the avenue, opened the door, jumped out while the carriage was still moving and walked into the avenue leading to the house. There was no one in the avenue; but looking to the right, he saw her. Her face was covered with a veil, but with joyful eyes he took in the special motion of her gait, peculiar to her alone, the curve of her shoulders, and the poise of her head, and immediately it was as if an electric current ran through his body. He felt his own self with new force, from the resilient movements of his legs to the movements of his lungs as he breathed, and something tickled his lips.

Coming up to him, she pressed his hand firmly.

'You're not angry that I sent for you? It was necessary for me to see you,' she said; and the serious and stern set of her lips, which he could see behind the veil, immediately changed his state of mind.

'I, angry! But how did you come, why here?'

'Never mind,' she said, putting her hand on his. 'Come, we must talk.'

He understood that something had happened, that this meeting would not be joyful. In her presence he had no will of his own: not knowing the reason for her anxiety, he already felt that this same anxiety had involuntarily communicated itself to him.

'What is it? What?' he asked, pressing her arm with his elbow and trying to read her thoughts in her face.

She walked a few steps in silence, gathering her courage, and suddenly stopped.

'I didn't tell you yesterday,' she began, breathing rapidly and heavily, 'that on the way home with Alexei Alexandrovich I told him everything . . . I said that I could not be his wife, that . . . I told him everything.'

He listened to her, involuntarily leaning his whole body towards her, as if wishing in this way to soften the difficulty of her situation. But as soon as she had said it, he suddenly straightened up and his face acquired a proud and stern expression.

'Yes, yes, it's better, a thousand times better! I understand how difficult it was,' he said.

But she was not listening to his words, she was reading his thoughts in the expression of his face. She could not have known that his expression reflected the first thought that occurred to him – that a duel was now inevitable. The thought of a duel had never entered her head and therefore she explained this momentary expression of sternness differently.

Having received her husband's letter, she already knew in the depths of her soul that everything would remain as before, that she would be unable to scorn her position, to leave her son and unite herself with her lover. The morning spent at Princess Tverskoy's had confirmed her still more in that. But all the same this meeting was extremely important for her. She hoped it would change their situation and save her. If at this news he should say to her resolutely, passionately, without a moment's hesitation: 'Abandon everything and fly away with me!' – she would leave her son and go with him. But the news did not produce in him what she expected: he only seemed insulted by something.

'It wasn't the least bit difficult. It got done by itself,' she said irritably. 'Here . . .' She took her husband's letter from her glove.

'I understand, I understand,' he interrupted, taking the letter without reading it and trying to calm her. 'I wished for one thing, I asked for one thing – to break up this situation, in order to devote my life to your happiness.'

'Why are you telling me that?' she said. 'Could I possibly doubt it? If I did . . .'

'Who's that coming?' Vronsky said suddenly, pointing at two ladies coming towards them. 'Maybe they know us,' and he hastened to turn down a side walk, drawing her after him.

'Oh, I don't care!' she said. Her lips were trembling. And it seemed to him that her eyes looked at him with a strange spite from behind the veil. 'As I said, that's not the point, I cannot doubt that, but here is what he writes to me. Read it.' She stopped again.

Again, as in the first moment, at the news of her break with her husband, Vronsky, while reading the letter, involuntarily yielded to the natural impression aroused in him by his attitude towards the insulted husband. Now, as he held his letter in his hands, he involuntarily pictured to himself the challenge he would probably find today or tomorrow at his place, and the duel itself, during which he would stand, with the same cold and proud expression that was now on his face, having fired into the air, awaiting the insulted husband's shot. And at once there flashed in his head the thought of what Serpukhovskoy had just said to him and what he himself had thought that morning – that it was better not to bind himself – and he knew that he could not tell her this thought.

Having read the letter, he raised his eyes to her, and there was no firmness in his look. She understood at once that he had already thought it over to himself. She knew that whatever he might tell her, he would not say everything he thought. And she understood that her last hope had been disappointed. This was not what she had expected.

'You see what sort of man he is,' she said in a trembling voice, 'he . . .'

'Forgive me, but I'm glad of it,' Vronsky interrupted. 'For God's sake, let me finish,' he added, his eyes begging her to give him time to explain his words. 'I'm glad, because it cannot, it simply cannot remain as he suggests.'

'Why not?' Anna asked, holding back her tears, obviously no longer attaching any significance to what he was going to say. She felt that her fate was decided.

Vronsky wanted to say that after the duel, in his opinion inevitable, this could not go on, but he said something else.

'It cannot go on. I hope you will leave him now. I hope,' he became confused and blushed, 'that you will allow me to arrange and think over our life. Tomorrow . . .' he began.

She did not let him finish.

'And my son?' she cried out. 'Do you see what he writes? I must leave him, and I cannot and will not do it.'

'But for God's sake, which is better? To leave your son or to go on in this humiliating situation?'

'Humiliating for whom?'

'For everyone and most of all for you.'

'You say "humiliating" . . . don't say it. Such words have no meaning for me,' she said in a trembling voice. She did not want him to say what was not true now. All she had left was his love, and she wanted to love him. 'You understand that from the day I loved you everything was changed for me. For me there is one thing only – your love. If it is mine, I feel myself so high, so firm, that nothing can be humiliating for me. I'm proud of my position, because . . . proud of . . . proud . . .' She did not finish saying what she was proud of. Tears of shame and despair stifled her voice. She stopped and burst into sobs.

He also felt something rising in his throat, tickling in his nose, and for the first time in his life he felt himself ready to cry. He could not have said precisely what moved him so; he pitied her, and he felt that he could not help her, and at the same time he knew that he was to blame for her unhappiness, that he had done something bad.

'Is divorce impossible?' he said weakly. She shook her head without replying. 'Can't you take your son and leave him anyway?'

'Yes, but it all depends on him. Now I must go to him,' she said drily. Her feeling that everything would remain as before had not deceived her.

'I'll be in Petersburg on Tuesday, and everything will be decided.'

'Yes,' she said. 'But let's not talk about it any more.'

Anna's carriage, which she had sent away and told to come to the gate of Vrede's garden, drove up. She took leave of him and went home.

XXIII

On Monday there was the usual meeting of the commission of June 2nd. Alexei Alexandrovich entered the meeting room, greeted the members and the chairman as usual, and took his seat, placing his hand on the papers prepared before him. Among these papers were the references he needed and the outline of the statement he intended to make. However, he did not need any references. He remembered everything and found it unnecessary to go over in his memory what he planned to say. He knew that when the time came and he saw the face of his adversary before him, vainly trying to assume an indifferent expression, his speech would flow of itself better than he could now prepare it. He felt that the content of his speech was so great that every word would be significant. Meanwhile, listening to the usual report, he had a most innocent, inoffensive look. No one, looking at his white hands with their swollen veins, their long fingers so tenderly touching both edges of the sheet of white paper lying before him, and his head bent to one side with its expression of fatigue, would have thought that from his mouth there would presently pour words that would cause a terrible storm, would make the members shout, interrupting each other, and the chairman call for order. When the report was over, Alexei Alexandrovich announced in his quiet, thin voice that he was going to give some of his reflections on the subject of the settlement of racial minorities. All attention turned to him. He cleared his throat and, without looking at his adversary, but choosing, as he always did when making a speech, the first person sitting in front of him – a mild little old man, who never expressed any opinion in the commission – began to expound his considerations. When it came to the fundamental and organic law, the adversary jumped up and began to object. Stremov, also a member of the commission and also cut to the quick, began to justify himself – and the meeting generally became stormy; but Alexei Alexandrovich triumphed, and his proposal was accepted; three new commissions were appointed, and the next day in a certain Petersburg circle there was no other talk than of this meeting. Alexei Alexandrovich's success was even greater than he had expected.

The next morning, Tuesday, on waking up, he recalled with pleasure the previous day's victory and could not help smiling, though he wished to look indifferent when the office manager, wishing to flatter him, told him about the rumours that had reached him concerning what had happened in the commission.

Busy with the office manager, Alexei Alexandrovich completely forgot that it was Tuesday, the day he had appointed for Anna Arkadyevna's arrival, and was unpleasantly surprised when a servant came to announce her arrival to him.

Anna arrived in Petersburg early in the morning; a carriage was sent to fetch her, in accordance with her telegram, and therefore Alexei Alexandrovich might have known of her arrival. But when she arrived, he did not meet her. She was told that he had not come out yet and was busy with the office manager. She asked that her husband be told of her arrival, went to her boudoir and began to unpack her things, expecting him to come to her. But an hour went by and he did not come. She went out to the dining room under the pretext of giving orders and spoke loudly on purpose, expecting him to come there; but he did not come, though she heard him walk to the door of the study to see the office manager off. She knew that he would soon leave for work, as usual, and she would have liked to see him before then, in order to have their relations defined.

After taking a few steps round the drawing room, she resolutely went to him. When she entered his study, he was sitting in his uniform, apparently ready to leave, leaning his elbows on the small table and gazing dejectedly in front of him. She saw him before he saw her, and she realized that he was thinking about her.

Seeing her, he made as if to get up, changed his mind, then his face flushed, something Anna had never seen before, and he quickly got up and went to meet her, looking not into her eyes but higher, at her forehead and hair. He went up to her, took her by the hand and asked her to sit down.

'I'm very glad you've come,' he said, sitting down next to her, and, obviously wishing to say something, he faltered. Several times he tried to begin speaking, but stopped. Although, while preparing herself for this meeting, she had taught herself to despise and accuse him, she did not know what to say and felt sorry for him. And the silence went on

like that for quite some time. 'Is Seryozha well?' he said and, without waiting for an answer, added: 'I won't dine at home today, and I must leave at once.'

'I wanted to go to Moscow,' she said.

'No, you did very, very well to come,' he said, and again fell silent.

Seeing that he was unable to begin talking, she began herself.

'Alexei Alexandrovich,' she said, looking up at him and not lowering her eyes under his gaze, directed at her hair, 'I am a criminal woman, I am a bad woman, but I am the same as I said I was then, and I've come to tell you that I cannot change anything.'

'I did not ask you about that,' he said suddenly, looking straight into her eyes, resolutely and with hatred, 'I had supposed as much.' Under the influence of anger, he apparently regained complete command of all his abilities. 'But, as I then said and wrote to you,' he went on in a sharp, thin voice, 'I now repeat that I am not obliged to know it. I ignore it. Not all wives are so kind as you are, to hasten to tell their husbands such *pleasant* news.' He especially emphasized the word 'pleasant'. 'I ignore it as long as it is not known to society, as long as my name is not disgraced. And therefore I only warn you that our relations must be such as they have always been and that only in the case of your *compromising* yourself would I have to take measures to protect my honour.'

'But our relations cannot be as they have always been,' Anna began in a timid voice, looking at him in fear.

When she saw again those calm gestures, heard that piercing, childlike and mocking voice, her loathing for him annihilated the earlier pity, and she was merely frightened, but wished at all costs to understand her situation.

'I cannot be your wife when I . . .' she began.

He laughed a spiteful, cold laugh.

'It must be that the sort of life you've chosen has affected your notions. I respect or despise the one and the other so much . . . I respect your past and despise the present . . . that I was far from the interpretation you have given to my words.'

Anna sighed and lowered her head.

'However, I do not understand, having as much independence as you do,' he went on, becoming excited, 'telling your husband straight out about your infidelity and finding nothing reprehensible in it, as it seems, how you find it reprehensible to fulfil the duties of a wife towards your husband.'

'Alexei Alexandrovich! What do you want from me?'

'I want that I not meet that man here, and that you behave in such a way that neither *society* nor *the servants* can *possibly* accuse you . . . that you not see him. It doesn't seem too much. And for that you will enjoy the rights of an honest wife, without fulfilling her duties. That is all I have to say to you. Now it is time for me to go. I will not dine at home.'

He got up and went to the door. Anna also got up. With a silent bow, he let her pass.

XXIV

The night Levin spent on the haystack was not wasted on him: the farming he had been engaged in he now came to loathe, and it lost all interest for him. Despite excellent crops, there had never been, or at least it seemed to him that there had never been, so many failures and so much animosity between him and the muzhiks as that year, and the cause of the failures and the animosity was now clear to him. The delight he had experienced in the work itself, the closeness with the muzhiks that had come from it, the envy of them and of their life that he had experienced, the wish to go over to that life, which that night had no longer been a dream for him but an intention, the fulfilment of which he had been thinking over in detail – all this had so changed his view of farming that he could no longer find any of his former interest in it and could not help seeing his own unpleasant attitude towards his workers, which was at the bottom of the whole thing. The herds of improved cows, the same as Pava, the earth all ploughed and fertilized, the nine equal fields planted round with willows, the three hundred acres of deeply ploughed-under dung, the seed drills and so on – all that would have been wonderful if it had been done by him alone, or with friends, people sympathetic to him. But he now saw clearly (his work on the book about agriculture, in which the fundamental element had to be the worker, had helped him greatly in this) – he saw clearly now that the farming he was engaged in was merely a cruel and persistent struggle between him and his workers, in which on the one side, his own, there was a constant, intense striving to remake everything after the best-considered fashion, and on the other there was the natural order of things. And in this struggle he saw that with the greatest straining of forces on his part and with no effort or even intention on the other, all that was achieved was that the farming did not go in any direction and that beautiful machines, beautiful cattle and soil were ruined for nothing. And above all – not only was the energy directed towards it completely wasted, but he could not help feeling, now that the meaning of this work had been laid bare for him, that the goal of his energy was a most unworthy one. What essentially did the struggle consist in? He stood for every penny he had (and could not do otherwise, because as soon as he slackened his energy, he would not have enough money to pay the workers), and they stood only for working quietly and pleasantly, that is, as they were accustomed to do. It was in his interest that each worker should do as much as possible, that he should keep his wits about him at the same time, that he should try not to break the winnowing machine, the horse-rake, the thresher, that he should try to think about whatever he was doing. The worker, however, wanted to work as pleasantly as possible, with rests, and above all – carelessly, obliviously, thoughtlessly. That summer Levin saw it at every step. He sent people to mow clover for hay, choosing the worst acres, overgrown with grass and wormwood, unfit for seed – they went and mowed down his best seeding acres, justifying themselves by shifting it on to the steward and comforting him with the excellence of the hay; but he knew the reason was that those acres were easier to mow. He sent out the hay-maker – it broke down in the first row, because the muzhik got bored sitting on the box under the turning blades. And they told him: 'Never fear, sir, the women will do it in a trice.' The ploughs were no good, because it did not occur to the worker to lower the raised shear and, resorting to force, he wore out the horses and ruined the soil; and they asked him not to worry. Horses were let into the wheat fields, because not one worker wanted to be night-watchman, and, despite orders to the contrary, the workers took turns looking after the horses at night, and some Vanka, after working all day, would fall asleep and then confess his sin, saying: 'Do as you like, sir.' The three best calves died from overfeeding, having been let out into a regrown clover field without being watered, and in no way would they believe that they became bloated by the clover, but told him in consolation how a neighbour had lost a hundred and twelve head in three days. All this was done not because anyone wished evil to Levin or his farming; on the contrary, he knew he was loved and considered a simple master (which was the highest praise); it was done only because of the wish to work merrily and carelessly, and his interests were not only foreign and incomprehensible to them, but fatally opposed to their own most just interests. For a long time Levin had felt displeased with his attitude towards farming. He had seen that his boat was leaking, but he could not find and did not look for the leak, perhaps deceiving himself on purpose. But now he could no longer deceive himself. The farming he had been engaged in not only ceased to interest him but disgusted him, and he could no longer be occupied with it.

To that was added the presence some twenty miles away of Kitty Shcherbatsky, whom he wanted to see and could not. Darya Alexandrovna Oblonsky, when he had visited her, had invited him to come: to come in order to renew his proposal to her sister, who, as she let him feel, would now accept him. Levin himself, when he saw Kitty Shcherbatsky, realized that he had never ceased to love her; but he could not go to the Oblonskys knowing that she was there. The fact that he had proposed and she had refused him put an insuperable obstacle between them. 'I can't ask her to be my wife only because she couldn't be the wife of the one she wanted,' he said to himself. The thought of it turned him cold and hostile towards her. 'I'd be unable to speak to her without a feeling of reproach, to look at her without anger, and she'll hate me still more, as she ought to. And then, too, how can I go to them now, after what Darya Alexandrovna told me? How can I not show that I know what she told me? And I'll come with magnanimity – to forgive, to show mercy to her. Me in the role of a man forgiving her and deigning to offer her his love! . . . Why did Darya Alexandrovna say that? I might have seen her accidentally, and then everything would have happened by itself, but now it's impossible, impossible!'

Darya Alexandrovna sent him a note, asking him for a side-saddle for Kitty. 'I've been told you have a side-saddle,' she wrote to him. 'I hope you'll bring it yourself.'

That he simply could not bear. How could an intelligent, delicate woman so humiliate her sister! He wrote ten notes, tore them all up, and sent the saddle without any reply. To write that he would come was impossible, because he could not come; to write that he could not come because something prevented him or he was leaving, was still worse. He sent the saddle without a reply and, with the awareness of doing something shameful, handed over his detested farming to the steward the very next day and left for a far-off district to visit his friend Sviyazhsky, who had excellent snipe marshes near by and who had written recently asking him to fulfil his long-standing intention of visiting him.

The snipe marshes in the Surov district had long tempted Levin, but he kept putting off the trip on account of farming matters. Now, though, he was glad to get away both from the Shcherbatskys' neighbourhood and, above all, from farming, precisely in order to hunt, which in all troubles served him as the best consolation.

XXV

There was no railway or post road to the Surov district, and Levin drove there with his own horses in the tarantass.

Half-way there he stopped for feeding at a wealthy muzhik's. A fresh, bald old man with a broad red beard, grey at the cheeks, opened the gates, pressing himself to the post to let the troika pass. Directing the coachman to a place under a shed in the big, clean and tidy new yard with fire-hardened wooden ploughs in it, the old man invited Levin in. A cleanly dressed young woman, galoshes on her bare feet, was bending over, wiping the floor in the new front hall. Frightened of the dog that came running in with Levin, she cried out, but immediately laughed at her fright, learning that the dog would not touch her. Pointing Levin to the inner door with her bared arm, she bent again, hiding her handsome face, and went on washing.

'The samovar, maybe?' she asked.

'Yes, please.'

The room was big, with a Dutch stove and a partition. Under the icons stood a table with painted decorations, a bench and two chairs. By the entrance was a small cupboard. The shutters were closed, the flies were few, and it was so clean that Levin took care that Laska, who had been running in the road and bathing in puddles, should not dirty the floor, pointing her to a place in the corner by the door. After looking round the room, Levin went out to the back yard. The comely young woman in galoshes, empty buckets swinging on the yoke, ran ahead of him to fetch water from the well.

'Look lively!' the old man shouted merrily after her and came up to Levin. 'Well, sir, are you on your way to see Nikolai Ivanovich Sviyazhsky? He stops here, too,' he began garrulously, leaning on the porch rail.

In the middle of the old man's story of his acquaintance with Sviyazhsky, the gates creaked again and the field workers drove into the yard with ploughs and harrows. The horses hitched to the ploughs and harrows were well fed and large. Two of the workers were apparently family members, young men in cotton shirts and peaked caps; the other two were hired men in hempen shirts – one an old man and the other a young lad. Leaving the porch, the old man went to the horses and began to unhitch them.

'What have you been ploughing?' asked Levin.

'Earthing up the potatoes. We've also got a bit of land. You, Fedot, don't turn the gelding loose, put him to the trough, we'll hitch up another one.'

'Say, father, what about those ploughshares I asked you to get, have you brought them?' asked a tall, strapping fellow, apparently the old man's son.

'There . . . in the sledge,' replied the old man, coiling the unhitched reins and throwing them on the ground. 'Set them up while we're having dinner.'

The comely young woman, with full buckets weighing down her shoulders, went into the front hall. Other women appeared from somewhere – young, beautiful, middle-aged, and old ugly ones, with and without children.

The samovar chimney hummed; the workers and family members, finished with the horses, went to have dinner. Levin got his own provisions from the carriage and invited the old man to have tea with him.

'Why, we've already had tea today,' said the old man, accepting the invitation with obvious pleasure. 'Or just for company.'

Over tea Levin learned the whole story of the old man's farming. Ten years ago the old man had rented three hundred and twenty acres from a lady landowner, and last year he had bought them and rented eight hundred more from a local landowner. A small portion of the land, the worst, he rented out, and he himself ploughed some hundred acres with his family and two hired men. The old man complained that things were going poorly. But Levin understood that he was complaining only for propriety's sake, and that his farm was flourishing. If it had been going poorly, he would not have bought land at forty roubles an acre, would not have got three sons and a nephew married, would not have rebuilt twice after fires, each time better than before. Despite the old man's complaints, it was clear that he was justifiably proud of his prosperity, proud of his sons, nephew, daughters-in-law, horses, cows, and especially that the whole farm held together. From talking with the old man,

Levin learned that he was also not against innovations. He had planted a lot of potatoes, and his potatoes, which Levin had noticed driving up, had already flowered and were beginning to set, while Levin's were just beginning to flower. He had ploughed for the potatoes with an iron plough, which he called a 'plougher', borrowed from the landowner. He sowed wheat. A small detail especially struck Levin, that as he thinned his rye he gave the thinned stalks to the horses. So many times, seeing this excellent feed go to waste, Levin had wanted to gather it; but it had always proved impossible. Yet with the muzhik it got done, and he could not praise this feed enough.

'Don't the womenfolk need work? They carry the piles to the road, and the cart drives up.'

'And for us landowners things go badly with our hired men,' said Levin, handing him a glass of tea.

'Thank you,' the old man replied, took the glass, but refused sugar, pointing to the nibbled lump he had left. 'Where are you going to get with hired men?' he said. 'It's sheer ruin. Take the Sviyazhskys even. We know their land – black as poppyseed, but they can't boast of their crops either. There's always some oversight!'

'But you do your farming with hired men?'

'That's between muzhiks. We can make do on our own. Bad work – out you go! We'll manage.'

'Father, Finogen says to fetch some tar,' the woman in galoshes said, coming in.

'So there, sir!' said the old man, getting up, and, crossing himself lengthily, he thanked Levin and left.

When Levin went into the kitchen side of the cottage to call his coachman, he saw all the men of the family at the table. The women served standing. The strapping young son, with his mouth full of kasha, was telling some funny story, and they were all laughing, and the woman in galoshes laughed especially gaily as she added more shchi to the bowl.

It might very well be that the comely face of the woman in galoshes contributed greatly to the impression of well-being that this peasant home made on Levin, but the impression was so strong that he could not get rid of it. And all the way from the old man to Sviyazhsky, he kept recalling this household, as if something in this impression called for his special attention.

XXVI

Sviyazhsky was the marshal of nobility in his district. He was five years older than Levin and long married. His young sister-in-law, a girl Levin found very sympathetic, lived in his house. And Levin knew that Sviyazhsky and his wife wished very much to marry this girl to him. He knew it indubitably, as these things are always known to young men, so-called suitors, though he would never have dared say it to anyone, and he also knew that even though he wanted to get married, even though by all tokens this quite attractive girl would make a wonderful wife, he was as little capable of marrying her, even if he had not been in love with Kitty Shcherbatsky, as of flying into the sky. And this knowledge poisoned for him the pleasure he hoped to have in visiting Sviyazhsky.

On receiving Sviyazhsky's letter with an invitation for hunting, Levin had thought of that at once, but in spite of it he had decided that Sviyazhsky's designs on him were only his own absolutely unfounded surmise, and therefore he would go all the same. Besides, in the depths of his soul he wanted to test himself, to measure himself against this girl again. The Sviyazhskys' domestic life was also pleasant in the highest degree, and Sviyazhsky himself, the best type of zemstvo activist that Levin had ever known, had always greatly interested him.

Sviyazhsky was one of those people, always astonishing to Levin, whose reasoning, very consistent though never independent, goes by itself, and whose life, extremely well defined and firm in its orientation, goes by itself, quite independent of and almost always contrary to their reasoning. Sviyazhsky was an extremely liberal man. He despised the nobility and considered all noblemen secret adherents of serfdom, who did not express themselves only out of timorousness. He considered Russia a lost country, something like Turkey, and the government of Russia so bad that he never allowed himself any serious criticism of its actions, but at the same time he served the state and was an exemplary marshal of nobility, and when he travelled he always wore a peaked cap with a red band and a cockade. He held that life was humanly possible only abroad, where he went to live at every opportunity, and along with that, in Russia he conducted a very complex and improved form of farming, followed everything with extreme interest and knew everything that was going on. He considered the Russian muzhik as occupying a transitional step of development between ape and man, and yet at zemstvo elections he was most willing to shake hands with muzhiks and listen to their opinions. He believed in neither God nor devil, but was very concerned about questions of improving the life of the clergy and the shrinking number of parishes, taking particular trouble over keeping up the church in his village.

In the woman question he was on the side of the extreme advocates of complete freedom for women, and especially of their right to work, but he lived with his wife in such a way that everyone admired the harmony of their childless family life; and he arranged his wife's existence so that she did not and could not do anything but concern herself, together with her husband, with how better and more gaily to pass the time.

If it had not been in Levin's nature to explain people to himself from the best side, Sviyazhsky's character would have presented no difficulty or problem for him; he would have said 'fool' or 'trash' to himself, and everything would have been clear. But he could not say 'fool' because Sviyazhsky was unquestionably not only a very intelligent but a very educated man and bore his education with extraordinary simplicity. There was no subject he did not know, but he showed his knowledge only when forced to. Still less could Levin say that he was trash, because Sviyazhsky was unquestionably an honest, kind, intelligent man, who cheerfully, energetically, ceaselessly did things highly appreciated by all around him and most certainly never consciously did or could do anything bad.

Levin tried but failed to understand and always looked on him and on his life as a living riddle.

He and Levin were friends, and therefore Levin allowed himself to probe Sviyazhsky, to try to get at the very foundations of his view of life; but it was always in vain. Each time Levin tried to penetrate further than the doors to the reception rooms of Sviyazhsky's mind, which were open to everyone, he noticed that Sviyazhsky became slightly embarrassed; his eyes showed a barely noticeable fear, as if he was afraid that Levin would understand him, and he gave a good-natured and cheerful rebuff.

Now, after his disappointment with farming, Levin found it especially pleasant to visit Sviyazhsky. Apart from the fact that the mere sight of these happy doves in their comfortable nest, so pleased with themselves and with everyone, had a cheering effect on him, he now wanted, since he felt so displeased with his own life, to get at the secret in Sviyazhsky which gave him such clarity, certainty and cheerfulness in life. Besides that, Levin knew that at Sviyazhsky's he would meet neighbouring landowners, and he was now especially interested in talking, in listening to those very farmers' conversations about crops, hiring help, and the like, which he knew were normally regarded as something low, but were now the only thing he found important. 'This may not have been important under serfdom, or may not be important in England. In both cases the conditions themselves are defined; but with us now, when all this has been overturned and is just beginning to settle, the question of how these conditions ought to be settled is the only important question in Russia,' thought Levin.

The hunting turned out worse than Levin had expected. The marsh had dried up and there were no snipe. He walked all day and brought back only three, but to make up for it he brought back, as always with hunting, an excellent appetite, excellent spirits, and that aroused state of mind which with him always accompanied strong physical movement. And while it would seem that he was not thinking of anything as he hunted, he again kept recalling the old man and his family, and it was as if this impression called not only for attention to itself, but for the resolution of something connected with it.

That evening over tea, in the company of two landowners who had come on some matter of custody, the interesting conversation that Levin had been hoping for sprang up.

Levin was sitting beside the hostess at the tea table and had to carry on a conversation with her and the sister-in-law, who sat facing him. The hostess was a short, round-faced, fair-haired woman, all beaming with smiles and dimples. Levin tried through her to probe for the answer to that important riddle which her husband represented for him; but he did not have full freedom of thought, because he felt painfully awkward. He felt painfully awkward because the sister-in-law sat facing him in a special dress, put on for his sake, as it seemed to him, cut in a special trapezoidal shape on her white bosom. This rectangular neckline, despite the fact that her bosom was very white, or precisely because of it, deprived Levin of his freedom of thought. He fancied, probably mistakenly, that this neckline had been made on his account, and considered that he had no right to look at it and tried not to look at it; but he felt that he was to blame for the neckline having been made at all. It seemed to Levin that he was deceiving someone, that he had to explain something, but that it was quite impossible to explain it, and therefore he blushed constantly, felt restless and awkward. His awkwardness also communicated itself to the pretty sister-in-law. But the hostess seemed not to notice it and purposely tried to draw her into the conversation.

'You say,' the hostess continued the conversation they had begun, 'that my husband cannot interest himself in things Russian. On the contrary, he may be cheerful abroad, but never so much as here. Here he feels in his element. There's so much to be done, and he has the gift of being interested in everything. Ah, you haven't been to our school?'

'I've seen it . . . That little vine-covered house?'

'Yes, it's Nastya's doing,' she said, pointing to her sister.

'Do you teach in it yourself?' asked Levin, trying to look past the neckline, but feeling that wherever he looked in that direction, he would see nothing else.

'Yes, I have taught and still do, but we have a wonderful young woman for a teacher. And we've introduced gymnastics.'

'No, thank you, I won't have more tea,' said Levin, and, feeling that he was being discourteous, but unable to continue the conversation any longer, he stood up, blushing. 'I hear a very interesting conversation,' he added and went to the other end of the table, where the host sat with the two landowners. Sviyazhsky was sitting sideways to the table, leaning his elbow on it and twirling a cup with one hand, while with the other he gathered his beard in his fist, put it to his nose as if sniffing it, and let it go again. His shining dark eyes looked straight at the excited landowner with the grey moustache, and he was obviously finding what he said amusing. The landowner was complaining about the peasantry. It was clear to Levin that Sviyazhsky had an answer to the landowner's complaints that would immediately destroy the whole meaning of what he said, but that from his position he was unable to give this answer, and therefore listened, not without pleasure, to the landowner's comic speech.

The landowner with the grey moustache was obviously an inveterate adherent of serfdom, an old countryman and passionate farmer. Levin saw tokens of it in his clothes – the old-fashioned, shabby frock coat, to which the landowner was obviously unaccustomed – and in his intelligent, scowling eyes, his well-turned Russian speech, his peremptory tone, obviously acquired through long experience, and the resolute movements of his big, handsome, sunburnt hands with a single old engagement ring on the ring-finger.

XXVII

'If only I wasn't sorry to drop what's been started . . . so much work has gone into it . . . I'd wave my hand at it all, sell it and go like Nikolai Ivanych . . . to hear *Hélène*,'[22] the landowner said, a pleasant smile lighting up his intelligent old face.

'Yes, but you don't drop it,' said Nikolai Ivanovich Sviyazhsky, 'which means it adds up to something.'

'All it adds up to is that I live at home, don't buy anything, don't rent anything. And one keeps hoping the peasantry will see reason. Otherwise you wouldn't believe it – the drunkenness, the depravity! Everybody's separate, not a horse, not a cow left. He may be starving to death, but hire him to work and he'll do his best to muck it up, and then go and complain to the justice of the peace.'[23]

'But you'll complain to the justice of the peace as well,' said Sviyazhsky.

'I'll complain? Not for anything in the world! There'd be so much talk, I'd be sorry I ever did! Look at that mill – they took the down-payment and left. And the justice of the peace? He acquitted them. It's all held together by the communal court and the headman. That one will give him a good old-fashioned whipping. If it wasn't for that – drop everything! Flee to the ends of the world!'

Obviously, the landowner was teasing Sviyazhsky, but Sviyazhsky not only did not get angry, but clearly found it amusing.

'Yes, and yet we carry on our farming without these measures,' he said, smiling, 'me, Levin, him.'

He pointed to the other landowner.

'Yes, things are going well for Mikhail Petrovich, but ask him how! Is it rational farming?' the landowner said, obviously flaunting the word 'rational'.

'My farming is simple,' said Mikhail Petrovich. 'Thank God. My method is just to make sure that the cash to pay the autumn taxes is there. The muzhiks come: Father, dear, help us out! Well, they're all neighbours, these muzhiks, I feel sorry for them. So I give them enough to pay the first third, only I say: Remember, boys, I helped you, so you help me when there's a need – sowing oats, making hay, harvesting – well, and I talk them into so much work for each tax paid. There's some of them are shameless, it's true.'

Levin, who had long known these patriarchal ways, exchanged glances with Sviyazhsky and interrupted Mikhail Petrovich, addressing the landowner with the grey moustache again.

'Then what do you think?' he asked. 'How should farming be done now?'

'Why, the same way Mikhail Petrovich does it: either let the land for half the crop, or rent it to the muzhiks. It can be done, but that way the common wealth of the state is ruined. Where with serf labour and good management my land produced ninefold, it will produce threefold when let for half the crop. The emancipation[24] has ruined Russia!'

Sviyazhsky glanced at Levin with smiling eyes and even gave him a barely noticeable mocking sign, but Levin did not find the landowner's words ridiculous – he understood them better than he did Sviyazhsky. And much of what the landowner went on to say, proving why Russia had been ruined by the emancipation, seemed to him very true, new and irrefutable. The landowner was obviously voicing his own thought, which happens rarely, and this thought had not been arrived at by a desire to somehow occupy an idle mind, but had grown out of the conditions of his own life, had been hatched out in his country solitude and considered on all sides.

'The point, kindly note, is that all progress is achieved by authority alone,' he said, apparently wishing to show that he was no stranger to education. 'Take the reforms of Peter, Catherine, Alexander.[25] Take European history. The more so with progress in agricultural methods. Take the potato – even it was introduced here by force. The wooden plough hasn't always been in use either. It was probably introduced before the tsars, and also introduced by force. Now, in our time, under serfdom, we landowners carried on our farming with improvements. Drying kilns, winnowers, the carting of dung, and all the tools – we introduced everything by our authority, and the muzhiks first resisted and then imitated us. Now, sirs, with the abolition of serfdom, our authority has been taken away, and our farming, where it was brought to a high level, is bound to sink to the most savage, primitive condition. That's how I understand it.'

'But why so? If it's rational, you can carry it on with hired help,' said Sviyazhsky.

'There's no authority. Who will I carry it on with, may I ask?'

'There it is – the work force, the chief element in farming,' thought Levin.

'With paid workers.'

'Workers don't want to do good work or to do good work with tools. Our worker knows one thing only – how to get drunk as a pig, and while drunk to break everything you give him. He'll overwater the horses, snap good harness, dismount a wheel with a tyre and sell it for drink, put a pintle into the thresher so as to break it. He loathes the sight of things that aren't to his liking. That causes the whole level of the farming to sink. Plots are abandoned, overgrown with wormwood or given up to muzhiks, and where millions of bushels used to be produced, now it's a few hundred thousand – the common wealth is diminished. If the same thing was done, only with calculation . . .'

And he began developing his own plan of liberation, which would have eliminated these inconveniences.

That did not interest Levin, but when he finished, Levin went back to his first proposition and said, addressing Sviyazhsky and trying to provoke him to voice his serious opinion:

'That the level of farming is sinking and that, given our relation to the workers, it is impossible to engage in rational farming profitably, is perfectly correct,' he said.

'I don't find it so,' Sviyazhsky retorted, seriously now. 'I only see that we don't know how to go about farming and that, on the contrary, the level of farming we carried on under serfdom was in fact not too high but too low. We have neither machines, nor good working stock, nor real management, nor do we know how to count. Ask any farm owner – he won't know what's profitable for him and what isn't.'

'Italian bookkeeping,' the landowner said ironically. 'No matter how you count, once they break everything, there won't be any profit.'

'Why break? A worthless thresher, that Russian treadle of yours, they will break, but not my steam thresher. A Russian horse – what's that breed? the Tosscan, good for tossing cans at – they'll spoil for you, but introduce Percherons, or at least our Bitiugs,[26] and they won't spoil them. And so with everything. We must raise our farming higher.'

'If only we could, Nikolai Ivanych! It's all very well for you, but I have a son at the university, the younger ones are in boarding school – I can't go buying Percherons.'

'That's what banks are for.'

'So that the last thing I have falls under the hammer? No, thank you!'

'I don't agree that the level of farming must and can be raised higher,' said Levin. 'I'm engaged in it, and I have the means, and I've been unable to do anything. I don't know what use the banks are. With me, at least, whatever I've spent money on in farming has all been a loss – the livestock were a loss, the machinery a loss.'

'That's true,' the landowner with the grey moustache confirmed, even laughing with pleasure.

'And I'm not the only one,' Levin went on. 'I can refer to all the farmers who conduct their business rationally; every one of them, with rare exceptions, operates at a loss. Tell me, now, is your farming profitable?' said Levin, and he immediately noticed in Sviyazhsky's eyes that momentary look of fear that he noticed whenever he wanted to penetrate beyond the reception rooms of Sviyazhsky's mind.

Besides, on Levin's part the question had not been asked in good conscience. Over tea the hostess had just told him that they had invited a German from Moscow that summer, an expert in bookkeeping, who for a fee of five hundred roubles had done the accounts of their farm and discovered that they were operating at a loss of three thousand and some roubles. She did not recall the exact figure, but it seems the German had it calculated down to the quarter kopeck.

The landowner smiled at the mention of the profits of Sviyazhsky's farming, apparently knowing what sort of gains his neighbour and marshal might have.

'Maybe it's not profitable,' Sviyazhsky replied. 'That only proves that I'm a bad manager, or that I spend the capital to increase the true rent.'

'Ah, the true rent!' Levin exclaimed with horror. 'Maybe true rent exists in Europe, where the land has been improved by the labour put into it; but with us the land all becomes worse from the labour put into it – that is, from being ploughed – and so there's no true rent.'

'What do you mean, no true rent? It's a law.'

'Then we're outside the law. True rent won't clarify anything for us; on the contrary, it will confuse things. No, tell us, how can the theory of true rent . . .'

'Would you like some curds? Masha, send us some curds here, or raspberries,' he turned to his wife. 'This year the raspberries went on remarkably late.'

And in a most pleasant state of mind, Sviyazhsky got up and left, apparently assuming that the conversation had ended, at the very place where Levin thought it was just beginning.

Deprived of his interlocutor, Levin went on talking with the landowner, trying to prove to him that all the difficulty came from our not knowing the properties and habits of our worker; but the landowner, like all people who think originally and solitarily, was slow to understand another man's thought and especially partial to his own. He insisted that the Russian muzhik was a swine and liked swinishness, and that to move him out of swinishness, authority was needed, and there was none, a stick was needed, and we suddenly became so liberal that we replaced the thousand-year-old stick with some sort of lawyers and lock-ups, in which worthless, stinking muzhiks are fed good soup and allotted so many cubic feet of air.

'Why do you think,' said Levin, trying to return to the question, 'that it's impossible to find relations with the workforce that would make work productive?'

'That will never be done with the Russian peasantry without a stick! There's no authority,' the landowner replied.

'How can new forms be found?' said Sviyazhsky, who, having eaten his curds and lit a cigarette, again came over to the arguers. 'All possible relations to the workforce have been defined and studied,' he said. 'That leftover of barbarism – the primitive community with its mutual guarantees – is falling apart of itself, serfdom is abolished, there remains only free labour, and its forms are defined and ready, and we must accept them. The hired worker, the day-labourer, the farmhand – you won't get away from that.'

'But Europe is dissatisfied with these forms.'

'Dissatisfied and searching for new ones. And she'll probably find them.'

'That's just what I'm talking about,' replied Levin. 'Why shouldn't we search for them on our own?'

'Because it's the same as inventing new ways of building railways. They're invented and ready.'

'But what if they don't suit us? What if they're stupid?' said Levin.

And again he noticed the look of fear in Sviyazhsky's eyes.

'Yes, right: we'll win at a canter, we've found what Europe's searching for! I know all that, but, pardon me, do you know what's been done in Europe about the question of workers' conditions?'

'No, very little.'

'This question now occupies the best minds in Europe. The Schulze-Delitsch tendency . . . Also all the vast literature on the workers question, on the most liberal Lassalle tendency . . . The Mulhouse system is already a fact, you surely know that.'[27]

'I have an idea, but a very vague one.'

'No, you only say so; you surely know it all as well as I do. Of course, I'm no social professor, but it once interested me, and if it interests you, you really should look into it.'

'But what did they arrive at?'

'Excuse me . . .'

The landowners got up, and Sviyazhsky, again stopping Levin in his unpleasant habit of prying beyond the reception rooms of his mind, went to see his guests off.

XXVIII

Levin was insufferably bored with the ladies that evening: he was troubled as never before by the thought that the dissatisfaction he now felt with farming was not his exceptional situation but the general condition of things in Russia, that to establish relations with workers so that they would work like the muzhik he had met half-way there was not a dream but a problem that had to be solved. And it seemed to him that this problem could be solved and that he must try to do it.

Having taken leave of the ladies and promised to stay the whole of the next day so that they could go together on horseback to look at an interesting landslide in the state forest, Levin stopped at his host's study before going to bed to take some books on the workers question that Sviyazhsky had offered him. Sviyazhsky's study was a huge room lined with bookcases and had two tables in it – one a massive desk that stood in the middle of the room, and the other a round one on which the latest issues of newspapers and magazines in different languages were laid out in a star-like pattern around a lamp. By the desk was a stand with boxes of all sorts of files marked with gilt labels.

Sviyazhsky got the books out and sat down in a rocking chair.

'What are you looking at?' he said to Levin, who stood by the round table looking through a magazine.

'Ah, yes, there's a very interesting article in it,' Sviyazhsky said of the magazine Levin was holding. 'It turns out,' he added with cheerful animation, 'that the chief culprit in the partition of Poland was not Frederick at all.[28] It turns out . . .'

And, with his particular clarity, he briefly recounted these new, very important and interesting discoveries. Despite the fact that Levin was now most occupied with the thought of farming, he kept asking himself as he listened to his host: 'What's got into him? And why, why is he interested in the partition of Poland?' When Sviyazhsky finished, Levin involuntarily asked: 'Well, what then?' But there was nothing. The only interesting thing was that 'it had turned out'. But Sviyazhsky did not explain or find it necessary to explain why he found it interesting.

'Yes, but I was very interested in the angry landowner,' Levin said with a sigh. 'He's intelligent and said many right things.'

'Ah, go on! An inveterate secret serf-owner, as they all are!' said Sviyazhsky.

'Of whom you are the marshal . . .'

'Yes, only I'm marshalling them in the other direction,' Sviyazhsky said, laughing.

'What interests me so much is this,' said Levin. 'He's right that our cause, that is, rational farming, doesn't work, that only usurious farming works, as with that silent one, or else the simplest kind. Who is to blame for that?'

'We are, of course. And besides, it's not true that it doesn't work. At Vassilchikov's it works.'

'A mill . . .'

'But all the same I don't know what you're surprised at. The peasantry stand at such a low level of both material and moral development that they apparently must oppose everything foreign to them. In Europe rational farming works because the peasantry are educated; which means that with us the peasantry have to be educated – that's all.'

'But how are we to educate the peasantry?'

'To educate the peasantry, three things are needed: schools, schools and schools.'

'But you said yourself that the peasantry stand at a low level of material development. How will schools help?'

'You know, you remind me of the anecdote about giving advice to a sick man: "Why don't you try a laxative?" "I did: got worse." "Try leeches." "Tried them: got worse." "Well, then, just pray to God." "Tried that: got worse." It's the same with you and me. I say political economy, and you say: worse. I say socialism – worse. Education – worse.'

'But how will schools help?'

'They'll give them different needs.'

'That's something I've never understood,' Levin objected hotly. 'How will schools help the peasantry to improve their material well-being? You say that schools, education, will give them new needs. So much the worse, because they won't be able to satisfy them. And how the knowledge of addition, subtraction and the catechism will help them to improve their material condition, I never could understand. The evening before last I met a woman with an infant at her breast and asked her where she had been. She said: "To the wise woman, because a shriek-hag has got into the child, so I took him to be treated." I asked how the wise woman treats the shriek-hag. "She puts the baby on a roost with the chickens and mumbles something."'

'Well, there you've said it yourself! We need schools so that she won't treat the shriek-hag by putting the baby on a roost . . .' Sviyazhsky said, smiling gaily.

'Ah, no!' Levin said in vexation. 'For me that treatment is like treating the peasantry with schools. The peasants are poor and uneducated, we see that as surely as the woman sees the shriek-hag because the baby shrieks. But why schools will help in this trouble – poverty and uneducation – is as incomprehensible as why chickens on a roost help against the shriek-hag. What must be helped is the cause of the poverty.'

'Well, in that at least you agree with Spencer,[29] whom you dislike so. He, too, says that education may result from a greater well-being and comfort in life – from frequent ablutions, as he says – but not from the ability to read and write . . .'

'Well, I'm very glad, or, on the contrary, very not-glad, that I agree with Spencer – only I've known it for a long time. Schools won't help, what will help is an economic system in which the peasantry will be wealthier, there will be more leisure – and then there will also be schools.'

'Nevertheless, all over Europe schools are now compulsory.'

'And how about you? Do you agree with Spencer?' asked Levin.

But a look of fear flashed in Sviyazhsky's eyes, and he said, smiling:

'Ah, but that shriek-hag is excellent! You actually heard it yourself?'

Levin saw that he was not going to find a connection between this man's life and his thoughts. Evidently it made absolutely no difference to him where his reasoning led him; he needed only the process of reasoning itself. And it was unpleasant for him when the process of reasoning led him to a dead end. That alone he disliked and avoided, turning the conversation to something pleasantly cheerful.

All the impressions of that day, starting with the muzhik half-way there, which seemed to serve as the fundamental basis for all that day's impressions and thoughts, stirred Levin deeply. This good Sviyazhsky, who kept his thoughts only for public use and evidently had some other bases of life, hidden from Levin, though at the same time he and that crowd whose name was legion guided public opinion with these thoughts that were alien to him; this embittered landowner, perfectly right in his reasoning which he had suffered through in his life, but not right in his bitterness against a whole class, and that the best class in Russia; his own dissatisfaction with his activity and the vague hope of finding a remedy for it – all this merged into a feeling of inner anxiety and the expectation of an imminent resolution.

Left alone in the room given him, lying on a spring mattress that unexpectedly tossed his arms and legs up with every movement, Levin did not fall asleep for a long time. Not one conversation with Sviyazhsky, though he had said many intelligent things, had interested Levin; but the landowner's arguments called for discussion. Levin involuntarily recalled all his words and in his imagination corrected his own replies.

'Yes, I should have said to him: "You say our farming doesn't work because the muzhiks hate all improvements and that they must be introduced by authority. Now, if farming didn't work at all without these improvements, you'd be right; but it does work, and it works only where the worker acts according to his habits, like that old man half-way here. Your and our common dissatisfaction with farming proves that either we or the workers are to blame. We've been pushing ahead for a long time in our own way, the European way, without asking ourselves about the properties of the workforce. Let's try to look at the work force not as an ideal *workforce* but as the *Russian muzhik* with his instincts, and organize our farming accordingly. Picture to yourself," I should have said to him, "that you do your farming like that old man, that you've found a way of getting the workers interested in the success of the work and found some midpoint in the improvements that they can recognize – and, without exhausting the soil, you'll bring in two or three times more than before. Divide it in two, give half to the workers; the difference you come out with will be greater and the workers will also come out with more. But to do that you have to lower the level of the farming and interest the workers in its success. How to do that is a matter of details, but there's no doubt that it's possible."'

This thought threw Levin into great agitation. He did not sleep half the night, thinking over the details for bringing the thought to realization. He had not intended to leave the next day, but now decided to go home early in the morning. Besides, this sister-in-law with her neckline produced in him a feeling akin to shame and repentance for having done something bad. Above all, it was necessary for him to leave without delay: he had to offer the new project to the muzhiks in time, before the winter sowing, so that the sowing could be done on a new basis. He decided to overturn all the old management.

XXIX

The carrying out of Levin's plan presented many difficulties; but he struggled with all his might and achieved, if not what he wished, at least something which, without deceiving himself, he could believe was worth the effort. One of the main difficulties was that the work was already in progress, that he could not stop everything and start over from the beginning, but had to retune the machine while it was running.

When, on returning home that same evening, he told the steward about his plans, the steward was obviously pleased to agree with the part of his speech which showed that everything done up to then was nonsense and unprofitable. The steward said that he had long been saying so, but no one had wanted to listen to him. As far as Levin's proposal was concerned – that he participate as a shareholder, along with the workers, in the whole farming enterprise – to this the steward responded only with great dejection and no definite opinion, and immediately began talking about the necessity of transporting the remaining sheaves of rye the next day and seeing to the cross-ploughing, so that Levin felt that now was not the time for it.

Talking with the peasants about the same thing and offering to lease them the land on new conditions, he also ran into the chief difficulty that they were so busy with the current day's work that they had no time to consider the advantages and disadvantages of the undertaking.

A naïve muzhik, Ivan the cowman, seemed to have fully understood Levin's proposal – that he and his family share in the profits of the cattle-yard – and was sympathetic with the undertaking. But when Levin impressed upon him his future advantages, Ivan's face showed alarm and regret that he could not listen to it all to the end, and he hastened to find something to do that could not be put off: taking the fork to finish heaping up hay from the cattle-yard, or fetching water, or clearing away manure.

Another difficulty lay in the peasants' invincible mistrust of any other purpose on the landowner's part than the desire to fleece them as much as possible. They were firmly convinced that his true goal, whatever he might tell them, would always lie in what he did not tell them. And they themselves, when they spoke, said many things, but never said what their true goal was. Besides that (Levin felt that the bilious landowner was right), the peasants put down as the first and immutable condition of any agreement whatsoever that they not be forced to employ new methods of farming or to make use of new tools. They agreed that the iron plough worked better, that the scarifier produced good results, but they found a thousand reasons why it was impossible for them to use either, and though he was convinced that he had to lower the level of farming, he was sorry to renounce improvements whose advantages were so obvious to him. But, despite all these difficulties, he had his way and by autumn things got going, or at least it seemed so to him.

In the beginning Levin thought of leasing the whole farm, as it was, to the peasants, workers and steward, on new conditions of partnership, but he soon became convinced that it was impossible, and he decided to subdivide the farming. The cattle-yard, orchards, kitchen gardens, meadows, fields, divided into several parts, were to constitute separate items. Naïve Ivan the cowman, who understood the matter best of all, as it seemed to Levin, chose an association for himself mainly from his own family, and became a participant in the cattle-yard. A far field that had lain fallow and overgrown for eight years was taken with the help of the clever carpenter Fyodor Rezunov by six muzhik families on the new associative terms, and the muzhik Shuraev leased all the kitchen gardens on the same conditions. The rest remained as before, but these three items were the beginning of a new system and fully occupied Levin.

True, in the cattle-yard things went no better than before, and Ivan strongly resisted the heating of the cow barn and making butter from fresh cream, maintaining that cows that are kept cold need less food and that sour-cream butter does you best, and he demanded a salary as in the old days, not concerned in the least that the money he got was not a salary but an advance against his share of the profit.

True, Fyodor Rezunov's company did not cross-plough their land before sowing, as had been agreed, justifying themselves by the shortness of time. True, the muzhiks of this company, though they had agreed to conduct business on the new basis, referred to the land not as common but as shared, and both the muzhiks of the association and Rezunov himself more than once said to Levin: 'If you'd take money for the land, it would put you at ease and unbind us.' Besides that, these muzhiks, under various pretexts, kept postponing the building of a cattle-yard and threshing barn on this land, as had been agreed, and dragged it on till winter.

True, Shuraev wanted to take the kitchen gardens leased to him and let them out in small parcels to the muzhiks. Evidently he had completely misunderstood and, it seemed, deliberately misunderstood, the conditions on which the land had been leased to him.

True, as he talked with the muzhiks, explaining all the advantages of the undertaking to them, Levin often felt that they were listening only to the music of his voice and knew firmly that, whatever he might say, they were not going to let him deceive them. He felt it especially when he talked with the smartest of the peasants, Rezunov, and noticed that play in his eyes which clearly showed both mockery of him and the firm conviction that, if anyone was going to be deceived, it was not he, Rezunov.

But, despite all that, Levin thought that things had got going and that, by strict accounting and having it his way, he would eventually prove to them the advantages of such a system, and then everything would go by itself.

These matters, along with the rest of the farming, which had been left in his hands, along with the study-work on his book, so occupied Levin's summer that he hardly ever went hunting. He learned at the end of August, from the man who brought back the side-saddle, that the Oblonskys had returned to Moscow. He felt that by not answering Darya Alexandrovna's letter, by his impoliteness, which he could not recall without a flush of shame, he had burned his boats and could never visit them again. He had done the same with the Sviyazhskys by leaving without saying goodbye. But he would never visit them again either. It made no difference to him now. The business of his new system of farming occupied him as nothing ever had before in his life. He read the books Sviyazhsky gave him, and, ordering what he did not have, also read books on political economy and socialism concerned with the same subject and, as he expected, found nothing that related to the business he had undertaken. In the politico-economic books – in Mill,[30] for instance, whom he studied at first with great fervour, hoping at any moment to find a solution to the questions that preoccupied him – he found laws deduced from the situation of European farming; but he simply could not see why those laws, not applicable in Russia, should be universal. He saw the same in the socialist books: these were either beautiful but inapplicable fantasies, such as he had been enthusiastic about while still a student, or corrections, mendings of the state of affairs in which Europe stood and with which Russian agriculture had nothing in common. Political economy said that the laws according to which European wealth had developed and was developing were universal and unquestionable. Socialist teaching said that development according to these laws led to ruin. And neither the one nor the other gave, not only an answer, but even the slightest hint of what he, Levin, and all Russian peasants and landowners were to do with their millions of hands and acres so that they would be most productive for the common good.

Once he got down to this matter, he conscientiously read through everything related to his subject and planned to go abroad in the autumn to study the matter on site, so that the same thing would not happen to him with this question as had happened so often with various other questions. Just as he was beginning to understand his interlocutor's thought and to explain his own, he would suddenly be told: 'And what about Kauffmann, and Jones, and Dubois, and Miccelli?[31] You haven't read them? You should – they've worked out this whole question.'

He now saw clearly that Kauffmann and Miccelli had nothing to tell him. He knew what he wanted. He saw that Russia had excellent land, excellent workers, and that in some cases, as with the muzhik half-way there, workers and land produced much, but in the majority of cases, when capital was employed European-style, they produced little, and that this came only from the fact that the workers wanted to work and to work well in the one way natural to them, and that their resistance was not accidental but constant and rooted in the spirit of the peasantry. He thought that the Russian peasantry, called upon to inhabit and cultivate vast unoccupied spaces, consciously kept to the methods necessary for it until all the lands were occupied, and that these methods were not at all as bad as was usually thought. And he wanted to prove it theoretically in his book and in practice on his estate.

XXX

At the end of September lumber was delivered for the building of the cattle-yard on the land allotted to the association, and the butter from the cows was sold and the profits distributed. The practical side of the farming was going excellently, or at least it seemed so to Levin. Now, to explain the whole thing theoretically and to finish his book, which, according to Levin's dreams, was not only to bring about a revolution in political economy but was to abolish that science altogether and initiate a new science – of the relation of the peasantry to the land – the only thing necessary was to go abroad and study on site everything that had been done there in that direction and to find convincing proofs that everything done there was not what was needed. Levin was waiting only for the delivery of the wheat, so as to get the money and go abroad. But rain set in, which prevented the harvesting of the remaining grain and potatoes and put a stop to all work, even the delivery of the wheat. Mud made the roads impassable; two mills were washed away by floods, and the weather was getting worse and worse.

On September 30th, the sun came out in the morning and, hoping for good weather, Levin resolutely began to prepare for departure. He ordered the wheat to be measured out, sent the steward to the merchant to get the money and went round the estate himself to give final orders before his departure.

Having done everything, wet from the streams that poured from his leather jacket either down his neck or into his boots, but in a most cheerful and excited mood, Levin returned home towards evening. The weather grew still worse towards evening, hail beat so painfully on his drenched horse that he walked sideways, twitching his ears and head; but Levin felt fine under his hood, and he glanced cheerfully around him, now at the turbid streams running down the ruts, now at the drops hanging on every bare twig, now at the white spots of unmelted hail on the planks of the bridge, now at the succulent, still-fleshy elm leaves that lay in a thick layer around the naked tree. Despite the gloom of the surrounding nature, he felt himself especially excited. Talks with the peasants in the distant village had shown that they were beginning to get used to their relations. The old innkeeper at whose place he stopped in order to dry off apparently approved of Levin's plan and himself offered to join the partnership to buy cattle.

'I need only persist in going towards my goal and I'll achieve what I want,' thought Levin, 'and so work and effort have their wherefore. This is not my personal affair, it is a question here of the common good. Agriculture as a whole, above all the position of the entire peasantry, must change completely. Instead of poverty – universal wealth, prosperity; instead of hostility – concord and the joining of interests. In short, a revolution, a bloodless but great revolution, first in the small circle of our own region, then the province, Russia, the whole world. Because a correct thought cannot fail to bear fruit. Yes, that is a goal worth working for. And the fact that it is I, Kostya Levin, the same one who came to the ball in a black tie and was rejected by Miss Shcherbatsky and is so pathetic and worthless in his own eyes – proves nothing. I'm sure that Franklin[32] felt as worthless and distrusted himself in the same way, looking back at his whole self. That means nothing. And he, too, surely had his Agafya Mikhailovna to whom he confided his projects.'

In such thoughts Levin rode up to the house when it was already dark.

The steward, who had gone to the merchant, came and brought part of the money for the wheat. The arrangement with the innkeeper was made, and the steward had found out on the way that wheat had been left standing in the fields everywhere, so that his own hundred and sixty stacks were nothing in comparison with what others had lost.

After dinner Levin sat down in his easy-chair with a book, as usual, and while reading continued to think about his forthcoming trip in connection with his book. Today the significance of what he was doing presented itself to him with particular clarity, and whole paragraphs took shape of themselves in his mind, expressing the essence of his thinking. 'This must be written down,' he thought. 'This should constitute the brief introduction that I considered unnecessary before.' He got up to go to his desk, and Laska, who lay at his feet, also got up, stretching herself, and looked back at him as if asking where to go. But there was no time to write it down, because the foremen of the work details came, and Levin went out to them in the front hall.

Having done the detailing – that is, given orders for the next day's work – and received all the muzhiks who had business with him, Levin went to his study and sat down to work. Laska lay under the desk; Agafya Mikhailovna settled in her place with a stocking.

Levin had been writing for some time when suddenly, with extraordinary vividness, he remembered Kitty, her refusal and their last encounter. He got up and began to pace the room.

'No point being bored,' Agafya Mikhailovna said to him. 'Well, why do you sit at home? Go to the hot springs, since you're all ready.'

'I'll go the day after tomorrow, Agafya Mikhailovna. I have business to finish.'

'Well, what's this business of yours? As if you haven't given the muzhiks enough already! They say, "Your master'll win favour with the tsar for that." It's even strange: why should you concern yourself with muzhiks?'

'I'm not concerned with them, I'm doing it for myself.'

Agafya Mikhailovna knew all the details of Levin's plans for the estate. Levin often told her his thoughts in fine detail and not infrequently argued with her and disagreed with her explanations. But this time she completely misunderstood what he said to her.

'It's a known fact, a man had best think of his own soul,' she said with a sigh. 'There's Parfen Denisych, illiterate as they come, but God grant everybody such a death,' she said of a recently deceased house servant. 'Took communion, got anointed.'[33]

'I'm not talking about that,' he said. 'I mean that I'm doing it for my own profit. The better the muzhiks work, the more profitable it is for me.'

'Whatever you do, if he's a lazybones, everything will come out slapdash. If he's got a conscience, he'll work, if not, there's no help for it.'

'Yes, but you say yourself that Ivan takes better care of the cattle now.'

'I say one thing,' Agafya Mikhailovna answered, evidently not at random but with a strictly consistent train of thought, 'you've got to get married, that's what!'

Agafya Mikhailovna's mention of the very thing he had just been thinking about upset and offended him. Levin frowned and, without answering her, sat down to his work, repeating to himself everything he thought about the significance of that work. Only occasionally he listened in the silence to the sound of Agafya Mikhailovna's needles and, recalling what he did not want to recall, winced again.

At nine o'clock they heard a bell and the dull heaving of a carriage through the mud.

'Well, here's guests coming to see you, so you won't be bored,' said Agafya Mikhailovna, getting up and going to the door. But Levin went ahead of her. His work was not going well now, and he was glad of a guest, whoever it might be.

XXXI

Having run half-way down the stairs, Levin heard the familiar sound of a little cough in the front hall; but he did not hear it clearly because of the noise of his footsteps and hoped that he was mistaken. Then he saw the whole long, bony, familiar figure, and it seemed no longer possible to deceive himself, yet he still hoped that he was mistaken and that this tall man taking off his fur coat and coughing was not his brother Nikolai.

Levin loved his brother, but being with him was always a torment. Now, under the influence of the thought that had come to him and of Agafya Mikhailovna's reminder, he was in a vague, confused state, and the imminent meeting with his brother seemed especially difficult. Instead of a cheerful, healthy stranger for a guest, who he hoped would divert him in his state of uncertainty, he had to confront his brother, who understood him thoroughly, who would call up all his innermost thoughts, would make him speak his whole mind. And that he did not want.

Angry with himself for this nasty feeling, Levin ran down to the front hall. As soon as he saw his brother up close, this feeling of personal disappointment vanished at once and was replaced by pity. Frightening as his brother Nikolai's thinness and sickliness had been before, he was now still thinner, still more wasted. He was a skeleton covered with skin.

He stood in the front hall, twitching his long, thin neck and tearing his scarf from it, and smiled with a strange pitifulness. Seeing this smile, humble and obedient, Levin felt his throat contract spasmodically.

'You see, I've come to visit you,' Nikolai said in a dull voice, not taking his eyes off his brother's face for a second. 'I've long been wanting to, but I wasn't feeling well. Now I'm much better,' he said, wiping his beard with big, thin palms.

'Yes, yes!' Levin replied. And he felt still more frightened when, as he kissed him, his lips felt the dryness of his brother's body and he saw his big, strangely glinting eyes up close.

A few weeks earlier Levin had written to his brother that, following the sale of a small, as yet undivided portion of their inheritance, he was now to receive his share, about two thousand roubles.

Nikolai said that he had come to receive the money and, above all, to visit his own nest, to touch the soil, in order to gather strength, as mighty heroes do, for future action. Despite his increasing stoop, despite his striking thinness in view of his height, his movements were, as usual, quick and impetuous. Levin led him to his study.

His brother changed with particular care, something he had never done before, combed his sparse, straight hair and, smiling, went upstairs.

He was in a most gentle and cheerful mood, as Levin had often remembered him in childhood. He even mentioned Sergei Ivanovich without anger. Seeing Agafya Mikhailovna, he joked with her and asked about the old servants. The news of the death of Parfen Denisych had an unpleasant affect on him. Fear showed in his face, but he recovered at once.

'Well, he was old,' he said and changed the subject. 'So, I'll live with you for a month or two, and then – to Moscow. You know, Miagkov has promised me a post, and I'll be going into the service. Now I'll arrange my life quite differently,' he went on. 'You know, I sent that woman away.'

'Marya Nikolaevna? Why, what for?'

'Ah, she's a nasty woman! She caused me a heap of troubles.' But he did not say what those troubles were. He could not say that he had chased Marya Nikolaevna out because the tea was weak, and above all because she looked after him as if he were an invalid. 'And then in general I want to change my life completely now. I've certainly committed some follies, like everybody else, but money is the least thing, I'm not sorry about it. As long as there's health – and my health, thank God, has improved.'

Levin listened and thought and could not think of anything to say. Nikolai probably felt the same. He began asking his brother about his affairs, and Levin was glad to talk about himself, because he could talk without pretending. He told his brother his plans and activities.

His brother listened but obviously was not interested.

These two men were so dear and close to each other that the slightest movement, the tone of the voice, told them both more than it was possible to say in words.

Now they both had one thought – Nikolai's illness and closeness to death – which stifled all the rest. But neither of them dared to speak of it, and therefore everything else they said, without expressing the one thing that preoccupied them, was a lie. Never had Levin been so glad when an evening ended and it was time to go to bed. Never with any stranger, on any official visit, had he been so unnatural and false as he had been that day. And his awareness of and remorse for this unnaturalness made him more unnatural still. He wanted to weep over his beloved dying brother, and he had to listen and keep up a conversation about how he was going to live.

As the house was damp and only one room was heated, Levin had his brother sleep in his own bedroom behind a screen.

His brother lay down and may or may not have slept, but, being a sick man, tossed, coughed and grumbled something when he was unable to clear his throat. Sometimes, when his breathing was difficult, he said, 'Ah, my God!' Sometimes, when phlegm choked him, he said vexedly, 'Ah! the devil!' Levin lay awake for a long time, listening to him. His thoughts were most varied, but the end of all his thoughts was one: death.

Death, the inevitable end of everything, presented itself to him for the first time with irresistible force. And this death, which here, in his beloved brother, moaning in his sleep and calling by habit, without distinction, now on God, now on the devil, was not at all as far off as it had seemed to him before. It was in him, too – he felt it. If not now, then tomorrow, if not tomorrow, then in thirty years – did it make any difference? And what this inevitable death was, he not only did not know, he not only had never thought of it, but he could not and dared not think of it.

'I work, I want to do something, and I've forgotten that everything will end, that there is – death.'

He was sitting on his bed in the dark, crouching, hugging his knees and thinking, holding his breath from the strain of it. But the more he strained to think, the clearer it became to him that it was undoubtedly so, that he had actually forgotten, overlooked in his life one small circumstance – that death would come and everything would end, that it was not worth starting anything and that nothing could possibly be done about it. Yes, it was terrible, but it was so.

'Yet I am still alive. And what am I to do now, what am I to do?' he said in despair. He lit the candle, got up carefully, went over to the mirror and began to examine his face and hair. Yes, there were grey hairs on his temples. He opened his mouth. The back teeth were beginning to go bad. He bared his muscular arms. Yes, good and strong. But Nikolenka, who was lying there breathing with the remains of his lungs, had also had a healthy body once. And he suddenly remembered how as children they had gone to bed at the same time and had only waited for Fyodor Bogdanych to leave before they started throwing pillows at each other and laughing, laughing irrepressibly, so that even the fear of Fyodor Bogdanych could not stop this overflowing and effervescent consciousness of life's happiness. 'And now this crooked and empty chest . . . and I, not knowing what will become of me or why . . .'

'Kha! Kha! Ah, the devil! What's this pottering about, why aren't you asleep?' his brother's voice called to him.

'I don't know, just insomnia.'

'And I slept well, I don't sweat now. Look, feel the shirt. No sweat?'

Levin felt it, went behind the partition, put out the candle, but did not sleep for a long time. He had just partly clarified the question of how to live, when he was presented with a new, insoluble problem – death.

'So he's dying, so he'll die towards spring, so how can I help him? What can I say to him? What do I know about it? I even forgot there was such a thing.'

XXXII

Levin had long ago observed that when things are made awkward by people's excessive compliance and submission, they are soon made unbearable by their excessive demandingness and fault-finding. He felt that this was going to happen with his brother. And indeed, brother Nikolai's meekness did not last long. The very next morning he became irritable and diligently applied himself to finding fault with his brother, touching the most sensitive spots.

Levin felt himself guilty and could do nothing about it. He felt that if they both had not pretended but had spoken, as the phrase goes, from the heart – that is, only what they both actually thought and felt – they would have looked into each other's eyes, and Konstantin would have said only, 'You're going to die, to die, to die!' and Nikolai would have answered only, 'I know I'm going to die, but I'm afraid, afraid, afraid!' And they would have said nothing else, if they had spoken from the heart. But it was impossible to live that way, and therefore Konstantin tried to do what he had tried to do all his life without succeeding, and what, in his observation, many could do so well, and without which it was impossible to live: he tried to say what he did not think, and kept feeling that it came out false, that his brother noticed it and was annoyed by it.

On the third day, Nikolai provoked his brother to tell him his plans again and began not only to condemn them, but deliberately to confuse them with communism.

'You've just taken other people's thought and distorted it, and you want to apply it where it's inapplicable.'

'But I'm telling you, the two have nothing in common. They deny the justice of property, capital, inheritance, while I, without denying this main stimulus' (Levin was disgusted with himself for using such words, but, ever since he had become involved in his work, he had inadvertently begun to use non-Russian words more and more often), 'only want to regulate labour.'

'That's the point, that you've taken other people's thought, lopped off everything that gives it force, and want to insist that it's something new,' said Nikolai, angrily twitching in his necktie.

'But my thought has nothing in common . . .'

'There,' said Nikolai Levin, with a malicious gleam in his eyes and an ironic smile, 'there at least there's a geometrical charm, so to speak – of clarity, of certainty. Maybe it's a utopia. But let's suppose it's possible to make a *tabula rasa* of the whole past: there's no property, no family, and so labour gets set up. While you have nothing . . .'

'Why do you confuse them? I've never been a communist.'

'But I have been, and I find that it's premature but reasonable, and that it has a future, like Christianity in the first centuries.'

'I only suppose that the work force must be considered from the point of view of natural science – that is, study it, recognize its properties, and . . .'

'But that's all useless. This force itself finds a certain way of action, according to its degree of development. Everywhere there were slaves, then *métayers*;* and with us, too, there's sharecropping, leasing, hired help – what are you seeking?'

Levin suddenly became aroused at these words because in the depths of his soul he was afraid it was true – true that he wanted to balance between communism and the established forms and that this was hardly possible.

* Tenant farmers.

'I'm seeking a productive way of working, both for my own sake and for the workers,' he answered hotly. 'I want to set up . . .'

'You don't want to set up anything, you simply want to be original, as you have all your life, to show that you don't simply exploit the muzhiks but do it with an idea.'

'Well, so you think – and let's drop it!' Levin replied, feeling the muscle on his left cheek quivering uncontrollably.

'You have no convictions and never had any, you only want to coddle your own vanity.'

'Well, splendid, then leave me alone!'

'And so I will! And it's high time, and you can go to the devil! I'm very sorry I came!'

No matter how Levin tried afterwards to calm his brother down, Nikolai would not listen to anything, saying that it was much better to part, and Konstantin saw that for his brother life had simply become unbearable.

Nikolai was already on the point of leaving when Konstantin came to him again and asked him in an unnatural manner to forgive him if he had offended him in any way.

'Ah, magnanimity!' Nikolai said and smiled. 'If you want to be in the right, I can give you that pleasure. You're right, but I'm still leaving!'

Only just before his departure Nikolai exchanged kisses with him and said, suddenly giving his brother a strangely serious look:

'Anyhow, don't think badly of me, Kostya!' and his voice trembled.

These were the only sincere words spoken. Levin understood that they implied: 'You see and know that I'm in a bad way and we may never see each other again.' Levin understood it, and tears gushed from his eyes. He kissed his brother once more, but there was nothing he could or knew how to say to him.

Three days after his brother's departure, Levin also left for abroad. Running into Shcherbatsky, Kitty's cousin, at the railway station, Levin amazed him with his gloominess.

'What's the matter with you?' Shcherbatsky asked him.

'Nothing, it's just that there's not much cheer in the world.'

'Not much? Come with me to Paris instead of some Mulhouse. You'll see how cheerful it is!'

'No, I'm finished. It's time for me to die.'

'A fine thing!' Shcherbatsky said, laughing. 'I'm just ready to begin.'

'I thought the same not long ago, but now I know that I'll die soon.'

Levin said what he had really been thinking lately. He saw either death or the approach of it everywhere. But his undertaking now occupied him all the more. He had to live his life to the end, until death came. Darkness covered everything for him; but precisely because of this darkness he felt that his undertaking was the only guiding thread in this darkness, and he seized it and held on to it with all his remaining strength.

Part Four

I

The Karenins, husband and wife, went on living in the same house, met every day, but were completely estranged from each other. Alexei Alexandrovich made it a rule to see his wife every day, so as to give the servants no grounds for conjecture, but he avoided dining at home. Vronsky never visited Alexei Alexandrovich's house, but Anna saw him elsewhere and her husband knew it.

The situation was painful for all three of them, and none of them would have been able to live even one day in that situation had they not expected that it would change and that it was only a temporary, grievous difficulty which would pass. Alexei Alexandrovich expected that this passion would pass, as all things pass, that everyone would forget about it and his name would remain undisgraced. Anna, upon whom the situation depended and for whom it was most painful of all, endured it because she not only expected but was firmly convinced that it would all resolve and clarify itself very soon. She decidedly did not know what would resolve this situation, but was firmly convinced that this something would now come very soon. Vronsky, involuntarily yielding to her, also expected something independent of himself which would clear up all the difficulties.

In the middle of winter Vronsky spent a very dull week. He was attached to a foreign prince who came to Petersburg,[1] and had to show him the sights of Petersburg. Vronsky himself was of impressive appearance; besides that, he possessed the art of bearing himself with dignified respect and was accustomed to dealing with people of this sort; that was why he had been attached to the prince. But he found the duty very burdensome. The prince wished to miss nothing of which he might be asked at home whether he had seen it in Russia; and he himself wished to take advantage, as far as possible, of Russian pleasures. Vronsky's duty was to be his guide in the one and the other. In the morning they went around seeing the sights; in the evening they partook of national pleasures. The prince enjoyed a health remarkable even among princes; by means of gymnastics and good care of his body, he had attained to such strength that, despite the intemperance with which he gave himself up to pleasure, he was as fresh as a big, green, waxy Dutch cucumber. The prince travelled a great deal and found that one of the main advantages of the modern ease of communication was the accessibility of national pleasures. He had been to Spain, where he had given serenades and become close with a Spanish woman who played the mandolin. In Switzerland he had shot a *Gemse*.* In England he had galloped over fences in a red tailcoat and shot two hundred pheasant for a bet. In Turkey he had visited a harem, in India he had ridden an elephant, and now in Russia he wished to taste all the specifically Russian pleasures.

Vronsky, who was, so to speak, his chief master of ceremonies, went to great lengths in organizing all the pleasures offered to the prince by various people. There were trotting races, and pancakes, and bear hunts, and troikas, and gypsies, and carousing with a Russian smashing of crockery. And the prince adopted the Russian spirit with extreme ease, smashed whole trays of crockery, sat gypsy girls on his knees and seemed to be asking: 'What else, or is this all that makes up the Russian spirit?'

In fact, of all Russian pleasures, the prince liked French actresses, a certain ballet dancer and champagne with the white seal best of all. Vronsky was accustomed to princes but, either because he himself had changed lately, or because he had been much too close to this prince, this week seemed terribly burdensome to him. During the whole week he kept feeling like a man attached to some dangerous lunatic, fearing the lunatic and at the same time, from his closeness to him, fearing for his own reason. Vronsky constantly felt the necessity of not relaxing his tone of official deference for a second, so as not to be insulted. The prince had a contemptuous manner of treating those very people who, to Vronsky's surprise, turned themselves inside out to supply him with Russian pleasures. His judgements of Russian women, whom he wished to study, more than once made Vronsky flush with indignation. But what made the prince especially burdensome was that Vronsky could

* Chamois.

not help seeing himself in him. And what he saw in that mirror was not flattering to his vanity. This was a very stupid, very self-confident, very healthy and very cleanly man, and nothing more. He was a gentleman – that was true, and Vronsky could not deny it. He was equable and unservile with his superiors, free and simple with his equals, and contemptuously good-natured with his inferiors. Vronsky was like that himself and considered it a great virtue; but with respect to the prince he was an inferior and this contemptuously good-natured attitude made him indignant.

'Stupid ox! Am I really like that?' he thought.

Be that as it may, when he said good-bye to him on the seventh day, before the prince's departure for Moscow, and received his thanks, he was happy to be rid of this awkward situation and unpleasant mirror. He said good-bye to him at the station, on the way back from a bear hunt, where they had spent the whole night in a display of Russian bravado.

II

On returning home, Vronsky found a note from Anna. She wrote: 'I am ill and unhappy. I cannot go out, but neither can I go on without seeing you. Come in the evening. At seven o'clock Alexei Alexandrovich is going to a meeting and will be there till ten.' After a moment's reflection about the strangeness of her summoning him directly to her home, despite her husband's demand that she not receive him, he decided to go.

That winter Vronsky had been promoted to colonel, had left regimental quarters and was living alone. After lunch he immediately lay down on the sofa and in five minutes the memories of the outrageous scenes he had witnessed over the last few days became confused and joined with the thought of Anna and the muzhik tracker who had played an important role in the bear hunt, and he fell asleep. He woke up in the dark, trembling with fear, and hastened to light a candle. 'What was that? What? What was that terrible thing I saw in my dream? Yes, yes. The muzhik tracker, I think, small, dirty, with a dishevelled beard, was bending down and doing something, and he suddenly said some strange words in French. Yes, that's all there was to the dream,' he said to himself. 'But why was it so horrible?' He vividly recalled the peasant again and the incomprehensible French words the peasant had uttered, and horror sent a chill down his spine.

'What is this nonsense!' thought Vronsky, and he glanced at his watch.

It was already half-past eight. He rang for his servant, hurriedly got dressed and went out to the porch, forgetting the dream entirely and suffering only over being late. Driving up to the Karenins' porch, he glanced at his watch and saw that it was ten minutes to nine. A tall, narrow carriage hitched to a pair of grey horses stood at the entrance. He recognized Anna's carriage. 'She's coming to me,' thought Vronsky, 'and that would be better. I don't like going into this house. But never mind, I can't start hiding,' he said to himself; and, with the manner habitual to him since childhood of one who has nothing to be ashamed of, Vronsky got out of the sleigh and went to the door. The door opened and the hall porter with a rug over his arm beckoned to the carriage. Vronsky, who was not in the habit of noticing details, nevertheless noticed the astonished expression with which the porter glanced at him. Just at the doorway he nearly ran into Alexei Alexandrovich. The gaslight fell directly on the bloodless, pinched face under the black hat and the white tie gleaming from inside the beaver coat. The immobile, dull eyes of Karenin fixed themselves on Vronsky's face. Vronsky bowed, and Alexei Alexandrovich, chewing his lips, raised his hand to his hat and passed by. Vronsky saw him get into the carriage without looking back, receive the rug and a pair of opera glasses, and disappear. Vronsky went into the front hall. His eyebrows frowned, his eyes gleamed with anger and pride.

'What a position!' he thought. 'If he'd fight, if he'd stand up for his honour, I'd be able to act, to express my feelings; but this weakness or meanness . . . He puts me in the position of a deceiver, which is something I never wanted and do not want to be.'

Since the time of his talk with Anna in Vrede's garden, Vronsky's thinking had changed greatly. Involuntarily submitting to the weakness of Anna, who had given herself to him entirely and expected the deciding of her fate from him alone, submitting to everything beforehand, he had long ceased to think that this liaison might end, as he had thought earlier. His ambitious plans retreated into the background again, and, feeling that he had left the circle of activity in which everything was definite, he gave himself wholly to his feeling, and this feeling bound him to her more and more strongly.

Still in the front hall, he heard her retreating footsteps. He realized that she had been waiting for him, listening, and had now returned to the drawing room.

'No!' she cried, seeing him, and at the first sound of her voice, tears came to her eyes. 'No, if it goes on like this, it will happen much, much sooner!'

'What is it, my love?'

'What? I've been waiting, suffering, one hour, two . . . No, I won't! . . . I cannot quarrel with you. Surely you couldn't help it. No, I won't!'

She placed both hands on his shoulders and gazed at him for a long time with a deep, rapturous and at the same time searching look. She studied his face to make up for the time in which she had not seen him. As at every meeting, she was bringing together her imaginary idea of him (an incomparably better one, impossible in reality) with him as he was.

III

'You met him?' she asked, when they sat down by the table under the lamp. 'That's your punishment for being late.'

'Yes, but how? Wasn't he supposed to be at the council?'

'He went and came back and went somewhere again. But never mind that. Don't talk about it. Where have you been? With the prince all the time?'

She knew all the details of his life. He wanted to say that he had not slept all night and had fallen asleep, but, looking at her excited and happy face, he felt ashamed. And he said that he had had to go and give a report about the prince's departure.

'But it's over now? He's gone?'

'Yes, thank God. You wouldn't believe how unbearable it was for me.'

'Why so? It's the usual life for all you young men,' she said, frowning, and taking up her crochet, which was lying on the table, she began extricating the hook from it without looking at Vronsky.

'I gave up that life long ago,' he said, surprised at the change of expression in her face and trying to penetrate its meaning. 'And I confess,' he said, his smile revealing his close-set white teeth, 'looking at that life all this week, it was as if I were seeing myself in a mirror, and I didn't like it.'

She held her crochet in her hands, not crocheting but looking at him with strange, shining and unfriendly eyes.

'This morning Liza came to see me – they're not afraid to visit me yet, in spite of Countess Lydia Ivanovna,' she put in. 'She told me about your Athenian night.[2] How vile!'

'I was just going to say that . . .'

She interrupted him:

'Was it the Thérèse you knew before?'

'I was going to say . . .'

'How vile you men are! How can you not imagine to yourselves that a woman cannot forget that?' she said, becoming increasingly angry and thereby betraying the cause of her vexation. 'Especially a woman who cannot know your life. What do I know? What did I know?' she said. 'Only what you tell me. And how do I know whether what you've told me is true . . .'

'Anna! That's insulting. Don't you believe me? Haven't I told you that I don't have a single thought that I wouldn't reveal to you?'

'Yes, yes,' she said, obviously trying to drive the jealous thoughts away. 'But if you knew how painful it is for me! I believe you, I do! . . . So what were you saying?'

But he could not immediately recall what he was going to say. These fits of jealousy, which had come over her more and more often lately, horrified him and, no matter how he tried to conceal it, made him cooler towards her, though he knew that the cause of her jealousy was her love for him. How many times he had told himself that her love was happiness; and here she loved him as only a woman can for whom love outweighs all that is good in life – yet he was much further from happiness than when he had followed her from Moscow. Then he had considered himself unhappy, but happiness was ahead of him; while now he felt that the best happiness was already behind. She was not at all as he had seen her in the beginning. Both morally and physically she had changed for the worse. She had broadened out, and her face, when she spoke of the actress, was distorted by a spiteful expression. He looked at her as a man looks at a faded flower he has plucked, in which he can barely recognize the beauty that had made him pluck and destroy it. And, despite that, he felt that when his love was stronger, he might have torn that love from his heart, had he strongly wished to do so, but now, when it seemed to him, as it did at that moment, that he felt no love for her, he knew that his bond with her could not be broken.

'Well, what did you want to tell me about the prince? I've driven him away, I've driven the demon away,' she added. The demon was their name for jealousy. 'Yes, what did you start to tell me about the prince? Why was it so burdensome for you?'

'Ah, unbearable!' he said, trying to catch the thread of his lost thought. 'He doesn't gain from closer acquaintance. If I were to define him, he's a superbly nourished animal, the sort that gets first prize at exhibitions, and nothing more,' he said with a vexation that she found interesting.

'No, how can you,' she objected. 'After all, he's seen a lot, he's educated, isn't he?'

'It's quite a different education – their education. You can see he's been educated only so that he can have the right to despise education, as they despise everything except animal pleasures.'

'But you all love those animal pleasures,' she said, and again he noticed her gloomy eyes, which avoided him.

'Why do you defend him so?' he said, smiling.

'I'm not defending him, it makes absolutely no difference to me; but I think that if you didn't like those pleasures yourself, you might have refused. But it gives you pleasure to look at Teresa in the costume of Eve . . .'

'Again, again the devil!' said Vronsky, taking the hand she had placed on the table and kissing it.

'Yes, but I can't bear it! You don't know how I suffered waiting for you! I don't think I'm jealous. I'm not jealous. I believe you when you're here with me, but when you're alone somewhere leading your life, which is incomprehensible to me . . .'

She drew back from him, finally extricated the hook from her crochet, and quickly, with the help of her index finger, began drawing stitches of white woollen yarn, shining in the lamplight, one after another, and quickly, nervously flicking her wrist in its embroidered cuff.

'Well, what then? Where did you meet Alexei Alexandrovich?' her voice suddenly rang unnaturally.

'We bumped into each other in the doorway.'

'And he bowed to you like this?' She pulled a long face and, half closing her eyes, quickly changed expression, folded her arms, and in her beautiful face Vronsky suddenly saw the very expression with which

Alexei Alexandrovich had bowed to him. He smiled, and she gaily laughed that lovely deep laugh that was one of her main charms.

'I decidedly do not understand him,' said Vronsky. 'If he had broken with you after your talk in the country, if he had challenged me to a duel . . . but this I do not understand: how can he bear such a situation? He suffers, it's obvious.'

'He?' she said with a laugh. 'He's perfectly content.'

'Why are we all tormented when everything could be so good?'

'Only not him. Don't I know him, the lie he's all steeped in? . . . Is it possible, if he has any feeling, to live with me as he does? He doesn't understand or feel anything. Can a man who has any feeling live in the same house with his "criminal" wife? Can he talk to her? Call her "my dear"?'

And again she involuntarily pictured him: '*Ma chère*, my Anna!'

'He's not a man, not a human being, he's a puppet! Nobody else knows it, but I do. Oh, if I were in his place, I'd have killed a wife like me long ago, I'd have torn her to pieces, I wouldn't say to her: "*Ma chère* Anna". He's not a man, he's an administrative machine. He doesn't understand that I'm your wife, that he's a stranger, that he's superfluous . . . Let's not, let's not talk! . . .'

'You're not right, not right, my love,' said Vronsky, trying to calm her. 'But never mind, let's not talk about him. Tell me, what have you been doing? What's wrong with you? What is this illness and what did the doctor say?'

She looked at him with mocking delight. Apparently she had found other ridiculous and ugly sides in her husband and was waiting for the moment to come out with them.

But he went on:

'My guess is that it's not illness but your condition. When is it to be?'

The mocking gleam in her eyes went out, but a different smile – of the knowledge of something he did not know and of a quiet sadness – replaced her former expression.

'Soon, soon. You said our situation is tormenting and we must resolve it. If you knew how painful it is for me, and what I would have given to be able to love you freely and boldly! I wouldn't be tormented and wouldn't torment you with my jealousy . . . And soon it will be so, but not the way we think.'

And at the thought of how it would be, she seemed so pitiful to herself that tears came to her eyes and she could not go on. She laid her hand, shining under the lamp with its rings and whiteness, on his sleeve.

'It will not be the way we think. I didn't want to tell you that, but you made me. Soon, soon everything will be resolved, we'll all, all be at peace and no longer tormented.'

'I don't understand,' he said, understanding her.

'You asked me when? Soon. And I won't survive it. Don't interrupt me!' and she began speaking hurriedly. 'I know this and know it for certain. I will die, and I'm very glad that I will die and deliver myself and you.'

Tears flowed from her eyes. He bent to her hand and began to kiss it, trying to conceal his anxiety, which he knew had no grounds, but which he was unable to control.

'There, that's better,' she said, pressing his hand with a strong movement. 'That is the one thing, the one thing left to us.'

He recovered and raised his head.

'What nonsense! What meaningless nonsense you're saying!'

'No, it's true.'

'What, what is true?'

'That I will die. I had a dream.'

'A dream?' Vronsky repeated and instantly recalled the muzhik in his dream.

'Yes, a dream,' she said. 'I had this dream long ago. I dreamed that I ran into my bedroom, that I had to get something there, to find something out – you know how it happens in dreams,' she said, her eyes wide with horror, 'and there was something standing in the bedroom, in the corner.'

'Ah, what nonsense! How can you believe . . .'

But she would not let herself be interrupted. What she was saying was much too important for her.

'And this something turned, and I saw it was a muzhik with a dishevelled beard, small and frightening. I wanted to run away, but he bent over a sack and rummaged in it with his hands . . .'

And she showed how he rummaged in the sack. There was horror in her face. And Vronsky, recalling his dream, felt the same horror filling his soul.

'He rummages and mutters in French, very quickly, and rolling the *r*s in his throat, you know: "*Il faut le battre le fer, le broyer, le pétrir* . . ."* And

* You must beat the iron, pound it, knead it.

I was so frightened that I wanted to wake up, and I woke up . . . but I woke up in a dream. And I wondered what it meant. And Kornei says to me: "You'll die in childbirth, dear, in childbirth . . ." And I woke up . . .'

'What nonsense, what nonsense!' Vronsky was saying, aware himself that there was no conviction in his voice.

'But let's not talk. Ring the bell, I'll order tea to be served. Wait, now, it won't be long, I . . .'

But suddenly she stopped. The expression on her face changed instantly. Terror and anxiety suddenly gave way to an expression of quiet, serious and blissful attention. He could not understand the meaning of this change. She had felt the stirring of new life inside her.

IV

After meeting Vronsky on his porch, Alexei Alexandrovich drove, as he had intended, to the Italian Opera. He sat out two acts there and saw everyone he had to. On returning home, he studied the coat-rack attentively and, observing that no military coat hung there, went to his rooms as usual. But, contrary to his habit, he did not go to bed but paced up and down his study till three o'clock in the morning. The feeling of wrath against his wife, who did not want to observe propriety and fulfil the only condition placed upon her – not to receive her lover at home – left him no peace. She had not fulfilled his request, and he must now carry out his threat – demand a divorce and take her son from her. He knew all the difficulties connected with this matter, but he had said that he would do it and now he had to carry out his threat. Countess Lydia Ivanovna had hinted to him that this was the best way out of his situation, and lately the practice of divorce had brought the matter to such perfection that Alexei Alexandrovich saw a possibility of overcoming the formal difficulties. Besides, misfortunes never come singly, and the cases of the settlement of the racial minorities and the irrigation of the fields in Zaraysk province had brought down on Alexei Alexandrovich such troubles at work that he had been extremely vexed all the time recently.

He did not sleep the entire night, and his wrath, increasing in a sort of enormous progression, by morning had reached the ultimate limits. He dressed hurriedly and, as if carrying a full cup of wrath and fearing to spill it, fearing to lose along with it the energy needed for a talk with his wife, went into her room as soon as he knew that she was up.

Anna, who thought she knew her husband so well, was struck by his look when he came in. His brow was scowling, and his grim eyes stared straight ahead, avoiding hers; his lips were tightly and contemptuously compressed. In his stride, in his movements, in the sound of his voice there were such resolution and firmness as his wife had never seen in him before. He came into the room without greeting her, made straight for her writing desk and, taking the keys, opened the drawer.

'What do you want?!' she cried.

'Your lover's letters,' he said.

'They're not here,' she said, closing the drawer; but by that movement he understood that he had guessed right and, rudely pushing her hand away, he quickly snatched the portfolio in which he knew she kept her most important papers. She tried to tear it from him, but he pushed her away.[3]

'Sit down! I must talk with you,' he said, putting the portfolio under his arm and pressing it so tightly with his elbow that his shoulder rose up.

Surprised and intimidated, she gazed at him silently.

'I told you that I would not allow you to receive your lover at home.'

'I had to see him, in order to . . .'

She stopped, unable to invent anything.

'I will not go into the details of why a woman needs to see her lover.'

'I wanted, I only . . .' she said, flushing. His rudeness annoyed her and gave her courage. 'Can't you feel how easy it is for you to insult me?' she said.

'One can insult an honest man or an honest woman, but to tell a thief that he is a thief is merely *la constatation d'un fait*.'*

'This cruelty is a new feature – I did not know it was in you.'

'You call it cruelty when a husband offers his wife freedom, giving her the honourable shelter of his name, only on condition that propriety is observed. Is that cruelty?'

'It's worse than cruelty, it's baseness, if you really want to know!' Anna cried out in a burst of anger and got up, intending to leave.

'No!' he shouted in his squeaky voice, which now rose a pitch higher than usual, and, seizing her arm so strongly with his big fingers that the

* The establishing of a fact.

bracelet he pressed left red marks on it, he forced her to sit down. 'Baseness? Since you want to use that word, it is baseness to abandon a husband and son for a lover and go on eating the husband's bread!'

She bowed her head. Not only did she not say what she had said the day before to her lover – that *he* was her husband and her husband was superfluous – but she did not even think it. She felt all the justice of his words and only said softly:

'You cannot describe my position as any worse than I myself understand it to be. But why are you saying all this?'

'Why am I saying this? Why?' he went on just as wrathfully. 'So that you know that since you have not carried out my wish with regard to observing propriety, I shall take measures to bring this situation to an end.'

'It will end soon anyway,' she said, and again, at the thought of her near and now desired death, tears came to her eyes.

'It will end sooner than you've thought up with your lover! You must satisfy your animal passions . . .'

'Alexei Alexandrovich! I will not say that it is not magnanimous, but it is not even respectable to hit someone who is down.'

'Yes, you're only mindful of yourself, but the suffering of the man who was your husband does not interest you. You are indifferent to the destruction of his whole life, to the suffering he has exple . . . expre . . . experimenced.'

Alexei Alexandrovich was speaking so quickly that he became confused and could not get the word out. He finally came out with 'experimenced'. She nearly laughed and at the same time felt ashamed that anything could make her laugh at such a moment. And for the first time, momentarily, she felt for him, put herself in his place and pitied him. But what could she say or do? She bowed her head and was silent. He, too, was silent for a while and then began to speak in a cold and less squeaky voice, emphasizing the arbitrarily chosen words, which had no particular importance.

'I've come to tell you . . .' he said.

She looked at him. 'No, I imagined it,' she thought, remembering the look on his face when he stumbled over the word 'experimenced', 'no, how can a man with those dull eyes, with that smug calm, feel anything?'

'There's nothing I can change,' she whispered.

'I've come to tell you that I am leaving for Moscow tomorrow and will not return to this house again, and you will be informed of my decision through my lawyer, to whom I shall entrust the matter of the divorce. My son will move to my sister's,' Alexei Alexandrovich said, trying hard to recall what he had wanted to say about the son.

'You need Seryozha in order to hurt me,' she said, looking at him from under her brows. 'You don't love him . . . Leave me Seryozha!'

'Yes, I've even lost my love for my son, because he is connected with my loathing for you. But all the same I will take him. Good-bye!'

And he turned to go, but this time she held him back.

'Alexei Alexandrovich, leave me Seryozha!' she whispered once again. 'I have nothing more to say. Leave me Seryozha till my . . . I will give birth soon, leave him with me!'

Alexei Alexandrovich turned red and, tearing his hand from hers, silently left the room.

V

The waiting room of the famous Petersburg lawyer was full when Alexei Alexandrovich entered it. Three ladies: an old one, a young one, and a merchant's wife; and three gentlemen: one a German banker with a signet ring on his finger, another a merchant with a beard, and the third an irate official in uniform with a decoration around his neck, had obviously been waiting for a long time already. Two assistants were writing at their desks, their pens scratching. The writing implements, of which Alexei Alexandrovich was a connoisseur, were exceptionally good. Alexei Alexandrovich could not help noticing it. One of the assistants, without getting up, narrowed his eyes and addressed Alexei Alexandrovich gruffly:

'What would you like?'

'I have business with the lawyer.'

'The lawyer's occupied,' the assistant said sternly, pointing with his pen at the waiting people, and went on writing.

'Could he not find time?' said Alexei Alexandrovich.

'He has no free time, he's always occupied. Kindly wait.'

'Then I shall trouble you to give him my card,' Alexei Alexandrovich said with dignity, seeing the necessity of abandoning his incognito.

The assistant took the card and, evidently disapproving of its content, went through the door.

Alexei Alexandrovich sympathized with open courts in principle, but he did not entirely sympathize with certain details of their application in our country, owing to higher official attitudes which were known to him, and he condemned them in so far as he could condemn anything ratified in the highest places. His whole life had been spent in administrative activity, and therefore, whenever he did not sympathize with anything, his lack of sympathy was softened by recognition of the inevitability of mistakes and the possibility of correcting them in each case. In the new court institutions he did not approve of the circumstances in which the legal profession had been placed.[4] But till now he had never dealt with lawyers and his disapproval had been merely theoretical, while now it was increased by the unpleasant impression he received in the lawyer's waiting room.

'He'll come at once,' the assistant said; and indeed, two minutes later the long figure of an old jurist who had been consulting with the lawyer appeared in the doorway, along with the lawyer himself.

The lawyer was a short, stocky, bald-headed man with a reddish-black beard, light and bushy eyebrows and a prominent forehead. He was dressed up like a bridegroom, from his tie and double watch-chain to his patent-leather boots. He had an intelligent, peasant-like face, but his outfit was foppish and in bad taste.

'Kindly come in,' said the lawyer, addressing Alexei Alexandrovich. And, gloomily allowing Karenin to pass, he closed the door.

'If you please?' He indicated an armchair by the paper-laden desk and himself sat down in the presiding seat, rubbing his small, stubby-fingered hands overgrown with white hairs and inclining his head to one side. But he had no sooner settled in this position than a moth flew over the desk. With a dexterity one would not have expected of him, the lawyer spread his arms, caught the moth, and resumed his former position.

'Before I begin talking about my case,' Alexei Alexandrovich said, his eyes following in surprise the lawyer's movement, 'I must observe that the matter I have to discuss with you must remain secret.'

A barely noticeable smile parted the lawyer's drooping reddish moustaches.

'I would not be a lawyer if I was unable to keep the secrets confided to me. But if you would like some assurance . . .'

Alexei Alexandrovich glanced at his face and saw that his grey, intelligent eyes were laughing and seemed to know everything already.

'You know my name?' Alexei Alexandrovich continued.

'I know you and your useful' – he caught another moth – 'activity, as every Russian does,' the lawyer said with a bow.

Alexei Alexandrovich drew a breath, gathering his courage. But, once resolved, he now went on in his squeaky voice, without timidity, without faltering, and emphasizing certain words.

'I have the misfortune,' Alexei Alexandrovich began, 'of being a deceived husband, and I wish to break relations with my wife legally – that is, to be divorced, but in such a way that my son does not stay with his mother.'

The lawyer's grey eyes tried not to laugh, but they leaped with irrepressible joy, and Alexei Alexandrovich could see that it was not only the joy of a man who was receiving a profitable commission – here there was triumph and delight, there was a gleam that resembled the sinister gleam he had seen in his wife's eyes.

'You desire my assistance in carrying through the divorce?'

'Yes, precisely,' said Alexei Alexandrovich, 'but I must warn you that I risk abusing your attention. I have come only to ask your advice in a preliminary way. I desire the divorce, but I give importance to the forms in which it is possible. It is very likely that, if the forms do not fit my requirements, I will renounce a formal suit.'

'Oh, that is always so,' said the lawyer, 'and it is always in your power.'

The lawyer dropped his eyes to Alexei Alexandrovich's feet, sensing that his look of irrepressible joy might offend his client. He saw a moth flying just in front of his nose and his hand jumped, but he did not catch it, out of respect for Alexei Alexandrovich's position.

'Although our statutes on this subject are known to me in general terms,' Alexei Alexandrovich continued, 'I would like to know the forms in which cases of this sort are most often carried through in practice.'

'You wish,' replied the lawyer, not raising his eyes, and adopting, not without pleasure, the tone of his client's speech, 'that I lay out for you the ways in which the fulfilment of your desire is possible.'

And, at an affirming nod of Alexei Alexandrovich's head, he continued, only giving a fleeting glance now and then at Alexei Alexandrovich's face, which was covered with red blotches.

'Divorce, according to our laws,' he said with a slight tinge of disapproval of our laws, 'is possible, as you know, in the following cases . . . Let them wait!' he said to the assistant who had thrust himself in the door, but nevertheless got up, said a few words and sat down again. 'In the following cases: physical defects in the spouses, or a five-year absence without communication,' he said, bending down his stubby, hair-covered fingers, 'or adultery' (he pronounced this word with visible pleasure). 'The subdivisions are the following' (he continued to bend down his fat fingers, though cases and subdivisions obviously could not be classified together): 'physical defects in husband or wife, and adultery of the husband or wife.' As he had run out of fingers, he unbent them all and went on. 'This is the theoretical view, but I suppose that you have done me the honour of appealing to me in order to find out about the practical application. And therefore, going by precedent, I must inform you that all cases of divorce come down to the following – there are no physical defects, I may take it? and no five-year absence either? . . .'

Alexei Alexandrovich inclined his head affirmatively.

'. . . come down to the following: adultery by one of the spouses and exposure of the guilty party by mutual agreement, or, lacking such agreement, by involuntary exposure. I must say that the latter case rarely occurs in practice,' the lawyer said and, glancing fleetingly at Alexei Alexandrovich, fell silent, like a seller of pistols who, having described the advantages of each of two weapons, waits for his purchaser's choice. But Alexei Alexandrovich was silent, and therefore the lawyer went on: 'The most usual, simple and sensible thing, I consider, is adultery by mutual consent. I would not have allowed myself to put it that way if I were talking with an undeveloped man,' said the lawyer, 'but I suppose we understand each other.'

Alexei Alexandrovich was so upset, however, that he did not understand at once the sensibleness of adultery by mutual consent, and his eyes expressed bewilderment; but the lawyer immediately came to his assistance:

'People cannot go on living together – there is a fact. And if they both agree in that, the details and formalities become a matter of indifference. And at the same time this is the simplest and surest method.'

Now Alexei Alexandrovich fully understood. But he had religious requirements that prevented him from accepting this measure.

'That is out of the question in the present case,' he said. 'Only one case is possible: involuntary exposure, confirmed by letters which I have in my possession.'

At the mention of letters, the lawyer pursed his lips and produced a high-pitched sound of pity and contempt.

'Kindly consider,' he began. 'Cases of this sort are decided, as you know, by the religious department; the reverend fathers are great lovers of the minutest details,' he said with a smile that showed his sympathy with the reverend fathers' taste. 'Letters undoubtedly could give partial confirmation; but the evidence must be obtained directly – that is, by witnesses. And, in general, if you do me the honour of granting me your trust, you should leave to me the choice of measures to be employed. He who wants results must allow for the means.'

'If so . . .' Alexei Alexandrovich began, suddenly turning pale, but at that moment the lawyer got up and went to the door to speak with the assistant, who had interrupted again.

'Tell her we don't give discounts!' he said and went back to Alexei Alexandrovich.

While returning to his place he inconspicuously caught another moth. 'Fine upholstery I'll have by summer!' he thought, frowning.

'And so, you were kindly saying . . .' he said.

'I shall inform you of my decision in writing,' said Alexei Alexandrovich, getting up and taking hold of the desk. After standing silently for a while, he said: 'I may thus conclude from your words that the carrying through of a divorce is possible. I should also like you to inform me of your terms.'

'Everything is possible, if you allow me complete freedom of action,' the lawyer said without answering the question. 'When may I expect to hear from you?' he asked, moving towards the door, his eyes and his patent-leather boots shining.

'In a week. And kindly give me an answer as to whether you will agree to undertake in this case and on what terms.'

'Very well, sir.'

The lawyer bowed deferentially, let his client out of the door and, left alone, gave himself up to his joyful feeling. He felt so merry that, contrary to his rules, he gave the bargaining lady a lower price and stopped catching moths, having decided finally that by next winter he would have to re-upholster the furniture in velvet, as at Sigonin's.

VI

Alexei Alexandrovich had won a brilliant victory at the meeting of the commission on August 17th, but the consequences of that victory crippled him. The new commission for the investigation into all aspects of the life of the racial minorities was appointed and sent to the scene with extraordinary swiftness and energy, inspired by Alexei Alexandrovich. Three months later a report was presented. The life of the minorities was investigated in its political, administrative, economic, ethnographic, material and religious aspects. All questions were furnished with excellent answers, and answers not open to doubt, since they were not the product of human thought, which is always subject to error, but were the products of institutional activity. The answers were all the result of official data, the reports of governors and bishops, based on the reports of regional superiors and vicars, based for their part on the reports of local officials and parish priests; and therefore all these answers were indubitable. All the questions, for instance, about why there were crop failures, why the populations clung to their beliefs, and so on – questions that would not and could not be resolved for centuries without the convenience of the institutional machine – now received a clear and indubitable resolution. The results were in favour of Alexei Alexandrovich's opinion. But when the reports of the commission were received, Stremov, feeling himself cut to the quick at the last meeting, employed a tactic that Alexei Alexandrovich did not expect. Drawing several other members with him, he suddenly went over to Alexei Alexandrovich's side, and not only hotly defended the carrying out of the measures suggested by Karenin, but offered additional measures, extreme ones, in the same spirit. These measures, intensified far beyond Alexei Alexandrovich's fundamental idea, were accepted, and then Stremov's tactic was revealed. These measures, carried to an extreme, suddenly proved to be so stupid that statesmen, and public opinion, and intelligent ladies and the newspapers all fell upon them at one and the same time, voicing their indignation both at the measures themselves and at their acknowledged father, Alexei Alexandrovich. Stremov then withdrew, pretending he had only been blindly following Karenin's plan and now was himself surprised and indignant at what had been done. This crippled Alexei Alexandrovich. But in spite of declining health, in spite of family woes, he did not give in. A split occurred in the commission. Some members, with Stremov at their head, justified their mistake by their trust in the inspection commission directed by Alexei Alexandrovich, which had presented the report, and said that the report of this commission was nonsense and nothing but waste paper. Alexei Alexandrovich, with a party of people who saw the danger of such a revolutionary attitude towards official papers, continued to support the data provided by the inspection commission. As a result, everything became confused in higher spheres and even in society, and, despite great interest on everyone's part, no one could make out whether the minorities were flourishing or were actually in need and perishing. Alexei Alexandrovich's position, as a result of that and partly as a result of the scorn that fell on him owing to his wife's infidelity, became quite shaky. And in that position Alexei Alexandrovich took an important decision. He announced, to the surprise of the commission, that he would request permission to go personally to investigate the matter on the spot. And, having received permission, Alexei Alexandrovich set out for the distant provinces.

Alexei Alexandrovich's departure caused a great stir, the more so as at his departure he officially returned under receipt the travelling money allotted him for twelve horses to take him to his destination.

'I find it very noble,' Betsy said of it to Princess Miagky. 'Why provide for post horses when everyone knows there are railways everywhere now?'

But Princess Miagky disagreed, and Princess Tverskoy's opinion even vexed her.

'It's all very well for you to talk,' she said, 'since you have I don't know how many millions, but I like it very much when my husband goes inspecting in the summer. It's very healthy and pleasant for him to ride around, and I make it a rule that the money goes for keeping a coach and coachman.'

On his way to the distant provinces Alexei Alexandrovich stopped for three days in Moscow.

The day after his arrival he went to visit the governor general. At the intersection of Gazetny Lane, where there is always a crowd of carriages and cabs, Alexei Alexandrovich suddenly heard his name called out in such a loud and merry voice that he could not help turning round. On the corner pavement, in a short, fashionable coat, with his short, fashionable hat cocked to one side, the gleam of a white-toothed smile between his red lips, merry, young and beaming, stood Stepan

Arkadyich, resolutely and insistently shouting and demanding that he stop. He was holding on with one hand to the window of a carriage that had stopped at the corner, out of which peered a woman's head in a velvet hat and two children's heads, and was smiling and beckoning to his brother-in-law with the other hand. The lady smiled a kindly smile and also waved her hand to Alexei Alexandrovich. It was Dolly with the children.

Alexei Alexandrovich did not want to see anyone in Moscow, least of all his wife's brother. He raised his hat and was about to drive on, but Stepan Arkadyich told his coachman to stop and ran to him across the snow.

'How wicked of you not to send word! Have you been here long? And I was at the Dussot yesterday and saw "Karenin" on the board, and it never occurred to me that it was you!' said Stepan Arkadyich, thrusting his head inside the carriage. 'Otherwise I'd have called on you. I'm so glad to see you!' he said, knocking one foot against the other to shake off the snow. 'How wicked of you not to let us know!' he repeated.

'I had no time, I'm very busy,' Alexei Alexandrovich replied drily.

'Let's go to my wife, she wants so much to see you.'

Alexei Alexandrovich removed the rug in which his chill-prone legs were wrapped and, getting out of the carriage, made his way over the snow to Darya Alexandrovna.

'What is it, Alexei Alexandrovich, why do you avoid us like this?' Dolly said, smiling sadly.

'I've been very busy. Very glad to see you,' he said, in a tone which showed clearly that he was upset by it. 'How are you?'

'And how is my dear Anna?'

Alexei Alexandrovich mumbled something and was about to leave. But Stepan Arkadyich stopped him.

'Here's what we'll do tomorrow. Dolly, invite him for dinner! We'll invite Koznyshev and Pestsov and treat him to the Moscow intelligentsia.'

'Yes, please do come,' said Dolly, 'we'll expect you at five, six if you like. Well, how is my dear Anna? It's so long since . . .'

'She's well,' Alexei Alexandrovich mumbled, frowning. 'Very glad to see you!' and he made for his carriage.

'Will you come?' Dolly called out.

Alexei Alexandrovich said something that Dolly could not make out in the noise of moving carriages.

'I'll drop in tomorrow!' Stepan Arkadyich called to him.

Alexei Alexandrovich got into his carriage and sank deep inside, so as not to see or be seen.

'An odd bird!' Stepan Arkadyich said to his wife and, looking at his watch, made a gesture in front of his face signifying love for his wife and children, and went off jauntily down the pavement.

'Stiva! Stiva!' Dolly called out, blushing.

He turned.

'I have to buy coats for Grisha and Tanya. Give me some money!'

'Never mind. Tell them I'll pay,' and he disappeared, nodding gaily to an acquaintance driving by.

VII

The next day was Sunday. Stepan Arkadyich called in on the ballet rehearsal at the Bolshoi Theatre and gave Masha Chibisova, a pretty dancer, newly signed on through his patronage, the coral necklace he had promised her the day before and, backstage, in the theatre's daytime darkness, managed to kiss her pretty face, brightened by the gift. Besides giving her the coral necklace, he had to arrange to meet her after the performance. Explaining to her that he could not be there for the beginning of the ballet, he promised to come by the last act and take her to supper. From the theatre Stepan Arkadyich went to the Okhotny Market, personally selected the fish and asparagus for dinner, and by noon was already at the Dussot, where he had to see three people who, fortunately for him, were staying at the same hotel: Levin, who was staying there after recently returning from abroad; his newly appointed superior, who had just taken over that high position and was inspecting Moscow; and his brother-in-law Karenin, to bring him to dinner without fail.

Stepan Arkadyich loved dining, but still more he loved giving a dinner, not a big dinner, but a refined one as to the food, the drinks and the selection of guests. The programme for today's dinner was very much to his liking: there would be live perch, asparagus and *la pièce de résistance* – a superb but simple roast beef – and the appropriate wines. So much for the food and drink. And as guests there would be Kitty and Levin, and, to make it less conspicuous, another girl cousin and the young Shcherbatsky, and *la pièce de résistance* among the guests – Sergei

Koznyshev and Alexei Alexandrovich – Muscovite philosopher and Petersburg politician. And he would also invite the well-known eccentric and enthusiast Pestsov, a liberal, a talker, a musician, a historian, and the dearest fifty-year-old boy, who would be like the gravy or garnish for Koznyshev and Karenin. He would rile them up and set them on each other.

The second instalment of the merchant's money for the wood had been received and was not yet all spent, Dolly had been very sweet and kind lately, and the thought of the dinner gladdened Stepan Arkadyich in all respects. He was in the merriest state of mind. There were two slightly unpleasant circumstances, but they both drowned in the sea of good-natured merriment that surged in his soul. These two circumstances were: first, that yesterday, when he met Alexei Alexandrovich in the street, he noticed that he was dry and stern with him, and, putting together the look on Alexei Alexandrovich's face, plus the fact that he had not called on them and had not let them know he was there, with the talk he had heard about Anna and Vronsky, Stepan Arkadyich guessed that something was wrong between the husband and wife.

That was one unpleasantness. The other slight unpleasantness was that his new superior, like all new superiors, already had the reputation of being a terrible man, who got up at six o'clock in the morning, worked like a horse, and demanded that his subordinates work in the same way. Besides, this new superior was also reputed to have the manners of a bear and, according to rumour, was a man of the completely opposite tendency from that to which the former superior had adhered and to which, till then, Stepan Arkadyich himself had also adhered. The day before, Stepan Arkadyich had come to work in his uniform and the new superior had been very amiable and had got to talking with him as with an acquaintance. Therefore Stepan Arkadyich felt obliged to call on him in a frock coat.[5] The thought that the new superior might not take it well was that second unpleasant circumstance. But Stepan Arkadyich felt instinctively that it would all *shape up* beautifully. 'They're human, they're people, just like us sinners: why get angry and quarrel?' he thought, going into the hotel.

'Greetings, Vassily,' he said, walking down the corridor with his hat cocked and addressing a servant he knew. 'So you're letting your side-whiskers grow? Levin's in number seven, eh? Take me there, please. And find out whether Count Anichkin' (that was the new superior) 'will receive me.'

'Very well, sir,' Vassily replied, smiling. 'You haven't been here for a long time.'

'I was here yesterday, only I used a different entrance. Is this number seven?'

Levin was standing in the middle of the room with a muzhik from Tver measuring a fresh bear-skin with a yardstick when Stepan Arkadyich came in.

'Ah, you shot it?' Stepan Arkadyich cried. 'A fine thing! A she-bear? Hello, Arkhip.'

He shook hands with the muzhik and sat down on a chair without taking off his coat and hat.

'But do take it off and stay a while,' said Levin, taking his hat off him.

'No, I have no time, I'll stay for one little second,' Stepan Arkadyich replied. He threw his coat open, but then took it off and sat for a whole hour talking with Levin about hunting and the most heartfelt subjects.

'Well, kindly tell me, what did you do abroad? Where did you go?' said Stepan Arkadyich, when the muzhik left.

'I was in Germany, in Prussia, in France, in England – not in the capitals, but in the manufacturing towns – and saw many new things. I'm glad I went.'

'Yes, I know your idea about setting up the workers.'

'Not at all: there can be no workers problem in Russia. In Russia there's a problem of the relation of working people to the land. It exists there, too, but there it's the repairing of something damaged, while here . . .'

Stepan Arkadyich listened attentively to Levin.

'Yes, yes!' he said. 'It's very possible that you're right,' he observed. 'But I'm glad you're in cheerful spirits – hunting bear, and working, and getting enthusiastic. Shcherbatsky told me he met you and that you were in some sort of despondency, kept talking about death . . .'

'And what of it? I haven't stopped thinking about death,' said Levin. 'It's true that it's time to die. And that everything is nonsense. I'll tell you truly: I value my thought and work terribly, but in essence – think about it – this whole world of ours is just a bit of mildew that grew over a tiny planet. And we think we can have something great – thoughts, deeds! They're all grains of sand.'

'But, my dear boy, that's as old as the hills!'

'Old, yes, but you know, once you understand it clearly, everything somehow becomes insignificant. Once you understand that you'll die today or tomorrow and there'll be nothing left, everything becomes so insignificant! I consider my thought very important, but it turns out to be as insignificant, even if it's carried out, as tracking down this she-bear. So you spend your life diverted by hunting or work in order not to think about death.'

Stepan Arkadyich smiled subtly and gently as he listened to Levin.

'Well, naturally! Here you're coming over to my side. Remember, you attacked me for seeking pleasures in life? "Be not so stern, O moralist"! . . .'[6]

'No, all the same there is this good in life that . . .' Levin became confused. 'But I don't know. I only know that we'll die soon.'

'Why soon?'

'And you know, there's less charm in life when you think about death – but it's more peaceful.'

'On the contrary, the last days are the merriest. Well, anyhow, it's time for me to go,' said Stepan Arkadyich, getting up for the tenth time.

'No, stay!' said Levin, trying to keep him. 'When are we going to see each other now? I'm leaving tomorrow.'

'I'm a fine one! That's what I came for . . . You must come to dinner with us tonight. Your brother will be there, and my brother-in-law Karenin.'

'Is he here?' said Levin, and he wanted to ask about Kitty. He had heard that she had been in Petersburg at the beginning of winter, staying with her sister, the diplomat's wife, and did not know if she had come back or not, but he changed his mind about asking. 'She'll be there or she won't be – it makes no difference.'

'So you'll come?'

'Well, naturally.'

'At five o'clock, then, and in a frock coat.'

And Stepan Arkadyich got up and went downstairs to see his new superior. Stepan Arkadyich's instinct had not deceived him. The terrible new superior turned out to be a very courteous man, and Stepan Arkadyich had lunch with him and stayed so long that it was past three o'clock before he got to Alexei Alexandrovich.

VIII

Alexei Alexandrovich, having come back from church, spent the whole morning at home. He was faced that morning with two tasks: first, to receive and send off to Petersburg a deputation from the racial minorities that was now in Moscow; and second, to write the promised letter to the lawyer. The deputation, though invited on his initiative, presented many inconveniences and even dangers, and Alexei Alexandrovich was very glad to have found it in Moscow. The members of the deputation had not the slightest idea of their role and responsibilities. They were naïvely convinced that their course consisted in explaining their needs and the true state of things and asking for government assistance, and they decidedly failed to understand that some of their statements and demands supported the hostile party and would therefore ruin the whole thing. Alexei Alexandrovich spent a long time with them, wrote a programme from which they were not to deviate, and, after dismissing them, wrote letters to Petersburg for the guidance of the deputation. His chief assistant in this matter was to be Countess Lydia Ivanovna. She was an expert in dealing with deputations and no one knew so well as she how to handle a deputation and guide it properly. Having finished that, Alexei Alexandrovich also wrote to the lawyer. Without the least hesitation, he gave him permission to act at his own discretion. In the letter he enclosed three notes from Vronsky to Anna which he had found in the portfolio he had taken from her.

Ever since Alexei Alexandrovich had left home with the intention of not returning to his family, and ever since he had seen the lawyer and told at least one person of his intention, especially since he had turned the matter of his life into a matter of papers, he had been growing more and more accustomed to his intention and now saw clearly the possibility of carrying it through.

He was sealing the envelope to his lawyer when he heard the loud sounds of Stepan Arkadyich's voice. Stepan Arkadyich was arguing with Alexei Alexandrovich's valet and insisting that he should be announced.

'It makes no difference,' thought Alexei Alexandrovich. 'So much the better: I'll declare my position regarding his sister now and explain why I cannot dine with them.'

'Show him in!' he said loudly, gathering up the papers and putting them into the blotter.

'You see, you're lying, he is at home!' Stepan Arkadyich's voice said to the lackey who had refused to let him in, and, taking his coat off as he went, Oblonsky entered the room. 'Well, I'm very glad I found you at home! So, I hope . . .' Stepan Arkadyich began merrily.

'I cannot come,' Alexei Alexandrovich said coldly, standing and not inviting his visitor to sit down.

Alexei Alexandrovich meant to enter at once into the cold relations he ought to have with the brother of a wife with whom he was beginning divorce proceedings; but he had not taken into account the sea of good-naturedness that overflowed the shores of Stepan Arkadyich's soul.

Stepan Arkadyich opened his shining, clear eyes wide.

'Why can't you? What do you mean to say?' he said perplexedly in French. 'No, you promised. And we're all counting on you.'

'I mean to say that I cannot come to your house, because the family relations that existed between us must cease.'

'What? I mean, how? Why?' Stepan Arkadyich said with a smile.

'Because I am starting divorce proceedings against your sister, my wife. I have been forced . . .'

But before Alexei Alexandrovich had time to finish what he was saying, Stepan Arkadyich acted in a way he had not expected at all. Stepan Arkadyich gasped and sank into an armchair.

'No, Alexei Alexandrovich, what are you saying!' cried Oblonsky, and suffering showed on his face.

'It's so.'

'Forgive me, but I can't, I simply can't believe it . . .'

Alexei Alexandrovich sat down, feeling that his words had not had the effect he anticipated, that it would be necessary for him to explain himself, and that whatever his explanations might be, his relations with his brother-in-law would remain the same.

'Yes, I am put under the painful necessity of demanding a divorce,' he said.

'I'll tell you one thing, Alexei Alexandrovich. I know you to be an excellent and just man, I know Anna – forgive me, I can't change my opinion of her – to be a wonderful, excellent woman, and therefore, forgive me, but I can't believe it. There's some misunderstanding here,' he said.

'Yes, if only it were a misunderstanding . . .'

'Excuse me, I do see,' Stepan Arkadyich interrupted. 'But, naturally . . . One thing: you mustn't be hasty. You mustn't, mustn't be hasty!'

'I am not being hasty,' Alexei Alexandrovich said coldly. 'And one cannot take anyone else's advice in such a matter. I am firmly decided.'

'This is terrible!' said Stepan Arkadyich with a deep sigh. 'There's one thing I'd do, Alexei Alexandrovich. I beg you to do it!' he said. 'The proceedings haven't started yet, as I understand. Before you start them, go and see my wife, talk with her. She loves Anna like a sister, she loves you, and she's an amazing woman. For God's sake, talk with her! Do it out of friendship for me, I beg you!'

Alexei Alexandrovich reflected, and Stepan Arkadyich looked at him sympathetically, without breaking his silence.

'Will you go and see her?'

'I don't know. That's why I didn't call on you. I suppose our relations must change.'

'Why so? I don't see it. Permit me to think that, apart from our family relations, you have for me, at least somewhat, the friendly feelings that I have always had for you . . . And true respect,' said Stepan Arkadyich, pressing his hand. 'Even if your worst suppositions are right, I do not and never will take it upon myself to judge either side, and I see no reason why our relations must change. But do it now, come and see my wife.'

'Well, we have different views of this matter,' Alexei Alexandrovich said coldly. 'However, let's not talk about it.'

'No, why shouldn't you come? Why not tonight for dinner? My wife is expecting you. Please come. And above all, talk it over with her. She's an amazing woman. For God's sake, I beg you on my knees!'

'If you want it so much – I'll come,' Alexei Alexandrovich said with a sigh.

And, wishing to change the subject, he asked about something that interested them both – Stepan Arkadyich's new superior, not yet an old man, who had suddenly been appointed to such a high position.

Alexei Alexandrovich had never liked Count Anichkin even before and had always differed with him in opinion, but now he could not refrain from the hatred, comprehensible among officials, of a man who has suffered a fiasco in the service for a man who has received a promotion.

'Well, have you seen him?' Alexei Alexandrovich said with a venomous grin.

'Of course, he came to our office yesterday. He seems to know his business perfectly and is very energetic.'

'Yes, but at what is his energy directed?' said Alexei Alexandrovich.

'At getting things done, or at redoing what has already been done? The misfortune of our government is paper administration, of which he is a worthy representative.'

'I really don't know what he can be faulted for. I don't know his tendency, but one thing I do know – he's an excellent fellow,' Stepan Arkadyich replied. 'I've just called on him and, really, he's an excellent fellow. We had lunch, and I taught him to make that drink – you know, wine with oranges. It's very refreshing. And remarkably enough, he didn't know it. He liked it very much. No, really, he's a nice fellow.'

Stepan Arkadyich looked at his watch.

'Heavens, it's past four and I still have to see Dolgovushin! So, please do come for dinner. Otherwise you don't know how upset my wife and I will be.'

Alexei Alexandrovich saw his brother-in-law off quite differently from the way he had met him.

'I've promised and I will come,' he answered glumly.

'Believe me, I appreciate it, and I hope you won't regret it,' Stepan Arkadyich replied, smiling.

And, putting on his coat as he left, he brushed the valet's head with his hand, laughed and went out.

'At five o'clock, and in a frock coat, please!' he called out once more, coming back to the door.

IX

It was past five and some of the guests had already arrived when the host arrived himself. He came in together with Sergei Ivanovich Koznyshev and Pestsov, who had bumped into each other on the doorstep. These were the two main representatives of the Moscow intelligentsia, as Oblonsky called them. They were both people respected for their character and intelligence. They respected each other but were in complete and hopeless disagreement on almost everything – not because they belonged to opposite tendencies, but precisely because they were from the same camp (their enemies mixed them up), but within that camp each had his own shade. And since there is nothing less conducive to agreement than a difference of thinking in half-abstract things, they not only never agreed in their opinions, but had long grown used to chuckling at each other's incorrigible error without getting angry.

They were going in the door, talking about the weather, when Stepan Arkadyich overtook them. Prince Alexander Dmitrievich, Oblonsky's father-in-law, young Shcherbatsky, Turovtsyn, Kitty and Karenin were already sitting in the drawing room.

Stepan Arkadyich saw at once that without him things were going badly in the drawing room. Darya Alexandrovna, in her smart grey silk dress, obviously preoccupied by the children's having to eat alone in the nursery and by her husband's absence, had not managed to mix this whole company without him. They all sat like a parson's daughters on a visit (in the old prince's expression), obviously perplexed at how they had wound up there, squeezing out words so as not to be silent. The good-natured Turovtsyn obviously felt out of his element, and the thick-lipped smile with which he met Stepan Arkadyich said in all but words: 'Well, brother, you've planted me among some clever ones! A drink at the Château des Fleurs is more in my line!' The old prince sat silently, glancing sidelong at Karenin with his shining little eyes, and Stepan Arkadyich could see that he had already thought up a little phrase to paste on this statesman, whom one was invited for as if he were a poached sturgeon. Kitty was looking at the door, plucking up her courage so as not to blush when Konstantin Levin came in. Young Shcherbatsky, who had not been introduced to Karenin, was trying to show that this did not embarrass him in the least. Karenin himself, by old Petersburg habit, coming to dinner with ladies, was wearing a tailcoat and white tie, and Stepan Arkadyich could see from his face that he had come only to keep his word and was performing a painful duty by being present in this company. He was the main cause of the chill that had frozen all the guests before Stepan Arkadyich's arrival.

On entering the drawing room, Stepan Arkadyich excused himself by explaining that he had been delayed by that prince who was the perennial scapegoat each time he was late or absent, and in a moment he got everyone acquainted with everyone else, and, putting Alexei Alexandrovich together with Sergei Koznyshev, slipped them the topic of the russification of Poland,[7] which they both seized upon at once, along with Pestsov. Patting Turovtsyn on the shoulder, he whispered something funny to him and sat him down with his wife and the prince. Then he told Kitty how beautiful she was that evening, and introduced Shcherbatsky to Karenin. In a moment he had kneaded this social dough so well that the drawing room was in fine form and ringing with voices.

Only Konstantin Levin was missing. But that was for the better, because, going out to the dining room, Stepan Arkadyich saw to his horror that the port and sherry had been bought at Deprez's and not at Levet's, and gave orders for the coachman to be sent to Levet's as soon as possible. Then he turned to go back to the drawing room.

In the dining room he met Konstantin Levin.

'I'm not late?'

'As if you could be anything else!' Stepan Arkadyich said, taking him under the arm.

'You have a lot of people? Who's here?' Levin asked, blushing, as he knocked the snow off his hat with his glove.

'All our own. Kitty's here. Let's go, I'll introduce you to Karenin.'

Despite his liberalism, Stepan Arkadyich knew that acquaintance with Karenin could not but be flattering and therefore treated his best friends to it. But just then Konstantin Levin was unable to feel all the pleasure of this acquaintance. He had not seen Kitty since that evening, so memorable for him, on which he had met Vronsky, unless he were to count the moment when he had seen her on the high road. In the depths of his soul he had known that he would see her here tonight. But, maintaining his inner freedom of thought, he tried to assure himself that he had not known it. Yet now, when he heard that she was there, he suddenly felt such joy, and at the same time such fear, that his breath was taken away and he could not bring out what he wanted to say.

'How is she? How? The way she was before, or the way she was in the carriage? And what if what Darya Alexandrovna said is true? Why shouldn't it be true?' he thought.

'Ah, do please introduce me to Karenin,' he barely uttered, and with a desperately determined step he went into the drawing room and saw her.

She was neither the way she had been before, nor the way she had been in the carriage; she was quite different.

She was frightened, timid, shamefaced, and all the more lovely because of it. She saw him the instant he came into the room. She had been waiting for him. She was joyful and so embarrassed by her joy that there was a moment – as he went up to the hostess and glanced at her again – when it seemed to her, and to him, and to Dolly, who saw it all, that she would not be able to stand it and would start to cry. She blushed, paled, blushed again and froze, her lips quivering a little, waiting for him. He came up to her, bowed and silently gave her his hand. Had it not been for the slight trembling of her lips and the moisture that came to her eyes, giving them an added brilliance, her smile would have been almost calm as she said:

'It's so long since we've seen each other!' and with desperate resolution pressed his hand with her cold hand.

'You haven't seen me, but I saw you,' said Levin, radiant with a smile of happiness. 'I saw you when you were driving to Yergushovo from the station.'

'When?' she asked with surprise.

'You were going to Yergushovo,' said Levin, feeling himself choking with the happiness that flooded his soul. And he thought to himself, 'How could I connect this touching being with the thought of anything not innocent! And, yes, it seems that what Darya Alexandrovna said is true.'

Stepan Arkadyich took him by the arm and brought him to Karenin.

'Allow me to introduce you.' He gave their names.

'Very pleased to meet you again,' Alexei Alexandrovich said coldly, shaking Levin's hand.

'You're acquainted?' Stepan Arkadyich asked in surprise.

'We spent three hours together on the train,' Levin said, smiling, 'but came away intrigued, as from a masked ball, or at least I did.'

'Really! This way, please,' Stepan Arkadyich said, pointing in the direction of the dining room.

The men went to the dining room and approached the table of hors d'oeuvres, set with six kinds of vodka and as many kinds of cheese with silver spreaders or without, with caviars, herring, various tinned delicacies and platters of sliced French bread.

The men stood by the fragrant vodkas and hors d'oeuvres, and the conversation between Koznyshev, Karenin and Pestsov about the russification of Poland began to die down in anticipation of dinner.

Sergei Ivanovich, who knew like no one else how to add some Attic salt[8] to the end of a most abstract and serious discussion and thereby change the mood of his interlocutors, did so now.

Alexei Alexandrovich maintained that the russification of Poland could be accomplished only as a result of higher principles, which ought to be introduced by the Russian administration.

Pestsov insisted that one nation could assimilate another only if it had a denser population.

Koznyshev acknowledged the one and the other, but with limitations.

To conclude the conversation, he said with a smile as they were leaving the drawing room:

'Therefore there is only one way of russifying the racial minorities – by breeding as many children as possible. There's where my brother and I are at our worst. And you married gentlemen, especially you, Stepan Arkadyich, are quite patriotic. How many do you have?' He turned with a gentle smile to his host and held out his tiny glass to him.

Everybody laughed, Stepan Arkadyich with particular gaiety.

'Yes, that's the best way!' he said, chewing some cheese and pouring some special sort of vodka into the held-out glass. The conversation indeed ceased on that joke.

'This cheese isn't bad. Would you care for some?' said the host. 'So you've gone back to doing exercises?' He turned to Levin, feeling his muscle with his left hand. Levin smiled, flexed his arm, and under Stepan Arkadyich's fingers a steely bump rose like a round cheese under the thin cloth of the frock coat.

'What a biceps! Samson!'

'I suppose it takes great strength to hunt bear,' said Alexei Alexandrovich, who had very foggy notions of hunting, spreading some cheese and tearing through the gossamer-thin slice of bread.

Levin smiled.

'None at all. On the contrary, a child can kill a bear,' he said with a slight bow, stepping aside before the ladies who, together with the hostess, were approaching the table of hors d'oeuvres.

'And you killed a bear, I'm told?' said Kitty, trying in vain to spear a disobedient, slippery mushroom with her fork and shaking the lace through which her arm showed white. 'Do you really have bears there?' she added, half turning her lovely head towards him and smiling.

It seemed there was nothing extraordinary in what she said, yet for him, what meaning, inexpressible in words, there was in every sound, in every movement of her lips, eyes, arm, as she said it! Here was a plea for forgiveness, and trust in him, and a caress, a tender, timid caress, and a promise, and hope, and love for him, in which he could not but believe and which choked him with happiness.

'No, we went to Tver province. On my way back I met your *beau-frère** on the train, or your *beau-frère*'s brother-in-law,' he said with a smile. 'It was a funny encounter.'

* Brother-in-law.

And he told, gaily and amusingly, how, after not sleeping all night, he had burst into Alexei Alexandrovich's compartment in his sheepskin jacket.

'The conductor, contrary to the proverb, judged me by my clothes and wanted to throw me out. But at that point I began talking in high-flown language, and ... you, too,' he said, forgetting Karenin's name as he turned to him, 'wanted to chase me out at first, judging by my jacket, but then stood up for me, for which I'm very grateful.'

'In general, passengers' rights in the choice of seats are rather vague,' said Alexei Alexandrovich, wiping the tips of his fingers with a handkerchief.

'I could see you were uncertain about me,' Levin said, smiling good-naturedly, 'but I hastened to start an intelligent conversation, so as to smooth over my sheepskin jacket.'

Sergei Ivanovich, continuing his conversation with the hostess while listening with one ear to his brother, cast a sidelong glance at him. 'What's got into him tonight? Such a triumphant look,' he thought. He did not know that Levin felt he had grown wings. Levin knew that she was listening to his words and liked listening to them. And that was the only thing that mattered to him. Not just in that room, but in all the world, there existed for him only he, who had acquired enormous significance, and she. He felt himself on a height that made his head spin, and somewhere below, far away, were all these kind, nice Karenins, Oblonskys, and the rest of the world.

Quite inconspicuously, without looking at them, but just like that, as if there were nowhere else to seat them, Stepan Arkadyich placed Levin and Kitty next to each other.

'Well, why don't you sit here,' he said to Levin.

The dinner was as good as the dinner ware, of which Stepan Arkadyich was a great fancier. The soup *Marie-Louise* succeeded splendidly; the pirozhki, which melted in the mouth, were irreproachable. The two servants and Matvei, in white ties, went about their duties with the food and wine quite unobtrusively, quietly and efficiently. On the material side, the dinner was a success; it was no less of a success on the non-material side. The conversation, now general, now particular, never lapsed and became so lively by the end of dinner that the men got up from the table still talking and even Alexei Alexandrovich grew animated.

X

Pestsov liked to argue to the end and was not satisfied with Sergei Ivanovich's words, the less so as he sensed the incorrectness of his own opinion.

'I never meant population density alone,' he said over the soup, addressing Alexei Alexandrovich, 'but as combined with fundamentals, and not with principles.'

'It seems to me,' Alexei Alexandrovich replied unhurriedly and listlessly, 'that they are one and the same thing. In my opinion, only that nation which is more highly developed can influence another, which . . .'

'But that's just the question,' Pestsov interrupted in his bass voice, always in a hurry to speak and always seeming to put his whole soul into what he said. 'What is this higher development supposed to be? The English, the French, the Germans – which of them stands on a higher level of development? Which will nationalize the other? We see the Rhine frenchified, yet the Germans are not on a lower level!' he cried. 'There's a different law here!'

'It seems to me that the influence always comes from the side of true education,' Alexei Alexandrovich said, raising his eyebrows slightly.

'But what should we take as signs of true education?' Pestsov said.

'I suppose that these signs are known,' said Alexei Alexandrovich.

'Are they fully known?' Sergei Ivanovich put in with a subtle smile. 'It is now recognized that a true education can only be a purely classical one; yet we see bitter disputes on one side and the other, and it cannot be denied that the opposing camp has strong arguments in its favour.'[9]

'You are a classicist, Sergei Ivanovich. May I pour you some red?' said Stepan Arkadyich.

'I am not expressing my opinion about either sort of education,' Sergei Ivanovich said with a smile of condescension, as if to a child, and held out his glass. 'I am merely saying that there are strong arguments on both sides,' he went on, turning to Alexei Alexandrovich. 'I received a classical education, but personally I can find no place for myself in this dispute. I see no clear arguments for preferring classical studies over the modern.'

'The natural sciences have as much pedagogical and developmental influence,' Pestsov picked up. 'Take astronomy alone, take botany or zoology, with its system of general laws!'

'I cannot fully agree with that,' Alexei Alexandrovich replied. 'It seems to me that one cannot but acknowledge the fact that the very process of studying the forms of languages has a particularly beneficial effect upon spiritual development. Besides, it cannot be denied that the influence of classical writers is moral in the highest degree, whereas the teaching of the natural sciences is unfortunately combined with those harmful and false teachings that constitute the bane of our time.'

Sergei Ivanovich was about to say something, but Pestsov with his dense bass interrupted him. He heatedly began proving the incorrectness of this opinion. Sergei Ivanovich calmly waited his turn, obviously ready with a triumphant retort.

'Yet,' said Sergei Ivanovich, turning to Karenin with a subtle smile, 'one cannot but agree that it is difficult to weigh fully all the advantages and disadvantages of both branches of learning, and the question of preference would not have been resolved so quickly and definitively if there had not been on the side of classical education that advantage you just mentioned: its moral or – *disons le mot** – anti-nihilistic[10] influence.'

'Undoubtedly.'

'If there had not been this advantage of an anti-nihilistic influence on the side of classical learning, we would have thought more, weighed the arguments on both sides,' Sergei Ivanovich went on with a subtle smile, 'and left room for the one tendency and the other. But now we know that the pills of classical education contain the healing power of anti-nihilism, and we boldly offer them to our patients . . . And what if there is no healing power?' he concluded, sprinkling his Attic salt.

Everybody laughed at Sergei Ivanovich's pills, Turovtsyn especially loudly and gaily, having at last been granted that something funny which was all he was waiting for as he listened to the conversation.

Stepan Arkadyich had made no mistake in inviting Pestsov. With Pestsov intelligent conversation could not die down even for a moment. No sooner had Sergei Ivanovich ended the conversation with a joke than Pestsov started up a new one.

'One cannot even agree,' he said, 'that the government has such a goal. The government is obviously guided by general considerations and remains indifferent to the influences its measures may have. For instance, the question of women's education ought to be regarded as pernicious, yet the government opens courses and universities for women.'

* Let us say the word.

And the conversation at once jumped over to the new subject of women's education.[11]

Alexei Alexandrovich expressed the thought that women's education was usually confused with the question of women's emancipation and could be considered pernicious only on that account.

'I would suppose, on the contrary, that these two questions are inseparably connected,' said Pestsov. 'It's a vicious circle. Women are deprived of rights because of their lack of education, and their lack of education comes from having no rights. We mustn't forget that the subjection of women is so great and so old that we often refuse to comprehend the abyss that separates them from us,' he said.

'You said "rights",' said Sergei Ivanovich, who had been waiting for Pestsov to stop talking, 'meaning the rights to take on the jobs of jurors, councillors, the rights of board directors, the rights of civil servants, members of parliament . . .'

'Undoubtedly.'

'But if women can, as a rare exception, occupy these positions, it seems to me that you have used the term "rights" incorrectly. It would be more correct to say "obligations". Everyone will agree that in doing the job of a juror, a councillor, a telegraph clerk, we feel that we are fulfilling an obligation. And therefore it would be more correct to say that women are seeking obligations, and quite legitimately. And one can only sympathize with this desire of theirs to help in men's common task.'

'Perfectly true,' Alexei Alexandrovich agreed. 'The question, I suppose, consists only in whether they are capable of such obligations.'

'They'll most likely be very capable,' Stepan Arkadyich put in, 'once education spreads among them. We can see that . . .'

'Remember the proverb?' said the old prince, who had long been listening to the conversation, his mocking little eyes twinkling. 'I can say it in front of my daughters: long hair, short . . .'[12]

'Exactly the same was thought of the negroes before the emancipation!' Pestsov said angrily.

'I merely find it strange that women should seek new obligations,' said Sergei Ivanovich, 'while unfortunately, as we see, men usually avoid them.'

'Obligations are coupled with rights. Power, money, honours – that's what women are seeking,' said Pestsov.

'The same as if I should seek the right to be a wet nurse and get offended that women are paid for it while I'm refused,' the old prince said.

Turovtsyn burst into loud laughter, and Sergei Ivanovich was sorry he had not said it himself. Even Alexei Alexandrovich smiled.

'Yes, but a man can't nurse,' said Pestsov, 'while a woman . . .'

'No, there was an Englishman who nursed his baby on a ship,' said the old prince, allowing himself this liberty in a conversation before his daughters.

'There will be as many women officials as there are such Englishmen,' Sergei Ivanovich said this time.

'Yes, but what will a girl do if she has no family?' Stepan Arkadyich interceded, remembering Chibisova, whom he had had in mind all the while he was sympathizing with Pestsov and supporting him.

'If you look into the girl's story properly, you'll find that she left her own family, or her sister's, where she could have had a woman's work,' Darya Alexandrovna said irritably, unexpectedly entering the conversation, probably guessing what girl Stepan Arkadyich had in mind.

'But we stand for a principle, an ideal!' Pestsov objected in a sonorous bass. 'Women want the right to be independent, educated. They are cramped and oppressed by their awareness that it is impossible.'

'And I'm cramped and oppressed that I can't get hired as a wet nurse in an orphanage,' the old prince said again, to the great joy of Turovtsyn, who laughed so much that he dropped the thick end of his asparagus into the sauce.

XI

Everybody took part in the general conversation except Kitty and Levin. At first, when the subject was the influence of one nation on another, Levin involuntarily began to consider what he had to say about it; but these thoughts, very important for him once, flashed through his head as in a dream and now had not the slightest interest for him. It even seemed strange to him that they should try so hard to talk about something that was of no use to anyone. In the same way, it would seem that what they were saying about the rights and education of women ought to have interested Kitty. How often she had thought of it, remembering Varenka, her friend abroad, and her painful dependence, how often she had wondered what would happen to her if she did not get married, and how many times she had argued about it with her sister! But now it did not interest her in the least. She and Levin were carrying on their own conversation, or not a conversation but some mysterious communication that bound them more closely together with every minute and produced in both of them a feeling of joyful fear before the unknown into which they were entering.

First, in response to Kitty's question of how he could have seen her in a carriage last year, Levin told her how he had met her on the high road as he was walking home from the mowing.

'It was very early in the morning. You must have just woken up. Your *maman* was asleep in her corner. It was a wonderful morning. I was walking along and thinking: Who is that in the coach-and-four? A fine four with little bells, and for an instant you flashed by, and I saw in the window – you were sitting like this, holding the ribbons of your bonnet with both hands and thinking terribly hard about something,' he said, smiling. 'How I longed to know what you were thinking about! Was it something important?'

'Wasn't I all dishevelled?' she thought. But seeing the rapturous smile that the recollection of these details evoked in him, she felt that, on the contrary, the impression she had made had been very good. She blushed and laughed joyfully.

'I really don't remember.'

'How nicely Turovtsyn laughs!' said Levin, admiring his moist eyes and shaking body.

'Have you known him long?' asked Kitty.

'Who doesn't know him!'

'And I see you think he's a bad man.'

'Not bad, but worthless.'

'That's not true! And you must immediately stop thinking so!' said Kitty. 'I had a very low opinion of him, too, but he – he is the dearest man, and remarkably kind. He has a heart of gold.'

'How could you know about his heart?'

'He and I are great friends. I know him very well. Last winter, soon after you . . . visited us,' she said with a guilty and at the same time trustful smile, 'Dolly's children all got scarlet fever, and he came to see her once. And can you imagine,' she said in a whisper, 'he felt so sorry for her that he stayed and began to help her look after the children. Yes, and he lived in their house for three weeks and looked after the children like a nurse.

'I'm telling Konstantin Dmitrich about Turovtsyn during the scarlet fever,' she said, leaning over to her sister.

'Yes, remarkable, charming!' said Dolly, glancing at Turovtsyn, who sensed that he was being talked about, and smiling meekly at him. Levin glanced at him once more and was surprised that he had not understood all the charm of this man before.

'I'm sorry, I'm sorry, and I'll never think badly of people again!' he said gaily, sincerely expressing what he then felt.

XII

In the conversation begun about the rights of women there were questions about the inequality of rights in marriage that it was ticklish to discuss in front of ladies. During dinner Pestsov had taken a fling at these questions several times, but Sergei Ivanovich and Stepan Arkadyich had carefully deflected him.

However, when they got up from the table and the ladies left, Pestsov did not follow them, but turned to Alexei Alexandrovich and began to explain the main cause of the inequality. The inequality of spouses, in his opinion, consisted in the fact that the unfaithfulness of a wife and the unfaithfulness of a husband were punished unequally by the law and public opinion.

Stepan Arkadyich hastened to Alexei Alexandrovich and offered him a cigar.

'No, I don't smoke,' Alexei Alexandrovich replied calmly and, as if deliberately wishing to show that he was not afraid of the conversation, turned to Pestsov with a cold smile.

'I suppose the grounds for such a view are in the very essence of things,' he said and was about to go to the drawing room; but here Turovtsyn suddenly spoke unexpectedly, addressing Alexei Alexandrovich.

'And have you heard about Pryachnikov?' Turovtsyn said, animated by the champagne he had drunk and having long waited for a chance to break the silence that oppressed him. 'Vasya Pryachnikov,' he said with a kindly smile of his moist and ruddy lips, mainly addressing the chief guest, Alexei Alexandrovich. 'I've just been told he fought a duel with Kvytsky in Tver and killed him.'

As one always seems to bump, as if on purpose, precisely on a sore spot, so now Stepan Arkadyich felt that, unluckily, the evening's conversation kept hitting Alexei Alexandrovich on his sore spot. He again wanted to shield his brother-in-law, but Alexei Alexandrovich himself asked with curiosity:

'What did Pryachnikov fight the duel over?'

'His wife. Acted like a real man! Challenged him and killed him!'

'Ah!' Alexei Alexandrovich said indifferently and, raising his eyebrows, proceeded to the drawing room.

'I'm so glad you came,' Dolly said to him with a frightened smile, meeting him in the anteroom. 'I must talk with you. Let's sit down here.'

With the same indifferent expression, produced by his raised eyebrows, Alexei Alexandrovich sat down beside Darya Alexandrovna and smiled falsely.

'The more so,' he said, 'as I, too, wanted to beg your pardon and bow out at once. I must leave tomorrow.'

Darya Alexandrovna was firmly convinced of Anna's innocence, and she felt herself growing pale and her lips trembling with wrath at this cold, unfeeling man who so calmly intended to ruin her innocent friend.

'Alexei Alexandrovich,' she said, looking into his eyes with desperate determination. 'I asked you about Anna and you didn't answer me. How is she?'

'It seems she's well, Darya Alexandrovna,' Alexei Alexandrovich replied without looking at her.

'Forgive me, Alexei Alexandrovich, I have no right . . . but I love and respect Anna like a sister; I beg you, I entreat you to tell me what's wrong between you? What do you accuse her of?'

Alexei Alexandrovich winced and, almost closing his eyes, bowed his head.

'I suppose your husband has told you the reasons why I consider it necessary to change my former relations with Anna Arkadyevna,' he said, not looking in her eyes and glancing with displeasure at Shcherbatsky who was passing through the drawing room.

'I don't believe it, I don't, I can't believe it!' said Dolly, clasping her bony hands before her with an energetic gesture. She got up quickly and placed her hand on Alexei Alexandrovich's sleeve. 'We'll be disturbed here. Please, let's go in there.'

Dolly's agitation affected Alexei Alexandrovich. He got up and obediently followed her to the schoolroom. They sat down at a table covered with oilcloth cut all over by penknives.

'I don't believe it, I just don't believe it!' said Dolly, trying to catch his eyes, which avoided hers.

'It's impossible not to believe facts, Darya Alexandrovna,' he said, stressing the word *facts*.

'But what has she done?' said Darya Alexandrovna. 'What precisely has she done?'

'She has scorned her obligations and betrayed her husband. That is what she has done,' he said.

'No, no, it can't be! No, for God's sake, you're mistaken!' said Dolly, touching her temples with her hands and closing her eyes.

Alexei Alexandrovich smiled coldly with his lips only, wishing to show her and himself the firmness of his conviction; but this ardent defence, though it did not shake him, rubbed salt into his wound. He spoke with increased animation.

'It is rather difficult to be mistaken, when the wife herself announces it to her husband. Announces that eight years of life and a son – that it was all a mistake and that she wants to live over again,' he said, sniffing angrily.

'Anna and vice – I can't put the two together, I can't believe it.'

'Darya Alexandrovna!' he said, now looking straight into Dolly's kind, agitated face and feeling that his tongue was involuntarily loosening. 'I would have paid dearly for doubt to be still possible. When I doubted, it was hard for me, but easier than now. When I doubted, there was hope; but now there is no hope and even so I doubt everything. I doubt everything so much that I hate my own son and sometimes do not believe that he is my son. I am very unhappy.'

He had no need to say it. Darya Alexandrovna understood it as soon as he looked into her face. She felt sorry for him, and her belief in her friend's innocence was shaken.

'Ah, it's terrible, terrible! But is it really true that you've decided on divorce?'

'I've decided on the final measure. There's nothing else for me to do.'

'Nothing to do, nothing to do . . .' she said with tears in her eyes. 'No, that's not so!' she said.

'The terrible thing in this sort of grief is that, unlike anything else – a loss, a death – one cannot simply bear one's cross. Here one must act,' he said, as if guessing her thought. 'One must get out of the humiliating position one has been put in: it is impossible to live as three.'

'I understand, I understand that very well,' said Dolly, and she bowed her head. She paused, thinking of herself, of her own family grief, and suddenly raised her head energetically and clasped her hands in a pleading gesture. 'But wait! You're a Christian. Think of her! What will become of her if you leave her?'

'I have been thinking, Darya Alexandrovna, and thinking a great deal,' Alexei Alexandrovich said. His face flushed in spots, his dull eyes looked straight at her. Darya Alexandrovna pitied him now with all her heart. 'That is what I did after she herself announced my disgrace to me. I left everything as it had been. I gave her the chance to reform. I tried to save her. And what? She did not fulfil the easiest of requirements – the observance of propriety,' he said heatedly. 'It is possible to save a person who does not want to perish. But if the whole nature is so corrupt, so perverted, that perdition itself looks like salvation, what can be done?'

'Anything, only not divorce!' Darya Alexandrovna replied.

'But what is this "anything"?'

'No, it's terrible! She'll be no one's wife, she'll be ruined!'

'What can I do?' said Alexei Alexandrovich, raising his shoulders and his eyebrows. The memory of his wife's last trespass vexed him so much that he again became cold, as at the beginning of their conversation. 'I thank you very much for your concern, but I must go,' he said, getting up.

'No, wait! You mustn't ruin her. Wait, I'll tell you about myself. I was married, and my husband deceived me. Angry, jealous, I wanted to abandon everything, I myself wanted . . . But I came to my senses – and who saved me? Anna saved me. And so I live. My children are growing up, my husband comes back to the family, he feels he wasn't right, becomes purer, better, and I live . . . I forgave, and you must forgive!'

Alexei Alexandrovich listened, but her words no longer affected him. In his soul there arose again all the anger of the day when he had decided on divorce. He shook himself and spoke in a shrill, loud voice:

'I cannot forgive, I do not want to, and I consider it unjust. I did everything for that woman, and she trampled everything in the mud that is so suitable to her. I am not a wicked man, I have never hated anyone, but her I hate with all the strength of my soul, and I cannot even forgive her, because I hate her so much for all the evil she has done me!' he said with tears of anger in his voice.

'Love those who hate you . . .' Darya Alexandrovna whispered shamefacedly.

Alexei Alexandrovich smiled contemptuously. He had long known that, but it could not be applied in his case.

'Love those who hate you, but to love those you hate is impossible. Forgive me for having upset you. Everyone has enough grief of his own!' And, having regained control of himself, Alexei Alexandrovich calmly said goodbye and left.

XIII

When they got up from the table, Levin wanted to follow Kitty into the drawing room, but he was afraid that she might be displeased by such all-too-obvious courtship of her on his part. He remained in the men's circle, taking part in the general conversation, but, without looking at Kitty, sensed her movements, her glances, and the place where she was in the drawing room.

He began at once, and without the slightest effort, to fulfil the promise he had given her – always to think well of all people and always to love everyone. The conversation turned to village communes, in which Pestsov saw some special principle which he called the choral principle.[13] Levin agreed neither with Pestsov nor with his brother, who had some way of his own of both agreeing and disagreeing with the significance of the Russian commune. But he talked with them, trying only to reconcile them and soften their objections. He was not the least bit interested in what he said himself, still less in what they said, and desired only one thing – that they and everyone should be nice and agreeable. He now knew the one important thing. And that one thing was at first there in the drawing room, and then began to move on and stopped by the door. Without turning round, he felt a gaze and a smile directed at him and could not help turning. She was standing in the doorway with Shcherbatsky and looking at him.

'I thought you were going to the piano,' he said, approaching her. 'That's what I lack in the country: music.'

'No, we were only coming to call you away, and I thank you,' she said, awarding him a smile as if it were a gift, 'for having come. What's all this love of arguing? No one ever convinces anyone else.'

'Yes, true,' said Levin, 'it most often happens that you argue hotly only because you can't understand what precisely your opponent wants to prove.'

Levin had often noticed in arguments between the most intelligent people that after enormous efforts, an enormous number of logical subtleties and words, the arguers would finally come to the awareness that what they had spent so long struggling to prove to each other had been known to them long, long before, from the beginning of the argument, but that they loved different things and therefore did not want to name what they loved, so as not to be challenged. He had often felt that sometimes during an argument you would understand what your opponent loves, and suddenly come to love the same thing yourself, and agree all at once, and then all reasonings would fall away as superfluous; and sometimes it was the other way round: you would finally say what you yourself love, for the sake of which you are inventing your reasonings, and if you happened to say it well and sincerely, the opponent would suddenly agree and stop arguing. That was the very thing he wanted to say.

She wrinkled her forehead, trying to understand. But as soon as he began to explain, she understood.

'I understand: you must find out what he's arguing for, what he loves, and then you can . . .'

She had fully divined and expressed his poorly expressed thought. Levin smiled joyfully: so striking did he find the transition from an intricate, verbose argument with his brother and Pestsov to this laconic and clear, almost wordless, communication of the most complex thoughts.

Shcherbatsky left them, and Kitty, going over to an open card table, sat down, took a piece of chalk in her hand and began to trace radiating circles on the new green cloth.

They resumed the conversation that had gone on at dinner about the freedom and occupations of women. Levin agreed with Darya Alexandrovna's opinion that a girl who did not get married could find feminine work for herself in her family. He supported it by saying that no family can do without a helper, that in every family, poor or rich, there are and must be nannies, hired or from the family.

'No,' said Kitty, blushing, but looking at him all the more boldly with her truthful eyes, 'a girl can be in such a position that she cannot enter a family without humiliation, while she herself . . .'

He understood from a hint.

'Oh! yes!' he said, 'yes, yes, yes, you're right, you're right!'

And he understood all that Pestsov had been maintaining at dinner about women's freedom, only because he saw the fear of spinsterhood and humiliation in Kitty's heart, and, loving her, he felt that fear and humiliation and at once renounced his arguments.

Silence ensued. She went on tracing on the table with the chalk. Her eyes shone with a quiet light. Obedient to her mood, he felt in his whole being the ever increasing tension of happiness.

'Ah! I've scribbled all over the table!' she said and, putting down the chalk, made a movement as if she wanted to get up.

'How can I stay alone . . . without her?' he thought with horror and he took the chalk. 'Wait,' he said, sitting down at the table. 'There's one thing I've long wanted to ask you.'

He looked straight into her tender though frightened eyes.

'Please do.'

'Here,' he said, and wrote the initial letters: w, y, a, m: t, c, b, d, i, m, n, o, t? These letters meant: 'When you answered me: "that cannot be", did it mean never or then?' There was no likelihood that she would be able to understand this complex phrase, but he watched her with such a look as if his life depended on her understanding these words.

She glanced at him seriously, then leaned her knitted brow on her hand and began to read. Occasionally she glanced at him, asking with her glance: 'Is this what I think?'

'I understand,' she said, blushing.

'What is this word?' he said, pointing to the *n* that signified the word *never*.

'That means the word *never*,' she said, 'but it's not true!'

He quickly erased what was written, gave her the chalk and got up. She wrote: t, I, c, g, n, o, a.

Dolly was completely consoled in her grief, caused by her conversation with Alexei Alexandrovich, when she saw these two figures: Kitty, chalk in hand, looking up at Levin with a timid and happy smile, and his handsome figure bent over the table, his burning eyes directed now at the table, now at her. He suddenly beamed: he had understood. It meant: 'Then I could give no other answer.'

He glanced at her questioningly, timidly.

'Only then?'

'Yes,' her smile replied.

'And n . . . And now?' he asked.

'Well, here, read this. I'll tell you what I would wish. Would wish very much!' She wrote the initial letters: t, y, c, f, a, f, w, h. It meant: 'that you could forgive and forget what happened'.

He seized the chalk with his tense, trembling fingers and, breaking it, wrote the initial letters of the following: 'I have nothing to forgive and forget, I have never stopped loving you.'

She glanced at him, the smile staying on her lips.

'I understand,' she said in a whisper.

He sat down and wrote a long phrase. She understood everything and, without asking him if she was right, took the chalk and replied at once.

For a long time he could not understand what she had written and kept glancing in her eyes. A darkening came over him from happiness. He simply could not pick out the words she had in mind; but in her lovely eyes shining with happiness he understood everything he needed to know! And he wrote three letters. But she was reading after his hand, and before he finished writing, she finished it herself and wrote the answer: 'Yes.'

'Playing *secrétaire*?' said the old prince, approaching. 'Well, come along, anyhow, if you want to make it to the theatre.'

Levin stood up and saw Kitty to the door.

In their conversation everything had been said – that she loved him, that she would tell her father and mother, that he would come tomorrow in the morning.

XIV

When Kitty had gone and Levin was left alone, he felt such anxiety without her and such an impatient desire to live quickly, the more quickly, till tomorrow morning, when he would see her again and be united with her for ever, that he became afraid, as of death, of those fourteen hours that he had to spend without her. He absolutely had to be with and talk to someone, so as not to remain alone, so as to cheat time. Stepan Arkadyich would have been the most agreeable company for him, but he was going, as he said, to an evening party, though actually to the ballet. Levin only had time to tell him that he was happy, that he loved him and would never, never forget what he had done for him. Stepan Arkadyich's eyes and smile showed Levin that he had understood this feeling in the right way.

'So it's no longer time to die?' said Stepan Arkadyich, pressing Levin's hand affectionately.

'No-o-o!' said Levin.

Darya Alexandrovna, saying good-bye to him, also said, as if congratulating him:

'How glad I am that you met Kitty again. One must cherish old friendships.'

But Levin found these words of Darya Alexandrovna unpleasant. She could not understand how lofty and inaccessible to her it all was, and she should not have dared to mention it.

Levin took leave of them, but, so as not to be left alone, latched on to his brother.

'Where are you going?'

'To a meeting.'

'Well, I'll go with you. May I?'

'Why not? Come along,' said Sergei Ivanovich, smiling. 'What's got into you tonight?'

'Into me? Happiness has got into me!' said Levin, letting down the window of the coach they were riding in. 'You don't mind? It's stuffy. Happiness has got into me! Why have you never married?'

Sergei Ivanovich smiled.

'I'm very glad, she seems to be a nice gi . . .' Sergei Ivanovich began.

'Don't speak, don't speak, don't speak!' Levin cried, seizing him by the collar of his fur coat with both hands and wrapping him up. 'She's a nice girl' was such a simple, such a low phrase, so out of harmony with his feeling.

Sergei Ivanovich laughed a merry laugh, which happened to him rarely.

'Well, anyhow I can say that I'm very glad of it.'

'Tomorrow, tomorrow you can, and no more of that! Never mind, never mind, silence!'[14] said Levin and, wrapping him in his fur coat once more, added: 'I love you very much! So, can I be present at the meeting?'

'Of course you can.'

'What are you discussing tonight?' Levin asked, without ceasing to smile.

They arrived at the meeting. Levin listened as the secretary haltingly read the minutes, which he evidently did not understand himself; but Levin could see by the face of this secretary what a sweet, kind and nice man he was. It could be seen from the way he became confused and embarrassed as he read the minutes. Then the speeches began. They argued about allotting certain sums and installing certain pipes, and Sergei Ivanovich needled two members and triumphantly spoke at length about something; and another member, having written something on a piece of paper, at first turned timid, but then responded to him quite venomously and sweetly. And then Sviyazhsky (he, too, was there) also said something ever so beautifully and nobly. Levin listened to them and saw clearly that neither those allotted sums nor the pipes existed, and that none of them was angry, they were all such kind, nice people and things all went so nicely and sweetly among them. They did not bother anyone, and everyone felt pleased. What Levin found remarkable was that he could see through them all that night, and by small tokens, inconspicuous before, could recognize the soul of each and see clearly that they were all kind. In particular it was him, Levin, that they all loved so much that night. It could be seen by the way they spoke to him and looked at him tenderly, lovingly, even all the strangers.

'Well, are you pleased?' Sergei Ivanovich asked him.

'Very. I never thought it could be so interesting! Fine, splendid!'

Sviyazhsky came up to Levin and invited him for tea at his place. Levin simply could not understand or recall what had displeased him in Sviyazhsky and what he had been looking for from him. He was an intelligent and remarkably kind man.

'Delighted,' he said and asked after his wife and sister-in-law. And by a strange filiation of ideas, since in his imagination the thought of Sviyazhsky's sister-in-law was connected with marriage, he decided that there could be no one better to tell of his happiness than Sviyazhsky's wife and sister-in-law, and he would be very glad to go and see them.

Sviyazhsky asked him about his work on the estate, as always, not allowing any possibility of finding anything not yet found in Europe, and now this was not the least bit unpleasant for Levin. On the contrary, he felt that Sviyazhsky was right, that the whole thing was worthless, and noted the surprisingly mild and gentle way in which Sviyazhsky avoided saying how right he was. Sviyazhsky's ladies were especially sweet. It seemed to Levin that they already knew everything and sympathized with him, and did not say so only out of delicacy. He stayed with them for an hour, two hours, three hours, talking about various subjects, but having in mind the one thing that filled his soul, and not noticing that he was boring them terribly and that it was long since time for them to go to bed. Sviyazhsky, yawning, saw him to the front hall, wondering at the strange state his friend was in. It was past one o'clock. Levin went back to his hotel and became frightened at the thought of how he, alone now with his impatience, was going to spend the remaining ten hours. The lackey on duty was not asleep, lit candles for him and was about to leave, but Levin stopped him. This lackey, Yegor, whom Levin had never noticed before, turned out to be a very intelligent and good man, and, above all, a kind one.

'So, Yegor, is it hard not sleeping?'

'No help for it. That's our job. It's easier in a master's house, but the reckoning's bigger here.'

It turned out that Yegor had a family, three boys and a daughter, a seamstress, whom he wanted to marry to a sales assistant in a saddler's shop.

Levin took this occasion to convey to Yegor his thought that the main thing in marriage was love, and that with love one was always happy, because happiness exists only in oneself.

Yegor heard him out attentively and evidently understood Levin's thought fully, but to corroborate it he made the observation, unexpected for Levin, that when he had lived with good masters he had always been pleased with them, and he was quite pleased with his master now, though he was a Frenchman.

'A remarkably kind man,' thought Levin.

'Well, and you, Yegor, when you got married, did you love your wife?'

'Of course I loved her,' answered Yegor.

And Levin saw that Yegor was also in a rapturous state and intended to voice all his innermost feelings.

'My life is also remarkable. Ever since I was little, I . . .' he began, his eyes shining, obviously infected by Levin's rapture, just as people get infected by yawning.

But at that moment the bell rang. Yegor went out, and Levin was left alone. He had eaten almost nothing at dinner, had declined tea and supper at the Sviyazhskys', but could not think of eating. He had not slept last night, but could not even think of sleeping. The room was cool, yet he felt stifled by the heat. He opened both vent-panes and sat on the table facing them. Beyond the snow-covered roof he could see an open-work cross with chains and rising above it the triangular constellation of the Charioteer with the bright yellowish Capella. He gazed first at the cross, then at the star, breathed in the fresh, frosty air that steadily entered the room, and followed, as in a dream, the images and memories that arose in his imagination. Towards four o'clock he heard footsteps in the corridor and looked out of the door. It was the gambler Myaskin, whom he knew, returning from the club. He was walking gloomily, scowling and clearing his throat. 'Poor, unfortunate man!' thought Levin, and tears came to his eyes from love and pity for the man. He wanted to talk to him, to comfort him; but, remembering that he had nothing on but a shirt, he changed his mind and again sat by the vent to bathe in the cold air and gaze at the wondrous form of the cross, silent but full of meaning for him, and at the soaring, bright yellow star. After six o'clock the floor polishers began to make noise, bells rang for some service and Levin felt that he was beginning to be cold. He closed the vent, washed, dressed and went out.

XV

The streets were still empty. Levin walked to the Shcherbatskys' house. The front door was locked and all was asleep. He walked back, went to his room and asked for coffee. The day lackey, not Yegor now, brought it to him. He wanted to get into conversation with the lackey, but they rang for him and he left. Levin tried to drink some coffee and put the roll in his mouth, but his mouth decidedly did not know what to do with it. He spat out the roll, put on his coat and again went out to walk around. It was past nine when he came to the Shcherbatskys' porch for the second time. In the house they were just getting up, and the cook had gone to buy provisions. He had to live through at least another two hours.

All that night and morning Levin had lived completely unconsciously and had felt himself completely removed from the conditions of material life. He had not eaten for a whole day, had not slept for two nights, had spent several hours undressed in the freezing cold, yet felt not only fresh and healthy as never before but completely independent of his body. He moved without any muscular effort and felt he could do anything. He was certain that he could fly into the air or lift up the corner of the house if need be. He spent the rest of the time walking the streets, constantly looking at his watch and gazing about him.

And what he saw then, he afterwards never saw again. He was especially moved by children going to school, the grey-blue pigeons that flew down from the roof to the pavement, and the white rolls sprinkled with flour that some invisible hand had set out. These rolls, the pigeons and the two boys were unearthly beings. All this happened at the same time: a boy ran up to a pigeon and, smiling, looked at Levin; the pigeon flapped its wings and fluttered off, sparkling in the sun amidst the air trembling with snowdust, while the smell of baked bread wafted from the window as the rolls appeared in it. All this together was so extraordinarily good that Levin laughed and wept from joy. Making a big circle along Gazetny Lane and Kislovka, he went back to his hotel again and, placing his watch in front of him, sat down to wait till twelve o'clock. In the next room they were saying something about machines and cheating, and coughing morning coughs. They did not realize that the hand was already approaching twelve. The hand reached twelve. Levin went out to the porch. The cabbies evidently knew everything. They surrounded him with happy faces, vying among themselves and offering their services. Trying not to offend the others and promising to ride with them, too, Levin hired one cabby and told him to go to the Shcherbatskys'. The cabby was charming, with his white shirt collar sticking out from under his caftan and buttoned tightly on his full, strong, red neck. This cabby's sleigh was high, smart, the like of which Levin never drove in again, and the horse was fine and tried to run, but did not move from the spot. The cabby knew the Shcherbatskys' house and, with particular deference to his fare, rounded his arms and shouted 'Whoa!' as he pulled up at the entrance. The Shcherbatskys' hall porter certainly knew everything. That could be seen by the smile of his eyes and the way he said:

'Well, you haven't been here for a long time, Konstantin Dmitrich!'

Not only did he know everything, but he was obviously exultant and was making efforts to hide his joy. Looking into his dear old eyes, Levin even understood something new in his happiness.

'Are they up?'

'Come in, please! You might leave it here,' he said, smiling, as Levin was about to go back for his hat. That must have meant something.

'To whom shall I announce you?' asked the footman.

The footman, though young and of the new sort, a dandy, was a very kind and good man, and also understood everything.

'The princess . . . The prince . . . The young princess . . .' said Levin.

The first person he saw was Mlle Linon. She passed through the room, her curls and face beaming. No sooner had he addressed her than the rustle of a dress was suddenly heard behind the door, and Mlle Linon vanished from Levin's sight, and the joyful terror of the nearness of his happiness communicated itself to him. Mlle Linon hastened away and, leaving him, went to the other door. As soon as she went out, there came the sound of quick, quick, light steps over the parquet, and his happiness, his life, he himself – better than his own self, that which he had sought and desired for so long – was quickly approaching him. She did not walk but by some invisible force rushed towards him.

He saw only her clear, truthful eyes, frightened by the same joy of love that filled his heart. Those eyes shone nearer and nearer, blinding him by their light of love. She stopped up close to him, touching him. Her arms rose and came down on his shoulders.

She had done all she could – she had run up to him and given all of herself, timidly and joyfully. He embraced her and pressed his lips to her mouth that sought his kiss.

She, too, had not slept all night and all morning had been waiting for him. Her mother and father had consented without question and were happy in her happiness. She had been waiting for him. She had wanted to be the first to announce to him her happiness and his. She had been preparing to meet him alone and rejoiced at the thought of it, and felt timid, and bashful, and did not know herself what she would do. She had heard his footsteps and voice and had waited behind the door till Mlle Linon left. Without thinking, without asking herself how or what, she had gone up to him and done what she had done.

'Let's go to mama!' she said, taking him by the hand. For a long time he could say nothing, not so much because he was afraid to spoil the loftiness of his feeling with words, as because each time he wanted to say something he felt that, instead of words, tears of happiness were about to burst out. He took her hand and kissed it.

'Can this be true?' he said finally in a muted voice. 'I can't believe you love me!'

She smiled at these words and at the timidity with which he glanced at her.

'Yes!' she said meaningly and slowly. 'I'm so happy!'

Without letting go of his hand, she went into the drawing room. The princess, seeing them, began breathing quickly and immediately broke down in tears, then immediately burst out laughing and, running to them with energetic strides that Levin would never have expected of her, embraced his head, kissed him and wetted his cheeks with tears.

'So it's all settled! I'm glad. Love her. I'm glad . . . Kitty!'

'That was quick work!' said the old prince, trying to be indifferent; but Levin noticed that his eyes were moist when he addressed him.

'I've long, I've always wished for this!' he said, taking Levin's hand and drawing him to him. 'Even then, when this flighty one took a notion . . .'

'Papa!' Kitty cried and covered his mouth with her hand.

'Well, all right!' he said. 'I'm very, very . . . hap . . . Ah! how stupid I am . . .'

He embraced Kitty, kissed her face, her hand, her face again, and made the sign of the cross over her.

And Levin was overcome by a new feeling of love for this man previously a stranger to him, the old prince, when he saw how long and tenderly Kitty kissed his fleshy hand.

XVI

The princess sat in an armchair, silent and smiling; the prince sat beside her. Kitty stood by her father's chair, still holding his hand. Everyone was silent.

The princess was the first to put names to things and translate all thoughts and feelings into questions of life. And it seemed equally strange and even painful to them all in the first moment.

'So, when? We must bless you and announce it. And when will the wedding be? What do you think, Alexandre?'

'He's the one,' said the old prince, pointing at Levin, 'he's the chief person here.'

'When?' said Levin, blushing. 'Tomorrow. If you ask me, in my opinion, the blessing today and the wedding tomorrow.'

'Come, come, *mon cher*, that's foolishness!'

'Well, in a week, then.'

'He's quite mad.'

'No, why?'

'Mercy!' said the mother, smiling joyfully at his haste. 'And the trousseau?'

'Will there really be a trousseau and all that?' Levin thought with horror. 'And yet, can the trousseau, and the blessing, and all that – can it spoil my happiness? Nothing can spoil it!' He glanced at Kitty and noticed that she was not the least bit offended at the thought of a trousseau. 'So it's necessary,' he thought.

'I really don't know anything, I only said what I wish,' he said, apologizing.

'Then we'll decide. We can give the blessing and make the announcement now. That's so.'

The princess went up to her husband, kissed him and was about to leave; but he held her back, embraced her and tenderly, like a young lover, smiling, kissed her several times. The old folk evidently got confused for a moment and could not quite tell whether it was they who were in love again, or only their daughter. When the prince and princess left, Levin went up to his fiancée and took her hand. He had now gained control of himself and could speak, and there was much that he needed to tell her. But he said not at all what he meant to.

'How I knew it would be so! I never hoped, but in my soul I was always sure,' he said. 'I believe it was predestined.'

'And I.' she said. 'Even when . . .' she stopped and then went on, looking at him resolutely with her truthful eyes, 'even when I pushed my happiness away from me. I always loved you alone, but I was infatuated. I must tell . . . Can you forget it?'

'Maybe it was for the better. You must forgive me many things. I must tell you . . .'

This was one of the things he had resolved to tell her. He had resolved to tell her two things in the very first days – one, that he was not as pure as she was, and the other, that he was an unbeliever. It was painful, but he considered that he ought to tell her both the one and the other.

'No, not now, later!' he said.

'Very well, later, but you absolutely must tell me. I'm not afraid of anything. I must know everything. It's settled now.'

He finished the phrase:

'Settled that you'll take me however I used to be, that you won't renounce me? Yes?'

'Yes, yes.'

Their conversation was interrupted by Mlle Linon, who, smiling falsely but tenderly, came to congratulate her favourite charge. Before she left, the servants came with their congratulations. Then relatives arrived, and that blissful tumult began from which Levin did not escape till the day after his wedding. Levin felt constantly awkward, bored, but the tension of happiness went on, ever increasing. He kept feeling that much that he did not know was demanded of him, and he did everything he was told and it all made him happy. He thought that his engagement would have nothing in common with others, that the ordinary conditions of engagement would spoil his particular happiness; but it ended with him doing the same things as others, and his happiness was only increased by it and became more and more special, the like of which had never been known and never would be.

'Now we'll have some sweets,' Mlle Linon would say, and Levin would go to buy sweets.

'Well, I'm very glad,' said Sviyazhsky. 'I advise you to buy flowers at Fomin's.'

'Must I?' And he went to Fomin's.

His brother told him that he would have to borrow money, because there would be many expenses, presents . . .

'Must there be presents?' And he galloped off to Fulde's.[15]

At the confectioner's, at Fomin's and at Fulde's he saw that they expected him, were glad to see him, and celebrated his happiness just as did everyone he had to deal with during those days. The extraordinary thing was not only that everyone loved him, but that all formerly unsympathetic, cold, indifferent people admired him and obeyed him in all things, treated his feeling with tenderness and delicacy, and shared his conviction that he was the happiest man in the world because his fiancée was the height of perfection. And Kitty felt the same. When Countess Nordston allowed herself to hint that she had wished for something better, Kitty flew into such a passion and proved so persuasively that nothing in the world could be better than Levin, that Countess Nordston had to admit it and never afterwards met Levin in Kitty's presence without a smile of admiration.

The explanation he had promised was the one painful event during that time. He discussed it with the old prince and, having obtained his permission, gave Kitty his diary, in which he had written down what tormented him. He had written this diary with his future fiancée in mind. Two things tormented him: his impurity and his unbelief. His confession of unbelief went unnoticed. She was religious, had never doubted the truths of religion, but his external unbelief did not affect her in the least. She knew his whole soul through love, and in his soul she saw what she wanted, and if such a state of soul was called unbelief, it made no difference to her. But the other confession made her weep bitterly.

It was not without inner struggle that Levin gave her his diary. He knew that there could not and should not be any secrets between them, and therefore he decided that it had to be so: but he did not realize how it might affect her, he did not put himself in her place. Only when he came to them that evening before the theatre, went to her room and saw her tear-stained, pathetic and dear face, miserable from the irremediable grief he had caused her, did he understand the abyss that separated his shameful past from her dove-like purity and feel horrified at what he had done.

'Take them, take these terrible books!' she said, pushing away the notebooks that lay before her on the table. 'Why did you give them to me! . . . No, all the same it's better,' she added, taking pity on his desperate face. 'But it's terrible, terrible!'

He bowed his head and was silent. There was nothing he could say.

'You won't forgive me,' he whispered.

'No, I've forgiven you, but it's terrible!'

However, his happiness was so great that this confession did not destroy it, but only added a new shade to it. She forgave him; but after that he considered himself still more unworthy of her, bowed still lower before her morally, and valued still more highly his undeserved happiness.

XVII

Involuntarily going over in his memory the impressions of the conversations during and after dinner, Alexei Alexandrovich went back to his lonely hotel room. Darya Alexandrovna's words about forgiveness produced nothing in him but vexation. The applicability or non-applicability of the Christian rule to his own case was too difficult a question, one about which it was impossible to speak lightly, and this question Alexei Alexandrovich had long ago decided in the negative. Of all that had been said, the words that had sunk deepest into his imagination were those of the stupid, kindly Turovtsyn: 'Acted like a real man; challenged him to a duel and killed him'. They all obviously sympathized with that, though out of politeness they did not say so.

'Anyhow, the matter's settled, there's no point in thinking about it,' Alexei Alexandrovich said to himself. And, thinking only of his impending departure and the inspection business, he went into his room and asked the porter who had accompanied him where his valet was; the porter said that the valet had just left. Alexei Alexandrovich asked to have tea served, sat down at the table and, taking up Froom,[16] began working out the itinerary of his trip.

'Two telegrams,' said the valet, coming back into the room. 'Excuse me, your excellency, I just stepped out.'

Alexei Alexandrovich took the telegrams and opened them. The first was the news of Stremov's appointment to the very post Karenin had desired. Alexei Alexandrovich threw down the dispatch and, turning red, got up and began to pace the room. '*Quos vult perdere dementat*,'* he said, meaning by *quos* those persons who had furthered this appointment. He was not vexed so much by the fact that it was not he who had obtained the post, that he had obviously been passed over; what he found incomprehensible and astonishing was how they could not see that the babbler, the phrase-monger Stremov was less fit for the job than anyone else. How could they not see that they were ruining themselves and their prestige by this appointment!

'Something else of the same sort,' he said biliously to himself, opening the second dispatch. The telegram was from his wife. Her signature in blue pencil – 'Anna' – was the first thing that struck his eyes. 'Am dying, beg, implore you come. Will die more peacefully with forgiveness,' he read. He smiled contemptuously and threw down the telegram. There could be no doubt, it seemed to him in that first moment, that this was a trick and a deception.

'She wouldn't stop at any deception. She's due to give birth. Maybe the illness is childbirth. But what is their goal? To legitimize the child, to compromise me and prevent the divorce,' he thought. 'But there's

* Those whom [God] would destroy he first makes mad.

something it says there – "Am dying . . ."' He reread the telegram; and suddenly the direct meaning of what it said struck him. 'And what if it's true?' he said to himself. 'If it's true that in the moment of suffering and near death she sincerely repents and I, taking it for deception, refuse to come? It would not only be cruel – and everybody would condemn me – but it would be stupid on my part.'

'Pyotr, cancel the coach. I'm going to Petersburg,' he said to the valet.

Alexei Alexandrovich decided that he would go to Petersburg and see his wife. If her illness was a deception, he would say nothing and go away. If she was really ill and dying, and wished to see him before she died, he would forgive her if he found her alive, and fulfil his final duty if he came too late.

For the whole way he gave no more thought to what he was to do.

With the feeling of fatigue and uncleanness that comes from a night on the train, in the early mist of Petersburg Alexei Alexandrovich drove down the deserted Nevsky and stared straight ahead, not thinking of what awaited him. He could not think of it because, when he imagined what was to be, he could not rid himself of the thought that death would resolve at a stroke all the difficulty of his situation. Bakers, locked-up shops, night cabs, caretakers sweeping the pavements, flashed past his eyes, and he observed it all, trying to stifle within himself the thought of what awaited him and what he dared not wish but wished all the same. He drove up to the porch. A cab and a coach with a sleeping coachman stood at the entrance. As he went into the front hall, Alexei Alexandrovich drew a resolution, as it were, from a far corner of his brain and consulted it. It read: 'If it is a deception, then calm contempt, and depart. If true, observe propriety.'

The hall porter opened the door even before Alexei Alexandrovich rang. The porter Petrov, also called Kapitonych, looked strange in an old frock coat, with no tie and in slippers.

'How is the mistress?'

'Safely delivered yesterday.'

Alexei Alexandrovich stopped and went pale. He now realized clearly how strongly he had desired her death.

'And her health?'

Kornei, in a morning apron, came running down the stairs.

'Very bad,' he answered. 'Yesterday there was a doctors' consultation, and the doctor is here now.'

'Take my things,' said Alexei Alexandrovich and, feeling slightly relieved at the news that there was after all some hope of death, he went into the front hall.

There was a military coat on the rack. Alexei Alexandrovich noticed it and asked:

'Who is here?'

'The doctor, the midwife and Count Vronsky.'

Alexei Alexandrovich walked into the inner rooms.

There was no one in the drawing room; at the sound of his footsteps the midwife came out of the boudoir in a cap with violet ribbons.

She went up to Alexei Alexandrovich and with the familiarity that comes from the nearness of death took him by the arm and led him to the bedroom.

'Thank God you've come! She talks only of you,' she said.

'Quickly fetch some ice!' the doctor's peremptory voice said from the bedroom.

Alexei Alexandrovich went into her boudoir. At her desk, his side to the back of the low chair, sat Vronsky, his face buried in his hands, weeping. At the sound of the doctor's voice he jumped up, took his hands away from his face, and saw Alexei Alexandrovich. Seeing the husband, he was so embarrassed that he sat down again, drawing his head down between his shoulders as if he wished to disappear somewhere; but he made an effort, stood up and said:

'She's dying. The doctors say there's no hope. I am entirely at your mercy, but allow me to be here . . . however, I shall do as you please, I . . .'

Alexei Alexandrovich, seeing Vronsky's tears, felt a surge of that inner disturbance that the sight of other people's suffering produced in him, and, averting his face, without waiting for him to finish, he hastily went to the door. From the bedroom came Anna's voice saying something. Her voice was gay, animated, with extremely distinct intonations. Alexei Alexandrovich went into the bedroom and approached the bed. She lay with her face turned towards him. Her cheeks were flushed red, her eyes shone, her small white hands, sticking out of the cuffs of her jacket, toyed with the corner of the blanket, twisting it. She seemed not only healthy and fresh but also in the best of spirits. She spoke quickly, sonorously, and with unusually regular and deep-felt intonations.

'Because Alexei – I am speaking of Alexei Alexandrovich (such a strange, terrible fate, that they're both Alexei, isn't it?) – Alexei wouldn't refuse me. I would have forgotten, he would have forgiven . . . But why doesn't he come? He's kind, he himself doesn't know how kind he is. Ah! My God, what anguish! Give me water, quickly! Ah, it will be bad for her, for my little girl! Well, all right, let her have a wet nurse! I agree, it's even better. He'll come, it will be painful for him to see her. Take her away.'

'Anna Arkadyevna, he has come. Here he is!' said the midwife, trying to draw her attention to Alexei Alexandrovich.

'Ah, what nonsense!' Anna went on, not seeing her husband. 'But give her to me, give me my little girl! He hasn't come yet. You say he won't forgive, because you don't know him. No one ever knew him. Only I did, and even for me it was hard. His eyes, you should know, Seryozha has the same eyes, that's why I can't look at them. Did Seryozha have his dinner? I know everybody will forget. He wouldn't have forgotten. You must move Seryozha to the corner room and ask Mariette to sleep with him.'

Suddenly she shrank, fell silent and fearfully, as if expecting to be struck, as if shielding herself, raised her hands to her face. She had seen her husband.

'No, no,' she began, 'I'm not afraid of him, I'm afraid of death. Alexei, come here. I'm hurrying because I have no time, I haven't long to live, I'll be feverish soon and won't understand anything. Now I do understand, I understand everything, I see everything.'

Alexei Alexandrovich's pinched faced acquired a suffering expression. He took her hand and wanted to say something, but was quite unable to speak; his lower lip trembled, but he kept struggling with his agitation and only occasionally glanced at her. And each time he glanced at her, he saw her eyes, which looked at him with such moved and rapturous tenderness as he had never seen in them before.

'Wait, you don't know . . . Wait, wait, all of you . . .' She stopped, as if trying to collect her thoughts. 'Yes,' she began. 'Yes, yes, yes. This is what I wanted to say. Don't be surprised at me. I'm the same . . . But there is another woman in me, I'm afraid of her – she fell in love with that man, and I wanted to hate you and couldn't forget the other one who was there before. The one who is not me. Now I'm real, I'm whole. I'm dying now, I know I'll die, ask him. I feel weights now – here they are – on my hands, my feet, my fingers. My fingers are like this – enormous! But it will all end soon . . . There's one thing I need: forgive me, forgive me completely! I'm terrible, but my nanny told me: that holy martyr – what was her name? – she was worse.[17] I'll go to Rome, too, there are deserts there, and then I won't bother anybody, I'll take only Seryozha and my little girl . . . No, you can't forgive me! I know this can't be forgiven! No, no, go away, you're too good!' With one hot hand she held his hand, and with the other she pushed him away.

Alexei Alexandrovich's inner disturbance kept growing and now reached such a degree that he ceased to struggle with it; he suddenly felt that what he had considered an inner disturbance was, on the contrary, a blissful state of soul, which suddenly gave him a new, previously unknown happiness. He was not thinking that the Christian law which he had wanted to follow all his life prescribed that he forgive and love his enemies; but the joyful feeling of love and forgiveness of his enemies filled his soul. He knelt down and, placing his head on the crook of her arm, which burned him like fire through her jacket, sobbed like a child. She embraced his balding head, moved closer to him, and raised her eyes with defiant pride.

'Here he is, I knew it! Now good-bye all, good-bye! . . . Again they've come, why don't they go away? . . . And do take these fur coats off me!'

The doctor took her arms away, carefully laid her back on the pillow and covered her shoulders. She lay back obediently and gazed straight ahead of her with radiant eyes.

'Remember one thing, that all I need is forgiveness, and I want nothing more, nothing . . . Why doesn't *he* come?' she said, addressing Vronsky through the door. 'Come here, come! Give him your hand.'

Vronsky came to the side of the bed and, seeing her, again covered his face with his hands.

'Uncover your face, look at him. He's a saint,' she said. 'No, uncover it, uncover your face!' she said crossly. 'Alexei Alexandrovich, uncover his face! I want to see him.'

Alexei Alexandrovich took Vronsky's hands and drew them away from his face, terrible in the expression of suffering and shame that was on it.

'Give him your hand. Forgive him.'

Alexei Alexandrovich gave him his hand, not holding back the tears that poured from his eyes.

'Thank God, thank God,' she said, 'now everything is ready. Just let me stretch my legs a little. There, that's wonderful. How tastelessly these flowers are done, quite unlike violets,' she said, pointing to the wallpaper. 'My God, my God! When will it end? Give me morphine. Doctor, give me morphine! Oh, my God, my God!'

And she began thrashing about in her bed.

*

The doctor and his colleagues said it was puerperal fever, which in ninety-nine cases out of a hundred ends in death. All day there was fever, delirium and unconsciousness. By midnight the sick woman lay without feeling and almost without pulse.

The end was expected at any moment.

Vronsky went home, but came in the morning to inquire, and Alexei Alexandrovich, meeting him in the front hall, said:

'Stay, she may ask for you,' and himself led him to his wife's boudoir.

Towards morning the excitement, liveliness, quickness of thought and speech began again, and again ended in unconsciousness. On the third day it was the same, and the doctors said there was hope. That day Alexei Alexandrovich came to the boudoir where Vronsky was sitting and, closing the door, sat down facing him.

'Alexei Alexandrovich,' said Vronsky, feeling that a talk was imminent, 'I am unable to speak, unable to understand. Spare me! However painful it is for you, believe me, it is still more terrible for me.'

He was about to get up. But Alexei Alexandrovich took his hand and said:

'I beg you to hear me out, it's necessary. I must explain my feelings to you, those that have guided me and those that will guide me, so that you will not be mistaken regarding me. You know that I had decided on a divorce and had even started proceedings. I won't conceal from you that, when I started proceedings, I was undecided, I suffered; I confess that I was driven by a desire for revenge on you and on her. When I received her telegram, I came here with the same feelings – I will say more: I wished for her death. But . . .' he paused, pondering whether to reveal his feelings to him or not. 'But I saw her and I forgave. And the happiness of forgiveness revealed my duty to me. I forgave her completely. I want to turn the other cheek, I want to give my shirt when my caftan is taken, and I only pray to God that He not take from me the happiness of forgiveness!' Tears welled up in his eyes, and their luminous, serene look struck Vronsky. 'That is my position. You may trample me in the mud, make me the laughing-stock of society, I will not abandon her, I will never say a word of reproach to you,' he went on. 'My duty is clearly ordained for me: I must be with her and I will be. If she wishes to see you, I will let you know, but now I suppose it will be better if you leave.'

He stood up, and sobs broke off his speech. Vronsky also got up and in a stooping, unstraightened posture looked at him from under his brows. He did not understand Alexei Alexandrovich's feelings. But he felt that this was something lofty and even inaccessible to him in his world-view.

XVIII

After his conversation with Alexei Alexandrovich, Vronsky went out to the porch of the Karenins' house and stopped, hardly remembering where he was and where he had to go or drive. He felt himself shamed, humiliated, guilty and deprived of any possibility of washing away his humiliation. He felt himself thrown out of the rut he had been following so proudly and easily till then. All the habits and rules of his life, which had seemed so firm, suddenly turned out to be false and inapplicable. The deceived husband, who till then had seemed a pathetic being, an accidental and somewhat comic hindrance to his happiness, had suddenly been summoned by her and raised to an awesome height, and on that height the husband appeared not wicked, not false, not ludicrous, but kind, simple and majestic. Vronsky could not but feel it. The roles had been suddenly changed. Vronsky felt Karenin's loftiness and his own abasement, Karenin's rightness and his own wrongness. He felt that the husband had been magnanimous even in his grief, while he had been mean and petty in his deceit. But this realization of his meanness before the man he had unjustly despised made up only a small part of his grief. He felt himself inexpressibly unhappy now, because his passion for Anna, which had been cooling, as it had seemed to him, in recent days, now, when he knew he had lost her for ever, had become stronger than it had ever been. He had seen the whole of her during her illness, had come to know her soul, and it seemed to him that he had never loved her before then. And now, when he had come to know her, to love her as he ought to have loved her, he had been humiliated before her and had lost her for ever, leaving her with nothing but a disgraceful memory of himself. Most terrible of all had been his ridiculous, shameful position when Alexei Alexandrovich tore his hands from his ashamed face. He stood on the porch of the Karenins' house like a lost man and did not know what to do.

'Shall I call a cab?' asked the porter.

'A cab, yes.'

Returning home after three sleepless nights, Vronsky lay face down on the sofa without undressing, his arms folded and his head resting on them. His head was heavy. Images, memories and the strangest thoughts followed one another with extreme rapidity and clarity: now it was the medicine he had poured for the sick woman, overfilling the spoon, now the midwife's white arms, now Alexei Alexandrovich's strange position on the floor beside the bed.

'Sleep! Forget!' he said to himself, with the calm certainty of a healthy man that, if he was tired and wanted to sleep, he would fall asleep at once. And indeed at that moment there was confusion in his head, and he began to fall into the abyss of oblivion. The waves of the sea of unconsciousness were already beginning to close over his head when suddenly – as if a strong electric shock was discharged in him – he gave such a start that his whole body jumped on the springs of the sofa and, propping himself with his arms, he got to his knees. His eyes were wide open, as if he had never slept. The heaviness of head and sluggishness of limb that he had experienced a moment before suddenly vanished.

'You may trample me in the mud.' He heard Alexei Alexandrovich's words and saw him before his eyes, and he saw Anna's face with its feverish flush and shining eyes, looking tenderly and lovingly not at him but at Alexei Alexandrovich; he saw his own stupid and ridiculous figure, as it seemed to him, when Alexei Alexandrovich drew his hands away from his face. He stretched his legs out again, threw himself on the sofa in the same position, and closed his eyes.

'Sleep! Sleep!' he repeated to himself. But with his eyes closed he saw still more clearly the face of Anna as it had been on that evening, so memorable for him, before the race.

'It is not and will not be, and she wishes to wipe it from her memory. And I cannot live without it. How, how can we be reconciled?' he said aloud, and began unconsciously to repeat these words. The repetition of the words held back the emergence of new images and memories which he felt thronging in his head. But not for long. Again, one after another, the best moments presented themselves with extreme rapidity, and together with them the recent humiliation. 'Take your hands away,' Anna's voice says. He takes his hands away and senses the ashamed and stupid look on his face.

He went on lying there, trying to fall asleep, though he felt that there was not the slightest hope, and he went on repeating in a whisper the accidental words of some thought, wishing to hold back the emergence of new images. He listened – and heard, repeated in a strange, mad whisper, the words: 'Unable to value, unable to enjoy; unable to value, unable to enjoy.'

'What is this? Or am I losing my mind?' he said to himself. 'Maybe so. Why else do people lose their minds, why else do they shoot themselves?' he answered himself and, opening his eyes, was surprised to see an embroidered pillow by his head, made by Varya, his brother's wife. He touched the pillow's tassel and tried to recall Varya and when he had seen her last. But to think of something extraneous was painful. 'No, I must sleep!' He moved the pillow and pressed his head to it, but he had to make an effort to keep his eyes closed. He sat up abruptly. 'That is finished for me,' he said to himself. 'I must think what to do. What's left?' His thought quickly ran through his life apart from his love for Anna.

'Ambition? Serpukhovskoy? Society? Court?' He could not fix on any of them. That had all had meaning once, but now nothing remained of it. He got up from the sofa, took off his frock coat, loosened his belt and, baring his shaggy chest in order to breathe more freely, paced up and down the room. 'This is how people lose their minds,' he repeated, 'and shoot themselves . . . so as not to be ashamed,' he added slowly.

He went to the door and closed it. Then with a fixed gaze and tightly clenched teeth he went to the table, took his revolver, examined it, turned it to a loaded chamber, and lapsed into thought. For a couple of minutes, his head bowed in an expression of mental effort, he stood motionless with the revolver in his hands and considered. 'Of course,' he said to himself, as if a logical, continuous and clear train of thought had brought him to an unquestionable conclusion. In fact, this 'of course' that he found so convincing was only the consequence of a repetition of exactly the same round of memories and notions that he had already gone through a dozen times within the hour. It was the same memory of happiness lost for ever, the same notion of the meaninglessness of everything he saw ahead of him in life, the same consciousness of his humiliation. The sequence of these notions and feelings was also the same.

'Of course,' he repeated, when his thought started for the third time on the same enchanted round of memories and thoughts, and, putting the revolver to the left side of his chest and forcefully jerking his whole hand as if clenching it into a fist, he pulled the trigger. He did not hear the sound of the shot, but a strong blow to his chest knocked him off his feet. He tried to catch hold of the edge of the table, dropped the revolver, staggered and sat down on the floor, looking around himself in surprise. He did not recognize his room as he looked from below at the curved legs of the table, the wastepaper basket and the tiger-skin rug. The quick, creaking steps of his servant, walking through the drawing room, brought him to his senses. He made a mental effort and understood that he was on the floor, and, seeing blood on the tiger-skin and on his hand, understood that he had tried to shoot himself.

'Stupid! I missed,' he said, groping for the revolver with his hand. The revolver was close by him, but he groped for it further away. Continuing to search, he reached out on the other side and, unable to keep his balance, fell over, bleeding profusely.

The elegant servant with side-whiskers, who had complained to his acquaintances more than once about the weakness of his nerves, was so frightened when he saw his master lying on the floor that he left him bleeding profusely while he ran for help. An hour later, Varya, his brother's wife, came and with the help of three doctors, whom she had summoned from all sides and who arrived at the same time, lay the wounded man in bed and stayed there to look after him.

XIX

The mistake Alexei Alexandrovich had made, while preparing to see his wife, in not taking into account the eventuality that her repentance would be sincere and he would forgive her, and then she would not die – this mistake presented itself to him in all its force two months after his return from Moscow. But the mistake came not only from his not having taken this eventuality into account, but also from the fact that, prior to the day when he saw his dying wife, he had not known his own heart. At his wife's bedside he had given himself for the first time in his life to that feeling of tender compassion which other people's suffering evoked in him, and which he had previously been ashamed of as a bad weakness. Pity for her, and repentance at having wished for her death, and above all the very joy of forgiveness, made it so that he suddenly felt not only relief from his suffering but also an inner peace that he had never experienced before. He suddenly felt that the very thing that had once been the source of his suffering had become the source of his spiritual joy, that what had seemed insoluble when he condemned, reproached and hated, became simple and clear when he forgave and loved.

He forgave his wife and pitied her for her sufferings and repentance. He forgave Vronsky and pitied him, especially after rumours reached him of his desperate act. He also pitied his son more than before, and now reproached himself for having been too little concerned with him. But for the newborn little girl he had some special feeling, not only of pity but also of tenderness. At first it was only out of compassion that he concerned himself with the newborn, weak little girl, who was not his daughter and who was neglected during her mother's illness and would probably have died if he had not looked after her – and he did not notice how he came to love her. He went to the nursery several times a day and sat there for a long while, so that the wet nurse and the nanny, who were intimidated at first, became used to him. He would sometimes spend half an hour silently gazing at the saffron-red, downy and wrinkled little face of the sleeping baby, watching the movements of her scowling forehead and plump little hands with curled fingers that rubbed her little eyes and nose with their backs. At such moments especially Alexei Alexandrovich felt utterly at peace and in harmony with himself, and saw nothing extraordinary in his situation, nothing that needed to be changed.

But the more time that passed, the more clearly he saw that, natural as this situation was for him now, he would not be allowed to remain in it. He felt that, besides the good spiritual force that guided his soul, there was another force, crude and equally powerful, if not more so, that guided his life, and that this force would not give him the humble peace he desired. He felt that everybody looked at him with questioning surprise, not understanding him and expecting something from him. In particular, he felt the precariousness and unnaturalness of his relations with his wife.

When the softening produced in her by the nearness of death passed, Alexei Alexandrovich began to notice that Anna was afraid of him, felt burdened by him, and could not look him straight in the eye. It was as if there were something she wanted but could not bring herself to say to him, and as if, also anticipating that their relations could not continue, she expected something from him.

At the end of February it happened that Anna's newborn daughter, who had also been named Anna, fell ill. Alexei Alexandrovich visited the nursery in the morning and, after giving orders to send for the doctor, went to the ministry. Having finished his work, he returned home towards four o'clock. On entering the front hall, he saw a handsome footman in galloons and a bear-skin cape, holding a white cloak of American dog.

'Who is here?' asked Alexei Alexandrovich.

'Princess Elizaveta Fyodorovna Tverskoy,' the footman replied, with what seemed to Alexei Alexandrovich like a smile.

Throughout that difficult time, Alexei Alexandrovich had noticed that his society acquaintances, especially the women, took a special interest in him and his wife. He had noticed that all these acquaintances had trouble concealing their joy over something, the same joy he had seen in the lawyer's eyes and now in the eyes of the footman. They were all as if delighted, as if they were getting somebody married. When meeting him, they would ask about his wife's health with barely concealed joy.

The presence of Princess Tverskoy, both by the memories associated with her and because he generally disliked her, was unpleasant for Alexei Alexandrovich, and he went directly to the nursery. In the first nursery Seryozha, his chest leaning on the desk and his legs on the chair, was drawing something and merrily talking away. The English governess, who had replaced the Frenchwoman during Anna's illness, was sitting by the boy crocheting *migniardise* and hastily rose and curtsied, giving Seryozha a tug.

Alexei Alexandrovich stroked the boy's hair with his hand, answered the governess's question about his wife's health, and asked what the doctor had said about the baby.

'The doctor said there was nothing dangerous, sir, and prescribed baths.'

'But she's still suffering,' said Alexei Alexandrovich, listening to the baby crying in the next room.

'I think the wet nurse is no good, sir,' the governess said resolutely.

'What makes you think so?' he asked, stopping.

'That's what happened with Countess Paul, sir. The baby was treated, but it turned out that it was simply hungry: the wet nurse had no milk, sir.'

Alexei Alexandrovich reflected and, after standing there for a few seconds, went through the other door. The little girl lay, her head thrown back, squirming in the wet nurse's arms, and refused either to take the plump breast offered to her or to be silent, despite the double shushing of the wet nurse and the nanny leaning over her.

'Still no better?' said Alexei Alexandrovich.

'She's very restless,' the nanny answered in a whisper.

'Miss Edwards says the wet nurse may have no milk,' he said.

'I've been thinking so myself, Alexei Alexandrovich.'

'Then why didn't you say so?'

'Who was I to say it to? Anna Arkadyevna's still unwell,' the nanny said, displeased.

The nanny was an old household servant. And in these simple words of hers Alexei Alexandrovich seemed to hear a hint at his situation.

The baby cried still louder, ran out of breath and choked. The nanny waved her hand, went over to her, took her from the wet nurse's arms and began rocking her as she walked.

'We must ask the doctor to examine the wet nurse,' said Alexei Alexandrovich.

The healthy-looking, well-dressed wet nurse, afraid that she might be dismissed, muttered something under her breath and, hiding away her big breast, smiled contemptuously at any doubt of her milkiness. In that smile Alexei Alexandrovich also detected mockery of his situation.

'Poor baby!' said the nanny, hushing the baby and continuing to walk.

Alexei Alexandrovich sat down on a chair and with a suffering, downcast face watched the nanny pacing back and forth.

When the baby, finally quieted, was lowered into the deep crib, and the nanny straightened the pillow and backed away, Alexei Alexandrovich got up and, walking with difficulty on tiptoe, went over to look. For a minute he stood silently with the same downcast face, but suddenly a smile, moving the hair and skin of his forehead, showed on his face, and he left the room just as quietly.

In the dining room he rang and told the servant who came to send for the doctor again. He was vexed with his wife for not taking care of this lovely baby, and he did not want to go to her in this irritated mood, nor did he want to see Princess Betsy; but his wife might wonder why he did not come to her as usual, and therefore he made an effort and went to her bedroom. Going over the soft carpet to her door, he inadvertently heard a conversation he did not want to hear.

'If he weren't going away, I would understand your refusal and his as well. But your husband ought to be above that,' Betsy was saying.

'I don't want it, not for my husband's sake but for my own. Don't say it!' Anna's agitated voice replied.

'Yes, but you can't not want to say goodbye to a man who shot himself on account of you . . .'

'That's why I don't want to.'

Alexei Alexandrovich stopped with a frightened and guilty expression and was about to go back unnoticed. But, considering that it would be unworthy of him, he turned again and, coughing, went towards the bedroom. The voices fell silent and he went in.

Anna, in a grey dressing gown, her short-cropped black hair growing again like a thick brush on her round head, was sitting on the couch. As always at the sight of her husband, the animation on her face suddenly vanished; she bowed her head and glanced round uneasily at Betsy. Betsy, dressed after the very latest fashion, in a hat that hovered somewhere over her head like a lampshade over a lamp, and in a dove-grey dress with sharp diagonal stripes going one way on the bodice and the other way on the skirt, was sitting by Anna. Holding her flat, tall figure erect and bowing her head, she met Alexei Alexandrovich with a mocking smile.

'Ah!' she said, as if surprised. 'I'm very glad you're home. You don't show yourself anywhere, and I haven't seen you since Anna became ill. I've heard all about your attentiveness. Yes, you are an amazing husband!' she said with a meaningful and benign look, as though conferring an order of magnanimity on him for his behaviour towards his wife.

Alexei Alexandrovich bowed coldly and, after kissing his wife's hand, asked about her health.

'I think I'm better,' she said, avoiding his eyes.

'But your face seems to have a feverish colour,' he said, emphasizing the word 'feverish'.

'We've talked too much,' said Betsy. 'I feel it's been egoism on my part, and I'm leaving.'

She stood up, but Anna, suddenly blushing, quickly seized her hand.

'No, stay a moment, please. I must tell you . . . no, you,' she turned to Alexei Alexandrovich, and the crimson spread over her neck and forehead. 'I cannot and do not wish to keep anything concealed from you,' she said.

Alexei Alexandrovich cracked his fingers and bowed his head.

'Betsy was saying that Count Vronsky wished to come here and say goodbye before he leaves for Tashkent.' She was not looking at her husband and was obviously hurrying to say everything, difficult as it was for her. 'I said I could not receive him.'

'You said, my friend, that it would depend on Alexei Alexandrovich,' Betsy corrected her.

'But no, I cannot receive him, and there's no point in . . .' She suddenly stopped and glanced questioningly at her husband (he was not looking at her). 'In short, I don't want to . . .'

Alexei Alexandrovich stirred and was about to take her hand.

Her first impulse was to pull her hand away from his moist hand with its big, swollen veins as it sought hers, but with an obvious effort she took it.

'I am very grateful for your confidence, but . . .' he said, feeling with embarrassment and vexation that what he could resolve easily and clearly in himself, he could not discuss in front of Princess Tverskoy, who was for him an embodiment of that crude force which was to guide his life in the eyes of the world and which prevented him from giving himself to his feeling of love and forgiveness. He stopped, looking at Princess Tverskoy.

'Well, good-bye, my lovely,' said Betsy, getting up. She kissed Anna and went out. Alexei Alexandrovich saw her off.

'Alexei Alexandrovich! I know you to be a truly magnanimous man,' said Betsy, stopping in the small drawing room and pressing his hand once more especially firmly. 'I am an outsider, but I love her and respect you so much that I will allow myself this advice. Receive him. Alexei Vronsky is the embodiment of honour, and he's leaving for Tashkent.'

'Thank you, Princess, for your concern and advice. But my wife will decide for herself the question of whether she can or cannot receive someone.'

He said this, out of habit, with a dignified raising of eyebrows, and at once reflected that, whatever his words might be, there could be no dignity in his position. And this he saw in the restrained, spiteful and mocking smile with which Betsy looked at him after his phrase.

XX

Alexei Alexandrovich bowed to Betsy in the reception room and went back to his wife. She was lying down, but, hearing his footsteps, hastily sat up in her former position and looked at him in fear. He saw that she had been crying.

'I am very grateful for your confidence in me.' He meekly repeated in Russian the phrase he had spoken in French when Betsy was there, and sat down next to her. When he spoke in Russian and used the intimate form of address, it was irrepressibly annoying to Anna. 'And I am very grateful for your decision. I, too, suppose that, since he's leaving, there's no need for Count Vronsky to come here. However . . .'

'But I've already said it, so why repeat it?' Anna suddenly interrupted him with an annoyance she had no time to restrain. 'No need,' she thought, 'for a man to come and say good-bye to the woman he loves, for whom he wanted to destroy and did destroy himself, and who cannot live without him. No need at all!' She pressed her lips together and lowered her shining eyes to his hands with their swollen veins, which were slowly rubbing each other.

'Let's not ever talk about it,' she added more calmly.

'I've left it for you to decide this question, and I'm very glad to see . . .' Alexei Alexandrovich began.

'That my wish coincides with yours,' she quickly finished, annoyed that he spoke so slowly, while she knew beforehand everything he was going to say.

'Yes,' he said, 'and Princess Tverskoy meddles quite inappropriately in the most difficult family matters. In particular, she . . .'

'I don't believe anything they say about her,' Anna said quickly. 'I know that she sincerely loves me.'

Alexei Alexandrovich sighed and fell silent. She played anxiously with the tassels of her dressing gown, glancing at him with that painful feeling of physical revulsion towards him for which she reproached herself and which she could not overcome. She now wished for only one thing – to be rid of his hateful presence.

'I've just sent for the doctor,' said Alexei Alexandrovich.

'I'm well – what do I need the doctor for?'

'No, the little one is crying, and they say the wet nurse doesn't have enough milk.'

'Then why didn't you let me nurse her when I begged to? Anyway' (Alexei Alexandrovich understood the meaning of this 'anyway'), 'she's a baby, and they'll be the death of her.' She rang and ordered the baby to be brought. 'I asked to nurse her, they didn't let me, and now I'm being reproached.'

'I'm not reproaching you . . .'

'Yes, you are! My God! Why didn't I die!' And she burst into sobs. 'Forgive me, I'm annoyed, I'm not being fair,' she said, recovering. 'But do go . . .'

'No, it cannot remain like this,' Alexei Alexandrovich said resolutely to himself, after leaving his wife.

The impossibility of his position in the eyes of the world, and his wife's hatred of him, and generally the power of that crude, mysterious force which, contrary to his inner mood, guided his life, demanding the carrying out of its will and a change in his relations with his wife, had never before been presented to him with such obviousness as now. He saw clearly that his wife and the whole of society demanded something of him, but precisely what, he could not understand. He felt how, in response to it, a spiteful feeling arose in his soul that destroyed his peace and all the worthiness of his deed. He considered that for Anna it would be better to break connections with Vronsky, but if they all regarded it as impossible, he was even prepared to allow these relations again, so long as the children were not disgraced and he was not deprived of them or forced to change his position. Bad as that was, it would still be better than a break-up, which would put her in a hopeless, shameful position and deprive him of everything he loved. But he felt powerless. He knew beforehand that everything was against him and that he would not be allowed to do what now seemed to him so natural and good, but would be forced to do what was bad but seemed to them the proper thing.

XXI

Betsy had not yet had time to leave the reception room when Stepan Arkadyich, just come from Yeliseev's,[18] where fresh oysters had been delivered, met her in the doorway.

'Ah, Princess! What a happy meeting!' he began. 'And I was just at your place.'

'A momentary meeting, because I'm on my way out,' said Betsy, smiling and putting on a glove.

'Wait, Princess, before you put your glove on, let me kiss your little hand. I'm grateful for nothing so much as the return of old fashions, such as the kissing of hands.' He kissed Betsy's hand. 'When shall we see each other?'

'You don't deserve it,' Betsy replied, smiling.

'No, I deserve it very much, because I've become a most serious man. I settle not only my own but other people's family affairs,' he said with a meaningful look on his face.

'Ah, I'm very glad!' Betsy replied, understanding at once that he was talking about Anna. And going back to the reception room, they stood in a corner. 'He'll be the death of her,' Betsy said in a meaningful whisper. 'It's impossible, impossible . . .'

'I'm very glad you think so,' said Stepan Arkadyich, shaking his head with a grave and painfully compassionate look on his face. 'I've come to Petersburg on account of that.'

'The whole town is talking about it,' she said. 'This is an impossible situation. She's wasting away. He doesn't understand that she's one of those women who can't trifle with their feelings. One of two things: he must either take her away, act energetically, or give her a divorce. But this is stifling her.'

'Yes, yes . . . precisely . . .' Oblonsky said, sighing. 'That's why I've come. That is, not essentially for that . . . I've been made a gentleman of the chamber, so I must show my gratitude. But above all, this has got to be settled.'

'Well, God help you!' said Betsy.

Having seen Princess Betsy to the front hall and kissed her hand above the glove, where the pulse beats, and having told her a heap of such unseemly drivel that she no longer knew whether to laugh or be angry, Stepan Arkadyich went to his sister. He found her in tears.

Despite the ebulliently merry mood he was in, Stepan Arkadyich naturally changed at once to the compassionate, poetically agitated tone that suited her mood. He asked about her health and how she had spent the night.

'Very, very badly. And the afternoon, and the morning, and all days past and to come,' she said.

'I think you're surrendering to dejection. You must shake yourself up, look at life straight on. I know it's hard, but . . .'

'I've heard that women love people even for their vices,' Anna suddenly began, 'but I hate him for his virtues. I cannot live with him. You understand, the look of him affects me physically, I get beside myself. I cannot, cannot live with him. What am I to do? I was unhappy and thought it was impossible to be more unhappy, but I could not have imagined the terrible state I live in now. Would you believe that, though I know he's a good and excellent man and I'm not worth his fingernail, I hate him even so? I hate him for his magnanimity. And I have nothing left, except . . .'

She was about to say 'death', but Stepan Arkadyich did not let her finish.

'You're ill and annoyed,' he said. 'Believe me, you exaggerate terribly. There's nothing so dreadful in it.'

And Stepan Arkadyich smiled. No one in Stepan Arkadyich's place, having to deal with such despair, would have allowed himself to smile (a smile would seem crude), but in his smile there was so much kindness and almost feminine tenderness that it could not be offensive. His quiet words and smiles worked softeningly and soothingly, like almond butter. And Anna soon felt it.

'No, Stiva,' she said. 'I'm lost, lost! Worse than lost. I'm not lost yet, I can't say it's all ended, on the contrary, I feel that it hasn't ended. I'm like a tightened string that's about to snap. It hasn't ended . . . and it will end horribly.'

'Never mind, the string can be gently loosened. There's no situation that has no way out.'

'I've been thinking and thinking. There's only one . . .'

Again he understood from her frightened eyes that this one way out, in her opinion, was death, and he did not let her finish.

'Not at all,' he said, 'excuse me. You can't see your situation as I can see it. Allow me to tell you frankly my opinion.' Again he warily smiled his almond-butter smile. 'I'll begin from the beginning: you married a man twenty years older than yourself. You married without love or not knowing what love is. That was a mistake, let's assume.'

'A terrible mistake!' said Anna.

'But I repeat: it's an accomplished fact. Then you had, let's say, the misfortune to fall in love with someone other than your husband. That is a misfortune, but it's also an accomplished fact. And your husband has accepted and forgiven it.' He paused after each sentence, expecting her to object, but she made no reply. 'That's so. The question now is:

can you go on living with your husband? Do you want that? Does he want it?'

'I don't know, I don't know anything.'

'But you said yourself that you can't stand him.'

'No, I didn't. I take it back. I don't know anything, I don't understand anything.'

'Yes, but excuse me . . .'

'You can't understand. I feel I'm flying headlong into some abyss, but I mustn't try to save myself. And I can't.'

'Never mind, we'll hold something out and catch you. I understand you, I understand that you can't take it upon yourself to speak your wish, your feeling.'

'There's nothing I wish for, nothing . . . only that it should all end.'

'But he sees it and knows it. And do you really think it's less burdensome for him than for you? You suffer, he suffers, and what on earth can come of it? Whereas a divorce would resolve everything.' Stepan Arkadyich, not without effort, spoke his main thought and looked at her meaningfully.

She made no reply and shook her cropped head negatively. But by the expression on her face, which suddenly shone with its former beauty, he saw that she did not want it only because to her it seemed an impossible happiness.

'I'm terribly sorry for you both! And how happy I'd be if I could settle it!' Stepan Arkadyich said, now with a bolder smile. 'No, don't say anything! If only God grants me to speak as I feel. I'll go to him.'

Anna looked at him with pensive, shining eyes and said nothing.

XXII

Stepan Arkadyich, with that somewhat solemn face with which he usually took the presiding chair in his office, entered Alexei Alexandrovich's study. Alexei Alexandrovich, his hands behind his back, was pacing the room and thinking about the same thing that Stepan Arkadyich had talked about with his wife.

'Am I disturbing you?' said Stepan Arkadyich, who, on seeing his brother-in-law, experienced what was for him an unaccustomed feeling of embarrassment. To hide this embarrassment he produced a cigarette case with a new-fangled clasp he had just bought, sniffed the leather and took out a cigarette.

'No. Is there something you need?' Alexei Alexandrovich replied reluctantly.

'Yes, I'd like . . . I need to dis . . . yes, to discuss something with you,' said Stepan Arkadyich, surprised at this unaccustomed feeling of timidity.

It was so unexpected and strange a feeling that Stepan Arkadyich did not believe it was the voice of his conscience, telling him that what he intended to do was bad. Stepan Arkadyich made an effort and conquered the timidity that had come over him.

'I hope you believe in my love for my sister and in my sincere attachment and respect for you,' he said, blushing.

Alexei Alexandrovich stopped and made no reply, but Stepan Arkadyich was struck by the look of the submissive victim on his face.

'I intended . . . I wanted to talk with you about my sister and your mutual situation,' said Stepan Arkadyich, still struggling with his unaccustomed shyness.

Alexei Alexandrovich smiled sadly, looked at his brother-in-law and, without replying, went over to the desk, took from it the beginning of a letter and handed it to him.

'I think continually of the same thing. And this is what I've begun to write, supposing that I will say it better in writing and that my presence annoys her,' he said, handing him the letter.

Stepan Arkadyich took the letter, looked with perplexed astonishment at the dull eyes gazing fixedly at him, and began to read.

> I see that my presence is burdensome to you. Painful as it was for me to become convinced of it, I see that it is so and cannot be otherwise. I do not blame you, and God is my witness that, seeing you during your illness, I resolved with all my soul to forget everything that had been between us and start a new life. I do not repent and will never repent of what I have done; but I desired one thing – your good, the good of your soul – and now I see that I have not achieved it. Tell me yourself what will give you true happiness and peace in your soul. I give myself over entirely to your will and your sense of justice.

Stepan Arkadyich handed the letter back and went on looking at his brother-in-law with the same perplexity, not knowing what to say. This silence was so awkward for them both that a painful twitch came to

Stepan Arkadyich's lips as he sat silently, not taking his eyes from Karenin's face.

'That is what I wanted to tell her,' Alexei Alexandrovich said, looking away.

'Yes, yes,' said Stepan Arkadyich, unable to answer for the tears that choked him. 'Yes, yes. I understand you,' he finally got out.

'I wish to know what she wants,' said Alexei Alexandrovich.

'I'm afraid she doesn't understand her situation herself. She's no judge,' Stepan Arkadyich said, recovering. 'She's crushed, precisely crushed by your magnanimity. If she reads this letter, she'll be unable to say anything, she'll only hang her head lower.'

'Yes, but in that case what? How to explain . . . how to find out her wish?'

'If you will allow me to express my opinion, I think it depends on you to point directly to the measures you find necessary in order to end this situation.'

'So you find that it must be ended?' Alexei Alexandrovich interrupted. 'But how?' he added, making an unaccustomed gesture with his hands in front of his eyes. 'I don't see any possible way out.'

'There's a way out of every situation,' Stepan Arkadyich said, standing up and becoming animated. 'There was a time when you wanted to break off . . . If you're now convinced that you can't make each other happy . . .'

'Happiness can be variously understood. But let's suppose that I agree to everything, that I want nothing. What is the way out of our situation?'

'If you want to know my opinion,' Stepan Arkadyich said, with the same softening, almond-butter smile with which he had spoken to Anna. His kind smile was so convincing that Alexei Alexandrovich, sensing his own weakness and giving in to it, was involuntarily prepared to believe what Stepan Arkadyich would say. 'She will never say it outright. But there is one possibility, there's one thing she may wish for,' Stepan Arkadyich went on, 'that is – to end your relations and all memories connected with them. I think that in your situation it's necessary to clarify your new mutual relations. And those relations can be established only with freedom on both sides.'

'Divorce,' Alexei Alexandrovich interrupted with repugnance.

'Yes, I suppose it means divorce. Yes, divorce,' Stepan Arkadyich repeated, blushing. 'For a couple in such relations as yours, it's the most intelligent way out in all respects. What's to be done if they've discovered that life together is impossible for them? That can always happen.' Alexei Alexandrovich sighed deeply and closed his eyes. 'There's only one consideration here: does either of them wish to enter into a new marriage? If not, it's very simple,' said Stepan Arkadyich, freeing himself more and more from his embarrassment.

Alexei Alexandrovich, pinched with agitation, murmured something to himself and made no reply. Everything that appeared so simple to Stepan Arkadyich, Alexei Alexandrovich had thought over thousands and thousands of times. And it all seemed to him not only not simple but utterly impossible. Divorce, the details of which he already knew, seemed impossible to him now because his sense of dignity and respect for religion would not permit him to take upon himself an accusation of fictitious adultery, still less to allow his wife, whom he had forgiven and loved, to be exposed and disgraced. Divorce seemed impossible for other, still more important reasons as well.

What would happen to his son in case of divorce? To leave him with his mother was impossible. The divorced mother would have her own illegitimate family, in which his position and upbringing as a stepson would in all likelihood be bad. To keep him with himself? He knew that this would be vengeance on his part, and he did not want that. But, apart from that, divorce seemed impossible to Alexei Alexandrovich, above all, because in consenting to a divorce he would be ruining Anna. What Darya Alexandrovna had said in Moscow – that in deciding on a divorce he was thinking only about himself and not thinking that by it he would be ruining her irretrievably – had sunk deeply into his soul. And, combining that with his forgiveness and his attachment to the children, he now understood it in his own way. To his mind, agreeing to a divorce, giving her freedom, meant depriving himself of his last tie to the life of the children he loved, and depriving her of her last support on the path to the good and casting her into perdition. If she were a divorced wife, he knew, she would join with Vronsky, and that liaison would be illegitimate and criminal, because according to Church law a woman may not remarry while her husband is alive. 'She'll join with him, and in a year or two either he will abandon her or she will enter a new liaison,' thought Alexei Alexandrovich. 'And, by agreeing to an illegitimate divorce, I would be to blame for her ruin.' He had thought it all over thousands of times and was convinced that the matter of a divorce was not only not very simple, as his brother-in-law said, but was completely impossible. He did not believe a single word Stepan

Arkadyich said, he had a thousand refutations for every word of it, yet he listened to him, feeling that his words expressed that powerful, crude force which guided his life and to which he had to submit.

'The only question is, on what conditions would you agree to grant a divorce. She wants nothing, she doesn't dare ask you, she leaves everything to your magnanimity.'

'My God! My God! Why this?' thought Alexei Alexandrovich, recalling the details of a divorce in which the husband had taken the blame upon himself, and, with the same gesture as Vronsky, he covered his face with his hands in shame.

'You're upset, I understand that. But if you think it over . . .'

'And to him who strikes you on the right cheek, offer the left, and to him who takes your caftan, give your shirt,' thought Alexei Alexandrovich.

'Yes, yes!' he cried in a shrill voice, 'I'll take the disgrace upon myself, I'll even give up my son, but . . . isn't it better to let things be? However, do as you like . . .'

And turning away from his brother-in-law, so that he would not see him, he sat on a chair by the window. He felt grieved; he felt ashamed. But along with grief and shame he experienced joy and tenderness before the loftiness of his humility.

Stepan Arkadyich was moved. He paused.

'Believe me, Alexei Alexandrovich, she will appreciate your magnanimity,' he said. 'But it looks as if it was the will of God,' he added and, having said it, felt that it was stupid, and barely managed to keep from smiling at his own stupidity.

Alexei Alexandrovich wanted to make some reply, but tears stopped him.

'It is a fatal misfortune and must be recognized as such. I recognize this misfortune as an accomplished fact and am trying to help her and you,' said Stepan Arkadyich.

When Stepan Arkadyich left his brother-in-law's room, he was moved, but that did not prevent him from being pleased at having successfully accomplished the deed, since he was sure that Alexei Alexandrovich would not take back his words. This pleasure was also mixed with a thought that had come to him, that when the deed was done, he would ask his wife and close acquaintances the question: 'What's the difference between me and the emperor? He makes alliances and no one benefits, I break alliances and three people benefit . . . Or, what's the similarity between me and the emperor? When . . . Anyhow, I'll come up with something better,' he said to himself with a smile.

XXIII

Vronsky's wound was dangerous, though it had missed the heart. He lay for several days between life and death. When he was able to speak for the first time, his brother's wife, Varya, was the only one in his room.

'Varya!' he said, looking sternly at her. 'I shot myself accidentally. And please never speak of it and tell everybody the same. Otherwise it's too stupid!'

Without replying to what he said, Varya leaned over him and looked into his face with a joyful smile. His eyes were clear, not feverish, but their expression was stern.

'Well, thank God!' she said. 'Does it hurt anywhere?'

'Here a little.' He pointed to his chest.

'Then let me change your bandage.'

Silently clenching his broad jaws, he gazed at her while she bandaged him. When she finished, he said:

'I'm not delirious: please make sure there's no talk of me shooting myself on purpose.'

'But nobody says that. Only, I hope you won't accidentally shoot yourself any more,' she said with a questioning smile.

'It must be that I won't, though it would be better . . .'

And he smiled gloomily.

Despite his words and smile, which frightened Varya so much, when the inflammation passed and he began to recover, he felt himself completely free of one part of his grief. By his act he had washed himself, as it were, of the shame and humiliation he had felt previously. He could think calmly now of Alexei Alexandrovich. He recognized all his magnanimity and no longer felt himself humiliated. Besides, he fell back into the old rut of his life. He saw the possibility of looking people in the eye without shame and could live under the guidance of his habits. The one thing he could not tear out of his heart, despite his constant struggle with this feeling, was the regret, reaching the point of despair, at having lost her for ever. That now, having redeemed his guilt before her husband, he had to renounce her and never again stand between her with her repentance and her husband, was firmly resolved in his heart; but he could not tear out of his heart the regret at the loss of her love, could not erase from his memory the moments of happiness he had known with her, which he had valued so little then and which now pursued him in all their enchantment.

Serpukhovskoy came up with an assignment for him in Tashkent, and Vronsky accepted the offer without the slightest hesitation. But the closer the time of departure came, the harder became the sacrifice he was offering to what he considered his duty.

His wound had healed and he was already up and about, making preparations for his departure for Tashkent.

'To see her once and then burrow in and die,' he thought and, while making his farewell visits, he voiced this thought to Betsy. With this mission Betsy went to Anna and brought him back a negative reply.

'So much the better,' thought Vronsky, on receiving the news. 'This was a weakness that would have destroyed my last strength.'

The next day Betsy herself came to him in the morning and announced that she had received positive news through Oblonsky that Alexei Alexandrovich was granting a divorce and that he could therefore see her.

Without even bothering to see Betsy to the door, forgetting all his resolutions, not asking when it was possible or where the husband was, Vronsky went at once to the Karenins'. He raced up the stairs, seeing nothing and no one, and with quick strides, barely keeping himself from running, entered her room. And without thinking, without noticing whether there was anyone in the room, he embraced her and began covering her face, hands and neck with kisses.

Anna had been preparing for this meeting, she had thought of what she was going to tell him, but she did not manage to say any of it: his passion seized her. She wanted to calm him, to calm herself, but it was too late. His feeling communicated itself to her. Her lips trembled so that for a long time she could not say anything.

'Yes, you possess me and I am yours,' she finally got out, pressing his hand to her breast.

'It had to be so!' he said. 'As long as we live, it must be so. I know it now.'

'It's true,' she said, growing paler and paler and embracing his head. 'Still, there's something terrible in it, after all that's happened.'

'It will pass, it will all pass, we'll be so happy! Our love, if it could possibly grow stronger, would grow stronger for having something terrible in it,' he said, raising his head and revealing his strong teeth in a smile.

And she could not help responding with a smile – not to his words but to his enamoured eyes. She took his hand and stroked herself with it on her cold cheeks and cropped hair.

'I don't recognize you with this short hair. You're so pretty. Like a boy. But how pale you are!'

'Yes, I'm very weak,' she said, smiling. And her lips trembled again.

'We'll go to Italy and you'll get better,' he said.

'Is it really possible that we'll be like husband and wife, alone, a family to ourselves?' she said, peering into his eyes from close up.

'I'm only surprised that it could ever have been otherwise.'

'Stiva says *he* consents to everything, but I can't accept *his* magnanimity,' she said, looking pensively past Vronsky's face. 'I don't want a divorce, it's all the same to me now. Only I don't know what he'll decide about Seryozha.'

He simply could not understand how, at this moment of their reunion, she could think about her son, about divorce. Was it not all the same?

'Don't talk about it, don't think,' he said, turning her hand in his own and trying to draw her attention to himself; but she still would not look at him.

'Ah, why didn't I die, it would be better!' she said, and tears streamed silently down both her cheeks; but she tried to smile so as not to upset him.

To decline a flattering and dangerous assignment to Tashkent would have been, to Vronsky's former way of thinking, disgraceful and impossible. But now he declined it without a moment's reflection and, noticing the disapproval of his act in high places, he at once resigned his commission.

A month later Alexei Alexandrovich was left alone in his apartment with his son, and Anna went abroad with Vronsky without obtaining a divorce and resolutely abandoning the idea.

Part Five

I

Princess Shcherbatsky thought that to have the wedding before Lent, which was only five weeks away, was impossible, because half of the trousseau would not be ready by then; but she could not help agreeing with Levin that after Lent would be too late, since Prince Shcherbatsky's old aunt was very ill and might die soon, and the mourning would delay the wedding still longer. And therefore, deciding to divide the trousseau into two parts, a larger and a smaller, the princess agreed to have the wedding before Lent. She decided to prepare the smaller part of the trousseau at once and send the larger part later, and she was very angry with Levin for being quite unable to tell her seriously whether he agreed to it or not. This disposition was the more convenient as immediately after the wedding the young people were going to the country, where the things in the larger trousseau would not be needed.

Levin continued in the same state of madness, in which it seemed to him that he and his happiness constituted the chief and only goal of all that existed, and that there was no longer any need for him to think or worry about anything, that everything was being and would be done for him by others. He even had no plans or goals for his future life; he left it for others to decide, knowing that it would all be wonderful. His brother Sergei Ivanovich, Stepan Arkadyich and the princess directed him in what he had to do. He was simply in complete agreement with everything suggested to him. His brother borrowed money for him, the princess advised leaving Moscow after the wedding, Stepan Arkadyich advised going abroad. He agreed to everything. 'Do as you like, if it amuses you. I'm happy, and my happiness can be no greater or smaller whatever you do,' he thought. When he told Kitty of Stepan Arkadyich's advice about going abroad, he was very surprised that she did not agree to it, but had certain requirements of her own regarding their future life. She knew that Levin had work in the country that he loved. He could see that she not only did not understand this work but had no wish to understand it. That did not prevent her, however, from considering this work very important. And therefore she knew that their home would be in the country and wanted to go, not abroad where she was not going to live, but where their home would be. This definitely expressed intention surprised Levin. But since it was all the same to him, he at once asked Stepan Arkadyich, as if it were his duty, to go to the country and arrange everything there as he knew how to do, with that taste of which he had so much.

'Listen, though,' Stepan Arkadyich asked Levin one day, after he came back from the country where he had arranged everything for the young people's arrival, 'do you have a certificate that you've been to confession?'

'No, why?'

'You can't go to the altar without it.'

'Ai, ai, ai!' Levin cried. 'I bet it's a good nine years since I last prepared for communion.[1] I never thought of it.'

'You're a fine one!' Stepan Arkadyich said, laughing. 'And you call me a nihilist! This won't do, however. You've got to confess and take communion.'

'But when? There are only four days left.'

Stepan Arkadyich arranged that as well. And Levin began to prepare for communion. For Levin, as an unbeliever who at the same time respected the beliefs of others, it was very difficult to attend and participate in any Church rituals. Now, in the softened mood he found himself in, sensitive to everything, this necessity to pretend was not only difficult for him but seemed utterly impossible. Now, in this state of his glory, his blossoming, he had either to lie or to blaspheme. He felt himself unable to do either the one or the other. But much as he questioned Stepan Arkadyich whether it might not be possible to get the certificate without going to confession, Stepan Arkadyich declared that it was impossible.

'And what is it to you – two days? And he's such a sweet, intelligent old fellow. He'll pull this tooth of yours before you notice it.'

Standing through the first liturgy, Levin tried to refresh in himself his youthful memories of the strong religious feeling he had experienced between the ages of sixteen and seventeen. But he could see at once that it was utterly impossible for him. He tried to look at it as a meaningless, empty custom, like the custom of paying visits; but he felt that he could not do that either. With regard to religion, Levin, like most of his contemporaries, was in a very uncertain position. He could not believe, yet at the same time he was not firmly convinced that it was all incorrect. And therefore, being unable either to believe in the meaningfulness of what he was doing or to look at it indifferently as at an empty formality, he experienced, all through this time of preparation, a feeling of awkwardness and shame at doing what he himself did not understand and therefore, as his inner voice kept telling him, something false and bad.

During the services, he first listened to the prayers, trying to ascribe a meaning to them that did not disagree with his views, then, feeling that he could not understand and had to condemn them, he tried not to listen, but occupied himself with his own thoughts, observations and memories, which during this idle standing in church wandered with extreme vividness through his head.

He stood through the liturgy, vigil and compline, and the next day, getting up earlier than usual, without having tea, went to the church at eight o'clock in the morning to hear the morning prayers and confess.

There was no one in the church except a begging soldier, two little old women and the clergy.

A young deacon, the two halves of his long back sharply outlined under his thin cassock, met him and, going over to a little table, began at once to read the prayers. As the reading went on, and especially at the frequent and rapid repetition of the same words, 'Lord have mercy,' which sounded like 'Lordamerse, Lordamerse,' Levin felt that his mind was locked and sealed and should not be touched or stirred now, otherwise confusion would come of it, and therefore, standing behind the deacon, without listening or fathoming, he went on having his own thoughts. 'Amazing how much expression there is in her hand,' he thought, recalling how they had sat at the corner table the day before. They found nothing to talk about, as almost always during that time, and she, placing her hand on the table, kept opening and closing it, and laughed as she watched its movement. He recalled kissing that hand and afterwards studying the merging lines on its pink palm. 'Again "Lordamerse,"' thought Levin, crossing himself, bowing and looking at the supple movement of the bowing deacon's back. 'Then she took my hand and studied the lines: "You have a nice hand," she said.' And he looked at his own hand and at the deacon's stubby hand. 'Yes, it will soon be over now,' he thought. 'No, it seems he's starting again,' he thought, listening to the prayers. 'No, it's the end; there he's bowing to the ground. That's always just before the end.'

The hand in its velveteen cuff having discreetly received a three-rouble note, the deacon said he would register it and, briskly stamping with his new boots over the flagstones of the empty church, went into the sanctuary. A moment later he peeked out and beckoned to Levin. The thought locked up till then in Levin's head began to stir, but he hastened to drive it away. 'It will work out somehow,' he reflected and walked to the ambo.[2] He went up the steps and, turning to the right, saw the priest. An elderly man with a thin, greying beard and tired, kindly eyes, he was standing by a lectern leafing through the service book. After bowing slightly to Levin, he at once began reading prayers in an accustomed voice. When he finished them, he bowed to the ground and turned to face Levin.

'Christ stands here invisibly and receives your confession,' he said, pointing to the crucifix. 'Do you believe everything that is taught by the holy apostolic Church?' the priest went on, turning his eyes from Levin's face and folding his hands under the stole.

'I have doubted, I doubt everything,' Levin said, in a voice he himself found unpleasant, and fell silent.

The priest waited a few seconds to see whether he would say anything more, and then, closing his eyes, in a quick, provincial patter with a stress on the *o*s, said:

'Doubts are in the nature of human weakness, but we must pray that God in His mercy will strengthen us. What particular sins do you have?' he added without the slightest pause, as if trying not to waste time.

'My chief sin is doubt. I doubt everything and for the most part live in doubt.'

'Doubt is in the nature of human weakness,' the priest repeated the same words. 'What is it that you doubt predominantly?'

'I doubt everything. I sometimes even doubt the existence of God,' Levin said involuntarily, and was horrified at the impropriety of what he had said. But Levin's words did not seem to make any impression on the priest.

'What doubts can there be of the existence of God?' he hastened to say with a barely perceptible smile.

Levin was silent.

'What doubt can you have of the existence of the Creator, when you behold His creations?' the priest went on in a quick, habitual manner.

'Who adorned the heavenly firmament with lights? Who clothed the earth in its beauty? How can it be without a creator?' he said, glancing questioningly at Levin.

Levin felt that it would be improper to enter into a philosophical debate with a priest, and therefore he said in answer only what had a direct bearing on the question.

'I don't know,' he said.

'You don't know? How then can you doubt that God created everything?' the priest said in merry perplexity.

'I don't understand anything,' Levin said, blushing and feeling that his words were stupid and could not help being stupid in such a situation.

'Pray to God and ask Him. Even the holy fathers had doubts and asked God to confirm their faith. The devil has great power, and we mustn't give in to him. Pray to God, ask Him. Pray to God,' he repeated hurriedly.

The priest was silent for a time, as if pondering.

'You are, as I have heard, about to enter into matrimony with the daughter of my parishioner and spiritual son, Prince Shcherbatsky?' he added with a smile. 'A wonderful girl!'

'Yes,' Levin answered, blushing for the priest. 'Why does he need to ask about it at confession?' he thought.

And the priest, as if answering his thought, said to him:

'You are about to enter into matrimony, and it may be that God will reward you with offspring, is it not so? Well, then, what sort of upbringing can you give your little ones, if you don't overcome in yourself the temptation of the devil who is drawing you into unbelief?' he said in mild reproach. 'If you love your child, then, being a good father, you will not desire only wealth, luxury and honour for him; you will desire his salvation, his spiritual enlightenment with the light of Truth. Is it not so? What answer will you give when an innocent child asks you: "Papa! Who created everything that delights me in this world – the earth, the waters, the sun, the flowers, the grass?" Will you really say to him, "I don't know"? You cannot not know, since the Lord God in His great mercy has revealed it to you. Or else your little one will ask you: "What awaits me in the life beyond the grave?" What will you tell him, if you don't know anything? How will you answer him? Will you leave him to the temptation of the world and the devil? That's not good!' he said and stopped, inclining his head to one side and looking at Levin with meek, kindly eyes.

Levin made no reply, now not because he did not want to get into an argument with a priest, but because no one had ever asked him such questions; and before his little ones asked him such questions, there was still time to think how to answer.

'You are entering upon a time of life,' the priest went on, 'when one must choose a path and keep to it. Pray to God that in His goodness He may help you and have mercy on you,' he concluded. 'May our Lord and God Jesus Christ, through the grace and bounties of His love for mankind, forgive you, child . . .' and, having finished the prayer of absolution, the priest blessed and dismissed him.

On returning home that day, Levin experienced the joyful feeling of having ended his awkward situation and ended it in such a way that he had not needed to lie. Apart from that, he was left with the vague recollection that what this kindly and nice old man had said was not at all as stupid as it had seemed to him at first, and that there was something in it that needed to be grasped.

'Not now, of course,' Levin thought, 'but some time later on.' Levin felt more than ever that there was something unclear and impure in his soul, and that with regard to religion he was in the same position that he so clearly saw and disliked in others and for which he reproached his friend Sviyazhsky.

Levin was especially happy that evening, which he spent with his fiancée at Dolly's, and, explaining his excited state to Stepan Arkadyich, said that he was as happy as a dog that has been taught to jump through a hoop and, having finally understood and done what was demanded of it, squeals, wags its tail, and leaps in rapture on to the tables and windowsills.

II

On the day of the wedding Levin, according to custom (the princess and Darya Alexandrovna strictly insisted on fulfilling all customs), did not see his fiancée and dined in his hotel with a chance gathering of three bachelors: Sergei Ivanovich, Katavasov, his university friend, now a professor of natural science, whom Levin had met in the street and dragged home with him, and Chirikov, one of his groomsmen, a Moscow justice of the peace, Levin's bear-hunting comrade. The dinner was very merry. Sergei Ivanovich was in the best of spirits and enjoyed Katavasov's originality. Katavasov, feeling that his originality was appreciated and understood, flaunted it. Chirikov gaily and good-naturedly supported all the conversations.

'See, now,' Katavasov said, drawing out his words, from a habit acquired at the lectern, 'what an able fellow our friend Konstantin Dmitrich used to be. I'm speaking of him as an absent man because he is no more. He loved science then, on leaving the university, and had human interests; but now half of his abilities are aimed at deceiving himself and the other half at justifying this deceit.'

'A more resolute enemy of marriage than you I've never yet seen,' said Sergei Ivanovich.

'No, not an enemy. I'm a friend of the division of labour. People who can't do anything should make people, and the rest should contribute to their enlightenment and happiness. That's how I understand it. The mixing of these trades is done by hosts of fanciers, of whom I am not one.'[3]

'How happy I'll be when I find out you've fallen in love!' said Levin. 'Kindly invite me to your wedding.'

'I'm already in love.'

'Yes, with the cuttlefish. You know,' Levin turned to his brother, 'Mikhail Semyonych is writing a work on the feeding and . . .'

'Well, don't go muddling things! It makes no difference what it's about. The point is that I really do love the cuttlefish.'

'But that won't prevent you loving a wife!'

'That won't prevent me, but the wife will.'

'Why so?'

'You'll find out. You, for instance, love farming and hunting – well, wait and see!'

'Arkhip came today and said there's no end of elk in Prudnoye, and two bears,' said Chirikov.

'Well, you'll have to bag them without me.'

'You see, it's true,' said Sergei Ivanovich. 'And from now on it's good-bye to bear hunting – your wife won't allow it!'

Levin smiled. The idea of his wife not allowing him pleased him so much that he was ready to renounce for ever the pleasure of seeing bears.

'Still, it's a pity those two bears will get bagged without you. Do you remember the last time in Khapilovo? We'd have great hunting,' said Chirikov.

Levin did not want to deprive him of the illusion that there could be anything good anywhere without her, and so he said nothing.

'This custom of bidding farewell to bachelor life was not established in vain,' said Sergei Ivanovich. 'However happy one may be, one still regrets one's freedom.'

'Confess, you do have that feeling of wanting to jump out of the window like the suitor in Gogol?'[4]

'Certainly he does, but he won't confess it!' Katavasov said and laughed loudly.

'Well, the window's open . . . Let's set off for Tver right now! One is a she-bear, so we can get to the den. Really, let's take the five o'clock train! And they can do as they like here,' said Chirikov, smiling.

'I'll tell you, by God,' Levin said, smiling, 'in my heart I can't find any feeling of regret for my freedom!'

'Ah, there's such chaos in your heart now that you couldn't find anything there,' Katavasov said. 'Wait till you sort things out, then you'll find it!'

'No, otherwise I'd have at least some slight sense that, besides my feeling' (he did not want to say 'of love' in front of him) '. . . and happiness, I was still sorry to lose my freedom . . . On the contrary, I'm glad precisely of this loss of freedom.'

'Bad! A hopeless specimen!' said Katavasov. 'Well, let's drink to his recovery, or else wish him that only a hundredth part of his dreams comes true. And that would already be such happiness as has never been on earth!'

The guests left soon after dinner so as to have time to change for the wedding.

Remaining alone and recalling the conversation of these bachelors, Levin once again asked himself: did he really feel in his heart this regret for his freedom that they had spoken of? He smiled at the question. 'Freedom? Why freedom? Happiness is only in loving and desiring, thinking her desires, her thoughts – that is, no freedom at all – that's what happiness is!'

'But do I know her thoughts, her desires, her feelings?' some voice suddenly whispered to him. The smile vanished from his face and he fell to thinking. And suddenly a strange sensation came over him. He was possessed by fear and doubt, doubt of everything.

'What if she doesn't love me? What if she's marrying me only so as to get married? What if she herself doesn't know what she's doing?' he asked himself. 'She may come to her senses and understand only after marrying that she does not and cannot love me.' And strange thoughts about her, of the very worst sort, began coming into his head. He was jealous of Vronsky, as he had been a year ago, as if that evening when he had seen her with Vronsky were yesterday. He suspected that she had not told him everything.

He quickly jumped up. 'No, it's impossible like this!' he said to himself in despair. 'I'll go to her, ask her, tell her for the last time: we're free, hadn't we better stop? Anything's better than eternal unhappiness, disgrace, infidelity!!' With despair in his heart and with anger at all people, at himself, at her, he left the hotel and drove to see her.

He found her in the back rooms. She was sitting on a trunk, making arrangements about something with a maid, with whom she was sorting out piles of many-coloured dresses laid over the backs of chairs and on the floor.

'Oh!' she cried when she saw him and lit up with joy. 'Why? What is it? How unexpected! And I'm here sorting out my girlhood dresses, which goes to whom . . .'

'Ah! that's very nice!' he said, looking gloomily at the maid.

'Run along, Dunyasha, I'll call you later,' said Kitty. 'What's the matter with you?' she asked, resolutely addressing him informally, as soon as the maid had left. She noticed his strange face, agitated and gloomy, and fear came over her.

'Kitty, I'm suffering! I can't suffer alone,' he said with despair in his voice, standing before her and looking at her imploringly. He already saw by her loving, truthful face that nothing could come of what he intended to say, but all the same he needed her reassurance. 'I've come to say that we still have time. It can all be cancelled and corrected.'

'What? I don't understand anything. What's the matter with you?'

'What I've told you a thousand times and can't help thinking . . . that I'm not worthy of you. You couldn't have agreed to marry me. Think. You've made a mistake. Think well. You can't love me . . . If . . . it's better to say it.' He talked without looking at her. 'I'll be unhappy. They can all say whatever they like – anything's better than unhappiness . . . Anything's better now, while there's time . . .'

'I don't understand,' she replied fearfully. 'You mean that you want to take back . . . that we shouldn't?'

'Yes, if you don't love me.'

'You're out of your mind!' she cried, flushing with vexation.

But his face was so pathetic that she held back her vexation and, throwing the dresses off a chair, sat closer to him.

'What are you thinking? Tell me everything.'

'I think that you cannot love me. What could you love me for?'

'My God! what can I . . . ?' she said, and burst into tears.

'Ah, what have I done!' he cried and, kneeling before her, he began kissing her hands.

When the princess came in five minutes later, she found them perfectly reconciled. Kitty had not only assured him that she loved him, but in answering his question about what she could love him for, had even explained to him what for. She had told him that she loved him because she thoroughly understood him, that she knew what he must love and that all that he loved, all of it, was good. And that seemed perfectly clear to him. When the princess came in, they were sitting side by side on the trunk, sorting out dresses and arguing over Kitty's wanting to give Dunyasha the brown dress she had been wearing when Levin proposed to her, while he insisted that that dress should not be given to anyone and that Dunyasha should get the light blue one.

'How can you not understand? She's a brunette and it won't suit her . . . I have it all worked out.'

On learning why he had come, the princess became angry half jokingly, half seriously, and sent him home to get dressed and not interfere with Kitty's having her hair done, because Charles would be coming presently.

'She's eaten nothing all these days and doesn't look well as it is, and here you come and upset her with your silliness,' she said to him. 'On your way, on your way, my dear man!'

Levin, guilty and ashamed, yet comforted, went back to his hotel. His brother, Darya Alexandrovna and Stepan Arkadyich, all fully dressed, were already waiting for him, to bless him with an icon. There was no time to linger. Darya Alexandrovna still had to go home to pick up her pomaded and curled son, who was to carry the icon for the bride.[5] Then one carriage had to be sent for the best man and another had to be sent back to pick up Sergei Ivanovich . . . Generally, there were a number of quite complicated considerations. One thing was beyond doubt – that they could not dawdle because it was already half-past six.

The blessing with the icon did not turn out well. Stepan Arkadyich assumed a comically solemn pose standing next to his wife, took the icon and, after telling Levin to bow to the ground, blessed him with a kind and mocking smile and kissed him three times. Darya Alexandrovna did the same, then hastened to leave at once and again became confused about the projected itineraries for the carriages.

'Well, here's what we'll do: you go and fetch him in our carriage, and Sergei Ivanovich, if he will be so kind, can go and then send the carriage back.'

'Why, I'll be very glad to.'

'And we'll go with him now. Have your things been sent?' said Stepan Arkadyich.

'Yes,' replied Levin, and he told Kuzma to prepare his clothes.

III

A crowd of people, especially women, surrounded the church which was lit up for the wedding. Those who had not managed to get into the middle crowded around the windows, shoving, arguing and looking through the grilles.

More than twenty carriages had already been ranged along the street by policemen. A police officer, disdainful of the frost, stood at the entrance in his dazzling uniform. More carriages kept driving up, and ladies in flowers, picking up the trains of their dresses, or men removing their caps or black hats, entered the church. Inside the church itself, both lustres were already lit as well as all the candles by the icons. The golden glow on the red background of the iconostasis,[6] the gilded carvings of the icon cases, the silver of the chandeliers and candle stands, the flagstones of the floor, the rugs, the banners up by the choirs, the steps of the ambo, the blackened old books, the cassocks and surplices – everything was flooded with light. To the right side of the heated church,[7] in the crowd of tailcoats and white ties, of uniforms and brocades, velvet, satin, hair, flowers, bared shoulders and arms and long gloves, there was subdued but lively talk, echoing strangely in the high cupola. Each time the door creaked open, the talking in the crowd hushed and everyone turned, expecting to see the bride and bridegroom enter. But the door had already opened more than ten times, and each time it was either a latecomer who joined the circle of invited guests to the right, or a spectator who had tricked or cajoled the police officer into letting her join the crowd of strangers to the left. The relatives and the strangers had already gone through all the phases of expectation.

At first it was supposed that the bride and bridegroom would come at any moment and no significance was ascribed to the delay. Then they began glancing more and more often at the door, talking about whether something might not have happened. Then the delay became awkward, and the relatives and guests tried to pretend that they were not thinking about the bridegroom but were taken up with their own conversations.

The protodeacon, as if to remind people of the value of his time, kept coughing impatiently, making the glass in the windows rattle. From the choir came the sounds now of voices warming up, now of bored singers blowing their noses. The priest was constantly sending the beadle or the deacon to see if the bridegroom had come and, in his purple cassock and embroidered belt, came out of the side door more and more often in expectation of the bridegroom. Finally one of the ladies, looking at her watch, said: 'It is odd, though!' and all the guests became agitated and began to voice their astonishment and displeasure. One of the groomsmen went to find out what had happened. Kitty, all the while, had long since been quite ready, in a white dress, a long veil and a coronet of orange blossoms, and stood with her sponsor and sister Natalie in the reception room of the Shcherbatsky house, looking out of the window, waiting in vain for word from her best man that the bridegroom had arrived at the church.

Levin, meanwhile, in his trousers but with no waistcoat or tailcoat, was pacing up and down his room, constantly thrusting himself out of the door and looking into the corridor. But the one he was expecting was not to be seen in the corridor, and, coming back in despair and throwing up his hands, he addressed the calmly smoking Stepan Arkadyich.

'Has any man ever been in such a terribly idiotic position!' he said.

'Yes, it's stupid,' Stepan Arkadyich agreed with a soothing smile. 'But calm down, they'll bring it in a moment.'

'No, really!' Levin said with suppressed rage. 'And these idiotic open-front waistcoats! Impossible!' he said, looking at the crumpled front of his shirt. 'And what if my things have already been taken to the station!' he cried in despair.

'Then you'll wear mine.'

'I should have done that long ago.'

'It's better not to look ridiculous . . . Wait! things will *shape up*.'

The trouble was that when Levin had asked for his clothes, Kuzma, his old servant, had brought the tailcoat, the waistcoat and everything needed.

'But where's the shirt!' cried Levin.

'The shirt is on you,' Kuzma replied with a calm smile.

It had not occurred to Kuzma to lay out a clean shirt and, on receiving the order to have everything packed and taken to the Shcherbatskys', from where the newlyweds were to set out that same night, he had done just that, packing everything except the dress suit. The shirt, worn since morning, was wrinkled and impossible with the now fashionable open-front waistcoat. It was too far to send to the Shcherbatskys'. They sent a footman to buy a shirt. He came back: everything was closed – it was Sunday. They sent to Stepan Arkadyich's for a shirt: it was impossibly wide and short. They finally sent to the Shcherbatskys' to have the luggage unpacked. The bridegroom was expected at the church and here he was, like an animal locked in a cage, pacing the room, poking his head out to the corridor and recalling with horror and despair all that he had said to Kitty and what she might be thinking now.

At last the guilty Kuzma, gasping for breath, came flying into the room with the shirt.

'Nearly missed them. They were already loading it on the cart,' Kuzma said.

Three minutes later, not looking at his watch so as not to rub salt into the wound, Levin went running down the corridor.

'That won't help now,' Stepan Arkadyich said with a smile, unhurriedly trotting after him. 'Things will *shape up*, things will *shape up*. . . I'm telling you.'

IV

'They've come!' 'Here he is!' 'Which one?' 'The younger one, is it?' 'And she, poor dear, is more dead than alive!' Voices came from the crowd, as Levin, having met his bride at the door, entered the church together with her.

Stepan Arkadyich told his wife the reason for the delay, and the guests, smiling, exchanged whispers. Levin did not notice anything or anyone; he gazed at his bride without taking his eyes off her.

Everyone said she had been looking very poorly over the last few days and at the altar was far less pretty than usual; but Levin did not find it so. He looked at her hair, dressed high under the long white veil and white flowers, at her high, stiff, fluted collar, which in an especially maidenly way covered her long neck at the sides and left it open in front, and at her amazingly slender waist, and it seemed to him that she was better than ever – not because these flowers, this veil, this gown ordered from Paris added anything to her beauty, but because, in spite of all the prepared magnificence of her attire, the expression of her dear face, her eyes, her lips, was still her own special expression of innocent truthfulness.

'I was thinking you wanted to run away,' she said and smiled at him.

'It's so stupid, what happened to me, I'm ashamed to speak of it!' he said, blushing, and he had to turn to the approaching Sergei Ivanovich.

'Your shirt story's a fine one!' Sergei Ivanovich said, shaking his head and smiling.

'Yes, yes,' Levin answered, not understanding what was said to him.

'Well, Kostya, now you've got to decide an important question,' said Stepan Arkadyich, with a look of mock fright. 'Precisely now you will be able to appreciate its full importance. I've been asked what candles to light, used ones or new ones?[8] It's a difference of ten roubles,' he added, drawing his lips into a smile. 'I decided, but was afraid you wouldn't give your consent.'

Levin realized that this was a joke, but was unable to smile.

'So, which is it – new or used? That is the question.'

'Yes, yes, new ones!'

'Well, I'm very glad. The question's decided!' Stepan Arkadyich said, smiling. 'How stupid people get in this situation, though,' he said to Chirikov, as Levin, giving him a lost look, moved nearer to his bride.

'See that you're the first to step on the rug,[9] Kitty,' Countess Nordston said, coming up. 'A fine one you are!' she turned to Levin.

'What, frightened?' said Marya Dmitrievna, her old aunt.

'You're not chilly? You look pale. Wait, bend down!' Kitty's sister Natalie said and, rounding her full, beautiful arms, she smilingly straightened the flowers on her head.

Dolly came over, tried to say something, but could not get it out, began to cry, then laughed unnaturally.

Kitty looked at everyone with the same absent gaze as Levin. To all that was said to her she could respond only with the smile of happiness that was now so natural to her.

Meanwhile the clergy had put on their vestments, and the priest and deacon came out to the lectern that stood inside the porch of the church.[10]

The priest turned to Levin and said something. Levin could not make out what the priest said.

'Take the bride's hand and lead her,' the best man said to Levin.

For a long time Levin could not understand what was required of him. For a long time they kept correcting him and were about to give it up – because he kept either taking the wrong hand or taking it with the wrong hand – when he finally understood that he had to take her right hand with his own right hand without changing position. When he finally took the bride by the hand as he was supposed to, the priest went a few steps ahead of them and stopped at the lectern. The crowd of relations and acquaintances moved after them with a buzz of talk and a rustle of skirts. Someone bent down and straightened the bride's train. The church became so still that the dripping of wax could be heard.

The little old priest, in a kamilavka,[11] with the silvery gleam of his grey locks of hair pulled back on both sides behind his ears, drew his small, old man's hands out from under his heavy chasuble, silver with a gold cross on the back, and fumbled with something at the lectern.

Stepan Arkadyich cautiously went up to him, whispered something, and, with a wink at Levin, went back again.

The priest lighted two candles adorned with flowers, holding them slantwise in his left hand so that the wax slowly dripped from them, and turned to face the young couple. He was the same priest who had confessed Levin. He looked wearily and sadly at the bride and bridegroom, sighed and, drawing his right hand out from under the chasuble, blessed the bridegroom and in the same way, but with a touch of careful tenderness placed his joined fingers over Kitty's bowed head. Then he handed them the candles and, taking the censer, slowly moved away from them.

'Can this be true?' Levin thought and looked at his bride. He could see her profile from slightly above, and by the barely perceptible movement of her lips and eyelashes he knew that she felt his gaze. She did not turn, but her high, fluted collar stirred, rising to her small pink ear. He could see that a sigh had stopped in her breast, and her small hand in its long glove trembled, holding the candle.

All the fuss over the shirt, over being late, the talking with acquaintances, relations, their displeasure, his ridiculousness – all suddenly vanished, and he felt joyful and frightened.

The handsome, tall protodeacon in a silver surplice, his brushed, curled locks standing out on either side, stepped briskly forward and, raising his stole in two fingers with an accustomed gesture, stopped in front of the priest.

'Ble-e-ess, ma-a-aster!' Slowly, one after the other, the solemn tones resounded, making the air ripple.

'Blessed is our God always, now, and ever, and unto ages of ages,' the old priest responded humbly and melodiously, continuing to fumble with something on the lectern. And, filling the whole church from windows to vaults, broadly and harmoniously, the full chord of the invisible choir rose, swelled, paused for a moment, and slowly died away.

The prayer was, as always, for the peace from above, for salvation, for the Synod,[12] for the emperor, and also for the servants of God Konstantin and Ekaterina, betrothed that day.

'That He will send down upon them perfect and peaceful love, and succour, let us pray to the Lord' – the whole church seemed to breathe through the protodeacon's voice.

Levin listened to the words and they struck him. 'How did they guess that it's succour, precisely succour?' he thought, remembering all his recent fears and doubts. 'What do I know? What can I do in this terrible matter,' he thought, 'without succour? It's precisely succour that I need now.'

When the deacon finished the litany, the priest turned with his book to the couple to be betrothed:

'O eternal God, who has brought into unity those who were sundered,' he read in a mild, melodious voice, 'and hast ordained for them an indissoluble bond of love; who didst bless Isaac and Rebecca and didst make them heirs of thy promise: bless also these thy servants, Konstantin and Ekaterina, guiding them unto every good work. For thou art a merciful God, who lovest mankind, and unto thee do we ascribe glory, to the Father, and to the Son, and to the Holy Spirit, now, and ever, and unto ages of ages.'

'A-a-men!' the invisible choir again poured into the air.

'"Who hast brought into unity those who were sundered, and hast ordained for them an indissoluble bond of love" – how profound these words are, and how well they correspond to what one feels at this moment!' thought Levin. 'Does she feel the same as I do?'

And, turning, he met her eyes.

And by the look in those eyes he concluded that she understood it as he did. But that was not so; she had almost no understanding of the words of the service and did not even listen during the betrothal. She was unable to hear and understand them: so strong was the one feeling that filled her soul and was growing stronger and stronger. That feeling was the joy of the complete fulfilment of that which had already been accomplished in her soul a month and a half ago and throughout all those six weeks had caused her joy and torment. On that day when, in her brown dress, in the reception room of their house on the Arbat, she had silently gone up to him and given herself to him – in her soul on that day and hour there was accomplished a total break with her entire former life, and there began a completely different, new life, totally unknown to her, while in reality the old one had gone on. Those six weeks had been a most blissful and tormenting time for her. All her life, all her desires and hopes were concentrated on this one man, still incomprehensible to her, with whom she was united by some feeling still more incomprehensible than the man himself, now drawing her to him, now repulsing her, and all the while she went on living in the circumstances of her former life. Living her old life, she was horrified at herself, at her total, insuperable indifference to her entire past: to things, to habits, to people who had loved and still loved her, to her mother, who was upset by this indifference, to her dear, tender father, whom she had once loved more than anyone in the world. First she would be horrified at this indifference, then she would rejoice over what had brought her to it. She could neither think nor desire anything outside her life with this man; but this new life had not begun yet, and she could not even picture it clearly to herself. There was nothing but expectation – the fear and joy of the new and unknown. And now the expectation, and the unknownness, and remorse at the renouncing of her former life – all this was about to end, and the new was to begin. This new could not help being frightening; but, frightening or not, it had already been accomplished six weeks earlier in her soul; now was merely the sanctifying of what had long ago been performed.

Turning back to the lectern, the priest took hold of Kitty's small ring with some difficulty and, asking for Levin's hand, placed it on the first joint of his finger. 'The servant of God, Konstantin, is betrothed to the handmaid of God, Ekaterina.' And, putting the big ring on Kitty's small, pink, pathetically frail finger, the priest repeated the same thing.

Several times the betrothed couple tried to guess what they had to do, and each time they were mistaken, and the priest corrected them in a whisper. Finally, having done what was necessary, having crossed them with the rings, he again gave Kitty the big one and Levin the little one; again they became confused and twice handed the rings back and forth, still without doing what was required.

Dolly, Chirikov and Stepan Arkadyich stepped forward to correct them. The result was perplexity, whispers and smiles, which did not alter the solemnly tender expression on the faces of the couple; on the contrary, while they confused their hands, their look was more serious and solemn than before, and the smile with which Stepan Arkadyich whispered that each of them should now put on the proper ring, involuntarily froze on his lips. He had the feeling that any smile would offend them.

'For thou, in the beginning, didst make them male and female,' the priest was reading, following the exchange of rings, 'and by thee is the woman joined unto the man as a helpmeet and for the procreation of the human race. Wherefore, O Lord our God, who has sent forth thy truth upon thine inheritance, and thy covenant unto thy servants our fathers, even thine elect, from generation to generation: look thou upon thy servant, Konstantin, and upon thy handmaid, Ekaterina, and establish their betrothal in faith, and in oneness of mind, in truth, and in love . . .'[13]

Levin felt more and more that all his thoughts about marriage, all his dreams of how he would arrange his life, were mere childishness, and that it was something he had not understood before, and now understood still less, though it was being accomplished over him; spasms were rising higher and higher in his breast, and disobedient tears were coming to his eyes.

V

All Moscow, family and acquaintances, was in the church. And during the rite of betrothal, in the brilliant illumination of the church, among the decked-out women, girls, and men in white ties, tailcoats and uniforms, the talk went on unceasingly in decently low tones, initiated mainly by the men, while the women were absorbed in watching all the details of the sacred ritual, which they always find so moving.

In the group nearest the bride were her two sisters: Dolly, and the eldest, the calm beauty Princess Lvov, who had come from abroad.

'Why is Marie wearing purple, almost like black, for a wedding?' said Mme Korsunsky.

'With her complexion it's the only salvation . . .' Mme Drubetskoy replied. 'I wonder why they're having the wedding in the evening. Like merchants . . .'

'It's more beautiful. I, too, was married in the evening,' Mme Korsunsky answered with a sigh, recalling how nice she had looked that day, how comically in love her husband had been, and how different everything was now.

'They say if anyone's been a best man more than ten times, he'll never marry. I wanted this to be my tenth time, to insure myself, but the job was taken,' Count Sinyavin said to the pretty princess Charsky, who had designs on him.

Princess Charsky answered him only with a smile. She was looking at Kitty, thinking of how and when she would be standing in Kitty's place with Count Sinyavin, and how she would remind him then of his present joke.

Shcherbatsky told the old lady-in-waiting, Mme Nikolaev, that he intended to put the crown on Kitty's chignon so that she would be happy.[14]

'She oughtn't to be wearing a chignon,' answered Mme Nikolaev, who had decided long ago that if the old widower she was trying to catch married her, the wedding would be the simplest. 'I don't like all this *faste*.'*

Sergei Ivanovich was talking with Darya Dmitrievna, jokingly assuring her that the custom of going away after the wedding was spreading because newlyweds are always a little ashamed.

'Your brother can be proud. She's wonderfully sweet. I suppose you're envious?'

'I've already been through that, Darya Dmitrievna,' he replied, and his face unexpectedly assumed a sad and serious expression.

Stepan Arkadyich was telling his sister-in-law his quip about separations.

'The coronet wants straightening,' she said, not listening to him.

'It's too bad she looks so poorly,' Countess Nordston said to Natalie. 'And all the same he's not worth her little finger. Isn't it so?'

'No, I like him very much. Not just because he's my future *beau-frère*,'

* Display.

Natalie replied. 'And how well he carries himself! It's so difficult: to carry oneself well in such a situation – not to be ridiculous. And he's not ridiculous, not tense, you can see he's moved.'

'It seems you were expecting this?'

'Almost. She's always loved him.'

'Well, let's see who steps on the rug first. I advised Kitty.'

'It makes no difference,' Natalie replied, 'we're all obedient wives, it runs in the family.'

'And I purposely stepped on it first, before Vassily. And you, Dolly?'

Dolly was standing next to them, heard them, but did not answer. She was moved. There were tears in her eyes, and she would have been unable to answer without weeping. She rejoiced over Kitty and Levin; going back in thought to her own wedding, she glanced at the beaming Stepan Arkadyich, forgetting all the present and recalling only her first innocent love. She remembered not only herself, but all women, her close friends and acquaintances; she remembered them at that uniquely solemn time for them, when they, just like Kitty, stood under the crown with love, hope and fear in their hearts, renouncing the past and entering into the mysterious future. Among all these brides who came to her mind, she also remembered her dear Anna, the details of whose presumed divorce she had heard recently. She, too, had stood pure in her orange blossom and veil. And now what? 'Terribly strange,' she murmured.

Not only did sisters, friends and relations follow all the details of the sacred ritual; women spectators, complete strangers, watched with breathless excitement, afraid to miss a single movement or facial expression of the bride and bridegroom, and irritably ignored or often did not hear the talk of the indifferent men, who made jocular and irrelevant observations.

'Why is she all in tears? Or is she marrying against her will?'

'Why against her will if he's such a fine fellow? A prince, isn't he?'

'Is that her sister in white satin? Well, listen to how the deacon's going to roar: "And the wife see that she reverence her husband."'[15]

'The Chudovsky choir?'

'The Synodal.'

'I asked the footman. He says he's taking her to his estate at once. He's awfully rich, they say. That's why they've married her to him.'

'No, they're a fine couple.'

'And you, Marya Vlasyevna, you argued that crinolines are now worn loose. Look at that one in puce – an ambassador's wife, they say – how hers is tucked up . . . Like this, and again like this.'

'What a sweetie the bride is, done up like a ewe-lamb! Say what you like, one feels pity for a sister.'

Such was the talk in the crowd of women spectators who had managed to slip through the doors of the church.

VI

When the rite of betrothal was finished, a verger spread a piece of pink silk in front of the lectern in the middle of the church, the choir began singing an artful and elaborate psalm[16] in which bass and tenor echoed each other, and the priest, turning, motioned the betrothed to the spread-out piece of pink cloth. Often and much as they had both heard about the belief that whoever is first to step on the rug will be the head in the family, neither Levin nor Kitty could recall it as they made those few steps. Nor did they hear the loud remarks and disputes that, in the observation of some, he had been the first, or, in the opinion of others, they had stepped on it together.

After the usual questions about their desire to enter into matrimony and whether they were promised to others, and their replies, which sounded strange to their own ears, a new service began. Kitty was listening to the words of the prayer, wishing to understand their meaning, but she could not. A feeling of triumph and bright joy overflowed her soul more and more as the rite continued and made it impossible for her to be attentive.

They prayed 'that there be granted unto them chastity and the fruit of the womb as is expedient for them, and be made glad with the sight of sons and daughters'. It was mentioned that God had created woman out of Adam's rib, 'for which cause a man will leave his father and mother and cleave unto his wife, and the two shall be one flesh', and that 'this is a great mystery'; it was asked that God grant them fruitfulness and blessing as He did to Isaac and Rebecca, Joseph, Moses and Sepphora, and that they see their children's children.[17] 'All this is very beautiful,' Kitty thought, listening to these words, 'all this cannot be otherwise,' and a smile of joy, which involuntarily communicated itself to everyone who looked at her, shone on her radiant face.

'Put it all the way on!' came the advice, when the priest put the crowns on them, and Shcherbatsky, his hand trembling in its three-buttoned glove, held the crown high over her head.

'Put it on!' she whispered, smiling.

Levin looked at her and was struck by the joyful glow of her face; and the feeling involuntarily communicated itself to him. He felt just as bright and happy as she did.

They were happy listening to the reading of the epistle and to the roll of the protodeacon's voice at the last verse, awaited with such impatience by the public outside. They were happy drinking the warm red wine mixed with water from the flat cup, and happier still when the priest, flinging back his chasuble and taking both their hands in his, led them around the lectern to the outbursts of the bass singing 'Rejoice, O Isaiah'.[18] Shcherbatsky and Chirikov, who followed them holding the crowns over their heads, getting tangled in the bride's train, also smiling and rejoicing at something, first lagged behind, then bumped into them each time the priest stopped. The spark of joy that had flared up in Kitty seemed to have communicated itself to everyone in the church. To Levin it seemed that both the priest and the deacon wanted to smile just as he did.

Having taken the crowns from their heads, the priest read the final prayer and congratulated the young couple. Levin looked at Kitty, and never before had he seen her like that. She was lovely with that new glow of happiness in her face. Levin wanted to say something to her, but he did not know if it was over yet. The priest resolved his difficulty. He smiled with his kindly mouth and said softly:

'Kiss your wife, and you kiss your husband,' and he took the candles from their hands.

Levin carefully kissed her smiling lips, offered her his arm and, feeling a new, strange closeness, started out of the church. He did not believe, he could not believe, that it was true. Only when their surprised and timid eyes met did he believe it, because he felt that they were already one.

After supper that same night the young couple left for the country.

VII

For three months Vronsky and Anna had been travelling together in Europe. They had visited Venice, Rome, Naples and had just arrived in a small Italian town where they wanted to stay for a while.

The handsome maître d'hôtel, his thick, pomaded hair parted from the nape up, wearing a tailcoat and a wide white cambric shirtfront, a bunch of charms on his round pot-belly, his hands thrust into his pockets, his eyes narrowed contemptuously, was sternly saying something in reply to a gentleman who stood before him. Hearing footsteps coming up the stairs from the other side of the entrance, the maître d'hôtel turned and, seeing the Russian count who occupied their best rooms, respectfully pulled his hands from his pockets and, inclining, explained that a messenger had come and that the matter of renting the palazzo had been settled. The manager was ready to sign the agreement.

'Ah! I'm very glad,' said Vronsky. 'And is the lady at home or not?'

'Madame went out for a walk but has now come back,' said the maître d'hôtel.

Vronsky removed his soft, wide-brimmed hat, took out a handkerchief and wiped his sweaty forehead and his hair, grown half-way over his ears and combed back to cover his bald spot. Glancing distractedly at the gentleman, who was still standing there studying him, he was about to go in.

'This gentleman is a Russian and has asked about you,' said the maître d'hôtel.

With a mixed feeling of vexation at being unable to get away from acquaintances and of desire to find at least some distraction from the monotony of his life, Vronsky glanced once again at the gentleman, who had moved aside and then stopped. The two men's eyes lit up simultaneously.

'Golenishchev!'

'Vronsky!'

It was indeed Golenishchev, Vronsky's comrade in the Corps of Pages. In the corps Golenishchev had belonged to the liberal party; he had left the corps with civil rank and had not served anywhere. The comrades had totally drifted apart after leaving the corps and had met only once since.

At that meeting Vronsky had understood that Golenishchev had chosen some high-minded liberal activity and as a result wanted to despise Vronsky's activity and rank. Therefore, on meeting Golenishchev, Vronsky had given him that cold and proud rebuff he knew how to give people, which meant: 'You may or may not like my way of life, it makes absolutely no difference to me: you must respect me if you want to know me.' Golenishchev, however, had been contemptuously indifferent to Vronsky's tone. That meeting ought, it would seem, to have estranged them still further. Now, however, they brightened up and exclaimed joyfully on recognizing each other. Vronsky had never expected that he could be so glad to see Golenishchev, but he probably did not know himself how bored he was. He forgot the unpleasant impression of their last meeting and with an open, joyful face offered his hand to his former comrade. The same expression of joy now replaced the earlier uneasy look on Golenishchev's face.

'I'm so glad to see you!' said Vronsky, baring his strong white teeth in a friendly smile.

'And I heard "Vronsky", but which Vronsky I didn't know. I'm very, very glad!'

'Let's go in. Well, what are you up to?'

'It's the second year I've been here. Working.'

'Ah!' Vronsky said with sympathy. 'But let's go in.'

And by a common Russian habit, so as not to say in Russian what he wanted to conceal from the servants, he began to speak in French.

'Do you know Mme Karenina? We're travelling together. I'm on my way to see her,' he said in French, peering intently into Golenishchev's face.

'Ah! I didn't know,' Golenishchev replied indifferently (though he did know). 'Have you been here long?' he added.

'I? Three days,' Vronsky replied, once again peering attentively into his comrade's face.

'Yes, he's a decent man and looks at the matter in the right way,' Vronsky said to himself, understanding the meaning of Golenishchev's look and the change of subject. 'I can have him meet Anna, he looks at it in the right way.'

In those three months he had spent with Anna abroad, Vronsky, on meeting new people, had always asked himself how this new person looked at his relations with Anna, and had found that the men, for the most part, understood it 'in the right way'. But if he or those men who understood it 'in the right way' had been asked what that understanding was, both he and they would have been in great difficulty.

In fact, those who understood it, to Vronsky's mind, 'in the right way', did not understand it in any way, but behaved generally as well-bred people do with regard to all the complicated and insoluble questions that surround life on all sides – decently, avoiding hints and unpleasant questions. They pretended to understand fully the significance and meaning of the situation, to acknowledge and even approve of it, but considered it inappropriate and unnecessary to explain it all.

Vronsky realized at once that Golenishchev was one of those people, and was therefore doubly glad to see him. Indeed, Golenishchev behaved himself with Anna, when brought to her, just as Vronsky would have wished. He avoided, obviously without the least effort, any conversation that might have led to awkwardness.

He had not known Anna before and was struck by her beauty and still more by the simplicity with which she accepted her situation. She blushed when Vronsky brought him in, and this childlike colour that came over her open and beautiful face he liked very much. But he especially liked that she at once, as if on purpose, called Vronsky simply Alexei, so that there could be no misunderstandings in the presence of a stranger, and said that they were moving together to a newly rented house, known locally as a palazzo. Golenishchev liked this direct and simple attitude to her position. Observing Anna's good-naturedly cheerful, energetic manner, and knowing both Alexei Alexandrovich and Vronsky, Golenishchev felt that he fully understood her. It seemed to him that he understood what she was quite unable to – namely, how it was that she, having caused the unhappiness of her husband, having abandoned him and their son, and having lost her own good name, could still feel energetically cheerful and happy.

'It's in the guidebook,' Golenishchev said of the palazzo Vronsky had rented. 'There's a splendid Tintoretto[19] there. From his last period.'

'You know what? The weather's splendid, let's go there and have another look,' said Vronsky, turning to Anna.

'I'd be very glad to. I'll go and put my hat on. You say it's hot?' she said, stopping at the door and looking questioningly at Vronsky, and again the bright colour came over her face.

Vronsky saw from her look that she did not know what relations he wanted to have with Golenishchev, and that she was afraid she might not be behaving as he would have wanted her to.

He gave her a long, tender look.

'No, not very,' he said.

And it seemed to her that she understood everything, above all that he was pleased with her; and, smiling at him, she went out with her quick step.

The friends looked at each other and there was perplexity in both their faces, as if Golenishchev, who obviously admired her, would have liked to say something about her but could not think what, while Vronsky wished and feared the same thing.

'So that's how it is,' Vronsky began, in order to begin some sort of conversation. 'So you've settled here? So you're still doing the same thing?' he went on, recalling that he had been told Golenishchev was writing something . . .

'Yes, I'm writing the second part of *The Two Origins*,' said Golenishchev, flushing with pleasure at the question. 'That is, to be precise, I'm not writing yet, but I'm preparing, collecting material. It will be much more extensive and cover almost all the questions. We in Russia don't want to understand that we are heirs of Byzantium.' He began a long, ardent explanation.[20]

At first Vronsky felt awkward, not knowing the first part of *The Two Origins*, which the author spoke of as something well known. But then, as Golenishchev began to explain his thoughts and Vronsky was able to follow him, though he did not know *The Two Origins*, he listened not without interest, for Golenishchev spoke well. But Vronsky was surprised and disturbed by the irritated excitement with which Golenishchev spoke of the subject that occupied him. The longer he spoke, the more his eyes burned, the more he hastened to object to imaginary opponents, and the more anxious and offended the expression of his face became. Remembering Golenishchev as a thin, lively, good-natured and noble boy, always the first student in the corps, Vronsky simply could not understand the causes of this irritation and disapproved of it. He especially disliked the fact that Golenishchev, a man from a good circle, put himself on the same level with some common scribblers who irritated him, and was angry with them. Was it worth it? That Vronsky did not like, but, in spite of it, he felt that Golenishchev was unhappy and he was sorry for him. Unhappiness, insanity almost, showed on this lively and quite handsome face as he went on hurriedly and ardently voicing his thoughts, not even noticing that Anna had come out.

When Anna appeared in her hat and wrap and paused by him, her beautiful hand playing in quick movements with her parasol, Vronsky tore himself with a sense of relief from the intent gaze of Golenishchev's complaining eyes, and with renewed love looked at his enchanting friend, full of life and joy. Golenishchev, recovering himself with difficulty, was at first dejected and glum, but Anna, kindly disposed towards everyone (as she was at that time), soon revived him with her simple and gay manner. After trying various topics of conversation, she brought him round to painting, about which he spoke very well, and listened to him attentively. They reached the rented house on foot and looked it over.

'I'm very glad of one thing,' Anna said to Golenishchev on their way back. 'Alexei will have a good *atelier.** You must certainly take that room, dear,' she said to Vronsky in Russian, addressing him familiarly, because she already understood that Golenishchev, in their seclusion, would be close to them and that there was no need to hide anything in front of him.

'So you paint?' asked Golenishchev, quickly turning to Vronsky.

'Yes, I took it up a long time ago and now I've begun a little,' Vronsky said, blushing.

'He has great talent,' Anna said with a joyful smile. 'Of course, I'm no judge. But judges who know have said the same thing.'

VIII

Anna, during this first period of her liberation and quick recovery, felt herself unpardonably happy and filled with the joy of life. The memory of her husband's unhappiness did not poison her happiness. This memory was, on the one hand, too terrible to think of. On the other hand, her husband's unhappiness had given her too great a happiness to be repentant. The memory of all that had happened to her after her illness: the reconciliation with her husband, the break-up, the news of Vronsky's wound, his appearance, the preparation for the divorce, the departure from her husband's house, the leavetaking from her son – all this seemed to her a feverish dream from which she had awakened abroad, alone with Vronsky. The memory of the evil done to her husband called up in her a feeling akin to revulsion and similar to that experienced

* Studio.

by a drowning man who has torn away another man clinging to him. That man drowned. Of course it was bad, but it was the only salvation, and it was better not to remember those dreadful details.

One soothing reflection about her behaviour had occurred to her then, in the first moment of the break-up, and now when she remembered all that had happened, she remembered that one reflection: 'It was inevitable that I would be this man's unhappiness,' she thought, 'but I don't want to take advantage of that unhappiness. I, too, suffer and will suffer: I'm deprived of all that I once valued most – my good name and my son. I did a bad thing and therefore I do not want happiness, I do not want a divorce, and will suffer from my disgrace and my separation from my son.' But however sincerely Anna wanted to suffer, she did not suffer. There was no disgrace. With the tact they both had so much of, they managed, by avoiding Russian ladies abroad, never to put themselves into a false position, and everywhere met people who pretended that they fully understood their mutual position far better than they themselves did. Even the separation from her son, whom she loved, did not torment her at first. The little girl, his child, was so sweet and Anna had become so attached to her, once this little girl was all she had left, that she rarely remembered her son.

The need to live, increased by her recovery, was so strong, and the conditions of life were so new and pleasant, that Anna felt herself unpardonably happy. The more she knew of Vronsky, the more she loved him. She loved him for himself and for his love of her. To possess him fully was a constant joy for her. His nearness was always pleasing to her. All the traits of his character, which she was coming to know more and more, were inexpressibly dear to her. His appearance, changed by civilian clothes, was as attractive to her as to a young girl in love. In everything he said, thought and did, she saw something especially noble and lofty. Her admiration for him often frightened her: she sought and failed to find anything not beautiful in him. She did not dare show him her awareness of her own nullity before him. It seemed to her that if he knew it, he would stop loving her sooner; and she feared nothing so much now, though she had no reason for it, as losing his love. But she could not help being grateful to him for his attitude towards her and showing him how much she appreciated it. He, who in her opinion had such a clear vocation for statesmanship, in which he ought to have played a prominent role, had sacrificed his ambition for her and never showed the slightest regret. He was more lovingly respectful of her than ever, and the thought that she must never be made to feel her awkward position did not leave him for a moment. He, manly as he was, not only never contradicted her, but had no will of his own, and seemed to be concerned only with anticipating her wishes. And she could not help appreciating it, though the very strain of his attentiveness towards her, the atmosphere of solicitude he surrounded her with, was sometimes burdensome to her.

Vronsky meanwhile, despite the full realization of what he had desired for so long, was not fully happy. He soon felt that the realization of his desire had given him only a grain of the mountain of happiness he had expected. It showed him the eternal error people make in imagining that happiness is the realization of desires. At first, after he had united with her and put on civilian clothes, he felt all the enchantment of freedom in general, which he had not known before, and of the freedom of love, and he was content, but not for long. He soon felt arise in his soul a desire for desires, an anguish. Independently of his will, he began to grasp at every fleeting caprice, taking it for a desire and a goal. Sixteen hours of the day had to be occupied by something, since they lived abroad in complete freedom, outside the sphere of conventional social life that had occupied their time in Petersburg. Of the pleasures of bachelor life that had diverted him during his previous trips abroad he could not even think, because one attempt of that sort, a late supper with acquaintances, had produced in Anna a dejection both unexpected and exaggerated. Contacts with local or Russian society, given the uncertainty of their position, were also impossible. Looking at places of interest, not to mention that they had already seen everything, did not have for him, a Russian and an intelligent man, the inexplicable importance that Englishmen are able to ascribe to it.

And as a hungry animal seizes upon every object it comes across, hoping to find food in it, so Vronsky quite unconsciously seized now upon politics, now upon new books, now upon painting.

Since he had had an ability for painting from an early age and, not knowing how to spend his money, had begun to collect engravings, he now chose painting, began studying it, and put into it that idle store of desires which called for satisfaction.

He had an ability to understand art and to imitate it faithfully, tastefully, and thought he had precisely what was needed for an artist. After some hesitation over what kind of painting he would choose – religious, historical, genre or realistic – he started to paint. He understood all kinds and could be inspired by one or another; but he could not imagine that one could be utterly ignorant of all the kinds of painting and be inspired directly by what was in one's soul, unconcerned whether what one painted belonged to any particular kind. Since he did not know that, and was inspired not directly by life but indirectly by life already embodied in art, he became inspired very quickly and easily, and arrived as quickly and easily at making what he painted look very much like the kind of art he wanted to imitate.

He liked the graceful and showy French manner more than any other, and in this manner he began painting a portrait of Anna in Italian costume, and to him and to everyone who saw it this portrait seemed very successful.

IX

The old, neglected palazzo, with stucco mouldings on its high ceilings and frescoes on its walls, with mosaic floors, heavy yellow damask curtains on its high windows, urns on consoles and mantelpieces, carved doors and sombre halls hung with pictures – this palazzo, once they had moved into it, by its very appearance maintained the agreeable illusion in Vronsky that he was not so much a Russian landowner, a chief equerry without a post, as an enlightened amateur and patron of the arts – and also a modest artist himself – who had renounced the world, connections, ambition for the woman he loved.

The role chosen by Vronsky with his move to the palazzo was a complete success and, having met some interesting people through Golenishchev's mediation, he was initially at peace. Under the guidance of an Italian professor of painting, he painted sketches from nature and studied medieval Italian life. Medieval Italian life had recently become so fascinating for Vronsky that he even began wearing his hat and a wrap thrown over his shoulder in a medieval fashion, which was very becoming to him.

'And here we live and know nothing,' Vronsky said when Golenishchev came to see him one morning. 'Have you seen Mikhailov's picture?' he asked, handing him a Russian morning newspaper and pointing to an article about a Russian painter who lived in the same town and had finished a picture of which rumours had long been going about and which had been purchased before completion. The article reproached the government and the Academy for leaving a remarkable painter without any encouragement or aid.

'I've seen it,' Golenishchev replied. 'He is certainly not without talent, but his tendency is completely false. The same old Ivanov-Strauss-Renan[21] attitude towards Christ and religious painting.'

'What does the picture represent?' asked Anna.

'Christ before Pilate. Christ is presented as a Jew with all the realism of the new school.'[22]

And, the question about the content of the picture having led him to one of his favourite themes, Golenishchev began to expound:

'I don't understand how they can be so grossly mistaken. Christ found His definitive realization in the art of the old masters. Which means, if they want to portray not God but some revolutionary or wise man, they should take someone from history – Socrates, Franklin, Charlotte Corday,[23] only not Christ. They take the very person who cannot be taken for art, and then . . .'

'And is it true that this Mikhailov lives in such poverty?' asked Vronsky, thinking that he, as a Russian Maecenas, ought to help the artist regardless of whether his picture was good or bad.

'Hardly. He's a remarkable portraitist. Have you seen his portrait of Mme Vassilchikov? But it seems he no longer wants to paint portraits, and perhaps he really is in need. What I'm saying is . . .'

'Couldn't we ask him to paint a portrait of Anna Arkadyevna?' said Vronsky.

'Why of me?' said Anna. 'I don't want any portrait after yours. Better of Annie' (so she called her little girl). 'And here she is,' she added, looking out the window at the beautiful Italian wet nurse who had taken the child to the garden, and at once glancing surreptitiously at Vronsky. This beautiful wet nurse, from whom Vronsky had painted the head for his picture, was the only secret grief in Anna's life. While painting her, he had admired her beauty and medievalness, and Anna did not dare admit to herself that she was afraid of being jealous of her, and therefore she especially pampered and spoiled both the woman and her little son.

Vronsky also glanced out the window and then into Anna's eyes, and, turning at once to Golenishchev, said:

'And do you know this Mikhailov?'

'I've met him. But he's an odd fellow and totally uneducated. You know, one of those wild new people you meet so often now, one of those freethinkers who are brought up *d'emblée** with notions of unbelief, negation and materialism. It used to be,' Golenishchev went on, not noticing or not wishing to notice that both Anna and Vronsky also wanted to talk, 'it used to be that a freethinker was a man who had been brought up with notions of religion, law, morality, and had arrived at freethinking by himself, through his own toil and struggle. But now a new type of self-made freethinkers has appeared, who grow up and never even hear that there were laws of morality, religion, that there were authorities, but who grow up right into notions of the negation of everything – that is, as wild men. He's like that. It seems he's the son of a Moscow major-domo and received no education. When he entered the Academy and made a reputation for himself, being far from stupid, he wanted to get educated. And he turned to what he thought was a source of education – the magazines. You understand, in older times a man who wanted to get educated, a Frenchman, let's say, would start by studying the classics – theologians, tragedians, historians, philosophers – and you can imagine all the mental labour that confronted him. But with us, now, he comes straight to nihilistic literature, very quickly learns the whole essence of its negative teaching, and there he is. And that's not all: some twenty years ago he'd have found signs of a struggle with authorities, with age-old views, in this literature, and from this struggle he'd have understood that something else existed; but now he comes straight to a literature that doesn't even deign to argue with the old views, but says directly: There is nothing, evolution, selection, the struggle for existence – and that's all. In my article I . . .'

'You know what,' said Anna, who had long been cautiously exchanging glances with Vronsky, and who knew that he was not interested in the artist's education but was concerned only with the thought of helping him and commissioning the portrait. 'You know what?' she resolutely interrupted the loquacious Golenishchev. 'Let's go and see him!'

Golenishchev recovered himself and willingly agreed. But since the artist lived in a remote quarter, they decided to take a carriage.

An hour later Anna, sitting beside Golenishchev and with Vronsky in the front seat, drove up to a new, ugly house in a remote quarter. Learning from the caretaker's wife, who came to meet them, that Mikhailov received people in his studio, but was now in his apartment two

* Straight off.

steps away, they sent her to him with their cards, asking permission to see his pictures.

X

The artist Mikhailov was working as usual when the cards of Count Vronsky and Golenishchev were brought to him. In the morning he had worked on the big picture in his studio. Returning home, he got angry with his wife for being unable to handle the landlady, who was demanding money.

'I've told you twenty times, don't get into explanations. You're a fool as it is, and when you start speaking Italian you come out a triple fool,' he told her, after a lengthy argument.

'You shouldn't let it go for so long, it's not my fault. If I had money . . .'

'Leave me alone, for God's sake!' Mikhailov exclaimed with tears in his voice and, stopping his ears, went to his workroom behind the partition and locked the door behind him. 'Witless woman!' he said to himself, sat down at the table, opened a portfolio, and at once set to work with particular ardour on a sketch he had begun.

He never worked so ardently and successfully as when his life was going badly, and especially after quarrelling with his wife. 'Ah, it can all go to blazes!' he thought as he went on working. He was making a sketch for the figure of a man in a fit of anger. There was an earlier sketch, but he had not been satisfied with it. 'No, that one was better . . . Where is it?' He went to his wife and, scowling, without looking at her, asked the older girl where the paper he had given them was. The paper with the discarded sketch was found, but it was dirty and spattered with stearin. All the same he took the drawing, placed it on his table and, stepping back and squinting, began to study it. Suddenly he smiled and joyfully threw up his hands.

'That's it, that's it!' he said and, taking up his pencil at once, began drawing quickly. A spot of stearin had given the man a new pose.

As he was drawing this new pose, he suddenly remembered the energetic face, with its jutting chin, of the shopkeeper he bought cigars from, and he drew that very face, that chin, for his man. He laughed with joy. The figure, from a dead, invented one, had come alive, and it was now impossible to change it. The figure lived and was clearly and unquestionably defined. He could correct it in keeping with what it demanded, could and even must place the legs differently, change the position of the left arm completely and have the hair thrown back. But in making these corrections, he did not alter the figure, but only cast off what concealed it. It was as if he removed the wrappings that kept it from being fully seen. Each new stroke only revealed more of the whole figure in all its energetic force, as it had suddenly appeared to him thanks to the spot of stearin. He was carefully finishing the figure when the cards were brought to him.

'One moment, one moment!'

He went to his wife.

'There now, Sasha, don't be angry!' he said to her, smiling timidly and tenderly. 'It was your fault. It was my fault. I'll settle everything.' And, having made peace with his wife, he put on an olive-green coat with a velvet collar and his hat and went to the studio. The successful figure was already forgotten. He was now gladdened and excited by the visit to his studio of these important Russians who had come in a carriage.

About his picture, which now stood on his easel, he had one judgement in the depths of his soul – that no one had ever painted such a picture. He did not think that his painting was better than any of Raphael's,[24] but he knew that what he wanted to convey and did convey in this picture no one had ever conveyed before. He knew that firmly and had known it for a long time, from the very moment he had begun painting it; nevertheless people's opinions, whatever they might be, were of great importance for him and stirred him to the bottom of his soul. Every observation, however insignificant, which showed that the judges saw at least a small part of what he saw in this picture, stirred him to the bottom of his soul. He always ascribed to his judges a greater depth of understanding than he himself had, and expected something from them that he himself did not see in his picture. And often in the opinions of viewers it seemed to him that he found it.

He approached the door of his studio with quick steps and, despite his excitement, was struck by the soft lighting on the figure of Anna, who was standing in the shadow of the porch and, while listening to Golenishchev vehemently telling her something, at the same time obviously wished to look at the approaching artist. He himself did not notice how, as he came up to them, he snatched and swallowed this impression, just as he had the chin of the shopkeeper who sold cigars, and hid it away somewhere where he could find it when it was needed. The visitors, disappointed in advance by what Golenishchev had told them about the artist, were still more disappointed by his appearance. Of average height, stocky, with a fidgety gait, Mikhailov, in his brown hat, olive-green coat and narrow trousers, when wide ones had long been in fashion, and especially with the ordinariness of his broad face and his combined expression of timidity and a desire to maintain his dignity, produced an unpleasant impression.

'Come in, please,' he said, trying to look indifferent and, going into the front hall he took a key from his pocket and unlocked the door.

XI

As he went into the studio, the artist Mikhailov looked his visitors over once again and also noted in his imagination the expression of Vronsky's face, especially his cheekbones. Though his artistic sense worked incessantly, collecting material, though he felt an ever increasing excitement because the moment for judgements of his work was approaching, he quickly and subtly formed an idea of these three people out of imperceptible tokens. This one (Golenishchev) was a local Russian. Mikhailov did not remember his last name or where he had met him and what they had talked about. He remembered only his face, as he did all the faces he had ever seen, but he also remembered that his was one of the faces laid away in his imagination in the huge department of the falsely important and poor in expression. A mass of hair and a very open forehead lent a superficial importance to the face, on which there was merely a small, childish, anxious expression, focused above the narrow bridge of the nose. Vronsky and Mme Karenina, in Mikhailov's conjecture, must have been noble and wealthy Russians who, like all wealthy Russians, understood nothing about art, but pretended to be amateurs and connoisseurs. 'They've probably already looked at all the old stuff, and now they're going around to the studios of the new ones – some German charlatan, some fool of a Pre-Raphaelite Englishman[25] – and have come to me only to complete the survey,' he thought. He knew very well the dilettantes' manner (which was worse the more intelligent they were) of going to look at the studios of contemporary artists with the sole aim of having the right to say that art has declined and that the more one looks at the new painters, the more one sees how inimitable the great old masters still are. He expected all that, he saw it in their faces, saw it in the indifferent nonchalance with which they talked among themselves, looked at the manikins and busts and strolled about freely, waiting for him to uncover the painting. But despite that, all the while he was turning over his sketches, raising the blinds and removing the sheet, he felt a strong excitement, the more so because, though to his mind all noble and wealthy Russians had to be brutes and fools, he liked Vronsky and especially Anna.

'Here, if you please?' he said, stepping aside with his fidgety gait and pointing to the picture. 'It's the admonition of Pilate. Matthew, chapter twenty-seven,' he said, feeling his lips beginning to tremble with excitement. He stepped back and stood behind them.

For a few seconds, as the visitors silently looked at the picture, Mikhailov also looked at it, and looked with an indifferent, estranged eye. For those few seconds he believed in advance that the highest, the fairest judgement would be pronounced by them, precisely by these visitors whom he had so despised a moment ago. He forgot everything he had thought before about his picture during the three years he had been painting it; he forgot all its virtues, which for him were unquestionable – he saw it with their indifferent, estranged, new eyes and found nothing good in it. He saw in the foreground the vexed face of Pilate and the calm face of Christ, and in the background the figures of Pilate's servants and the face of John, peering at all that was going on. Each face, grown in him with its own particular character after so much searching, after so many errors and corrections, each face that had brought him so much pain and joy, and all of them rearranged so many times to preserve the whole, the nuances of colour and tone achieved with such difficulty – all this together, seen through their eyes, now seemed to him a banality repeated a thousand times. The dearest face of all, the face of Christ, the focus of the picture, which had delighted him so when he discovered it, was quite lost for him when he looked at the picture through their eyes. He saw a well-painted (or even not so well-painted – he now saw clearly a heap of defects) repetition of the endless Christs of Titian, Raphael, Rubens, with the same soldiers and Pilate. All this was banal, poor, old, and even badly painted – gaudy and weak. They would be right to speak falsely polite phrases in the artist's presence, and to pity him and laugh at him when they were alone.

This silence became too painful for him (though it lasted no more than a minute). To break it and show that he was not excited, he took himself in hand and addressed Golenishchev.

'I believe I had the pleasure of meeting you,' he said to him, anxiously turning to look now at Anna, now at Vronsky, so as not to miss a single detail in the expressions on their faces.

'Why, yes! We met at Rossi's, remember, the evening of the recital by that young Italian lady, the new Rachel,'[26] Golenishchev replied freely, taking his eyes from the picture without the least regret and turning to the artist.

Noticing, however, that Mikhailov was waiting for an opinion on the picture, he said:

'Your picture has progressed considerably since I last saw it. And now, as then, I find the figure of Pilate extraordinarily striking. One understands the man so well – a kind, nice fellow, but a functionary to the bottom of his soul, who knows not what he does. But it seems to me . . .'

The whole of Mikhailov's mobile face suddenly beamed; his eyes lit up. He wanted to say something but could not speak from excitement, and pretended he was coughing. Little as he valued Golenishchev's ability to understand art, trivial as was the correct observation about the rightness of Pilate's expression as a functionary, offensive as it might have seemed to voice such a trivial observation first, while more important things were ignored, Mikhailov was delighted with this observation. He himself thought the same about the figure of Pilate as Golenishchev did. That this opinion was one of a million opinions which, as Mikhailov well knew, would all be correct, did not diminish for him the significance of Golenishchev's observation. He loved Golenishchev for it, and from a state of dejection suddenly went into ecstasy. The whole painting at once came to life before him with all the complexity of everything that lives. Mikhailov again tried to say that he understood Pilate the same way; but his lips trembled disobediently and he could not get the words out. Vronsky and Anna were also saying something in those soft voices in which people usually talk at exhibitions, partly so as not to insult the artist, partly so as not to say some foolishness aloud, as it is so easy to do when talking about art. It seemed to Mikhailov that the picture had made an impression on them as well. He went over to them.

'How astonishing Christ's expression is!' said Anna. Of all she saw, she liked that expression most; she felt it was the centre of the picture, and therefore that praise of it would please the artist. 'One can see he pities Pilate.'

This was again one of the million correct opinions that could be held about his picture and the figure of Christ. She said he pitied Pilate. In Christ's expression there had to be pity, because there was in him the expression of love, unearthly peace, readiness for death and an awareness of the vanity of words. Of course, there was the expression of a functionary in Pilate and of pity in Christ, because one embodied carnal and the other spiritual life. All this and many other things flashed in Mikhailov's thoughts. And again his face beamed with ecstasy.

'Yes, and the way the figure's done, so much air. You can walk around it,' said Golenishchev, obviously indicating by this observation that he did not approve of the content and idea of the figure.

'Yes, amazing mastery!' said Vronsky. 'How those figures in the background stand out! That's technique,' he said, turning to Golenishchev and alluding to a previous conversation between them about Vronsky's despair of acquiring such technique.

'Yes, yes, amazing!' Golenishchev and Anna agreed. In spite of the agitated state he was in, the remark about technique grated painfully on Mikhailov's heart and, glancing angrily at Vronsky, he suddenly scowled. He had often heard this word 'technique' and decidedly did not understand what it implied. He knew that it implied a mechanical ability to paint and draw, completely independent of content. He had often noticed, as in this present praise, that technique was opposed to inner virtue, as if it were possible to make a good painting of something bad. He knew that great attention and care were needed to remove the wrappings without harming the work itself, and to remove all the wrappings; but there was no art of painting, no technique here. If what he saw had also been revealed to a little child or to his kitchen-maid, they too would have been able to lay bare what they saw. But the most experienced and skilful painter-technician would be unable, for all his mechanical ability, to paint anything unless the boundaries of the content were first revealed to him. Besides, he saw that if one were to speak of technique he could not be praised for it. In all his paintings, present and past, his eye was struck by defects that came from the carelessness with which he had removed the wrappings and that he could no longer correct without marring the whole work. And he still saw on almost all the figures and faces the remains of wrappings not yet completely removed, which marred the painting.

'One thing might be said, if you will allow me to make an observation . . .' Golenishchev observed.

'Oh, please do, I'll be very glad,' said Mikhailov, smiling falsely.

'It is that you have made him a man-God and not a God-man.[27] However, I know that's what you meant to do.'

'I could not paint a Christ whom I do not have in my soul,' Mikhailov said sullenly.

'Yes, but in that case, if you will allow me to say what I think . . . Your picture is so good that my observation cannot harm it, and besides it's my personal opinion. With you it's different. The motif itself is different. But let's take Ivanov. I think that if Christ is to be reduced to the level of a historical figure, it would have been better if Ivanov had selected a different historical theme, something fresh, untouched.'

'But what if this is the greatest theme available to art?'

'If one seeks, one can find others. But the thing is that art doesn't suffer argument and reasoning. And in front of Ivanov's painting a question arises both for the believer and for the unbeliever – is he God or not? – and destroys the unity of the impression.'

'Why so? It seems to me,' said Mikhailov, 'that for educated people the question can no longer exist.'

Golenishchev disagreed with that and, keeping to his first thought about the unity of impression necessary for art, crushed Mikhailov.

Mikhailov was excited but unable to say anything in defence of his thinking.

XII

Anna and Vronsky had long been exchanging glances, regretting the clever loquacity of their friend, and Vronsky finally moved on, without waiting for his host, to another smaller picture.

'Ah, how charming, what a charming thing! A marvel! How charming!' they said with one voice.

'What is it they like so much?' thought Mikhailov. He had forgotten this picture, painted three years ago, forgotten all the agonies and ecstasies he had lived through with this picture, when it alone had occupied him persistently for several months, day and night; forgotten it as he always forgot finished pictures. He did not even like looking at it and had put it out only because he was expecting an Englishman who wanted to buy it.

'It's just an old study,' he said.

'How good!' said Golenishchev, who had obviously fallen under the charm of the painting as well.

Two boys were fishing in the shade of a willow. One, the elder, had just dropped his line in and was carefully drawing the bobber from behind a bush, all absorbed in what he was doing; the other, slightly younger, was lying in the grass, his dishevelled blond head resting on his hands, gazing into the water with pensive blue eyes. What was he thinking about?

The admiration for this picture stirred the former excitement in Mikhailov's soul, but he feared and disliked this idle feeling for the past, and therefore, though glad of the praise, he wanted to distract his visitors with a third picture.

But Vronsky asked if the picture was for sale. Mikhailov, excited by his visitors, now found the talk of money very unpleasant.

'It was put out to be sold,' he replied, scowling darkly.

When the visitors had gone, Mikhailov sat down facing the picture of Pilate and Christ and went over in his mind what had been said, or not said but implied, by these visitors. And, strangely, what had carried such weight for him when they were there and when he put himself mentally into their point of view, suddenly lost all meaning for him. He began to look at his picture with his full artistic vision and arrived at that state of confidence in the perfection and hence the significance of his picture which he needed for that tension, exclusive of all other interests, which alone made it possible for him to work.

The foreshortening of Christ's leg was still not quite right. He took his palette and set to work. As he corrected the leg, he kept studying the figure of John in the background, which the visitors had not noticed but which he knew to be the height of perfection. After finishing the leg, he wanted to get to this figure, but he felt himself too excited for it. He was equally unable to work when he was cold and when he was too receptive and saw everything too well. There was only one step in this transition from coldness to inspiration at which work was possible. But today he was too excited. He was about to cover the painting, but stopped and, holding the sheet in his hand, gazed for a long time and with a blissful smile at the figure of John. Finally, as if sadly tearing himself away, he lowered the sheet and went home, weary but happy.

Vronsky, Anna and Golenishchev, on their way back, were especially animated and merry. They talked about Mikhailov and his paintings. The word 'talent', which they understood as an inborn and almost physical ability, independent of mind and heart, and which they wanted to apply to everything the artist experienced, occurred particularly often in their conversation, since they needed it in order to name something they had no idea of, but wanted to talk about. They said that it was impossible to deny his talent, but that his talent had been unable to develop for lack of education – a common misfortune of our Russian artists. But the painting with the boys stuck in their memory and every now and then they went back to it.

'So charming! He succeeded so well and so simply! He doesn't understand how good it is. Yes, we must buy it and not let it slip,' said Vronsky.

XIII

Mikhailov sold Vronsky his little painting and agreed to do Anna's portrait. On the appointed day he came and set to work.

From the fifth sitting the portrait struck everyone, especially Vronsky, not only by its likeness but by its special beauty. It was strange how Mikhailov was able to find this special beauty in her. 'One would have to know her and love her as I do to find that sweetest inner expression of hers,' thought Vronsky, though he had learned of that sweetest inner expression of hers only from this portrait. But the expression was so true that he and others thought they had always known it.

'I've been struggling for so long and have done nothing,' he said of his own portrait, 'and he just looked and started painting. That's what technique means.'

'It will come,' Golenishchev comforted him. To his mind, Vronsky had talent and, above all, education, which gives one an exalted view of art. Golenishchev's conviction of Vronsky's talent was also supported by the fact that he needed Vronsky's sympathy and praise for his articles and thoughts, and felt that praise and support ought to be mutual.

In other people's houses, and especially in Vronsky's palazzo, Mikhailov was quite a different man than he was at home in his studio. He showed an unfriendly deference, as if wary of getting close to people he did not respect. He called Vronsky 'your highness' and, despite Anna's and Vronsky's invitations, never stayed for dinner, but came only for the sittings. Anna was nicer to him than to others, and was grateful for her portrait. Vronsky was more than polite, and was obviously interested in the artist's opinion of his painting. Golenishchev never missed an opportunity to instil true notions of art into Mikhailov. But Mikhailov remained equally cold to them all. Anna felt from his eyes that he liked looking at her; but he avoided talking with her. To Vronsky's talk about his art he remained stubbornly silent, and he remained as stubbornly silent when he was shown Vronsky's picture and, obviously burdened by Golenishchev's talk, did not contradict him.

Generally, once they got to know him better, they very much disliked Mikhailov, with his reserved and unpleasant, as if hostile, attitude. And they were glad when the sittings were over, the wonderful portrait was left with them and he stopped coming.

Golenishchev was the first to voice a thought they all had – namely, that Mikhailov was simply envious of Vronsky.

'Or let's say, not envious, because he has *talent*; but it vexes him that a courtier and a wealthy man, who is also a count (they do hate all that), without much effort does the same, if not better, as he who has devoted his life to it. Above all, it's education that he lacks.'

Vronsky defended Mikhailov, but in the depths of his soul he believed it, because to his mind a man of a different, inferior world had to be envious.

Anna's portrait, the same subject painted from nature by himself and by Mikhailov, ought to have shown Vronsky the difference between himself and Mikhailov. But he did not see it. He merely stopped painting Anna's portrait after Mikhailov finished, deciding that it was now superfluous. However, he went on with his painting from medieval life. And he himself, and Golenishchev, and especially Anna, found it very good because it looked much more like famous pictures than Mikhailov's picture did.

Mikhailov, meanwhile, though he had been much taken up with the portrait of Anna, was even more glad than they were when the sittings ended and he did not have to listen to Golenishchev's talk about art any more and could forget about Vronsky's painting. He knew it was impossible to forbid Vronsky to toy with painting; he knew that he and all the dilettantes had every right to paint whatever they liked, but he found it unpleasant. It was impossible to forbid a man to make a big wax doll and kiss it. But if this man with the doll came and sat in front of a man in love and began to caress his doll the way the man in love caressed his beloved, the man in love would find it unpleasant. Mikhailov experienced the same unpleasant feeling at the sight of Vronsky's painting; he felt it ridiculous, vexing, pathetic and offensive.

Vronsky's enthusiasm for painting and the Middle Ages did not last long. He had enough taste for painting to be unable to finish his picture. The picture came to a stop. He vaguely felt that its defects, little noticeable in the beginning, would become striking if he went on. The same thing happened with him as with Golenishchev, who felt he had nothing to say and kept deceiving himself by saying that his thought had not ripened, that he was nurturing it and preparing his materials. But Golenishchev was embittered and tormented by it, while Vronsky could not deceive and torment himself, still less become embittered. With his peculiar resoluteness of character, without explaining anything or justifying himself, he ceased to occupy himself with painting.

But without this occupation his life and Anna's, who was surprised by his disappointment, seemed so boring to him in this Italian town, the palazzo suddenly became so obviously old and dirty, so unpleasant the sight of the stains on the curtains, the cracks in the floors, the chipped stucco of the cornices, and so boring became this ever-the-same Golenishchev, the Italian professor, and the German traveller, that a change of life was necessary. They decided to go to Russia, to the country. In Petersburg Vronsky intended to make a division of property with his brother, and Anna to see her son. The summer they planned to spend on Vronsky's big family estate.

XIV

Levin had been married for three months. He was happy, but not at all in the way he had expected. At every step he found disenchantment with his old dream and a new, unexpected enchantment. He was happy, but, having entered upon family life, he saw at every step that it was not what he had imagined. At every step he felt like a man who, after having admired a little boat going smoothly and happily on a lake, then got into this boat. He saw that it was not enough to sit straight without rocking; he also had to keep in mind, not forgetting for a minute, where he was going, that there was water underneath, that he had to row and his unaccustomed hands hurt, that it was easy only to look at, but doing it, while very joyful, was also very difficult.

As a bachelor, seeing the married life of others, their trifling cares, quarrels, jealousy, he used only to smile scornfully to himself. In his own future married life, he was convinced, there not only could be nothing like that, but even all its external forms, it seemed to him, were bound to be in every way completely unlike other people's lives. And suddenly, instead of that, his life with his wife did not form itself in any special way, but was, on the contrary, formed entirely of those insignificant trifles he had scorned so much before, but which now, against his will, acquired an extraordinary and irrefutable significance. And Levin saw that to arrange all those trifles was by no means as easy as it had seemed to him before. Though he had thought that he had the most precise notions of family life, he had, like all men, involuntarily pictured it to himself only as the enjoyment of love, which nothing should hinder and from which trifling cares should not detract. He was supposed, as he understood it, to do his work and to rest from it in the happiness of love. She was supposed to be loved and only that. But, like all men, he had forgotten that she also needed to work. And he was surprised at how she, this poetic, lovely Kitty, in the very first, not weeks, but days of married life, could think, remember and fuss about tablecloths, furniture, mattresses for guests, about a tray, the cook, the dinner and so on. While still her fiancé, he had been struck by the definitiveness with which she had renounced going abroad and decided to go to the country, as if she knew something necessary and, besides her love, could still think of extraneous things. This had offended him then, and now, too, her petty fussing and cares several times offended him. But he saw that she needed it. And loving her as he did, though he did not understand why, though he chuckled at those cares, he could not help admiring them. He chuckled at her arranging the furniture brought from Moscow, decorating her room and his in a new way, hanging curtains, assigning future quarters for guests, for Dolly, setting up quarters for her new maid, giving the old cook orders for dinner, getting into arguments with Agafya Mikhailovna, dismissing her from her charge of the provisions. He saw how the old cook smiled, admiring her and listening to her inexperienced, impossible orders; he saw how Agafya Mikhailovna thoughtfully and gently shook her head at the young mistress's new instructions in the pantry; he saw how extraordinarily sweet Kitty was when she came to him, laughing and crying, to tell him that the maid Masha kept treating her like a young girl and because of it no one listened to her. It seemed sweet to him but strange, and he thought it would have been better without it.

He did not know that feeling of change she was experiencing after living at home, where she would sometimes want cabbage with kvass or sweets, and could not have either, while now she could order whatever she liked, buy heaps of sweets, spend any amount of money and order any pastry she wanted.

She now dreamed joyfully of Dolly's coming with the children, especially because she was going to order each child's favourite pastry, and Dolly would appreciate all her new arrangements. She did not know why or what for, but housekeeping attracted her irresistibly. Instinctively sensing the approach of spring and knowing there would also be bad weather, she was building her nest as best she could, hastening both to build it and to learn how it was done.

This trifling preoccupation of Kitty's, so opposite to Levin's ideal of the exalted happiness of the initial period, was one of his disenchantments; yet this sweet preoccupation, the meaning of which he did not understand but which he could not help loving, was one of his new enchantments.

Their quarrels were another disenchantment and enchantment. Levin never imagined that there could be any other relations between himself and his wife than tender, respectful, loving ones, and suddenly, in the very first days, they quarrelled, and she told him he did not love her, loved only himself, wept and waved her hands.

This first quarrel occurred because Levin went to a new farmstead and came back half an hour late, having lost his way trying to take a shortcut. He was returning home thinking only of her, of her love, of his happiness, and the closer he came to home the more ardent his tenderness for her grew. He rushed into the room with the same feeling and even stronger than when he had gone to the Shcherbatskys' to propose. And suddenly he was met with a sullen expression he had never seen in her. He wanted to kiss her, but she pushed him away.

'What's the matter?'

'You're having fun . . .' she began, trying to be calmly venomous.

But she no sooner opened her mouth than reproachful words of senseless jealousy, all that had tortured her during the half hour she had spent sitting motionless at the window, burst from her. Only then did he understand clearly for the first time what he had not understood when he had led her out of the church after the wedding. He understood not only that she was close to him, but that he no longer knew where she ended and he began. He understood it by the painful feeling of being split which he experienced at that moment. He was offended at first, but in that same instant he felt that he could not be offended by her, that she was him. In the first moment he felt like a man who, having suddenly received a violent blow from behind, turns with vexation and a desire for revenge to find out who did it, and realizes that he has accidentally struck himself, that there is no one to be angry with and he must endure and ease the pain.

Never afterwards did he feel it so strongly, but this first time it took him long to recover. Natural feeling demanded that he vindicate himself, prove to her that she was wrong; but to prove that she was wrong would mean to upset her still more and make the breach that had caused all the trouble still wider. One habitual feeling urged him to shift the blame from himself to her; another, stronger one urged him quickly, as quickly as possible, to smooth over the breach and keep it from growing bigger. To remain under so unjust an accusation was tormenting, but to hurt her by vindicating himself was still worse. Like a man suffering from pain while half asleep, he wanted to tear off, to throw away the sore spot and, coming to his senses, found that the sore spot was himself. He could only try to help the sore spot to suffer through it, and that he did.

They made peace. Realizing that she was wrong, but not saying so, she became more tender towards him, and they experienced a new, redoubled happiness in their love. But that did not keep such confrontations from being repeated and even quite frequently, for the most unexpected and insignificant causes. These confrontations also often took place because they did not yet know what was important for the other and because during this initial time they were both often in bad spirits. When one was in good and the other in bad spirits, the peace was not broken, but when both happened to be in bad spirits, confrontations occurred for such incomprehensibly insignificant reasons that afterwards they were simply unable to remember what they had quarrelled over. True, when both were in good spirits, their joy of life was doubled. But all the same this initial period was a difficult time for them.

Throughout this time they sensed especially keenly the tension, the tugging to one side and the other, of the chain that bound them. Generally, that honeymoon – that is, the month following the wedding, from which, by tradition, Levin had expected so much – not only had no honey in it, but remained in both their memories as the most difficult and humiliating time of their life. They both tried equally in later life to cross out of their recollections all the ugly, shameful circumstances of that unhealthy time when they were rarely in a normal state, were rarely themselves.

Only in the third month of marriage, after their return from Moscow where they had gone for a month, did their life become smoother.

XV

They had only just come back from Moscow and were glad of their solitude. He was sitting at the desk in his study writing. She, in that dark lilac dress she had worn in the first days after their marriage and had now put on again, and which was especially memorable and dear to him, was sitting on the sofa, that same old leather sofa that had always stood in the study of Levin's father and grandfather, and doing broderie anglaise. He thought and wrote, rejoicing all the while at the feeling of her presence. He had not given up work either on the estate or on his book, which was to explain the principles of a new way of farming; but as this work and thought had once appeared small and insignificant to him compared to the darkness that covered his whole life, so now, too, they appeared unimportant and small compared to the life flooded with the bright light of happiness that lay before him. He continued his occupations, but he now felt that the centre of gravity of his attention had shifted elsewhere, and owing to that he looked at his work quite differently and more clearly. Formerly his work had been a salvation from life for him. Formerly he had felt that without it his life would have been too bleak. But now this work was necessary to him so that life would not be so uniformly bright. Taking up his papers again, rereading what he had written, he was pleased to find that the thing was worth working on. It was new and useful. Many of his former thoughts seemed superfluous and extreme, but many gaps became clear to him as he refreshed the whole thing in his memory. He was now writing a new chapter on the reasons for the unprofitable state of agriculture in Russia. He maintained that Russia's poverty came not only from an incorrect distribution of landed property and a false orientation, but had recently been contributed to by an alien civilization abnormally grafted on to Russia, particularly by the means of communication and the railways, entailing a centralization in cities, the development of luxury and, as a result of that, to the detriment of agriculture, the development of factory industry, of credit and its companion – the stock exchange. It seemed to him that when the wealth of a state develops normally, all these phenomena occur only after considerable labour has already been invested in agriculture, after it has arrived at the correct or at least at definite conditions; that the wealth of a country should grow uniformly and, in particular, so that other branches of wealth do not outstrip agriculture; that, in conformity with a given state of agriculture, there should exist corresponding means of communication, and that considering our incorrect use of the land, the railways, brought about not by economic but by political necessity, were premature and, instead of contributing to agriculture, which was what they were expected to do, had outstripped agriculture and halted it, causing the development of industry and credit, and that therefore, just as the one-sided and premature development of one organ in an animal would hinder its general development, so credit, the means of communication, the increase of factory industry – though undoubtedly necessary in Europe, where their time had come – here in Russia only harmed the general development of wealth by setting aside the main, immediate question of the organization of agriculture.

While he was doing his writing, she was thinking of how unnaturally attentive her husband had been to the young prince Charsky, who had very tactlessly bantered with her on the eve of their departure. 'He's jealous,' she thought. 'My God, how sweet and silly he is! He's jealous of me! If he only knew that they're all the same as Pyotr the cook for me,' she thought, gazing at his nape and red neck with a proprietary feeling strange to her. 'Though it's a pity to distract him from his work (but he'll have time to do it!), I must look at his face. Will he feel me looking at him? I want him to turn round . . . I want him to!' And she opened her eyes wide, wishing thereby to increase the effect of her gaze.

'Yes, they draw all the juices off to themselves and lend a false glitter,' he muttered, stopped writing and, feeling her looking at him and smiling, turned to her.

'What?' he asked, smiling and getting up.

'He turned,' she thought.

'Nothing, I just wanted you to turn to me,' she said, looking at him and trying to see whether he was annoyed that she had distracted him.

'How good it is for us here together! For me, that is,' he said, going to her and beaming with a smile of happiness.

'It's so good for me! I won't go anywhere, especially not to Moscow!'

'And what have you been thinking?'

'Me? I was thinking . . . No, no, go and write, don't get distracted,' she said, puckering her lips. 'And I've got to cut out these little holes now, see?'

She took the scissors and began to cut.

'No, tell me what,' he said, sitting down beside her and watching the circular movement of the small scissors.

'Ah, what was I thinking? I was thinking about Moscow, about the nape of your neck.'

'Precisely why have I been given such happiness? It's unnatural. Too good,' he said, kissing her hand.

'For me, on the contrary, the better it is, the more natural it seems.'

'And you've got a little strand here,' he said, carefully turning her head. 'A little strand. See, right here. No, no, we're busy with our work.'

But the work no longer went on, and they guiltily jumped away from each other when Kuzma came to announce that tea was served.

'Have they come from the city?' Levin asked Kuzma.

'They've just arrived; they're unpacking.'

'Come quickly,' she said as she left the study, 'or I'll read the letters without you. And then let's play four hands.'

Left alone, he put his notebooks into the new briefcase she had bought and began washing his hands at the new washstand with its elegant new accessories that had also appeared with her. Levin smiled at his thoughts and shook his head at them disapprovingly; he suffered from a feeling akin to remorse. There was something shameful, pampered, Capuan,[28] as he called it to himself, in his present life. 'It's not good to live like this,' he thought. 'It will soon be three months and I'm not doing anything. Today is almost the first time I seriously got down to work – and what? I no sooner started than I dropped it. Even my usual occupations – I've all but abandoned them, too. My farming – I almost don't go to look after it. I either feel sorry to leave her or see that she's bored. And here I used to think that life before marriage was just so, anyhow, didn't count, and that real life started after marriage. And it will soon be three months, and I've never spent my time so idly and uselessly. No, it's impossible. I must get started. Of course, it's not her fault. There's nothing to reproach her for. I must be firmer myself, must fence off my male independence. Or else I may get into the habit and teach it to her . . . Of course, it's not her fault,' he said to himself.

But it is hard for a discontented man not to reproach someone else, especially the very one who is closest to him, for his discontent. And it vaguely occurred to Levin, not that she was at fault (she could not be at fault for anything), but that her upbringing was at fault, was too superficial and frivolous ('that fool Charsky: I know she'd have liked to stop him, but she didn't know how'). 'Yes, besides an interest in the house (that she does have), besides her clothes and her broderie anglaise, she has no serious interests. No interest in my work, in farming, in the muzhiks, nor in music, which she's quite good at, nor in reading. She's not doing anything and is quite content.' In his soul Levin disapproved of that and did not yet understand that she was preparing for the period of activity which was to come for her, when she would be at one and the same time the wife of her husband, the mistress of the house, and would bear, nurse and raise her children. He did not understand that she knew it intuitively and, while preparing for this awesome task, did not reproach herself for the moments of insouciance and the happiness of love that she enjoyed now, while cheerfully building her future nest.

XVI

When Levin came upstairs, his wife was sitting at the new silver samovar by the new tea set and, having seated old Agafya Mikhailovna before a full cup of tea, was reading a letter from Dolly, with whom she was in constant and frequent correspondence.

'See, your lady seated me, she told me to sit with her,' Agafya Mikhailovna said, smiling amiably at Kitty.

In these words of Agafya Mikhailovna Levin read the denouement of the drama that had been going on lately between Agafya Mikhailovna and Kitty. He saw that despite all the grief caused Agafya Mikhailovna by the new mistress, who had taken the reins of government from her, Kitty had still prevailed and made the old woman love her.

'See, I also read your letter,' said Kitty, handing him an illiterate letter. 'It's from that woman, I think, your brother's . . .' she said. 'I didn't really read it. And this is from my family and from Dolly. Imagine! Dolly took Grisha and Tanya to a children's ball at the Sarmatskys'. Tanya was a marquise.'

But Levin was not listening to her. Flushing, he took the letter from Marya Nikolaevna, his brother Nikolai's former mistress, and started to read it. This was now the second letter from Marya Nikolaevna. In the first letter she had written that his brother had driven her out through no fault of her own, and had added with touching naïvety that though she was again destitute, she did not ask or wish for anything, only that the thought of Nikolai Dmitrich perishing without her on account of the weakness of his health was killing her, and she asked his brother to look after him. Now she wrote something else. She had found Nikolai Dmitrich, had been with him again in Moscow, and had gone with him to a provincial capital where he had been given a post. But he had quarrelled with his superior there and was returning to Moscow, only on the way had become so ill that it was unlikely he would ever get back on his feet – so she wrote. 'He keeps mentioning you, and we also have no more money.'

'Read it, Dolly writes about you,' Kitty began, smiling, but suddenly stopped, noticing the changed expression of her husband's face.

'What's the matter? What is it?'

'She writes that my brother Nikolai is dying. I'll go.'

Kitty's countenance suddenly changed. Her thoughts about Tanya as a marquise, about Dolly, all vanished.

'When will you go?' she said.

'Tomorrow.'

'And I'll go with you, may I?' she said.

'Kitty! What on earth?' he said in reproach.

'Why not?' she said, offended that he seemed to take her suggestion reluctantly and vexedly. 'Why shouldn't I go? I won't bother you. I . . .'

'I'm going because my brother is dying,' said Levin. 'Why should you . . .'

'Why? For the same reason as you.'

'At such an important moment for me,' thought Levin, 'she thinks only about being bored by herself.' And that pretext in such an important matter made him angry.

'It's impossible,' he said sternly.

Agafya Mikhailovna, seeing that things were heading for a quarrel, quietly put down her cup and left. Kitty did not even notice her. The tone in which her husband had spoken the last words offended her, especially since he obviously did not believe what she had said.

'And I tell you that if you go, I'll go with you, I'll certainly go,' she said hastily and wrathfully. 'Why is it impossible? Why do you say it's impossible?'

'Because to go God knows where, on what roads, with what inns . . . You'd be a hindrance to me,' said Levin, trying to preserve his equanimity.

'Not in the least. I don't need anything. Where you can be, I, too . . .'

'Well, if only because this woman will be there, with whom you cannot associate.'

'I do not know or wish to know anything about who or what is there. I know that my husband's brother is dying, and that my husband is going to him, and I am going with my husband, so that . . .'

'Kitty! Don't be angry. But just think, this is such an important matter that it pains me to think you're mixing it up with a feeling of weakness, a reluctance to stay by yourself. Well, if it's boring for you to be alone, then go to Moscow.'

'There, you *always* ascribe bad, mean thoughts to me,' she began, with tears of offence and anger. 'It's nothing to do with me, no weakness, nothing . . . I feel it's my duty to be with my husband when my husband is in distress, and you purposely want to hurt me, you purposely don't want to understand . . .'

'No, this is terrible. To be some sort of slave!' Levin cried out, standing up and no longer able to hold back his vexation. But in the same instant he felt that he was striking himself.

'Why did you get married, then? You could be free. Why, if you regret it now?' she said, jumped up and ran to the drawing room.

When he went to her there, she was sobbing.

He began talking, wishing to find words that might not so much dissuade her as merely calm her down. But she would not listen and would not agree with anything. He bent down and took her resisting hand. He kissed her hand, kissed her hair, kissed her hand again – she kept silent. But when he took her face in both his hands and said 'Kitty!' she suddenly recovered herself, wept a little more and made peace.

It was decided that they would go together the next day. Levin told his wife that he believed she wanted to go only in order to be of use, agreed that Marya Nikolaevna's presence at his brother's side did not present any impropriety; but in the depths of his soul he went away displeased with her and with himself. He was displeased with her for being unable to bring herself to let him go when it was necessary (and how strange it was for him to think that he, who so recently had not dared to believe in the happiness of her loving him, now felt unhappy because she loved him too much!), and displeased with himself for not standing firm. Still less did he agree in the depths of his soul that she was not concerned about the woman who was with his brother, and he thought with horror of all the confrontations that might occur. The fact alone that his wife, his Kitty, would be in the same room with a slut already made him shudder with revulsion and horror.

XVII

The hotel in the provincial capital where Nikolai Levin lay was one of those provincial hotels that are set up in accordance with new, improved standards, with the best intentions of cleanliness, comfort and even elegance, but which, because of their clients, turn extremely quickly into dirty pot-houses with a pretence to modern improvements, and by that very pretence become still worse than the old hotels that were simply dirty. This hotel had already reached that state; the soldier in a dirty uniform, smoking a cigarette at the entrance, who was supposed to represent the doorman, the gloomy and unpleasant wrought-iron stairway, the casual waiter in a dirty tailcoat, the common room with a dusty bouquet of wax flowers adorning the table, the dirt, dust and slovenliness everywhere in the hotel, and with that some sort of new, modern-railwayish, smug preoccupation – gave the Levins, after their newlywed life, a most painful feeling, especially as the false impression made by the hotel could not be reconciled with what awaited them.

As always, after the question of how much they wanted to pay for a room, it turned out that there were no good rooms: one of the good rooms was occupied by a railway inspector, another by a lawyer from Moscow, and the third by Princess Astafyev coming from her estate. There remained one dirty room, with an adjacent room which they were told would be vacated by evening. Vexed with his wife because what he had anticipated was coming true – namely, that at the moment of arrival, when his heart was seized with agitation at the thought of his brother, he had to be concerned with her instead of running to him at once – Levin brought her to the room they had been given.

'Go, go!' she said, giving him a timid, guilty look.

He silently went out the door and straight away ran into Marya Nikolaevna, who had learned of his arrival and had not dared to enter his room. She was exactly the same as he had seen her in Moscow: the same woollen dress with no collar or cuffs, the same kindly, dull, pockmarked face, grown slightly fuller.

'Well, what? How is he?'

'Very bad. Bedridden. He's been waiting for you. He . . . Are you . . . with your wife?'

Levin did not understand at first what made her embarrassed, but she explained it to him at once.

'I'll leave, I'll go to the kitchen,' she managed to say. 'He'll be glad. He's heard, and he knows her and remembers her from abroad.'

Levin understood that she meant his wife and did not know what to answer.

'Let's go, let's go!' he said.

But just as he started off, the door of his room opened and Kitty peeked out. Levin flushed from shame and vexation with his wife for putting herself and him in this painful situation; but Marya Nikolaevna flushed even more. She shrank all over and flushed to the point of tears, and, seizing the ends of her kerchief with both hands, twisted them in her red fingers, not knowing what to say or do.

For the first moment Levin saw an expression of eager curiosity in the look Kitty gave this, for her, incomprehensible and terrible woman; but it lasted only an instant.

'Well? How is he?' she turned to her husband and then to her.

'We really can't start talking in the corridor!' Levin said, turning crossly to look at a gentleman who, as if on his own business, was just then walking down the corridor with a jerky gait.

'Well, come in then,' said Kitty, addressing Marya Nikolaevna, who had now recovered; but she added, noticing her husband's frightened face, 'or else go, go and send for me later,' and returned to the room. Levin went to his brother.

He had in no way expected what he saw and felt there. He had expected to find the same state of self-deception that, he had heard, occurs so often with consumptives and that had struck him so strongly during his brother's visit in the autumn. He had expected to find the physical signs of approaching death more definite – greater weakness, greater emaciation – but still almost the same condition. He had expected that he himself would experience the same feeling of pity at losing his beloved brother and of horror in the face of death that he had experienced then, only to a greater degree. And he had been preparing himself for that; but he found something else entirely.

In a small, dirty room, with bespattered painted panels on the walls, divided by a thin partition behind which voices could be heard, in an atmosphere pervaded with a stifling smell of excrement, on a bed moved away from the wall, lay a blanket-covered body. One arm of this body lay on top of the blanket, and an enormous, rake-like hand was in some incomprehensible way attached to the long arm-bone, thin and straight from wrist to elbow. The head lay sideways on the pillow. Levin could see the sweaty, thin hair on the temples and the taut, as if transparent, forehead.

'It cannot be that this terrible body is my brother Nikolai,' Levin thought. But he came nearer, saw the face, and doubt was no longer possible. Despite the terrible change in the face, Levin had only to look into those living eyes raised to him as he entered, notice the slight movement of the mouth under the matted moustache, to realize the terrible truth, that this dead body was his living brother.

The shining eyes looked sternly and reproachfully at the brother coming in. And that look at once established a living relation between the living. Levin at once felt the reproach in the glance directed at him and remorse for his own happiness.

When Konstantin took his hand, Nikolai smiled. The smile was faint, barely perceptible, and, in spite of it, the stern expression of the eyes did not change.

'You didn't expect to find me like this,' he brought out with difficulty.

'Yes . . . no,' said Levin, stumbling over his words. 'Why didn't you let me know earlier, I mean back at the time of my wedding? I made inquiries everywhere.'

He had to speak so as not to be silent, but he did not know what to say, especially as his brother did not respond but only stared without taking his eyes off him, apparently trying to grasp the meaning of each word. Levin told his brother that his wife had come with him. Nikolai expressed satisfaction but said he was afraid to frighten her by his condition. A silence followed. Suddenly Nikolai stirred and began to say something. From the expression of his face, Levin expected something especially meaningful and important, but Nikolai spoke of his health. He accused the doctor, regretted that the famous Moscow doctor was not there, and Levin realized that he still had hope.

Profiting from the first moment of silence, Levin stood up, wishing to get rid of the painful feeling at least for a moment, and said he would go and bring his wife.

'Very well, and I'll have things cleaned up here. It's dirty here and I suppose it stinks. Masha, tidy up here!' the sick man said with difficulty. 'And once you've finished, go away,' he added, looking questioningly at his brother.

Levin made no reply. He went out to the corridor and stopped. He had said he would bring his wife, but now, aware of the feeling he had experienced, he decided, on the contrary, to try to persuade her not to go to see the sick man. 'Why should she suffer as I do?' he thought.

'Well, how is he?' Kitty asked with a frightened face.

'Ah, it's terrible, terrible! Why did you come?' said Levin.

Kitty was silent for a few seconds, looking timidly and pityingly at her husband; then she went up to him and took him by the elbow with both hands.

'Kostya, take me to him, it will be easier with two of us. Just take me there, take me, please, and leave,' she began. 'You must understand that for me to see you and not see him is much harder. There I might perhaps be of use to you and to him. Please, let me!' she implored her husband, as if the happiness of her life depended on it.

Levin had to consent, and, recovering himself and forgetting all about Marya Nikolaevna, he went back to his brother with Kitty.

With a light tread, glancing constantly at her husband and showing him a brave and compassionate face, she went into the sick man's room and, turning without haste, noiselessly closed the door behind her. With inaudible steps she quickly approached the sick man's bed, and, placing herself so that he would not have to turn his head, at once took in her fresh, young hand the skeleton of his enormous hand, pressed it, and began talking to him with that unoffending and sympathetic animation peculiar only to women.

'We met at Soden but didn't become acquainted,' she said. 'You never thought I'd be your sister.'

'Would you have recognized me?' he said, lighting up with a smile as she came in.

'Yes, I would. You were so right to let us know! There wasn't a day when Kostya didn't remember you and worry about you.'

But the sick man's animation did not last long.

Before she finished speaking, his face became set again in the stern, reproachful expression of a dying man's envy of the living.

'I'm afraid it's not very nice for you here,' she said, turning away from his intent gaze and looking round the room. 'We must ask the innkeeper for a different room,' she said to her husband, 'and also for us to be closer.'

XVIII

Levin could not look calmly at his brother, could not be natural and calm in his presence. When he entered the sick man's room, his eyes and attention would unconsciously become veiled, and he did not see or distinguish the details of his brother's condition. He smelled the terrible stench, saw the filth, the disorder, and the painful posture and groaning, and felt that it was impossible to be of help. It did not even occur to him to look into the details of the sick man's state, to think of how this body lay there under the blanket, how the emaciated shins, legs, back lay bent there and whether they could not be laid out better, to do something, if not to improve things, at least to make them less bad. A chill went down his spine when he began to think of these details. He was certain beyond doubt that nothing could be done to prolong his life or alleviate his suffering. But the sick man sensed his awareness that he considered all help impossible and was annoyed by it. And that made it still harder for Levin. To be in the sick-room was torture for him, not to be there was still worse. And, on various pretexts, he kept going out and coming back again, unable to stay alone.

But Kitty thought, felt and acted quite differently. At the sight of the sick man, she felt pity for him. And pity in her woman's soul produced none of the horror and squeamishness it did in her husband, but a need to act, to find out all the details of his condition and help with them. As she did not have the slightest doubt that she had to help him, so she had no doubt that it was possible, and she got down to work at once. Those same details, the mere thought of which horrified her husband, at once attracted her attention. She sent for the doctor, sent to the pharmacy, ordered Marya Nikolaevna and the maid who had come with her to sweep, dust, scrub, washed and rinsed something herself, put something under the blanket. On her orders things were brought in and carried out of the sick man's room. She went to her room several times, paying no attention to the passing gentlemen she met, to fetch and bring sheets, pillowcases, towels, shirts.

The waiter, who was serving dinner to some engineers in the common room, several times came at her call with an angry face, but could not help carrying out her orders, because she gave them with such gentle insistence that it was simply impossible to walk away from her. Levin disapproved of it all; he did not believe it could be of any use to the sick man. Most of all he feared that his brother would get angry. But, though he seemed indifferent, he did not get angry but only embarrassed, and generally appeared interested in what she was doing to him. Coming back from the doctor, to whom Kitty had sent him, Levin opened the door and found the sick man at the moment when, on Kitty's orders, his underwear was being changed. The long, white frame of his back, with enormous protruding shoulder blades, the ribs and vertebrae sticking out, was bare, and Marya Nikolaevna and the waiter had got tangled in a shirt sleeve, unable to put the long, dangling arm into it. Kitty, who hastily closed the door behind Levin, was not looking in that direction; but the sick man moaned and she quickly went to him.

'Hurry up,' she said.

'Don't come here,' the sick man said crossly, 'I myself . . .'

'What's that?' Marya Nikolaevna asked.

But Kitty heard and understood that he found it embarrassing and unpleasant to be naked in front of her.

'I'm not looking, I'm not looking!' she said, putting the arm right. 'Marya Nikolaevna, go around to the other side and put it right,' she added.

'Go, please, there's a vial in my small bag,' she turned to her husband, 'you know, in the side pocket. Bring it, please, while they straighten everything up here.'

When he returned with the vial, Levin found the sick man lying down and everything around him completely changed. The heavy smell was replaced by the smell of vinegar and scent, which Kitty, her lips pursed and her red cheeks puffed out, was spraying through a little pipe. No dust could be seen anywhere; there was a rug beside the bed. Vials and a carafe stood neatly on the table, where the necessary linen lay folded, along with Kitty's broderie anglaise. On the other table, by the sick-bed, were drink, a candle and powders. The sick man himself, washed and combed, lay on clean sheets, on high-propped pillows, in a clean shirt, its white collar encircling his unnaturally thin neck, and looked at Kitty, not taking his eyes off her, with a new expression of hope.

The doctor brought by Levin, who had found him at his club, was not the one who had treated Nikolai Levin and with whom he was displeased. The new doctor took out a little tube and listened to the patient's chest, shook his head, wrote a prescription, and explained with particular thoroughness, first, how to take the medicine, then what diet to observe. He advised eggs, raw or slightly boiled, and seltzer water with fresh milk at a certain temperature. When the doctor left, the sick man said something to his brother; but Levin heard only the last words: 'your Katia', and by the look he gave her, Levin understood that he was praising her. He beckoned to Katia, as he called her, to come over.

'I'm much better already,' he said. 'With you I'd have recovered long ago. How nice!' He took her hand and drew it towards his lips, but, as if fearing it would be unpleasant for her, changed his mind, let go and only stroked it. Kitty took his hand in both of hers and pressed it.

'Now turn me on my left side and go to bed,' he said.

No one made out what he said, only Kitty understood him. She understood, because her thought constantly followed what he needed.

'On the other side,' she said to her husband, 'he always sleeps on that side. Turn him, it's unpleasant to call the servants. I can't do it. Can you?' she turned to Marya Nikolaevna.

'I'm scared,' answered Marya Nikolaevna.

Frightening as it was for Levin to put his arms around that frightening body, to hold those places under the blanket that he did not want to know about, he yielded to his wife's influence, made the resolute face she knew so well, put his arms under the blanket and took hold of him, but, in spite of his strength, he was amazed at the strange heaviness of those wasted limbs. As he turned him over, feeling an enormous, emaciated arm around his neck, Kitty quickly, inaudibly, turned the pillow over, plumped it up, and straightened the sick man's head and his thin hair, again stuck to his temple.

The sick man kept his brother's hand in his own. Levin felt that he wanted to do something with his hand and was drawing it somewhere. Levin yielded with a sinking heart. Yes, he drew it to his mouth and kissed it. Levin shook with sobs and, unable to get a word out, left the room.

XIX

'Hidden from the wise and revealed unto babes and the imprudent.'[29] So Levin thought about his wife as he talked with her that evening.

Levin was thinking of the Gospel saying not because he considered himself wise. He did not consider himself wise, but he could not help knowing that he was more intelligent than his wife or Agafya Mikhailovna, and he could not help knowing that when he thought about death, he thought about it with all the forces of his soul. He also knew that many great masculine minds, whose thoughts about it he had read, had pondered death and yet did not know a hundredth part of what his wife and Agafya Mikhailovna knew about it. Different as these two women were – Agafya Mikhailovna and Katia, as his brother Nikolai called her and as Levin now especially liked to call her – they were perfectly alike in this. Both unquestionably knew what life was and what death was, and though they would have been unable to answer and would not even have understood the questions that presented themselves to Levin, neither had any doubt about the meaning of this phenomenon and looked at it in exactly the same way, not only between themselves, but sharing this view with millions of other people. The proof that they knew firmly what death was lay in their knowing, without a moment's doubt, how to act with dying people and not being afraid of them. While Levin and others, though they could say a lot about death, obviously did not know, because they were afraid of death and certainly had no idea what needed to be done when people were dying. If Levin had been alone now with his brother Nikolai, he would have looked at him with horror, and would have waited with still greater horror, unable to do anything else.

Not only that, but he did not know what to say, how to look, how to walk. To speak of unrelated things seemed to him offensive, impossible; to speak of death, of dark things – also impossible. To be silent – also impossible. 'If I look, I'm afraid he'll think I'm studying him; if I don't look, he'll think I'm thinking of something else. If I walk on tiptoe, he'll be displeased; if I stomp around, it's embarrassing.' But Kitty obviously did not think about herself and had no time to; she thought about him, because she knew something, and it all turned out well. She told him about herself and about her wedding, and smiled, and pitied, and caressed him, and spoke of cases of recovery, and it all turned out well;

which meant that she knew. The proof that what she and Agafya Mikhailovna did was not instinctive, animal, unreasoning, was that, besides physical care, the alleviation of suffering, both Agafya Mikhailovna and Kitty demanded something more important for the dying man, something that had nothing in common with physical conditions. Agafya Mikhailovna, speaking of an old man who had died, said: 'Well, thank God, he took communion, got anointed, God grant everybody such a death.' In the same way Katia, besides all her cares about linen, bedsores, drink, persuaded the sick man on the very first day of the need to take communion and be anointed.

When he left the sick man and went to his own rooms for the night, Levin sat, his head bowed, not knowing what to do. Not to mention having supper, settling for the night, thinking about what they were going to do, he could not even speak to his wife: he was abashed. But Kitty, on the contrary, was more active than usual. She was even more animated than usual. She ordered supper, unpacked their things herself, helped to make the beds, and did not forget to sprinkle them with Persian powder. She had in her that excitement and quickness of judgement that appear in men before a battle, a struggle, in dangerous and decisive moments of life, those moments when once and for all a man shows his worth and that his whole past has not been in vain but has been a preparation for those moments.

Everything she did went well, and it was not yet midnight when all the things were unpacked, cleanly and neatly, somehow specially, so that the room began to resemble her home, her rooms: beds made, brushes, combs, mirrors laid out, doilies spread.

Levin found it inexcusable even now to eat, sleep, talk, and felt that his every movement was improper. Yet she was sorting her brushes, doing it in such a way that there was no offence in it.

They could not eat anything anyway, and for a long time they could not fall asleep; it was even a long time before they went to bed.

'I'm very glad I persuaded him to be anointed tomorrow,' she said, sitting in a dressing jacket before her folding mirror and combing her soft, fragrant hair with a fine comb. 'I've never seen it done, but mama told me all the prayers are about healing.'

'Do you really think he can get well?' Levin said, looking at the narrow parting at the back of her round little head, which kept closing the moment she drew her comb forward.

'I asked the doctor: he says he can't live more than three days. But can they really know? All the same, I'm very glad I persuaded him,' she said, looking sideways at her husband from behind her hair. 'Anything can happen,' she added, with the special, somewhat sly expression she usually had on her face when she talked about religion.

Since their conversation about religion while they were still engaged, neither he nor she had ever started speaking of it, but she always observed her rituals of going to church and saying her prayers with the same calm awareness that it was necessary. Despite his assurances to the contrary, she was firmly convinced that he was as good a Christian as she was, or even better, and that everything he said about it was one of those ridiculous male quirks, like what he said about broderie anglaise: that good people mend holes, while she cut them on purpose, and so on.

'Yes, that woman, Marya Nikolaevna, couldn't have arranged it all,' said Levin. 'And . . . I must admit that I'm very, very glad you came. You're such purity that . . .' He took her hand and did not kiss it (to kiss that hand in this presence of death seemed improper to him) but only pressed it with a guilty air, looking into her brightened eyes.

'It would be so painful for you alone,' she said, and raising her arms high so that they hid her cheeks, blushing from pleasure, she twisted her braids on the back of her head and pinned them up. 'No,' she went on, 'she didn't know . . . Fortunately, I learned a lot in Soden.'

'Can there have been such sick people there?'

'Worse.'

'For me the terrible thing is that I can't help seeing him as he was when he was young . . . You can't imagine what a lovely youth he was, but I didn't understand him then.'

'I believe it very, very much. I do feel that I *would have been* friends with him,' she said, and became frightened at what she had said, turned to look at her husband, and tears came to her eyes.

'Yes, *would have been*,' he said sadly. 'He's precisely one of those people of whom they say that they're not meant for this world.'

'However, we've got many days ahead of us, it's time for bed,' said Kitty, looking at her tiny watch.

XX

DEATH

The next day the sick man took communion and was anointed. During the rite, Nikolai Levin prayed fervently. His big eyes, directed at an icon set on a card table covered with a flowery napkin, expressed such passionate entreaty and hope that Levin was terrified to look at them. Levin knew that this passionate entreaty and hope would make it still harder for him to part with life, which he loved so much. Levin knew his brother and the train of his thought; he knew that his unbelief had come not because it was easier for him to live without faith, but because his beliefs had been supplanted step by step by modern scientific explanations of the phenomena of the world, and therefore he knew that his present return was not legitimate, accomplished by way of the same thinking, but was only temporary, self-interested, done in the mad hope of recovery. Levin also knew that Kitty had strengthened that hope by accounts of extraordinary healings she had heard of. Levin knew all that, and it was tormentingly painful for him to look at those pleading eyes filled with hope, that emaciated hand rising with difficulty to make the sign of the cross on the taut skin of the forehead, at the protruding shoulders and the gurgling, empty chest that could no longer contain the life that the sick man was asking for. During the sacrament Levin also prayed and did what he, as an unbeliever, had done a thousand times. He said, addressing God: 'If You exist, make it so that this man is healed (for that very thing has been repeated many times), and You will save him and me.'

After the anointing the sick man suddenly felt much better. He did not cough even once for a whole hour, smiled, kissed Kitty's hand, thanking her tearfully, saying that he was well, that there was no pain anywhere and that he felt appetite and strength. He even sat up by himself when soup was brought for him and also asked for a cutlet. Hopeless as he was, obvious as it was from one look at him that he could not recover, during this hour Levin and Kitty shared the same excitement, happy yet fearful of being mistaken.

'He's better.' 'Yes, much.' 'Amazing.' 'Not amazing at all.' 'He's better, anyhow,' they said in a whisper, smiling at each other.

This illusion did not last long. The sick man fell peacefully asleep, but half an hour later was awakened by coughing. And suddenly all hope vanished in those around him and in himself. The actuality of suffering destroyed it without question, along with all memory of former hopes, in Levin, in Kitty and in the sick man himself.

Not even mentioning what he had believed half an hour earlier, as if it were embarrassing even to remember it, he asked to be given iodine for inhalation in a vial covered with perforated paper. Levin handed him the jar, and the same look of passionate hope with which he had been anointed was now directed at his brother, demanding that he confirm the doctor's words that inhaling iodine worked miracles.

'Katia's not here?' he croaked, looking around, when Levin had reluctantly repeated the doctor's words. 'Well, then I can say it . . . I performed that comedy for her. She's so sweet, but it's impossible for you and me to deceive ourselves. This is what I believe in,' he said, and, clutching the vial with his bony hand, he began breathing over it.

Between seven and eight in the evening Levin and his wife were having tea in their room when Marya Nikolaevna, out of breath, came running to them. She was pale, her lips were trembling.

'He's dying!' she whispered. 'I'm afraid he'll die any minute.'

They both ran to him. He had got up and was sitting on the bed, propped on his elbows, his long back bent and his head hanging low.

'What do you feel?' Levin asked in a whisper, after some silence.

'I feel I'm going,' Nikolai said with difficulty, but with extreme certainty, slowly squeezing the words out. He did not raise his head but only looked upwards, his gaze not reaching his brother's face. 'Katia, go away!' he also said.

Levin jumped up and in a peremptory whisper made her leave.

'I'm going,' he said again.

'Why do you think so?' said Levin, just to say something.

'Because I'm going,' he repeated, as if he liked the expression. 'It's the end.'

Marya Nikolaevna went up to him.

'Lie down, you'll feel better,' she said.

'I'll soon lie still,' he said. 'Dead,' he added jeeringly and angrily. 'Well, lay me down if you like.'

Levin laid his brother on his back, sat down beside him and with bated breath looked at his face. The dying man lay with his eyes closed, but on his forehead the muscles twitched from time to time, as with a man who is thinking deeply and intensely. Levin involuntarily thought with him about what was now being accomplished in him, but, despite all his mental efforts to go with him, he saw from the expression of that calm, stern face and the play of a muscle over one eyebrow, that for the dying man something was becoming increasingly clearer which for him remained as dark as ever.

'Yes, yes, it's so,' the dying man said slowly, distinctly. 'Wait.' Again he was silent. 'So!' he suddenly drew out peacefully, as if everything had been resolved for him. 'Oh Lord!' he said and sighed heavily.

Marya Nikolaevna felt his feet.

'Getting cold,' she whispered.

For a long time, a very long time, it seemed to Levin, the sick man lay motionless. But he was still alive and sighed now and then. Levin was weary now from mental effort. He felt that in spite of it all, he could not understand what was *so*. He felt that he lagged far behind the dying man. He could no longer think about the question of death itself, but thoughts came to him inadvertently of what he was to do now, presently: close his eyes, dress him, order the coffin. And, strangely, he felt completely cold and experienced neither grief, nor loss, nor still less pity for his brother. If he had any feeling for him now, it was rather envy of the knowledge that the dying man now had but that he could not have.

He sat over him like that for a long time waiting for the end. But the end did not come. The door opened and Kitty appeared. Levin stood up to stop her. But as he stood up, he heard the dead man stir.

'Don't go,' said Nikolai, and reached out his hand. Levin gave him his own and angrily waved at his wife to go away.

With the dead man's hand in his, he sat for half an hour, an hour, another hour. Now he was no longer thinking about death at all. He was thinking about what Kitty was doing, and who lived in the next room, and whether the doctor had his own house. He wanted to eat and sleep. He carefully freed his hand and felt the sick man's feet. The feet were cold, but the sick man was breathing. Levin was again about to leave on tiptoe, but the sick man stirred and said:

'Don't go.'

Day broke; the sick man's condition was the same. Levin, quietly freeing his hand, not looking at the dying man, went to his room and fell asleep. When he woke up, instead of the news of his brother's death that he had expected, he learned that the sick man had reverted to his earlier condition. He again began to sit up, to cough, began to eat again, to talk, and again stopped talking about death, again began to express hope for recovery and became still more irritable and gloomy than before. No one, neither his brother nor Kitty, could comfort him. He was angry with everyone and said unpleasant things to everyone, reproached everyone for his suffering and demanded that a famous doctor be brought to him from Moscow. To all questions about how he felt, he replied uniformly with an expression of spite and reproach:

'I'm suffering terribly, unbearably!'

The sick man suffered more and more, especially from bedsores, which would no longer heal over, and was more and more angry with those around him, reproaching them for everything, especially for not bringing him a doctor from Moscow. Kitty tried her best to help him, to comfort him; but it was all in vain, and Levin could see that she herself was physically and morally exhausted, though she would not admit it. That sense of death evoked in them all by his farewell to life on the night he summoned his brother was destroyed. They all knew he would die inevitably and soon, that he was already half dead. They all desired only one thing – that he die as soon as possible – yet, concealing it, they gave him medicine from vials, went looking for medicines and doctors, and deceived him, and themselves, and each other. All this was a lie, a foul, insulting and blasphemous lie. And Levin, by a peculiarity of his character, and because he loved the dying man more than anyone else did, felt this lie especially painfully.

Levin, who had long been occupied with the thought of reconciling his brothers, if only in the face of death, had written to his brother Sergei Ivanovich and, having received a reply from him, read this letter to the sick man. Sergei Ivanovich wrote that he could not come himself, but in moving words asked his brother's forgiveness.

The sick man said nothing.

'What shall I write to him?' asked Levin. 'You're not angry with him, I hope?'

'No, not in the least!' Nikolai replied vexedly to this question. 'Write to him to send me a doctor.'

Three more days of torment went by; the sick man was in the same condition. A desire for his death was now felt by everyone who saw him: the servants in the hotel, its proprietor, all the lodgers, the doctor, Marya Nikolaevna, and Levin and Kitty. The sick man alone did not express this feeling, but, on the contrary, was angry that the doctor had not been brought, went on taking medicine and talked about life. Only in rare moments, when the opium made him momentarily forget his incessant suffering, did he sometimes say in half sleep what was stronger in his soul that in anyone else's: 'Ah, if only this were the end!' Or: 'When will it end!'

Suffering, steadily increasing, did its part in preparing him for death. There was no position in which he did not suffer, no moment when he was oblivious, no part or limb of his body that did not hurt, that did not torment him. Even this body's memories, impressions and thoughts now evoked in him the same revulsion as the body itself. The sight of other people, their conversation, his own memories – all this was sheer torment to him. Those around him felt it and unconsciously forbade themselves any free movement, conversation, expression of their wishes. His whole life merged into one feeling of suffering and the wish to be rid of it.

A turnabout was obviously taking place that was to make him look at death as the satisfaction of his desires, as happiness. Formerly each separate desire caused by suffering or privation, such as hunger, fatigue, thirst, had been satisfied by a bodily function that gave pleasure; but now privation and suffering received no satisfaction, and the attempt at satisfaction caused new suffering. And therefore all his desires merged into one – the desire to be rid of all sufferings and their source, the body. But he had no words to express this desire for liberation, and therefore did not speak of it, but out of habit demanded the satisfaction of desires that could no longer be fulfilled. 'Turn me on the other side,' he would say, and immediately afterwards would demand to be turned back as before. 'Give me some bouillon. Take the bouillon away. Say something, don't all be silent!' And as soon as they began talking, he would close his eyes and show fatigue, indifference and disgust.

On the tenth day after their arrival in the town, Kitty fell ill. She had a headache, vomited and could not leave her bed the whole morning.

The doctor explained that the illness came from fatigue and worry, and prescribed inner peace.

After dinner, however, Kitty got up and, bringing her handwork, went to the sick man as usual. He gave her a stern look when she came in, and smiled contemptuously when she said she had been ill. That day he blew his nose incessantly and moaned pitifully.

'How do you feel?' she asked him.

'Worse,' he said with difficulty. 'It hurts!'

'Where does it hurt?'

'Everywhere.'

'It will end today, you'll see,' Marya Nikolaevna said in a whisper, but loudly enough for the sick man, whose hearing, as Levin had noticed, was very keen, to hear her. Levin shushed her and looked at his brother. Nikolai had heard, but the words made no impression on him. He had the same tense and reproachful look.

'Why do you think so?' Levin asked when she followed him out to the corridor.

'He's begun plucking at himself,' said Marya Nikolaevna.

'How, plucking?'

'Like this,' she said, pulling down the folds of her woollen dress. Indeed, he had noticed that the sick man had been clutching at himself all that day, as if wanting to pull something off.

Marya Nikolaevna's prediction proved correct. By nightfall Nikolai was already too weak to raise his arms and only looked straight ahead without changing the intently concentrated expression of his gaze. Even when his brother or Kitty leaned over him so that he could see them, his look was the same. Kitty sent for a priest to read the prayers for the dying.

While the priest was reading the prayers, the dying man showed no signs of life; his eyes were closed. Levin, Kitty and Marya Nikolaevna stood by the bed. Before the priest finished reading, the dying man stretched out, sighed and opened his eyes. The priest finished the prayers, put the cross to the cold forehead, then slowly wrapped it in his stole and, after standing silently a minute or two longer, he touched the enormous, cold and bloodless hand.

'It is ended,' said the priest, and he was about to step aside; but suddenly the dead man's matted moustache stirred and clearly in the silence there came from the depths of his chest the sharply distinct sounds:

'Not quite . . . Soon.'

And a moment later his face brightened, a smile showed under the moustache, and the assembled women began to busy themselves with laying out the deceased.

The sight of his brother and the proximity of death renewed in Levin's soul that feeling of horror at the inscrutability and, with that, the nearness and inevitability of death, which had seized him on that autumn evening when his brother had come for a visit. The feeling was now stronger than before; he felt even less capable than before of understanding the meaning of death, and its inevitability appeared still more horrible to him; but now, thanks to his wife's nearness, the feeling did not drive him to despair: in spite of death, he felt the necessity to live and to love. He felt that love saved him from despair and that under the threat of despair this love was becoming still stronger and purer.

No sooner had the one mystery of death been accomplished before his eyes, and gone unfathomed, than another arose, equally unfathomed, which called to love and life.

The doctor confirmed his own surmise about Kitty. Her illness was pregnancy.

XXI

From the moment when Alexei Alexandrovich understood from his talks with Betsy and Stepan Arkadyich that only one thing was required of him, that he leave his wife alone and not bother her with his presence, and that his wife herself wished it, he felt so lost that he could decide nothing by himself, not knowing what he wanted now, and, giving himself into the hands of those who took such pleasure in looking after his affairs, he agreed to everything. Only when Anna had already left his house and the English governess had sent to ask him if she was to dine with him or separately did he understand his situation clearly for the first time, and it horrified him.

The most difficult thing in that situation was that he simply could not connect and reconcile his past with what there was now. It was not the past when he had lived happily with his wife that puzzled him. He had already suffered through the transition from that past to the knowledge of his wife's unfaithfulness; that state had been painful but comprehensible to him. If his wife, declaring her unfaithfulness, had then left him, he would have been grieved, unhappy, but he would not have been in this hopeless, incomprehensible situation which he now felt himself to be in. He simply could not reconcile his recent forgiveness, his tenderness, his love for his sick wife and another man's child, with what there was now – that is, when he, as if in reward for it all, found himself alone, disgraced, derided, needed by none and despised by all.

For the first two days after his wife's departure, Alexei Alexandrovich received petitioners, his office manager, went to the committee, and came out to eat in the dining room as usual. Without realizing why he was doing it, he strained all his inner forces during those two days merely to look calm and even indifferent. In response to questions about what to do with Anna Arkadyevna's rooms and belongings, he made great efforts to give himself the look of a man for whom what had happened had not been unforeseen and had nothing extraordinary about it, and he achieved his goal: no one could notice any signs of despair in him. But on the third day after her departure, when Kornei handed him a bill from a fashion shop that Anna had forgotten to pay, and reported that the shop assistant was there himself, Alexei Alexandrovich ordered the assistant to be shown in.

'Excuse me, your excellency, for venturing to trouble you. But if you would prefer to have us deal with her excellency, be so kind as to inform us of her address.'

Alexei Alexandrovich fell to pondering, as it seemed to the shop assistant, and suddenly turned and sat down at his desk. His head lowered on to his hands, he sat for a long time in that position, made several attempts to start talking and stopped.

Understanding his master's feelings, Kornei asked the assistant to come some other time. Left alone again, Alexei Alexandrovich realized that he was no longer able to maintain the role of firmness and calmness. He cancelled the waiting carriage, ordered that no one be received, and did not appear for dinner.

He felt that he could not maintain himself against the general pressure of contempt and callousness that he saw clearly in the face of this assistant, and of Kornei, and of everyone without exception that he had met in those two days. He felt that he could not divert people's hatred from himself, because the reason for that hatred was not that he was bad (then he could have tried to be better), but that he was shamefully and repulsively unhappy. For that, for the very fact that his heart was wounded, they would be merciless towards him; people would destroy him, as dogs kill a wounded dog howling with pain. He knew that the only salvation from people was to conceal his wounds from them, and for two days he had tried unconsciously to do that, but now he felt that he was no longer able to keep up this unequal struggle.

His despair was increased by the awareness that he was utterly alone with his grief. Not only did he not have a single person in Petersburg to whom he could tell all that he felt, who would pity him not as a high official, not as a member of society, but simply as a suffering person, but he had no such person anywhere.

Alexei Alexandrovich had grown up an orphan. They were two

brothers. They did not remember their father; their mother had died when Alexei Alexandrovich was ten. The fortune was small. Their uncle Karenin, an important official and once a favourite of the late emperor, had brought them up.

Having finished his school and university studies with medals, Alexei Alexandrovich, with his uncle's help, had set out at once upon a prominent career in the service, and since then had devoted himself exclusively to his service ambitions. Neither at school, nor at the university, nor afterwards in the service had Alexei Alexandrovich struck up any friendly relations. His brother had been the person closest to his heart, but he had served in the ministry of foreign affairs and had always lived abroad, where he died shortly after Alexei Alexandrovich's marriage.

During his governorship, Anna's aunt, a rich provincial lady, had brought the already not-so-young man but young governor together with her niece and put him in such a position that he had either to declare himself or to leave town. Alexei Alexandrovich had hesitated for a long time. There were then as many reasons for this step as against it, and there was no decisive reason that could make him abandon his rule: when in doubt, don't.[30] But Anna's aunt insinuated through an acquaintance that he had already compromised the girl and that he was honour-bound to propose. He proposed and gave his fiancée and wife all the feeling he was capable of.

The attachment he experienced for Anna excluded from his soul the last need for heartfelt relations with people. And now, among all his acquaintances, there was no one who was close to him. There were many of what are known as connections, but there were no friendly relations. Alexei Alexandrovich had many people whom he could invite for dinner, ask to participate in an affair that interested him or to solicit for some petitioner, and with whom he could candidly discuss the actions of other people and the higher government; but his relations with these people were confined to one sphere, firmly defined by custom and habit, from which it was impossible to depart. There was one university comrade with whom he had become close afterwards and with whom he could have talked about a personal grief, but he was a school superintendent in a remote district. Of people living in Petersburg, the closest and most likely were his office manager and his doctor.

Mikhail Vassilyevich Slyudin, the office manager, was a simple, intelligent, good and moral man, and Alexei Alexandrovich sensed that he was personally well disposed towards him; but their five years of work together had placed between them a barrier to heartfelt talks.

Alexei Alexandrovich, having finished signing papers, sat silently for a long time, glancing at Mikhail Vassilyevich, and tried several times to start talking, but could not. He had already prepared the phrase: 'You have heard of my grief?' But he ended by saying, as usual: 'So you will prepare this for me' – and dismissed him.

The other man was the doctor, who was also well disposed towards him; but they had long ago come to a tacit agreement that they were both buried in work and always in a hurry.

Of his female friends, and of the foremost of them, Countess Lydia Ivanovna, Alexei Alexandrovich did not think. All women, simply as women, were frightening and repulsive to him.

XXII

Alexei Alexandrovich had forgotten Countess Lydia Ivanovna, but she had not forgotten him. At this most difficult moment of lonely despair, she came to see him and walked into his study unannounced. She found him in the same position in which he had been sitting, resting his head on both hands.

'*J'ai forcé la consigne*,'* she said, coming in with rapid steps and breathing heavily from agitation and quick movement. 'I've heard everything! Alexei Alexandrovich! My friend!' she went on, firmly pressing his hand with both hands and looking into his eyes with her beautiful, pensive eyes.

Alexei Alexandrovich, frowning, got up and, freeing his hand from hers, moved a chair for her.

'If you please, Countess. I am not receiving because I am ill,' he said, and his lips trembled.

'My friend!' repeated Countess Lydia Ivanovna, not taking her eyes off him, and suddenly the inner tips of her eyebrows rose, forming a triangle on her forehead; her unattractive yellow face became still more unattractive; but Alexei Alexandrovich could feel that she pitied him and was ready to weep. He was deeply moved: he seized her plump hand and began to kiss it.

* I have forced my way in.

'My friend!' she said in a voice faltering with agitation. 'You mustn't give way to grief. Your grief is great, but you must find comfort.'

'I'm broken, I'm destroyed, I'm no longer a human being!' Alexei Alexandrovich said, letting go of her hand, but continuing to look into her tear-filled eyes. 'My position is the more terrible in that I can find no foothold in myself or anywhere.'

'You will find a foothold. Seek it not in me, though I beg you to believe in my friendship,' she said with a sigh. 'Our foothold is love, the love that He left us. His burden is light,'[31] she said with that rapturous look that Alexei Alexandrovich knew so well. 'He will support you and help you.'

Though there was in these words that tenderness before her own lofty feelings, and that new, rapturous, mystical mood which had recently spread in Petersburg,[32] and which Alexei Alexandrovich had considered superfluous, he now found it pleasant to hear.

'I'm weak. I'm annihilated. I foresaw nothing and now I understand nothing.'

'My friend,' Lydia Ivanovna repeated.

'It's not the loss of what isn't there now, it's not that,' Alexei Alexandrovich went on. 'I don't regret it. But I can't help feeling ashamed before people for the position I find myself in. It's wrong, but I can't help it, I can't help it.'

'It was not you who accomplished that lofty act of forgiveness, which I admire along with everyone, but He, dwelling in your heart,' Countess Lydia Ivanovna said, raising her eyes rapturously, 'and therefore you cannot be ashamed of your action.'

Alexei Alexandrovich frowned and, bending his hands, began cracking his fingers.

'One must know all the details,' he said in a high voice. 'There are limits to a man's strength, Countess, and I've found the limits of mine. I had to spend the whole day today making arrangements, arrangements about the house, resulting' (he emphasized the word 'resulting') 'from my new solitary situation. The servants, the governess, the accounts . . . These petty flames have burned me up, I couldn't endure it. Over dinner . . . yesterday I almost left the dinner table. I couldn't stand the way my son looked at me. He didn't ask me what it all meant, but he wanted to ask, and I couldn't endure that look. He was afraid to look at me, but that's not all . . .'

Alexei Alexandrovich wanted to mention the bill that had been brought to him, but his voice trembled and he stopped. He could not recall that bill, on blue paper, for a hat and ribbons, without pitying himself.

'I understand, my friend,' said Countess Lydia Ivanovna. 'I understand everything. Help and comfort you will not find in me, but all the same I've come only so as to help you if I can. If I could take from you these petty, humiliating cares . . . I understand that you need a woman's word, a woman's order. Will you entrust me with it?'

Alexei Alexandrovich pressed her hand silently and gratefully.

'We'll look after Seryozha together. I'm not strong in practical matters. But I'll take it up, I'll be your housekeeper. Don't thank me. It is not I who am doing it . . .'

'I cannot help thanking you.'

'But, my friend, don't give in to that feeling you spoke of – of being ashamed of what is the true loftiness of a Christian: "He that humbleth himself shall be exalted".[33] And you cannot thank me. You must thank Him and ask Him for help. In Him alone shall we find peace, comfort, salvation and love,' she said and, raising her eyes to heaven, began to pray, as Alexei Alexandrovich understood from her silence.

Alexei Alexandrovich listened to her now, and these expressions that had once seemed not exactly unpleasant but unnecessary, now seemed natural and comforting. He had not liked the new rapturous spirit. He was a believer who was interested in religion mostly in a political sense, and the new teaching that allowed itself some new interpretations was disagreeable to him on principle, precisely because it opened the door to debate and analysis. His former attitude to this new teaching had been cold and even inimical, and he had never argued with Countess Lydia Ivanovna, who was enthusiastic about it, but had carefully passed over her challenges in silence. But now for the first time he listened to her words with pleasure and did not inwardly object to them.

'I'm very, very grateful to you, both for your deeds and for your words,' he said, when she had finished praying.

Countess Lydia Ivanovna once more pressed both her friend's hands.

'Now I shall get down to work,' she said with a smile, after a pause, wiping the remaining tears from her face. 'I am going to Seryozha. I shall turn to you only in extreme cases.' And she got up and went out.

Countess Lydia Ivanovna went to Seryozha's rooms and there, drenching the frightened boy's cheeks with tears, told him that his father was a saint and his mother was dead.

*

Countess Lydia Ivanovna kept her promise. She indeed took upon herself all the cares of managing and running Alexei Alexandrovich's house. But she was not exaggerating when she said that she was not strong in practical matters. All her orders had to be changed, they were unfeasible as they were, and the one who changed them was Kornei, Alexei Alexandrovich's valet, who, unnoticed by anyone, began to run the entire Karenin household and, while dressing his master, calmly and carefully reported to him what was needed. But all the same Lydia Ivanovna's help was in the highest degree effective: she gave Alexei Alexandrovich moral support in the awareness of her love and respect for him, and especially, as she found it comforting to think, in that she had almost converted him to Christianity – that is, turned him from an indifferent and lazy believer into an ardent and firm adherent of that new explanation of Christian doctrine that had lately spread in Petersburg. Alexei Alexandrovich easily became convinced of it. Like Lydia Ivanovna and other people who shared their views, he was totally lacking in depth of imagination, in that inner capacity owing to which the notions evoked by the imagination become so real that they demand to be brought into correspondence with other notions and with reality. He did not see anything impossible or incongruous in the notion that death, which existed for unbelievers, did not exist for him, and that since he possessed the fullest faith, of the measure of which he himself was the judge, there was no sin in his soul and he already experienced full salvation here on earth.

It is true that Alexei Alexandrovich vaguely sensed the levity and erroneousness of this notion of his faith, and he knew that when, without any thought that his forgiveness was the effect of a higher power, he had given himself to his spontaneous feeling, he had experienced greater happiness than when he thought every moment, as he did now, that Christ lived in his soul and that by signing papers he was fulfilling His will; but it was necessary for him to think that way, it was so necessary for him in his humiliation to possess at least an invented loftiness from which he, despised by everyone, could despise others, that he clung to his imaginary salvation as if it were salvation indeed.

XXIII

Countess Lydia Ivanovna had been given in marriage as a young, rapturous girl to a rich, noble, very good-natured and very dissolute bon vivant. In the second month her husband abandoned her and responded to her rapturous assurances of tenderness only with mockery and even animosity, which people who knew the count's kind heart and saw no defects in the rapturous Lydia were quite unable to explain. Since then, though not divorced, they had lived apart, and whenever the husband met his wife, he treated her with an invariable venomous mockery, the reason for which was impossible to understand.

Countess Lydia Ivanovna had long ceased to be in love with her husband, but she never ceased being in love with someone. She was in love with several people at the same time, both men and women; she was in love with almost everyone who was particularly distinguished in some way. She was in love with all the new princesses and princes who had come into the tsar's family. She was in love with one metropolitan, one bishop and one priest. She was in love with one journalist, with three Slavs, with Komisarov,[34] with one minister, one doctor, one English missionary, and with Karenin. All these loves, now waning, now waxing, filled her heart, gave her something to do, but did not keep her from conducting very extensive and complex relations at court and in society. But once she took Karenin under her special patronage after the misfortune that befell him, once she began toiling in his house, looking after his well-being, she felt that all the other loves were not real, and that she was now truly in love with Karenin alone. The feeling she now experienced for him seemed stronger to her than all her former feelings. Analysing it and comparing it with the former ones, she saw clearly that she would not have been in love with Komisarov if he had not saved the emperor's life, would not have been in love with Ristich-Kudzhitsky if there had been no Slavic question,[35] but that she loved Karenin for himself, for his lofty, misunderstood soul, the high sound of his voice, so dear to her, with its drawn-out intonations, his weary gaze, his character, and his soft, white hands with their swollen veins. She was not only glad when they met, but sought signs in his face of the impression she made on him. She wanted him to like her not only for what she said, but for her whole person. For his sake she now took greater care with her toilette than ever. She caught herself dreaming of what might have happened if she were not married and he were free. She blushed with excitement when he came into the room; she could not suppress a smile of rapture when he said something pleasant to her.

For several days now Countess Lydia Ivanovna had been in the greatest agitation. She had learned that Anna and Vronsky were in Petersburg. Alexei Alexandrovich had to be saved from meeting her, he had to be saved even from the painful knowledge that this terrible woman was in the same town with him and that he might meet her at any moment.

Lydia Ivanovna, through her acquaintances, gathered intelligence about what those *loathsome people*, as she called Anna and Vronsky, intended to do, and tried during those days to direct her friend's every movement so that he would not meet them. The young adjutant, Vronsky's friend, through whom she obtained information and who hoped to obtain a concession through Countess Lydia Ivanovna, told her that they had finished their business and were leaving the next day. Lydia Ivanovna was beginning to calm down when the next morning she was brought a note and with horror recognized the handwriting. It was the handwriting of Anna Karenina. The envelope was of thick paper, like birch bark; the oblong yellow sheet bore an enormous monogram and the letter gave off a wonderful scent.

'Who brought it?'

'A messenger from a hotel.'

It was some time before Countess Lydia Ivanovna could sit down and read the letter. Excitement had given her an attack of the shortness of breath she suffered from. When she calmed down, she read the following, written in French:

Mme la Comtesse: The Christian feelings that fill your heart inspire in me what is, I feel, the unpardonable boldness of writing to you. I am unhappy in being separated from my son. I beg you to allow me to see him once before my departure. Forgive me for reminding you of myself. I am addressing you and not Alexei Alexandrovich only because I do not want to make that magnanimous man suffer from any reminder of me. Knowing your friendship for him, you will understand me. Will you send Seryozha to me, or shall I come to the house at a certain appointed time, or will you let me know where I can see him outside the house? I do not anticipate a refusal, knowing the magnanimity of the person upon whom it depends. You cannot imagine the longing I have to see him, and therefore you cannot imagine the gratitude your help will awaken in me.

Anna.

Everything in this letter annoyed Countess Lydia Ivanovna: the content, the reference to magnanimity and especially what seemed to her the casual tone.

'Tell him there will be no reply,' Countess Lydia Ivanovna said and at once, opening her blotting pad, wrote to Alexei Alexandrovich that she hoped to see him between twelve and one for the felicitations at the palace.

'I must discuss an important and sad matter with you. We will arrange where when we meet. Best of all would be my house, where I shall prepare *your* tea. It is necessary. He imposes the cross. He also gives the strength,' she added, so as to prepare him at least a little.

Countess Lydia Ivanovna usually wrote two or three notes a day to Alexei Alexandrovich. She liked this process of communicating with him, as having both elegance and mystery, which were lacking in her personal relations.

XXIV

The felicitations were coming to an end. On their way out, people met and discussed the latest news of the day, the newly bestowed awards, and the transfers of important officials.

'What if Countess Marya Borisovna got the ministry of war, and Princess Vatkovsky was made chief of staff?' a grey-haired little old man in a gold-embroidered uniform said, addressing a tall, beautiful lady-in-waiting who had asked about the transfers.

'And I an aide-de-camp,' the lady-in-waiting said, smiling.

'You already have an appointment. In the religious department. And for your assistant – Karenin.'

'How do you do, Prince!' said the old man, shaking hands with a man who came over.

'What did you say about Karenin?' asked the prince.

'He and Putyatov got the Alexander Nevsky.'[36]

'I thought he already had it.'

'No. Just look at him,' said the old man, pointing with his embroidered hat to Karenin in his court uniform, a new red sash over his shoulder, standing in the doorway of the reception room with an influential member of the State Council. 'Happy and pleased as a new copper penny,' he added, stopping to shake hands with a handsome, athletically built gentleman of the bed-chamber.

'No, he's aged,' the gentleman of the bed-chamber said.

'From worry. He keeps writing projects nowadays. He won't let that unfortunate fellow go now until he's told him everything point by point.'

'Aged? *Il fait des passions.** I think Countess Lydia Ivanovna is now jealous of his wife.'

'Come, come! Please don't say anything bad about Countess Lydia Ivanovna.'

'But is it bad that she's in love with Karenin?'

'And is it true that Madame Karenina's here?'

'That is, not here in the palace, but in Petersburg. I met them yesterday, her and Alexei Vronsky, *bras dessus, bras dessous*,† on Morskaya.'

'*C'est un homme qui n'a pas* . . .'‡ the gentleman of the bed-chamber began, but stopped, making way and bowing to a person of the tsar's family passing by.

So people talked ceaselessly of Alexei Alexandrovich, judging him and laughing at him, while he, standing in the way of a State Council member he had caught, explained his financial project to him point by point, not interrupting his explanation for a moment, so as not to let him slip away.

At almost the same time that his wife had left him, the bitterest of events for a man in the service had also befallen Alexei Alexandrovich – the cessation of his upward movement. This cessation was an accomplished fact and everyone saw it clearly, but Alexei Alexandrovich himself was not yet aware that his career was over. Whether it was the confrontation with Stremov, or the misfortune with his wife, or simply that Alexei Alexandrovich had reached the limit destined for him, it became obvious to everyone that year that his official career had ended. He still occupied an important post, was a member of many commissions and committees, but he was an entirely spent man from whom nothing more was expected. Whatever he said, whatever he proposed, he was listened to as though it had long been known and was the very thing that was not needed.

But Alexei Alexandrovich did not feel this and, on the contrary, being removed from direct participation in government activity, now saw more

* He's a success with the ladies.

† Arm in arm.

‡ He's a man who has no . . .

clearly than before the shortcomings and faults in the work of others and considered it his duty to point out the means for correcting them. Soon after his separation from his wife, he began writing a proposal about the new courts, the first in an endless series of totally unnecessary proposals which he was to write on all branches of administration.

Alexei Alexandrovich not only did not notice his hopeless position in the official world or feel upset by it, but was more satisfied with his activity than ever.

'He that is married careth for the things that are of the world, how he may please his wife, he that is unmarried careth for the things that belong to the Lord, how he may please the Lord,' said the apostle Paul,[37] and Alexei Alexandrovich, who was now guided by the Scriptures in all things, often recalled this text. It seemed to him that since he had been left without a wife, he had, by these very projects, served the Lord more than before.

The obvious impatience of the Council member, who wished to get away from him, did not embarrass Alexei Alexandrovich; he stopped explaining only when the member, seizing his chance when a person of the tsar's family passed, slipped away from him.

Left alone, Alexei Alexandrovich bowed his head, collecting his thoughts, then looked around absentmindedly and went to the door, where he hoped to meet Countess Lydia Ivanovna.

'And how strong and physically fit they are,' Alexei Alexandrovich thought, looking at the powerful gentleman of the bed-chamber with his brushed-up, scented side-whiskers and at the red neck of the prince in his tight-fitting uniform, whom he had to pass by. 'It is rightly said that all is evil in the world,' he thought again, casting another sidelong glance at the calves of the gentleman of the bed-chamber.

Moving his feet unhurriedly, Alexei Alexandrovich, with his usual look of weariness and dignity, bowed to these gentlemen who had been talking about him and, looking through the doorway, sought Countess Lydia Ivanovna with his eyes.

'Ah! Alexei Alexandrovich!' said the little old man, his eyes glinting maliciously, as Karenin came abreast of them and nodded his head with a cold gesture. 'I haven't congratulated you yet,' he said, pointing to his newly received sash.

'Thank you,' Alexei Alexandrovich replied. 'What a *beautiful* day today,' he added, especially emphasizing the word 'beautiful', as was his habit.

That they laughed at him he knew, but he did not expect anything except hostility from them; he was already used to it.

Catching sight of the yellow shoulders rising from the corset of Countess Lydia Ivanovna, who was coming through the door, and of her beautiful, pensive eyes summoning him, Alexei Alexandrovich smiled, revealing his unfading white teeth, and went up to her.

Lydia Ivanovna's toilette had cost her much trouble, as had all her toilettes of late. The purpose of it was now quite the opposite of the one she had pursued thirty years ago. Then she had wanted to adorn herself with something, and the more the better. Now, on the contrary, the way she felt obliged to adorn herself was so unsuited to her years and figure that her only concern was that the contrast of the adornments with her appearance should not be too terrible. And as far as Alexei Alexandrovich was concerned, she achieved it and looked attractive to him. For him she was the one island not only of kindly disposition but of love amidst the sea of hostility and mockery that surrounded him.

Passing between the rows of mocking eyes, he was naturally drawn to her amorous eyes, as a plant is to the light.

'Congratulations,' she said to him, indicating the sash with her eyes.

Suppressing a smile of satisfaction, he shrugged his shoulders and closed his eyes, as if to say it was no cause for rejoicing. Countess Lydia Ivanovna knew very well that it was one of his chief joys, though he would never admit it.

'How is our angel?' asked Countess Lydia Ivanovna, meaning Seryozha.

'I can't say I'm entirely pleased with him,' Alexei Alexandrovich said, raising his eyebrows and opening his eyes. 'And Sitnikov is not pleased with him either.' (Sitnikov was the teacher entrusted with Seryozha's secular education.) 'As I told you, there is some coldness in him towards those very chief questions which ought to touch the soul of every person and every child.' Alexei Alexandrovich began to explain his thoughts about the only question that interested him apart from the service – his son's education.

When Alexei Alexandrovich, with the help of Lydia Ivanovna, returned anew to life and action, he felt it his duty to occupy himself with the education of the son left on his hands. Never having concerned himself with questions of education before, Alexei Alexandrovich devoted some time to the theoretical study of the subject. And, after reading several books on anthropology, pedagogy and didactics, he made himself a plan of education and, inviting the best pedagogue in Petersburg for guidance, got down to business. And this business occupied him constantly.

'Yes, but his heart? I see his father's heart in him, and with such a heart a child cannot be bad,' Countess Lydia Ivanovna said rapturously.

'Yes, perhaps . . . As for me, I am fulfilling my duty. That is all I can do.'

'You shall come to my house,' Countess Lydia Ivanovna said after a pause, 'we must talk about a matter that is sad for you. I'd have given anything to deliver you from certain memories, but other people do not think that way. I have received a letter from *her*. *She* is here, in Petersburg.'

Alexei Alexandrovich gave a start at the mention of his wife, but his face at once settled into that dead immobility which expressed his utter helplessness in the matter.

'I was expecting that,' he said.

Countess Lydia Ivanovna looked at him rapturously, and tears of admiration at the grandeur of his soul came to her eyes.

XXV

When Alexei Alexandrovich entered Countess Lydia Ivanovna's small, cosy boudoir, filled with antique porcelain and hung with portraits, the hostess herself was not there. She was changing.

On a round table covered with a tablecloth stood a Chinese tea service and a silver spirit-lamp tea-kettle. Alexei Alexandrovich absentmindedly glanced around at the numberless familiar portraits that adorned the boudoir, and, sitting down at the desk, opened the Gospel that lay on it. The rustle of the countess's silk dress diverted him.

'Well, there, now we can sit down quietly,' Countess Lydia Ivanovna said with a nervous smile, hurriedly squeezing between the table and the sofa, 'and have a talk over tea.'

After a few words of preparation, Countess Lydia Ivanovna, breathing heavily and flushing, handed Alexei Alexandrovich the letter she had received.

Having read the letter, he was silent for a long time.

'I don't suppose I have the right to refuse her,' he said, timidly raising his eyes.

'My friend! You see no evil in anyone!'

'On the contrary, I see that everything is evil. But is it fair? . . .'

There was indecision in his face, a seeking for counsel, support and guidance in a matter incomprehensible to him.

'No,' Countess Lydia Ivanovna interrupted him. 'There is a limit to everything. I can understand immorality,' she said, not quite sincerely, because she never could understand what led women to immorality, 'but I do not understand cruelty – and to whom? To you! How can she stay in the same town with you? No, live and learn. And I am learning to understand your loftiness and her baseness.'

'And who will throw the stone?'[38] said Alexei Alexandrovich, obviously pleased with his role. 'I forgave everything and therefore cannot deprive her of what for her is a need of love – love for her son . . .'

'But is it love, my friend? Is it sincere? Granted, you forgave, you forgive . . . but do we have the right to influence the soul of this angel? He considers her dead. He prays for her and asks God to forgive her sins . . . And it's better that way. Otherwise what will he think?'

'I hadn't thought of that,' said Alexei Alexandrovich, obviously agreeing.

Countess Lydia Ivanovna covered her face with her hands and remained silent. She was praying.

'If you ask my advice,' she said, finishing her prayer and uncovering her face, 'I advise you not to do it. Can't I see how you're suffering, how it has opened all your wounds? But suppose you forget about yourself, as always. What can it lead to? To new sufferings on your part, to torment for the child? If there's anything human left in her, she herself should not wish for that. No, I have no hesitation in advising against it, and, if you allow me, I will write to her.'

Alexei Alexandrovich consented, and Countess Lydia Ivanovna wrote the following letter in French:

Dear Madam: A reminder of you may lead to questions on the part of your son which could not be answered without instilling into the child's soul a spirit of condemnation of what should be holy for him, and therefore I beg you to take your husband's refusal in the spirit of Christian love. I pray the Almighty to be merciful to you.

Countess Lydia.

This letter achieved the secret goal that Countess Lydia Ivanovna had concealed from herself. It offended Anna to the depths of her soul.

Alexei Alexandrovich, for his part, on returning home from Lydia Ivanovna's, was unable for the rest of the day to give himself to his usual occupations and find that peace of mind of a saved and believing man which he had felt before.

The memory of the wife who was so guilty before him and before whom he was so saintly, as Countess Lydia Ivanovna had rightly told him, should not have upset him; yet he was not at peace: he could not understand the book he was reading, could not drive away the painful memories of his relations with her, of those mistakes that he, as it now seemed to him, had made regarding her. The memory of how he had received her confession of unfaithfulness on the way back from the races (and in particular that he had demanded only external propriety from her and had made no challenge to a duel), tormented him like remorse. The memory of the letter he had written her also tormented him, and in particular his forgiveness, needed by no one, and his taking care of another man's child, burned his heart with shame and remorse.

And he now experienced exactly the same sense of shame and remorse, going over all his past with her and remembering the awkward words with which, after long hesitation, he had proposed to her.

'But in what am I to blame?' he said to himself. And this question always called up another question in him – whether they feel differently, love differently, marry differently, these other people, these Vronskys and Oblonskys . . . these gentlemen of the bed-chamber with their fat calves. And he pictured a whole line of these juicy, strong, undoubting people, who, against his will, had always and everywhere attracted his curious attention. He drove these thoughts away; he tried to convince himself that he lived not for this temporary life here and now but for eternal life, and that there was peace and love in his soul. Yet the fact that in this temporary, negligible life he had made, as it seemed to him, some negligible mistakes tormented him as though that eternal salvation in which he believed did not exist. But this temptation did not last long, and soon the tranquillity and loftiness were restored in Alexei Alexandrovich's soul thanks to which he was able to forget what he did not want to remember.

XXVI

'Well, Kapitonych?' said Seryozha, red-cheeked and merry, coming back from a walk on the eve of his birthday and giving his pleated jacket to the tall old hall porter, who smiled down at the little fellow from his great height. 'Did the bandaged official come today? Did papa receive him?'

'He did. As soon as the manager came out, I announced him,' the porter said with a merry wink. 'I'll take it off, if you please.'

'Seryozha!' said the Slav tutor,[39] pausing in the inside doorway. 'Take it off yourself.'

But Seryozha, though he heard the tutor's weak voice, paid no attention. He stood holding on to the porter's sash and looking into his face.

'And did papa do what he wanted him to?'

The porter nodded affirmatively.

The bandaged official, who had already come seven times to petition Alexei Alexandrovich for something, interested both Seryozha and the hall porter. Seryozha had come upon him once in the front hall and had heard him pitifully asking the porter to announce him, saying that he and his children were sure to die.

Since then Seryozha had taken an interest in the official, having met him in the front hall another time.

'And was he very glad?' he asked.

'How could he not be! He was all but skipping when he left.'

'And has anything come?' asked Seryozha, after a pause.

'Well, sir,' the porter said in a whisper, shaking his head, 'there's something from the countess.'

Seryozha understood at once that the porter was talking about a present for his birthday from Countess Lydia Ivanovna.

'Is there really? Where?'

'Kornei took it to your papa's. Must be something nice!'

'How big is it? Like this?'

'A bit smaller, but it's nice.'

'A book?'

'No, a thing. Go, go, Vassily Lukich is calling,' the porter said, hearing the steps of the approaching tutor and, carefully unclasping the little hand in the half-removed glove that was holding on to his sash, he winked and nodded towards Vunich.

'Coming, Vassily Lukich!' Seryozha answered with that merry and loving smile that always won over the dutiful Vassily Lukich.

Seryozha was too merry, everything was too happy, for him not to tell his friend the porter about another family joy, which he had learned of during his walk in the Summer Garden from Countess Lydia Ivanovna's niece. This joy seemed especially important to him, as it fell in with the joy of the official and his own joy about the toys that had come. It seemed to Seryozha that this was a day when everybody must be glad and merry.

'You know papa got the Alexander Nevsky?'

'How could I not know? People have already come to congratulate him.'

'And is he glad?'

'How could he not be glad of the tsar's favour! He must have deserved it,' the porter said sternly and seriously.

Seryozha reflected, peering into the porter's face, which he had studied in the smallest detail, particularly his chin, hanging between grey side-whiskers, which no one saw except Seryozha, because he always looked at it from below.

'Well, and has your daughter been to see you lately?'

The porter's daughter was a ballet dancer.

'When could she come on weekdays? They've also got to study. And you, too, sir. Off you go!'

When he came to his room, instead of sitting down to his lessons, Seryozha told his tutor his guess that what had been brought must be an engine. 'What do you think?' he asked.

But Vassily Lukich thought only that the grammar lesson had to be learned for the teacher, who was to come at two o'clock.

'No, but just tell me, Vassily Lukich,' he asked suddenly, already sitting at his desk and holding the book in his hands, 'what's bigger than the Alexander Nevsky? You know papa got the Alexander Nevsky?'

Vassily Lukich replied that the Vladimir was bigger than the Alexander Nevsky.

'And higher?'

'The highest of all is Andrew the First-called.'[40]

'And higher than Andrew?'

'I don't know.'

'What, even you don't know?' And Seryozha, leaning on his elbow, sank into reflection.

His reflections were most complex and varied. He imagined how his father would suddenly get both the Vladimir and the Andrew, and how as a result of that he would be much kinder today at the lesson, and how he himself, when he grew up, would get all the decorations, and the one they would invent that was higher than the Andrew. No sooner would they invent it than he would deserve it. They would invent a still higher one, and he would also deserve it at once.

The time passed in such reflections, and when the teacher came, the lesson about the adverbial modifiers of time, place and manner was not prepared, and the teacher was not only displeased but also saddened. The teacher's sadness touched Seryozha. He did not feel himself to blame for not having learned the lesson; but try as he might, he was quite unable to do it: while the teacher was explaining it to him, he believed and seemed to understand, but once he was on his own, he was simply unable to remember and understand that such a short and clear word as 'thus' was *an adverbial modifier of manner*. But all the same he was sorry that he had made his teacher sad and wanted to comfort him.

He chose a moment when the teacher was silently looking in the book.

'Mikhail Ivanych, when is your name-day?' he asked suddenly.

'You'd better think about your work. Name-days mean nothing to intelligent beings. Just like any other day when we have to work.'

Seryozha looked attentively at the teacher, his sparse little beard, his spectacles which had slipped down below the red mark on his nose, and lapsed into thought so that he heard nothing of what his teacher explained to him. He realized that his teacher was not thinking about what he said, he felt it by the tone in which it was spoken. 'But why have they all decided to say it in the same way, everything that's most boring and unnecessary? Why does he push me away from him? Why doesn't he love me?' he asked himself with sorrow, and could think of no answer.

XXVII

After the teacher there was a lesson with his father. Waiting for his father, Seryozha sat at the desk playing with his penknife and began to think. Among his favourite occupations was looking for his mother during his walk. He did not believe in death generally and especially not in her death, though Lydia Ivanovna had told him and his father had confirmed it, and therefore, even after he was told that she was dead, he looked for her during his walks. Any full-bodied, graceful woman with dark hair was his mother. At the sight of such a woman, a feeling of tenderness welled up in his soul, so strong that he choked and tears came to his eyes. And he expected her to come up to him at any moment and lift her veil. Her whole face would be visible, she would smile, embrace him, he would smell her smell, feel the tenderness of her hand, and weep happily, as he had one evening when he lay at her feet and she tickled him, and he laughed and bit her white hand with its rings. Later, when he learned by chance from the nanny that his mother was not dead, and his father and Lydia Ivanovna explained to him that she was dead for him, because she was not good (which he simply could not believe, because he loved her), he kept looking and waiting for her in the same way. Today in the Summer Garden there was a lady in a purple veil whom he watched with a sinking heart, expecting it to be her as she approached them on the path. This lady did not reach them but disappeared somewhere. Today Seryozha felt stronger surges of love for her than ever, and now, forgetting himself, while waiting for his father, he cut up the whole edge of the desk with his knife, staring straight ahead with shining eyes and thinking of her.

'Papa is coming!' Vassily Lukich distracted him.

Seryozha jumped up, approached his father and, after kissing his hand, looked at him attentively, searching for signs of joy at getting the Alexander Nevsky.

'Did you have a nice walk?' Alexei Alexandrovich said, sitting down in his armchair, moving the book of the Old Testament to him and opening it. Though Alexei Alexandrovich had told Seryozha many times that every Christian must have a firm knowledge of sacred history, he often consulted the Old Testament himself, and Seryozha noticed it.

'Yes, it was great fun, papa,' said Seryozha, sitting sideways on the chair and rocking it, which was forbidden. 'I saw Nadenka' (Nadenka was Lydia Ivanovna's niece, whom she was bringing up). 'She told me you've been given a new star. Are you glad, papa?'

'First of all, don't rock, please,' said Alexei Alexandrovich. 'And second, what is precious is not the reward but the work. And I wish you to understand that. If you work and study in order to get a reward, the work will seem hard to you; but when you work,' Alexei Alexandrovich said, recalling how he had sustained himself by a sense of duty that morning in the dull work of signing a hundred and eighteen papers, 'if you love the work, you will find your reward in that.'

Seryozha's eyes, shining with tenderness and gaiety, went dull and lowered under his father's gaze. This was the same long-familiar tone in which his father always addressed him and which he had learned to fall in with. His father always talked to him – so he felt – as if he were addressing some imaginary boy, one of those that exist in books, but quite unlike him. And he always tried, when with his father, to pretend he was that book boy.

'You understand that, I hope?' said his father.

'Yes, papa,' Seryozha replied, pretending to be the imaginary boy.

The lesson consisted in learning several verses from the Gospel by heart and going over the beginning of the Old Testament. Seryozha knew the Gospel verses quite well, but as he was reciting them, he got so lost in contemplating the bone of his father's forehead, which curved sharply at the temple, that he got confused by a repetition of the same word and moved the ending of one verse to the beginning of another. It was obvious to Alexei Alexandrovich that he did not understand what he was saying, and that annoyed him.

He frowned and began to explain what Seryozha had already heard many times and could never remember, because he understood it all too clearly – the same sort of thing as 'thus' being an adverbial modifier of manner. Seryozha looked at his father with frightened eyes and thought of one thing only: whether or not his father would make him repeat what he said, as sometimes happened. And this thought frightened him so much that he no longer understood anything. But his father did not make him repeat it and went on to the lesson from the Old Testament. Seryozha recounted the events themselves quite well, but when he had to answer questions about what some of the events foreshadowed, he knew nothing, though he had already been punished for this lesson. The place where he could no longer say anything and mumbled, and cut the table, and rocked on the chair, was the one where he had to speak of the antediluvian patriarchs. He knew none of them except Enoch, who had been taken alive to heaven.[41] He had remembered the names before, but now he had quite forgotten them, especially because Enoch was his favourite person in all the Old Testament, and Enoch's having been taken alive to heaven was connected in his mind with a whole long train of thought to which he now gave himself, staring with fixed eyes at his father's watch chain and a waistcoat button half-way through the buttonhole.

In death, which he had been told about so often, Seryozha totally refused to believe. He did not believe that the people he loved could die, and especially that he himself would die. For him that was perfectly impossible and incomprehensible. Yet he had been told that everyone would die; he had even asked people he trusted and they had confirmed it; his nanny had also confirmed it, though reluctantly. But Enoch had not died, which meant that not everyone died. 'And why can't everyone be deserving in the same way before God and get taken alive to heaven?' thought Seryozha. The bad ones – that is, those whom Seryozha did not like – they could die, but the good ones should all be like Enoch.

'Well, so who are the patriarchs?'

'Enoch, Enos.'

'You've already said that. Bad, Seryozha, very bad. If you don't try to learn what's most necessary for a Christian,' his father said, getting up, 'what else can interest you? I'm displeased with you, and Pyotr Ignatyich' (the chief pedagogue) 'is displeased with you . . . I will have to punish you.'

The father and the pedagogue were both displeased with Seryozha, and indeed he studied very badly. But it was quite impossible to say that he was an incapable boy. On the contrary, he was much more capable than the boys whom the pedagogue held up as examples to Seryozha. As his father saw it, he did not want to learn what he was taught. But in fact, he could not learn it. He could not, because there were demands in his soul that were more exacting for him than those imposed by his father and the pedagogue. These demands were conflicting, and he fought openly with his educators.

He was nine years old, he was a child; but he knew his own soul, it was dear to him, he protected it as the eyelid protects the eye, and did not let anyone into his soul without the key of love. His educators complained that he did not want to learn, yet his soul was overflowing with a thirst for knowledge. And he learned from Kapitonych, from his nurse, from Nadenka, from Vassily Lukich, but not from his teachers. The water that his father and the teacher had expected to turn their mill-wheels had long since seeped away and was working elsewhere.

His father punished Seryozha by not letting him visit Nadenka, Lydia Ivanovna's niece; but this punishment turned out to be lucky for Seryozha. Vassily Lukich was in good spirits and showed him how to make windmills. They spent the whole evening working and dreaming of how to make a windmill so that you could turn round with it: hold on to the wings, or be tied to them, and turn. Seryozha did not think of his mother all evening, but when he went to bed, he suddenly remembered her and prayed in his own words that, for his birthday tomorrow, his mother would stop hiding and come to him.

'Vassily Lukich, do you know what extra I prayed for besides?'

'To study better?'

'No.'

'Toys?'

'No. You'll never guess. It's splendid, but secret! If it comes true, I'll tell you. You can't guess?'

'No, I can't. You'll have to tell me,' Vassily Lukich said, smiling, which rarely happened with him. 'Well, lie down, I'm putting the candle out.'

'And I can see what I prayed for better without the candle. Now I've nearly told you the secret!' said Seryozha, laughing gaily.

When the candle was taken away, he heard and felt his mother. She stood over him and caressed him with her loving eyes. But windmills came, a penknife came, everything got confused, and he fell asleep.

XXVIII

On arriving in Petersburg, Vronsky and Anna stayed in one of the best hotels. Vronsky separately on the lower floor, Anna upstairs with the baby, the wet nurse and the maid, in a big four-room suite.

The day they arrived Vronsky went to see his brother. There he found his mother, who had come from Moscow on her own business. His mother and sister-in-law met him as usual; they asked him about his trip abroad, spoke of mutual acquaintances, and did not say a word about his liaison with Anna. But his brother, when he came to Vronsky the next day, asked about her himself, and Alexei Vronsky told him straight out that he considered his liaison with Mme Karenina a marriage; that he hoped to arrange for a divorce and then marry her; and till then he considered her just as much his wife as any other wife and asked him to convey that to his mother and his wife.

'If society doesn't approve of it, that's all the same to me,' said Vronsky, 'but if my family wants to have family relations with me, they will have to have the same relations with my wife.'

The elder brother, who had always respected the opinions of the younger, could not quite tell whether he was right or wrong until society decided the question; he himself, for his own part, had nothing against it and went together with Alexei to see Anna.

In his brother's presence, as in everyone else's, Vronsky addressed Anna formally and treated her as a close acquaintance, but it was implied that the brother knew of their relations, and mention was made of Anna going to Vronsky's estate.

Despite all his social experience, Vronsky, owing to the new position in which he found himself, was strangely deluded. It seems he ought to have understood that society was closed to him and Anna; but some vague arguments were born in his head, that it had been so only in olden times, while now, progress being so quick (without noticing it he had become an advocate of every sort of progress), society's outlook had changed and the question of their being received in society was still to be decided. 'Naturally,' he thought, 'court society will not receive her, but closer acquaintances can and must understand it in the right way.'

A man can spend several hours sitting cross-legged in the same position if he knows that nothing prevents him from changing it; but if he knows that he has to sit with his legs crossed like that, he will get cramps, his legs will twitch and strain towards where he would like to stretch them. That was what Vronsky felt with regard to society. Though in the depths of his soul he knew that society was closed to them, he tested whether it might change now and they might be received. But he very soon noticed that, though society was open to him personally, it was closed to Anna. As in the game of cat and mouse, arms that were raised for him were immediately lowered before Anna.

One of the first ladies of Petersburg society whom Vronsky saw was his cousin Betsy.

'At last!' she greeted him joyfully. 'And Anna? I'm so glad! Where are you staying? I can imagine how awful our Petersburg must seem to you after your lovely trip; I can imagine your honeymoon in Rome. What about the divorce? Has that all been done?'

Vronsky noticed that Betsy's delight diminished when she learned that there had been no divorce as yet.

'They'll throw stones at me, I know,' she said, 'but I'll go to see Anna. Yes, I'll certainly go. Will you be here long?'

And, indeed, she went to see Anna that same day; but her tone was now quite unlike what it used to be. She was obviously proud of her courage and wished Anna to appreciate the faithfulness of her friendship. She stayed less than ten minutes, talking about society news, and as she was leaving said:

'You haven't told me when the divorce will be. Granted I've thrown my bonnet over the mills, but other starched collars will blow cold on you until you get married. And it's so simple now. *Ça se fait.** So you leave on Friday? A pity we won't see more of each other.'

From Betsy's tone Vronsky could understand what he was to expect from society; but he made another attempt with his family. He had no hopes for his mother. He knew that she, who had so admired Anna when they first became acquainted, was now implacable towards her for having brought about the ruin of her son's career. But he placed great hopes in Varya, his brother's wife. He thought that she would not throw stones and would simply and resolutely go to see Anna and receive her.

The day after his arrival Vronsky went to her and, finding her alone, voiced his wish directly.

'You know, Alexei,' she said, after hearing him out, 'how much I love you and how ready I am to do anything for you. But I have kept silent because I know I cannot be useful to you and Anna Arkadyevna,' she said, articulating 'Anna Arkadyevna' with special care. 'Please don't think that I condemn her. Never. It may be that in her place I would have done the same thing. I do not and cannot go into the details,' she said, glancing timidly at his sullen face. 'But one must call things by their names. You want me to see her, to receive her, and in that way to rehabilitate her in society, but you must understand that I *cannot* do it. I have growing daughters, and I must live in society for my husband's sake. If I go to see Anna Arkadyevna, she will understand that I cannot invite her or must do it so that she does not meet those who would take a different view of it, and that will offend her. I cannot raise her . . .'

'I don't consider that she has fallen any more than hundreds of other women whom you do receive!' Vronsky interrupted her still more sullenly, and silently got up, realizing that his sister-in-law's decision was not going to change.

'Alexei! Don't be angry with me. Please understand that it's not my fault,' said Varya, looking at him with a timid smile.

'I'm not angry with you,' he said just as sullenly, 'but it doubles my

* It's done.

pain. What also pains me is that it breaks up our friendship. Or let's say it doesn't break it up, but weakens it. You realize that for me, too, it cannot be otherwise.'

And with that he left her.

Vronsky understood that further attempts were futile and that they would have to spend those few days in Petersburg as in a foreign city, avoiding all contacts with their former society so as not to be subjected to insults and unpleasantnesses, which were so painful for him. One of the most unpleasant things about the situation in Petersburg was that Alexei Alexandrovich and his name seemed to be everywhere. It was impossible to begin talking about anything without the conversation turning to Alexei Alexandrovich; it was impossible to go anywhere without meeting him. At least it seemed so to Vronsky, as it seems to a man with a sore finger that he keeps knocking into everything, as if on purpose, with that finger.

The stay in Petersburg seemed the more difficult to Vronsky because all that time he saw some new, incomprehensible mood in Anna. At one moment she appeared to be in love with him, at another she became cold, irritable and impenetrable. She was suffering over something and concealing something from him, and seemed not to notice those insults that poisoned his life and that for her, with her subtle perceptiveness, ought to have been still more painful.

XXIX

For Anna one of the objects of the trip to Russia was to see her son. Since the day she left Italy, the thought of seeing him had not ceased to excite her. And the closer she came to Petersburg, the greater became the joy and significance of this meeting for her. She never asked herself the question of how to arrange it. To her it seemed natural and simple to see her son when she was in the same town with him; but on arriving in Petersburg, she suddenly saw her present position in society clearly and realized that it would be difficult to arrange the meeting.

She had already been in Petersburg for two days. The thought of her son had never left her for a moment, but she still had not seen him. She felt she did not have the right to go directly to the house, where she might encounter Alexei Alexandrovich. She might be insulted and turned away. As for writing and entering into relations with her husband, it was painful even to think of it: she could be at peace only when not thinking of her husband. To find out when and where her son went for his walks and see him then, was not enough for her: she had been preparing so long for this meeting, she had so much to tell him, she wanted so much to embrace him, to kiss him. Seryozha's old nanny might have helped her and instructed her. But the nanny no longer lived in Alexei Alexandrovich's house. In these hesitations and in the search for the nanny, two days passed.

Learning of the close relations between Alexei Alexandrovich and Countess Lydia Ivanovna, Anna decided on the third day to write her a letter, which cost her great effort, in which she said deliberately that permission to see her son depended on her husband's magnanimity. She knew that if her husband were shown the letter, he, pursuing his role of magnanimity, would not refuse her.

The messenger who had carried the letter brought her a most cruel and unexpected reply – that there would be no reply. She had never felt so humiliated as in that moment when, having summoned the messenger, she heard from him a detailed account of how he had waited and how he had then been told: 'There will be no reply.' Anna felt herself humiliated, offended, but she saw that from her own point of view Countess Lydia Ivanovna was right. Her grief was the stronger because it was solitary. She could not and did not want to share it with Vronsky. She knew that for him, though he was the chief cause of her unhappiness, the question of her meeting her son would be a most unimportant thing. She knew that he would never be able to understand all the depth of her suffering; she knew that she would hate him for his cold tone at the mention of it. She feared that more than anything in the world, and so she concealed everything from him that had to do with her son.

She spent the whole day at home, inventing means for meeting her son, and arrived at the decision to write to her husband. She was already working on the letter when Lydia Ivanovna's letter was brought to her. The countess's silence had humbled and subdued her, but the letter, everything she could read between its lines, annoyed her so much, its malice seemed so outrageous compared with her passionate and legitimate tenderness for her son, that she became indignant with them and stopped accusing herself.

'This coldness is a pretence of feeling,' she said to herself. 'All they want is to offend me and torment the child, and I should submit to them!

Not for anything! She's worse than I am. At least I don't lie.' And she decided then and there that the next day, Seryozha's birthday itself, she would go directly to her husband's house, bribe the servants, deceive them, but at all costs see her son and destroy the ugly deceit with which they surrounded the unfortunate child.

She went to a toy store, bought lots of toys, and thought over her plan of action. She would come early in the morning, at eight o'clock, when it was certain that Alexei Alexandrovich would not be up yet. She would have money with her, which she would give to the hall porter and the footman so that they would let her in, and, without lifting her veil, she would tell them she had come from Seryozha's godfather to wish him a happy birthday and had been charged with putting the toys by the boy's bed. The only thing she did not prepare was what she would say to her son. However much she thought about it, she could not think of anything.

The next day, at eight o'clock in the morning, Anna got out of a hired carriage by herself and rang at the big entrance of her former home.

'Go and see what she wants. It's some lady,' said Kapitonych, not dressed yet, in a coat and galoshes, looking out of the window at a lady in a veil who was standing just at the door.

The porter's helper, a young fellow Anna did not know, opened the door for her. She came in and, taking a three-rouble bill from her muff, hurriedly put it into his hand.

'Seryozha . . . Sergei Alexeich,' she said and started forward. Having examined the bill, the porter's helper stopped her at the inside glass door.

'Who do you want?' he asked.

She did not hear his words and made no reply.

Noticing the unknown woman's perplexity, Kapitonych himself came out to her, let her in the door and asked what she wanted.

'I've come from Prince Skorodumov, to see Sergei Alexeich,' she said.

'He's not up yet,' the porter said, looking at her intently.

Anna had never expected that the totally unchanged interior of the front hall of the house in which she had lived for nine years would affect her so strongly. One after another, joyful and painful memories arose in her soul, and for a moment she forgot why she was there.

'Would you care to wait?' said Kapitonych, helping her off with her fur coat.

After taking her coat, Kapitonych looked into her face, recognized her and silently made a low bow.

'Please come in, your excellency,' he said to her.

She wanted to say something, but her voice refused to produce any sound; giving the old man a look of guilty entreaty, she went up the stairs with quick, light steps. All bent over, his galoshes tripping on the steps, Kapitonych ran after her, trying to head her off.

'The tutor's there and may not be dressed. I'll announce you.'

Anna went on up the familiar stairs, not understanding what the old man was saying.

'Here, to the left please. Excuse the untidiness. He's in the former sitting room now,' the porter said breathlessly. 'Allow me, just a moment, your excellency, I'll peek in,' he said, and, getting ahead of her, he opened the tall door and disappeared behind it. Anna stood waiting. 'He's just woken up,' the porter said, coming out the door again.

And as the porter said it, Anna heard the sound of a child's yawn. From the sound of the yawn alone she recognized her son and could see him alive before her.

'Let me in, let me in, go away!' she said, and went through the tall doorway. To the right of the door stood a bed, and on the bed a boy sat upright in nothing but an unbuttoned shirt, his little body arched, stretching and finishing a yawn. As his lips came together, they formed themselves into a blissfully sleepy smile, and with that smile he slowly and sweetly fell back again.

'Seryozha!' she whispered, approaching him inaudibly.

While they had been apart, and with that surge of love she had been feeling all the time recently, she had imagined him as a four-year-old boy, the way she had loved him most. Now he was not even the same as when she had left him; he was still further from being a four-year-old, was taller and thinner. What was this! How thin his face was, how short his hair! How long his arms! How he had changed since she left him! But this was he, with his shape of head, his lips, his soft neck and broad shoulders.

'Seryozha!' she repeated just over the child's ear.

He propped himself on his elbow, turned his tousled head from side to side as if looking for something, and opened his eyes. For several seconds he gazed quietly and questioningly at his mother standing motionless before him, then suddenly smiled blissfully and, closing his sleepy eyes again, fell, not back now, but towards her, towards her arms.

'Seryozha! My sweet boy!' she said, choking and putting her arms around his plump body.

'Mama!' he said, moving under her arms, so as to touch them with different parts of his body.

Smiling sleepily, his eyes still shut, he shifted his plump hands from the back of the bed to her shoulders, snuggled up to her, enveloping her with that sweet, sleepy smell and warmth that only children have, and began rubbing his face against her neck and shoulders.

'I knew it,' he said, opening his eyes. 'Today's my birthday. I knew you'd come. I'll get up now.'

And he was falling asleep again as he said it.

Anna looked him over greedily; she saw how he had grown and changed during her absence. She did and did not recognize his bare feet, so big now, sticking out from under the blanket, recognized those cheeks, thinner now, those locks of hair cut short on the back of his neck, where she had so often kissed them. She touched it all and could not speak; tears choked her.

'What are you crying for, mama?' he said, now wide awake. 'Mama, what are you crying for?' he raised his tearful voice.

'I? I won't cry . . . I'm crying from joy. I haven't seen you for so long. I won't, I won't,' she said, swallowing her tears and turning away. 'Well, it's time you got dressed,' she added after a pause, recovering herself; and without letting go of his hand, she sat by his bed on a chair where his clothes were lying ready.

'How do you get dressed without me? How . . .' She wanted to begin talking simply and cheerfully, but could not and turned away again.

'I don't wash with cold water, papa told me not to. And did you see Vassily Lukich? He'll come. And you sat on my clothes!' Seryozha burst out laughing.

She looked at him and smiled.

'Mama, darling, dearest!' he cried, rushing to her again and embracing her. As if it were only now, seeing her smile, that he understood clearly what had happened. 'No need for that,' he said, taking her hat off. And, as if seeing her anew without a hat, he again began kissing her.

'But what have you been thinking about me? You didn't think I was dead?'

'I never believed it.'

'Didn't you, my love?'

'I knew it, I knew it!' He repeated his favourite phrase and, seizing her hand, which was caressing his hair, he pressed her palm to his mouth and began to kiss it.

XXX

Meanwhile Vassily Lukich, who did not understand at first who this lady was, and learning from the conversation that she was the same mother who had left her husband and whom he did not know because he had come to the house after she left, was in doubt whether to go in or to inform Alexei Alexandrovich. Considering finally that his duty was to get Seryozha up at a certain time and that therefore he had no need to determine who was sitting there, the mother or someone else, but had to fulfil his duty, he got dressed, went to the door and opened it.

But the caresses of the mother and son, the sounds of their voices, and what they were saying – all this made him change his mind. He shook his head and closed the door with a sigh. 'I'll wait another ten minutes,' he said to himself, clearing his throat and wiping away his tears.

Just then there was great commotion among the domestic servants. Everyone had learned that the mistress had come, that Kapitonych had let her in, and that she was now in the nursery; and meanwhile the master always went to the nursery himself before nine o'clock, and everyone realized that a meeting between the spouses was impossible and had to be prevented. Kornei, the valet, went down to the porter's lodge and began asking who had let her in and how, and on learning that Kapitonych had met her and shown her in, he reprimanded the old man. The porter remained stubbornly silent; but when Kornei told him that he deserved to be sacked for it, Kapitonych leaped towards him and, waving his arms in front of Kornei's face, said:

'Yes, and you wouldn't have let her in! Ten years' service, seeing nothing but kindness from her, and then you'd go and say: "Kindly get out!" Subtle politics you've got! Oh, yes! You mind yourself, robbing the master and stealing racoon coats!'

'Old trooper!' Kornei said contemptuously and turned to the nanny, who had just arrived. 'Look at that, Marya Efimovna: he let her in, didn't tell anybody,' Kornei went on. 'Alexei Alexandrovich will come out presently and go to the nursery.'

'Such goings-on!' said the nanny. 'Listen, Kornei Vassilyevich, why don't you delay somehow – the master, I mean – while I go and somehow lead her away. Such goings-on!'

When the nanny went into the nursery, Seryozha was telling his mother how he and Nadenka fell while they were sliding and rolled over three times. She listened to the sound of his voice, saw his face and the play of its expression, felt his hand, but did not understand what he was saying. She had to go, she had to leave him – that was all she thought and felt. She heard the steps of Vassily Lukich as he came to the door and coughed, she also heard the steps of the nanny approaching; but she sat as if turned to stone, unable either to begin talking or to get up.

'Mistress, dearest!' the nanny started to say, going up to Anna and kissing her hand and shoulders. 'What a God-sent joy for our little one's birthday! You haven't changed at all.'

'Ah, nanny, dear, I didn't know you were in the house,' said Anna, coming to her senses for a moment.

'I don't live here, I live with my daughter, I came to wish him a happy birthday, Anna Arkadyevna, dearest!'

The nanny suddenly wept and started kissing her hand again.

Seryozha, with radiant eyes and smile, holding his mother with one hand and his nanny with the other, stamped his fat little bare feet on the rug. He was delighted with his beloved nanny's tenderness towards his mother.

'Mama! She often comes to see me, and when she comes . . .' he began, but stopped, noticing that the nanny was whispering something to his mother, and that his mother's face showed fear and something like shame, which was so unbecoming to her.

She went up to him.

'My dear one!' she said.

She could not say *goodbye*, but the look on her face said it, and he understood. 'Dear, dear Kutik!' She said the name she had called him when he was little. 'You won't forget me? You . . .' but she was unable to say more.

How many words she thought of later that she might have said to him! But now she did not and could not say anything. Yet Seryozha understood all that she wanted to tell him. He understood that she was unhappy and that she loved him. He even understood what the nanny had said to her in a whisper. He had heard the words 'always before nine' and understood that this referred to his father and that his mother and father must not meet. But one thing he could not understand: why did fear and shame appear on her face? . . . She was not guilty, but she was afraid of him and ashamed of something. He wanted to ask the question that would have cleared up this doubt, but did not dare to do it: he saw that she was suffering and he pitied her. He silently pressed himself to her and said in a whisper:

'Don't go yet. He won't come so soon.'

His mother held him away from her, to see whether he had thought of what he was saying, and in his frightened expression she read that he was not only speaking of his father but was, as it were, asking her how he should think of him.

'Seryozha, my dear,' she said, 'love him, he is better and kinder than I, and I am guilty before him. When you grow up, you will decide.'

'No one's better than you! . . .' he cried through tears of despair, and seizing her by the shoulders, he pressed her to him, his arms trembling with the strain.

'My darling, my little one!' said Anna, and she started crying as weakly, as childishly, as he.

Just then the door opened and Vassily Lukich came in. Steps were heard at the other door, and the nanny said in a frightened whisper:

'He's coming,' and gave Anna her hat.

Seryozha sank down on the bed and sobbed, covering his face with his hands. Anna took his hands away, kissed his wet face once more and with quick steps went out of the door. Alexei Alexandrovich was coming towards her. Seeing her, he stopped and bowed his head.

Though she had just said that he was better and kinder than she, feelings of loathing and spite towards him and envy about her son came over her as she glanced quickly at him, taking in his whole figure in all its details. With a swift movement she lowered her veil and, quickening her pace, all but ran out of the room.

She had had no time to take out the toys she had selected with such love and sadness in the shop the day before, and so brought them home with her.

XXXI

Strongly as Anna had wished to see her son, long as she had been thinking of it and preparing for it, she had never expected that seeing him would have so strong an effect on her. On returning to her lonely suite in the hotel, she was unable for a long time to understand why she was there. 'Yes, it's all over and I'm alone again,' she said to herself and, without taking off her hat, she sat down in an armchair by the fireplace. Staring with fixed eyes at the bronze clock standing on the table between the windows, she began to think.

The French maid, brought from abroad, came in to suggest that she dress. She looked at her in surprise and said:

'Later.'

The footman offered her coffee.

'Later,' she said.

The Italian wet nurse, having changed the baby, came in with her and gave her to Anna. The plump, well-nourished baby, as always, seeing her mother, turned over her bare little arms, which looked as if they had string tied round them, and, smiling with a toothless little mouth, began rowing with her hands palm down like a fish with its fins, making the starched folds of her embroidered frock rustle. It was impossible not to smile, not to kiss the little girl, not to give her a finger, which she seized, squealing and bouncing with her whole body; it was impossible not to offer her a lip, which she, as if in a kiss, took into her mouth. And Anna did all this, took her in her arms, got her to jump, and kissed her fresh cheek and bare little elbows; but the sight of this child made it still clearer that her feeling for her, compared to what she felt for Seryozha, was not even love. Everything about this little girl was sweet, but for some reason none of it touched her heart. To the first child, though of a man she did not love, had gone all the force of a love that had not been satisfied; the girl, born in the most difficult conditions, did not receive a hundredth part of the care that had gone to the first child. Besides, in this little girl everything was still to come, while Seryozha was almost a person, and a loved person; thoughts and feelings already struggled in him; he understood her, he loved her, he judged her, she thought, remembering his words and looks. And she was forever separated from him, not only physically but also spiritually, and it was impossible to remedy that.

She gave the girl to the wet nurse, dismissed her, and opened a locket which held a portrait of Seryozha when he was nearly the same age as the girl. She got up and, after removing her hat, took an album from a little table in which there were photographs of her son at other ages. She wanted to compare the photographs and began taking them out of the album. She took them all out. One remained, the last, the best picture. He was sitting astride a chair, in a white shirt, his eyes sulky and his mouth smiling. This was his most special, his best expression. With her small, deft hands, which today moved their thin, white fingers with a peculiar strain, she picked at the corner several times, but the picture was stuck and she could not get it out. As there was no paper-knife on the table, she took out the picture next to it (it was a picture of Vronsky in a round hat and with long hair, taken in Rome) and pushed her son's picture out with it. 'Yes, here he is!' she said, glancing at the picture of Vronsky, and she suddenly remembered who had been the cause of her present grief. She had not thought of him once all morning. But now suddenly, seeing that noble, manly face, so familiar and dear to her, she felt an unexpected surge of love for him.

'But where is he? Why does he leave me alone with my sufferings?' she suddenly thought, with a feeling of reproach, forgetting that she herself had concealed from him everything to do with her son. She sent to him asking him to come to her at once; with a sinking heart she waited for him, thinking up the words in which she would tell him everything, and the expressions of love with which he would comfort her. The messenger came back with the reply that he had a visitor but would come presently, and with the question whether she could receive him with Prince Yashvin, who had come to Petersburg. 'He won't come alone, and yet he hasn't seen me since dinner yesterday,' she thought. 'He won't come so that I can tell him everything, but will come with Yashvin.' And suddenly a strange thought occurred to her: what if he had stopped loving her?

And, going over the events of the last few days, it seemed to her that she found the confirmation of this horrible thought in everything: in the fact that he had dined out the previous evening, and that he had insisted they stay separately in Petersburg, and that even now he was not coming to her alone, as if to avoid meeting her tête-à-tête.

'But he ought to tell me that. I need to know that. If I knew it, then I know what I'd do,' she said to herself, unable to imagine the position she would be in once she became convinced of his indifference. She thought he had stopped loving her, she felt herself close to despair, and as a result she became peculiarly agitated. She rang for the maid and went to her dressing room. As she dressed, she paid more attention to her toilette than she had all those days, as if, having ceased to love her, he might start loving her again because she was wearing a dress or had done her hair in a way more becoming to her.

She heard the bell ring before she was ready.

When she came out to the drawing room, it was not his but Yashvin's eyes that met hers. Vronsky was looking at the photographs of her son, which she had forgotten on the table, and was in no hurry to look at her.

'We're acquainted,' she said, putting her small hand into the enormous hand of Yashvin, whose embarrassment went strangely with his huge stature and coarse face. 'Since last year, at the races. Give them to me,' she said, and with a quick movement she took from Vronsky the pictures of her son that he had been looking at, glancing at him meaningfully with her shining eyes. 'Were the races good this year? I watched the races at the Corso in Rome instead. However, you don't like life abroad,' she said, smiling gently. 'I know you and know all your tastes, though we've met so seldom.'

'I'm very sorry for that, because my tastes are mostly bad,' Yashvin said, biting the left side of his moustache.

Having talked for a while and noticing that Vronsky was glancing at the clock, Yashvin asked her how long she would be in Petersburg and, unbending his enormous figure, took his cap.

'Not long, it seems,' she said in perplexity, glancing at Vronsky.

'So we won't see more of each other?' said Yashvin, standing up and addressing Vronsky. 'Where will you dine?'

'Come and dine with me,' Anna said resolutely, as if angry with herself for her embarrassment, but blushing as she always did when she revealed her position to a new person. 'The dinners aren't good here, but at least you'll see each other. Of all his comrades in the regiment, there's no one Alexei loves more than you.'

'Delighted,' Yashvin said with a smile, by which Vronsky could see that he liked Anna very much.

Yashvin bowed and left. Vronsky stayed behind.

'You're going, too?' she asked him.

'I'm late already,' he answered. 'Go on! I'll catch up with you in a minute,' he called to Yashvin.

She held his hand and gazed at him, not taking her eyes away, searching her mind for something to say that would keep him there.

'Wait, I must tell you something,' and, taking his short hand, she pressed it to her neck. 'So it's all right that I asked him to dinner?'

'You did splendidly,' he said with a calm smile, revealing his solid row of teeth, and kissed her hand.

'Alexei, you haven't changed towards me?' she said, pressing his hand with both of hers. 'Alexei, I'm suffering here. When will we leave?'

'Soon, soon. You wouldn't believe how painful our life here is for me, too,' he said, and withdrew his hand.

'Well, go, go!' she said, offended, and quickly left him.

XXXII

When Vronsky came home, Anna was not yet there. He was told that some lady had come to see her shortly after he left and they had gone off together. The fact that she had gone without saying where, that she was still away, that she had also gone somewhere in the morning without telling him anything – all this, along with the strangely excited expression of her face that morning and the memory of the hostile tone with which, in Yashvin's presence, she had all but torn the photographs of her son out of his hands, made him ponder. He decided that it was necessary to have a talk with her. And he waited for her in her drawing room. But Anna did not come back alone; she brought her aunt with her, an old maid, Princess Oblonsky. This was the same one who had come in the morning and with whom Anna had gone shopping. Anna seemed not to notice Vronsky's concerned and questioning expression and cheerfully told him what she had bought that morning. He saw that something peculiar was going on in her: her shining eyes, when they fleetingly rested on him, showed a strained attention, and her talk and movements had that nervous quickness and grace that in the first time of their intimacy had so delighted him and now troubled and alarmed him.

Dinner was set for four. They were all about to go to the small dining room when Tushkevich arrived with a message for Anna from Princess Betsy. Princess Betsy apologized for not coming to say goodbye; she was not well but asked Anna to come to her between half-past six and nine. At this specification of the time, showing that measures had been taken so that she would not meet anyone, Vronsky glanced at Anna; but Anna seemed not to notice it.

'I regret that between half-past six and nine is precisely when I cannot come,' she said, smiling slightly.

'The princess will be very sorry.'

'I am, too.'

'You must be going to hear Patti?'[42] said Tushkevich.

'Patti? That gives me an idea. I would go if I could get a box.'

'I can get one,' Tushkevich volunteered.

'I'd be very, very grateful to you,' said Anna. 'And would you care to dine with us?'

Vronsky gave a barely noticeable shrug. He utterly failed to understand what Anna was doing. Why had she brought this old princess, why had she asked Tushkevich to stay for dinner, and, most surprising, why was she sending him to get a box? Was it thinkable in her situation to go to a subscription performance by Patti, when all her society acquaintances would be there? He gave her a serious look, but she answered with the same defiant look, something between cheerful and desperate, the meaning of which he could not fathom. During dinner Anna was aggressively cheerful: she seemed to flirt with both Tushkevich and Yashvin. When they got up from the table, Tushkevich went for the box, while Yashvin went to smoke. Vronsky accompanied him to his room. Having stayed for some time, he ran back upstairs. Anna was already dressed in a light-coloured gown of silk and velvet with a low-cut neck that had been made for her in Paris, and had costly white lace on her head, which framed her face and showed off her striking beauty to particular advantage.

'Are you really going to the theatre?' he said, trying not to look at her.

'Why do you ask so fearfully?' she said, again offended that he was not looking at her. 'Why shouldn't I go?'

It was as if she did not understand the meaning of his words.

'Of course, there's no reason at all,' he said, frowning.

'That's just what I say,' she said, deliberately not understanding the irony of his tone and calmly rolling up a long, perfumed glove.[43]

'Anna, for God's sake, what's the matter with you?' he said, trying to wake her up, in the same way that her husband had once spoken to her.

'I don't understand what you're asking.'

'You know it's impossible to go.'

'Why? I'm not going alone. Princess Varvara has gone to dress; she will go with me.'

He shrugged his shoulders with a look of bewilderment and despair.

'But don't you know . . .' he tried to begin.

'I don't even want to know!' she almost shouted. 'I don't. Do I repent of what I've done? No, no, no! If it were all to be done over again, it would be the same. For us, for me and for you, only one thing matters: whether we love each other. There are no other considerations. Why do we live separately here and not see each other? Why can't I go? I love you, and it makes no difference to me,' she said in Russian, glancing at him with eyes that had a peculiar, incomprehensible gleam, 'as long as you haven't changed. Why don't you look at me?'

He looked at her. He saw all the beauty of her face and of her attire, which had always been so becoming to her. But now it was precisely her beauty and elegance that irritated him.

'My feeling cannot change, you know that, but I ask you not to go, I implore you,' he said again in French, with a tender plea in his voice, but with coldness in his eyes.

She did not hear the words but saw the coldness of his eyes and answered with irritation:

'And I ask you to tell me why I shouldn't go.'

'Because it may cause you to be . . .' he faltered.

'I understand nothing. Yashvin *n'est pas compromettant*,* and Princess Varvara is no worse than others. And here she is.'

XXXIII

Vronsky experienced for the first time a feeling of vexation, almost of anger, with Anna for her deliberate refusal to understand her position. This feeling was intensified by his being unable to explain to her the cause of his vexation. If he had told her directly what he thought, he would have said: 'To appear in the theatre in that attire and with that notorious princess is not only to acknowledge your position as a ruined woman but also to throw down a challenge to society – that is, to renounce it for ever.'

He could not say that to her. 'But how can she not understand it, and what is going on inside her?' he said to himself. He felt that his respect for her was decreasing at the same time as his consciousness of her beauty increased.

Frowning, he returned to his rooms and, sitting down by Yashvin, who had stretched his long legs out on a chair and was drinking cognac with seltzer water, ordered the same for himself.

'You mentioned Lankovsky's Powerful. A fine horse, I advise you to buy him,' Yashvin said, glancing at his friend's gloomy face. 'He's got a

* Is not compromising.

low-slung rump, but for legs and head you couldn't ask for better.'

'I think I'll take him,' replied Vronsky.

The conversation about horses interested him, but he did not forget Anna for a moment, involuntarily listened for the sound of steps in the corridor and kept glancing at the clock on the mantelpiece.

'Anna Arkadyevna asked me to tell you, sir, that she has gone to the theatre.'

Yashvin, having poured another glass of cognac into the fizzy water, drank it and got up, buttoning his jacket.

'Well, shall we go?' he said, smiling slightly under his moustache, and showing by this smile that he understood the reason for Vronsky's gloominess but attached no importance to it.

'I'm not going,' Vronsky said gloomily.

'But I have to go, I promised. Well, good-bye. Or else come to the stalls, you can take Krasinsky's seat,' Yashvin added on his way out.

'No, I've got things to do.'

'A wife's a worry, a non-wife's even worse,' thought Yashvin as he left the hotel.

Vronsky, left alone, got up from his chair and began pacing the room.

'What's today? The fourth subscription ... Yegor's there with his wife, and probably my mother. That means all Petersburg is there. She's gone in now, taken off her fur coat, come out to the light. Tushkevich, Yashvin, Princess Varvara ...' he pictured it to himself. 'What about me? Am I afraid, or did I pass it on to Tushkevich to chaperone her? However you look at it, it's stupid, stupid ... And why does she put me in such a position?' he said, waving his arm.

In that movement he brushed against the little table on which the seltzer water and decanter of cognac stood and almost knocked it over. He went to catch it, dropped it, kicked the table in vexation, and rang the bell.

'If you want to work for me,' he said to the valet as he came in, 'then remember your duty. No more of this. You must clean it up.'

The valet, feeling that it was not his fault, was about to vindicate himself but, glancing at his master, realized from his look that he had better keep silent; squirming, he hastily got down on the rug and began sorting out the whole glasses and bottles from the broken.

'That's not for you to do. Send a lackey to clean up, and lay out a tailcoat for me.'

*

Vronsky entered the theatre at half-past eight. The performance was in full swing. An old usher helped Vronsky off with his fur coat and, recognizing him, called him 'your highness' and suggested that he not take a tag but simply ask for Fyodor. There was no one in the bright corridor except the usher and two lackeys with fur coats in their hands, listening by the door. From behind the closed door came the sounds of the orchestra's careful staccato accompaniment and one female voice distinctly pronouncing a musical phrase. The door opened to allow the usher to slip in, and the concluding phrase clearly struck Vronsky's ear. The door closed at once and he did not hear the end of the phrase or the cadenza, but he could tell by the thunder of applause behind the door that it was over. When he entered the hall, brightly lit by chandeliers and bronze gas brackets, the noise still continued. On stage the singer, her bare shoulders and diamonds gleaming, bent over and, with the help of the tenor who held her hand, smilingly picked up the bouquets that had been awkwardly thrown across the footlights, then went over to a gentleman with glistening, pomaded hair parted in the middle, who reached his long arms across the footlights, holding out something or other – and all the audience in the stalls as well as in the boxes stirred, stretched forward, shouted and applauded. The conductor on his podium helped to hand it on and straightened his white tie. Vronsky went into the middle of the stalls, stopped and began to look around. Tonight he paid less attention than ever to the habitual surroundings, to the stage, to the noise, to this whole familiar, uninteresting, motley flock of spectators in the tightly packed theatre.

As usual, there were the same sort of ladies in the boxes with the same sort of officers behind them; the same multi-coloured women, uniforms, frock coats, God knows who they were; the same dirty crowd in the gallery; and in all this crowd, in the boxes and front rows, there were about forty *real* men and women. And to these oases Vronsky at once paid attention, and with them he at once entered into contact.

The act ended as he came in, and therefore, without going to his brother's box, he walked up to the front row and stopped by the footlights with Serpukhovskoy, who, bending his knee and tapping his heel against the wall, had seen him from a distance and summoned him with a smile.

Vronsky had not yet seen Anna; he purposely did not look her way. But from the direction of all eyes he knew where she was. He looked around surreptitiously, but not for her; expecting the worst, his eyes were seeking Alexei Alexandrovich. To his good fortune, Alexei Alexandrovich was not in the theatre this time.

'How little of the military is left in you!' Serpukhovskoy said to him. 'A diplomat, an artist, something of that sort.'

'Yes, I put on a tailcoat as soon as I got home,' Vronsky replied, smiling and slowly taking out his opera-glasses.

'In that, I confess, I envy you. When I come back from abroad and put this on,' he tapped his epaulettes, 'I regret my lost freedom.'

Serpukhovskoy had long since given up on Vronsky's career, but he loved him as before and now was especially amiable with him.

'Too bad you were late for the first act.'

Vronsky, listening with one ear, transferred his opera-glasses from the *baignoire* to the dress circle and scanned the boxes. Next to a lady in a turban and a bald old man, who blinked angrily into the lenses of the moving opera-glasses, Vronsky suddenly saw Anna's head, proud, strikingly beautiful, and smiling in its frame of lace. She was in the fifth *baignoire*, twenty steps away from him. She was sitting at the front and, turning slightly, was saying something to Yashvin. The poise of her head on her beautiful, broad shoulders, the glow of restrained excitement in her eyes and her whole face reminded him of her exactly as he had seen her at the ball in Moscow. But his sense of this beauty was quite different now. His feeling for her now had nothing mysterious in it, and therefore her beauty, though it attracted him more strongly than before, at the same time offended him. She was not looking in his direction, but Vronsky could sense that she had seen him.

When Vronsky again looked in that direction through his opera-glasses, he noticed that Princess Varvara was especially red, laughed unnaturally and kept turning to look at the neighbouring box, while Anna, tapping on the red velvet with a folded fan, gazed off somewhere and did not see or want to see what was happening in that box. Yashvin's face wore the expression it had when he was losing at cards. He sulkily put the left side of his moustache further and further into his mouth, glancing sidelong at the same neighbouring box.

In this box to the left were the Kartasovs. Vronsky knew them and knew that Anna was acquainted with them. Mme Kartasov, a thin, small woman, was standing in her box, her back turned to Anna, and putting on a cape that her husband was holding for her. Her face was pale and cross, and she was saying something excitedly. Kartasov, a fat, bald gentleman, kept looking round at Anna and trying to calm his wife.

When his wife left, the husband lingered for a long time, his eyes seeking Anna's, apparently wishing to bow to her. But Anna, obviously ignoring him on purpose, turned round and was saying something to Yashvin, who leaned his cropped head towards her. Kartasov went out without bowing, and the box was left empty.

Vronsky did not understand precisely what had taken place between the Kartasovs and Anna, but he realized that it had been humiliating for Anna. He realized it both from what he had seen and, most of all, from Anna's look. He knew she had gathered her last forces in order to maintain the role she had taken upon herself. And in this role of ostensible calm she succeeded fully. People who did not know her and her circle, and who had not heard all the expressions of commiseration, indignation and astonishment from women that she should allow herself to appear in society and appear so conspicuously in her lace attire and in all her beauty, admired the calm and beauty of this woman and did not suspect that she was experiencing the feelings of a person in the pillory.

Knowing that something had happened but not knowing precisely what, Vronsky felt a tormenting anxiety and, hoping to find something out, went to his brother's box. On his way, deliberately choosing the aisle in the stalls on the side opposite Anna's box, he ran into the commander of his former regiment, who was talking with two acquaintances. Vronsky heard the name Karenina spoken, and noticed how the commander hastened to address him loudly, with a meaningful glance at the speakers.

'Ah, Vronsky! When will you visit the regiment? We can't let you go without a banquet. You're one of us,' said the commander.

'Can't stop, very sorry, another time,' Vronsky said and ran up the stairs to his brother's box.

The old countess, Vronsky's mother, with her steely little curls, was in his brother's box. Varya and the young princess Sorokin met him in the corridor of the dress circle.

After taking Princess Sorokin to his mother, Varya gave her brother-in-law her hand and at once began talking to him about what interested him. He had rarely seen her so agitated.

'I find it mean and nasty, and Mme Kartasov had no right. Anna Arkadyevna . . .' she began.

'But what? I don't know.'

'You mean you haven't heard?'

'You know I'll be the last to hear of it.'

'Is there a wickeder creature than that Mme Kartasov?'

'But what did she do?'

'My husband told me . . . She insulted Anna Arkadyevna. Her husband began talking to her across the box, and Mme Kartasov made a scene. They say she said something insulting and walked out.'

'Count, your *maman* is calling you,' said Princess Sorokin, looking out the door of the box.

'And I've been waiting for you all this time,' his mother said to him with a mocking smile. 'One sees nothing of you.'

Her son noted that she could not suppress a smile of joy.

'Good evening, *maman*. I was coming to see you,' he said coldly.

'Why don't you go *faire la cour à madame Karenine*?'* she said, when Princess Sorokin stepped away. '*Elle fait sensation. On oubli la Patti pour elle*.'†

'*Maman*, I asked you not to talk to me about that,' he answered, frowning.

'I'm only saying what everybody says.'

Vronsky made no reply and, after saying a few words to Princess Sorokin, left. In the doorway he ran into his brother.

'Ah, Alexei!' said his brother. 'What nastiness! A fool, nothing more . . . I was just about to go to her. Let's go together.'

Vronsky was not listening. He went downstairs with quick steps: he felt he had to do something but did not know what. Vexation with her for putting herself and him in such a false position, along with pity for her suffering, agitated him. He went down to the stalls and made straight for Anna's *baignoire*. Stremov stood there talking with her:

'There are no more tenors. *La moule en est brisé*.'‡

Vronsky bowed to her and paused to greet Stremov.

'It seems you got here late and missed the best aria,' Anna said to Vronsky, looking at him mockingly, as it seemed to him.

'I'm a poor connoisseur,' he said, looking sternly at her.

'Like Prince Yashvin,' she said, smiling, 'who finds that Patti sings too loud. Thank you,' she added, her small hand in its long glove taking the playbill Vronsky had picked up, and suddenly at that instant her beautiful face twitched. She rose and went to the back of the box.

* Pay court to Mme Karenina.

† She's caused a sensation. La Patti is forgotten on her account.

‡ Their mould has been broken.

Noticing that her box remained empty during the next act, Vronsky, provoking a hissing in the audience, which was hushed to the sounds of the cavatina, left the stalls and drove home.

Anna was already there. When Vronsky came in, she was alone, still wearing the same dress she had worn to the theatre. She was sitting in the first chair by the wall, staring straight ahead of her. She glanced at him and at once resumed her former position.

'Anna,' he said.

'You, you're to blame for it all!' she cried, getting up, with tears of despair and anger in her voice.

'I asked you, I implored you not to go. I knew it would be unpleasant . . .'

'Unpleasant!' she cried. 'Terrible! I won't forget it as long as I live. She said it was a disgrace to sit next to me.'

'A foolish woman's words,' he said. 'But why risk, why provoke . . .'

'I hate your calmness. You shouldn't have driven me to that. If you loved me . . .'

'Anna! What does the question of my love have to do . . .'

'Yes, if you loved as I do, if you suffered as I do . . .' she said, looking at him with an expression of fear.

He felt sorry for her, and still he was vexed. He assured her of his love, because he saw that that alone could calm her now, and he did not reproach her in words, but in his soul he did reproach her.

And those assurances of love, which seemed so banal to him that he was ashamed to utter them, she drank in and gradually grew calm. The next day, completely reconciled, they left for the country.

Part Six

I

Darya Alexandrovna was spending the summer with her children in Pokrovskoe at her sister Kitty Levin's. On her own estate the house had completely fallen apart, and Levin and his wife had persuaded her to spend the summer with them. Stepan Arkadyich highly approved of this arrangement. He said he was very sorry that his duties prevented him from spending the summer in the country with his family, which would have been the greatest happiness for him, and he remained in Moscow, occasionally going to the country for a day or two. Besides the Oblonskys, with all the children and the governess, the old princess also stayed with the Levins that summer, considering it her duty to look after her inexperienced daughter, who was in a 'certain condition'. Besides that, Varenka, Kitty's friend from abroad, had kept her promise to visit Kitty when she was married and was now her friend's guest. These were all relations and friends of Levin's wife. And though he loved them all, he slightly regretted his Levin world and order, which was smothered under this influx of the 'Shcherbatsky element', as he kept saying to himself. Of his own relations only Sergei Ivanovich stayed with him that summer, but even he was a man not of the Levin but of the Koznyshev stamp, so that the Levin spirit was completely annihilated.

In Levin's long-deserted house there were now so many people that almost all the rooms were occupied, and almost every day the old princess had to count them as they sat down at the table and seat the thirteenth granddaughter or grandson at a separate table. And for Kitty, who diligently occupied herself with the household, there was no little bother over procuring chickens, turkeys and ducks, of which, considering the summer appetites of guests and children, a great many were needed.

The whole family was sitting at dinner. Dolly's children were making plans with the governess and Varenka about where to go mushrooming. Sergei Ivanovich, whose intellect and learning enjoyed a respect among all the guests amounting almost to veneration, surprised them all by mixing into the conversation about mushrooms.

'Take me with you. I like mushrooming very much,' he said, looking at Varenka. 'I find it a very good occupation.'

'Why, we'd be very glad to,' Varenka said, blushing. Kitty exchanged meaningful glances with Dolly. The suggestion of the learned and intelligent Sergei Ivanovich that he go mushrooming with Varenka confirmed some of Kitty's surmises, which had occupied her very much of late. She hastened to address her mother, so that her glances would not be noticed. After dinner Sergei Ivanovich sat with his cup of coffee at the drawing-room window, continuing a conversation he and his brother had begun and glancing towards the door through which the children who were going mushrooming were supposed to come. Levin sat on the window-seat beside his brother.

Kitty stood near her husband, obviously waiting for the end of the conversation, which did not interest her, so that she could tell him something.

'You've changed in many ways since you got married, and for the better,' said Sergei Ivanovich, smiling at Kitty and obviously not much interested in the conversation they had begun, 'but you've remained loyal to your passion for defending the most paradoxical themes.'

'Katia, it's not good for you to stand,' her husband said to her, moving a chair over for her and giving her a meaningful look.

'Well, yes, and anyway there's no time,' Sergei Ivanovich added, seeing the children run out.

Ahead of them all came Tanya in her tight stockings, galloping sideways, waving her basket and Sergei Ivanovich's hat and running straight towards him.

Having boldly run up to Sergei Ivanovich, her eyes shining, so like her father's beautiful eyes, she handed him his hat and made as if to put it on him, softening her liberty with a timid and tender smile.

'Varenka's waiting,' she said, carefully putting the hat on his head, seeing by Sergei Ivanovich's smile that it was allowed.

Varenka stood in the doorway, having changed into a yellow cotton dress, with a white kerchief tied on her head.

'Coming, coming, Varvara Andreevna,' said Sergei Ivanovich, finishing his cup of coffee and putting his handkerchief and cigar-case in his pockets.

'How lovely my Varenka is, isn't she?' Kitty said to her husband, as soon as Sergei Ivanovich got up. She said it so that Sergei Ivanovich could hear her, which she obviously wanted. 'And how beautiful she is, how nobly beautiful! Varenka!' Kitty shouted, 'will you be in the mill wood? We'll meet you there.'

'You quite forget your condition, Kitty,' the old princess said, hurrying out of the door. 'You mustn't shout like that.'

Varenka, hearing Kitty's voice and her mother's reprimand, quickly came up to her with a light step. Her quickness of movement, the colour that suffused her animated face, all showed that something extraordinary was taking place in her. Kitty knew what this extraordinary thing was and observed her closely. She had called Varenka now only so as to bless her mentally for the important event which, in Kitty's mind, was to take place after dinner today in the forest.

'Varenka, I'll be very happy if a certain thing happens,' she said in a whisper, kissing her.

'And will you come with us?' Varenka said to Levin, embarrassed and pretending not to have heard what had been said to her.

'I will, but only as far as the threshing floor, and I'll stay there.'

'Now, what have you got to do there?' said Kitty.

'I must look over the new wagons and do some figures,' said Levin. 'And where will you be?'

'On the terrace.'

II

The entire company of women gathered on the terrace. They generally liked to sit there after dinner, but today they also had things to do. Besides the sewing of little shirts and the knitting of baby blankets, with which they were all occupied, jam was being made there according to a method new to Agafya Mikhailovna, without the addition of water. Kitty was introducing this new method which they used at home. Agafya Mikhailovna, who had been in charge of it before, considering that nothing done in the Levins' house could be bad, had put water in the strawberry and wild strawberry jam all the same, insisting that it could not be done otherwise; she had been caught at it, and now raspberry jam was being made in front of everyone, and Agafya Mikhailovna had to be brought to believe that jam without water could turn out well.

Agafya Mikhailovna, with a flushed and upset face, her hair tousled, her thin arms bared to the elbows, rocked the basin in circular movements over the brazier and stared gloomily at the raspberry jam, wishing with all her heart that it would thicken before it was cooked through. The princess, feeling that Agafya Mikhailovna's wrath must be directed at her, as the chief adviser on making raspberry jam, tried to pretend she was busy with something else and not interested in the jam, talked about unrelated things, but kept casting sidelong glances at the brazier.

'I always buy dresses for my maids myself, at a discount,' the princess said, continuing the conversation they had begun . . . 'Shouldn't you skim it now, dear?' she added, addressing Agafya Mikhailovna. 'It's quite unnecessary for you to do it yourself – and it's hot,' she stopped Kitty.

'I'll do it,' said Dolly, and, getting up, she began drawing the spoon carefully over the foaming sugar, tapping it now and then to knock off what stuck to it on to a plate, which was already covered with the bright-coloured yellow-pink scum, with an undercurrent of blood-red syrup. 'How they'll lick it up with their tea!' She thought of her children, remembering how she herself, as a child, had been surprised that grown-ups did not eat the best part – the scum.

'Stiva says it's much better to give them money,' Dolly meanwhile continued the interesting conversation they had begun about the best way of giving presents to servants, 'but . . .'

'How can you give money!' the princess and Kitty said with one voice. 'They appreciate presents so.'

'Last year, for instance, I bought not poplin exactly but something like it for our Matryona Semyonovna,' said the princess.

'I remember, she wore it for your name-day party.'

'The sweetest pattern – so simple and noble. I'd have liked to make it for myself, if she hadn't had it. Like Varenka's. So sweet and inexpensive.'

'Well, it seems to be ready now,' said Dolly, pouring the syrup off the spoon.

'When it leaves a tail, it's ready. Cook it a little longer, Agafya Mikhailovna.'

'These flies!' Agafya Mikhailovna said crossly. 'It'll be all the same,' she added.

'Ah, how sweet he is, don't frighten him!' Kitty said suddenly, looking at a sparrow that had alighted on the railing and, turning over a raspberry stem, began pecking at it.

'Yes, but you keep away from the brazier,' said her mother.

'*À propos de* Varenka,' Kitty said in French, which they had been speaking all the while so that Agafya Mikhailovna would not understand them. 'You know, *maman*, for some reason I expect a decision today. You understand what I mean. How good it would be!'

'What an expert matchmaker, though!' said Dolly. 'How carefully and skilfully she brings them together . . .'

'No, tell me, *maman*, what do you think?'

'What is there to think? He' ('he' meaning Sergei Ivanovich) 'could always make the foremost match in Russia; he's not so young any more, but I know that many would marry him even now . . . She's very kind, but he could . . .'

'No, mama, you must understand why one couldn't think of anything better for him or for her. First, she's lovely!' Kitty said, counting off one finger.

'He likes her very much, it's true,' Dolly confirmed.

'Then, he occupies such a position in society that he has absolutely no need for a wife with a fortune or social position. He needs one thing – a good and sweet wife, a peaceful one.'

'Yes, with her he can be peaceful,' Dolly confirmed.

'Third, that she should love him. And that's there . . . I mean, it would be so good! . . . I'm just waiting for them to come back from the forest and everything will be decided. I'll see at once from their eyes. I'd be so glad! What do you think, Dolly?'

'Don't get excited. You must never get excited,' said her mother.

'But I'm not excited, mama. I think he'll propose today.'

'Ah, it's so strange, when and how a man proposes . . . There's some obstacle, and suddenly it's broken through,' said Dolly, smiling pensively and recalling her past with Stepan Arkadyich.

'Mama, how did papa propose to you?' Kitty asked suddenly.

'There was nothing extraordinary, it was quite simple,' replied the princess, but her face became all bright at the memory.

'No, but how? Anyway, you loved him before you were allowed to talk?'

Kitty felt a special charm in being able to talk with her mother as an equal about these most important things in a woman's life.

'Of course I loved him. He used to visit us in the country.'

'But how did it get decided? Mama?'

'You probably think you invented something new? It was all the same: it got decided by looks, by smiles . . .'

'How well you put it, mama! Precisely by looks and smiles,' Dolly confirmed.

'But what words did he say?'

'What did Kostya say to you?'

'He wrote with chalk. It was amazing . . . It seems so long ago!' she said.

And the three women fell to thinking about the same thing. Kitty was the first to break the silence. She recalled that whole last winter before her marriage and her infatuation with Vronsky.

'One thing . . . that former passion of Varenka's,' she said, recalling it by a natural train of thought. 'I wanted somehow to tell Sergei Ivanovich, to prepare him. They – all men,' she added, 'are terribly jealous of our past.'

'Not all,' said Dolly. 'You're judging by your husband. He still suffers from the memory of Vronsky. Yes? It's true?'

'It is,' Kitty replied, smiling pensively with her eyes.

'Only I don't know,' the princess-mother defended her motherly supervision of her daughter, 'what past of yours could bother him? That Vronsky courted you? That happens to every girl.'

'Well, that's not what we mean,' Kitty said, blushing.

'No, excuse me,' her mother went on, 'and then you yourself didn't want to let me have a talk with Vronsky. Remember?'

'Oh, mama!' Kitty said with a suffering look.

'Nowadays there's no holding you back . . . Your relations couldn't go further than was proper: I myself would have called him out. However, it won't do for you to get excited, my dear. Please remember that and calm yourself.'

'I'm perfectly calm, *maman*.'

'How happily it turned out for Kitty that Anna came then,' said Dolly, 'and how unhappily for her. Precisely the opposite,' she added, struck by the thought. 'Anna was so happy then, and Kitty considered herself unhappy. How completely opposite! I often think about her.'

'A fine one to think about! A vile, disgusting woman, quite heartless,' said the mother, unable to forget that Kitty had married not Vronsky but Levin.

'Who wants to talk about that,' Kitty said in vexation. 'I don't think about it and I don't want to think . . . And I don't want to think,' she repeated, hearing her husband's familiar footsteps on the terrace stairs.

'And I don't want to think – about what?' asked Levin, coming out on the terrace.

But no one answered him, and he did not repeat the question.

'I'm sorry I've disturbed your women's kingdom,' he said, looking around at them all with displeasure, realizing that they had been talking about something that they would not have talked about in his presence.

For a second he felt that he shared Agafya Mikhailovna's feeling – displeasure that the raspberry jam had been made without water, and in general with the alien Shcherbatsky influence. He smiled, however, and went over to Kitty.

'Well, how are you?' he asked, looking at her with the same expression with which everyone now addressed her.

'Oh, fine,' said Kitty, smiling, 'and you?'

'They hold three times more than a cart. So, shall we go for the children? I told them to harness up.'

'What, you want to take Kitty in the wagonette?' her mother said reproachfully.

'But at a walk, Princess.'

Levin never called the princess *maman*, as sons-in-law do, and that displeased her. But, though he loved and respected the princess very much, Levin could not call her that without profaning his feelings for his dead mother.

'Come with us, *maman*,' said Kitty.

'I don't want to witness this folly.'

'I'll go on foot, then. It's good for me.' Kitty got up, went over to her husband and took him by the hand.

'Good, but everything in moderation,' said the princess.

'Well, Agafya Mikhailovna, is the jam done?' said Levin, smiling at Agafya Mikhailovna and wishing to cheer her up. 'Is it good the new way?'

'Must be good. We'd say it's overcooked.'

'So much the better, Agafya Mikhailovna, it won't get mouldy. Our ice has all melted by now and there's nowhere to keep it,' said Kitty, understanding her husband's intention at once and addressing the old woman with the same feeling. 'Besides, your pickling is so good, my mama says she's never tasted the like anywhere,' she added, smiling and straightening the old woman's kerchief.

Agafya Mikhailovna looked crossly at Kitty.

'Don't comfort me, mistress. I just look at you and him and I feel cheered,' she said, and this crude expression 'him' instead of 'the master' touched Kitty.

'Come mushrooming with us, you can show us the places.' Agafya Mikhailovna smiled and shook her head, as if to say: 'I'd gladly be angry with you, but it's impossible.'

'Please do as I advise you,' said the old princess, 'cover the jam with a piece of paper and wet it with rum: it will never get mouldy, even without ice.'

III

Kitty was especially glad of the chance to be alone with her husband, because she had noticed a shadow of chagrin cross his face, which reflected everything so vividly, when he had come out on the terrace, asked what they were talking about and received no answer.

When they went on foot ahead of the others and were out of sight of the house on the hard-packed, dusty road strewn with ears and grains of rye, she leaned more heavily on his arm and pressed it to her. He had already forgotten the momentary, unpleasant impression, and alone with her now, when the thought of her pregnancy never left him for a moment, he experienced what was for him a new and joyful delight, completely free of sensuality, in the closeness of a loved woman. There was nothing to say, but he wanted to hear the sound of her voice, which had changed now with her pregnancy, as had her look. In her voice, as in her look, there was a softness and seriousness such as occurs in people who are constantly focused on one beloved task.

'So you won't get tired? Lean more on me,' he said.

'No, I'm so glad of the chance to be alone with you, and I confess, good as it is for me to be with them, I miss our winter evenings together.'

'That was good, and this is still better. Both are better,' he said, pressing her arm to him.

'Do you know what we were talking about when you came?'

'Jam?'

'Yes, about jam, too. But also about how men propose.'

'Ah!' said Levin, listening more to the sound of her voice than to what she was saying, and thinking all the while about the road, which now took them through the woods, and avoiding places where she might stumble.

'And about Sergei Ivanych and Varenka. Have you noticed? . . . I wish it very much,' she went on. 'What do you think about it?' And she looked into his face.

'I don't know what to think,' Levin replied, smiling. 'I find Sergei very strange in that respect. I did tell you . . .'

'Yes, that he was in love with that girl who died . . .'

'That was when I was a child; I know it by hearsay. I remember him then. He was amazingly nice. But since then I've been observing him with women: he's courteous, he likes some of them, but you feel that they're simply people for him, not women.'

'Yes, but now with Varenka . . . It seems there's something . . .'

'Maybe there is . . . But you have to know him . . . He's a special, astonishing man. He lives only a spiritual life. He's an exceedingly pure and high-minded man.'

'How do you mean? Will it lower him?'

'No, but he's so used to living only a spiritual life that he can't reconcile himself with actuality, and Varenka is after all an actuality.'

Levin was used now to speaking his thought boldly, without troubling to put it into precise words; he knew that his wife, in such loving moments as this, would understand what he wanted to say from a hint, and she did understand him.

'Yes, but it's not the same actuality in her as in me. I can understand that he could never love me. She's all spiritual . . .'

'Ah, no, he loves you so, and it always pleases me that my people love you.'

'Yes, he's good to me, but . . .'

'But not like the late Nikolenka . . . you really fell in love with each other,' Levin finished. 'Why not speak of it?' he added. 'I sometimes reproach myself: one ends by forgetting. Ah, what a terrible and lovely man he was . . . Yes, what were we talking about?' Levin said after a pause.

'You think he's unable to fall in love,' said Kitty, translating it into her own language.

'Not exactly unable,' said Levin, smiling, 'but he doesn't have the weakness necessary . . . I've always envied him, and I still envy him even now, when I'm so happy.'

'You envy him for being unable to fall in love?'

'I envy him for being better than I am,' said Levin, smiling. 'He doesn't live for himself. His whole life is subordinated to duty. And therefore he can be calm and satisfied.'

'And you?' said Kitty, with a mocking, loving smile.

She would never have been able to express the train of thought that made her smile; but the final conclusion was that her husband, in admiring his brother and demeaning himself before him, was insincere. Kitty knew that this insincerity came from his love for his brother, from his embarrassment at being too happy, and especially from the desire to be better, which never left him – she loved that in him, and so she smiled.

'And you? What are you dissatisfied with?' she asked with the same smile.

Her disbelief in his dissatisfaction with himself delighted him, and he unconsciously provoked her to give the reasons for her disbelief.

'I'm happy, but dissatisfied with myself . . .' he said.

'How can you be dissatisfied if you're happy?'

'I mean, how shall I tell you? . . . In my heart I wish for nothing except that you shouldn't stumble now. Ah, no, you mustn't jump like that!' He interrupted his talk with a reproach, because she had made too quick a movement stepping over a branch that lay in the path. 'But when I consider myself and compare myself with others, especially with my brother, I feel that I'm bad.'

'But in what?' Kitty went on with the same smile. 'Don't you also do things for others? And your farmsteads, and your farming, and your book? . . .'

'No, I feel – especially now, and it's your fault,' he said, pressing her arm to him, 'that that is not it. I do it casually, lightly. If I could love all this as I love you . . . but lately I've been doing it as a set task.'

'Well, what would you say of papa?' asked Kitty. 'Is he bad, too, since he's done nothing for the common cause?'

'He? No. But one must have the simplicity, clarity and kindness that your father has, and do I have that? I do nothing and I suffer. It's all your doing. When there was no you and no *this*,' he said, with a glance at her stomach, which she understood, 'I put all my strength into my work. But now I can't and I'm ashamed; I do it just like a set task, I pretend . . .'

'Well, and would you like to change places with Sergei Ivanych now?' said Kitty. 'Would you like to work for this common cause and love this set task as he does, and only that?'

'Of course not,' said Levin. 'Anyhow, I'm so happy that I don't understand anything. And you really think he's going to propose today?' he added after a pause.

'I do and don't. Only I want it terribly. Wait a second.' She bent down and picked a wild daisy by the roadside. 'Here, count: he will propose, he won't propose,' she said, handing him the daisy.

'He will, he won't,' Levin said, tearing off the narrow, white, grooved petals.

'No, no!' Kitty, who was excitedly watching his fingers, seized his hand. 'You've torn off two.'

'Well, but this little one doesn't count,' said Levin, tearing off a short, undeveloped petal. 'And here's the wagonette catching up with us.'

'Aren't you tired, Kitty?' the princess shouted.

'Not in the least.'

'You could get in, if the horses stay quiet and walk slowly.'

But it was not worthwhile getting in. They were nearly there, and everybody went on foot.

IV

Varenka, with her white kerchief over her dark hair, surrounded by children, good-naturedly and cheerfully occupied with them, and apparently excited by the possibility of a declaration from a man she liked, was very attractive. Sergei Ivanovich walked beside her and kept admiring her. Looking at her, he recalled all the nice conversation he had heard from her, all the good he had heard about her, and realized more and more that the feeling he had for her was something special, which he had experienced long, long ago, and only once, in his early youth. The feeling of joy at her nearness, ever increasing, reached the point where, as he put into her basket a huge mushroom he had found, with a slender foot and upturned edge, he glanced into her eyes and, noticing the blush of joyful and frightened excitement that spread over her face, became confused himself and silently smiled to her the sort of smile that says all too much.

'If it's so,' he said to himself, 'I must think it over and decide, and not give myself like a boy to some momentary infatuation.'

'I'll go now and gather mushrooms on my own, otherwise my acquisitions won't be noticed,' he said and went alone away from the edge of the wood, where they were walking over silky, low grass among sparse old birches, towards the depths of the wood, where grey aspen trunks and dark hazel bushes showed among the white birch trunks. Going some forty paces away and stepping behind a spindle-tree in full bloom with its pinkish-red catkins, Sergei Ivanovich stopped, knowing he could not be seen. Around him it was perfectly still. Only the flies made a ceaseless noise like a swarm of bees in the tops of the birches he was standing under, and now and then the children's voices reached him. Suddenly, from the edge of the wood not far away, he heard Varenka's contralto calling Grisha, and a joyful smile lit up Sergei Ivanovich's face. Conscious of this smile, Sergei Ivanovich shook his head disapprovingly at the state he was in and, taking out a cigar, began to light it. For a long time he was unable to strike a match against the birch trunk. The tender film of the white bark stuck to the phosphorus and the flame went out. Finally a match flared up, and the strong-scented smoke of the cigar, clearly outlined in a broad, undulating sheet, spread forward and up over the bush under the hanging birch branches. Following the strip of smoke with his eyes, Sergei Ivanovich walked on at a slow pace, reflecting on his state.

'And why not?' he thought. 'If it were a momentary flash or passion, if I experienced only this attraction – this mutual attraction (I may call it "mutual") – but felt that it went against my whole mode of life, if I felt that in yielding to this attraction I would betray my calling and my duty . . . but it's not so. The only thing I can say against it is that, when I lost Marie, I told myself I would remain faithful to her memory. That is all I can say against my feeling . . . That's important,' Sergei Ivanovich said to himself, feeling at the same time that for him personally this consideration could have no importance at all, but would only spoil his poetic role in the eyes of others. 'But apart from that, search as I may, I won't find anything to say against my feeling. If I were to choose with my mind alone, I couldn't find anything better.'

He recalled any number of women and girls he knew, but could not recall one who would combine to such a degree all, precisely all, the qualities that he, reasoning coldly, would wish to see in his wife. She had all the loveliness and freshness of youth, yet she was not a child, and if she loved him, she loved him consciously, as a woman should love: that was one thing. Another: she was not only far from worldliness, but obviously had a loathing for the world, yet at the same time she knew that world and had all the manners of a woman of good society, without which a life's companion was unthinkable for Sergei Ivanovich. Third: she was religious, and not unaccountably religious and good, like a child, like Kitty, for instance, but her life was based on religious convictions. Even to the smallest details, Sergei Ivanovich found in her everything he could wish for in a wife: she was poor and alone, so she would not bring a heap of relations and their influence into the house, as he saw with Kitty, but would be obliged to her husband in all things, which he had also always wished for his future family life. And this girl, who combined all these qualities in herself, loved him. He was modest, but he could not fail to see it. And he loved her. One negative consideration was his age. But his breed was long-lived, he did not have a single grey hair, no one would have taken him for forty, and he remembered Varenka saying that it was only in Russia that people considered themselves old at the age of fifty, that in France a fifty-year-old man considered himself *dans la force de l'âge*,* and a forty-year-old *un jeune homme*.† But what did the counting of years mean if he felt himself young in his soul, as he had been twenty years ago? Was it not youth, the feeling he experienced now, when, coming out to the edge of the wood again from the other side, he saw in the bright light of the sun's slanting rays Varenka's graceful figure, in a yellow dress and with her basket, walking with a light step past the trunk of an old birch, and when this impression from the sight of Varenka merged with the sight, which struck him with its beauty, of a yellowing field of oats bathed in the slanting light, and of an old wood far beyond the field, spotted with yellow, melting into the blue distance? His heart was wrung with joy. A feeling of tenderness came over him. He felt resolved. Varenka, who had just crouched down to pick a mushroom, stood up with a supple movement and looked over her shoulder. Throwing his cigar away, Sergei Ivanovich walked towards her with resolute strides.

* In the prime of life.

† A young man.

V

'Varvara Andreevna, when I was still very young, I made up for myself an ideal of the woman I would love and whom I would be happy to call my wife. I have lived a long life, and now for the first time I have met in you what I have been seeking. I love you and offer you my hand.'

Sergei Ivanovich was saying this to himself when he was just ten steps away from Varenka. Kneeling down and protecting a mushroom from Grisha with her hands, she was calling little Masha.

'Here, here! There are small ones! Lots!' she said in her sweet, mellow voice.

Seeing Sergei Ivanovich approaching, she did not get up and did not change her position, but everything told him that she felt him approaching and was glad of it.

'So, did you find any?' she asked, turning her beautiful, quietly smiling face to him from behind the white kerchief.

'Not one,' said Sergei Ivanovich. 'And you?'

She did not answer him, busy with the children around her.

'That one, too, by the branch.' She pointed Masha to a small mushroom, its resilient pink cap cut across by a dry blade of grass it had sprung up under. She stood up when Masha picked the mushroom, breaking it into two white halves. 'This reminds me of my childhood,' she added, stepping away from the children with Sergei Ivanovich.

They went on silently for a few steps. Varenka saw that he wanted to speak. She guessed what it was about and her heart was gripped by the excitement of joy and fear. They went far enough away so that no one could hear them, and still he did not begin to speak. It would have been better for Varenka to remain silent. After a silence it would have been easier to say what they wanted to say than after talking about mushrooms; but against her own will, as if inadvertently, Varenka said:

'So you didn't find any? But then there are always fewer inside the wood.'

Sergei Ivanovich sighed and made no answer. He was vexed that she had begun talking about mushrooms. He wanted to bring her back to her first words about her childhood; but, as if against his will, after being silent for a while, he commented on her last words.

'I've heard only that the white boletus grows mostly on the edge, though I'm unable to identify it.'

Several more minutes passed, they went still further away from the children and were completely alone. Varenka's heart was pounding so that she could hear it, and she felt herself blush, then turn pale, then blush again.

To be the wife of a man like Koznyshev, after her situation with Mme Stahl, seemed to her the height of happiness. Besides, she was almost certain that she was in love with him. And now it was to be decided. She was frightened. Frightened that he would speak, and that he would not.

He had to declare himself now or never; Sergei Ivanovich felt it, too. Everything in Varenka's gaze, colour, lowered eyes, showed painful expectation. Sergei Ivanovich saw it and pitied her. He even felt that to say nothing now would be to insult her. In his mind he quickly repeated all the arguments in favour of his decision. He also repeated to himself the words in which he wished to express his proposal; but instead of those words, by some unexpected consideration that occurred to him, he suddenly asked:

'And what is the difference between a white boletus and a birch boletus?'

Varenka's lips trembled as she answered:

'There's hardly any difference in the caps, but in the feet.'

And as soon as these words were spoken, both he and she understood that the matter was ended, and that what was to have been said would not be said, and their excitement, which had reached its highest point just before then, began to subside.

'In the birch boletus, the foot resembles a two-day growth of beard on a dark-haired man,' Sergei Ivanovich said, calmly now.

'Yes, that's true,' Varenka replied, smiling, and the direction of their walk changed inadvertently. They began going towards the children. Varenka was both hurt and ashamed, but at the same time she had a sense of relief.

On returning home and going through all the arguments, Sergei Ivanovich found that his reasoning had been wrong. He could not betray the memory of Marie.

'Quiet, children, quiet!' Levin shouted angrily at the children, standing in front of his wife in order to protect her, when the bunch of children came flying to meet them with shrieks of joy.

After the children, Sergei Ivanovich and Varenka also came out of the wood. Kitty had no need to ask Varenka; from the calm and somewhat embarrassed expressions on both their faces, she understood that her plans had not worked out.

'Well, what happened?' her husband asked, as they went back home.

'Didn't bite,' said Kitty, her smile and manner of speaking resembling her father's, something Levin often noticed in her with pleasure.

'Didn't bite, meaning what?'

'Like this,' she said, taking her husband's hand, putting it to her mouth, and touching it with unopened lips. 'Like kissing a bishop's hand.'

'But which of them didn't bite?' he said, laughing.

'Neither. And it should have been like this . . .'

'There are muzhiks coming . . .'

'No, they didn't see.'

VI

During the children's tea the grown-ups sat on the balcony talking as if nothing had happened, though they all knew very well, Sergei Ivanovich and Varenka especially, that something important, though negative, had happened. They both experienced an identical feeling, similar to that of a pupil after failing an examination, staying in the same class or being expelled from the institution for good. Everyone present, also feeling that something had happened, talked animatedly about unrelated subjects. Levin and Kitty felt particularly happy and amorous that evening. And the fact that they were happy in their love contained in itself an unpleasant allusion to those who wanted but could not have the same – and they were embarrassed.

'Mark my words: Alexandre won't come,' said the old princess.

Stepan Arkadyich was expected on the train that evening, and the old prince had written that he, too, might come.

'And I know why,' the princess went on. 'He says that a young couple should be left alone at first.'

'But papa has left us alone. We haven't seen him,' said Kitty. 'And what kind of young couple are we? We're already so old.'

'Only if he doesn't come, I, too, will say good-bye to you, children,' said the princess, sighing sadly.

'Well, what is it to you, mama!' Both daughters fell upon her.

'But think, how is it for him? You see, now . . .'

And suddenly, quite unexpectedly, the old princess's voice trembled. Her daughters fell silent and exchanged glances. '*Maman* always finds something sad for herself,' they said with these glances. They did not know that, good as it was for the princess to be at her daughter's, and useful as she felt herself there, it had been painfully sad for her and for her husband since they had given away their last beloved daughter in marriage and the family nest had been left empty.

'What is it, Agafya Mikhailovna?' Kitty suddenly asked Agafya Mikhailovna, who stood there with a mysterious look and an important face.

'About supper.'

'Well, that's wonderful,' said Dolly. 'You go and give the orders, and I'll go with Grisha to hear his lesson. Otherwise he'll have done nothing today.'

'That's a lesson for me! No, Dolly, I'll go,' said Levin, jumping up.

Grisha, already enrolled in school, had to go over his lessons during the summer. Darya Alexandrovna, who had studied Latin with her son while still in Moscow, had made it a rule when she came to the Levins' to go over the most difficult lessons in arithmetic and Latin with him at least once a day. Levin had volunteered to replace her; but the mother had heard Levin's lesson once and, noticing that he did not do it in the same way as the teacher in Moscow, embarrassed and trying not to offend him, had told him resolutely that it was necessary to go by the book, as the teacher did, and that she had better do it again herself. Levin was vexed both with Stepan Arkadyich, who in his carelessness left it to the mother to look after the teaching, of which she understood nothing, instead of doing it himself, and with the teachers for teaching children so poorly; but he promised his sister-in-law that he would conduct the lessons as she wished. And he went on tutoring Grisha, not in his own way now but by the book, and therefore did it reluctantly and often missed the time of the lesson. So it happened that day.

'No, I'll go, Dolly, and you sit,' he said. 'We'll do everything properly, by the book. Only when Stiva comes and we go hunting, then I'll skip.'

And Levin went to Grisha.

Varenka said the same thing to Kitty. Even in the happy, comfortable home of the Levins, Varenka was able to be useful.

'I'll order supper, and you sit,' she said and got up to go with Agafya Mikhailovna.

'Yes, yes, they probably couldn't find any chickens. Our own, then . . .' Kitty said.

'We'll decide, Agafya Mikhailovna and I.' And Varenka disappeared with her.

'What a dear girl!' said the princess.

'Not dear, *maman*, but as lovely as can be.'

'So you're expecting Stepan Arkadyich today?' asked Sergei Ivanovich, obviously unwilling to continue the conversation about Varenka. 'It's hard to find two brothers-in-law less alike than your husbands,' he said with a subtle smile. 'One all movement, living in society like a fish in water, the other, our Kostya, alive, quick, sensitive to everything, but the moment he's in society, he either freezes or thrashes about senselessly like a fish on dry land.'

'Yes, he's very light-minded,' said the princess, turning to Sergei Ivanovich. 'I precisely wanted you to tell him that it's impossible for her, for Kitty, to stay here, that she must come to Moscow. He talks of sending for a doctor . . .'

'*Maman*, he'll do everything, he'll agree to everything,' said Kitty, vexed with her mother for inviting Sergei Ivanovich to judge in the matter.

In the midst of their conversation they heard a snorting of horses and the sound of wheels on the gravel of the drive.

Before Dolly had time to get up and go to meet her husband, Levin jumped out the window of the downstairs room where Grisha studied and helped Grisha out.

'It's Stiva!' Levin shouted from under the balcony. 'We finished, Dolly, don't worry!' he added and, like a boy, went running to meet the carriage.

'*Is, ea, id, ejus, ejus, ejus*,'* cried Grisha, skipping down the drive.

'And somebody else. Must be papa!' Levin cried out, stopping at the entrance to the drive. 'Kitty, don't go down the steep stairs, go around.'

But Levin was mistaken in taking the one sitting in the carriage with Oblonsky for the old prince. When he got close to the carriage, he saw beside Stepan Arkadyich not the prince but a handsome, stout young man in a Scotch cap with long ribbons hanging down behind. This was Vasenka Veslovsky, the Shcherbatskys' cousin twice removed, a brilliant

* He, she, it, his, hers, its.

man around Petersburg and Moscow – 'a most excellent fellow and a passionate hunter', as Stepan Arkadyich introduced him.

Not put out in the least at the disappointment he caused by replacing the old prince with himself, Veslovsky gaily greeted Levin, reminding him of their former acquaintance, and, taking Grisha up into the carriage, lifted him over the pointer that Stepan Arkadyich had brought along.

Levin did not get into the carriage but walked behind. He was slightly vexed that the old prince, whom he loved more the more he knew him, had not come, and that this Vasenka Veslovsky, a completely alien and superfluous man, had appeared. He seemed all the more alien and superfluous in that, when Levin came up to the porch where the whole animated crowd of grown-ups and children had gathered, he saw Vasenka Veslovsky kiss Kitty's hand with an especially gentle and gallant air.

'Your wife and I are cousins, as well as old acquaintances,' said Vasenka Veslovsky, again pressing Levin's hand very, very firmly.

'Well, is there any game?' Stepan Arkadyich turned to Levin, having barely had time to say hello to everyone. 'He and I have come with the cruellest intentions. Of course, *maman*, they haven't been to Moscow since. Well, Tanya, there's something for you! Get it from the back of the carriage, please,' he spoke in all directions. 'How fresh you look, Dollenka,' he said to his wife, kissing her hand again, keeping it in his own and patting it with his other hand.

Levin, who a minute ago had been in the merriest spirits, now looked darkly at everyone and did not like anything.

'Who did he kiss yesterday with those lips?' he thought, gazing at Stepan Arkadyich's tenderness with his wife. He looked at Dolly and did not like her either.

'She doesn't believe in his love. Then why is she so glad? Revolting!' thought Levin.

He looked at the princess, who had been so dear to him a moment ago, and did not like the manner in which she welcomed this Vasenka with his ribbons, as if she were in her own home.

Even Sergei Ivanovich, who also came out on to the porch, seemed unpleasant to him in the sham friendliness with which he met Stepan Arkadyich, when Levin knew that his brother neither liked nor respected Oblonsky.

And Varenka, too, was disgusting to him, with her look of a *sainte* *nitouche*,* as she made the acquaintance of this gentleman, while all she thought about was getting married.

And most disgusting of all was Kitty, the way she yielded to the tone of merriment with which this gentleman regarded his arrival in the country as a festive occasion for himself and everyone, and particularly unpleasant was the special smile with which she responded to his smiles.

Talking noisily, they all went into the house; but as soon as they all sat down, Levin turned round and left.

Kitty saw that something was wrong with her husband. She wanted to snatch a moment and talk to him alone, but he hastened away from her, saying he had to go to the office. It was long since his farm affairs had seemed so important to him as they did right then. 'It's all a holiday for them,' he thought, 'but these are no holiday affairs, they won't wait and without them life is impossible.'

VII

Levin returned home only when they sent to call him to supper. Kitty and Agafya Mikhailovna were standing on the stairs, conferring about the wines.

'Why make such a fuss? Serve what you usually do.'

'No, Stiva won't drink . . . Kostya, wait, what's the matter?' Kitty began to say, running after him, but he mercilessly strode off to the dining room without waiting for her and at once got into the animated general conversation that Vasenka Veslovsky and Stepan Arkadyich were carrying on there.

'Well, what about it, shall we go hunting tomorrow?' said Stepan Arkadyich.

'Yes, please, let's go,' said Veslovsky, shifting his chair and sitting on it sideways, tucking his fat leg under him.

'I'll be very glad to. And have you already gone hunting this year?' Levin said to Veslovsky, studying his leg attentively, but with an assumed pleasantness that Kitty knew so well and that was so unbecoming to him. 'I don't know if we'll find any great snipe, but there are plenty of

* Holy touch-me-not.

snipe. Only we'll have to start early. You won't be tired? Aren't you tired, Stiva?'

'Me tired? I've never been tired yet. Let's not sleep all night! Let's go for a walk.'

'Yes, really, let's not sleep! Excellent!' agreed Veslovsky.

'Oh, we're quite sure of that, that you can go without sleep and keep others from sleeping,' Dolly said to her husband with that barely noticeable irony with which she almost always treated him now. 'And I think it's now time . . . I'm off to bed, I won't have supper.'

'No, stay here, Dollenka,' said Stepan Arkadyich, going round to her side of the big table at which they were having supper. 'I have lots more to tell you!'

'Nothing, I'm sure.'

'You know, Veslovsky's been to see Anna. And he's going there again. They're less than fifty miles from us. I'll certainly go, too. Veslovsky, come here!'

Vasenka moved over to the ladies and sat down beside Kitty.

'Ah, tell us, please! So you've been to see her? How is she?' Darya Alexandrovna turned to him.

Levin stayed at the other end of the table and, without ceasing to talk with the princess and Varenka, saw that an animated and mysterious conversation was going on between Dolly, Kitty and Veslovsky. Not only was a mysterious conversation going on, but he could see in his wife's face an expression of serious feeling as she gazed into the handsome face of Vasenka, who was animatedly telling them something.

'It's very nice at their place,' Vasenka was saying about Vronsky and Anna. 'Naturally, I don't take it upon myself to judge, but in their house you feel as if you're in a family.'

'And what do they intend to do?'

'It seems they want to go to Moscow for the winter.'

'How nice it would be for us all to get together at their place! When are you going?' Stepan Arkadyich asked Vasenka.

'I'll spend July with them.'

'And will you go?' Stepan Arkadyich turned to his wife.

'I've long wanted to go and certainly will,' said Dolly. 'I pity her, and I know her. She's a wonderful woman. I'll go alone after you leave, and I won't be in anyone's way. It will even be better without you.'

'Well, splendid,' said Stepan Arkadyich. 'And you, Kitty?'

'Me? Why should I go?' said Kitty, flushing all over. And she turned to look at her husband.

'Are you acquainted with Anna Arkadyevna?' Veslovsky asked her. 'She's a very attractive woman.'

'Yes,' Kitty, turning still more red, replied to Veslovsky, got up and went to her husband.

'So you're going hunting tomorrow?' she said.

His jealousy had gone far in those few minutes, especially after the blush that had covered her cheeks as she talked with Veslovsky. Listening to her words, he now understood them in his own way. Strange as it was for him to recall it later, it seemed clear to him now that if she asked him whether he was going hunting, she was interested only in knowing whether he would give this pleasure to Vasenka Veslovsky, with whom, to his mind, she was already in love.

'Yes, I am,' he replied in an unnatural voice that he himself found disgusting.

'No, better if you stay at home tomorrow, since Dolly hasn't seen her husband at all, and go the day after,' said Kitty.

Levin now interpreted the meaning of Kitty's words as follows: 'Don't part me from *him*. I don't care if you leave, but let me enjoy the company of this charming young man.'

'Oh, if you wish, we can stay at home tomorrow,' Levin replied with special pleasantness.

Vasenka meanwhile, not in the least suspecting all the suffering his presence caused, got up from the table after Kitty and followed her with a smiling, gentle gaze.

Levin saw this gaze. He paled and could not catch his breath for a moment. 'How can he allow himself to look at my wife like that!' seethed in him.

'Tomorrow, then? Let's go, please,' said Vasenka, sitting down on a chair and again tucking his leg under, as was his habit.

Levin's jealousy had gone further still. He already saw himself as a deceived husband, needed by his wife and her lover only to provide them with life's conveniences and pleasures . . . But, despite that, he courteously and hospitably questioned Vasenka about his hunting, guns, boots and agreed to go the next day.

Fortunately for Levin, the old princess put an end to his agony by getting up herself and advising Kitty to go to bed. But here, too, it did not pass without new suffering for Levin. Saying good-night to his hostess, Vasenka again went to kiss her hand, but Kitty, blushing, with a naïve rudeness for which she was later reprimanded by her mother, drew back her hand and said:

'That's not done in our house.'

In Levin's eyes she was to blame for having permitted such relations, and still more to blame for showing so awkwardly that she did not like them.

'Well, who cares about sleep!' said Stepan Arkadyich, who, after drinking several glasses of wine at dinner, was in his sweetest, most poetical mood. 'Look, Kitty, look!' he said, pointing to the moon rising from behind the lindens. 'How lovely! Veslovsky, it's time for a serenade. You know, he has a fine voice; he and I sang together on our way here. He's brought some wonderful romances along, two new ones. We should sing with Varvara Andreevna.'

When they had all dispersed, Stepan Arkadyich and Veslovsky paced up and down the drive for a long time, and their voices could be heard singing a new romance together.

Listening to those voices, Levin sat scowling in the armchair in his wife's bedroom and to her questions about what was the matter maintained an obstinate silence; but when she finally asked with a timid smile: 'Was it something you disliked about Veslovsky?' – he burst out and said everything. What he said was insulting to himself and therefore irritated him still more.

He stood before her, his eyes flashing terribly from under his scowling eyebrows, pressing his strong hands to his chest, as if straining with all his might to hold himself back. The expression on his face would have been stern and even cruel had it not at the same time expressed suffering, which touched her. His jaw was twitching, and his voice broke.

'You understand that I'm not jealous: it's a vile word. I cannot be jealous, or believe that . . . I cannot say what I'm feeling, but it's terrible . . . I'm not jealous, but I'm offended, humiliated that someone dares to think, dares to look at you with such eyes . . .'

'What eyes?' said Kitty, trying as conscientiously as she could to recall all the words and gestures of that evening and all their nuances.

In the depths of her soul she found that there had been something of the sort, precisely at the moment when he had gone after her to the other end of the table, but she dared not confess it even to herself, much less venture to tell it to him and so increase his suffering.

'But what can be attractive in me the way I am? . . .'

'Ah!' he cried, clutching his head. 'Hear what she says! . . . So, if you were attractive . . .'

'No, Kostya, wait, listen!' she said, looking at him with an expression of suffering commiseration. 'What can you be thinking? When nobody exists for me, nobody, nobody! . . . Do you want me not to see anyone?'

In the first moment his jealousy offended her; she was vexed that the smallest diversion, and the most innocent, was forbidden her; but now she would gladly have sacrificed not just such trifles but everything to deliver him from the suffering he was going through.

'You understand the horror and comicality of my position,' he went on in a desperate whisper, 'that he's in my house, that he essentially did nothing improper, except for this casualness and tucking his leg under. He considers it the best tone, and so I have to be courteous to him.'

'But, Kostya, you're exaggerating,' said Kitty, who in the depths of her soul rejoiced at the strength of his love which was now expressing itself in his jealousy.

'The most terrible thing is that you – the way you always are, and now, when you're so sacred to me and we're so happy, so especially happy, and suddenly this trash . . . Not trash, why do I abuse him? I don't care about him. But why should my happiness, your happiness . . . ?'

'You know, I understand how it happened,' Kitty began.

'How? How?'

'I saw the way you looked as we were talking over dinner.'

'Ah, yes, yes!' Levin said fearfully.

She told him what they had been talking about. And as she told it, she was breathless with agitation. Levin remained silent, then looked closer at her pale, frightened face and suddenly clutched his head.

'Katia, I'm tormenting you! Darling, forgive me! It's madness! Katia, it's my fault all round. How could I suffer so over such stupidity?'

'No, I'm sorry for you.'

'For me? For me? What am I? A madman! . . . But why you? It's terrible to think that any outsider can upset our happiness.'

'Of course, that's the offensive thing . . .'

'No, but, on the contrary, I'll have him stay with us all summer, on purpose, and I'll overflow with courtesy,' Levin said, kissing her hands. 'You'll see. Tomorrow . . . Ah, right, tomorrow we're leaving.'

VIII

The next day, before the ladies were up, the hunting carriages, carts and a small wagon stood at the entrance, and Laska, who since morning had understood that they were going hunting, having squealed and jumped her fill, got into the cart beside the driver, looking at the doorway through which the hunters had yet to come with excitement and disapproval of the delay. The first to come out was Vasenka Veslovsky, in big, new boots that reached half-way up his fat haunches, in a green blouse tied at the waist with a cartridge belt smelling of new leather, and in his cap with ribbons, carrying a new English gun with no swivel or sling. Laska bounded over to him, jumped up to greet him, asked him in her own way whether the others were coming out, but, receiving no answer, went back to her lookout post and again froze, her head cocked and one ear pricked up. Finally the door opened with a bang, out flew Krak, Stepan Arkadyich's golden and white pointer, spinning and turning in the air, and then Stepan Arkadyich himself came out with a gun in his hands and a cigar in his mouth. 'Good boy, good boy, Krak!' he called tenderly to the dog, who put his paws on his stomach and chest, clawing at the game bag. Stepan Arkadyich was dressed in brogues and leggings, tattered trousers and a short coat. On his head was the wreck of some hat, but his new-system gun was a jewel, and his game bag and cartridge belt, though worn, were of the best quality.

Vasenka Veslovsky had not previously understood this true hunter's dandyism – to wear rags but have hunting gear of the best make. He understood it now, looking at Stepan Arkadyich, shining in those rags with the elegance of his well-nourished, gentlemanly figure, and decided that before the next hunting season he would be sure to set himself up in the same way.

'Well, and what about our host?' he asked.

'A young wife,' Stepan Arkadyich said, smiling.

'Yes, and such a lovely one.'

'He was already dressed. He must have run back to her.'

Stepan Arkadyich had guessed right. Levin had run back to his wife to ask her once more if she had forgiven him for yesterday's foolishness, and also to beg her for the Lord's sake to be more careful. Above all, to keep further away from the children – they could always bump into her.

Then he had to have her confirm once again that she was not angry with him for leaving for two days, and also to ask her to be sure to send a mounted messenger the next morning with a note, to write just two words so that he would know she was well.

Kitty, as always, was pained at having to be parted from her husband for two days, but seeing his animated figure, which seemed particularly big and strong in hunting boots and a white blouse, and with the glow of some hunting excitement incomprehensible to her, she forgot her own distress because of his joy and cheerfully said good-bye to him.

'Sorry, gentlemen!' he said, running out to the porch. 'Did they put the lunch in? Why is the chestnut on the right? Well, never mind. Laska, enough, go and sit down!'

'Put them in with the heifers,' he turned to the cow-man, who had been waiting by the porch with a question about some bullocks. 'Sorry, here comes another villain.'

Levin jumped down from the cart in which he was already seated to meet the hired carpenter, who was walking up to the porch with a ruler.

'You see, you didn't come to the office yesterday and now you're holding me up. Well, what is it?'

'Let me make another turn, sir. To add three more steps. And we'll fit it right in. It'll be much more convenient.'

'You should have listened to me,' Levin replied with vexation. 'I told you to put up the string boards and then cut in the steps. You can't fix it now. Do as I told you – make a new one.'

The thing was that the carpenter had spoiled the staircase in the wing that was being built, having constructed it separately and miscalculated the height, so that when it was installed all the steps were aslant. Now he wanted to leave the same stairs in place and add three more steps.

'It will be much better.'

'But where will it come out with these three steps?'

'If you please, sir,' the carpenter said with a scornful smile. 'It'll go just right. I mean, it'll start out below,' he said with a persuasive gesture, 'and go up and up and come out just right.'

'But three steps will also add to the length . . . Where will it end?'

'Like I said, it'll start below and come out just right,' the carpenter said stubbornly and persuasively.

'It will come out under the ceiling and into the wall.'

'If you please. She'll start below. She'll go up and up and come out just right.'

Levin took a ramrod and began drawing a stairway in the dust for him.

'There, you see?'

'As you wish,' said the carpenter, with suddenly bright eyes, obviously understanding the whole thing at last. 'Looks like I'll have to make a new one.'

'Well, then make it the way you were told!' Levin shouted, getting up on the cart. 'Drive! Hold the dogs, Filipp!'

Levin, having left all his family and farming cares behind, now experienced such a strong sense of the joy of life and expectation that he did not want to talk. Besides, he had that feeling of concentrated excitement that every hunter experiences as he nears the place of action. If anything concerned him now, it was only the questions of whether they would find anything in the Kolpeno marsh, how Laska would perform in comparison with Krak and how successful his own shooting would be that day. What if he disgraced himself in front of the new man? What if Oblonsky outshot him? – also went through his head.

Oblonsky had similar feelings and was also untalkative. Only Vasenka Veslovsky kept cheerfully talking away. Listening to him now, Levin was ashamed to remember how unfair he had been to him yesterday. Vasenka was indeed a nice fellow, simple, good-natured and very cheerful. If Levin had met him while still a bachelor, he would have become friends with him. He found his holiday attitude towards life and his sort of loose-mannered elegance slightly disagreeable. As if he considered himself lofty and unquestionably important for having long fingernails and a little hat and the rest that went with it; but that could be excused on account of his kind-heartedness and decency. Levin liked in him his good upbringing, his excellent pronunciation of French and English, and the fact that he was a man of his own world.

Vasenka was extremely taken with the left outrunner, a Don Steppe horse. He kept admiring it.

'How good it must be to gallop over the steppe on a steppe horse! Eh? Am I right?' he said.

He imagined there was something wild and poetic in riding a steppe horse, though nothing came of it; but his naïvety, especially combined with his good looks, sweet smile, and gracefulness of movement, was very attractive. Either because Veslovsky's nature was sympathetic to him, or because he was trying to find everything good in him in order to redeem yesterday's sin, Levin enjoyed being with him.

Having gone two miles, Veslovsky suddenly discovered that his cigars and wallet were missing and did not know whether he had lost them or left them on the table. There were three hundred and seventy roubles in his wallet, and it could not be left like that.

'You know what, Levin, I'll ride back on this Don outrunner. That will be splendid. Eh?' he said, preparing to mount up.

'No, why?' replied Levin, who reckoned that Vasenka must weigh no less than two hundred pounds. 'I'll send my coachman.'

The coachman went on the outrunner, and Levin drove the pair himself.

IX

'Well, what's our itinerary? Tell us all about it,' said Stepan Arkadyich.

'The plan is the following: right now we're going as far as Gvozdevo.[1] In Gvozdevo there's a marsh with great snipe on the near side, and beyond Gvozdevo there are wonderful snipe marshes, with occasional great snipe. It's hot now, but we'll arrive towards evening (it's twelve miles) and do the evening field. We'll spend the night, and tomorrow we'll go to the big marsh.'

'And there's nothing on the way?'

'There is, but that would delay us, and it's hot. There are two nice spots, though it's not likely there'll be anything.'

Levin himself would have liked to stop at those spots, but they were close to home, he could do them any time, and they were small – three men would have no room to shoot. And so it was with some duplicity that he said it was not likely there would be anything. Coming to the small marsh, he was going to pass by, but the experienced hunter's eye of Stepan Arkadyich at once spotted rushes that were visible from the road.

'Won't we try there?' he said, pointing to the marsh.

'Levin, please! how splendid!' Vasenka Veslovsky started begging, and Levin had to consent.

No sooner had they stopped than the dogs, vying with each other, were already racing for the marsh.

'Krak! Laska! . . .'

The dogs came back.

'It's too small for three. I'll stay here,' said Levin, hoping they would find nothing but the lapwings that had been stirred up by the dogs and, swaying as they flew, wept plaintively over the marsh.

'No! Come on, Levin, let's go together!' called Vasenka.

'It's really too small. Here, Laska! Here! You don't need two dogs, do you?'

Levin stayed by the wagonette and watched the hunters with envy. They went all around the marsh. Except for a water hen and some lapwings, one of which Vasenka bagged, there was nothing there.

'So you see, it wasn't that I grudged you this marsh,' said Levin, 'it was just a loss of time.'

'No, it was fun all the same. Did you see?' said Vasenka Veslovsky, awkwardly getting up on the cart with his gun and the lapwing in his hands. 'I bagged this one nicely! Isn't it true? Well, how soon will we get to the real place?'

Suddenly the horses gave a start. Levin hit his head against the barrel of somebody's gun and a shot rang out. So it seemed to Levin, but in fact the shot came first. The thing was that Vasenka Veslovsky, while uncocking the hammers, had his finger on one trigger as he eased off the other. The shot struck the ground, doing no one any harm. Stepan Arkadyich shook his head and laughed reproachfully at Veslovsky. But Levin did not have the heart to reprimand him. First, any reproach would seem to be caused by the danger he had escaped and the bump swelling on his forehead; and second, Veslovsky began by being so naïvely upset and then laughed so good-naturedly and enthusiastically at the general commotion that it was impossible not to laugh with him.

When they drove up to the second marsh, which was quite big and was bound to take a long time, Levin tried to persuade them not to go in, but Veslovsky again insisted. Again, since the marsh was narrow, Levin, as a hospitable host, stayed by the carriages.

Krak made straight for the hummocks. Vasenka Veslovsky was the first to run after the dog. And before Stepan Arkadyich had time to get close, a great snipe had already flown up. Veslovsky missed and the snipe landed in an unmowed meadow. This snipe was left to Veslovsky. Krak found it again, pointed, Veslovsky shot it and went back to the carriages.

'Now you go and I'll stay with the horses,' he said.

Hunter's envy was beginning to take hold of Levin. He handed the reins to Veslovsky and went into the marsh.

Laska, who had long been squealing pitifully and complaining at the injustice, rushed ahead, straight to some trusty hummocks, familiar to Levin, where Krak had not yet gone.

'Why don't you stop her?' cried Stepan Arkadyich.

'She won't scare them,' replied Levin, delighted with the dog and hurrying after her.

Laska's search became more serious the closer she came to the familiar hummocks. A small marsh bird distracted her only for an instant. She made one circle in front of the hummocks, began another, suddenly gave a start and froze.

'Here, here, Stiva!' cried Levin, feeling his heart pounding faster, and it was as if some latch had suddenly opened in his strained hearing, and sounds, losing all measure of distance, began to strike him haphazardly but vividly. He heard Stepan Arkadyich's footsteps and took them for the distant clatter of horses, heard the crunching sound made by the corner of a hummock that he tore off with its roots as he stepped on it and took the sound for the flight of a great snipe. He also heard, not far behind him, some splashing in the water which he could not account for.

Picking his way, he moved towards the dog.

'Flush it!'

Not a great snipe but a snipe tore up from under the dog. Levin followed it with his gun, but just as he was taking aim, that same noise of splashing water increased, came nearer, and was joined by the strangely loud voice of Veslovsky shouting something. Levin saw that he was aiming his gun behind the snipe, but he fired anyway.

After making sure he had missed, Levin turned round and saw that the horses and cart were no longer on the road but in the swamp.

Veslovsky, anxious to see the shooting, had driven into the swamp and mired the horses.

'What the devil got into him!' Levin said to himself, going back to the mired cart. 'Why did you drive in here?' he said drily and, calling the coachman, started freeing the horses.

Levin was vexed because his shooting had been disturbed, and because his horses were stuck in the mud, and above all because neither Stepan Arkadyich nor Veslovsky helped him and the coachman to unharness the horses and get them out, neither of them having the slightest understanding of harnessing. Saying not a word in reply to Vasenka's assurances that it was quite dry there, Levin silently worked with the coachman to free the horses. But then, getting into the heat of the work, and seeing how diligently and zealously Veslovsky pulled the cart by the splash-board, so that he even broke it off, Levin reproached himself for being too cold towards him under the influence of yesterday's feeling, and tried to smooth over his dryness by being especially amiable. When everything was put right and the cart was back on the road, Levin ordered lunch to be served.

'*Bon appétit – bonne conscience! Ce poulet va tomber jusqu'au fond de mes bottes.*'* Vasenka, merry again, joked in French as he finished a second chicken. 'So, now our troubles are over; now everything's going to go well. Only, for my sins I ought to sit on the box. Isn't that right? Eh? No, no, I'm an Automedon.[2] You'll see how I get you there!' he said, not letting go of the reins when Levin asked him to let the coachman drive. 'No, I must redeem my sins, and I feel wonderful on the box.' And he drove on.

Levin was a bit afraid that he would wear out the horses, especially the chestnut on the left, whom he was unable to control; but he involuntarily yielded to his merriment, listened to the romances that Veslovsky, sitting on the box, sang along the way, or to his stories and his imitation of the proper English way of driving a four-in-hand; and after lunch, in the merriest spirits, they drove on to the Gvozdevo marsh.

X

Vasenka drove the horses at such a lively pace that they reached the marsh too early, while it was still hot.

Having arrived at the serious marsh, the main goal of the trip, Levin involuntarily thought about how to get rid of Vasenka and move about unhindered. Stepan Arkadyich obviously wished for the same thing, and Levin saw on his face the preoccupied expression that a true hunter always has before the start of a hunt and a certain good-natured slyness all his own.

'How shall we proceed? I see it's an excellent marsh, and there are hawks,' said Stepan Arkadyich, pointing at two big birds circling over the sedge. 'Where there are hawks, there must be game as well.'

* A good appetite means a good conscience! This chicken is going to drop right to the bottom of my boots [that is, go down very well].

'So you see, gentlemen,' said Levin, pulling up his boots and examining the percussion caps on his gun with a slightly glum expression. 'You see that sedge?' He pointed to a little black-green island showing dark against the huge, half-mowed wet meadow that stretched to the right side of the river. 'The swamp begins there, right in front of us, where it's greener. From there it goes to the right, where those horses are; it's hummocky and there are great snipe; and then around the sedge to that alder grove over there and right up to the mill. See, where that creek is. That's the best spot. I once shot seventeen snipe there. We'll split up in two directions with the two dogs and meet there at the mill.'

'Well, who goes right and who left?' asked Stepan Arkadyich. 'It's wider to the right, the two of you go that way, and I'll go left,' he said as if casually.

'Excellent! We'll outshoot him. Well, let's go, let's go!' Vasenka picked up.

Levin could not but consent, and they went their separate ways.

As soon as they entered the marsh, both dogs began searching together and drew towards a rusty spot. Levin knew this searching of Laska's, cautious and vague; he also knew the spot and was expecting a wisp of snipe.

'Walk beside me, Veslovsky, beside me!' he said in a muted voice to his comrade, who was splashing behind him through the water, and the direction of whose gun, after the accidental shot by the Kolpeno marsh, involuntarily interested him.

'No, I don't want to hamper you, don't think about me.'

But Levin could not help remembering Kitty's words as he parted from her: 'See that you don't shoot each other.' The dogs came closer and closer, passing by each other, each following its own thread; the expectation was so intense that the sucking of his own boot as he pulled it out of the rusty water sounded to Levin like the call of a snipe, and he tightened his grip on the stock of his gun.

'Bang! bang!' rang out by his ear. It was Vasenka shooting at a flock of ducks that was circling above the swamp, far out of range, and just then came flying over the hunters. Levin had barely turned to look when a snipe creeched, then another, a third, and some eight more rose one after the other.

Stepan Arkadyich brought one down just as it was about to start zigzagging and the snipe fell like a lump into the mire. Oblonsky unhurriedly aimed at another that was still flying low towards the sedge, and that snipe dropped; it could be seen thrashing about in the mowed sedge, beating its unhurt wing, white underneath.

Levin was not so lucky: his first snipe was too close when he fired, and he missed; he aimed at it again as it flew up, but just then another flew out from under his feet and distracted him, and he missed a second time.

While they were reloading their guns another snipe rose, and Veslovsky, who had had time to reload, sent another two charges of small shot over the water. Stepan Arkadyich picked up his snipe and glanced at Levin with shining eyes.

'Well, let's split up now,' said Stepan Arkadyich, and, limping slightly on his left leg and holding his gun ready, he whistled to his dog and went off in one direction. Levin and Veslovsky went in the other.

It always happened with Levin that when the first shots were unsuccessful, he would become angry, vexed, and shoot badly all day. That was happening now. There were a great many snipe. Snipe kept flying up from under the dog, from under the hunters' feet, and Levin might have recovered; but the more shots he fired, the more he disgraced himself in front of Veslovsky, who merrily banged away, in and out of range, hit nothing and was not the least embarrassed by it. Levin rushed, could not control himself, became more and more feverish and finally reached the point of shooting almost without hope of hitting anything. Even Laska seemed to understand it. She began searching more lazily and glanced back at the hunters as if in perplexity or reproach. Shots came one after another. Powder smoke hung about the hunters, yet in the big, roomy net of the hunting bag there were only three small, light snipe. And of those one had been shot by Veslovsky and another by them both. Meanwhile, along the other side of the swamp, the infrequent but, as it seemed to Levin, significant shots of Stepan Arkadyich rang out, followed almost each time by: 'Fetch, Krak, fetch!'

This upset Levin still more. Snipe kept circling in the air over the sedge. Creeching close to the ground and croaking higher up came ceaselessly from all sides; snipe flushed out earlier raced through the air and alighted just in front of the hunters. Not two but dozens of hawks, whimpering, circled over the marsh.

Having gone through the greater part of the marsh, Levin and Veslovsky reached a place where the muzhiks' meadow was divided into long strips running down to the sedge, marked out here by trampled strips, there by thin rows of cut grass. Half of these strips had already been mowed.

Though there was little hope of finding as many in the unmowed grass as in the mowed, Levin had promised to meet Stepan Arkadyich and went further on down the mowed and unmowed strips with his companion.

'Hey, hunters!' one of the muzhiks, sitting by an unhitched cart, shouted to them. 'Come and have a bite with us! Drink a glass!'

Levin turned.

'Come on, it's all right!' a merry, bearded muzhik with a red face shouted, baring his white teeth and raising a glittering green bottle in the sun.

'*Qu'est-ce qu'ils disent?*'* asked Veslovsky.

'They're inviting us to drink vodka. They've probably been dividing up the meadows. I'd go and have a drink,' said Levin, hoping Veslovsky would be tempted by the vodka and go to them.

'Why do they want to treat us?'

'Just for fun. You really ought to join them. You'd be interested.'

'*Allons, c'est curieux.*'†

'Go on, go on, you'll find the way to the mill!' Levin shouted and, looking back, was pleased to see Veslovsky, hunched over, his weary legs stumbling, his gun in his outstretched hand, making his way out of the marsh towards the peasants.

'You come, too!' the muzhik cried to Levin. 'Why not? Have a bit of pie! Eh!'

Levin badly wanted a drink of vodka and a piece of bread. He felt weak, so that it was hard for him to pull his faltering legs from the mire, and for a moment he hesitated. But the dog pointed. And at once all fatigue vanished, and he stepped lightly over the mire towards the dog. A snipe flew up at his feet; he shot and hit it – the dog went on pointing. 'Fetch!' Another rose just in front of the dog. Levin fired. But it was an unlucky day; he missed, and when he went to look for the one he had shot, he could not find it either. He searched everywhere in the sedge, but Laska did not believe he had shot it, and when he sent her to search, she did not really search but only pretended.

Even without Vasenka, whom Levin blamed for his failure, things did not improve. There were many snipe here, too, but Levin missed time after time.

The slanting rays of the sun were still hot; his clothes were soaked

* What are they saying?

† Let's go, it's curious.

through with sweat and clung to his body; his left boot, filled with water, was heavy and sloshy; drops of sweat rolled down his face, grimy with the soot of gunpowder; there was a bitter taste in his mouth, the smell of powder and rust in his nose, and in his ears the ceaseless creeching of the snipe; the gun barrels were too hot to touch; his heart pounded in short, quick beats; his hands shook from agitation, and his weary legs stumbled and tripped over the hummocks and bog; but he went on and kept shooting. Finally, after a shameful miss, he threw down his gun and hat.

'No, I must come to my senses!' he said to himself. He picked up the gun and hat, called Laska to heel and left the marsh. Coming to a dry spot, he sat down on a hummock, took off his boot, poured the water out of it, then went back to the marsh, drank some rusty-tasting water, wetted the burning gun barrels and rinsed his face and hands. Having refreshed himself, he moved back to the spot where the snipe had landed, with the firm intention of not getting agitated.

He wanted to keep calm, but it was the same thing all over again. His finger pulled the trigger before the bird was in his sights. It all went worse and worse.

There were only five birds in his game bag when he came out of the marsh to the alder grove where he was to meet Stepan Arkadyich.

Before he saw Stepan Arkadyich, he saw his dog. Krak leaped from behind the upturned roots of an alder, all black with the stinking slime of the marsh, and with a victorious look began sniffing Laska. Behind Krak the stately figure of Stepan Arkadyich appeared in the shade of the alders. He came towards Levin, red, sweaty, his collar open, still limping in the same way.

'Well, so? You did a lot of shooting!' he said, smiling gaily.

'And you?' asked Levin. But there was no need to ask, because he already saw the full game bag.

'Not too bad.'

He had fourteen birds.

'A fine marsh! Veslovsky must have hampered you. It's inconvenient for two with one dog,' said Stepan Arkadyich, softening his triumph.

XI

When Levin and Stepan Arkadyich came to the cottage of the muzhik with whom Levin always stayed, Veslovsky was already there. He was sitting in the middle of the cottage, holding on with both hands to a bench from which a soldier, the brother of the mistress of the house, was pulling him by the slime-covered boots, and laughing his infectiously gay laugh.

'I've just come. *Ils ont été charmants.** Imagine, they wined me and dined me. Such bread, a wonder! *Délicieux!* And the vodka – I never drank anything tastier! And they absolutely refused to take money. And they kept saying "No offence", or something.'

'Why take money? They were treating you. As if they'd sell their vodka!' said the soldier, finally pulling off the wet boot and the blackened stocking along with it.

Despite the filth in the cottage, muddied by the hunters' boots and the dirty dogs licking themselves, the smell of marsh and powder that filled it, and the absence of knives and forks, the hunters drank their tea and ate dinner with a relish that only comes from hunting. Washed and clean, they went to the swept-out hay barn where the coachmen had prepared beds for the masters.

Though it was already dark, none of the hunters wanted to sleep.

After wavering between reminiscences and stories about shooting, about dogs, about previous hunts, the conversation hit upon a subject that interested them all. Prompted by Vasenka's repeated expressions of delight at the charm of the night and the smell of the hay, at the charm of the broken cart (it seemed broken to him because its front end had been detached), the affability of the muzhiks who had given him vodka, the dogs who lay each at its master's feet, Oblonsky told about the charm of the hunting at Malthus's place, which he had taken part in during the past summer. Malthus was a well-known railway magnate. Stepan Arkadyich told about the marshlands this Malthus had bought up in Tver province, and how he kept them as a reserve, and what carriages – dog-carts – the hunters drove in, and the tent they set up for lunch by the marsh.

'I don't understand you,' said Levin, sitting up on his hay. 'How is it

* They were charming.

you're not disgusted by those people? I understand that Lafite with lunch is very agreeable, but aren't you disgusted precisely by that luxury? All those people make their money, as our old tax farmers[3] used to, in a way that earns them people's contempt. They ignore it and then use their dishonestly earned money to buy off the former contempt.'

'Absolutely right!' responded Vasenka Veslovsky. 'Absolutely! Of course, Oblonsky does it out of *bonhomie*, and the others say, "Well, if Oblonsky goes there . . ." '

'Not a bit of it,' Levin sensed Oblonsky's smile as he said it. 'I simply don't consider him more dishonest than any other wealthy merchant or nobleman. He and they both make money by the same hard work and intelligence.'

'Yes, but where's the hard work? Is it work to get a concession and resell it?'

'Of course it's work. It's work in this sense, that if it weren't for him and others like him, there wouldn't be any railways.'

'But it's not the same as the work of a muzhik or a scholar.'

'Granted, but it is work in the sense that it produces a result – railways. But then you think railways are useless.'

'No, that's another question. I'm prepared to admit they're useful. But any acquisition that doesn't correspond to the labour expended is dishonest.'

'But who defines the correspondence?'

'Acquisition by dishonest means, by cunning,' said Levin, feeling that he was unable to draw a clear line between honest and dishonest, 'like the acquisitions of banks,' he went on. 'This evil, the acquisition of huge fortunes without work, as it used to be with tax farming, has merely changed its form. *Le roi est mort, vive le roi!** Tax farming was no sooner abolished than railways and banks appeared: the same gain without work.'

'Yes, all that may be true and clever . . . Lie down, Krak!' Stepan Arkadyich called to the dog, who was scratching and churning up all the hay. He was obviously convinced of the justice of his theme, and therefore spoke calmly and unhurriedly. 'But you haven't drawn the line between honest and dishonest work. That I receive a higher salary than my chief clerk, though he knows the business better than I do – is that dishonest?'

* The king is dead, long live the king.

'I don't know.'

'Well, then I'll tell you: that you get, say, a surplus of five thousand for your farm work, while the muzhik here, our host, however hard he works, will get no more than fifty roubles, is as dishonest as my getting more than my chief clerk, and Malthus getting more than a railway engineer. On the other hand, I see some hostile, absolutely unfounded attitude of society towards those people, and it seems to me there's envy here . . .'

'No, that's unjust,' said Veslovsky. 'There can be no envy, and there's something unclean in this whole business.'

'No, excuse me,' Levin went on. 'You say it's unjust that I get five thousand and a muzhik gets fifty roubles. That's true, it is unjust, and I feel it, but . . .'

'Indeed it is. Why do we eat, drink, hunt, do nothing, while he's eternally, eternally working?' said Vasenka, apparently thinking about it clearly for the first time in his life, and therefore quite sincerely.

'Yes, you feel it, and yet you don't give him your property,' said Stepan Arkadyich, as if deliberately provoking Levin.

Lately some sort of secret antagonism had been established between the two brothers-in-law: as if a rivalry had arisen between them, since they had married two sisters, as to whose life was set up better, and that antagonism now showed itself in the conversation, which was beginning to acquire a personal nuance.

'I don't give it to him because no one demands it of me, and I couldn't if I wanted to,' replied Levin, 'and there's nobody to give it to.'

'Give it to this muzhik; he won't refuse.'

'Yes, but how am I going to give it to him? Shall I go and draw up a deed of purchase with him?'

'I don't know, but if you're convinced that you have no right . . .'

'I'm not at all convinced. On the contrary, I feel that I don't have the right to give it up, that I have responsibilities to the land and to my family.'

'No, excuse me, but if you think this inequality is unjust, why don't you act that way? . . .'

'I do act, only negatively, in the sense that I'm not going to try to increase the difference of situation that exists between him and me.'

'No, excuse me now: that is a paradox.'

'Yes, it's a somewhat sophistic explanation,' Veslovsky confirmed.

'Ah, it's our host!' he said to the muzhik, who opened the creaking barn door and came in. 'You're not asleep yet?'

'No, what sleep! I thought you gentlemen were asleep, but then I heard you talking. I need to get a hook here. He won't bite?' he added, stepping cautiously with bare feet.

'And where are you going to sleep?'

'We're going to night pasture.'

'Ah, what a night!' said Veslovsky, looking at the end of the cottage and the unharnessed cart, visible in the faint light of the afterglow, through the big frame of the now open door. 'Listen, those are women's voices singing, and not badly at that. Who's singing, my good man?'

'Those are farm girls not far from here.'

'Let's take a stroll! We're not going to fall asleep anyway. Come on, Oblonsky!'

'If only it was possible to stay lying down and still go,' Oblonsky answered, stretching. 'It's wonderful to be lying down.'

'Then I'll go by myself,' said Veslovsky, getting up quickly and putting his boots on. 'Goodbye, gentlemen. If it's fun, I'll call you. You treated me to game, and I won't forget you.'

'Isn't he a nice fellow?' said Oblonsky, when Veslovsky was gone and the muzhik had closed the door behind him.

'Yes, nice,' said Levin, still thinking about the subject of their conversation. It seemed to him that he had expressed his thoughts and feelings as clearly as he could, and yet the two of them, sincere and not stupid people, had told him in one voice that he was comforting himself with sophisms. That puzzled him.

'There it is, my friend. It has to be one or the other: either admit that the present social arrangement is just and then defend your own rights, or admit that you enjoy certain unjust advantages, as I do, and enjoy them with pleasure.'

'No, if it was unjust, you wouldn't be able to enjoy those benefits with pleasure, at least I wouldn't be able to. For me the main thing is to feel that I'm not at fault.'

'But why not go, in fact?' said Stepan Arkadyich, obviously weary from the strain of thinking. 'We won't sleep anyway. Really, let's go!'

Levin did not reply. The remark he had made in their conversation, about acting justly only in the negative sense, preoccupied him. 'Can one be just only negatively?' he asked himself.

'How strong the fresh hay smells, though!' Stepan Arkadyich said, getting up. 'I wouldn't sleep for anything. Vasenka's on to something there. Can you hear him laughing and talking? Why not go? Come on!'

'No, I won't go,' replied Levin.

'Can that also be on principle?' Stepan Arkadyich said with a smile, searching for his cap in the dark.

'Not on principle, but why should I go?'

'You know, you're going to make trouble for yourself,' said Stepan Arkadyich, finding his cap and standing up.

'Why?'

'Don't I see how you've set things up with your wife? I heard how it's a question of the first importance with you whether or not you go hunting for two days. That's all well and good as an idyll, but it's not enough for a whole lifetime. A man must be independent, he has his manly interests. A man must be masculine,' Oblonsky said, opening the door.

'Meaning what? To go courting farm girls?' asked Levin.

'Why not, if it's fun? *Ça ne tire pas à conséquence.** My wife will be none the worse for it, and I'll have fun. The main thing is to preserve the sanctity of the home. Nothing like that in the home. But don't tie your own hands.'

'Maybe,' Levin said drily and turned over on his side. 'Tomorrow we must get an early start, and I'm not going to wake anybody up, I'll just set out at dawn.'

'*Messieurs, venez vite!*'† said Veslovsky, coming in again. '*Charmante!* I discovered her. *Charmante*, a perfect Gretchen,[4] and we've already become acquainted. The prettiest little thing, really!' he went on with an approving look, as if she had been made pretty especially for him and he was pleased with the one who had done it for him.

Levin pretended to be asleep, but Oblonsky, having put on his shoes and lit a cigar, left the barn, and their voices soon died away.

Levin could not fall asleep for a long time. He heard his horses munching hay, then the host and his older son getting ready and going out to the night pasture; then he heard the soldier settling down to sleep at the other end of the barn with his nephew, the host's smaller son; he

* It won't lead to anything.

† Gentlemen, come quickly.

heard the boy telling his uncle in a thin little voice his impression of the dogs, who seemed huge and fearsome to him; then the boy asking him what the dogs would catch, and the soldier telling him in a hoarse and sleepy voice that the hunters would go to the marsh tomorrow and shoot off their guns, and after that, to have done with the boy's questions, he said: 'Sleep, Vaska, sleep or else!' and soon he was snoring, and everything quieted down; the only sounds were the neighing of horses and the croaking of snipe. 'Can it be only negative?' he repeated to himself. 'Well, and what then? It's not my fault.' And he started thinking about the next day.

'Tomorrow I'll go early in the morning and make it a point not to get excited. There's no end of snipe. And great snipe, too. I'll come back and there'll be a note from Kitty. Yes, maybe Stiva's right: I'm not manly enough with her, I've gone soft . . . But what's to be done! Negative again!'

Through sleep he heard Veslovsky's and Stepan Arkadyich's laughter and merry talk. He opened his eyes for an instant: the moon had risen, and in the open doorway, in the bright light of the moon, they stood talking. Stepan Arkadyich was saying something about the girl's freshness, comparing it to a fresh, just-shelled nut, and Veslovsky, laughing his infectious laugh, repeated something, probably what the muzhik had said to him: 'You get yourself one of your own!' Levin murmured drowsily:

'Tomorrow at daybreak, gentlemen!' and fell asleep.

XII

Waking up in the early dawn, Levin tried to rouse his comrades. Vasenka, lying on his stomach, one stockinged foot thrust out, was so fast asleep that he could get no response from him. Oblonsky refused through his sleep to go so early. Even Laska, who slept curled up at the edge of the hay, got up reluctantly, lazily straightening and stretching her hind legs, first one and then the other. Levin put on his boots, took his gun and, carefully opening the creaking barn door, went out. The coachmen were sleeping by their carriages, the horses were dozing. Only one was lazily eating oats, scattering them all over the trough with its muzzle. It was still grey outside.

'What are you doing up so early, dearie?' the muzhik's old woman, stepping out of the cottage, addressed him amicably as a good old acquaintance.

'Going hunting, auntie. Is this the way to the marsh?'

'Straight through the back yards, past our threshing floor, my dear man, and then the hemp field – there's a footpath.'

Stepping carefully with her tanned bare feet, the old woman showed him to the fence of the threshing floor and opened it for him.

'Straight on and you'll hit the marsh. Our boys took the horses there last night.'

Laska gaily ran ahead on the path; Levin followed her with a quick, light step, constantly glancing at the sky. He did not want the sun to come up before he reached the marsh. But the sun did not tarry. The moon, which was still shining when he set out, now merely gleamed like a bit of quicksilver; the morning star, which could not be missed earlier, now had to be looked for; the spots on the distant field, indistinct before, were now clearly visible. They were shocks of rye. Still invisible without the sun's light, the dew on the tall, fragrant hemp, from which the heads had already been plucked, wetted Levin's legs and his blouse above the waist. In the transparent stillness of morning the slightest sounds could be heard. A bee whizzed past Levin's ear like a bullet. He looked closer and saw another, then a third. They all flew out from behind the wattle fence of the apiary and disappeared in the direction of the marsh. The path led him straight to the marsh. It could be recognized by the steam rising from it, thicker in some places, thinner in others, so that the sedge and some small willow bushes, like islands, wavered in this steam. At the edge of the marsh and the road, the boys and muzhiks who had spent the night with the horses all lay, having fallen asleep under their caftans before dawn. Not far from them, three hobbled horses moved about. One of them clanked its chains. Laska walked beside her master, looking about and asking to run ahead. As he walked past the sleeping muzhiks and came up to the first marshy patch, Levin checked his caps and let the dog go. One of the horses, a sleek chestnut two-year-old, saw the dog, shied, tossed its tail and snorted. The others also became frightened and, splashing their hobbled legs in the water, their hoofs making a sound like clapping as they pulled them from the thick clay, began leaping their way out of the marsh. Laska stopped, looking mockingly at the horses and questioningly at Levin. Levin patted her and whistled the signal for her to start.

Laska ran with a gay and preoccupied air over the bog that yielded under her.

Running into the marsh, Laska at once picked up, amidst the familiar smells of roots, marsh grass, rust, and the alien smell of horse dung, the bird smell spread all through the place, that same strong-smelling bird that excited her more than anything else. Here and there over the moss and marsh burdock this smell was very strong, but it was impossible to tell in which direction it grew stronger or weaker. To find the direction she had to go further downwind. Not feeling her legs under her, moving at a tense gallop so that she could stop at each leap if necessary, Laska ran to the right, away from the morning breeze blowing from the east, and then turned upwind. Breathing in the air with flared nostrils, she sensed at once that there were not only tracks but *they* themselves were there, and not one but many. She slowed the speed of her run. They were there, but precisely where she was still unable to tell. She had already begun a circle to find the place when her master's voice suddenly distracted her. 'Here, Laska!' he said, pointing in a different direction. She paused briefly, as if to ask if it would not be better to finish what she had begun. But he repeated the order in an angry voice, pointing to a water-flooded hummocky spot where there could not be anything. She obeyed him, pretending to search in order to give him pleasure, ran all over the hummocks and then went back to the former place, and immediately sensed them again. Now, when he was not hindering her, she knew what to do, and, not looking where she put her feet, stumbling in vexation over high hummocks and getting into the water, but managing with her strong, supple legs, she began the circle that would make everything clear to her. *Their* smell struck her more and more strongly, more and more distinctly, and suddenly it became perfectly clear to her that one of them was there, behind that hummock, five steps away from her. She stopped and her whole body froze. On her short legs she could see nothing ahead of her, but she knew from the smell that it was sitting no more than five steps away. She stood, sensing it more and more and delighting in the anticipation. Her tense tail was extended and only its very tip twitched. Her mouth was slightly open, her ears pricked up a little. One ear had got folded back as she ran, and she was breathing heavily but cautiously, and still more cautiously she turned more with her eyes than her head to look at her master. He, with his usual face but with his ever terrible eyes, was coming, stumbling over hummocks, and extremely slowly as it seemed to her. It seemed to her that he was moving slowly, yet he was running.

Noticing the special way Laska was searching, pressed flat to the ground, as if raking it with her hind legs in big strides, and with her mouth slightly open, Levin understood that she was after great snipe, and, praying to God in his heart that he would be successful, especially with the first bird, he ran to her. Coming right up to her, he began looking in front of him from his height and saw with his eyes what she had seen with her nose. In a space between two hummocks, close to one of them, he made out a great snipe. It was listening, its head turned. Then, fluffing its wings slightly and folding them again, it wagged its behind clumsily and disappeared round the corner.

'Flush it, flush it,' cried Levin, nudging Laska from behind.

'But I can't flush anything,' thought Laska. 'Where will I flush it from? I can sense them from here, but if I move forward, I won't be able to tell where they are or what they are.' Yet here he was nudging her with his knee and saying in an excited whisper: 'Flush it, Lasochka, flush it!'

'Well, if that's what he wants, I'll do it, but I can't answer for myself any more,' she thought and tore forward at full speed between the hummocks. She no longer smelled anything, but only saw and heard, without understanding anything.

Ten steps from the former place, with a thick creech and the swelling noise of wings peculiar to its kind, a single great snipe flew up. And following a shot it plopped down heavily, its white breast against the wet bog. Another did not wait but flew up behind Levin without the dog.

When Levin turned to it, it was already far away. But the shot reached it. Having flown some twenty yards, the second snipe suddenly jerked upwards and, tumbling like a thrown ball, fell heavily on to a dry patch.

'That'll do nicely!' thought Levin, putting the two plump, warm birds into his game bag. 'Eh, Lasochka, won't it do nicely?'

By the time Levin reloaded his gun and started off again, the sun, though still invisible behind the clouds, was already up. The crescent moon, having lost all its brilliance, showed white like a cloud in the sky; there was no longer a single star to be seen. The marshy patches, silvery with dew earlier, now became golden. The rustiness turned to amber. The blue of the grass changed to yellowish green. Little marsh birds pottered by the brook, in bushes glistening with dew and casting long shadows. A hawk woke up and sat on a haystack, turning its head from side to side, looking with displeasure at the marsh. Jackdaws flew into the fields, and a barefoot boy was already driving the horses towards an old man, who had got up from under his caftan and was scratching himself. Smoke from the shooting, like milk, spread white over the green grass.

One of the boys came running to Levin.

'Uncle, there were ducks here yesterday!' he cried to him and followed him at a distance.

And in the sight of this boy, who expressed his approval, Levin took a double pleasure in straight away killing three more snipe, one after the other.

XIII

The hunters' omen proved true, that if the first beast or bird was taken the field would be lucky.

Tired, hungry, happy, Levin returned towards ten o'clock, having walked some twenty miles on foot, with nineteen pieces of fine game and one duck, which he tied to his belt because there was no room for it in his game bag. His comrades had long been awake and had had time to get hungry and have breakfast.

'Wait, wait, I know it's nineteen,' said Levin, counting for a second time the snipe and great snipe, doubled up and dry, caked with blood, their heads twisted to the side, no longer looking as impressive as when they flew.

The count was correct, and Levin was pleased at Stepan Arkadyich's envy. He was also pleased to find on his return that the messenger had already arrived with a note from Kitty.

'I am quite well and cheerful. If you are afraid for me, you may be more at ease than ever. I have a new bodyguard, Marya Vlasyevna' (this was the midwife, a new, important person in Levin's family life). 'She came to see how I am. She found me perfectly well, and we are having her stay until you come. Everyone is cheerful and well, so please don't you be in a hurry, and if the hunting is good, stay another day.'

These two joys, the lucky hunting and the note from his wife, were so great that the two minor unpleasantnesses that occurred afterwards passed easily for him. One was that the chestnut outrunner, evidently overworked the day before, was off her feed and looked dull. The coachman said she had been strained.

'She was overdriven yesterday, Konstantin Dmitrich,' he said. 'Of course, she was pushed hard those seven miles!'

The other unpleasantness that upset his good mood at first, but at which he later laughed a great deal, was that of all the provisions, which Kitty had sent with them in such abundance that it seemed they could not have been eaten in a week, nothing remained. Coming back from the hunt tired and hungry, Levin had been dreaming so specifically of pirozhki that, as he approached their quarters, he could already feel their smell and taste in his mouth, the way Laska could sense game, and he at once ordered Filipp to serve them. It turned out that there were not only no pirozhki but no chicken either.

'Quite an appetite!' said Stepan Arkadyich, laughing and pointing at Vasenka Veslovsky. 'I don't suffer from lack of appetite myself, but this is astonishing . . .'

'*Mais c'était délicieux.*'* Veslovsky praised the beef he had just eaten.

'Well, nothing to be done!' said Levin, giving Veslovsky a dark look. 'Serve some beef, then, Filipp.'

'The beef got eaten. I gave the bone to the dogs,' Filipp replied.

Levin was so upset that he said vexedly:

'You might have left me at least something!' and nearly wept.

'Clean the game,' he said to Filipp in a trembling voice, trying not to look at Vasenka, 'and layer it with nettles. And fetch me some milk at least.'

Later on, when he had drunk his fill of milk, he felt ashamed at having shown vexation to a stranger, and he started laughing at his hungry anger.

That evening they hunted in yet another field, where Veslovsky also shot several birds, and at night they returned home.

The way back was as merry as the way there. Veslovsky sang, then recalled with pleasure his exploits with the muzhiks who had treated him to vodka and said 'No offence', then his night's exploits with the nuts and the farm girl, and the muzhik who had asked him whether he was married or not and, on learning that he was not, had told him: 'Don't you go looking at other men's wives; you'd best get one of your own.' These words especially made Veslovsky laugh.

'All in all I'm terribly pleased with our trip. And you, Levin?'

'I'm very pleased,' Levin said sincerely, especially glad not only that

* But it was delicious.

he did not feel the hostility he had felt towards Vasenka Veslovsky at home, but that, on the contrary, he felt the most friendly disposition towards him.

XIV

The next day at ten o'clock, having already made the round of the farm, Levin knocked at the door of Vasenka's bedroom.

'*Entrez*,' Veslovsky called to him. 'Excuse me, I've just finished my ablutions,' he said, smiling, standing before him in nothing but his underwear.

'Please don't be embarrassed.' Levin sat down by the window. 'Did you sleep well?'

'Like a log. What a good day for hunting!'

'Yes. Will you take tea or coffee?'

'Neither one. I'll wait for lunch. I'm ashamed, really. The ladies must be up already? It would be splendid to take a stroll around. You can show me your horses.'

After strolling in the garden, visiting the stables, and even doing some exercises together on the bars, Levin and his guest returned to the house and went into the drawing room.

'We had excellent hunting and so many impressions!' Veslovsky said, going up to Kitty, who was sitting by the samovar. 'It's a pity ladies are deprived of such pleasures!'

'Well, so what? He has to find something to talk about with his hostess,' Levin said to himself. Again it seemed to him there was something in the smile and the victorious expression with which his guest had addressed Kitty . . .

The princess, who was sitting at the other end of the table with Marya Vlasyevna and Stepan Arkadyich, called Levin over and started a conversation with him about moving to Moscow for Kitty's confinement and getting an apartment ready. As Levin had found all the preparations for the wedding unpleasant, insulting in their insignificance to the grandeur of what was taking place, so he found still more insulting the preparations for the future confinement, the date of which was somehow being counted out on their fingers. He tried all the time not to hear those conversations about the ways of swaddling the future baby, tried to turn away and not see some sort of mysterious, endless knitted strips, some sort of linen triangles, to which Dolly attached some special significance, and so on. The event of his son's birth (he was sure it would be a son), which he had been promised but in which he still could not believe – so extraordinary did it seem to him – appeared on the one hand as such an enormous and therefore impossible happiness, and on the other as such a mysterious event, that this imaginary knowledge of what was going to be and, consequently, the preparation for it as for something ordinary, done by these same people, seemed to him outrageous and humiliating.

But the princess did not understand his feelings and explained his unwillingness to think and talk about it as light-mindedness and indifference, and therefore would not leave him in peace. She had charged Stepan Arkadyich with seeing about the apartment, and now she called Levin over.

'I don't know a thing, Princess. Do as you like,' he said.

'You must decide when you'll move.'

'I really don't know. I know there are millions of children born without Moscow and doctors . . . why then . . .'

'But if that's . . .'

'But no, it's as Kitty wants.'

'It's impossible to discuss it with Kitty! Do you want me to frighten her? This spring Natalie Golitsyn died because of a bad doctor.'

'I will do whatever you say,' he said sullenly.

The princess began telling him, but he was not listening to her. Though the conversation with the princess upset him, he became gloomy not because of that conversation, but because of what he saw by the samovar.

'No, this is not possible,' he thought, glancing again and again at Vasenka, who was leaning towards Kitty, talking to her with his handsome smile, and then at her, blushing and excited.

There was something impure in Vasenka's pose, in his glance, in his smile. Levin even saw something impure in Kitty's pose and glance. And again everything went dark in his eyes. Again, as yesterday, suddenly, without the least transition, he felt himself thrown down from the height of happiness, peace, dignity, into an abyss of despair, anger and humiliation. Again everyone and everything became repulsive to him.

'Do as you like, then, Princess,' he said, turning round again.

'Heavy is the hat of Monomakh!'[5] Stepan Arkadyich joked, obviously alluding not only to the conversation with the princess but to the cause of Levin's agitation, which he had noticed. 'How late you are today, Dolly!'

Everyone rose to greet Darya Alexandrovna. Vasenka rose for a moment and, with that lack of courtesy peculiar to the new young men, bowed slightly and went on with his conversation, laughing at something.

'Masha has worn me out. She slept poorly and has been very capricious all day,' said Dolly.

The conversation Vasenka had begun with Kitty was again on yesterday's subject, on Anna and whether love can be above social conventions. Kitty found this conversation unpleasant. It upset her by its content and by the tone in which it was carried on, and especially by the effect she now knew it would have on her husband. But she was too simple and innocent to be able to stop the conversation or even to hide the external pleasure the young man's obvious attention gave her. She wanted to stop it, but she did not know how. She knew that whatever she did would be noticed by her husband and interpreted in a bad sense. And indeed, when she asked Dolly what was the matter with Masha, and Vasenka, waiting for that discussion, which he found dull, to be over, began gazing indifferently at Dolly, the question seemed to Levin an unnatural, disgusting ruse.

'What do you say, shall we go mushrooming today?' asked Dolly.

'Let's go, please, and I'll go, too,' said Kitty, and blushed. She wanted, out of politeness, to ask Vasenka if he would go, but did not. 'Where are you going, Kostya?' she asked her husband, with a guilty look, as he walked past her with resolute strides. That guilty expression confirmed all his suspicions.

'The mechanic came in my absence. I haven't seen him yet,' he said without looking at her.

He went downstairs, but before he had time to leave his study, he heard the familiar steps of his wife, who was coming to him with incautious haste.

'What is it?' he said drily. 'We're busy.'

'Excuse me,' she turned to the German mechanic, 'I must say a few words to my husband.'

The German was going to leave, but Levin said:

'Don't bother.'

'The train's at three?' asked the German. 'I don't want to be late.'

Levin did not reply and stepped out of the room with his wife.

'Well, what do you have to say to me?' he said in French.

He was not looking in her face and did not want to see that she, in her condition, stood with her face all trembling and looked pitiful and crushed.

'I . . . I want to say that it's impossible to live this way, that it's torture . . .' she said.

'There are people in the pantry here,' he said angrily, 'kindly do not make a scene.'

'Let's go in here then!'

They were standing in a passage. Kitty wanted to go into the next room, but the governess was giving Tanya a lesson there.

'Then let's go to the garden!'

In the garden they came upon a muzhik who was weeding the path. And no longer considering that the muzhik might see her tear-stained and his troubled face, not considering that they had the look of people fleeing some disaster, they went on with quick steps, feeling that they had to say everything and reassure each other, to be alone together and rid themselves of the suffering they were both experiencing.

'It's impossible to live this way! It's torture! I'm suffering, you're suffering. Why?' she said, when they finally reached a solitary bench at the corner of a linden alley.

'But tell me yourself: was there something indecent, impure, humiliatingly terrible in his tone?' he said, standing before her again, fists on his chest, in the same pose as the other night.

'There was,' she said in a trembling voice. 'But don't you see, Kostya, that it's not my fault? All morning I wanted to set a certain tone, but these people . . . Why did he come? We were so happy!' she said, choking with sobs that shook her whole filled-out body.

The gardener saw with surprise that, though no one had chased them and there had been nothing to flee from, and though they could not have found anything especially joyful on that bench – they returned home past him with calmed, radiant faces.

XV

After taking his wife upstairs, Levin went to Dolly's side of the house. Darya Alexandrovna, for her part, was very upset that day. She was pacing the room and saying angrily to the girl who stood in the corner howling:

'And you'll stand in the corner all day, and have dinner alone, and won't see a single doll, and I won't make you a new dress,' she said, not knowing how else to punish her.

'No, she's a nasty little girl!' She turned to Levin. 'Where did she get these vile inclinations?'

'But what did she do?' Levin said rather indifferently. He had wanted to consult her about his own affairs and was therefore vexed that he had come at the wrong moment.

'She and Grisha went into the raspberry bushes, and there . . . I can't even tell you what she did there. Such nasty things. I'm a thousand times sorry Miss Elliot's not here. This woman doesn't look after anything, she's a machine . . . *Figurez-vous, que la petite* . . .'*

And Darya Alexandrovna related Masha's crime.

'That doesn't prove anything. It's not vile inclinations, it's simply a prank,' Levin comforted her.

'But you're upset about something? Why did you come?' asked Dolly. 'What's going on there?'

And in the tone of this question Levin heard that it would be easy for him to say what he meant to say.

'I wasn't there, I was alone in the garden with Kitty. It's the second time we've quarrelled since . . . Stiva arrived.'

Dolly looked at him with intelligent, understanding eyes.

'Well, tell me, hand on heart, wasn't there . . . not in Kitty, but in that gentleman, a tone that could be unpleasant – not unpleasant but terrible, insulting for a husband?'

'That is, how shall I put it to you . . . Stay, stay in the corner,' she said to Masha, who, seeing a barely noticeable smile on her mother's lips, had begun to stir. 'Society's view would be that he's behaving as all young men behave. *Il fait la cour à une jeune et jolie femme*,† and a worldly husband should be flattered by it.'

* Imagine, the little girl . . .

† He's courting a young and pretty woman.

'Yes, yes,' Levin said gloomily, 'but you did notice?'

'Not only I, but Stiva noticed. He told me just after tea: "*Je crois que Veslovsky fait un petit brin de cour à Kitty.*"'*

'Well, splendid, now I'm at peace. I shall throw him out,' said Levin.

'What, have you lost your mind?' Dolly cried in horror. 'No, Kostya, come to your senses!' she said, laughing. 'Well, you can go to Fanny now,' she said to Masha. 'No, if you want, I'll tell Stiva. He'll take him away. He can say you're expecting guests. Generally, he doesn't fit in with us.'

'No, no, I'll do it myself.'

'But you're going to quarrel? . . .'

'Not at all. It will be great fun for me,' said Levin, his eyes indeed sparkling merrily. 'Well, forgive her, Dolly! She won't do it again,' he said, referring to the little criminal, who would not go to Fanny and stood hesitantly before her mother, looking expectantly from under her brows and seeking her eyes.

The mother looked at her. The girl burst into sobs, buried her face in her mother's lap, and Dolly placed her thin hand tenderly on her head.

'And what do we and he have in common?' thought Levin, and he went to look for Veslovsky.

Passing through the front hall, he ordered the carriage harnessed to go to the station.

'A spring broke yesterday,' the footman replied.

'The tarantass, then, but quickly. Where's the guest?'

'The gentleman has gone to his room.'

Levin found Vasenka at a moment when, having taken his things from the suitcase and laid out the new song music, he was trying on his leggings for horseback riding.

Either there was something special in Levin's face, or Vasenka himself sensed that the *petit brin de cour* he had started was out of place in this family, but he was somewhat embarrassed (as much as a worldly man could be) by Levin's entrance.

'You wear leggings when you ride?'

'Yes, it's much cleaner,' said Vasenka, putting his fat leg on a chair, fastening the lower hook, and smiling cheerfully and good-naturedly.

He was undoubtedly a nice fellow, and Levin felt sorry for him and ashamed for himself, the master of the house, when he noticed the timidity in Vasenka's eyes.

* I believe Veslovsky's courting Kitty a bit.

On the table lay a piece of a stick they had broken that morning during gymnastics, when they had tried to raise the jammed bars. Levin took the piece in his hands and started breaking off the splintered end, not knowing how to begin.

'I wanted . . .' He fell silent, but suddenly, remembering Kitty and all that had taken place, he said, looking him resolutely in the eye: 'I've ordered the horses to be harnessed for you.'

'How's that?' Vasenka began in surprise. 'To go where?'

'You are going to the station,' Levin said darkly, splintering the end of the stick.

'Are you leaving, or has something happened?'

'It happens that I am expecting guests,' said Levin breaking off the splintered ends of the stick more and more quickly with his strong fingers. 'No, I am not expecting guests, and nothing has happened, but I am asking you to leave. You may explain my discourtesy in any way you like.'

Vasenka drew himself up.

'I ask *you* to explain to me . . .' he said with dignity, having understood at last.

'I cannot explain to you,' Levin spoke softly and slowly, trying to hide the quivering of his jaw. 'And it is better that you not ask.'

And as the splintered ends were all broken off, Levin took the thick ends in his fingers, snapped the stick in two and carefully caught one end as it fell.

Probably it was the sight of those nervously tensed arms, those same muscles that he had felt that morning during the gymnastics, and the shining eyes, the soft voice and quivering jaw, that convinced Vasenka more than any words. He shrugged his shoulders and bowed with a contemptuous smile.

'May I see Oblonsky?'

The shrug of the shoulders and the smile did not annoy Levin. 'What else can he do?' he thought.

'I'll send him to you presently.'

'What is this senselessness?' said Stepan Arkadyich, on learning from his friend that he was being chased out of the house, and finding Levin in the garden, where he was strolling, waiting for his guest's departure. '*Mais c'est ridicule!** What fly has bitten you? *Mais c'est du dernier*

* But this is ridiculous!

*ridicule!** What are you imagining to yourself, if a young man . . .'

But the place where the fly had bitten Levin was evidently still sore, because he turned pale again when Stepan Arkadyich wanted to explain the reason and hastily interrupted him:

'Please, don't explain any reasons! I could not do otherwise! I am very ashamed before you and before him. But for him I don't think it will be a great misfortune to leave, while for me and my wife his presence is disagreeable.'

'But it's insulting to him! *Et puis c'est ridicule!*'

'And for me it's both insulting and painful! And I'm not at fault in anything, and there's no need for me to suffer!'

'Well, I never expected this from you! *On peut être jaloux, mais à ce point, c'est du dernier ridicule!*'†

Levin turned quickly, walked away from him into the depths of the alley and went on pacing back and forth alone. Soon he heard the clatter of the tarantass and through the trees saw Vasenka, sitting on some hay (as luck would have it there was no seat on the tarantass), in his Scotch cap, bobbing with the bumps as they rolled down the drive.

'What's this now?' thought Levin, when a footman ran out of the house and stopped the tarantass. It was the mechanic, whom Levin had completely forgotten. The mechanic bowed and said something to Veslovsky; then he got into the tarantass and they drove off together.

Stepan Arkadyich and the princess were indignant at Levin's act. And he himself felt that he was not only *ridicule* in the highest degree, but also guilty and disgraced all round; but, recalling what he and his wife had suffered through, he asked himself how he would act another time and replied that he would do exactly the same thing.

Despite all that, towards the end of the day everybody except the princess, who could not forgive Levin this act, became extremely animated and merry, like children after being punished or grown-ups after a difficult official reception, and that evening, in the princess's absence, Vasenka's banishment was talked about like a long-past event. And Dolly, who had inherited her father's gift for comic storytelling, made Varenka roll with laughter when she told for the third or fourth time, always with new humorous additions, how she had been about to put on some new ribbons for the guest and come out to the drawing room,

* But this is the height of ridiculousness!

† One can be jealous, but to such an extent, it's the height of ridiculousness!

when she suddenly heard the noise of the old rattletrap. And who was in the old rattletrap but Vasenka himself, with his Scotch cap, and his romances, and his leggings, sitting on the hay.

'You might at least have had the carriage harnessed! But no, and then I hear: "Wait!" Well, I think, they've taken pity on him. I look, and they put the fat German in with him and drive off . . . And my ribbons all went for naught! . . .'

XVI

Darya Alexandrovna carried out her intention and went to see Anna. She was very sorry to upset her sister and cause her husband unpleasantness; she understood how right the Levins were in not wishing to have any connections with Vronsky; but she considered it her duty to visit Anna and show her that her feelings could not change, despite the change in Anna's situation.

So as not to depend on the Levins for the trip, Darya Alexandrovna sent to the village to hire horses; but Levin, learning of it, came to reprimand her.

'Why do you think your trip is unpleasant for me? And even if it was unpleasant, it is still more unpleasant that you're not taking my horses,' he said. 'You never once told me you had decided on going. And to hire in the village is, first of all, unpleasant for me, but the main thing is that they'll promise to get you there and won't do it. I have horses. And if you don't want to upset me, you'll take mine.'

Darya Alexandrovna had to consent, and on the appointed day Levin prepared a four-in-hand and a relay, assembling it from work and saddle horses, not very handsome, but capable of getting Darya Alexandrovna there in a day. Now, when horses were needed both for the departing princess and for the midwife, this was difficult for Levin, but by the duty of hospitality he could not allow Darya Alexandrovna to hire horses while in his house, and, besides, he knew that the twenty roubles Darya Alexandrovna would be asked to pay for the trip were very important for her; and he felt Darya Alexandrovna's money matters, which were in a very bad state, as if they were his own.

On Levin's advice, Darya Alexandrovna started out before dawn. The road was good, the carriage comfortable, the horses ran at a merry pace, and on the box beside the coachman sat the clerk, whom Levin sent along instead of a footman for safety's sake. Darya Alexandrovna dozed off and woke up only as they were approaching an inn where the horses were to be changed.

After having tea with the same rich muzhik-proprietor with whom Levin had stayed on his way to Sviyazhsky's, and talking with the women about children and with the old man about Count Vronsky, whom he praised very much, Darya Alexandrovna set off again at ten o'clock. At home, busy with the children, she never had time to think. But now, during this four-hour drive, all the previously repressed thoughts suddenly came crowding into her head, and she thought about the whole of her life as never before, and from all different sides. She herself found her thoughts strange. First she thought of her children, about whom she still worried, though the princess, and above all Kitty (she relied more on her), had promised to look after them. 'What if Masha starts her pranks again, and what if Grisha gets kicked by a horse, and what if Lily's stomach gets still more upset?' But then the questions of the present were supplanted by questions of the near future. She began thinking that they ought to rent a new apartment in Moscow for the next winter, the furniture in the drawing room should be changed and a fur coat should be made for the oldest daughter. Then came thoughts of the more distant future: how she was going to send the children into the world. 'Never mind about the girls – but the boys?

'Very well, I can busy myself with Grisha now, but that's because I'm now free myself, I'm not pregnant. Naturally, there's no counting on Stiva. With the help of good people, I will send them out; but if there's another child . . .' And it occurred to her how incorrect the saying was about a curse being laid upon woman, that in pain she would bring forth children.[6] 'Never mind giving birth, but being pregnant – that's the pain,' she thought, picturing her last pregnancy and the death of that last child. And she remembered her conversation with the young peasant woman at the inn. To the question whether she had children, the beautiful young woman had cheerfully replied:

'I had one girl, but God freed me, I buried her during Lent.'

'And aren't you very sorry about her?' Darya Alexandrovna had asked.

'Why be sorry? The old man has lots of grandchildren. Nothing but trouble. No work, no nothing. Just bondage.'

This answer had seemed repulsive to Darya Alexandrovna, despite the young woman's good-natured prettiness, but now she inadvertently recalled those words. Cynical as they were, there was some truth in them.

'And generally,' thought Darya Alexandrovna, looking back at the whole of her life in those fifteen years of marriage, 'pregnancy, nausea, dullness of mind, indifference to everything, and, above all, ugliness. Kitty, young and pretty Kitty, even she has lost her good looks, but when I'm pregnant I get ugly, I know it. Labour, suffering, ugly suffering, that last moment . . . then nursing, the sleepless nights, the terrible pains . . .'

Darya Alexandrovna shuddered at the mere recollection of the pain from cracked nipples that she had endured with almost every child. 'Then the children's illnesses, this eternal fear; then their upbringing, vile inclinations' (she remembered little Masha's crime in the raspberries), 'education, Latin – all of it so incomprehensible and difficult. And on top of it all, the death of these same children.' And again there came to her imagination the cruel memory, eternally gnawing at her mother's heart, of the death of her last infant boy, who had died of croup, his funeral, the universal indifference before that small, pink coffin, and her own heart-rending, lonely pain before the pale little forehead with curls at the temples, before the opened, surprised little mouth she had glimpsed in the coffin just as it was covered by the pink lid with the lace cross.

'And all that for what? What will come of it all? That I, having not a moment's peace, now pregnant, now nursing, eternally angry, grumpy, tormented myself and tormenting others, repulsive to my husband, will live my life out and bring up unfortunate, poorly educated and destitute children. Even now, if we weren't with the Levins, I don't know how we'd live. Of course, Kostya and Kitty are so delicate that we don't notice it; but it can't go on. They'll start having children and won't be able to help us; they're in tight straits even now. Is papa, who has kept almost nothing for himself, to help us? And so I can't set my children up myself, but only with the help of others, in humiliation. Well, and if we take the most fortunate outcome: the children won't die any more, and I'll bring them up somehow. At best they simply won't turn out to be scoundrels. That's all I can wish for. And for that so much torment, so much work . . . A whole life ruined!' Again she recalled what the young peasant woman had said, and again the recollection was vile to her; but she could not help admitting that there was a dose of crude truth in those words.

'Is it far now, Mikhaila?' Darya Alexandrovna asked the clerk, to get her mind off these thoughts that frightened her.

'Five miles from this village, they say.'

The carriage drove down the village street on to a bridge. Along the bridge, with cheerful, ringing talk, went a crowd of merry peasant women with plaited sheaf-binders on their shoulders. The women stopped on the bridge, gazing curiously at the carriage. The faces turned to her all seemed healthy and cheerful to Darya Alexandrovna, taunting her with the joy of life. 'Everybody lives, everybody enjoys life,' she went on thinking, going past the women and on up the hill at a trot, again rocking pleasantly on the soft springs of the old carriage, 'and I, released, as if from prison, from a world that is killing me with cares, have only now come to my senses for a moment. Everybody lives – these women, and my sister Natalie, and Varenka, and Anna, whom I am going to see – and only I don't.

'And they all fall upon Anna. What for? Am I any better? I at least have a husband I love. Not as I'd have wanted to love, but I do love him, and Anna did not love hers. How is she to blame, then? She wants to live. God has put that into our souls. I might very well have done the same. Even now I don't know if I did the right thing to listen to her that terrible time when she came to me in Moscow. I ought to have left my husband then and started life over from the beginning. I might have loved and been loved in a real way. And is it better now? I don't respect him. He's necessary to me,' she thought about her husband, 'and so I put up with him. Is that better? I could still have been liked then, I still had some of my beauty,' Darya Alexandrovna went on thinking and wanted to look in the mirror. She had a travelling mirror in her bag and would have liked to take it out; but looking at the backs of the coachman and the rocking clerk, she felt she would be embarrassed if one of them turned round, and so she did not take the mirror out.

But even without looking in the mirror she thought it was still not too late. She remembered Sergei Ivanovich, who was especially amiable towards her, and Stiva's friend, the kindly Turovtsyn, who had helped her take care of her children when they had scarlet fever and was in love with her. And there was also one quite young man who, as her husband had told her jokingly, found her the most beautiful of all the sisters. And Darya Alexandrovna pictured the most passionate and impossible love affairs. 'Anna acted splendidly, and I am not going to reproach her. She's happy, she makes another person happy, and she's not downtrodden the way I am, but is probably as fresh, intelligent and open to everything as ever,' she thought, and a sly, contented smile puckered her lips, particularly because, as she thought about Anna's love affair, she imagined, parallel to it, an almost identical love affair of her own, with an imaginary collective man who was in love with her. She confessed everything to her husband, just as Anna had done. And Stepan Arkadyich's astonishment and perplexity at the news made her smile.

In such reveries she reached the turning from the high road that led to Vozdvizhenskoe.

XVII

The coachman reined in the four-in-hand and looked to the right, at a field of rye, where some muzhiks were sitting by a cart. The clerk was about to jump down, then changed his mind and shouted peremptorily to a muzhik, beckoning him over. The breeze they had felt during the drive became still when they stopped; horseflies covered the sweaty horses, who angrily tried to shake them off. The metallic ring of a scythe blade being hammered beside the cart became still. One of the muzhiks stood up and came over to the carriage.

'See how rusty he is!' the clerk shouted angrily at the barefooted muzhik stepping slowly over the bumps of the dry, untrampled road. 'Come on, you!'

The curly-headed old man, his hair tied with a strip of bast, his hunched back dark with sweat, quickened his pace, came up to the carriage and placed his sunburnt hand on the splash-board.

'Vozdvizhenskoe? The master's house? The count's?' he repeated. 'Just beyond that little rise. There's a left turn. Straight down the havenue and you run smack into it. Who is it you want? Himself?'

'And are they at home, my dear man?' Darya Alexandrovna said vaguely, not even knowing how to ask the muzhik about Anna.

'Should be,' said the muzhik, shifting his bare feet and leaving a clear, five-toed footprint in the dust. 'Should be,' he repeated, obviously willing to strike up a conversation. 'There's more guests came yesterday. No end of guests . . . What is it?' He turned to a lad who shouted something to him from the cart. 'Ah, yes! They just passed here on horseback to go and look at a reaper. They should be home by now. And where are you from? . . .'

'Far away,' said the coachman, getting up on the box. 'So it's near by?'

'I told you, it's right here. Just beyond . . .' he said, moving his hand on the splash-board.

A young, hale, strapping fellow also came over.

'Is there any work at the harvesting?' he asked.

'I don't know, my dear.'

'So just go left and you come straight to it,' said the muzhik, obviously wishing to talk and reluctant to let the travellers go.

The coachman started, but they had no sooner made the turn than they heard the muzhik shouting:

'Wait! Hey, wait, man!' two voices cried.

The coachman stopped.

'It's them coming! There they are!' cried the muzhik. 'See them coming along!' he said, pointing to four people on horseback and two in a *char à banc* moving along the road.

It was Vronsky with his jockey, Veslovsky and Anna on horseback, and Princess Varvara and Sviyazhsky in the *char à banc*. They had gone for a ride and to see some newly arrived reaping machines at work.

When the carriage stopped, the riders came on at a slow pace. At their head rode Anna beside Veslovsky. Anna rode calmly on a short, sturdy English cob with a cropped mane and short tail. Her beautiful head with black hair escaping from under the top hat, her full shoulders, her slender waist in the black riding habit, and her whole calm, graceful bearing struck Dolly.

In the first moment it seemed improper to her that Anna should be on horseback. To Darya Alexandrovna's mind, the notion of ladies on horseback was connected with the notion of light, youthful coquetry, which in her opinion did not suit Anna's situation; but when she saw her closer up, she at once became reconciled with her horseback riding. In spite of her elegance, everything in Anna's bearing and dress and movement was so simple, calm and dignified that nothing could have been more natural.

Beside Anna on a fiery grey cavalry horse rode Vasenka Veslovsky, in his Scotch cap with its flying ribbons, his fat legs stretched forward, obviously admiring himself, and Darya Alexandrovna, recognizing him, could not suppress a gay smile. Behind them rode Vronsky. Under him was a dark bay thoroughbred, obviously excited from galloping. He worked the reins, trying to hold it back.

After him rode a small man in a jockey's outfit. Sviyazhsky and the princess, in a new *char à banc* drawn by a big black trotter, were overtaking the riders.

Anna's face suddenly lit up with a joyful smile as she recognized the small figure huddled in the corner of the old carriage as Dolly. She gave a cry, sat up in the saddle and touched her horse into a gallop. Coming up to the carriage, she jumped down unassisted and, holding the skirts of her riding habit, ran to meet Dolly.

'I thought so but didn't dare think it. What a joy! You can't imagine what a joy it is for me!' she said, first pressing her face to Dolly's and kissing her, then drawing back and looking at her with a smile.

'What a joy, Alexei!' she said, turning to Vronsky, who had dismounted and was coming towards them.

Vronsky, having taken off his tall grey hat, approached Dolly.

'You won't believe how glad we are that you've come,' he said, giving the words he spoke a special significance and revealing his strong white teeth in a smile.

Vasenka Veslovsky, without dismounting, took his cap off and greeted the visitor, joyfully waving the ribbons over his head.

'That is Princess Varvara,' Anna responded to Dolly's questioning look, as the *char à banc* drove up.

'Ah!' said Darya Alexandrovna, and her face involuntarily showed displeasure.

Princess Varvara was her husband's aunt; she had known her for a long time and had no respect for her. She knew that Princess Varvara had spent her whole life as a sponger on wealthy relations, but the fact that she was now living off Vronsky, a man who was a stranger to her, offended her feelings for her husband's family. Anna noticed the look on Dolly's face, became embarrassed, blushed, lost hold of her skirt and tripped over it.

Darya Alexandrovna went over to the halted *char à banc* and greeted Princess Varvara coldly. Sviyazhsky was also an acquaintance. He asked how his eccentric friend and his young wife were doing and, after a fleeting glance at the ill-matched horses and the carriage with its patched splash-boards, invited the ladies to ride in the *char à banc*.

'And I'll go in that *vehicle*,' he said. 'The horse is quiet, and the princess is an excellent driver.'

'No, you stay as you were,' said Anna, coming over, 'and we'll go in the carriage.' And, taking Dolly by the arm, she led her away.

Darya Alexandrovna stared wide-eyed at that elegant equipage, the like of which she had never seen before, at those superb horses, at the elegant, shining faces that surrounded her. But she was struck most of all by the change that had taken place in her familiar and beloved Anna. Another less attentive woman, one who had not known Anna before, and above all one who had not been thinking what Darya Alexandrovna had been thinking on the way, would not have noticed anything special about Anna. But Dolly was struck by that temporary beauty which women have in moments of love and which she now found in Anna's face. Everything in her face – the distinctness of the dimples on her cheeks and chin, the set of her lips, the smile that seemed to flit about her face, her shining eyes, the gracefulness and quickness of her movements, the fullness of the sound of her voice, even the manner in which she replied with angry indulgence to Veslovsky, who asked permission to ride her cob in order to teach him to gallop on the right leg – everything was especially attractive, and it seemed that she herself knew it and rejoiced in it.

When the two women got into the carriage, both were suddenly overcome with embarrassment. Anna was embarrassed by the attentively inquisitive way Dolly looked at her; Dolly because, after Sviyazhsky's words about the 'vehicle', she felt involuntarily ashamed of the dirty old carriage that Anna got into with her. The coachman Filipp and the clerk felt the same way. To conceal his embarrassment, the clerk bustled about, helping the ladies in, but Filipp the coachman turned glum and prepared himself ahead of time not to submit to this external superiority. He smiled ironically, glancing at the black trotter, and had already made up his mind that this black one of the *char à banc* was good only for 'permenading', and would not even make twenty-five miles in hot weather, harnessed singly.

The muzhiks all got up from the cart and curiously and merrily watched the visitor's reception, making their own observations.

'They're glad, too, haven't seen each other in a long while,' said the curly-headed old man tied with bast.

'Say, Uncle Gerasim, with that black stallion to haul sheaves, we'd step lively!'

'Looky there. Is that one in britches a woman?' said one of them, pointing at Vasenka Veslovsky, who was mounting a side-saddle.

'Naw, it's a man. See how sprightly he hopped up!'

'Well, boys, does it look like we'll have our nap?'

'Forget it!' said the old man, with a sidelong glance at the sun. 'It's already past noon! Take the hooks and get started!'

XVIII

Anna looked at Dolly's thin, worn face with dust caught in its wrinkles and was about to say what she was thinking – namely, that Dolly had grown thinner; but remembering that she herself had become prettier and that Dolly's eyes told her so, she sighed and began talking about herself.

'You look at me,' she said, 'and think, can she be happy in her situation? Well, and what? It's embarrassing to admit it, but I . . . I'm unforgivably happy. Something magical has happened to me, like a dream, when you feel frightened, creepy, and suddenly wake up and feel that all those fears are gone. I woke up. I lived through the torment and fear, and for a long time now, especially since we came here, I've been so happy! . . .' she said, looking at Dolly with a timid, questioning smile.

'How glad I am!' Dolly said with a smile, involuntarily speaking more coldly than she meant to. 'I'm very glad for you. Why didn't you write to me?'

'Why? . . . Because I didn't dare . . . you forget my situation . . .'

'To me? You didn't dare? If you knew how I . . . I consider . . .'

Darya Alexandrovna wanted to tell Anna about her thoughts from that morning, but for some reason the moment seemed inappropriate to her.

'Anyhow, of that later. What are all these buildings?' she asked, wishing to change the subject and pointing to the red and green roofs visible through the green quickset hedge of acacia and lilac. 'Just like a little town.'

But Anna did not reply.

'No, no! What's your opinion of my situation? What do you think?' she asked.

'I suppose . . .' Darya Alexandrovna began, but just then Vasenka Veslovsky, who had got the cob going on the right leg, galloped past them in his short jacket, bouncing heavily against the suede of the side-saddle.

'He's caught on, Anna Arkadyevna!' he shouted.

Anna did not even look at him; but again it seemed awkward to Darya Alexandrovna to start this long conversation in the carriage, and so she abridged her thought.

'I have no opinion,' she said, 'but I've always loved you, and when you love someone, you love the whole person, as they are, and not as you'd like them to be.'

Anna turned her glance from her friend's face and, narrowing her eyes (this was a new habit that Dolly had not known in her), pondered, wishing to fully understand the meaning of those words. Then, evidently having understood them as she wanted, she looked at Dolly.

'If you have any sins,' she said, 'they should all be forgiven you for your coming and for those words.'

And Dolly saw tears come to Anna's eyes. She silently pressed her hand.

'So what are these buildings? There are so many of them!' She repeated her question after a moment's silence.

'Those are the employees' houses, the stud farm, the stables,' replied Anna. 'And here the park begins. It had all run to seed, but Alexei has renovated everything. He loves this estate very much and, something I never expected, he's passionately interested in managing it. But then, his is such a rich nature! Whatever he does, he does splendidly. He's not only not bored, but he takes it up passionately. Besides all I've known of him, he's become a shrewd and excellent manager. He's even stingy in his management, but only then. Where it's a matter of tens of thousands, he doesn't count,' she said with that joyfully sly smile with which women often speak of the secret qualities of a beloved man, revealed only to them. 'You see that big building? It's a new hospital. I think it will cost more than a hundred thousand. It's his *dada** now. And do you know what it came from? It seems the muzhiks asked him to lower the rent for some meadows, but he refused, and I reproached him for stinginess. Of course, it wasn't just from that, but from everything together – he began on this hospital, you see, in order to show that he wasn't stingy. *C'est une petitesse*† if you like; but I love him the more for it. And now you'll see the house. It's an ancestral house, and nothing on the outside has been altered.'

'How fine!' said Dolly, gazing with involuntary astonishment at the

* Hobby-horse.

† It's a petty thing.

beautiful house with its columns emerging from amidst the varied greens of the old trees in the garden.

'Isn't it? And the view from the house, from upstairs, is wonderful.'

They drove into a courtyard covered with gravel and adorned with flowers, where two workmen were placing uncut porous stones around a freshly turned flower bed, and stopped under a covered portico.

'Ah, they're here already!' said Anna, looking at the saddle horses which were just being led away from the porch. 'Isn't that a fine horse? He's a cob. My favourite. Bring him here and get me some sugar. Where's the count?' she asked of the two liveried footmen who came running out. 'Ah, here he is!' she said, seeing Vronsky and Veslovsky coming to meet them.

'Where will you put the princess?' Vronsky said in French, addressing Anna, and without waiting for an answer he greeted Darya Alexandrovna again, this time kissing her hand. 'In the big bedroom with the balcony, I assume?'

'Oh, no, it's too far away! Better in the corner room, we'll see more of each other. Well, come along,' said Anna, giving her favourite horse the sugar that the footman had brought her.

'*Et vous oubliez votre devoir,*'* she said to Veslovsky, who also came out to the porch.

'*Pardon, j'en ai tout plein les poches,*'† he said, smiling and putting his fingers into his waistcoat pocket.

'*Mais vous venez trop tard,*'‡ she said, wiping with a handkerchief the hand that the horse had wetted as he took the sugar. Anna turned to Dolly: 'How long will you stay? One day? That's impossible!'

'That's what I promised, and the children . . .' said Dolly, feeling embarrassed both because she had to take her handbag from the carriage and because she knew that her face must be quite covered with dust.

'No, Dolly, darling . . . Well, we'll see. Come along, come along!' And Anna took Dolly to her room.

This room was not the fancy one Vronsky had suggested, but one for which Anna said that Dolly must excuse her. And this room for which excuses were offered was filled with such luxury as Dolly had never lived in and reminded her of the best hotels abroad.

'Well, darling, how happy I am!' said Anna, sitting down in her riding

* And you're forgetting your duty.

† Excuse me, I've got my pockets full.

‡ But you've come too late.

habit for a moment beside Dolly. 'Tell me about your family. I saw Stiva in passing, but he can't talk about the children. How's my favourite, Tanya? A big girl, I suppose?'

'Yes, very big,' Darya Alexandrovna replied curtly, surprised at herself for answering so coldly about her children. 'We're having a wonderful stay with the Levins.'

'If only I'd known you don't despise me . . .' said Anna. 'You could all come to stay with us. Stiva is an old and great friend of Alexei's,' she added and suddenly blushed.

'Yes, but we're so nicely . . .' Dolly replied, embarrassed.

'Yes, anyhow I'm talking foolishly from joy. One thing, darling, is that I'm so glad you've come!' Anna said, kissing her again. 'You haven't told me yet how and what you think of me, and I want to know everything. But I'm glad you'll see me as I am. Above all, I wouldn't want people to think that I want to prove anything. I don't want to prove anything, I simply want to live; to cause no evil to anyone but myself. I have that right, haven't I? However, that's a long conversation, and we'll still have a good talk about it all. Now I'll go and dress, and I'll send you a maid.'

XIX

Left alone, Darya Alexandrovna looked round her room with a housewifely eye. Everything she had seen while approaching the house and passing through it, and now in her own room, gave her an impression of opulence and display and that new European luxury she had only read about in English novels but had never seen in Russia, let alone in the country. Everything was new, from the new French wallpaper to the carpet that covered the entire floor. The bed had springs and a mattress, a special headboard, and little pillows with raw-silk slips. The marble washstand, the dressing table, the couch, the tables, the bronze clock on the mantelpiece, the curtains on the windows and doors – it was all expensive and new.

The smart maid who came to offer her services, her dress and coiffure more fashionable than Dolly's, was as new and expensive as the rest of the room. Darya Alexandrovna liked her politeness, neatness and obliging manner, but she felt ill at ease with her; she was embarrassed before her for the patched chemise which, as ill luck would have it, she had packed by mistake. She was ashamed of those very patches and mendings which she had been so proud of at home. At home it was clear that for six chemises she needed seventeen yards of nainsook at ninety kopecks a yard, which would come to over fifteen roubles, besides the work and the trimmings, and these were fifteen roubles gained. But in front of the maid she felt not so much ashamed as ill at ease.

It was a great relief for Darya Alexandrovna when her old acquaintance, Annushka, came into the room. The smart maid was needed by her mistress, and Annushka stayed with Darya Alexandrovna.

Annushka was obviously very glad of the lady's arrival and talked incessantly. Dolly noticed that she wanted to give her opinion of her mistress's situation, especially of the count's love and devotion for Anna, but Dolly took care to interrupt her each time she began to speak of it.

'I grew up with Anna Arkadyevna, she's dearest of all to me. So it's not for us to judge. And, you'd think, to love like that . . .'

'So, please send this to be washed, if possible,' Darya Alexandrovna interrupted her.

'Very well, ma'am. We have two women especially for small laundry, but the linen's all done by machine. The count sees to everything himself. What husband would . . .'

Dolly was glad when Anna came in and by her arrival interrupted Annushka's chatter.

Anna had changed into a very simple cambric dress. Dolly looked attentively at this simple dress. She knew what such simplicity meant and what money was paid for it.

'An old acquaintance,' Anna said of Annushka.

Anna was no longer embarrassed. She was perfectly free and calm. Dolly saw that she had now fully recovered from the impression her arrival had made on her, and had assumed that tone of superficial indifference which indicated that the door to the compartment in which she kept her feelings and innermost thoughts was locked.

'Well, and how is your little girl, Anna?' asked Dolly.

'Annie?' (So she called her daughter Anna.) 'Quite well. She's gained a lot of weight. Would you like to see her? Come, I'll show her to you. There's been terrible trouble with the nannies,' she began to tell the story. 'We have an Italian wet nurse. Good, but so stupid! We wanted to send her away, but the child is so used to her that we still keep her.'

'But how did you arrange . . . ?' Dolly began to ask about what name the girl would have; but, noticing Anna's sudden frown, she changed the sense of the question. 'How did you arrange about weaning her?'

But Anna understood.

'That's not what you wanted to ask. You wanted to ask about her name, didn't you? That torments Alexei. She has no name. That is, she's Karenina,' said Anna, narrowing her eyes so that only her joined eyelashes could be seen. 'However,' her face suddenly brightened, 'we'll talk about all that later. Come, I'll show her to you. *Elle est très gentille.** She crawls already.'

In the nursery the luxury that had struck Darya Alexandrovna everywhere in the house struck her still more. Here were carriages ordered from England, and contraptions for learning to walk, and a specially designed couch, like a billiard table, for crawling, and rocking chairs and special new baths. It was all of English make, sturdy, of good quality, and obviously very expensive. The room was big, very high-ceilinged and bright.

When they came in the little girl was sitting on a chair at the table in just her shift, drinking bouillon, which she spilled all down her front. The child was being fed by a Russian maid who served in the nursery and who apparently ate with her. Neither the wet nurse nor the nanny was there; they were in the next room, where they could be heard talking in a strange French, the only language in which they could communicate with each other.

On hearing Anna's voice, a tall, well-dressed English governess with an unpleasant face and an impure expression came through the door, hastily shaking her blond curls, and at once began justifying herself, though Anna had not accused her of anything. To Anna's every word the governess hastily chimed 'Yes, my lady' several times.

Darya Alexandrovna liked the dark-browed, dark-haired, ruddy-cheeked little girl very much, with her sturdy red body and taut, goose-fleshed skin, despite the stern expression with which she looked at the new person. She even envied her healthy look. She also liked very much the way the girl crawled. None of her children had crawled like that. This girl, when she was sitting on the rug with her dress tucked behind her, was very sweet. She looked at the grown-ups with shining, dark eyes, like a little animal, obviously glad to be admired; smiling and turning her legs sideways, she leaned energetically on her hands and

* She is very nice.

quickly lifted her whole bottom up, then again moved her little hands forward.

But Darya Alexandrovna very much disliked the general spirit of the nursery, and the governess in particular. How Anna, with her knowledge of people, could have engaged such an unsympathetic, unrespectable governess for her child, she could explain to herself only by the fact that a good one would not have come to such an irregular family as Anna's. Moreover, she could tell at once, from a few words, that Anna, the wet nurse, the nanny and the baby did not get on together, and that the mother's visit was an unusual thing. Anna wanted to give her little girl a toy, but could not find it.

Most surprising of all was that, when asked how many teeth the girl had, Anna was mistaken and knew nothing about the two latest teeth.

'It pains me sometimes that I seem so superfluous here,' said Anna, leaving the nursery and picking up her train so as to avoid the toys lying by the door. 'It wasn't like that with my first.'

'I thought the opposite,' Darya Alexandrovna said timidly.

'Oh, no! You know, I saw him – Seryozha,' Anna said, narrowing her eyes as if peering at something in the distance. 'However, we'll talk about it later. You wouldn't believe it, I'm like a hungry person who suddenly has a full meal put in front of her and doesn't know where to start. The full meal is you and the conversations I'm going to have with you, which I haven't been able to have with anybody; and I don't know which conversation to get to first. *Mais je ne vous ferai grâce de rien.** I have to say everything. Ah, yes, I should describe for you the company you'll find here,' she began. 'I'll begin with the ladies. Princess Varvara. You know her, and I know your and Stiva's opinion of her. Stiva says the whole aim of her life consists in proving her superiority to Aunt Katerina Pavlovna. It's all true, but still she's kind and I'm so grateful to her. There was a moment in Petersburg when I needed a chaperone. And she came along. But, really, she's kind. She made my situation a lot easier. I see you don't realize all the difficulty of my situation . . . there, in Petersburg,' she added. 'Here I'm perfectly calm and happy. Well, about that later. I must go on with the list. Then there's Sviyazhsky. He's the marshal and a very decent man, but he wants something from Alexei. You see, with his wealth, now that we've settled in the country, Alexei could have great influence. Then there's Tushkevich – you've seen

* But I won't let you off anything.

him, he was hanging around Betsy. Now he's been dismissed and he's come to us. As Alexei puts it, he's one of those people who are quite agreeable if taken as they would like to appear, *et puis, il est comme il faut*,* as Princess Varvara says. Then there's Veslovsky . . . that one you know. A very nice boy,' she said, and a sly smile puckered her lips. 'What's this wild story with Levin? Veslovsky told Alexei, but we can't believe it. *Il est très gentil et naïf*,'† she said, again with the same smile. 'Men need diversion, and Alexei needs an audience, so I value this whole company. We must keep it gay and animated, so that Alexei won't wish for anything new. Then you'll meet the steward. A German, very nice and knows his business. Alexei values him highly. Then the doctor, a young man, not an outright nihilist, but, you know, eats with his knife. But a very good doctor. Then the architect . . . *Une petite cour*.'‡

XX

'Well, here's Dolly for you, Princess, you wanted so much to see her,' said Anna, coming out with Darya Alexandrovna to the big stone terrace, where Princess Varvara was sitting in the shade over her embroidery frame, making a chair seat for Count Alexei Kirillovich. 'She says she wants nothing before dinner, but you order lunch to be served and I'll go and find Alexei and bring them all here.'

Princess Varvara received Dolly benignly and somewhat condescendingly, and at once began explaining to her that she was living with Anna because she had always loved Anna more than had her sister Katerina Pavlovna, the one who had brought Anna up, and now, when everyone had abandoned Anna, she considered it her duty to help her in this most difficult transitional period.

'Her husband will give her a divorce, and then I shall go back into my seclusion, but now I can be of use and, however hard it is for me, I shall fulfil my duty – not like some others. And how nice of you, what a good thing you've done, to come! They live just like the best of couples. It's for God to judge them, not us. Aren't Biriuzovsky and Mme Avenyev . . . And Nikandrov himself, and Vassilyev and Mme Mamonov, and

* And then, he's proper enough.

† He is very nice and simple.

‡ A little court.

Liza Neptunov . . . And has anyone ever said anything? And it ended with everyone receiving them. And then, *c'est un intérieur si joli, si comme il faut. Tout-à-fait à l'anglaise. On se réunit le matin au breakfast et puis on se sépare.** Everyone does what he likes till dinner. Dinner is at seven. Stiva did very well to send you. He must stick by them. You know, through his mother and brother he can do anything. And then they do so much good. Hasn't he told you about his hospital? *Ce sera admirable*† – everything comes from Paris.'

Their conversation was interrupted by Anna, who had found the men gathered in the billiard room and returned with them to the terrace. There was still a long time till dinner and, as the weather was fine, several ways were suggested for passing the remaining two hours. There were a great many ways of passing the time in Vozdvizhenskoe, and they were all different from what was done at Pokrovskoe.

'*Une partie de lawn tennis*,'‡ Veslovsky suggested, smiling his handsome smile. 'We can be partners again, Anna Arkadyevna.'

'No, it's too hot. Better to stroll in the garden and go for a boat ride, to show Darya Alexandrovna the banks,' suggested Vronsky.

'I'm agreeable to everything,' said Sviyazhsky.

'I think Dolly would like most to take a stroll, isn't that right? And then go for a boat ride,' said Anna.

So it was decided. Veslovsky and Tushkevich went to the bathing house, and promised to get the boat ready there and wait for them.

They walked down the path in two pairs, Anna with Sviyazhsky and Dolly with Vronsky. Dolly was slightly embarrassed and worried in the totally new milieu in which she found herself. Abstractly, theoretically, she not only justified but even approved of what Anna had done. Weary of the monotony of a moral life, as irreproachably moral women in general often are, she not only excused criminal love from a distance but even envied it. Besides, she loved Anna from the heart. But in reality, seeing her among these people she found so alien, with their good tone that was so new for her, she felt awkward. It was especially unpleasant for her to see Princess Varvara, who forgave them everything for the sake of the comfort she enjoyed.

In general, abstractly, Dolly approved of what Anna had done, but to

* It's such a pretty interior, in such good taste. Quite in the English style. We get together in the morning for breakfast and then go our separate ways.

† It will be wonderful.

‡ A game of lawn tennis.

see the man for whose sake she had done it was unpleasant for her. Besides, she had never liked Vronsky. She considered him very proud and saw nothing in him that he could be proud of except his wealth. But, against her will, here, in his own house, he impressed her still more than before, and she could not be comfortable with him. She felt with him as she had felt with the maid about her chemise. As she had felt not so much ashamed as ill at ease with the maid about the patches, so with him she felt not so much ashamed as ill at ease about herself.

Dolly felt embarrassed and searched for a topic of conversation. She thought that he, with his pride, was sure to find praise of his house and garden displeasing but, unable to come up with anything else, she told him all the same that she liked his house very much.

'Yes, it's a very handsome building and in the good old style,' he said.

'I like the courtyard in front of the porch very much. Is that how it was?'

'Oh, no!' he said, and his face lit up with pleasure. 'You should have seen that courtyard in the spring!'

And, cautiously at first, but then more and more enthusiastically, he began to draw her attention to various details of the embellishment of the house and garden. One could see that, having devoted much work to improving and embellishing his estate, Vronsky felt a need to boast of it before a new person and was heartily glad of Darya Alexandrovna's praise.

'If you're not tired and would like to have a look at the hospital, it's not far. Let's go,' he said, glancing at her face to be sure she was indeed not bored.

'Will you come, Anna?' he turned to her.

'Yes, we'll come. Won't we?' She turned to Sviyazhsky. '*Mais il ne faut pas laisser le pauvre Veslovsky et Tushkevich se morfondre là dans le bateau.** Send somebody to tell them. Yes, he'll leave it behind as a memorial,' said Anna, turning to Dolly with the same sly, knowing smile as when she had spoken of the hospital earlier.

'Oh, a capital affair!' said Sviyazhsky. But to avoid seeming to fall in with Vronsky, he at once added a slightly deprecatory observation. 'I'm astonished, though, Count,' he said, 'that you, who are doing so much for the people in the sanitary respect, are so indifferent to schools.'

* But we mustn't leave poor Veslovsky and Tushkevich to languish there in the boat.

'*C'est devenu tellement commun, les écoles!*'* said Vronsky. 'It's not because of that, you understand, I just got carried away. This way to the hospital.' He turned to Darya Alexandrovna, pointing to a side path off the avenue.

The ladies opened their parasols and went down the side path. After making several turns and passing through a gate, Darya Alexandrovna saw on a rise before her a large, red, fancifully designed and nearly completed building. The still unpainted iron roof shone dazzlingly in the bright sun. Beside the completed building, another one, surrounded by scaffolding, was under construction, and on the planks workmen in aprons were laying bricks, taking mortar from troughs and smoothing it with trowels.

'How quickly your work's going!' said Sviyazhsky. 'The last time I was here, there was no roof yet.'

'It will all be done by the autumn. The interior's nearly finished now,' said Anna.

'And what's this new one?'

'This will house the doctor and the dispensary,' Vronsky replied and, seeing the architect in his short coat coming towards them, he excused himself to the ladies and went to meet him.

Sidestepping a trough from which the workmen took lime, he stopped with the architect and heatedly began telling him something.

'The pediment still comes out too low,' he answered Anna, who had asked him what was the matter.

'I kept saying the foundation had to be raised,' said Anna.

'Yes, certainly, that would have been better, Anna Arkadyevna,' said the architect, 'but it's too late now.'

'Yes, I'm very interested in it,' Anna replied to Sviyazhsky, who had expressed surprise at her knowledge of architecture. 'The new building ought to correspond to the hospital. But it was thought of later and begun without a plan.'

When he finished talking with the architect, Vronsky joined the ladies and showed them into the hospital.

Though they were still working on the cornices outside, and the ground floor was still being painted, upstairs almost everything was done. Having climbed the wide cast-iron stairway to the landing, they went into the first big room. The walls had been plastered to look like

* They've become so common, these schools!

marble, enormous plate-glass windows had already been installed, only the parquet floor was not yet finished, and the joiners, who were planing a square they had removed, stopped work and took off their headbands to greet the gentlefolk.

'This is the reception room,' said Vronsky. 'It will have a desk, a table, a cupboard, and that's all.'

'Here, come this way. Don't go near the window,' said Anna, testing whether the paint was dry. 'The paint's already dry, Alexei,' she added.

From the reception room they went into the corridor. Here Vronsky showed them the new ventilation system he had installed. Then he showed them marble baths, beds with extraordinary springs. Then, one after the other, he showed them the wards, the store room, the linen room, then stoves of some new construction, then special carts that would make no noise when conveying necessary things through the corridors, and much more. Sviyazhsky appreciated it all like one familiar with all the new improvements. Dolly was simply surprised at what she had never seen before and, wishing to understand it all, asked about everything in great detail, which obviously pleased Vronsky very much.

'Yes, I think this will be the only quite properly set-up hospital in Russia,' said Sviyazhsky.

'And won't you have a maternity ward?' asked Dolly. 'It's so needed in the country. I often . . .'

In spite of his courtesy, Vronsky interrupted her.

'This is not a maternity home, it's a hospital, and meant for all illnesses except infectious ones,' he said. 'And take a look at this . . .' He wheeled a newly ordered convalescent chair up to Darya Alexandrovna. 'Watch now.' He sat in the chair and began moving it. 'He can't walk, he's weak or has bad legs, but he needs air, and so he wheels himself about in it . . .'

Darya Alexandrovna was interested in it all, liked it all very much, but most of all she liked Vronsky himself, with his natural, naïve passion. 'Yes, he's a very nice, good man,' she thought occasionally, not listening to him but trying to penetrate his expression and mentally putting herself inside Anna. She now liked him so much in his animation that she understood how Anna could fall in love with him.

XXI

'No, I think the princess is tired, and horses don't interest her,' Vronsky said to Anna, who had suggested strolling over to the stud farm, where Sviyazhsky wanted to see the new stallion. 'You go and I'll take the princess home, and we can talk,' he said, 'if you'd like that.' He turned to her.

'I understand nothing about horses and shall be very glad,' said Darya Alexandrovna, slightly surprised.

She saw by Vronsky's face that he wanted something from her. Nor was she mistaken. As soon as they went back through the gate into the garden, he looked in the direction Anna had gone and, having made sure that she could not hear or see them, began:

'You've guessed that I wanted to talk with you?' he said, looking at her with laughing eyes. 'I'm not mistaken in thinking that you're Anna's friend.' He removed his hat, took out a handkerchief, and wiped his balding head.

Darya Alexandrovna made no reply and only looked fearfully at him. Now that she was left alone with him, she suddenly became frightened: his laughing eyes and the stern expression of his face scared her.

The most varied suppositions as to the subject of his talk with her flashed through her head: 'He's going to ask me to come and stay here with my children, and I'll have to say no to him; or to become part of Anna's circle in Moscow . . . Or is it about Vasenka Veslovsky and his relations with Anna? Maybe about Kitty, about how he feels himself guilty?' She foresaw only unpleasantness, but failed to guess what he wanted to talk with her about.

'You have such influence on Anna, and she loves you so,' he said. 'Help me.'

Darya Alexandrovna looked with questioning timidity at his energetic face, which kept moving into sunlit gaps in the shade of the lindens, then was darkened again by the shade, and waited for what more he would say; but he walked silently beside her, his stick grazing the gravel.

'If you have come to us, you, the only woman among Anna's former friends – I don't count Princess Varvara – I understand that you've done it not because you consider our situation normal, but because, realizing all the difficulty of that situation, you still love her and want to help her. Have I understood you rightly?' he asked, turning to look at her.

'Oh, yes,' Darya Alexandrovna replied, folding her parasol, 'but . . .'

'No,' he interrupted and stopped involuntarily, forgetting that he was thereby putting her into an awkward position, so that she had to stop as well. 'No one feels all the difficulty of Anna's situation more fully or strongly than I do. And that is understandable, if you do me the honour of considering me a man who has a heart. I am the cause of that situation, and that is why I feel it.'

'I understand,' said Darya Alexandrovna, involuntarily admiring him for having said it so sincerely and firmly. 'But precisely because you feel yourself the cause of it, I'm afraid you exaggerate,' she said. 'Her situation in society is difficult, I understand that.'

'It's hell in society!' he said quickly, with a dark frown. 'It's impossible to imagine moral torments worse than those she lived through for two weeks in Petersburg . . . I beg you to believe that.'

'Yes, but here, so long as neither Anna . . . nor you feel any need of society . . .'

'Society!' he said scornfully. 'What need can I have of society?'

'Then for so long – and that may mean for ever – you'll be happy and at peace. I can see that Anna is happy, perfectly happy, she's already had time to tell me so,' Darya Alexandrovna said, smiling; and now, as she said it, she involuntarily doubted whether Anna was indeed happy.

But Vronsky, it seemed, did not doubt it.

'Yes, yes,' he said. 'I know she has revived after all her sufferings; she's happy. She's happy in the present. But I? . . . I'm afraid of what awaits us . . . Sorry, would you like to move on?'

'No, it makes no difference.'

'Let's sit down here then.'

Darya Alexandrovna sat down on a garden bench in the corner of the avenue. He stood in front of her.

'I see that she's happy,' he repeated, and the doubt whether she was happy struck Darya Alexandrovna still more strongly. 'But can it go on like this? Whether what we did was good or bad is another question. The die is cast,' he said, going from Russian to French, 'and we're bound for our whole life. We're united by the bonds of love, which are the most sacred thing for us. We have a child, we may have more children. But the law and all the conditions of our situation are such that thousands of complications exist that she doesn't see and doesn't want to see now, as she rests her soul after all her sufferings and ordeals. And that is understandable. But I can't help seeing them. My daughter, according to the law, is not my daughter, she is – Karenin's. I do not want this deceit!' he said with an energetic gesture of negation, and he gave Darya Alexandrovna a gloomily questioning look.

She made no reply and only looked at him. He went on:

'And tomorrow a son will be born, my son, and by law he is a Karenin, he is heir neither to my name nor to my fortune, and however happy we may be in our family and however many children we may have, there will be no connection between me and them. They are Karenins. You can understand the burden and horror of this situation! I've tried to say it to Anna. It annoys her. She doesn't understand, and I can't say everything to *her*. Now look at it from the other side. I'm happy in her love, but I must be occupied. I have found an occupation, and I am proud of that occupation and consider it nobler than the occupations of my former comrades at court and in the service. And I certainly would never exchange it for what they do. I work here, staying put, and I'm happy, content, and we need nothing more for happiness. I love this activity. *Cela n'est pas un pis-aller*,* on the contrary . . .'

Darya Alexandrovna noticed that at this point of his explanation he became confused, and she did not quite understand this digression, but she sensed that once he had begun talking about his innermost attitudes, which he could not talk about with Anna, he would now say everything, and that the question of his activity on the estate belonged to the same compartment of innermost thoughts as the question of his relations with Anna.

'And so, to continue,' he said, recovering himself. 'The main thing is that, as I work, I must be sure that my work will not die with me, that I will have heirs – and that is not the case. Imagine the situation of a man who knows beforehand that his children by the woman he loves will be not his but someone else's, someone who hates them and does not want to know them. It's terrible!'

He fell silent, obviously in great agitation.

'Yes, of course, I understand that. But what can Anna do?' asked Darya Alexandrovna.

'Yes, that brings me to the point of what I'm saying,' he said, making an effort to calm down. 'Anna can do something, it depends on her . . . A divorce is necessary even in order to petition the emperor for adoption. And that depends on Anna. Her husband agreed to a divorce – at that

* This is not making the best of a bad thing.

time your husband had it all but arranged. And even now, I know, he would not refuse. It would only take writing to him. His answer then was that if she expressed the wish, he would not refuse. Of course,' he said gloomily, 'this is one of those pharisaic cruelties that only such heartless men are capable of. He knows what torment any remembrance of him costs her, and, knowing her, he demands a letter from her. I understand that it torments her. But the reasons are so important that she must *passer par-dessus toutes ces finesses de sentiment. Il y va du bonheur et de l'existence d'Anne et de ses enfants.** I'm not speaking of myself, though it's hard for me, very hard,' he said, with a look as if he were threatening someone for making it so hard. 'And so, Princess, I am shamelessly seizing upon you as an anchor of salvation. Help me to talk her into writing to him and demanding a divorce!'

'Yes, of course,' Darya Alexandrovna said pensively, vividly remembering her last meeting with Alexei Alexandrovich. 'Yes, of course,' she repeated resolutely, remembering Anna.

'Use your influence on her, make her write to him. I don't want to talk with her about it and almost cannot.'

'Very well, I'll talk with her. But how is it she doesn't think of it herself?' said Darya Alexandrovna, at the same time suddenly recalling for some reason Anna's strange new habit of narrowing her eyes. And she remembered that Anna had narrowed her eyes precisely when it was a matter of the most intimate sides of life. 'As if she narrows her eyes at her life in order not to see it all,' thought Dolly. 'I'll be sure to talk with her, for my own sake and for hers,' Darya Alexandrovna replied to his look of gratitude.

They got up and went towards the house.

XXII

Finding Dolly already at home, Anna looked attentively into her eyes, as if asking about the conversation she had had with Vronsky, but she did not ask in words.

'I think it's time for dinner,' she said. 'We haven't seen each other at

* One must pass over all these fine points of feeling. The happiness and the existence of Anna and her children depend on it.

all yet. I'm counting on the evening. Now I must go and dress. You, too, I think. We all got dirty at the construction site.'

Dolly went to her room and felt like laughing. She had nothing to change into because she had already put on her best dress; but to mark her preparations for dinner in some way, she asked the maid to brush her dress, changed the cuffs and the bow, and put lace on her head.

'This is all I could do,' she said, smiling, to Anna, who came out to her in a third, again extremely simple, dress.

'Yes, we're very formal here,' she said, as if apologizing for being dressed up. 'Alexei is rarely so pleased with anything as he is with your visit. He's decidedly in love with you,' she added. 'But aren't you tired?'

There was no time to talk about anything before dinner. Coming into the drawing room, they found Princess Varvara and the men in their black frock coats already there. The architect was wearing a tailcoat. Vronsky introduced the doctor and the steward to his guest. She had already met the architect at the hospital.

The fat butler, his round, clean-shaven face and the starched bow of his white tie gleaming, announced that the meal was ready, and the ladies rose. Vronsky asked Sviyazhsky to give Anna Arkadyevna his arm, and went over to Dolly himself. Veslovsky got ahead of Tushkevich in offering his arm to Princess Varvara, so that Tushkevich, the steward and the doctor went in by themselves.

The dinner, the dining room, the dinnerware, the servants, the wine and the food were not only in keeping with the general tone of new luxury in the house, but seemed even newer and more luxurious than all the rest. Darya Alexandrovna observed this luxury, which was new to her, and, being herself the mistress of a house – though with no hope of applying to her own house anything of what she saw, so far did its luxury exceed her style of life – involuntarily took note of all the details, asking herself who had done it all and how. Vasenka Veslovsky, her own husband, and even Sviyazhsky, and many other people she knew, never gave it a thought, and took for granted what any decent host wishes his guests to feel – namely, that everything he had arranged so well had cost him, the host, no trouble and had got done by itself. But Darya Alexandrovna knew that not even the porridge for the children's breakfast got done by itself and that therefore such a complicated and excellent arrangement had required someone's close attention. And from the look of Alexei Kirillovich as he inspected the table, nodded to the butler, and offered her a choice between cold borscht and soup, she understood that everything was done and maintained through the care of the host himself. It obviously depended no more on Anna than on Veslovsky. She, Sviyazhsky, the princess and Veslovsky were guests alike, cheerfully enjoying what had been prepared for them.

Anna was hostess only in conducting the conversation. And that task – quite difficult for a hostess at a small table in the presence of people like the steward and the architect, people from a completely different world, trying not to be intimidated by the unaccustomed luxury and unable to take part for long in a general conversation – Anna performed with her usual tact, naturalness and even pleasure, as Darya Alexandrovna noticed.

The conversation turned to how Tushkevich and Veslovsky had gone for a boat ride alone, and Tushkevich began telling them about the last race at the Petersburg Yacht Club. But Anna, after a suitable pause, turned at once to the architect, to draw him out of his silence.

'Nikolai Ivanovich was struck,' she said of Sviyazhsky, 'by how the new building has grown since he was here last; but I'm there every day, and every day I'm surprised at how quickly it goes.'

'It's good working with his excellency,' the architect said with a smile (he was a quiet and deferential man with a sense of his own dignity). 'A far cry from dealing with the provincial authorities. Where we'd fill out a stack of papers with them, I just report to the count, we discuss it, and in three words it's done.'

'American methods,' Sviyazhsky said, smiling.

'Yes, sir, building's done rationally there . . .'

The conversation turned to government abuses in the United States, but Anna immediately turned it to a different subject, so as to draw the steward out of his silence.

'Have you ever seen these harvesting machines?' She turned to Darya Alexandrovna. 'We were coming from looking at them when we met you. It was the first time I'd seen them myself.'

'How do they work?' asked Dolly.

'Just like scissors. A board and a lot of little scissors. Like this.'

Anna took a knife and fork in her beautiful, white, ring-adorned hands and began to demonstrate. She obviously could see that her explanation would not make anything understood, but, knowing that her speech was pleasant and her hands were beautiful, she went on explaining.

'Rather like penknives,' Veslovsky said playfully, never taking his eyes off her.

Anna gave a barely noticeable smile, but did not reply to him.

'Isn't it just like scissors, Karl Fedorych?' She turned to the steward.

'*Oh, ja,*' the German answered. '*Es ist ein ganz einfaches Ding,*'* and he began explaining the construction of the machine.

'Too bad it doesn't bind. I saw one at an exhibition in Vienna that binds with wire,' said Sviyazhsky. 'They'd be more profitable.'

'*Es kommt drauf an... Der Preis vom Draht muss ausgerechnet werden.*'† And the German, roused from his silence, addressed Vronsky: '*Das lässt sich ausrechnen, Erlaucht.*'‡ The German was about to go to his pocket, where he had a pencil in a little notebook in which he calculated everything, but, remembering that he was sitting at dinner and noticing Vronsky's cold gaze, he checked himself. '*Zu kompliziert, macht zu viel Troubles,*'§ he concluded.

'*Wünscht man Roubles, so hat man auch Troubles,*'¶ said Vasenka Veslovsky, teasing the German. '*J'adore l'allemand.*'** He turned to Anna again with the same smile.

'*Cessez,*'†† she said to him with mock severity.

'And we hoped to find you in the fields, Vassily Semyonych,' she turned to the doctor, a sickly man. 'Were you there?'

'I was, but I evaporated,' the doctor replied with gloomy jocularity.

'So you got some good exercise?'

'Magnificent!'

'Well, and how's the old woman's health? I hope it's not typhus.'

'Typhus or no, her condition is not of the most advantageous.'

'What a pity!' said Anna, and having granted due courtesy to the people of the household, she turned to her own friends.

'But still, it would be difficult to build a machine from your description, Anna Arkadyevna,' Sviyazhsky said jokingly.

'No, why?' Anna replied with a smile which said that she knew there had been something endearing in the way she had explained the construction of the machine, something Sviyazhsky had noticed as well. This new feature of youthful coquetry struck Dolly unpleasantly.

* It's quite a simple thing.

† That depends . . . The cost of the wire must be taken into account.

‡ It can be calculated, your excellency.

§ Too complicated, makes too much troubles.

¶ A man who wants roubles will also have troubles.

** I love German.

†† Stop it.

'On the other hand, Anna Arkadyevna's knowledge of architecture is amazing,' said Tushkevich.

'That it is! Yesterday I heard Anna Arkadyevna say "in strobilus" and "plinths",' said Veslovsky. 'Am I saying it right?'

'There's nothing amazing about it when one has seen and heard so much,' said Anna. 'And you probably don't even know what houses are made of!'

Darya Alexandrovna saw that Anna was displeased with that playful tone between her and Veslovsky but involuntarily fell into it herself.

Vronsky in this case acted not at all like Levin. He obviously did not attach any significance to Veslovsky's chatter and, on the contrary, encouraged these jokes.

'So, tell us, Veslovsky, what holds the bricks together?'

'Cement, naturally.'

'Bravo! And what is cement?'

'Just some sort of paste . . . no, putty,' said Veslovsky, provoking general laughter.

The conversation among the diners, except for the doctor, the architect, and the steward, who were sunk in gloomy silence, never flagged, now gliding along smoothly, now touching and cutting someone to the quick. On one occasion Darya Alexandrovna was cut to the quick and got so excited that she even turned red and later tried to recall whether she had said anything out of place or unpleasant. Sviyazhsky had started talking about Levin, telling of his strange opinions about machines being only harmful for Russian farming.

'I don't have the pleasure of knowing this Mr Levin,' Vronsky said, smiling, 'but he has probably never seen the machines he denounces. And if he has seen and tried one, it was not of foreign make but some Russian version. And what views can there be here?'

'Turkish views, generally,' Veslovsky said with a smile, turning to Anna.

'I cannot defend his opinions,' Darya Alexandrovna said, flushing, 'but I can tell you that he's a very educated man, and if he were here he would know how to answer you, though I'm unable to.'

'I like him very much and we're great friends,' said Sviyazhsky, smiling good-naturedly. '*Mais pardon, il est un petit peu toqué*:* for instance, he maintains that the zemstvo and the local courts – that it's all unnecessary, and he doesn't want to participate in any of it.'

* But, excuse me, he's a bit cracked.

'That's our Russian apathy,' said Vronsky, pouring water from a chilled carafe into a thin glass with a stem, 'not to feel the responsibilities imposed on us by our rights and thus to deny those responsibilities.'

'I don't know a man more strict in fulfilling his responsibilities,' said Darya Alexandrovna, annoyed by Vronsky's superior tone.

'I, on the contrary,' Vronsky went on, evidently touched to the quick for some reason by this conversation, 'I, on the contrary, such as I am, feel very grateful for the honour done me, thanks to Nikolai Ivanych here' (he indicated Sviyazhsky), 'in electing me an honourable justice of the peace. I think that for me the responsibility of attending the sessions, of judging the case of a muzhik and his horse, is as important as anything I can do. And I will consider it an honour if I'm elected to the council. That is the only way I can pay back the benefits I enjoy as a landowner. Unfortunately, people don't understand the significance major landowners ought to have in the state.'

Darya Alexandrovna found it strange to hear how calmly in the right he was, there at his own table. She remembered Levin, who thought the opposite, being just as resolute in his opinions at his own table. But she loved Levin and was therefore on his side.

'So we can rely on you, Count, for the next session?' said Sviyazhsky. 'But you must leave early so as to be there by the eighth. Why don't you honour me with a visit first?'

'And I'm somewhat in agreement with your *beau-frère*,' said Anna. 'Only not in the same way,' she added with a smile. 'I'm afraid we've had too many of these social responsibilities lately. Just as there used to be so many officials that there had to be an official for every case, so now it's all social activists. Alexei's been here six months and he's already a member of five or six social institutions – he's a trustee, a judge, a councillor, a juror, and something to do with horses. *Du train que cela va*,* all his time will be spent on it. And I'm afraid when there's such a host of these affairs, it's all just form. How many places are you a member of, Nikolai Ivanych?' She turned to Sviyazhsky. 'More than twenty, isn't it?'

Anna spoke playfully, but irritation could be felt in her voice. Darya Alexandrovna, who was observing Anna and Vronsky very closely, noticed it at once. She also noticed that Vronsky's face during this conversation immediately acquired a serious and stubborn expression.

* At this rate.

Noticing this and the fact that, to change the subject, Princess Varvara at once began talking hurriedly of some Petersburg acquaintances, and recalling Vronsky's stray remarks in the garden about his activities, Dolly understood that the question of social activity was connected with some private quarrel between Anna and Vronsky.

The dinner, the wines, the table – it was all very fine, but it was all the same as Darya Alexandrovna had seen at big formal dinners and balls, which she had become unused to, and had the same impersonal and strained character; and therefore, on an ordinary day and in a small circle, it all made an unpleasant impression on her.

After dinner they sat on the terrace for a while. Then they began to play lawn tennis. The players, dividing into two groups, installed themselves on a carefully levelled and rolled croquet-ground, on either side of a net stretched between two gilded posts. Darya Alexandrovna tried to play, but at first she could not understand the game, and by the time she did understand it, she was so tired that she sat down with Princess Varvara and merely watched. Her partner, Tushkevich, also dropped out; but the others went on with the game for a long time. Sviyazhsky and Vronsky both played very well and seriously. They kept a sharp eye on the ball sent to them, ran to it adroitly, without haste or delay, waited for it to bounce and, hitting the ball squarely and firmly with the racket, sent it back over the net. Veslovsky played worse than the others. He got too excited, but, to make up for it, he enlivened the other players with his merriment. His laughter and shouting never ceased. With the ladies' permission, he removed his frock coat, as did the other men, and his big, handsome figure in white shirtsleeves, with his red, sweaty face and brisk movements, etched itself in the memory.

When Darya Alexandrovna went to bed that night, the moment she closed her eyes she saw Vasenka Veslovsky dashing about the croquet-ground.

But during the game Darya Alexandrovna was not happy. She did not like the playful relations between Vasenka Veslovsky and Anna, which went on all the while, and that general unnaturalness of grown-ups when they play at a children's game by themselves, without children. But, so as not to upset the others and to pass the time somehow, she joined the game again, after resting, and pretended to have fun. All that day she had had the feeling that she was playing in the theatre with actors better than herself and that her poor playing spoiled the whole thing.

She had come with the intention of spending two days if all went well. But that same evening, during the game, she decided to leave the next day. Those painful cares of motherhood that she had hated so on her way there, now, after a day spent without them, presented themselves to her in a different light and drew her to them.

When, after the evening tea and a late boat ride, Darya Alexandrovna went to her room alone, got undressed and sat down to do her thin hair for the night, she felt great relief.

It was even unpleasant for her to think that Anna would shortly come to her. She wanted to be alone with her thoughts.

XXIII

Dolly was about to get into bed when Anna came in dressed for the night.

During the day Anna had several times begun talking about her intimate affairs and had stopped each time after a few words. 'Later, when we're alone, we'll discuss everything. There's so much I must tell you,' she had said.

Now they were alone and Anna did not know what to talk about. She sat by the window, looking at Dolly and going through all that seemingly inexhaustible store of intimate conversation, and found nothing. It seemed to her just then that everything had already been said.

'Well, how's Kitty?' she said, sighing heavily and looking guiltily at Dolly. 'Tell me the truth, Dolly, is she angry with me?'

'Angry? No,' Darya Alexandrovna said, smiling.

'But she hates me, despises me?'

'Oh, no! But, you know, such things don't get forgiven.'

'Yes, yes,' said Anna, turning away and looking out of the open window. 'But it wasn't my fault. And whose fault was it? What does "fault" mean? Could it have been otherwise? What do you think? Could you not be Stiva's wife?'

'I really don't know. But tell me this . . .'

'Yes, yes, but we haven't finished about Kitty. Is she happy? He's a wonderful man, they say.'

'To say he's wonderful isn't enough. I don't know a better man.'

'Ah, I'm so glad! I'm very glad! To say he's a wonderful man isn't enough,' she repeated.

Dolly smiled.

'But tell me about yourself. I must have a long talk with you. I spoke with . . .' Dolly did not know what to call him. She felt awkward calling him either the count or Alexei Kirillych.

'With Alexei,' Anna said. 'I know you did. But I wanted to ask you directly – what do you think about me, about my life?'

'How can I say so suddenly? I really don't know.'

'No, tell me all the same . . . You see my life. But don't forget you're seeing us in the summer, on a visit, and that we're not by ourselves . . . But we came in early spring, we lived completely alone, and we shall live alone, and I don't wish for anything better than that. But imagine me living alone without him, alone – and it will happen . . . Everything tells me that it will be repeated often, that he will spend half his time away from home,' she said, getting up and moving closer to Dolly.

'Of course,' she interrupted Dolly, who was about to object, 'of course, I can't keep him by force. And I'm not keeping him now. There's a race today, his horses are in it, off he goes. I'm very glad. But think of me, imagine my position . . . Ah, why speak of that!' She smiled. 'So, what did he talk about with you?'

'He talked about what I myself want to talk about, and it's easy for me to be his advocate: about whether it mightn't be possible, whether you couldn't . . .' Darya Alexandrovna faltered, 'improve your situation, put it right . . . You know how I look at . . . But all the same, if possible, you should get married . . .'

'Meaning a divorce?' said Anna. 'You know, the only woman who came to see me in Petersburg was Betsy Tverskoy. Do you know her? *Au fond c'est la femme la plus dépravée qui existe.** She had a liaison with Tushkevich, deceiving her husband in the nastiest way. And she told me that she didn't want to know me as long as my situation was irregular. Don't think I'm comparing . . . I know you, my darling. But I happened to remember . . . Well, so what did he tell you?' she repeated.

'He said he suffers for you and for himself. You may say it's egoism, but it's such legitimate and noble egoism! He would like, first of all, to

* At bottom, she's the most depraved woman in the world.

legitimize his daughter and to be your husband, to have the right to you.'

'What wife, what slave, can be so much a slave as I am, in my situation?' she interrupted gloomily.

'And the main thing he wants . . . he wants you not to suffer.'

'That's impossible! Well?'

'Well, and the most legitimate thing – he wants your children to have a name.'

'What children?' said Anna, not looking at Dolly and narrowing her eyes.

'Annie, and the future . . .'

'He can rest easy about that, I won't have any more children.'

'How can you say you won't have any more? . . .'

'I won't, because I don't want it.'

And, despite all her excitement, Anna smiled, noticing the naïve look of curiosity, astonishment and horror on Dolly's face.

'The doctor told me after my illness . . . .
. . . .'

'It can't be!' said Dolly, wide-eyed. For her it was one of those discoveries the consequences and conclusions of which are so enormous that for the first moment one feels only that it is impossible to grasp it all, but that one must think about it a great, great deal.

This discovery, which suddenly explained for her all those formerly incomprehensible families with only one or two children, called up in her so many thoughts, reflections and contradictory feelings that she was unable to say anything and only looked at Anna with wide-eyed astonishment. This was the very thing she had dreamed of that morning on her way there, but now, on learning that it was possible, she was horrified. She felt it was a much too simple solution of a much too complicated question.

'*N'est-ce pas immoral?*'* was all she said, after a pause.

'Why? Consider, I have to choose between the two: either to become pregnant, meaning ill, or to be a friend, a companion for my husband, or the same as my husband,' Anna said in a deliberately superficial and frivolous tone.

'Ah, yes, yes,' Darya Alexandrovna repeated, listening to the very

* Isn't it immoral?

same arguments she had produced for herself and finding them no longer convincing.

'For you, for others,' Anna said, as if guessing her thoughts, 'there may still be doubt, but for me . . . Understand, I'm not a wife. He loves me as long as he loves me. And what then, how am I to keep his love? With this?'

She held her white arms out in front of her stomach.

Thoughts and memories came crowding into Darya Alexandrovna's head with extraordinary quickness, as happens in moments of excitement. 'I didn't make myself attractive to Stiva,' she thought. 'He left me for other women, and the first one he betrayed me for did not keep him by being always beautiful and gay. He dropped her and took another. And is this how Anna is going to attract and keep Count Vronsky? If he's looking for that, he'll find clothes and manners that are still more gay and attractive. And however white, however beautiful her bare arms, however attractive her full bosom, her flushed face against that dark hair, he'll find still better ones, as my disgusting, pathetic and dear husband seeks and finds them.'

Dolly made no answer and only sighed. Anna noticed her sigh, which showed disagreement, and went on. She had more arguments in store, such strong ones that it was impossible to answer them.

'You say it's not good? But you must consider,' she went on. 'You forget my situation. How can I want children? I'm not talking about the suffering, I'm not afraid of that. But think, who will my children be? Unfortunate children, who will bear another man's name. By their very birth they'll be placed in the necessity of being ashamed of their mother, their father, their birth.'

'That's just why you must get divorced.'

But Anna did not hear her. She wanted to voice the same arguments with which she had so often persuaded herself.

'Why have I been given reason, if I don't use it so as not to bring unfortunate children into the world?'

She looked at Dolly, but went on without waiting for an answer:

'I would always feel guilty before those unfortunate children,' she said. 'If they don't exist, at least they won't be unfortunate, and if they're unfortunate, I alone am to blame.'

These were the same arguments Darya Alexandrovna had produced for herself, but now she listened to them and could not understand them. 'How can she be guilty before beings who don't exist?' she wondered.

And suddenly a thought came to her: could it be better in any possible case for her favourite, Grisha, if he had never existed? And it seemed so wild to her, so strange, that she shook her head to scatter this whirling confusion of mad thoughts.

'No, I don't know, it's not good,' she merely said, with a squeamish look on her face.

'Yes, but don't forget what you are and what I am . . . And besides,' Anna added, as if, despite the wealth of her arguments and the poverty of Dolly's, she still admitted that it was not good, 'don't forget the main thing, that I'm not in the same situation now as you are. For you the question is whether you do not want to have any more children, and for me it's whether I want to have them. And that is a big difference. You see, I can't want it in my situation.'

Darya Alexandrovna did not object. She suddenly felt she had become so distant from Anna that there were questions between them which they would never agree on and of which it was better not to speak.

XXIV

'Then you need all the more to settle your situation, if possible,' said Dolly.

'Yes, if possible,' Anna said suddenly, in a completely different, soft and sad voice.

'Is divorce impossible? I was told your husband has agreed.'

'Dolly! I don't want to talk about it.'

'Well, then we won't,' Darya Alexandrovna hastened to say, noticing the look of suffering on Anna's face. 'I only see that you look at things too darkly.'

'Me? Not a bit. I'm very cheerful and content. You've noticed, *je fais des passions*.* Veslovsky . . .'

'Yes, to tell the truth, I didn't like Veslovsky's tone,' Darya Alexandrovna said, wishing to change the subject.

'Ah, not a bit! It tickles Alexei, that's all; but he's a boy and he's entirely in my hands; you understand, I control him as I please. He's the same as your Grisha . . . Dolly!' she suddenly changed her tone, 'you say

* I'm a success with men.

I look at things too darkly. You cannot understand. It's too terrible. I try not to look at all.'

'But I think you must. You must do everything possible.'

'But what is possible? Nothing. You say marry Alexei and that I don't think about it. I don't think about it!!' she repeated, and colour came to her face. She rose, drew herself up, sighed deeply, and began pacing the room with her light step, pausing every now and then. 'I don't think? There isn't a day or an hour that I don't think of it and don't reproach myself for that thinking . . . because the thought of it could drive me mad. Drive me mad,' she repeated. 'When I think of it, I can't fall asleep without morphine. But, very well. Let's talk calmly. Divorce, I'm told. First of all, *he* won't grant me a divorce. *He* is now under the influence of Countess Lydia Ivanovna.'

Darya Alexandrovna, drawn up straight on her chair, with a suffering and sympathetic face, kept turning her head as she watched Anna pacing.

'You must try,' she said softly.

'Suppose I try. What does it mean?' She was obviously saying something she had thought over a thousand times and learned by heart. 'It means that I, who hate him but still acknowledge myself guilty before him – and I consider him magnanimous – that I must humiliate myself by writing to him . . . Well, suppose I make an effort and do it. I'll either get an insulting reply or his consent. Good, so I get his consent . . .' Just then Anna was at the far end of the room, and she stopped there, doing something to the window curtain. 'I get his consent, but my . . . my son? They won't give him to me. He'll grow up despising me, with the father I abandoned. You must understand that I love two beings – equally, I think, but both more than myself – Seryozha and Alexei.'

She came to the middle of the room and stopped in front of Dolly, her arms pressed to her breast. In the white peignoir her figure seemed especially big and wide. She bowed her head and with shining wet eyes looked from under her brows at the small, thin Dolly, trembling all over with agitation, pathetic in her mended chemise and night-cap.

'I love only these two beings, and the one excludes the other. I can't unite them, yet I need only that. And if there isn't that, the rest makes no difference. It all makes no difference. And it will end somehow, and so I can't, I don't like talking about it. Don't reproach me, then, don't judge me for anything. You with your purity can't understand all that I suffer over.'

She went up to Dolly, sat down beside her and, peering into her face with a guilty expression, took her by the hand.

'What are you thinking? What do you think of me? Don't despise me. I'm not worthy of being despised. I'm just unhappy. If anyone is unhappy, I am,' she said and, turning away, she wept.

Left alone, Dolly prayed and went to bed. She had pitied Anna with all her soul while talking with her; but now she was unable to make herself think about her. Memories of her home and children arose in her imagination with some new radiance, some special loveliness she had not known before. That world of hers now seemed so precious and dear to her that she did not want to spend an extra day outside it for anything and decided to leave the next morning without fail.

Anna meanwhile, on returning to her boudoir, took a glass and into it put a few drops of medicine, of which morphine made up a significant part, and after drinking it and sitting motionless for a time, grown quiet, she went to the bedroom in calm and cheerful spirits.

When she came into the bedroom, Vronsky looked at her attentively. He sought traces of the conversation which he knew she must have had with Dolly, since she had stayed so long in her room. But in her expression, excitedly restrained and concealing something, he found only that beauty which, familiar as it was, still captivated him, and her awareness of that beauty and her desire that it affect him. He did not want to ask her what they had talked about, but hoped she would say something herself. But all she said was:

'I'm glad you like Dolly. You do, don't you?'

'But I've known her for a long time. She's very kind, I think, *mais excessivement terre-à-terre.** But still, I'm very glad of her visit.'

He took Anna's hand and looked questioningly into her eyes.

She, understanding that look differently, smiled at him.

The next morning, despite her hosts' entreaties, Darya Alexandrovna made ready to leave. Levin's driver, in his none-too-new caftan and something half resembling a post-boy's hat, with his ill-matched horses, gloomily and resolutely drove the carriage with patched splash-boards under the covered, sand-strewn portico.

Taking leave of Princess Varvara and the men was unpleasant for Darya Alexandrovna. After a day together, both she and her hosts clearly

* But excessively down-to-earth.

felt that they were unsuited to each other and that it was better for them not to get together. Only Anna felt sad. She knew that now, with Dolly's departure, there would be no one to stir up in her soul those feelings that had been aroused in her at this meeting. To stir up those feelings was painful for her; but she knew all the same that that was the best part of her soul and that it was quickly being overgrown in the life she led.

Driving out into the fields, Dolly felt pleasantly relieved, and she was about to ask the servants how they had liked it at Vronsky's when the driver, Filipp, suddenly spoke himself:

'Maybe they're rich, but they only gave the horses three measures of oats. They cleaned the bottom before cockcrow. What's three measures? Just a snack. Nowadays innkeepers sell oats for forty-five kopecks. At home we give visitors as much as they can eat.'

'A miserly master,' the clerk agreed.

'Well, and did you like their horses?' asked Dolly.

'Horses is the word. And the food's good. Found it a bit boring otherwise, Darya Alexandrovna, I don't know about you,' he said, turning his handsome and kindly face to her.

'I thought so, too. Well, will we get there by evening?'

'Ought to.'

On returning home and finding everyone quite well and especially nice, Darya Alexandrovna told them about her trip with great animation, about how well she had been received, the luxury and good taste of the Vronskys' life, their amusements, and would not let anyone say a word against them.

'You have to know Anna and Vronsky – I've come to know him better now – to understand how sweet and touching they are,' she said, now with perfect sincerity, forgetting the vague sense of dissatisfaction and discomfort that she had experienced there.

XXV

Vronsky and Anna spent the whole summer and part of the autumn in the country, in the same conditions, without taking any measures towards a divorce. It was decided between them that they would not go anywhere; but they both sensed, the longer they lived alone, especially in the autumn and without guests, that they would not be able to endure that life and would have to change it.

Life, it seemed, was such that it was impossible to wish for better: there was abundance, there was health, there was the child, and they both had their occupations. Anna paid attention to herself in the same way without guests, and was also very much taken up with reading – of novels and the serious books that were in vogue. She ordered all the books that were mentioned with praise in the foreign newspapers and magazines she received, and read them with that concentration that one only finds in solitude. Moreover, by means of books and special journals, she studied all the subjects that interested Vronsky, so that he often turned directly to her with questions of agronomy, architecture and, occasionally, even horse-breeding and sports. He was amazed at her knowledge, her memory, and, being doubtful at first, wanted corroboration; and she would find what he had asked about in her books and show it to him.

The setting up of the hospital also occupied her. She not only helped but also arranged and devised many things herself. But her chief concern was still her own self – herself, in so far as she was dear to Vronsky, in so far as she was able to replace for him all that he had abandoned. Vronsky appreciated this desire, which had become the only goal of her life, not only to be liked by him but to serve him, yet at the same time he found those amorous nets in which she tried to ensnare him a burden. The more time that passed, the more often he saw himself ensnared in those nets, and the more he wanted not so much to get out of them as to test whether they hampered his freedom. Had it not been for this ever strengthening desire to be free, not to have a scene every time he had to go to town for a meeting or a race, Vronsky would have been quite content with his life. The role he had chosen, the role of the rich landowner, of whom the nucleus of the Russian aristocracy ought to consist, not only proved entirely to his taste, but now, after living that way for half a year, gave him an ever increasing pleasure. And his affairs, which occupied and engaged him more and more, went splendidly. Despite the enormous amount of money that the hospital, the machines, the cows ordered from Switzerland and many other things had cost him, he was certain that he was not wasting but increasing his fortune. Wherever it was a matter of income, of selling timber, grain, wool, of leasing land, Vronsky was hard as flint and knew how to stick to his price. In matters of large-scale farming, on this and other estates, he kept to the simplest, least risky ways, and was shrewd and frugal to the highest degree in small household matters. Despite all the cleverness and cunning of the German, who tried to get him involved in buying and presented every estimate in such a way that it was necessary to begin by investing more, but then calculated that he could do the same thing for less and have an immediate profit, Vronsky never yielded to him. He listened to the steward, asked questions, and agreed with him only when the things he ordered and set up were of the newest sort, still unknown in Russia and capable of causing amazement. Besides that, he would decide upon a major expenditure only when he had some extra money and, in making this expenditure, went into all the details and insisted on getting the best for his money. So that, by the way he conducted his affairs, it was clear that he had not wasted but increased his fortune.

In the month of October, there were elections among the nobility of Kashin province, where the estates of Vronsky, Sviyazhsky, Koznyshev, Oblonsky, and a small part of Levin's estate, were located.

These elections, owing to many circumstances, including the people taking part in them, attracted public attention. They were much talked about and prepared for. People from Moscow, Petersburg and abroad, who never attended elections, came for them.

Vronsky had long ago promised Sviyazhsky that he would attend.

Before the elections Sviyazhsky, who often visited Vozdvizhenskoe, drove over for Vronsky.

On the eve of that day Vronsky and Anna had almost quarrelled over this proposed trip. It was the most boring, difficult autumn time in the country, and therefore Vronsky, preparing for a fight, announced his departure with a stern and cold expression on his face which he had never had before when talking to her. But, to his surprise, Anna took the news very calmly and only asked when he would come back. He looked at her attentively, not understanding this calm. She smiled at his look. He knew this ability she had of withdrawing into herself, and he knew that it happened only when she had decided on something in herself without telling him her plans. He feared it, but he wished so much to avoid a scene that he pretended to believe, and in part sincerely believed, in what he would have liked to believe in – her reasonableness.

'You won't be bored, I hope?'

'I hope,' said Anna. 'Yesterday I received a box of books from Gautier.[7] No, I won't be bored.'

'She wants to take this tone, and so much the better,' he thought, 'otherwise it would be the same thing all over again.'

And so, without challenging her to a frank explanation, he went off to the elections. It was the first time since the start of their liaison that he had parted from her without talking it all through. On the one hand, this troubled him; on the other, he found it better this way. 'At first it will be like now, something vague, hidden, but then she'll get used to it. In any case, I can give her everything, but not my male independence,' he thought.

XXVI

In September Levin moved to Moscow for Kitty's confinement. He had already spent a whole month in Moscow doing nothing, when Sergei Ivanovich, who owned an estate in Kashin province and took great interest in the question of the forthcoming elections, got ready to attend them. He invited his brother, who had a ballot for the Seleznev district, to go with him. Besides that, Levin had business in Kashin, of the utmost importance for his sister, who lived abroad, to do with settling the matter with the trusteeship and obtaining a quittance.

Levin was still undecided, but Kitty, who saw that he was bored in Moscow, advised him to go and, without asking, ordered him a nobleman's uniform that cost eighty roubles. And the eighty roubles spent on the uniform were the main thing that made Levin go. He went to Kashin.

Levin had been in Kashin for six days already, attending the meetings every day and busying himself with his sister's affairs, which did not go well. The marshals were all occupied with the elections and it was impossible to settle the very simple matter which depended on the trusteeship. The other business – obtaining the money – met with obstacles in the same way. After long efforts to have the freeze lifted, the money was ready to be paid; but the notary, a most obliging man, could not issue the cheque because the chairman's signature was needed, and the chairman, without handing over his duties, was attending the session. All this bustling, going about from place to place, talking with very kind, good people, who well understood the unpleasantness of the petitioner's position but were unable to help him – all this tension, while producing no results, gave Levin a painful feeling similar to that vexing impotence one experiences in dreams when one tries to use physical force. He felt it often, speaking with his good-natured attorney. This attorney did everything possible, it seemed, and strained all his mental powers to get Levin out of the quandary. 'Try this,' he said more than once, 'go to this place and that place,' and the attorney would make a whole plan for getting round the fatal principle that was hindering everything. Then he would add at once, 'They'll hold it up anyway, but try it.' And Levin tried, visited, went. Everybody was kind and courteous, but it always turned out that what had been got round re-emerged in the end and again barred the way. In particular it was offensive that Levin simply could not understand with whom he was struggling, who profited from the fact that his case never came to an end. This no one seemed to know; the attorney did not know either. If Levin could have understood it, as he understood why he could not get to the ticket window at the station otherwise than by waiting in line, he would not have felt offended and vexed; but no one could explain to him why the obstacles he encountered in his case existed.

However, Levin had changed greatly since his marriage; he was patient, and if he did not understand why it was all arranged that way, he said to himself that he could not judge without knowing everything, that it probably had to be that way, and he tried not to be indignant.

Now, being present at the elections and taking part in them, he tried in the same way not to condemn, not to argue, but to understand as well as he could this business, which honest and good people, whom he respected, took up with such seriousness and enthusiasm. Since marrying, so many new, serious aspects had been revealed to him, which formerly, because of his light-minded attitude towards them, had seemed insignificant, that he assumed and sought a serious meaning in the business of the elections as well.

Sergei Ivanovich explained to him the meaning and importance of the revolution that was supposed to take place at the elections. The provincial marshal of nobility, in whose hands the law placed so many important social matters – trusteeships (the same from which Levin was now suffering), the huge funds of the nobility, high schools for girls and boys, the military school, public education as prescribed by the new legislation and, finally, the zemstvo – the provincial marshal, Snetkov, was a man of the old noble cast, who had run through a huge fortune, a good man, honest in his way, but who failed completely to understand the demands of the new time. He always took the side of the nobility in everything, directly opposed the spread of public education, and to the zemstvo, which was supposed to have such enormous significance, attributed a class character. It was necessary that he be replaced by a fresh, modern, practical man, completely new, and that things be conducted in such a way as to gain from the rights granted to the nobility, not as nobility but as an element of the zemstvo, every possible benefit of self-government. In the rich Kashin province, which always led the others in everything, such forces had now accumulated that, if matters were conducted properly, it could serve as an example for other provinces, for the whole of Russia. And therefore the whole matter was of great significance. The plan was that Snetkov be replaced as marshal of nobility either by Sviyazhsky or, better still, by Nevedovsky, a former professor, a remarkably intelligent man and a great friend of Sergei Ivanovich's.

The assembly was opened by the governor, who delivered a speech to the noblemen, saying that they should elect people to posts not out of partiality, but by merit and for the good of the fatherland, and that he hoped the honourable nobility of Kashin would fulfil their duty religiously, as they had done in previous elections, thus justifying the high trust of the monarch.

Having finished his speech, the governor left the room, and the noblemen noisily and animatedly, some even rapturously, followed him and surrounded him just as he was putting on his coat and talking amicably with the provincial marshal. Levin, wishing to understand everything and not miss anything, stood there in the crowd and heard the governor say: 'Please tell Marya Ivanovna that my wife is very sorry but she must go to the orphanage.' And after that the gentlemen cheerfully took their coats and went to the cathedral.

In the cathedral Levin, lifting his hand and repeating the words of the archpriest along with the others, swore with the most terrible oaths to fulfil all the governor's hopes. Church services always had an effect on him, and when he uttered the words, 'I kiss the cross,'[8] and turned to look at the crowd of young and old people repeating the same thing, he felt himself moved.

On the second and third days the discussions concerned the matters of the funds raised by the nobility and of the girls' school, which, as Sergei Ivanovich explained, were of no importance, and Levin, occupied with his business, did not follow them. On the fourth day, the auditing of the provincial accounts lay on the provincial table. And here for the first time a confrontation took place between the new party and the old. The commission entrusted with verifying the accounts reported to the assembly that all was in order. The provincial marshal rose to thank the gentlemen for their trust and waxed tearful. The nobility loudly cheered him and shook his hand. But at that moment one of the gentlemen from Sergei Ivanovich's party said he had heard that the commission had not audited the accounts, considering auditing an insult to the provincial marshal. One of the members of the commission imprudently confirmed it. Then one small, very young-looking, but very venomous gentleman started to say that it would probably be a pleasure for the provincial marshal to give a report of the accounts and that the excessive delicacy of the members of the commission deprived him of that moral satisfaction. Then the members of the commission withdrew their statement, and Sergei Ivanovich began to demonstrate logically that the accounts must be acknowledged as either audited or not audited, and developed this dilemma in detail. Some speaker from the opposing party objected to Sergei Ivanovich. Then Sviyazhsky spoke, and then again the venomous gentleman. The debate went on for a long time and ended with nothing. Levin was surprised that they argued about it for so long, especially since, when he asked Sergei Ivanovich if he thought the money had been embezzled, Sergei Ivanovich answered:

'Oh, no! He's an honest man. But this old-fashioned, patriarchal, family-like way of running the affairs of the nobility has to be shaken up.'

On the fifth day came the election of district marshals. In some districts this was a very stormy day. For the Seleznev district Sviyazhsky was elected unanimously without a vote, and there was a dinner that day at his house.

XXVII

On the sixth day the provincial elections were to be held. The rooms, big and small, were filled with noblemen in various uniforms. Many had come for that day only. Acquaintances who had not seen each other for a long time, some from the Crimea, some from Petersburg, some from abroad, met in those rooms. By the governor's table, beneath the portrait of the emperor, a debate was under way.

The noblemen in both big and small rooms grouped themselves by camps, and from the hostility and mistrustfulness of the glances, from the hushing of talk whenever an outsider approached, from the fact that people went off to a far corridor to whisper, one could see that each side had secrets from the other. In outward appearance, the noblemen were sharply divided into two sorts: the old and the new. The old were for the most part either in the old-style buttoned-up uniforms of the nobility, with swords and hats, or in their particular navy, cavalry, or infantry uniforms. The uniforms of the old noblemen were of an outmoded cut, with the sleeves puffed up at the shoulders; they were obviously too small, short at the waist and tight, as if their wearers had outgrown them. The young were in unbuttoned noblemen's uniforms, low-waisted and wide at the shoulders, with white waistcoats, or in uniforms with the black collars and embroidered laurels of the Ministry of Justice. To the young also belonged the court uniforms that adorned the crowd here and there.

But the division into young and old did not coincide with the division into parties. Some of the young, by Levin's observation, belonged to the old party and, on the contrary, some of the oldest noblemen whispered with Sviyazhsky and were apparently ardent supporters of the new party.

Levin stood in the small room for smoking and refreshments, by a group of his own people, listening to what they were saying and uselessly straining his mental powers to understand it. Sergei Ivanovich was the centre around which the others grouped themselves. He was now listening to Sviyazhsky and Khliustov, the marshal of another district, who belonged to their party. Khliustov would not agree to go with his district and ask Snetkov to stand, but Sviyazhsky was trying to persuade him to do it, and Sergei Ivanovich approved of the plan. Levin did not understand why the opposition party should ask the marshal to stand when they intended to vote him down.

Stepan Arkadyich, having just had a snack and a drink, wiping his mouth with a perfumed cambric handkerchief with a border, came over to them in his uniform of a gentleman of the bedchamber.

'Positioning yourself, Sergei Ivanych!' he said, smoothing down his side-whiskers.

And, after listening to the conversation, he confirmed Sviyazhsky's opinion.

'One district will be enough, and Sviyazhsky's obviously already in the opposition,' he said in words that everyone except Levin could understand.

'So, Kostya, it seems you've acquired a taste for it, too?' he added, turning to Levin and taking him under the arm. Levin would even have been glad to acquire a taste for it, but he could not understand what the point was and, moving a few steps away from the talkers, he voiced his perplexity to Stepan Arkadyich as to why the provincial marshal should be nominated.

'*O sancta simplicitas*,'[9] said Stepan Arkadyich, and he explained the matter briefly and clearly to Levin.

'If all the districts nominated the provincial marshal, as at the previous elections, he would be elected unanimously. That must not happen. Now eight districts have agreed to nominate him. If the other two refuse to nominate him, Snetkov may refuse to stand. And then the old party may choose someone else from among themselves, and all our calculations will go for naught. But if Sviyazhsky's district alone does not nominate him, Snetkov will stand. He will even be chosen, and they will purposely give him more votes to mislead the opposition, and when our candidate is put forward, they will give him more votes.'

Levin understood, but not completely, and was about to ask a few more questions, when everyone suddenly started talking and moving noisily into the big room.

'What is it? What? Whom? A warrant? For whom? What? They refute it? There's no warrant. Flerov's not admitted. What if he is on trial? That way no one will be admitted. It's mean. The law!' came from all sides, and along with the rest, who hurried from everywhere and were afraid of missing something, Levin went to the big room and, jostled by the noblemen, approached the governor's table, around which a heated discussion was going on between the provincial marshal, Sviyazhsky and other leaders.

XXVIII

Levin was standing quite far away. Beside him stood one nobleman who was wheezing and breathing heavily and another whose thick soles creaked, preventing him from hearing well. He could only hear the marshal's soft voice from afar, then the shrill voice of the venomous nobleman, and then Sviyazhsky's voice. They were arguing, as far as he could gather, about the meaning of an article of the law and especially of the words: 'being under investigation'.

The crowd parted to make way as Sergei Ivanovich approached the table. Sergei Ivanovich, after waiting for the venomous nobleman to finish his speech, said it seemed to him that the right thing to do would be to consult the article of the law, and he asked the secretary to find it. In the article it said that in case of disagreement there should be a vote.

Sergei Ivanovich read the article and began to explain its meaning, but here a tall, fat, slightly stooping landowner with a dyed moustache, in a tight uniform with a collar that propped his neck up from behind, interrupted him. He came up to the table and, rapping on it with his signet ring, shouted loudly: 'To the vote! Cast your ballots! No point talking! Cast your ballots!'

Here several voices started talking, and the tall nobleman with the signet ring, growing more and more angry, shouted louder and louder. But it was impossible to make out what he was saying.

He was saying the same thing that Sergei Ivanovich had suggested; but he obviously hated him and his whole party, and that feeling of hatred communicated itself to the whole party and provoked a response of the same anger, though more decent, from the other side. Shouts arose, and for a moment everything was so confused that the provincial marshal had to call for order.

'To the vote! To the vote! Every nobleman will understand. We shed our blood . . . The monarch's trust . . . Don't count the marshal, he's no one to give orders . . . That's not the point . . . The vote, if you please! Disgusting! . . .' Angry, furious cries came from all sides. The looks and faces were still more angry and furious than the talk. They expressed irreconcilable hatred. Levin had no idea what it was all about and was astonished at the passion with which they discussed the question of whether the opinion about Flerov should or should not be put to the vote. As Sergei Ivanovich later explained to him, he had forgotten the syllogism that for the common good it was necessary to bring down the provincial marshal; to bring down the provincial marshal, a majority of the votes was necessary; for a majority of the votes, Flerov had to be given the right to a voice; to have Flerov's eligibility recognized, they had to explain how to understand the article of the law.

'One vote could decide the whole thing, and you must be serious and consistent if you want to serve the common cause,' Sergei Ivanovich concluded.

But Levin had forgotten that, and it was painful for him to see these good people, whom he respected, in such unpleasant, angry agitation. To rid himself of that painful feeling, he went to the other room without waiting for the end of the debate. No one was there except the servants at the buffet. Seeing the servants busily wiping platters and setting out plates and glasses, seeing their calm, animated faces, Levin experienced a sudden feeling of relief, as if he had gone from a stinking room into the fresh air. He began pacing up and down, looking with pleasure at the servants. He liked it very much when one servant with grey side-whiskers, showing his contempt for the younger ones who kept teasing him, taught them how to fold napkins. Levin was about to get into conversation with the old servant when the secretary of the noblemen's trust, a little old man whose specialty was knowing all the noblemen of the province by name and patronymic, distracted him.

'If you please, Konstantin Dmitrich,' he said to him, 'your brother is looking for you. The question is being put to the vote.'

Levin went into the room, was given a little white ball and, following his brother Sergei Ivanovich, approached the table at which Sviyazhsky stood with a significant and ironic face, gathering his beard in his fist and sniffing it. Sergei Ivanovich thrust his hand into the box, put his ballot somewhere and, yielding his place to Levin, stayed right there. Levin came up, but forgetting what it was all about and becoming embarrassed, he turned to Sergei Ivanovich and asked: 'Where shall I put it?' He asked it softly, while there was talk around him, and hoped his question would not be heard. But the talkers fell silent, and his improper question was heard. Sergei Ivanovich frowned.

'That is a matter of individual conviction,' he said sternly.

A few smiled. Levin blushed, hastily put his hand under the cloth and placed the ballot to the right, since it was in his right hand. Then he remembered that he should also have put his left hand in, and put it in as well, but too late, and, still more embarrassed, hurriedly retreated to the farthest rows.

'One hundred and twenty-six in favour! Ninety-eight against!' the voice of the secretary, who swallowed his *r*s, rang out. Laughter followed: a button and two nuts had been found in the box. The nobleman was admitted, and the new party was victorious.

But the old party did not consider itself defeated. Levin heard that

Snetkov was being asked to stand, and saw a crowd of noblemen surround the provincial marshal, who was saying something. Levin went closer. In answer to the noblemen, Snetkov spoke of the confidence of the nobility, of their love for him, which he did not deserve, for his whole merit consisted in his being loyal to the nobility, to whom he had devoted twelve years of service. Several times he repeated the words: 'I have served with all my strength, truly and loyally, I appreciate and thank you,' and suddenly he stopped, choked by tears, and walked out of the room. Whether those tears were caused by awareness of the injustice done him, or by his love for the nobility, or by the strained position he was in, feeling himself surrounded by enemies, his emotion communicated itself, the majority of the noblemen were moved and Levin felt a tenderness for Snetkov.

In the doorway the provincial marshal ran into him.

'I'm sorry, please excuse me,' he said to him, as to a stranger; but recognizing Levin, he smiled timidly. It seemed to Levin that he wanted to say something, but could not because of the emotion. The expression of his face and of his whole figure in the uniform, the crosses and white trousers with galloons, the hurried way he walked, reminded Levin of a hunted beast who sees that things are going badly for him. Levin found the expression on the marshal's face especially touching because only yesterday he had called on him at his home on the matter of the trusteeship and had seen him in all the grandeur of a good family man. The big house with its old family furniture; the unfashionable and slightly shabby but deferential old servants, apparently former house serfs who had never changed masters; the fat and good-natured wife in a lace cap and Turkish shawl, caressing a pretty little grandchild, her daughter's daughter; the fine fellow of a son, a sixth-grade student on holiday from school, who kissed his father's big hand in greeting; the host's imposing, benign conversation and gestures – all this had involuntarily called up respect and sympathy in Levin the day before. Now he found the old man touching and pitiful, and he wanted to say something nice to him.

'So you're to be our marshal again,' he said.

'Hardly,' said the marshal, looking round fearfully. 'I'm tired and old. There are others worthier and younger than I. Let them serve.'

And the marshal disappeared through the side door.

The most solemn moment arrived. The elections were about to begin. The leaders of both parties were tallying white and black ballots on their fingers.

The debate over Flerov had given the new party not only Flerov's one vote but also a gain in time, so that three noblemen who had been kept from participating in the elections by the machinations of the old party could be brought in. Two of these noblemen, who had a weakness for wine, had been made drunk by Snetkov's minions, and the third had had his uniform stolen.

Learning of it, the new party managed, during the debate over Flerov, to send two of their people in a cab to furnish the one nobleman with a uniform and bring one of the two drunk men to the meeting.

'I poured water over one and brought him,' said the landowner who had gone on the errand, coming up to Sviyazhsky. 'Never mind, he'll do.'

'He's not too drunk? He won't fall down?' Sviyazhsky said, shaking his head.

'No, he's fine. As long as they don't give him any more to drink here . . . I told the barman on no account to serve him.'

XXIX

The narrow room for smoking and refreshments was filled with noblemen. The excitement kept mounting, and anxiety could be noticed on all faces. Especially excited were the leaders, who knew all the details and the count of all the ballots. They were the directors of the impending battle. The rest, like rank-and-file soldiers, though readying themselves before the fight, meanwhile sought distraction. Some ate and drank, standing up or sitting at the table; others paced up and down the long room, smoking cigarettes and talking with friends they had not seen for a long time.

Levin did not want to eat and did not smoke; he also did not want to mix with his own people, that is, with Sergei Ivanovich, Stepan Arkadyich, Sviyazhsky and the others, because Vronsky was standing with them in his equerry's uniform, engaged in an animated conversation. Levin had noticed him at the elections the day before and had carefully avoided him, not wishing to meet him. He went over to the window and sat down, looking at the groups and listening to what was being said around him. He felt sad, especially because he could see that everyone was animated, preoccupied and busy, and he alone, along with one extremely old, toothless man in a navy uniform, who sat next to him chewing his gums, had no interest and nothing to do.

'He's such a rogue! I told him, but no. Really! In three years he couldn't collect it,' a short, stooping landowner, with pomaded hair that hung over the embroidered collar of his uniform, was saying energetically, stomping solidly with the heels of his new boots, evidently donned for the elections. And, casting a displeased glance at Levin, he abruptly turned away.

'Yes, it's dirty work, say what you will,' the little landowner said in a high voice.

After them a whole crowd of landowners, surrounding a fat general, hurriedly came towards Levin. The landowners were obviously looking for a place to talk without being overheard.

'How dare he say I ordered his trousers stolen! He drank them up, I suppose. I spit on him and his princely rank. He daren't say that, it's swinishness!'

'I beg your pardon! They're basing it on the article,' voices came from another group, 'the wife must be on record as a noblewoman.'

'The devil I care about the article! I'm speaking from the soul. That's what makes us nobility. There has to be trust.'

'Come, your excellency, there's *fine champagne*.'*

Another crowd followed after a nobleman who was loudly shouting something: he was one of the three who had been made drunk.

'I always advised Marya Semyonovna to lease it, because she can't make any profit,' a grey-moustached landowner in the uniform of a colonel of the old general headquarters said in a pleasant voice. This was the landowner Levin had met at Sviyazhsky's. He recognized him at once. The landowner also looked closer at Levin, and they greeted each other.

'Delighted! Of course! I remember very well. Last year at Marshal Nikolai Ivanovich's.'

'Well, how goes the farming?' asked Levin.

'The same – still at a loss,' the landowner, stopping near Levin, answered with a resigned smile, but with an expression of calm conviction that it had to be so. 'And how have you wound up in our province?' he asked. 'Come to take part in our *coup d'état*?' he said, pronouncing the French words firmly but poorly. 'All Russia's assembled here:

* Superior cognac.

gentlemen of the bedchamber and all but ministers.' He pointed to the impressive figure of Stepan Arkadyich, in white trousers and the uniform of a gentleman of the bedchamber, walking about with a general.

'I must confess that I have a very poor understanding of the significance of these elections among the nobility,' said Levin.

The landowner looked at him.

'What's there to understand? There is no significance. An obsolete institution that goes on moving only by the force of inertia. Look at the uniforms – even they tell you: this is an assembly of justices of the peace, of permanent members and so on, and not of the nobility.'

'Then why do you come?' asked Levin.

'Out of habit, that's all. And one must also keep up one's connections. A moral responsibility in a sense. And then, to tell the truth, there is a certain interest. My son-in-law wants to stand as a permanent member; they're not well-to-do people and I must help him win. But why do these people come?' he said, pointing to the venomous gentleman who had spoken at the governor's table.

'That's the new generation of nobility.'

'New it is. But not nobility. They are landlords, and we are landowners. As nobility, they're committing suicide.'

'But you yourself say that it's an outdated institution.'

'Outdated it is, but still it ought to be treated more respectfully. Take Snetkov . . . Good or not, we've been a thousand years growing. You know, when you want to make a garden in front of your house, you have to lay it out, and there's a hundred-year-old tree growing in that spot . . . Though it's old and gnarled, you still won't cut the old-timer down for the sake of your flower beds, you'll lay them out so as to include the tree. It can't be grown in a year,' he said cautiously, and immediately changed the subject. 'Well, and how's your estate?'

'Not so good. About five per cent.'

'Yes, but you're not counting yourself. You're also worth something. I'll tell you about myself. Before I took up farming, I had a salary of three thousand roubles in the service. Now I work more than in the service, and like you I get five per cent, and thank God for that. And my work is done free.'

'Then why do it, if it's an outright loss?'

'You just do! What can I say? A habit, and also knowing that you have to do it. I'll tell you more,' the landowner went on, leaning his elbow on the windowsill and warming to the subject. 'My son has no interest in farming. It's obvious he'll be a scholar. So there won't be anybody to carry on. And still you do it. I've just planted a garden.'

'Yes, yes,' said Levin, 'it's perfectly true. I always feel that there's no real economy in my farming, and yet I do it . . . You feel a sort of responsibility towards the land.'

'Here's what I'll tell you,' the landowner went on. 'I had a merchant for a neighbour. We took a walk round my farm, my garden. "No," he says, "Stepan Vassilyich, you've got everything going in good order, but your little garden's neglected." Though my garden's in quite good order. "If it was me, I'd cut those lindens down. Only the sap must have risen. You've got a thousand lindens here, and each one would yield two good pieces of bast.[10] Bast fetches a nice price these days, and you can cut a good bit of lumber out of the lindens."'

'And he'd use the money to buy cattle or land for next to nothing and lease it out to muzhiks,' Levin finished with a smile, obviously having met with such calculations more than once. 'And he'll make a fortune. While you and I – God help us just to hang on to what's ours and leave it to our children.'

'You're married, I hear?' said the landowner.

'Yes,' Levin replied with proud satisfaction. 'Yes, it's a strange thing,' he went on. 'The way we live like this without reckoning, as if we've been appointed, like ancient vestals,[11] to tend some sort of fire.'

The landowner smiled under his white moustache.

'There are also some among us – our friend Nikolai Ivanych, for instance, or Count Vronsky, who's settled here now – they want to introduce industry into agronomy; but that hasn't led to anything yet except the destroying of capital.'

'But why don't we do as the merchants do? Cut down the lindens for bast?' said Levin, going back to a thought that had struck him.

'It's tending the fire, as you say. No, that's no business for noblemen. And our noblemen's business isn't done here at the elections, but there in our own corner. There's also the instinct of your class, what's done and what isn't done. And the muzhiks are the same, to look at them sometimes: a good muzhik just takes and rents as much land as he can. No matter how poor it is, he ploughs away. Also without reckoning. For an outright loss.'

'Just like us,' said Levin. 'It's been very, very nice to meet you again,' he added, seeing Sviyazhsky approaching them.

'And here we've just met for the first time since we were at your place,' said the landowner, 'so we fell to talking.'

'Well, have you denounced the new ways?' Sviyazhsky said with a smile.

'That, too.'

'Unburdened our souls.'

XXX

Sviyazhsky took Levin under the arm and went with him to their people.

Now it was impossible to avoid Vronsky. He stood with Stepan Arkadyich and Sergei Ivanovich and looked straight at the approaching Levin.

'Delighted! I believe I had the pleasure of meeting you . . . at Princess Shcherbatsky's,' he said, holding out his hand to Levin.

'Yes, I remember our meeting very well,' said Levin and, flushing crimson, he turned away at once and began talking with his brother.

Vronsky smiled slightly and went on talking with Sviyazhsky, evidently having no wish to get into conversation with Levin; but Levin, while talking with his brother, kept looking back at Vronsky, trying to think up something to say to him to smooth over his rudeness.

'What comes next?' asked Levin, looking at Sviyazhsky and Vronsky.

'Next is Snetkov. He must either refuse or accept,' replied Sviyazhsky.

'And what about him, has he accepted or not?'

'The thing is that he's done neither,' said Vronsky.

'And if he refuses, who's going to stand?' asked Levin, who kept looking at Vronsky.

'Whoever wants to,' said Sviyazhsky.

'Will you?' asked Levin.

'Certainly not,' said Sviyazhsky, embarrassed and casting a fearful glance at the venomous gentleman who was standing by Sergei Ivanovich.

'Who, then? Nevedovsky?' said Levin, feeling himself at a loss.

But that was worse still. Nevedovsky and Sviyazhsky were the two candidates.

'Not I, in any case,' the venomous gentleman replied.

This was Nevedovsky himself. Sviyazhsky introduced him to Levin.

'What, has it got under your skin, too?' said Stepan Arkadyich, winking at Vronsky. 'It's like a race. We could bet on it.'

'Yes, it does get under your skin,' said Vronsky. 'And once you take something up, you want to go through with it. It's a battle!' he said, frowning and clenching his strong jaws.

'What a mover Sviyazhsky is! Everything's so clear to him.'

'Ah, yes,' Vronsky said distractedly.

Silence followed, during which Vronsky – since one had to look at something – looked at Levin, at his feet, at his uniform, then at his face, and noticing the sullen look directed at him, said, in order to say something:

'And how is it that you are a permanent country-dweller and not a justice of the peace? You're not wearing the uniform of a justice of the peace.'

'Because I think the local court is an idiotic institution,' Levin replied sullenly, though he had been waiting all along for a chance to strike up a conversation with Vronsky in order to smooth over his initial rudeness.

'I don't think so, on the contrary,' Vronsky said with calm astonishment.

'It's a game,' Levin interrupted him. 'We don't need justices of the peace. I haven't had a single case in eight years. And when I did have one, it was decided inside-out. The justice of the peace lives twenty-five miles from me. I have to send an attorney who costs fifteen roubles on business that's worth two.'

And he told them how a muzhik stole flour from a miller, and when the miller told him about it, the muzhik sued him for slander. This was all inappropriate and stupid, and Levin felt it himself as he spoke.

'Oh, what an original!' said Stepan Arkadyich with his most almond-buttery smile. 'But come, I think they're voting . . .'

And they dispersed.

'I don't understand,' said Sergei Ivanovich, who had observed his brother's awkward escapade, 'I don't understand how it's possible to be deprived of political tact to such a degree. That's what we Russians lack. The provincial marshal is our opponent and you are *ami cochon** with him and ask him to stand. And Count Vronsky . . . I'm not going to be friends with him – he's invited me to dinner; I won't go – but he's one

* Fast friends.

of us. Why make an enemy of him? And then you ask Nevedovsky if he's going to stand. It isn't done.'

'Ah, I don't understand any of it! And it's all trifles,' Levin replied sullenly.

'You say it's all trifles and then you muddle everything up.'

Levin fell silent and together they went into the big room.

The provincial marshal, though he felt that a dirty trick was in the air, prepared for him, and though not everyone had asked him, still decided to stand. The whole room fell silent; the secretary announced stentoriously that Captain of the Guards Mikhail Stepanovich Snetkov was standing for provincial marshal.

The district marshals began circulating with little plates of ballots, from their own tables to the governor's, and the elections began.

'Put it on the right,' Stepan Arkadyich whispered to Levin, as he and his brother followed the marshal to the table. But just then Levin forgot the calculation that had been explained to him and feared that Stepan Arkadyich was mistaken when he said 'to the right'. For Snetkov was the enemy. As he approached the box, he held the ballot in his right hand, but, thinking he was mistaken, he shifted it to his left hand and then, obviously, put it on the left. An expert who was standing near the box and could tell just from the movement of the elbow where the ballot had been put, winced with displeasure. There was nothing for him to exercise his perspicacity on.

Everyone kept silent and the counting of the ballots could be heard. Then a single voice announced the numbers for and against.

The marshal was elected by a large majority. A hubbub arose and everybody rushed headlong for the door. Snetkov came in and the nobility surrounded him, offering congratulations.

'Well, is it over now?' Levin asked Sergei Ivanovich.

'It's just beginning,' Sviyazhsky, smiling, answered for Sergei Ivanovich. 'The new candidate for marshal may get more votes.'

Again Levin had quite forgotten about that. Only now did he remember that there was some subtlety here, but he found it boring to recall what it was. He was overcome with dejection and wanted to get out of the crowd that instant.

Since no one paid any attention to him and he seemed not to be needed by anyone, he quietly went to the smaller room where refreshments were served and felt greatly relieved to see the servants again. The little old servant offered him something, and Levin accepted. After eating a cutlet with beans and discussing the servant's former masters with him, Levin, unwilling to enter the big room where he felt so uncomfortable, went for a stroll in the gallery.

The gallery was filled with smartly-dressed women who leaned over the balustrade trying not to miss a word of what was being said below. Beside the ladies sat or stood elegant lawyers, bespectacled high-school teachers and officers. The talk everywhere was about the elections, and how tormenting it was for the marshal, and how good the debate had been. In one group Levin heard his brother praised. A lady said to a lawyer:

'I'm so glad I heard Koznyshev! It was worth going without dinner. Charming! So lucid. And one can hear everything! In your courts no one ever speaks like that. Only Meidel, and even he is far less eloquent.'

Finding free space by the balustrade, Levin leaned over and began to look and listen.

All the noblemen sat behind their partitions, by districts. In the middle of the room a man in a uniform stood and announced in a loud, high voice:

'Now standing for provincial marshal of the nobility is Cavalry Staff-Captain Evgeny Ivanovich Opukhtin!'

A dead silence ensued, and one weak old man's voice was heard:

'Decline!'

'Now standing is Court Councillor Pyotr Petrovich Bohl,' the voice began again.

'Decline!' a shrill young voice rang out.

The same thing again, and again a 'decline'. It went on that way for about an hour. Levin, leaning on the balustrade, looked and listened. At first he was surprised and wanted to understand what it meant; then, realizing that he was unable to understand it, he became bored. Then, remembering the agitation and anger he had seen on all faces, he felt sad. He decided to leave and went downstairs. Passing through the corridor behind the gallery, he met a dejected high-school student with puffy eyes pacing up and down. And on the stairs he met a couple: a lady running quickly on her high-heeled shoes and a light-footed assistant prosecutor.

'I told you you wouldn't be late,' the prosecutor said just as Levin stepped aside to let the lady pass.

Levin was already on the main stairway and taking the tag for his coat from his waistcoat pocket, when the secretary caught up with him. 'Please come, Konstantin Dmitrich, we're voting.'

The so resolutely declining Nevedovsky was now standing as a candidate.

Levin came to the door of the big room: it was locked. The secretary knocked, the door opened, and two red-faced landowners whisked out past Levin.

'I can't stand any more,' said one red-faced landowner.

After him, the face of the provincial marshal stuck itself out. Exhaustion and fear gave this face a dreadful look.

'I told you not to let them out!' he shouted to the doorkeeper.

'I was letting them in, your excellency!'

'Lord!' And with a heavy sigh, the provincial marshal, shuffling wearily in his white trousers, his head bowed, walked across the room to the governor's table.

Nevedovsky got the majority of votes, as had been calculated, and became the provincial marshal. Many were amused, many were pleased, happy, many were delighted, many were displeased and unhappy. The provincial marshal was in despair, which he was unable to conceal. As Nevedovsky left the big room, the crowd surrounded him and followed him out, just as it had followed the governor on the first day when he had opened the elections, and just as it had followed Snetkov when he had been elected.

XXXI

The newly elected provincial marshal and many from the victorious party of the new dined that day at Vronsky's.

Vronsky had come to the elections because he was bored in the country and had to assert his right to freedom before Anna, and in order to repay Sviyazhsky with support at the elections for all the trouble he had taken for him at the zemstvo elections, and most of all in order to strictly fulfil all the responsibilities of the position of nobleman and landowner that he had chosen for himself. But he had never expected that this business of the elections could get him so involved, could so touch him to the quick, or that he could do it so well. He was a completely new man in the circle of the noblemen, but he was obviously a success, and he was not mistaken in thinking that he had already gained influence among them. Contributing to that influence were: his wealth and high birth;

his splendid lodgings in town, which his old acquaintance, Shirkov, a financial dealer who had established a flourishing bank in Kashin, allowed him to use; an excellent chef, whom Vronsky had brought along from the country; his friendship with the governor, who had been Vronsky's comrade, and a patronized comrade at that; and most of all his simple, equable treatment of everyone, which very soon made most of the noblemen change their opinion about his supposed pride. He himself felt that, apart from the crack-brained gentleman married to Kitty Shcherbatsky, who, *à propos de bottes*,* had told him, with ridiculous anger, heaps of totally inappropriate inanities, every nobleman whose acquaintance he had made had ended by becoming his adherent. He saw clearly, and others admitted it as well, that he had contributed greatly to Nevedovsky's success. And now, at his own table, celebrating Nevedovsky's victory, he experienced a pleasant feeling of triumph for the man of his choice. The elections themselves enticed him so much that, should he be married by the end of the three-year term, he was thinking of standing himself – in the same way as, after winning a prize through a jockey, he would always wish he had raced himself.

But now the jockey's victory was being celebrated. Vronsky sat at the head of the table; to his right sat the young governor, a general at imperial headquarters. For everyone else he was the master of the province, who had solemnly opened the elections, delivered a speech, and inspired both respect and servility in many, as Vronsky could see; but for Vronsky he was Katie Maslov – as he had been nicknamed in the Corps of Pages – who felt abashed before him and whom Vronsky tried to *mettre à son aise*.† To the left of him sat Nevedovsky, with his youthful, unshakable and venomous face. With him Vronsky was simple and respectful.

Sviyazhsky bore his failure cheerfully. It was not even a failure for him, as he said himself, addressing Nevedovsky with a glass: it was impossible to find a better representative of that new direction which the nobility must follow. And therefore all that was honest, as he said, stood on the side of the present success and celebrated it.

Stepan Arkadyich was also glad that he was having a merry time and that everyone was pleased. Over an excellent dinner they recalled

* Apropos of nothing.

† Set at ease.

episodes from the elections. Sviyazhsky comically imitated the marshal's tearful speech and observed, turning to Nevedovsky, that his excellency would have to find a different method, more complicated than tears, for auditing the books. Another jocular nobleman told them that stockinged lackeys had been summoned for the provincial marshal's ball, and that now they would have to be sent back, unless the new provincial marshal gave a ball with stockinged lackeys.

During dinner Nevedovsky was constantly addressed with the words 'our provincial marshal' and 'your excellency'.

This was done with the same pleasure as when a young woman is addressed as 'madame' and with her husband's last name. Nevedovsky pretended that he was not only indifferent to but even scorned the title, yet it was obvious that he was happy and only kept a tight rein on himself so as not to express a delight unsuited to the new liberal milieu in which they all found themselves.

Over dinner several telegrams were sent to people interested in the course of the elections. And Stepan Arkadyich, who was very merry, sent Darya Alexandrovna a telegram with the following content: 'Nevedovsky won by twelve votes. Congratulations. Spread news.' He dictated it aloud, observing: 'They must share the glad tidings.' When she received the telegram, Darya Alexandrovna merely sighed over the waste of a rouble, realizing that it must have been the end of the dinner. She knew that Stiva had a weakness for *faire jouer le télégraphe** at the end of a good dinner.

Everything, including the excellent dinner and the wines (not from Russian wine merchants but bottled abroad), was very noble, simple and merry. The circle of twenty people had been selected by Sviyazhsky from like-minded new liberal activists who were at the same time witty and respectable. Toasts were drunk, also half in jest, to the new provincial marshal, to the governor, to the bank director, and to 'our gentle host'.

Vronsky was pleased. He had never expected such nice tone in the provinces.

At the end of dinner things grew merrier still. The governor asked Vronsky to attend a concert for the benefit of the *brothers*,[12] arranged by his wife, who wished to make his acquaintance.

* Bringing the telegraph into play.

'There will be a ball, and you'll see our beauty. In fact, she's remarkable.'

'Not in my line,' Vronsky answered in English, having a fondness for the expression, but he smiled and promised to come.

Before leaving the table, when everyone had already begun to smoke, Vronsky's butler came to him with a letter on a tray.

'By messenger from Vozdvizhenskoe,' he said with a significant look.

'It's amazing how much he resembles the assistant prosecutor Sventitsky,' one of the guests said in French, referring to the butler, while Vronsky read the letter with a frown.

The letter was from Anna. He knew its contents even before reading it. Supposing the elections would be over in five days, he had promised to be home on Friday. Today was Saturday, and he knew the letter contained reproaches for his not having come on time. The letter he had sent the previous evening probably had not yet reached her.

The contents were just as he had expected, but the form was unexpected and particularly disagreeable to him. 'Annie is very sick, the doctor says it may be an infection. Alone I lose my head. Princess Varvara is not a help but a hindrance. I expected you two days ago, then yesterday, and now I'm sending to find out where and how you are. I wanted to come myself but changed my mind, knowing it would displease you. Give me some answer so that I know what to do.'

Their child was sick, and she wanted to come herself. Their daughter was sick, and there was this hostile tone.

The innocent merriment of the elections and that gloomy, oppressive love he had to go back to struck Vronsky by their contrast. But he had to go, and that night he took the first train home.

XXXII

Before Vronsky left for the elections, Anna, considering that the scenes repeated each time he left might only make him colder and not bind him to her, decided to try as hard as she could to calmly endure her separation from him. But the cold, stern look he gave her when he came to announce that he was leaving offended her, and even before he left her calm was already broken.

Later, when she was alone, she thought about that look, which expressed his right to freedom, and arrived, as always, at one thing – the awareness of her humiliation. 'He has the right to go off wherever and whenever he wants. Not only to go off but to abandon me. He has all the rights and I have none. But, knowing that, he shouldn't have done it. And yet what did he do? . . . He looked at me with a cold, stern expression. Of course, that is indefinable, intangible, but it wasn't so before, and that look means a lot,' she thought. 'That look shows that the cooling off has begun.'

And though she was convinced that the cooling off had begun, still there was nothing she could do, she could not change anything in her relations with him. Just as before, she could only try to keep him by her love and her attractiveness. And as before, by being occupied during the day and taking morphine at night, she could stifle the terrible thoughts of what would happen if he stopped loving her. True, there was one other means, not to keep him – for that she wanted nothing but his love – but to get so close to him, to be in such a position, that he could not abandon her. That means was divorce and marriage. And she began to wish for it, and decided to agree to it the very first time he or Stiva brought it up.

In such thoughts she spent five days without him, those days when he intended to be away.

Walks, conversations with Princess Varvara, visits to the hospital and, above all, reading, reading one book after another, occupied her time. But on the sixth day, when the coachman came back without him, she felt that she no longer had the strength to stifle her thoughts of him and of what he was doing there. Just then her daughter became sick. Anna began to look after her, but that did not distract her either, particularly as the sickness was not dangerous. Much as she tried, she could not love this girl, nor could she pretend to love her. Towards evening of that day, left alone, Anna felt such fear about him that she almost decided to go to town, but, thinking better of it, wrote that contradictory letter which Vronsky received and, without rereading it, sent it with a messenger. The next morning she received his letter and regretted her own. She anticipated with horror the repetition of that stern look he had cast at her as he was leaving, especially when he discovered that the girl was not dangerously sick. But all the same she was glad she had written to him. Anna now admitted to herself that he was burdened by her, that he would regret parting with his freedom and coming back to her, but in spite of that she was glad of his coming. Let him be burdened, but let him be there with her, so that she could see him and know his every move.

She was sitting in the drawing room, under a lamp, with a new book by Taine,[13] reading and listening to the noise of the wind outside, and expecting the carriage to arrive any moment. Several times she thought she heard the sound of wheels, but was mistaken; at last she heard not only the sound of wheels but the driver's shouts and the hollow sound under the portico. Even Princess Varvara, who was playing patience, confirmed it, and Anna, flushing, got up, but instead of going downstairs as she had already done twice, she stopped. She suddenly felt ashamed of her lie, but frightened most of all at how he was going to greet her. The offended feeling was gone now; she only feared he would show his displeasure. She remembered that their daughter had already been well for two days. She was even vexed that she had recovered just as the letter was sent. Then she remembered him, that he was there, all of him, with his hands, his eyes. She heard his voice. And, forgetting everything, she joyfully ran to meet him.

'Well, how's Annie?' he said timidly from below, looking at Anna running down to him.

He was sitting in a chair, and the footman was pulling off one of his warm boots.

'All right, she's better.'

'And you?' he said, giving himself a shake.

She took his hand in both of hers and drew it to her waist, not taking her eyes off him.

'Well, I'm very glad,' he said, coldly looking at her, her hair, the dress he knew she had put on for him.

He liked it all, but he had already liked it so many times! And the stony, stern expression she had been so afraid of settled on his face.

'Well, I'm very glad. And are you well?' he said, wiping his wet beard with a handkerchief and kissing her hand.

'It makes no difference,' she thought, 'as long as he's here, and when he's here he can't, he daren't not love me.'

The evening passed happily and cheerfully in the presence of Princess Varvara, who complained to him that without him Anna took morphine.

'What was I to do? I couldn't sleep . . . My thoughts troubled me. When he's here I never take it. Almost never.'

He told her about the elections, and Anna, with her questions, was able to guide him to the very thing that cheered him – his success. She told him about everything that interested him at home. And all her news was most cheerful.

But late at night, when they were alone, Anna, seeing that she was again in full possession of him, wished to wipe away the painful impression of that look owing to the letter. She said:

'But confess, you were vexed to get the letter and didn't believe me?'

As soon as she said it, she realized that however amorously disposed he was towards her now, he had not forgiven her for it.

'Yes,' he said. 'The letter was so strange. First Annie's sick, and then you want to come yourself.'

'It was all true.'

'I don't doubt that.'

'Yes, you do. You're displeased, I can see.'

'Not for one minute. I'm only displeased, it's true, that you seem not to want to admit there are responsibilities . . .'

'Responsibilities to go to a concert . . .'

'Let's not talk about it,' he said.

'And why not talk about it?' she said.

'I merely wish to say that business may come up, something necessary. Now, you see, I'll have to go to Moscow to do with the house . . . Ah, Anna, why are you so irritable? Don't you know I can't live without you?'

'If so,' said Anna, in a suddenly changed voice, 'then this life is a burden to you . . . Yes, you'll come for a day and then go, as men do . . .'

'Anna, that's cruel. I'm ready to give my whole life . . .'

But she was not listening to him.

'If you go to Moscow, I'll go, too. I won't stay here. Either we separate or we live together.'

'You know that that is my only wish. But for that . . .'

'A divorce is necessary? I'll write to him. I see that I can't live like this . . . But I will go with you to Moscow.'

'It's as if you're threatening me. Yet there's nothing I wish more than not to be separated from you,' Vronsky said, smiling.

But the look that flashed in his eyes as he spoke those tender words was not only the cold, angry look of a persecuted and embittered man.

She saw that look and correctly guessed its meaning.

'If it is like this, it is a disaster!' said the look. It was a momentary impression, but she never forgot it.

Anna wrote a letter to her husband asking him for a divorce, and at the end of November, having parted with Princess Varvara, who had to go to Petersburg, she moved to Moscow with Vronsky. Expecting a reply from Alexei Alexandrovich any day, to be followed by a divorce, they now settled together like a married couple.

Part Seven

I

The Levins were already living for the third month in Moscow. The term was long past when, by the surest calculations of people who knew about such things, Kitty ought to have given birth; and yet she was still expecting, and there was no indication that the time was nearer now than two months ago. The doctor, the midwife, Dolly, her mother, and Levin especially, who could not think of the approaching event without horror, were beginning to feel impatient and anxious; Kitty alone was perfectly calm and happy.

She was now clearly aware of the new feeling of love being born in her for the future child who, for her, was already partly present, and she delighted in attending to this feeling. It was no longer wholly a part of her now, but sometimes lived its own life independent of her. It often caused her pain, but at the same time made her want to laugh with a strange new joy.

Everyone she loved was with her, and everyone was so kind to her, took such care of her, she saw so much of sheer pleasantness in all that was offered to her, that if she had not known and felt that it must soon end, she could not even have wished for a better or more pleasant life. The one thing that spoiled the charm of that life for her was that her husband was not the way she loved him and the way he used to be in the country.

She loved his calm, gentle, and hospitable tone in the country. But in the city he was constantly anxious and wary, as if fearing someone might offend him and, above all, her. There, in the country, obviously knowing he was where he belonged, he did not hurry anywhere and was never unoccupied. Here in the city he was constantly in a hurry, as though he might miss something, and he had nothing to do. And she pitied him.

To others, she knew, he did not look pitiful; on the contrary, when Kitty watched him in company, as one sometimes watches a person one loves, trying to see him as a stranger, to define the impression he makes on others, she saw, even with fear of her own jealousy, that he was not only not pitiful but very attractive in his decency, his rather old-fashioned, bashful politeness with women, his powerful figure, and his – as it seemed to her – particularly expressive face. But she saw him not from the outside but from inside; she saw that here he was not his real self; there was no other way she could define his condition. Sometimes she reproached him in her heart for not knowing how to live in the city; sometimes she also admitted that it was truly difficult for him to arrange his life here in a satisfying way.

Indeed, what was there for him to do? He did not like to play cards. He did not go to the club. To keep company with merry men like Oblonsky – she now knew what that meant . . . it meant drinking and going somewhere afterwards. She could not think without horror of where men went on such occasions. To go out in society? But for that she knew that one had to take pleasure in meeting young women, and she could not wish for that. To sit at home with her and her mother and sister? But however pleasant and enjoyable she found those ever identical conversations – 'Alines and Nadines', as the old prince called these conversations between sisters – she knew they had to be boring for him. What was left for him to do? To go on writing his book? He did try to do that, and in the beginning went to the library to take notes and references; but, as he told her, the longer he did nothing, the less time he had left. And besides, he complained to her that he had talked too much about his book here, and as a result all his thoughts about it had become confused and he had lost interest in them.

One advantage of this city life was that here in the city they never had any quarrels. Either because city conditions were different, or because they had both become more prudent and sensible in that respect, in Moscow they had no quarrels because of jealousy, something they had been very much afraid of when they moved to the city.

There even occurred an event that was very important for them both – namely, Kitty's meeting with Vronsky.

The old princess Marya Borisovna, Kitty's godmother, who had always loved her, wanted to see her without fail. Kitty, who in her condition never went anywhere, did go with her father to see the venerable old woman, and there met Vronsky.

The only thing Kitty could reproach herself with in that meeting was that, when she recognized that once so familiar figure in his civilian clothes, her breath was taken away, the blood rushed to her heart, and bright colour (she could feel it) came to her face. But that lasted only a few seconds. Before her father, who purposely addressed Vronsky in a loud voice, had finished what he was saying, she was fully prepared to look at him, to talk with him, if necessary, just as she talked with Princess Marya Borisovna, and, above all, so that everything to the very last intonation and smile could have been approved of by her husband, whose invisible presence she seemed to feel above her at that moment.

She said a few words to him, even smiled calmly at his joke about the elections, which he called 'our parliaments'. (She had to smile to show that she understood the joke.) But she immediately turned away to Princess Marya Borisovna and never once glanced at him until he got up to leave; then she looked at him, but obviously only because it was impolite not to look at a man when he was bowing to you.

She was grateful to her father for not saying anything about meeting Vronsky; but by his special tenderness after the visit, during their usual walk, she saw that he was pleased with her. She was pleased with herself. She had never expected that she would have the strength to hold down somewhere deep in her heart all memories of her former feeling for Vronsky, and not only to seem but to be quite indifferent and calm towards him.

Levin flushed much more than she did when she told him she had met Vronsky at Princess Marya Borisovna's. It was very hard for her to tell him about it, and still harder for her to go on talking about the details of the meeting, since he did not ask but only looked frowning at her.

'It's too bad you weren't there,' she said. 'That is, not that you weren't in the room . . . I wouldn't have been so natural with you there . . . Now I'm blushing much more, much, much more,' she said, blushing to tears. 'But that you couldn't have looked through a crack.'

Her truthful eyes told Levin that she was pleased with herself, and, despite her blushing, he calmed down at once and began asking questions, which was just what she wanted. When he had learned everything, even to the detail that she could not help flushing in the first second, but after that had felt as simple and easy as with anybody at all, Levin cheered up completely and said he was very glad of it and that now he would not behave as stupidly as he had at the elections, but would try at the very first meeting with Vronsky to be as friendly as possible.

'It's so tormenting to think that there's a man who is almost an enemy, whom it's painful to meet,' said Levin. 'I'm very, very glad.'

II

'So please call on the Bohls,' Kitty said to her husband, when he came to see her at eleven o'clock, before going out. 'I know you're dining at the club, papa signed you up. And what are you doing in the morning?'

'I'm just going to visit Katavasov,' answered Levin.

'Why so early?'

'He promised to introduce me to Metrov. I'd like to discuss my work with him. He's a well-known Petersburg scholar,' said Levin.

'Yes, wasn't it his article that you praised so much? Well, and then?' said Kitty.

'I may also go to the court on my sister's business.'

'And to the concert?' she asked.

'As if I'd go alone!'

'No, do go. They perform these new things . . . You were so interested. I wouldn't miss it.'

'Well, in any case I'll call in at home before dinner,' he said, looking at his watch.

'Put on your frock coat, so that you can call on Countess Bohl on the way.'

'But is it absolutely necessary?'

'Oh, absolutely! He called on us. Well, what will it cost you? You'll go, talk about the weather for five minutes, get up and leave.'

'Well, you won't believe it, but I'm so unaccustomed to these things that it makes me ashamed. How is it? A stranger comes, sits down, stays for no reason, bothers them, upsets himself, and then leaves.'

Kitty laughed.

'You paid calls when you were a bachelor, didn't you?' she said.

'I did, but I was always ashamed, and now I'm so unaccustomed to it that, by God, I'd rather go two days without dinner than pay this call. Such shame! I keep thinking they'll be offended and say: "Why come for no reason?"'

'No, they won't be offended. I can answer for that,' said Kitty, looking into his face and laughing. She took his hand. 'Well, good-bye . . . Please go.'

He was just about to kiss her hand and leave when she stopped him.

'Kostya, you know, I only have fifty roubles left.'

'Well, then I'll go and get some from the bank. How much?' he said, with an expression of displeasure familiar to her.

'No, wait.' She held on to his hand. 'Let's talk, this bothers me. I don't think I spend on anything unnecessary, but the money just goes. We're doing something wrong.'

'Not at all,' he said, clearing his throat and looking at her from under his eyebrows.

She knew that clearing of his throat. It was a sign that he was strongly displeased, not with her, but with himself. He was indeed displeased, not that a lot of money had been spent, but that he was reminded of something which he, knowing that things were not right, had wished to forget.

'I've told Sokolov to sell the wheat and take money in advance for the mill. In any case, we'll have money.'

'No, but I'm afraid it's generally too much . . .'

'Not at all, not at all,' he repeated. 'Well, good-bye, darling.'

'No, really, I'm sometimes so sorry I listened to mama. It was so good in the country! And here I've worn you all out, and we're spending money . . .'

'Not at all, not at all. Not once since I've been married have I said it would have been better otherwise than it is . . .'

'Truly?' she said, looking into his eyes.

He had said it without thinking, just to comfort her. But when he glanced at her and saw those dear, truthful eyes fixed questioningly on him, he repeated the same thing from the bottom of his heart. 'I'm decidedly forgetting her,' he thought. And he remembered what so soon awaited them.

'Soon now? How do you feel?' he whispered, taking both her hands.

'I've thought it so many times that now I don't think or know anything.'

'And you're not afraid?'

She smiled scornfully.

'Not a bit,' she said.

'So, if anything happens, I'm at Katavasov's.'

'No, nothing will happen, don't even think of it. I'll go for a stroll on the boulevard with papa. We'll stop at Dolly's. I'll be expecting you before dinner. Ah, yes! Do you know that Dolly's situation is becoming quite impossible? She's in debt all around, and she has no money. Yesterday I talked with mama and Arseny' (so she called Prince Lvov, her sister's husband), 'and we decided to set him and you on Stiva. This is quite impossible. One can't talk to papa about it . . . But if you and he . . .'

'But what can we do?' asked Levin.

'Still, while you're at Arseny's, talk to him; he'll tell you what we decided.'

'Well, with Arseny I'll agree to everything beforehand. I'll call on him. By the way, if I do go to the concert, I'll go with Natalie. Well, good-bye.'

At the porch Kuzma, the old servant from his bachelor days, who was handling their town arrangements, stopped him.

'Beau' (this was the left shaft-horse, brought from the country) 'has been re-shod, but he still limps,' he said. 'What are your orders?'

At the beginning of their life in Moscow, Levin had concerned himself with the horses he brought from the country. He had wanted to arrange that part as well and as cheaply as possible; but it turned out that keeping his own horses was more expensive than hiring, and they hired cabs anyway.

'Send for the horse doctor, it may be a sore.'

'Well, and for Katerina Alexandrovna?' asked Kuzma.

Levin was no longer struck now, as he had been at the beginning of their life in Moscow, that to go from Vozdvizhenka to Sivtsev Vrazhek it was necessary to hitch a pair of strong horses to a heavy carriage, take that carriage less than a quarter of a mile through snowy mush, and let it stand there for four hours, having paid five roubles for it. Now it seemed natural to him.

'Tell the cabby to bring a second pair for our carriage,' he said.

'Yes, sir.'

And having solved so simply and easily, thanks to town conditions, a difficulty which in the country would have called for so much personal effort and attention, Levin went out on the porch, hailed a cab, got into it and drove to Nikitskaya. On the way he no longer thought about money, but reflected on how he was going to make the acquaintance of a Petersburg scholar, a specialist in sociology, and talk to him about his book.

Only during his very first days in Moscow had Levin been struck by those unproductive but inevitable expenses, so strange for a country-dweller, that were demanded of him on all sides. Now he had grown used to them. What had happened to him in this respect was what they say happens with drunkards: the first glass is a stake, the second a snake, and from the third on it's all little birdies. When Levin changed the first hundred-rouble note to buy liveries for his footman and hall porter, he calculated that these liveries – totally useless but inevitable and necessary, judging by the princess's and Kitty's astonishment at his hint that they might be dispensed with – would cost as much as two summer workers, meaning about three hundred workdays from Easter to Advent, each one a day of hard work from early morning till late in the evening – and that hundred-rouble note still went down like a stake. But the next one, broken to buy provisions for a family dinner that had cost twenty-eight roubles, though it had called up in Levin the recollection that twenty-eight roubles meant about seventy-two bushels of oats which, with much sweating and groaning, had been mowed, bound, carted, threshed, winnowed, sifted and bagged – this next one all the same had gone a little more easily. And now the notes he broke had long ceased to call up such thoughts and flew off like little birdies. Whether the labour spent in acquiring money corresponded to the pleasure afforded by what was bought with it was a long-lost consideration. The economic consideration that there was a certain price below which a certain kind of grain could not be sold, was also forgotten. His rye, the price of which he had insisted on for such a long time, was sold at fifty kopecks less per measure than had been offered a month earlier. Even the consideration that with such expenses it would be impossible to get through the year without going into debt no longer had any significance. Only one thing was required: to have money in the bank, without asking where it came from, so as always to know how to pay for the next day's beef. And so far he had observed that consideration: he had always had money in the bank. But now the money in the bank had come to an end and he did not quite know where to get more. It was this that upset him for a moment when Kitty reminded him about money; but he had no time to think of it. He drove on, thinking about Katavasov and the impending meeting with Metrov.

III

During his stay in Moscow Levin had again become close with his former university friend, Professor Katavasov, whom he had not seen since his marriage. He liked Katavasov for the clarity and simplicity of his world-view. Levin thought that the clarity of Katavasov's world-view came from the poverty of his nature, and Katavasov thought that the inconsistency of Levin's thought came from a lack of mental discipline; but Levin liked Katavasov's clarity, and Katavasov liked the abundance of Levin's undisciplined thoughts, and they loved to get together and argue.

Levin read some parts of his writing to Katavasov, and he liked them. The day before, meeting Levin at a public lecture, Katavasov had told him that the famous Metrov, whose article Levin had liked so much, was in Moscow and was very interested in what Katavasov had told him about Levin's work, and that Metrov would be calling on him the next day at eleven o'clock and would be very glad to make his acquaintance.

'You're decidedly improving, my friend, it's nice to see it,' said Katavasov, meeting Levin in the small drawing room. 'I heard the bell and thought: can it be he's on time? . . . Well, how about these Montenegrins? Born fighters.'[1]

'What about them?' asked Levin.

Katavasov told him the latest news in a few words, then, going into the study, introduced Levin to a short, stocky man of very pleasant appearance. This was Metrov. The conversation dwelt for a brief time on politics and on what view was taken of the latest events in the highest Petersburg spheres. Metrov told them the words, which he had from a reliable source, supposedly uttered on that occasion by the emperor and one of his ministers. Katavasov had heard, also reliably, that the emperor had said something quite different. Levin tried to conceive of circumstances in which both things could have been said, and the conversation on that subject ceased.

'So he's almost finished a book on the natural conditions of the worker in relation to the land,' said Katavasov. 'I'm no expert, but what I liked about it, as a natural scientist, was that he doesn't consider mankind as something outside zoological laws, but, on the contrary, regards it as dependent on the environment and looks for the laws of development within that dependence.'

'That is very interesting,' said Metrov.

'I actually began writing a book on agriculture, but involuntarily, in concerning myself with the main tool of farming, the worker,' Levin said, blushing, 'I arrived at totally unexpected results.'

And carefully, as if testing the ground, Levin began to explain his view. He knew that Metrov had written an article against the commonly accepted political-economic theory, but how far he could expect him to be sympathetic to his new views he did not know and could not guess from the scholar's calm and intelligent face.

'But what do you see as the special properties of the Russian worker?' asked Metrov. 'His zoological properties, so to speak, or the conditions in which he finds himself?'

Levin saw that this question already implied a thought he disagreed with; but he continued to explain his own thought, which was that the Russian worker had a view of the land that differed completely from that of other peoples. And to prove this point he hastened to add that in his opinion this view of the Russian people came from their awareness of being called upon to populate the enormous unoccupied spaces of the east.

'It is easy to be led into error by drawing conclusions about a people's general calling,' Metrov said, interrupting Levin. 'The worker's condition will always depend on his relation to the land and to capital.'

And not letting Levin finish his thought, Metrov began explaining to him the particularity of his own theory.

What the particularity of his theory was Levin did not understand, because he did not bother to understand; he saw that Metrov, just like the others, despite his article in which he refuted the teaching of the economists, still regarded the position of the Russian worker only from the point of view of capital, wages and income. Though he had to admit that in the greater part of Russia, the eastern part, income was still zero, that for nine-tenths of the Russian population of eighty million wages were only at subsistence level, and that capital did not exist otherwise than as the most primitive tools – he still regarded all workers from that point of view alone, though he disagreed with economists on many points and had his own new theory about wages, which he explained to Levin.

Levin listened reluctantly and began by objecting. He wanted to interrupt Metrov in order to tell him his thought, which in his opinion would make further explanations superfluous. But then, convinced that they looked at the matter so differently that they would never understand each other, he stopped contradicting and merely listened. Despite the fact that he was no longer interested in what Metrov was saying, he nevertheless experienced a certain satisfaction in listening to him. It flattered his vanity that such a learned man was telling him his thoughts so eagerly, with such attention and confidence in his knowledge of the subject, sometimes referring to whole aspects of the matter by a single allusion. He ascribed it to his own merit, unaware that Metrov, having talked about it with everyone around him, was especially eager to talk on the subject with each new person, and generally talked eagerly with everyone about the subject, which interested him but was as yet unclear to him.

'We're going to be late, though,' said Katavasov, glancing at his watch, as soon as Metrov finished his explanation.

'Yes, today there's a meeting of the Society of Amateurs to commemorate Svintich's fiftieth birthday,'[2] Katavasov replied to Levin's question. 'Pyotr Ivanych and I intend to go. I promised to speak about his works on zoology. Come with us, it's very interesting.'

'Yes, in fact it's time,' said Metrov. 'Come with us, and from there to my place, if you wish. I'd like very much to hear your work.'

'No, really. It's still so unfinished. But I'll be glad to go to the meeting.'

'Say, my friend, have you heard? They've proposed a separate opinion,' said Katavasov, who was putting on his tailcoat in the other room.

And a conversation began on the university question.[3]

The university question was a very important event in Moscow that winter. Three old professors on the council had not accepted the opinion of the young ones; the young ones had proposed a separate opinion. That opinion, in the view of some, was terrible, and, in the view of others, was very simple and correct, and so the professors had split into two parties.

Some, including Katavasov, saw falsity, denunciation and deceit in the opposing side; the others – puerility and disrespect for authority. Levin, though he did not belong to the university, had already heard and talked about this matter several times since coming to Moscow and had formed his own opinion about it. He took part in the conversation, which continued outside as the three men walked to the old university building.

The meeting had already begun . . . Around the baize-covered table at which Katavasov and Metrov seated themselves, six men were sitting, and one of them, bending close to a manuscript, was reading something.

Levin sat in one of the vacant chairs that stood around the table and in a whisper asked a student who was sitting there what was being read. The student looked Levin over with resentment and said:

'The biography.'

Though Levin was not interested in the scientist's biography, he listened involuntarily and learned some interesting and new things about the life of the famous man.

When the reader had finished, the chairman thanked him and read a poem by the poet Ment,[4] sent to him for this jubilee, with a few words of gratitude to the author. Then Katavasov, in his loud, piercing voice, read his note on the learned works of the man being honoured.

When Katavasov finished, Levin looked at his watch, saw that it was already past one o'clock, and reflected that he would not have time to read his work to Metrov before the concert, and besides he no longer wanted to. During the reading he had also been thinking about their conversation. It was now clear to him that, while Metrov's thought might be important, his own thoughts were also important; these thoughts might be clarified and lead to something only if each of them worked separately on his chosen way, and nothing could come from communicating these thoughts to each other. And, having decided to decline Metrov's invitation, Levin went over to him at the end of the meeting. Metrov introduced Levin to the chairman, with whom he was discussing the political news. Metrov told the chairman the same thing he had told Levin, and Levin made the same observations he had already made that morning, but for diversity offered a new opinion that had just occurred to him. After that the talk on the university question started up again. Since Levin had already heard it all, he hastened to tell Metrov that he was sorry he could not accept his invitation, made his bows and went to see Lvov.

IV

Lvov, who was married to Kitty's sister Natalie, had spent all his life in the capitals and abroad, where he had been educated and served as a diplomat.

A year ago he had left the diplomatic service, not owing to unpleasantness (he never had any unpleasantness with anyone), and gone to serve in the palace administration in Moscow, in order to give the best education to his two boys.

Despite the sharpest contrast in habits and views, and the fact that Lvov was older than Levin, they had become very close that winter and grown to love each other.

Lvov was at home, and Levin went in without being announced.

Lvov, wearing a belted house jacket and suede boots, was sitting in an armchair, a pince-nez with blue lenses on his nose, reading a book propped on a lectern, carefully holding out in a shapely hand a cigar half turned to ash.

His handsome, fine, and still-young face, to which his curly, shining silver hair lent a still more thoroughbred appearance, brightened with a smile when he saw Levin.

'Excellent! And I was about to send to you. Well, how's Kitty? Sit here, it's more comfortable . . .' He got up and moved a rocking chair over. 'Have you read the latest circular letter in the *Journal de St-Pétersbourg*?[5] I find it splendid,' he said with a slight French accent.

Levin told him what he had heard from Katavasov about the talk in Petersburg and, after discussing politics, told of his making the acquaintance of Metrov and going to the meeting. Lvov became very interested in that.

'I envy you your entry into that interesting world of learning,' he said. And, warming to the subject, he switched, as usual, to French, which suited him better. 'True, I also have no time. My service and the children's education deprive me of that; and besides, I'm not ashamed to say that my education is much too deficient.'

'I don't think so,' Levin said with a smile, touched as always by his low opinion of himself, by no means affected out of a desire to seem or even be modest, but perfectly sincere.

'Ah, yes! I feel now how little learning I have. For my children's education I even have to refresh my memory a good deal and simply study. Because it's not enough to have teachers, there must also be a supervisor, just as in your farming you need workers and an overseer. See what I'm reading?' he pointed to Buslaev's grammar[6] on the lectern. 'It's required of Misha, and it's so difficult . . . Explain this to me now. He says here . . .'

Levin tried to explain to him that one cannot understand it but must simply learn it; but Lvov did not agree with him.

'Yes, see how you laugh at it!'

'On the contrary, you can't imagine how, by looking at you, I always learn what's in store for me – I mean children's education.'

'There certainly isn't anything to learn,' said Lvov.

'I only know,' said Levin, 'that I've never met better-brought-up children than yours and couldn't wish for better myself.'

Lvov obviously wanted to restrain himself and not show his joy, but he simply beamed all over.

'As long as they're better than I am. That's all I wish for. You don't know all the trouble yet,' he began, 'with boys who, like mine, were neglected in that life abroad.'

'You'll catch up on it all. They're such capable children. Above all – moral education. That's what I learn from looking at your children.'

'Moral education, you say. It's impossible to imagine how hard it is! You've just prevailed on one side when something else crops up, and the struggle starts again. Without support from religion – remember, we talked about it – no father, using only his own resources, would be able to bring up a child.'

This conversation, which always interested Levin, was interrupted by the entrance of the beautiful Natalya Alexandrovna, already dressed to go out.

'I didn't know you were here,' she said, obviously not only not sorry but even glad to have interrupted this, for her, long-familiar and boring conversation. 'Well, how's Kitty? I'm dining with you today. Now then, Arseny,' she turned to her husband, 'you will take the carriage . . .'

And a discussion began between husband and wife about how they were going to spend the day. Since the husband had to go and meet someone to do with his work, and the wife had to go to a concert and a public meeting of the South-Eastern Committee, there was much to be decided and thought over. Levin, as one of the family, had to take part in the planning. It was decided that Levin would go with Natalie to the concert and the public meeting, and from there the carriage would be sent to the office for Arseny, and he would come to fetch her and take her to Kitty's; or, if he was still busy, he would send the carriage and Levin would go with her.

'The man spoils me,' he said to his wife, 'he assures me that our children are wonderful, when I know how much bad there is in them.'

'Arseny goes to extremes, as I always say,' said the wife. 'If you look for perfection, you'll never be content. It's true what papa says, that when we were being brought up there was one extreme – we were kept in the attic, while the parents lived on the first floor; now it's the opposite – the parents go to the store-room and the children to the first floor. Parents mustn't have any life now, everything's given to the children.'

'Why not, if they like it?' Lvov said, smiling his handsome smile and touching her hand. 'Anyone who didn't know you would think you were not a mother but a stepmother.'

'No, extremes aren't good in anything,' Natalie said calmly, putting his paper-knife in its proper place on the desk.

'Well, come here now, you perfect children,' he said to the handsome boys who came in and, after bowing to Levin, went over to their father, evidently wishing to ask him about something.

Levin would have liked to talk with them, to hear what they said to their father, but Natalie turned to him, and just then Lvov's colleague, Makhotin, in a court uniform, came into the room to fetch him, so that they could go together to meet someone, and now an endless conversation started about Herzegovina, Princess Korzinsky, the duma, and the unexpected death of Mme Apraksin.

Levin quite forgot about the errand he had been given. He remembered it only on his way to the front hall.

'Ah, Kitty told me to discuss something about Oblonsky with you,' he said, when Lvov stopped on the stairs, seeing his wife and Levin out.

'Yes, yes, *maman* wants us, *les beaux-frères*, to fall upon him,' he said, blushing and smiling. 'But, after all, why me?'

'Then I'll fall upon him,' Natalie said, waiting in her white dog-fur *rotonde* for the conversation to end. 'Well, come along!'

V

Two very interesting things were offered at the matinée concert.

One was a fantasia, *King Lear on the Heath*,[7] the other a quartet dedicated to the memory of Bach. Both pieces were new and in the new spirit, and Levin wanted to form his own opinion of them. Having taken his sister-in-law to her seat, he installed himself by a column and resolved to listen as closely and conscientiously as possible. He tried not to get distracted and spoil his impression by looking at the arm-waving of the white-tied conductor, which is always such an unpleasant distraction of musical attention, or at the ladies in hats, who had carefully tied ribbons over their ears especially for the concert, or at all the faces, either unoccupied by anything or occupied by interests quite other than music. He tried to avoid meeting musical connoisseurs and talkers, and stood with lowered eyes, listening.

But the longer he listened to the *King Lear* fantasia, the further he felt from any possibility of forming some definite opinion for himself. The musical expression of feeling was ceaselessly beginning, as if gathering itself up, but it fell apart at once into fragments of new beginnings of musical expressions and sometimes into extremely complex sounds, connected by nothing other than the mere whim of the composer. But these fragments of musical expressions, good ones on occasion, were unpleasant because they were totally unexpected and in no way prepared for. Gaiety, sadness, despair, tenderness and triumph appeared without justification, like a madman's feelings. And, just as with a madman, these feelings passed unexpectedly.

All through the performance Levin felt like a deaf man watching people dance. He was in utter perplexity when the piece ended and felt great fatigue from such strained but in no way rewarded attention. Loud applause came from all sides. Everybody stood up, began walking, talking. Wishing to explain his perplexity by means of other people's impressions, Levin began to walk about, looking for connoisseurs, and was glad to see one well-known connoisseur talking with Pestsov, whom he knew.

'Amazing!' Pestsov's dense bass said. 'Good afternoon, Konstantin Dmitrich. Particularly graphic and, so to speak, sculptural and rich in colour is the place where you feel Cordelia approaching, where a woman, *das ewig Weibliche*,*[8] enters the struggle with fate. Don't you think?'

'But what does Cordelia have to do with it?' Levin asked timidly, forgetting completely that the fantasia portrayed King Lear on the heath.

'Cordelia comes in . . . here!' said Pestsov, tapping his fingers on the satiny playbill he was holding and handing it to Levin.

Only then did Levin remember the title of the fantasia, and he hastened to read Shakespeare's verses in Russian translation, printed on the back of the bill.

'You can't follow without it,' said Pestsov, addressing Levin, since his interlocutor had left and there was no one else for him to talk to.

During the entr'acte an argument arose between Levin and Pestsov

* The eternal feminine.

about the virtues and shortcomings of the Wagnerian trend in music.[9] Levin maintained that the mistake of Wagner and all his followers lay in their music wishing to cross over to the sphere of another art, just as poetry is mistaken when it describes facial features, something that should be done by painting, and he gave as an example of such a mistake a sculptor who decided to carve in marble the phantoms of poetic images emerging around the figure of a poet on a pedestal.[10] 'The sculptor gave these phantoms so little of the phantasmic that they're even holding on to the stairs,' said Levin. He liked the phrase, but he did not remember whether he might not have used it before, and precisely with Pestsov, and having said it, he became embarrassed.

Pestsov maintained that art is one and that it can reach its highest manifestations only by uniting all its forms.

The second part of the concert Levin could not hear at all. Pestsov stood next to him and spent almost the whole time talking to him, denouncing the piece for its superfluous, cloying, affected simplicity and comparing it with the Pre-Raphaelites in painting. On the way out Levin met still more acquaintances, with whom he talked about politics, music and mutual acquaintances. Among others he met Count Bohl, whom he had completely forgotten to visit.

'Well, you can go now,' Natalie said to him when he told her of it. 'Maybe they won't receive you, and then you can come and fetch me at the meeting. I'll still be there.'

VI

'Perhaps they're not receiving?' said Levin, entering the front hall of Countess Bohl's house.

'They are. Please come in,' said the porter, resolutely helping him out of his coat.

'How annoying,' thought Levin, sighing as he removed a glove and shaped his hat. 'Well, why am I going? And what shall I talk about with them?'

Passing through the first drawing room, Levin met Countess Bohl in the doorway. With a preoccupied and stern face, she was ordering a servant to do something. Seeing Levin, she smiled and invited him into the next small drawing room, from which voices came. In this drawing room, in armchairs, sat the countess's two daughters and a Moscow colonel of Levin's acquaintance. Levin went up to them and, after the greetings, sat down by the sofa, holding his hat on his knee.

'How is your wife's health? Were you at the concert? We couldn't go. Mama had to be at a panikhida.'[11]

'Yes, I heard . . . Such a sudden death,' said Levin.

The countess came in, sat on the sofa and also asked about his wife and the concert.

Levin answered her and repeated the remark about the suddenness of Mme Apraksin's death.

'Though she always had weak health.'

'Did you go to the opera yesterday?'

'Yes, I did.'

'Lucca was very good.'[12]

'Yes, very good,' he said, and as he was totally indifferent to what they thought of him, he began to repeat what he had heard hundreds of times about the singer's special talent. Countess Bohl pretended to listen. Then, when he had talked enough and fell silent, the colonel, silent up to then, began to speak. The colonel also talked about the opera and the lighting. Finally, having mentioned the planned *folle journée**[13] at Tiurin's, the colonel started laughing, got up noisily and left. Levin also got up, but noticed from the countess's face that it was too early for him to leave. Another couple of minutes were called for. He sat down.

But as he kept thinking how stupid it was, he could find nothing to talk about and remained silent.

'You're not going to the public meeting? They say it's very interesting,' the countess began.

'No, I promised my *belle-soeur* I'd come and fetch her,' said Levin.

Silence ensued. Mother and daughter exchanged glances once more.

'Well, I suppose now is the time,' thought Levin, and he got up. The ladies shook hands with him and asked him to convey *mille choses*† to his wife.

As he held his coat for him, the porter asked:

'Where are you staying, if you please?' and wrote it down at once in a big, well-bound book.

'Of course, it makes no difference to me, but still it's embarrassing

* Crazy day.

† All their best.

and terribly stupid,' Levin reflected, comforting himself with the thought that everyone did it; and he drove to the public meeting of the Committee, where he was to find his sister-in-law and take her home with him.

There were many people, including almost the whole of society, at the public meeting of the Committee. Levin managed to catch the summary, which, as everyone said, was very interesting. When the reading of the summary was over, society got together, and Levin met Sviyazhsky, who insisted on inviting him that evening to the Agricultural Society, where a celebrated lecture would be read, and Stepan Arkadyich, who was just back from the races, and many other acquaintances, and Levin talked more and listened to various opinions about the meeting, about the new music, and about a certain trial. But, probably owing to the flagging attention he was beginning to experience, when he talked about the trial he made a blunder, and later he recalled that blunder several times with vexation. Speaking of the impending sentencing of a foreigner who was on trial in Russia, and about how wrong it would be to sentence him to exile abroad,[14] Levin repeated what he had heard the day before from an acquaintance.

'I think that exiling him abroad is the same as punishing a pike by throwing it into the water,' Levin said. Only later did he remember that this thought, which he seemed to pass off as his own and had really heard from an acquaintance, came from one of Krylov's fables,[15] and his acquaintance had repeated it from a newspaper *feuilleton*.

After taking his sister-in-law home with him, and finding Kitty happy and well, Levin went to the club.

VII

Levin arrived at the club just in time. Guests and members were driving up as he arrived. Levin had not been to the club in a very long while, not since he had lived in Moscow and gone out in society after leaving the university. Though he remembered the club, the external details of its arrangement, he had completely forgotten the impression it used to make on him. But as soon as he drove into the wide, semi-circular courtyard and stepped out of the cab on to the porch, where a porter in a sash soundlessly opened the door for him and bowed; as soon as he saw in the porter's lodge the galoshes and coats of the members who understood that it was less trouble to take off their galoshes downstairs than to go up in them; as soon as he heard the mysterious bell ringing to announce him, saw the statue on the landing as he went up the low carpeted steps of the stairway, and saw in the doorway above a third familiar though aged porter in club livery, promptly but unhurriedly opening the door while looking the visitor over, he was enveloped by the long-past impression of the club – an impression of restfulness, contentment and propriety.

'Your hat, please,' the porter said to Levin, who had forgotten the club rule about leaving hats in the porter's lodge. 'It's a long time since you were here. The prince signed you in yesterday. Prince Stepan Arkadyich has not arrived yet.'

The porter knew not only Levin but all his connections and family and at once mentioned people close to him.

Going through the first big room with screens and another to the right where there was a fruit buffet, overtaking a slow-walking old man, Levin entered a dining room full of noisy people.

He walked among almost completely occupied tables, looking the guests over. Here and there he saw the most diverse people, old and young, familiar or barely known to him. There was not a single angry or worried face. It seemed they had all left their anxieties and cares in the porter's lodge together with their hats and were now about to enjoy the material blessings of life at their leisure. Sviyazhsky, and Shcherbatsky, and Nevedovsky, and the old prince, and Vronsky and Sergei Ivanovich were all there.

'Ah! Why so late?' said the prince, smiling and giving him his hand over his shoulder. 'How's Kitty?' he added, straightening the napkin that he had tucked behind a waistcoat button.

'Quite well, thanks. The three of them are dining at home.'

'Ah, Alines and Nadines. Well, we have no room here. Go to that table and quickly take a seat,' said the prince and, turning away, he carefully accepted a plate of burbot soup.

'Levin, over here!' a good-natured voice called from a bit further off. It was Turovtsyn. He was sitting with a young military man, and next to them two chairs were tipped forward. Levin gladly joined them. He had always liked the good-natured carouser Turovtsyn – his proposal to Kitty was connected with him – but now, after so many strained intellectual conversations, he found Turovtsyn's good-natured air especially agreeable.

'These are for you and Oblonsky. He'll be here any minute.'

The very straight-backed military man with merry, always laughing eyes was the Petersburger Gagin. Turovtsyn introduced them.

'Oblonsky's eternally late.'

'Ah, here he is.'

'Have you just arrived?' said Oblonsky, quickly coming up to them. 'Greetings! Had vodka? Well, come on!'

Levin got up and went with him to the big table set with all kinds of vodka and a great variety of hors d'oeuvres. It seemed that out of two dozen kinds he might have chosen one to his taste, but Stepan Arkadyich ordered something special and a liveried servant who was standing there immediately brought what he had ordered. They drank a glass each and went back to the table.

Right then, still over the fish soup, Gagin was served champagne and had four glasses poured. Levin did not refuse the wine he was offered and ordered another bottle. He was hungry, and ate and drank with great pleasure, and with still greater pleasure took part in the gay and simple conversation of his companions. Gagin, lowering his voice, told a new Petersburg joke which, though indecent and stupid, was so funny that Levin burst out laughing loudly enough to make his neighbours turn to look at him.

'It's the same kind as "That I simply cannot bear!" Do you know that one?' asked Stepan Arkadyich. 'Ah, it's lovely! Bring us another bottle,' he said to the waiter and began telling the joke.

'Compliments of Pyotr Ilyich Vinovsky,' interrupted Stepan Arkadyich's old footman, bringing over two thin glasses of still-bubbling champagne and addressing Stepan Arkadyich and Levin. Stepan Arkadyich took a glass and, exchanging glances with a balding, red-haired man with a moustache at the other end of the table, nodded to him and smiled.

'Who's that?' asked Levin.

'You met him once at my house, remember? A nice fellow.'

Levin did as Stepan Arkadyich had done and took his glass.

Stepan Arkadyich's joke was also very amusing. Levin told a joke of his own, which was enjoyed too. Then the conversation turned to horses, to the day's races and how dashingly Vronsky's Satiny had won the first prize. Levin did not notice how the dinner went by.

'Ah, here they are!' Stepan Arkadyich said when dinner was already over, turning across the back of his chair and holding out his hand to

Vronsky, who was coming towards them with a tall colonel of the guards. Vronsky's face also shone with the general merry good humour of the club. He merrily leaned on Stepan Arkadyich's shoulder, whispering something to him, and with the same merry smile gave his hand to Levin.

'Very glad to see you,' he said. 'I looked for you back at the elections, but was told you had already left.'

'Yes, I left that same day. We've just been talking about your horse. Congratulations,' said Levin. 'That's very fast riding.'

'I believe you also keep horses.'

'No, my father did. But I remember and know about them.'

'Where did you dine?' asked Stepan Arkadyich.

'We're at the second table, behind the columns.'

'He's been congratulated,' said the tall colonel. 'His second imperial prize – if only I had such luck at cards as he has with horses! . . . Well, no use wasting precious time. I'm off to the inferno,' said the colonel, and he walked away from the table.

'That's Yashvin,' Vronsky answered Turovtsyn and sat down in a place that had been vacated next to them. After drinking the glass he was offered, he ordered a bottle. Levin, influenced either by the impression of the club or by the wine he had drunk, got into a conversation with Vronsky about the best breeds of cattle and was very glad to feel no hostility towards the man. He even told him, among other things, that his wife had mentioned meeting him at Princess Marya Borisovna's.

'Ah, Princess Marya Borisovna, she's lovely!' said Stepan Arkadyich, and he told a joke about Marya Borisovna that made everybody laugh. Vronsky, in particular, burst into such good-natured laughter that Levin felt completely reconciled with him.

'So, all done?' said Stepan Arkadyich, getting up and smiling. 'Let's go!'

VIII

Leaving the table, feeling his arms swinging with a special rightness and ease as he went, Levin walked with Gagin through the high-ceilinged rooms towards the billiard room. Going through the main hall, he ran into his father-in-law.

'Well, so? How do you like our temple of idleness?' the prince said, taking him under the arm. 'Come, let's take a stroll.'

'I also wanted to have a look round. It's interesting.'

'Yes, for you it's interesting. But my interest is different from yours. You look at these little old men,' he said, indicating a club member with a bent back and a hanging lower lip who walked towards and then past them, barely moving his feet in their soft boots, 'and you think they were born such sloshers.'

'Why sloshers?'

'See, you don't even know the word. It's our club term. You know, when you're rolling hard-boiled eggs, an egg that's been rolled a lot gets all cracked and turns into a slosher. It's the same with our kind: we keep coming and coming to the club and turn into sloshers. Yes, you may laugh, but our kind have to watch out that we don't wind up with the sloshers. You know Prince Chechensky?' asked the prince, and Levin could see from his look that he was going to tell some funny story.

'No, I don't.'

'Well, really! I mean the famous Prince Chechensky. Well, it makes no difference. He's always playing billiards. Some three years ago he was still a fine fellow and not one of the sloshers. He even called other men sloshers. Only one day he comes and our porter . . . you know Vassily? Well, that fat one. He's a great wit. So Prince Chechensky asks him, "Well, Vassily, who's here? Any sloshers?" And he says to him "You're the third." Yes, brother, so it goes!'

Talking and greeting the acquaintances they met, Levin and the prince passed through all the rooms: the main one, where card tables were already set up and habitual partners were playing for small stakes; the sitting room, where people were playing chess and Sergei Ivanovich sat talking with someone; the billiard room, where, around the sofa in the curve of the room, a merry company, which included Gagin, had gathered with champagne; they also looked into the inferno, where many gamblers crowded round a single table at which Yashvin was already sitting. Trying not to make any noise, they went into the dim reading room where, under shaded lamps, a young man with an angry face sat flipping through one magazine after another and a bald-headed general was immersed in reading. They also went into a room which the prince called the 'clever room'. In this room three gentlemen were hotly discussing the latest political news.

'If you please, Prince, we're ready,' one of his partners said, finding him there, and the prince left. Levin sat and listened for a while, but, recalling all the conversations of that day, he suddenly felt terribly bored. He got up quickly and went to look for Oblonsky and Turovtsyn, with whom he felt merry.

Turovtsyn was sitting with a tankard of drink on a high-backed sofa in the billiard room, and Stepan Arkadyich was talking about something with Vronsky by the doorway in the far corner of the room.

'It's not that she's bored, it's the uncertainty, the undecidedness of the situation,' Levin heard and was about to retreat hastily, but Stepan Arkadyich called to him.

'Levin!' said Stepan Arkadyich, and Levin noticed that his eyes, though not tearful, were moist, as always happened with him when he was drinking or very moved. This time it was both. 'Levin, don't go,' he said and held him tightly by the elbow, obviously not wishing him to leave for anything.

'This is my truest, maybe even my best friend,' he said to Vronsky. 'You, too, are even nearer and dearer to me. And I want you to be and know that you should be close friends, because you're both good people.'

'Well, all that's left is for us to kiss,' Vronsky said with good-natured humour, giving him his hand.

Levin quickly took the proffered hand and pressed it firmly.

'I'm very, very glad,' he said.

'Waiter, a bottle of champagne,' said Stepan Arkadyich.

'I'm very glad, too,' said Vronsky.

But, despite Stepan Arkadyich's wishes, and their own wishes, they had nothing to talk about and they both felt it.

'You know, he's not acquainted with Anna?' Stepan Arkadyich said to Vronsky. 'And I absolutely want to take him to her. Let's go, Levin!'

'Really?' said Vronsky. 'She'll be very glad. I'd go home now,' he added, 'but I'm worried about Yashvin and want to stay till he's finished.'

'What, is it bad?'

'He keeps losing and I'm the only one who can hold him back.'

'How about a little game of pyramids? Levin, will you play? Well, splendid!' said Stepan Arkadyich. 'Set it up for pyramids.' He turned to the marker.

'It's been ready for a long time,' replied the marker, who had set the balls into a triangle long ago and was knocking the red one around to amuse himself.

'Let's begin.'

After the game, Vronsky and Levin joined Gagin's table and Levin, at Stepan Arkadyich's suggestion, began betting on aces. Vronsky first sat by the table, surrounded by acquaintances who were constantly coming up to him, then went to the inferno to visit Yashvin. Levin experienced a pleasant rest from the mental fatigue of the morning. He was glad of the cessation of hostilities with Vronsky, and the feeling of peacefulness, propriety and contentment never left him.

When the game was over, Stepan Arkadyich took Levin under the arm.

'Well, shall we go to Anna? Now? Eh? She's at home. I've long been promising to bring you. Where were you going to spend the evening?'

'Nowhere in particular. I promised Sviyazhsky I'd go to the Agricultural Society. But all right, let's go,' said Levin.

'Excellent! Off we go! Find out if my carriage has arrived,' Stepan Arkadyich turned to a footman.

Levin went to the table, paid the forty roubles he had lost betting on aces, paid his club expenses, known in some mysterious way to the little old footman who stood by the door, and, with a special swing of the arms, walked through all the rooms to the exit.

IX

'The Oblonsky carriage!' shouted the porter in a gruff bass. The carriage pulled up and they got in. Only at the beginning, while the carriage was driving through the gates of the club, did Levin continue to feel the impression of the club's peace, contentment, and the unquestionable propriety of the surroundings; but as soon as the carriage drove out to the street and he felt it jolting over the uneven road, heard the angry shout of a driver going the other way, saw in the dim light the red signs over a pot-house and a shop, that impression was destroyed, and he began to reflect on his actions, asking himself if he was doing the right thing by going to Anna. What would Kitty say? But Stepan Arkadyich did not let him ponder and, as if guessing his doubts, dispersed them.

'I'm so glad,' he said, 'that you'll get to know her. You know, Dolly has long been wanting it. And Lvov has called on her and keeps dropping in. Though she's my sister,' Stepan Arkadyich went on, 'I can boldly say that she's a remarkable woman. You'll see. Her situation is very trying, especially now.'

'Why especially now?'

'We're discussing a divorce with her husband. And he consents. But there's a difficulty here about her son, and the matter, which should have been concluded long ago, has been dragging on for three months. As soon as she gets the divorce, she'll marry Vronsky. It's so stupid, this old custom of marching in a circle, "Rejoice, O Isaiah,"[16] which nobody believes in and which hinders people's happiness!' Stepan Arkadyich added. 'Well, and then her situation will be as definite as mine, as yours.'

'What's the difficulty?' said Levin.

'Ah, it's a long and boring story! It's all so indefinite in this country. But the point is that, while waiting for the divorce, she's been living here in Moscow for three months, where everybody knows them both. She doesn't go anywhere, doesn't see any women except Dolly, because, you understand, she doesn't want them to come to her out of kindness. That fool, Princess Varvara – even she found it improper and left. And so, in that situation another woman wouldn't be able to find resources in herself. She, though, you'll see how she's arranged her life, how calm and dignified she is. To the left, into the lane, across from the church!' Stepan Arkadyich shouted, leaning out of the window of the carriage. 'Pah, what heat!' he said, opening his already unbuttoned coat still more, though it was twelve degrees below zero.

'But she has a daughter; mustn't she keep her busy?' said Levin.

'You seem to picture every woman as a mere female, *une couveuse*,'* said Stepan Arkadyich. 'If she's busy, it must be with children. No, she's bringing her up splendidly, it seems, but we don't hear about her. She's busy, first of all, with writing. I can already see you smiling ironically, but you shouldn't. She's writing a book for children and doesn't tell anybody about it, but she read it to me, and I gave the manuscript to Vorkuev . . . you know, that publisher . . . a writer himself, it seems. He's a good judge, and he says it's a remarkable thing. But you'll think she's a woman author? Not a bit of it. Before all she's a woman with heart, you'll see that. Now she has a little English girl and a whole family that she's occupied with.'

'What is it, some sort of philanthropy?'

'See, you keep looking at once for something bad. It's not philanthropy,

* A broody hen.

it's heartfelt. They had – that is, Vronsky had – an English trainer, a master of his trade, but a drunkard. He's drunk himself up completely, delirium tremens, and the family's abandoned. She saw them, helped them, got involved, and now the whole family's on her hands; and not patronizingly, not with money, but she herself is helping the boys with Russian in preparation for school, and she's taken the girl to live with her. You'll see her there.'

The carriage drove into the courtyard, and Stepan Arkadyich loudly rang the bell at the entrance, where a sleigh was standing.

And, without asking the servant who opened the door whether anyone was at home, Stepan Arkadyich went into the front hall. Levin followed him, more and more doubtful whether what he was doing was good or bad.

Looking in the mirror, Levin noticed that he was flushed; but he was sure that he was not drunk, and he walked up the carpeted stairway behind Stepan Arkadyich. Upstairs Stepan Arkadyich asked the footman, who bowed to him as a familiar of the house, who was with Anna, and received the answer that it was Mr Vorkuev.

'Where are they?'

'In the study.'

Passing through a small dining room with dark panelled walls, Stepan Arkadyich and Levin crossed a soft carpet to enter the semi-dark study, lit by one lamp under a big, dark shade. Another lamp, a reflector, burned on the wall, throwing its light on to a large, full-length portrait of a woman, to which Levin involuntarily turned his attention. This was the portrait of Anna painted in Italy by Mikhailov. While Stepan Arkadyich went behind a trellis-work screen and the male voice that had been speaking fell silent, Levin gazed at the portrait, stepping out of its frame in the brilliant light, and could not tear himself away from it. He even forgot where he was and, not listening to what was said around him, gazed without taking his eyes from the astonishing portrait. It was not a painting but a lovely living woman with dark, curly hair, bare shoulders and arms, and a pensive half smile on her lips, covered with tender down, looking at him triumphantly and tenderly with troubling eyes. Only, because she was not alive, she was more beautiful than a living woman can be.

'I'm very glad,' he suddenly heard a voice beside him, evidently addressing him, the voice of the same woman he was admiring in the portrait. Anna came to meet him from behind the trellis, and in the half light of the study Levin saw the woman of the portrait in a dark dress of various shades of blue, not in the same position, and not with the same expression, but at the same height of beauty that the artist had caught. She was less dazzling in reality, but in the living woman there was some new attractiveness that was not in the portrait.

X

She had risen to meet him, not concealing her joy at seeing him. And in the calmness with which she gave him her small and energetic hand, introduced him to Vorkuev and pointed to the pretty, red-haired girl who was sitting there over her work, referring to her as her ward, Levin saw the familiar and agreeable manners of a high-society woman, always calm and natural.

'Very, very glad,' she repeated, and on her lips these words for some reason acquired a special meaning for Levin. 'I've long known of you and loved you, both for your friendship with Stiva and for your wife . . . I knew her for a very short time, but she left me with the impression of a lovely flower, precisely a flower. And now she'll soon be a mother!'

She spoke freely and unhurriedly, shifting her eyes now and then from Levin to her brother, and Levin felt that the impression he made was good, and he at once found it light, simple and pleasant to be with her, as if he had known her since childhood.

'Ivan Petrovich and I settled in Alexei's study,' she said, in answer to Stepan Arkadyich's question whether he might smoke, 'precisely in order to smoke.' And with a glance at Levin, instead of asking if he smoked, she moved a tortoise-shell cigar case towards her and took out a cigarette.

'How are you feeling today?' her brother asked.

'All right. Nerves, as usual.'

'Remarkably well done, isn't it?' Stepan Arkadyich said, noticing that Levin kept glancing at the portrait.

'I've never seen a better portrait.'

'And isn't it a remarkable likeness?' said Vorkuev.

Levin glanced from the portrait to the original. A special glow lit up Anna's face the moment she felt his eyes on her. Levin blushed and to hide his embarrassment was about to ask if it was long since she had seen Darya Alexandrovna, but just then Anna spoke:

'Ivan Petrovich and I were just talking about Vashchenkov's latest pictures. Have you seen them?'

'Yes, I have,' Levin replied.

'But excuse me, I interrupted you, you were about to say . . .'

Levin asked if it was long since she had seen Dolly.

'She came yesterday. She's very angry with the school on account of Grisha. It seems the Latin teacher was unfair to him.'

'Yes, I've seen the paintings. I didn't much like them,' Levin went back to the conversation she had begun.

Now Levin spoke not at all with that workaday attitude towards things with which he had spoken that morning. Each word of conversation with her acquired a special meaning. It was pleasant to talk to her and still more pleasant to listen to her.

Anna spoke not only naturally and intelligently, but intelligently and casually, without attaching any value to her own thoughts, yet giving great value to the thoughts of the one she was talking to.

The conversation turned to the new trend in art, to the new Bible illustrations by a French artist.[17] Vorkuev accused the artist of realism pushed to the point of coarseness. Levin said that the French employed conventions in art as no one else did, and therefore they saw particular merit in the return to realism. They saw poetry in the fact that they were no longer lying.

Never had anything intelligent that Levin had said given him so much pleasure as this. Anna's face lit up when she suddenly saw his point. She laughed.

'I'm laughing,' she said, 'as one laughs seeing a very faithful portrait. What you've said perfectly characterizes French art now, painting and even literature: Zola, Daudet.[18] But perhaps it always happens that people first build their *conceptions* out of invented, conventionalized figures, but then – once all the *combinaisons* are finished – the invented figures become boring, and they begin to devise more natural and correct figures.'

'That's quite right!' said Vorkuev.

'So you were at the club?' She turned to her brother.

'Yes, yes, what a woman!' thought Levin, forgetting himself and gazing fixedly at her beautiful, mobile face, which now suddenly changed completely. Levin did not hear what she said as she leaned towards her brother, but he was struck by the change in her expression. So beautiful before in its calmness, her face suddenly showed a strange curiosity, wrath and pride. But that lasted only a moment. She narrowed her eyes as if remembering something.

'Ah, yes, however, it's not interesting for anyone,' she said, and turned to the English girl:

'Please order tea in the drawing room.'

The girl got up and went out.

'Well, did she pass her examination?' asked Stepan Arkadyich.

'Splendidly. She's a very capable girl and with a sweet nature.'

'You'll end by loving her more than your own.'

'That's a man talking. There is no more or less love. I love my daughter with one love and her with another.'

'I was just telling Anna Arkadyevna,' said Vorkuev, 'that if she spent at least a hundredth of the energy she puts into this English girl on the common cause of the education of Russian children, Anna Arkadyevna would be doing a great and useful thing.'

'Say what you like, I can't do it. Count Alexei Kirillych strongly encouraged me' (in pronouncing the words 'Count Alexei Kirillych', she gave Levin a pleadingly timid look, and he involuntarily responded with a respectful and confirming look) '– encouraged me to occupy myself with the village school. I went several times. They're very nice, but I couldn't get caught up in it. Energy, you say. Energy is based on love. And love can't be drawn from just anywhere, it can't be ordered. I love this English girl, I myself don't know why.'

And again she glanced at Levin. Her eyes, her smile, everything told him that she was addressing what she said to him, valuing his opinion and at the same time knowing beforehand that they understood each other.

'I understand that perfectly,' Levin replied. 'One cannot put one's heart into a school or generally into institutions of that sort, and that is precisely why I think these philanthropic institutions always produce such meagre results.'

She kept silent and then smiled.

'Yes, yes,' she agreed. 'I never could. *Je n'ai pas le coeur assez large** to love a whole orphanage of nasty little girls. *Cela ne m'a jamais réussi.*† There are so many women who have made themselves a *position sociale* that way. And the less so now,' she said with a sad, trustful expression,

* My heart isn't big enough.

† I've never succeeded in it.

ostensibly addressing her brother but obviously speaking only to Levin, 'now, when I so need some occupation, I cannot do it.' And, frowning suddenly (Levin understood that she was frowning at herself for talking about herself), she changed the subject. 'What I know about you,' she said to Levin, 'is that you're a bad citizen, and I've defended you the best I could.'

'How have you defended me?'

'Depending on the attack. But wouldn't you like some tea?' She rose and picked up a morocco-bound book.

'Give it to me, Anna Arkadyevna,' said Vorkuev, pointing to the book. 'It's well worth it.'

'Oh, no, it's all so unfinished.'

'I told him,' Stepan Arkadyich said to his sister, pointing to Levin.

'You shouldn't have. My writing is like those little carved baskets made in prisons that Liza Mertsalov used to sell me. She was in charge of prisons in that society,' she turned to Levin. 'And those unfortunates produced miracles of patience.'

And Levin saw another new feature in this woman whom he found so extraordinarily to his liking. Besides intelligence, grace, beauty, there was truthfulness in her. She did not want to conceal from him all the difficulty of her situation. Having said this, she sighed, and it was as if her face, acquiring a stern expression, suddenly turned to stone. With this expression she was still more beautiful than before; but this was a new look; it was outside the realm of the expressions, radiant with happiness and giving happiness, which the artist had caught in the portrait. Levin glanced once more at the portrait and then at her figure as she took her brother's arm and walked with him through the high doorway, and felt a tenderness and pity for her that surprised him.

She asked Levin and Vorkuev to go to the drawing room and stayed behind to talk about something with her brother. 'About the divorce, about Vronsky, about what he's doing at the club, about me?' thought Levin. And he was so excited by the question of what she was talking about with Stepan Arkadyich that he hardly listened to what Vorkuev was telling him about the merits of the children's novel Anna Arkadyevna had written.

Over tea the same pleasant, meaningful conversation continued. Not only was there not a single moment when it was necessary to search for a subject of conversation but, on the contrary, there was a feeling of having no time to say what one wanted and of willingly restraining oneself in order to hear what the other was saying. And whatever was said, not only by her but by Vorkuev, by Stepan Arkadyich, acquired a special significance, as it seemed to Levin, owing to her attention and observations.

As he followed the interesting conversation, Levin admired her all the while – her beauty, her intelligence, her education, and with that her simplicity and deep feeling. He listened, talked, and all the while thought about her, about her inner life, trying to guess her feelings. And he who had formerly judged her so severely, now, by some strange train of thought, justified her and at the same time pitied her, and feared that Vronsky did not fully understand her. After ten, when Stepan Arkadyich got up to leave (Vorkuev had left earlier), it seemed to Levin as if he had just come. He, too, regretfully got up to leave.

'Good-bye,' she said, holding his hand and looking into his eyes with an appealing gaze. 'I'm very glad *que la glace est rompue*.'*

She let go of his hand and narrowed her eyes.

'Tell your wife that I love her as before, and if she cannot forgive me my situation, I wish her never to forgive me. In order to forgive, one must have lived through what I have lived through, and may God spare her that.'

'Certainly, yes, I'll tell her . . .' said Levin, blushing.

XI

'What an amazing, dear and pitiful woman,' he thought, going out with Stepan Arkadyich into the frosty air.

'Well, so? I told you,' Stepan Arkadyich said to him, seeing that Levin was completely won over.

'Yes,' Levin replied pensively, 'an extraordinary woman! Not just her intelligence, but her heart. I'm terribly sorry for her!'

'God grant it will all be settled soon now. Well, so don't go judging beforehand,' said Stepan Arkadyich, opening the carriage doors. 'Good-bye. We're not going the same way.'

Never ceasing to think about Anna, about all those most simple conversations he had had with her, and at the same time remembering

* That the ice is broken.

all the details of her facial expression, entering more and more into her situation and pitying her, Levin arrived at home.

At home Kuzma told Levin that Katerina Alexandrovna was well, that her sisters had left her only recently, and handed him two letters. Levin read them right there in the front hall, so as not to be distracted later. One was from his steward, Sokolov. Sokolov wrote that it was impossible to sell the wheat, that the offer was only five and a half roubles, and there was nowhere else to get money. The other letter was from his sister. She reproached him for still not having taken care of her business.

'So we'll sell it for five-fifty, since they won't pay more.' Levin resolved the first question at once, with extraordinary ease, though it had seemed so difficult to him before. 'It's amazing how all one's time is taken up here,' he thought about the second letter. He felt guilty before his sister for still not having done what she had asked him to do. 'Again today I didn't go to court, but today I really had no time.' And, having decided that he would do it the next day without fail, he went to his wife. On his way, Levin quickly ran through the whole day in his memory. The day's events were all conversations: conversations he had listened to and taken part in. They had all been about subjects which he, had he been alone and in the country, would never have bothered with, but here they were very interesting. And all the conversations had been nice; only in two places had they not been so nice. One was what he had said about the pike, the other that there was something *not right* in the tender pity he felt for Anna.

Levin found his wife sad and bored. The dinner of the three sisters had gone very cheerfully, but afterwards they had waited and waited for him, they had all became bored, the sisters had gone home, and she had been left alone.

'Well, and what did you do?' she asked, looking into his eyes, which somehow had a peculiarly suspicious shine. But, so as not to hinder his telling her everything, she hid her attentiveness and listened with an approving smile as he told her how he had spent his evening.

'Well, I was very glad that I met Vronsky. I felt very easy and simple with him. You see, now I shall try never to meet him again, but since that awkwardness is over . . .' he said and, recalling that, *trying never to meet him again*, he had at once gone to see Anna, he blushed. 'We go around saying that the people drink; I don't know who drinks more, the people or our own class; the people at least drink on feast days, but . . .'

But Kitty was not interested in his thoughts about the people drinking. She had seen him blush and wished to know why.

'Well, and where did you go after that?'

'Stiva was terribly insistent on going to see Anna Arkadyevna.'

Having said that, Levin blushed still more, and his doubts about whether he had done a good or a bad thing by going to see Anna were finally resolved. He now knew that he should not have done it.

Kitty's eyes opened especially wide and flashed at the name of Anna, but with effort she concealed her agitation and deceived him.

'Ah!' was all she said.

'You surely won't be angry that I went. Stiva asked me to, and Dolly also wanted it,' Levin continued.

'Oh, no,' she said, but he saw the effort in her eyes, which boded him no good.

'She's a very nice, a very, very pitiful and good woman,' he said, telling her about Anna, her occupations, and what she had asked him to tell her.

'Yes, to be sure, she's very pitiful,' said Kitty, when he had finished. 'Who was your letter from?'

He told her and, believing in her calm tone, went to undress.

Coming back, he found Kitty in the same armchair. When he went up to her, she looked at him and burst into tears.

'What is it? What is it?' he asked, already knowing *what*.

'You've fallen in love with that nasty woman. She's bewitched you. I saw it in your eyes. Yes, yes! What can come of it? You drank at the club, drank, gambled, and then went . . . to whom? No, let's go away . . . Tomorrow I'm going away.'

It took Levin a long time to calm his wife down. When he finally did, it was only by confessing that the feeling of pity, along with the wine, had thrown him off guard and made him yield to Anna's cunning influence, and that he was going to avoid her. The one thing he confessed most sincerely of all was that, living so long in Moscow, just talking, eating and drinking, he had got befuddled. They talked till three o'clock in the morning. Only at three o'clock were they reconciled enough to be able to fall asleep.

XII

After seeing her guests off, Anna began pacing up and down the room without sitting down. Though for the whole evening (lately she had acted the same way towards all young men) she had unconsciously done everything she could to arouse a feeling of love for her in Levin, and though she knew that she had succeeded in it, as far as one could with regard to an honest, married man in one evening, and though she liked him very much (despite the sharp contrast, from a man's point of view, between Levin and Vronsky, as a woman she saw what they had in common, for which Kitty, too, had loved them both), as soon as he left the room, she stopped thinking about him.

One and only one thought relentlessly pursued her in various forms. 'If I have such an effect on others, on this loving family man, why is *he* so cold to me? . . . or not really cold, he loves me, I know that. But something new separates us now. Why was he gone all evening? He sent word with Stiva that he could not leave Yashvin and had to watch over his gambling. Is Yashvin a child? But suppose it's true. He never tells lies. But there's something else in this truth. He's glad of an occasion to show me that he has other responsibilities. I know that, I agree with it. But why prove it to me? He wants to prove to me that his love for me shouldn't hinder his freedom. But I don't need proofs, I need love. He ought to have understood all the difficulty of my life here in Moscow. Do I live? I don't live, I wait for a denouement that keeps being postponed. Again there's no answer! And Stiva says he can't go to Alexei Alexandrovich. And I can't write again. I can't do anything, start anything, change anything. I restrain myself, wait, invent amusements for myself – the Englishman's family, writing, reading – but it's all only a deception, the same morphine again. He ought to pity me,' she said, feeling tears of self-pity come to her eyes.

She heard Vronsky's impetuous ring and hastily wiped her tears, and not only wiped them but sat down by the lamp and opened the book, pretending to be calm. She had to show him that she was displeased that he had not come back as he had promised, only displeased, but in no way show him her grief and least of all her self-pity. She might have pity for herself, but not he for her. She did not want to fight, she reproached him for wanting to fight, but involuntarily she herself assumed a fighting position.

'Well, you weren't bored?' he said, coming up to her, cheerful and animated. 'What a terrible passion – gambling!'

'No, I wasn't bored, I learned long ago not to be bored. Stiva was here, and Levin.'

'Yes, they wanted to come and see you. Well, how do you like Levin?' he said, sitting beside her.

'Very much. They left not long ago. What did Yashvin do?'

'He was winning – seventeen thousand. I called him. He was just about to leave. But he went back and now he's losing again.'

'What good was your staying then?' she asked, suddenly raising her eyes to him. The expression on her face was cold and inimical. 'You told Stiva you were staying to take Yashvin away. And you left him there.'

The same expression of cold readiness for a fight also showed on his face.

'First of all, I didn't ask him to convey anything to you; second, I never tell lies. And the main thing is that I wanted to stay and so I did,' he said, frowning. 'Anna, why, why?' he said, after a moment's silence, leaning towards her and opening his hand, hoping she would put her hand in it.

She was glad of this invitation to tenderness. But some strange power of evil would not allow her to yield to her impulse, as if the conditions of the fight did not allow her to submit.

'Of course, you wanted to stay and so you did. You do whatever you like. But why do you tell that to me? Why?' she said, becoming still angrier. 'Does anyone dispute your rights? No, you want to be right, so be right.'

His hand closed, he drew back, and his face assumed a still more stubborn expression than before.

'For you it's a matter of obstinacy,' she said, looking intently at him and suddenly finding the name for that annoying expression on his face, 'precisely of obstinacy. For you it's a question of whether you are victorious over me, but for me . . .' Again she felt pity for herself and she all but wept. 'If you knew what it is for me! When I feel, as I do now, that you look at me with hostility – yes, with hostility – if you knew what that means for me! If you knew how close I am to disaster in these moments, how afraid I am, afraid of myself!' And she turned away, hiding her sobs.

'But what is this all about?' he said, horrified at the expression of her despair and, leaning towards her again, he took her hand and kissed it.

'Why? Do I look for outside amusements? Don't I avoid other women's company?'

'I should hope so!' she said.

'Well, tell me, what must I do to set you at peace? I'm ready to do anything to make you happy,' he said, moved by her despair. 'There's nothing I won't do to deliver you from such grief as now, Anna!' he said.

'Never mind, never mind!' she said. 'I myself don't know: maybe it's the lonely life, nerves . . . Well, let's not speak of it. How was the race? You haven't told me,' she asked, trying to hide her triumph at the victory, which after all was on her side.

He asked for supper and began telling her the details of the race; but in his tone, in his eyes, which grew colder and colder, she saw that he did not forgive her the victory, that the feeling of obstinacy she had fought against was there in him again. He was colder to her than before, as if he repented of having given in. And, recalling the words that had given her the victory – 'I'm close to terrible disaster and afraid of myself' – she realized that this was a dangerous weapon and that she could not use it a second time. She felt that alongside the love that bound them, there had settled between them an evil spirit of some sort of struggle, which she could not drive out of his heart and still less out of her own.

XIII

There are no conditions to which a person cannot grow accustomed, especially if he sees that *everyone* around him lives in the same way. Levin would not have believed three months earlier that he could fall peacefully asleep in circumstances such as he was in now; that, living an aimless, senseless life, a life also beyond his means, after drunkenness (he could not call what had happened at the club by any other name), an awkward friendliness shown to a man with whom his wife had once been in love, and a still more awkward visit to a woman who could be called nothing other than fallen, and having been attracted to that woman, thus upsetting his wife – that in such circumstances he could fall peacefully asleep. But under the influence of fatigue, a sleepless night and the wine he had drunk, he slept soundly and peacefully.

At five o'clock he was awakened by the creak of an opening door. He sat up and looked around. Kitty was not in bed beside him. But there was a light moving behind the partition, and he heard her steps.

'What? . . . What is it?' he asked, half awake. 'Kitty! What is it?'

'Nothing,' she said, coming from behind the partition with a candle in her hand. 'Nothing. I wasn't feeling well,' she said, smiling with an especially sweet and meaningful smile.

'What? It's starting? Is it starting?' he said fearfully. 'We must send . . .' And he hastily began to get dressed.

'No, no,' she said, smiling and holding him back. 'It's probably nothing. I just felt slightly unwell. But it's over now.'

And, coming to the bed, she put out the candle, lay down and was quiet. Though he was suspicious of that quietness, as if she were holding her breath, and most of all of the expression of special tenderness and excitement with which she had said 'Nothing' to him, as she came from behind the partition, he was so sleepy that he dozed off at once. Only later did he remember the quietness of her breathing and understand what had been going on in her dear, sweet soul while she lay beside him, without stirring, awaiting the greatest event in a woman's life. At seven o'clock he was awakened by the touch of her hand on his shoulder and a soft whisper. It was as if she were struggling between being sorry to awaken him and the wish to speak to him.

'Kostya, don't be frightened. It's nothing. But I think . . . We must send for Lizaveta Petrovna.'

The candle was burning again. She was sitting on the bed holding her knitting, which she had busied herself with during the last few days.

'Please don't be frightened, it's nothing. I'm not afraid at all,' she said, seeing his frightened face, and she pressed his hand to her breast, then to her lips.

He hastily jumped out of bed, unaware of himself and not taking his eyes off her, put on his dressing gown, and stood there, still looking at her. He had to go, but he could not tear himself from her eyes. Not that he did not love her face and know her expression, her gaze, but he had never seen her like that. When he remembered how upset she had been yesterday, how vile and horrible he appeared to himself before her as she was now! Her flushed face, surrounded by soft hair coming from under her night-cap, shone with joy and resolution.

However little unnaturalness and conventionality there was in Kitty's character generally, Levin was still struck by what was uncovered to him now, when all the veils were suddenly taken away and the very core of her soul shone in her eyes. And in that simplicity and nakedness she, the very one he loved, was still more visible. She looked at him and smiled; but suddenly her eyebrows twitched, she raised her head and, quickly going up to him, took his hand and pressed all of herself to him, so that he could feel her hot breath on him. She was suffering and seemed to be complaining to him of her suffering. And by habit, in the first moment, he thought that he was to blame. But there was a tenderness in her eyes that said she not only did not reproach him but loved him for these sufferings. 'If it's not I, then who is to blame for this?' he thought involuntarily, looking for the one to blame in order to punish him; but there was no one to blame. No one was to blame, but then was it not possible simply to help her, to free her? But that, too, was impossible, was not needed. She suffered, complained and yet triumphed in these sufferings, and rejoiced in them, and loved them. He saw that something beautiful was being accomplished in her soul, but what – he could not understand. It was above his understanding.

'I've sent for mama. And you go quickly for Lizaveta Petrovna . . . Kostya! . . . Never mind, it's over.'

She moved away from him and rang the bell.

'Well, go now. Pasha's coming. I'm all right.'

And with surprise Levin saw her take up the knitting she had brought during the night and begin to knit again.

As he was going out of one door, he heard the maid come in the other. He stopped in the doorway and heard Kitty give detailed orders to the maid and help her to start moving the bed.

He got dressed and, while the horse was being harnessed, since there were no cabs yet, again ran to the bedroom, not on tiptoe but on wings, as it seemed to him. Two maids with a preoccupied air were moving something in the bedroom. Kitty was walking and knitting, quickly throwing over the stitches as she gave orders.

'I'm going for the doctor now. They've sent for Lizaveta Petrovna, but I'll call there, too. Do we need anything else? Ah, yes, shall I send for Dolly?'

She looked at him, obviously not listening to what he was saying.

'Yes, yes. Go, go,' she said quickly, frowning and waving her hand at him.

He was going into the drawing room when he suddenly heard a pitiful, instantly fading moan from the bedroom. He stopped and for a long time could not understand.

'Yes, it's she,' he said to himself and, clutching his head, he ran down the stairs.

'Lord, have mercy, forgive us, help us!' he repeated words that somehow suddenly came to his lips. And he, an unbeliever, repeated these words not just with his lips. Now, in that moment, he knew that neither all his doubts, nor the impossibility he knew in himself of believing by means of reason, hindered him in the least from addressing God. It all blew off his soul like dust. To whom was he to turn if not to Him in whose hands he felt himself, his soul and his love to be?

The horse was still not ready, but feeling in himself a special straining of physical powers and of attention to what he was going to do, so as not to lose a single minute, he started on foot without waiting for the horse, telling Kuzma to catch up with him.

At the corner he met a speeding night cab. In the small sleigh sat Lizaveta Petrovna in a velvet cloak, with a kerchief wrapped round her head. 'Thank God, thank God,' he said, recognizing with delight her small blond face, which now wore an especially serious, even stern, expression. He ran back alongside her without telling the driver to stop.

'So it's been about two hours? Not more?' she asked. 'You'll find Pyotr Dmitrich, only don't rush him. And get some opium at the apothecary's.'

'So you think it may be all right? Lord have mercy and help us!' said Levin, seeing his horse come through the gate. Jumping into the sleigh beside Kuzma, he told him to go to the doctor's.

XIV

The doctor was not up yet, and the footman said he 'went to bed late and was not to be awakened, but would be getting up soon'. The footman was cleaning the lamp-glasses and seemed to be very absorbed in it. His attention to the glasses and indifference to what was happening at home at first astounded Levin, but, thinking better, he realized at once that no one knew or was obliged to know his feelings, and that his actions had to be all the more calm, thoughtful and resolute, so as to break through this wall of indifference and achieve his goal. 'Don't rush and don't overlook anything,' Levin said to himself, feeling a greater and greater upsurge of physical strength and attentiveness to all he was going to do.

Having learned that the doctor was not up yet, Levin, out of all the plans he could think of, settled on the following: Kuzma would go with a note to another doctor; he himself would go to the pharmacy to get the opium, and if, when he came back, the doctor was still not up, he would bribe the footman or, if he refused, awaken the doctor by force at all costs.

At the apothecary's a lean dispenser, with the same indifference with which the footman had cleaned the glasses, was compressing powders into pills for a waiting coachman and refused him the opium. Trying not to hurry or become angry, Levin began persuading him, giving him the names of the doctor and the midwife and explaining what the opium was needed for. The dispenser asked in German for advice about providing the medicine and, getting approval from behind a partition, took out a bottle and a funnel, slowly poured from the big bottle into a small one, stuck on a label, sealed it, despite Levin's requests that he not do so, and also wanted to wrap it up. That was more than Levin could bear; he resolutely tore the bottle from his hands and ran out through the big glass door. The doctor was not up yet, and the footman, now occupied with spreading a carpet, refused to wake him. Levin unhurriedly took out a ten-rouble note and, articulating the words slowly, yet wasting no time, handed him the note and explained that Pyotr Dmitrich (how great and significant the previously unimportant Pyotr Dmitrich now seemed to Levin!) had promised to come at any time, that he would certainly not be angry, and therefore he must wake him at once.

The footman consented and went upstairs, inviting Levin into the consulting room.

Through the door Levin could hear the doctor coughing, walking about, washing and saying something. Some three minutes passed; to Levin they seemed more like an hour. He could not wait any longer.

'Pyotr Dmitrich, Pyotr Dmitrich!' he said in a pleading voice through the open door. 'For God's sake, forgive me. Receive me as you are. It's already been more than two hours.'

'Coming, coming!' replied the voice, and Levin was amazed to hear the doctor chuckle as he said it.

'For one little moment . . .'

'Coming!'

Two more minutes went by while the doctor put his boots on, and another two minutes while he put his clothes on and combed his hair.

'Pyotr Dmitrich!' Levin began again in a pitiful voice; but just then the doctor came out, dressed and combed. 'These people have no shame,' thought Levin, 'combing his hair while we perish!'

'Good morning!' the doctor said to him, holding out his hand, as if teasing him with his calmness. 'Don't be in a hurry. Well, sir?'

Trying to be as thorough as possible, Levin began to give all the unnecessary details of his wife's condition, constantly interrupting his story with requests that the doctor come with him at once.

'Don't you be in a hurry. You see, I'm probably not even needed, but I promised and so I'll come if you like. But there's no hurry. Sit down, please. Would you care for some coffee?'

Levin looked at him, asking with his eyes whether he was laughing at him. But the doctor never even thought of laughing.

'I know, sir, I know,' the doctor said, smiling, 'I'm a family man myself; but in these moments we husbands are the most pathetic people. I have a patient whose husband always runs out to the stable on such occasions.'

'But what do you think, Pyotr Dmitrich? Do you think it may end well?'

'All the evidence points to a good outcome.'

'Then you'll come now?' said Levin, looking spitefully at the servant who brought the coffee.

'In about an hour.'

'No, for God's sake!'

'Well, let me have some coffee first.'

The doctor began on his coffee. The two were silent.

'The Turks are certainly taking a beating, though. Did you read yesterday's dispatch?' the doctor said, chewing his roll.

'No, I can't stand it!' said Levin, jumping up. 'So you'll be there in a quarter of an hour?'

'In half an hour.'

'Word of honour?'

When Levin returned home, he drove up at the same time as the princess, and together they went to the bedroom door. There were tears in the princess's eyes and her hands were trembling. Seeing Levin, she embraced him and wept.

'What news, darling Lizaveta Petrovna?' she said, seizing the hand of Lizaveta Petrovna, who came out to meet them with a radiant and preoccupied face.

'It's going well,' she said. 'Persuade her to lie down. It will be easier.'

From the moment he had woken up and realized what was happening, Levin had prepared himself to endure what awaited him, without reflecting, without anticipating, firmly locking up all his thoughts and feelings, without upsetting his wife, but, on the contrary, calming and supporting her. Not allowing himself even to think of what would happen, of how it would end, going by his inquiries about how long it usually lasts, Levin had prepared himself in his imagination to endure and keep his heart under control for some five hours, and that seemed possible to him. But when he came back from the doctor's and again saw her sufferings, he began to repeat more and more often: 'Lord, forgive us and help us,' to sigh and lift up his eyes, and he was afraid that he would not hold out, that he would burst into tears or run away. So tormenting it was for him. And only one hour had passed.

But after that hour another hour passed, two, three, all five hours that he had set for himself as the furthest limit of his endurance, and the situation was still the same; and he still endured, because there was nothing else he could do, thinking every moment that he had reached the final limit of endurance and that his heart was about to break from compassion.

But more minutes passed, hours and more hours, and his feelings of suffering and dread grew and became more intense.

All the ordinary circumstances of life, without which nothing could be imagined, ceased to exist for Levin. He lost awareness of time. Sometimes minutes – those minutes when she called him to her and he held her sweaty hand, which now pressed his with extraordinary force, now pushed him away – seemed like hours to him, and sometimes hours seemed like minutes. He was surprised when Lizaveta Petrovna asked him to light a candle behind the screen, and he discovered that it was already five o'clock in the evening. If he had been told that it was now only ten o'clock in the morning, he would have been no more surprised. Where he had been during that time he did not know, any more than he knew when things had happened. He saw her burning face, bewildered and suffering, then smiling and comforting him. He saw the princess, red, tense, her grey hair uncurled, biting her lips in an effort to hide her tears; he saw Dolly, and the doctor smoking fat cigarettes, and Lizaveta Petrovna with her firm, resolute and comforting face, and the old prince pacing the reception room with a frown. But how they all came and went, and where they were, he did not know. The princess was now with the doctor in the bedroom, now in the study where a laid table had appeared; then it was not she but Dolly. Then Levin remembered being sent somewhere. Once he was sent to move a table and a sofa. He did it zealously, thinking it was for her, and only later learned that he had prepared his own bed. Then he was sent to the study to ask the doctor something. The doctor answered and then began talking about the disorders in the Duma. Then he was sent to the princess's bedroom to fetch an icon in a gilded silver casing, and with the princess's old maid he climbed up to take it from the top of a cabinet and broke the icon lamp; the princess's maid comforted him about his wife and the icon lamp, and he brought the icon and put it by Kitty's head, carefully tucking it behind the pillow. But where, when, and why all this happened, he did not know. Nor did he know why the princess took him by the hand and, gazing pitifully at him, asked him to calm down, why Dolly kept telling him to eat something and leading him out of the room, and even the doctor looked at him gravely and commiseratingly and offered him some drops.

He knew and felt only that what was being accomplished was similar to what had been accomplished a year ago in a hotel in a provincial capital, on the deathbed of his brother Nikolai. But that had been grief and this was joy. But that grief and this joy were equally outside all ordinary circumstances of life, were like holes in this ordinary life, through which something higher showed. And just as painful, as tormenting in its coming, was what was now being accomplished; and just as inconceivably, in contemplating this higher thing, the soul rose to such heights as it had never known before, where reason was no longer able to overtake it.

'Lord, forgive us and help us,' he constantly repeated to himself, feeling, in spite of so long and seemingly so complete an estrangement, that he was turning to God just as trustfully and simply as in his childhood and early youth.

All this time he had two separate moods. One away from her presence, with the doctor, who smoked one fat cigarette after another, putting them out against the edge of the full ashtray, with Dolly and the prince, where they talked of dinner, politics, Marya Petrovna's illness, where Levin would suddenly forget what was happening for a moment and feel as if he were waking up; and the other in her presence, by her head, where his heart was ready to burst from compassion but would not burst, and he prayed to God without ceasing. And each time he was brought out of momentary oblivion by a cry reaching him from the bedroom, he fell into the same strange delusion that had come over him at the first moment; each time, hearing a cry, he jumped up and ran to vindicate himself, remembering on the way that he was not to blame, and then he longed to protect and help her. But, looking at her, he again saw that it was impossible to help, and he was horrified and said: 'Lord, forgive us and help us.' And the more time that passed, the stronger the two moods became: the calmer he became, even forgetting her completely, away from her presence, and the more tormenting became her sufferings and his own helplessness before them. He would jump up, wishing to run away somewhere, and run to her.

Sometimes, when she called him again and again, he blamed her. But seeing her obedient, smiling face and hearing the words, 'I've worn you out,' he blamed God, then, remembering God, he at once asked Him to forgive and have mercy.

XV

He did not know whether it was late or early. The candles were all burning low. Dolly had just come to the study to suggest that the doctor lie down. Levin sat there listening to the doctor tell about a quack mesmerist and watching the ashes of his cigarette. It was a period of rest and he had become oblivious. He had entirely forgotten what was going on now. He listened to the doctor's story and understood it. Suddenly there was a scream unlike anything he had ever heard. The scream was so terrible that Levin did not even jump up, but, holding his breath, gave the doctor a frightened, questioning look. The doctor cocked his head to one side, listened, and smiled approvingly. It was all so extraordinary that nothing any longer astonished Levin: 'Probably it should be so,' he thought and went on sitting. Whose scream was it? He jumped up, ran on tiptoe to the bedroom, went round Lizaveta Petrovna and the princess, and stood in his place at the head of the bed. The screaming had ceased, but something was changed now. What – he did not see or understand, nor did he want to see and understand. But he saw it from Lizaveta Petrovna's face: her face was stern and pale and still just as resolute, though her jaws twitched a little and her eyes were fixed on Kitty. Kitty's burning, tormented face, with a strand of hair stuck to her sweaty forehead, was turned to him and sought his eyes. Her raised hands asked for his. Seizing his hands in her sweaty hands, she started pressing them to her face.

'Don't leave, don't leave! I'm not afraid, I'm not afraid!' she spoke quickly. 'Mama, take my earrings. They bother me. You're not afraid? Soon, Lizaveta Petrovna, soon . . .'

She spoke quickly, quickly, and tried to smile. But suddenly her face became distorted, and she pushed him away from her.

'No, it's terrible! I'll die, I'll die! Go, go!' she cried, and again came that scream that was unlike anything in the world.

Levin clutched his head and ran out of the room.

'Never mind, never mind, it's all right!' Dolly said after him.

But whatever they said, he knew that all was now lost. Leaning his head against the doorpost, he stood in the next room and heard a shrieking and howling such as he had never heard before, and he knew that these cries were coming from what had once been Kitty. He had long ceased wishing for the child. He now hated this child. He did not even wish for her to live now; he only wished for an end to this terrible suffering.

'Doctor! What is it? What is it? My God!' he said, seizing the doctor by the arm as he came in.

'It's nearly over,' said the doctor. And the doctor's face was so serious as he said it that Levin understood this 'nearly over' to mean she was dying.

Forgetting himself, he ran into the bedroom. The first thing he saw was Lizaveta Petrovna's face. It was still more stern and frowning. Kitty's face was not there. In place of it, where it used to be, was something dreadful both in its strained look and in the sound that came from it. He leaned his head against the wooden bedstead, feeling that his heart was bursting. The terrible screaming would not stop, it became still more terrible and then, as if reaching the final limit of the terrible, it suddenly stopped. Levin did not believe his ears, but there could be no doubt: the screaming stopped, and there was a quiet stirring, a rustle and quick breathing, and her faltering, alive, gentle and happy voice softly said: 'It's over.'

He raised his head. Her arms resting strengthlessly on the blanket, remarkably beautiful and quiet, she silently looked at him and tried but was unable to smile.

And suddenly from that mysterious and terrible, unearthly world in which he had lived for those twenty-two hours, Levin felt himself instantly transported into the former, ordinary world, but radiant now with such a new light of happiness that he could not bear it. The taut strings all snapped. Sobs and tears of joy, which he could never have foreseen, rose in him with such force, heaving his whole body, that for a long time they prevented him from speaking.

Falling on his knees beside the bed, he held his wife's hand to his lips, kissing it, and the hand responded to his kisses with a weak movement of the fingers. And meanwhile, there at the foot of the bed, in the deft hands of Lizaveta Petrovna, like a small flame over a lamp, wavered the life of a human being who had never existed before and who, with the same right, with the same importance for itself, would live and produce its own kind.

'Alive! Alive! And it's a boy! Don't worry!' Levin heard the voice of Lizaveta Petrovna, who was slapping the baby's back with a trembling hand.

'Mama, is it true?' said Kitty's voice.

She was answered only by the princess's sobs.

And amidst the silence, as the indubitable reply to the mother's question, a voice was heard, quite different from all the subdued voices speaking in the room. It was the bold, brazen cry, not intent on understanding anything, of a new human being who had appeared incomprehensibly from somewhere.

Earlier, if Levin had been told that Kitty had died and that he had died with her, and that they had angels for children, and that God was there before them – none of it would have surprised him; but now, having come back to the world of reality, he made great mental efforts to understand that she was alive and well, and that the being shrieking so desperately was his son. Kitty was alive, her sufferings were over. And he was inexpressibly happy. That he understood, and in that he was fully happy. But the baby? Whence, why, and who was he? . . . He simply could not understand, could not get accustomed to this thought. It seemed to him something superfluous, an over-abundance, and for a long time he could not get used to it.

XVI

Towards ten o'clock the old prince, Sergei Ivanovich and Stepan Arkadyich were sitting at Levin's and, after talking about the new mother, had begun talking about other things as well. Levin listened to their talk and, involuntarily recalling the past, the way things had been before that morning, also recalled himself as he had been yesterday before it all. It was as if a hundred years had passed since then. He felt himself on some inaccessible height, from which he tried to climb down so as not to offend those with whom he was talking. He talked and never stopped thinking about his wife, about the details of her present condition, and about his son, trying to get used to the thought of his existence. The whole world of women, which had acquired a new, previously unknown significance for him after his marriage, now rose so high in his estimation that he was unable to encompass it in imagination. He listened to the conversation about yesterday's dinner at the club and thought, 'What's going on with her now? Is she sleeping? How is she? What is she thinking about? Is our son Dmitri crying?' And in the middle of the conversation, in the middle of a phrase, he jumped up and started out of the room.

'Send me word if she can be seen,' said the prince.

'Very well, one moment,' replied Levin and without pausing he went to her room.

She was not sleeping but was talking softly with her mother, making plans for the future christening.

Tidied up, her hair combed, in a fancy cap trimmed with something light blue, her arms on top of the blanket, she was lying on her back, and her eyes, meeting his, drew him to her. Her eyes, bright to begin with, brightened still more as he approached her. In her face there was the same change from earthly to unearthly that occurs in the faces of the dead; but there it is a farewell, here it was a meeting. Again an emotion like that which he had experienced at the moment of the birth welled up in his heart. She took his hand and asked whether he had slept. He was unable to respond and kept turning away, certain of his own weakness.

'And I dozed off, Kostya!' she said to him. 'And I feel so good now.'

She was looking at him, but suddenly her expression changed.

'Give him to me,' she said, hearing the baby squealing. 'Give him here, Lizaveta Petrovna, and he can look at him, too.'

'Well, there, let papa have a look,' said Lizaveta Petrovna, picking up and bringing to him something red, strange and wobbly. 'Wait, we'll tidy ourselves up first.' And Lizaveta Petrovna put this wobbly and red thing on the bed, began unwrapping and wrapping the baby, lifting and turning him with one finger and dusting him with something.

Levin, gazing at this tiny, pathetic being, made vain efforts to find some trace of paternal feeling in his soul. All he felt for him was squeamishness. But when he saw him naked, and glimpsed the thin, thin little arms, the legs, saffron-coloured, with toes and even with a big toe different from the others, and when he saw Lizaveta Petrovna press down those little arms, which kept popping up like soft springs, confining them in the linen clothes, he was overcome with such pity for this being, and such fear that she might harm him, that he held back her hand.

Lizaveta Petrovna laughed.

'Don't be afraid, don't be afraid!'

When the baby was tidied up and turned into a stiff little doll, Lizaveta Petrovna rocked him once, as if proud of her work, and drew back so that Levin could see his son in all his beauty.

Kitty, not taking her eyes away, looked sidelong in the same direction.

'Give him here, give him here!' she said and even rose slightly.

'No, no, Katerina Alexandrovna, you mustn't make such movements! Wait, I'll bring him. Here, we'll show papa what a fine fellow we are!'

And Lizaveta Petrovna held out to Levin on one hand (the other merely propping the unsteady head with its fingers) this strange, wobbly, red being whose head was hidden behind the edge of the swaddling-clothes. There was also a nose, crossed eyes and smacking lips.

'A beautiful baby!' said Lizaveta Petrovna.

Levin sighed with dismay. This beautiful baby inspired only a feeling of squeamishness and pity in him. It was not at all the feeling he had expected.

He turned away while Lizaveta Petrovna was putting him to the unaccustomed breast.

Suddenly laughter made him raise his head. It was Kitty laughing. The baby had taken the breast.

'Well, enough, enough!' said Lizaveta Petrovna, but Kitty would not let go of him. The baby fell asleep in her arms.

'Look now,' said Kitty, turning the baby towards him so that he could see him. The old-looking face suddenly wrinkled still more, and the baby sneezed.

Smiling and barely keeping back tears of tenderness, Levin kissed his wife and left the darkened room.

What he felt for this small being was not at all what he had expected. There was nothing happy or joyful in this feeling; on the contrary, there was a new tormenting fear. There was an awareness of a new region of vulnerability. And this awareness was so tormenting at first, the fear lest this helpless being should suffer was so strong, that because of it he scarcely noticed the strange feeling of senseless joy and even pride he had experienced when the baby sneezed.

XVII

Stepan Arkadyich's affairs were in a bad state.

The money for two-thirds of the wood had already been run through, and he had taken from the merchant, after a discount of ten per cent, almost all the money for the final third. The merchant would not give more, especially since that winter Darya Alexandrovna, claiming a direct right to her own fortune for the first time, had refused to put her signature to the receipt of the money for the last third of the wood. His entire salary went on household expenses and the paying of small, ever present debts. They had no money at all.

This was unpleasant, awkward, and could not go on, in Stepan Arkadyich's opinion. The reason for it, to his mind, was that his salary was too small. The post he occupied had obviously been very good five years ago, but now it was no longer so. Petrov, a bank director, earned twelve thousand; Sventitsky, a company director, earned seventeen thousand; Mitin, founder of a bank, earned fifty thousand. 'I evidently fell asleep and they forgot me,' Stepan Arkadyich thought to himself. And he began to keep his ears and eyes open, and by the end of winter had picked out a very good post and mounted an attack on it, first from Moscow, through aunts, uncles, friends, and then, in the spring, as the affair ripened, he himself went to Petersburg. This was one of those cushy bribery posts, with salaries ranging from a thousand to fifty thousand a year, which had now become more numerous than before; it was a post as member of the commission of the United Agency for Mutual Credit Balance of the Southern Railway Lines and Banking Institutions.[19] This post, like all such posts, called for such vast knowledge and energy as could hardly be united in one person. And since the person in whom all these qualities could be united did not exist, it would be better in any case if the post were occupied by an honest man rather than a dishonest one. And Stepan Arkadyich was not only an honest man (without emphasis), but was also an hónest man (with emphasis), with that special significance which the word has in Moscow, when they say: an hónest politician, an hónest writer, an hónest journal, an hônest institution, an hónest tendency – which signifies not only that the man or institution is not dishonest, but that they are capable on occasion of sticking a pin into the government. Stepan Arkadyich belonged to those circles in Moscow in which this word had been introduced, was considered an hónest man in them, and therefore had more rights to this post than others did.

The post brought from seven to ten thousand a year, and Oblonsky could occupy it without leaving his government post. It depended on two ministers, one lady and two Jews; and, though they had been primed already, Stepan Arkadyich still had to see them all in Petersburg. Besides that, Stepan Arkadyich had promised his sister Anna to get a decisive answer from Karenin about the divorce. And so, having begged fifty roubles from Dolly, he went to Petersburg.

Sitting in Karenin's study and listening to his proposal on the causes of the bad state of Russian finances, Stepan Arkadyich only waited for the moment when he would finish, so that he could speak about his own affairs and about Anna.

'Yes, that's very true,' he said, when Alexei Alexandrovich, taking off his pince-nez, without which he was now unable to read, looked questioningly at his former brother-in-law, 'it's very true in detail, but all the same the principle of our time is freedom.'

'Yes, but I put forward another principle that embraces the principle of freedom,' said Alexei Alexandrovich, emphasizing the word 'embraces' and putting his pince-nez on again in order to reread to his listener the passage where that very thing was stated.

And, looking through the beautifully written, huge-margined manuscript, Alexei Alexandrovich reread the persuasive passage.

'I oppose systems of protection, not for the sake of the profit of private persons, but for the common good – for lower and upper classes equally,' he said, looking at Oblonsky over his pince-nez. 'But *they* cannot understand it, *they* are concerned only with personal interest and have a passion for phrases.'

Stepan Arkadyich knew that when Karenin started talking about what *they* did and thought, the same ones who did not want to accept his proposals and were the cause of all the evil in Russia, it meant that he was near the end; and therefore he now willingly renounced the principle of freedom and fully agreed with him. Alexei Alexandrovich fell silent, thoughtfully leafing through his manuscript.

'Ah, by the way,' said Stepan Arkadyich, 'I wanted to ask you, when you happen to see Pomorsky, to mention to him that I would like very much to get that vacant post as member of the commission of the United Agency for Mutual Credit Balance of the Southern Railway Lines.'

Stepan Arkadyich had become accustomed to the title of this post so near his heart and pronounced it quickly, without making a mistake.

Alexei Alexandrovich inquired into the activity of this new commission and fell to thinking. He was trying to make out whether there was anything in the activity of this commission that was contrary to his proposals. But since the activity of this new institution was extremely complex, and his proposals embraced an extremely vast area, he could not make it all out at once and, taking off his pince-nez, said:

'Doubtless I can speak to him. But why in fact do you want to get that post?'

'The salary's good, as much as nine thousand, and my means . . .'

'Nine thousand,' Alexei Alexandrovich repeated and frowned. The high figure of the salary reminded him that this aspect of Stepan Arkadyich's intended activity was contrary to the main sense of his proposals, which always tended towards economy.

'I find, and I've written a memorandum about it, that in our time these huge salaries are signs of the false economic *assiette** of our administration.'

'But what do you want?' said Stepan Arkadyich. 'Well, suppose a bank director gets ten thousand – but he deserves it. Or an engineer gets twenty thousand. It's a living matter, like it or not!'

'I think that a salary is payment for value received, and it should be subject to the law of supply and demand. And if the appointed salary departs from that law, as when I see two engineers graduate from an institute, both equally capable and knowledgeable, and one gets forty thousand and the other contents himself with two, or when lawyers or

* Policy.

hussars who have no special professional knowledge are made directors of banking companies, I conclude that salaries are appointed not by the law of supply and demand but directly by personal influence. And there is an abuse here, important in itself and with an adverse effect on government functions. I believe . . .'

Stepan Arkadyich hastened to interrupt his brother-in-law.

'Yes, but you must agree that a new, unquestionably useful institution is being opened. Like it or not, it's a living matter! They especially value things being done hónestly,' Stepan Arkadyich said with emphasis.

But the Moscow meaning of 'honesty' was incomprehensible to Alexei Alexandrovich.

'Honesty is merely a negative quality,' he said.

'But you'll do me a great favour in any case,' Stepan Arkadyich said, 'if you mention it to Pomorsky. Just in passing . . .'

'Though it depends more on Bolgarinov, I think,' said Alexei Alexandrovich.

'Bolgarinov, for his part, is in complete agreement,' Stepan Arkadyich said, blushing.

Stepan Arkadyich blushed at the mention of Bolgarinov because he had called on the Jew Bolgarinov that same morning, and the visit had left him with an unpleasant memory. Stepan Arkadyich was firmly convinced that the business he wanted to serve was new, alive and honest; but that morning, when Bolgarinov, obviously on purpose, had made him wait for two hours with the other petitioners in the anteroom, he had suddenly felt awkward.

Whether it was that he, Prince Oblonsky, a descendant of Rurik,[20] had waited for two hours in a Jew's anteroom, or that for the first time in his life he was not following the example of his ancestors by serving the state but was setting out on a new path, in any case he had felt very awkward. During those two hours of waiting at Bolgarinov's, Stepan Arkadyich had pertly strutted about the anteroom, smoothing his side-whiskers, striking up conversations with the other petitioners, and devising a pun he intended to tell about how he had had much ajew with a Jew, at pains all the while to conceal his feelings from everyone else and even from himself.

But all that time he had felt vexed and awkward without knowing why: whether because nothing came of the pun, 'I had *much a-jew* with *a Jew*,' or for some other reason. When Bolgarinov had finally received him with the utmost courtesy, obviously triumphant at his humiliation, and all but refused him, Stepan Arkadyich had hastened to forget it as soon as he could. And remembering it only now, he blushed.

XVIII

'Now there's another matter, and you know which one. About Anna,' said Stepan Arkadyich, after pausing briefly to shake off the unpleasant impression.

The moment Oblonsky pronounced Anna's name, Alexei Alexandrovich's face changed completely: instead of the former animation, it expressed fatigue and deadness.

'What in fact do you want from me, sir?' he said, turning in his chair and snapping shut his pince-nez.

'A decision, some sort of decision, Alexei Alexandrovich. I am addressing you now' (Stepan Arkadyich was going to say 'not as an offended husband' but, for fear of thereby ruining everything, he replaced the phrase) 'not as a statesman' (which came out inappropriately) 'but simply as a man, a good man and a Christian. You must take pity on her,' he said.

'But for what, in fact?' Karenin said softly.

'Yes, take pity on her. If you had seen her as I have – I've spent the whole winter with her – you would take pity on her. Her situation is awful, simply awful.'

'It seems to me,' Alexei Alexandrovich replied in a higher, almost shrieking voice, 'that Anna Arkadyevna has everything she herself wanted.'

'Ah, Alexei Alexandrovich, for God's sake, let's not have any recriminations! What's past is past, and you know what she wishes and is waiting for – a divorce.'

'But I took it that Anna Arkadyevna renounced divorce in case I demanded a pledge that our son be left with me. I replied in that sense and thought the matter was ended. And I consider that it is ended,' Alexei Alexandrovich shrieked.

'For God's sake, don't get angry,' said Stepan Arkadyich, touching his brother-in-law's knee. 'The matter is not ended. If you will allow me to recapitulate, the matter stood like this: when you parted, you were great, you could not have been more magnanimous; you granted her everything – freedom, and even a divorce. She appreciated that. Don't think she didn't. She precisely appreciated it. So much so that in those first moments, feeling herself guilty before you, she did not and could not think it all over. She renounced everything. But reality and time have shown her that her situation is tormenting and impossible.'

'Anna Arkadyevna's life cannot interest me,' Alexei Alexandrovich interrupted, raising his eyebrows.

'Allow me not to believe that,' Stepan Arkadyich objected softly. 'Her situation is tormenting to her and that without the slightest profit to anyone. She has deserved it, you will say. She knows that and asks nothing of you; she says directly that she dares not ask anything. But I, and all the family, all those who love her, beseech you. Why must she suffer? Who is the better for it?'

'Excuse me, sir, but you seem to be putting me in the position of the accused,' said Alexei Alexandrovich.

'No, no, not at all. Do understand me,' said Stepan Arkadyich, touching his hand, as if he were sure that this touching would soften his brother-in-law. 'I'm saying only one thing: her situation is tormenting, and you can relieve it, and you won't lose anything. I'll arrange it all for you so that you won't even notice. You did promise.'

'The promise was given earlier. And I thought that the question of our son had settled the matter. Besides, I hoped that Anna Arkadyevna would be magnanimous enough . . .' Pale, his lips trembling, Alexei Alexandrovich barely got the words out.

'She leaves it all to your magnanimity. She begs, she beseeches you for one thing – to bring her out of the impossible situation in which she finds herself. She no longer asks to have the boy. Alexei Alexandrovich, you are a kind man. Put yourself in her situation for a moment. The question of divorce in her situation is for her a question of life and death. If you hadn't given your promise earlier, she would have reconciled herself to her situation, she would be living in the country. But you promised, she wrote to you and moved to Moscow. And now for six months she's been living in Moscow, where every meeting is like a stab in the heart, waiting each day for the decision to come. It's like keeping a man condemned to death for months with a noose around his neck, promising him maybe death, maybe mercy. Take pity on her, and then I undertake to arrange everything so that . . . *Vos scrupules** . . .'

* Your scruples.

'I'm not speaking of that, not of that . . .' Alexei Alexandrovich interrupted squeamishly. 'But I may have promised what I had no right to promise.'

'So you refuse what you promised?'

'I have never refused to do what was possible, but I would like to have time to consider how far what was promised is possible.'

'No, Alexei Alexandrovich!' Oblonsky said, jumping up. 'I won't believe it! She's as unhappy as a woman can be, and you can't deny her such a . . .'

'How far what was promised is possible. *Vous professez d'être un libre penseur.** But I, as a believer, cannot act contrary to the Christian law in such an important matter.'

'But in Christian societies, and even in ours as far as I know, divorce is permitted,' said Stepan Arkadyich. 'Divorce is also permitted by our Church. And we see . . .'

'Permitted, but not in this sense.'

'Alexei Alexandrovich, I don't recognize you,' Oblonsky said, after a silence. 'Wasn't it you (and didn't we all appreciate it?) who forgave everything and, moved precisely by Christian feeling, were ready to sacrifice everything? You yourself talked about "giving a caftan when your shirt was taken", and now . . .'

'I beg you, sir,' Alexei Alexandrovich said, pale and with a trembling jaw, in a squeaky voice, suddenly getting to his feet, 'I beg you to stop, to stop . . . this conversation.'

'Oh, no! Well, forgive me, forgive me if I've upset you,' Stepan Arkadyich said, smiling abashedly and holding out his hand, 'but in any case, as an ambassador, I have merely conveyed my message.'

Alexei Alexandrovich gave him his hand, reflected a little, and said:

'I must think it over and look for guidance. I'll give you a decisive answer the day after tomorrow,' he added, having thought of something.

* You profess to be a freethinker.

XIX

Stepan Arkadyich was about to leave when Kornei came in and announced:

'Sergei Alexeich!'

'Who is Sergei Alexeich?' Stepan Arkadyich was about to ask, but remembered at once.

'Ah, Seryozha!' he said. '"Sergei Alexeich" – I thought it was the director of some department.' And he remembered, 'Anna did ask me to see him.'

He recalled the timorous, pitiful expression with which Anna had said, as she let him go, 'Anyway, try to see him. Find out in detail where he is and who is with him. And, Stiva . . . if it's possible! Could it be possible?' Stepan Arkadyich understood what this 'if it's possible' meant – if it was possible to arrange the divorce so that the son would go to her . . . Now Stepan Arkadyich could see that there was no question of that, but anyway he was glad to see his nephew.

Alexei Alexandrovich reminded his brother-in-law that the boy never heard any mention of his mother and asked him not to say even one word about her.

'He was very ill after that meeting with his mother, which had not been an-ti-ci-pated,' said Alexei Alexandrovich. 'We even feared for his life. But sensible treatment and sea bathing in the summer restored him to health, and now, on the doctor's advice, I have sent him to school. Indeed, the influence of his comrades has had a beneficial effect on him, and he is now completely well and a good student.'

'What a fine fellow he's become! Indeed no Seryozha, but a full Sergei Alexeich!' Stepan Arkadyich said with a smile, looking at the handsome, broadly built boy in a dark-blue jacket and long trousers who briskly and casually strode into the room. The boy had a healthy and cheerful look. He bowed to his uncle as to a stranger, but, recognizing him, blushed and quickly turned away from him, as if offended or angered by something. The boy went up to his father and handed him a report of the marks he had received at school.

'Well, that's decent enough,' said his father. 'You may go.'

'He's grown thinner and taller and stopped looking like a child. He's become a real boy. I like that,' said Stepan Arkadyich. 'Do you remember me?'

The boy glanced quickly at his father.

'Yes, *mon oncle*,' he said, looking at his uncle and then looking down again.

His uncle called the boy to him and took him by the hand.

'Well, so, how are things?' he said, wishing to start talking and not knowing what to say.

The boy blushed and did not answer, but kept pulling his hand cautiously from his uncle's. As soon as Stepan Arkadyich let go of his hand, the boy, like a released bird, shot a questioning glance at his father and with quick steps walked out of the room.

It was a year since Seryozha had last seen his mother. Since then he had never heard of her again. That same year he was sent to school and came to know and love his comrades. Those dreams and memories of his mother which, after meeting her, had made him ill, no longer interested him. When they came, he tried to drive them away, considering them shameful and fit only for girls, not for a boy and a comrade. He knew that there had been a quarrel between his father and mother that had separated them, knew that he was to stay with his father, and tried to get used to the thought.

Seeing his uncle, who looked like his mother, was unpleasant for him because it called up in him those very memories that he considered shameful. It was the more unpleasant since, from the few words he had heard while waiting by the door of the study, and especially from the expression on his father's and uncle's faces, he guessed that they must have been talking about his mother. And so as not to judge his father, with whom he lived and on whom he depended, and, above all, not to give in to his sentiments, which he considered so humiliating, Seryozha tried not to look at this uncle who had come to disrupt his tranquillity and not to think about what he reminded him of.

But when Stepan Arkadyich, who followed him out, saw him on the stairs, called him back, and asked him how he spent the time between classes at school, Seryozha, away from his father's presence, got to talking with him.

'We've got a railway going now,' he said, in answer to the question. 'It's like this: two of us sit on a bench. They're the passengers. And one stands up on the same bench. And everybody else gets in harness. You can do it with hands or with belts, and they start moving through all the rooms. The doors are opened ahead of them. And it's very hard to be the conductor!'

'That's the one who's standing up?' Stepan Arkadyich asked, smiling.

'Yes, he's got to be brave and agile, especially if they stop all of a sudden or somebody falls down.'

'Yes, that's no joke,' said Stepan Arkadyich, sadly studying those animated eyes, his mother's, no longer those of a child, no longer wholly innocent. And though he had promised Alexei Alexandrovich not to speak of Anna, he could not help himself.

'Do you remember your mother?' he asked suddenly.

'No, I don't,' Seryozha said quickly and, turning bright red, looked down. And the uncle could get nowhere with him any more.

The Slav tutor found his charge on the stairway half an hour later and for a long time could not tell whether he was angry or crying.

'You must have fallen and hurt yourself?' said the tutor. 'I told you it's a dangerous game. The director must be informed.'

'Even if I did hurt myself, nobody would have noticed. That's for certain.'

'What's wrong, then?'

'Let me be! Remember, don't remember . . . What business is it of his? Why should I remember? Leave me alone!' he said, not to the tutor now, but to the whole world.

XX

Stepan Arkadyich, as always, did not idle away his time in Petersburg. In Petersburg, besides the business of his sister's divorce and the post, he had, as always, to refresh himself, as he put it, after the stuffiness of Moscow.

Moscow, in spite of its *cafés chantants* and omnibuses, was, after all, a stagnant swamp. That Stepan Arkadyich had always felt. Living in Moscow, especially around his family, he felt he was losing his spirits. When he lived in Moscow for a long time without leaving, he reached the point of worrying about his wife's bad moods and reproaches, his children's health and education, the petty concerns of his service; he even worried about having debts. But he needed only to go and stay for a while in Petersburg, in the circle to which he belonged, where people lived – precisely lived, and did not vegetate as in Moscow – and immediately all these thoughts vanished and melted away like wax before the face of fire.[21]

Wife? . . . Only that day he had been talking with Prince Chechensky. Prince Chechensky had a wife and family – grown-up boys serving as pages – and there was another illegitimate family, in which there were also children. Though the first family was good as well, Prince Chechensky felt happier in the second family. And he had brought his eldest son into the second family, and kept telling Stepan Arkadyich that he found it useful for the boy's development. What would they have said to that in Moscow?

Children? In Petersburg children did not hinder their father's life. Children were brought up in institutions, and there existed nothing like that wild idea spreading about Moscow – as with Lvov, for instance – that children should get all the luxuries of life and parents nothing but toil and care. Here they understood that a man is obliged to live for himself, as an educated person ought to live.

Service? Here the service was also not that persistent, unrewarded drudgery that it was in Moscow; here there was interest in it. An encounter, a favour, an apt word, an ability to act out various jokes – and a man's career was suddenly made, as with Briantsev, whom Stepan Arkadyich had met yesterday and who was now a leading dignitary. Such service had some interest in it.

But the Petersburg view of money matters had an especially soothing effect on Stepan Arkadyich. Bartniansky, who had run through at least fifty thousand, judging by his *train*,* had spoken a remarkable word to him about it yesterday.

In a conversation before dinner, Stepan Arkadyich had said to Bartniansky:

'It seems to me that you're close to Mordvinsky; you might do me a favour and kindly put in a word for me. There's a post I'd like to get. Member of the Agency . . .'

'Well, I won't remember it anyway . . . Only who wants to get into all these railway affairs with the Jews? . . . As you wish, but all the same it's vile!'

Stepan Arkadyich did not tell him that it was a living matter; Bartniansky would not have understood it.

'I need money, I have nothing to live on.'

* Style of life.

'You do live, though?'

'I live, but in debt.'

'Really? How deep?' Bartniansky said with sympathy.

'Very deep – about twenty thousand.'

Bartniansky burst into merry laughter.

'Oh, lucky man!' he said. 'I owe a million and a half and have nothing, and, as you see, I can still live.'

And Stepan Arkadyich could see that it was true not only in words but in reality. Zhivakhov had debts of three hundred thousand and not a kopeck to his name, and yet he lived, and how! The requiem had long been sung for Count Krivtsov, yet he kept two women. Petrovsky ran through five million and lived the same as ever, and was even a financial director and received a salary of twenty thousand. But, besides that, Petersburg had a physically pleasant effect on Stepan Arkadyich. It made him younger. In Moscow he sometimes looked at his grey hair, fell asleep after dinner, stretched, climbed the stairs slowly, breathing heavily, became bored in the company of young women, did not dance at balls. In Petersburg he always felt he had shaken off ten years.

He experienced in Petersburg the same thing that he had been told only yesterday by the sixty-year-old prince Pyotr Oblonsky, just returned from abroad.

'Here we don't know how to live,' Pyotr Oblonsky had said. 'Would you believe, I spent the summer in Baden. Well, really, I felt myself quite a young man. I'd see a young woman, and thoughts . . . You dine, drink a little – strength, vigour. I came to Russia – had to see my wife, and also the estate – well, you wouldn't believe it, two weeks later I got into my dressing gown, stopped changing for dinner. No more thinking about young lovelies! Turned into a real old man. Only thing left was saving my soul. Went to Paris – rallied again.'

Stepan Arkadyich felt exactly the same difference as Pyotr Oblonsky. In Moscow he went so much to seed that, in fact, if he lived there long enough, he would, for all he knew, reach the point of saving his soul; in Petersburg he felt himself a decent human being again.

Between Princess Betsy Tverskoy and Stepan Arkadyich there existed long-standing and quite strange relations. Stepan Arkadyich had always jokingly paid court to her and told her, also jokingly, the most indecent things, knowing that that was what she liked most. The day after his talk with Karenin, Stepan Arkadyich, calling on her, felt so young that he inadvertently went too far in this jocular courtship and bantering, and did not know how to get out of it, for, unfortunately, he not only did not like her but found her repulsive. They fell into this tone because she liked him very much. So that he was very glad of the arrival of Princess Miagky, which put a timely end to their tête-à-tête.

'Ah, you're here, too,' she said when she saw him. 'Well, how is your poor sister? Don't look at me like that,' she added. 'Though everybody's fallen upon her, when they're all a thousand times worse than she is, I find that she acted very beautifully. I can't forgive Vronsky for not letting me know when she was in Petersburg. I'd have called on her and gone everywhere with her. Please send her my love. Well, tell me about her.'

'Yes, her situation is difficult, she . . .' Stepan Arkadyich began, in the simplicity of his soul, taking her words at face value when Princess Miagky said, 'Tell me about your sister.' Princess Miagky interrupted him at once, as was her habit, and began talking herself.

'She did no more than what everybody, except me, does but keeps hidden. She didn't want to deceive and she did splendidly. And she did better still by abandoning that half-witted brother-in-law of yours. You must excuse me. Everybody kept saying he's intelligent, he's intelligent, and I alone said he was stupid. Now that he's got himself associated with Lydia and Landau, everybody says he's half-witted, and I'd be glad to disagree with them all, but this time I can't.'

'But explain to me, please,' said Stepan Arkadyich, 'what is the meaning of this? Yesterday I went to see him on my sister's business and asked for a decisive answer. He gave me no answer and said he would think, and this morning, instead of an answer, I received an invitation to come to Countess Lydia Ivanovna's this evening.'

'Well, so there!' Princess Miagky said joyfully. 'They're going to ask Landau what he says.'

'Landau? Why? What is Landau?'

'You mean you don't know Jules Landau, *le fameux Jules Landau, le clairvoyant*? He's half-witted, too, but your sister's fate depends on him. That's what happens when you live in the provinces: you don't know anything. You see, Landau was a *commis** in a shop in Paris, and he went to the doctor. In the doctor's office he fell asleep and in sleep started giving all the patients advice. Remarkable advice, too. Then Yuri Meledinsky's wife – he's ill, you know? – found out about this Landau

* Salesman.

and brought him to her husband. He's been treating her husband. Hasn't done him any good, in my opinion, because he's still as paralysed as ever, but they believe in him and take him everywhere. And they brought him to Russia. Here everybody fell upon him and he started treating everybody. He cured Countess Bezzubov, and she likes him so much that she's adopted him.'

'Adopted him?'

'Yes, adopted him. He's no longer Landau, he's Count Bezzubov. But that's not the point, it's that Lydia – I love her very much, but she's off her head – naturally fell upon this Landau, and now neither she nor Alexei Alexandrovich can decide anything without him, and so your sister's fate is now in the hands of this Landau, alias Count Bezzubov.'[22]

XXI

After an excellent dinner and a great quantity of cognac, drunk at Bartniansky's, Stepan Arkadyich, only a little later than the appointed time, entered Countess Lydia Ivanovna's house.

'Who else is with the countess? The Frenchman?' Stepan Arkadyich asked the hall porter, looking at the familiar overcoat of Alexei Alexandrovich and a strange, naïve overcoat with clasps.

'Alexei Alexandrovich Karenin and Count Bezzubov,' the porter replied sternly.

'Princess Miagky guessed right,' thought Stepan Arkadyich, going up the stairs. 'Strange! However, it would be nice to get friendly with her. She has enormous influence. If she'd put in a word for me with Pomorsky, it would be a sure thing.'

It was still broad daylight outside, but in Countess Lydia's small drawing room the blinds were already drawn and the lamps lit.

At a round table under a lamp the countess and Alexei Alexandrovich sat talking about something in low voices. A short, lean man with womanish hips and knock-kneed legs, very pale, handsome, with beautiful, shining eyes and long hair falling over the collar of his frock coat, stood at the other end, studying the portraits on the wall. Having greeted the hostess and Alexei Alexandrovich, Stepan Arkadyich involuntarily looked again at the unknown man.

'Monsieur Landau!' The countess addressed the man with a softness and carefulness that struck Oblonsky. And she introduced them.

Landau hastily turned, approached and, smiling, placed his inert, sweaty hand into the extended hand of Stepan Arkadyich and immediately went back and began looking at the portraits. The countess and Alexei Alexandrovich exchanged meaningful looks.

'I'm very glad to see you, especially today,' said Countess Lydia Ivanovna, pointing Stepan Arkadyich to the place next to Karenin.

'I introduced him to you as Landau,' she said in a low voice, glancing at the Frenchman and then at once at Alexei Alexandrovich, 'but in fact he is Count Bezzubov, as you probably know. Only he doesn't like the title.'

'Yes, I've heard,' Stepan Arkadyich replied. 'They say he cured Countess Bezzubov completely.'

'She called on me today. She's so pitiful!' The countess turned to Alexei Alexandrovich. 'This parting is terrible for her. Such a blow!'

'And he's definitely leaving?' asked Alexei Alexandrovich.

'Yes, he's leaving for Paris. He heard a voice yesterday,' said Countess Lydia Ivanovna, looking at Stepan Arkadyich.

'Ah, a voice!' Oblonsky repeated, feeling that he had to be as careful as possible in this company where something special had taken place, or was about to take place, to which he did not yet have the key.

A momentary silence followed, after which Countess Lydia Ivanovna, as if approaching the main subject of conversation, said to Oblonsky with a subtle smile:

'I've known you for a long time and am very glad to get to know you more closely. *Les amis de nos amis sont nos amis.** But to be someone's friend, one has to penetrate the friend's state of soul, and I'm afraid you have not done so with regard to Alexei Alexandrovich. You understand what I am talking about,' she said, raising her beautiful, pensive eyes.

'In part, Countess, I understand that Alexei Alexandrovich's position . . .' Oblonsky said, not understanding very well what the matter was and therefore wishing to speak in general.

'The change is not in his external position,' Countess Lydia Ivanovna said sternly, at the same time following Alexei Alexandrovich with amorous eyes as he got up and went over to Landau. 'His heart has changed, a new heart has been given him, and I'm afraid you haven't quite perceived the change that has taken place in him.'

* The friends of our friends are our friends.

'That is, in general terms I can picture the change to myself. We've always been friends, and now . . .' Stepan Arkadyich said, responding to the countess's gaze with a tender gaze of his own and trying to make out which of the two ministers she was closer to, so as to know which one to ask her about.

'The change that has taken place in him cannot weaken his feelings of love for his neighbours; on the contrary, the change that has taken place in him can only increase his love. But I'm afraid you don't understand me. Would you like some tea?' she said, indicating with her eyes the servant who was offering tea on a tray.

'Not entirely, Countess. Of course, his misfortune . . .'

'Yes, a misfortune that turned into the greatest good fortune, when his heart became new, fulfilled in Him,' she said, gazing amorously at Stepan Arkadyich.

'I think I could ask her to put in a word with both of them,' thought Stepan Arkadyich.

'Oh, of course, Countess,' he said, 'but I think these changes are so intimate that no one, not even the closest person, likes to speak of them.'

'On the contrary! We must speak and help one another.'

'Yes, no doubt, but there are such differences of conviction, and besides . . .' Oblonsky said with a soft smile.

'There can be no difference in matters of sacred truth.'

'Ah, yes, of course, but . . .' And, embarrassed, Stepan Arkadyich became silent. He realized that they had got on to religion.

'I think he's about to fall asleep,' Alexei Alexandrovich said in a meaningful whisper, coming up to Lydia Ivanovna.

Stepan Arkadyich turned. Landau was sitting by the window, leaning on the back and armrest of his chair, his head bowed. Noticing the eyes directed at him, he raised his head and smiled a childishly naïve smile.

'Don't pay any attention,' said Lydia Ivanovna, and with a light movement she pushed a chair towards Alexei Alexandrovich. 'I've noticed . . .' she was beginning to say something when a footman came in with a letter. Lydia Ivanovna quickly scanned the note and, apologizing, wrote an extremely quick reply, handed it over and returned to the table. 'I've noticed,' she continued the conversation she had begun, 'that Muscovites, the men especially, are quite indifferent to religion.'

'Oh, no, Countess, I believe the Muscovites have a reputation for being quite staunch,' Stepan Arkadyich replied.

'But, as far as I understand, you, unfortunately, are among the indifferent,' Alexei Alexandrovich said, turning to him with a weary smile.

'How can one be indifferent!' said Lydia Ivanovna.

'In that respect, I'm not really indifferent, but expectant,' said Stepan Arkadyich, with his most soothing smile. 'I don't think the time for these questions has come for me.'

Alexei Alexandrovich and Lydia Ivanovna exchanged glances.

'We can never know whether the time has come for us or not,' Alexei Alexandrovich said sternly. 'We mustn't think whether we're ready or not: grace is not guided by human considerations; it sometimes descends not upon the labourers but upon the unprepared, as it did upon Saul.'[23]

'No, not just yet, it seems,' said Lydia Ivanovna, who had been following the Frenchman's movements all the while.

Landau got up and came over to them.

'Will you allow me to listen?' he said.

'Oh, yes, I didn't want to disturb you,' said Lydia Ivanovna, looking at him tenderly. 'Sit down with us.'

'One need only not close one's eyes, so as not to be deprived of light,' Alexei Alexandrovich went on.

'Ah, if you knew the happiness we experience, feeling His constant presence in our souls!' said Lydia Ivanovna, smiling beatifically.

'But sometimes a man may feel himself unable to rise to that height,' said Stepan Arkadyich, not forthrightly, acknowledging the loftiness of religion, but at the same time not daring to acknowledge his freethinking before the person who, by saying one word to Pomorsky, could provide him with the desired post.

'That is, you mean to say that sin prevents him?' said Lydia Ivanovna. 'But that is a false view. There is no sin for believers; sin is already redeemed. *Pardon*,' she added, looking at the footman, who came in again with another note. She read it and responded verbally: 'Say tomorrow at the Grand Duchess's. There is no sin for a believer,' she continued the conversation.

'Yes, but faith without works is dead,' said Stepan Arkadyich, recalling this phrase from the catechism, defending his independence only with his smile.

'There it is, from the Epistle of the Apostle James,'[24] said Alexei Alexandrovich, addressing Lydia Ivanovna somewhat reproachfully, evidently to do with something they had talked about more than once. 'How much harm the wrong interpretation of that passage has done! Nothing so turns people from faith as this interpretation: "I have no works, I cannot believe," when that is said nowhere. What is said is the opposite.'

'To labour for God, to save your soul by works, by fasting,' Countess Lydia Ivanovna said with squeamish contempt, 'these are the wild notions of our monks . . . Whereas that is said nowhere. It is much simpler and easier,' she added, looking at Oblonsky with the same encouraging smile with which, at court, she encouraged young maids-of-honour bewildered by their new situation.

'We are saved by Christ, who suffered for us. We are saved by faith,' Alexei Alexandrovich confirmed, approving of her words with his eyes.

'*Vous comprenez l'anglais?*'* Lydia Ivanovna asked and, receiving an affirmative answer, stood up and began looking through the books on the shelf.

'I want to read *Safe and Happy*, or *Under the Wing*?'[25] she said, with a questioning look at Karenin. And, having found the book and sat down again, she opened it. 'It's very short. It describes the way in which faith is acquired and the happiness beyond all earthly things which then fills the soul. A believer cannot be unhappy, because he is not alone. You'll see now.' She was about to read when the footman came in again. 'Mme Borozdin? Say tomorrow at two o'clock. Yes,' she said, holding the place in the book with her finger, sighing and gazing before her with her beautiful, pensive eyes. 'That is the effect of true faith. Do you know Marie Sanin? Do you know about her misfortune? She lost her only child. She was in despair. Well, and what then? She found this Friend, and now she thanks God for the death of her child. That is the happiness that faith gives!'

'Ah, yes, that's very . . .' said Stepan Arkadyich, pleased that she was going to read and give him time to recover a little. 'No,' he thought, 'looks as if it would be better not to ask for anything this time. So long as I can get out of here without messing things up.'

'It will be boring for you,' said Countess Lydia Ivanovna, turning to Landau, 'you don't know English. But it's short.'

'Oh, I shall understand,' Landau said with the same smile and closed his eyes.

Alexei Alexandrovich and Lydia Ivanovna exchanged meaningful glances, and the reading began.

* Do you understand English?

XXII

Stepan Arkadyich felt completely baffled hearing this talk, which was new and strange to him. The complexity of Petersburg life generally had an exhilarating effect on him, lifting him out of his Moscow stagnation; but he liked and understood those complexities in spheres that were close and familiar to him, while in this alien milieu he was baffled, dumbfounded, and could not grasp it all. Listening to Countess Lydia Ivanovna and sensing Landau's beautiful eyes – naïve or sly, he did not know which – fixed on him, Stepan Arkadyich began to feel some peculiar heaviness in his head.

The most diverse thoughts were tangled in his head. 'Marie Sanin is glad her child died . . . Would be nice to smoke now . . . To be saved, one need only believe, and the monks don't know how to do it, but Countess Lydia Ivanovna does . . . And why is there such a heaviness in my head? From the cognac, or because it's all so strange? Anyhow, I don't think I've done anything improper yet. But, still, it's impossible to ask for her help now. I've heard they make people pray. What if they make me pray? That would be too stupid. And what's this nonsense she's reading, albeit with good enunciation? Landau is Bezzubov. Why is he Bezzubov?' Suddenly Stepan Arkadyich felt his lower jaw beginning to contract irrepressibly before a yawn. He smoothed his side-whiskers, concealing the yawn, and shook himself. But next he felt he was already asleep and about to snore. He woke up just as the voice of Countess Lydia Ivanovna said, 'He's asleep.'

Stepan Arkadyich woke up in fear, feeling guilty and exposed. But he was reassured at once, seeing that the words 'He's asleep' referred not to him but to Landau. The Frenchman had fallen asleep as had Stepan Arkadyich. But while Stepan Arkadyich's sleep, as he thought, would have offended them (however, he did not think even that, so strange everything seemed to him), Landau's sleep delighted them in the extreme, Countess Lydia Ivanovna especially.

'*Mon ami*,' said Lydia Ivanovna, carefully picking up the folds of her silk dress so as not to rustle, and in her excitement calling Karenin '*mon ami*' now instead of Alexei Alexandrovich, '*donnez-lui la main. Vous voyez?** Shh!' she shushed the footman, who came in again. 'Receive no one.'

* Give him your hand. You see?

The Frenchman slept, or pretended to sleep, his head resting on the back of the armchair, and made feeble movements with the sweaty hand that lay on his knee, as if attempting to catch something. Alexei Alexandrovich got up, trying to be careful but brushing against the table, went over and put his hand into the Frenchman's hand. Stepan Arkadyich also got up and, opening his eyes wide, wishing to waken himself in case he was asleep, looked now at the one man, now at the other. It was all real. Stepan Arkadyich felt that his head was getting worse and worse.

'*Que la personne qui est arrivée la dernière, celle qui demande, qu'elle sorte! Qu'elle sorte!*'* the Frenchman said, without opening his eyes.

'*Vous m'excuserez, mais vous voyez . . . Revenez vers dix heures, encore mieux demain.*'†

'*Qu'elle sorte!*' the Frenchman impatiently repeated.

'*C'est moi, n'est-ce pas?*'‡

And, receiving an affirmative reply, Stepan Arkadyich, forgetting about what he had wanted to ask Lydia Ivanovna, and also forgetting about his sister's business, with the sole desire of quickly getting out of there, left on tiptoe and, as if it were a plague house, ran out to the street and spent a long time talking and joking with a cabby, hoping the sooner to come to his senses.

At the French Theatre, where he arrived for the last act, and then over champagne at the Tartars', Stepan Arkadyich caught his breath a little in an atmosphere more suitable to him. But even so he felt quite out of sorts that evening.

Returning home to Pyotr Oblonsky's, where he was staying in Petersburg, Stepan Arkadyich found a note from Betsy. She wrote that she wished very much to finish the conversation they had started and invited him to come the next day. No sooner had he read the note and winced at it than he heard downstairs the heavy footsteps of people carrying some weighty object.

Stepan Arkadyich went out to look. It was the rejuvenated Pyotr Oblonsky. He was so drunk that he was unable to climb the stairs; but he ordered them to stand him on his feet when he saw Stepan Arkadyich,

* The person who came last, the one who is asking for something, must get out! Get out!

† You will excuse me, but you can see . . . Come back at around ten, or better still tomorrow.

‡ That's me, isn't it?

and, hanging on to him, went with him to his room, there began telling about how he had spent the evening, and fell asleep on the spot.

Stepan Arkadyich was in low spirits, which rarely happened to him, and could not fall asleep for a long time. Everything he recalled, everything, was vile, but vilest of all was the recollection, as if of something shameful, of the evening at Countess Lydia Ivanovna's.

The next day he received from Alexei Alexandrovich a definitive refusal to divorce Anna and understood that this decision was based on what the Frenchman had said in his real or feigned sleep.

XXIII

In order to undertake anything in family life, it is necessary that there be either complete discord between the spouses or loving harmony. But when the relations between spouses are uncertain and there is neither the one nor the other, nothing can be undertaken.

Many families stay for years in the same old places, hateful to both spouses, only because there is neither full discord nor harmony.

For both Vronsky and Anna, Moscow life in the heat and dust, when the sun no longer shone as in spring but as in summer, and all the trees on the boulevards had long been in leaf, and the leaves were already covered with dust, was unbearable. But instead of moving to Vozdvizhenskoe, as they had long ago decided to do, they went on living in the Moscow they both hated, because lately there had been no harmony between them.

The irritation that divided them had no external cause, and all attempts to talk about it not only did not remove it but increased it. This was an inner irritation, which for her was based on the diminishing of his love, and for him on his regret at having put himself, for her sake, in a difficult situation, which she, instead of making easier, made still more difficult. Neither of them spoke of the causes of their irritation, but each considered the other in the wrong and tried to prove it at every opportunity.

For her, all of him, with all his habits, thoughts, desires, with his entire mental and physical cast, amounted to one thing: love for women. And that love, which, as she felt, should have been concentrated on her alone, had diminished. Therefore, she reasoned, he must have transferred part of it to other women, or to another woman – and she was jealous. She was jealous not of any one woman, but of the diminishing of his love. Having as yet no object for her jealousy, she was looking for one. Following the slightest hint, she transferred her jealousy from one object to another. Now she was jealous of those coarse women with whom he could so easily associate himself thanks to his bachelor connections; then she was jealous of the society women he might meet, or again of some imaginary girl he wanted to marry after breaking the liaison with her. And this last jealousy tormented her most of all, especially as he himself, in a moment of candour, had imprudently told her that his mother understood him so little that she allowed herself to insist that he should marry Princess Sorokin.

And, being jealous, Anna was indignant with him and sought pretexts for indignation in everything. She blamed him for everything that was difficult in her situation. The painful state of expectation, between heaven and earth, in which she lived in Moscow, Alexei Alexandrovich's slowness and indecision, her seclusion – she ascribed it all to him. If he loved her, he would understand the full difficulty of her situation and would take her out of it. The fact that she was living in Moscow and not in the country was also his fault. He could not live buried in the country, as she wanted to. Society was necessary for him, and he put her into that terrible position, the difficulty of which he did not wish to understand. And it was he again who was to blame for her being for ever separated from her son.

Even the rare moments of tenderness that occurred between them did not bring her peace: in his tenderness she now saw a tinge of tranquillity, of assurance, which had not been there before and which irritated her.

It was already dark. Alone, waiting for him to come back from a bachelors' dinner he had gone to, Anna paced up and down his study (the room where the noise of the street was heard least) and mentally went through the nuances of yesterday's quarrel in all their detail. Going further back from the memorably insulting words of the argument to what had caused them, she finally came to the beginning of their conversation. For a long time she could not believe that the quarrel had begun from such a harmless conversation, not close to either of their hearts. Yet it was really so. It had all begun with him laughing at women's high schools, which he considered unnecessary, and her defending them. He referred disrespectfully to women's education in general and said that Hannah, Anna's English protégée, did not need any knowledge of physics.

That irritated Anna. She saw it as a contemptuous allusion to her concerns. And she devised and spoke a phrase that would pay him back for the pain he had caused her.

'I don't expect you to be mindful of me or my feelings as a loving man would be, but I do expect simple tactfulness,' she said.

And indeed he turned red with vexation and said something unpleasant. She did not remember what reply she made to him, but only that he, obviously also wishing to cause her pain, responded by saying:

'It's true I'm not interested in your concern for this girl, because I can see it's unnatural.'

The cruelty with which he destroyed the world she had so laboriously built up for herself in order to endure her difficult life, the unfairness with which he accused her of being false and unnatural, made her explode.

'I am very sorry that only coarse and material things seem understandable and natural to you,' she said and walked out of the room.

When he came to her that evening, they did not mention the quarrel that had taken place, but they both felt that, though it had been smoothed over, it was still there.

Today he had not been home all day, and she felt so lonely and so pained to have quarrelled with him that she wanted forget it all, to forgive and make peace with him, wanted to accuse herself and justify him.

'It's my own fault, I'm irritable, I'm senselessly jealous. I'll make peace with him, we'll leave for the country, I'll be calmer there,' she said to herself.

'Unnatural' – she suddenly remembered the most offensive thing, not the word so much as the intention to cause her pain.

'I know what he wanted to say. He wanted to say that it's unnatural for me to love someone else's child when I don't love my own daughter. What does he understand about the love for children, about my love for Seryozha, whom I have sacrificed for him? But this wish to cause me pain! No, he loves another woman, it can't be anything else.'

And seeing that, while wishing to calm herself, she had gone round the circle she had already completed so many times and come back to her former irritation, she was horrified at herself. 'Is it really impossible? Can I really not take it upon myself?' she said to herself, and began again from the beginning. 'He's truthful, he's honest, he loves me. I love him, the divorce will come any day now. What more do we need? We need peace, trust, and I'll take it upon myself. Yes, now, when he comes, I'll tell him it was my fault, though it wasn't, and we'll leave.'

And so as not to think any more and not to yield to irritation, she rang the bell and ordered the trunks to be brought in order to pack things for the country.

At ten o'clock Vronsky arrived.

XXIV

'So, did you have a good time?' she asked, coming out to meet him with a guilty and meek expression on her face.

'As usual,' he replied, understanding at a glance that she was in one of her good moods. He had become used to these changes, and was especially glad of it today, because he himself was in the best of spirits.

'What's this I see! That's good!' he said, pointing to the trunks in the hallway.

'Yes, we must leave. I went for a ride, and it's so nice that I wanted to go to the country. Nothing's keeping you?'

'It's my only wish. I'll come at once and we'll talk, I only have to change. Send for tea.'

And he went to his study.

There was something offensive in his saying 'That's good,' as one speaks to a child when it stops misbehaving; still more offensive was the contrast between her guilty and his self-assured tone; and for a moment she felt a desire to fight rising in her; but, making an effort, she suppressed it and met Vronsky just as cheerfully.

When he came out to her, she told him, partly repeating words she had prepared, about her day and her plans for departure.

'You know, it came to me almost like an inspiration,' she said. 'Why wait for the divorce here? Isn't it the same in the country? I can't wait any longer. I don't want to hope, I don't want to hear anything about the divorce. I've decided it's no longer going to influence my life. Do you agree?'

'Oh, yes!' he said, looking uneasily into her excited face.

'And what were you all doing there? Who came?' she said after a pause.

Vronsky named the guests.

'The dinner was excellent, and the boat race and all that was quite nice, but in Moscow they can't do without the *ridicule*. Some lady appeared, the queen of Sweden's swimming teacher, and demonstrated her art.'

'How? She swam?' Anna said, frowning.

'In some red *costume de natation*,* old, ugly. So, when do we leave?'

'What a stupid fantasy! Does she swim in some special way?' Anna said without answering.

'Certainly nothing special. That's what I'm saying – terribly stupid. So, when do you think of leaving?'

Anna shook her head as if wishing to drive some unpleasant thought away.

'When? The sooner the better. We won't be ready tomorrow. The day after tomorrow.'

'Yes . . . no, wait. The day after tomorrow is Sunday, I must call on *maman*,' Vronsky said, embarrassed, because as soon as he mentioned his mother, he felt her intent, suspicious look fixed on him. His embarrassment confirmed her suspicions. She flushed and drew away from him. Now it was no longer the queen of Sweden's teacher that Anna pictured to herself, but Princess Sorokin, who lived on Countess Vronsky's country estate near Moscow.

'Can't you go tomorrow?' she said.

'No, I can't! The business I'm going for, the warrant and the money, won't have come by tomorrow,' he replied.

'In that case, we won't leave at all.'

'But why not?'

'I won't go later. Monday or never!'

'But why?' Vronsky said as if in surprise. 'It makes no sense!'

'For you it makes no sense, because you don't care about me at all. You don't want to understand my life. The only thing that has occupied me here is Hannah. You say it's all pretence. You did say yesterday that I don't love my daughter but pretend to love this English girl and that it's unnatural. I'd like to know what kind of life can be natural for me here!'

* Swimming costume.

For a moment she recovered herself and was horrified at having failed in her intention. But, even knowing that she was ruining herself, she could not hold back, could not keep from showing him how wrong he was, could not submit to him.

'I never said that. I said that I did not sympathize with this sudden love.'

'Since you boast of your directness, why don't you tell the truth?'

'I never boast, and I never say anything that isn't true,' he said softly, holding back the anger that was surging up in him. 'It's a great pity if you don't respect . . .'

'Respect was invented to cover the empty place where love should be. But if you don't love me, it would be better and more honest to say so.'

'No, this is becoming unbearable!' Vronsky cried, getting up from his chair. And, stopping in front of her, he said slowly, 'Why do you try my patience?' He looked as if he could have said many other things, but restrained himself. 'It does have limits.'

'What do you mean by that?' she cried, staring with horror at the clear expression of hatred that was on his whole face, especially in his cruel, menacing eyes.

'I mean . . .' he began, but stopped. 'I must ask you what you want of me.'

'What can I want? The only thing I can want is that you not abandon me, as you're thinking of doing,' she said, understanding all that he had left unsaid. 'But that's not what I want, that's secondary. I want love and there is none. Which means it's all over!'

She went towards the door.

'Wait! Wa-a-ait!' said Vronsky, not smoothing the grim furrow of his brows, but stopping her by the arm. 'What's the matter? I said we should put off our departure for three days and to that you said that I was lying, that I'm a dishonest man.'

'Yes, and I repeat that a man who reproaches me by saying he has sacrificed everything for me,' she said, recalling the words of a previous quarrel, 'is still worse than a dishonest man – he's a man with no heart!'

'No, patience has its limits!' he cried, and quickly let go of her arm.

'He hates me, it's clear,' she thought, and silently, without looking back, she left the room with faltering steps.

'He loves another woman, that's clearer still,' she said to herself, going into her room. 'I want love and there is none. Which means it's all over,' she repeated the words she had said, 'and I must end it.'

'But how?' she asked herself, and sat down on a chair in front of the mirror.

Thoughts of where she would go now – to the aunt who had brought her up, to Dolly, or simply abroad alone – and of what *he* was doing now, alone in his study, and whether this quarrel was the final one or reconciliation was still possible, and of what all her former Petersburg acquaintances would say about her now, and how Alexei Alexandrovich would look at it, and many other thoughts of what would happen now, after the break-up, came to her mind, but she did not give herself wholeheartedly to these thoughts. In her soul there was some vague thought which alone interested her, yet she was unable to bring it to consciousness. Having remembered Alexei Alexandrovich once again, she also remembered the time of her illness after giving birth, and the feeling that would not leave her then. 'Why didn't I die?' – she remembered the words she had said then and the feeling she had had then. And she suddenly understood what was in her soul. Yes, this was the thought which alone resolved everything. 'Yes, to die! . . .

'The shame and disgrace of Alexei Alexandrovich and of Seryozha, and my own terrible shame – death will save it all. To die – and he will repent, pity, love and suffer for me.' With a fixed smile of compassion for herself, she sat in the chair, taking off and putting on the rings on her left hand, vividly imagining from all sides his feelings after her death.

Approaching steps, his steps, distracted her. As if occupied with arranging her rings, she did not even turn to him.

He went up to her, took her hand and said softly:

'Anna, let's go the day after tomorrow, if you like. I agree to everything.'

She was silent.

'What is it?' he asked.

'You know yourself,' she said, and at the same moment, unable to restrain herself any longer, she burst into sobs.

'Leave me, leave me!' she repeated between sobs. 'I'll go away tomorrow . . . I'll do more. What am I? A depraved woman. A stone around your neck. I don't want to torment you, I don't! I'll release you. You don't love me, you love another woman!'

Vronsky implored her to calm herself and assured her that there was not the shadow of a reason for her jealousy, that he had never stopped and never would stop loving her, that he loved her more than ever.

'Anna, why torment yourself and me like this?' he said, kissing her hands. There was tenderness in his face now, and it seemed to her that she heard the sound of tears in his voice and felt their moisture on her hand. And instantly Anna's desperate jealousy changed to a desperate, passionate tenderness; she embraced him and covered his head and neck and hands with kisses.

XXV

Feeling that their reconciliation was complete, in the morning Anna briskly began preparing for departure. Though it had not been decided whether they would go on Monday or on Tuesday, since they had kept yielding to each other the night before, Anna actively prepared for departure, now completely indifferent to whether they left a day earlier or later. She was standing in her room over an open trunk, sorting things, when he, already dressed, came into her room earlier than usual.

'I'm going to see *maman* right now. She can send me the money through Yegorov. And tomorrow I'll be ready to leave.'

Good as her state of mind was, the mention of going to his mother's country house stung her.

'No, I won't be ready myself,' she said, and at once thought, 'So he could have arranged to do it the way I wanted.' 'No, do it the way you wanted. Go to the dining room, I'll come presently, as soon as I've sorted out the things I don't need,' she said, putting something else over Annushka's arm, where a pile of clothes already hung.

Vronsky was eating his beefsteak when she came out to the dining room.

'You wouldn't believe how sick I am of these rooms,' she said, sitting down beside him over her coffee. 'There's nothing more terrible than these *chambres garnies*.* They have no face to them, no soul. This clock, these curtains, above all this wallpaper – a nightmare. I think of Vozdvizhenskoe as a promised land. You're not sending the horses yet?'

'No, they'll go after us. Are you going out somewhere?'

'I wanted to go to Mrs Wilson, to take her some dresses. So it's tomorrow for certain?' she said in a cheerful voice; but suddenly her face changed.

* Furnished rooms.

Vronsky's valet came to ask for a receipt for a telegram from Petersburg. There was nothing special in Vronsky's receiving a telegram, but he, as if wishing to hide something from her, said that the receipt was in the study and quickly turned to her.

'I'll certainly be done with everything by tomorrow.'

'Who was the telegram from?' she asked, not listening to him.

'Stiva,' he answered reluctantly.

'Why didn't you show it to me? What secrets can there be between Stiva and me?'

Vronsky called the valet back and told him to bring the telegram.

'I didn't want to show it because Stiva has a passion for sending telegrams. Why send telegrams if nothing's been decided?'

'About the divorce?'

'Yes, but he writes: "Unable to obtain anything yet. Decisive answer promised in a day or two." Read here.'

With trembling hands Anna took the telegram and read the same thing Vronsky had said. At the end there was also added: 'Little hope, but will do everything possible and impossible.'

'I said yesterday that I'm totally indifferent to when I get the divorce, or even whether I get it at all,' she said, flushing. 'There was no need to hide it from me.' And she thought, 'In the same way he can and does conceal his correspondence with women from me.'

'And Yashvin wanted to come this morning with Voitov,' said Vronsky. 'It seems he's won everything from Pevtsov, even more than he can pay – about sixty thousand.'

'No,' she said, irritated that by this change of subject he should make it so obvious to her that she was irritated, 'why do you think this news interests me so much that you even have to conceal it? I said I don't want to think about it, and I wish you were as little interested in it as I am.'

'I'm interested because I like clarity,' he said.

'Clarity is not in form but in love,' she said, getting more and more irritated, not by his words but by the tone of calm tranquillity in which he spoke. 'What do you want that for?'

'My God,' he thought, wincing, 'again about love.'

'You know what for: for you and for the children to come,' he said.

'There won't be any children.'

'That's a great pity,' he said.

'You need it for the children, but you don't think about me?' she said, completely forgetting or not hearing that he had said '*for you* and for the children'.

The question about the possibility of having children had long been in dispute and it irritated her. She explained his wish to have children by the fact that he did not value her beauty.

'Ah, I did say "for you". For you most of all,' he repeated, wincing as if from pain, 'because I'm sure that the greater part of your irritation comes from the uncertainty of your situation.'

'Yes, now he's stopped pretending and I can see all his cold hatred of me,' she thought, not listening to his words, but gazing with horror at the cold and cruel judge who looked out of his eyes, taunting her.

'That's not the cause,' she said, 'and I do not even understand how the fact that I am completely in your power can be a cause of irritation, as you put it. What is uncertain in my situation? On the contrary.'

'It's a great pity you don't want to understand,' he interrupted her, stubbornly wishing to express his thought. 'The uncertainty consists in the fact that to you it seems I'm free.'

'Concerning that you may be perfectly at ease,' she said and, turning away, began to drink her coffee.

She raised her cup, holding out her little finger, and brought it to her lips. After taking several sips, she glanced at him and, from the expression on his face, clearly understood that he was disgusted by her hand, and her gesture, and the sound her lips made.

'I am perfectly indifferent to what your mother thinks and how she wants to get you married,' she said, setting the cup down with a trembling hand.

'But we're not talking about that.'

'Yes, precisely about that. And believe me, a woman with no heart, whether she's old or not, your mother or someone else's, is of no interest to me, and I do not care to know her.'

'Anna, I beg you not to speak disrespectfully of my mother.'

'A woman whose heart cannot tell her what makes for the happiness and honour of her son, is a woman with no heart.'

'I repeat my request: do not speak disrespectfully of my mother, whom I respect,' he said, raising his voice and looking sternly at her.

She did not reply. Gazing intently at him, at his face, his hands, she remembered in all its details the scene of yesterday's reconciliation and his passionate caresses. 'Those caresses, exactly the same as he has lavished, and will lavish, and wants to lavish on other women,' she thought.

'You don't love your mother. It's all words, words, words!' she said, looking at him with hatred.

'In that case, we must . . .'

'We must decide, and I have decided,' she said and was about to leave, but just then Yashvin came into the room. Anna greeted him and stopped.

Why, when there was a storm in her soul and she felt she was standing at a turning point in her life that might have terrible consequences, why at such a moment she should have to pretend in front of a stranger, who would learn everything sooner or later anyway, she did not know; but having instantly calmed the storm within her, she sat down and began talking with the visitor.

'Well, how are things? Did you get what was owed you?' she asked Yashvin.

'Oh, things are all right. It seems I won't be getting the whole sum, and I have to leave on Wednesday. And when are you leaving?' said Yashvin, narrowing his eyes and glancing at Vronsky, obviously guessing that a quarrel had taken place.

'The day after tomorrow, I think,' said Vronsky.

'You've been intending to for a long time, though.'

'But now it's decided,' said Anna, looking straight into Vronsky's eyes, with a stare meant to tell him that he should not even think of the possibility of a reconciliation.

'Aren't you sorry for this poor Pevtsov?' she went on talking with Yashvin.

'I've never asked myself whether I'm sorry or not, Anna Arkadyevna. Just as in war you don't ask whether you're sorry or not. My whole fortune is here,' he pointed to his side pocket, 'and I'm a rich man now. But tonight I'll go to the club and maybe leave it a beggar. The one who sits down with me also wants to leave me without a shirt, as I do him. So we struggle, and that's where the pleasure lies.'

'Well, and if you were married,' said Anna, 'how would your wife feel?'

Yashvin laughed.

'That must be why I never married and never wanted to.'

'And Helsingfors?' said Vronsky, entering the conversation, and he glanced at the smiling Anna.

Meeting his glance, Anna's face suddenly assumed a coldly stern expression, as if she were telling him: 'It's not forgotten. It's as it was.'

'Can you have been in love?' she said to Yashvin.

'Oh, Lord, more than once! But you see, one man can sit down to cards, but be able to get up when the time comes for a rendezvous. Whereas I can be busy with love, but not be late for a game in the evening. That's how I arrange it.'

'No, I'm not asking about that, but about the present.' She was going to say 'Helsingfors', but did not want to say the word Vronsky had said.

Voitov came, the purchaser of the stallion. Anna got up and walked out.

Before leaving the house, Vronsky came to her room. She was about to pretend to be looking for something on the table but, ashamed of pretending, she looked straight into his face with cold eyes.

'What do you want?' she asked him in French.

'Gambetta's papers. I've sold him,' he replied, in a tone that said more clearly than words, 'I have no time to talk, and it gets us nowhere.'

'I'm not guilty before her in anything,' he thought. 'If she wants to punish herself, *tant pis pour elle*.'* But, as he went out, he thought she said something, and his heart was suddenly shaken with compassion for her.

'What, Anna?' he asked.

'Nothing,' she replied in the same cold and calm voice.

'If it's nothing, then *tant pis*,' he thought, growing cold again, and he turned and went out. As he was leaving, he saw her face in the mirror, pale, with trembling lips. He would have liked to stop and say something comforting to her, but his legs carried him out of the room before he could think of what to say. He spent the whole day away from home, and when he came back late in the evening, the maid told him that Anna Arkadyevna had a headache and asked him not to come to her.

XXVI

Never before had a quarrel lasted a whole day. This was the first time. And it was not a quarrel. It was an obvious admission of a complete cooling off. How could he look at her as he had when he came into the

* Too bad for her.

room to get the papers? Look at her, see that her heart was breaking with despair, and pass by silently with that calmly indifferent face? He had not simply cooled towards her, he hated her, because he loved another woman – that was clear.

And, remembering all the cruel words he had said, Anna also invented the words he obviously had wished to say and might have said to her, and she grew more and more irritated.

'I am not holding you,' he might have said. 'You may go wherever you like. You probably did not want to divorce your husband so that you could go back to him. Go back, then. If you need money, I will give it to you. How many roubles do you need?'

All the cruellest words a coarse man could say, he said to her in her imagination, and she could not forgive him for them, as if he had actually said them to her.

'And wasn't it only yesterday that he swore he loved me, he, a truthful and honest man? Haven't I despaired uselessly many times before?' she said to herself after that.

All that day, except for the visit to Mrs Wilson, which took two hours, Anna spent wondering whether everything was finished or there was hope of a reconciliation, and whether she ought to leave at once or see him one more time. She waited for him the whole day, and in the evening, going to her room and giving the order to tell him she had a headache, she thought, 'If he comes in spite of what the maid says, it means he still loves me. If not, it means it's all over, and then I'll decide what to do! . . .'

In the evening she heard the sound of his carriage stopping, his ring, his footsteps and conversation with the maid: he believed what he was told, did not want to find out any more, and went to his room. Therefore it was all over.

And death presented itself to her clearly and vividly as the only way to restore the love for her in his heart, to punish him and to be victorious in the struggle that the evil spirit lodged in her heart was waging with him.

Now it made no difference whether they went to Vozdvizhenskoe or not, whether she got the divorce from her husband or not – none of it was necessary. The one thing necessary was to punish him.

When she poured herself the usual dose of opium and thought that she had only to drink the whole bottle in order to die, it seemed so easy and simple to her that she again began to enjoy thinking how he would suffer, repent, and love her memory when it was too late. She lay in bed with her eyes open, looking at the moulded cornice of the ceiling and the shadow of a screen extending over part of it in the light of one burnt-down candle, and she vividly pictured to herself what he would feel when she was no more and had become only a memory for him. 'How could I have said those cruel words to her?' he would say. 'How could I have left the room without saying anything? But now she's no more. She's gone from us for ever. She's there . . .' Suddenly the shadow of the screen wavered, spread over the whole cornice, over the whole ceiling; other shadows from the other side rushed to meet it; for a moment the shadows left, but then with renewed swiftness came over again, wavered, merged, and everything became dark. 'Death!' she thought. And she was overcome with such terror that for a long time she could not understand where she was, and her trembling hands were unable to find a match and light another candle in place of the one that had burned down and gone out. 'No, anything – only to live! I do love him. He does love me. It was and it will be no more,' she said, feeling tears of joy at the return of life running down her cheeks. And to save herself from her fear, she hastily went to him in the study.

He was in the study fast asleep. She went over to him and, lighting his face from above, looked at him for a long time. Now, when he was asleep, she loved him so much that, looking at him, she could not keep back tears of tenderness; but she knew that if he woke up he would give her a cold look, conscious of his own rightness, and that before talking to him of her love, she would have to prove to him how guilty he was before her. She went back to her room without waking him up and, after a second dose of opium, towards morning fell into a heavy, incomplete sleep, in which she never lost awareness of herself.

In the morning a dreadful nightmare, which had come to her repeatedly even before her liaison with Vronsky, came to her again and woke her up. A little old muzhik with a dishevelled beard was doing something, bent over some iron, muttering meaningless French words, and, as always in this nightmare (here lay its terror), she felt that this little muzhik paid no attention to her, but was doing this dreadful thing with iron over her, was doing something dreadful over her. And she awoke in a cold sweat.

When she got up, she recalled the previous day as in a fog.

'There was a quarrel. There was what had already happened several times. I said I had a headache, and he didn't come in. Tomorrow we're leaving, I must see him and get ready for the departure,' she said to herself. And, learning that he was in his study, she went to him. As she passed through the drawing room she heard a vehicle stop by the entrance, and, looking out the window, she saw a carriage with a young girl in a violet hat leaning out of it and giving orders to the footman who was ringing at the door. After negotiations in the front hall, someone came upstairs, and Vronsky's steps were heard by the drawing room. He was going downstairs with quick steps. Anna went to the window again. Now he came out on the steps without a hat and went up to the carriage. The young girl in the violet hat handed him a package. Vronsky, smiling, said something to her. The carriage drove off; he quickly ran back up the stairs.

The fog that had covered everything in her soul suddenly cleared. Yesterday's feelings wrung her aching heart with a new pain. She could not understand now how she could have lowered herself so far as to spend a whole day with him in his house. She went into his study to announce her decision to him.

'That was Mme Sorokin and her daughter calling by to bring me money and papers from *maman*. I couldn't get them yesterday. How's your head? Better?' he said calmly, not wishing to see or understand the gloomy and solemn expression on her face.

She stood silently in the middle of the room, gazing fixedly at him. He glanced at her, frowned momentarily, and went on reading a letter. She turned and slowly started out of the room. He could still bring her back, but she reached the door, he remained silent, and only the rustle of the turning page was heard.

'Ah, incidentally,' he said, when she was already in the doorway, 'we're definitely going tomorrow, aren't we?'

'You are, but I'm not,' she said, turning to him.

'Anna, we can't live like this . . .'

'You are, but I'm not,' she repeated.

'This is becoming unbearable!'

'You . . . you will regret that,' she said and walked out.

Frightened by the desperate look with which these words were spoken, he jumped up and was about to run after her, but, recollecting himself, sat down again, clenched his teeth tightly and frowned. This improper – as he found it – threat of something irritated him. 'I've tried everything,' he thought, 'the only thing left is to pay no attention,' and he began getting ready to go to town and again to his mother's, whose signature he needed on the warrant.

She heard the sound of his steps in the study and the dining room. He stopped by the drawing room. But he did not turn to her, he only gave orders to hand the stallion over to Voitov in his absence. Then she heard the carriage being brought, the door opening, him going out again. But now he was back in the front hall, and someone was running up the stairs. It was his valet running to fetch the gloves he had forgotten. She went to the window and saw him take the gloves without looking, touch the driver's back and say something to him. Then, without looking at the windows, he assumed his usual posture in the carriage, his legs crossed, and, pulling on a glove, disappeared round the corner.

XXVII

'He's gone. It's over!' Anna said to herself, standing at the window. And in response to this question the impressions of the horrible dream and of the darkness when the candle had gone out merged into one, filling her heart with cold terror.

'No, it can't be!' she cried out and, crossing the room, loudly rang the bell. She was now so afraid of staying alone that, without waiting for the servant to come, she went to meet him.

'Find out where the count went,' she said.

The servant replied that the count had gone to the stables.

'He said to tell you that the carriage will return at once, if you would like to go out.'

'Very well. Wait. I'll write a note. Send Mikhaila to the stables with the note. Quickly.'

She sat down and wrote:

'I am to blame. Come home, we must talk. For God's sake come, I'm frightened!'

She sealed it and gave it to the servant.

She was afraid to stay alone now. She left the room after the servant and went to the nursery.

'No, this isn't right, it's not him! Where are his blue eyes, his sweet and timid smile?' was her first thought when she saw her plump, red-cheeked little girl with curly hair instead of Seryozha, whom, in the confusion of her thoughts, she had expected to see in the nursery. The girl, sitting at the table, was loudly and persistently banging on it with a stopper, looking senselessly at her mother with two black currants – her eyes. Having said, in reply to the governess's question, that she was quite well and was going to the country the next day, Anna sat down with the girl and began twirling the stopper of the carafe in front of her. But the child's loud, ringing laughter and the movement she made with her eyebrow reminded her so vividly of Vronsky that she hastily got up, stifling her sobs, and left. 'Is it really all over? No, it can't be,' she thought. 'He'll come back. But how will he explain to me that smile, that animation after talking with her? But even if he doesn't explain, I'll still believe him. If I don't, there is only one thing left for me – and I don't want it.'

She looked at the clock. Twelve minutes had passed. 'He has received the note now and is coming back. It won't be long, another ten minutes ... But what if he doesn't come? No, that can't be. He mustn't see me with tearful eyes. I'll go and wash. Ah, and did I do my hair or not?' she asked herself. And could not remember. She felt her head with her hand. 'Yes, my hair's been done, but I certainly don't remember when.' She did not even believe her hand and went to the pier-glass to see whether her hair had indeed been done or not. It had been, but she could not remember when she had done it. 'Who is that?' she thought, looking in the mirror at the inflamed face with strangely shining eyes fearfully looking at her. 'Ah, it's me,' she realized, and looking herself all over, she suddenly felt his kisses on her and, shuddering, moved her shoulders. Then she raised her hand to her lips and kissed it.

'What is this? I'm losing my mind.' And she went to her bedroom, where Annushka was tidying up.

'Annushka,' she said, stopping before the maid and looking at her, not knowing what she was going to say to her.

'You wanted to go to Darya Alexandrovna's,' said the maid, as if she understood.

'To Darya Alexandrovna's? Yes, I'll go.'

'Fifteen minutes there, fifteen minutes back. He's on his way, he'll be here at any moment.' She took out her watch and looked at it. 'But how could he go away and leave me in such a state? How can he live without making it up with me?' She went to the window and began to look out. In terms of time, he could already be back. But her calculation could be wrong, and again she started recalling when he had left and counting the minutes.

As she was going to the big clock to check her watch, someone drove up. Looking out of the window, she saw his carriage. But no one came up the stairs and voices could be heard below. This was the messenger, who had come back in the carriage. She went down to him.

'I didn't find the count. He left for the Nizhni Novgorod railway.'

'What are you doing? What . . .' she said to the merry, red-cheeked Mikhaila, who was handing her note back to her.

'Ah, yes, he didn't get it,' she remembered.

'Take this note to Countess Vronsky's country estate. You know it? And bring an answer at once,' she said to the messenger.

'And I, what shall I do?' she thought. 'Ah, I'm going to Dolly's, that's right, otherwise I'll go out of my mind. Ah, I can also send a telegram.' And she wrote a telegram:

'*I absolutely must talk with you, come at once.*'

Having sent the telegram, she went to get dressed. Dressed and with her hat on, she again looked into the eyes of the plump, placid Annushka. Obvious compassion could be seen in those small, kind, grey eyes.

'Annushka, dear, what am I to do?' Anna said, sobbing, as she sank helplessly into an armchair.

'Why worry so, Anna Arkadyevna! It happens. You go and take your mind off it,' said the maid.

'Yes, I'll go,' said Anna, recollecting herself and getting up. 'And if a telegram comes while I'm gone, send it to Darya Alexandrovna's . . . No, I'll come back myself.

'Yes, I mustn't think, I must do something, go out, first of all – leave this house,' she said, listening with horror to the terrible turmoil in her heart, and she hurriedly went out and got into the carriage.

'Where to, ma'am?' asked Pyotr, before climbing up on the box.

'To Znamenka, to the Oblonskys'.'

XXVIII

The weather was clear. All morning there had been a fine, light drizzle, but now it had cleared up. The iron roofs, the flagstones of the pavements, the cobbles of the roadway, the wheels and leather, copper and tin of the carriages – everything glistened brightly in the May sun. It was three o'clock and the liveliest time in the streets.

Sitting in the corner of the comfortable carriage, barely rocking on its resilient springs to the quick pace of the greys, again going over the events of the last few days, under the incessant clatter of the wheels and the quickly changing impressions of the open air, Anna saw her situation quite differently from the way it had seemed to her at home. Now the thought of death no longer seemed to her so terrible and clear, and death itself no longer appeared inevitable. Now she reproached herself for stooping to such humiliation. 'I begged him to forgive me. I submitted to him. I acknowledged myself guilty. Why? Can't I live without him?' And, not answering the question of how she would live without him, she began reading the signboards. 'Office and Warehouse. Dentist. Yes, I'll tell Dolly everything. She doesn't like Vronsky. It will be shameful, painful, but I'll tell her everything. She loves me, and I'll follow her advice. I won't submit to him; I won't allow him to teach me. Filippov, Baker. They say he also sells his dough in Petersburg. Moscow water is so good. The Mytishchi springs and the pancakes.' And she remembered how long, long ago, when she was just seventeen years old, she had gone with her aunt to the Trinity Monastery.[26] 'One still went by carriage. Was that really me with the red hands? How much of what then seemed so wonderful and unattainable has become insignificant, and what there was then is now for ever unattainable. Would I have believed then that I could come to such humiliation? How proud and pleased he'll be when he gets my note! But I'll prove to him . . . How bad that paint smells. Why are they always painting and building? Fashions and Attire,' she read. A man bowed to her. It was Annushka's husband. 'Our parasites,' she remembered Vronsky saying. 'Ours? Why ours? The terrible thing is that it's impossible to tear the past out by the roots. Impossible to tear it out, but possible to hide the memory of it. And I will hide it.' Here she remembered her past with Alexei Alexandrovich and how she had wiped him from her memory. 'Dolly will think I'm leaving a second husband and so I'm probably in the wrong. As if I want to be right! I can't be!' she said, and wanted to cry. But she at once began thinking what those two young girls could be smiling at. 'Love, probably? They don't know how joyless it is, how low . . . A boulevard and children. Three boys running, playing horses. Seryozha! And I'll lose everything and not get him back. Yes, I'll lose everything if he doesn't come back. Maybe he was late for the train and is back by now. Again you want humiliation!' she said to herself. 'No, I'll go to Dolly and tell her straight out: I'm unhappy, I deserve it, I'm to blame, but even so I'm unhappy, help me.

These horses, this carriage – how loathsome I am to myself in this carriage – it's all his. But I won't see them any more.'

Thinking of the words she was going to say to Dolly, and deliberately chafing her own heart, Anna went up the steps.

'Is anyone here?' she asked in the front hall.

'Katerina Alexandrovna Levin,' the footman replied.

'Kitty! The same Kitty that Vronsky was in love with,' thought Anna, 'the one he remembered with love. He regrets not having married her. And me he remembers with hatred, and he regrets having become intimate with me.'

When Anna arrived, the two sisters were having a consultation about nursing. Dolly came out alone to meet her guest, who had just interrupted their conversation.

'You haven't left yet? I wanted to come and see you myself,' she said. 'I received a letter from Stiva today.'

'We also received a telegram,' Anna replied, looking past her for Kitty.

'He writes that he can't understand precisely what Alexei Alexandrovich wants, but that he won't leave without an answer.'

'I thought there was someone with you. May I read the letter?'

'Yes, it's Kitty,' Dolly said, embarrassed. 'She stayed in the nursery. She's been very ill.'

'I heard. May I read the letter?'

'I'll bring it at once. But he doesn't refuse. On the contrary, Stiva has hopes,' said Dolly, pausing in the doorway.

'I have no hope, and don't even wish it,' said Anna.

'What is it?' thought Anna, left alone. 'Does Kitty consider it humiliating to meet me? Maybe she's right. But it's not for her, who was once in love with Vronsky, it's not for her to show it to me, even if it's true. I know that not a single decent woman can receive me in my position. I know that from the first moment I sacrificed everything to him! And this is the reward! Oh, how I hate him! And why did I come here? It's still worse, still harder.' She heard the voices of the sisters talking in the other room. 'And what shall I say to Dolly now? Shall I comfort Kitty with my unhappiness, submit to her patronizing? No, and Dolly won't understand anything either. And I have nothing to tell her. It would only be interesting to see Kitty and show her how I despise everyone and everything, and how it makes no difference to me now.'

Dolly came with the letter. Anna read it and silently handed it back.

'I knew all that,' she said. 'And it doesn't interest me in the least.'

'But why? On the contrary, I'm hopeful,' said Dolly, looking at Anna with curiosity. She had never seen her in such a strange, irritated state. 'When are you leaving?' she asked.

Anna looked straight ahead with narrowed eyes and did not answer her.

'So is Kitty hiding from me?' she said, looking towards the door and blushing.

'Oh, what nonsense! She's nursing and it's not going well, so I advised her . . . She's very glad. She'll come at once,' Dolly said awkwardly, not knowing how to tell an untruth. 'And here she is.'

Learning that Anna was there, Kitty did not want to come out, but Dolly persuaded her to. Gathering her strength, Kitty came out and, blushing, went to her and held out her hand.

'I'm very glad,' she said in a trembling voice.

Kitty was confused by the struggle going on inside her between animosity towards this bad woman and the wish to be lenient with her; but as soon as she saw Anna's beautiful, sympathetic face, all her animosity disappeared at once.

'I wouldn't have been surprised if you didn't want to meet me. I've grown used to everything. You've been ill? Yes, you've changed,' said Anna.

Kitty felt that Anna was looking at her with animosity. She explained this animosity by the awkward position that Anna, who had once patronized her, now felt herself to be in, and she felt sorry for her.

They talked about her illness, about the baby, about Stiva, but obviously nothing interested Anna.

'I came to say good-bye to you,' she said, getting up.

'When are you leaving?'

But Anna, again without answering, turned to Kitty.

'Yes, I'm very glad to have seen you,' she said with a smile. 'I've heard so much about you from all sides, even from your husband. He visited me, and I liked him very much,' she added, obviously with ill intent. 'Where is he?'

'He went to the country,' Kitty said, blushing.

'Be sure to give him my regards.'

'I'll be sure to!' Kitty naïvely repeated, looking into her eyes with compassion.

'Farewell then, Dolly!' and having kissed Dolly and shaken Kitty's hand, Anna hastily went out.

'The same as always and just as attractive. Such a handsome woman!' said Kitty, when she was alone with her sister. 'But there's something pathetic about her! Terribly pathetic!'

'No, today there was something peculiar about her,' said Dolly. 'When I saw her off in the front hall, I thought she was going to cry.'

XXIX

Anna got into the carriage in a still worse state than when she had left the house. To the former torment was now added the feeling of being insulted and cast out, which she clearly felt when she met Kitty.

'Where to, ma'am? Home?' asked Pyotr.

'Yes, home,' she said, not even thinking of where she was going.

'How they looked at me as if at something frightful, incomprehensible and curious. What can he be talking about so ardently with the other one?' she thought, looking at two passers-by. 'Is it really possible to tell someone else what one feels? I wanted to tell Dolly, and it's a good thing I didn't. How glad she would be of my unhappiness! She would hide it, but her main feeling would be joy that I've been punished for the pleasures she envied me. Kitty, she would be even more glad. How I see right through her! She knows that I was more than usually friendly to her husband. And she's jealous, and she hates me. And also despises me. In her eyes I'm an immoral woman. If I were an immoral woman, I could get her husband to fall in love with me . . . if I wanted to. And I did want to. This one is pleased with himself,' she thought of a fat, red-cheeked gentleman who, as he drove by in the opposite direction, took her for an acquaintance and raised a shiny hat over his bald, shiny head and then realized he was mistaken. 'He thought he knew me. And he knows me as little as anyone else in the world knows me. I don't know myself. I know my appetites, as the French say. Those two want that dirty ice cream. That they know for certain,' she thought, looking at two boys who had stopped an ice-cream man, who was taking the barrel down from his head and wiping his sweaty face with the end of a towel. 'We all want something sweet, tasty. If not candy, then dirty ice cream. And Kitty's the same: if not Vronsky, then Levin. And she envies me. And hates me. We all hate each other. I Kitty, Kitty me. That's the truth.

Twitkin, Coiffeur . . . *Je me fais coiffer par Twitkin . . .** I'll tell him when he comes,' she thought and smiled. But at the same moment she remembered that she now had no one to tell anything funny to. 'And there isn't anything gay or funny. Everything is vile. The bells ring for vespers and this merchant crosses himself so neatly! As if he's afraid of dropping something. Why these churches, this ringing and this lie? Only to hide the fact that we all hate each other, like these cabbies who quarrel so spitefully. Yashvin says, "He wants to leave me without a shirt, and I him." That's the truth!'

In these thoughts, which carried her away so much that she even stopped thinking about her situation, she pulled up at the entrance of her house. Only on seeing the hall porter coming out to meet her did she remember that she had sent the note and the telegram.

'Is there an answer?' she asked.

'I'll look at once,' said the porter and, glancing at the desk, he picked up the thin, square envelope of a telegram and handed it to her. 'I cannot come before ten. Vronsky,' she read.

'And the messenger hasn't come back yet?'

'No, ma'am,' replied the porter.

'Ah, in that case I know what to do,' she said, and, feeling a vague wrath surge up in her, and a need for revenge, she ran upstairs. 'I'll go to him myself. Before going away for ever, I'll tell him everything. I've never hated anyone as I do this man!' she thought. Seeing his hat on the coat rack, she shuddered with revulsion. She did not realize that his telegram was a reply to her telegram and that he had not yet received her note. She imagined him now, calmly talking with his mother and Princess Sorokin and rejoicing at her suffering. 'Yes, I must go quickly,' she said to herself, still not knowing where to go. She wanted to get away quickly from the feelings she experienced in that terrible house. The servants, the walls, the things in the house – it all gave her a feeling of revulsion and anger and pressed her down with its weight.

'Yes, I must go to the railway station, and if I don't find him, I'll go there myself and expose him.' Anna looked up the train schedule in the newspaper. The evening train left at 8:02. 'Yes, I can make it.' She ordered other horses to be harnessed and began packing her travelling bag with the things necessary for several days. She knew she would not come back there any more. Among other plans that entered her head,

* I have my hair done by Twitkin.

she also vaguely decided that after whatever happened there at the station or at the countess's estate, she would take the Nizhni Novgorod railway to the first town and stay there.

Dinner was on the table; she went up to it, smelled the bread and cheese and, convinced that the smell of all food disgusted her, ordered the carriage to be brought and went out. The house already cast its shadow across the whole street, and the clear evening was still warm in the sun. Annushka, who accompanied her with her things, and Pyotr, who put them into the carriage, and the obviously disgruntled driver – they all disgusted her and irritated her with their words and movements.

'I don't need you, Pyotr.'

'And what about your ticket?'

'Well, as you like, it makes no difference to me,' she said with vexation.

Pyotr jumped up on the box and, arms akimbo, told the driver to go to the railway station.

XXX

'Here it is again! Again I understand everything,' Anna said to herself as soon as the carriage set off, rocking and clattering over the small cobbles, and again the impressions began changing one after another.

'Yes, what was that last thing I thought about so nicely?' she tried to remember. 'Twitkin, Coiffeur? No, not that. Yes, it was what Yashvin said: the struggle for existence and hatred – the only thing that connects people. No, you're going in vain,' she mentally addressed a company in a coach-and-four who were evidently going out of town for some merriment. 'And the dog you're taking with you won't help you. You won't get away from yourselves.' Glancing in the direction in which Pyotr had just turned, she saw a half-dead-drunk factory worker with a lolling head being taken somewhere by a policeman. 'Sooner that one,' she thought. 'Count Vronsky and I didn't find that pleasure either, though we expected so much from it.' And now for the first time Anna turned the bright light in which she saw everything upon her relations with him, which she had avoided thinking about before. 'What was he looking for in me? Not love so much as the satisfaction of his vanity.' She remembered his words, the expression on his face, like an obedient pointer, in the early days of their liaison. And now everything confirmed it. 'Yes, there was the triumph of successful vanity in him. Of course, there was love, too, but for the most part it was the pride of success. He boasted of me. Now it's past. Nothing to be proud of. Not proud but ashamed. He took all he could from me, and I'm of no use to him any more. I'm a burden to him, and he tries not to be dishonourable towards me. He let it slip yesterday – he wants the divorce and marriage in order to burn his boats. He loves me – but how? *The zest is gone*,' she said to herself in English. 'This one wants to astonish everybody and is very pleased with himself,' she thought, looking at a red-cheeked sales clerk riding a rented horse. 'Yes, I no longer have the same savour for him. If I leave him, at the bottom of his heart he'll be glad.'

This was not a supposition. She saw it clearly in that piercing light which now revealed to her the meaning of life and of people's relations.

'My love grows ever more passionate and self-centred, and his keeps fading and fading, and that's why we move apart,' she went on thinking. 'And there's no help for it. For me, everything is in him alone, and I demand that he give his entire self to me more and more. While he wants more and more to get away from me. We precisely went towards each other before our liaison, and after it we irresistibly move in different directions. And it's impossible to change that. He tells me I'm senselessly jealous, and I've told myself that I'm senselessly jealous, but it's not true. I'm not jealous, I'm dissatisfied. But . . .' She opened her mouth and shifted her place in the carriage from the excitement provoked by the thought that suddenly occurred to her. 'If I could be anything else but a mistress who passionately loves only his caresses – but I cannot and do not want to be anything else. And by this desire I provoke his disgust, and he provokes my anger, and it cannot be otherwise. Don't I know that he would not deceive me, that he doesn't have any intentions towards Princess Sorokin, that he is not in love with Kitty, that he will not be unfaithful to me? I know all that, but it's none the easier for me. If he is kind and gentle towards me out of *duty*, without loving me, and I am not to have what I want – that is a thousand times worse even than anger! It's hell! And that is what we have. He has long ceased loving me. And where love stops, hatred begins. I don't know these streets at all. Some sort of hills, and houses, houses . . . And in the houses people, people . . . So many, no end of them, and they all hate each other. Well, so let me think up for myself what I want in order to be happy. Well? I get the divorce, Alexei Alexandrovich gives me Seryozha, and I marry Vronsky.' Remembering Alexei Alexandrovich, she immediately pictured him with extraordinary vividness as if he were standing before her, with his meek, lifeless, extinguished eyes, the blue veins on his white hands, his intonations, the cracking of his fingers, and, remembering the feeling there had been between them, which was also called love, she shuddered with disgust. 'Well, I'll get the divorce and be Vronsky's wife. What, then? Will Kitty stop looking at me as she did today? No. And will Seryozha stop asking or thinking about my two husbands? And between me and Vronsky what new feeling will I think up? Is anything – not even happiness but just not torment – possible? No, nothing!' she answered herself now without the least hesitation. 'Impossible! Our lives are parting ways, and I have become his unhappiness and he mine, and it's impossible to remake either him or me. All efforts have been made; the screw is stripped. Ah, a beggar woman with a child. She thinks she's to be pitied. Aren't we all thrown into the world only in order to hate each other and so to torment ourselves and others. Students going by, laughing. Seryozha?' she remembered. 'I also thought I loved him and used to be moved by my own tenderness. But I did live without him, exchanged him for another love, and didn't complain of the exchange as long as I was satisfied by that love.' And with disgust she remembered what it was that she called 'that love'. And she was glad of the clarity with which she now saw her own and everyone else's life. 'So it is with me, and with Pyotr, with the driver Fyodor, and that merchant, and all the people living there on the Volga, where these announcements invite one to go, and everywhere and always,' she thought, as she drove up to the low building of the Nizhni Novgorod station and the attendants came running to meet her.

'A ticket to Obiralovka?' said Pyotr.

She had completely forgotten where and why she was going, and only with great effort was able to understand the question.

'Yes,' she said, handing him her purse and, with her small red bag on her arm, she got out of the carriage.

Walking through the crowd into the first-class waiting room, she gradually recalled all the details of her situation and the decisions among which she had been hesitating. And first hope, then despair over old hurts again began to chafe the wounds of her tormented, terribly fluttering heart. Sitting on a star-shaped sofa and waiting for the train, looking with revulsion at the people coming in and going out (they all disgusted her), she thought of how she would arrive at the station, write a note to him, and of what she would write, then of how he was now complaining to his mother (not understanding her suffering) about his situation, and how she would come into the room and what she would say to him. Then she thought of how life could still be happy, and how tormentingly she loved and hated him, and how terribly her heart was pounding.

XXXI

The bell rang, some young men went by, ugly, insolent and hurried, and at the same time conscious of the impression they produced; Pyotr also crossed the room in his livery and gaiters, with a dull, animal face, and came up to her in order to escort her to the train. The noisy men quieted down when she passed them on the platform, and one whispered something about her to another – something nasty, to be sure. She mounted the high step and sat by herself in a compartment, on a soiled, once white, spring seat. Her bag bounced on the springs and lay still. Outside the window, Pyotr, with a foolish smile, raised his gold-braided cap in a sign of farewell; an insolent conductor slammed the door and latched it. An ugly lady with a bustle (Anna mentally undressed the woman and was horrified at her hideousness) and a little girl, laughing unnaturally, ran by under the window.

'Katerina Andreevna has it, she has everything, *ma tante*!' cried the girl.

'The little girl – even she is ugly and affected,' Anna thought. So as not to see anyone, she quickly got up and sat at the opposite window in the empty carriage. A dirty, ugly muzhik in a peaked cap, his matted hair sticking out from under it, passed by the window, bending down to the wheels of the carriage. 'There's something familiar about that hideous muzhik,' thought Anna. And recalling her dream, she stepped away to the opposite door, trembling with fear. The conductor was opening the door, letting in a husband and wife.

'Would you like to get out?'

Anna did not reply. Neither the conductor nor the people who entered noticed the expression of terror on her face under the veil. She went back to her corner and sat down. The couple sat on the opposite side, studying her dress attentively but surreptitiously. Anna found both husband and wife repulsive. The husband asked whether she would allow him to smoke, obviously not in order to smoke, but in order to strike up a conversation with her. Having received her consent, he began talking with his wife in French about things he needed to talk about still less than he needed to smoke. They said foolish things in an affected way only so that she would overhear them. Anna saw clearly how sick they were of each other and how they hated each other. And it was impossible not to hate such pathetically ugly people.

The second bell rang and was followed by the moving of luggage, noise, shouting, laughter. It was so clear to Anna that no one had anything to be glad about, that this laughter irritated her painfully, and she would have liked to stop her ears so as not to hear it. Finally the third bell rang, the whistle sounded, the engine screeched, the chain jerked and the man crossed himself. 'It would be interesting to ask him what he means by that,' thought Anna, looking at him spitefully. She was gazing out of the window past the lady at the people who, as if rolling backwards, were standing on the platform seeing the train off. Rhythmically jolting over the joints of the tracks, the carriage in which Anna sat rolled past the platform, the brick wall, the signal disc, other carriages; the well-oiled, smooth-rolling wheels rang slightly over the rails, the window lit up with bright evening sunlight, and the breeze played with the curtain. Anna forgot her companions in the carriage and, to the slight rocking of the train, breathing in the fresh air, again began to think.

'Yes, where did I leave off? At the fact that I'm unable to think up a situation in which life would not be suffering, that we're all created in order to suffer, and that we all know it and keep thinking up ways of deceiving ourselves. But if you see the truth, what can you do?'

'Man has been given reason in order to rid himself of that which troubles him,' the lady said in French, obviously pleased with her phrase and grimacing with her tongue between her teeth.

The words were like a response to Anna's thought.

'To rid himself of that which troubles,' Anna repeated. And, glancing at the red-cheeked husband and the thin wife, she realized that the sickly wife considered herself a misunderstood woman and that her husband deceived her and supported her in this opinion of herself. It was as if Anna could see their story and all the hidden corners of their souls, turning her light on them. But there was nothing interesting there, and she went on with her thinking.

'Yes, troubles me very much, and reason was given us in order to rid ourselves of it. So I must rid myself of it. Why not put out the candle, if there's nothing more to look at, if it's vile to look at it all? But how? Why was that conductor running along the footboard? Why are those young men in the other carriage shouting? Why do they talk? Why do they laugh? It's all untrue, all a lie, all deceit, all evil! . . .'

When the train arrived at the station, Anna got off in a crowd of other passengers and, shunning them like lepers, stopped on the platform, trying to remember why she had come there and what she had intended to do. Everything that had seemed possible to her earlier was now very hard for her to grasp, especially in the noisy crowd of all these hideous people who would not leave her alone. Attendants came running up to her offering their services; young men, stomping their heels on the boards of the platform and talking loudly, looked her over; the people she met stepped aside the wrong way. Remembering that she wanted to go further if there was no answer, she stopped an attendant and asked whether there was a coachman there with a note for Count Vronsky.

'Count Vronsky? There was someone here from him just now. Meeting Princess Sorokin and her daughter. What is the coachman like?'

As she was speaking with the attendant, the coachman Mikhaila, red-cheeked, cheerful, in smart blue jacket with a watch chain, obviously proud of having fulfilled his errand so well, came up to her and handed her a note. She opened it, and her heart sank even before she read it.

'I'm very sorry the note did not find me. I'll be back at ten,' Vronsky wrote in a careless hand.

'So! I expected that!' she said to herself with a spiteful smile.

'Very well, you may go home,' she said softly, addressing Mikhaila. She spoke softly because the quick beating of her heart interfered with her breathing. 'No, I won't let you torment me,' she thought, addressing her threat not to him, not to herself, but to the one who made her suffer, and she walked along the platform past the station-house.

Two maids who were pacing the platform bent their heads back, looking at her and voicing their thoughts about her clothes. 'The real thing,' they said of the lace she was wearing. The young men would not leave her alone. They passed by again, peering into her face, laughing and shouting something in unnatural voices. The stationmaster, as he passed by, asked whether she would be getting on the train. A boy selling kvass could not take his eyes off her. 'My God, where to go?' she thought, walking further and further down the platform. At the end of it she stopped. Some ladies and children, who were laughing and talking loudly as they met a gentleman in spectacles, fell silent and looked her over as she went past them. She quickened her pace and walked away from them to the edge of the platform. A goods train was coming. The platform shook, and it seemed to her that she was on the train again.

And suddenly, remembering the man who was run over the day she first met Vronsky, she realized what she must do. With a quick, light step she went down the stairs that led from the water pump to the rails and stopped close to the passing train. She looked at the bottoms of the carriages, at the bolts and chains and big cast-iron wheels of the first carriage slowly rolling by, and tried to estimate by eye the midpoint between the front and back wheels and the moment when the middle would be in front of her.

'There!' she said to herself, staring into the shadow of the carriage at the sand mixed with coal poured between the sleepers, 'there, right in the middle, and I'll punish him and be rid of everybody and of myself.'

She wanted to fall under the first carriage, the midpoint of which had drawn even with her. But the red bag, which she started taking off her arm, delayed her, and it was too late: the midpoint went by. She had to wait for the next carriage. A feeling seized her, similar to what she experienced when preparing to go into the water for a swim, and she crossed herself. The habitual gesture of making the sign of the cross called up in her soul a whole series of memories from childhood and girlhood, and suddenly the darkness that covered everything for her broke and life rose up before her momentarily with all its bright past joys. Yet she did not take her eyes from the wheels of the approaching second carriage. And just at the moment when the midpoint between the two wheels came even with her, she threw the red bag aside and, drawing her head down between her shoulders, fell on her hands under the carriage, and with a light movement, as if preparing to get up again at once, sank to her knees. And in that same instant she was horrified at what she was doing. 'Where am I? What am I doing? Why?' She wanted to rise, to throw herself back, but something huge and implacable pushed at her head and dragged over her. 'Lord, forgive me for everything!' she said, feeling the impossibility of any struggle. A little muzhik, muttering to himself, was working over some iron. And the candle by the light of which she had been reading that book filled with anxieties, deceptions, grief and evil, flared up brighter than ever, lit up for her all that had once been in darkness, sputtered, grew dim, and went out for ever.

Part Eight

I

Nearly two months had gone by. It was already the middle of the hot summer, and Sergei Ivanovich was only now preparing to leave Moscow.

During that time, Sergei Ivanovich had his own events going on in his life. His book, the fruit of six years of toil, entitled *An Essay in Survey of the Principles and Forms of Statehood in Europe and Russia*, had been finished a year ago. Some sections of the book and the introduction had been printed in periodical publications and other parts had been read by Sergei Ivanovich to people of his circle, so that the ideas of the work could no longer be quite new to the public; but all the same Sergei Ivanovich expected the appearance of the book to make a serious impression in society and cause, if not a revolution in scholarship, at least a great stir in the scholarly world.

This book, after careful polishing, had been published last year and sent out to the booksellers.

Asking no one about it, responding with reluctance and feigned indifference to his friends' questions about how the book was doing, not even asking the booksellers how the sales were, Sergei Ivanovich watched keenly and with strained attention for the first impression his book would make in society and in literature.

But a week went by, a second, a third, and there was no noticeable impression in society. His friends, the specialists and scholars, sometimes mentioned it, evidently out of politeness. But his other acquaintances, not interested in a book of learned content, did not speak to him about it at all. And in society, which especially now was busy with other things, there was complete indifference. In literature, too, for a whole month there was not a word about the book.

Sergei Ivanovich calculated in detail the time needed to write a review, but a month went by, then another, and there was the same silence.

Only in the *Northern Beetle*,[1] in a humorous *feuilleton* about the singer Drabanti, who had lost his voice, were a few scornful words said in passing about Koznyshev's book, indicating that it had long since been condemned by all and handed over to general derision.

Finally in the third month a critical article appeared in a serious journal. Sergei Ivanovich knew the author of the article. He had met him once at Golubtsov's.

The author was a very young and sickly *feuilletonist*, quite pert as a writer, but with extremely little education and timid in his personal relations.

Despite his complete contempt for the author, Sergei Ivanovich set about with complete respect to read the article. The article was terrible.

The *feuilletonist* had obviously understood the whole book deliberately in a way in which it could not possibly be understood. But he had selected his quotations so cleverly that for those who had not read the book (and obviously almost no one had read it) it was completely clear that the whole book was nothing but a collection of highflown words, which were also used inappropriately (this was indicated by question marks), and that the author of the book was a completely ignorant man. And it was all so witty that Sergei Ivanovich would not have minded displaying such wit himself. That was the terrible thing.

Despite the complete conscientiousness with which Sergei Ivanovich tested the correctness of the reviewer's arguments, he did not linger for a moment over the shortcomings and mistakes that were being ridiculed – it was too obvious that it had all been selected on purpose – but at once began involuntarily to recall in the smallest detail his meeting and conversation with the author of the article.

'Did I offend him in some way?' Sergei Ivanovich asked himself.

And remembering that, when they had met, he had corrected the young man in the use of a word that showed his ignorance, he found the explanation of the article's meaning.

After this article came a dead silence, both printed and oral, about the book, and Sergei Ivanovich saw that his work of six years, elaborated with such love and effort, had gone by without leaving a trace.

His situation was the more difficult because, once he finished the book, he no longer had the intellectual work that formerly had taken up the greater part of his time.

Sergei Ivanovich was intelligent, educated, healthy, energetic and did not know where to apply his energy. Conversations in drawing rooms, conferences, meetings, committees, wherever one could talk, took up part of his time; but as an inveterate city-dweller, he did not allow himself to be totally consumed by talking, as his inexperienced brother did when he was in Moscow; he was still left with considerable leisure and mental force.

Fortunately for him, at this most trying time of his book's failure, the questions of racial minorities, American friends, famine in Samara, the Exposition, and spiritism came to be replaced by the Slavic question,[2] previously only smouldering in society, and Sergei Ivanovich, one of those who had previously raised this question, gave himself wholly to it.

In the milieu to which Sergei Ivanovich belonged, nothing else was talked or written about at that time but the Slavic question and the Serbian war. All that an idle crowd usually does to kill time was now done for the benefit of the Slavs. Balls, concerts, dinners, speeches, ladies' dresses, beer, taverns – all bore witness to a sympathy with the Slavs.

With much of what was said and written on this subject Sergei Ivanovich did not agree in detail. He saw that the Slavic question had become one of those fashionable fads which, supplanting one another, always serve as a subject of concern for society; he also saw that there were many people who concerned themselves with it for vain, self-interested purposes. He recognized that the newspapers printed a great many useless and exaggerated things with one aim – to draw attention to themselves and out-shout the rest. He saw that in this general upsurge of society the ones who leaped to the forefront and shouted louder than the rest were all the failures and the aggrieved: commanders-in-chief without armies, ministers without ministries, journalists without journals, party chiefs without partisans. He saw that much here was frivolous and ridiculous; but he also saw and recognized the unquestionable, ever growing enthusiasm which united all classes of society, with which one could not but sympathize. The slaughter of co-religionists and brother Slavs awakened sympathy for the sufferers and indignation against the oppressors. And the heroism of the Serbs and Montenegrins, fighting for a great cause, generated in the whole nation a desire to help their brothers not in word now but in deed.

But with that came another phenomenon that made Sergei Ivanovich rejoice: this was the manifestation of public opinion. Society definitely expressed its wish. The nation's soul was given expression, as Sergei Ivanovich liked to put it. And the more involved he became in it, the more obvious it seemed to him that this was a cause that would attain vast proportions, that would mark an epoch.

He devoted himself completely to the service of this great cause and forgot all about his book.

His time was now wholly taken up, so that he was even unable to respond to all the letters and requests addressed to him.

Having spent the entire spring and part of the summer working, it was only in the month of July that he decided to go to his brother's in the country.

He was going for a two-week rest in the very holy of holies of the people, the depths of the country, there to revel in the sight of that upsurge of popular spirit of which he and all the inhabitants of the capital and other cities were fully convinced. Katavasov, who had long wanted to fulfil his promise to visit Levin, went with him.

II

Sergei Ivanovich and Katavasov had only just driven up to the Kursk railway station, particularly alive with people that day, climbed out of the carriage, and looked round for the footman who was coming after them with the luggage, when the volunteers[3] arrived in four hired cabs. Ladies with bouquets met them and, accompanied by the crowd that poured after them, they went into the station.

One of the ladies who had met the volunteers addressed Sergei Ivanovich as she came out of the waiting room.

'You've also come to see them off?' she asked in French.

'No, Princess, I'm travelling myself. For a rest at my brother's. Do you always see them off?' Sergei Ivanovich said with a barely perceptible smile.

'One couldn't possibly!' replied the princess. 'Is it true that we've already sent eight hundred men? Malvinsky didn't believe me.'

'More than eight hundred. If we count those who weren't sent directly from Moscow, it's over a thousand,' said Sergei Ivanovich.

'Well, there. Just what I said!' the lady agreed joyfully. 'And it's true that nearly a million has been donated now?'

'More, Princess.'

'And how about today's telegram? The Turks have been beaten again.'

'Yes, I read it,' replied Sergei Ivanovich. They were speaking of the latest telegram confirming that for three days in a row the Turks had been beaten at all points and had fled, and that the decisive battle was expected the following day.

'Ah, yes, you know, there's a certain young man, a wonderful one, who wants to volunteer. I don't know why they made difficulties. I know him and wanted to ask you please to write a note. He's been sent from Countess Lydia Ivanovna.'

Having asked what details the princess knew about the volunteering young man, Sergei Ivanovich went to the first-class waiting room, wrote a note to the person on whom it depended, and gave it to the princess.

'You know, Count Vronsky, the famous one . . . is going on this train,' said the princess, with a triumphant and meaningful smile, when he found her again and handed her the note.

'I heard he was going but didn't know when. On this train, is it?'

'I saw him. He's here. His mother is the only one seeing him off. All in all, it's the best thing he could do.'

'Oh, yes, of course.'

While they were talking, the crowd poured past them towards the dining table. They also moved there and heard the loud voice of one gentleman who, with a glass in his hand, delivered a speech to the volunteers. 'Serve for the faith, for humanity, for our brothers,' the gentleman spoke, constantly raising his voice. 'Mother Moscow blesses you for a great deed. *Zhivio!*'* he concluded loudly and tearfully.

Everyone shouted '*Zhivio!*' and another new crowd poured into the room, all but knocking the princess off her feet.

'Ah, Princess! How about all this!' said Stepan Arkadyich, who suddenly appeared in the midst of the crowd, beaming with a joyful smile. 'He put it so nicely, so warmly, didn't he? Bravo! And Sergei Ivanych! Why don't you say something for your part – a few words, you know, an encouragement. You do it so well,' he added with a gentle, respectful and cautious smile, pushing Sergei Ivanovich lightly by the arm.

'No, I'm just leaving.'

'Where for?'

'The country, my brother's place,' replied Sergei Ivanovich.

'You'll see my wife, then. I've written to her, but you'll see her before;

* 'Viva' in Serbian.

please tell her you've seen me and it's *all right*. She'll understand. Anyhow, be so good as to tell her that I've been appointed a member of the commission of the United . . . Well, she'll understand! You know, *les petites misères de la vie humaine*,'* he turned to the princess, as if in apology. 'And Princess Miagky, not Liza but Bibish, is really sending a thousand guns and twelve nurses. Did I tell you?'

'Yes, I heard that,' Koznyshev said reluctantly.

'It's a pity you're leaving,' said Stepan Arkadyich. 'Tomorrow we're giving a dinner for two departing friends – Diemer-Bartniansky from Petersburg, and our own Veselovsky, Grisha. They're both going. Veselovsky got married recently. A fine fellow! Right, Princess?' he turned to the lady.

The princess, without replying, looked at Koznyshev. But the fact that both Sergei Ivanovich and the princess seemed to want to be rid of him did not embarrass Stepan Arkadyich in the least. Smiling, he looked now at the feather in the princess's hat, now all around him, as if trying to remember something. Seeing a lady passing by with a cup, he called her over and put a five-rouble note into it.

'I can't look calmly at those cups as long as I've got money,' he said. 'And how do you like today's dispatch? Fine fellows, the Montenegrins!'

'You don't say so!' he exclaimed, when the princess told him that Vronsky was going on this train. For a moment Stepan Arkadyich's face showed sadness; but a minute later, when, springing at each step and smoothing his side-whiskers, he went into the room where Vronsky was, Stepan Arkadyich had already quite forgotten his desperate sobs over his sister's body and saw Vronsky only as a hero and an old friend.

'With all his shortcomings it's impossible not to do him justice,' said the princess to Sergei Ivanovich, as soon as Oblonsky left them. 'His is precisely a fully Russian, Slavic nature! Only I'm afraid Vronsky won't find it pleasant to see him. Whatever you say, that man's fate moves me. Talk to him on the way,' said the princess.

'Yes, maybe, if I have the chance.'

'I never liked him. But this redeems a lot. He's not only going himself, but he's equipping a squadron at his own expense.'

'Yes, I heard.'

The bell rang. Everyone crowded towards the door.

'There he is!' said the princess, pointing to Vronsky, in a long coat

* The little miseries of human life.

and wide-brimmed black hat, walking arm in arm with his mother. Oblonsky was walking beside him, saying something animatedly.

Vronsky, frowning, was looking straight ahead of him, as if not hearing what Stepan Arkadyich was saying.

Probably at Oblonsky's indication, he glanced over to where the princess and Sergei Ivanovich were standing and silently raised his hat. His face, aged and full of suffering, seemed made of stone.

Going out on the platform, Vronsky silently let his mother pass and disappeared into the carriage.

From the platform came 'God Save the Tsar,' then shouts of 'Hurrah!' and '*Zhivio!*' One of the volunteers, a tall and very young man with a sunken chest, bowed especially conspicuously, waving a felt hat and a bouquet over his head. From behind him, also bowing, peeped two officers and an older man with a big beard and a greasy peaked cap.

III

Having taken leave of the princess, Sergei Ivanovich and Katavasov, who now rejoined him, got into the packed carriage together, and the train started.

At the Tsaritsyn station[4] the train was met by a harmonious choir of young people singing 'Glory Be'. Again the volunteers bowed and stuck their heads out the windows, but Sergei Ivanovich paid no attention to them; he had dealt with the volunteers so much that he knew their general type and it did not interest him. But Katavasov, busy with his learned occupations, had had no chance to observe the volunteers, was very interested in them and questioned Sergei Ivanovich about them.

Sergei Ivanovich advised him to go to second class and talk with them himself. At the next station Katavasov followed that advice.

At the first stop he went to second class and made the acquaintance of the volunteers. They were sitting apart in a corner of the carriage, talking loudly, obviously aware that the attention of the passengers and of the entering Katavasov was turned on them. The loudest talker of all was the young man with the sunken chest. He was obviously drunk and was recounting some episode that had happened at his school. Opposite him sat an officer, no longer young, wearing an Austrian military jacket from the uniform of the guards. He listened, smiling, to the narrator and kept interrupting him. The third, in an artillery uniform, sat on a suitcase next to them. The fourth was asleep.

Getting into conversation with the young man, Katavasov learned that he was a wealthy Moscow merchant who had squandered a large fortune before he was twenty-two. Katavasov disliked him for being pampered, spoiled, and of weak health; he was obviously convinced, especially now, after drinking, that he was performing a heroic deed, and he boasted in a most disagreeable manner.

The second, the retired officer, also made an unpleasant impression on Katavasov. One could see that this was a man who had tried everything. He had worked for the railway, and as a steward, and had started his own factory, and talked about it all using learned words needlessly and inappropriately.

The third, the artilleryman, on the contrary, Katavasov liked very much. He was a modest, quiet man, who obviously admired the knowledge of the retired guardsman and the heroic self-sacrifice of the merchant and did not say anything about himself. When Katavasov asked him what had moved him to go to Serbia, he replied modestly:

'Why, everybody's going. We must help the Serbs. It's a pity.'

'Yes, they're especially short of you artillerymen,' said Katavasov.

'I didn't serve long in the artillery. Maybe they'll send me to the infantry or the cavalry.'

'Why the infantry when artillerymen are needed most of all?' said Katavasov, calculating from the artilleryman's age that he must be of significant rank.

'I didn't serve long in the artillery, I retired as a cadet,' he said, and began to explain why he had not passed the examination.

All this together made an unpleasant impression on Katavasov, and when the volunteers got out at the station to have a drink, he wanted to talk with someone and share his unfavourable impression. One passenger, a little old man in a military overcoat, had been listening all the while to his conversation with the volunteers. Left alone with him, Katavasov addressed him.

'What a variety of situations among all the men going there,' Katavasov said vaguely, wishing to voice his opinion and at the same time to find out what the old man's opinion was.

The old man was a soldier who had done two campaigns. He knew what it was to be a soldier, and from the look and talk of these gentlemen, from the dashing way they applied themselves to the flask as they went, he considered them poor soldiers. Besides, he lived in a provincial town and wanted to tell how a discharged soldier in his town had volunteered, a drunkard and a thief whom no one would even hire as a worker. But knowing from experience that, in the present mood of society, it was dangerous to express an opinion contrary to the general one, and particularly to denounce the volunteers, he also searched out Katavasov.

'Well, they need people there. I've heard the Serbian officers aren't any good.'

'Oh, yes, and these will make fine soldiers,' Katavasov said, laughing with his eyes. And they began to talk about the latest war news, each concealing from the other his perplexity as to whom the next day's battle was to be fought with, if, according to the latest news, the Turks had been beaten at all points. And so they parted, neither of them having voiced his opinion.

Katavasov went to his carriage and, involuntarily dissembling, told Sergei Ivanovich his observations on the volunteers, from which it turned out that they were excellent fellows.

At a large town station the volunteers were again met with singing and shouting, again men and women appeared with collection cups, and the provincial ladies offered bouquets to the volunteers and followed them to the buffet; but all this was considerably weaker and smaller than in Moscow.

IV

During the stop in the provincial capital Sergei Ivanovich did not go to the buffet but started pacing up and down the platform.

The first time he walked past Vronsky's compartment, he noticed that the window was curtained. But, walking past it a second time, he saw the old countess at the window. She called him over to her.

'You see, I'm accompanying him as far as Kursk,' she said.

'Yes, I heard,' said Sergei Ivanovich, pausing by her window and looking inside. 'What a handsome gesture on his part!' he added, noticing that Vronsky was not in the compartment.

'But after his misfortune what was he to do?'

'Such a terrible occurrence!' said Sergei Ivanovich.

'Ah, what I've lived through! But do come in . . . Ah, what I've lived through!' she repeated, when Sergei Ivanovich came in and sat down beside her on the seat. 'You can't imagine! For six weeks he didn't speak to anyone and ate only when I begged him to. And he couldn't be left alone for a single moment. We took away everything he might have used to kill himself; we lived on the ground floor, but we couldn't predict anything. You know, he already tried to shoot himself because of her,' she said, and the old lady's brows knitted at the memory of it. 'Yes, she ended as such a woman should have ended. Even the death she chose was mean and low.'

'It's not for us to judge, Countess,' Sergei Ivanovich said with a sigh, 'but I understand how hard it was for you.'

'Ah, don't even say it! I was living on my estate and he was with me. A note was brought to him. He wrote a reply and sent it back. We had no idea that she was right there at the station. In the evening I had just gone to my room when my Mary told me that some lady at the station had thrown herself under a train. It was as if something hit me! I knew it was she. The first thing I said was: "Don't tell him." But he had already been told. His coachman was there and saw it all. When I came running into his room, he was no longer himself – it was terrible to look at him. He galloped off to the station without saying a word. I don't know what happened there, but he was brought back like a dead man. I wouldn't have recognized him. *Prostration complète*, the doctor said. Then came near frenzy.

'Ah, what is there to say!' the countess went on, waving her hand. 'A terrible time! No, whatever you say, she was a bad woman. Well, what are these desperate passions! It's all to prove something special. So she proved it. Ruined herself and two fine men – her husband and my unfortunate son.'

'And what about her husband?' asked Sergei Ivanovich.

'He took her daughter. At first Alyosha agreed to everything. But now he suffers terribly for having given his daughter to a stranger. But he can't go back on his word. Karenin came to the funeral. But we tried to make it so that he wouldn't meet Alyosha. For him, for the husband, it's easier after all. She set him free. But my poor son gave her all of himself. He abandoned everything – career, me – and even so she took no pity on him but deliberately destroyed him completely. No, whatever you say, her death was itself the death of a vile, irreligious woman. God forgive me, but I can't help hating her memory, looking at the ruin of my son.'

'But how is he now?'

'This is God's help to us, this Serbian war. I'm an old woman, I don't understand anything about it, but it's been sent him by God. Of course, as a mother I'm afraid, and above all they say *ce n'est pas très bien vu à Pétersbourg.** But what can be done! It's the only thing that could have lifted him up again. Yashvin – his friend – lost everything at cards and decided to go to Serbia. He came to see him and talked him into it. Now he's taken up with it. Talk to him, please, I want him to be distracted. He's so sad. And, as ill luck would have it, he's got a toothache. He'll be very glad to see you. Please talk to him, he's walking on that side.'

Sergei Ivanovich said he would be very glad to, and went over to the other side of the train.

V

In the slanted evening shadow of the sacks piled on the platform, Vronsky, in his long coat, his hat pulled down over his eyes, his hands in his pockets, was pacing like a caged animal, turning abruptly every twenty steps. As Sergei Ivanovich approached, it seemed to him that Vronsky saw him but pretended to be unseeing. That made no difference to Sergei Ivanovich. He was above keeping any personal accounts with Vronsky.

In Sergei Ivanovich's eyes, Vronsky was at that moment an important actor in a great cause, and he considered it his duty to encourage him and show his approval. He went up to him.

Vronsky stopped, peered, recognized him and, taking a few steps towards him, gave him a very firm handshake.

'Perhaps you didn't wish to see me,' said Sergei Ivanovich, 'but may I not be of some use to you?'

'There is no one it would be less unpleasant for me to see than you,' said Vronsky. 'Forgive me. Nothing in life is pleasant for me.'

'I understand, and I wanted to offer you my services,' said Sergei Ivanovich, peering into Vronsky's obviously suffering face. 'Might you need a letter to Ristich, or to Milan?'[5]

'Oh, no!' said Vronsky, as though he had difficulty understanding. 'If you don't mind, let's walk a bit more. It's so stuffy on the train. A letter?

* It's not very well regarded in Petersburg.

No, thank you. One needs no recommendations in order to die. Unless it's to the Turks . . .' he said, smiling with his lips only. His eyes kept their expression of angry suffering.

'Yes, but perhaps it will be easier for you to enter into relations, which are necessary in any case, with someone who has been prepared. However, as you wish. I was very glad to hear of your decision. There are so many attacks on the volunteers that a man like you raises them in public opinion.'

'As a man,' said Vronsky, 'I'm good in that life has no value for me. And I have enough physical energy to hack my way into a square and either crush it or go down – that I know. I'm glad there's something for which I can give my life, which is not so much needless as hateful to me. It will be useful to somebody.' And he made an impatient movement with his jaw, caused by an incessant, gnawing toothache, which even prevented him from speaking with the expression he would have liked.

'You'll come back to life, I predict it,' said Sergei Ivanovich, feeling moved. 'Delivering one's brothers from the yoke is a goal worthy of both death and life. May God grant you outward success – and inner peace,' he added and held out his hand.

Vronsky firmly pressed Sergei Ivanovich's hand.

'Yes, as a tool I may prove good for something. But as a human being I am a wreck,' he said measuredly.

The nagging pain in the strong tooth, filling his mouth with saliva, prevented him from speaking. He fell silent, peering into the wheels of a tender rolling slowly and smoothly towards him on the rails.

And suddenly a quite different feeling, not pain but a general, tormenting inner discomfort, made him forget his toothache for a moment. As he looked at the tender and the rails, influenced by the conversation with an acquaintance he had not met since his misfortune, he suddenly remembered *her* – that is, what was left of her when he came running like a madman into the shed of the railway station: on a table in the shed, sprawled shamelessly among strangers, lay the blood-covered body, still filled with recent life; the intact head with its heavy plaits and hair curling at the temples was thrown back, and on the lovely face with its half-open red lips a strange expression was frozen, pitiful on the lips and terrible in the fixed, unclosed eyes, as if uttering the words of that terrible phrase – that he would regret it – which she had spoken to him when they had quarrelled.

And he tried to remember her as she had been when he first met her, also at a station, mysterious, enchanting, loving, seeking and giving happiness, and not cruelly vengeful as he remembered her in the last moment. He tried to remember his best moments with her, but those moments were for ever poisoned. He remembered only her triumphant, accomplished threat of totally unnecessary but ineffaceable regret. He ceased to feel the toothache, and sobs distorted his face.

After silently walking past the sacks a couple of times and regaining control of himself, he calmly addressed Sergei Ivanovich:

'Have you had any telegrams since yesterday's? Yes, they were beaten for a third time, but tomorrow the decisive battle is expected.'

And having talked more about Milan being proclaimed king and the enormous consequences it might have, they went back to their carriages after the second bell.

VI

As he had not known when he would be able to leave Moscow, Sergei Ivanovich had not telegraphed his brother in order to be met. Levin was not at home when Katavasov and Sergei Ivanovich, dusty as Moors, in a little tarantass hired at the station, drove up to the porch of the Pokrovskoe house at around noon. Kitty, who was sitting on the balcony with her father and sister, recognized her brother-in-law and ran down to meet him.

'Shame on you for not letting us know,' she said, giving Sergei Ivanovich her hand and offering her forehead.

'We had a wonderful ride, and without bothering you,' replied Sergei Ivanovich. 'I'm so dusty I'm afraid to touch you. I've been so busy I didn't know when I'd be able to get away. And you, as ever,' he said, smiling, 'are enjoying quiet happiness far from all the currents in your quiet backwater. And our friend Fyodor Vassilyevich also finally decided to come.'

'And I'm no Negro – I'll wash and look like a human being,' Katavasov said with his usual jocularity, giving her his hand and smiling, his teeth gleaming especially on account of his black face.

'Kostya will be very glad. He's gone out to the farmstead. He ought to be home any time now.'

'Still busy with the farming. Precisely in backwaters,' said Katavasov.

'And we in the city see nothing but the Serbian war. Well, what's my friend's attitude? Surely something unlike other people's?'

'No, not really, the same as everyone else's,' Kitty replied, looking with some embarrassment at Sergei Ivanovich. 'I'll send for him, then. And we have papa with us. He came from abroad not long ago.'

And, giving orders that Levin be sent for and that her dust-covered guests be taken to wash, one to the study, the other to Dolly's former room, and that lunch be prepared for them, she ran out to the balcony, exercising her right to move quickly, which she had been deprived of during her pregnancy.

'It's Sergei Ivanovich and Katavasov, a professor,' she said.

'Ah, it's hard in such heat!' said the prince.

'No, papa, he's very nice, and Kostya loves him very much,' said Kitty, smiling, as if persuading him of something, having noticed the mocking look on her father's face.

'Oh, don't mind me.'

'Go to them, darling,' Kitty said to her sister, 'and entertain them. They met Stiva at the station. He's well. And I'll run to Mitya. Poor thing, I haven't nursed him since breakfast. He's awake now and must be crying.' And, feeling the influx of milk, she went with quick steps to the nursery.

Indeed, it was not that she guessed (her bond with the baby had not been broken yet), but she knew for certain by the influx of milk in her that he needed to be fed.

She knew he was crying even before she came near the nursery. And he was indeed crying. She heard his voice and quickened her pace. But the quicker she walked, the louder he cried. It was a good, healthy, but hungry and impatient voice.

'Has he been crying long, nanny?' Kitty said hurriedly, sitting down on a chair and preparing to nurse him. 'Give him to me quickly. Ah, nanny, how tiresome you are – no, you can tie the bonnet afterwards!'

The baby was in a fit of greedy screaming.

'That's not the way, dearie,' said Agafya Mikhailovna, who was almost always there in the nursery. 'He must be tidied up properly. Coo, coo!' she sang over him, paying no attention to the mother.

The nanny brought the baby to the mother. Agafya Mikhailovna followed them, her face melting with tenderness.

'He knows me, he does. It's God's truth, dearest Katerina Alexandrovna, he recognized me!' Agafya Mikhailovna out-shouted the baby.

But Kitty did not listen to what she said. Her impatience kept growing along with the baby's.

Owing to that impatience, it was a long time before matters were put right. The baby grabbed the wrong thing and got angry.

Finally, after a desperate, gasping cry and empty sucking, matters were put right, mother and baby simultaneously felt pacified, and both quieted down.

'He's all sweaty, too, poor little thing,' Kitty said in a whisper, feeling the baby. 'Why do you think he recognizes you?' she added, looking sideways at the baby's eyes, which seemed to her to be peeping slyly from under the pulled-down bonnet, at his regularly puffing cheeks and his hand with its red palm, with which he was making circular movements.

'It can't be! If he recognized anyone, it would be me,' Kitty said in response to Agafya Mikhailovna's observation, and she smiled.

She smiled because, though she had said he could not recognize anything, she knew in her heart that he not only recognized Agafya Mikhailovna but knew and understood everything, knew and understood much else that no one knew and which she, his mother, had herself learned and begun to understand only thanks to him. For Agafya Mikhailovna, for his nanny, for his grandfather, even for his father, Mitya was a living being who required only material care; but for his mother he had long been a moral creature with whom she had a whole history of spiritual relations.

'Once he wakes up, God willing, you'll see for yourself. I do like this, and he just beams all over, the darling. Beams all over, like a sunny day,' said Agafya Mikhailovna.

'Well, all right, all right, we'll see then,' whispered Kitty. 'Go now, he's falling asleep.'

VII

Agafya Mikhailovna tiptoed out; the nanny lowered the blind, chased away the flies from under the muslin bed curtain and a hornet that was beating against the window-pane, and sat down, waving a wilting birch branch over the mother and baby.

'Ah, this heat, this heat! If only God would send a little rain,' she said.

'Yes, yes, shh . . .' was Kitty's only reply, as she rocked slightly and gently pressed down the plump arm, as if tied with a thread at the wrist, which Mitya kept waving weakly, now closing, now opening his eyes. This arm disturbed Kitty: she would have liked to kiss it but was afraid to, lest she waken the baby. The little arm finally stopped moving and the eyes closed. Only from time to time, going on with what he was doing, the baby raised his long, curling eyelashes slightly and glanced at his mother with his moist eyes, which seemed black in the semi-darkness. The nanny stopped waving and dozed off. From upstairs came the rumble of the old prince's voice and Katavasov's loud laughter.

'They must have struck up a conversation without me,' thought Kitty. 'But all the same it's vexing that Kostya's not here. He must have gone to the apiary again. Though it's sad that he goes there so often, I'm glad all the same. It diverts him. Now he's begun to be more cheerful and better than in the spring. Then he was so gloomy and tormented, I began to be frightened for him. What a funny man!' she whispered, smiling.

She knew what tormented her husband. It was his unbelief. Although, if she had been asked whether she supposed that in the future life he would perish for his unbelief, she would have had to agree that he would, his unbelief did not make her unhappy; and while she acknowledged that there was no salvation for an unbeliever, and she loved her husband's soul more than anything in the world, she smiled as she thought about his unbelief and said to herself that he was funny.

'Why has he been reading all sorts of philosophies for a whole year?' she thought. 'If it's all written in those books, then he can understand them. If it's not true, why read them? He says himself that he'd like to believe. Then why doesn't he believe? Probably because he thinks so much. And he thinks so much because of his solitude. Alone, always alone. With us he can't talk about everything. I think he'll like having these guests, especially Katavasov. He likes discussing things with him,' she thought, and at once turned her mind to where it would be best to put Katavasov – in a separate room, or together with Sergei Ivanovich. And here a thought suddenly came to her that made her start with agitation and even disturb Mitya, who gave her a stern look for it. 'I don't think the laundress has brought the washing yet, and the bed linen for guests has all been used. If I don't see to it, Agafya Mikhailovna will give Sergei Ivanovich unwashed linen' – and the very thought of it brought the blood rushing to Kitty's face.

'Yes, I'll see to it,' she decided and, going back to her previous thoughts, remembered that she had not finished thinking about something important, intimate, and she began to remember what it was. 'Yes, Kostya's an unbeliever,' she remembered again with a smile.

'So, he's an unbeliever! Better let him stay that way than be like Mme Stahl, or like I wanted to be that time abroad. No, he's not one to pretend.'

And a recent instance of his kindness appeared vividly to her. Two weeks ago Dolly had received a repentant letter from Stepan Arkadyich. He implored her to save his honour, to sell her estate in order to pay his debts. Dolly was in despair, hated her husband, despised him, pitied him, resolved to divorce him, to refuse him, but ended by agreeing to sell part of her estate. Then Kitty, with an involuntary smile of tenderness, remembered her husband's embarrassment, his several awkward approaches to the matter in question, and how, having thought up the one and only way of helping Dolly without insulting her, he had suggested that Kitty give up her part of the estate, something she had not thought of before.

'What kind of unbeliever is he? With his heart, with that fear of upsetting anyone, even a child! Everything for others, nothing for himself. Sergei Ivanovich simply thinks it's Kostya's duty to be his steward. His sister, too. Now Dolly and her children are in his care. And there are all these muzhiks who come to him every day as if it were his business to serve them.'

'Yes, be just like your father, be just like him,' she said, handing Mitya to the nanny and touching his cheek with her lips.

VIII

From that moment when, at the sight of his beloved brother dying, Levin had looked at the questions of life and death for the first time through those new convictions, as he called them, which imperceptibly, during the period from twenty to thirty-four years of age, had come to replace his childhood and adolescent beliefs, he had been horrified, not so much at death as at life without the slightest knowledge of whence it came, wherefore, why, and what it was. The organism, its decay, the indestructibility of matter, the law of the conservation of energy, development, were the words that had replaced his former faith. These words and the concepts connected with them were very well suited to intellectual purposes, but they gave nothing for life, and Levin suddenly felt himself in the position of a person who has traded his warm fur coat for muslin clothing and, caught in the cold for the first time, is convinced beyond question, not by reasoning but with his whole being, that he is as good as naked and must inevitably die a painful death.

From that moment on, though not accounting for it to himself and continuing to live as before, Levin never ceased to feel that fear at his ignorance.

Moreover, he felt vaguely that what he called his convictions were not only ignorance but were a way of thinking that made the knowledge he needed impossible.

At first his marriage, the new joys and responsibilities he came to know, completely stifled these thoughts; but lately, after his wife gave birth, while he was living idly in Moscow, Levin began to be faced more and more often, more and more urgently, by this question that demanded an answer.

The question for him consisted in the following: 'If I do not accept the answers that Christianity gives to the questions of my life, then which answers do I accept?' And nowhere in the whole arsenal of his convictions was he able to find, not only any answers, but anything resembling an answer.

He was in the position of a man looking for food in a toymaker's or a gunsmith's shop.

Involuntarily, unconsciously, he now sought in every book, in every conversation, in every person, a connection with these questions and their resolution.

What amazed and upset him most of all was that the majority of people of his age and circle, who had replaced their former beliefs, as he had, with the same new beliefs as he had, did not see anything wrong with it and were perfectly calm and content. So that, besides the main question, Levin was tormented by other questions: Are these people sincere? Are they not pretending? Or do they not understand somehow differently, more clearly, than he the answers science gives to the questions that concerned him? And he diligently studied both the opinions of these people and the books that expressed these answers.

One thing he had discovered since he began to concern himself with these questions was that he had been mistaken in supposing, from memories of his youthful university circle, that religion had outlived its day and no longer existed. All the good people close to him were believers. The old prince, and Lvov, whom he had come to love so much, and Sergei Ivanovich, and all the women were believers, and his wife believed as he had believed in early childhood, and ninety-nine hundredths of all the Russian people, that people whose life inspired the greatest respect in him, were believers.

Another thing was that, after reading many books, he became convinced that those who shared the same views with him saw nothing else implied in them and, without explaining anything, simply dismissed the questions which he felt he could not live without answering, and tried to resolve completely different questions, which could not be of interest to him – for instance, about the development of the organism, about the mechanical explanation of the soul, and so on.

Besides that, while his wife was giving birth an extraordinary thing had happened to him. He, the unbeliever, had begun to pray, and in the moment of praying he had believed. But that moment had passed, and he was unable to give any place in his life to the state of mind he had been in then.

He could not admit that he had known the truth then and was now mistaken, because as soon as he began to think calmly about it, the whole thing fell to pieces; nor could he admit that he had been mistaken then, because he cherished his state of soul of that time, and by admitting that it had been due to weakness he would have profaned those moments. He was in painful discord with himself and strained all the forces of his soul to get out of it.

IX

These thoughts wearied and tormented him now less, now more strongly, but they never left him. He read and pondered, and the more he read and pondered, the further he felt himself from the goal he was pursuing.

Recently in Moscow and in the country, convinced that he would not find an answer in the materialists, he reread, or read for the first time, Plato, and Spinoza, Kant, Schelling, Hegel and Schopenhauer – the philosophers who gave a non-materialistic explanation of life.[6]

Their thoughts seemed fruitful to him when he was either reading or devising refutations of other teachings, especially that of the materialists; but as soon as he read or himself devised answers to the questions, one and the same thing always repeated itself. Following the given definitions of vague words such as *spirit*, *will*, *freedom*, *substance*, deliberately falling into the verbal trap set for him by the philosophers or by himself, he seemed to begin to understand something. But he had only to forget the artificial train of thought and refer back from life itself to what had satisfied him while he thought along a given line – and suddenly the whole artificial edifice would collapse like a house of cards, and it would be clear that the edifice had been made of the same words rearranged, independent of something more important in life than reason.

Once, reading Schopenhauer, he substituted *love* for his *will*,[7] and this new philosophy comforted him for a couple of days, until he stepped back from it; but it collapsed in the same way when he later looked at it from life, and turned out to be warmthless muslin clothing.

His brother Sergei Ivanovich advised him to read the theological works of Khomiakov.[8] Levin read the second volume of Khomiakov's writings and, despite the elegant and witty polemical tone, which put him off at first, was struck by their teaching about the Church. He was struck first by the thought that it is not given to man to comprehend divine truths, but it is given to an aggregate of men united by love – the Church. He rejoiced at the thought of how much easier it was to believe in the presently existing, living Church, which constitutes the entire faith of men, which has God at its head and is therefore holy and infallible, and from it to receive one's beliefs about God, creation, the fall, redemption, than to begin with God, the distant, mysterious God, creation, and so on. But later, having read a history of the Church by a Catholic writer and a history of the Church by an Orthodox writer, and seeing that the two Churches, infallible in their essence, rejected each other, he became disappointed in Khomiakov's teaching about the Church as well, and this edifice fell to dust just as the philosophical edifices had done.

All that spring he was not himself and lived through terrible moments.

'Without knowing what I am and why I'm here, it is impossible for me to live. And I cannot know that, therefore I cannot live,' Levin would say to himself.

'In infinite time, in the infinity of matter, in infinite space, a bubble-organism separates itself, and that bubble holds out for a while and then bursts, and that bubble is – me.'

This was a tormenting untruth, but it was the sole, the latest result of age-long labours of human thought in that direction.

This was the latest belief on which all researches of the human mind in almost all fields were built. This was the reigning conviction, and out of all other explanations it was precisely this one that Levin, himself not knowing when or how, had involuntarily adopted as being at any rate the most clear.

But it was not only untrue, it was the cruel mockery of some evil power, evil and offensive, which it was impossible to submit to.

It was necessary to be delivered from this power. And deliverance was within everyone's reach. It was necessary to stop this dependence on evil. And there was one means – death.

And, happy in his family life, a healthy man, Levin was several times so close to suicide that he hid a rope lest he hang himself with it, and was afraid to go about with a rifle lest he shoot himself.

But Levin did not shoot himself or hang himself and went on living.

X

When Levin thought about what he was and what he lived for, he found no answer and fell into despair; but when he stopped asking himself about it, he seemed to know what he was and what he lived for, because he acted and lived firmly and definitely; recently he had even lived much more firmly and definitely than before.

Returning to the country in the middle of June, he also returned to his usual occupations. Farming, relations with the muzhiks and his neighbours, running the household, his sister's and brother's affairs, which were in his hands, relations with his wife and family, cares about the baby, the new interest in bees he had acquired that last spring, took up all his time.

These things occupied him, not because he justified them to himself by some general views as he had done formerly; on the contrary, now, disappointed by the failure of his earlier undertakings for the general good, on the one hand, and, on the other hand, too occupied with his thoughts and the very quantity of things that piled upon him from all sides, he completely abandoned all considerations of the common good, and these things occupied him only because it seemed to him that he had to do what he was doing – that he could not do otherwise.

Formerly (it had begun almost from childhood and kept growing till full maturity), whenever he had tried to do something that would be good for everyone, for mankind, for Russia, for the district, for the whole village, he had noticed that thinking about it was pleasant, but the doing itself was always awkward, there was no full assurance that the thing was absolutely necessary, and the doing itself, which at the start had seemed so big, kept diminishing and diminishing, dwindling to nothing; while now, after his marriage, when he began to limit himself more and more to living for himself, though he no longer experienced any joy at the thought of what he was doing, he felt certain that his work was necessary, saw that it turned out much better than before and that it was expanding more and more.

Now, as if against his will, he cut deeper and deeper into the soil, like a plough, so that he could no longer get out without turning over the furrow.

For the family to live as their fathers and grandfathers had been accustomed to live – that is, in the same cultural conditions and with the same upbringing of children – was undoubtedly necessary. It was as necessary as dinner when one was hungry; and just as for that it was necessary to prepare dinner, so it was necessary to run the farming mechanism of Pokrovskoe in such a way as to produce income. As undoubtedly as it was necessary to pay debts, it was also necessary to maintain the family land in such condition that when his son inherited it he would thank his father, as Levin had thanked his grandfather for everything he had built and planted. And for that it was necessary not to lease the land, but to do the farming personally, to keep cattle, to manure the fields, to plant trees.

It was as impossible not to take care of Sergei Ivanovich's affairs, the affairs of his sister and of all the muzhiks who came for advice and were accustomed to do so, as it was impossible to drop a baby one is already holding in one's arms. It was necessary to see to the comfort of his invited sister-in-law and her children, and of his wife and baby, and it was impossible not to spend at least a small part of the day with them.

All that, together with hunting and the new interest in bees, filled that entire life of Levin's which had no meaning for him when he thought.

But besides the fact that Levin firmly knew *what* he had to do, he knew just as well *how* he had to do it all and which matter was more important than another.

He knew that he had to hire workers as cheaply as possible, but that he should not put them in bondage by paying them in advance at a cheaper rate than they were worth, though it was very profitable. He could sell the muzhiks straw when there was a shortage, though he felt sorry for them; but the inn and the pot-house, even though they brought income, had to be eliminated. For felling timber he had to punish them as severely as possible, but he could not fine them for cattle that strayed into his pastures, and though it upset the watchmen and eliminated fear, it was impossible not to return the stray cattle.

Pyotr, who was paying ten per cent a month to a moneylender, had to be given a loan to redeem him; but it was impossible to let go or postpone the payment of quit-rent for non-paying muzhiks. The steward could not be let off if a small meadow was left unmowed and the grass went to waste; yet he could not mow the two hundred acres where a young forest had been planted. He could not excuse a worker who went home during a work period because his father had died, no matter how sorry he felt for him, and he had to pay him less for the costly months he missed; but it was impossible not to give monthly payments to old, useless household serfs.

Levin also knew that, on returning home, he must first of all go to his wife, if she was unwell, and that the muzhiks who had been waiting for three hours could wait longer; and he knew that, despite all the pleasure he experienced when hiving a swarm, he would have to give up that pleasure and let the old man hive the swarm without him, and go to talk with the peasants who had come looking for him at the apiary.

Whether he was acting well or badly he did not know, and not only would not start proving it now but even avoided talking or thinking about it.

Reasoning led him into doubt and kept him from seeing what he should and should not do. Yet when he did not think, but lived, he constantly felt in his soul the presence of an infallible judge who decided which of two possible actions was better and which was worse; and whenever he did not act as he should, he felt it at once.

So he lived, not knowing and not seeing any possibility of knowing what he was and why he was living in the world, tormented by this ignorance to such a degree that he feared suicide, and at the same time firmly laying down his own particular, definite path in life.

XI

The day Sergei Ivanovich arrived at Pokrovskoe was one of Levin's most tormenting days.

It was the most pressing work time, when all the peasants show such an extraordinary effort of self-sacrifice in their labour as is not shown in any other conditions of life, and which would be highly valued if the people who show this quality valued it themselves, if it were not repeated every year, and if the results of this effort were not so simple.

To mow and reap rye and oats and cart them, to mow out the meadows, to cross-plough the fallow land, to thresh the seed and sow the winter crops – it all seems simple and ordinary; but to manage to get it all done, it was necessary that all the village people, from oldest to youngest, work ceaselessly during those three or four weeks, three times more than usual, living on kvass, onions and black bread, threshing and transporting the sheaves by night and giving no more than two or three hours a day to sleep. And every year this was done all over Russia.

Having lived the major part of his life in the country and in close relations with the peasantry, Levin always felt during the work period that this general peasant excitement communicated itself to him as well.

In the morning he went to the first sowing of the rye, then to the oats, which he helped to cart and stack. Returning by the time his wife and sister-in-law got up, he had coffee with them and left on foot for the farmstead, where they had to start the newly set-up threshing machine for preparing the seed.

That whole day, talking with the steward and the muzhiks, and at home talking with his wife, with Dolly, with her children, with his father-in-law, Levin thought about the one and only thing that occupied him during this time, apart from farm cares, and sought in everything a link to his questions: 'What am I? And where am I? And why am I here?'

Standing in the cool of the newly covered threshing barn, with fragrant leaves still clinging to the hazel rods pressed to the freshly peeled aspen rafters of the thatched roof, Levin gazed now through the open doorway in which the dry and bitter dust of the threshing hovered and sparkled, at the grass of the threshing floor lit by the hot sun and the fresh straw just taken from the barn, now at the white-breasted swallows with multi-coloured heads that flew peeping under the roof and, fluttering their wings, paused in the opening of the door, now at the people pottering about in the dark and dusty threshing barn, and thought strange thoughts.

'Why is all this being done?' he thought. 'What am I standing here and making them work for? Why are they all bustling about and trying to show me their zeal? Why is this old woman toiling so? (I know her, she's Matryona, I treated her when a beam fell on her during a fire),' he thought, looking at a thin woman who, as she moved the grain with a rake, stepped tensely with her black-tanned bare feet over the hard, uneven threshing floor. 'That time she recovered; but today or tomorrow or in ten years they'll bury her and nothing will be left of her, nor of that saucy one in the red skirt who is beating the grain from the chaff with such a deft and tender movement. She'll be buried, too, and so will this piebald gelding – very soon,' he thought, looking at the heavy-bellied horse, breathing rapidly through flared nostrils, that was treading the slanted wheel as it kept escaping from under him. 'He'll be buried, and Fyodor, the feeder, with his curly beard full of chaff and the shirt torn on his white shoulder, will also be buried. And now he's ripping the sheaves open, and giving orders, and yelling at the women, and straightening the belt on the flywheel with a quick movement. And above all, not only they, but I, too, will be buried and nothing will be left. What for?'

He thought that and at the same time looked at his watch to calculate how much had been threshed in an hour. He had to know that in order to set the day's quota by it.

'It will soon be an hour, and they've only just started on the third stack,' Levin thought, went over to the feeder and, shouting above the noise of the machine, told him to feed more slowly.

'You stuff in too much, Fyodor! See – it gets choked, that's why it's slow. Even it out!'

Blackened by the dust sticking to his sweaty face, Fyodor shouted something in reply, but went on doing it not as Levin wanted.

Levin went up to the drum, motioned Fyodor aside, and began feeding himself.

Working till the muzhiks' dinner-time, which was not far off, he left the threshing barn together with the feeder and got into conversation with him, stopping by a neat yellow rick of harvested rye stacked on the seed-threshing floor.

The feeder came from a distant village, the one where Levin used to lease land on collective principles. Now it was leased to an innkeeper.

Levin got into conversation about that land with Fyodor and asked whether Platon, a wealthy and good muzhik from the same village, might rent it next year.

'The price is too dear, Platon wouldn't make enough, Konstantin Dmitrich,' said the muzhik, picking ears of rye from under his sweaty shirt.

'Then how does Kirillov make it pay?'

'Mityukha' (so the muzhik scornfully called the innkeeper) 'makes it pay right enough, Konstantin Dmitrich! He pushes till he gets his own. He takes no pity on a peasant. But Uncle Fokanych' (so he called old Platon), 'he won't skin a man. He lends to you, he lets you off. So he comes out short. He's a man, too.'

'But why should he let anyone off?'

'Well, that's how it is – people are different. One man just lives for his own needs, take Mityukha even, just stuffs his belly, but Fokanych – he's an upright old man. He lives for the soul. He remembers God.'

'How's that? Remembers God? Lives for the soul?' Levin almost shouted.

'Everybody knows how – by the truth, by God's way. People are different. Now, take you even, you wouldn't offend anybody either . . .'

'Yes, yes, goodbye!' said Levin, breathless with excitement, and, turning, he took his stick and quickly walked off towards home.

A new, joyful feeling came over him. At the muzhik's words about Fokanych living for the soul, by the truth, by God's way, it was as if a host of vague but important thoughts burst from some locked-up place and, all rushing towards the same goal, whirled through his head, blinding him with their light.

XII

Levin went in big strides along the main road, listening not so much to his thoughts (he still could not sort them out) as to the state of his soul, which he had never experienced before.

The words spoken by the muzhik had the effect of an electric spark in his soul, suddenly transforming and uniting into one the whole swarm of disjointed, impotent, separate thoughts which had never ceased to occupy him. These thoughts, imperceptibly to himself, had occupied him all the while he had been talking about leasing the land.

He felt something new in his soul and delightedly probed this new thing, not yet knowing what it was.

'To live not for one's own needs but for God. For what God? For God. And could anything more meaningless be said than what he said? He said one should not live for one's needs – that is, one should not live for what we understand, for what we're drawn to, for what we want – but for something incomprehensible, for God, whom no one can either comprehend or define. And what then? Didn't I understand those meaningless words of Fyodor's? And having understood, did I doubt their rightness? Did I find them stupid, vague, imprecise?

'No, I understood him, and in absolutely the same way that he understands, I understood fully and more clearly than I understand anything else in life, and never in my life have I doubted or could I doubt it. And not I alone, but everybody, the whole world, fully understands this one thing, and this one thing they do not doubt and always agree upon.

'Fyodor says that Kirillov the innkeeper lives for his belly. That is clear and reasonable. None of us, as reasonable beings, can live otherwise than for our belly. And suddenly the same Fyodor says it's bad to live for the belly and that one should live for the truth, for God, and I understand him from a hint! And I and millions of people who lived ages ago and are living now, muzhiks, the poor in spirit, and the wise men who have thought and written about it, saying the same thing in their vague language – we're all agreed on this one thing: what we should live for and what is good. I and all people have only one firm, unquestionable and clear knowledge, and this knowledge cannot be explained by reason – it is outside it, and has no causes, and can have no consequences.

'If the good has a cause, it is no longer the good; if it has a consequence – a reward – it is also not the good. Therefore the good is outside the chain of cause and effect.

'And I know it, and we all know it.

'But I looked for miracles, I was sorry that I'd never seen a miracle that would convince me. And here it is, the only possible miracle, ever existing, surrounding me on all sides, and I never noticed it!

'What miracle can be greater than that?

'Is it possible that I've found the solution to everything, is it possible that my sufferings are now over?' thought Levin, striding along the dusty road, noticing neither heat nor fatigue, and experiencing a feeling of relief after long suffering. This feeling was so joyful that it seemed incredible to him. He was breathless with excitement and, unable to walk any further, went off the road into the woods and sat down on the unmowed grass in the shade of the aspens. He took the hat from his sweaty head and lay down, propping himself on his elbow in the succulent, broad-bladed forest grass.

'Yes, I must collect myself and think it over,' he thought, looking intently at the untrampled grass before him and following the movements of a little green bug that was climbing a stalk of couch-grass and was blocked in its ascent by a leaf of angelica. 'From the very beginning,' he said to himself, holding back the leaf of angelica so that it no longer hindered the bug and bending down some other plant so that the bug could get over on to it. 'What makes me so glad? What have I discovered?

'I used to say that in my body, in the body of this plant and of this bug (it didn't want to go over to that plant, it spread its wings and flew away), an exchange of matter takes place according to physical, chemical and physiological laws. And that in all of us, along with the aspens, and the clouds, and the nebulae, development goes on. Development out of what? Into what? An infinite development and struggle? . . . As if there can be any direction or struggle in infinity! And I was astonished that in spite of the greatest efforts of my thinking along that line, the meaning of life, the meaning of my impulses and yearnings, was still not revealed to me. Yet the meaning of my impulses is so clear to me that I constantly live by it, and was amazed and glad when a muzhik voiced it for me: to live for God, for the soul.

'I haven't discovered anything. I've only found out what I know. I've understood that power which not only gave me life in the past but is giving me life now. I am freed from deception, I have found the master.'

And he briefly repeated to himself the whole train of his thought during those last two years, the beginning of which was the clear, obvious thought of death at the sight of his beloved, hopelessly ill brother.

Understanding clearly then for the first time that for every man and for himself nothing lay ahead but suffering, death and eternal oblivion, he decided that it was impossible to live that way, that he had either to explain his life so that it did not look like the wicked mockery of some devil, or shoot himself.

But he had done neither the one nor the other, and had gone on living, thinking and feeling, and had even married at that same time and experienced much joy, and was happy whenever he did not think about the meaning of his life.

What did it mean? It meant that his life was good, but his thinking was bad.

He lived (without being aware of it) by those spiritual truths that he had drunk in with his mother's milk, yet he thought not only without admitting those truths but carefully avoiding them.

Now it was clear to him that he was able to live only thanks to the beliefs in which he had been brought up.

'What would I be and how would I live my life, if I did not have those beliefs, did not know that one should live for God and not for one's needs? I would rob, lie, kill. Nothing of what constitutes the main joys of my life would exist for me.' And, making the greatest efforts of imagination, he was still unable to imagine the beastly being that he himself would be if he did not know what he lived for.

'I sought an answer to my question. But the answer to my question could not come from thought, which is incommensurable with the question. The answer was given by life itself, in my knowledge of what is good and what is bad. And I did not acquire that knowledge through anything, it was given to me as it is to everyone, *given* because I could not take it from anywhere.

'Where did I take it from? Was it through reason that I arrived at the necessity of loving my neighbour and not throttling him? I was told it as a child, and I joyfully believed it, because they told me what was in my soul. And who discovered it? Not reason. Reason discovered the struggle for existence and the law which demands that everyone who hinders the satisfaction of my desires should be throttled. That is the conclusion of reason. Reason could not discover love for the other, because it's unreasonable.

'Yes, pride,' he said to himself, rolling over on his stomach and beginning to tie stalks of grass into a knot, trying not to break them.

'And not only the pride of reason, but the stupidity of reason. And, above all – the slyness, precisely the slyness, of reason. Precisely the swindling of reason,' he repeated.

XIII

And Levin remembered a recent scene with Dolly and her children. The children, left alone, started roasting raspberries over the candles and squirting streams of milk into their mouths. Their mother, catching them at it, tried to impress upon them, in Levin's presence, how much work the things they destroyed had cost the grown-ups, and that this work had been done for them, and that if they started breaking cups they would have nothing to drink tea out of, and if they started spilling milk they would have nothing to eat and would die of hunger.

And Levin was struck by the quiet, glum mistrust with which the children listened to their mother. They were merely upset that their amusing game had been stopped and did not believe a word of what she said to them. And they could not believe it, because they could not imagine the full scope of what they enjoyed and therefore could not imagine that they were destroying the very thing they lived by.

'That all goes without saying,' they thought, 'and there's nothing interesting or important about it, because it has always been so and always will be. And it's always the same thing over and over. There's no point in us thinking about it, it's all ready-made. We'd like to think up some new little thing of our own. So we thought up putting raspberries in a cup and roasting them over a candle, and squirting milk in streams straight into each other's mouths. It's fun and new and no worse than drinking from cups.'

'Don't we do the same thing, didn't I, when I sought the significance of the forces of nature and the meaning of human life with reason?' he went on thinking.

'And don't all philosophical theories do the same thing, leading man by a way of thought that is strange and unnatural to him to the knowledge of what he has long known and known so certainly that without it he would not even be able to live? Is it not seen clearly in the development of each philosopher's theory that he knows beforehand, as unquestionably as the muzhik Fyodor and no whit more clearly than he, the chief meaning of life, and only wants to return by a dubious mental path to what everybody knows?

'Go on, leave the children alone to provide for themselves, to make the dishes, do the milking and so on. Would they start playing pranks? They'd starve to death. Go on, leave us to ourselves, with our passions and thoughts, with no notion of one God and Creator! Or with no notion of what the good is, with no explanation of moral evil.

'Go on, try building something without those notions!

'We destroy only because we're spiritually sated. Exactly like children!

'Where do I get the joyful knowledge I have in common with the muzhik, which alone gives me peace of mind? Where did I take it from?

'Having been brought up with the notion of God, as a Christian, having filled my whole life with the spiritual blessings that Christianity gave me, filled with those blessings myself and living by them, but, like the children, not understanding them, I destroy – that is, want to destroy – what I live by. And as soon as an important moment comes in my life, like children who are cold and hungry, I go to Him, and even less than children scolded by their mother for their childish pranks do I feel that my childish refusal to let well enough alone is not to my credit.

'Yes, what I know, I do not know by reason, it is given to me, it is revealed to me, and I know it by my heart, by faith in that main thing that the Church confesses.

'The Church? The Church!' Levin repeated, turned over on his other side and, leaning on his elbow, began looking into the distance, at the herd coming down to the river on the other bank.

'But can I believe in everything the Church confesses?' he thought, testing himself and thinking up everything that might destroy his present peace. He began purposely to recall all the teachings of the Church that had always seemed to him the most strange and full of temptation. 'Creation? And how do I account for existence? By existence? By nothing? The devil and sin? And how am I to explain evil? . . . The Redeemer? . . .

'But I know nothing, nothing, and can know nothing but what I've been told along with everybody else.'

And it now seemed to him that there was not a single belief of the Church that violated the main thing – faith in God, in the good, as the sole purpose of man.

In place of each of the Church's beliefs there could be put the belief in serving the good instead of one's needs. And each of them not only did not violate it but was indispensable for the accomplishment of that chief miracle, constantly manifested on earth, which consists in it being possible for each person, along with millions of the most diverse people, sages and holy fools, children and old men – along with everyone, with some peasant, with Lvov, with Kitty, with beggars and kings – to understand one and the same thing with certainty and to compose that life of the soul which alone makes life worth living and alone is what we value.

Lying on his back, he was now looking at the high, cloudless sky. 'Don't I know that it is infinite space and not a round vault? But no matter how I squint and strain my sight, I cannot help seeing it as round and limited, and despite my knowledge of infinite space, I am undoubtedly right when I see a firm blue vault, more right than when I strain to see beyond it.'

Levin had stopped thinking and was as if only listening to the mysterious voices that spoke joyfully and anxiously about something among themselves.

'Can this be faith?' he wondered, afraid to believe his happiness. 'My God, thank you!' he said, choking back the rising sobs and with both hands wiping away the tears that filled his eyes.

XIV

Levin looked before him and saw the herd, then he saw his own little gig with Raven harnessed to it, and the coachman, who drove up to the herd and said something to the herdsman; then, already close to him, he heard the sound of wheels and the snorting of the sleek horse; but he was so absorbed in his thoughts that he did not even think why the coachman was coming to him.

He remembered it only when the coachman, having driven up quite close to him, called out.

'The mistress sent me. Your brother has come and some other gentleman with him.'

Levin got into the gig and took the reins.

As if roused from sleep, Levin took a long time coming to his senses. He looked at the sleek horse, lathered between the thighs and on the neck where a strap rubbed it, looked at the coachman, Ivan, who was sitting beside him, and remembered that he had been expecting his brother, that his wife was probably worried by his long absence, and tried to guess who the visitor was who had come with his brother. He now pictured his brother, and his wife, and the unknown visitor differently than before. It seemed to him that his relations with all people would now be different.

'With my brother now there won't be that estrangement there has always been between us, there won't be any arguments; with Kitty there will be no more quarrels; with the visitor, whoever he is, I'll be gentle and kind; and with the servants, with Ivan, everything will be different.'

Keeping a tight rein on the good horse, who was snorting with impatience and begging to run free, Levin kept looking at Ivan, who sat beside him not knowing what to do with his idle hands and constantly smoothing down his shirt, and sought a pretext for starting a conversation with him. He wanted to say that Ivan should not have tightened the girth so much, but that seemed like a reproach and he wanted to have a loving conversation. Yet nothing else came to his mind.

'Please bear to the right, sir, there's a stump,' said the coachman, guiding Levin by the reins.

'Kindly do not touch me and do not instruct me!' said Levin, vexed by this interference from the coachman. This interference vexed him just as it always had, and at once he sadly felt how mistaken he had been in supposing that his inner state could instantly change him in his contacts with reality.

About a quarter of a mile from home, Levin saw Grisha and Tanya running to meet him.

'Uncle Kostya! Mama's coming, and grandpapa, and Sergei Ivanych, and somebody else,' they said, climbing into the gig.

'Who is it?'

'He's terribly scary! And he goes like this with his arms,' said Tanya, standing up in the gig and imitating Katavasov.

'But is he old or young?' Levin asked, laughing, reminded of someone by Tanya's imitation. 'Ah,' he thought, 'I only hope it's not somebody unpleasant!'

Only when he turned round the bend of the road and saw them coming to meet him did Levin recognize Katavasov in his straw hat, walking along waving his arms just as Tanya had imitated him.

Katavasov was very fond of talking about philosophy, taking his notion of it from natural scientists who never studied philosophy, and in Moscow recently Levin had had many arguments with him.

One of those conversations, in which Katavasov had thought he had gained the upper hand, was the first thing that Levin remembered when he recognized him.

'No, I'm not going to argue and speak my thoughts light-mindedly, not for anything,' he thought.

Getting down from the gig and greeting his brother and Katavasov, Levin asked about his wife.

'She's taken Mitya to Kolok' (that was a wood near the house). 'She wanted to settle him there, it's hot in the house,' said Dolly.

Levin had always advised his wife against taking the baby to the wood, which he considered dangerous, and the news displeased him.

'She rushes from place to place with him,' the prince said, smiling. 'I advised her to try taking him to the ice-cellar.'

'She wanted to go to the apiary. She thought you were there. That's where we're going,' said Dolly.

'Well, what are you up to?' said Sergei Ivanovich, lagging behind the others and walking side by side with his brother.

'Nothing special. Busy with farming, as usual,' Levin answered. 'And you, can you stay long? We've been expecting you all this while.'

'A couple of weeks. There's so much to do in Moscow.'

At these words the brothers' eyes met, and Levin, despite his usual and now especially strong desire to be on friendly and, above all, simple terms with his brother, felt it awkward to look at him. He lowered his eyes and did not know what to say.

Going over subjects of conversation that would be agreeable for Sergei Ivanovich and would distract him from talking about the Serbian war and the Slavic question, which he had hinted at in mentioning how busy he was in Moscow, Levin spoke of Sergei Ivanovich's book.

'Well, have there been reviews of your book?' he asked.

Sergei Ivanovich smiled at the deliberateness of the question.

'Nobody's interested in it, and I least of all,' he said. 'Look, Darya Alexandrovna, it's going to rain,' he added, pointing with his umbrella at some white clouds that appeared over the aspen tops.

And these words were enough to re-establish between the brothers the not hostile but cool relations that Levin was trying to avoid.

Levin went over to Katavasov.

'How nice that you decided to come,' he said to him.

'I've long been meaning to. Now we'll talk and see. Have you read Spencer?'

'No, I didn't finish,' Levin said. 'However, I don't need him now.'

'How so? That's interesting. Why?'

'I mean I've finally become convinced that I won't find in him and those like him the solution to the questions that interest me. Now . . .'

But he was suddenly struck by the calm and cheerful expression on Katavasov's face, and was so sorry to have disturbed his own mood with this conversation, as he obviously had, that, recalling his intention, he stopped.

'However, we'll talk later,' he added. 'If we're going to the apiary, it's here, down this path,' he said, addressing everyone.

Having come by a narrow path to an unmowed clearing, covered on one side with bright cow-wheat thickly interspersed with tall, dark-green clumps of hellebore, Levin placed his guests in the dense, fresh shade of the young aspens, on a bench and on stumps especially prepared for visitors to the apiary who were afraid of bees, and went to the enclosure to fetch bread, cucumbers, and fresh honey for the children and grown-ups.

Trying to make as few quick movements as possible and listening to the bees flying past him more and more frequently, he went down the path as far as the cottage. Just at the front door a bee whined, tangled in his beard, but he carefully freed it. Going into the shady front hall, he took down his net that hung from a peg in the wall, put it on, and, hands in pockets, went out to the fenced apiary where, in the middle of a mowed space, in even rows, tied to stakes with strips of bast, the old hives stood – all of them familiar to him, each with its own story – and, along the wattle fence, the young ones started that year. Bees and drones played, dizzying the eye, before the flight holes, circling and swarming in one spot, and among them the worker bees flew, all in the same direction, out to the blossoming lindens in the forest and back to the hives with their booty.

His ears were ceaselessly filled with various sounds, now of a busy worker bee flying quickly by, now of a trumpeting, idle drone, now of alarmed, sting-ready sentry bees guarding their property against the enemy. On the other side of the fence, the old man was shaving a hoop and did not see Levin. Levin stopped in the middle of the apiary without calling to him.

He was glad of the chance to be alone, in order to recover from reality, which had already brought his mood down so much.

He remembered that he had already managed to get angry with Ivan, to show coldness to his brother, and to talk light-mindedly with Katavasov.

'Can it have been only a momentary mood that will pass without leaving a trace?' he thought.

But in that same moment, returning to his mood, he felt with joy that something new and important had taken place in him. Reality had only veiled for a time the inner peace he had found, but it was intact within him.

Just as the bees now circling around him, threatening and distracting him, deprived him of full physical ease, made him shrink to avoid them, so the cares that had surrounded him from the moment he got into the gig had deprived him of inner freedom; but that lasted only as long as he was among them. As his bodily strength was wholly intact in him, despite the bees, so, too, was his newly realized spiritual strength intact.

XV

'And do you know, Kostya, whom Sergei Ivanovich travelled with on the way here?' Dolly asked, after distributing the cucumbers and honey among the children. 'Vronsky! He's going to Serbia.'

'And not alone – he's taking a squadron at his own expense!' said Katavasov.

'That suits him well,' said Levin. 'And are the volunteers still going?' he added, glancing at Sergei Ivanovich.

Sergei Ivanovich, without replying, was carefully probing with a blunt knife in the bowl, where a square of white honeycomb lay, for a still-living bee stuck in the liquid honey.

'And how they are! You should have seen what went on at the station yesterday!' said Katavasov, noisily crunching on a cucumber.

'Well, how are we to understand that? For Christ's sake, Sergei Ivanovich, explain to me where all these volunteers go, who are they fighting?' asked the old prince, evidently continuing a conversation started without Levin.

'The Turks,' Sergei Ivanovich replied with a calm smile, having liberated the bee, dark with honey and helplessly waving its legs, and transferred it from the knife to a sturdy aspen leaf.

'But who declared war on the Turks? Ivan Ivanych Ragozov and Countess Lydia Ivanovna, along with Mme Stahl?'

'No one declared war, but people sympathize with the suffering of their neighbours and want to help them,' said Sergei Ivanovich.

'But the prince is not talking about help,' said Levin, interceding for his father-in-law, 'but about war. The prince is saying that private persons cannot take part in a war without the permission of the government.'

'Kostya, look, it's a bee! We'll really get stung!' said Dolly, waving away a wasp.

'It's not a bee, it's a wasp,' said Levin.

'Well, sir, what's your theory?' Katavasov said to Levin with a smile, obviously challenging him to an argument. 'Why do private persons not have the right?'

'My theory is this. On the one hand, war is such a beastly, cruel and terrible thing that no man, to say nothing of a Christian, can personally take upon himself the responsibility for starting a war. That can only be done by a government, which is called to it and is inevitably drawn into war. On the other hand, according to both science and common sense, in state matters, especially the matter of war, citizens renounce their personal will.'

Sergei Ivanovich and Katavasov began talking simultaneously with ready-made objections.

'That's the hitch, my dear, that there may be occasions when the government does not carry out the will of the citizens, and then society declares its will,' said Katavasov.

But Sergei Ivanovich obviously did not approve of this objection. He frowned at Katavasov's words and said something different.

'The question shouldn't be put that way. There is no declaration of war here, but simply the expression of human, Christian feeling. They're killing our brothers, of the same blood, of the same religion. Well, suppose they weren't even our brothers, our co-religionists, but simply children, women, old men; indignation is aroused, and the Russian people run to help stop these horrors. Imagine yourself going down the street and seeing some drunk beating a woman or a child, I don't think you'd start asking whether war had or had not been declared on the man, but would fall upon him and protect the victim.'

'But I wouldn't kill him,' said Levin.

'Yes, you would.'

'I don't know. If I saw it, I would yield to my immediate feeling, but I can't say beforehand. And there is not and cannot be such an immediate feeling about the oppression of the Slavs.'

'Maybe not for you. But for others there is,' said Sergei Ivanovich, with a frown of displeasure. 'There are stories alive among the people about Orthodox Christians suffering under the yoke of the "infidel Hagarenes".[9] The people heard about their brothers' suffering and spoke out.'

'Maybe so,' Levin said evasively, 'but I don't see it. I'm the people myself, and I don't feel it.'

'Neither do I,' said the prince. 'I was living abroad and reading the newspapers, and I confess, before the Bulgarian atrocities I simply couldn't understand why the Russians all suddenly loved their brother Slavs so much, while I felt no love for them. I was very upset, thought I was a monster, or that Karlsbad affected me that way. But I came here and was reassured – I see there are people interested just in Russia and not in our brother Slavs. Konstantin for one.'

'Personal opinions mean nothing here,' said Sergei Ivanovich. 'It's no matter of personal opinions when all Russia – the people – has expressed its will.'

'Forgive me. I just don't see that. The people know nothing about it,' said the prince.

'No, papa . . . how could they not? What about Sunday in church?' said Dolly, who was listening to the conversation. 'Give me a napkin, please,' she said to the old man, who was looking at the children with a smile. 'It can't be that everybody . . .'

'And what about Sunday in church? The priest was told to read it. He read it. They understood nothing, sighed, as they do at every sermon,' the prince went on. 'Then they were told the church would take up a collection for a charitable cause, and so they each got out a kopeck and gave. But for what, they themselves didn't know.'

'The people cannot help knowing. A consciousness of their destiny always exists among the people, and in such moments as the present it becomes clear to them,' Sergei Ivanovich said, glancing at the old beekeeper.

The handsome old man with streaks of grey in his black beard and thick silver hair stood motionless, holding a bowl of honey, looking down gently and calmly from his height upon the masters, obviously neither understanding nor wishing to understand anything.

'That's quite so,' he said to Sergei Ivanovich's words, shaking his head significantly.

'There, just ask him. He doesn't know or think anything,' said Levin. 'Have you heard about the war, Mikhailych?' He turned to him. 'What they read about in church? What do you think? Should we go to war for the Christians?'

'What's there for us to think? Alesander Nikolaich, the emperor, has thought on us, and he'll think on us in everything. He knows better . . . Shall I bring more bread? For the lad?' he asked Darya Alexandrovna, pointing to Grisha, who was finishing the crust.

'I have no need to ask,' said Sergei Ivanovich. 'We have seen and still see how hundreds and hundreds of people, abandoning everything to serve a just cause, come from all ends of Russia and directly and clearly state their thought and aim. They bring their kopecks or go themselves and directly say why. What does that mean?'

'In my opinion,' said Levin, beginning to get excited, 'it means that, among eighty million people, there are always to be found, not hundreds like now, but tens of thousands of people who have lost their social position, reckless people, who are always ready – to join Pugachev's band, to go to Khiva, to Serbia . . .'[10]

'I tell you, they are not hundreds and not reckless people, but the best representatives of the nation!' said Sergei Ivanovich, with such irritation as if he were defending his last possession. 'And the donations? Here the whole people directly expresses its will.'

'This word "people" is so vague,' said Levin. 'District clerks, teachers, and maybe one muzhik in a thousand know what it's about. And the remaining eighty million, like Mikhailych, not only don't express their will, but don't have the slightest notion what they should express their will about. What right then do we have to say it's the will of the people?'

XVI

Experienced in dialectics, Sergei Ivanovich, without objecting, at once shifted the conversation to a different area.

'Yes, if you want to learn the spirit of the people in an arithmetical way, that is certainly very difficult to achieve. Voting has not been introduced among us, and it cannot be introduced, because it does not express the will of the people. But there are other ways of doing it. It is felt in the air, it is felt in the heart. Not to mention those undercurrents that have stirred up the stagnant sea of the people and are clear to any unprejudiced person. Look at society in the narrow sense. All the most diverse parties in the world of the intelligentsia, so hostile before, have merged into one. All discord has ended, all social organs are saying one and the same thing, everyone has felt the elemental power that has caught them up and is carrying them in one direction.'

'It's the newspapers that all say the same thing,' said the prince. 'That's true. And it's so much the same that it's like frogs before a thunderstorm. You can't hear anything on account of them.'

'Frogs or no frogs, I don't publish the newspapers and don't want to defend them. I'm talking about the one-mindedness of the world of the intelligentsia,' said Sergei Ivanovich, turning to his brother.

Levin was about to reply, but the old prince interrupted him.

'Well, about this one-mindedness something else might be said,' he observed. 'There's this dear son-in-law of mine, Stepan Arkadyich, you know him. He's now getting a post as member of the committee of the commission and whatever else, I don't remember. Only there's nothing to do there – what, Dolly, it's not a secret! – and the salary's eight thousand. Try asking him whether his work is useful and he'll prove to you that it's very much needed. And he's a truthful man. But then it's impossible not to believe in the usefulness of eight thousand.'

'Yes, he asked me to tell Darya Alexandrovna that he got the post,' Sergei Ivanovich said with displeasure, thinking that the prince had spoken beside the point.

'And it's the same with the one-mindedness of the newspapers. It's been explained to me: as soon as there's a war, their income doubles. How can they not think that the destiny of the people and the Slavs . . . and all the rest of it?'

'There are many newspapers I don't like, but that is unfair,' said Sergei Ivanovich.

'I would make just one condition,' the prince went on. 'Alphonse Karr put it splendidly before the war with Prussia.[11] "You think war is necessary? Fine. Send anyone who preaches war to a special front-line legion – into the assault, into the attack, ahead of everyone!" '

'The editors would be a fine sight,' Katavasov said with a loud laugh, picturing to himself the editors he knew in this select legion.

'Why, they'd run away,' said Dolly, 'they'd just be a hindrance.'

'If they run, get them from behind with canister-shot or Cossacks with whips,' said the prince.

'That's a joke, and not a very nice joke, if you'll forgive me, Prince,' said Sergei Ivanovich.

'I don't see it as a joke, it's . . .' Levin began, but Sergei Ivanovich interrupted him.

'Each member of society is called upon to do what is proper to him,' he said. 'Thinking people do their work by expressing public opinion. And the unanimity and full expression of public opinion is the merit of the press, and at the same time a joyous fact. Twenty years ago we would have been silent, but now we hear the voice of the Russian people, ready to rise as one man and sacrifice themselves for their oppressed brothers. That is a great step and a pledge of strength.'

'But it's not just to sacrifice themselves, it's also to kill Turks,' Levin said timidly. 'The people sacrifice and are always prepared to sacrifice themselves for their soul, not for murder,' he added, involuntarily connecting the conversation with the thoughts that occupied him so much.

'How, for the soul? You understand that for a natural scientist that is a troublesome expression. What is this soul?' Katavasov said, smiling.

'Ah, you know!'

'By God, I haven't the slightest idea!' Katavasov said with a loud laugh.

' "I have brought not peace but a sword," says Christ,'[12] Sergei Ivanovich objected on his side, simply quoting, as if it were the most understandable thing, the very passage of the Gospel that had always disturbed Levin most of all.

'That's quite so,' the old man, who was standing near them, again repeated, responding to the accidental glance cast at him.

'No, my dear, you're demolished, demolished, completely demolished!' Katavasov cried merrily.

Levin flushed with vexation, not because he was demolished, but because he had not restrained himself and had begun to argue.

'No, I can't argue with them,' he thought, 'they're wearing impenetrable armour, and I am naked.'

He saw that his brother and Katavasov were not to be persuaded, and still less did he find it possible for himself to agree with them. What they preached was that very pride of reason which had nearly ruined him. He could not agree with the idea that dozens of people, his brother among them, had the right, on the basis of what was told them by some hundreds of fine-talking volunteers coming to the capitals, to say that they and the newspapers expressed the will and thought of the people, a thought that expressed itself in revenge and murder. He could not agree with it, because he did not see the expression of these thoughts in the people among whom he lived, nor did he find these thoughts in himself (and he could not consider himself anything else but one of those persons who made up the Russian people), and above all because, while neither he nor the people knew or could know what the common good consisted in, he knew firmly that it was only possible to attain that common good by strictly fulfilling the law of the good that was open to every man, and therefore he could not desire war and preach it for any common purposes whatsoever. He said, together with Mikhailych and the people, who expressed their thought in the legend about the calling of the Varangians:[13] 'Be our princes and rule over us. We joyfully promise full obedience. All labours, all humiliations, all sacrifices we take upon ourselves, but we will not judge or decide.' And now, according to Sergei Ivanovich's words, the people had renounced this right purchased at so dear a cost.

He also wanted to say that if public opinion is an infallible judge, then why was a revolution or a commune not as legitimate as the movement in defence of the Slavs? But these were all thoughts that could not decide anything. Only one thing could unquestionably be seen – that in that present moment the argument irritated Sergei Ivanovich and therefore it was bad to argue; and Levin fell silent and drew his visitors' attention to the fact that clouds were gathering and that they had better go home before it rained.

XVII

The prince and Sergei Ivanovich got into the gig and drove; the rest of the company, quickening their pace, went home on foot.

But the storm clouds, now white, now black, came on so quickly that they had to walk still faster to get home ahead of the rain. The advancing clouds, low and dark as sooty smoke, raced across the sky with extraordinary speed. They were still about two hundred paces from the house, but the wind had already risen, and a downpour could be expected at any moment.

The children ran ahead with frightened, joyful shrieks. Darya Alexandrovna, struggling hard with the skirts that clung to her legs, no longer walked but ran, not taking her eyes off the children. The men, holding on to their hats, walked with long strides. They were just at the porch when a big drop struck and broke up on the edge of the iron gutter. The children, and the grown-ups after them, ran under the cover of the roof with merry chatter.

'Katerina Alexandrovna?' Levin asked Agafya Mikhailovna, who met them in the front hall with cloaks and wraps.

'We thought she was with you.'

'And Mitya?'

'They must be in Kolok, and the nanny's with them.'

Levin seized the wraps and ran to Kolok.

During that short period of time the centre of the cloud had covered the sun so that it became as dark as during a solar eclipse. The stubborn wind, as if insisting on its own, kept stopping Levin and, tearing off leaves and linden blossoms and baring the white birch boughs in an ugly and strange way, bent everything in one direction: acacias, flowers, burdock, grass and treetops. Farm girls who had been working in the garden ran squealing under the roof of the servants' quarters. The white curtain of pouring rain had already invaded all the distant forest and half the nearby field and was moving quickly towards Kolok. The dampness of rain breaking up into fine drops filled the air.

Lowering his head and struggling against the wind, which tore the shawls from his arms, Levin was already running up to Kolok and could see something white showing beyond an oak, when suddenly everything blazed, the whole earth caught fire and the vault of the sky seemed to crack overhead. Opening his dazzled eyes and peering through the thick curtain of rain that now separated him from Kolok, Levin first saw with horror the strangely altered position of the familiar oak's green crown in the middle of the wood. 'Can it have snapped off?' Levin barely managed to think, when, moving more and more quickly, the oak's crown disappeared behind the other trees, and he heard the crash of a big tree falling.

The flash of the lightning, the sound of the thunder, and the feeling of his body being instantly doused with cold, merged in Levin into one impression of horror.

'My God! My God, not on them!' he said.

And though he immediately thought how senseless his request was that they should not be killed by an oak that had already fallen, he repeated it, knowing that he could do nothing better than this senseless prayer.

He ran to the spot where they usually went, but did not find them there.

They were at the other end of the wood, under an old linden, and calling to him. Two figures in dark dresses (they were actually light) stood bending over something. They were Kitty and the nanny. The rain was already letting up and it was growing lighter as Levin raced towards them. The lower part of the nanny's dress was dry, but Kitty's dress was soaked through and clung to her body all over. Though it was no longer raining, they went on standing in the same position they had assumed when the storm broke, bent over the carriage, holding a green umbrella.

'Alive? Safe? Thank God!' he said, splashing through the puddles in his flopping, water-filled shoes, and running up to them.

Kitty's rosy and wet face was turned to him and smiled timidly from under her now shapeless hat.

'Well, aren't you ashamed? I don't understand how you can be so imprudent!' He fell upon his wife in vexation.

'I swear it's not my fault. I was just going to leave when he began acting up. We had to change him. We just . . .' Kitty began excusing herself.

Mitya was safe, dry, and had slept through it all.

'Well, thank God! I don't know what I'm saying!'

They gathered up the wet napkins; the nanny took the baby out and carried him. Levin walked beside his wife and, guilty on account of his vexation, squeezed her hand in secret from the nanny.

XVIII

Throughout the day, during the most varied conversations, in which he took part as if only with the external part of his mind, Levin, despite his disappointment in the change that was supposed to take place in him, never ceased joyfully sensing the fullness of his heart.

After the rain it was too wet to go for a walk; besides, the storm clouds never left the horizon and, now here, now there, passed thundering and black across the edges of the sky. The whole company spent the rest of the day at home.

No more arguments started, and, on the contrary, after dinner everyone was in the best of spirits.

Katavasov first made the ladies laugh with his original jokes, which people always liked so much on first making his acquaintance, but then, prompted by Sergei Ivanovich, he told them his very interesting observations on the differences of character and even of physiognomy between female and male house flies and on their life. Sergei Ivanovich was also merry and over tea, prompted by his brother, expounded his view of the future of the Eastern question,[14] so simply and well that everyone listened with delight.

Only Kitty could not listen to the end. She was called to bathe Mitya.

A few minutes after Kitty had left, Levin, too, was called to her in the nursery.

Leaving his tea, and also regretting the interruption of the interesting conversation, and at the same time worrying about why he had been called, since that happened only on important occasions, Levin went to the nursery.

In spite of his great interest in Sergei Ivanovich's plan – something completely new to him and which he had not heard to the end – for how the liberated forty millions of the Slavic world, together with Russia, were to start a new epoch in history, and in spite of his curiosity and alarm about why he had been called, as soon as he left the drawing room and was alone he at once remembered his morning thoughts. And all those considerations about the meaning of the Slavic element in world history seemed so insignificant to him compared with what was happening in his soul that he instantly forgot it all and was transported into the same mood he had been in that morning.

He did not recall his whole train of thought now, as he had done before (he did not need to). He was immediately transported into the feeling that guided him, which was connected with those thoughts, and he found that feeling still stronger and more definite in his soul than before. What had happened to him before, when he had invented some reassurance and had had to restore the whole train of thought in order to recover the feeling, did not happen now. On the contrary, now the feeling of joy and reassurance was all the more alive, and his thought could not keep up with it.

He walked across the terrace and looked at two stars appearing in the already darkening sky, and suddenly remembered: 'Yes, when I was looking at the sky and thinking that the vault I see is not an untruth, there was something I didn't think through, something I hid from myself,' he thought. 'But whatever it was, there can be no objection. I only have to think and everything will be explained!'

As he was going into the nursery, he remembered what he had hidden from himself. It was that if the main proof of the Deity is His revelation of what is good, then why was this revelation limited to the Christian Church alone? What relation did the beliefs of the Buddhists, the Mohammedans, who also confess and do good, have to that revelation?

It seemed to him that he had the answer to that question, but before he had time to formulate it for himself, he was already in the nursery.

Kitty was standing with her sleeves rolled up beside the tub with the baby splashing in it and, hearing her husband's steps, turned her face to him and called him with her smile. With one hand she supported the head of the plump baby, who was floating on his back, his little legs squirming, and with the other, smoothly tensing her muscles, she squeezed out a sponge over him.

'Look, look here!' she said, when her husband came up to her. 'Agafya Mikhailovna's right. He recognizes us.'

The thing was that Mitya, that day, obviously, unquestionably, had begun to recognize all his own people.

As soon as Levin came up to the bath, an experiment was performed for him, and it succeeded perfectly. The scullery maid, invited for the purpose, took Kitty's place and bent over the baby. He frowned and wagged his head negatively. Kitty bent over him and he lit up with a smile, put his hands to the sponge and bubbled with his lips, producing such a pleased and strange sound that not only Kitty and the nanny but Levin, too, went into unexpected raptures.

The baby was taken out of the tub with one hand, doused with water, wrapped in a sheet, dried off and, after a piercing shout, handed to his mother.

'Well, I'm glad you're beginning to love him,' Kitty said to her husband, after settling calmly in her usual place with the baby at her breast. 'I'm very glad. Because it was beginning to upset me. You said you felt nothing for him.'

'No, did I say I felt nothing? I only said I was disappointed.'

'What, disappointed in him?'

'Not in him but in my own feeling. I expected more. I expected that a new, pleasant feeling would blossom in me like a surprise. And suddenly, instead of that, there was squeamishness, pity . . .'

She listened to him attentively over the baby, replacing on her slender fingers the rings she had taken off in order to wash Mitya.

'And, above all, there's much more fear and pity than pleasure. Today, after that fear during the thunderstorm, I realized how much I love him.'

Kitty smiled radiantly.

'Were you very frightened?' she said. 'I was, too, but I'm more afraid now that it's past. I'll go and look at the oak. And how nice Katavasov is! And generally the whole day was so pleasant. And you're so good with Sergei Ivanovich when you want to be . . . Well, go to them. It's always so hot and steamy here after the bath . . .'

XIX

Leaving the nursery and finding himself alone, Levin at once remembered that thought in which there was something unclear.

Instead of going to the drawing room, where voices could be heard, he stopped on the terrace and, leaning on the rail, began looking at the sky.

It was already quite dark, and in the south, where he was looking, there were no clouds. The clouds stood on the opposite side. From there came flashes of lightning and the roll of distant thunder. Levin listened to the drops monotonously dripping from the lindens in the garden and looked at the familiar triangle of stars and the branching Milky Way passing through it. At each flash of lightning not only the Milky Way but the bright stars also disappeared, but as soon as the lightning died out they reappeared in the same places, as if thrown by some unerring hand.

'Well, what is it that disturbs me?' Levin said to himself, feeling beforehand that the resolution of his doubts, though he did not know it yet, was already prepared in his soul.

'Yes, the one obvious, unquestionable manifestation of the Deity is the laws of the good disclosed to the world by revelation, which I feel in myself, and by acknowledging which I do not so much unite myself as I am united, whether I will or no, with others in one community of believers which is called the Church. Well, but the Jews, the Mohammedans, the Confucians, the Buddhists – what are they?' He asked himself the same question that had seemed dangerous to him. 'Can these hundreds of millions of people be deprived of the highest good, without which life has no meaning?' He pondered, but at once corrected himself. 'What am I asking?' he said to himself. 'I'm asking about the relation to the Deity of all the various faiths of mankind. I'm asking about the general manifestation of God to the whole world with all these nebulae. What am I doing? To me personally, to my heart, unquestionable knowledge is revealed, inconceivable to reason, and I stubbornly want to express this knowledge by means of reason and words.

'Don't I know that the stars don't move?' he asked himself, looking at a bright planet that had already changed its position over the topmost branch of a birch. 'Yet, looking at the movement of the stars, I cannot picture to myself the turning of the earth, and I'm right in saying that the stars move.

'And would the astronomers be able to understand or calculate anything, if they took into account all the various complex movements of the earth? All their astonishing conclusions about the distances, weights, movements and disturbances of the heavenly bodies are based solely on the visible movement of the luminaries around the fixed earth, on that very movement which is now before me, which has been that way for millions of people throughout the ages, and has been and will always be the same and can always be verified. And just as the conclusions of astronomers that were not based on observations of the visible sky in relation to the same meridian and the same horizon would be idle and lame, so my conclusions would be idle and lame if they were not based on that understanding of the good which always has been and will be the same for everyone, and which is revealed to me by Christianity and can always be verified in my soul. And I don't have the right or possibility of resolving the question of other beliefs and their attitude to the Deity.'

'Ah, you haven't gone?' the voice of Kitty suddenly said. She was walking the same way towards the drawing room. 'What, are you upset about something?' she said, studying his face attentively by the light of the stars.

But she would still have been unable to see his face if lightning, again hiding the stars, had not lit it up. By its light she made out his face and, seeing that he was calm and joyful, she smiled at him.

'She understands,' he thought. 'She knows what I'm thinking about. Shall I tell her or not? Yes, I'll tell her.' But just as he was about to begin speaking, she also started to speak.

'Listen, Kostya, do me a favour,' she said. 'Go to the corner room and see how they've arranged everything for Sergei Ivanovich. I'm embarrassed to. Did they put in the new washstand?'

'Very well, I'll make sure,' said Levin, getting up and kissing her.

'No, I won't tell her,' he thought, as she walked on ahead of him. 'It's a secret that's necessary and important for me alone and inexpressible in words.

'This new feeling hasn't changed me, hasn't made me happy or suddenly enlightened, as I dreamed – just like the feeling for my son. Nor was there any surprise. And faith or not faith – I don't know what it is – but this feeling has entered into me just as imperceptibly through suffering and has firmly lodged itself in my soul.

'I'll get angry in the same way with the coachman Ivan, argue in the same way, speak my mind inappropriately, there will be the same wall between my soul's holy of holies and other people, even my wife, I'll accuse her in the same way of my own fear and then regret it, I'll fail in the same way to understand with my reason why I pray, and yet I will pray – but my life now, my whole life, regardless of all that may happen to me, every minute of it, is not only not meaningless, as it was before, but has the unquestionable meaning of the good which it is in my power to put into it!'

The End

Notes

The following notes are indebted to the commentaries in the twenty-two-volume edition of Tolstoy's works published by Khudozhestvennaya Literatura (Volumes VIII and IX, Moscow, 1981–2) and to Vladimir Nabokov's notes to Part One of *Anna Karenina*, in *Lectures on Russian Literature* (London and New York, 1981). Biblical quotations, unless otherwise specified, are from the King James version.

Epigraph

Romans 12:19. St Paul refers to Deuteronomy 32:35: 'To me belongeth vengeance, and recompence.'

Part One

1 **Il mio tesoro:** Probably the aria '*Il mio tesoro*' sung by Don Ottavio in Act II, scene ii of Mozart's *Don Giovanni*.
2 **physiology:** *Reflexes of the Brain*, by I. M. Sechenov (1829–1905), was published in 1863. There was widespread interest at the time in materialistic physiology, even among those who knew of it only by hearsay.
3. **newspaper:** Stepan Arkadyich probably reads *The Voice*, edited by A. Kraevsky, the preferred newspaper of liberal functionaries, known as 'the barometer of public opinion', or possibly, as Nabokov suggests, the mildly liberal *Russian Gazette*.
4 **Rurik:** Chief (d. 879) of the Scandinavian rovers known as Varangians, he founded the principality of Novgorod at the invitation of the local populace, thus becoming the ancestor of the oldest Russian nobility. The dynasty of Rurik ruled from 862 to 1598; it was succeeded by the Romanovs.
5 **Bentham and Mill:** Jeremy Bentham (1748–1832), English philosopher and jurist, founded the English utilitarian school of philosophy. John Stuart Mill (1806–73), philosopher and economist of the experimental school, was the

author of the influential *Principles of Political Economy*, published in 1848.
6 **Count Ferdinand von Beust:** (1809–86), prime minister of Saxony and later chancellor of the Austro-Hungarian empire, a political opponent of Bismarck, he was frequently mentioned in the press. Wiesbaden, capital of the German province of Hesse, was famous for its hot springs. Von Beust visited Wiesbaden in February 1872 (see Nabokov's extensive note).
7 **kalatch:** A very fine white yeast bread shaped like a purse with a handle; pl. kalatchi.
8 **zertsalo:** A three-faced glass pyramid bearing an eagle and certain edicts of the emperor Peter the Great (1682–1725) which stood on the desk in every government office.
9 **kammerjunker:** The German title ('gentleman of the bed-chamber') was adopted by the Russian imperial court.
10 **zemstvo:** An elective provincial council for purposes of local administration, established in Russia in 1865 by the emperor Alexander II (1818–81).
11 **his opinion:** Levin expresses a widely shared opinion of the time, that zemstvo activists commonly abused their position in order to make money.
12 **psychological and physiological phenomena:** In 1872–3 there was a heated debate in the magazine *The Messenger of Europe* about the relations between psychological and physiological phenomena, one side saying there was no known connection (but possibly a 'parallelism') between the two, the other that all psychic acts are reflexes subject to physiological study. Tolstoy, like Levin, took his distance from both sides.
13 **origin of man:** In the early 1870s works by Charles Darwin (1809–82) were published in Russian and his theories of natural selection and the descent of man from the animals were discussed in all Russian magazines and newspapers.
14 **Wurst, Knaust, Pripasov:** Tolstoy invented these names for comic and parodic effect; they mean, respectively, 'sausage', 'stingy' and 'provisions'.
15 **leaning on chairs:** Chairs on runners were provided for beginners and occasionally for ladies to hold on to or be pushed around in.
16 **Tartars:** One of the 'racial minorities' of the Russian empire, they are a people originally native to Central Asia east of the Caspian Sea. Tolstoy seems to have no special intention in having them work as waiters in the Hotel Anglia (an actual hotel of the time, located on Petrovka, which enjoyed a dubious reputation as a place for aristocratic assignations).
17 **shchi:** Cabbage soup, and kasha, a sort of thick gruel made from various grains, most typically buckwheat groats, are the two staple foods of Russian peasants.
18 **Levins are wild:** In a letter to his aunt Alexandra A. Tolstoy (1817–1904), his elder by only ten years, Tolstoy spoke of the 'Tolstoyan wildness' characteristic of 'all the Tolstoys', meaning originality of behaviour and freedom from conventional rules. She in turn used to call him 'roaring Leo'.
19 **'Bold steeds . . .':** Oblonsky quotes (imprecisely) the poem 'From Anacreon'

(1835), by Alexander Pushkin (1799–1837). Later he will quote it, again imprecisely, in a conversation with Vronsky.

20 **'with disgust reading over my life . . .':** Levin now quotes Pushkin's poem 'Remembrance' (1828), one of Tolstoy's own favourites.

21 **'Himmlisch ist's . . .':** 'Heavenly it would be to conquer/My earthly lusts;/But though I've not succeeded,/I still have lots of pleasure' – a stanza from the libretto of *Die Fledermaus*, an operetta with music by Johann Strauss (1825–99).

22 **lovely fallen creatures:** The words are a paraphrase from a speech by Walsingham in Pushkin's 'little tragedy' *The Feast During the Plague* (1830).

23 **words . . . misused** They are referring to Luke 7:47: 'Wherefore I say unto thee, Her sins, which are many, are forgiven; for she loved much' – a passage often quoted out of context as a justification for loose behaviour.

24 **threw all difficult questions over his right shoulder . . . :** Refers to a character by the name of Mr John Podsnap in Charles Dickens's novel *Our Mutual Friend* (1865).

25 **two loves:** The two loves discussed by the participants in Plato's *Symposium* are typified by two aspects of the goddess Aphrodite: earthly, sensual love (Aphrodite Pandemos) and heavenly love free of sensual desire (Aphrodite Urania). The latter came to be known as 'platonic love'.

26 **some sort of courses:** In 1872 a school of continuing education for women was opened in Moscow, where girls with a high-school diploma could study literature, history, art history and the history of civilization, foreign languages, physics, mathematics and hygiene.

27 **table-turning and spirits:** Tolstoy was very interested in the fashion of spiritualism, which reached Russia in the 1870s. His earliest criticism of it appears here in Levin's argument with Vronsky; in 1890 he wrote a satirical comedy on spiritualism entitled *The Fruits of Enlightenment*, performed in 1892 by the Maly Theatre in Moscow. (See Nabokov's delightful note to this same place.)

28 **Corps of Pages:** An elite military school connected to the imperial household, made up of one hundred and fifty boys drawn mostly from the court nobility. After four or five years in the Corps of Pages, those who passed the examination were accepted as officers in whatever regiment they chose, and the top sixteen pupils each year were attached to various members of the imperial family. Enrolment in the Corps of Pages was thus considered the start of a brilliant career in the service.

29 **bezique:** A card game (*bésique* in French), introduced in the seventeenth century, that came back into fashion in the 1860s.

30 **Château des Fleurs:** The name of a Moscow restaurant and amusement spot featuring singers, dancers, cyclists, gymnasts and the like.

31 **Honi soit . . . :** 'Shamed be he who thinks evil of it' – motto of the Order of the Garter, the highest order of English knighthood, founded by Edward III *c.* 1344.

32 sole provider . . . : Frequent and spectacular accidents in the early days caused widespread public fear of the railways, whose owners were not required to pay indemnities to victims or their families. These problems were much debated in the press of the time.

33 cast a stone: 'He that is without sin among you, let him first cast a stone at her' (John 8:7).

34 public theatre: The first public theatre was opened in Moscow in 1873. Prior to that, the theatres of Moscow and Petersburg all functioned under the control of the Department of Imperial Theatres.

35 without cuffs or collar: A sign of poverty. Women's dresses had detachable cuffs and collars, which could be changed and laundered frequently. A woman would normally have a good supply of them in her wardrobe.

36 Nikolai Dmitrich: Nabokov notes that Masha addresses Nikolai Levin formally, by his first name and patronymic (and in the second person plural), as a respectful petty bourgeois wife would address her husband, while an aristocratic woman like Dolly, when she refers to her husband in the same way, deliberately chooses it as the most distant and estranged way to speak of him.

37 Sunday schools: In the early 1870s revolutionaries organized Sunday schools in the factories to give workers the rudiments of education. In 1874 strict control over these schools was introduced, and many students were expelled from the universities for participating in them.

38 rug sleigh: 'A type of rustic comfortable sleigh which looked as if it consisted of a rug on runners' (Nabokov).

39 book by Tyndall: John Tyndall (1820–93), British physicist; in 1872, Tolstoy read his book *Heat as a Mode of Motion* (1863), translated and published in Petersburg in 1864.

40 third bell . . . sleeping car: Three bells signalled the departure of a train in Russian stations: the first fifteen minutes before, the second five minutes before, and the third at the moment of departure. (See Nabokov's detailed note on Russian sleeping cars and first-class night travel.)

41 Petersburg face: The soft water of the Neva and the salt air of Petersburg were considered good for the complexion.

42 Pan-Slavist: The Pan-Slavists saw the future of Russia in an eastward-looking political and spiritual union of all the Slavs, rather than in a closer rapprochement with the West. This is referred to in Part Eight as 'the Eastern question'.

43 Duc de Lille: The name Tolstoy gives to the poet is a play on the name of the French poet Leconte de Lisle (1818–94), leader of the Parnassian school; the title of the book also parodies the titles of a number of French books of the time, including Baudelaire's *Les Fleurs du mal*. For the fullest expression of Tolstoy's dislike of the new art of his time see his *What Is Art?* (1898).

44 slave-girl Rebecca genre: That is, the Semitic type of beauty, which had became fashionable in the nineteenth century as an alternative to the classical type.

Part Two

1 **Great Lent:** The forty-day fast period preceding Holy Week and Easter in the Orthodox liturgical calendar, called 'great' to distinguish it from several 'lesser' fasts at other times of the year.
2 **famous singer:** The singer, as we learn later, is Swedish soprano Christiane Nilsson (1843–1927). She had great success on the stages of the Bolshoi Theatre in Moscow and the Mariinsky Theatre in Petersburg between 1872 and 1885.
3 **Blessed are the peacemakers . . . :** Cf. Matthew 5:9: 'Blessed are the peacemakers: for they shall be called the children of God.'
4 **young men are out driving . . . :** The story that follows was told to Tolstoy by his brother-in-law, Alexander Bers. Tolstoy found it 'a charming story in itself' and asked permission to use it in his novel.
5 **titular councillor and councilloress:** Titular councillor was ninth of the fourteen ranks of the imperial civil service established by Peter the Great, equivalent to the military rank of staff-captain.
6 **Talleyrand:** Charles-Maurice de Talleyrand-Périgord (1754–1838), French diplomat and political figure, served in a number of important capacities throughout the period of the revolution, the empire and the restoration, perhaps most brilliantly at the Congress of Vienna (1814–15).
7 **unable to continue standing:** There are no pews in Orthodox churches; people stand through the services, which can be very long.
8 **Kaulbach:** The German painter Wilhelm Kaulbach (1805–74), director of the Münich Academy of Art, was considered the last representative of idealism. Actors and opera singers of the time studied his monumental biblical and historical compositions in order to learn stage gestures and movements.
9 **diable rose:** In 1874 the French Theatre in Petersburg produced a play by E. Grange and L. Thiboux entitled *Les Diables roses* (*The Pink Devils*).
10 **a man deprived of a shadow:** There is no such tale in the collection of the Brothers Grimm. The motif of the lost shadow belongs to *The Extraordinary Adventures of Peter Schlemihl*, by Adalbert Chamisso (Adalbert de Chamisso de Boncourt, 1781–1838), a German Romantic writer of French origin. But Princess Miagky may be thinking of 'The Shadow', by Hans Christian Andersen (1805–75), published in Russian translation in 1870.
11 **. . . some French verse:** An almost literal translation of '*Nul n'est content de sa fortune, ni mécontent de son esprit*', a line by the French pastoral poet Mme Antoinette Déshoulières (1637–94).
12 **Bouffe:** Opera bouffe (from the Italian *opera buffa*, 'comic opera') became popular in the eighteenth century. The *Opéra-bouffe* in Paris was opened at the Théâtre Montmartre in 1847. In 1870 a French comic opera theatre called the Opera Bouffe was opened in Petersburg.
13 **Rambouillet . . . graces and muses:** The literary salon at the Hôtel Rambouillet,

presided over by the Marquise de Rambouillet (1588–1665), was the most influential of its day, bringing together important writers, poets, artists and politicians – the 'taste-makers' of their age.

14 **conscription:** The new military regulations of 1874 replaced the twenty-five-year term of service by a maximum six-year term and abolished the privilege of exemption from military service enjoyed until then by the nobility. The plans for this reform were debated in the press during the early 1870s.

15 **seven below:** On the Réaumur scale, which was used in Russia at that time, a temperature of –7° is the equivalent of –9° C (16° F).

16 **Krasnaya Gorka:** In Russian popular tradition, the day known as Krasnaya Gorka (literally 'Pretty Little Hill'), the Tuesday following St Thomas's Sunday (the first Sunday after Easter), is a day of commemoration of the dead.

17 **ploughs and harrows:** Russian peasants used ploughs and harrows of hardened wood – hence the knock of axes. Tolstoy will later show Levin's frustration at their resistance to the introduction of iron implements.

18 **before Lent:** That is, two months earlier.

19 **polotok:** Polotok is split and dried or smoked chicken; like home-made herb liqueurs and nettle soup, it is typical of Russian country fare.

20 **preserves:** Fruit preserves (more liquid than our jams) were commonly served in little dishes after dinner with coffee or tea.

21 **Ossianic:** That is, like the heroines of the Romantic forgery *Fragments of Ancient Poetry* (1760), which the author, James Macpherson (1736–96), claimed he had translated from the Gaelic of a bard named Ossian.

22 **'To count the sands . . .':** Oblonsky quotes, not quite accurately, from the famous ode 'God', by Gavrila Derzhavin (1743–1816), the major Russian poet of the age preceding Pushkin.

23 **icon:** According to custom, every room in a Russian house should have an icon, if not several icons, usually in the corner to far right of the door. Lower-class people, merchants and tradesmen, would still look for the icon and cross themselves on entering a room, a habit enlightened aristocrats like Oblonsky and Levin have lost.

24 **electric light everywhere:** In the early 1870s electric light was still a great rarity and was generally considered impracticable. However, it could be found as a technical novelty in some amusement establishments.

25 **Wertherian:** Werther is the hero of *The Sorrows of Young Werther*, a semi-autobiographical novel in letters about unhappy love and suicide, by the German poet Johann Wolfgang von Goethe (1749–1832).

26 **Krasnoe Selo:** 'Beautiful Village', originally some fifteen miles southwest of Petersburg, by 1973 was incorporated into the city itself. At the turn of the nineteenth century, wooden palaces were built there for members of the imperial family; the imperial residences of Tsarskoe Selo and Gatchina were also near by. From 1823 until the revolution, the village housed a military school and a guards corps (hence Vronsky's presence). In 1861 a racetrack was built there and

the place became a fashionable summer suburb for the Petersburg aristocracy.

27 **Thule:** Or Ultima Thule, was the Greek and Latin name of a legendary land some six days' sail north of Britain, thought to be the northernmost place in the world. The line is from the opera *Faust*, by French composer Charles Gounod (1818–93), based on Goethe's monumental drama of the same title.

28 **Peterhof:** An imperial residence and park on the Bay of Kronstadt, built in 1711 by Peter the Great.

29 **. . . thought of her son . . . :** In Russia before the revolution divorce was granted by an ecclesiastical court and was very difficult to obtain. Only the injured party could sue for divorce, and the offending party was denied custody of the children and the right to remarry.

30 **provincial marshal:** The provincial marshal of nobility was the highest elective office in a Russian province; governors and other administrative officers were appointed by the tsar.

31 **Widows' Home:** A philanthropic institution for poor, sick and old widows opened in Moscow and Petersburg in 1803.

32 **Slavonic:** Church Slavonic, linguistically based on Old Bulgarian, was and remains the liturgical and scriptural language of the Orthodox Church in Slavic countries.

33 **. . . turn the other cheek . . . :** Loose paraphrase of Luke 6:29: 'And unto him that smiteth thee on the one cheek offer also the other; and him that taketh away thy cloke forbid not to take thy coat also' (cf. Matthew 5:39–40).

34 **Pietists:** Pietism was a seventeenth-century reform movement within the Lutheran Church, but the prince is referring here to a more general current of piety in the Russian aristocracy of the time, favouring inner peace and prayer over external ritual, with more than a touch of smug sanctimoniousness.

35 **they've beaten everybody:** The colonel is referring to the series of Prussian military successes, culminating in the victory over France in the Franco-Prussian War (1870–71), through which Bismarck consolidated the German empire.

Part Three

1 **St Peter's:** That is, the feast of Sts Peter and Paul on 29 June.

2 **council member:** A member of the zemstvo council.

3 **criminal courts:** Open courts and trial by jury were first introduced in Russia by the judicial reforms of 1864.

4 **day of the Trinity:** The Russian name for the feast of Pentecost, on the occasion of which churches and homes are decorated with flowers and branches of greenery.

5 **Lafite:** Château Lafite, one of the finest red Bordeaux wines.

6 **kvass:** A sort of home-made beer made from fermented rye.

7 **corvée:** Under serfdom, the unpaid labour owed by serfs to the lord.

8 not received communion for more than a year: At that time, the normal practice was to take communion twice a year – at Christmas and Easter. Dolly's children have missed two Easters and one Christmas, and have thus gone an unusually long time without communion.

9 three fasts: The child was born before St Peter's fast the previous year and was thus nursed through three fast periods – St Peter's in June, the Dormition fast in August, and the Advent fast in November – and weaned before the beginning of the Great Lent. (See note 1, Part Two.)

10 visit often: It was a common situation for peasant men to be hired in a local town, in the provincial capital, or even in another province, wherever there were jobs to be had. Hence Dolly's question about visiting.

11 St Philip's: St Philip's day, 14 November, is the eve of the forty-day Advent fast. Since weddings are not permitted during fast periods, the boy got married just before.

12 La Belle Hélène: An operetta by Jacques Offenbach (1819–80), based on the story of Helen of Troy; Menelaus is of course the cuckolded husband. The operetta had been performed recently in Petersburg.

13 Eugubine Tables: Seven bronze tablets inscribed in Umbrian and Latin, dating back to the second or first century BC, discovered in Gubbio, Italy (ancient Iguvium, later Eugubium), in 1444. In 1874 the French *Revue des deux mondes* published an article on the Eugubine Tables, which may be what Karenin is reading.

14 Zaraysk province: Tolstoy may have in mind the numerous projects for irrigating the fields in Samara province after the famine of 1873, which drew large government subsidies regardless of their practicability.

15 settling of racial minorities: Abuses were widespread in cases of the resettlement of unoccupied lands, for instance the thirty million acres belonging to the Bashkir people in Orenburg province. In the 1860s the government began to encourage the leasing of Bashkir land to displaced peoples from Central Asia, which led to shady speculations involving officials in the provincial administration itself.

16 Les sept merveilles du monde: The seven wonders of the world, the seven most remarkable works of antiquity: the pyramids of Egypt, the hanging gardens of Semiramis in Babylon, the statue of Olympian Zeus by Phidias, the Colossus of Rhodes, the temple of Artemis in Ephesus, the mausoleum of Halicarnassus, and the lighthouse of Alexandria. The Petersburg circle adopted this name in hyperbole.

17 unexpected young guest . . . : This unnamed guest, as Tolstoy's son Sergei observed in his memoirs, was apparently one of the young grand dukes, the sons of the emperor, on whose entrance even elderly ladies were required to rise.

18 Decembrist: The sudden death of the emperor Alexander I on 19 November 1825 was followed by a period of confusion about the succession. A conspiratorial group of officers and noblemen, opposed to imperial absolutism and favouring a constitutional monarchy or even a republican government, seized the occasion and gathered their forces in the Senate Square of Petersburg on 14 December 1825. Hence the name 'Decembrists'. The uprising was promptly quashed by loyal contingents of the Imperial Guard; one hundred and twenty-one men were arrested, of whom five were executed and the rest stripped of their rights and fortunes and exiled to Siberia.

19 one of the most expensive regiments: A commanding officer received symbolic pay and was expected to outfit his regiment at his own expense.

20 Serpukhovskoy . . . back from Central Asia: In 1873 the Khiva khanate was united with Russia. Events in Central Asia, judging by the press of the time, aroused considerable international interest. Quick and brilliant military careers could be made in the Turkestan of the 1870s, of which Serpukhovskoy is a typical example.

21 Russian communists: Various radical groups of the 1860s, including the followers of the writer N. G. Chernyshevsky (1828–89), advocated forms of communism based on the theories of French socialists such as Charles Fourier (1772–1837) and Saint-Simon (1760–1825), prior to the emergence of Marxian communism.

22 Hélène: See note 12, Part Three.

23 justice of the peace: The legal reform of 1864 handed all local civil disputes over to the justices of the peace. Their hearings were open, contentious, oral and equitable. The nobility considered this a loss of power, and complaints about justices of the peace were common among landowners of the time.

24 serf . . . emancipation: The Russian serfs were emancipated by the emperor Alexander II in 1861.

25 Peter, Catherine, Alexander: The emperors Peter the Great (1672–1725) and Alexander II (1818–81) and the empress Catherine the Great (1729–96) were the most important reformers of the Russian empire. The potato, for instance, was forcibly introduced by Catherine the Great. The period 'before the tsars' was that of the princedoms of Novgorod, Kiev and Moscow.

26 Tosscan . . . Bitiug: 'Tosscan' appears to come from 'Toscan' (i.e. 'Tuscan'), punningly distorted by Nikolai Ivanych. Percherons are a great breed of work and draft horses from La Perche in Normandy; the Bitiug, named after an affluent of the Don, is a Russian breed of strong, heavy-set cart horses.

27 Mulhouse system: In the 1850s the German economist Hermann Schulze-Delitsch (1808–83) proposed an arrangement of independent banks and cooperatives, with the idea of reconciling the interests of workers and owners. Companies organized on his principles appeared in Russia in 1865. Ferdinand Lassalle (1825–64), a German socialist, was the founder of the German Universal Workers' Union. Instead of Schulze-Delitsch cooperatives, he favoured manufacturing associations supported by the state. The 'Mulhouse system' refers to a society for the improvement of workers' lives founded by a factory-owner named Dolfuss in the Alsatian city of Mulhouse. A commercial undertaking with philanthropic aims, it built houses which were sold to workers on credit.

28 **Frederick:** Poland was first partitioned between Russia, Austria and Prussia in 1772. The king of Prussia at that time was Frederick the Great (1712–86).

29 **Spencer:** British philosopher Herbert Spencer (1820–1903), founder of the evolutionary school, believed that education does not lead to national prosperity but that prosperity is a necessary condition for the development of education. A Russian translation of an article by Spencer on education was published in 1874.

30 **Mill:** See note 5, Part One. Mill's book on political economy was translated into Russian by the radical writer N. G. Chernyshevsky (see note 21, Part Three), author of the influential novel *What Is to Be Done?* (1863).

31 **Kauffmann, Jones, Dubois, Miccelli:** These are invented names, parodying the pedantic manner of referring to obscure authorities.

32 **Franklin:** Benjamin Franklin (1706–90), American writer, inventor, patriot and statesman. As a young man, Tolstoy kept a diary in the manner of Franklin's, in which he chronicled his own moral shortcomings and exhorted himself to improve.

33 **anointed:** The Orthodox sacrament of the anointing of the sick is a sacrament of healing which, like the Roman Catholic sacrament of extreme unction, has come to be associated with terminal illness.

Part Four

1 **foreign prince . . . to Petersburg:** In January–February 1874, Petersburg was host to princes from Germany, England and Denmark, invited on the occasion of the wedding of Alfred, Duke of Edinburgh, to Maria Alexandrovna, daughter of Alexander II.

2 **Athenian night:** The Roman writer Aulus Gellius (second century AD) was the author of a collection of dialogues on various branches of knowledge known as *Athenian* (or *Attic*) *Nights*, the title of which in Russian became proverbial for gatherings marked by licentious behaviour.

3 **portfolio . . . pushed her away:** According to the law of that time, Karenin, as head of the family, had the right to read the correspondence of his wife and any other member of his household.

4 **legal profession . . . placed:** The legal profession emerged in Russia together with the institution of open courts, as a result of the judicial reforms of 1864. Lawyers became prominent public figures and their profession both profitable and fashionable.

5 **in a frock coat:** That is, dressed more casually, not in the formal tailcoat usually called for on such occasions.

6 **'Be not so stern . . .':** A jumbled quotation of the first two lines of the poem

'From Hafiz' by Afanasy Fet (1820–92), a friend of Tolstoy's and one of his favourite poets.

7 **russification of Poland:** Portions of Poland came under Russian domination through the three partitions of 1772, 1793 and 1798. The national insurrections that broke out in 1830 and 1863 were cruelly repressed, and 'Russian' Poland remained under Russian domination until 1914.

8 **Attic salt:** Refined wit thought to be typical of Athenian conversation, as represented in the many 'dialogues' of classical and Hellenistic literature.

9 **education . . . disputes . . . :** In 1871 the Russian minister of national education, Count D. A. Tolstoy, proposed establishing two sorts of schools, so-called 'real' high schools and classical gymnasiums. The distinction was intended to limit the teaching of natural science, which was seen as a source of dangerous materialistic and atheistic notions. It was hoped that classical studies would cure young people of revolutionary ideas.

10 **anti-nihilistic:** The term 'nihilism', first used philosophically in German (*Nihilismus*) to signify annihilation, a reduction to nothing (attributed to Buddha), or the rejection of religious beliefs and moral principles, came via the French *nihilisme* to Russian, where it acquired a political meaning, referring to the doctrine of the younger generation of socialists of the 1860s, who advocated the destruction of the existing social order without specifying what should replace it. The great Russian lexicographer V. I. Dahl (1801–72), normally a model of restraint, defines 'nihilism' in his *Interpretive Dictionary of the Living Russian Language* as 'an ugly and immoral doctrine which rejects everything that cannot be palpated'.

11 **women's education:** In the 1860s women were allowed education only as teachers or midwives, but by the 1870s women's struggle for intellectual and social independence had been clearly expressed and higher studies in many fields were opened to them. (See note 26, Part One.)

12 **long hair, short . . . :** The full saying is: 'Long on hair, short on brains'.

13 **choral principle:** Pestsov here borrows a favourite notion of the Slavophiles, proponents of Russian national culture and Orthodoxy, originally expressed by the writer K. S. Aksakov (1817–60), about the peasant village commune being a sort of 'moral chorus' in which each voice is heard, but in harmony with all other voices.

14 **. . . never mind, silence!:** Levin quotes, consciously or unconsciously, the unmistakable words of the lovelorn and mad Mr Poprishchin in *The Diary of a Madman*, by Nikolai Gogol (1809–52).

15 **Fomin's . . . Fulde's:** Fomin's was an actual florist's shop in Moscow, and Fulde's was an actual jewellery shop.

16 **Froom:** That is, *Froom's Railway Guide for Russia and the Continent of Europe*, published in English in 1870.

17 **that holy martyr . . . :** Anna is thinking of St Mary of Egypt, a fifth-century saint much venerated in the Orthodox Church, a prostitute who converted to

Christianity and withdrew to the Egyptian desert, where she spent more than forty years in solitude and repentance.
18 Yeliseev's: The Yeliseev brothers owned famous delicatessen shops in Petersburg and Moscow which have survived to this day.

Part Five

1 prepared for communion: Only practising Orthodox Christians could be married in the Orthodox Church. To be a practising Christian meant to receive communion, and the necessary preparation for communion was the confession of one's sins.
2 the ambo: A raised platform leading from the body of the church to the doors of the sanctuary.
3 The mixing of these trades . . . : The sentence is a slightly altered quotation from the comedy *Woe from Wit* by the Russian poet, playwright and diplomat Alexander Griboedov (1795–1829).
4 suitor in Gogol: The suitor Ivan Kuzmich Podkolesin, in Gogol's comedy *The Wedding*, jumps out the window and flees just before he is expected to propose.
5 icon for the bride: In the Orthodox wedding ceremony, the bride and groom enter the church preceded by two children carrying icons – an icon of the Saviour for the groom and of the Mother of God for the bride.
6 the iconostasis: In an Orthodox church this is an icon-bearing partition with three doors that separates the body of the church from the sanctuary.
7 the heated church: City churches are often very large and only part of them can be kept warm in winter. This wedding, since it is before the Great Lent, is taking place in the very early spring.
8 new ones?: Specially painted and decorated candles are held by the bride and groom in an Orthodox wedding. They are often kept afterwards, but, as they are costly and burn down very little during the service, they may also be given back to the church.
9 step on the rug: A small piece of fine cloth is placed in the middle of the church for the bride and groom to stand on during the actual marriage ceremony. There is a popular belief that whoever steps on it first will be the dominant partner in the marriage.
10 porch of the church: The Orthodox marriage service has two parts: the betrothal and the marriage proper (the 'crowning', during which attendants hold crowns over the heads of the bride and groom). The betrothal takes place in the porch of the church, the crowning inside the church itself.
11 kamilavka: A special round velvet hat worn by Orthodox priests; the Russian word is a distortion of the Greek *kalimavka*, meaning 'beautiful hat'.
12 the Synod: At the death of the patriarch Adrian in 1700, Peter the Great reorganized the administration of the Russian Orthodox Church, appointing a

Holy Synod of bishops, instead of a new patriarch, to preside over Church affairs, headed by a Chief Procurator who was a layman answerable to the tsar. The Church was thus regarded not as a divine institution but as a department of the state. This 'synodal' period of Russian church history lasted until 1917, when an all-church council elected a new patriarch, Tikhon (now St Tikhon).

13 **'For thou . . . in love':** The extracts from the Orthodox marriage service in this chapter are taken from *The Service Book of the Holy Orthodox-Catholic Apostolic Church*, compiled, translated and arranged by Isabel Florence Hapgood with the endorsement of the patriarch Tikhon, published since 1918 in a number of editions.

14 **. . . would be happy:** Another popular belief concerning the marriage ceremony. The crowns are customarily held above the heads of the bride and groom during the service, but it was thought that if the crown was actually put on the person's head, it would help to make the person happy in married life.

15 **'. . . reverence her husband':** Ephesians 5:33. The Slavonic version reads 'fear' instead of the milder 'reverence' of the King James version.

16 **elaborate psalm:** Psalm 128, beginning: 'Blessed is every one that feareth the Lord; that walketh in his ways.'

17 **see their children's children:** Tolstoy quotes snippets from prayers and petitions in the marriage service (see note 13, Part Five).

18 **'Rejoice, O Isaiah':** At this central moment in the marriage service, the priest takes the bride and groom by the hand and leads them three times around the lectern, the attendants following them holding the crowns over their heads, while the choir sings certain verses, the best known beginning 'Rejoice, O Isaiah'.

19 **Tintoretto:** Jacopo Robusti, known as Tintoretto (1518–94), was an Italian painter of the Venetian school.

20 **The Two Origins . . . explanation:** The Slavophiles (see note 13, Part Four) often touched on the notion of the two origins – Catholic and Orthodox, rational and spiritual, Western and Eastern – of Russian culture. A. S. Khomiakov (1804–60), religious philosopher and poet, an important representative of the Slavophile movement, wrote about the Byzantine origin of Russian history. At the end of the novel, Levin will be 'disappointed in Khomiakov's teaching about the Church'.

21 **Ivanov-Strauss-Renan:** A. A. Ivanov (1806–58), an artist of the 'Wanderers' group, was the founder of the historical school of Russian painting; his most famous work was 'Christ Shown to the People' (1858). David Strauss (1808–74), German theologian and philosopher, wrote a famous 'historical' *Life of Jesus*, as did the French religious historian and lapsed Catholic Ernest Renan (1823–92).

22 **new school:** The artist I. N. Kramskoy (1837–87), also a 'Wanderer', met Tolstoy in 1873 and may have told him about his plans for a painting on the subject of the mocking of Christ. The 'new school' treated traditional religious

subjects with the techniques of realism. Tolstoy thought they had taken a wrong turn; his preference went neither to the traditionally 'religious' nor to the new 'realistic', but to a 'moral' treatment of the subject (see his *What Is Art?*).

23 **Charlotte Corday:** Charlotte Corday d'Armont (1768–93) became famous for assassinating the French revolutionary politician Jean-Paul Marat (1743–93), a Montagnard, in revenge for the 'September massacres' of the Girondin party, which he instigated. She went to the guillotine.

24 **Raphael's:** Raphael Sanzio (1483–1520), one of the greatest painters of the Florentine school, was commonly regarded in the nineteenth century as the supreme master of the art of painting. It was his 'idealizing' influence above all that the new historical school rejected.

25 **Pre-Raphaelite Englishman:** The Pre-Raphaelite Brotherhood, a group of English painters that emerged in the mid-nineteenth century, W. Holman-Hunt (1827–1910), J. E. Millais (1829–96) and D. G. Rossetti (1828–82) chief among them, revolted against the imitation of nature and favoured convention in art. They held up the Italian masters before Raphael, particularly Giotto and Botticelli, as models. The influential critic John Ruskin (1819–1900) championed their work.

26 **Rachel:** The Swiss-born actress Eliza Félix (1820–58), known as Mlle Rachel, contributed greatly to the revival of French classical tragedy on the nineteenth-century stage.

27 **. . . man-God . . . God-man:** According to Christian dogma, God became man in the 'God-man' Christ. Golenishchev implies that Mikhailov, in portraying a Christ whose divinity he denies, is in fact turning man into a god. (Kirillov makes the same reversal in Dostoevsky's *Demons*.)

28 **Capuan:** According to Livy (59 BC–AD 17) in his history of Rome, after spending the winter in Capua, near Naples, during the second Punic War, Hannibal's army became physically and morally soft and was subsequently defeated. In journalism of the 1870s, the name 'Capua' was often applied to the Paris of Napoleon III, but the use of 'Capuan' here is peculiar to Tolstoy: in his diaries he referred to his own periods of inactivity as 'Capua'.

29 **'Hidden from the wise . . .':** A misquotation of Matthew 11:25: '. . . thou hast hid these things from the wise and prudent, and hast revealed them unto babes'. (See also Luke 10:21.)

30 **when in doubt . . . :** A literal translation of the French proverb: *Dans le doute abstiens-toi*, which was Tolstoy's favourite saying.

31 **burden is light:** Cf. Matthew 11:30: 'For my yoke is easy, and my burden is light.'

32 **mystical mood . . . in Petersburg:** See note 34, Part Two.

33 **'He that humbleth himself . . .':** See Luke 14:11.

34 **Komisarov:** In April 1866 a certain O. I. Komissarov (1838–92), a peasant hatter from Kostroma (Tolstoy spells the name with one *s*), turned up by chance near the fence of the Summer Garden in Petersburg and inadvertently hindered

Karakozov's attempt to assassinate Alexander II. For that he was granted nobility and became socially fashionable for a time. He eventually drank himself into obscurity.

35 **Ristich-Kudzhitsky:** That is, Yovan Ristich (1831–99), a Serbian political activist who opposed Turkish and Austrian influence in Serbia. His name was well known in Russia. The 'Slavic question' was the question of freeing the Slavic peoples from the Ottoman yoke, one of the most important political issues of the 1870s. In 1875 a popular revolt broke out in Bosnia and Herzegovina, in 1876 in Montenegro. Serbia declared war on Turkey that same year. Bulgaria placed its hopes in Russia. In 1877 Russia declared war on Turkey, and there was talk of 'taking Constantinople' in revenge for the Russian defeat in the Crimean War (1854–6).

36 **the Alexander Nevsky:** That is, the Order of Alexander Nevsky, created by Peter the Great in 1722, named after St Alexander Nevsky (1220–63), a prince whose victories over the Swedes and the Teutonic knights made him a national hero.

37 **'He that is married . . .':** Cf. 1 Corinthians 7:32–3. Karenin inverts the two halves of the sentence.

38 **throw the stone:** See note 33, Part One.

39 **Slav tutor:** It was traditional to have an English or French tutor; Karenin follows the new fashion in having his son learn Russian from a Slav tutor.

40 **the Vladimir . . . Andrew the First-called:** That is, the Order of St Vladimir, named after Prince Vladimir of Kiev (956?–1015), who laid the foundations of the Kievan state and in 988 converted his people to Christianity, and the Order of St Andrew the apostle, patron saint of Russia, traditionally known as 'the first-called' from the account of his calling in John 1:37–40.

41 **Enoch . . . alive to heaven:** See Genesis 5:18–24 and Hebrews 11:5.

42 **Patti:** Carlotta Patti (1835–89), Italian opera singer, elder sister of the more famous Adelina Patti (1843–1919), toured in Russia from 1872 to 1875.

43 **perfumed glove:** The long, tight-fitting gloves fashionable at the time could only be put on by first being rolled up like a stocking.

Part Six

1 **Gvozdevo . . . near side:** The topography of Pokrovskoe resembles that of Tolstoy's estate Yasnaya Polyana down to the smallest details. The marsh where Tolstoy used to hunt was divided in two by railway tracks; that is why Levin says 'on the near side'.

2 **Automedon:** Achilles' charioteer in the *Iliad*.

3 **tax farmers:** private persons authorized by the state to collect taxes in exchange for a fixed fee. The practice was obviously open to abuse, and tax farmers could

become extremely wealthy, though never quite respectable. The practice was abolished in the 1860s by the reforms of Alexander II.

4 **Gretchen:** Diminutive of Margarete, a peasant girl in Goethe's *Faust* who is seduced and abandoned by Faust.

5 **hat of Monomakh:** A slightly altered quotation from Pushkin's historical drama *Boris Godunov*. The 'hat of Monomakh' is the hereditary crown of the Russian tsars, named after Prince Vladimir Monomakh (1053–1126).

6 **bring forth children:** See Genesis 3:16 (Revised Standard Version).

7 **Gautier:** An actual bookshop in Moscow, owned by V. I. Gautier, located on Kuznetsky Bridge.

8 **'... kiss the cross':** It was customary to seal an oath by kissing the cross.

9 **'... sancta simplicitas':** 'O holy simplicity' – words said to have been spoken by the Czech reformer Jan Hus (1369–1415), as he was being burned at the stake, to an old woman who came up to add a stick to the fire.

10 **bast:** The flexible inner bark of the linden, which had many uses (as roofing material, fibre for binding, material for shoes) in rural Russia.

11 **vestals:** The Vestal Virgins were priestesses who tended the sacred fire in the temple of Vesta, goddess of the hearth and household, in ancient Rome.

12 **the brothers:** That is, 'brother Slavs' – Serbians, Bulgarians, Montenegrins – whose struggle for independence drew sympathy and aid from Russian society (see note 35, Part Five).

13 **Taine:** Hippolyte Taine (1828–93), French philosopher, historian and critic. His book *Intelligence* was published in 1870. In *What Is Art?* Tolstoy includes him among the futile reasoners about beauty.

Part Seven

1 **Montenegrins ... fighters:** Over the course of some six centuries Montenegro never ceased its resistance to Turkish rule. In 1876 the Montenegrins formed bands and embarked on a guerrilla war in the mountains, which was followed closely in the European press.

2 **Svintich's fiftieth birthday:** An ironic reference to the celebrating of all sorts of anniversaries that became fashionable in the 1870s.

3 **the university question:** The January 1875 issue of the *Russian Herald*, in which the first chapters of *Anna Karenina* were published, also contained an article by Professor N. Liubimov on 'The University Question'. Liubimov, who opposed the autonomy of the universities, was accused by young professors of handing them over to the government.

4 **Ment:** The name of the poet Ment, which means '[he] lies' in French, is Tolstoy's invention, as is the name of the scholar Metrov, from 'metre' or 'measure'.

5 Journal de St-Pétersbourg: A semi-official magazine published in French from 1842, reflecting the political views of the higher aristocratic circles.

6 Buslaev's grammar: F. I. Buslaev (1818–97), Russian scholar and philologist, was the author of two fundamental works of historical grammar.

7 King Lear on the Heath: This fantasia is Tolstoy's parody of the programme music that had become popular in nineteenth-century concert halls, which he disapproved of (see *What Is Art?*). Two Russian composers used Shakespeare's *King Lear* as a subject: M. A. Balakirev (1837–1910) in his *King Lear* (1860), and P. I. Tchaikovsky (1840–93) in *The Storm* (1874). Tolstoy believed that the need for adjusting music to literature or literature to music destroyed creative freedom.

8 das ewig Weibliche: The notion of the *ewig Weibliche* comes from the finale of Goethe's *Faust*.

9 Wagnerian trend . . . : Like Levin, Tolstoy considered the operas of Richard Wagner (1813–83) and the musical 'trend' that followed from them another form of programme music. His strongest attack on Wagner and his theory of the *Gesamtkunstwerk* (total or composite work of art) appears in *What Is Art?*

10 . . . poet on a pedestal: Tolstoy has in mind the model for a monument to Pushkin by the sculptor M. M. Antokolsky (1843–1902), which was exhibited in the Academy of Art in 1875. Pushkin was shown sitting on a rock with the heroes of his works coming up some stairs towards him, the intention being to illustrate Pushkin's lines: 'Now an invisible swarm of guests comes to me,/ Familiar of old, the fruits of my dream.'

11 panikhida: A memorial service for the dead.

12 Lucca: Paulina Lucca (1841–1908), an Italian-born opera singer who made her career in Austria, visited Russia in the early 1870s. She had great successes as Zerlina in Mozart's *Don Giovanni* and Carmen in Bizet's *Carmen*.

13 folle journée: The French phrase, taken from the comedy *La Folle journée, ou le Mariage de Figaro*, by Beaumarchais (1732–99), came to be applied to all sorts of carnivals and festive evenings.

14 foreigner . . . to exile abroad: In October 1875 a commercial credit bank in Moscow was suddenly closed, and its directors and board members were arrested. The chief cause of the scandal was a certain foreign negotiator whose fraudulent dealings led to the bank's collapse. His trial lasted until November 1876, when he was found guilty and banished from Russia, a 'punishment' which aroused widespread indignation.

15 Krylov's fables: The poet Ivan Krylov (1769–1843) was the father of the Russian fable. Levin's phrase is modelled on the line, 'And the pike was thrown into the river', from the fable 'The Pike', in which a corrupt court punishes the guilty pike by throwing it into the river.

16 'Rejoice, O Isaiah': See note 18, Part Five.

17 Bible illustrations . . . : The French graphic artist Gustave Doré (1832–83) is most famous as an illustrator of classics such as *The Divine Comedy*, *Don*

Quixote, and *Gargantua and Pantagruel*. In 1875 a luxury edition of the Bible with Doré's illustrations went on sale in Russia. Tolstoy disapproved of Doré's illustrations for being 'merely aesthetic'.

18 Zola, Daudet: Tolstoy is thinking of the naturalist movement in French literature in the latter half of the nineteenth century, headed by Émile Zola (1840–1902), based on the exact reproduction of life and the total absence of novelistic fiction. For a time Alphonse Daudet (1840–97) was also an adherent of naturalism. Tolstoy criticized the movement for its lack of 'spiritualizing' ideas.

19 United Agency . . . Banking Institutions: The title of the post is a parody conflating the names of two actually existing institutions of the time: The Society of Mutual Land Credit and The Society of Southwestern Railways.

20 Rurik: See note 4, Part One.

21 . . . face of fire: The simile is borrowed from Psalm 68:2: 'as wax melteth before the fire, so let the wicked perish at the presence of God' – which is sung in the Orthodox Easter service and has thus become proverbial.

22 Landau . . . Bezzubov: Influential mediums were a feature of society life at that time. Landau resembles the medium Douglas Hume, who travelled and 'prophesied' in America and Europe, enjoyed the sympathy of Napoleon III and was received at the court of Alexander II. Hume had surprising success in Russia, married the daughter of Count Bezborodko ('Beardless') and thus became a count himself. Tolstoy parodies his success by having Landau adopted by Countess Bezzubov ('Toothless').

23 Saul: The reference is to the conversion of Saul (the apostle Paul) recounted in Acts 9:3–9.

24 Apostle James: Oblonsky quotes from James 2:26: 'For as the body without the spirit is dead, so faith without works is dead also.' This teaching seems to be a contradiction of St Paul's notion of 'justification by faith' (see Romans 4, Galatians 3), so much so that Martin Luther, who (like Karenin and Countess Lydia Ivanovna) preached justification by faith, wanted to have the Epistle of James removed from the Bible. The two apparently contradictory assertions are in fact complementary.

25 . . . Under the Wing: Titles, which Tolstoy gives in English, of pious tracts in the spirit of the 'new mystical trend' connected with the sermons of the Protestant missionary Lord Radstock (Granville Augustus William Waldgrave, Lord Radstock, 1831–1913), who visited Russia twice, in 1874 and 1878, and was a popular figure in the high-society salons of Moscow and Petersburg. Lord Radstock, a graduate of Eton and Oxford, was invited to Russia by Countess Chertkov, the mother of Vladimir Chertkov, who later became the most important of Tolstoy's 'disciples'.

26 Trinity Monastery: The Trinity-St Sergius Monastery, some thirty miles north of Moscow, is a spiritual centre and place of pilgrimage founded in the fourteenth century by St Sergius of Radonezh (*c.* 1314–92).

Part Eight

1 **Northern Beetle:** The title is a parody of the *Northern Bee*, a reactionary newspaper edited by Faddey Bulgarin (1789–1859), who was also a bad novelist and a secret agent specializing in the denunciation of writers, Pushkin among them.

2 **American friends . . . Slavic question:** After the failed attempt on the life of Alexander II in 1866, an American diplomatic mission arrived in Petersburg and presented the tsar with an expression of sympathy and respect on the part of all the American people. The 'American friends' were met with receptions and banquets in the capital. In 1871–2 there was drought in Samara province, followed in 1873 by famine. Committees were organized for relief of the peasants there, and Tolstoy was one of the first to respond with a large donation. For the 'Slavic question' see note 35, Part Five.

3 **volunteers:** 'Slavic Committees' appeared in Russia soon after the outbreak of the Serbian war in 1876, recruiting volunteers to send to the aid of Serbia. Prior to Russia's entry into the war, only retired officers like Yashvin and Vronsky could serve as volunteers.

4 **Tsaritsyn station:** The name of Tsaritsyn, a major city on the Volga, was changed to Volgograd in 1925, then to Stalingrad, and has now been changed back to Volgograd.

5 **Ristich . . . Milan:** For Ristich, see note 35, Part Five. Milan Obrenovich (1852–1901), prince of Serbia, declared war on Turkey in 1876 with the promise of Russian support. Serbia achieved complete independence in 1878, and in 1882 the country was made a kingdom with Milan Obrenovich as king. In 1889 he abdicated in favour of his son Alexander I.

6 **Plato . . . life:** Before and during his work on *Anna Karenina*, Tolstoy assiduously studied philosophy, convinced that it gave the best answers to questions about the meaning of life and death. Like Levin, he was particularly interested in the works of Plato, Kant, Schopenhauer and Spinoza.

7 **love . . . will:** Tolstoy was both fascinated and repulsed by the philosophy of the German thinker Arthur Schopenhauer (1788–1860), who maintained that a blind will underlies phenomena, in opposition to the representation of the world produced by the intelligence. Tolstoy considered his views hopeless, dark and pessimistic; hence Levin's attempt to substitute *love* for *will*.

8 **Khomiakov:** See note 20, Part Five.

9 **'infidel Hagarenes':** That is, the Muslims, reputed to be descendants of Hagar, concubine of Abraham and mother of Ishmael (Genesis 16).

10 **Pugachev . . . Khiva:** Emelian Pugachev (*c.* 1742–75), a Cossack and impostor, claimed to be the tsar Peter III and led an uprising in an attempt to take the throne. He was defeated and executed. For Khiva, see note 20, Part Three.

11 **Karr . . . Prussia:** Alphonse Karr (1808–90), a witty Parisian journalist

and pamphleteer who wrote for the collection *Guêpes* (*Wasps*), published anti-military pamphlets before the Franco-Prussian War in 1870.

12 **'. . . not peace but a sword':** A slight misquotation of Matthew 10:34: 'Think not that I am come to send peace on earth: I came not to send peace, but a sword.'

13 **Varangians:** See note 4, Part One.

14 **the Eastern question:** See note 42, Part One.

Contemporary Services Marketing Management

A Reader

Contemporary Services Marketing Management

A Reader

Edited by
Mark Gabbott and Gillian Hogg

The Dryden Press
Harcourt Brace & Company Limited
London Fort Worth New York Orlando
Philadelphia San Diego Toronto Sydney Tokyo

The Dryden Press
24–28 Oval Road
London NW1 7DX

This book is printed on acid-free paper.

ISBN 0-03-099035-1

Typeset by Mackreth Media Services, Hemel Hempstead, Herts
Printed in Great Britain by WBC Book Manufacturers, Bridgend, Mid Glamorgan

Contents

Introduction

Mark Gabbott and Gillian Hogg

Considerable effort has been expended by academics over the last twenty years in establishing that services are different to other products and that these differences present special challenges to the service marketer. In their review of the development of services marketing literature Fisk, Brown and Bitner (1993) use an evolutionary metaphor. They identify a period of 'crawling out' as services marketing emerged from the goods marketing paradigm, through a 'scurrying about' phase to the present, where services marketing is 'walking erect' and demonstrating empirical and theoretical rigour. At the same time, the cross disciplinary and international nature of services research has become apparent. The nature of services and the value of taking a service orientated approach to management has been recognised outwith the specific discipline of services marketing. In this text we attempt not only to provide readers with some of the most interesting and stimulating examples of current services research, but also to provide a summary of where the discipline has come from, with a section on the Classics from the crawling out phase, which set the parameters of services research. By concentrating, in the main, on contemporary articles (which we define as since 1990) we hope to indicate where the discipline of services marketing is today. By way of an introduction it is, however, worthwhile rehearsing the basis of services marketing and reviewing the foundations upon which it is built.

DEFINITIONS OF SERVICES

The first problem with discussing service products, rather that goods, lies in defining what a service is. There is no single universally accepted definition of the term, Grönroos (1990) lists a selection of 11 definitions of the term dating from 1960 before, reluctantly, arriving at a definition which he describes as a 'blend' of those suggested by Lehtinen and Lehtinen (1982), Kotler and Bloom (1984) and Gummesson (1987):

> A service is an activity or series of activities of more or less intangible nature that normally, but not necessarily, take place in interactions between the customer and the service employee and/or physical resources or goods and/or systems of the service provider, which are provided as solutions to customer problems.
>
> Grönroos (1990) p. 27

The complexity and rather convoluted nature of this definition illustrates the problem in succinctly defining services. Gummesson (1987), referring to an unidentified source, suggests an alternative definition that is more of a criticism of attempts to find an acceptable definition

> Services are something which can be bought and sold but which you can not drop on your foot
>
> Gummesson (1987) p. 22

There is still not agreement amongst some academics as to whether the differences between goods and services are significant enough to justify the distinction. Levitt (1976) states that there are no such thing as service industries, only industries where the service component is greater or less than those in other industries. Similarly Shostack (1977) argues that there are very few 'pure' goods or services preferring a product continuum from tangible dominant goods to intangible dominant services. Any distinction is between products where the core of what is being sold is a service, with possible accompanying goods, and products where the core is a physical good where the service element is used as a product augmentation for competitive advantage.

An alternative way of regarding the definition problem in service products is presented by Rust and Oliver (1994) who conceptualise all business transactions as services, which may or may not involve a physical product. This argument is based on the idea that all products deliver some form of service, for example, a washing machine washes clothes, the washing machine is bought to deliver that service. Along with the physical product the buyer also receives service delivery, i.e. the experience of buying the washing machine, the service environment (the shop in which it is bought) and the service product which they define as the specifications of the offering. All products are, therefore, made up of these elements, centred around the physical product which is present in goods and absent in pure services. The case for considering services marketing as a separate entity is based on the belief that there are a number of common characteristics of service products which distinguish them from goods. Although the conceptualisation of the term 'services' is difficult, all products have characteristics, or attributes, that define the nature of the offering. For services these can be identified as intangibility, heterogeneity, inseparability, perishability and the concept of ownership (see, for instance, Lovelock, 1981 and Grönroos, 1978).

CHARACTERISTICS OF SERVICES

Intangibility is one of the most important characteristics of services, they do not have a physical dimension. Often services are described using tangible nouns but this obscures the fundamental nature of the service which remains intangible. Shostack (1987) points out by way of example that 'airline' means air transportation, 'hotel' means lodging rental. Berry (1980) describes a good as 'an object, a device, a thing', in contrast to a service which is 'a deed, a performance, an effort'. He argues that even though the performance of most services is supported by tangibles the essence of what is purchased is a performance; therefore, as McLuhan (1964) points out, it is the process of delivering a service which comprises the product. The implication of this argument is that consumers cannot see, touch, hear, taste or smell a service they can only experience the performance of it (Carman and Uhl, 1973; Sasser *et al.*, 1978). This makes the perception of a service a highly subjective and abstract concept.

The second characteristic of services is the inseparability of the production and consumption aspects of the transaction. The service is a performance, in real time, in which the purchaser cooperates with the provider. According to Thomas (1978) the degree of this involvement is dependent upon the extent to which the service is people based or equipment based. The inference of this distinction is that people based services tend to be less standardised than equipment based services or goods producing activities. Goods are produced, sold and then consumed, whereas services are sold and then produced and consumed simultaneously (Regan, 1963; Cowell, 1984). The inseparability of the role of service provider and consumer also relates to the lack of standardisation since the purchaser can alter both the way in which the service is delivered, as well as what is delivered, which has important implications for both the management and the evaluation of the service product.

The heterogeneity of services is also a function of human involvement in the delivery and consumption process. It refers to the fact that services are delivered by individuals and therefore each service encounter will be different by virtue of the participants or time of performance. As a consequence each purchaser is likely to receive a different service experience. The perishability of services describes the real time nature of the product. Services cannot be stored unlike goods and the absence of the ability to build and maintain stocks of the product means that fluctuations in demand cannot be accommodated in the same way as goods, i.e. in periods of excess demand more product cannot be utilised. For the purchaser of services the time at which he/she chooses to use the service may be critical to its performance and therefore to the consumers' experience. Kelley, Donnelly and Skinner (1990) make the observation that consumption is inextricably linked to the presence of other consumers and their presence can influence the service outcome.

To the above characteristics of services, Wyckham *et al.* (1975) and Kotler (1986) have identified the concept of ownership as a distinguishing feature of services. With the sale of a good the purchaser generally obtains ownership of it. By contrast in the case of a service the purchaser only has temporary access or use of it: what is owned is the benefit of the service, not the service itself, e.g. in terms of a holiday the purchaser has the benefit of the flight, hotel and beach but does not own them. The absence of ownership stresses the finite nature of services for purchasers, there is no enduring involvement in the product, only in the benefit.

PROCESS AND OUTCOME

In discussing the service product it is important to make a distinction between two principal components of the service product, the outcome, i.e. what the service is designed to achieve, and the process of delivery, i.e. how the service is delivered. It is frequently more difficult for a supplier to differentiate the outcome; for example, an accounting audit must achieve certain criteria; the outcome, audited accounts, are not easily differentiated. The purchaser requires reliability of the outcome, differentiation takes place at the process dimension, how the accounts are audited. In many services this outcome is difficult for the purchaser to evaluate, even after the service has been delivered. It is possible for the purchaser to know that the service has been delivered, but difficult to assess whether it has been delivered in the most effective way. The purchaser may not know whether the accounts were audited in the most efficient or cost effective manner; in these circumstances the way the audit takes place, the process of auditing is used to assess the competence of the auditors, i.e. financial competence is implied from the manner in which the audit is conducted. Whereas the reliability of the outcome is essential, the service supplier must deliver the core service, much of the competition in service industries takes place at the process level.

Other models have been presented which have similar bases, despite different terminology, and they all describe a process and outcome form. For instance, Grönroos (1990) refers to technical versus functional aspects, Zeithaml (1988) uses an intrinsic versus extrinsic distinction, Iacobucci *et al.* (1994) describe 'core' and 'peripheral' aspects of the service. The word pairs are not exactly interchangeable but there are strong conceptual parallels. The key factor is that in service products it is important to make a distinction between what is delivered and how it is delivered. The relationship between these two aspects is considered throughout the articles in this reader and it is the basis of most of the work on service quality and satisfaction included in Section III.

STRUCTURE OF THE READER

The reader is divided into five sections reflecting different aspects of services research. However, the sections are not intended to be inclusive, they merely provide a convenient way of presenting contemporary services research. The first section, The Classics, is the basis of the consideration of services as a separate discipline with some of the most important and, for their time, ground-breaking articles on services. This is where services research is coming from, the starting point for the subject and the foundation for the reader. The following sections, however, are reflective of current services marketing thought, in effect we have 'jumped' the intervening years. This is not to imply that the years between have not produced interesting and exciting services marketing research; readers may wish to look at Solomon, Surprenant, Czepiel and Gutman (1985) and Bitner, Boom and Tetreault's (1990) work on service encounters, Guiltinan's (1987) article on the pricing of services or Levitt's (1972 and 1976) work on services, to name but a few. However, these articles have been extensively reprinted and included in other texts; see for example, Bateson (1995). In this text we are attempting to illustrate where the discipline is in the mid 1990s and the articles chosen are all illustrative of current research in the field.

As Fisk *et al.* (1993) point out, the battle for services to be considered a separate discipline has now been won. The number of publications, conferences, teaching programmes and research centres bears witness to the fact that services are now recognised as an important and developing research area. We are now in the 'walking erect' stage of the evolution metaphor as we hope is demonstrated by the range and scope of the research represented in this reader.

REFERENCES

Bateson, J. (1995) *Managing Services Marketing*, 3rd Edn. London: Dryden Press.

Berry, L. L. (1980) 'Service Marketing Is Different', *Business* (May–June): 24–29.

Bitner, M. J., Booms, B. and Tetreault, B. (1990) 'The Service Encounter: Diagnosing Favourable and Unfavourable Incidents'. *Journal of Marketing* **54**: 71–84.

Carman, J. and Uhl, K. (1973) *Marketing: Principles and Methods.* Homewood, Ill: Irwin.

Cowell, D. (1984) *The Marketing of Services.* London: Heinemann.

Fisk, R., Brown, S. and Bitner, M. J. (1993) 'Tracking the Evolution of Services Marketing Literature'. *Journal of Retailing* **69** (No. 1): 61–103.

Grönroos, C. (1978) 'A Service Orientated Approach to Marketing Services'. *European Journal of Marketing* **12** (8), 588–601.

Grönroos, C. (1990) *Service Management and Marketing: Managing The Moments of Truth in Service Competition.* Lexington Marketing Association, Maxwell Macmillan.

Guiltinan, J. (1987) 'The Price Bundling of Services: A Normative Framework'. *Journal of Marketing* **31** (April): 74–85.

Gummesson, E. (1987) 'Lip services – A Neglected Area in Services Marketing'. *Journal of Services Marketing* (No. 1): 22.

Iacobucci, D., Grayson, K. and Ostrom, A. (1994) 'The Calculus of Service Quality and Customer Satisfaction: Theoretical and Empirical Differentiation and Integration'. *Advances in Services Marketing and Management* **3**: 1–67.

Kelley, S. W., Donnelly, J. H. and Skinner, S. J. (1990) 'Customer Participation in Service Production and Delivery'. *Journal of Retailing* **66** (No. 3): 315–335.

Kotler, P. (1986) *Principles of Marketing*, 3rd Edn. Englewood Cliffs, New Jersey: Prentice-Hall International.

Kotler, P. and Bloom, P. (1984) *Marketing Professional Services.* Englewood Cliffs NJ: Prentice Hall.

Lehtinen, U. and Lehtinen, J. (1982) *Service Quality: A Study of Dimensions.* Research Report, Helsinki, Finland.

Levitt, T. (1972) 'The Production Line Approach to Service'. *Harvard Business Review* (September/October): 41–52.

Levitt, T. (1976) 'The Industrialisation of Service'. *Harrrvard Business Review* (Sept–Oct) 63–74.

Lovelock, C. (1981) 'Why Marketing Management Needs to Be Different for Services'. In *Marketing of Services* (J. H. Donnelly and W. R. George, eds). American Marketing Association, Chicago.

Regan, W. J. (1963) 'The Service Revolution', *Journal of Marketing* 27 (July): 57–62.

Rust, R. T. and Oliver, R. L. (1994) 'Service Quality: Insights and Managerial Implications Form The Frontier'. In *Service Quality: New Directions in Theory and Practice* (R. Rust and R. Oliver, Eds). California: Sage.

Sasser, W. E., Olsen, R. P., and Wyckoff, D. D. (1978) *The Management of Service Operations.* Boston, MA: Allyn and Bacon.

Solomon, M., Surprenant, C., Czepiel, J. and Gutman, E. (1985) 'Service Encounters: An Overview'. In *The Service Encounter: Managing Employee/Customer Interaction in Service Businesses* (J. Czepiel, M. Solomon and C. Surprenant, Eds). MA: Lexington Books, 3–15.

Thomas, D. R. E. (1978) 'Strategy Is Different in Service Business'. *Harvard Business Review* (July–August): 158–165.

Wyckham, R. G., Fitzroy, P. and Mandry, G. (1975) 'Marketing of Services: An Evaluation of The Theory'. *European Journal of Marketing* **9**: 59-67.

Zeithaml, V. (1988) 'Consumer Perceptions of Price, Quality and Value: A Means-End Model and Synthesis'. *Journal of Marketing* **52** (July): 2–22.

Section I

The Classics

Services marketing management has now reached a stage in its development which demands a recognition of the special characteristics of the service product. However, this was not always the case. Academics and practitioners struggled for some time against the view that services were no different to any other class of product. As the services sector emerged in the Western economies, it was clear that new marketing tools were needed in assisting the development of a newly conceptualised product class and this is where our reader starts. We have included in this section five articles which for us represent the emergence of the services discipline and provide a necessary reference point for the consideration of more contemporary material.

The paper by Shostack (1977) has been recognised as one of the first major service marketing works. It presents a number of key ideas which have become cornerstones of the discipline. The article tackles the difficult issue of marketing semantics as an attempt to differentiate services from the dominance of the 'product orientation'. As far as the author undoubtedly moved the debate forward, the issue of definitions is still a debating point in classes and seminars across the world. The crux of the argument is the issue of 'tangibility' and Shostack argues coherently that to conceptualise services and physical products as the same, apart from intangibility, is to argue that apples are no different from oranges apart from their 'appleness'. A simple example perhaps, but one which went to the core(!) of the debate in the late 1970s and highlights the 'breaking free' aspect of this work.

The middle section of this article continues to take 'pot shots' at the prevailing marketing paradigm and this part of the work has relevance even beyond services. However, the re-conceptualisation of products as combinations of discrete elements formed into a molecular model neatly side-stepped the arguments about the classification of individual products and services. Shostack presents an holistic approach based upon a tangible/intangible continuum and this has become a classic in its own right. In the final section of the article, the author goes on to provide some suggestions about how marketers need to compensate for the problems presented by intangibility by managing peripheral cues; those things consumers experience through their five senses which characterise for them the reality of the service experience. The term 'tangibilising the intangible' changes through the discussion of physical/tangible evidence as Shostack applies it to different services contexts and their representation through advertising. In total this article summarises many of the main themes of the services marketing literature and is still considered a classic.

Unlike Shostack, the paper by Lovelock (1983) is concerned primarily with classification and has been included here to lead on from the Shostack article. Whereas Shostack dealt with services in a general way, looking for a normative approach, the work by Lovelock recognises the diversity within services and approaches the problem inductively by trying to establish commonalities across service products. This is then used as a means of engendering a cross fertilisation of ideas and activities to define some sort of boundary for services marketing. This article marks the beginning of a services classification theme in the literature continued by Lovelock, Gummesson, and Grönroos etc. While some have argued that this is a distraction from the main issues facing services, and contributes very little to the development of practice or research, the article by Lovelock is more than just a classification exercise. The statement of the five questions about services highlights some of the key issues for marketing in the services context. The matrices and accompanying text provide a great deal of clarity and detail to some of the issues highlighted by Shostack. By concentrating upon the nature of the services act, the type of relationship, degree of customisation, nature of demand and supply and finally delivery, Lovelock is able to explore a series of sub-questions through an 'insights and implications' structure. The value of this article is not so much in the classifications derived from the asking of the five questions but through the portrayal of similar services across dimensions allowing for practitioners to look beyond their own experience and draw from the experiences and activities of others.

Zeithaml (1981) presents a different perspective by concentrating upon service consumers. If one accepts the contention that service products and services marketing activity is different to that of physical products, then we must accept that consumers' responses to products are also likely to be different. This argument is still strangely alien even now in the 1990s and the amount of published research on service consumption is still relatively sparse compared to research on service products. The article presents for the first time, an attempt to explain some inherent differences in how consumers use and evaluate services as opposed to physical products. Zeithaml uses a search, experience, credence framework derived from the work of Nelson (1974) and Darby and Karni (1973). It argues that the characteristics of services suggest that they are high in experience and credence qualities but low in search qualities representing an increased difficulty for consumers in evaluation. We can criticise the framework for inadequate conceptualisation. For instance by an insufficient distinction between search and experience (i.e. when do experiences, especially of other consumers become searchable?) and between experience and credence (i.e. to what extent is there a reliance upon experience in determining credence?). However, this framework has been influential in guiding research on consumer behaviour and services in general and service evaluation in particular. The article is structured around eleven hypotheses which Zeithaml presents as axiomatic for the service consumers. In the absence of any empirical work the hypotheses remain in their propositional form, but have intuitive appeal. These hypotheses are grouped into information search, evaluative criteria, size and composition of the evoked set, perceived risk, adoption of innovations, brand loyalty and attribution of dissatisfaction which covers a considerable amount of consumer behaviour of interest to marketers. The article finishes with a series of recommendations for service marketers in respect of the hypotheses.

Grönroos (1978) provides insights from services companies as to how the marketing mix is planned and applied bearing in mind the characteristics of the service product. The article is also notable for its observations about service marketing management which, even though it was written nearly twenty years ago, are still relevant today. The article presents three dimensions which the author believes are central to the development of a contextualised marketing mix. It uses a series of three case studies to provide supporting evidence for the importance of accessibility, the human element in service delivery and the provision of auxiliary (or augmented) service offerings. It is suggested that these elements relate directly to the consumer's experience of the service product and must therefore be integral to the task of marketing planning.

The final article by Rathmell is truly a classic, being published in 1966. Its status though is not just in terms of its age, for the content of this article shows quite clearly how the early debate over the definition and classification of services was framed. It is included here as an example of the early service marketing research formulated as a discussion of issues related to service products. Many of the ideas which subsequently became important in services research are contained here, such as the difficulty in conceptualising products comprising both goods and services, the nature of service satisfaction, and the goods–service continuum. The final section of the article identifies a number of service characteristics which can still guide current debate and a call for research in the area which has certainly been responded to.

CONTENTS

1

Breaking Free from Product Marketing

G. Lynn Shostack

New concepts are necessary if service marketing is to succeed. Service marketing is an uncharted frontier. Despite the increasing dominance of services in the US economy, basic texts still disagree on how services should be treated in a marketing context.[1]

The heart of this dispute is the issue of applicability. The classic marketing 'mix', the seminal literature, and the language of marketing all derive from the manufacture of physical goods. Practicing marketers tend to think in terms of products, particularly mass-market consumer goods. Some service companies even call their output 'products' and have 'product' management functions modeled after those of experts such as Procter and Gamble.

Marketing seems to be overwhelmingly product-oriented. However, many service-based companies are confused about the applicability of product marketing, and more than one attempt to adopt product marketing has failed.

Merely adopting product marketing's labels does not resolve the question of whether product marketing can be overlaid on service businesses. Can corporate banking services really be marketed according to the same basic blueprint that made *Tide* a success? Given marketing's historic tenets, there is simply no alternative.

Could marketing itself be 'myopic' in having failed to create relevant paradigms for the service sector? Many marketing professionals who transfer to the services arena find their work fundamentally 'different', but have a difficult time articulating how and why their priorities and concepts have changed. Often, they also find to their frustration and bewilderment that 'marketing' is treated as a peripheral function or is confused with one of its components, such as research or advertising, and kept within a very narrow scope of influence and authority.[2]

This situation is frequently rationalized as being due to the 'ignorance' of senior management in service businesses. 'Education' is usually recommended as the solution. However, an equally feasible, though less comforting, explanation is that service industries have been slow to integrate marketing into the mainstream of decision-making and control because marketing offers no guidance, terminology, or practical rules that are clearly *relevant* to services.

Reprinted with permission from *Journal of Marketing*, Vol. 41, April, pp. 73–80

MAKING ROOM FOR INTANGIBILITY

The American Marketing Association cites both goods *and* services as foci for marketing activities. Squeezing services into the Procrustean phrase 'intangible products',[3] is not only a distortion of the AMA's definition but also a complete contradiction in terms.

It is wrong to imply that services are just like products 'except' for intangibility. By such logic, apples are just like oranges, except for their 'appleness'. Intangibility is not a modifier; it is a state. Intangibles may come with tangible trappings, but no amount of money can buy physical ownership of such intangibles as 'experience' (movies), 'time' (consultants), or 'process' (dry cleaning). A service is rendered. A service is experienced. A service cannot be stored on a shelf, touched, tasted or tried on for size. 'Tangible' means 'palpable', and 'material'. 'Intangible' is an antonym, meaning '*im*palpable', and '*not* corporeal'.[4] This distinction has profound implications. Yet marketing offers no way to treat intangibility as the core element it is, nor does marketing offer usable tools for managing, altering, or controlling this amorphous core.

Even the most thoughtful attempts to broaden the definition of 'that which is marketed' away from product synonymity suffer from an underlying assumption of tangibility. Not long ago, Philip Kotler argued that 'values' should be considered the end result of 'marketing'.[5] However, the text went on to imply that 'values' were created by 'objects' and drifted irredeemably into the classic product axioms.

To truly expand marketing's conceptual boundaries requires a framework which accommodates intangibility instead of denying it. Such a framework must give equal descriptive weight to the components of 'service' as it does to the concept of 'product'.

The complexity of marketed entities

What kind of framework would provide a new conceptual viewpoint? One unorthodox possibility can be drawn from direct observation of the marketplace and the nature of the market 'satisfiers' available to it. Taking a fresh look, it seems that there are really very few, if any, 'pure' products or services in the marketplace.

Examine, for instance the automobile. Without question, one might say, it is a physical object, with a full range of tangible features and options. But another, equally important element is marketed in tandem with the steel and chrome – i.e. the service of transportation. Transportation is an *independent* marketing element; in other words, it is not car-dependent, but can be marketed in its own right. A car is only *one* alternative for satisfying the market's transportation needs.

This presents a semantic dilemma. How should the automobile be defined? Is General Motors marketing a *service*, a service that happens to include a *by*-product called a car? Levitt's classic 'Marketing Myopia' exhorts businessmen to think in exactly this generic way about what they market.[6] Are automobiles 'tangible services'? It cannot be denied that both elements – tangible and intangible – exist and are vigorously marketed. Yet they are, by definition, different qualities, and to attempt to compress them into a single word or phrase begs the issue.

Conversely, how shall a service such as airline transportation be described?

Although the service itself is intangible, there are certain very real things that belong in any description of the total entity, including such important tangibles as interior decor, food and drink, seat design, and overall graphic continuity from tickets to attendants' uniforms. These items can dramatically affect the 'reality' of the service in the consumer's mind. However, there is no accurate way to lump them into a one-word description.

If 'either-or' terms (products vs. service) do not adequately describe the true nature of marketed entities, it makes sense to explore the usefulness of a new *structural* definition. This broader concept postulates that market entities are, in reality, *combinations of discrete elements* which are linked together in molecule-like wholes. Elements can be either tangible or intangible. The entity may have either a tangible or intangible nucleus. But the whole can only be described as having a certain dominance.

Molecular model

A 'molecular' model offers opportunities for visualization and management of a total market entity. It reflects the fact that a market entity can be partly tangible *and* partly intangible, without diminishing the importance of either characteristic. Not only can the potential be seen for picturing and dealing with multiple *elements*, rather than a *thing*, but the concept of dominance can lead to enriched considerations of the priorities and approach that may be required of a marketer. Moreover, the model suggests the scientific analogy that if market entities have multiple elements, a deliberate or inadvertent change in a *single* element may completely alter the entity, as the simple switching of FE_3O_2 to FE_2O_3 creates a new substance. For this reason, a marketer must carefully manage all the elements, especially those for service-based entities, which may not have been considered previously within his domain.

DIAGRAMMING MARKET ENTITIES

A simplified comparison demonstrates the conceptual usefulness of a molecular modeling system. In Figure 1, automobiles and airline travel are broken down into their major elements. As shown, these two entities have different nuclei. They also differ in dominance.

Clearly, airline travel is intangible-dominant; that is, it does not yield physical ownership of a tangible good. Nearly all of the other important elements in the entity are intangible as well. Individual elements and their combinations represent unique satisfiers to different market segments. Thus:

- For some markets – students, for example – pure transport takes precedence over all other considerations. The charter flight business was based on this element. As might be expected during lean economic times, 'no frills' flights show renewed emphasis on this nuclear core.
- For business travelers, on the other hand, schedule frequency may be paramount.
- Tourists, a third segment, may respond most strongly to the combination of in-flight and post-flight services.

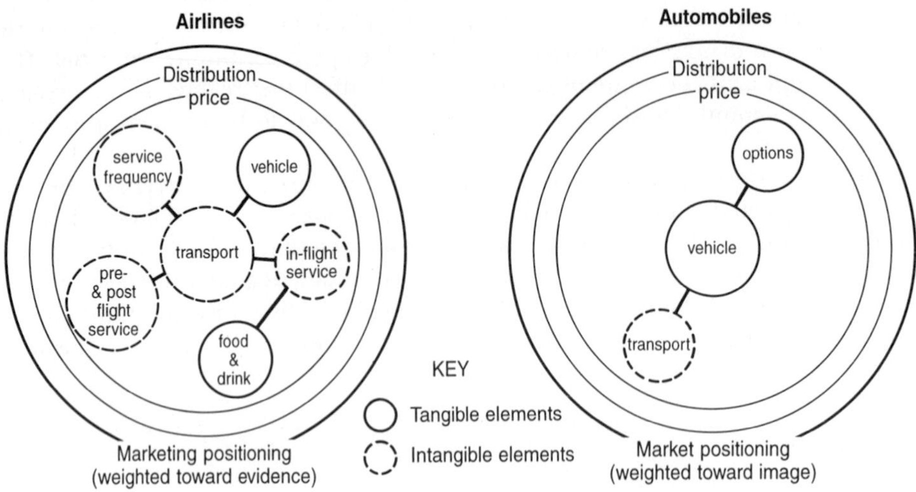

Figure 1. Diagram of market entities.

As the market entity of airline travel has evolved, it has become more and more complex. Ongoing reweighting of elements can be observed, for example, in the marketing of airline food, which was once a battleground of quasi-gourmet offerings. Today, some airlines have stopped marketing food altogether, while others are repositioning it primarily to the luxury markets.

Airlines vs. automobiles

In comparing airlines to automobiles, one sees obvious similarities. The element of transportation is common to both, as it is to boats, trains, buses, and bicycles. Tangible decor also plays a role in both entities. Yet in spite of their similarities, the two entities are not the same, either in configuration or in marketing implications.

In some ways, airline travel and automobiles are mirror opposites. A car is a physical possession that renders a service. Airline travel, on the other hand, cannot be physically possessed. It can only be experienced. While the inherent 'promise' of a car is service, airline transportation often promises a Lewis Carroll version of '*product*', i.e. *destination*, which is marketed as though it were physically obtainable. If only tropical islands and redwood forests *could* be purchased for the price of an airline ticket!

The model can be completed by adding the remaining major marketing elements in a way that demonstrates their function vis-a-vis the organic core entity. First, the total entity is ringed and defined by a set value or price. Next, the valued entity is circumscribed by its distribution. Finally, the entire entity is encompassed according to its core configuration, by its public 'face', i.e. its positioning to the market.

The molecular concept makes it possible to describe and array market entities along a continuum, according to the weight of the 'mix' of elements that comprise them. As Figure 2 indicates, teaching services might be at one end of such a scale,

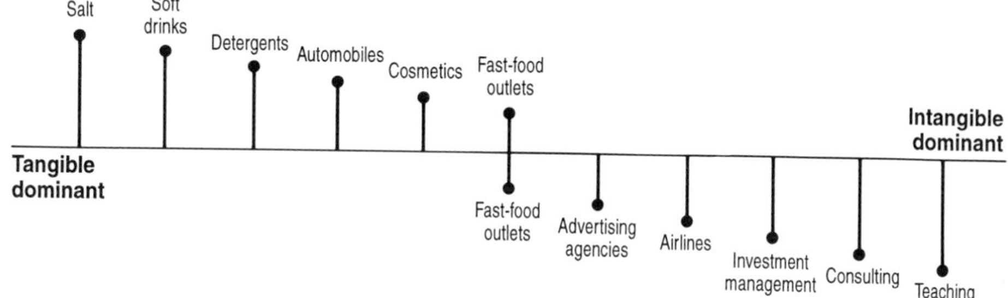

Figure 2. Scale of market entities.

intangible or I-dominant, while salt might represent the other extreme, *tangible or T-dominant.* Such a scale accords intangible-based entities a place and weight commensurate with their true importance. The framework also provides a mechanism for comparison and market positioning.

In one of the handful of books devoted to services, the author holds that 'the more intangible the service, the greater will be the difference in the marketing characteristics of the service.'[7] Consistent with an entity scale, this axiom might now be amended to read: *the greater the weight of intangible elements in a market entity, the greater will be the divergence from product marketing in priorities and approach.*

Implications of the molecular model

The hypothesis proposed by molecular modeling carries intriguing potential for rethinking and reshaping classic marketing concepts and practices. Recognition that service-dominant entities differ from product-dominant entities allows consideration of other distinctions which have been intuitively understood, but seldom articulated by service marketers.

A most important area of difference, is immediately apparent, i.e. that service 'knowledge' and product 'knowledge' cannot be gained in the same way.

A *product* marketer's first task is to 'know' his product. For tangible-dominant entities this is relatively straight-forward. A tangible object can be described precisely. It is subject to physical examination or photographic reproduction or quantitative measure. It can not only be exactly replicated, but also modified in precise and duplicate ways.

It is not particularly difficult for the marketer of *Coca-Cola,* for example, to summon all the facts regarding the product itself. He can and does make reasonable assumptions about the product's behavior, e.g. that it is consistent chemically to the taste, visually to the eye, and physically in its packaging. Any changes he might make in these three areas can be deliberately controlled for uniformity since they will be tangibly evident. In other words, the marketer can take the product's 'reality' for granted and move on to considerations of price, distribution, and advertising or promotion.

To gain *service* 'knowledge', however, or knowledge of a service element, where does one begin? It has been pointed out that intangible elements are dynamic, subjective, and ephemeral. They cannot be touched, tried on for size, or displayed on a shelf. They are exceedingly difficult to quantify.

Reverting to airline travel, precisely what *is* the service of air transportation to the potential purchaser? What 'percent' of airline travel is comfort? What 'percent' is fear or adventure? What *is* this service's 'reality' to its market? And how does that reality vary from segment to segment? Since this service exists only during the time in which it is rendered, the entity's true 'reality' must be defined experientially, not in engineering terms.

A new approach to service definition

Experiential definition is a little-explored area of marketing practice. A product-based marketer is in danger of assuming he understands an intangible-dominant entity when, in fact, he may only be projecting his *own* subjective version of 'reality'. And because there is no documented guidance on acquiring service-knowledge, the changes for error are magnified.

Case example

One short-lived mistake (with which the author is familiar) occurred recently in the trust department of a large commercial bank. The department head, being close to daily operations, understood 'investment management' as the combined work of hundreds of people, backed by the firm's stature, resources, and long history, With this 'reality' in mind, he concluded that the service could be better represented by professional salesmen, than through the traditional, but interruptive use of the portfolio manager as main client contact.

Three salesmen were hired, and given a training course in investments. They failed dismally, both in maintaining current client relationships and in producing new business for the firm. In hindsight, it became clear that the department head misunderstood the service's 'reality' as it was being experienced by his clients. To the clients, 'investment *management*' was found to mean 'investment *manager*', i.e. a single human being upon whom they depended for decisions and advice. No matter how well prepared, the professional salesman was not seen as an acceptable substitute by the majority of the market.

Visions of reality

Clearly, more than one version of 'reality' may be found in a service market. Therefore, the crux of service-knowledge is the description of the major *consensus realities* that define the service entity to various market segments. The determination of consensus realities should be a high priority for service marketers, and marketing should offer more concrete guidance and emphasis on this subject than it does.

To define the market-held 'realities' of a service requires a high tolerance for subjective, 'soft' data, combined with a rigidly objective attitude toward that data. To understand what a service entity is to a market, the marketer must undertake more initial research than is common in product marketing. More important, it will be research of a different kind than is the case in product marketing. The marketer must rely heavily on the tools and skills of psychology, sociology and other behavioral sciences – tools that in product marketing usually come into play in determining *image*, rather than fundamental 'reality'.

In developing the blueprint of a service entity's main elements, the marketer might find, for instance, that although tax return preparation is analogous to 'accurate mathematical computation' within his firm, it means 'freedom from responsibility' to one segment of the consuming public 'opportunity for financial savings' to another segment, and 'convenience' to yet a third segment.

Unless these 'realities' are documented and ranked by market importance, no sensible plan can be devised to represent a service effectively or deliberately. And in *new* service development, the importance of the service-research function is even more critical, because the successful development of a new service – a molecular collection of intangibles – is so difficult it makes new-product development look like child's play.

Image vs. evidence – the key

The definition of consensus realities should not be confused with the determination of 'image'. Image is a method of *differentiating* and *representing* an entity to its target market. Image is not 'product', nor is it 'service'. As was suggested in Figure 1, there appears to be a critical difference between the way tangible- and intangible-dominant entities are best represented to their markets. Examination of actual cases suggests a common thread among effective representations of services that is another mirror-opposite contrast to product techniques.

In comparing examples, it is clear that consumer product marketing often approaches the market by enhancing a physical object through abstract associations. *Coca-Cola*, for example, is surrounded with visual, verbal and aural associations with authenticity and youth. Although *Dr. Pepper* would also be physically categorized as a beverage, its *image* has been structured to suggest 'originality' and 'risk-taking', while *7-up* is 'light' and 'buoyant'. A high priority is placed on linking these abstract images to physical items.

But a service is already abstract. To compound the abstraction dilutes the 'reality' that the marketer is trying to enhance. Effective service representations appear to be turned 180° *away* from abstraction. The reason for this is that service images, and even service 'realities', appear to be shaped to a large extent by the things that the consumer can comprehend with his five senses – tangible things. But a service itself cannot be tangible, so reliance must be placed on *peripheral* clues.

Tangible clues are what allow the detective in a mystery novel to surmise events at the scene of a crime without having been present. Similarly, when a consumer attempts to judge a service, particularly before using or buying it, that service is 'known' by the tangible clues, the tangible evidence, that surround it.

The management of tangible evidence is not articulated in marketing as a primary priority for service marketers. There has been little in-depth exploration of the *range* of authority that emphasis on tangible evidence would create for the service marketer. In product marketing, tangible evidence is primarily the product itself. But for services, tangible evidence would encompass broader considerations in contrast to product marketing, *different* considerations than are typically considered marketing's domain today.

Focusing on the evidence

In *product* marketing, many kinds of evidence are beyond the marketer's control and are consequently omitted from priority consideration in the market positioning process. Product marketing tends to give first emphasis to creating *abstract* associations.

Service marketers, on the other hand, should be focused on enhancing and differentiating 'realities' through manipulation of *tangible* clues. The management of evidence comes first for service marketers, because service 'reality' is arrived at by the consumer mostly through a process of deduction, based on the total impression that the evidence creates. Because of product marketing's biases, service marketers often fail to recognize the unique forms of evidence that they *can* normally control and fail to see that they should be part of marketing's responsibilities.

MANAGEMENT OF THE ENVIRONMENT

Environment is a good example. Since product distribution normally means shipping to outside agents, the marketer has little voice in structuring the environment in which the product is sold. His major controllable impact on the environment is usually product packaging. Services, on the other hand, are often fully integrated with environment; that is, the setting in which the service is 'distributed' *is* controllable. To the extent possible, management of the physical environment should be one of a service marketer's highest priorities.

Setting can play an enormous role in influencing the 'reality' of a service in the consumer's mind. Marketing does not emphasize this rule for services, yet there are numerous obvious examples of its importance.

Physician's offices provide an interesting example of intuitive environmental management. Although the quality of medical service may be identical, an office furnished in teak and leather creates a totally different 'reality' in the consumer's mind from one with plastic slipcovers and inexpensive prints. Carrying the example further, a marketer could expect to cause change in the service's image simply by painting a physician's office walls neon pink or silver, instead of white.

Similarly, although the services may be identical, the consumer's differentiation between 'Bank A Service' and 'Bank B Service' is materially affected by whether the environment is dominated by butcher-block and bright colors or by marble and polished brass.

By understanding the importance of evidence management, the service marketer can make it his business to review and take control of this critical part of his 'mix'. Creation of environment can be deliberate, rather than accidental or as a result of leaving such decisions in the hands of the interior decorators.

Integrating evidence

Going beyond environment, evidence can be integrated across a wide range of items. Airlines, for example, manage and coordinate tangible evidence, and do it better than almost any large service industry. Whether by intuition or design, airlines do *not* focus attention on trying to explain or characterize the service itself. One never sees an ad that attempts to convey 'the slant of takeoff', 'the feel of acceleration', or 'the aerodynamics of lift'. Airline transport is given shape and form through consistency of a firm's identification, its uniforms, the decor of its planes, its graphics, and its advertising. Differentiation among airlines, though they all provide the same service, is a direct result of differences in 'packages' of evidence.

Some businesses in which tangible and intangible elements carry equal weight emphasize abstractions and evidence in about equal proportions. McDonald's is an excellent example. The food *product* is associated with 'nutritious' (two all-beef, etc.), 'fun' (Ronald McDonald) and 'helpful' ('We Do it All for You', 'You Deserve a Break Today'). The main *service* element, i.e. fast food preparation, is tangibly distinguished by uniformity of environment, color, and style of graphics and apparel, consistency of delivery (young employees), and the ubiquitous golden arches.

Using the scale developed in Figure 2, this concept can be postulated as a principle for service representation. As shown in Figure 3, once an entity has been analyzed and positioned on the scale, the degree to which the marketer will focus on either tangible evidence or intangible abstractions for market positioning will be found to be *inversely related to the entity's dominance.*

The more intangible elements there are, the more the marketer must endeavor to stand in the consumer's shoes, thinking through and gaining control of *all* the inputs to the consumer's mind that can be classified as material evidence.

Some forms of evidence can seem trivial until one recognizes how great their impact can be on service perception. Correspondence is one example. Letters, statements, and the like are sometimes the main conveyers of the 'reality' of a service to its market; yet often these are treated as peripheral to any marketing plan. From the grade of paper to the choice of colors, correspondence is visible evidence that conveys a unique message. A mimeographed, non-personalized, cheaply offset letter

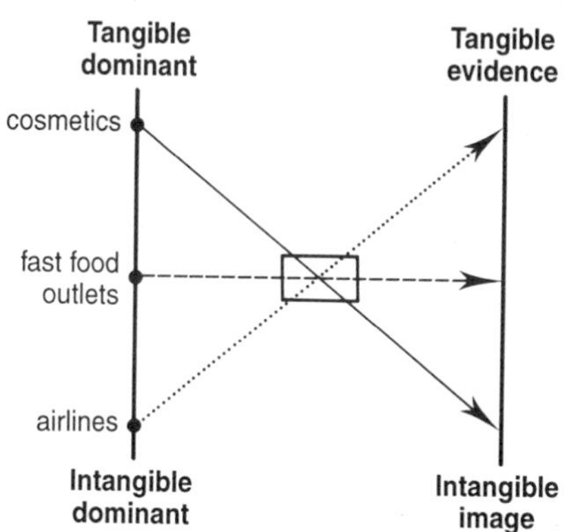

Figure 3. Principle of market positioning emphasis.

contradicts any words about service quality that may appear in the text of that letter. Conversely, engraved parchment from the local dry cleaner might make one wonder about their prices.

Profile as evidence

As was pointed out in the investment management example, services are often inextricably entwined with their human representatives. In many fields, a person is perceived to *be* the service. The consumer cannot distinguish between them. Product marketing is myopic in dealing with the issue of *people as evidence* in terms of market positioning. Consumer marketing often stops at the production of materials and programs for salesmen to use. Some service industries, on the other hand, have long intuitively managed human evidence to larger ends.

Examples of this principle have been the basis for jokes, plays, and literature. 'The Man in the Grey Flannel Suit', for example, was a synonym for the advertising business for many years. Physicians are uniformly 'packaged' in smocks. Lawyers and bankers are still today known for pin-stripes and vests. IBM representatives were famous for adhering to a 'White Shirt' policy. Going beyond apparel, as mentioned earlier, McDonald's even achieves age uniformity – an extra element reinforcing its total market image.

These examples add up to a serious principle when thoughtfully reviewed. They are particularly instructive for service marketers. None of the above examples were the result of deliberate market planning. McDonald's, for instance, backed into age consistency as a result of trying to keep labor costs low. Airlines are the single outstanding example of consciously-planned standards for uniformity in human representation. The power of the human evidence principle is obvious, and the potential power of more deliberately controlling or structuring this element is clear.

Lest this discussion be interpreted as an advocacy of regimentation, it should be pointed out that management of human evidence can be as basic as providing nametags to service representatives or as complex as the 'packaging' of a political candidate, whose very words are often chosen by committee and whose hair style can become a critical policy issue. Or, depending upon what kind of service 'reality' the marketer wishes to create, human representation can be encouraged to display *non-*conformity, as is the case with the 'creative' departments of advertising agencies. The point is that service marketers should be charged with tactics and strategy in this area, and must consider it a management responsibility.

SERVICES AND THE MEDIA

As has been previously discussed, service elements are abstract. Because they are abstract, the marketer must work hard at making them 'real', by building a case from tangible evidence. In this context, media advertising presents a particularly difficult problem.

The problem revolves around the fact that media (television, radio, print) are one step removed from tangibility. Media, by its McLuhanesque nature, abstracts the physical.

Even though product tangibility provides an anchor for media representation because a product can be *shown*, media still abstract products. A photograph is only a two-dimensional version of a physical object, and may be visually misleading. Fortunately, the consumer makes the mental connection between seeing a product in the media and recognizing it in reality. This is true even when a product is substantially distorted. Sometimes, only part of a product is shown. Occasionally, as in recent commercials for *7-up*, the product is *not* shown. However, the consumer remembers past experience. He has little difficulty recognizing *7-up* by name or remembered appearance when he sees it or wants to buy it.

Thus, media work *with* the creation of product image and *help* in adding abstract qualities to tangible goods. Cosmetics, for example, are often positioned in association with an airbrushed or soft-focus filmed *ideal* of beauty. Were the media truly accurate, the wrinkles and flaws of the flesh, to which even models are heir, might not create such an appealing product association.

Making services more concrete

Because of their abstracting capabilities, the media often make service entities more *hazy*, instead of more *concrete*, and the service marketer must work *against* this inherent effect. Unfortunately, many marketers are so familiar with product-oriented thinking that they go down precisely the wrong path and attempt to represent services by dealing with them in abstractions.

The pages of the business press are filled with examples of this type of misconception in services advertising. In advertisements for investment management, for instance, the worst examples attempt to describe the already intangible service with *more* abstractions such as 'sound analysis', 'careful portfolio monitoring', 'strong research capability', etc. Such compounded abstractions do *not* help the consumer form a 'reality', do *not* differentiate the service and do *not* achieve any credibility, much less any customer 'draw'.

The best examples are those which attempt to associate the service with some form of *tangible evidence*, working against the media's abstracting qualities. Merrill Lynch, for instance, has firmly associated itself with a clear visual symbol of bulls and concomitant bullishness. Where Merrill Lynch does not use the visual herd, it uses photographs of *tangible physical booklets*, and invites the consumer to write for them.

Therefore, the final principle offered for service marketers would hold that *effective media representation of intangibles is a function of establishing non-abstract manifestations of them.*

CONCLUSION

This article has presented several market-inspired thoughts toward the development of new marketing concepts, and the evolution of relevant service marketing principles. The hypotheses presented here do not by any means represent an exhaustive analysis of the subject. No exploration was done, for example, on product vs. service pricing or product vs. service distribution. Both areas offer rich potential for creative new approaches and analysis.

It can be argued that there are many grey areas in the molecular entity concept, and that diagramming and managing according to the multiple-elements schema could present considerable difficulties by virtue of its greater complexity. It might also be argued that some distinctions between tangible and intangible-dominant entities are so subtle as to be unimportant.

The fact remains that service marketers are in urgent need of concepts and priorities that are relevant to their actual experience and needs, and that marketing has failed in evolving to meet that demand. However unorthodox, continuing exploration of this area must be encouraged if marketing is to achieve stature and influence in the new post-Industrial Revolution services economy.

NOTES

1. See, for example, McCarthy, E. J. (1971) *Basic Marketing: A Managerial Approach,* 4th edn. Homewood, IL: Richard D. Irwin, p. 303, compared to Stanton, W. J. (1971) *Fundamentals of Marketing,* 3rd edn. New York: McGraw-Hill, p. 567.
2. See George, W. R. and Barksdale, H. C. (1974) 'Marketing Activities in the Service Industries'. *Journal of Marketing* **38** (October, No. 4): 65–70.
3. *The Meaning and Sources of Marketing Theory* (1965) Marketing Science Institute Series. New York: McGraw-Hill, p. 88.
4. *Webster's New Collegiate Dictionary* (1974) Springfield, MA: G&C Merriam Company.
5. Kotler, P. (1972) 'A Generic Concept of Marketing'. *Journal of Marketing* **36** (April, No. 2): 46–54.
6. Levitt, T. H. (1960) 'Marketing Myopia'. *Harvard Business Review* **38** (July–August): 45–46.
7. Wilson, A. (1972) *The Marketing of Professional Services.* New York: McGraw-Hill, p. 8.

2

Classifying Services to Gain Strategic Marketing Insights

Christopher H. Lovelock

INTRODUCTION

Developing professional skills in marketing management requires the ability to look across a broad cross-section of marketing situations, to understand their differences and commonalities, and to identify appropriate marketing strategies in each instance. In the manufacturing sector many experienced marketers have worked for a variety of companies in several different industries, often including both consumer goods and industrial firms. As a result, they have a perspective that transcends narrow industry boundaries.

But exposure to marketing problems and strategies in different industries is still quite rare among managers in the service sector. Not only is the concept of a formalized marketing function still relatively new to most service firms, but service industries have historically been somewhat inbred. The majority of railroad managers, for instance, have spent their entire working lives within the railroad industry – even within a single company. Most hoteliers have grown up in the hotel industry. And most hospital or college administrators have remained within the confines of health care or higher education, respectively. The net result of such narrow exposure is that it restricts a manager's ability to identify and learn from the experience of organizations facing parallel situations in other service industries – and, of course, from marketing experience in the manufacturing sector. Conversely, marketers from the manufacturing sector who take positions in service businesses often find that their past experience has not prepared them well for working on some of the problems that regularly challenge service marketers (Knisely, 1979; Lovelock, 1981; Shostack, 1977).

This article argues that development of greater sophistication in services marketing will be aided if we can find new ways to group services other than by current industry classifications. A more useful approach may be to segment services into clusters that share certain relevant marketing characteristics – such as the nature of the relationship between the service organization and its customers or patterns of demand relative to supply – and then to examine the implications for marketing action.

Reprinted with permission from *Journal of Marketing*, Vol. 47, Summer, pp. 9–20

After briefly reviewing the value of classification schemes in marketing, the article summarizes past proposals for classifying services. This is followed by presentation and discussion of five classification schemes based on past proposals, or on clinical research. In each instance examples are given of how various services fall into similar or different categories, and an evaluation is made of the resulting marketing insights and what they imply for marketing strategy development.

THE VALUE OF CLASSIFICATION IN MARKETING

Hunt (1976) has emphasized the usefulness of classification schemes in marketing. Various attempts have been made in the past by marketing theorists to classify goods into different categories. One of the most famous and enduring is Copeland's (1923) classification of convenience, shopping and speciality goods. Not only did this help managers obtain a better understanding of consumer needs and behavior, it also provided insights into the management of retail distribution systems. Bucklin (1963) and others have revised and refined Copeland's original classification and thereby been able to provide important strategic guidelines for retailers. Another major classification has been between durable and nondurable goods. Durability is closely associated with purchase frequency, which has important implications for development of both distribution and communications strategy. Yet another classification is consumer goods versus industrial goods: this classification relates both to the type of goods purchased (although there is some overlap) and to product evaluation, purchasing procedures and usage behavior. Recognition of these distinctions by marketers has led to different types of marketing strategy being directed at each of these groups. Through such classification the application of marketing management tools and strategies in manufacturing has become a professional skill that transcends industry divisions.

By contrast, service industries remain dominated by an operations orientation that insists that each industry is different. This mind set is often manifested in managerial attitudes that suggest, for example, that the marketing of airlines has nothing at all in common with that of banks, insurance, motels, hospitals or household movers. But if it can be shown that some of these services do share certain marketing relevant characteristics, then the stage may be set for some useful cross-fertilization of concepts and strategies.

How might services be classified?

Various attempts have been proposed in the past for classifying services and are outlined, with brief commentaries, in Table 1. But developing classification schemes is not enough. If they are to have managerial value, they must offer strategic insights. That is why it is important to develop ways of analyzing services that highlight the characteristics they have in common, and then to examine the implications for marketing management.

This article builds on past research by examining characteristics of services that transcend industry boundaries and are different in degree or kind from the

Table 1. Summary of previously proposed schemes for classifying services

Author	Proposed classification schemes	Comment
Judd (1964)	(1) Rented goods services (right to own and use a good for a defined time period) (2) Owned goods services (custom creation, repair or improvement of goods owned by the customer) (3) Nongoods services (personal experiences or 'experiential possession')	First two are fairly specific, but third category is very broad and ignores services such as insurance, banking, legal advice and accounting.
Rathmell (1974)	(1) Type of seller (2) Type of buyer (3) Buying motives (4) Buying practice (5) Degree of regulation	No specific application to services – could apply equally well to goods.
Shostack (1977)[a] Sasser *et al.*[a] (1978)	Proportion of physical goods and intangible services contained within each product 'package'	Offers opportunities for multiattribute modeling. Emphasizes that there are few pure goods or pure services.
Hill (1977)	(1) Services affecting persons vs. those affecting goods (2) Permanent vs. temporary effects of the service (3) Reversibility vs. nonreversibility of these effects (4) Physical effects vs. mental effects (5) Individual vs. collective services	Emphasizes nature of service benefits and (in 5), variations in the service delivery/consumption environment.
Thomas (1978)	(1) Primarily equipment based (a) automated (e.g. car wash) (b) monitored by unskilled operators (e.g. movie theater) (c) operated by skilled personnel (e.g. airline) (2) Primarily people-based (a) unskilled labor (e.g. lawn care) (b) skilled labor (e.g. repair work) (c) professional staff (e.g. lawyers, dentists)	Although operational rather than marketing in orientation, provides a useful way of understanding product attributes.
Chase (1978)	Extent of customer contact required in service delivery (a) high contact (e.g. health care, hotels, restaurants) (b) low contact (e.g. postal service, wholesaling)	Recognizes that product variability is harder to control in high contact services because customers exert more influence on timing of demand and service features, due to their greater involvement in the service process.
Kotler (1980)	(1) People-based vs. equipment-based (2) Extent to which client's presence is necessary (3) Meets personal needs vs. business needs (4) Public vs. private, for-profit vs. nonprofit	Synthesizes previous work, recognizes differences in purpose of service organization.

Continued overleaf

Table 1. – *(continued)*

Author	Proposed classification schemes	Comment
Lovelock (1980)	(1) Basic demands characteristics – object served (persons vs. property) – extent of demand/supply imbalances – discrete vs. continuous relationships between customers and providers (2) Service content and benefits – extent of physical goods content – extent of personal service content – single service vs. bundle of services – timing and duration of benefits (3) Service delivery procedures – multisite vs. single site delivery – allocation of capacity (reservations vs. first come, first served) – independent vs. collective consumption – time defined vs. task defined transactions – extent to which customers must be present during service delivery	Synthesizes previous classifications and adds several new schemes. Proposes several categories within each classification. Concludes that defining object served is most fundamental classification scheme. Suggests that valuable marketing insights would come from combining two or more classification schemes in a matrix.

[a]These were two independent studies that drew broadly similar conclusions.

categorization schemes traditionally applied to manufactured goods. Five classification schemes have been selected for presentation and discussion, reflecting their potential for affecting the way marketing management strategies are developed and implemented. Each represents an attempt to answer one of the following questions:

1. What is the nature of the service act?
2. What type of relationship does the service organization have with its customers?
3. How much room is there for customization and judgment on the part of the service provider?
4. What is the nature of demand and supply for the service?
5. How is the service delivered?

Each question will be examined on two dimensions, reflecting my conclusion in an earlier study (Lovelock, 1980) that combining classification schemes in a matrix may yield better marketing insights than classifying service organizations on one variable at a time.

WHAT IS THE NATURE OF THE SERVICE ACT?

A service has been described as a 'deed, act or performance' (Berry, 1980). Two fundamental issues are at whom (or what) is the act directed, and is this act tangible or intangible in nature?

As shown in Figure 1, these two questions result in a four-way classification

What is the nature of the service act?	Who or what is the direct recipient of the service?	
	People	Things
Tangible actions	Services directed at people's bodies: • health care • passenger transportation • beauty salons • exercise clinics • restaurants • haircutting	Services directed at goods and other physical possessions: • freight transportation • industrial equipment repair and maintenance • janitorial services • laundry and dry cleaning • landscaping/lawn care • veterinary care
Intangible actions	Services directed at people's minds: • education • broadcasting • information services • theaters • museums	Services directed at intangible assets: • banking • legal services • accounting • securities • insurance

Figure 1. Understanding the nature of the service act.

scheme involving (1) tangible actions to people's bodies, such as airline transportation, haircutting and surgery; (2) tangible actions to goods and other physical possessions, such as air freight, lawn mowing and janitorial services; (3) intangible actions directed at people's minds, such as broadcasting and education; and (4) intangible actions directed at people's intangible assets, such as insurance, investment banking and consulting.

Sometimes a service may seem to spill over into two or more categories. For instance, the delivery of educational, religious or entertainment services (directed primarily at the mind) often entails tangible actions such as being in a classroom, church or theater: the delivery of financial services may require a visit to a bank to transform intangible financial assets into hard cash; and the delivery of airline services may affect some travelers' states of mind as well as physically moving their bodies from one airport to another. But in most instances the core service act is confined to one of the four categories, although there may be secondary acts in another category.

Insights and implications

Why is this categorization scheme useful to service marketers? Basically it helps answer the following questions:

1. Does the customer need to be *physically* present:
   (a) throughout service delivery?
   (b) only to initiate or terminate the service transaction (e.g. dropping off a car for repair and picking it up again afterwards)?
   (c) not at all (the relationship with the service supplier can be at arm's length through the mails, telephone or other electronic media)?

2. Does the customer need to be *mentally* present during service delivery? Can mental presence be maintained across physical distances through mail or electronic communications?
3. In what ways is the target of the service act 'modified' by receipt of the service? And how does the customer benefit from these 'modifications'?

It is not always obvious what the service is and what it does for the customer because services are ephemeral. By identifying the target of the service and then examining how it is 'modified' or changed by receipt of the service act, we can develop a better understanding of the nature of the service product and the core benefits that it offers. For instance, a haircut leaves the recipient with shorter and presumably more appealingly styled hair, air freight gets the customer's goods speedily and safely between two points, a news radio broadcast updates the listener's mind about recent events, and life insurance protects the future value of the insured person's assets.

If customers need to be physically present during service delivery, then they must enter the service 'factory' (whether it be a train, a hairdressing salon, or a hospital at a particular location) and spend time there while the service is performed. Their satisfaction with the service will be influenced by the interactions they have with service personnel, the nature of the service facilities, and also perhaps by the characteristics of other customers using the same service. Questions of location and schedule convenience assume great importance when a customer has to be physically present or must appear in person to initiate and terminate the transaction.

Dealing with a service organization at arm's length, by contrast, may mean that a customer never sees the service facilities at all and may not even meet the service personnel face-to-face. In this sort of situation, the outcome of the service act remains very important, but the process of service delivery may be of little interest, since the customer never goes near the 'factory'. For instance, credit cards and many types of insurance can be obtained by mail or telephone.

For operational reasons it may be very desirable to get the customer out of the factory and to transform a 'high-contact' service into a 'low-contact' one (Chase, 1978). The chances of success in such an endeavor will be enhanced when the new procedures also offer customers greater convenience. Many services directed at *things* rather than at people formerly required the customer's presence but are now delivered at arm's length. Certain financial services have long used the mails to save customers the inconvenience of personal visits to a specific office location. Today, new electronic distribution channels have made it possible to offer instantaneous delivery of financial services to a wide array of alternative locations. Retail banking provides a good example, with its growing use of such electronic delivery systems as automatic teller machines in airports or shopping centers, pay-by-phone bill paying, or on-line banking facilities in retail stores.

By thinking creatively about the nature of their services, managers of service organizations may be able to identify opportunities for alternative, more convenient forms of service delivery or even for transformation of the service into a manufactured good. For instance, services to the mind such as education do not necessarily require attendance in person since they can be delivered through the mails of electronic media (Britain's Open University, which makes extensive use of television and radio broadcasts, is a prime example). Two-way communication hook-ups can make it possible for a physically distant teacher and students to interact directly where this is necessary to the educational process (one recent Bell System advertisement featured a chamber music class in a small town being taught by an instructor several hundred miles away). Alternatively, lectures can be packaged and sold as books, records or videotapes. And in programmed learning exercises can be developed in computerized form, with the terminal serving as a Socratic surrogate.

WHAT TYPE OF RELATIONSHIP DOES THE SERVICE ORGANIZATION HAVE WITH ITS CUSTOMERS?

With very few exceptions, consumers buy manufactured goods at discrete intervals, paying for each purchase separately and rarely entering into a formal relationship with the manufacturer. (Industrial purchasers, by contrast, often enter into long-term relationships with suppliers and sometimes receive almost continuous delivery of certain supplies).

In the service sector both household and institutional purchasers may enter into ongoing relationships with service suppliers and may receive service on a continuing basis. This offers a way of categorizing services. We can ask, does the service organization enter into a 'membership' relationship with its customers – as in telephone subscriptions, banking and the family doctor – or is there no formal relationship? And is service delivered on a continuous basis – as in insurance, broadcasting and police protection – or is each transaction recorded and charged separately? Figure 2 shows the 2 × 2 matrix resulting from this categorization, with some additional examples in each category.

Insights and implications

The advantage to the service organization of a membership relationship is that it knows who its current customers are and, usually, what use they make of the services

Nature of service delivery	Type of relationship between the service organization and its customers	
	Membership relationship	No formal relationship
Continuous delivery of service	insurance telephone subscription college enrollment banking American Automobile Association	radio station police protection lighthouse public highway
Discrete transactions	long-distance phone calls theater series subscription commuter ticket or transit pass	car rental mail service toll highway pay phone movie theater public transportation restaurant

Figure 2. Relationships with customers.

offered. This can be valuable for segmentation purposes if good records are kept and the data are readily accessible in a format that lends itself to computerized analysis. Knowing the identities and addresses of current customers enables the organization to make effective use of direct mail, telephone selling and personal sales calls – all highly targeted marketing communications media.

The nature of service relationships also has important implications for pricing. In situations where service is offered on an ongoing basis, there is often just a single periodic charge covering all services contracted for. Most insurance policies fall in this category, as do tuition and board fees at a residential college. The big advantage of this package approach is its simplicity. Some memberships, however, entail a series of separate and identifiable transactions with the price paid being tied explicitly to the number and type of such transactions. While more complex to administer, such an approach is fairer to customers (whose usage patterns may vary widely) and may discourage wasteful use of what are perceived as 'free' services. In such instances, members may be offered advantages over casual users, such as discounted rates (telephone subscribers pay less for long-distance calls make from their own phones than do pay phone users) or advance notification and priority reservations (as in theater subscriptions). Some membership services offer certain services (such as rental of equipment or connection to a public utility system) for a base fee and then make incremental charges for each separate transaction above a defined minimum.

Profitability and customer convenience are central issues in deciding how to price membership services. Will the organization generate greater long term profits by tying payment explicitly to consumption, by charging a flat rate regardless of consumption, or by unbundling the components of the service and charging a flat rate for some and an incremental rate for others? Telephone and electricity services for instance, typically charge a base fee for connection to the system and rental of equipment, plus a variety of incremental charges for consumption above a defined minimum. On the other hand, Wide Area Telephone Service (WATS) offers the convenience of unlimited long-distance calling for a fixed fee. How important is it to customers to have the convenience of paying a single periodic fee that is known in advance? For instance, members of the American Automobile Association (AAA) can obtain information booklets, travel advice and certain types of emergency road services free of additional charges. Such a package offers elements of both insurance and convenience to customers who may not be able to predict their exact needs in advance.

Where no formal relationship exists between supplier and customer, continuous delivery of the product is normally found only among that class of services that economists term 'public goods' – such as broadcasting, police and lighthouse services, and public highways – where no charge is made for use of a service that is continuously available and financed from tax revenues. Discrete transactions, where each usage involves a payment to the service supplier by an essentially 'anonymous' consumer, are exemplified by many transportation services, restaurants, movie theaters, show repairs and so forth. The problem of such services is that marketers tend to be much less well-informed about who their customers are and what use each customer makes of the service than their counterparts in membership organizations.

Membership relationships usually result in customer loyalty to a particular service supplier (sometimes there is no choice because the supplier has a monopoly). As a marketing strategy, many service businesses seek ways to develop formal, ongoing relations with customers in order to ensure repeat business and/or ongoing financial support. Public radio and television broadcasters, for instance, develop membership clubs for donors and offer monthly program guides in return: performing arts organizations sell subscription series: transit agencies offer monthly passes; airlines create clubs for high mileage fliers; and hotels develop 'executive service plans' offering priority reservations and upgraded rooms for frequent guests. The marketing task here is to determine how it might be possible to build sales and revenues through such memberships but to avoid requiring membership when this would result in freezing out a large volume of desirable casual business.

HOW MUCH ROOM IS THERE FOR CUSTOMIZATION AND JUDGMENT?

Relatively few consumer goods nowadays are built to special order, most are purchased 'off the shelf'. The same is true for a majority of industrial goods, although by permutating options it is possible to give the impression of customization. Once they have purchased their goods, of course, customers are usually free to use them as they see fit.

The situation in the service sector, by contrast, is sharply different. Because services are created as they are consumed, and because the customer is often actually involved in the production process, there is far more scope for tailoring the service to meet the needs of individual customers. As shown in Figure 3, customization can proceed along at least two dimensions. The first concerns the extent to which the characteristics of the service and its delivery system lend themselves to customization; the second relates to how much judgment customer contact personnel are able to exercise in defining the nature of the service received by individual customers.

Some service concepts are quite standardized. Public transportation, for instance, runs over fixed routes on predetermined schedules. Routine appliance repairs typically involve a fixed charge, and the customer is responsible for dropping of the item at a given retail location and picking it up again afterwards. Fast food

Extent to which customer contact personnel exercise judgment in meeting individual customer needs	Extent to which service characteristics are customized	
	High	Low
High	legal services health care/surgery architectural design executive search firm real estate agency taxi service beautician plumber education (tutorials)	education (large classes) preventative health programs
Low	telephone service hotel services retail banking (excl. major loans) good restaurant	public transportation routine appliance repair fast food restaurant movie theater spectator sports

Figure 3. Customization and judgment in service delivery.

restaurants have a small, set menu; few offer the customer much choice in how the food will be cooked and served. Movies, entertainment and spectator sports place the audience in a relatively passive role, albeit a sometimes noisy one.

Other services offer customers a wide choice of options. Each telephone subscriber enjoys an individual number and can use the phone to obtain a broad array of different services – from receiving personal calls, from a next-door neighbor to calling a business associate on the other side of the world, and from data transmission to dial-a-prayer. Retail bank accounts are also customized, with each check or bank card carrying the customer's name and personal code. Within the constraints set down by the bank, the customer enjoys considerable latitude in how and when the account is used and receives a personalized monthly statement. Good hotels and restaurants usually offer their customers an array of service options from which to choose, as well as considerable flexibility in how the service product is delivered to them.

But in each of these instances, the role of the customer contact personnel (if there are any) is somewhat constrained. Other than tailoring their personal manner to the customer and answering straightforward questions, contact personnel have relatively little discretion in altering the characteristics of the service they deliver; their role is basically that of operator or order taker. Judgment and discretion in customer dealings is usually reserved for managers or supervisors who will not normally become involved in service delivery unless a problem arises.

A third category of services gives the customer contact personnel wide latitude in how they deliver the service, yet these individuals do not significantly differentiate the characteristics of their service between one customer and another. For instance, educators who teach courses by lectures and give multiple choice, computer scored exams expose each of their students to a potentially similar experience, yet one professor may elect to teach a specific course in a very different way from a colleague at the same institution.

However, there is a class of services that not only involves a high degree of customization but also requires customer contact personnel to exercise judgment concerning the characteristics of the service and how it is delivered to each customer. Far from being reactive in their dealings with customers, these service personnel are often prescriptive: users (or clients) look to them for advice as well as for customized execution. In this category the locus of control shifts from the user to the supplier – a situation that some customers may find disconcerting. Consumers of surgical services literally place their lives in the surgeon's hands (the same, unfortunately, is also true of taxi services in many cities). Professional services such as law, medicine, accounting and architecture fall within this category. They are all white collar 'knowledge industries', requiring extensive training to develop the requisite skills and judgment needed for satisfactory service delivery. Deliverers of such services as taxi drivers, beauticians and plumbers are also found in this category. Their work is customized to the situation at hand and in each instance, the customer purchases the expertise required to devise a tailor-made solution.

Insights and implications

To a much greater degree than in the manufacturing sector, service products are 'custom-made'. Yet customization has its costs. Service management often represents an ongoing struggle between the desires of marketing managers to add value and the goals of operations managers to reduce costs through standardization. Resolving such disputes, a task that may require arbitration by the general manager, requires a good understanding of consumer choice criteria, particularly as these relate to price/value trade-offs and competitive positioning strategy. At the present time, most senior managers in service businesses have come up through the operations route: hence, participation in executive education programs may be needed to give them the necessary perspective on marketing to make balanced decisions.

Customization is not necessarily important to success. As Levitt (1972, 1976) has pointed out, industrializing a service to take advantage of the economies of mass production may actually increase consumer satisfaction. Speed, consistency and price savings may be more important to many customers than customized service. In some instances, such as spectator sports and the performing arts, part of the product experience is sharing the service with many other people. In other instances the customer expects to share the service facilities with other consumers, as in hotels or airlines, yet still hopes for some individual recognition and custom treatment. Allowing customers to reserve specific rooms or seats in advance, having contact personnel address them by name (it is on their ticket or reservation slip), and providing some latitude for individual choice (room service and morning calls, drinks and meals) are all ways to create an image of customization.

Generally, customers like to know in advance what they are buying – what the product features are, what the service will do for them. Surprises and uncertainty are not normally popular. Yet when the nature of the service requires a judgment-based, customized solution, as in a professional service, it is not always clear to either the customer or the professional what the outcome will be. Frequently, an important dimension of the professional's role is diagnosing the nature of the situation, then designing a solution.

In such situations those responsible for developing marketing strategy would do well to recognize that customers may be uneasy concerning the prior lack of certainty about the outcome. Customer contact personnel in these instances are not only part of the product but also determine what that product should be.

One solution to this problem is to divide the product into two separate components, diagnosis and implementation of a solution, that are executed and paid for separately. The process of diagnosis can and should be explained to the customer in advance, since the outcome of the diagnosis cannot always be predicted accurately. However, once that diagnosis has been made, the customer need not proceed immediately with the proposed solution: indeed, there is always the option of seeking a second opinion. The solution 'product', by contrast, can often be spelled out in detail beforehand, so that the customer has a reasonable idea of what to expect. Although there may still be some uncertainty, as in legal actions or medical treatment, the range of possibilities should be narrower by this point, and it may be feasible to assign probabilities to specified alternative outcomes.

Marketing efforts may need to focus on the process of client-provider interactions. It will help prospective clients make choices between alternative suppliers, especially where professionals are concerned, if they know something of the organization's (or individual's) approach to diagnosis and problem-solving, as well as client-relationship style. These are considerations that transcend mere statements of qualification in an advertisement or brochure. For instance, some pediatricians allow new parents time for a free interview before any commitments are made. Such a trial encounter has the advantage of allowing both parents to decide whether or not a good match exists.

WHAT IS THE NATURE OF DEMAND AND SUPPLY FOR THE SERVICE?

Manufacturing firms can inventory supplies of their products as a hedge against fluctuations in demand. This enables them to enjoy the economies derived from operating plants at a steady level of production. Service businesses cannot do this because it is not possible to inventory the finished service. For instance, the potential income from an empty seat of an airline flight is lost forever once that flight takes off, and each hotel daily room vacancy is equally perishable. Likewise, the productive capacity of an auto repair shop is wasted if no one brings a car for servicing on a day when the shop is open. Conversely, if the demand for a service exceeds supply on a particular day, the excess business may be lost. Thus, if someone cannot get a seat on one airline, another carrier gets the business or the trip is cancelled or postponed. If an accounting firm is too busy to accept tax and audit work from a prospective client, another firm will get the assignment.

But demand and supply imbalances are not found in all service situations. A useful way of categorizing services for this purpose is shown in Figure 4. The horizontal axis classifies organizations according to whether demand for the service fluctuates widely or narrowly over time; the vertical axis classifies them according to whether or not capacity is sufficient to meet peak demand.

Organization in Box 1 could use increases in demand outside peak periods, those in Box 2 must decide whether to seek continued growth in demand and capacity or to continue the status quo, while those in Box 3 represent growing organizations that may need temporary demarketing until capacity can be increased to meet or exceed current demand levels. But service organizations in Box 4 face an ongoing problem of trying to smooth demand to match capacity, involving both stimulation and discouragement of demand.

Extent to which supply is constrained	Extent of demand fluctuations over time	
	Wide	Narrow
Peak demand can usually be met without a major delay	1 electricity natural gas telephone hospital maternity unit police and fire emergencies	2 insurance legal services banking laundry and dry cleaning
Peak demand regularly exceeds capacity	4 accounting and tax preparation passenger transportation hotels and motels restaurants theaters	3 services similar to those in 2 but which have insufficient capacity for their base level of business

Figure 4. What is the nature of demand for the service relative to supply?

Insights and implications

Managing demand is a task faced by nearly all marketers, whether offering goods or services. Even where the fluctuations are sharp, inventories cannot be used to act as a buffer between supply and demand, it may still be possible to manage capacity in a service business – for instance, by hiring part time employees or renting extra facilities at peak periods. But for a substantial group of service organizations, successfully managing demand fluctuations through marketing actions is the key to profitability.

To determine the most appropriate strategy in each instance, it is necessary to seek answers to some additional questions:

1. What is the typical cycle period of these demand fluctuations?
   - predictable (i.e. demand varies by hour of the day, day of the week or month, season of the year).
   - random (i.e. no apparent pattern to demand fluctuations).
2. What are the underlying causes of these demand fluctuations?
   - customer habits or preferences (could marketing efforts change these?)
   - actions by third parties (for instance, employers set working hours, hence marketing efforts might usefully be directed at those employers).
   - nonforecastable events, such as health symptoms, weather conditions, acts of God and so forth – marketing can do only a few things about these, such as offering priority services to members and disseminating information about alternative services to other people.

One way to smooth out the ups and downs of demand is through strategies that encourage customers to change their plans voluntarily, such as offering special discount prices or added product value during periods of low demand. Another approach is to ration demand through a reservation or queuing system (which basically inventories demand rather than supply). Alternatively, to generate demand in period of excess capacity, new business development efforts might be targeted at prospective customers with a countercyclical demand pattern. For instance, an accounting firm with a surfeit of work at the end of each calendar year might seek new customers whose financial year ended on June 30 or September 30.

Determining what strategy is appropriate requires an understanding of who or what is the target of the service (as discussed in an earlier section of this article). If the service is delivered to customers in person there are limits to how long a customer will wait in line: hence strategies to inventory or ration demand should focus on adoption of reservation systems (Sasser, 1976). But if the service is delivered to goods or to intangible assets, then a strategy of inventorying demand should be more feasible (unless the good is a vital necessity such as a car, in which case reservations may be the best approach).

HOW IS THE SERVICE DELIVERED?

Understanding distribution issues in service marketing requires that two basic issues be addressed. The first relates to the method of delivery. Is it necessary for the customer to be in direct physical contact with the service organization (customers may have to go to the service organization, or the latter may come to the former), or can transactions be completed at arm's length? And does the service organization maintain just a single outlet or does it serve customers through multiple outlets at different sites? The outcome of this analysis can be seen in Figure 5, which consists of six different cells.

Nature of interaction between customer and service organization	Availability of service outlets	
	Single site	Multiple set
Customer goes to service organization	theater barbershop	bus service fast food chain
Service organization comes to customer	lawn care service pest control service taxi	mail delivery AAA emergency repairs
Customer and service organization transact at arm's length (mail or electronic communications)	credit card company local TV station	broadcast network telephone company

Figure 5. Method of service delivery.

Insights and implications

The convenience of receiving service is presumably lowest when a customer has to come to the service organization and must use a specific outlet. Offering service through several outlets increases the convenience of access for customers but may start to raise problems of quality control as convenience of access relates to the consistency of the service product delivered. For some types of services the organization will come to the customer. This is, of course, essential when the target of the service is some immovable physical item (such as a building that needs repairs or pest control treatment, or a garden that needs landscaping). But since it is usually more expensive to take service personnel and equipment to the customer than vice versa, the trend has been away from this approach to delivering consumer services (e.g., doctors no longer like to make house calls). In many instances, however, direct contact between customers and the service organization is not necessary; instead, transactions can be handled at arm's length by mail or electronic communications. Through the use of 800 numbers many service organizations have found that they can bring their services as close as the nearest telephone, yet obtain important economies from operating out of a single physical location.

Although not all services can be delivered through arm's length transactions, it may be possible to separate certain components of the service from the core product and to handle them separately. This suggests an additional classification scheme: categorizing services according to whether transactions such as obtaining information, making reservations and making payment can be broken out separately from delivery of the core service. If they can be separated, then the question is whether or not is is advantageous to the service firm to allow customers to make these peripheral transactions through an intermediary or broker.

For instance, information about airline flights, reservations for such flights and purchases of tickets can all be made through a travel agent as well as directly through the airline. For those who prefer to visit in person, rather than conduct business by telephoning, this greatly increases the geographic coverage of distribution, since there are usually several travel agencies located more conveniently than the nearest airline office. Added value from using a travel agent comes from the 'one-stop shopping' aspect of travel agents; the customer can inquire about several airlines and make car rental and hotel reservations during the same call. Insurance brokers and theater ticket agencies are also examples of specialist intermediaries that represent a number of different service organizations. Consumers sometimes perceive such intermediaries as more objective and more knowledgeable about alternatives than the various service suppliers they represent. The risk to the service firm of working through specialist intermediaries is, of course, that they may recommend use of a competitor's product!

DISCUSSION

Widespread interest in the marketing of services among both academics and practitioners is a relatively recent phenomenon. Possibly this reflects the fact that marketing expertise in the service sector has significantly lagged behind that in the manufacturing sector. Up to now most academic research and discussion has centered on the issue, 'How do services differ from goods?' A number of authors including Shostack (1977). Bateson (1979) and Berry (1980) have argued that there are significant distinctions between the two and have proposed several generalizations for management practice. But others such as Enis and Roering (1981) remain unconvinced that these differences have meaningful strategic implications.

Rather than continue to debate the existence of this broad dichotomy, it seems more useful to get on with the task of helping managers in service businesses do a better job of developing and marketing their products. We need to recognize that the service sector, particularly in the United States, is becoming increasingly competitive (Langeard *et al.*, 1981), reflecting such developments as the partial or complete deregulation of several major service industries in recent years, the removal of professional association restrictions on using marketing techniques (particularly advertising), the replacement (or absorption) of independent service units by franchise chains, and the growth of new electronic delivery systems. As competition intensifies within the service sector, the development of more effective marketing efforts becomes essential to survival.

The classification schemes proposed in this article can contribute usefully to management practice in two ways. First, by addressing each of the five questions posed earlier, marketing managers can obtain a better understanding of the nature of their product, of the types of relationships their service organizations have with customers, of the factors underlying any sharp variations in demand, and of the characteristics of their service delivery systems. This understanding should help them identify how these factors shape marketing problems and opportunities and thereby affect the nature of the marketing task. Second, by recognizing which characteristics their own service shares with other services, often in seemingly unrelated industries, managers will learn to look beyond their immediate competitors for new ideas as to how to resolve marketing problems that they share in common with firms in other service industries.

Recognizing that the products of service organizations previously considered as 'different' actually face similar problems or share certain characteristics in common can yield valuable managerial insights. Innovation in marketing, after all, often reflects a manager's ability to seek out and learn from analogous situations in other contexts. These classification schemes should also be of value to researchers to whom they offer an alternative to either broad-brush research into services or an industry-by-industry approach. Instead, they suggest a variety of new ways of looking at service businesses, each of which may offer opportunities for focused research efforts. Undoubtedly there is also room for further refinement of the schemes proposed.

REFERENCES

Bateson, J. E. G. (1979) 'Why We Need Service Marketing'. In *Conceptual and Theoretical Developments in Marketing* (O. C. Ferrell, S. W. Brown and C. W. Lamb, Eds). Chicago: American Marketing Association, pp. 131–146.

Berry, L. L. (1980) 'Services Marketing is Different'. *Business Week* (May–June): 24–29.

Bucklin, L. (1963) 'Retail Strategy and the Classification of Consumer Goods'. *Journal of Marketing* **27** (January): 50.

Chase, R. B. (1978) 'Where Does the Customer Fit in a Service Operation?'. *Harvard Business Review* **56** (November–December): 137–142.

Copeland, M. T. (1923) 'The Relation of Consumers' Buying Habits to Marketing Methods'. *Harvard Business Review* **1** (April): 282–289.

Enis, B. M. and Roering, K. J. (1981) 'Services Marketing: Different Products, Similar Strategies'. In *Marketing of Services* (J. H. Donnelly and W. R. George, Eds). Chicago: American Marketing Association.

Hill, T. P. (1977) 'On Goods and Services'. *Review of Income and Wealth* **23** (December): 315–338.

Hunt, S. D. (1976) *Marketing Theory*. Columbus, OH: Grid.

Judd, R. C. (1964) 'The Case for Redefining Services'. *Journal of Marketing* **28** (January): 59.

Knisely, G. (1979) 'Marketing and the Services Industry'. *Advertising Age* (January 15), 47–50; (February 19), 54–60; (March 19), 58–62; (May 15), 57–58.

Kotler, P. (1980) *Principles of Marketing*. Englewood Cliffs, NJ: Prentice-Hall, Inc.

Langeard, E., Bateson, J. E. G., Lovelock, C. H. and Eiglier, P. (1981) *Services Marketing: New Insights from Consumers and Managers*. Cambridge, MA: Marketing Science Institute.

Levitt, T. (1972) 'Production Line Approach to Service'. *Harvard Business Review* **50** (September–October): 41.

Levitt, T. (1976) 'The Industrialization of Service'. *Harvard Business Review* **54** (September–October): 63–74.

Lovelock, C. H. (1980) 'Towards a Classification of Services'. In *Theoretical Developments in Marketing* (C. W. Lamb and P. M. Dunne, Eds) Chicago: American Marketing Association, pp. 72–76.

Lovelock, C. H. (1981) 'Why Marketing Management Needs to Be Different for Services'. In *Marketing of Services* (J. H. Donnelly and W. R. George, Eds). Chicago, IL: American Marketing Association.

Rathmell, J. M. (1974) *Marketing in the Service Sector*. Cambridge, MA: Winthrop.

Sasser, W. E. Jr. (1976) 'Match Supply and Demand in Service Industries'. *Harvard Business Review* **54** (November–December): 133.

Sasser, W. E. Jr., Olsen, R. P. and Wyckoff, D. D. (1978) *Management of Service Operations: Text and Cases*. Boston: Allyn & Bacon.

Shostack, G. L. (1977) 'Breaking Free from Product Marketing'. *Journal of Marketing* **41** (April): 73–80.

Thomas, D. R. E. (1978) 'Strategy Is Different in Service Businesses'. *Harvard Business Review* **56** (July–August): 158–165.

3

How Consumer Evaluation Processes Differ Between Goods and Services

Valarie A. Zeithaml

Services account for a large and growing proportion of economic activity. Providers of medical and legal services, haircuts, day care, entertainment, and education, among others, will proliferate to meet the growing demands for leisure and spending which accompany a rising standard of living. The primary objective of these service producers will be identical to that of all marketers: to develop and provide offerings that satisfy consumer needs, thereby ensuring their own economic survival.

To achieve this objective, service providers will need to understand how consumers choose and evaluate their offerings. Unfortunately, most of what is known about consumer evaluation processes pertains specifically to goods. The assumption appears to be that services, if not identical to goods, are at least similar enough in the consumer's mind that they are chosen and evaluated in the same manner. I propose to refute this assumption by showing that services' unique characteristics necessitate different consumer evaluation processes from those used when assessing goods.

SERVICES: SEARCH VERSUS EXPERIENCE VERSUS CREDENCE PROPERTIES?

One framework for isolating differences in evaluation processes between goods and services is the classification of qualities of goods proposed by economists Philip Nelson (1970) and Darby and Karni (1973). Nelson distinguishes between two categories of qualities of consumer goods: *search qualities*, attributes which a consumer can determine prior to purchasing a product; and *experience qualities*, attributes which can only be discerned after purchase or during consumption. Search qualities include attributes such as color, style, price, fit, feel, hardness, smell, while experience qualities include characteristics such as taste, wearability, purchase satisfaction. Some goods (e.g. clothing, furniture, and jewelry) are high in search qualities, for their attributes can be almost completely determined and evaluated prior to purchase. Other goods and services (e.g. vacations and restaurant meals) are

Reprinted with permission from *Marketing of Services* (James H. Donnelly and William R. George, Eds), pp. 39–47 high in experience qualities, for their attributes cannot be known or assessed until they have been purchased and are being consumed. Darby and Karni (1973) add to Nelson's two-way classification system a third category of qualities of goods, *credence qualities*, which are characteristics which the consumer may find impossible to evaluate even after purchase and consumption. Examples of offerings high in credence qualities include appendix operations and brake relinings on automobiles. Few consumers possess medical or mechanical skills sufficient to evaluate whether these services are necessary or are performed properly, even after they have been prescribed and produced by the seller.

Figure 1 arrays goods and services high in search, experience and credence qualities along a continuum of evaluation ranging from 'easy to evaluate' to 'difficult to evaluate'. At the left end of the continuum are goods high in search qualities, easiest to evaluate even before purchase. In the center are goods and services high in experience qualities, more difficult to evaluate because they must be purchased and consumed before assessment is possible. At the right end of the continuum are goods and services high in credence qualities, most difficult to evaluate because the consumer may be unaware of or may lack sufficient knowledge to appraise whether the offerings satisfy given wants or needs even after consumption.

The major premise of this paper is that most goods fall to the left of this continuum, while most services fall to the right due to three distinguishing characteristics. These distinguishing characteristics – intangibility, nonstandardization, and inseparability of production and consumption – make services more difficult to evaluate than goods. Difficulty in evaluation, in turn, forces consumers to rely on different cues and processes when evaluating services.

Several scholars detail the characteristics which distinguish services from products (Bessom, 1973; Rathmell, 1974; Eiglier *et al.*, 1977). *Intangibility* pertains to the

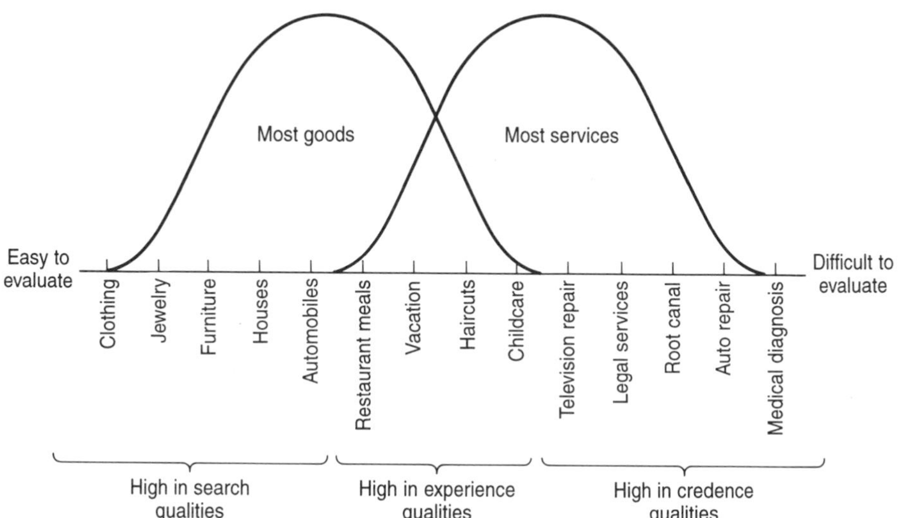

Figure 1. Continuum of evaluation for different types of products.

inability of services to be seen, felt, tasted, or touched in the same manner in which goods can be sensed. Services cannot be displayed, physically demonstrated or illustrated; therefore, they possess few search qualities and many experience qualities. *Nonstandardization* entails the inability of a producer to provide consistent performance and quality with a service. Since services cannot be inventoried, performance depends to some extent on level of demand; in periods of high demand, a service provider may not spend as much time or exert as much effort as in periods of low demand. Quality also may change from day to day because different employees perform the service, or because each employee's skills and moods vary. Nonstandardization results in high experience qualities, for consumers cannot be certain about performance on any given day, even if they use the same service provider on a regular basis. *Inseparability of production and consumption* constitutes the final characteristic which distinguishes goods and services. While tangible goods are produced, sold, and then consumed, services are sold, then produced and consumed simultaneously (Regan, 1963). Because of this inseparability, the buyer usually participates in producing the service, thereby affecting the performance and quality of the service. A doctor's accurate diagnosis, the desired haircut from a salon, effective stain removal from a dry cleaner – all these depend on the consumer's specification, communication, and participation in the production of the service. The quality of most services, and their ability to satisfy the consumer, depend not only on how well the service provider performs, but also on how well the consumer performs.

In sum, the inseparability, nonstandardization, and tangibility of services lead them to possess few search qualities and many experience qualities. Credence qualities also dominate in many services, especially those provided by professionals and specialists. While consumers may find it easy to evaluate the performance of everyday services (e.g. restaurant meals, housekeeping, or lawn care) prior to consumption, they may find it impossible to judge those performed by professionals and specialists with extensive training or experience in a specialized skill (e.g. medical diagnosis, television repair, or estate settlement).

SERVICES; SOME HYPOTHESES ABOUT CONSUMER EVALUATION PROCESSES

Because experience and credence qualities dominate in services, consumers may employ different evaluation processes than those they use with goods, where search qualities dominate. Specific areas where characteristics of services may lead to divergent evaluation processes are: information search, evaluative criteria, size and composition of the evoked set of alternatives, perceived risk, adoption of innovations, brand loyalty, and attribution of dissatisfaction.

Information search

Consumers obtain information about products and services from personal sources (e.g. friends or experts) and from nonpersonal sources (e.g. mass or selective media). When purchasing goods, consumers employ both personal and nonpersonal sources since both effectively convey information about search qualities.

When purchasing services, on the other hand, consumers may seek and rely to a greater extent on personal sources for several reasons. First, mass and selective media can convey information about search qualities but can communicate little about experience qualities. By asking friends or experts about services, however, the consumer can obtain information vicariously about experience qualities. Second, nonpersonal sources may not be available because: (1) many service providers are local, independent merchants with neither the experience nor the funds for advertising; (2) 'cooperative' advertising, or advertising funded jointly by the retailer and the manufacturer, is used rarely with services since most local providers are both producer and retailer of the service; and (3) professional associations banned advertising for so many years that some professionals and consumers tend to resist its use even though it is now permitted. Third, since consumers can discover few attributes prior to purchase of a service, they may feel greater risk to be associated with selecting an alternative. Given this risk, they may depend to a greater extent on sources such as word-of-mouth which they may perceive to be more credible and less biased.

Researchers suggest that personal sources might be more appropriate in situations where experience qualities dominate. Robertson (1971) claimed that personal influence becomes pivotal as product complexity increases and when objective standards by which to evaluate the product decrease (i.e. when experience qualities are high). Eiglier and Langeard *et al.* (1977) revealed that managers in four service industries believe word-of-mouth to have a great influence in services. Finally, many researchers (among them Perry and Hamm, 1969; Cunningham, 1967; Arndt, 1967) confirmed that the credibility of personal sources encourages their use in situations of high perceived risk.

> *Hypothesis 1:* Consumers seek and rely more on information from personal sources than from nonpersonal sources when evaluating services prior to purchase.

Consumers may find post-purchase evaluation more essential with services than with goods because services possess experience qualities which cannot be adequately assessed prior to purchase. The dissonance-attribution model of audience response to communication (Ray, 1973) describes the situation which frequently occurs when consumers select services: (1) the consumer selects from among virtually indistinguishable alternatives; (2) through experience, the consumer develops an attitude toward the service; and (3) after the development of an attitude, the consumer learns more about the service by paying attention to messages supporting his choice. In contrast both to the learning response model and the low-involvement model (Ray, 1973), where consumers seek information and evaluate products prior to purchase, as they do with tangible goods, the dissonance-response model represents the case of services where most evaluation follows purchase.

> *Hypothesis 2:* Consumers engage in greater post-purchase evaluation and information seeking with services than with products.

> *Hypothesis 3:* Consumers engage in most post-purchase evaluation than pre-purchase evaluation when selecting and consuming services.

Criteria for evaluating quality

When purchasing goods, the consumer employs multiple cues to judge quality, among them style, color, label, feel, package, brand name, and price. When purchasing services, the consumer is limited to a small number of cues; in many cases, the only cues available on which to judge quality are the service's price and the physical facilities which house the service.

Plumbing, housekeeping, and lawn care are examples of services where price may be the only pre-purchase indicator of quality. Research (Tull, 1964; Olander, 1970; McConnell, 1968) demonstrates that when the price is the only information available, consumers use it to assess quality.

With other services (e.g. haircuts, legal aid, dental services, and weight reduction), consumers may base decisions about quality on the tangible evidence of the services: the physical facilities. Thus they may examine the offices, personnel, equipment, and paraphernalia used to perform the service in order to evaluate quality. The importance of physical facilities for this purpose has been emphasized by Eiglier *et al.* (1977), Bessom (1973), and others.

Hypothesis 4: Consumers use price and physical facilities as the major cues to service quality.

Evoked set

The evoked set of alternatives, that group of products which a consumer considers acceptable options in a given product category, is likely to be smaller with services than with goods. One reason for the reduced set involves differences in retailing between goods and services. To purchase goods, consumers generally shop in retail stores which display competing products in close proximity, clearly demonstrating the alternatives from which a consumer may select. To purchase services, on the other hand, the consumer visits a retail establishment (e.g. a bank, a dry cleaner, or a hair salon) which offers only a single 'brand' for sale. A second reason for the smaller evoked set is that consumers are unlikely to find more than one or two stores providing the same services in a given geographic area, whereas they may find numerous retail establishments in that same area carrying the identical manufacturer's product. A third reason for a smaller evoked set is the difficulty of obtaining adequate pre-purchase information about services.

Faced with the difficult task of collecting and evaluating experience qualities, consumers may satisfice by selecting the first acceptable alternative rather than maximize by considering and evaluating all available alternatives.

Hypothesis 5: The consumer's evoked set of alternatives is smaller with services than with products.

For nonprofessional services, consumers' decisions often entail choices between performing the services for themselves and hiring someone else to perform them. Working wives may choose between cleaning their own homes or hiring housekeepers, between altering their families' clothes or taking them to a tailor, even between staying home to take care of the children or engaging a day care center to provide child care. Many other services, including lawn care, tax preparation, and restaurant meals, involve decisions where consumers may consider themselves as sources of supply.

> *Hypothesis 6:* For many nonprofessional services, the consumer's evoked set frequently includes self-provision of the service.

Innovation diffusion

The rate of diffusion of an innovation depends on consumer's perceptions of the innovation with regard to five characteristics: relative advantage, compatibility, communicability, divisibility, and complexity (Rogers, 1962). A product which has a relative advantage over existing or competing products, that is compatible with existing norms, values, and behaviors, that is communicable, and that is divisible (i.e. that can be tried or tested on a limited basis) diffuses more quickly than others. A product which is complex, i.e. difficult to understand or use, diffuses more slowly than others.

Considered as a group, services are less communicable, less divisible, more complex, and probably less compatible than goods. They are less communicable because they are intangible (e.g. their features cannot be displayed, illustrated, or compared) and because they are often unique to each buyer (as in a medical diagnosis or dental care). Services are less divisible because they are usually impossible to sample or test on a limited basis (e.g. how does one 'sample' a medical diagnosis? a lawyer's services in settling a divorce? even a haircut?). Services are frequently more complex than goods because they are composed of a bundle of different attributes, not all of which will be offered to every buyer on each purchase.

Finally, services may be incompatible with existing values and behaviors, especially if consumers are accustomed to providing the services for themselves. As an illustration, consider a novel day care center which cooks breakfast for children so that parents can arrive at work early. Mothers accustomed to performing this service for their children may resist adopting the innovation because it requires a change in habit, in behavior, even in values.

> *Hypothesis 7:* Consumers adopt innovations in services more slowly than they adopt innovations in goods.

Perceived risk

Eiglier *et al.* (1977) report that French managers believe the level of perceived risk to be higher for consumers purchasing services as opposed to physical goods. While some degree of perceived risk probably accompanies all purchase transactions, more risk would appear to be involved in the purchase of services than in the purchase of goods because services are intangible, nonstandardized, and are usually sold without guarantees or warranties.

First, the intangible nature of services and their high levels of experience qualities imply that services generally must be selected on the basis of less pre-purchase information than is the case for products. Since research (Cox and Rich, 1967; Spence *et al.*, 1970; and others) suggests that a decrease in the amount and/or quality of information usually is accompanied by a concomitant increase in perceived risk, the purchasing of services may involve more perceived risk than the purchasing of goods.

Second, consumers may perceive more risk to be associated with the purchase of services because they are nonstandardized. Even though a consumer may have purchased the same service (e.g. haircut) many times in his or her lifetime, there will always be recurring uncertainty about the outcome and consequences each time the service is purchased.

Third, service purchases may involve more perceived risk than product purchases because, with few exceptions, services are not accompanied by warranties or guarantees. Dissatisfied service purchasers can rarely 'return' a service, since they have already consumed it by the time they realize their dissatisfaction.

Finally, many services (e.g. medical diagnosis or pest control) are so technical or specialized that consumers possess neither the knowledge nor the experience to evaluate whether they are satisfied, even after they have consumed the service.

> *Hypothesis 8:* Consumers perceive greater risks when buying services than when buying products.

Brand loyalty

The degree to which consumers are committed to particular brands of goods or services depends on a number of factors: costs of changing brands, the availability of substitutes, the perceived risk associated with the purchase, and the degree to which they have obtained satisfaction in the past. Because it may be more costly to change brands of services, because it may be more difficult to be aware of the availability of substitutes, and because higher risks may accompany services, consumers may tend to be more brand loyal with services than with goods.

Greater search costs and monetary costs may be involved in changing brands of services than in changing brands of goods. Because of the difficulty of obtaining information about services, consumers may be unaware of alternatives or substitutes to their brands, and may be uncertain about the ability of alternatives to increase satisfaction over present brands. Monetary fees may accompany brand switching in many services: Physicians often require complete physicals on the initial visit; dentists sometimes demand new X-rays; and day care centers frequently charge 'membership fees' at the outset to obtain long-term commitments from consumers.

If consumers perceive greater risks with services, as is hypothesized above, they probably depend on brand loyalty to a greater extent than when they purchase products. Bauer (in Cox, 1967) stated that brand loyalty is a 'means of economizing decision effort by substituting habit for repeated, deliberate decisions' and suggested that it functions as a device for reducing the risks of consumer decisions. He predicted a strong correlation between degree of perceived risk and brand loyalty, and his prediction has been supported by research in perceived risk (Cunningham, 1967; Roselius, 1971; Sheth and Venkatesan, 1968).

A final reason why consumers may be more brand loyal with services is the recognition of the need for repeated patronage in order to obtain optimum satisfaction from the seller. Becoming a 'regular customer' allows the seller to gain knowledge of the consumer's tastes and preferences, ensures better treatment, and encourages more interest in the consumer's satisfaction. Therefore, a consumer may exhibit greater brand loyalty in order to cultivate a satisfying relationship with the seller.

Hypothesis 9: Brand switching is less frequent with services than with products.

Attribution of dissatisfaction

When consumers are disappointed with purchases – because the products did not fulfill the given needs, because they did not perform satisfactorily, or because they were not worth the prices – they may attribute their dissatisfaction to a number of different sources, among them the producers, the retailers, or themselves. Because consumers participate to a greater extent in the definition and production of services, they may feel more responsible for this dissatisfaction when they purchase services than when they purchase goods. As an example, consider a female consumer purchasing a haircut; receiving the cut she desires depends in part upon her clear specification of her needs to the stylist. If disappointed she may blame either the stylist (for lack of skill) or herself (for choosing the wrong stylist or for not communicating her own needs clearly).

The quality of many services depends on consumer definition: a doctor's accurate, diagnosis requires a conscientious case history and a clear articulation of symptoms; a dry-cleaner's success in removing a spot depends on the customer's knowledge of its cause; and a tax preparer's satisfactory performance relies on the receipts saved by the consumer. Failure to obtain satisfaction with any of these services may not be blamed completely on the retailer or producer, since the consumer must adequately perform his or her part in the production process also.

With products, on the other hand, a consumer's main form of participation is the act of purchase. The consumer may attribute failure to receive satisfaction to her own decision-making error, but she holds the producer responsible for product performance. Goods usually carry warranties or guarantees with purchase, emphasizing that the producer believes that if something goes wrong, it is not the fault of the consumer.

Hypothesis 10: Consumers attribute some of their dissatisfaction with services to their own inability to specify or perform their part of the service.

Hypothesis 11: Consumers may complain less frequently about services than about products due to their belief that they themselves are partly responsible for their dissatisfaction.

SERVICES: STRATEGIC IMPLICATIONS FOR MARKETERS

If research confirms that hypotheses about services, service providers may need to alter their marketing mixes to recognize different consumer evaluation processes. The high levels of experience and credence qualities postulated to be characteristic of services require alternative approaches to information provision, pricing, new service introduction, and other marketing strategies.

Information provision. If consumers employ personal sources more frequently than nonpersonal sources when seeking information about services prior to purchase, the marketer's task may be to reduce the proportion of advertising in the promotional mix. Alternatively, the marketer may want to use advertising to stimulate and simulate word-of-mouth communication (e.g. through testimonial advertisements or by developing advertising high in controversial value) (Kotler, 1980). If consumers seek more post-purchase information with services, the marketer's task may be to concentrate communication efforts to reduce dissonance after purchase.

Quality image. The potential importance of price and physical facilities as indicators of service quality suggests that marketers should manipulate these cues to their own advantage. If marketers desire to position services as high-quality offerings, for example, they may need to set a price above that of competing services. They might also want to match their physical facilities to the desired impression of quality (Bessom, 1973) so that the tangible evidence of the service provides the appropriate atmosphere.

The consumer as competitor. Nonprofessional service providers today must recognize that they often replace or compete with the consumer, which may imply more exacting standards from the consumer and more individualized, personal attention from the service provider. Consumers know what they expect from providers of housecleaning or lawn care or day care because they know what they are accustomed to providing for themselves. The alert service marketer will be certain to research consumers' expectations and demands in such situations.

Innovation diffusion. Marketers may need to concentrate on incentives to trial when introducing new services. The awareness–interest–evaluation stages of the adoption process may best be bypassed because of the difficulty and inefficiency of communicating information about intangibles. Offering free visits, dollars-off coupons, and samples may be appropriate strategies to speed diffusion of innovations in services.

Reduction of perceived risk. The hypothesized increase in perceived risk involved in purchasing services suggests the use of strategies designed to reduce risk. Where appropriate, guarantees of satisfaction may be offered. To the extent possible, service providers should emphasize employee training and other procedures to standardize their offerings, so that consumers learn to expect a given level of quality and satisfaction.

Implications of strong brand loyalty. The fact that one's own customers may be brand loyal with services is not a problem; the fact that the customers of one's competitors may be difficult to capture, however, may create special challenges. Marketers may need to direct communications and strategy to the customers of competitors, emphasizing attributes and strengths which one firm possesses and its competitors lack.

SUMMARY AND CONCLUSION

Service's unique characteristics of intangibility, nonstandardization, and inseparability lead them to possess high levels of experience and credence properties, which, in turn, make them more difficult to evaluate than tangible goods. Eleven specific hypotheses about differences in consumer evaluation processes between services and goods were offered, accompanied by strategic implications for marketers.

REFERENCES

Arndt, J. (1967). 'Word-of-Mouth Advertising and Information Communication'. In *Risk Taking and Information Handling in Consumer Behavior* (D. F. Cox, Ed.). Boston: Division of Research, Harvard University.

Bessom, R. M. (1973) 'Unique Aspects of Marketing Services'. *Arizona Business Bulletin* **9**(November): 8–15.

Cox, D. F. and Rich, S. U. (1967) 'Perceived Risk and Consumer Decision Making – The Case of Telephone Shopping'. In *Risk Taking and Information Handling in Consumer Behavior* (D. F. Cox, Ed.). Boston: Division of Research, Harvard University.

Cunningham, S. M. (1967) 'Perceived Risk in Information Communications'. In *Risk Taking and Information Handling in Consumer Behavior* (D. F. Cox, Ed.). Boston: Division of Research, Harvard University.

Darby, M. R. and Karni, E. (1973) 'Free Competition and the Optimal Amount of Fraud'. *Journal of Law and Economics* **16** (April): 67–86.

Eiglier, P., Langeard, E., Lovelock, C. H., Bateson, E. G. and Young, R. F. (1977). *Marketing Consumer Services: New Insights.* Cambridge, MA: Marketing Science Institute.

Kotler, P. (1980) *Marketing Management: Analysis, Planning and Control.* Englewood Cliffs, NJ: Prentice Hall.

McConnell, J. D. (1968) 'Effect of Pricing on Perception of Product Quality'. *Journal of Applied Psychology* **52** (August): 300–303.

Nelson, P. (1970) 'Advertising as Information'. *Journal of Political Economy* **81** (July–August): 729–754.

Olander, F. (1970) 'The Influence of Price on the Consumer's Evaluation of Products'. In *Pricing Strategy* (B. Taylor and G. Wills, Eds). Princeton, NJ: Auerbach Publishers.

Perry, M. and Hamm, B. C. (1969) 'Canonical Analysis of the Relationship Between Socioeconomic Risk and Personal Influence in Purchase Decisions'. *Journal of Marketing Research* **6** (August): 351–354.

Rathmell, J. M. (1974). *Marketing in the Service Sector.* Cambridge, MA: Winthrop.

Ray, M. L. (1973) 'Marketing Communications: The Hierarchy-of-Effects'. Unpublished research paper 180, Stanford University, August.

Regan, W. J. (1963) 'The Service Revolution'. *Journal of Marketing* **27** (July): 57–62.

Robertson, T. S. (1971). *Innovative Behavior and Communication.* New York: Holt, Rinehart and Winston.

Roselius, T. 'Consumer Rankings of Risk Reduction Methods'. *Journal of Marketing* **35**: (January): 56–61.

Rogers, E. M. (1962). *Diffusion of Innovations.* New York: The Free Press.

'Service Industries: Growth Field of '80's'. (1980). *U.S. News and World Report,* March 17, 80–84.

Sheth, J. N. and Venkatesan, M. (1968) 'Risk-Reduction Processes in Repetitive Consumer Behavior'. *Journal of Marketing* **5** (August): 307–310.

Spence, H. E., Engel, J. F. and Blackwell, R. D. (1970) 'Perceived Risk in Mail-Order and Retail Store Buying'. *Journal of Marketing Research* **5** (August): 307–310.

Tull, D., Boring, R. A. and Gonsoir, M. H. (1964) 'A Note on the Relationship of Price and Imputed Quality'. *Journal of Business* **37** (April): 186–191.

4

A Service-Orientated Approach to Marketing of Services

Christian Grönroos

THE PROBLEM

Service companies are less marketing-orientated than firms which are marketing physical goods, according to reports on service marketing.[1] Some prominent Swedish firms have recently, after several meetings in 1975 and 1976, reported that there are severe marketing problems in the service sector in comparison with goods marketing.[2] The main difference between marketing goods and services was found to be the difficulty of developing a concrete, tangible service offering. Most marketing problems discussed by the service companies came out of this conclusion.

It has even been said that service marketing has failed.[3] The research which I have been conducting among companies in several service industries in Sweden and in Finland has confirmed the view that marketing services is a difficult task. Moreover, it has also been said that the existing marketing literature has little aid to offer companies in service industries. This view should not be surprising. Marketing literature and research almost completely take their examples from goods industries. Therefore, the problems relevant to this area of business have been investigated very thoroughly indeed. Marketing scholars have, however, been very little interested in the problems of firms in service industries. Examples of the marketing problems and the marketing planning situation of these industries are very seldom discussed by researchers or treated in marketing texts.

The service sector has thus been forgotten to a great extent.[4] The re-defining of the product concept seems to be the only radical development of service marketing. Products became goods and services indicating that services are by no means without interest. However, this may have been quite fatal. It seems as if marketing scholars have been tempted to deal with service marketing and goods marketing using the same concepts, models and frames of reference. As marketing focusing on the problems of companies producing physical goods has been developed to a high degree of sophistication, marketers seem to have come to believe that this progress

Reprinted with permission from *European Journal of Marketing*, Vol. 12, No. 8, pp. 588–601

would be a gain to service firms as well. Many writers do, however, point out that service marketing must differ from goods marketing, but, nevertheless, no radical effort to develop a marketing theory, or even some marketing concepts, for service firms aiming at solving their problems seems to have been made.[5] I think that companies in the service industries deserve a better treatment by marketing scholars.

The purpose of this article

A good deal of the marketing problems of service companies may be caused by the lack of a theory of its own for service marketing. The purpose of the present article is to discuss this matter and to suggest a hypothetical framework for an important part of such a theory, i.e. the marketing mix planning. Some empirical evidence supporting the hypotheses will also be accounted for.

The most severe problems of service marketing are, in my opinion, to be found in connection with the planning of a marketing mix. I believe that this part of marketing planning is the main victim of the goods-orientation in marketing research. In this context I am mainly concentrating on *the development of a concrete service offering as part of a service marketing mix planning process*, whereas the marketing variables not to be considered part of the offering – the 'product' of service firms – are not discussed in any detail. Moreover, I am mainly interested in marketing services to consumer markets.

MARKETING OF SERVICES – THE MARKETING MYOPIA OF TODAY

The service marketing confusions

There are, in my opinion, at least three confusions of service marketing, which can to a great extent be blamed for the situation of service marketing. I believe that marketing of services can be labelled the marketing myopia of today. Yet the proportion of GNP coming from the service industries, and the proportion of all employees working in this sector of business, is approaching 50% in most developed societies, and the percentage is in fact over 50% in the most developed ones.

These confusions of service marketing are (1) the faltering service concept, (2) the opinion that everybody is in service, and (3) the view that marketing research helping companies in goods industries would help service firms equally well.

The service concept itself is confusing. No distinction is made between services as objects of marketing and services as marketing variables, i.e. as means of competition when marketing goods. Such a distinction must, in my opinion, definitely be made. Marketing of services concerns services in the first sense of the concept. The service is the *object* of marketing, i.e. *the company is selling the service as the core of its market offering.* When services are treated as a means of competition, the core of the selling proposition is a physical good, not a service. Then it is not service marketing, and the planning situation can be coped with by means of the traditional concepts and models of marketing literature.

The faltering service concept may well be a result of the idea of a goods–service continuum. All offerings may, it is said, be described by the continuum with pure goods at one extreme and pure services at the other, and with most offerings falling somewhere between these points.[6] This continuum concept mixes the two service concepts separated above. From a marketing planning point-of-view the continuum does not exist, or at least it is highly misguiding to the marketer. It gives the impression that every offering basically is the same, and can be planned in a similar manner applying the same planning instruments. In my opinion an offering concerns either goods, with or without service support (transport, maintenance, repair, etc.), or services, which may be pure services which make it possible to use goods or which are accompanied by goods (car rental, hotel, inclusive tours, etc.).

The same company may, of course, be engaged in both goods marketing and service marketing. Every firm must, however, in every planning situation, analyse the planning problem, and try to find out whether it is developing a service offering or a goods offering. A definite borderline between these two kinds of offerings cannot be drawn in a goods-service continuum. The problem must be solved *in situ* by the marketer.

Sometimes combinations of equally important goods and service elements are marketed. This marketing planning situation, systems selling, is, however, out of the scope of the present article.

Is everybody really in service?

It has become popular to consider all marketing to be service marketing. Consumers, it is said, are not buying goods or services, but the value satisfaction of offerings.[7] Consequently, there are no goods industries or service industries, but industries with varying degrees of service components, and, thus, everybody is in service.[8]

This seems to be another confusion of service marketing. The present marketing literature normally maintains that there is nothing like marketing of goods and marketing of services, but there is just marketing of goods (and services). So it also, although not on the same grounds, supports the view that everybody is in the same sort of business. Yet companies in the service sector still seem to be in trouble with their marketing.

It is, of course, reasonable to consider both goods and services to be bought by consumers in order to give some service or value satisfaction. And companies marketing physical goods would certainly many times be better off by concentrating more on the needs of the consumers and less on the tangible good itself in their marketing planning. Every consumer can perhaps be said to be in service, but certainly not every enterprise. To state that every industry is a service industry would indicate, from a marketing planning point-of-view, that the planning situation, and the tools, concepts, and models used are the same for service companies as for firms marketing goods. But, the marketing planning situation is, in my opinion, different when marketing services than when marketing physical goods.

If the marketing planning situation differs between service industries and goods industries, which I think it does, *the planning instruments developed to assist in solving the problems of goods industries may well not be applicable when planning service marketing.* However, it is most frequently said that the concepts and models used by companies in goods industries can equally well be applied by service firms. I think that there is enough empirical evidence to prove this opinion to be wrong and just another confusion of service marketing. A theory of service marketing is needed. The traditional marketing does not offer service companies appropriate planning tools.

Characteristics of services

I do not intend to add a definition of my own to the range of more or less unsatisfactory definitions already existing. I believe that it is quite impossible to find one final definition. One can, for instance, use a rather traditional one suggested by Judd in the 1960s:

> Marketed Services – A market transaction by an enterprise of an entrepreneur where the object of the market transaction is *other than* the transfer of ownership (or title, if any) of a tangible commodity.[9]

In my opinion, it would be more fruitful to find out in what respects services differ from goods, and to examine the implications for marketing planning caused by the characteristics of services.

Several characteristics can be found, but I am here going to stress only three, which I think are vital to service marketing planning. Perhaps the most important characteristic of a service is its *intangibility*. The customer cannot feel, taste, smell, or see a service before he buys it. One cannot make a thorough evaluation of a service. However, such an evaluation seems often to be desirable for most consumers, so they evaluate what they can: the interior of a restaurant, the appearance of the air hostesses, the behaviour of the bank clerks.[10]

Of course, it is not always easy to evaluate physical goods either, but the point is that they can be physically evaluated, i.e. there is something tangible to evaluate. Services cannot be evaluated as such, so they must be transformed to concrete offerings, which can be evaluated and compared to those of the competitors. If the firm does not manage this process, the customers will, in an unguided manner, pick out tangible attributes which *are* the service in the customers' mind.

Another essential characteristic of services is the *production/consumption interaction* in most service businesses. Services cannot be separated from the producer, and the producer and the seller are the same organisation.[11] A service is considered to be consumed as it is produced. Thus, producing and marketing are very interactive processes, too. Both activities are simultaneously performed by the same persons in a service company. Moreover, the inseparability of services is said to make only direct distribution possible. In fact, no normal distribution could be possible, as there is nothing tangible to distribute using the usual channels of distribution.[12]

A third characteristic of services is the *lack of ownership and transaction of ownership* when dealing with services. One does not own anything, when one has purchased a service. One is only given the right to use things, and as symbols of the lack of ownership one may get tickets, certificates, value coupons, etc.

As a summary, it seems obvious that services do differ from goods as objects of marketing. Therefore, services cannot be treated like goods in a marketing planning context. *A new service marketing mix concept is needed.*

Weaknesses of the traditional goods-orientated marketing mix concept

As a simultaneous analysis of all marketing variables in the same context is not usually possible, the marketing mix models, like McCarthy's four P's and Lipson and Darling's subcomponent model, have been developed. Different submixes are thought to be planned separately, and, finally, blended into a total marketing mix. Only the product mix must, in some way, be already shaped, before detailed pricing, distribution, and communication planning can take place.

This is a way of planning an efficient marketing mix for physical goods, and the models are developed for goods marketing. No matter how sophisticated such models are, they take for granted that it is possible to plan submixes, which afterwards can be co-ordinated into one total mix. This is possible, if there is a tangible product involved. Then there is something to develop, to price, to distribute, and to communicate about. That is, in goods marketing there is a tangible core around which the offering can be developed in a manner reflected by the traditional marketing mix models. In service marketing there is no such tangible core. It simply is not possible to plan separate submixes, which can be blended into one total marketing mix. Therefore, the traditional marketing mix concept developed for goods marketing is likely to fail in service marketing planning. This may be the main reason why service firms are less marketing-orientated than other companies.

PLANNING THE SERVICE OFFERING

The accessibility of services

Only direct distribution was earlier mentioned to be possible for service firms, because of the close production/consumption interaction. It may seem so when viewing the matter strictly in the goods sense of the distribution concept. I do believe, however, that a more innovative approach to distribution of services is called for. It seems to me as if the traditional concept ought not to be applied to service marketing at all. Instead of being a useful means of competition it becomes an unnecessary burden to the marketer.

In my opinion *the accessibility of a service* is a much more promising concept for service firms. Resources influencing accessibility are, for example, human resources, machines, offices, buildings, and other physical things as well as extra services. These resources can be managed by the marketer, and they are all aimed at making the service quickly and conveniently accessible to the consumers.

The difference between the concept of distribution channels and the concept of physical distribution does not seem meaningful in the context of services. For example, a guide may be considered part of the channel of distribution for inclusive tours. Without him much experience and many views and facts, which are part of the tours, would not be accessible to the consumers. At the same time he also distributes this part of the service; that is, he performs physical distribution.

Applying the traditional concept it may be difficult to view a person like the guide as a part of the channel of distribution, and he certainly is not performing any physical distribution, because there is nothing tangible to distribute. In terms of accessibility, the guide is, however, a manageable resource making it possible for the customers to consume the service.

I believe that the concept of accessibility can improve the understanding of service marketing in at least two ways. First, it stresses all parts of the service offering, which the consumers may recognise as the service. The service itself is intangible, but the resources – both human and non-human – influencing the accessibility transform the service into a concrete offering, which is accessible to the consumers and can be evaluated by them in comparison with competing offerings. These resources can therefore be labelled *bearers of the service*, because they bring out the service to the market.

Such elements of the service offering are, for instance, the location of a bank, the interior of a bank office or travel agency office, means of transportation and their condition, the interior and exterior of a restaurant, the waiters, ticket-collectors on buses and trains, bank clerks and cashiers, barbers, cheques, pass-books, tickets, computer and telecommunication networks, etc. These elements are indeed of many kinds but they all have two essential features in common: they promote the accessibility of the services, and they can be managed and used as a means of competition by the marketer.

Secondly, I believe that by applying the accessibility concept, service marketing has a chance of breaking free from the burden of the traditional distribution concept.[13] Direct distribution will then by no means be the only way of making the service accessible to the consumers. Insurance vending machines and franchise arrangements used by hotel and catering enterprises are examples of an innovative development of the resources influencing the accessibility.[14]

The human resources

The consumers of a service will almost always see and meet some representative of the service firm sometimes during the purchasing and/or consumption process. Nearly all employees, irrespective of their place in the organisation, will, on the other hand, at least occasionally get in touch with the customers. Therefore, the manner in which the bank manager, the bank clerk, the travel agency representative, the telephone receptionist, the tour guide, the barber, or the waiter treats the customers, what he says, and how he behaves are very critical to the view of the service which the consumers get. *Almost every single person in a service firm is, therefore, acting as a salesman and is engaged in the personal market communication efforts of the company.*

The human resources of a service firm are also part of the accessibility system of a service, and this fact makes the personnel even more vital to the company and its marketing planning. Thus, *the administration of the human resources must be considered an important means of competition in service marketing.* Marketing training – especially concerning communication and selling – is a much greater task and involves many more people in service industries than in goods industries. For a company producing and marketing physical goods it is satisfactory if the marketing staff is properly trained and the salesmen know how to sell. In a service company almost every employee belongs to the 'marketing department'. This is a fact that must be recognised, e.g. when engaging employees and planning personnel training programmes. And this goes for the financial manager of a bank as well as for the waiter of a restaurant and the telephone receptionist of an airline company.

As so many people in service firms are engaged in marketing tasks, their behaviour influences the success of the company to a great extent. Therefore, it is important to be aware of the *internal marketing task of service firms,* i.e. a service must first be successfully marketed to the personnel, so that the employees accept the service offering and thoroughly engage in performing their marketing duties. Otherwise the service may easily turn out to be a failure in relation to its ultimate target markets.

The importance of the administration of the personnel and of the internal marketing process to the success of service companies is not, I believe, quite recognised today. Frequently the employees have not been engaged to perform any marketing tasks but merely to produce the services. Therefore, it will not be an easy task for a service firm to manage its human resources in a more marketing-orientated manner. First the attitude of the personnel must be changed so that the employees accept that they are not only producers of a service, but, simultaneously, are also engaged in selling the very same service.

The personal market communication and selling tasks performed by the personnel are bearers of the service as well as the resources influencing the accessibility, because the performance of the representatives of the firm is also an element of the service offering, which brings out the intangible service to the market and can be considered by the consumers instead of the service itself.

Auxiliary services

The accessibility of a service may be influenced by offering extra services. For instance, the bank clerk may fill out forms and supermarkets may offer large parking areas in order to help the customers. But, furthermore, services can be offered as separate means of competition. Such auxiliaries are, for example, hotel booking and inclusive tours arrangements offered by airline companies and coffee offered by barbers' shops.

Sometimes a service may be an extra service influencing the accessibility for one consumer and an auxiliary service for another. Someone may choose to go by train instead of by bus, because he can have his lunch in the restaurant of the train, whereas someone else may take the train just because he enjoys the excellent meals served. But he does not actually have to eat anything.

An auxiliary service is not a bearer of the service, because it does not bring out the service to the market. But it is promoting the service, and it is certainly considered part of the service offering by the consumers.

Intra-corporate elements of the service

In the marketing planning process service firms cannot separate the different kinds of marketing mix variables, as frequently is done in marketing of physical goods. In particular, the personal market communication, as part of the administration of human resources, and the resources influencing the accessibility are extremely close to each other and to the intangible service itself.

As a matter of fact, the personal communication and the accessibility of services may be viewed as parts of the service offered to the target markets, i.e. as parts of the 'product' of service industries. They fulfil the function as bearers of the service, which bring out the intangible service to the markets as a concrete service offering, i.e. as a product. Moreover, the auxiliary services offered are from the consumers' point-of-view also part of the service offering. They are, too, shaping the service which the customers evaluate and eventually perhaps buy.

The bearers of the service and the auxiliary services are *intra-corporate elements of the service*, because the marketer can maintain full control over them. Figure 1 shows how the bearers and the auxiliary services are linked together and to the core of the offering, i.e. to the intangible idea of the service.

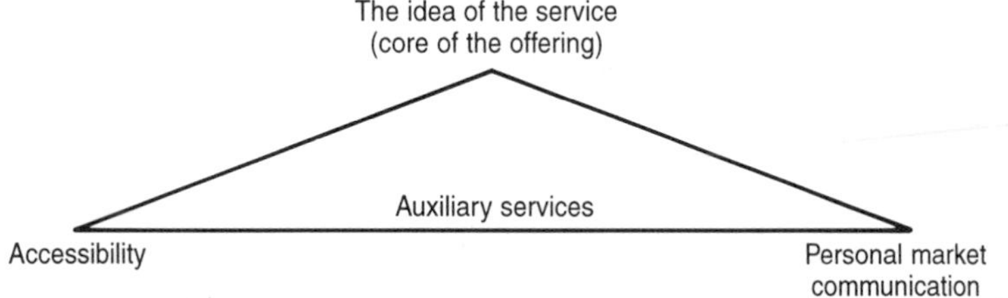

Figure 1. Intra-corporate elements of the service.

The figure illustrates how integrated the planning of marketing variables must be in service marketing. Product development is in fact quite another task than one usually thinks about, when applying the product development concept to service marketing in the goods-orientated sense of the concept.

Companies in service industries have to recognise that product development involves many more activities than one traditionally believes it does. *Development of the resources influencing the accessibility, the administration of human resources, and the development of auxiliary services are parts of the product development process.*[15] By accepting such a view services companies can, I believe, achieve considerable improvements in their marketing performance.

THE CONSUMERS AS ACTIVE PARTICIPANTS IN MARKETING

Usually the consumers are only considered to have needs which are unknown to them or relatively badly satisfied by existing products, and they either buy the product offered to them or do not buy it. They take part in the product development process only in a *passive* manner by having unsatisfied needs. They are not considered as actively shaping the product. Consumer tests and test marketing may be used, but these are actually rather passive ways in which the consumers can influence the product. Only the competitors on the market are thought of as actively influencing the performance of marketing.

When marketing services the situation of the marketer is, however, somewhat different. The traditional view of the consumers' role in the marketplace is an unnecessary restriction on the development of marketing. While this view may express the situation of a goods marketer, service companies have to make other considerations as far as the behaviour of the consumer is concerned.

The consumers are actively taking part in shaping the service offering, i.e. in product development.[16] This is due to the production/consumption interaction, which is characteristic of the service industries, and to the fact that several consumers and/or potential consumers simultaneously are on the same spot either consuming, purchasing, or planning to purchase the service. The consumers influence both the accessibility of a service and the communication about the service, and their influence can be either desirable or undesirable.

A consumer may, for instance, cause queues in a bank, thus causing the quality of the bank's services to deteriorate, or he may be part of the atmosphere in a music hall, thus improving the quality of the concert. He may also be telling potential consumers of, for instance, the restaurant of a hotel, that he, by experience, knows that it is a dull place, thus changing the communication about the restaurant in an unfavourable manner. He may on the other hand enthusiastically encourage others to visit the hotel restaurant, thus making a desirable impact on the communication.

Companies in service industries should, therefore, consider the consumers, not only the competitors, to be elements in the market actively influencing marketing planning. From the consumers' point-of-view, the other consumers, who simultaneously are making their purchasing decision and/or consuming the service, are part of the service itself. The service marketer has to recognise this fact, and include also this active role of the consumers in his marketing planning.

Moreover, the consumer himself can be considered part of the service he buys and consumes. His expectations and acting certainly influence the behaviour of the human representatives of the service firm. Thus, the quality of the service varies according to the behaviour of the consumer. The attitude of the consumers towards the service and towards the organisation producing and marketing the service must from the very beginning be kept favourable, and if the consumer happens to become disappointed, immediate action is called for.

Such activities are also important means of competition in the service industries. And the consumers of a service can be considered *extra-corporate elements of the service.* In Figure 2 these elements have been added to the intra-corporate dimensions of services.

The continuous line in the figure connecting the idea of the service, the accessibility, the personal market communication, and the auxiliary services with each other indicates that these elements of the service can be directly controlled and managed by the marketer. The dotted line connecting the consumers with the two bearers of the service shows that the consumers may influence both of them, but that the behaviour of the consumers can be controlled only indirectly by the marketer. But the line also stresses the point that the behaviour of the consumer is still, in some way, manageable.

The marketer can in advance anticipate possible patterns of behaviour of the consumers in order to be able to eliminate undesirable effects on both the accessibility and the communication.[17] And he should also be prepared to take advantage of favourable consumer influence, which is improving the quality of the service.

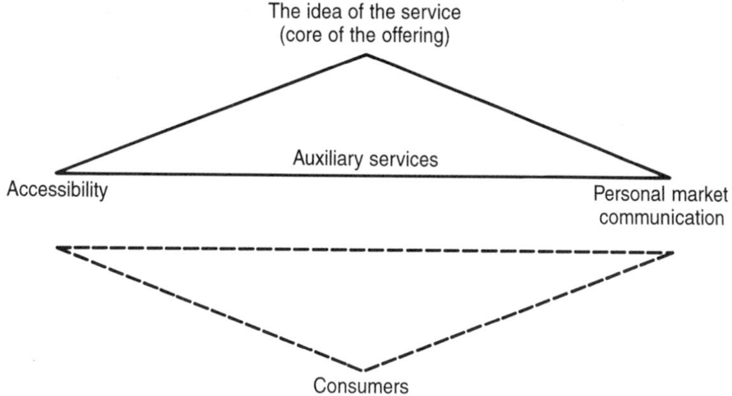

Figure 2. An extensive view of the service.

SOME EMPIRICAL SUPPORT

The study

In order to test the hypothetical view of the service offering put forward in this article, I have during the winter 1976/77 made twelve case studies of marketing planning procedures of successful companies in several service industries in Sweden and in Finland. The information was gathered by means of a two-stage interviewing procedure. First a questionnaire was mailed to the firms, and, in the second stage, the answers were supplemented by personal interviews with the persons responsible for the marketing planning.

My case studies reveal an amazingly uniform picture of the problems of the service firms, and, moreover, of the planning behaviour and the marketing variables applied by the firms. Every company, *irrespective of industry*, seems to have similar problems, mainly those of the intangibility of the services and of developing a concrete offering out of the intangible service. The tools used were also very similar, although varying terms were used.

I am not going to account for all case studies in this article. I will just present two cases, here labelled *inclusive tours marketing* and *barber's shop marketing*. Adding more cases to these would not give any new empirical evidence.

The case of inclusive tours marketing

A company offering inclusive tours for holidaymakers is operating around an intangible idea of, for example, recreation, change of milieu, experiences, excitement, and adventures. 'We sell a week of power. The consumer purchases a position where he can order others to serve him, where he is the employer, not the employee'.

In order to transform the intangible service into concrete offerings varying kinds of means are used. These means usually also make the service accessible to the consumers, but some of them are mere auxiliary services. The traditional ticket has been replaced by a travel certificate, which is issued and printed out by a computer, at the time when the tour is ordered. The computer facilitates quick and detailed booking information with a minimum of mistakes, thus giving the consumers an impression of exactness and security. 'People are not sure of what service they actually will get. In this way we give them, in advance, a concrete written specification of which services they have bought.' The travel certificate serves as an allround ticket, thus not only in a tangible manner symbolising the service, but also minimising the amount of papers and forms usually needed and, therefore, making the service more conveniently and easily accessible to the consumers.

The hotel, the airline company, and the type of aircraft used, as well as various kinds of auxiliary services, such as meals included in the tour and trips arranged on destination, are also part of the service which the company offers. Because of these resources the inclusive tours become accessible to the consumers. They are thus shaping the service, which the consumers get.

The human resources of the company are considered vitally important to the marketing performance. For example, the manager, the people behind the desk in the booking offices, and the guides are essential to the accessibility. The employees are carefully selected and trained. The performance of the personnel is considered to a great extent to shape the service which is offered. The guides are especially vital, 'because it is the guide who sells the next tour'. As long as the tour lasts the guides are in contact with the consumers, and they are more or less the last contact which the consumers have with the service and the company. If something goes wrong, it is the guides who, as representatives of the firm, have to be capable of reshaping the service so that quality is maintained and the consumers will remain satisfied.

The employees of the firm are performing market communication and selling tasks, and the better they know the destination of a tour, the better they sell. Clearly, the administration of the human resources of the company and the training of the personnel are important to marketing.

The consumers are considered part of the service offering. 'Our image keeps drinkers away, which makes the tours more comfortable to the other consumers'. The consumers also sometimes take part in the communication about the services. One single person may get all the others to complain of something without really having any reason. 'But there can be a person, who gets everybody on an auxiliary trip by enthusiastically telling them that he was on that trip last time and it was marvellous'.

The corporate image is considered important to marketing, because consumers buy the company as well as a certain tour. A favourable and attractive image is vital to the accessibility. If the image is unfavourable, the consumers may not even be interested in recognising other means of competition used by the firm.

To sum up, one can in this case notice the importance of the bearers of the intangible service to marketing. The resources influencing the accessibility and the personal market communication and selling by the personnel, as well as the auxiliary services offered, are marketing variables shaping the service offerings. Furthermore, the consumers are actively influencing the services and taking part in the communication about it.

The case of barber's shop marketing

A barber's shop offers intangible services concerning personal care, relaxation, etc. In order to transform the intangible services to concrete offerings various means are used.

It is important that the shop is located near people, on busy streets. The interior and exterior of the shop are also vital to the success of the firm. The windows of the shop are not covered, so that the people passing by can easily see what is going on inside the shop. This is a way of making the services of the barber's shop more concrete. 'We wish to create an atmosphere which pleases the customers. Our customers shall enjoy their stay with us'. Colours and music are important to the milieu and used in order to achieve the right atmosphere.

The people working in the shop and their capability of doing a good job according to the taste and wishes of the customers are perhaps the most important part of the accessibility of the services. They have to be well-trained, but, moreover, their appearance is also considered vital. They are uniformly dressed, and the uniforms are now and then changed.

The behaviour of the personnel is important too: not only how they do the job, but also what they are talking about and how they are doing it. The human resources are part of the service which the consumers get, and the administration of these resources is important to the success of the barber's shop. 'If our employees are satisfied with their job and enjoy the place, they will do a better job, and then our customers will enjoy our services even more'.

Auxiliary services are offered to some extent. Coffee is served and magazines are available. To minimise the waiting time, the shop actively tries to get its customers to book time in advance. This diminishes the risks of getting irritated customers and of lost business because of queues in the shop.

As a summary, one can notice the extreme importance of the bearers of the intangible barber services. The location, the way in which the shop is planned, the employees and their behaviour as producers and salesmen of the services are all parts of the services, which the consumers buy. Moreover, auxiliary services are offered, and the behaviour of the consumers is to some extent managed by the barber's shop.

CONCLUSIONS

The concepts and models for marketing mix planning of today do not seem applicable to companies in service industries. The case studies, both those presented here and the other studies, too, point out how much more integrated the planning of the marketing variables must be in comparison to the traditional marketing mix models. The 'product' of service firms is extremely complicated, and, therefore, the product development process involves elements normally not considered when discussing the topic.

The bearers of the service, i.e. the resources influencing the accessibility of the service and the personal market communication, are integrated parts of the service as well as possible auxiliary services. This fact makes the planning of these intra-corporate elements of the service offering parts of product development. Furthermore, the service is also shaped by the consumers, thus actively, as an extra-corporate element of the service, having an impact on the marketing planning.

The corporate image seems to be very important to service firms, because the consumers almost always get in touch with the very company offering the service. The image is thus part of the accessibility and one of the very first things the consumers may think about. A favourable image may be vital for the firm's attempts to attract customers, whereas an undesirable image may keep people from even being interested in noticing other means of competition.

Marketing variables, which do not seem to be part of the service, have not been considered in this article. However, I believe that they can be grouped into two main categories labelled *pricing* and *non-interactive market communication,* which mainly consists of advertising, publicity, and other possible means of communication where there is no production/consumption interaction between representatives of the service company and the consumers.

A lot of research has still to be done; e.g. a consumer study, the purpose of which will be to find out whether consumers really evaluate and purchase the same service offerings as indicated by the hypothetical view of the elements of the service put forward in this article and supported by the present case studies.

NOTES AND REFERENCES

1. George, W. R. and Barksdale, H. C. (1974) 'Marketing Activities in the Service Industries'. *Journal of Marketing* (October) 65; Bessom, R. M. and Jackson, D. R., Jr. (1975) 'Service Retailing: A Strategic Marketing Approach'. *Journal of Retailing* (Summer): 84; and Holloway, R. J. and Hancock, R. S. (1973) *Marketing in a Changing Environment.* New York: John Wiley & Sons, pp. 55–56: 'Marketing has not yet become an important function for most service institutions . . . Perhaps we will see the service industries become more marketing-conscious in the decade ahead.'
2. Back, R. (Ed.) (1975) *Erfagruppverksamheten.* Report from Marknadstekniskt Centrum, Stockholm, Sweden, 1976.
3. Levitt, T. (1972) 'Product-line Approach to Service'. *Harvard Business Review* (September–October): 43.
4. Wilson, A. (1975) *Professional Services and the Market Place,* Report from Marknadstekniskt Centrum, No. 4, Stockholm, Sweden, p. 5.
5. There are some efforts to create new concepts, though: for example, the suggestion of a concept of marketing intermediaries in the context of services by Donnelly, J. H., Jr. (1976) 'Marketing Intermediaries in Channels of Distribution for Services'. *Journal of Marketing* (January): 57.
6. Rathmell, J. M. (1966) 'What is Meant by Services?' *Journal of Marketing* (October): 33–34.
7. Levitt, T. (1974) *Marketing for Business Growth.* New York: McGraw-Hill, p. 8.
8. Levitt, T. 'Product-Line Approach to Service', *op, cit.*, pp. 41–42.
9. Judd, R. C. (1964) 'The Case for Redefining Services'. *Journal of Marketing* (January): 59. This definition makes it possible to distinguish between the three main categories of services: the right to possess and use a product (Rented Goods Services); or 2, the customer creation of, repair, or improvement of a product (Owned Goods Services); or 3, no product element but rather an experience or what might be termed experimental possession (Non-Goods Services).' (*ibid.*, p. 59). Marketing of services should only be concerned with services of the first and third category. Owned Goods Services are normally, but not necessarily always, means of competition when marketing goods.

10. Wyckham, R. G., Fitzroy, P. T. and Mandy, G. D. (1975) 'Marketing of Services: An Evaluation of the Theory'. *European Journal of Marketing* No. 1: p. 61.
11. Stanton, W. J. (1975) *Fundamentals of Marketing.* Tokyo: McGraw-Hill Kogakusha, p. 551.
12. George and Barksdale, *op. cit.*, p. 67.
13. Donnelly, J. H. Jr. *op. cit.* Intermediaries replacing the goods-orientated distribution concept suggested by Donnelly are any extra-corporate entity between the producer and the consumers which makes the service available and/or more convenient for the consumers. This certainly is a contribution to service marketing, but he does not, however, include intra-corporate resources with the same purpose, which, in my opinion, is too restricting when expanding the distribution concept in order to help service firms.
14. A very important part of the service firm is the corporate image. Consumers of physical goods seldom have to see or meet the producing company. Normally they deal with wholesalers and retailers. But the consumers of services nearly always get in touch with the service producing firm. This makes the firm part of the accessibility of the service. Therefore, the corporate image of the service firm may be of vital importance to marketing. If the consumers do not consider the image favourable and attractive, they will perhaps not even be interested in noticing the other means of competition of the company.
15. In some cases personal market communication can be viewed solely in a communication context and not as part of the service. The performance of a professional salesman, who is only thought of as a salesman by the customers, and not as part of the accessibility system, may be planned separately in the same context as advertising and other means of impersonal communication. However, in marketing to consumer markets personal communication is rarely just communicating about the service offering; it is almost always also shaping the service itself.
16. See Eiglier, P. and Langeard, E. (1976) *Principes de politique marketing pour les enterprises de services,* L'Institute d'Administration des Enterprises, Université d'Aix-Marseille, Decembre, who make this interesting suggestion.
17. For instance, the *demarketing* concept suggested by Kotler, P. and Levy, S. J. (1971) 'Demarketing, yes, demarketing'. *Harvard Business Review* (November–December) could be applied in this context.

5

What is Meant by Services?

John M. Rathmell

Certain concepts and phrases still exist in conventional marketing thought without their meaning being challenged, even though conditions surrounding their origin have changed. The classification of consumer goods into convenience, shopping, and specialty categories is one example;[1] channels of distribution is another.[2]

The ubiquitous phrase 'goods and services' is a special example. Most marketers have some idea of the meaning of the term 'goods'; these are tangible economic products that are capable of being seen and touched and may or may not be tasted, heard, or smelled.

But 'services' seem to be everything else; and an understanding of them is not clear. For example, convenience foods have 'built-in services'. Are they services in contrast with goods? A business publication refers to a giant retailer's new services: leased beauty salons and restaurants, telephone ordering, and in-home selling. Are these institutional rearrangements really services?

And what about service businesses that do not require heavy investment in plant and equipment? Railroads? Light and power utilities?

MARKETING'S 'GOODS' ORIENTATION

The marketing discipline has a strong 'goods' orientation. In academic courses in marketing, tangible goods are considered, but rarely services to any extent. Yet services represent an area of economic activity that accounts for 30 to 40% of consumer dollar expenditures!

Similarly, many retailers and manufacturers tend to think only in terms of tangible goods; relatively few have broadened their conception of a product to include services. There are exceptions, of course: Sears, Roebuck & Company's entry into the insurance industry, mutual funds, and interior-decorating; the automobile manufacturer's interest in repairing, financing, and leasing.

So, it is refreshing that in recent years American Marketing Association national

Reprinted with permission from *Journal of Marketing*, Vol. 30, October, pp. 32–36

conferences have included sessions on utility and financial marketing, and that the Association also has sponsored special-interest conferences in these areas of marketing.

Also, others have prescribed usage of terms rightfully marketing's responsibility. Thus, the US Department of Agriculture continues to include food-processing costs as a marketing expense, even though this practice was challenged many years ago.[3] The US Department of Commerce has assumed responsibility for blocking out the 'services' category, and thus has made a useful contribution to our knowledge of economic activity. However, does its distinction between 'goods and services' hold up from the marketing viewpoint?[4] How about the following distinctions?

- Food and clothing are goods; housing is a service.
- Automobiles are goods; airline tickets represent a purchase of a service.
- Fuel oil is a good; gas is a service.
- Religious and welfare activities contributions are services.

GOODS AND SERVICES DISTINGUISHED

A useful distinction can be made between (1) *rented-goods services*; (2) *owned-goods services*; and (3) *non-goods services*. Also we might think of *marketed services* as market transactions by an enterprise or entrepreneur where the object is other than the transfer of ownership of a tangible commodity.[5]

One implicit distinction is to consider a good to be a noun and a service a verb – a good is a thing and a service is an act. The former is an object, an article, a device, or a material, whereas the latter is a deed, a performance, or an effort. When a good is purchased, the buyer acquires an asset; when a service is purchased, the buyer incurs an expense.

Another test to distinguish a good from a service is the nature of the product's utility. Does the utility for the consumer lie in the physical characteristics of the product, or in the nature of the action or performance?

Applying this test, there are very few pure products and pure services. The satisfaction, or utility, deriving from a work of art, such as a painting or sculpture, lies solely in the good itself. The benefit, or utility, arising from legal counsel proceeds exclusively from the service rendered. In the former, no act is performed; in the latter, no good is involved.

Apart from these extremes, most goods, whether consumer or industrial, require supporting services in order to be useful; most services require supporting goods in order to be useful.

GOODS–SERVICES CONTINUUM

Economic products lie along a goods–service continuum, with pure goods at one extreme and pure services at the other, but with most of them falling between these two extremes.

This mixed characteristic is suggested by both Table 1 and Figure 1, even though quite broad categories are considered. Some are primarily goods with service support, whereas others are primarily services with goods support. Most goods are a complex of goods and facilitating services; most services are a complex of services and facilitating goods.

Table 1. Personal consumption expenditures by type of product[a]

	1959 %	1964 %
Food and tobacco:		
Goods	100.0	100.0
Services	0.0	0.0
Clothing, accessories, and jewelry:		
Goods	89.1	89.8
Services	10.9	10.2
Personal care:		
Goods	55.3	56.8
Services	44.7	43.2
Housing:		
Goods	0.0	0.0
Services	100.0	100.0
Household operation:		
Goods	59.1	57.9
Services	40.9	42.1
Medical care and death expenses:		
Goods	23.3	21.4
Services	76.7	78.6
Personal business:		
Goods	0.0	0.0
Services	100.0	100.0
Transportation:		
Goods	75.5	77.2
Services	24.5	22.8
Recreation:		
Goods	66.4	68.5
Services	33.6	31.5
Private education and research:		
Goods	0.0	0.0
Services	100.0	100.0
Religious and welfare activities:		
Goods	0.0	0.0
Services	100.0	100.0
Foreign travel and remittances *net*:		
Goods	50.3	39.5
Services	49.7	60.5
Total personal consumption expenditures:		
Goods	61.4	59.2
Services	38.6	40.8

[a]Derived from *Survey of Current Business*, Vol. 45 (November, 1965), pp. 20–23.

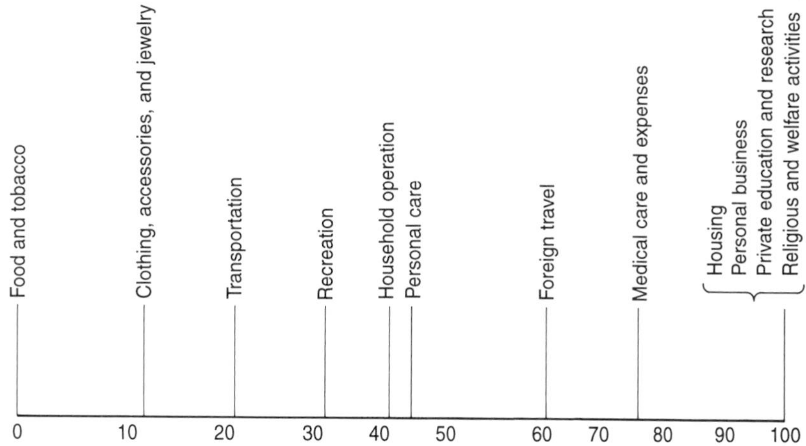

Figure 1. Per cent of major classes of personal consumption expenditures allocated to services, 1964. (Source: *Survey of Current Business*, Vol. 45 (November, 1965), pp. 20–23).

This mixed nature of most economic products is well illustrated by the leasing transaction. If a product is purchased, it is a good; but if it is rented or leased, the rentee or lessee acquires a service.

Yet for the service to have any meaning whatever a goods component must also be present. Service would contribute time and place utility; the good would be the physical commodity made available and the service would be the act of making it available for a prescribed period of time as an alternative to outright purchase.

MARKETING CHARACTERISTICS OF SERVICES

The basic question is – *What are the marketing characteristics of services?* Here are 13 answers:

1. Unlike a good, where monetary values are stated in terms of a price, services are more likely to be expressed as *rates, fees, admissions, charges, tuition, contributions, interest, and the like.*
2. In many types of service transactions, *the buyer is a client rather than a customer of the seller*; the client, when buying a service, figuratively or literally places himself 'in the hands' of the seller of the service. Consider, for example, the relationship between the student and the college, the patient and the hospital or physician, the passenger and the carrier. The buyer is not free to use the service as he wishes, as would be the case in the purchase of a good; he must abide by certain prescripts laid down by the seller in order for the service to make any contribution.[6]
3. The various marketing systems in the services category have taken on *highly differentiated characteristics.* Although contrasts do exist in those marketing systems that have evolved for different types of physical goods, they are primarily differences of degree. In the case of services, the marketing of recreation bears

little resemblance to the marketing of medical service. As additional examples, there is no apparent relationship between the marketing system for shoe-repair service and for hospital service.

4. Since services are acts or processes and are produced as they are consumed, they *cannot be inventoried,* and there can be no merchant middleman since only 'direct' sales are possible. In a number of instances, agent intermediaries are utilized in the marketing of services: insurance and travel agents, for example.
5. The question may be raised as to *the economic nature* of certain products in the services category, for example, payments to charitable and religious bodies and non-profit educational institutions. Are the church on the corner, the college on the hill, and the United Fund Agency downtown economic entities on the supply side? Certainly they compete for the consumer's dollar.
6. There appears to be a *more formal* or *professional approach to the marketing of many services* (not all, by any means) – for example, financial, medical, legal, and educational services.
7. Because services cannot be mass-produced, *standards cannot be precise.* Although service producers may be standardized, their actual implementation will vary from buyer to buyer. Perhaps there will be a standardization of services through the increasing use of service technology at the expense of personalized service, especially in medicine and education; and this would mean that services will follow goods from custom to mass production and standardization.[7]
8. *'Price-making' practices vary greatly* within the services category. Utility and transportation rates are rigidly controlled by public agencies; interest rates display characteristics of price leadership; and some service charges are established on the basis of what the traffic will bear.
9. Economic concepts of supply and demand and costs are difficult to apply to a service because of its *intangible nature.* Moreover, values of some services are difficult to fix. What is the value of the service of a lawyer or a physician in a losing cause as compared with a successful one?
10. *Most fringe benefits* take the form of services: pensions, insurance, unemployment benefits, eye and dental care, psychiatric service; seldom are benefits in the form of goods (such as turkeys at Christmas).[8] If benefits are created by the employer, in a marketing sense he is selling a product (in lieu of higher wages) to a market segment, his own employees. If the service is created by an outside specialist, such as a life insurance company, the employer is an agent (in a marketing sense) between the seller–creator of the service and the buyer–consumer.
11. There appears to be *limited concentration in the services sector of the economy.* There are few service chains; carriers and utilities are regulated.
12. Until recently, *service firms failed to differentiate between the production and marketing of services.* Performance was equivalent to marketing the service.
13. In the case of services, *symbolism derives from performance* rather than from possession.

Industrial services

The significance of industrial services in the economy is indicated in the data in Table 2.

Table 2. Magnitude of some industrial services[a]

Type of service	Gross and personal expenditures	Industrial expenditures
Engineering and other professional services		$2 966 000 000
Business services (not elsewhere classified)		$8 492 000 000
Corporate sales: telephone, telegraph, etc.	$10 929 000 000	
Less personal consumption expenditures: telephone, telegraph, etc.	−4 720 000 000	$6 209 000 000
Corporate sales: electric and gas utilities	$20 197 000 000	
Less personal consumption expenditures: electricity and gas	−8 422 000 000	$11 775 000 000
Corporate sales: railroads	$10 382 000 000	
Less personal consumption expenditures: railway (including commutation)	−454 000 000	$9 928 000 000

[a] *Survey of Current Business*, Vol. 44 (July, 1964), pp. 16 and 28. Net figures represent corporate sales not only to business but also to government, institutions, agriculture, etc.

Services of government

The greatest marketer of services in the United States is government. The public sector is becoming a major supplier of that which was once the domain of private enterprises or private institutions. Consider Medicare, urban renewal and slum clearance, public parks and recreational areas, public higher education, and publicly-owned utilities.

Moreover, private sellers of many services are much more controlled by public agencies than are private sellers of goods. It is not much of an exaggeration to say that the mixed economy is divided on a goods–service axis. It is conceivable that most consumer services (excluding personal-care services) eventually will be purchased from public bodies, whereas consumer goods will continue to be purchased from private enterprise.

THE SERVICE CHALLENGE FOR MARKETING

Table 1 shows services are a major component in the economy. McKittrick sees them not only diverting income flow away from manufacturing but also pressuring wages upward because of their relatively greater price increases.[9] Others have cited the lower efficiency in the personal-services sector because of the lower quality of labor in services production, as compared with goods production, and because of the limited opportunities for mechanization.[10]

The distribution of goods is within the province of marketing. But is there the same consensus regarding amusements, health services, and hotels? Should they be treated vertically, within the respective industries and professions – or horizontally, under the marketing umbrella?

In this connection: How are the public services marketed? Are there public marketing institutions and procedures? When is the transaction completed? What is the price? What are the terms of sale? The recent promotion campaign to sell the voluntary provision in Medicare to 20 million eligible citizens represents one of the first major attempts to market a government service.

CONCLUSION

The increasing percentage of consumer expenditures allocated to intangibles deserves special attention. This is especially true of the marketing of services by public agencies.

But what are services? Certainly any comprehensive approach to the study of services marketing must begin at the conceptual level.

NOTES AND REFERENCES

1. Holton, R. H. (1958) 'The Distinctions Between Convenience Goods, Shopping Goods, and Specialty Goods'. *Journal of Marketing* **23** (July): 53–56, and (1959) 'What is Really Meant by "Specialty Goods"?' *Journal of Marketing* **24** (July): 64–66; Luck, D. J. (1959) 'On the Nature of Specialty Goods'. *Journal of Marketing* **24** (July): 61–64.
2. McVey, P. (1960) 'Are Channels of Distribution What the Textbooks Say?' *Journal of Marketing* **24** (January): 61–65.
3. Beckman, T. N. and Buzzell, R. D. (1955) 'What is the Marketing Margin for Agricultural Products?' *Journal of Marketing* **20** (October): 166–168.
4. *Survey of Current Business* (1964) **44** (July): 16.
5. Judd, R. C. (1964) 'The Case for Redefining Services'. *Journal of Marketing* **28** (January): 58–59, at p. 59.
6. For an interesting discussion of relations between clients and client-serving organizations see Bidwell, C. E. and Vreeland, R. S. (1963) 'Authority and Control in Client-serving Organizations'. *The Sociological Quarterly* **4** (Summer): 231–242.
7. Regan, W. J. (1963) 'The Service Revolution'. *Journal of Marketing* **27** (July): 57–62, at pp. 61–62.
8. 'Why Union Eyes Are on Fringes'. (1964) *Business Week* (September 12): 60.
9. McKittrick, J. B. (1962) 'The Nature of the Involvement of Marketing Management in the Profit Failure'. In *Marketing Precision and Executive Action* (C. H. Hindersman, Ed.). Chicago: American Marketing Association, pp. 75–88, at pp. 81–82.
10. 'Why Service Workers are Less Productive'. (1964) *Business Week* (November 14): 156.

Section II

The Service Experience

In this section of the reader we present some contemporary work considering elements of the service experience. It has been argued that services are no more than an experience, and as such the management of the service experience is the essence of service management. In the first article by Grove, Fisk and Bitner (1992) the authors present a means of understanding experiences based upon a drama perspective referred to as dramaturgy. This approach uses a theatrical metaphor to explore elements of the consumer's service experience. After identifying a number of parallels between the service product and drama, which includes the existence of roles, scripts and actors in both settings, the authors go on to consider how the drama metaphor can be used to investigate the delivery of the service product. By focusing upon four critical dimensions – the actors, the setting, the audience and the performance – this article is able to demonstrate that the metaphor can be meaningfully extended to the development of service strategy. The attraction of this work is the holistic nature of the framework which allows for an informed analysis of the consumer's service experience. It also presents opportunities for both a new descriptive vocabulary and a means of classifying elements of the service product. In total, this approach has many attractions not least the ease of access to service terminology. However, the authors also provide a caution. First, that the dramaturgy approach does not have universal application and second, that the notion of acting can sometimes be confused with insincerity. It may be, for instance, that total rehearsal of the performance removes an important part of experience such as variation, customisation and the need to be individually responsive. Continuing the metaphor, why pay more for first and last nights if all performances are the same?

There has been an almost implicit acceptance that services are 'riskier' than physical goods due to their intangibility and the nature of their delivery. But when looking for evidence of this in the large perceived risk and uncertainty literature there appears to be almost no mention of it. The article by Murray and Schlacter (1990) presents for the first time evidence that services do indeed invoke heightened perceptions of risk and perceptions of variability. The article draws upon perceived risk literature associated with physical products to present a series of eight hypotheses which are then sequentially examined through empirical work based upon an experimental methodology. The importance of this work is in the rigorous examination of risk as applied to service products and in the presentation of the conclusions. The first outcome of the research results is that risk reduction strategies associated with service products must be focused upon employees, encouraging continuity of personal relationships and thereby reducing the perception of variability. Second, that the methodology adopted allows for some operationalisation of 'goods' and 'services' constructs and finally that there exists differentiation among service products in consumers minds, i.e. that they are not a generic class.

The theme of differential responses by consumers is continued in the paper by Hui and Bateson (1991). The authors explore in some detail components of the service encounter in order to explain the impact of the physical setting upon consumer evaluations. The article concerns the role of perceived control which is described as the perceived ability to demonstrate competence, superiority and mastery over the environment. It is argued that this is a crucial variable in mediating the consumer's emotional and behavioural response to both the physical environment in which a service is delivered and the service personnel. The authors use two situational variables to pursue their hypotheses – consumer density (crowding) and consumer choice (degree of discretion) – to investigate the evaluation of the encounter and to assess approach–avoidance response. For those with a quantitative leaning the mechanics of the analysis are worth the effort in terms of understanding the basis of the proposed model. For those without such a leaning the article presents an integrated model which supports the contention that perceived control does have explanatory power in explaining the effects of consumer choice and consumer density on consumer evaluations of the service. The article ends with a discussion of the possible managerial responses to the conclusions drawn and an agenda for research concentrated upon the investigation of pleasurable versus unpleasurable experiences.

The paper by Gabbott and Hogg (1994) is intended as a general review of the main issues facing researchers and practitioners in locating the study of service consumption. Its inclusion here is to present evidence that consumers' experiences are highly dependent upon how and what they perceive. This is achieved by taking the defining characteristics of services and examining their impact upon information search, comparison and evaluation. The general issues are then used to provide some indication of the practical problems facing consumers when interacting with service products and in evaluating their service experiences. In the first section it is proposed that objective prepurchase information about services is difficult to obtain and there is a natural tendency for consumers to look to others to provide detail on the service experience as a source of both additional and verification information. In the second section the article re-emphasises the importance of peripheral or tangible cues used to approximate missing product information. Finally the article turns to the problem of evaluation, specifically the issue of credence and the role of experience in building credence. In conclusion the article provides a discussion of both consumer and service provider responses to the identified issues.

The final paper in this section, by Bitner, Booms and Mohr (1994), considers one of the most important elements in the service experience for consumers: the service employee. The basis of the article is that in order to fully understand the service encounter behaviour needs to be analysed from both the employee's and the customer's perspective in order to establish the events and types of behaviours which contribute to satisfaction and dissatisfaction. Apart from tackling the immensely complex area of interpersonal behaviour the authors also adopt an unusual but highly effective methodology. The authors present a theoretical perspective based upon how people use role expectation and scripts to formalise their behaviours, pointing to the importance of both as variables in explaining differences in expectations between customers and employees. Similarly the existence of self-serving attribution bias would also partially explain differences in perceptions of the encounter between groups. The critical incident methodology highlights a number of important differences in perception between the encounter participants and focuses upon the issue of 'problem customers' both in terms of their impact upon staff and their own encounter. The article finishes with a good discussion of the managerial implications of the research which points to the central importance of front-line staff in mediating the consumer's experience.

CONTENTS

6

Dramatizing the Service Experience: A Managerial Approach

Stephen J. Grove, Raymond P. Fisk and Mary Jo Bitner

INTRODUCTION

The growth of the services economy has been widely documented and discussed. Seventy-one percent of the US GNP is produced by service industries (US Bureau of Census, 1988). Furthermore, 'service sector jobs are now a soaring seventy-two percent of all US employment' (Heskett, 1986, p. 3). The expanding interest in services marketing and management is partially related to economic trends such as the deregulation of various service industries, the growth of franchising, the relaxation of professional association standards, and computerization and technological innovation (Lovelock, 1984, 1988).

Services managers have recognized that they face several challenges unique to the nature of service products. First, supply and demand management is much more difficult than in physical goods industries (Lovelock, 1984; Sasser, 1976; Zeithaml, Parasuraman and Berry, 1985). Second, quality control in services marketing is elusive due to the inability to standardize and imperfect human performance (Bateson, 1989; Bitner and Zeithaml, 1988; Brown and Swartz, 1989; Parasuraman, Zeithaml and Berry, 1988; Zeithaml, Berry and Parasuraman, 1988; Ziethaml, Parasuraman and Berry, 1985). Third, it is difficult to calculate the costs of services, which makes pricing services a formidable task (Dearden, 1978; Guiltinan, 1987; Zeithaml, Parasuraman and Berry, 1985). Other contemporary services marketing issues include concerns over how to organize service systems (Kingman-Brundage, 1989; Shostack, 1984a, 1984b, 1987), how to portray the service encounter (Czepiel, Solomon and Surprenant, 1985; Solomon *et al.*, 1985), how to understand the service environment (Baker, 1987), how to personalize services (Surprenant and Solomon, 1985, 1987) and how to incorporate internal marketing strategies (Grönroos, 1985, 1990).

The search for services marketing generalizations has lagged behind the investigation of specific service industry issues. In 1985, only 17% (340 of 1991) of

Reprinted with permission from *Advances in Services Marketing and Management*, Vol. 1, pp 91–121.

the American Marketing Association's services marketing bibliography (Fisk and Tansuhaj, 1985) addressed general conceptual insights while 83% was industry specific. In a recent computerized expansion of the services marketing bibliography (Fisk, Tansuhaj and Crosby, 1988) the general conceptual literature had eroded to slightly less than 15% (574 of 3910) of total services marketing literature. In short, conceptualizations and frameworks are needed that demonstrate common characteristics across services, distinguish services from physical goods marketing and address what Shostack (1984a) has termed 'descriptive language problems'. In addition, new taxonomies are needed that serve to summarize existing knowledge and provide direction for future research (e.g. Murphy and Enis, 1986). Also, conceptualizations and frameworks are needed that can facilitate the understanding and control of services marketing.

In recent years, several marketing scholars have acknowledged the 'drama-related' dimensions associated with services marketing. For instance, Lovelock (1981) argued that services marketers must perform several 'roles', among which are the services marketer as 'dramatist' and 'choreographer'. Berry (1981) detailed the efficacy of the Disney Corporation's practice of using show business terms such as 'cast member', 'onstage' and 'show' to describe its various operations at Disneyland and Walt Disney World. In addition, Grönroos (1985) has suggested that services are essentially 'performances', a sentiment echoed by Berry, Zeithaml and Parasuraman (1985) who argue that 'the manner in which the service is performed can be a crucial component of the service from the consumer's point of view' (p. 46). Others (Lovelock *et al.*, 1981; Booms and Bitner, 1982) have stressed the often subtle, yet pervasive influence of a service's physical 'setting'. In fact, 'it plays much the same role as packaging does for manufactured goods' (Booms and Bitner, 1982, p. 39). In short, many 'drama' aspects of services marketing can be recognized and ultimately managed.

The goal of this article is to demonstrate that (1) the drama metaphor is applicable to the marketing management of service organizations and (2) the drama metaphor framework can be utilized to enhance the understanding and control of services marketing and management. The drama metaphor is uniquely suited to managing services marketing phenomena because it captures the dynamics of the human interactions that occur. First, the drama metaphor is presented and explained. Second, an approach to dramatizing the services marketing mix that emerges from a '7 Ps' approach to services (Booms and Bitner, 1981) is presented. Third, two strategic models are developed that apply the drama tools, and service industry examples are explicated to clarify the applications of the strategic models. Fourth, strategic guidelines for services managers are presented. Finally, several contributions to services marketing thought, as well as several cautions concerning the drama framework, are discussed.

METAPHOR

A metaphor is described by Nisbet (1969, p. 4) as a way of proceeding from the known to the unknown by transferring the qualities of familiar objects to objects that are unfamiliar due to their remoteness or complexity. Poets, philosophers, socio-linguists and others have long recognized the power of the metaphor as a descriptive and analytical device. By presenting a symbolically rich message that evokes from its receiver details or 'chunks' of information lacking in a literal translation of the message, the metaphor creates a vivid mental image. As such, the metaphor often succeeds at capturing and communicating the experiential and/or processual characteristics of many phenomena that resist comprehension through logic and words alone. Whether it is applying the concept of a 'machine' to an organization structure, categorizing stock market investors as 'bulls' and 'bears', or depicting the researcher as a 'detective', the metaphor moves beyond the literal to describe and connect unfamiliar topics (Ortony 1975), generate analysis and hypotheses (Morgan, 1980) and, in some instances, serve as the basis for entire schools of thought (Arndt, 1985; Morgan, 1980). The next sections explore the drama metaphor, marketing metaphors and drama as a marketing metaphor for services.

The drama metaphor

The proposition that human behavior is drama has a rich historical tradition. Centuries ago, William Shakespeare (1600) accentuated the theatrical nature of human behavior when he wrote, 'All the world's a stage, and all the men and women merely players.' More recently, writers such as Kenneth Burke (1945, 1950, 1968), Erving Goffman (1959, 1967, 1974), R. S. Perinbanayagam (1974), Gregory Stone (1962) and a host of others have described the dramatic aspects of social interaction. Implicit in these observations is the perspective that people are symbol users who interact with others based on the meanings assigned to different features present at a behavioral setting.

The drama metaphor does not 'seek to discover or to impute to human behavior causal kinds of relations ... the concern is simply to describe the process of human behaving' (Brissett and Edgley, 1975, p. 4). In a manner similar to that of actors in a theatrical production, people utilize various dramatic devices in their everyday interactions to convey desired information. As such, any object or action, including properties of the physical environment, language, gestures, expressions, etc., may be used to influence another's perception and assessment of an interactive situation and, ultimately, his/her response to it. Just as one's understanding of a movie or theatrical production develops as the plot unfolds, one's definitions of reality emerge as actions occur and meanings are assigned to the many signs and symbols found in the behavioral setting. Social reality, then, is not simply like drama – it *is* drama insofar as it is a communication and symbolic discourse that involves articulation, definition and interactive processes (Perinbanayagam, 1974, p. 533).

Within the discipline of sociology the metaphor of human behavior as drama serves as the basis for the general school of thought called 'dramaturgy'. Perhaps best articulated through the networks of Goffman (1959, 1967, 1974), dramaturgy has spawned a depiction of social behavior as theatrical 'performances' among 'actors' who present themselves and their actions in such a way as to create a desired 'impression' one 'gives' and 'gives off' before an 'audience', in what is termed 'the front region'. Through the 'rehearsal' of performances away from the audience's view in the 'back region', aspects of the social 'actors' presentation are worked out, so a general coherence exists among 'the settings, appearance and manner' (Goffman,

1959, p. 25) that ultimately contributes to an authentic, sincere and/or believable performance.

In essence, the drama metaphor argues that the development and maintenance of a definition of an interaction relies on the audience's input as well as the actors' presentation. Through all of this, performances are viewed as tenuous, fragile processes, which can be disrupted by even minor mishaps such as unintended gestures or slips of behavior.

Marketing metaphors

Marketers have only recently begun to explore the use of metaphors as conceptual tools (Arndt, 1985; Zikmund, 1982; Stern, 1988), despite the fact that the use of metaphors is common in marketing (Zikmund, 1982). For example, phenomena such as the evolution of retailing, the pattern of a product's sales over time, the path that a product takes as it moves to market and the desired combination of marketing variables are vividly and compactly represented by the metaphors of a '*wheel* of retailing', a 'product *life cycle*', a '*channel* of distribution' and a 'marketing *mix*', respectively. A recent metaphor, which has gained significant popularity within the business literature, is the depiction of the marketing enterprise as warfare (e.g. Duro and Sandstrom, 1987; Kotler and Singh, 1981; Michaelson, 1987; Ries and Trout, 1986).

Drama as a marketing metaphor for services

Several parallels can be easily drawn between the concerns of a services manager and the proposition that drama is a metaphor for human behavior. For example, both are concerned with the strategies and tactics employed by participants to create and maintain a desirable impression before an audience, and both recognize that one way to accomplish this is through the careful management of 'expressions given and given off' by the actors and the physical setting of their behavior. Paralleling the insights of many services marketing scholars, Goffman (1959) observes that performances serve

> ...mainly to express characteristics of the task that is performed and not the characteristics of the performers. Thus, one finds that service personnel, whether in profession, bureaucracy, business, or craft enliven their manner with movements which express proficiency and integrity, but whether this manner conveys about them, often its major purpose is to establish a favorable definition of their services or product (p. 77).

Can the drama metaphor provide a way to understand and control service experiences? The remainder of this article argues that due to numerous similarities between the characteristics of service experiences and the elements comprising dramatic analysis, depicting services via the drama metphor is a logical and stimulating exercise that provides both a vocabulary and a conceptual framework for communicating and understanding services marketing and management.

DRAMATIZING THE SERVICES MARKETING MIX

The notion of the marketing mix refers to the tools or activities that are essential to marketing and that enable an enterprise to communicate with and satisfy its target markets. More specifically, the 'mix' term is intended to convey the importance of blending these tools in various desirable combinations. Traditionally, the marketing mix has been conceived as consisting of '4 Ps': *product, price, promotion* and *place* (McCarthy, 1960).

Booms and Bitner (1981) argued for the expansion of the marketing mix for services beyond the original '4 Ps'. Because services are often produced and consumed simultaneously and because customers frequently interact directly with the organization's personnel, the service manager has additional controllable elements with which to communicate and satisfy customers. Booms and Bitner (1981) proposed that these additional variables should be recognized in a broader marketing mix for services that captures the social and physical context of services by adding three additional 'Ps' (p. 48):

- *Participants* – 'All human actors who play a part in service delivery and thus influence the buyer's perceptions' (personnel and other customers).
- *Physical evidence* – 'The environment in which the service is assembled and where the firm and the customer interact.'
- *Process of service assembly* – 'The actual procedures, mechanisms, and flow of activities by which the service is delivered.'

It has become generally accepted that the services marketing mix is different from the traditional marketing mix. Cowell (1985) included Booms and Bitner's '3 New Ps' in his services marketing textbook. Meanwhile, Magrath (1986) has proposed '3 New Ps' for services marketing that are quite similar (personnel, physical facilities and process management) to those of Booms and Bitner. Prus and Frisby (1987) have also advocated two similar new Ps: people and process. In addition, continued support for the '3 New Ps' for services marketing has come from Bitner and Zeithaml (1988). The drama metaphor helps clarify the unique marketing management significance of the '3 New Ps' as proposed by Booms and Bitner.

Major drama concepts are analogous to the '3 New Ps' and can be utilized to operationalize their management. As shown in Table 1, the term 'participants' is analogous to the theatrical terms of 'actors' and 'audience', 'physical evidence' is analogous, to the 'setting' and 'process of service assembly' is analogous to the 'performance'. As with many marketing management concepts, these drama concepts embody a strong change agent orientation. Moreover, Bell (1981) has

Table 1. Drama analogues to 'Three New Ps'

Three new Ps	Drama
Participants	Actors/Audience
Physical evidence	Setting
Process of service assembly	Performance

argued that services are uniquely suited to remixing the marketing mix during the consumption of the service. The most easily remixed elements of the services marketing mix are the '3 New Ps': *participants, physical evidence* and *process of service assembly*. The drama perspective provides a framework uniquely suited for remixing these '3 New Ps' of the services marketing mix.

But will the use of these drama analogues facilitate operationalizing the management of the '3 New Ps?' Two strategic models will assist in the investigation of this question.

STRATEGIC MODELS

In approaching the service experience as drama four critical drama elements need examination: (1) the actors (personnel) whose presence and actions define the service; (2) the audience (customers) to whom the service is directed; (3) the physical setting in which the experience occurs; and (4) the service performance itself. Each of these elements represents an essential component that contributes to the service experience. Drama is the product of actors and the enactment of their roles, the scenery and staging of the action, and the audience and its involvement; the service experience is defined by similar features. First, strategic models that incorporate these drama elements are presented. Second, each drama element is examined in detail, which includes consideration of how these elements are commonly manifested in various service industries and examples of how specific service organizations have distinguished themselves by emphasizing one or more of the drama elements.

The service experience as drama

Figure 1 presents a generic model of the service experience as drama. The broadest level of the model is the setting. The setting is basically the background to the model

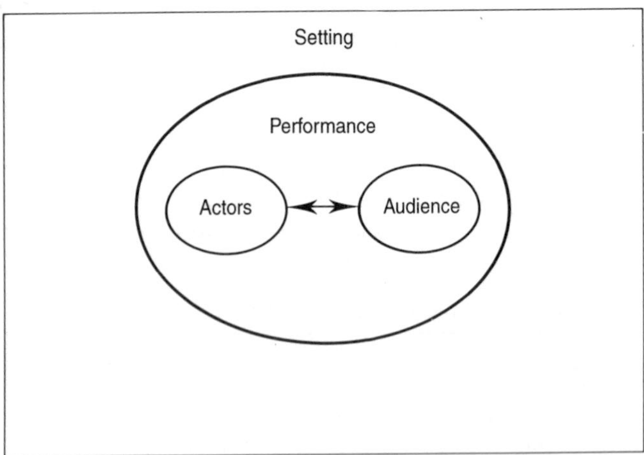

Figure 1. The service experience as drama.

and it encompasses all the dimensions embodied in the service's physical environment. The remaining components of the model represent the foreground. As depicted, the foreground concerns people and represents the social context of the model. The actors and audience are positioned at the model's center to emphasize that a service performance is largely a product of their interaction within the context of a particular setting. The bi-directional arrow between actors and audience represents the interdependence of the two entities in determining the service performance. The service performance is a unique type of restricted marketing exchange (Bagozzi, 1975) in which the actors' offering is both a response to and determinant of the audience behavior and vice versa.

While any service that involves face-to-face contact between the service provider(s) and the customer(s) within a market-controlled environment can be represented by Figure 1 (e.g. hospitals, hotels, restaurants, airlines, etc.), it is the strategic combination of these components that characterizes the nature of a particular service. For example, one hotel may strive to create an upscale service experience through careful attention to the setting's physical evidence and atmospherics, well-rehearsed scripts on the part of the actors, and a concerted effort to monitor and control the audience. Another hotel might seek a low-priced, 'no frills' service performance by reducing or altering its emphasis on the theatrical elements.

The service performance cube

Figure 2 presents a model that depicts the relative importance of the three theatrical elements comprising a service performance using a three-dimensional plus – minus structure (a '+' indicates more importance while a '−' indicates less importance). In this context, importance refers to the degree of significance that can be attributed to the drama element. The 'service performance' embraces and is a function of the

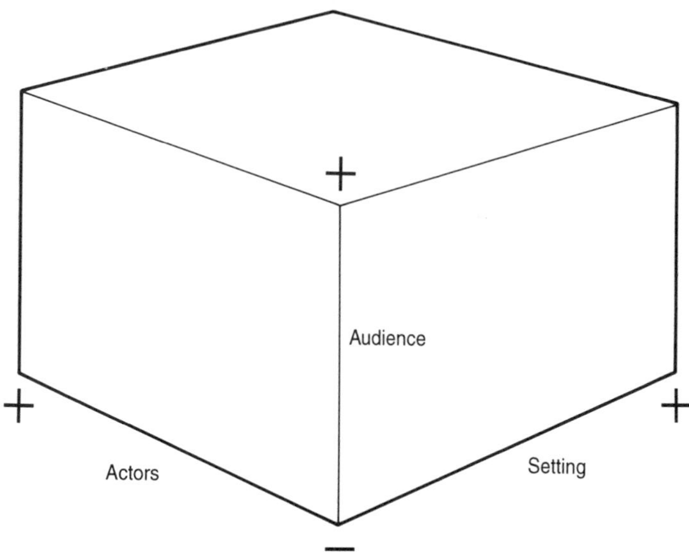

Figure 2. The service performance cube.

dimensions of actors, audience and setting. Hence, the management of these three theatrical elements affects the nature of the service performance. Each part of the 'service performance cube' can be managed before the performance begins. For any given service organization, managers may employ varying degrees of emphasis on the three dimensions of the cube. For example, until recently, women giving birth were served by hospitals that delivered babies in sterile settings, without the father present and with the physician in complete control of the delivery. Women demanded better 'settings' and more involvement of family 'audience' members and the health care system slowly responded. Today, a woman is more likely to deliver her baby by natural childbirth methods in a hospital's 'birthing' room resplendent with reminders of home. In addition, the father is typically present and assisting during the delivery. This contemporary version of childbirth represents a 'dramatically' different position on the service performance cube than the older method.

While variations in the relative importance of the various theatrical elements may be recognized within specific service industries, it is possible to identify modal responses to the elements that distinguish one service industry from another. For example, restaurants typically must attend to the potential impact of each of the theatrical components of a service experience while most motion picture theaters – despite requiring similar attention to the setting and audience components – probably are not as directly affected by the impact of the actor component (ticket takers, ushers, etc).

The 'service performance cube' offers potential insights into the positioning of services organizations. An organization may 'position' itself in terms of its emphasis on actors, audience or setting. Moreover, the 'service performance cube' can be used to facilitate identifying market niches for new services or adaptations of existing services.

The following discussion further explicates the drama elements of actors, audience, setting and performance and provides numerous specific service organization examples to clarify the many ways these drama elements can be manifested.

The actors

Just as the success of a theatrical production relies largely on the expertise and credibility of those on stage, a satisfying service experience for many services is determined largely by the service's contact personnel. From the audience's (consumer's) perspective, those delivering the service may represent the service itself; their 'technical skills' (what they do) and their 'functional skills' (how they do it) are observed and evaluated and become prime indicators of the service's quality (Grönroos, 1985). Consequently, just as theatrical performers must attend to a variety of considerations in the interest of a successful show, service 'actors' are obliged to attend to several critical dimensions of their role in the service's performance to foster the proper impression or desired definitions of the service.

Among the dramaturgical dimensions of the contact personnel that are particularly relevant for a service's evaluation are the actors': (1) appearance and manner, termed 'personal front' by Goffman (1959); (2) skill in playing their parts or performing their routines in the service's delivery; and (3) commitment to the service performance. The actors' appearance and manner consist of such personal information as dress, grooming and demeanor, which help to form the identity, mood and/or attitudes conveyed to others (Solomon, 1985; Stone, 1962). Attention to these aspects of the service personnel's presentation is one means of 'tangibilizing' a service (Berry, 1980) and can help establish consumer expectations prior to a service's performance. The skill displayed by the actors in fulfilling their service roles refers to a myriad of considerations such as competence, courtesy, knowledge, reliability and communicative abilities, all of which have been identifed as important determinants of service quality (Parasuraman, Zeithaml and Berry, 1985). How the contact personnel perform their parts in the service production contributes to the consumer's total impression of the service reality (Shostack, 1977; Zeithaml, Parasuraman and Berry, 1985).

Intimately related to one's skillful service role enactment is one's level of commitment to the service's performance. Commitment may be evidenced by the actor's determination to learn his/her part correctly, to sustain the service's impression even under conditions of personal duress and to recognize, plan for and respond to the audience's particular needs or desires (Bitner, Booms and Tetreault, 1990). Motivation for such a commitment may be the by-product of a service organization's 'internal marketing' effort (Berry, 1980; Grönroos, 1985; Sasser and Arbeit, 1978), which instills a consumer-orientation and stresses the sanctity of producing a quality service. When combined, these three dimensions of the actors' presentation affect the audience's perception of the service delivery process, a determination that ultimately influences the assessment of the service's excellence (Berry, 1980; Parasuraman, Zeithaml and Berry, 1985; Sasser, Olsen and Wyckoff, 1978; Surprenant and Solomon, 1985).

Since services typically vary with respect to the degree of direct personal contact between the service personnel and the consumer, the relative importance of the actors and their attention to dramaturgical dimensions will vary commensurately. Service organizations such as hospitals, restaurants, resorts and the like, which offer a high degree of contact between the service employees and consumers, are particularly affected by the actors' dramaturgical acumen. Services, such as public utility companies or automatic transfer machines (ATMs), which involve little or no direct personal contact between the service and the customer are obviously less affected. Furthermore, it is likely that the actors' impact will be felt more greatly in those services characterized by repeated contact with the customer, such as banking or medical services, or those services in which there is little or no other contact with the organization other than interaction with an employee at the organization's boundary, such as is the case with express mail companies and travel and insurance agencies. It is also quite important to recognize the potentially great impact of the actors' dramaturgical presentation in those services in which the contact personnel have discretion in determining the nature of the service and how it is delivered, such as education, medical services, legal services and the like. In each of these circumstances, the actors are likely to be scrutinized closely by their audience as evidence tangibilizing the service and determining its excellence.

It is apparent from this discussion that many industries exist in which the actors or contact personnel are inherently important in determining customer perceptions of the service. For example, a patient's evaluation of medical service received in a hospital is closely tied to perceptions of physician and nursing staff technical expertise as well as the functional, or process quality, of interactions with these same contact personnel. In the case of hospitals, it is almost impossible to separate the patient's evaluation of the service from his/her perceptions of the actors who deliver it. Indeed, as far as the patient is concerned, the actors, doctors, nurses, etc.) *are* the service.

In other industries, the importance of the actor may not be as obvious as it is with medical services. In such industries, an opportunity for an organization often arises to distinguish itself from its competitors by emphasizing the role of contact personnel in determining service quality. This is a notion discussed by Berry, Parasuraman and Zeithaml (1988) as the 'people factor'. Scandinavian Airlines System (SAS) has successfully implemented this approach and has gained competitive strength by stressing the personal service component of the marketing mix. SAS has accomplished this by allowing its employees far greater discretion than is typical in the airline industry (Carlzon, 1987). SAS employees are trained to 'serve the customer' and are given almost free reign to interpret what that means for each customer. The result is more satisfied customers and happier employees. Clearly, SAS has demonstrated the importance of the actor component of the services marketing mix.

The audience

A second strategic component in the depiction of the service experience as drama is the audience in whose presence the service is delivered. Since the customer must be present for many services to occur (e.g. airlines, dental treatment, etc.), one of the often cited characteristics of services is the inseparability of production from consumption (Berry, 1980; Judd, 1964; Lovelock, 1981, 1983; Regan, 1963; Shostack, 1977). As Berry, Zeithaml and Parasuraman (1985) contend, for many services, customers are 'in the factory' where they observe and 'consume' the service firsthand as it is delivered.

The condition of inseparability underscores the impact an audience may have on a service performance. The customer receiving the service or other customers present at the service experience may exercise a profound influence over a service's delivery and/or outcome (Booms and Bitner, 1981; Carman and Langeard, 1980; Langeard *et al.*, 1981; Lovelock, 1983; Martin and Pranter, 1989; Parasuraman, Zeithaml and Berry, 1985, 1988). Crowding, unruly or unanticipated behavior on the part of others sharing the service or an unwillingness or inability to cooperate with the service production on the part of the individual customer can destroy a service performance.

In short, just as the audience of a theatrical production has a responsibility to participate in the staging of the show by accepting certain rules or standards of behavior, the customers of a service are similarly obliged. As a member of the audience, not only must the customer refrain from undermining another's service experience, but he or she must also strive to enable the actors to perform at their best. This means that the customer must be informed and educated as to the expectations and requirements demanded of one as a service participant (e.g. the proper protocol and procedures to evoke a satisfying service) and cooperate accordingly (e.g. provide service personnel with the necessary inputs to perform their tasks adequately) (Bowen, 1986; Mills and Morris, 1986). Whether it is learning how to use an ATM correctly, giving a physician an accurate account of one's symptoms or responding to the rights and privileges of others sharing a service, the audience plays an active role in the service production. Through it all, the service customer – like his/her theater patron counterpart – is expected to accept tacitly the dramaturgical rule that the 'show must go on' by tolerating minor imperfections of the service performance in the interest of the overall production.

As the strategic component, the audience is an important element to consider under several conditions. Beyond those circumstances in which a high degree of direct contact with the service is involved (as discussed previously), the audience's importance also increases when a self-service feature is added to the service (ATMs, fast-food, etc.). In such cases, the audience is instrumental in determining the service's outcome (Lovelock and Young, 1979; Silpakit and Fisk, 1985). The importance of the audience is similarly evident in those services characterized as requiring a high degree of personalization (insurance, legal advice) since the audience must provide the proper inputs (e.g. communication of needs, special wants, etc.) to ensure a satisfying performance by the actors (Berry, 1983). Increased audience importance is also found among those services that cater to several or many customers simultaneously (restaurants, entertainment, etc.) since other customers can influence one's service experience and satisfaction (Grove and Fisk, 1983; Lovelock, 1983; Martin and Pranter, 1989).

Organizations skillful in their management of customer participation and customer–customer interactions can improve the value of the service from the customer's point of view. In cases when a high degree of customer participation is required, organizations can embrace their service by teaching customers their role in the service script. Bateson (1985) has argued that a clear understanding of the service script and one's part in it will increase consumers' perceptions of control of the situation insofar as they can predict the unfolding of events. Ultimately, an increased sense of control results in more satisfied customers.

Many successful service organizations have recognized the importance of educating their customers to ensure correct performance of the script. Obvious examples include various self-service restaurants where signs and verbal directions from employees help to move customers through the different steps required to create their meals. Signs on tables and doors help to ensure that customers will also clean up after themselves. Another example is the extensive effort that was required to educate bank customers in the proper use of ATMs when the devices were first introduced. To enhance their adoption, it was necessary to familiarize customers with the new technology properly, as well as aid them in overcoming the depersonalization of a formerly personal service.

Less obvious examples of customer education occur in many professional services in which clients must provide accurate information to the professional in order to receive the service they need. Professional organizations that do a good job communicating the service script and what is required of the client go a long way toward ensuring quality service outcomes. For example, an individual who goes to Hyatt Legal Services to have a will written enacts a different script than one who seeks the assistance of a 'downtown' law firm for the same purpose. In either case, clear communication of the client role is essential to the service outcome. Another interesting example in the professional service area occurs with hospital surgery services. Many hospitals now thoroughly educate the patient prior to surgery regarding post-surgery events, including how he or she will feel following surgery and the procedures that will be used. Knowing what will happen and knowing one's role in the process may increase a patient's sense of perceived control and satisfaction.

The other issue faced in managing the 'audience' or the participants relates to managing customer–customer interactions. Presumably, if all customers understand the script and enact their parts properly, there should be no conflicts among participants. A good example is the Benihana restaurant chain where interaction among customers is part of the service concept. Customers are seated in groups of eight to 10 around a central cooking area where the Japanese chef prepares each meal. Often, customers are seated next to complete strangers – a circumstance that might cause social distress in some other situations. Yet, this is the accepted 'script' at Benihana and a distinguishing characteristic of the restaurant's success.

However, many service organizations atract a variety of market segments that may each be enacting slightly different scripts. This is often the case for recreational and hospitality services such as ski resorts and hotels, among others. A hotel may be simultaneously serving a large trade show convention, a group of businesswomen, families on vacation and newleywed couples on their honeymoons. Each of these customer types has different needs and purposes for being at the hotel and probably contrasting scripts as well. To minimize potential clashes among their different customer groups, many hotels try to separate physically the market segments or encourage them to use the hotel at different times. Education of the customers as to the various scripts that may be operating may also help. For example, letting the businesswomen know what time of day the trade show conventioneers will be checking out and offering them an alternative check-out time might avoid unnecessary delays and complaints.

The setting

A third strategic component in the model of services as theater is the physical setting in which the service performance occurs. As in the staging of a theatrical production that relies on scenery, props and other physical cues to create desired impressions, a service may employ a myriad of devices to do likewise. In the words of Shostack (1977), the 'setting can play an enormous role in influencing the "reality" of a service in the consumer's mind' (p. 78).

As depicted in Figure 1, the setting embraces various features which surround the service interaction that transpires between the actors and the audience. Marketers have long recognized the potential importance of the physical environment for defining and facilitating the service exchange (Baker, 1987; Booms and Bitner, 1982; Grove and Fisk, 1983; Sherowksi, 1983; Shostack, 1977; Upah and Fulton, 1985; Zeithaml, 1981; Zeithaml, Parasuraman and Berry, 1985). Among a setting's features that may influence the character of a service are the colors or brightness of the service's surroundings; the volume and pitch of sounds employed/present within the setting; the scents, movement, freshness and temperature of the air; the use of space; the style and comfort of the furnishings; the setting's design and cleanliness; and a host of other 'atmospherics' (Kotler, 1973). All these represent evidence or tangible clues that help determine a service's reality.

Just as conditions exist under which the strategic components of service actors and audience become more important, conditions arise under which the service's setting increases in its impact. For example, the setting is likely to be more important when the time a consumer spends in the organization's environment is substantial, as may be the case with hospitals, hotels/resorts or air travel. A longer duration of contact with the service environment amplifies the potential effect of the setting's features.

The setting also increases in importance when the nature of a service may be distinguished by its environment. For instance, although they represent the same generic services, Motel 6 and Westin Hotels, Steak and Ale and Ponderosa Steakhouses, or Hyatt Legal Services and a 'downtown' law firm are usually perceived as quite different, partially due to setting characteristics. Relatedly, the importance of the setting increases when an intended market segment may be identified through a service's physical environment, as is often attempted by retail stores, restaurants or hotels. In such a circumstance, the setting provides cues that are designed to attract and appeal to a specific type of audience. For example, the settings of Chuck E. Cheese versus Pizza Hut pizza parlors are created to target quite different audiences.

Finally, a service's setting may prove to be extremely important for those special cases in which the audience is unfamiliar with the service offered and/or have few (if any) other cues upon which to judge the service. Organizations that market new service concepts are wise to rely on physical cues to simplify, tangibilize and communicate information about their offerings. In such circumstances, the physical environment may provide valuable information and indicators of quality that can facilitate consumer understanding of the service in question.

In summary, much like the theatrical production that relies on scenery and other physical cues to help define the stage action, the nature of a service in many cases is intimately tied to the environment in which it occurs. Recognizing and responding to this proposition may better enable service marketers to devise and implement the service reality they desire.

Despite the potential impact of environmental design on the audience's perceptions of the service, most design decisions are based on aesthetics from a professional designer's point of view) or on operational efficiencies. The customer, or ultimate user of the facility, is rarely consulted directly. Yet the 'atmospherics' of a service may be as important in determining the image of the organization as any variable in the services marketing mix. Many successful service organizations have recognized this power and have distinguished themselves by creative management of their physical facilities. Physical facilities can be used effectively to accomplish a variety of marketing goals, including communicating a new concept, repositioning an organization in the eyes of its target market or attracting new market segments (Booms and Bitner, 1982).

For example, when Speedi Lube started in Seattle, Washington, the owners knew they were offering an unfamiliar service to consumers. The concept of an efficient 10-minute, no-appointment-necessary, efficient car lubrication and oil change was unknown to car owners. To communicate clearly the new concept to potential customers, Speedi Lube made use of every element of physical evidence at its disposal. It communicated efficiency through crisp and clear exterior signage, tidy employee uniforms and an organized shop area painted in bright colors. It also tangibilized its service through use of a graphic schematic on the waiting room wall that showed customers exactly what was being done to their car. Further tangible evidence was provided in a checklist given to the customer showing all services performed. All this was very different from what most car owners were used to finding at corner service stations, and it served to make a new service concept a reality.

Many service organizations have been successful in repositioning themselves through skillful use of physical evidence. Facing increasing competition, a number of banks have hired retail consultants to help reposition themselves as consumer-oriented organizations with a variety of services to offer. Bank One is an example of this approach (Weiner, 1986). Bank One's interior space is no longer divided between a row of tellers on one side and imposing desks on the other, the traditional layout for a bank. Rather, a number of smaller boutiques, similar to a retail store, separate real estate services from stock brokerage, from travel services, etc. On the other side of the bank are the bank's core services: three tellers, an automated teller machine and a new accounts desk. Creative packaging of products and appealing displays are used to attract new market segments and to increase business and loyalty among old customers. All these changes in the physical decor and layout are intended to reposition the bank as a multi-service 'store' rather than a traditional bank. Thus, the setting of the service's delivery helps to define its dramatic performance.

The performance

Applying the drama metaphor to services marketing depicts the service experience as a performance in which the dramaturgical components of actors, audience and setting combine to create and sustain a service definition. Since services are processual in nature, the service definition emerges over time in response to the blending of the various components and their manifestations (see Figure 1). In the quest to present a credible and forceful service performance, it is important to coordinate the evidence provided by the actors and the setting and involve the audience adequately in the service's staging. A theatrical production adorned by magnificent scenery is likely to fail if the actors' skills are poor, just as the artful enactment of actors' roles may be for naught if the production's staging is remiss. So too, a service performance is doomed if key dramatic components do not support one another or are not responsive to the audience. It is also important to seek consistency among the dramaturgical elements over the duration of a service encounter and from one encounter to the next. Maintaining congruity between the actors' manner, actions and appearance and the cues from the service's physical environment in the performance can help establish a clear defination of a service. For example, a retail bank seeking an image of stability and competence is advised to determine from the audience's perspective the appropriate aspects to stress in the actors' and setting's contribution to a service performance that articulate such a definition. These should then be implemented so as to complement one another and fashion a single service reality. Service organizations such as McDonald's and Marriott are good examples of operations with well-defined images of service excellence based largely on the coordination and consistency of the dramaturgical components.

Further contributing to a quality performance is a strong customer-orientation as evidenced, among other things, by actively monitoring and adapting to the audience's responses to the unfolding service drama. This involves the willingness and capacity of the service actors (contact personnel and those working in the back region) to recognize the subtle (or not so subtle) cues of the audience's satisfaction with various aspects of the emerging service action and adjust the performance accordingly. Whether it is altering one's role, playing down aspects of one's service presentation, adjusting the physical environment or undertaking some other action in response to perceived audience desires, such adaptations reflect the adaptive character of a service performance.

DRAMA STRATEGY GUIDELINES

The underlying premise of the '3 New Ps' (*participants, physical evidence* and *process of service delivery*) is that each of the new Ps can aid in achieving marketing goals and thus should be managed as elements of the organization's strategy (Booms and Bitner, 1981). Given that the drama metaphor is analogous actors'/audience' roles, the setting and the performance are developed in this section as a means to improving management of the '3 New Ps'. This section also offers strategic guidelines for international services marketing.

The drama metaphor offers numerous conceptual insights that foster managerial direction and control of the drama dimensions of service organizations. Considerable managerial preparation is possible to address the actors'/audience's roles as well as service setting concerns. The service performance is harder to frame and requires careful managerial monitoring of the service experience as it unfolds.

Improving the actors'/audience's roles

Five strategies for improving the actors'/audience's roles are suggested: (1) audition the service actors; (2) employ scripting; (3) train and rehearse; (4) develop performance teams; and (5) select and train the audience.

Audition the service actors

Like holding an audition for a play, the service organization should develop methods of employee selection that go beyond the simple interview. Possible approaches include using simulation techniques (Schneider and Schecter, 1988) and having prospective employees role play job behaviors, particularly interactions with customers. A related method of employee selection might utilize videotapes to present prospective service actors with role playing situations similar to ones they may encounter on the job (Jones and Decotiis, 1986). An important aspect of 'auditioning' service worker actors is the recognition that some people are not right for parts that put them in front of an audience (Davidson, 1978; Hogan, Hogan and Busch, 1984; Schneider and Schecter, 1988).

Employ scripting

In some situations, careful scripting of plans and procedures for service actors can be implemented. In this context, a script would consist of a detailed plot of the appropriate behavior(s) in a given situation, yet not necessarily the exact words to be spoken. Determination of the various enactments to include among the scripts would be based largely on the audience's expectations (Smith and Houston, 1983, 1985; Surprenant and Solomon, 1987) and the behaviors necessary to fashion a credible performance. Such scripts would be especially useful for routine service behaviors. For example, a life insurance firm could create a script of procedures for day-to-day office activities. Also, emergency scripts would be quite circumspect to ensure a satisfactory service performance under conditions of duress. For instance, it might be advisable for insurance firms to create emergency scripts of procedures for handling the unexpected death of a policyholder. Overall, the service organization might find it valuable to develop a repertoire of scripts for each service actor, as well as for anticipated service encounters.

Train and rehearse

When theatrical actors are training and rehearsing, they have the goal of flawless performances. The actors engage in intensive rehearsals to reach this goal. Following this example, services marketers should consider developing elaborate training and rehearsal procedures for service actors. This could include extending the training process beyond simply the indoctrination of new service workers. In addition, the training and rehearsal should focus on those service employees who operate backstage, as well as those whose actions are visible to the audience in the front region. While some service organizations want their employees to perform identical behaviors for all customers, others expect their employees to be able to adapt to the needs of the customer (Surprenant and Solomon, 1987). Both circumstances require training; however, as a general rule, more complex services necessitate improvisation by the service actors. Jazz improvisation makes a good analogy here. The best jazz improvisation is not done by novices but by experienced musicians. Service organizations that expect their employees to improvise should invest in considerable training. Relatedly, the service actors who succeed at delivering a superb performance are likely to have spent some time rehearsing their parts.

Develop performance teams

Another way to enhance a service production is to create and nurture performance teams that combine the talents of highly skilled service actors (mentors) with those new to the service arena (apprentices). A similar approach is to organize the work force into a small cast of highly skilled service workers, some of whom are designated as primary players while others are supporting players (Hare, 1985). For some more complex services it might also be beneficial to utilize an 'understudy' arrangement in which the new service worker is afforded the opportunity to develop his/her skills 'at the feet' of one more experienced. This would be done prior to casting the new service actor in a frontstage part and would ostensibly increase the likelihood of a successful production by the performance team when the neophyte enters the service stage. In essense, developing teamwork requires the service organization to invest time, money and confidence in its employees. An important aspect of the performance team is the development and coordination of clearly defined parts/routines that each member of the team performs. Managing this effort is similar to directing the stage production.

Select and train the audience

Every service organization wants to select an appreciative audience for its performances. Many traditional marketing ideas are available that facilitate the selection of a target market and the promotion to it. Also, once an audience has been selected, it may become necessary to train it in order to support the performance (Bowen, 1986; Mills and Morris, 1986). As Zeithaml (1981) has stated, 'The quality of most services and their ability to satisfy the consumer depend not only on how well the service provider performs, but also on how well the consumer performs' (p. 187).

For many services, knowledgeable and cooperative participation by the audience is as much a factor affecting service performance as the service's setting or actors. For example, a successful outcome from one's encounter with an ATM or a self-service gas pump depends on one's willingness and ability to use the technology. Furthermore, a doctor's diagnosis or a hair stylist's perm relies on accurate information provided by the service customer. The willingness of the audience members to cooperate among themselves can have an impact also (Martin and Pranter, 1989). Knowledge of and adherence to the rules of conduct and protocol concerning appropriate audience behavior is necessary to enhance the service experience for one and all (e.g. airline service, restaurants, etc.). Nevertheless, few service organizations actually train their patients, clients, patrons, customers, etc.

One approach to training the audience might involve identifying those customers who have not previously patronized the service. If customers are new, efforts can be made to educate them as to customer role expectations in the service production. Enhancing the first service experience for new customers is likely to increase the probability of their repeat patronage. A variety of props, setting changes and other devices are available to enhance the customers' orientation to the service (Wener, 1985) and their role in its performance (Lovelock and Young, 1979; Martin and Pranter, 1989; Solomon *et al.*, 1985).

Improving the setting

Three strategies for improving the services setting can be applied: (1) experimenting with the service setting; (2) frontstage versus backstage decisions; and (3) managing tangible evidence.

Experimenting with the service setting

Because the setting is managerially controllable, service providers can experimentally test variations in setting just as manufacturers of physical goods spend millions of dollars to test product improvements and variations (Farrell, 1984). Field testing new setting choices in local markets may be possible for many nationwide service organizations. Field tests have the advantage of providing a 'real world' test of the setting. Where actual field tests are not feasible, the use of full-size experimental models, scale models, computer models, drawings, slides or photographic simulations can be used to gather customer input prior to design implementation. As an example, the Marriott Corporation tested preliminary design concepts for the Marriott Courtyard Hotels in a warehouse. It is crucial that the design of service settings should be a function of a customer and employee orientation and not just the orientations of architects, interior designers and service firm managers. In all cases, the setting should be sufficiently versatile to allow for growth and change in service delivery. The service setting needs to work for both customers and employees (Baker, Berry and Parasuraman, 1988).

Frontstage versus backstage decisions

The services manager must decide which aspects of the organization's service should be performed on the frontstage (in the audience's full view) and which should be attended to backstage (away from the audience's inspection). In those service operations where it is difficult to meet customer expectations of frontstage service delivery excellence, service managers may find it prudent to move such aspects to the back region. A niche may be developed in this manner also (e.g. the fabled automat restaurants). If a service organization wants to move backstage dimensions of service production to the frontstage, it requires greater attention to other performance components, such as the actors' roles and their scripts, the audience's participation and the setting's physical cues. Moving backstage activities to the frontstage has proven a successful strategy for restaurants that offer self-serve salad bars or that cook food in view of the customers. Benihana Restaurants (discussed previously) has established a competitive niche by having the chef cook the food at the table. Not surprisingly, food preparation at Benihana has become an elaborately staged performance.

Managing tangible evidence

The goal in managing tangible evidence should be the presentation of a cohesive, coherent image. One important component of the tangible evidence is the physical appearance of service employees. Many service organizations (airlines, hotels, restaurants, hospitals, law firms, etc.) have uniforms (costumes) their employees are expected to wear (Solomon, 1985). Few of these organizations have actively researched how their customers and employees respond to these uniforms. A second important component is the use of props. Every service industry has certain props that readily identify its business. Consider how easy it is to identify the service industry that is associated with the following props: stethoscope, chalkboard, bar tray and scissors. While props may seem trivial, they are actually an effective means of symbolically creating the image of the service, as well as instrumentally delivering it. Service organizations can search for props that provide both the most powerful images and the most effective means of delivering the service. As an example, life insurance firms that invest in portable computers for their agents, allowing them to do all calculations and procedures while visiting clients' homes, are using props effectively.

Improving performance

Three procedures for improving performance are available: (1) test new performances; (2) document performances; and (3) critique performances.

Test new performances

It may be expensive to test new performance alternatives, but it is less expensive than a full-scale launch of a new service performance without a 'dress rehearsal'. The goal here is to develop an organizational tradition of constantly testing 'new routines'. Such an approach may be compared to that of a comedian who regularly tests new jokes because the old jokes have become too familiar. Few service organizations can afford the complacency of a static service performance. It may take the public longer to become bored with an old service performance than an old joke, but eventually it will happen.

Document performances

Services organizations should seek to document the performances of their employees. One of the simplest methods of doing this is the use of observation by management, similar to what Peters and Austin (1985) discuss as 'Management by Wandering Around' and 'naive listening'. The biggest hazard of this approach is that the manager's observation may disrupt the service performance. Perhaps a more effective and objective observational technique would be the use of audio and/or videotaping to document the service performance. Audio and videotaping have the advantage of providing a relatively permanent and unbiased record of the service performance. The audio or videotape can be closely examined to determine strengths or weaknesses in the service production. One caveat, however, concerns the appropriateness of observing customers without their knowledge or permission. The ethics related to such documentation should be carefully considered. As an effective substitute for observation, customer recollection of critical service performances can be used to document and track performance (Bitner, Booms and Tetreault, 1990).

Critique performances

The goal of critiquing performances is to maximize the performance of all service employees. As a result, two practices are desirable: (1) reward excellent performance and (2) correct poor performance. Rewarding excellent performance is a powerful motivator not only to the excellent performer but also to those employees who aspire to excellent performance. The reward can be modest and the recongition enthusiastic. A plaque or a small cash gift is probably sufficient. Correcting poor performance is more difficult. When a service employee makes a mistake it can have dangerous consequences. The rash strategy would be to fire the employee in an extremely public way. This would serve to terrorize the remaining staff. The wiser strategy would be privately showing the employee how to avoid the mistake. Most employees want to perform well and give good service (Schneider, 1980).

International guidelines

The drama metaphor can also be employed to develop services marketing guidelines for the many service organizations that are heavily engaged in international services trade. Drama is an ancient art form and is universally practiced in modern cultures. Hence, the drama metaphor is readily communicable across cultural boundaries. Furthermore, the drama metaphor may make it conceptually easier for services marketers to understand the importance of adapting the 'play' to different cultures.

All the drama strategy guidelines presented previously in this section can be applied internationally. The general drama structure will not change, but the management of actors, audience, setting and performances will need to vary in different cultures. Goffman (1959) noted the tremendous dramaturgical variation from one culture to the next. The common vocabulary offered by the drama framework may serve as a basis for analyzing and adapting services marketing systems from one cultural setting to the next.

CONTRIBUTIONS AND CAUTIONS

Four contributions from adopting the drama metaphor are advanced and four cautionary warnings are raised.

Contributions

The drama metaphor offers four contributions to services marketing and management thought and practice by providing a (1) holistic framework; (2) design tool; (3) classification scheme; and (4) descriptive vocabulary.

Holistic framework

The drama model offers managers a holistic framework that simultaneously combines all '3 New Ps' – participants, physical evidence and process of service assembly – into the services marketing mix. Much like the original metaphor of the marketing 'mix', the drama model suggests a combination of ingredients that can be optimally blended to achieve different goals. The drama framework is then a multidimensional tool for comprehending and evaluating the service experience. The drama model offers an appealing representation of marketing transactions as persuasive and entertaining without sacrificing the ability to control the transaction.

Design tool

The drama metaphor can serve as a tool for planning, coordinating and implementing specific service designs. A major approach to service design is blueprinting (Kingman-Brundage, 1989; Shostack, 1984a, 1984b, 1987). While not part of the drama metaphor, blueprinting is a powerful tool for making the various drama components (actors, audience, setting, performance, etc.) more transparent. In addition, used in conjunction with blueprinting, the drama metaphor offers managers directions for (1) the different emphases to place on service components (e.g. low contact services should stress 'setting' to increase perceptions of service quality); (2) the amount and type of attention to devote to recruiting, selecting, training and controlling service workers (e.g. high contact services need actors with strong dramatic skills); (3) the influence that customer expectations have on service quality levels (e.g. patrons demanding high quality dictate a greater attention to detail in service delivery).

Classification scheme

A third contribution is the provision of a structural model that may be applied across different services, thereby responding to a need identified by several services scholars (Lovelock, 1983; Shostack, 1984a; Upah, Berry and Shostack, 1983). The 'service performance cube' (see Figure 2) provides a basis for analyzing and grouping similar services (e.g. those services that emphasize elaborate settings compared to those with minimal investment in setting, those services that require highly trained actors versus those requiring minimally trained actors and those services that are performed before an active audience rather than a passive audience), potentially leading to a cross-fertilization of concepts and strategies (Lovelock, 1983). In addition, this classification scheme facilitates the identification of unserved market niches and offers assistance in manipulating the services mix to capture the niche.

Descriptive vocabulary

Finally, the drama metaphor offers a vocabulary for translating and communicating the various characteristics of any particular service, thereby fostering an understanding of its nature. For example, the metaphor can be used to describe a specific service as one in which standardized 'routines' are important as a marketing technique, one in which skilled actors contribute greatly to the credibility of the 'performance' and so on. Furthermore, used as a training device, the drama framework provides a working vocabulary derived from a social phenomenon familiar to most individuals and easy to communicate to service employees.

Cautions

Four serious cautions are necessary concerning adopting the drama metaphor: the importance of authenticity, the need for adaptability, the need for appropriateness and the range of applicability.

The importance of authenticity

To many people, the drama metaphor may carry the dangerous connotation of superficial 'just acting' behaviors. The 'Have a Nice Day' phrase so dutifully mouthed by the employees of many service businesses is woefully insincere. It is imperative that the customer believes in the performance. If the public believes that a service business is presenting a 'false front', it will quickly take its patronage elsewhere. Services marketers should recognize the importance of honest actors and authentic performances.

The need for adaptability

A second hazardous connotation of the drama metaphor is that of 'canned' performances. Many dramas are rigidly scripted and may convey the image of a fixed product. Managers should consider the need for adaptability and should pursue strategies that maximize the adaptability of the service experience. Service organizations can best fulfill the marketing concept by striving to maintain the adaptability of an 'ethic of service' rather than the precision of an 'ethic of efficiency' (Schneider and Bowen, 1984). Whenever possible, rather than following a fixed script, the service worker should be encouraged to adapt the performance to the needs of the audience.

The need for appropriateness

Third, services marketers and managers should recognize the need for appropriateness. Grotesque, grating or vulgar performances are likely to yield negative consumer reviews and may 'close early'. Attractive, soothing or refined performances are likely to be 'held over by popular demand'. In short, service performances must be well tailored to the tastes and expectations of the service audience.

The range of applicability

As a last caution, the drama metaphor does not apply equally well to all services. Grove and Fisk (1989) argue that the range of applicability of the drama metaphor to services marketing management is determined by the size of the consumer audience and the degree of contact between the service performer and the consumer. Hence, the drama metaphor is weakly applicable to those services whose consumers are physically removed from the service provider and interacting via mail, telephone or computer. However, the drama metaphor applies quite well to services serving large consumer audiences and/or providing significant contact between service performer and consumer.

CONCLUSION

The drama metaphor and the application of its theatrical constructs to service experiences unites the '3 New Ps' of Booms and Bitner (1981) and can be utilized to operationalize the management of them. As was shown in Table 1, the term 'participants' is analogous to the theatrical terms of 'actors' and 'audience', 'physical evidence' is analogous to the 'setting', 'process of service assembly' is analogous to the 'performance'. Two strategic models were proposed that facilitate understanding the applications of drama constructs to services marketing and numerous strategic guidelines were offered.

As a conceptual tool, the drama framework addresses many well-known services marketing issues by demonstrating the implicit and explicit relationships among the service organization, its customers, its employees and its physical properties. As with any metaphor, the description of services in dramatic terms facilitates communication and analysis of the phenomenon at hand and can be used to generate researchable propositions. Ultimately, application of the drama metaphor to services marketing provides a holistic framework, a design tool, a classification scheme and a vocabulary for promoting the understanding and management of service experiences.

ACKNOWLEDGMENTS

The authors thank Jerry Goolsby, University of South Florida, Carol Surprenant, University of Rhode Island, and Joshua Wiener, Oklahoma State University for their helpful comments on earlier drafts of this article.

REFERENCES

Arndt, J. (1985) 'On Making Marketing Science More Scientific: Role of Orientations, Paradigms, Metaphors and Puzzle Solving'. *Journal of Marketing* **49** (Summer): 11–23.

Bagozzi, R. (1975) 'Marketing as Exchange'. *Journal of Marketing* **39** (October): 32–39.

Baker, J. (1987) 'The Role of the Environment in Marketing Services: The Consumer Perspective'. In *The Services Challenge: Integrating for Competitive Advantage* (J. Czepiel, C. Congram and J. Shanahan, Eds). Chicago: American Marketing Association, pp. 79–84.

Baker, J., Berry, L. and Parasuraman, A. (1988) 'The Marketing Impact of Branch Facility Design'. *Journal of Retail Banking* **10** (2): 33–42.

Bateson, J. (1985) 'Perceived Control and the Service Encounter'. In *The Service Encounter: Managing Employee/Customer Interaction in Service Businesses* (J. Czepiel, M. Solomon and C. Surprenant, Eds). Lexington, MA: Lexington Books, pp. 67–82.

Bateson, J. (1989) *Managing Services Marketing: Text and Readings.* Hinsdale, IL: Dryden Press.

Bell, M. (1981) 'Tactical Service Marketing and the Process of Remixing'. In *Marketing of Services* (J. Donnelly and W. George, Eds). Chicago: American Marketing Association, pp. 163–167.

Berry, L. (1980) 'Services Marketing is Different'. *Business* **30** (May–June): 24–29.

Berry, L. (1981) 'The Employee as Customer'. *Journal of Retail Banking* **3** (March): 33–40.

Berry, L. (1983) 'Relationship Marketing'. In *Emerging Perspectives in Services Marketing* (L. Berry, G. Shostack and G. Upah, Eds). Chicago: American Marketing Association, pp. 25–28.

Berry, L., Ziethaml, V. and Parasuraman, A. (1985) 'Quality Counts in Services, Too'. *Business Horizons* **28** (May–June): 44–52.

Berry, L., Parasuraman, A. and Zeithaml, V. (1988) 'The Service-Quality Puzzle'. *Business Horizons* **31** (September–October): 35–43.

Bitner, M. and Zeithaml, V. (1988) 'Fundamentals in Services Marketing'. In *Add Value to Your Service* (C. Surprenant, ed.). Chicago: American Marketing Association, pp. 7–12.

Bitner, M., Booms, B. and Stanfield Tetreault, M. (1990) 'The Service Encounter: Diagnosing Favorable and Unfavorable Incidents'. *Journal of Marketing* **54** (January): 71–84.

Booms, B. and Bitner, M. (1981) 'Marketing Strategies and Organizational Structures for Service Firms'. In *Marketing of Services* (J. Donnelly and W. George, Eds), Chicago: American Marketing Association, 47–51.

Booms, B. and Bitner, M. (1982) 'Marketing Services by Managing the Environment'. *The Cornell Hotel and Restaurant Administration Quarterly* **23** (May): 35–39.

Bowen, D. (1986) 'Managing Customers as Human Resources in Service Organizations'. *Human Resource Management* 25: 371–383.

Brissett, D. and Edgley, C. (1975) *Life As Theatre: A Dramaturgical Sourcebook.* Chicago: Aldine Publishing Co.

Brown, S. and Swartz, T. (1989) 'A Gap Analysis of Professional Service Quality'. *Journal of Marketing* **53** (April): 92–98.

Burke, K. (1945) *A Grammar of Motives.* New York: Prentice-Hall, Inc.

Burke, K. (1950) *A Rhetoric of Motives.* New York: Prentice-Hall, Inc.

Burke, K. (1968) 'Dramatism'. In *International Encyclopedia of the Social Sciences, VII.* New York: Macmillan, pp. 445–452.

Carlzon, J. (1987) *Moments of Truth.* Cambridge, MA: Ballinger Publishing Company.

Carman, J. and Langeard, E. (1980) 'Growth Strategies for Service Firms'. *Strategic Management Journal* **1** (January–March): 7–22.

Cowell, D. (1985) *The Marketing of Services.* London: W. Heinemann.

Czepiel, J., Solomon, M. and Surprenant, C. (Eds) (1985) *The Service Encounter: Managing Employee/Customer Interaction in Service Businesses.* Lexington, MA: Lexington Books.

Davidson, D. (1978) 'How to Succeed in a Service Industry: Turn the Organization Chart Upside Down'. *Management Review* **67** (April): 13–16.

Dearden, J. (1978), 'Cost Accounting Comes to Service Industries'. *Harvard Business Review,* **56** (September–October): 132–140.

Duro, R. and Sandstrom, B. (1987) *The Basic Principles of Marketing Warfare.* Chichester, England: John Wiley & Sons.

Eiglier, P. and Langeard, E. (1977) 'A New Approach to Service Marketing', in *Marketing Consumer Services: New Insights* (P. Eiglier, E. Langeard, C. Lovelock, J. Bateson and R. Young, Eds). Cambridge, MA: Marketing Science Institute, pp. 31–58.

Farrell, K. (1984) 'Franchise Prototypes'. *Venture* (January): 108–113.

Fisk, R., Tansuhaj, P. and Crosby, L. A. (eds) (1985) *Services Marketing: An Annotated Bibliography.* Chicago: American Marketing Association.

Fisk, R., Tansuhaj, P. and Crosby, L. A. (eds) (1988) *SERVMARK: The Electronic Bibliography of Services Marketing Literature.* Tempe, AZ: First Interstate Center for Services Marketing, Arizona State University.

Goffman, E. (1959) *The Presentation of Self in Everyday Life.* New York: Doubleday and Co.

Goffman, E. (1967) *Interactional Ritual.* Garden City, NJ: Doubleday and Co.

Goffman, E. (1974) *Frame Analysis: An Essay on the Organization of Experience.* New York: Harper and Row.

Grönroos (1985) '*Internal Marketing* – Theory and Practice'. In *Services Marketing in a Changing*

Environment (T. Bloch, G. Upah and V. Zeithaml, Eds). Chicago: American Marketing Association, pp. 41–47.

Grönroos, C. (1990) *Service Management and Marketing: Managing the Moments of Truth in Service Competition.* Lexington, MA: Lexington Books.

Grove, S. and Fisk, R. (1983) 'The Dramaturgy of Services Exchange: An Analytical Framework for Services Marketing'. In *Emerging Perspectives on Services Marketing* (L. Berry, G. Shostack and G. Upah, Eds). Chicago: American Marketing Association, pp. 45–49.

Grove, S. and Fisk, R. (1989) 'Impression Management in Services Marketing: A Dramaturgical Perspective'. In *Impression Management in the Organization* (R. Giacalone and P. Rosenfeld, Eds). Hillsdale, NJ: Lawrence Erlbaum Associates, pp. 427–438.

Guiltinan, J. (1987) 'The Price Bundling of Services: A Normative Framework'. *Journal of Marketing* **51** (April): 74–85.

Hare, A. (1985) *Social Interaction as Drama.* Beverly Hills, CA: Sage Publications, Inc.

Heskett, J. (1986) *Managing in the Service Economy.* Boston: Harvard Business School Press.

Hogan, J., Hogan, R. and Busch, C. (1984) 'How to Measure Service Orientation'. *Journal of Applied Psychology* **69** (1): 167–173.

Johnson, E. (1969) 'Are Goods and Services Different? An Exercise in Marketing Theory', Ph.D. Dissertation, Washington University.

Jones, C. and Decotiis, T. (1986) 'A Better Way to Select Service Employees: Video-Assisted Testing'. *Cornell Hotel and Restaurant Administration Quarterly* **27** (August): 68–73.

Judd, R. (1964) 'The Case for Redefining Services'. *Journal of Marketing* **28** (January): 58–59.

Kingman-Brundage, J. (1989) 'The ABC's of Service System Blueprinting'. In *Designing a Winning Service Strategy* (M. Bitner and L. Crosby, Eds). Chicago: American Marketing Association, pp. 30–33.

Kotler, P. (1973) 'Atmospherics as a Marketing Tool'. *Journal of Retailing* **49** (Winter): 48–64.

Kotler, P. and Singh, R. (1981) 'Marketing Warfare'. *Journal of Business Strategy* 1(Winter): 30–41.

Langeard, E., Bateson, J. Lovelock, C., and Eiglier, P. (eds) (1981) *Marketing of Services: New Insights from Consumers and Managers.* Cambridge, MA: Marketing Science Institute.

Lovelock, C. (1981) 'Why Marketing Management Needs to be Different for Services'. In *Marketing of Services* (J. Donnelly and W. George, Eds). Chicago: American Marketing Association, pp. 5–9.

Lovelock, C. (1983) 'Classifying Services to Gain Strategic Marketing Insights'. *Journal of Marketing* **47** (Summer): 9–20.

Lovelock, C. (1984) *Services Marketing: Text, Cases, and Readings.* Englewood Cliffs, NJ: Prentice-Hall, Inc.

Lovelock, C. (1988) *Managing Services: Marketing Operations, and Human Resources.* Englewood Cliffs, NJ: Prentice-Hall, Inc.

Lovelock, C. and Young, R. (1979) 'Look to Consumers to Increase Productivity'. *Harvard Business Review* **57** (May–June): 168–178.

Lovelock, C., Langeard, E., Bateson, J. and Eiglier, P. (1981) 'Some Organization Problems Facing Marketing in the Services Sector'. In *Marketing of Services* (J. Donnelly and W. George, Eds). Chicago: American Marketing Association, pp. 168–171.

Magrath, A. J. (1986) 'When Marketing Services, 4 Ps Are Not Enough'. *Business Horizons* **29** (May–June): 44–50.

Martin, C. and Pranter, C. (1989) 'Compatibility Management: Customer-to-Customer Relationships in Service Environments'. *Journal of Services Marketing* **3** (Summer): 6–15.

McCarthy, E. (1960) *Basic Marketing: A Managerial Approach.* Homewood, IL: Richard D. Irwin, Inc.

Michaelson, G. (1987) *Winning the Marketing War.* Lantham, MD: Abt Books.

Mills, P. and Morris, J. (1986) 'Clients as Partial Employees of Service Organizations: Role Development in Client Participation'. *Academy of Management Review* **11** (4): 726–735.

Morgan, G. (1980) 'Paradigms, Metaphors, and Puzzle Solving in Organizational Theory'. *Administrative Science Quarterly* **25** (December): 605–622.

Murphy, P. and Enis, B. (1986) 'Classifying Products Strategically'. *Journal of Marketing* **50** (July): 24–42.

Nisbet, R. (1969) *Social Change and History*. London: Oxford University Press.

Ortony, A. (1975) 'Why Metaphors are Necessary and Not Just Nice'. *Educational Theory* **25** (Winter): 45–53.

Parasuraman, A., Berry, L. and Zeithaml, V. (1983) 'Service Firms Need Marketing Skills'. *Business Horizons* **26** (November–December): 28–31.

Parasuraman, A., Zeithaml, V. and Berry, L. (1985) 'A Conceptual Model of Service Quality and Its Implications for Future Research'. *Journal of Marketing* **49** (Fall): 41–50.

Parasuraman, A., Zeithaml, V. and Berry, L. (1988), 'SERVQUAL: A Multiple-Item Scale for Measuring Consumer Perceptions of Service Quality'. *Journal of Retailing* **64** (Spring): 12–40.

Perinbanayagam, R. S. (1974) 'The Definition of the Situation: An Analysis of the Ethnomethodological and Dramaturgical View'. *The Sociological Quarterly* **15** (Autumn): 521–541.

Peters, T. and Austin, N. (1986) *A Passion for Excellence*. New York: Warner Books.

Prus, R. and Frisby, W. (1987) 'Marketplace Dynamics: The P's of 'People' and 'Process'. In *Advances in Consumer Research* (M. Wallendorf and P. Anderson, Eds). Provo, UT: Association for Consumer Research. pp. 61–65.

Regan, W. J. (1963) 'The Service Revolution'. *Journal of Marketing* **27** (July): 57–62.

Ries, A. and Trout, J. (1986) *Marketing Warfare*. New York: McGraw-Hill, Inc.

Sasser, W. (1976) 'Match Supply and Demand in Service Industries'. *Harvard Business Review* **54** (November–December): 133–140.

Sasser, W. and Arbeit, S. (1978) 'Selling Jobs in the Service Sector'. *Business Horizons* 19 (June): 61–65.

Sasser, W., Olsen, R. and Wyckoff, D. (1978) *Management of Service Operations: Text, Cases, and Readings*. Boston: Allyn and Bacon.

Schneider, B. (1980) 'The Service Organization: Climate is Crucial'. *Organizational Dynamics* **9** (Autumn): 52–65.

Schneider, B. and Bowen, D. (1984) 'New Services Design, Development and Implementation and the Employee'. In *Developing New Services* (W. George and C. Marshall, Eds). Chicago, IL: American Marketing Association, pp. 82–101.

Schneider, B. and Schecter, D. (1991) 'The Development of a Personnel System for Service Jobs'. In *Service Quality: Multidisciplinary and Multinational Perspectives* (S. Brown, E. Gummesson, B. Edvardsson and B. Gustavsson, Eds). Lexington, MA: Lexington Books.

Shakespeare, W. [1600](1954) *As You Like It* (S. C. Burchell, Ed.). New Haven, CT: Yale University Press.

Sherowski, H. (1983) 'Marketing Through Facilities Design'. In *Emerging Perspectives on Services Marketing* (L. Berry, G. Shostack and G. Upah, Eds). Chicago: American Marketing Association, pp. 134–136.

Shostack, G. (1977) 'Breaking Free From Product Marketing'. *Journal of Marketing* **41** (April): 73–80.

Shostack, G. (1984a) 'A Framework for Services Marketing'. In *Marketing Theory: Distinguished Contributions* (S. Brown and R. Fisk, Eds). New York: John Wiley and Sons, pp. 250–261.

Shostack, G. (1984b) 'Designing Services that Deliver'. *Harvard Business Review* **62** (January–February): 133–139.

Shostack, G. (1987) 'Service Positioning Through Structural Change'. *Journal of Marketing* **51** (January): 34–43.

Silpakit, P. and Fisk, R. (1985) ''Participatizing' the Service Process: A Theoretical Framework'. In *Services Marketing In A Changing Environment* (T. Bloch, G. Upah and V. Zeithaml, Eds). Chicago: American Marketing Association, pp. 117–121.

Smith, R. (1985) 'A Psychometric Assessment of Measures of Scripts in Consumer Memory'. *Journal of Consumer Research* **12** (September): 214–224.

Smith, R. and Houston, M. (1983) 'Script-Based Evaluations of Satisfaction With Services'. In *Emerging Perspectives on Services Marketing* (L. Berry, G. Shostack and G. Upah, Eds). Chicago: American Marketing Association, pp. 59–62.

Solomon, M. (1985) 'Packaging the Service Provider'. *Service Industries Journal* **5** (March), 64–72.

Solomon, M. *et al.* (1985) 'A Role Theory Perspective on Dyadic Interactions: The Service Encounter'. *Journal of Marketing* **49** (Winter): 99–111.

Stern, B. (1988) 'Medieval Allegory: Roots of Advertising Strategy for the Mass Market'. *Journal of Marketing* **52** (July): 84–94.

Stone, G. (1962) 'Appearance and the Self'. In *Human Behavior and Social Process* (A. Rose, Ed.). Boston: Houghton-Mifflin, pp. 86–117.

Surprenant, C. and Solomon, M. (1985) 'Dimensions of Personalization'. In *Services Marketing In A Changing Environment* (T. Bloch, G. Upah and V. Zeithaml, Eds). Chicago: American Marketing Association, pp. 56–59.

Surprenant, C. and Solomon, M. (1987) 'Predictability and Personalization in the Service Encounter'. *Journal of Marketing* **51** (April): 86–96.

Upah, G. and Fulton, J. (1985) 'Situation Creation in Services Marketing'. In *The Service Encounter: Managing Employee/Customer Interaction in Service Businesses.* (J. Czepiel, M. Solomon and C. Surprenant, Eds). Lexington, MA: Lexington Books, pp. 255–263.

Upah, G., Berry, L. and Shostack, G. (1983) 'Emerging Themes and Directions for Services Marketing'. In *Emerging Perspectives on Services Marketing* (L. Berry, G. Shostack and G. Upah, Eds). Chicago: American Marketing Association, pp. 139–141.

US Bureau of the Census (1988). *Statistical Abstract of the United States: 1989.* 109th edition, Washington, DC.

Weiner, S. (1986) 'Banks Hire Retailing Consultants for Help in Becoming Financial-Products 'Stores''. *Wall Street Journal* May 20: 33.

Wener, R. (1985) 'The Environmental Psychology of Service Encounters'. In *The Service Encounter: Managing Employee/Customer Interaction in Service Businesses* (J. Czepiel, M. Solomon and C. Surprenant, Eds). Lexington, MA: Lexington Books, pp. 101–112.

Zeithaml, V. (1981) 'How Consumer Evaluation Processes Differ Between Goods and Services'. In *Marketing of Services* (J. Donnelly and W. George, Eds). Chicago: American Marketing Association, pp. 186–190.

Zeithaml, V. (1982) 'The Acquisition, Meaning and Use of Price Information by Consumers of Professional Services'. In *Marketing Theory: Philosophy of Science Perspectives* (R. Bush and S. Hunt, Eds). Chicago: American Marketing Association, pp. 237–241.

Zeithaml, V., Parasuraman, A. and Berry, L. (1985) 'Problems and Strategies in Services Marketing'. *Journal of Marketing* **49** (Spring): 33–46.

Zeithaml, V., Berry, L. and Parasuraman, A. (1988) 'Communication and Control Processes in the Delivery of Service Quality'. *Journal of Marketing* **52** (April): 35–48.

Zikmund, W. (1982) 'Metaphors as Methodology'. In *Marketing Theory: Philosophy of Science Perspectives* (R. Bush and S. Hunt, Eds). Chicago: American Marketing Association, pp. 75–77.

7

The Impact of Services versus Goods on Consumers' Assessment of Perceived Risk and Variability

Keith B. Murray and John L. Schlacter

INTRODUCTION

In view of the dominant role of the service sector in the industrialized economies of the world, services marketing represents a phenomenon of substantial interest. To date, however, much of the attention in services has been concerned with making a theoretical case that services are conceptually different from goods and that these differences point to special marketing management considerations (Eiglier and Langeard, 1977; Judd, 1964; Rathmell, 1966; Lovelock, 1983; Ziethaml, Parasuraman and Berry, 1985). Unfortunately, the empirical – in contrast to theoretical – basis for distinguishing key differences in substance or marketing strategy is limited.

Despite the call for a balance between qualitative and quantitative approaches to theory construction and validation (Arndt, 1985; Bagozzi, 1984; Brinberg and Hirschman, 1986; Deshpande, 1983), the development of services marketing thought has been heavily dependent on conceptual elaborations. Furthermore, empirical demonstration and verification of service marketing literature has been largely confined to nonexperimental research (Biehal, 1983; Swartz and Stephens, 1984). Compared to empirical research involving nonservice products, experimentation which examines service marketing phenomena appears to be derived from operationally ad hoc definitions and spontaneous operationalizations of the service construct (e.g. Guseman, 1981; George, Weinberger and Kelly, 1985; George *et al.*, 1984; Lewis, 1976; Weinberger and Brown, 1977). Thus, conclusions from experimental data, such as they exist, are divergent and the opportunity for replication is problematic.

Clearly, then, what is needed – as the discipline matures in this area – is a more rigorous research approach regarding services, one which can provide a process for replication and verification (Uhl and Upah, 1983). To this end, the present research

K. B. Murray and J. L. Schlacter, *Journal of the Academy of Marketing Science*, Vol. 18, No. 1, pp. 51–65,

contributes to our understanding of goods/services, in three ways. First, an issue of considerable importance to marketers, perceived risk, is addressed. While a rich literature exists which examines this concept in the context of traditional product marketing, far less effort has been devoted to the examination of perceived risk as it relates to services. No research has attempted to bridge the gap between goods and services marketing by examining the relationship of consumers' perceived risk for service relative to goods.

Second, this research extends extant services marketing thought by introducing a technique for operationalizing the service construct, for validating the construct and for using the construct in an experimentally controlled design to examine the phenomenon of perceived risk in a goods/services context. This approach responds specifically to the discipline's call for empirical examination of services marketing.

Finally, the independent variable in this study, goods/services products, is empirically determined based upon a market definition of product. Research results offer support for the notion that (1) products exist along a goods/services continuum (Johnson, 1969; Levitt, 1980; Shostack, 1977), and (2) that services are perceived by consumers as possessing inherently more risk and variability.

REVIEW OF THE LITERATURE

An elaborate marketing literature exists in which perceived risk is recognized as a fundamental concept in consumer behavior (Bauer, 1960; Bettman, 1973; Cox, 1967; Jacoby and Kaplan, 1972; Kaplan, Szybillo and Jacoby, 1974; Lutz and Reilly, 1973; Perry and Hamm, 1969; Roselius, 1971; Ross, 1972; Shiffman, 1972). Although there has been evidence that consumers may evaluate and purchase services in a different manner, compared to goods (Davis, Guiltinan and Jones, 1979; Johnson, 1969; Lewis, 1976; Weinberger and Brown, 1977), there has been relatively limited research published which examines the relative risk perceptions of services. The results of only two studies (Guseman, 1981; George *et al.*, 1984; George, Weinberger and Kelly, 1985) have been disseminated in marketing publications which address this important topic and indicate that some consumer-related differences may occur. However, these research findings point to conflicting conclusions and neither empirical approach is without qualifications in terms of the research design employed.

The early Guseman (1981) study points to a difference in risk perception between services and goods, with services found to be riskier. In this particular study, the risk perceptions of ten goods (hosiery, butter/margarine, cough drops, felt-tip markers, tape recorders, bed mattresses, small personal leather goods, paint brush roller, wood stands, and typewriters) were contrasted to ten services (appliance repair, motel lodging, medical treatment, commercial bank services, clothes cleaning, motion pictures, spectator sports, dance instruction, auto rental, and apartment rental). Using a mail questionnaire directed to 'the lady of the home' and a total sample of 192 women, Guseman (1981) found significant differences between types of products in an aggregate measure of risk.

While Guseman's (1981) findings are consistent with theoretical predictions of marketing scholars (e.g. Ziethaml, 1981) there are signiciant problems with the experimental design of the study. First, the stimulus products, although selected at random from the Standard Industrial Classification Code Book, lack homogeneity in terms of several key, consumer-relevant considerations. Intuitive analysis of both within- and between-product group comparisons strongly suggests large differences in terms of importance, cost, involvement, and familiarity to the consumer. It is not unreasonable to expect that such differences, as they may occur, would have a significant impact on the evaluative and risk perceptions of subjects (e.g. Claxton, Fry and Portis, 1974; Jacoby and Kaplan, 1972). Specifically, it is possible to attribute significant perceived risk differences between product groupings in this study to any or all of these other rival influences on the product evaluation by subjects. Furthermore, Guseman's (1981) study exerts little experimental control over subject behavior with respect to questionnaire completion. Generalizations, such as may be possible, are only applicable to female perceptions of risk. Also, although the study is laudable in its focus on a significant topic, more specific measures of perceived risk are available and relevant.

In a later study, George, Weinberger and Kelly (1985) and George *et al.* (1984) attempt to examine risk perceptions between goods and services using a mall intercept format whereby 94 subjects rated eight products (four goods and four services) on seven risk dimensions. Attempting to control for 'homogeneity' of products on a 'tangible/intangible continuum', four product 'sets' were designated by the researchers (eye glasses/eye exam; color TV/TV repair; carpeting/carpet cleaning; quartz watch/watch repair) whereby each paired 'good' and 'service' was presumably equivalent and equidistant (relative to an assumed continuum of products) with regards to tangibility/intangibility considerations. These research findings suggest that earlier generalizations about services being higher on all risk categories may not be entirely justified, that risk differences between goods and services may not exist.

The empirical approach of this study (George, Weinberger and Kelly, 1985; George *et al.*, 1984), while addressing some of the previous experimental shortcomings of Guseman (1981), merits careful examination. Specification, the study, by fiat, declares that certain product stimuli are 'services' and others are 'goods'. While there is some face validity associated with each respective designation, the stimuli are clearly vulnerable to debate. An intuitive selection of product stimuli belies an absence of explicit criteria associated with operationalizing the construct for either goods or services. Lacking an objective means of construct determination, it is arguable that several operationalizations are such that the declared 'service' retains a 'goods' component, and vice versa. Furthermore, the derivation of a product 'continuum' lacks explication and also appears to be strictly intuitive in nature, thus making replication – a hallmark of the scientific process – difficult.

While pairwise comparisons suggest a degree of 'relatedness' among the selected products, several problems encountered by Guseman (1981) persist. An absence of experimental and/or statistical controls is evident and may have significantly influenced the data. Several aspects merit brief mention: expected cost differences between pairwise products were not explicitly identified nor controlled for, despite evidence that financial cost considerations have been shown to influence risk perceptions (Jacoby and Kaplan, 1972); no specific control for subject familiarity of product experience is reported; sample composition considerations appear to have been minimized, despite the call for more uniform, homogeneous samples in cases involving theory validation/falsification (Calder, Phillips and Tybout, 1981); and, the lack of sufficient context for the rating task required of the subjects.

In short, the need for additional research which addresses the process and criteria for the inclusion of product stimuli in a test of perceived differences between goods and services is apparent. Consequently, this article will address this aspect of services marketing research and will proceed to describe the findings of an experiment which focuses on the perceived risk and perceived variability of goods and services.

Conceptualization of goods and services in marketing research

While a good can be conceptualized, at least in part, as a physical entity composed of tangible attributes which buyers purchase to satisfy specific wants and needs, the problems associated with the definition of a service have persisted to plague services research. Nonetheless, services marketing theorists have established a fairly broad consensus as to what characterizes service products (for example, Zeithaml, Parasuraman, and Berry, 1985). Generalizations characterizing services include intangibility, simultaneity of production and consumption, inseparability, and nonstandardization. As an outgrowth of these conceptualizations, marketing thought has implicitly pointed to (1) the existence of an intrinsic dichotomy between market offerings of goods and services; and (2) the notion that marketing knowledge is inherently biased toward the marketing of goods and, therefore, not necessarily applicable in the service sector of marketing (for example, Bateson, 1977; Lovelock 1979; Shostack 1977).

Despite the persuasive character of services marketing literature, some argue that there are few substantive differences between services and a generic concept of product marketing (Brown and Fern, 1981; Wyckham, Fitzroy and Mandry, 1975). Scholars have proposed that consumers make expenditures not for goods and/or services but, instead, for value satisfactions they believe are bestowed by what they are buying (Enis and Roering, 1981; Hollander, 1979; Levitt, 1969, 1980) and that products have varying degrees of tangibility–intangibility and 'service' associated with them (Levitt, 1981). Proponents of this view argue that goods-type and service-type products are not necessarily mutually exclusive.

One approach to resolving the conflict between traditional marketing thought and services marketing literature is to suggest a model that proposes the arrangement of all products along a continuum based on dimensions by which classical goods–services distinctions theoretically are made. Since *all* products can be observed to possess common properties, or dimensions (e.g. Johnson, 1969), the difference between products conventionally referred to as 'goods; or 'services' lies in the relative proportions that a particular product may have of each specific dimension (e.g. intangibility, nonstandardization, etc.) as well as the perceived dominance of each dimension relative to all other dimensions involved in defining products. Indeed, marketing scholars support the concept of a spectrum to meaningfully arrange products, based on their perceived attributes (Aspinwall, 1961; Rathmell, 1966; Shostack, 1977).

In short, a simple characterization of services qua services (and, implicitly, goods qua goods) is, at best, a crude generalization of the true nature of products and it is imperative that empirical research efforts in the services area explicitly recognize and incorporate measures which address this issue. Thus, this paper proposes that (1) there is a continuous range of products, rather than a simple, categorical dichotomy, and (2) premised on consumer perceptions, products can be meaningfully arrayed to reflect important marketing/purchase differences (Shostack, 1977).

THEORY AND HYPOTHESES: SERVICE RISK AND VARIABILITY

Perceived risk is a multi-dimensional construct (e.g. Jacoby and Kaplan, 1972; Kaplan, Szybillo and Jacoby, 1974; Roselius, 1971) which implies that consumers experience pre-purchase uncertainty as to type and degree of expected loss resulting from the purchase and use of a product (Bauer, 1960; Cox, 1967). Types of risk include financial performance, physical, psychological, social and convenience loss (e.g. Jacoby and Kaplan, 1972; Kaplan, Szybillo and Jacoby, 1974; Roselius, 1971). In risk theory literature, degree of risk is determined using a variety of approaches (Ross, 1972) and essentially involves the expected relative risk associated with a product purchase.

A number of predictions can be made which directly flow from the service marketing and consumer behavior literature with respect to risk and product variability. As noted previously, services have been typically associated with greater degrees of intangibility, simultaneity of production and consumption, and direct provider–consumer contact and, indirectly, nonstandardization (e.g. Johnson, 1969; Rathmell, 1966; Zeithaml, 1981; Zeithaml, Parasuraman and Berry, 1985). In view of these elements, the amount and/or quality of information available for services is diminished, and the amount of perceived risk is expected to be elevated (e.g. Cox and Rich, 1964; Spence, Engel and Blackwell, 1970). While there is necessarily some degree of risk which accompanies all purchases, it is predicted that more risk is associated with services than with goods (Guseman, 1981; Lewis, 1976; Zeithaml, 1981). The following hypothesis, therefore, is offered:

H_1: Consumers will perceive greater overall pre-choice risk for services than for goods.

In contrast to goods, many services typically involve costs which cannot be fully determined by the consumer in advance of the purchase decision, contributing to the uncertainty of outcome and, at the very least, a heightened degree of financial loss to the consumer. For virtually all nonservice market offerings, price is established prior to the purchase event and consumption; for services, however, this is not always possible, since many services are associated with variable completion times and/or component elements that are not completely identifiable in advance of the completion of the product, both of which might affect product cost.

For services where the price is standardized in advance of the purchase event, the actual benefits of the transaction are nonetheless variable. While the cost may be known prior to the decision to buy, actual product benefits are difficult to fully ascertain prior to purchase. Thus, even for services when costs are fixed, the nonstandardization of services leads to uncertainty with respect to the real costs and performance of the product. Consequently, the following predictions are possible:

H_2: Consumers will perceive greater pre-choice financial risk for services than for goods.
H_3: Consumers will perceive greater pre-choice performance risk for services than for goods.

Although not true for all services, most entail some degree of human involvement as an integral part of the product. Furthermore, in addition to possible direct contact between the service provider and consumer, the service environment typically can include other individuals as well. Contact with others increases the opportunity for interactions of a sensitive or potentially embarrassing nature (e.g. consumer uneasiness at expressing dissatisfaction or indecision, consumer fear of asking nairve or foolish questions). For many purchases associated with nonservice products, the potential for this type of conflict is reduced, if for no other reason than the fact that the consumption of the product is not frequently at the purchase or provision site. Thus, it can be predicted that the relatively high degree of provider/customer involvement associated with simultaneity of production and consumption for services leads to the increased opportunity for social risk, the potential loss of esteem, respect, and/or friendship offered to the consumer by other individuals. Therefore,

H_4: Consumers will perceive greater social risk for services than for goods.

Several remaining types of risk have not been specifically addressed in current services marketing literature. These forms of risk include convenience, physical, and psychological loss. Convenience risk addresses loss of time and effort associated with achieving satisfaction with a purchase; physical risk addresses product safety and possible danger or harm related to product purchase or use; and, psychological risk relates to possible loss of self-image or self-concept as a result of product purchase or use. Without clear evidence in the literature for these remaining dimensions of perceived risk, the following predictions can be tested against acceptance of the null hypothesis:

H_5: Consumers will perceive no difference in pre-choice convenience risk between services and goods.
H_6: Consumers will perceive no difference in pre-choice physical risk between services and goods.
H_7: Consumers will perceive no difference in pre-choice psychological risk between services and goods.

Closely related to the concept of perceived risk is the notion of product benefit variability. Benefit variability can be associated with the inability to standardize many services (Booms and Bitner, 1981). From a managerial perspective, factors influencing product variability include channel length and distribution configuration, the demand level, involvement of new or different service personnel and/or other customers in the service system, consumer cooperation, and other similar factors (Bateson, 1979; Eiglier and Langeard, 1977; Lovelock, 1981; Sasser, 1976). Mills and Margulies (1980) attribute this nonstandardization of services to the inability of service providers to isolate the 'technical' core of the 'manufacturing process' of services.

Thus, despite the opportunity for customized, individual-specific product benefits, other factors influence the ability of the provider to render benefits in a consistent, uniform nature. Consequently, there is expected to be particular uncertainty on the part of the consumer relative to the degree of positive and/or negative utility associated with a service (Berry, 1984; Rathmell, 1974). Therefore, it is predicted that

H_8: Consumers will perceive services to have greater variability than goods.

These hypotheses are intended to test the prediction that goods and services are associated with important consumer differences with respect to specific risk and product variation perceptions. Collectively they represent a synthesis of current marketing literature with respect to services marketing concepts.

METHODOLOGY

Previous experimental service marketing studies have assumed a priori products are 'services' and that others are 'goods' (e.g. Guseman, 1981; Weinberger and Brown, 1977; George, Weinberger and Kelly, 1985). However, research efforts predicated on this approach to product definition present theoretical difficulties (Peter, 1981), since conclusions premised on assumed operationalizations are necessarily suspect. Consequently, procedures are required whereby a respondent sample evaluates products in advance of the experiemental manipulation, in order to determine whether the products are typically perceived as goods or services. To that end, a survey was undertaken to establish a range of products against which to subsequently test hypotheses relating to consumer risk perceptions of goods and services.

Phase 1: pre-experimental study

Selection of products for the main study. A large population of products was identified to be subsequently rated in terms of their respective goods/services components. Sources for the initial list of products included *The Simmons Study of Media and Markets*, the consumer *Yellow Pages* of a large US urban metropolitan area, and the *US Census Standard Industrial Classification.* Products were selected on the basis of their inclusion in consumer product categories for both goods and services as defined by each of the sources. A judgment sample of 235 product categories was collected.

A sample of 145 consumers, drawn from the population of the main study was asked to rate products, irrespective of any designation as 'goods' or 'services', in terms of their relative goods or services qualities on a seven-point fixed interval scale from 'Has extreme "goods" properties' to 'Has extreme "service" properties'. An arithmetic mean was computed for each rated product which permitted the arrangement of the entire sample of products to be rank–ordered in terms of their relative placement along a goods–services continuum. Product ratings took place after subjects had been given a brief description of six criteria (relative to tangibility, simultaneity of production and consumption, standardization, buyer participation, importance of the producer and perishability (see Murray, 1986)) by which marketing literature typically distinguishes goods from services. To diminish respondent fatigue and bias, survey subjects were asked to rate sequentially a random subsample of no more than 50 products of the 235 initially identified.

To increase the precision of the product construct factors, pre-experimental subjects were asked to rate the perceived monetary value, or expected financial cost, associated with each product in terms of a seven point interval scale. In the determination of the factors of the subsequent experiment, the specific selection of products was limited to those falling in the expected cost range of $20 to $50. Since there is a direct correlation between cost and overall risk (e.g. Jacoby and Kaplan, 1972), this was expected to increase control of an important extraneous risk factor. To further increase experimental precision, the degree of a subject's familiarity with each product was measured by his or her rating on a seven-point interval scale. Only those products for which respondents expressed at least moderate familiarity were included in the final sample of products.

Products falling within the specific monetary value and familiarity range were arrayed along a goods–services continuum based on the mean score for each product. For purposes of this study, services were considered to be those products receiving a rating greater than 6.0 on a seven-point scale; goods were considered to be those products receiving a score of less than 2.0. Products characterized by roughly equal degrees of goods and service attributes were those falling in a mid-range of 3.5 to 4.5. Five goods, five services, and five 'mixed' products were then selected as the independent variables for the study. The use of a sample of products was intended to increase the stability of the dependent measures (Minium, 1978).

Table 1 shows a partial array of the survey data for these critical regions and, specifically, the products selected as factors of the independent variable.

Phase 2: controlled experiment

The purpose of this phase of the research was to experiementally assess the differing impact of goods and services on consumer perception of risk and expected product variability.

Experimental design

The specific formulation proposed in this study is that of a completely balanced block (repeated measures) design with nested factors in a hierarchical arrangement. From an experimental perspective, this design minimizes error variance and obtains a relatively precise estimate of treatment effects, thereby obtaining a more powerful test of a false null hypothesis (Green, 1973; Kirk, 1982). Pretests of the data collection instrument showed that confounding effects atributable to reactivity or order effects were not present with the design employed.

Sample

A total of 273 experimental sets were distributed to university students at a large, urban university in the southwestern US. However, 17 questionnaire forms were not

Table 1. Partial pre-test product rating data

Product	Good–service continuum value (1–7)	Expected product cost ($)
Low perceived service identity level of independent variable		
Windbreaker jacket	1.3	25.00
Tennis racket	1.4	41.40
Barbecue grill	1.4	47.70
Small elecric vacuum cleaner	1.5	39.60
Pocket camera	1.6	21.30
Mean product value:	1.4	35.00
Moderate perceived service identity level of independent variable		
Auto re-upholstery (including installation)	3.5	43.40
Smoke detector/alarm	3.5	25.30
Furniture rental, sofa	3.6	31.50
Auto muffler (including installation)	3.8	49.10
Restaurant meal	4.3	21.50
Mean product value:	3.7	34.16
High perceived service identity level of independent variable		
Teeth cleaning by a dentist or hygienist	6.0	35.40
Income tax advice and preparation	6.1	39.50
Auto wheel alignment	6.1	24.60
Professional interior decoration advice	6.3	37.30
Eye exam	6.6	36.50
Mean product value:	6.2	34.66

completed, properly, resulting in 256 acceptable response sets for tabulation and analysis. Of the sample, 120 subjects were males (46.9%) and 136 females (53.1%). The mean age of the sample subject was 23.8 years, with a standard deviation of 3.4.

Sample size for the proposed study was derived using an estimation approach based on expected mean differences of dependent measure scores with an adjusted confidence level of 95% and a 0.05 bound on the error of estimation. Table 2 shows the layout of the design and the accompanying sample utilized.

Procedures

To test the proposed hypotheses, the sample of young adult consumers was administered written purchase scenarios involving consumer products systematically varied and randomly selected from the 15 product stimuli isolated in the pre-test survey. Three levels of the independent variable (that is, product groups varying in goods/services characteristics) were administered to each subject in a role-playing context.

The hypothetical purchase scenario employed was adapted from Lutz and Reilly (1973) and Locander and Hermann (1979) and conforms to Bettman's (1972) concept of inherent risk for products varying in service attributes. The decision context of the purchase scenario was of a non-emergency nature, since purchase

Table 2. Experimental design: balanced complete block with repeated measures

	Level of service characteristics of product administered as the independent variable[a]															
	High 5 products					Moderate 5 products					Low 5 products					
Number of respondents	1	2	3	4	5	6	7	8	9	10	11	12	13	14	15	n
1–47	•					•					•					47
48–96		•					•					•				49
97–151			•					•					•			55
152–209				•					•					•		58
210–256					•					•					•	47
																$n = 256$
Replications:	47	49	55	58	47	47	49	55	58	47	47	49	55	58	47	= 768

[a]Products represent empirically determined stimuli used as the independent variable in the study. Five product stimuli were selected from three disparate portions of a goods–services continuum. Subjects corresponding to numbers in left-most column were exposed to one product stimulus from each sample of five for each level. The product stimuli correspond to those identified in Table 1.

decisions reflecting emergency circumstances may involve abbreviated information search processes (Wright, 1974). While scenario stimuli are employed in current marketing research (e.g. Jackson, Keith and Burdick, 1984; Mowen *et al.*, 1985; Puto, Patton and King, 1985), a number of considerations specifically favored the use of a role-playing methodology. This approach offered the opportunity to (1) incorporate existing and accepted risk operationalizations and scales (e.g. Bettman, 1972, 1973; Jacoby and Kaplan, 1972; Locander and Hermann, 1979; Lutz and Reilly, 1973; Perry and Hamm, 1969; Peter and Ryan, 1976; Zikmund and Scott, 1973); (2) use advanced statistical analysis of the data, including the assessment of the reliability and validity of dependent measures (e.g. Churchill, 1979b; Leigh, 1983; Smith, 1982) and their interactions (e.g. Punj and Stewart, 1983); and (3) to implement a repeated measures MANOVA design, thus maximizing the degree of experimental control over a wide range of important consumer purchase determinants.

The experimental treatments consisted of three levels of the independent variable from five potential product stimuli for each level, resulting in hypothetical situations. The sets of 15 feasible treatments were identical except for the product to be 'purchased'. Respondents were randomly assigned to treatment order of the independent variable and were presented with one factor from each level of the independent variable. Thus, respondents engaged in a projective purchase task for three products systematically varied in terms of relative 'serviceness'.

Statistical analysis

The data of this research were analyzed by multivariate analysis of variance (MANOVA) procedure. As an extension of the classical MANOVA model to cases in which more than a single criterion variable is involved. MANOVA permits tests of differences involving correlated, multiple response variables, precluding the need to meet the assumption of compound symmetry required by the conventional analysis of a repeated measures design (LaTour and Miniard, 1983). The merits of this statistical technique for this type of research have been explained in detail and cogently defined by Green (1973), Wind and Denny (1974), and Green and Tull (1978) and implemented by Locander and Hermann (1979). SPSSX statistical software was used to carry out these procedures.

Measures of the dependent variables

Immediately following exposure to each of the three projective purchase scenarios, subjects completed a self-administered questionnaire designed to measure product risk and variability for each respective product stimulus. Each construct was assessed using multiple measures to enhance conceptual validity (e.g. Cook and Campbell, 1975; Campbell and Fiske, 1959). Specifically, questionnaire items measured subject response on 14 dependent variables: seven measures of perceived product risk (financial, performance, social, psychological, convenience, physical, and overall loss) and perceived product return (financial, performance social psychological, convenience, physical, and overall gain). Covariate measures of respondent age, sex and experience with the product class were also collected. in addition, the data collection instrument included appropriate manipulation checks to verify the intended effect of the independent variable.

Perceived risk. Although the literature reflects a wide variety of measures of perceived risk, the measures employed in this research were intended to collect data on inherent risk (Bettman, 1973). Consistent with other risk research (e.g. Jacoby and Kaplan, 1972; Perry and Hamm, 1969; Reselius, 1971; Schiffman, 1972; Zikmund and Scott, 1973), this study involved a number of specific factors associated with perceived risk in the purchase decision-making process. Perceived risk measures were derived from previous risk research literature (e.g. Jacoby and Kaplan, 1972; Peter and Tarpey, 1975; Roselius, 1971), although it was necessary to slightly modify item statements to accommodate products of a service nature. Six fixed interval scales were constructed and scored 1 to 7 (low to high loss). Overall perceived risk scores were obtained by summing across each of the six loss dimensions for each respondent relative to each product type rated.

Product variability. A measure of product variability is derived from the net perceived return model of Peter and Tarpey (1975) which proposes that consumer decision-making strategies are motivated by not only minimization of risk, but also the maximization of positive utility. A perceived return model is formulated identically to the perceived risk model, except for a focus on positive instead of negative utilities; conceptually, however, the two models are independent. While the net perceived gain model of Peter and Tarpey (1975) suggests that consumer decisions are based on net valences between positive and negative factors associated with a product or brand, this study, by contrast, adapts the net return model to reflect the absolute perceived valences associated with a product. In effect, this model is a combination of the risk and return models, the purpose of which is to quantify the perceived variability of the product utility. Products with comparatively greater degrees of both positive and/or negative valence imply greater respondent 'uncertainty' with regard to product perception and, implicitly, the expectation of variability. Products with minimal perceived risk and/or gain are expected to be associated with small values of product variability. Bettman (1973) provides support for this inference.

Based on Peter and Tarpey (1975), items measuring specific types of perceived return were composed of six fixed interval scales and scored 1 to 7 and measure perceived financial, social, psychological, convenience, physical, and performance gain. Overall product return was obtained by summing across each of the six gain dimensions with respect to each hypothetical product purchase.

In addition to dependent measures associated with risk and variability, covariate measures tapping respondent gender, age and product experience were employed.

RESULTS

Analysis of the experimental manipulations

To test the efficacy of the product factors identified in pre-test procedures in terms of relative service attributes, a manipulation check of the independent variable showed that the factor levels of products had been significantly varied in the context of the experimental setting. Using a seven point scale, the ratings of each group of products were 6.32, 3.77, and 1.75 for service products, service-good product combinations, and goods products, respectively. Across all factors of the independent variable, the MANOVA F value for difference among the three levels of the independent variable was significant (F = 1290.00, $p < .000$) as were all planned comparisons using a Bonferroni multiple comparison t test approach for contrasts among the three means.

A seven point fixed response scale was used to measure respondent familiarity with the factors of the independent variable included in the research. The product familiarity mean score across all subjects and factors was 4.58 with a standard deviation of 1.653. Familiarity scores were 4.44, 4.44, and 4.85, respectively, for high, moderate, and low levels of the independent variable. These data suggest that the sample of products used in the experimental setting were familiar to the respondents.

Although the economic risk with respect to the perceived cost of each experimental operationalization (that is, each product stimulus) was not specifically examined in the experimental setting due to questionnaire length and subject fatigue considerations, the pre-test data indicated that the average perceived product cost for high, moderate, and low-service-attribute products was \$35.66, \$34.16, and \$35.00, respectively. These data suggest that for the population sampled the economic risk across factors associated with the levels of the independent variable was controlled for with respect to approximate perceived cost equivalence.

Measurement validation

Since multiple items were used to measure risk and variability constructs, the reliability of each measurement scale was assessed consistent with the assumptions of domain sampling theory (Churchill, 1979a). Coefficient alpha data for perceived risk, perceived return, and respondent product experience were computed. All values revealed acceptable correlations with true scores and were consistent with Nunnally's (1967) alpha values for these operationalizations. These data are summarized in Table 3.

Table 3. Validation analysis of dependent and covariate measures

Service level	Model components	Cronbach's alpha
A. Internal consistency estimates of perceived risk		
High	Mean risk	.861
Moderate	Mean risk	.797
Low	Mean risk	.802
Across all levels	Financial loss	.522
	Performance loss	.577
	Physical loss	.412
	Psychological loss	.607
	Social loss	.525
	Convenience loss	.764
	Overall mean	.877
B. Internal consistency estimates of perceived benefit		
High	Mean return	.804
Moderate	Mean return	.839
Low	Mean return	.814
Across all levels	Financial gain	.600
	Performance gain	.576
	Physical gain	.639
	Psychological gain	.475
	Social gain	.644
	Convenience gain	.723
	Overall mean	.878
C. Internal consistency estimates of subjects' product experience		
High		.924
Moderate		.895
Low		.905
	Mean coefficient alpha value	.817

FINDINGS

The study hypotheses were concerned with the effects of goods and services on respondents' perception of general and specific measures of risk as well as perception of product variability.

Overall perceived risk

Hypothesis 1 predicted that overall perceived risk would be greater for services than for goods. MANOVA procedures indicated that services were associated with greater perceived risk (F = 15.44, $p < .000$). Bonferroni t tests to compare dependent measures among all levels of the independent variable were performed, with the overall alpha level set at .05 for each set of comparisons. The results of this test indicated that no significant differences were detected between the low and moderate levels of the independent variable, although there was directional support for the hypothesis. There were significant differences between the moderate and high levels of the independent variable ($t = 4.18$, $p < .000$) and between the low and high levels ($t = 5.40$, $p < .000$).

Thus support for Hypothesis 1 was encountered, leading to the rejection of the null hypothesis that there are no risk differences between goods and services.

Expected financial risk

Hypothesis 2 predicted that services would be associated with greater perceived financial risk than would goods. This variable was assessed with a measure derived from previous research examining risk phenomena (Brooker, 1984; Jacoby and Kaplan, 1972; Kaplan, Szybillo and Jacoby, 1974). While there was directional support for this prediction, the analysis failed to provide statistical (F = 2.106, $p < .124$) support at the $a < .05$ level.

Expected performance risk

Hypothesis 3 predicted that expected performance risk would be greater for services than for goods. This variable was assessed with a measure derived from previous research examining risk phenomena (Brooker, 1984; Jacoby and Kaplan, 1972; Kaplan, Szybillo and Jacoby, 1974). The MANOVA statistical analysis failed to support the stated hypothesis (F = 1.075, $p < .343$). Although the data points of the dependent variable suggest a nonlinear relationship, there is some directional support for the outcome predicted.

Expected social risk

Hypothesis 4 proposed that services are associated with greater social risk than goods. This variable was assessed with a measure derived from previous research examining risk phenomena (Brooker, 1984; Jacoby and Kaplan, 1972; Kaplan, Szybillo and Jacoby, 1974). Results of the MANOVA analysis indicate that services are associated with greater expected social risk ($F = 4.713$, $p < .010$). Bonferroni t tests between the low and moderate level of the independent variable were not significant. However, the comparisons between moderate and high ($t = 2.990$, $p < .001$) and low and high ($t = 2.430$, $p < .008$) were statistically significant.

Expected convenience risk

Hypothesis 5 tests the null hypothesis that there are no differences in perceived convenience risk between goods and services. This variable was assessed with a measure derived from previous research relative to convenience risk phenomena (Roselius, 1971). The null hypothesis was rejected in view of a significant MANOVA *F* statistic ($F = 16.574$, $p < .000$). Bonferroni *t* test statistics were not significant at the $a = .05$ level between low and moderate levels of the independent variable ($t = .630$, $p < .250$). However, contrasts between the moderate and high levels ($t = 4.919$, $p < .000$) and low and high levels ($t = 5.173$, $p < .000$) of the independent variable were significant.

Expected physical risk

Hypothesis 6 predicts that subjects would not perceive a difference in expected physical risk between goods and services. This variable was assessed with a measure derived from previous research examining perceived physical risk (Brooker, 1984; Jacoby and Kaplan, 1972; Kaplan, Szybillo and Jacoby, 1974). The MANOVA *F* test ($F = 27.452$, $p < .000$) was significant as were the Bonferroni *t* tests of planned comparisons among all means. These findings preclude acceptance of the null hypothesis and provide support for the notion that respondents perceive services as having greater perceived physical risk.

Expected psychological risk

Hypothesis 7 tests the null hypothesis with respect to differences in perceived psychological risk between goods and services. This variable was assessed with a measure derived from previous research examining perceived psychological risk (Brooker, 1984; Jacoby and Kaplan, 1972; Kaplan, Szybillo and Jacoby, 1974). Statistical analysis of the data indicates a significant MANOVA *F* value ($F = 7.966$, $p < .000$). Bonferroni *t* tests among means show a significant difference at the .05 level among all means. Consequently, the null hypothesis was rejected, suggesting that services are associated with greater perceived psychological risk.

Perceived product variability

Hypothesis 8 makes the prediction that subjects perceive services to have greater variability than goods. The measure of the dependent variable in this test is the sum of the absolute ratings of respondents for perceived loss and perceived gain across all six measures of risk and return.

The MANOVA *F* test ($F = 9.410$, $p < .000$) was significant, indicating that goods and services are associated with differences in perceived product variability. Thus, the prediction of the hypothesis was supported by the data, that services are associated with greater perceived variability. Bonferroni *t* tests among the means reveal no significant differences between the low and moderate lives of the independent variable. However, significant *t* tests were found between the moderate and high ($t = 3.323$, $p < .000$) and low and high ($t = 4.377$, $p < .000$) levels of the independent variable.

A summary of the stated hypotheses and mean response scores for Hypotheses 1 through 8 is shown in Table 4.

Table 4. Review of hypotheses focus and experimental results

A. Summary of the empirical findings of the service variables

Hypothesis	Focus of prediction	Empirical evidence that service products effect significant differences
1	Overall risk	Yes
2	Financial risk	No, despite directional support
3	Performance risk	No, despite directional support
4	Social risk	Yes
5	Convenience risk	Yes
6	Physical risk	Yes
7	Psychological risk	Yes
8	Product variability	Yes

B. Summary of the statistical results

Variable	Level of independent variable: Low	Medium	High	MANOVA *F* value	Significance level	Bonferroni *t* test ($p < .05$) L-M	M-H	L-H
Type of risk								
Overall	3.456	3.544	3.931	15.449	.000	No	Yes	Yes
Financial	4.185	4.225	4.454	2.106	.124	–	–	–
Performance	4.480	4.394	4.583	1.075	.343	–	–	–
Social	2.520	2.409	2.830	4.713	.010	No	Yes	Yes
Convenience	4.074	4.152	4.762	16.575	.000	No	Yes	Yes
Physical	2.669	3.157	3.630	27.452	.000	Yes	Yes	Yes
Psychological	2.777	2.965	3.293	7.966	.000	No	Yes	Yes
Perceived product variability	3.675	3.722	3.938	9.410	.000	No	Yes	Yes

DISCUSSION

This research suggests that product attributes can influence risk perceptions. That respondents would find services to have greater risk than goods, Hypothesis 1, was supported by that data. Consistent with the predictions of Zeithaml (1981) these data indicate that consumers make significant risk distinctions based on product attributes vis-a-vis a goods–services continuum. Although these findings have been previously suggested by services marketing literature, this research offers empirical support with experimental evidence.

Hypotheses 2 and 3 predicted, respectively, that greater financial risk and performance risk would be associated with services. Though these hypotheses did not achieve statistical significance, there was directional support for the predictions. Post hoc analysis using a model which included the covariate of respondent product experience did reject the hypothesis for respondents with low product experience in the case of both predictions. Specifically, it was found that for respondents who reported low-product experience, perceived performance and financial risk was significantly elevated for services compared to goods. Alternatively, high product experience respondents perceived no significant differences for these types of risk across all levels of the independent variable. These findings are consistent with the theoretical implications of the model proposed by Zeithaml (1981), which, for naive consumers, points to the absence of search qualities for services.

Hypothesis 4 predicts that services are associated with increased social risk. The data confirmed this expectation and are consistent with service marketing literature which points to direct provider-consumer contact which, in turn, suggests the potential for conflict (Bateson, 1979; Eiglier and Langeard, 1977).

Hypotheses 5, 6 and 7 test the null hypothesis and predict no difference in perceived risk with respect to convenience, physical safety, and psychological risk, respectively. For each dimension of risk, the null hypothesis was rejected and the data point to significantly increased perceived convenience, safety, and psychological risk associated with the purchase of services.

Hypothesis 8 predicts that the perceived loss/gain variability is greater for services than for goods. This hypothesis was confirmed in support of the theoretical expectation that services are associated with increased nonstandarization in comparison to goods (Bateson, 1979; Booms and Bitner, 1981; Eiglier and Langeard, 1977).

CONCLUSIONS AND RECOMMENDATIONS

The findings of this research indicate that consumers perceive services to be more risky than goods across several types of risk and more variable in nature. A number of managerial and theoretical implications flow from these conclusions.

Managerial implications

In view of significant differences in consumers' perceived risk, the data suggest a prolonged consumer adoption and diffusion process for services and implicitly point to a need for marketing activities specifically intended to reduce risk. Several examples of marketing considerations are offered. Since services are frequently associated with greater levels of human interaction, the management of customer-contact personnel seems to be a particularly appropriate focus of marketers to decrease the opportunity for social and/or psychological loss to the consumer. The data suggest the need for service marketers to develop personnel screening and supervision techniques which specifically focus on identifying and cultivating skilled service providers who will minimize social risk for consumers.

In view of the role of experience in diminishing some types of perceived risk, service marketers may need to adopt strategies which specifically encourage consumer trial of the service product. Such strategies imply the need to offer services of an introductory nature, ideally at a reduced cost. Exposure to the service product of even a limited nature would permit the service consumer to acquire some 'experience' in evaluating personnel, product benefit, and the purchase context generally, thus reducing uncertainty and perceived risk. This strategy by the service provider would specifically address financial and performance risk considerations. This approach is consistent with Zeithaml (1981) and Young (1981) who argue that consumers find post-purchase evaluation more essential with services than with goods, since services possess experience qualities, which cannot be adequately assessed in advance of purchase.

Because of consumer perception of higher variability associated with services, a marketing mix strategy for services demands special attention to increased product uniformity. While the nature of many services is dependent upon the environment and other individuals in the service system benefit uniformity can be advanced by ensuring the standardization of key factors in the service delivery process. These factors would include provider emphasis on promoting uniformity of the service context in terms of the physical setting and environmental conditions, generally. Insofar as possible, the service firm should seek to facilitate the continuity of interpersonal relationships between provider and consumer, thus diminishing the opportunity for the service customer to attribute variation in the service product to involvement with new or unfamiliar personnel. Also, since tangible cues appear to be relevant to the consumer prior to service purchase, tangible cues provided to the consumer after the service sale may be surrogate indicators of product uniformity. Examples of 'tangibilized', post-purchase cues include a documented 'personalized' financial plan (in the case of financial services), printed suggestions to be carried out by the consumer which serve to enhance the service benefit (following consultation with a physician, landscape architect, or tax advisor), a trinket or memento symbolizing a pleasant visit (to a restaurant, pediatrician, sports event, etc.), or a before-sleep snack in the form of a chocolate mint placed on a turned-down pillow (by a hotel or cruise firm).

Efforts to smooth product variation – and the perception of variation – should be complemented by measures which ensure minimal satisfaction levels to consumers by means of guarantees, money back offers, and similar augmented product strategies. Such measures would diminish financial risk in the face of heightened levels of uncertainty concerning product variability and, ultimately, utility for the prospective service consumer. Beyond these measures, service providers need to subtly yet consciously seek to manage expectations in such a way that consumer expectancies will be consistent with the delivered service utility.

Theoretical implications

While services marketing literature suggests that services are more risky, this study represents an advance in a test of risk differences between services and goods and provides experimental evidence that services are perceived to be more risky across several specific dimensions. These specific measures go beyond previous research and extend the discipline's understanding of consumer risk perceptions across goods and services. When respondent product experience is accounted for, the data show that all risk factors are significantly elevated for services. Thus, the study offers specific empirical evidence of differential consumer risk for all dimensions across a wide range of goods and services. In addition, confirmation of the prediction that services are perceived to be associated with greater variability represents a further substantiation of extant marketing theory.

The contributions of the present study are significant in view of the attempt of this research to quantitatively and empirically define service and goods products and the subsequent effort to experimentally assess the influence of such types of products on consumer perception and behavior. While there have been few attempts at empirical research in this area, the literature in this regard has been largely conceptual in nature and has not empirically identified products and services. However, this study is significant in its application of an experimental methodology to a research area in which conceptual or survey approaches have predominated, or in which the operationalization and control of the service variable from the perspective of the consumer lacks definitional and operational rigor. Specifically, this research demonstrates that it is possible to operationalize the concept of 'services' and 'goods' with sufficient articulation so that (1) as a variable it can be manipulated and (2) its variation as an independent variable can be reliably verified by naive subjects.

Second, in contrast to dependence on a single product or product class, the present research was able to incorporate a wide range, or 'sample', of products in the experimental paradigm. Since the experimental factors were not drawn from a defined universe, theoretical 'generalizations' of the findings, in a strict sense, are not possible. However, the use of many different products to operationalize the independent variable suggests a wider application of the findings than would otherwise be possible with other, more narrowly focused research paradigms.

Third, the degree of experimental and statistical control associated with this paradigm is noteworthy. Control of the product factors in terms of perceived cost and respondent familiarity represents an important step in not only service marketing research, but also research associated with consumer risk perception. The analytic procedures represent a significant contribution to specifically controlling important individual differences which otherwise exert a confounding influence on dependent measures.

Future research directions

More experimental research in consumer behavior with respect to services is needed. A key issue relates to the development of adequate measures of consumer behavior involving services. Further study in the area should also seek to extend the scope of this study to include other product factors and sample populations from other consumer goods. While the findings here seem to show some consistency within the samples of factors of the independent variable and with the sample of subjects, the tentative conclusions with respect to perceived risk and variability need to be tested for their applicability to other factors and use groups.

It is also important that these findings be tested in a real world setting (that is, in terms of actual purchases of real products) to determine their true implications. A research context for evaluating actual consumer responses would conceivably entail the collection of data from a large sample of consumers with respect to their perceptions and behavior toward products varying in service attributes. With proper data collection and statistical controls, as suggested by this study, it would be possible to make a more deliberate determination of the importance of these data, based on actual purchase behavior of consumers.

REFERENCES

Arndt, J. (1985) 'On Making Marketing Science More Scientific: Role of Orientations, Paradigms, Metaphors, and Puzzle Solving'. *Journal of Marketing* **49**: 11–23.

Aspinwall, L. (1961) *Four Marketing Theories*. Boulder, CO: University of Colorado.

Bagozzi, R. P. (1984) 'A Prospectus for Theory Construction in Marketing'. *Journal of Marketing* **48**: 11–29.

Bateson, J. E. G. (1977) 'Do We Need Service Marketing'. In *Marketing Consumer Services: New Insights* (P. Eiglier, E. Langeard, C. H. Lovelock, J. E. G. Bateson and R. F. Young Eds). Cambridge, MA: Marketing Science Institute.

Bateson, J. E. G. (1979) 'Why We Need Service Marketing'. In *Conceptual and Theoretical Developments in Marketing* (O. C. Ferrell, S. W. Brown and C. W. Lamb, Jr., Eds). Chicago: American Marketing Association.

Bauer, R. A. (1960) 'Consumer Behavior As Risk-taking'. In *Dynamic Marketing for a Changing World*. Chicago: American Marketing Association, 389–393. Cited by Donald F. Cox (Ed.), *Risk-taking and Information-handling in Consumer Behavior*. Boston: Harvard University Press, 1967.

Berry, L. L. (1984) 'Services Marketing is Different'. In *Services Marketing* (C. H. Lovelock, Ed.). Englewood Cliffs, NJ: Prentice-Hall.

Berry, L. L., Shostack, G. L. and Upah, G. D. (1983) 'Preface'. In *Emerging Perspectives on Services Marketing* (L. L. Berry, G. L. Shostack and G. D. Upah, Eds). Chicago: American Marketing Association.

Bettman, J. R. (1972) Perceived Risk: A Measurement Methodology and Preliminary Findings'. In *Proceedings*, Third Annual Conference of the Advances in Consumer Research (M. Venkatesan, Ed.). College Park, MD: Association for Consumer Research.

Bettman, J. R. (1973) 'Perceived Risk and Its Components: A Model and Empirical Test'. *Journal of Marketing Research* **10**: 184–189.

Bettman, J. R. (1979) *An Information Processing Theory of Consumer Choice*. Reading, MA: Addison-Wesley.

Biehal, G. J. (1983) 'Consumers' Prior Experience and Perceptions in Auto Repair Choice'. *Journal of Marketing* **47**: 82–91.

Booms, B. H. and Bitner, M. J. (1981) 'Marketing Strategies and Organization Structures for Service Firms'. In *Marketing of Services* (J. H. Donnelly and W. R. George, Eds). Chicago: American Marketing Association.

Brinberg, D. and Hirschman, E. C. (1986) 'Multiple Orientations for the Conduct of Marketing Research: An Analysis of the Academic/Practitioner Distinction'. *Journal of Marketing* **50**: 161–173.

Brooker, George, (1984) 'An Assessment of an Expected Measure of Perceived Risk'. In *Advances in Consumer Research* Vol. 11 (T. C. Kinnear, Ed.). Urbana, IL: Association for Consumer Research.

Brown, J. R. and Fern, E. F. (1981) 'Goods vs. Services Marketing: A Divergent Perspective'. In *Conceptual and Theoretical Developments in Marketing* (O. C. Ferrell, S. W. Brown and C. W. Lamb, Jr, Eds). Chicago: American Marketing Association.

Calder, B. J., Phillips, L. W. and Tybout, A. M. (1981) 'Designing Research for Application'. *Journal of Consumer Research* **8**: 197–207.

Campbell, D. and Fiske, D. (1959) 'Convergent and Disciminant Validation by the Multitrait-Multimethod Matrix'. *Psychological Bulletin* **56**: 81–105.

Churchill, G. A., Jr. (1979a) *Marketing Research*. Hinsdale, IL: Dryden Press.

Churchill, G. A., Jr. (1979b) 'A Paradigm for Developing Better Measures of Marketing Constructs'. *Journal of Marketing Research* **16**: 64–73.

Claxton, J. D., Fry, J. N. and Portis, B. (1974) 'A Taxonomy of Prepurchase Information Gathering Patterns'. *Advances in Consumer Behavior* **1**: 35–42.

Cook, T. and Campbell, D. (1975) 'The Design and Conduct of Experiment and Quasi-Experiments in Field Settings'. In *Handbook of Industrial and Organizational Research* (M. Dunnette, Ed.). Chicago: Rand McNally & Company, pp. 233–321.

Cox, D. F. (1967) *Risk-taking and Information Handling in Consumer Behavior.* Boston: Harvard University.

Cox, D. F. and Rich, S. V. (1964) 'Perceived Risk and Consumer Decision-making – The Case of Telephone Shopping'. *Journal of Marketing Research* **1**: 32–39.

Eiglier, P. and Langeard, E. (1977) 'A New Approach to Service Marketing'. In *Marketing Consumer Services: New Insights* (P. Eiglier, E. Langeard, C. H. Lovelock, J. E. G. Bateson and R. F. Young, Eds). Cambridge, MA: Marketing Science Institute, pp. 33–58.

Enis, B. M. and Roering, K. J. (1981) 'Services Marketing: Different Products, Similar Strategy'. In *Marketing of Services* (J. H. Donnelly and W. R. George, Eds). Chicago: American Marketing Association, pp. 1–4.

Davis, D. L., Guiltinan, J. P. and Jones, W. H. (1979) 'Service Characteristics, Consumer Search, and the Classification of Retail Services'. *Journal of Retailing* **3**: 3–23.

Deshpande, R. (1983) '"Paradigms Lost". On Theory and Method in Research in Marketing'. *Journal of Marketing* **47**: 101–110.

George, W. R., Weinberger, M. G., Tsou, B. and Kelly, J. P. (1984) 'Risk Perceptions: A Reexamination of Services Versus Goods'. In *Proceedings* (D. M. Kline and A. E. Smith, Eds). Boca Raton, FL: The Southern Marketing Association and Florida Atlantic University.

George, W. R., Weinberger, M. G. and Kelly, J. P. (1985) 'Consumer Risk Perceptions: Managerial Tool for the Service Encounter'. In *The Service Encounter: Managing Employee/Customer Interaction in Service Businesses* (J. A. Czepiel, M. R. Solomon and C. F. Surprenant, Eds). Lexington, MA: Lexington Books.

Green, P. E. (1973) 'On the Design of Multiattribute Choice Experiments Involving Large Number of Factors or Factor Levels'. In *Advances in Consumer Research, Vol. 1* (S. Ward and P. Wright, Eds). Urbana, IL: Association for Consumer Research.

Green, P. E. and Tull, D. S. (1978) *Research for Marketing Decisions.* Englewood, NJ: Prentice-Hall, Inc.

Guseman, D. S. (1981) 'Risk Perception and Risk Reduction in Consumer Services'. In *Marketing of Services* (J. H. Donnelly and W. R. George, Eds). Chicago: American Marketing Association, pp. 200–204.

Hollander, S. C. (1979) 'Is There a Generic Demand for Services?'. *MSU Business Topics* **3**: 41–46.

Jacoby, J. and Kaplan, L. B. (1972) 'The Components of Perceived Risk'. In *Proceedings, Third Annual Conference* (M. Venkatesan Ed.). Urbana, IL: Association for Consumer Research.

Jackson, D. W., Jr., Keith, J. E. and Burdick, R. K. (1984) 'Purchasing Agents' Perceptions of Industrial Buying Center Influence: A Situational Approach'. *Journal of Marketing* **48**: 75–83.

Johnson, M. E. (1969) Are Goods and Services Different? An Exercise in Marketing Theory. Unpublished dissertation. Washington University.

Judd, R. C. (1964) 'The Case for Redefining Services'. *Journal of Marketing* **28**: 58–59.

Kaplan, L., Szybillo, G. J. and Jacoby, J. (1974) 'Components of Perceived Risk in Product Purchase: A Cross-Validation'. *Journal of Applied Psychology* **59**: 287–291.

Kirk, R. E. (1982) *Experimental Design: Procedures for the Behavioral Sciences,* Belmont, CA: Brooks/Cole Publishing.

Langeard, E. (1983) 'Service Marketing in Europe and the USA'. In *Emerging Perspectives on Services Marketing* (L. L. Berry, G. L. Shostack, and G. D. Upah, Eds). Chicago: American Marketing Association, pp. 5–8.

LaTour, S. A. and Miniard, P. W. (1983) 'The Misuse of Repeated Measures Analysis in Marketing Research'. *Journal of Marketing Research* **20**: 45–57.

Leigh, J. H. (1983) 'Reliability and Validity Assessment of Patterns of Information Source Usage'. In *Advances in Consumer Research, Vol. 10,* (R. P. Bagozzi and A. Tybout, Eds). Ann Arbor, MI: Association for Consumer Research, pp. 673–678.

Levitt, T. (1969) 'Improving Sales Through Product Augmentation'. *European Business* **21**: 5–12.

Levitt, T. (1980) 'Marketing Success Through Differentiation – Anything'. *Harvard Business Review* **58**: 83–92.

Levitt, T. (1981) 'Marketing Intangible Products and Product Intangibles'. *Harvard Business Review* **59**: 94–102.

Lewis, W. F. (1976) An Empirical Investigation of the Relationship Between Services and Products in Terms of Perceived Risk. Unpublished dissertation. University of Cincinnati, OH.

Locander, W. B. and Hermann, P. W. (1979) 'The Effects of Self-Confidence and Anxiety on Information Seeking in Consumer Risk Reduction'. *Journal of Marketing Research* **16**: 268–278.

Lovelock, C. L. (1979) 'Theoretical Contributions from Services and Nonbusiness Marketing'. In *Conceptual and Theoretical Developments in Marketing* (O. C. Ferrell, S. W. Brown and C. W. Lamb, Jr., Eds). Chicago: American Marketing Association, pp. 147–163.

Lovelock, C. L. (1981) 'Why Marketing Management Needs to Be Different for Services'. In *Marketing Services* (J. H. Donnelly and W. R. George, Eds). Chicago: American Marketing Association, pp. 5–9.

Lovelock, C. H. (1983) 'Classifying Services to Gain Strategic Marketing Insights'. *Journal of Marketing* **47**: 9–20.

Lutz, R. J. and Reilly, P. J. (1973) 'An Exploration of the Effects of Perceived Social and Performance Risk on Consumer Information Acquisition'. In *Advances in Consumer Research, Vol. 1* (S. Ward and P. Wright, Eds). Urbana, IL: Association for Consumer Research, pp. 393–405.

Mills, P. K. and Margulies, N. (1980) 'Toward a Core Typology of Service Organization'. *Academy of Management Review* **5**: 255–265.

Minium, E. W. (1978) *Statistical Reasoning in Psychology and Education.* New York: John Wiley & Sons.

Mowen, J. C., Keith, J. E., Brown, S. W. and Jackson, D. W. Jr. (1985) 'Utilizing Effort and Task Difficulty Information in Evaluating Salespeople'. *Journal of Marketing Research* **22**: 185–191.

Murray, K. B. (1986) 'An Empirical Determination of Service Products and Consumer Perception of Their Relative Risk'. Working Paper 86–50, College of Business Administration, Northeastern University.

Nunnally, J. C. (1967) *Psychometric Theory.* New York: McGraw-Hill.

Park, C. (1976) 'The Effect of Individual and Situation-related Factors on Consumer Selection-related Factors on Consumer Selection of Judgmental Models'. *Journal of Marketing Research* **13**: 144–151.

Perry, M. and Hamm, B. C. (1969) 'Canonical Analysis of Relations Between Socioeconomic Risk and Personal Influence in Purchase Decisions'. *Journal of Marketing Research* **6**: 351–354.

Peter, J. (1979) 'Reliability: A Review of Psychometric Basics and Recent Marketing Practices'. *Journal of Marketing Research* **6**: 351–354.

Peter, J. (1981) 'Construct Validity: A Review of Basic Issues and Marketing Practices'. *Journal of Marketing* **18**: 133–145.

Peter, J. and Ryan, M. J. (1976) 'An Investigation of Perceived Risk at the Brand Level'. *Journal of Marketing Research* **13**: 184–188.

Peter, J. and Tarpey, L. X. (1975) 'A Comparative Analysis of Three Consumer Decision Strategies'. *Journal of Consumer Research* **2**: 29–37.

Punj, G. N. and Stewart, D. W. (1983) 'An Interaction Framework of Consumer Decision Making'. *Journal of Consumer Research* **10**: 181–196.

Puto, C. P., Patton, W. E. III and King, R. H. (1985). 'Risk Handling Strategies in Industrial Vendor Selection Decisions'. *Journal of Marketing* **49**: 89–98.

Rathmell, J. M. (1966) 'What is Meant by Services'. *Journal of Marketing* **30**: 32–36.

Rathmell, J. M. (1974) 'Marketing in the Services Sector, Cambridge, MA: Winthrop.

Roselius, T. (1971) 'Consumer Rankings of Risk Reduction Methods'. *Journal of Marketing* **35**: 56–61.

Ross, I. (1972) 'Perceived Risk and Consumer Behavior: A Critical Review'. In *Advances in Consumer Research, Vol. 2* (M. J. Schlinger Ed.). Urbana, IL: Association for Consumer Research, pp. 1–19.

Sasser, W. E. (1976) 'Match Supply and Demand in Service Industries'. *Harvard Business Review* **54**: 133–141.

Schiffman, L. G. (1972) 'Perceived Risk in New Product Trial by Elder Consumers'. *Journal of Marketing Research* **9**: 106–108.

Shostack, G. L. (1977) 'Breaking Free from Product Marketing'. *Journal of Marketing* **41**: 73–80.

Shostack, G. L. (1978) 'The Service Marketing Frontier'. In *Annual Review of Marketing 1978* (G. Zaltman, Ed.). Chicago: American Marketing Association, pp. 373–388.

Smith, S. M. (1982) 'Providing Information for the Consumer Search Process'. In *Advances in Consumer Research, Vol. 9* (A. Mitchell, Ed.). Ann Arbor, MI: Association for Consumer Research, pp. 244–246.

Spence, H. E., Engel, J. F. and Blackwell, R. D. (1970) 'Perceived Risk in Mail-order and Retail Store Buying'. *Journal of Marketing Research* **7**: 364–369.

Swartz, T. A. and Stephens, N. (1984) 'Information Search for Services: The Maturity Segment'. In *Advances in Consumer Research, Vol. 11* (T. C. Kinnear, Ed.). Provo, UT: Association for Consumer Research, pp. 244–249.

Uhl, K. P. and Upah, G. D. (1983) 'The Marketing of Services: Why and How Is It Different?'. In *Research in Marketing, Vol. 6* (J. N. Sheth, Ed.). Greenwich, CT: JAI Press, pp. 231–257.

Weinberger, M. G. and Brown, S. W. (1977) 'Difference in Information Influences: Services vs. Goods'. *Journal of the Academy of Marketing Science* **5**: 389–402.

Wind, Y. and Denny, J. (1974) 'Multivariate Analysis of Variance in Research on the Effectiveness of TV Commercials'. *Journal of Marketing Research* **11**: 136–142.

Wright, P. (1974) 'The Harassed Decision Maker: Time Pressures, Distractions, and the Use of Evidence'. *Journal of Applied Psychology* **59**: 555–561.

Wyckham, R. G., Fitzroy, P. T. and Mandry, G. D. (1975) 'Marketing of Services: An Evaluation of Theory'. *European Journal of Marketing* **9**: 59–67.

Young, R. F. (1981) 'The Advertising of Consumer Services and the Hierarchy of Effects'. In *Marketing of Services* (J. H. Donnelly and W. R. George Eds). Chicago: American Marketing Association, pp. 196–199.

Zeithaml, V. A. (1981) 'How Consumer Evaluation Processes Differ Betweem Goods and Services'. In *Marketing of Services* (J. H. Donnelly and W. R. George, Chicago: American Marketing Association, pp. 186–190.

Zeithaml, V., Parasuraman, A. and Berry, L. L. (1985) 'Problems and Strategies in Services Marketing'. *Journal of Marketing* **49**: 33–46.

Zikmund, W. G. and Scott, J. E. (1973) 'A Multivariate Analysis of Perceived Risk, Self-confidence and Information Sources'. In *Proceedings of the Fourth Annual Convention of the Association for Consumer Research* (S. Ward and P. Wright, Eds). Urbana, IL: Association for Consumer Research, pp. 406–416.

8

Perceived Control and the Effects of Crowding and Consumer Choice on the Service Experience

Michael K. Hui and John E. G. Bateson

The production and consumption of services generally involve a series of interactions between consumers and both the contact personnel and the settings that are provided by service organizations (Eiglier and Langeard, 1977). From these interpersonal (contact personnel and consumer) and human–environment (consumer and service setting) interactions, consumers attempt to get their needs and wants satisfied. This organization–consumer interface is commonly known as the service encounter (Czepiel, Solomon and Surprenant, 1985). We draw the distinction between this tangible series of interactions and the service experience, which is defined as the consumer's emotional feelings during the service encounter.

It has been suggested that perceived control is a crucial determinant of the quality of the two types of interactions (interpersonal and human environment) that institute the service encounter. For example, Schutz (1966) has proposed that human social behaviors are driven by three kinds of interpersonal needs, including control. He suggests that a feeling of control is essential to having satisfactory interactions with other people. Similarly, in environmental psychology, Proshansky, Ittelson and Rivlin (1974) have suggested that people tend to feel and behave more positively when they perceive that there is more control in the environment.

Drawing heavily from environmental psychology, this article explores and empirically demonstrates the contribution of the perceived-control concept to understanding the service experience and explaining the effects of consumer density (the number of consumers that are present in a service setting) and consumer choice (whether it is a person's own decision to enter into and stay in a service encounter) on the service experience. We conducted an experimental study to test the basic proposition that the consumer's perceived control in the service encounter has considerable impact on the service experience. Two situational features of the service encounter, consumer density and consumer choice, were manipulated in the experiment, and their effects on the consumer's emotional and behavioral responses to the encounter were examined. All the hypothesized relationships were integrated into a single theoretical model. The model provides substantial insights in explaining consumer's favorable or unfavorable responses to the service encounter and their reactions to crowding in different service settings.

PERCEIVED CONTROL AND THE SERVICE EXPERIENCE

Control is widely accepted as a human driving force and has often been defined as the need to demonstrate one's competence, superiority, and mastery over the environment (White, 1959). According to Averill (1973), the concept of control has been operationalized in three different ways: behavioral control, cognitive control, and decisional control. Behavioral control refers to the 'availability of a response which may directly influence or modify the objective characteristics of an event' (Averill, 1973, p. 293). Cognitive control has been broken down into predictability and cognitive reinterpretation of a situation. Finally, decisional control refers to 'choice in the selection of outcomes or goal' (Averill, 1973, p. 289).

Empirical evidence has shown that increased perceived control exerts a significant, positive impact on human physical and psychological well-being; this includes physiological responses (see, e.g. Szpiler and Epstein, 1976), task performance (see, e.g. Burger 1987), tolerance of pain and frustration (see, e.g. Sherrod *et al.*, 1977), self-report of distress and anxiety (see, e.g. Staub, Tursky and Schwartz, 1971), and physiological well-being (see, e.g. Langer and Rodin, 1976). A review of these studies (e.g. Langer, 1983) indicates that, in environmental psychology, the concept of perceived control has been used in both laboratory and field settings. From the perspective of the service encounter, the most relevant studies have been those experiments that were performed in hospitals, homes for the aged, and supermarkets.

In studies of both hospitals and homes for the aged, the dependent measures have been physiological and psychological well-being. For example, Langer, Janis and Wolfer (1975) related experimentally manipulated cognitive control to the pre- and postoperative stress of surgical patients. They showed that control-enhancing manipulations, such as cognitive reappraisal of anxiety-provoking events, had positive benefits for well-being. Langer and Rodin (1976) showed that enhanced personal responsibility (behavioral and decisional control), such as opportunity to control time of eating and visitors, resulted in happier and more active nursing-home residents. In a follow-up study, the control-induced residents were found to live longer as well (Rodin and Langer, 1977). Langer and Saegart (1977), in their pioneering field quasi experiment, manipulated perceived control and then measured emotional (e.g. satisfaction) and behavioral (e.g. success in shopping) outcomes. Although they did not measure perceived control directly, they argued that their manipulations of density and warnings about the effects of density would directly influence control. All of the studies described above suggest that a consumer's perceived control can have considerable impact on the service experience (Bateson, 1985) and lead to our first hypothesis.

H_1: In the service encounter, any situational or interpersonal characteristic that increases consumers' perceived control will positively affect emotional and, in turn, behavioral responses to the encounter.

To test such a hypothesis requires the selection of suitable situational or interpersonal characteristics that influence the consumer's perceived control. For this study, we have chosen to focus on two situational characteristics: consumer choice and consumer density. Because of the very limited use of the perceived control concept in consumer behavior settings (and, therefore, a lack of data to guide us), it was important to choose characteristics that had proven impact in environmental psychology and that could reasonably be adapted to consumer settings. The next section reviews the theoretical pedigree of the chosen variables.

CONSUMER CHOICE AND CONSUMER DENSITY

Consumer choice

Existing literature suggests that perceived choice (the perception that an experience or outcome is caused by a person's own decision) can result in positive psychological and behavioral outcomes (Wortman, 1975). As noted earlier, Averill (1973) has argued that perceived choice is one important type of control, or, in his terms 'decisional control'. Thus, providing choice can increase perceived decisional control that should in turn increase the amount of overall perceived control. According to this model, therefore, any emotional or behavioral effects that are caused by the availability of alternative choices can be considered as outcomes of perceived control. In environmental psychology, choice has commonly been operationalized as whether it is a person's own decision to enter into or stay in a situation (Averill, 1973). Accordingly, our second hypothesis is formulated as follows.

H_2: Providing the consumer with a choice of whether to stay in the service situation will result in higher perceptions of control.

Consumer density

Stokols (1972) has asserted that there is a need to distinguish between the terms 'density' and 'crowding'. Density refers to the physical condition, 'in terms of spatial parameters' (Stokols, 1972, p. 275). On the other hand, perceived crowding is an unpleasant feeling that is experienced by an individual. More important, perceived control has been argued as a key intervening variable between density and crowding (Schmidt and Keating, 1979).

Proshansky *et al.* (1974) have suggested that density is a key determinant of an individual's perceived control in a particular setting. Density can facilitate or obstruct desired behaviors; the influence it has will then determine the individual's perception of crowding. For example, Rodin, Solomon and Metcalf (1978) have shown that high perceived crowding results when density reduces an individual's ability to perform a desired action. Nonetheless, there is considerable evidence showing that perceived crowding is also a direct function of density (e.g. Langer and Saegart, 1977). This finding is not unexpected since perceived crowding refers to the 'the negative subjective experience of certain density levels' (Rapoport, 1975, p. 134). Our third hypothesis captures all the above-mentioned relationships.

> H_3: In a service setting, density affects consumers' perceived crowding directly and indirectly through perceived control.

In line with the existing conceptualization that perceived crowding is a negative subjective experience (e.g. Stokols, 1972), the fourth hypothesis relates perceived crowding to emotional and behavioral outcomes.

> H_4: In a service encounter, consumers' perceived crowding negatively affects emotional and, in turn, behavioral responses to the encounter.

A summary of hypotheses 1–4 can be represented by a model as presented in Figure 1. Empirical evidence has shown that the relationship between density and pleasure can vary between different settings (McClelland and Auslander, 1978). A high-density bar or restaurant is interpreted as less unpleasant than a high-density bank or retail outlet. According to Figure 1, one possible explanation for the above finding is that perceived control as a function of density varies between settings. Our fifth hypothesis captures this relationship.

> H_5: The relationship between density and perceived control varies with the service setting.

The hypothesized model (Figure 1) also suggests a more stringent test of the intervening role of perceived control between density and perceived crowding. Given that perceived crowding is a function of perceived control, any situational determinant of the consumer's perceived control (e.g. consumer choice) is expected

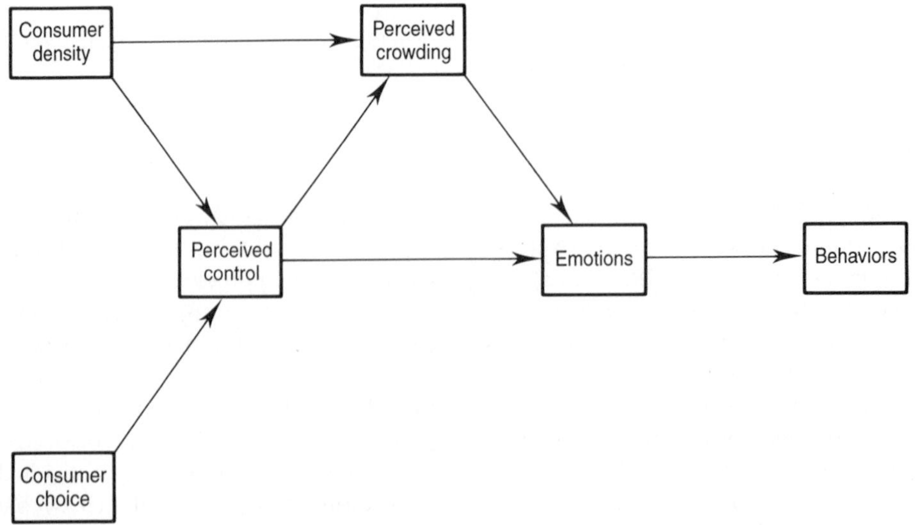

Figure 1. Effects of consumer density and consumer choice on the service experience.

to influence the consumer's perceived crowding. The sixth hypothesis is therefore formulated as follows:

> H_6: In a service setting of any density level, consumers' perceived crowding is a function of any situational determinant of perceived control.

METHOD

Research design

An experimental study was conducted to test our six research hypotheses. In the study, consumer choice in the service encounter and consumer density of the service setting were manipulated independently, and their effects on the consumer's psychological and behavioral responses to the service encounter were examined. The manipulation of these two characteristics of the encounter provides a more powerful test of hypothesis 1. If a simple one-characteristic relationship can be mediated by a change in another characteristic, and this can be shown to be due to changes in perceived control, then the true intervening nature of perceived control is demonstrated.

To test hypothesis 5, we also included two service settings, a bank and a bar, in the study. Results of a pilot study indicated that people tend to believe that consumer density has less negative impact on the service experience in a bar setting than in a bank setting. Most respondents said that they would not mind staying in a high-density bar but that they would definitely try to avoid a high-density bank. In short, a 3 (consumer density: high, medium, and low) × 2 (consumer choice: choice and no choice) × 2 (service setting: bank and bar) experimental factorial design was employed. Consumer density and consumer choice were nonrepeated factors whereas service setting was a repeated factor.

Consumer density was operationalized through color slides that portrayed three different numbers of consumers in a medium-sized branch of a bank and a country bar. Prior studies have shown that slides can adequately represent the environment (e.g. Hershberger and Cass, 1974). To encompass known peaks and troughs in the number of consumers, a total of 50 slides were taken by a camera fixed at a corner of the bank. Since the camera was fixed at the same position, the only difference between the slides was the number of consumers that were inside the bank. Another 50 slides were also taken in the bar by the same method.

The consumer-density level represented in each of the 100 slides (50 from each setting) was determined by a procedure adapted from McClelland and Auslander (1978). Three individuals rated all the slides on two physical dimensions: number of people (in absolute number) and number of people per unit area (1–10 rating). Of the 100 slides, the interrater reliability, estimated by the Spearman–Brown formula (Tinsley and Weiss, 1975), was .94 for number of people and .96 for number of people per unit area. For each slide, raters' scores were summed for each of the two physical dimensions. A linear composite of the two-dimension scores then determined the consumer-density level that was represented in the slide. Finally, the three bank slides showing the highest, average, and lowest density levels were used in the experimental study to represent the high-, medium-, and low-density settings, respectively. Three bar slides were chosen in the same way.

Written scenarios were employed to operationalize the choice treatments and to describe the features of various service situations. To illustrate how the choice manipulation was created, consider the two bank scenarios used in the study.

Bank scenario 1 (choice). 'It is quarter to three on Friday afternoon and Mr Y is in a bank to transfer money from his saving to his checking account. The transfer can also be done through the cash dispensing machine outside the bank but he decides to use the cashier. Of course, he can always change his mind and use the machine instead or he can come back next week because the money is not urgently needed. However, he sticks to his original decision and stays in the bank until the transfer is done. The slide we are going to show you depicts the interior of the bank while Mr Y is there.'

Bank scenario 2 (no choice). 'It is quarter to three on Friday afternoon and Mr Y is in a bank to transfer money from his deposit to his current account. The transfer can also be done through the cash dispensing machine outside the bank but the machine is temporarily out of service. He can't come back later because the bank is going to close and the money is desparately needed to cover a check he has already written. Hence, he has to use the cashier and stay in the bank until the transfer is done. The slide we are going to show you depicts the interior of the bank while Mr Y is there.'

In the context of a laboratory experiment, it is very difficult to manipulate perceived choice in the service encounter directly. Decisions to 'come back later' are difficult to operationalize. Instead, all respondents saw the given density situation, and the scenarios were used to manipulate their perceived choice. The situations described by the written scenarios can be regarded as service-encounter analogues of Glass and Singer's (1972) manipulation of choice. In their studies, a stressful stimulus (e.g. electric shock) was delivered to all subjects. Half of the subjects, however, were given an option to avoid or escape from the stimulus, but they were asked not to do so as long as they found the stimulus bearable. As a result, no subject selected the escape or avoid option and, therefore, both the choice and no-choice subjects experienced the same stressful stimulus. Nonetheless, the findings indicated that the choice subjects felt and behaved significantly better than the no-choice subjects.

The same principle was employed in designing the written scenarios. Despite the fact that Mr Y ends up facing the same crowd of people, his presence in the service situation is more his own decision in the choice scenario than it is in the no-choice scenario. According to hypothesis 2, the two written scenarios are expected to produce a difference in the subjects' perceived choice and, hence, perceived control. A similar approach was adopted in the development of the two bar scenarios (see the Appendix).

The use of a hypothetical figure in the scenarios is based on the work of Havlena and Holbrook (1986). They suggest that there are two advantages to using hypothetical consumers (e.g. Mr Y, as in the bank scenarios) in written scenarios: '(a) to provide a projective task and thereby to discourage social desirability effects, and (b) to avoid problems involving individual differences in reactions to specific types of activities' (Havlena and Holbrook, 1986, p. 396).

The benefit of using hypothetical consumers was confirmed in a pretest of the written scenarios. When a projective task was not used, a number of respondents complained that the described situations would never happen to them and, hence, that it was difficult for them to judge their reactions to the situations.

Methodology

Subjects were recruited from various churches and a public housing estate located in London, England, and through an advertisement in a free local newspaper. A total of 115 people between the ages of 25 and 40 participated in the study.

Concurrent experimental sessions were conducted in three different lecture rooms that were of similar size and design. In each room, two envelopes were left in front of each available seat. Each envelope contained a questionnaire, the front page of which consisted of either a choice scenario or a no-choice scenario as described above. Each subject was randomly assigned to a seat in one of the three experimental rooms.

At the beginning of each experimental session, the experimenter announced that the main objective of the study was to examine human reactions to daily social situations. The subjects were asked to open the first envelope and read the scenario on the first page of the questionnaire. After one minute, the first slide, showing the same service setting that was described in the scenario at one of the three (high, medium, and low) consumer-density levels, was projected on a screen. The subjects then reported the hypothetical consumer's feelings in the situation as described by the scenario and shown in the slide. After the last subject had finished, the whole procedure was repeated again for the second service situation. Each session lasted from 50 to 70 minutes.

Dependent measures

A self-administered questionnaire measured the five dependent variables: perceived choice, perceived control, perceived crowding, pleasure, and approach-avoidance. The last two variables were drawn from the Mehrabian and Russell (1974) model of environmental reactions to represent the consumer's emotional and behavioral responses to the service encounter, respectively. Three emotional dimensions (pleasure–displeasure, dominance–submissiveness, arousal–unarousal) are included in the model, but existing evidence reveals that pleasure–displeasure tends to be the dimension that produces the most direct and strongest effect on approach-avoidance (Donovan and Rossiter, 1982; Mehrabian and Russell, 1974).

Perceived choice was measured using two simple questions. For the bank setting, the two questions were: 'How much choice do you think Mr Y has in deciding when to transfer the money?' and 'How much choice do you think Mr Y has in deciding how to transfer the money?' These questions were used as a manipulation check of the choice treatments.

Five seven-point semantic differential scales were included in one section of the questionnaire. Mehrabian and Russell's (1974) scale of dominance and Glass and Singer's (1972) scale of helplessness were combined as a semantic differential indicator of perceived control (CTL1). Both dominance and helplessness have been considered as closely associated with or alternative labels for perceived control (Russell and Mehrabian, 1976; Seligman, 1975). This section also contained Mehrabian and Russell's (1974) scale of pleasure (PLE1), a scale of perceived crowding (CRD) that was developed from review of the crowding literature (stuffy–not stuffy, cramped–uncramped, crowded–uncrowded, free to move–restricted, and spacious–confined), and a single item (choice–no choice) that was used as a second measure of perceived choice (PCHOICE2). To avoid response bias, the direction of half of the items in each scale was reversed. The items were mixed and the order of presentation was randomized.

Another section of the questionnaire consisted of three seven-point Likert-type scales. One of the scales, adapted from the studies conducted by Newcomb and Harlow (1986) and Fleming, Baum and Weiss (1987), was included as the second measure of perceived control (CTL2). Two other scales, adapted from Mehrabian and Russell's (1974) scale of approach-avoidance, measured desire to stay (DSTAY) and desire to affiliate (DAFF). The final scale was a third measure of perceived choice (PCHOICE3). This scale, developed from the choice literature, included statements like, 'It is his own decision to stay in the situation.'

In the last section of the questionnaire, 27 emotional terms were given. The respondents were asked to describe the service experience that was shown and described in the written scenario by checking a seven-point scale (from 'not at all' to 'extremely so') for each term. Twenty-four of the terms were used by Havlena and Holbrook (1986) to measure the eight basic emotion components that were identified by Plutchik (1980); each component was operationalized by three emotional terms. One more component, comfort, was added to this study. This component was also operationalized by three emotional terms: calm, peaceful, and relaxed. The 27 emotional terms form a perfect two-dimensional (pleasure–displeasure; arousing–unarousing) circumplex model as proposed by Russell and Pratt (1980). The terms were mixed, and the order of presentation was randomized. The ratings obtained on the pleasure dimension were converted into a second indicator of pleasure (PLE2) through Bush's (1972) successive-interval scales of adjectives denoting feelings.

RESULTS

The experiemental sessions produced 107 and 112 completed questionnaires for the bank and the bar settings, respectively. A two-way analysis of variance of perceived choice as a function of the two experimental variables revealed a significant choice main effect in both settings. The two choice scenarios produced significantly higher perceived-choice ratings than did the two no-choice scenarios in both settings (for the bank, $F(1,101) = 175.18$, $p < .001$; for the bar, $F(1,106) = 112.51$, $p < .001$). Neither the density main effect nor the interaction was significant. The findings indicated that the choice manipulation was effective.

The data were then analyzed through the structural equations model shown in Figure 2. The model was proved to be identified through a procedure suggested by

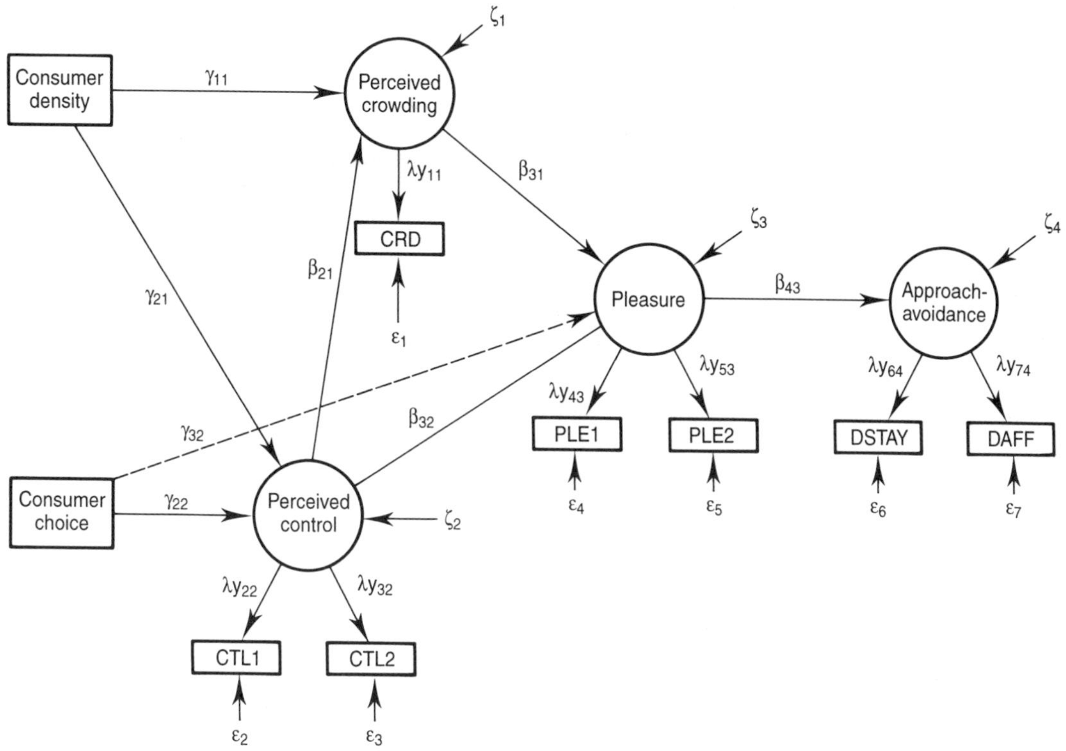

Figure 2. Structural equations model. The dashed line signifies a relationship not included in the hypothesized model (M-1) but found to be significant in the analysis (M-2).

Bagozzi (1980). Perceived choice was omitted for a more parsimonious model and because of the powerful manipulation check. With either set of data, a Cronbach α of .9 was obtained for the one scale used to measure perceived crowding (CRD). Therefore, the measurement error (ϵ_1) and correspondence loading (λ_{y11}) of CRD were fixed at .10 ($1 - \alpha$) and .95 (the square root of α), respectively, in the analysis.

Testing the hypothesized model

Multisample LISREL (Jöreskog and Sörbom, 1989) was used to test the hypothesized model. This method allowed simultaneous analysis of the data that were obtained from the two settings, and, hence, any similarity or difference in the estimated values of the parameters between the two settings could be explored. The structural equation model (M-1) gave a chi-square value of 63.89 ($df = 50$; $p = .090$), a goodness-of-fit index (GFI) of .936, and a root mean square residual (RMR) of .039 for the bank setting, and a GFI of .946 and a RMR of .031 for the bar setting. The findings suggested that M-1 produced a reasonable fit in both settings (Bagozzi and Yi, 1988).

Rival model A

A modification index of significant size, however, was obtained for the paramter γ_{32} (the causal path between choice and pleasure) in both settings. This finding suggested that there may exist a direct choice effect on pleasure. The parameter γ_{32} was therefore set free in another multisample LISREL analysis. The modified model produced a chi-square value of 50.03 ($df = 48$; $p = .393$). Compared with M-1, the modified model (M-2) has two degrees of freedom less, but its chi-square value was also 13.86 smaller. Since the difference between the chi-square values of two nested models also forms a chi-square distribution (Bagozzi, 1980), we can therefore conclude that M-2 is a better model than M-1 ($\chi^2 = 13.86$, $df = 2$, $p < .01$). A direct choice effect on pleasure (represented by the dotted line in Figure 2) was therefore added to our original hypothesized model in the subsequent analysis. A conceptual rationalization for this path is included in the Discussion.

Rival model B

As shown in Figure 2, no direct relationship is hypothesized between perceived control and approach-avoidance responses. Pleasure is assumed to be an intervening variable through which perceived control influences approach-avoidance. We made two changes to M-2 to test this assumption. First, the causal path between perceived control and approach-avoidance was set free. Second, the causal path between perceived control and pleasure was fixed at zero. The rival model produced a chi-square value of 175.03 ($df = 48$, $p < .000$), which indicated a poor fit. Therefore, a direct relationship from perceived control to approach-avoidance was not supported by our findings.

Rival model C

Another interesting rival model draws from the argument that the direction of causality between perceived control and perceived crowding may, in fact, be reversed. In other words, a strong correlation between the two variables may indicate that perceived control is a function of perceived crowding rather than the opposite, as we hypothesized. The causal path between perceived crowding and perceived control was therefore reversed in another multisample LISREL analysis, but the modified model (M-4) produced a poor fit with the data ($\chi^2 = 79.29$, $df = 48$, $p = .003$). Accordingly, the argument that high perceived crowding causes low perceived control was not supported.

Comparison between two settings

This part of the analysis was concerned with the stability of the estimated parameters across the two settings. When the values of all the parameters were constrained to be identical between the two settings, the structural equations model (M-5) produced a chi-square value of 82.30 ($df = 69$, $p = .131$). A less restrictive model (M-6), one that allowed the values of all the γ parameters to vary between the two settings, produced a chi-square value of 68.14 ($df = 65$, $p = .371$). The two chi-square values suggested that M-6 produced a significantly better fit than did M-5 ($\chi^2 = 14.16$, $df = 4$, $p < .01$).

Estimated values of parameters

A summary of all the multisample LISREL models that were tested in our analysis is presented in Table 1. Two of the models, M-2 and M-6, undoubtedly produce the best fit with our data. Note that the only difference between M-2 and M-6 is that, in the latter model, all the parameters, other than the γ's, were constrained to be identical between the two settings. Since the chi-square difference between M-2 and M-6 was not significant ($\chi^2 = 18.11$, $df = 17$, p = NS) and for the sake of simplicity, we therefore used the LISREL estimates of M-6 (Table 2) in testing our six hypotheses.

As shown in Table 2, except γ_{21} of the bar setting, the estimated values of all the other path coefficients are significantly different from zero at least at the .05 level. The two path coefficients, β_{32} and β_{43}, confirm that perceived control is a positive determinant of pleasure, which, in turn, exerts a positive effect on approach-

Table 1. Goodness-of-fit indicators for the structural equation models

Model	Description	χ^2	*df*	*p*	GFI	RMR
M-1	Hypothesized model	63.89	50	.090	.946[a] .936[b]	.031[a] .039[b]
M-2	M-1 plus a direct choice effect on pleasure	50.03	48	.393	.948[a] .957[b]	.032[a] .033[b]
M-3	Modification of M-2; a direct effect from perceived control to approach-avoidance	175.03	48	.000	.872[a] .875[b]	.121[a] .079[b]
M-4	Modification of M-2; perceived control as a function of perceived crowding	79.29	48	.003	.922[a] .936[b]	.130[a] .099[b]
M-5	Modification of M-2; all the parameters are constrained to be identical between the two samples	82.30	69	.131	.920[a] .922[b]	.074[a] .067[b]
M-6	Modification of M-2; except the γ's, all the parameters are constrained to be identical between the two samples	68.14	65	.371	.931[a] .938[b]	.043[a] .047[b]

GFI = goodness-of-fit index; RMR - root mean square residual.
[a]Data are for bar scenarios.
[b]Data are for bank scenarios.

Table 2. LISREL estimates of M-6

Parameters	Estimated values
λ_{y11}	.950[a]
λ_{y22}	1.000
λ_{y32}	.901 (15.78)***
λ_{y43}	1.000
λ_{y53}	.991 (24.56)***
λ_{y64}	1.000
λ_{y74}	.749 (9.63)***
β_{12}	−.661 (−10.25)***
β_{31}	−.126 (−2.78)*
β_{32}	.781 (10.93)***
β_{43}	.863 (17.11)***
γ_{11}:	
Bar	.529 (7.42)***
Bank	.398 (5.35)***
γ_{21}:	
Bar	.128 (1.76)+
Bank	−.218 (−2.92)*
γ_{22}:	
Bar	.604 (8.04)***
Bank	.446 (5.82)***
γ_{32}:	
Bar	.126 (2.32)*
Bank	.194 (3.82)***

Data are maximum likelihood estimates. For the sake of simplicity, only the estimated values of the λ_y, β, and γ parameters are presented. Numbers inside the parentheses are the t values of the estimates. Estimates without a t value are fixed parameters.
[a]A Cronbach α of .9 is obtained for the scale of perceived crowding. The λ_{y11} is fixed at a value equal to the square root of the obtained α value.
+$p < .10$.
*$p < .05$.
***$p < .001$.

avoidance (Hypothesis 1). A highly significant γ_{22} also indicates that perceived control is a positive function of consumer choice (Hypothesis 2).

The excellent fit of the structural equations model also supports the hypothesis that perceived crowding is both a direct and an indirect function of consumer density (Hypothesis 3). Moreover, a significant negative β_{31} and a significant positive β_{43} support the hypothesized relationships between perceived crowding, pleasure, and approach-avoidance (Hypothesis 4). The estimated values of γ_{21} confirm that density has a different impact on perceived control in the bar setting than in the bank setting (Hypothesis 5). In fact, a negative estimate of the parameter is obtained with the bank data, while a positive estimate, although only marginally significant ($t = 1.76$, $p < .10$), is obtained with the bar data.

Finally, the LISREL results show that perceived crowding is a negative function of perceived control (β_{12}), which, in turn, is a positive function of consumer choice (γ_{22}). Accordingly, perceived crowding is expected to be a negative function of consumer density (Hypothesis 6). As shown in Table 3, in either the bank or the bar setting, the choice subjects reported significantly lower perceived crowding than did their no-choice counterparts at all three density levels (for the bank, $F(1,101) = 13.50$, $p < .001$; for the bar, $F(1,106) = 18.73$, $p < .001$).

Table 3. Mean scores of perceived crowding as a function of density and choice

Consumer density	Choice	No choice
Bank:[a]		
Low	3.96	4.88
Medium	5.21	5.87
High	5.73	6.35
Bar:[b]		
Low	3.58	4.31
Medium	4.01	5.50
High	5.00	5.60

Perceived crowding measured with a 1–7 rating. Higher score indicates higher perceived crowding.

[a]Choice main effect: $F(1,101) = 13.50$, $p < .001$; density main effect: $F(2,101) = 22.85$, $p < .001$; choice-density interaction: $F(2,101) = .22$, NS.

[b]Choice main effect: $F(1,106) = 18.73$, $p < .001$; density main effect: $F(2,101) = 14.69$, $p < .001$; choice-density interaction: $F(2,106) = 1.67$, NS.

DISCUSSION AND CONCLUSIONS

The findings of this study strongly support the hypothesized model (Figure 1) and confirm the power of concept of perceived control in explaining the effects of consumer choice and consumer density on the emotional and behavioral outcomes of the service encounter.

Perceived control and consumer emotions and behaviors

Variation in the subject's perceived control that was caused by consumer choice and consumer density was found to exert a considerable effect on pleasure and approach-avoidance. Moreover, the fact that choice can mediate the influence of density on perceived crowding and pleasure adds support to the significance of perceived control and vindicates the use of two manipulations of perceived control.

The confirmation of Hypothesis 1 suggests that the perceived-control concept can contribute to exploring different ways to create a more pleasant service experience. Giving more choice to the consumer in the service encounter is one alternative. For example, drawing heavily from the concepts of control and choice, Mills and Krantz (1979) have allowed blood donors to choose which arm is used. This manipulation has been found to ameliorate significantly donors' experiences in blood transfusion centers. In fact, greater consumer choice is considered to be one crucial benefit of service customization, a common competitive strategy that is employed by service organizations (Surprenant and Solomon, 1987).

One limitation of this study is that the service experience was examined in a rather narrow context, in the sense that only two particular features of the service encounter were manipulated. To confirm the role of perceived control as a crucial dimension of the service experience, researchers need to investigate the power of the concept in explaining a wide variety of pleasant and unpleasant service experiences.

Perceived control and crowding

Our results also demonstrate that perceived control is a powerful concept in explaining the consumer's reactions to consumer density in the service environment. The confirmation of Hypothesis 6 suggests that any negative outcomes of high consumer density can be minimized by returning some control to the consumer. Our results show that a greater degree of choice can lower the consumer's perceived crowding in the service encounter. Other authors have suggested that similar effects can be obtained from providing situational and emotional information (Baum, Fisher and Solomon, 1981), distraction and attribution (Worchel, 1978), and architectural and interior design (Baum and Valins, 1977).

Perceived control can also be used to explain the previous finding that density produces positive emotional and behavioral effects in some settings and negative effects in other settings (Freedman, 1975). In both the bank and bar settings, there is a positive relationship between density and perceived crowding (γ_{11}), and a negative relationship between perceived control and perceived crowding (β_{12}). However, the sign of the relationship between density and perceived control (γ_{21}) varies with the setting. In the bank setting, high density is associated with lower perceived control, but in the bar setting, high density is associated with higher control. Thus, density can directly influence pleasure in a negative manner, but this can be counteracted by a positive association through perceived control.

Two existing theories can be used to explain a positive relationship between density and perceived control. According to manning theory (Wicker, 1984), every setting requires an optimal number of occupants to function effectively; then the setting is said to be adequately 'manned'. A high-density bar may be more adequately manned than a low-density bar and, hence, may offer higher levels of perceived control. The concept of behavior–environment fit (Michelson, 1970) provides an alternative explanation. People may feel that they have more control in the high-density bar simply because the setting is more compatible with their situational goals, say, to have an exciting evening after a monotonous day of hard work (Argyle, Furnham and Graham, 1980).

A possible confounding effect

The only unexpected finding obtained in this study is a direct relationship between choice and pleasure. Conceptually, this finding can be attributed to a possible confounding effect that was created by the two choice scenarios. When the subjects were told that Mr X decides to stay in the noisy bar or Mr Y decides to use the cashier, they might infer that the hypothetical consumer is a person who enjoys disco music or prefers to deal with human tellers. The two no-choice scenarios, on the other hand, did not contain any clues about the personal disposition of the hypothetical consumer (Jones and Davis, 1965).

The subjects' conditioned responses to the situations that were described in the scenarios might also contribute to a direct choice effect on pleasure. For example, subjects might have learned from previous experience that a situation like a cash-dispensing machine temporarily out of service is unpleasant. Consequently, spontaneous negative responses may have been likely when a similar service situation was described to the subjects during the experimental sessions.

APPENDIX

Bar scenarios used in the experimental study

Bar scenario 1 (choice). 'It is eight o'clock on Thursday evening, and Mr X is with one of his friends in a country pub for a drink and a chat. Disco music is being played in one of the two separated lounges in the pub. When they first arrive, Mr X and his friend decide to stay in the music lounge. Since the music is very noisy, they know beforehand they have to shout when chatting with each other in the lounge. Of course, they can always change their minds and go the quieter lounge but they stay in the music lounge until they leave an hour later. The slide we are going to show you depicts the interior of the lounge while Mr X and his friend are there.'

Bar scenario 2 (no choice). 'It is eight o'clock ... a chat. There are two lounges in the pub. Disco music is being played in both lounges so that they have to shout when chatting with each other. It is impossible for them to go to another pub because it is the only one in the area. They stay there for an hour as Mr X's friend is very keen for a drink. The slide we are ... are there.'

ACKNOWLEDGMENTS

The authors wish to thank Russell Belk for his comments on an earlier draft of this article, and three anonymous reviewers for their patience and insights. This research was funded by a grant from the Marketing Science Institute.

REFERENCES

Argyle, M., Furnham, A. and Graham, J. A. (1980) *Social Situations.* Cambridge: Cambridge University Press.

Averill, J. R. (1973) 'Personal Control over Aversive Stimuli and Its Relationship to Stress'. *Psychological Bulletin* **80** (4): 286–303.

Bagozzi, R. P. (1980) *Causal Models in Marketing.* New York: Wiley.

Bagozzi, R. P. and Yi, Y. (1988) 'On the Evaluation of Structural Equation Models'. *Journal of Academy of Marketing Science* **16** (1): 74–94.

Bateson, J. E. G. (1985) 'Perceived Control and the Service Encounter'. In *The Service Encounter: Managing Employee/Customer Interaction in Service Business* (J. A. Czpiel *et al.*, Eds). Lexington, MA: Lexington, 67–82.

Baum, A. and Valins, S. (1977) *Architecture and Social Behavior: Psychological Studies of Social Density.* Hillsdale, NJ: Erlbaum.

Baum, A., Fisher, J. D. and Solomon, S. K. (1981) 'Type of Information, Familiarity, and the Reduction of Crowding Stress'. *Journal of Personality and Social Psychology* **40** (1): 11–23.

Burger, Jerry M. (1987) 'Increased Performance with Increased Personal Control: A Self-Presentation Interpretation'. *Journal of Experimental Social Psychology* **23** (4): 350–360.

Bush, L. E. II (1972) 'Successive-Intervals Scaling of Adjectives Denoting Feelings'. *JSAS Catalog of Selected Documents in Psychology* **2**: 140.

Czepiel, J. A., Solomon, M. R. and Surprenant, C. F. (1985) *The Service Encounter: Managing Employee/Customer Interaction in Service Businesses.* Lexington, MA: Lexington.

Donovan, R. J. and Rossiter, J. R. (1982) 'Store Atmosphere: An Environmental Psychology Perspective'. *Journal of Retailing* **58** (Spring): 34–57.

Eiglier, P. and Langear, E. (1977) 'Services as Systems: Marketing Implications'. In *Marketing Consumer Services: New Insights* (P. Eiglier *et al.*, Eds). Cambridge, MA: Marketing Science, pp. 83–103.

Flemming, I., Baum, A. and Weiss, L. (1987) 'Social Density and Perceived Control as Mediators of Crowding Stress in High-Density Residential Neighborhoods'. *Journal of Personality and Social Psychology*, **52** (5), 899–906.

Freedman, J. L. (1975) *Crowding and Behavior.* San Francisco: Freeman.

Glass, D. C. and Singer, J. E. (1972) *Urban Stress: Experiments on Noise and Social Stressors.* New York: Academic Press.

Havlena, W. J. and Holbrook, M. B. (1986) 'The Varieties of Consumption Experience: Comparing Two Typologies of Emotion in Consumer Behavior'. *Journal of Consumer Research* **13** (December): 394–404.

Hershberger, R. G. and Cass, R. C. (1974) 'Predicting User Responses to Buildings'. In *Man-Environment Interactions: Evaluations and Applications, Part II* (D. H. Carson, Ed). Stroudsbury, PA: Dowden, Hutchison & Ross, pp. 117–134.

Jones, E. E. and Davis, K. (1965) 'From Acts to Dispositions: The Attribution Process in Person Perception'. In *Advances in Experimental Social Psychology*, Vol. 2 (L. Berkowitz, Ed.). New York: Academic Press, pp. 219–266.

Jöreskog, K. G. and Sörbom, D. (1989) *LISREL 7 User's Reference Guide.* Mooresville, IN: Scientific Software.

Langer, E. J. (1983) *The Psychology of Control.* Beverly Hills, CA: Sage.

Langer, E. J. and Rodin, J. (1976) 'The Effects of Choice and Enhanced Personal Responsibility for the Aged: A Field Experiment in an Institutional Setting'. *Journal of Personality and Social Psychology* **34** (2): 191–198.

Langer, E. J. and Saegart, S. (1977) 'Crowding and Cognitive Control'. *Journal of Personality and Social Psychology*, **35** (3): 175–182.

Langer, E. J., Janis, I. L. and Wolfer, J. A. (1975) 'Reduction of Psychological Stress in Surgical Patients'. *Journal of Experimental Social Psychology* **11** (2): 156–165.

McClelland, L. and Auslander, N. (1978) 'Perceptions of Crowding and Pleasantness in Public Settings'. *Environment and Behavior* **10** (4): 535–553.

Mehrabian, A. and Russell, J. A. (1974) *An Approach to Environmental Psychology.* Cambridge, MA: MIT Press.

Michelson, W. (1970) *Man and His Urban Environment: A Sociological Approach.* Reading, MA: Addison-Wesley.

Mills, R. T. and Krantz, D. S. (1979) 'Information, Choice and Reactions to Stress: A Field Experiment in a Blood Bank with Laboratory Analogue'. *Journal of Personality and Social Psychology* **37** (4): 608–620.

Newcomb, M. D. and Harlow, L. L. (1986) 'Life Events and Substance Use among Adolescents:

Mediating Effects of Perceived Loss of Control and Meaninglessness in Life'. *Journal of Personality and Social Psychology* **51** (3): 564–577.

Plutchik, R. (1980) *Emotion: A Psychoevolutionary Synthesis.* New York: Harper & Row.

Proshansky, H. M., Ittelson, W. H. and Rivlin, L. G. (1974) 'Freedom of Choice and Behavior in a Physical Setting'. In *Environmental Psychology* (H. M. Proshansky *et al.*, Eds). New York: Holt, Rinehart & Winston, pp. 170–181.

Rapoport, A. (1975) 'Toward a Redefinition of Density'. *Environment and Behavior* **7** (2): 133–158.

Rodin, J. and Langer, E. J. (1977) 'Long-Term Effects of a Control-relevant Intervention'. *Journal of Personality and Social Psychology* **35** (12): 897–902.

Rodin, J., Solomon, S. K. and Metcalf, J. (1978) 'Role of Control in Mediating Perceptions of Density'. *Journal of Personality and Social Psychology* **36** (9): 988–999.

Russell, J. A. and Mehrabian, A. (1976) 'Some Behavioral Effects of the Physical Environment'. In *Experiencing the Environment* (S. Wapner, S. B. Cohen and B. Kaplan, Eds). New York: Plenum, pp. 5–18.

Russell, J. A. and Pratt, G. (1980) 'A Description of the Affective Quality Attributed to Environment'. *Journal of Personality and Social Psychology* **38** (2): 311–322.

Schmidt, D. E. and Keating, J. P. (1979) 'Human Crowding and Personal Control: An Integration of Research'. *Psychological Bulletin* **86** (4): 680–700.

Schutz, W. C. (1966) *The Interpersonal Underworld.* Palo Alto, CA: Science & Behavior.

Seligman, M. E. P. (1975) *Helplessness.* San Francisco: Freeman.

Sherrod, D. R., Hage, J. N., Halpern, P. L. and More, B. S. (1977) 'Effects of Personal Causation and Perceived Control on Responses to an Aversive Environment: The More Control, The Better'. *Journal of Experimental Social Psychology* **13** (1): 14–27.

Staub, E., Tursky, B. and Schwartz, G. E. (1971) 'Self-Control and Predictability: Their Effects on Reactions to Aversive Stimulation'. *Journal of Personality and Social Psychology* **18** (2): 157–162.

Stokols, D. (1972) 'On the Distinction between Density and Crowding: Some Implications for Future Research'. *Psychological Review* **79** (3): 275–278.

Surprenant, C. F. and Solomon, M. R. (1987) 'Predictability and Personalization in the Service Encounter'. *Journal of Marketing* **51** (April): 86–96.

Szpiler, J. A. and Epstein, S. (1976) 'Availability of an Avoidance Response as Related to Autonomic Arousal'. *Journal of Abnormal Psychology* **85** (1): 73–82.

Tinsley, H. E. A. and Weiss, D. J. (1975) 'Inter-rater Reliability and Agreement of Subjective Judgements'. *Journal of Counseling Psychology* **22** (4): 358–376.

White, R. W. (1959) 'Motivation Reconsidered: The Concept of Competence'. *Psychological Review* **66** (5): 297–333.

Wicker, A. W. (1984) *An Introduction to Ecological Psychology.* Monterey, CA: Brooks/Cole.

Worchel, S. (1978) 'Reducing Crowding without Increasing Space: Some Application of an Attributional Theory of Crowding'. *Journal of Population* **1** (3): 216–230.

Wortman, C. B. (1975) 'Some Determinants of Perceived Control'. *Journal of Personality and Social Psychology* **31** (2): 282–294.

9

Consumer Behaviour and Services: A Review

Mark Gabbott and Gillian Hogg

INTRODUCTION

Since the early work of Judd (1964), Rathwell (1966) and Levitt (1972) there has been increasing attention paid to the marketing of services. This interest has been motivated by a recognition of the importance of the 'services sector' and a need to understand the problems of marketing services more explicitly. Early work by Sasser *et al.* (1978) provided a clear articulation of the characteristics of services which distinguished them from goods and these provided an agenda for considering how the nature of services marketing differed from that of goods, as well as highlighting some of the problems associated with adopting goods marketing terminology and concepts.

The dominant feature of the existing literature on the marketing of services is its implicit management orientation, a concentration on how services are, or should be, marketed. This approach makes a fundamental assumption which this article seeks to challenge, specifically that consumer behavior is unaffected by the nature of the product. While research into the consumption of services is sparse, this literature has already established a number of areas where the characteristics of services make accepted forms of consumer behaviour problematic. This article reviews the current services and consumer behaviour literature in order to clarify the main issues for consumers in obtaining information about services, comparing alternative service provision and evaluating the service encounter. Until the mid-1980s the dominant theoretical paradigm in consumer behaviour was the information processing approach. More recently, experiential and behavioural perspectives have been recognized as providing realistic alternatives to the information processing approach. While these perspectives may provide a means to amplify our understanding of consumer behaviour and services, the discussion in this article will take place using the information processing model in order to provide a means to synthesize service marketing and consumer behaviour literatures. This analysis highlights a number of aspects of consumer behaviour which need to be considered by service marketers.

PRODUCTS, GOODS AND SERVICES

As a first stage it is necessary to make a distinction between products, goods and

Reprinted with permission from *Journal of Marketing Management*, Vol. 10, No. 4, pp. 311–324.

services. Marketing theory has been dominated by concepts and terminology derived from the marketing of goods. This orientation has endured despite a recognition that services have a number of unique characteristics. In as much as goods and services both provide benefits and customer satisfaction, they have both been described as products in the widest sense of the word (Cowell, 1991; Enis and Reoring, 1981) which has allowed services literature to develop based upon a sound marketing literature. However there has also been a tendency to use the terms 'goods' and 'products' interchangeably with little attention paid to the service dimension which may have far-reaching implications for marketers. If it is accepted that services do have distinguishing characteristics, such as those identified by Lovelock (1981) and Booms and Bitner (1981) for example, then it is necessary to restate and understand the differences between a product, which can include both a good and service element, and a good which is defined purely in terms of its physical properties.

Most definitions of services are still framed in terms of differences with goods. The distinction is provided on the basis of a comparison of the dominant characteristics of each (Schifman and Kanuk, 1991; Regan, 1963; and Blois, 1974). However, as Foxall (1985) points out, if services are seen not as a separate entity but only as a different type of product, the differences identified between goods and services are not fundamental but merely classificatory. What is needed is an appreciation of the dimensions of services which place different demands on both the purchaser and the provider.

As a way of highlighting the inadequacy of discriminating between goods and services Levitt (1972) argues that there is no such thing as a service industry, only industries where service components are greater. The distinction is between suppliers where the core of what they are selling is a service and suppliers that use a service element associated with a goods element as a competitive advantage, a theme developed by Gronroos (1978). The corollary of this argument is that all purchases of goods involve an element of service. Shostack (1977) argues that there are very few 'pure' products or services and describes a product continuum from tangible dominant goods to intangible dominant services. However, even within this approach there is a service element which is still indistinct from the good. Kotler (1991) provides structure to the continuum by identifying four distinct categories of offer: purely tangible goods, tangible goods with accompanying services, a major service with accompanying goods and services and pure services. A common feature of these approaches is a recognition that services have a number of distinguishing characteristics. These characteristics have been identified as: intangibility, inseparability, heterogeneity, perishability and ownership (Sasser *et al.*, 1978; Shostack, 1977; Grönroos, 1978).

SERVICE CHARACTERISTICS

Intangibility is one of the most important characteristics of services, they do not have a physical dimension. Often services are described using tangible nouns but this obscures the fundamental nature of the service which remains intangible. Shostack (1987) for instance points out that 'airline' means air transportation, 'hotel' means lodging rental. Berry (1980) argues that even although the performance of most services is supported by tangibles the essence of what is purchased is a performance, therefore as McLuhan (1964) points out, it is the process of delivering a service which comprises the product. The implication of this argument is that consumers cannot see, touch, hear, taste or smell a service they can only experience the performance of it (Carman and Uhl, 1973; Sasser *et al.*, 1978). The second characteristic of services is the inseparability of the production and consumption aspects of the transaction. The service is a performance, in real time, in which the consumer cooperates with the provider, Bell (1981). According to Thomas (1978) the degree of this involvement is dependent upon the extent to which the service is people-based or equipment-based. The inference of this distinction is that people-based services tend to be less standardized than equipment-based services or goods producing activities. Goods are produced, sold and then consumed, whereas services are sold and then produced and consumed simultaneously (Regan, 1963; Cowell, 1984). The inseparability of the role of service provider and consumer also refers to the lack of standardization since the consumer can alter both the way in which the service is delivered, as well as what is delivered, which has important implications for the process of evaluation.

The heterogeneity of services is also a function of human involvement in the delivery and consumption process. It refers to the fact that services are delivered by individuals to individuals and therefore each service encounter will be different by virtue of the participants or time of performance. As a consequence each consumer is likely to receive a different service experience. The perishability of services describes the real time nature of the product. Services cannot be stored unlike goods and the absence of the ability to build and maintain stocks of the product means that fluctuations in demand cannot be accommodated in the same way as goods, i.e. in periods of excess demand more product cannot be utilized. For the consumer of services the time at which the consumer chooses to use the service may be critical to its performance and therefore the consumers experience. Kelley *et al.* (1990) make the observation that consumption is inextricably linked to the presence of other consumers and their presence can influence the service outcome.

To the above characteristics of services, Judd (1964), Wyckham *et al.* (1975) and Kotler (1982) have identified the concept of ownership as a distinguishing feature of services. With the sale of a good the purchaser generally obtains ownership of it. By contrast in the case of a service the purchaser only has temporary access or use of it: what is owned is the benefit of the service, not the service itself, i.e. in terms of a holiday the consumer has the benefit of the flight, hotel and beach but does not own them. The absence of ownership stresses the finite nature of services for consumers, there is no enduring involvement in the product only in the benefit.

These separate characteristics which distinguish a service from a good have formed the basis of most analyses of services marketing. However, very few attempts have been made to consider these characteristics together in order to investigate their joint effect upon consumers' behaviour. Simply, we know that intangibility creates a problem for consumers in evaluation and choice, we also know that heterogeneity presents an impediment to learning and routinizing behaviour but the combined effect of service characteristics are still not clearly understood.

CONSUMER BEHAVIOUR AND SERVICES

With the developing interest in services and services marketing it might be expected that the consumer behaviour literature would include references to the evaluation and consumption of intangibles. However, there are very few examples of published work which refer explicitly to the consumption characteristics of services. There would appear to be an assumption, consistent with the interchangeability of terminology, that consumer behaviour related to goods is the same as that related to products, i.e. the difference between goods and services is insignificant. In the case of products where the 'good' element is dominant this may be a valid assumption, but for products where the dominant characteristic is the service intangibility this assumption denies the significant impact upon consumption behaviour of the characteristics identified above.

As a vehicle for examining likely differences in consumer behaviour and services, a simple process model of consumer behaviour will be used, drawn from the dominant information processing perspective. This view implies that consumers first search for information about possible alternatives and attributes, selected alternatives are then compared on the basis of these attributes and once consumption has occurred the product is re-evaluated. Under each of these three process headings the services and consumer behaviour literature will be reviewed in order to provide some indication of the likely consumer responses to the problems presented by services.

Information search

The literature on consumer information activity in relation to goods is large and concentrates upon classifying the various sources of information (e.g. Beales *et al.*, 1981; Engel *et al.*, 1986; Westbrook and Fornell, 1979; Fletcher, 1987), the ability to assimilate information from these sources (e.g. Jacoby *et al.*, 1974; Miller, 1956; Keller and Staelin, 1987; Summers, 1974; Wilkie, 1974; Jacoby, 1984; Muller, 1984); the motivation for external search behaviour and the extent of that behaviour (e.g. Johnson and Russo, 1984; Urbany *et al.*, 1989; Bucklin, 1966; Moore and Lehlann, 1980). The characteristics of services which we believe place an additional information burden on consumers are associated with information sources used, the nature of information available from each source and the consumers response to that information.

Commonly two types of consumer information sources are referred to: internal and external sources. The search of internal sources of information is characterized by Bettman (1979b) as a scan of memory. When faced with a purchase decision consumer first examine memory for information which may be relevant to the decision (Jacoby *et al.*, 1978). This information may be the result of previous experiences, which constitute a body of knowledge about, or an attitude toward, a product or a product class. If previous service experience is available this is an extremely credible source even if it is recognized that the experiences which comprise this information are event-specific and may not provide any clear indication as to future performance. The work carried out by Murray (1991) provided some support for this and pointed to a preference for internal sources of information in evaluating services.

Where information gained from previous experience is not available to consumers, or the information already held is considered insufficient to discriminate between different offerings, then the consumer may be motivated to search for information externally. This external information search implies a conscious recognition of the need for more decision-relevant information. The extent of external search is said to be dependent upon a number of factors, such as product category experience, product complexity or the degree of buyer uncertainty. On each of these dimensions, services are likely to prompt significant external search effort. In itself, this does not indicate any specific differences in the consumption behaviour related to services with that of goods. An alternative approach suggested by Murray (1991) is that in considering the degree of external information search it is inadequate to merely analyse the absolute number of sources used but more productive to assess source effectiveness.

The effectiveness of information available from external sources is related to the nature of services. Nelson (1970) identifies experience and search qualities of products where search qualities are those product attributes which can be almost completely determined and evaluated prior to purchase, for example, colour, size, price, etc. Experience qualities are those attributes which cannot be known or assessed prior to purchase but are determined during or after consumption. The more tangible the product the more dominant are the search qualities and the more intangible the less information is available before consumption. Services are therefore high in experience qualities and low in search qualities.

The implication for the consumer is that experiential information is perhaps the most difficult to obtain pre-purchase. The only sources of this type of information are pre-purchase trial, observation or reliance upon the experiences of others (Locander and Hermann, 1979). Pre-purchase trial is not an option in the case of services since they are produced as they are consumed and they therefore have to be experienced in total before they can be assessed, for instance it is not possible to try a haircut before purchase. Observation is equally unreliable as a source of information since the service is intangible and the participation of any other individual gives no guarantee of a repeated performance. As a consequence a number of authors (e.g. Murray, 1991) suggest that consumers look towards personal sources of information. This positions is supported by Zeithaml (1981) who suggests that the need for experience information of the service prompts a reliance upon word-of-mouth sources as they are perceived to be more credible and less biased. This is also consistent with the work of Robertson (1970), Eiglier *et al.* (1977) and Urbany and Weilbacker (1987) who indicate that word-of-mouth sources are pivotal in relation to services. As a consequence we can say that where service is a dominant element of a product, consumers face a number of problems, primarily in acquiring and using their own knowledge and also that the external environment cannot provide appropriate objective information. The likely response is an increased reliance on personal sources of information.

Comparison

The process of information search leads the consumer to an evoked set of alternatives that will form the basis of comparison and choice. The difficulties of obtaining effective pre-purchase information about services is likely to result in a smaller evoked set in services than goods. Zeithaml (1981) suggests that because of the nature of services and the difficulties in obtaining effective information consumers tend to be more loyal once they have found an acceptable alternative, for instance in the case of professional services like solicitors; indeed, if the consumer has previous experience of a service the evoked set may be as small as one (see Johnston and Bonama 1981). However if the internal information is negative or the consumer does not have experience on which to base the choice then the size of evoked set will be dependent upon the effectiveness of the external information that was available. There are various models of how consumers choose between available alternatives in different situations, such as Bettman (1979a), Grether and Wilde (1984), Wright (1975) and Fletcher and Hastings (1983). The common component of these models is a set of attributes. There are two identifiable problems for consumers in defining attribute sets in relation to services, problems of identifying attributes and problems of making comparisons on the basis of these attributes.

All products have attributes or defining characteristics, in the case of goods these attributes are tangible, can be determined in advance of purchase and common to all consumers purchasing the product. By contrast in the case of services the attributes of provision are intangible, cannot be determined in advance of purchase and are not common to all consumers, i.e. the individual consumers' needs are accommodated by their involvement in the service delivery, for example, in the case of hairdressing where the consumer is involved in describing and modifying the service outcome. In the absence of any tangible indications of what the service will be like consumers must use other means of comparing services in the pre-purchase phase. Shostack (1977) and Berry (1980) point to the subsequent reliance upon peripheral tangible cues to predict quality. The more intangible dominant the service the fewer clues are likely to be available, Levitt (1981) suggests that in these circumstances it is necessary for consumers to establish metaphors for tangibility or cues that help them to 'tangibilize the intangible', in order that they may create a credible expectation. Various authors have pointed to the role of the environment in which the consumption of the service takes place in providing these metaphors or cues such as Bitner (1992) or Lewis (1991). These would include corporate wear, decor, appearance of service providers, standard of equipment or furnishing and all may be used to approximate the missing tangible product information (Gabbott, 1991). The key problem for the consumer is identifying the cues which will most accurately predict the nature of the service experience.

The second issue for consumers is in comparing service alternatives on the basis of common attributes. Services cannot be compared simultaneously, but can only be compared in series, not parallel, i.e. a consumer cannot put two services side by side at any one time. Added to this time dimension is the problem of heterogeneity. The absence of truly common attributes implies that services are non-comparable products. Johnson (1984) suggests that faced with non-comparable product alternatives the consumer will search for the basis of a comparison by moving to more abstract product attributes, e.g. necessity, social status or entertainment value. In the case of services non-comparability is likely to evoke a reverse form of abstraction where services are compared on increasingly material or tangible criteria until there is little left to compare other than the service provider as the ultimate physical embodiment of the service.

Another characteristic of service dominant products is that some attributes are bargainable in the sense that they are determined between provider and consumer. Brucks and Shurr (1990) define bargaining as a process whereby two or more parties mutually define one or more attribute values for a product. For instance, in the case of insurance services the terms of the offering are negotiated before delivery. The bargainable nature of some service attributes serves to emphasize the uncertainty of the comparison process. This factor also has implication for the number of alternatives compared where bargainability reduces the number of alternatives as well as significantly reducing the number of attributes used in the comparison process.

Evaluation

A critical stage in the consumption process is the evaluation of the product after consumption as a means of building experience and knowledge as well as learning about the product class. Any product is evaluated on the basis of whether it fulfils the pre-determined need and whether the outcome meets the consumer's expectations about how the need should have been fulfilled. In this sense there is a pre-determined standard against which to compare the outcome. Several researchers have made a distinction between objective and perceived quality in evaluating products, e.g. Zeithaml (1988). Objective quality refers to the technical superiority or excellence of a product against measurable and verifiable standards. Garvin (1983) describes this as evaluation based upon amounts of specific attributes or ingredients, for example, weight, colour or size. Perceived quality can be defined as the consumers' judgement about a product's overall excellence or superiority. Quality is defined solely in terms of the consumer's perception which is a much more use-orientated approach to evaluation and is closer to the definition of service quality proposed by Zeithaml *et al.* (1990) as 'meeting or exceeding customer expectations'. The determination of satisfaction or dissatisfaction is therefore on the basis of a comparison between perceived quality and expected quality of the service experience.

Parasuraman *et al.* (1991) suggest that there is a fundamental expectation of a service; which is that it provides what it promises, i.e. accountants produce accurate accounts and dry cleaners produce clean clothes. This fundamental expectation has been described as a reliability dimension of service by Parasuraman *et al.* (1991) and by Gronroos (1991) as the technical quality dimension. This basic expectation generally relates to the more tangible elements of a product and as such it can be measured by the consumer in a reasonably objective manner. Swan and Comb (1976) make a similar point using the term instrumental performance to describe a minimum level of quality.

In the case of goods, what has been received is evident before its performance is evaluated. By comparison services are produced as they are consumed therefore the difference between goods and service elements of a product is that the consumer of a service evaluates how a service is received before it is clear what has been received. Once the service performance is complete it is conceivable that satisfaction with how the service was delivered will be reviewed. This makes the process of evaluating performance, i.e. determining satisfaction or dissatisfaction much more complex in the case of services.

The problem with this approach comes when consumers do not have the knowledge or experience to evaluate what they have received or that their expectations of what they wanted from the service are not clear. Darby and Karni (1973) refer to these as the credence qualities, these are characteristics of a product that the consumer finds difficult to evaluate even after purchase and consumption. In these circumstances how a service was delivered may be used to evaluate what was delivered, this is referred to by Gronroos as the functional quality, or by Swan and Comb (1976) as expressive performance. Parasuraman *et al.* (1991) refer to both as process dimensions and argue that these dimensions are usually evaluated as the service is delivered. Process dimensions have been described as service responsiveness (willingness to help), assurance (knowledge and courtesy of providers), and empathy (the caring individualized relationship between provider and consumer) and the signs, symbols and artifacts of delivery (signposting, decor, personal presentation) (Zeithaml, 1981; Bitner, 1992). These dimensions added to the reliability of the delivered service and form five dimensions of service quality identified by Zeithaml *et al.* (1990). This research suggests that although reliability ('the what') is important in meeting customer expectations the process dimensions ('the how') are the most important in exceeding customer expectations. The 'how' dimensions are almost invariably associated with the individual service provider.

In terms of satisfaction, the way in which the consumer participates in the service will influence his evaluation of the service received. Customers may be required to participate in the definition and production of the service and may therefore feel personally involved in the success or failure of the outcome (Zeithaml, 1981). If a consumer cannot or does not clearly articulate or understand their own requirements, or has formed unrealistic expectations of the service then they may feel that some responsibility for the failure was their own. Therefore the process of evaluating services in terms of satisfaction and dissatisfaction is a shared responsibility between provider and consumer.

DISCUSSION

This article has suggested that acquiring information, choice and the evaluation of services present a number of problems for consumers. These problems are derived from the nature of services in particular their intangibility and their heterogeneity. In the first stage of the simple process model, information is difficult to obtain since the service is intangible and there is no objective information that the consumer can obtain other than relying upon personal experience. However, since service experiences vary across consumers and across time so experience information either from self or others can only be a guide to future performance rather than a predictor. Other information gained from search has to be tempered by the evaluation of the source of the information. As such information effectiveness for the consumer of services is questionable.

The second problem for consumers is in comparing service alternatives. Again intangibility and heterogeneity present the main impediments to the effective assessment of future performance. What is being assessed in the case of a service is the perceived benefit from the service rather than the service itself. The consumer is choosing between their own subjective assessments of the likely service outcome. Comparison is hampered further by the heterogeneity of service provision and the difficulties in identifying or generating attributes upon which to base a choice. Finally, once the service has been initiated either by purchase, by acceptance or instruction there are problems in evaluating what is being, or what has been provided. In this context the role of expectations are pivotal. It has been argued that failure to achieve satisfaction from a service is as much the responsibility of the consumer as the provider in not identifying precise needs, yet it must also be recognized that consumers may not have a precise set of needs to communicate and this is central to the delivery of satisfaction and benefit.

The description of services as problematic for consumers is a theme which is common across a broad range of literature. Most suggestions propose marketing responses tackling some of the fundamental characteristics of services. These include making services appear less intangible by focusing upon physical dimensions, or less heterogeneous through standardized delivery or by recognizing the importance of word-of-mouth information sources using such techniques as personal endorsement. However, little attention has been paid to the likely consumer responses to the problems presented by services.

Responses

It is generally accepted that consumers are ultimately seeking to simplify or routinize their purchase decisions at the same time as minimizing the level of risk attached to the outcome. In relation to goods two key responses have been identified: first, the reliance upon product cues which are used to approximate missing information or predict likely outcomes and second, the reliance upon inertia or loyalty built upon satisfaction in order to routinize the consumption decision. However, both these responses need to be examined in the light of the characteristics of services.

Existing work on product cues associated with goods has tended to concentrate upon the identification of cues used by the consumer. A number of studies have identified brand name, origin or price as active cues. The basis of this analysis is that goods have a finite number of available attributes which can serve as pre-purchase clues for the consumer. In the case of services the range of cues is much wider since they are present in all tangible accompaniments to the service, i.e. provider, artifacts, premises or goods components. If the range of cues available pre-purchase is wider than that associated with goods and the cues are also uniquely associated with each service. The presence of variable cues both within service products and across service products do not provide support for the simplification function of cues for the consumer. A second implicit assumption associated with product cues is the ability to justify or prove their worth. Since tangible cues vary from provider to provider and form a small part of the service experience, the effectiveness of individual cues is likely to vary from provider to provider. Finally, product cues in relation to goods are used pre-purchase and their value assessed post-purchase. Where services are concerned the delivery may take place at a different time, with a different provider, with different tangibles or in a different place to the purchase transaction. As a result cues used to evaluate a service pre-purchase may be different to those used to evaluate during delivery or even after delivery has taken place.

The second response of consumers in relation to goods is brand or product loyalty which is one form of routinizing purchase behaviour. In the case of services loyalty can only be placed with the provider of the service rather than the service itself, i.e. it is theoretically impossible to obtain the same service from a different provider. Loyalty is built up from a series of successful service encounters with the same provider and the number of consumers with successful encounters builds reputation. An aspect of loyalty in relation to services which is different to that of goods is the potential to cement a relationship between customer and provider. We have identified above the inability in some circumstances of the consumer to accurately vocalize or identify needs and expectations. Subsequent service encounters allow needs and expectations of the consumer to be synchronized with the abilities and performance of the provider. This process of repeat purchasing is likely to result in the continued and increment strengthening of service relationships where the consumer is able to take full advantage of the potential benefits offered. In the case of goods the relationship is likely to plateau once all benefits have been experienced and may in some circumstances start to decline. It is evident that this continued relationship also produces a sense of ownership over the service with consumers referring to 'my accountant', 'my hairdresser', or 'my mechanic'. Equally this may have an impact upon attribution in the case of failure. The amount of investment in the relationship may lead consumers to rationalize failures on the basis of 'just a bad day', since they have experienced better or that it is their own fault in not correctly communicating needs. Either way relationships are likely to be more stable in the case of services than goods.

CONCLUSION

This article has investigated the implications for consumer behaviour presented by services as opposed to goods. It has concluded that services present a number of problems for consumers and also that suggested consumer responses in relation to goods may not be applicable to services. Specifically that there is a body of knowledge which explains consumer behaviour in relation to goods and that this body of knowledge suggest problems for consumers in choosing and evaluating services. It also suggests a number of responses to these problems which are again derived from this goods perspective. The final consideration is that the whole argument is being framed within the rational information processing perspective of consumer behaviour. Either consumer problems in relation to services need to be more fully explored within this framework or research will need to move outside this perspective perhaps towards examining the personal relationship between provider and consumer such as the degree of empathy or sympathy or explore the alternative behavioural perspectives. These may provide a means to integrate service design, service encounter and service consumption which emerge as crucial to service marketing. This article has endeavoured to concentrate upon consumer behaviour rather than re-iterate the managerial implications of service characteristics which form the basis of a substantial part of the services literature. It is our contention that unless consumer behaviour and in particular consumer responses to the problems associated with service are clarified, service marketing may be in danger of pursuing provider-oriented solutions to the problems perceived to be faced by consumers rather than truly understanding the nature of consumer decision processes or the reality of consumer behaviour.

REFERENCES

Beales, H., Mazis, M. Salop, S. and Staelin, R. (1981) 'Consumer Search and Public Policy'. *Journal of Consumer Research* **8** (June): 11–22.

Bell, M. L. (1981) 'A Matrix Approach to the Classification of Marketing Goods and Services'. In *Marketing of Services* (J. H. Donnelly and W. R. George, Eds). Chicago: AMA.

Berry, L. L. (1980) 'Services Marketing is Different'. *Business* (May–June): 24–29.

Bettman, J. R. (1979a) *An Information Processing Theory of Consumer Choice.* Massachusetts, Addison Wesley.

Bettman, J. R. (1979b) 'Memory Factors in Consumer Choice: A Review'. *Journal of Marketing* **43**: 37–53.

Bitner, M. J. (1992) 'Servicecapes: The Impact of Physical Surroundings on Customers and Employees'. *Journal of Marketing* **56**: 57–71.

Blois, K. J. (1974) 'The Marketing of Services: An Approach'. *European Journal of Marketing* **8** (Summer): 137–145.

Booms, B. H. and Bitner, M. J. (1981) 'Marketing Strategies and Organizational Structures for Service Firms'. In *Marketing of Services* (J. H. Donnelly and W. R. George, Eds). Chicago: AMA.

Brucks, M. and Schurr, P. (1990) 'The Effects of Bargainable Attributes and Attribute Range Knowledge on Consumer Choice Processes'. *Journal of Consumer Research* **16** (March): 409–419.

Bucklin, L. (1966) 'Testing Propensities to Shop'. *Journal of Marketing* **30** (January): 22–27.

Carman, J. and Uhl, K. (1973) *Marketing: Principles and Methods.* Homewood, IL: Irwin.

Cowell, D. (1984). *The Marketing of Services.* London: Heinemann.

Cowell, D. W. (1991) 'Marketing Services'. In *The Marketing Book* (M. J. Baker Ed.). Oxford, Butterworth Heinemann.

Darby, M. R. and Karni, E. (1973) 'Free Competition and the Optimal Amount of Fraud'. *Journal of Law and Economics* **16** (April): 67–86.

Eiglier, P., Langeard, E., Lovelock, C., Bateson, J. and Young, R. (1977) *Marketing Consumer Services: New Insights.* Cambridge, MA: Marketing Science Institute.

Engel, J., Blackwell, R. and Miniard, P. (1986) *Consumer Behaviour.* New York: Dryden.

Enis, B. M. and Roering, K. (1981) 'Services Marketing: Different Products, Similar Strategies'. In *Marketing of Services* (J. H. Donnelly and W. R. George, Eds). Chicago: AMA.

Fletcher, K. and Hastings, W. (1983) 'The Relevance of the Fishbein Model to Insurance Buying'. *Service Industries Journal* **3** (No. 3): 296–307.

Fletcher, K. (1987) 'Consumers Use and Perceptions of Retailer Controlled Information Sources'. *International Journal of Retailing* **2** (No. 3): 59–66.

Foxall, G. (1985) 'Marketing is Service Marketing'. In *Marketing in the Service Industries.* London: Frank Cass.

Gabbott, M. (1991) 'The Role of Product Cues in Assessing Risk in Second Hand Markets'. *European Journal of Marketing* **25** (No. 9): 38–50.

Garvin, D. (1983) 'Quality on the Line'. *Harvard Business Review* **61** (Sept–Oct): 65–73.

Grether, D. and Wilde, L. (1984) 'An Analysis of Conjunctive Choice: Theory and Experiments'. *Journal of Consumer Research* **10** (March): 373–385.

Gronroos, C. (1978) 'A Service Orientated Approach to Marketing Services'. *European Journal of Marketing* **12** (No. 8): 589.

Gronroos, C. (1991) *Strategic Management and Marketing in the Services Sector.* Studentlitteratur: Lund, Sweden.

Jacoby, J. (1984) 'Perspectives on Information Overload'. *Journal of Consumer Research* **10** (March).

Jacoby, J., Chestnut, R. and Fisher, W. (1978) 'A Behavioural Process Approach to Information Acquisition in Nondurable Purchasing'. *Journal of Marketing Research* **15** (No. 3, August): 532–544.

Jacoby, J., Speller, D. and Berning, C. (1974) 'Brand Choice Behaviour as a Function of Information Load: Replication and Extension'. *Journal of Consumer Research* **1**: 33–42.

Johnson, E. and Russo, J. E. (1984) 'Product Familiarity and Learning New Information'. *Journal of Consumer Research* **11** (June): 542–550.

Johnson, M. (1984) 'Consumer Choice Strategies for Comparing Noncomparable Alternatives'. *Journal of Consumer Research* **11** (December): 741–753.

Johnston, W. and Bonoma, T. (1981) 'Purchase Process for Capital Equipment and Services'. *Industrial Marketing* **4**: 253–264.

Judd, R. C. (1964) 'The Case for Redefining Services'. *Journal of Marketing* **28**: 59–73.

Keller, K. and Staelin, R. (1987) 'Effects of Quality and Quantity of Information on Decision Effectiveness'. *Journal of Consumer Research* **14** (September): 200–213.

Kelley, S. W., Donnelly, J. H. and Skinner, S. J. (1990) 'Customer Participation in Service Production and Delivery'. *Journal of Retailing* **66** (No. 3): 315–335.

Kotler, P. (1982) *Principles of Marketing*. New Jersey: Prentice-Hall.

Kotler, P. (1991) *Marketing Management*. New Jersey: Prentice-Hall.

Levitt, T. (1972) 'Production-line Approach to Service'. *Harvard Business Review* (Sept–Oct): 41–52.

Levitt, T. (1981) 'Marketing Intangible Products and Product Intangibles'. *Harvard Business Review* **59** (May–June): 94–102.

Lewis, B. (1991) 'Service Quality: An International Comparison of Bank Customers' Expectations and Perceptions'. *Journal of Marketing Management* **7**: 47–62.

Locander, W. and Hermann, P. (1979) 'The Effect of Self-confidence and Anxiety on Information Seeking in Consumer Risk Reduction'. *Journal of Marketing Research* **19**: 268–274.

Lovelock, C. (1981) 'Why Marketing Management Needs to be Different for Services'. In *Marketing of Services* (J. H. Donnelly, and W. R. George, Eds). Chicago: AMA.

McLuhan, M. (1964) *Understanding Media*. New York: McGraw-Hill.

Miller, G. (1956) 'The Magical Number Seven Plus or Minus Two, Some limitations on our Capacity for Processing Information'. *Psychological Review* **63** (No. 2).

Moore, W. L. and Lehmann, D. (1980) 'Individual Differences in Search Behaviour for a Nondurable'. *Journal of Consumer Research* **7** (December): 296–307.

Muller, T. (1984) 'Buyer Response to Variation in Product Information Load'. *Journal of Applied Psychology* **69** (No. 2, May).

Murray, K. (1991) 'A Test of Services Marketing Theory: Consumer Information Acquisition Activities'. *Journal of Marketing* **55** (January): 10–25.

Nelson, P. (1974) 'Advertising as Information'. *Journal of Political Economy* **81** (July–August): 729–754.

Parasuraman, A., Berry, L. and Ziethaml, V. (1991) 'Understanding Customer Expectations of Service'. *Sloan Management Review* (Spring): 39–48.

Rathwell, J. M. (1966) 'What is Meant by Services?' *Journal of Marketing* **30**: 32–36.

Rathwell, J. M. (1974) *Marketing in the Services Sector*. Cambridge, MA: Winthrop.

Regan, W. J. (1963) 'The Service Revolution'. *Journal of Marketing* **27** (July): 57–62.

Robertson, T. S. (1970) *Innovative Behaviour and Communication*. New York: Holt, Rheinhart and Winston.

Sasser, W. E., Olsen, R. P. and Wyckoff, D. D. (1978) *The Management of Service Operations*. Boston, MA: Allyn & Bacon.

Schiffman, L. and Kanuk, L. (1991) *Consumer Behaviour*, 4th Edition. New Jersey: Prentice-Hall.

Shostack, G. L. (1977) 'Breaking Free From Product Marketing'. *Journal of Marketing* **41**: 73–80.

Shostack, G. L. (1987) 'Service Positioning Through Structural Change'. *Journal of Marketing* **51**: 34–43.

Summers, J. (1974) 'Less Information is Better'. *Journal of Marketing Research* **XI** (November): 467–468.

Swan, J. and Comb, L. (1976) 'Product Performance and Consumer Satisfaction: A New Concept;. *Journal of Marketing* **40** (April): 25–33.

Thomas, D. R. E. (1978) 'Strategy is Different in Service Businesses'. *Harvard Business Review* (July–August): 158–165.

Urbany, J. and Weilbacker, D. (1987) 'A Critical Examination of Nelson's Theory of Information and Consumer Behaviour'. In *AMA Educators Conference Proceedings* (S. Douglas *et al.* Eds). Chicago: AMA.

Urbany, J., Dickson, P. and Wilkie, W. (1989) 'Buyer Uncertainty and Information Search'. *Journal of Consumer Research* **16** (September): 208–215.

Westbrook, R. A. and Fornell, C. (1979) 'Patterns of Information Source Usage Among Durable Goods Buyers'. *Journal of Marketing Research* **16** (August): 303–312.

Wilkie, W. L. (1974) 'Analysis of Effects of Information Load'. *Journal of Marketing Research* **XI** (November): 462–466.

Wright, P. (1975) 'Consumer Choice Strategies: Simplifying or Optimising'. *Journal of Marketing Research* **12** (February): 60–67.

Wyckham, R., Fitzroy, P. and Mandry, G. (1975) 'Marketing of Services: An Evaluation of Theory'. *European Journal of Marketing* **9** (No. 1): 59–67.

Zeithaml, V. (1988) 'Consumer Perceptions of Price, Quality and Value: A Means–End Model and Synthesis'. *Journal of Marketing* **52** (July): 2–22.

Zeithaml, V. (1981) 'How Consumer Evaluation Processes Differ Between Goods and Services'. In *Marketing of Services* (J. H. Donnelly and W. R. George, Eds). Chicago: AMA.

Zeithaml, V., Parasuraman, A. and Berry, L. (1990) *Delivering Quality Service.* New York: Collier Macmillan.

10

Critical Service Encounters: The Employee's Viewpoint

Mary Jo Bitner, Bernard H. Booms and Lois A. Mohr

The worldwide quality movement that has swept the manufacturing sector over the last decade is beginning to take shape in the service sector (*Business Week*, 1991; Crosby, 1991). According to some, the shift to a quality focus is essential to the competitive survival of service businesses, just as it has become essential in manufacturing (Heskett *et al.*, 1994; Schlesinger and Heskett, 1991).

Service quality researchers have suggested that 'the proof of service [quality] is in its flawless performance' (Berry and Parasuraman, 1991, p. 15), a concept akin to the notion of 'zero defects' in manufacturing. Others have noted that 'breakthrough' service managers pursue the goal of 100% defect-free service (Heskett, Sasser and Hart, 1990). From the customer's point of view, the most immediate evidence of service occurs in the service encounter or the 'moment of truth' when the customer interacts with the firm. Thus, one central goal in the pursuit of 'zero defects' in service is to work toward 100% flawless performance in service encounters. Here, flawless performance is not meant to imply rigid standardization, but rather 100% satisfying performance from the customer's point of view. The cost of not achieving flawless performance is the 'cost of quality', which includes the costs associated with redoing the service or compensating for poor service, lost customers, negative word of mouth, and decreased employee morale.

Although more firms are realizing the importance of service quality and customer satisfaction, it is not always clear how to achieve these goals. Situations arise in which quality is low and the problem is recognized by both the firm (i.e. employees) and the customer, but there may be disagreement on the causes of the problem and the appropriate solutions. In service encounters such disagreements, sure to diminish customer satisfaction, underscore the importance of understanding the types of events and behaviours that cause customers to be satisfied or dissatisfied. Because the service encounter involves at least two people, it is importance to understand the encounter from multiple perspectives. Armed with such understanding, firms are better able to design processes and educate both employees and customers to achieve quality in service encounters.

Reprinted with permission from *Journal of Marketing*, Vol. 58, October, pp. 95–106

Previous research in the context of the restaurant, hotel, and airline industries identified categories of events and behaviors that underlie critical service encounters from the customer's point of view (Bitner, Booms and Tetreault, 1990; hereafter BBT). The primary purpose of this study is to examine the contact employee's perspective of critical service encounters and to understand, in the context of the same three industries, the kinds of events and behaviors that employees believe underlie customer satisfaction. The employee perspective is then compared with BBT to gain insight into any disparities in perspectives. A second purpose of the study is to evaluate the usefulness of the classification scheme developed by BBT (1990). If the scheme is conceptually robust, it should hold for different respondent groups.

The research is guided by the following questions:

- From the contact employee's point of view, what kinds of events lead to satisfying service encounters for the customer? What causes these events to be remembered favorably?
- From the contact employee's point of view, what kinds of events lead to dissatisfying service encounters for the customer? What causes these events to be remembered with distaste?
- Do customers and employees report the same kinds of events and behaviors leading to satisfaction and dissatisfaction in service encounters?

Before presenting the empirical study, we discuss relevant research and theory.

CUSTOMER AND CONTACT EMPLOYEE VIEWPOINTS

Frontline personnel are a critical source of information about customers. There are two basic ways that customer knowledge obtained by contact employees is used to improve service: (1) Such knowledge is used by the contact employees themselves to facilitate their interactions with customers and (2) It is used by the firm for making decisions. First, employees often modify their behavior from moment to moment on the basis of feedback they receive while serving customers. Schneider (1980) argues that people who choose to work in service occupations generally have a strong desire to give good service. To the extent that this is true, contact personnel can be expected to look frequently for cues that tell them how their service is received by customers. The more accurate their perceptions are, the more likely their behavioral adjustments are to improve customer satisfaction.

Second, because contact personnel have frequent contact with customers, they serve a boundary-spanning role in the firm. As a result, they often have better understanding of customer needs and problems than others in the firm. Researchers have theorized and found some evidence that open communication between frontline personnel and managers is important for achieving service quality (Parasuraman, Berry, and Zeithaml, 1990; Zeithaml, Berry and Parasuraman, 1988). Schneider and Bowen (1984) argue that firms should use information gathered from contact personnel in making strategic decisions, especially decisions regarding new service development and service modifications.

It seems reasonable to conclude that accurate employee understanding of customers enables both the employee and the firm to adjust appropriately to customer needs. However, previous research correlating customer and employee views of service is sparse and offers mixed conclusions. Schneider and Bowen (1985) and Schneider, Parkington and Buxton (1990) found high correlations ($r = .63$ and $r = .67$, respectively) between employee and customer attitudes about overall service quality in a bank setting. Their results are contradicted, however, in a study by Brown and Swartz (1989). These researchers gathered data on patient experiences with their physicians and compared them with the physicians' perceptions of their patient's experiences. The differences they found were rather large and inversely related to overall patient satisfaction.

Another study of 1300 customers and 900 customer service professionals conducted by Development Dimensions International found differences in perceptions between the two groups (*Services Marketing Newsletter*, 1989). Customer service professionals in that study consistently rated the importance of particular service skills and competencies and their actual performance higher than customers rated the same skills and competencies. Similarly, Langeard and colleagues (1981) found that field managers at two banks tended to overestimate (compared with customer ratings) the importance of six broad service delivery dimensions. Other studies have found differences when comparing customer and employee evaluations of business situations using scenarios and role playing in product failure contexts (Folkes and Kotsos, 1986), a complaint context (Resnik and Harmon, 1983), and the context of retailer respondents to customer problems (Dornoff and Dwyer, 1981).

We would therefore expect, on the basis of these studies, to find similarities in employee and customer views of the service encounter, but we would expect significant differences as well. Role, script, and attribution theories provide conceptual bases for these expectations.

THEORETICAL EXPLANATIONS

Role and script theories

Similarities in how customers and employees view service encounters are most likely when the two parties share common rule expectations and the service script is well defined (Mohr and Bitner, 1991; Solomon *et al.*, 1985). A *role* is the behavior associated with a socially defined position (Solomon *et al.*, 1985), and *role expectations* are the standards for role behavior (Biddle, 1986). In many routine service encounters, particularly for experienced employees and customers, the roles are well defined and both the customer and employee know what to expect from each other.

In addition, many types of service encounters, such as seating customers in a restaurant, are repeated frequently throughout a person's life, resulting in strong, standardized, and well-rehearsed scripts (i.e. structures that describe appropriate sequences of role behaviors) (Schank and Abelson, 1977). When service encounters have strong scripts, the employee and customer are likely to share expectations about the events that will occur and the order of occurrence. They are less likely to share ideas about subscripts, which are prescriptions for handling what Schank and Abelson describe as 'obstacles and errors', two types of interferences that may occur in otherwise predictable scripts.

Role and script theory, combined with the routine nature of many service encounters, suggests that customers and employees are likely to share a common perspective on service experiences. It is also clear that differences in perspective may arise when roles are less defined, a participant is unfamiliar with expected behaviors, or interferences require the enactment of complex or less routine subscripts.

Attribution theory

Dissimilarities in viewpoint may arise when service encounter partners have conflicting views of the underlying causes behind the events, that is, when their attributions differ. Research shows that there are many biases in the attribution process (Fiske and Taylor, 1984). Most clearly relevant for the perception of service providers and customers is the self-serving attribution bias. This is the tendency for people to take credit for success (i.e. to give internal attributions for their successes, a self-enhancing bias) and deny responsibility for failure (i.e. to blame failure on external causes, a self-protecting bias). Given these biases we would expect employees to blame the system or the customer for service failures, whereas the customer would be more likely to blame the system or the employee. The result would be different views of the causes of service dissatisfaction. It is less clear that this bias would operate in the case of a service encounter success. Although the desire for self-enhancement might lead both the employee and customer to give themselves credit for the success, the fact that the customer is paying the firm for a service would probably preclude the bias on the customer's side. Overall, then, the self-serving attribution bias leads to the expectation that the perspectives of the employee and customer will differ more in service failure than in service success situations.

Both empirical research and theory suggest that similarities as well as differences in perspectives are likely to occur between service encounter participants. Role and script theories suggest that in relatively routine situations such as the ones studied, there will be strong similarities in perspective. However, attribution biases suggest that there will also be significant differences in viewpoint. We explore to what extent the perspectives of contact personnel and those of customers are different. And, to the degree that they are different, the data provide insight into the nature of these disparities.

METHOD AND ANALYSIS

Data collection

Data were collected using the critical incident technique (CIT), a systematic procedure for recording events and behaviors that are observed to lead to success or failure on a specific task (Ronan and Latham, 1974), in this case, satisfying the customer. (For more detailed discussions of the method, see BBT; Flanagan, 1954; Wilson-Pessano, 1988): Using the CIT, data are collected through structured, open-ended questions, and the results are context analyzed. Respondents are asked to report specific events from the recent past (within 6 to 12 months). These accounts provide rich details of firsthand experiences in which customers have been satisfied or dissatisfied. Because respondents are asked about specific events rather than generalities, interpretation, or conclusions, this procedure meets criteria established by Ericsson and Simon (1980) for providing valuable, reliable information about cognitive processes. Researchers have concluded that when used appropriately (Flanagan, 1954; Wilson-Pessano, 1988), the critical incident method is reliable in terms of stability of the categories identified across judges, valid with respect to the content identified, and relevant in that the behaviors illuminated have proven to be important to the success or failure of the task in question (Ronan and Latham, 1974; White and Locke, 1981).

Hotel, restaurant, and airline employees were interviewed and asked to recall critical service encounters that caused satisfaction or dissatisfaction for customers of their firms. Thirty-seven trained student interviewers collected the data – 781 total incidents. Each one recruited a minimum of ten employees from among the same three industries studied in BBT, asking each employee to describe one incident that was satisfactory and one that was dissatisfactory from the customer's point of view.

Because all the interviewers were employed in the hospitability sector, they recruited fellow employees and employees of establishments with which they were familiar. They were instructed not to interview fellow students. The refusal rate was negligible. The incident sample represented 58 hotels, 152 restaurants, and 4 airlines. On average, the employees providing the incidents had 5.5 years of working experience in their respective industries. The employees ranged in age from 16 to 64 (mean age 27) and were 55% female and 45% male. The instructions to the employees being interviewed were as follows:

> Put yourself in the shoes of customers of your firm. In other words, try to see your firm through your customers' eyes.
> Think of a recent time when a customer of your firm had a particularly satisfying (dissatisfying) interaction with yourself or a fellow employee. Describe the situation and exactly what happened.

They were then asked the following questions:

1. When did the incident happen?
2. What specific circumstances led up to this situation?
3. Exactly what did you or your fellow employee say or do?
4. What resulted that made you feel the interaction was satisfying (dissatisfying) from the customer's point of view?
5. What should you or your fellow employee have said or done? (for dissatisfying incident only)

To be used in the analysis, an incident was required to (1) involve employee-customer interaction, (2) by very satisfying or dissatisfying from the customer's point of view, (3) be a discrete episdoe, and (4) have sufficient detail to be visualized by the interviewer. Seven incidents failed to meet these criteria, leaving 774 incidents (397 satisfactory and 377 dissatisfactory).

Classification of incidents

The incident classification system developed by BBT was used as a starting point for sorting the data with the assumption that, to the degree that customers and employees remember satisfying and dissatisfying encounters in the same way, the same classification system should be appropriate. Incidents that could not be classified within the original scheme would then provide evidence for differences in perspective.

One researcher trained in the classification scheme coded the incidents. Any that did not fit into the scheme were put aside. This researcher and a second then worked together on categorizing this group of 86 incidents (11% of the total). These incidents were read and sorted, combined, and resorted until a consistent coding scheme was developed that combined similar incidents into distinct, meaningful categories. When the new categories were labeled and the two researchers achieved concensus on assignment of the incidents, the new cateogires (one major group with four sub-categories) were added to the original classification system.

A set of complete coding instructions was then written (see Appendix A). They included general instructions for coders, operational definitions of each category, and decision rules for assigning incidents to categories. These are procedures recommended by Perreault and Leigh (1989) for improving the reliability of judgment-based data. The coding instructions were used to train a third researcher who had not participated in the categorization decisions. This researcher then coded the 774 employee incidents, providing an interjudge reliability check on the classification system. Discrepancies between the first and third researchers' assignments were resolved by the second researcher.

The interjudge agreement between the first and third researchers was 84% for the satisfying incidents and 85% for the dissatisfying incidents. These figures are respectably high, especially considering that the classification system in this study contains 16 categories. The percentage agreement statistic probably underestimates interjudge reliability in this case because this statistic is influenced by the number of coding categories (i.e. the more categories, the lower the percentage agreement is likely to be) (Perreault and Leigh, 1989). For this reason, two other measures of interjudge reliability were calculated. Cohen's κ, which corrects for the likelihood of chance agreement between judges, was found to be .816 for the satisfying and .823 for the dissatisfying incidents. Perreault and Leigh (1989) argue, however, that κ is an overly conservative measure of reliability because it assumes an a priori knowledge of the likely distribution of responses across categories. To correct for this they designed an alternative index of reliability, I_r, appropriate for marketing data. Rather than contrasting interjudge agreement with an estimate of chance agreement, I_r is based on a model of the level of agreement that might be expected given a true (population) level of reliability. Furthermore, the index focuses on the reliability of the whole coding process, not just on the agreement between judges. I_r was found to be .911 and .914 for the satisfying and dissatisfying incidents, respectively.

RESULTS AND DISCUSSION

The categories of events and behaviors that employees believe underlie their customers' satisfaction and dissatisfaction in service encounters are identified and discussed first. Then the results are compared with customer perceptions using the BBT data.

Classification of employee-reported incidents

The critical incident classification system based on incidents gathered from customers (BBT) consists of three major groups of employee behaviors that account for all satisfactory and dissatisfactory incidents: (1) employee response to service delivery system failures, (2) employee response to customer needs and requests, and (3) unprompted and unsolicited employee actions. Of the 774 employee incidents, 668 were classified into one of these three groups and the 12 categories within them. The incidents were very similar in detail to those provided by customers. (See BBT for detailed descriptions of the groups and categories and sample incidents.)

Eighty-six encounters (11% of the total) did not fit any of the predetermined groups. These incidents were categorized into one major group labeled 'problem customer behavior' and they were added to the categorization scheme as 'Group 4'. In these cases, the coders could not attribute the satisfaction and dissatisfaction to an action or attitude of the employee – instead, the root cause was the customer. Such customers were basically uncooperative, that is, unwilling to cooperate with the service provider, other customers, industry regulations, and/or laws. These situations created problems for the employees, and rarely were they able to deal with them in such a way as to bring about customer satisfaction; only three of these incidents were satisfactory.

Within the problem customer behavior group, four categories emerged (Table 1 provides examples of incidents from the four new categories):

1. *Drunkenness* – The employee perceives the customer to be clearly intoxicated and creating problems such as harassing other customers nearby, giving the employee a hard time, or disrupting the atmosphere of the establishment:;
2. *Verbal and physical abuse* – The customer verbally and/or physically abuses either the employee or other customers;
3. *Breaking company policies or laws* – The customer refuses to comply with policies or laws, and the employee attempts to enforce compliance; and
4. *Uncooperative customers* – The customer is generally rude and uncooperative or unreasonably demanding. From the employee's perspective, the customer is unwilling to be satisfied, no matter what is done for him or her.

The employee's view of satisfactory versus dissatisfactory encounters

Here we examine the frequencies and proportions of employee accounts in the four groups and 16 categories as shown in Table 2. It should be noted that the frequencies and proportions shown in the table reflect numbers of reported events. The actual frequency of occurrence of the type of event represented by a particular group or category cannot be inferred from the data. Nor can greater importance be inferred by greater frequencies in a particular category (Wilson-Pessano, 1988). The data are shown in full in Table 2; however, our discussion focuses on the four major groups. To facilitate understanding, the employee-reported incidents are

Table 1. Group 4 sample incidents: problem customers

Dissatisfactory	Satisfactory
A. Drunkenness	
An intoxicated man began pinching the female flight attendants. One attendant told him to stop, but he continued and then hit another passenger. The copilot was called and asked the man to sit down and leave the others alone, but the passenger refused. The copilot then 'decked' the man, knocking him into his seat.	A person who became intoxicated on a flight started speaking loudly, annoying the other passengers. The flight attendant asked the passenger if he would be driving when the plane landed and offered him coffee. He accepted the coffee and became quieter and friendlier.
B. Verbal and physical abuse	
While a family of three was waiting to order dinner, the father began hitting his child. Another customer compalined about this to the manager who then, in a friendly and sympathetic way, asked the family to leave. The father knocked all the plates and glasses off the table before leaving.	None
C. Breaking company policies or laws	
Five guests were in a hotel room two hours past checkout time. Because they would not answer the phone calls or let the staff into the room, hotel security staff finally broke in. They found the guests using drugs and called the police.	None
D. Uncooperative customer	
When a man was shown to his table in the nonview dining area of the restaurant, he became extremely angry and demanded a window table. The restaurant was very busy, but the hostess told him he could get a window seat in a half hour. He refused to wait and took his previously reserved table, but he complained all the way through the dinner and left without tipping.	None

Table 2. Group and category classification by type of incident outcome (employees only)

Group and category	Type of Incident Outcome					
	Satisfactory		Dissatisfactory		Row total	
	No.	%	No.	%	No.	%
Group 1. Employee-responses to service-delivery system failures						
A. To unavailable service	31	7.8	37	9.8	68	8.8
B. To unreasonably slow service	23	6.0	48	12.7	71	9.2
C. To other core service failures	55	13.9	110	29.2	165	21.3
Subtotal, Group 1	109	27.5	195	51.7	304	39.3
Group 2. Employee responses to customer needs and requests						
A. To 'special needs' customers	80	20.2	14	3.7	94	12.1
B. To customer preferences	99	24.9	43	11.4	142	18.3
C. To admitted customer error	11	2.8	0	0.0	11	1.4
D. To potentially disruptive others	6	1.5	5	1.3	11	1.4
Subtotal, Group 2	196	49.4	62	16.4	258	33.3
Group 3. Unprompted and unsolicited employee actions						
A. Attention paid to customer	43	10.8	6	1.6	49	6.3
B. Truly out-of-the ordinary employee behavior	25	6.3	28	7.4	53	6.8
C. Employee behaviors in the context of cultural norms	7	1.8	3	.8	10	1.3
D. Gestalt evaluation	0	0.0	0	0.0	0	0.0
E. Performance under adverse circumstances	14	3.5	0	0.0	14	1.8
Subtotal, Group 3	89	22.4	37	9.8	126	16.3
Group 4. Problematic customer behavior						
A. Drunkenness	3	0.8	16	4.2	19	2.5
B. Verbal and Physical Abuse	0	0.0	9	2.4	9	1.2
C. Breaking company policies or laws	0	0.0	16	4.2	16	2.1
D. Uncooperative customer	0	0.0	42	11.1	42	5.4
Subtotal, Group 4	3	0.8	83	22.0	86	11.1
Column total	397	51.3	377	48.7	774	100%

summarized and ranked according to the percentage of incidents in the four major incident groups:

Distribution of dissatisfactory incidents

Rank order	Group:	*Percentage*
1	Group 1: Response to failures	51.7
2	Group 4: Problem customers	22.0
3	Group 2: Response to requests	16.4
4	Group 3: Unprompted action	9.8

Distribution of satisfactory incidents

Rank order	Group:	*Percentage*
1	Group 2: Response to requests	49.4
2	Group 1: Response to failures	27.5
3	Group 3: Unprompted action	22.4
4	Group 4: Problem customers	.8

When employees were asked to report incidents resulting in customer dissatisfaction, they tended to describe problems with external causes such as the delivery system or inappropriate customer behaviors. By far the largest number of dissatisfactory incidents were categorized in Group 1 (response to delivery system failures), with the next largest proportion falling into Group 4 (problem customers). These results are not unexpected given what attribution theory suggests. When things go wrong, people are more likely to blame external, situational factors than to attribute the failing to their own shortcomings. A modest number of dissatisfactory incidents were found in Group 2. In many of these cases, the employees implied that they were unable to satisfy customer needs due to constraints placed on them by laws of their own organization's rules and procedures, again placing the blame on an external source. The smallest percentage of dissatisfactory incidents were classified in Group 3, which reflects spontaneous negative employee behaviors (e.g. rudeness, lack of attention). Again, this is consistent with the bias toward not blaming oneself for failures.

The largest proportion of satisfactory incidents, from the employee's point of view, occurred in response to customer needs and requests (Group 2). Almost half of particularly satisfying customer encounters reported by employees resulted from their ability to adjust the system to accommodate customer needs and requests. Success is attributed in these cases to the employee's own ability and willingness to adjust. The next largest proportion of satisfactory incidents were categorized in Group 1. This is an interesting set of incidents, because each one began as a failure but ended as a success because of the ability of the employee to recover. Employees clearly remember their ability to recover in failure situations as a significant cause for ultimate customer satisfaction. A relatively modest (when compared with the customer view) number of satisfactory incidents were categorized as unprompted and unsolicited employee actions (Group 3). Perhaps employees do not view their own behavior as 'spontaneous', but they instead remember them in association with a specific external cause (e.g. a customer need, a service failure). Finally, there were virtually no satisfactory incidents categorized in the problem customer group (Group 4). This makes sense, because it is difficult to imagine a very problematic customer leaving the encounter feeling satisfied except under highly unusual circumstances.

Comparing customer and employee views

Table 3 combines data from the current study with the original BBT data for purposes of comparison. Because the employees and customers in these two studies all described different incidents, conclusions from employee–customer comparisons are exploratory, and the explanations are somewhat speculative. Although we rely on role and attribution theories to explain the differences we observed, it is possible that these differences could be due to sampling variations of differences in the incident pool from which the two groups drew. However, given the care taken in collecting the data to avoid systematic biases, that both studies were conducted in the same city using the same three industries, and that many of the same firms were the source of incidents in both studies, we have confidence in our theoretical explanations of the results.

Table 3. Comparison of employee and customer responses: incident classification by type of incident outcome[a]

	Type of Incident Outcome					
	Satisfactory		Dissatisfactory		Row total	
Groups	No.	%	No.	%	No.	%
Group 1. Employee responses to service delivery system failures						
Employee Data	109	27.5	195	51.7	304	39.3
Customer Data	81	23.3	151	42.9	232	33.2
Group 2. Employee responses to customer needs and requests						
Employee Data	196	49.4	62	16.4	258	33.3
Customer Data	114	32.9	55	15.6	169	24.2
Group 3. Unprompted and unsolicited employee actions						
Employee Data	89	22.4	37	9.8	126	16.3
Customer Data	152	43.8	146	41.5	298	42.6
Group 4. Problematic customer behavior						
Employee Data	3	0.8	83	22.0	86	11.1
Customer Data	0	0.0	0	0.0	0	0.0
Column total						
Employee Data	397	51.3	377	48.7	774	100%
Customer Data	347	49.6	352	50.4	699	100%

[a]Customer response data from Bitner, Booms and Tetreault (1990).

A large majority of the employee incidents from the current study could be categorized in the original three groups and 12 categories, suggesting strong similarities in the way employees and customers report the sources of satisfaction and dissatisfaction in service encounters. Recall that these are relatively routine service encounters and in both studies the respondents were experienced service participants. Even so, the addition of a fourth group and the significant differences in frequencies and proportions of incidents found in the groups suggest that there are dissimilarities in what they report as well. Hierarchical log-linear analysis of Table 3 shows a significant three-way interaction between group (1, 2, 3, or 4), type of outcome (satisfactory or dissatisfactory), and incident source (employee or customer) (LR χ^2 change = 8.17; p = .04). There is also a significant two-way interaction between group and incident source (LR χ^2 change = 263.31; $p < .0001$). Because of the significant three-way interaction, the results are discussed separately for satisfactory and dissatisfactory incidents.

Within the dissatisfactory incident classifications, customers and employees have relatively similar proportions in Groups 1 and 2. The significant interaction is caused by Group 3, which is dominated by customer incidents, and Group 4, which contains incidents reported by employees only. These results are very consistent with expectations based on attribution biases. Employees are highly unlikely to describe customer dissatisfaction as being caused by their own predispositions, attitudes, or spontaneous behaviors. Customers, on the other hand, will be likely to blame the employee rather than anything they themselves might have contributed. This is clearly reflected in the observation that customers report no dissatisfactory incidents caused by their own problem behaviors (Group 4).

The differences in how customers and employees report satisfactory encounters are provocative as well, albeit less exteme. Again, this is consistent with attribution theory, which predicts larger differences in perceptions in failure than in success situations. Within the satisfactory incidents, Groups 1 and 4 are equally represented for both customers and employees. The significant interaction is the result of Group 2 being dominated by employee incidents and Group 3 being dominated by customer incidents.

IMPLICATIONS FOR RESEARCHERS

Generalizability of the service encounter classification scheme

The importance and usefulness of robust classification schemes for theory development and practical application have been discussed by social scientists (e.g. McKelvey, 1982) and marketing scholars (e.g. Hunt, 1991; Lovelock, 1983). Yet we have few such frameworks in marketing, primarily because the classification schemes that have been proposed have rarely been subjected to empirical validation across times and contexts.

This study represents one contribution in a program of research designed to test the validity and generalizability of a scheme for categorizing sources of service encounter satisfaction and dissatisfaction (BBT). If the scheme holds in different settings (e.g. different industry contexts, or in internal as well as external encounters) and across different respondents (e.g. customers versus providers, customers in different cultures), then the scheme can be viewed as more robust and of greater theoretical as well as practical value. Other studies have reported that the three major groups of behaviors identified by BBT are also found in a retail context (Kelley, Hoffman and Davis, 1993) and a study of 16 consumer services (Gremler and Bitner, 1992). Through replication, the framework becomes more valuable in identifying generalizable 'service behaviors'.

The results of our research indicate that all the categories found in the original customer-perspective study were also found when employees were asked to report except 'problem customers'. The addition of this new group provides a more complete classification system that can be further examined in other contexts.

Problem customers

A primary contribution of this research effort is the empirically based finding that unsatisfactory service encounters may be due to inappropriate customer behaviors – the notion that sometimes customers are wrong. Others have suggested the existence of problem customers (e.g. Lovelock, 1994; Schrage, 1992; Zemke and Anderson, 1990). Lovelock for example, suggests the term 'jaycustomers' to label customers who 'misconsume' in a manner similar to jaywalkers who cross streets in unauthorized places. Our research provides empirical evidence that these difficult customer types do exist and in fact can be the source of their own dissatisfaction.

Although no one really believes customers are always right, firms have policies that pretend this is so, and managers urge and demand that customer contact employees treat customers as if they are always right. Needless to say, such avoidance leads to stresses and strains for managers and frontline personnel alike and potentially bigger problems for firms. (See Hochschild, 1983, for a discussion of personal and organizational impacts of nonauthentic ways of dealing with customers). With a better understanding of problem customers can come better methods for eliminating or dealing with the underlying causes of the problems.

This area is ripe with important research questions, such as the following: What types of problems do customers cause? What are the most frequent problems? What types of customers tend to be problem customers? Under what circumstances do customers create either more or fewer problems? And, from a management viewpoint, what can be done to identify problem customers, and how can and should employees deal with them?

This initial research represents a start at addressing some of these questions and the beginnings of a typology of problem customer behaviors. The categories of behaviors discovered are not surprising given the nature of the industries studied. Each service involves the possible serving of food and drink – including alcoholic beverages. In each service the customers are in close physical proximity for extended periods of time. Restaurant, airline, and hotel customers are many times in tight public spaces that put them cheek to jowl with other customers. Personal social interactions are carried out in front of other customers who are most often strangers. And, as mentioned previously, the types of encounters studied here are all relatively routine and commonly experienced. Finally, customers frequently have transaction-based encounters with the service personnel rather than long-term relationship-based encounters. It is assumed that these circumstances influenced the nature of the subcategories of problems identified in Group 4. Thus, although we believe that the major problem customer group will surface whenever employees are asked to relate instances of dissatisfactory encounters, further research is needed to identify other subcategories within the group and relate problem types to service industry conditions, circumstances, and customer segments.

Although we have identified problem customers by exploring the sources of customer dissatisfaction, there may be other types of 'wrong customers'. For example, even when customers do not misbehave, they may not be good relationship customers for the organization because they do not meet the target market profile, they are not profitable in the long term, or in some cases they may not be compatible with the service provider in terms of personality or work style (Lovelock, 1994; Zeithaml and Bitner, 1995). It is beyond the scope of this article to discuss the full conceptualization of wrong customers, but it may be fruitful for researchers in the future to incorporate the misbehaving customers we have identified into this more extensive conceptual scheme.

Theory implications

Role and script theories suggest that customers and employees in routine, well-understood service transactions will share parallel views of their roles and the expected sequence of events and behaviors. The types of service encounters studied here and in the original study do represent frequently encountered and routine services. Shared views of the encounter should result in common notions of the sources of customer satisfaction and dissatisfaction. The fact that 89% of the employee incidents could be classified in the original classification scheme suggests that customers and employees do indeed report incidents with most of the same sources of satisfaction and dissatisfaction.

An interesting issue for further research is whether the overall strong similarity of views between customers and employees would result if the industries studied were ones in which the scripts were less routine and well practiced.

Results of the study indicate that though employees and customers do report many of the same sources of customer satisfaction and dissatisfaction, there are also significant differences. These disparities show up in the distribution of incidents across the major groups, and the differences were most dramatic for the dissatisfactory service encounters. The self-serving attribution bias suggests explanations for why some of these differences were observed.

MANAGERIAL IMPLICATIONS

Using the classification scheme

One purpose of this study was to evaluate the soundness of the classification scheme developed by BBT in a distinctive context. Through the addition of the problem customer grouping, the framework is now more complete, and the scheme itself can provide a starting point for a company or industry to begin identifying with greater specificity the events and behaviors peculiar to its own setting. For example, the framework has been used for proprietary purposes in medical and travel agent contexts. In these cases, the companies began with the existing groups in the classification scheme and fleshed out the categories with useful specifics that could be employed in service training or service re-design.

The customer is not always right

In the industries studied here, problem customers were the source of 22% of the dissatisfactory incidents. This group may be even larger in industries in which the customer has greater input into the service delivery process (e.g. health care, education, legal services).

Several implications are suggested by the problem customer group. First, managers must acknowledge that the customer is not always right, nor will he or she always behave in acceptable ways. Contact employees who have been on the job any period of time know this, but frequently they are being told that the 'customer is king' and are not given the appropriate training and tools to deal with problem customers. Employees need appropriate coping and problem-solving skills to handle customers as well as their own personal feelings in these situations. Employees can also be taught to recognize characteristics of situations (e.g. unexpected peaks in demand, inordinate delays) and anticipate the moods of their customers so that some potential problem situations can be avoided completely or alleviated before they accelerate.

To provide employees with the appropriate training and skills for working with problem customers, the organization must clarify its position regarding such customers. A basic problem customer strategy might be conceptualized as ranging along a continuum from 'refuse to serve them' to 'satisfy them at all costs'. For example, some car rental companies have attempted to refuse customers with bad driving histories by checking records in advance and rejecting bad-risk drivers (Dahl, 1992). In a different context, some Madison Avenue ad agencies say that 'some accounts are so difficult to work with that they simply cannot – or will not – service them' (Bird, 1993). Although organizations have intuitively recognized that not all customer segments are right for the firm and that each individual customer is not right all the time, some are beginning to acknowledge these facts more explicitly and are attempting to quantify the impact of problem or 'wrong' customers on profitability and organizational stress.

Beyond the need to develop employee skills, there is the need for 'training' customers so that they will know what to expect and appropriate behaviors in given situations. For example, some upscale resorts that offer highly discounted rates in nonpeak seasons find that their discount customers, who may not be accustomed to the 'rules of behavior' appreciate information on what to wear and other expected behaviors while at the resort. In other more complex and less familiar service situations (e.g. professional services), customers may truly appreciate knowing more about their role in the service process and the behaviors and information that are needed from them to make the service succeed (Bloom, 1984). It has been suggested that by treating customers as 'partial employees' they can learn to contribute to the service in ways that will enhance their own satisfaction (Bowen, 1986).

Employees as sources of customer data

Previous research has suggested that contact employees are good sources of information on customer attitudes (Schneider and Bowen, 1985; Schneider. Parkington and Buxton, 1980). Our study confirms these findings insofar as employees of hotels, restaurants, and airlines report all the same categories of customer satisfaction and dissatisfaction reported by customers in the same industries. However, we would caution against relying too much on contact employee interpretations of customer satisfaction for two reasons. First, although they report the same basic categories, the proportions of incidents found in the categories are significantly different from those reported by customers. Second, in some industries in which service encounters are less routine, contact employees may not be as accurate in their assessment of customer expectations and satisfaction (see Brown and Swartz, 1989).

Employee desire for knowledge and control

It is apparent in reading the incidents that contact employees *want* to provide good service and are very proud of their abilities to do so. This pride comes through in the large percentage of satisfactory incidents found in Group 2, in which employees' own skills, abilities, and willingness to accommodate customer needs were the sources of customer satisfaction. Balancing out this sense of pride are a large number of frustrating incidents in which employees believe they cannot for some reason recover from a service failure or adjust the system to accommodate a customer need. These reasons usually stem from lack of basic knowledge of the system and its contraints, inability to provide a logical explanation to the customer, cumbersome bureaucratic procedures, poorly designed systems or procedures, or the lack of authority to do anything.

Reliability is critical

The data show that a majority of the dissatisfactory incidents reported by employees resulted from inadequate responses to service delivery system failures. This result, together with other research reporting service reliability as the single most important dimension used by consumers to judge service quality (Parasuraman, Zeithaml and Berry, 1988, 1990), implies a need for service process and system analysis to determine the root causes of system failures (Kingman-Brundage, 1989; Shostack, 1984, 1987). Systems can then be redesigned and processes implemented to ensure higher reliability from the customer's point of view. The best way to ensure satisfaction, however, is not to have a failure in the first place.

CONCLUSION

The research suggests that many frontline employees do have a true customer orientation and do identify with and understand customer needs in service encounter situations. They have respect for customers and a desire to deliver excellent service. Oftentimes the inability to do so is governed by inadequate or poorly designed systems, poor or nonexistent recovery strategies, or lack of knowledge. When employees have the skills and tools to deliver high-quality service, they are proud of their ability to do so.

We also learned from employees that customers can be the source of their own dissatisfaction through inappropriate behavior or being unreasonably demanding. We suspect that this new group of dissatisfactory incidents caused by problem customers would surface in any service industry and that its existence represents a strategic challenge for the organization as well as an operational real-time challenge for service employees. In a time when 'customer is king' is the stated philsophy of most forward-thinking organizations, acknowledgment that wrong customers exist, coupled with creative thinking about customer roles and management of customer expectations, may considerably deepen understanding of and ability to cultivate customer relationships.

APPENDIX A: INSTRUCTIONS FOR CODERS

Overview

1. You will be provided with a set of written critical service encounter events. Each 'story' or 'event' is recorded on a standardized questionnaire. Two types of questionnaires were used, one for satisfying interactions and one for dissatisfying interactions.
2. Each service encounter questionnaire reflects the events and behaviors associated with an encounter that is memorable because it is either particularly satisfying or particularly dissatisfying. The respondents were employees of restaurants, airlines and hotels. However, they were asked to take the customer's point of view in responding to the questions. Thus, the data reflect employees' remembrances of times when customers had particularly dis/satisfying encounters with their firms.
3. You will be asked to categorize each incident into one of 16 categories, based on the key factor that triggered the dis/satisfactory incident. Sorting rules and definitions of categories are detailed below.
4. It is suggested that you read through each entire service encounter before you attempt to categorize it. If an incident does not appear to fit within any of the 16 categories, put it aside. In addition, do not attempt to categorize incidents that do not meet the basic criteria. An incident must: (A) include employee-customer interaction, (B) by very satisfying or dissatisfying from the customer's point of view, (C) be a discrete episode, and (D) have sufficient detail to be visualized by the interviewer.

Coding rules

Each incident should be categorized within one category only. Once you have read the incident, you should begin asking the following questions in order to determine the apropriate category. Definitions of the categories are attached.

1. Is there a service delivery system failure? That is, is there an initial failure of the core service that causes the employee to respond in some way? Is it the employee's response that causes the event to be remembered as highly satisfactory or dissatisfactory?

If the answer is *yes*, place the incident in Group 1. Then ask, what type of failure? (A) unavailable service; (B) unreasonably slow service; (C) other core service failures.

If the answer is *no*, go on to question 2.

2. Is there an explicit or implicit request or need for accommodation or extra services? That is, is the customer asking (either explicitly or implicitly) that the system be somehow adjusted to accommodate him/her? Is it the employee's response that causes the event to be remembered as highly satisfactory or dissatisfactory?

If the answer is *yes*, place the incident in Group 2. Then ask what type of need/request is triggering the incident: (A) 'special needs' customer, (B) customer preferences; (C) admitted customer error; (D) potentially disruptive other customers.

If the answer is *no*, go on to question 3.

3. Is there an unprompted and unsolicited action on the part of the employee that causes the dis/satisfaction? That is, does a spontaneous action or attitude of the employee cause the dis/satisfaction? (Since this follows rules 1 and 2, it obviously implies that there is no service failure and no explicit/implicit request.)

If the answer is *yes*, place the incident in Group 3. Then, ask what type of unprompted and unsolicited action took place: (A) attention paid to customer; (B) truly out-of-the-ordinary action; (C) employee behaviors in the context of cultural norms; (D) gestalt evaluation; (E) exemplary performance under adverse circumstances.

If the answer is *no*, go to question 4.

4. Does the dis/satisfaction stem from the actions/attitudes/behaviors of a 'problem customer'? That is, rather than the dis/satisfaction being attributable to an action or attitude of the employee, is the root cause actually the customer?

If the answer is *yes*, place the incident in Group 4. Then, ask what type of behavior is causing the problem: (A) drunkenness; (B) verbal/physical abuse; (C) breaking/resisting company policies or laws; (D) uncooperative customer.

If the answer is *no*, put the incident aside.

CIT classification system – definitions

Group 1. Employee response to service delivery system failure (failure in the core service, e.g. the hotel room, the restaurant meal service, the flight, system failures).

A. Response to unavailable service (services that should be available are lacking or absent, e.g. lost hotel room reservation, overbooked airplane, unavailable reserved window table).
B. Response to unreasonably slow service (services or employee performances are perceived as inordinately slow). (Note: When service is both slow and unavailable, use the *triggering* event).
C. Response to other core service failures (e.g. hotel room not clean, restaurant meal cold or improperly cooked, damaged baggage).

Group 2. Employee response to customer needs and requests (when the customer requires the employee to adapt, the service delivery system to suit his/her unique needs; contains either an explicit or inferred request for customized (from the customer's point of view) service).

A. Response to 'special needs' customers (customers with medical, dietary, psychological, language, or sociological difficulties; children; elderly customers).
B. Response to customer preferences (when the customer makes 'special' requests due to personal preferences; this includes times when the customer requests a level of service customization clearly beyond the scope of or in violation of policies or norms).
C. Response to admitted customer error (Triggering event is a customer error that strains the service encounter, e.g. lost tickets, incorrect order, missed reservations).
D. Response to potentially disruptive others (when other customers exhibit behaviors that potentially strain the encounter, e.g. intoxication, rudeness, deviance).

Group 3. Unprompted and unsolicited employee actions (events and behaviors that are truly unexpected from the customer's point of view, not triggered by a service failure, and show no evidence of the customer having a special need or making a special request).

A. Attention paid to customer (e.g. making the customer feel special or pampered, ignoring or being impatient with the customer).
B. Truly out-of-the-ordinary employee behavior (particularly extraordinary actions or expressions of courtesy, or profanity, inappropriate touching, violations of basic etiquette, rudeness).
C. Employee behaviors in the context of cultural norms (norms such as equality, honesty, fairness, discrimination, theft, lying, or refraining from the above when such behavior was expected).
D. Gestalt evaluation (no single feature stands out, instead 'everything went right' or 'everything went wrong'.
E. Exemplary performance under adverse circumstances (when the customer is particularly impressed or displeased with the way an employee handles a stressful situation).

Group 4. Problematic customer behavior (customer is unwilling to cooperate with laws, regulations, or the service provider; this includes rudeness, abusiveness, or a general unwillingness to indicate satisfaction with the service regardless of the employees' efforts).

A. Drunkenness (in the employee's perception, the customer is clearly intoxicated and creating problems, and the employee has to handle the situation).
B. Verbal and physical abuse (the customer verbally and/or physically abuses either the employee or other customers, and the employee has to handle the situation).
C. Breaking/resisting company policies or laws (the customer refuses to comply with policies (e.g. showing airplane ticket to the flight attendant before boarding) or laws (e.g. use of illegal drugs in the hotel room), and the employee has to enforce compliance).
D. Uncooperative customer (customer is generally rude and uncooperative or extremely demanding; any efforts to compensate for a perceived service failure are rejected; customer may appear unwilling to be satisfied; and the employee has to handle the situation).

ACKNOWLEDGMENTS

The authors gratefully acknowledge the support of the First Interstate Center for Services Marketing and the College of Business, Arizona State University, in conducting this research. The helpful comments of three anonymous *JM* reviewers are also appreciated.

REFERENCES

Berry, L. L. and Parasuraman, A. (1991) *Marketing Services.* New York: The Free Press.

Biddle, B. J. (1986) 'Recent Developments in Role Theory'. *Annual Review of Sociology* **12**: 67–92.

Bird, L. (1993) 'The Clients That Exasperate Madison Avenue'. *Wall Street Journal* (November 2): B1.

Bitner, M. J., Booms, B. H. and Tetreault, M. S. (1990) 'The Service Encounter: Diagnosing Favorable and Unfavorable Incidents'. *Journal of Marketing* **54** (January): 71–84.

Bloom, P. N. (1984) 'Effective Marketing for Professional Services'. *Harvard Business Review* (September/October): 102–110.

Bowen, D. E. (1986) 'Managing Customers as Human Resources in Service Organizations'. *Human Resource Management* **25** (3): 371–383.

Brown, S. W. and Swartz, T. A. (1989) "A Gap Analysis of Professional Service Quality'. *Journal of Marketing* **53** (April): 92–98.

Business Week (199), Special Issue on Quality.

Crosby, L. A. (1991) 'Expanding the Role of CSM in Total Quality'. *International Journal of Service Industry Management* **2** (2): 5–19.

Dahl, J. (1992) 'Rental Counters Reject Drivers Without Good Records'. *Wall Street Journal* (October 23): B1.

Dornoff, R. J. and Dwyer, F. R. (1981) 'Perceptual Differences in Market Transactions Revisited: A Waning Source of Consumer Frustration'. *The Journal of Consumer Affairs* **15** (Summer): 146–157.

Ericsson, K. A. and Simon, H. A. (1980) 'Verbal Reports as Data'. *Psychological Review* **87** (May): 215–250.

Fiske, S. T. and Taylor, S. E. (1984) *Social Cognition.* Reading, MA: Addison-Wesley.

Flanagan, J. C. (1954) 'The Critical Incident Technique'. *Psychological Bulletin* **51** (July): 327–358.

Folkes, V. S. and B. Kotsos (1986) 'Buyers and Sellers' Explanations for Product Failure: Who Done It?'. *Journal of Marketing* **50** (April): 74–80.

Gremler, D. and Bitner, M. J. (1992) 'Classifying Service Encounter Satisfaction Across Industries'. In *Marketing Theory and Applications* (C. T. Allen *et al.*, Eds). Chicago: American Marketing Association, pp. 111–118.

Heskett, J. L., Jones, T. O., Loveman, G. W., Earl Sasser, Jr., W. and Schlesinger, L. A. (1994) 'Putting the Service-Profit Chain to Work'. *Harvard Business Review* (March/April): 164–172.

Heskett, J. L., Earl Sasser, Jr., W. and Hart , C. W. L. (1990) *Service Breakthrough.* New York: The Free Press.

Hochschild, A. R. (1983) *The Managed Heart.* Berkeley, CA: University of California Press.

Hunt, S. (1991) *Modern Marketing Theory.* Cincinnati, OH: South-Western Publishing Company.

Kelley, S. W., Hoffman, K. D. and Davis, M. A. (1993) 'A Typology of Retail Failures and Recoveries'. *Journal of Retailing* **69** (4): 429–452.

Kingman-Brundage, J. (1989) 'The ABC's of Service System Blueprinting'. In *Designing a Winning Service Strategy* (M. J. Bitner and L. A. Crosby, Eds). Chicago: American Marketing Association, pp. 30–33.

Langeard, E., Bateson, J. E. G., Lovelock, C. H. and Eiglier, P. (1981) *Services Marketing: New Insights from Consumers and Managers.* Cambridge, MA: Marketing Science Institute.

Lovelock, C. (1983) 'Classifying Services to Gain Strategic Marketing Insights'. *Journal of Marketing* **47** (Summer): 9–20.

Lovelock, C. (1994) *Product Plus.* New York: McGraw-Hill.

McKelvey, B. (1982) *Organizational Systematics: Taxonomy, Evolution, Classification.* Berkeley, CA: University of California Press.

Mohr, L. A. and Bitner, M. J. (1991) 'Mutual Understanding Between Customers and Employees in Service Encounters'. In *Advances in Consumer Research,* Vol. 18, R. H. Holman and M. R. Solomon, Eds. Provo, UT: Association for Consumer Research, 611–617.

Parasuraman, A., Berry, L. L. and Zeithaml, V. A. (1991) 'Refinement and Reassessment of the SERVQUAL Scale'. *Journal of Retailing* **67** (4): 420–450.

Parasuraman, A., Zeithaml, V. and Berry, L. L. (1988) 'SERVQUAL: A Multiple-Item Scale for Measuring Consumer Perception of Service Quality'. *Journal of Retailing* **64** (Spring): 12–40.

Parasuraman, A., Zeithaml, V. and Berry, L. L. (1990) 'An Empirical Examination of Relationships in an Extended Service Quality Model'. Report No. 90–122. Cambridge, MA: Marketing Science Institute.

Perreault, W. D., Jr. and Leigh, L. E. (1989) 'Reliability of Nominal Data Based on Qualitative Judgments'. *Journal of Marketing Research* **26** (May): 135–148.

Resnik, A. J. and Harmon, R. R. (1983) 'Consumer Complaints and Managerial Response: A Holistic Approach'. *Journal of Marketing* **47** (Winter): 86–97.

Ronan, W. W. and Latham, G. P. (1974) 'The Reliability and Validity of the Critical Incident Technique: A Closer Look'. *Studies in Personnel Psychology* **6** (Spring): 53–64.

Schank, R. C. and Abelson, R. P. (1977) *Scripts, Plans, Goals and Understanding.* New York: John Wiley and Sons, Inc.

Schlesinger, L. A. and Heskett, J. L. (1991) 'The Service-Driven Service Company'. *Harvard Business Review* (September/October): 71–81.

Schneider, B. (1980) 'The Service Organization: Climate is Crucial'. *Organizational Dynamics* (Autumn): 52–65.

Schneider, B. and Bowen, D. E. (1984) 'New Services Design, Development and Implementation and the Employee'. In *Developing New Services* (W. R. George and C. Marshall, Eds). Chicago: American Marketing Association, 82–101.

Schneider, B. and Bowen, D. E. (1985) 'Employee and Customer Perceptions of Services in Banks: Replication and Extension'. *Journal of Applied Psychology* **70** (3): 423–433.

Schneider, B., Parkington, J. J. and Buxton, V. M. (1980) 'Employee and Customer

Perceptions of Service in Banks'. *Administrative Science Quarterly* **25** (June): 252–267.
Schrage, M. (1992) 'Fire Your Customers'. *Wall Street Journal* (March 16): A8.
Services Marketing Newsletter (1989) 'Recent Study Shows Gap Between Customers and Service Employees on Customer Service Perceptions'. 5 (Summer), 1.
Shostack, G. L. (1984) 'Designing Services That Deliver'. *Harvard Business Review* (January/February): 133–139.
Shostack, G. L. (1987) 'Service Positioning Through Structural Change'. *Journal of Marketing* **51** (January): 34–43.
Solomon, M. R., Surprenant, C., Czepiel, J. A. and Gutman, E. G. (1985) 'A Role Theory Perspective on Dyadic Interactions: The Service Encounter'. *Journal of Marketing* **49** (Winter): 99–111.
White, F. M. and Locke, E. A. (1981) 'Perceived Determinants of High and Low Productivity in Three Occupational Groups: A Critical Incident Study'. *Journal of Management Studies* **18** (4): 375–387.
Wilson-Pessano, S. R. (1988) 'Defining Professional Competence: The Critical Incident Technique 40 Years Later'. American Institutes for Research, invited address to the Annual Meeting of the American Educational Research Association, New Orleans.
Zeithaml, V. A., Berry, L. L. and Parasuraman, A. (1988) 'Communication and Control Processes in the Delivery of Service Quality'. *Journal of Marketing* **52** (April): 35–48.
Zeithaml, V. A. and Bitner, M. J. (1995) *Services Marketing*. New York: McGraw-Hill.
Zemke, R. and Anderson, K. (1990) 'Customers From Hell'. *Training* (February): 25–33.

Section III

Service Quality and Satisfaction

Service quality is at the centre of any discussion about service marketing management. The conceptualisation of service quality, its relationship to satisfaction, and methods of measuring it, have been a central theme of the services literature over the past 15 years. Whilst there may be general agreement that the evaluation of services is more subjective than tangible goods and, therefore, that an understanding of consumers is central to understanding service quality, there has been less agreement about how to operationalise service quality as a construct. Service quality remains illusive, difficult to define and measure. There is not even general agreement about the meaning of quality. In particular, the close conceptual links between satisfaction and quality have led to considerable disagreement about whether and how these two dimensions are related. Much of this debate had centred around the direction of causality, i.e. whether service quality is an antecedent to satisfaction or whether it is a wider concept, developed as a result of a number of satisfying experiences over time. As Parasuraman (1993) pointed out, the issue is complicated by the fact that the terms are often used interchangeably and have both been operationalised using the same disconfirmation of expectations paradigm (i.e. the idea that customers hold expectations about a service and their subsequent evaluations are based on whether these expectations are confirmed or not). The relationship between satisfaction and quality is raised in a number of the articles in this section and is representative of a recurrent theme in the service quality literature. Holbrook (1994) goes so far as to suggest that 'issues regarding the meaning of the word "quality" appear to pose considerable barriers to clear thinking. In order to remove some of these barriers, this section considers two main themes of service quality research, the development of a measurement tool that can be used by firms to assess the quality of the service they provide, and the relationship between operatinalisations of service quality and customer evaluations.

We start by presenting the most commonly used, and abused, service quality measurement tool: SERVQUAL. The impact of Parasuraman, Zeithaml and Berry's work on contemporary service management literature cannot be underestimated. The central idea of their work is the notion of 'gaps' between the expectations of service and subsequent perceptions of what is delivered. These gaps are located throughout the organisation between front line staff, customers and managers. The identification of ten dimensions of service quality, later refined to five – reliability, assurance, tangibles, empathy and responsiveness (RATER) – has dominated the literature in the field of service quality. Much of the research in this area since Parasuraman, Zeithaml and Berry introduced SERVQUAL in 1988 has been concerned with validating or challenging the construct. Two key articles that challenge the gaps model are included in this section: Cronin and Taylor's (1992) paper, which argues for performance based measures and presents a variant SERVPERF scale, and an article by Teas (1993), who questions the conceptual and operational validity of the perceptions minus expectations framework. However, you may wish to refer to the January 1994 edition of the *Journal of Marketing* in which Parasuraman, Zeithaml and Berry respond to these criticisms and Cronin and Taylor and Teas reply.

In contrast, Frank Buttle's (1996) review of SERVQUAL concentrates on systematically examining the theoretical, operational and statistical criticisms of the SERVQUAL scale and raises a number of directions for future research in the area of service quality measurement. These discussions represent marketing academics grappling with the intricacies of service quality in order to present a recognised and accepted basis for the advancement of research and the improvement of practice.

The following two articles in this section address an alternative perspective on the service quality debate, the extent to which consumers behavioural intentions are influenced by the service quality that they receive. Boulding *et al.* (1993) are concerned with identifying the ways in which customer expectations are formed and the consequences of these upon purchase behaviour. In contrast Bolton and Drew (1991) consider how customers assess value and suggest a multi-stage model of service evaluation. The model proposes that service satisfaction, quality perception and value are interlinked into an overall evaluation which is affected by actual performance. These streams of service quality research are not independent and taken together provide an overview of current conceptualisations of service quality research in the consumer arena. The final article considers quality in the context of industrial services, specifically how industrial buyers can build relationships via service quality. The importance of quality as a factor in relationship building is the basis of much of the literature on relationship marketing (see, for instance, Christopher, Payne and Ballantyne 1991). The Holmlund and Kock (1995) article in this section discusses this in terms of the level of quality necessary to meet the firm's goals. The authors stress the economic service quality dimension which is of vital importance in industrial situations and permeates all business transactions.

CONTENTS

11

SERVQUAL: A Multiple-Item Scale for Measuring Consumer Perceptions of Service Quality

A. Parasuraman, Valarie A. Zeithaml and Leonard L. Berry

Intensifying competition and rapid deregulation have led many service and retail businesses to seek profitable ways to differentiate themselves. One strategy that has been related to success in these businesses is the delivery of high service quality (Rudie and Wansley, 1985; Thompson, DeSouza and Gale, 1985). Delivering superior service quality appears to be a prerequisite for success, if not survival, of such businesses in the 1980s and beyond.

Unlike goods quality, which can be measured objectively by such indicators as durability and number of defects (Crosby, 1979; Garvin, 1983), service quality is an abstract and elusive construct because of three features unique to services: intangibility, heterogeneity, and inseparability of production and consumption (Parasuraman, Zeithaml and Berry, 1985). In the absence of objective measures, an appropriate approach for assessing the quality of a firm's service to measure consumers' perceptions of quality. As yet, however, no quantitative yardstick is available for gauging these perceptions.

The purpose of this article is twofold: (1) to describe the development of a multiple-item scale for measuring service quality (called SERVQUAL) and (2) to discuss the scale's properties and potential applications. The basic steps employed in constructing the scale closely parallel procedures recommended in Churchill's (1979) paradigm for developing better measures of marketing constructs. Figure 1 provides an overview of the steps.

This article is divided into five sections. The first section delimits the domain of the service-quality construct and describes the generation of scale items (Steps 1, 2 and 3 in Figure 1). The second section presents the data-collection and scale-purification procedures (Steps 4 through 9) while the third section provides an evaluation of the scale's reliability and factor structure (Step 10). The next section deals with assessment of the scale's validity (Step 11). The final section discusses potential applications of the scale.

Reprinted with permission from *Journal of Retailing*, Vol. 64, No. 1, pp. 12–40.

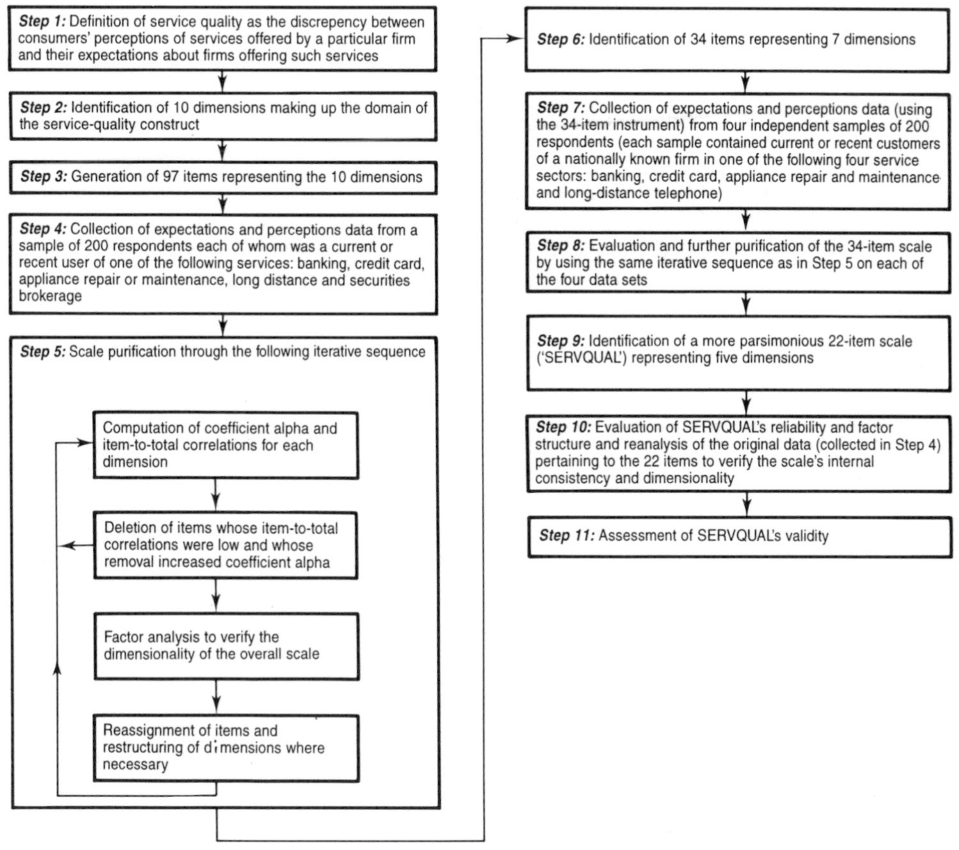

Figure 1. Summary of steps employed in developing the service quality scale.

DOMAIN OF THE SERVICE-QUALITY CONSTRUCT

In deploring the inadequacy of measurement procedures used in the marketing discipline Jacoby (1978) wrote:

> Many of our measures are developed at the whim of a researcher with nary a thought given to whether or not it is meaningfully related to an explicit conceptual statement or the phenomena or variable in question. In most instances, our concepts have no identity apart from the instrument or procedures used to measure them. (p. 92).

The need for scale development to be preceded by, and rooted in, a sound conceptual specification of the construct being scaled has been emphasized by other scholars as well (e.g. Churchill, 1979; Peter, 1981). The conceptual foundation for the SERVQUAL scale was derived from the works of a handful of researchers who have examined the meaning of service quality (Sasser, Olsen and Wyckoff, 1978; Gronroos, 1982; Lehtinen and Lehtinen, 1982) and from a comprehensive qualitative research study that defined service quality and illuminated the dimensions along which consumers perceive and evaluate service quality (Parasuraman, Zeithaml and Berry, 1985).

Conceptualization of service quality

The construct of quality as conceptualized in the services literature and as measured by SERVQUAL, the scale that is the focus of this article, involves perceived quality. Perceived quality is the consumer's judgment about an entity's overall excellence or superiority (Zeithaml, 1987). It differs from objective quality (as defined by, for example, Garvin, 1983 and Hjorth-Anderson, 1984); it is a form of attitude, related but not equivalent to satisfaction, and results from a comparison of expectations with perceptions of performance.

Perceived quality versus objective quality

Researchers (Garvin, 1983; Dodds and Monroe, 1984; Holbrook and Corfman, 1985; Jacoby and Olson, 1985; Zeithaml, 1987) have emphasized the difference between objective and perceived quality. Holbrook and Corfman (1985), for example, note that consumers do not use the term quality in the same way as researchers and marketers, who define it conceptually. The conceptual meaning distinguishes between mechanistic and humanistic quality: 'mechanistic (quality) involves an objective aspect or feature of a thing or event; humanistic (quality) involves the subjective response of people to objects and is therefore highly relativistic phenomenon that differs between judges' (Holbrook and Corfman, 1985, p. 33). Garvin (1983) discusses five approaches to define quality, including two (product-based and manufacturing-based) that refer to objective quality and one (user-based) that parallels perceived quality.

Quality as attitude

Olshavsky (1985) views quality as a form of overall evaluation of a product, similar in many ways to attitude. Holbrook concurs, suggesting that quality acts as a relatively global value judgment. Exploratory research conducted by Parasuraman, Zeithaml and Berry (1985) supports the notion that service quality is an overall evaluation similar to attitude. The researchers conducted a total of twelve focus group interviews with current or recent consumers of four different services – retail banking, credit card, securities brokerage, and product repair and maintenance. The discussions centred on issues such as the meaning of quality in the context of the service in question, the characteristics the service and the provider should possess in order to project a high quality image, and the criteria customers use in evaluating service quality. Comparison of the findings from the focus groups revealed that, regardless of the type of service, customers used basically the same general criteria in arriving at an evaluative judgement about service quality.

Quality versus satisfaction

Oliver (1981) summarizes current thinking on satisfaction in the following definition: '[satisfaction is a] summary psychological state resulting when the emotion surrounding disconfirmed expectations is coupled with the consumer's prior feelings about the consumption experience' (p. 27). This and other definitions (e.g Howard and Sheth, 1969; Hunt, 1979) and most all measures of satisfaction relate to a specific transaction. Oliver (1981) summarizes the transaction-specific nature of satisfaction, and differentiates it from attitude, as follows:

> Attitude is the consumer's relatively enduring affective orientation for a product, store, or process (e.g. customer service) while satisfaction is the emotional reaction following a disconfirmation experience which acts on the base attitude level and is consumption-specific. Attitude is therefore measured in terms more general to product or store and is less situationally oriented. (p. 42).

Consistent with the distinction between attitude and satisfaction, is a distinction between service quality and satisfaction: perceived service quality is a global judgment, or attitude, relating to the superiority of the service, whereas satisfaction is related to a specific transaction. Indeed, in the twelve focus group interviews included in the exploratory research conducted by Parasuraman, Zeithaml and Berry (1985), respondents gave several illustrations of instances when they were satisfied with a specific service but did not feel the service firm was of high quality. In this way, the two constructs are related, in that incidents of satisfaction over time result in perceptions of service quality. In Oliver's (1981) words, 'satisfaction soon decays into one's overall attitude toward purchasing products'.

Expectations compared to perceptions

The writings of Sasser, Olsen and Wyckoff (1978); Gronroos (1982); and Lehtinen and Lehtinen (1982), and the extensive focus group interviews conducted by Parasuraman, Zeithaml and Berry (1985), unambiguously support the notion that service quality, as perceived by consumers, stems from a comparison of what they feel service firms should offer (i.e. from their expectations) with their perceptions of the performance of firms providing the services. Perceived service quality is therefore viewed as the degree and direction of discrepancy between consumers' perceptions and expectations.

The term 'expectations' as used in the service quality literature differs from the way it is used in the consumer satisfaction literature. Specifically, in the satisfaction literature, expectations are viewed as *predictions* made by consumers about what is likely to happen during an impending transaction or exchange. For instance, according to Oliver (1981), 'It is generally agreed that expectations are consumer-defined probabilities of the occurrence of positive and negative events if the consumer engages in some behavior' (p. 33). In contrast, in the service quality literature, expectations are viewed as desires or wants of consumers, i.e. what they feel a service provider *should* offer rather than *would* offer.

Dimensions of service quality

Exploratory research of Parasuraman, Zeithaml and Berry (1985) revealed that the criteria used by consumers in assessing service quality fit 10 potentially overlapping dimensions. These dimensions were tangibles, reliability, responsiveness, communication, credibility, security, competence, courtesy, understanding/knowing the customer, and access (a description of the dimensions can be found in Parasuraman, Zeithaml and Berry, 1985, p. 47). These 10 dimensions and their descriptions served as the basic structure of the service-quality domain from which items are derived for the SERVQUAL scale.

Generation of scale items

Items representing various facets of the 10 service-quality dimensions were generated to form the initial item pool for the SERVQUAL instrument. This process resulted in the generation of 97 items (approximately 10 items per dimension). Each item was recast into two statements – one to measure expectations about firms in general within the service category being investigated and the other to measure perceptions about the particular firm whose service quality was being assessed. Roughly half of the statement pairs were worded positively and the rest were worded negatively, in accordance with recommended procedures for scale development (Churchill, 1979). A seven-point scale ranging from 'Strongly Agree' (7) to 'Strongly Disagree' (1), with no verbal labels for scale points 2 through 6, accompanied each statement (scale values were reversed for negatively worded statements prior to data analysis). The expectation statements were grouped together and formed the first half of the instrument. The corresponding perception statements formed the second half. An abbreviated version of the instrument, containing a set of expectation statements (labeled as E's) and a corresponding set of perception statements (labeled as P's), along with directions for responding to them, is included in the appendix. Negatively worded statements are identified by a minus sign within parentheses in the appendix.

DATA COLLECTION AND SCALE PURIFICATION

The 97-item instrument was subjected to two stages of data collection and refinement. The first stage focused on: (1) condensing the instrument by retaining only those items capable of discriminating well across respondents having differing quality perceptions about firms in several categories, and (2) examining the dimensionality of the scale and establishing the reliabilities of its components. The second stage was primarily confirmatory in nature and involved re-evaluating the condensed scale's dimensionality and reliability by analyzing fresh data from four independent samples. Some further refinements to the scale occurred in this stage.

Data collection, first stage

Data for initial refinement of the 97-item instrument were gathered from a quota sample of 200 adult respondents (25 years of age or older) recruited by a marketing research firm in a shopping mall in a large metropolitan area in the

Southwest of the USA. The sample size of 200 was chosen because other scale developers in the marketing area had used similar sample sizes to purify initial instruments containing about the same number of items as the 97-item instrument (e.g. Churchill, Ford and Walker, 1974; Saxe and Weitz, 1982). The sample was about equally divided between males and females. Furthermore, the respondents were spread across five different service categories – appliance repair and maintenance, retail banking, long-distance telephone, securities brokerage, and credit cards. These categories were chosen to represent a broad cross-section of services that varied along key dimensions used by Lovelock (1980, 1983) to classify services. For each service category, a quota of 40 recent users of the service was established. To qualify for the study, respondents had to have used the service in question during the past three months.

Screened and qualified respondents self administered a two-part questionnaire consisting of a 97-statement expectations part followed by a 97-statement perceptions part. For the first part, respondents were instructed to indicate the level of service that should be offered by firms within the service category in question. For the second part, respondents were first asked to name a firm (within the service category) that they had used and with which they were most familiar. Respondents were then instructed to express their perceptions about the firm.

Scale purification, first stage

The 97-item instrument was refined by analyzing pooled data (i.e. data from all five service categories considered together). The pooling data was deliberate and appropriate because the basic purpose of this research stage was to develop a concise instrument that would be reliable and meaningful in assessing quality in a variety of service sectors. In other words, the purpose was to produce a scale that would have general applicability.

Purification of the instrument began with the computation of coefficient alpha (Cronbach, 1951), in accordance with Churchill's (1979) recommendation. Because of the multidimensionality of the service-quality construct, coefficient alpha was computed separately for the 10 dimensions to ascertain the extent to which items making up each dimension shared a common core.

The raw data used in computing coefficient alpha (and in subsequent analyses) were in the form of difference scores. Specifically, for each item a difference score Q (representing perceived quality along that item) was defined as $Q = P - E$, where P and E are the ratings on the corresponding perception and expectation statements, respectively. The idea of using difference scores in purifying a multiple-item scale is not new. This approach has been used in developing scales for measuring constructs such as role conflict (Ford, Walker and Churchill, 1975).

The values of coefficient alpha ranged from .55 to .78 across the 10 dimensions and suggested that deletion of certain items from each dimension would improve the alpha values. The criterion used in deciding whether to delete an item was the item's corrected item-to-total correlation (i.e. correlation between the score on the item and the sum of scores on *all other* items making up the dimension to which the item was assigned). The corrected item-to-total correlations were plotted in descending order for each dimension. Items with very low correlations and/or those whose correlations produced a sharp drop in the plotted pattern were discarded. Recomputations of alpha values for the reduced sets of statements and examination of the new corrected item-to-total correlations led to further deletion of items whose elimination improved the corresponding alpha values. The iterative sequence of computing alphas and item-to-total correlations, followed by deletion of items, was repeated several times and resulted in a set of 54 items, with alpha values ranging from .72 to .83 across the 10 dimensions.

Examining the dimensionality of the 54-item scale was the next task in this stage of scale purification and was accomplished by factor analyzing the difference scores on the 54 items. The principal axis factoring procedure (Harman, 1967) was used and the analysis was constrained *a priori* to 10 factors. When the 10-factor solution was rotated orthogonally, no clear factor pattern emerged. Many of the items had high loadings on several factors, thereby implying that the factors may not be independent of one another. Moreover, some degree of overlap among the 10 conceptual dimensions was anticipated by the researchers who initially identified and labeled the dimensions (Parasuraman, Zeithaml and Berry, 1985). Therefore the 10-factor solution was subjected to oblique rotation (using the OBLIMIN procedure in SPSS-X) to allow for intercorrelations among the dimensions and to facilitate easy interpretation.

The oblique rotation produced a factor-loading matrix that was by and large easy to interpret. However, several items still had high loadings on more than one factor. When such items were removed from the factor-loading matrix, several factors themselves became meaningless because they had near-zero correlations with the remaining items, thereby suggesting a reduction in the presumed dimensionality of the service-quality domain. Furthermore, the highest loadings of a few of the remaining items were on factors to which they were not originally assigned. In other words, the factor loading suggested reassignment on some items.

The deletion of certain items (and the resultant reduction in the total number of factors or clusters of items) and the reassignment of certain others necessitated the recomputation of alphas and item-to-total correlations and the reexamination of the factor structure of the reduced item pool. This iterative sequence of analyses (Step 5 in Figure 1) was repeated a few times and resulted in a final pool of 34 items representing seven distinct dimensions. The alpha values and factor loadings pertaining to the 34-item instrument are summarized in Table 1.

As shown in Table 1, five of the original 10 dimensions – tangibles, reliability, responsiveness, understanding/knowing customers, and access – remained distinct. The remaining five dimensions – communication, credibility, security, competence, and courtesy – collapsed into two distinct dimensions (D4 and D5), each consisting of items from several of the original five dimensions. The average pairwise correlation among the seven factors following oblique rotation was .27. This relatively low correlation, along with the relatively high factor loadings shown in Table 1, suggested that service quality might have seven fairly unique facets.

The high alpha values indicated good internal consistency among items within each dimension. Moreover, the combined reliability for the 34-item scale, computed by using the formula for the reliability of linear combinations (Nunnally, 1978), was

Table 1. Summary of results from first stage of scale purification

Dimension	Label	Reliability coefficients (alphas)	Number of items	Factor loadings of items on dimensions to which they belong[a]
Tangibles	D1	.72	4	63 75 62 47
Reliability	D2	.83	5	74 56 73 71 47
Responsiveness	D3	.84	5	60 73 59 76 66
Communication Credibility Security Competence Courtesy	D4	.79	4	35 53 66 56
	D5	.85	7	41 62 47 50 75 52 54
Understanding/ Knowing Customers	D6	.85	4	80 76 62 77
Access	D7	.78	5	57 50 75 52 71
Reliability of linear combination (Total-scale reliability)		.94		

[a]Numbers are the magnitudes of the factor loadings multiplied by 100. The loadings of items on dimensions to which they did not belong were all less than .3. The percentage of variance extracted by the seven factors was 61.7%.

quite high (.94). Therefore, the 34-item instrument was considered to be ready for further testing with data from new samples.

Data collection, second stage

To further evaluate the 34-item scale and its psychometric properties, data were collected pertaining to the service quality of four nationally known firms: a bank, a credit-card company, a firm offering appliance repair and maintenance services, and a long-distance telephone company. For each firm, an independent shopping-mall sample of 200 customers 25 years-of-age or older were recruited by a marketing research firm in a major metropolitan area in the East. To qualify for the study, respondents had to have used the services of the firm in question within the past three months. Each sample was divided about equally between males and females. As in the first stage of data collection, questionnaires were self-administered by qualified respondents.

Scale purification, second stage

A major objective of this stage was to evaluate the robustness of the 34-item scale when used to measure the service quality of the four firms. Therefore the data from each of the four samples analyzed separately to obtain alpha values (along with corrected item-to-total correlations) and a factor-loading matrix following oblique rotation of a seven-factor solution. The results from each sample facilitated cross-validation of the results from the other samples.

The results of the four sets of analyses were quite consistent, but differed somewhat from the first-stage findings summarized in Table 1. Specifically, two differences emerged. First, the corrected item-to-total correlations for several items (particularly among items making up the dimension labeled D4 and D7 in Table 1) and the alphas for the corresponding dimensions were lower than those obtained from the first stage. Second, the factor-loading matrices obtained from all four analyses showed much greater overlap between dimensions D4 and D5, and between dimensions D6 and D7. Because these differences occurred consistently across four independent samples and data sets, further purification of the 34-item scale was deemed necessary.

A few items with relatively low item-to-total correlations were deleted. Furthermore, as suggested by the factor analyses, the items remaining in D4 and D5, as well as those in D6 and D7, were combined to form two separate dimensions. For each sample, alpha values were recomputed for the reduced set of five dimensions and a factor analysis (involving extraction of five factors followed by olique rotation) was performed. In examining the results of these analyses, an iterative sequence similar to the one shown in Step 5 in Figure 1 was followed. This procedure resulted in a refined scale ('SERVQUAL') with 22 items spread among five dimensions (D1, D2, D3, a combination of D4 and D5, and a combination of D6 and D7). The expectation and perception statements in the final SERVQUAL instrument are shown in the appendix.

An examination of the content of the final items making up each of SERVQUAL's five dimensions (three original and two combined dimensions) suggested the following labels and concise definitions for the dimensions:

Tangibles:	Physical facilities, equipment, and appearance of personnel
Reliability:	Ability to perform the promised service dependably and accurately
Responsiveness:	Willingness to help customers and provide prompt service
Assurance:	Knowledge and courtesy of employees and their ability to inspire trust and confidence
Empathy:	Caring, individualized attention the firms provides its customers

The last two dimensions (assurance and empathy) contain items representing seven original dimensions – communication, credibility, security, competence, courtesy, understanding/knowing customers, and access – that did not remain distinct after the two stages of scale purification. Therefore, while SERVQUAL has only five distinct dimensions, they capture facets of all 10 originally conceptualized dimensions.

SERVQUAL'S RELIABILITY AND FACTOR STRUCTURE

Table 2 shows the component and total reliabilities of SERVQUAL for each of the four samples. The reliabilities are consistently high across all four samples, with the possible exception of a couple of values pertaining to the tangible dimension. The total-scale reliability (i.e. reliability of linear combination) is close to .9 in each of the four instances.

Results of the factor analyses of data from the four samples are summarized in Table 3. The overall patterns of factor loading are remarkably similar across the four independent sets of results. With few exceptions, items assigned to each dimension consistently have high loadings on only one of the five factors extracted. The distinctiveness of SERVQUAL's five dimensions implied by the results in Table 3 was further supported by relatively low intercorrelations among the five factors – the average pairwise correlations between factors following oblique rotation were .21, .24, .26 and .23 for the bank, credit card, repair and maintenance, and long-distance telephone samples, respectively.

As an additional verification of the reliabilities and factor structure of SERVQUAL, the first-stage data set that resulted in the 34-item instrument with seven dimensions was reanalyzed after deleting the 12 items that dropped out during the second stage of scale purification. The results of this reanalysis are summarized in Table 4 and reconfirm the high reliabilities and dimensional distinctiveness of the scale. The average pairwise correlation among the five factors following oblique rotation was .35.

It is worth noting that the interative procedure used to refine the initial instrument was guided by empirical criteria and by the goal of obtaining a concise scale whose items would be meaningful to a variety of service firms. The reliabilities and factor structures indicate that the final 22-item scale and its five dimensions have sound and stable psychometric properties. Moreover, by design, the iterative procedure retained only those items that are common and relevant to all service

Table 2. Internal consistencies of the five service-quality dimensions following second stage of scale purification

Dimension	Label	Number of items	Reliability coefficients (alphas)[a] B	CC	R&M	LDT	Items[b]
Tangibles	F1	4	.52	.62	.64	.64	Q1 Q2 Q3 Q4
Reliability	F2	5	.80	.78	.84	.74	Q5 Q5 Q6 Q7 Q8 Q9
Responsiveness	F3	4	.72	.69	.76	.70	Q10 Q11 Q12 Q13
Assurance	F4	4	.84	.80	.87	.84	Q14 Q15 Q16 Q17
Empathy	F5	5	.71	.80	.72	.76	Q18 Q19 Q20 Q21 Q22
Reliability of Linear Combination (Total-Scale Reliability)			.87	.89	.90	.88	

[a] B = bank; CC = credit card company; R&M = repair and maintenance company; LDT = long distance telephone company.

[b] The item numbers correspond to those of the expectation and perception statements in the appendix.

firms included in the study. However, by the same token, this procedure may have deleted certain 'good' items relevant to some but not all firms. Therefore, while SERVQUAL can be used in its present form to assess and compare service quality across a wide variety of firms or units within a firm, appropriate adaptation of the instrument may be desirable when only a single service is investigated. Specifically, items under each of the five dimensions can be suitably reworded and/or augmented to make them more germane to the context in which the instrument is to be used.

Table 3. Factor loading matrices following oblique rotation of five-factor solutions[a]

	FACTOR LOADINGS																			
	Bank					Credit card company					Repair and maintenance company					Long distance telephone company				
Items	F1	F2	F3	F4	F5	F1	F2	F3	F4	F5	F1	F2	F3	F4	F5	F1	F2	F3	F4	F5
Q1	34	28	–	–	–	36	–	35	–	–	34	–	–	–	–	42	–	–	–	–
Q2	64	–	–	–	–	70	–	–	–	–	70	–	–	–	–	72	–	–	–	–
Q3	39	–	–	28	–	52	–	–	–	–	53	–	–	–	–	51	–	–	–	–
Q4	28	–	–	28	–	52	–	–	–	–	65	–	–	–	–	59	–	–	30	–
Q5	–	72	–	–	–	–	54	–	–	–	–	73	–	–	–	–	52	–	–	–
Q6	–	63	–	–	–	–	43	27	–	–	–	51	–	–	–	–	40	–	–	–
Q7	–	71	–	–	–	–	87	–	–	–	–	84	–	–	–	–	79	–	–	–
Q8	–	80	–	–	–	–	83	–	–	–	–	88	–	–	–	–	59	–	–	–
Q9	–	39	–	–	–	–	49	–	–	–	–	29	–	30	–	–	54	–	–	–
Q10	–	–	37	–	–	–	–	43	–	26	–	–	56	–	–	–	–	39	–	–
Q11	–	–	55	–	–	–	–	48	–	–	–	–	52	–	–	–	–	43	–	–
Q12	–	–	62	–	–	–	–	54	–	–	–	–	74	–	–	–	–	92	–	–
Q13	–	–	69	–	–	–	–	33	–	–	–	–	71	–	–	–	–	53	–	–
Q14	–	–	–	68	–	–	–	–	65	–	–	–	–	86	–	–	–	–	69	–
Q15	–	–	–	84	–	–	–	–	76	–	–	–	–	89	–	–	–	–	81	–
Q16	–	–	–	72	–	–	–	–	73	–	–	–	–	65	–	–	–	–	61	–
Q17	–	–	–	64	–	–	–	–	61	–	–	–	–	64	–	–	–	–	66	–
Q18	–	–	–	–	37	–	–	–	–	64	–	–	–	–	42	–	–	–	–	59
Q19	–	–	–	–	48	–	–	–	–	72	–	–	–	–	61	–	–	–	–	79
Q20	–	–	–	–	41	–	–	–	–	63	–	28	34	–	46	–	–	–	–	55
Q21	–	–	–	–	33	–	–	–	–	59	–	–	–	–	32	–	–	–	–	36
Q22	–	–	–	–	68	–	–	–	–	64	–	–	–	–	61	–	–	–	–	59

[a] All numbers in the table are magnitudes of the factor loadings multiplied by 100. Loadings that are .25 of less are not shown. The percentage of variance extracted by five factors in the bank, credit card, repair and maintenance, and long-distance telephone samples were 56.0%, 57.5%, 61.6%, and 56.2%, respectively.

Table 4. Reanalysis of first stage data for the five-dimensional scale

Dimension	Label	Number of items	Reliability coefficients (alphas)	Items	Factor loadings of items on dimensions to which they belong[a]
Tangibles	F1	4	.72	Q1	69
				Q2	68
				Q3	64
				Q4	51
Reliability	F2	5	.83	Q5	75
				Q6	63
				Q7	71
				Q8	75
				Q9	50
Responsiveness	F3	4	.82	Q10	51
				Q11	77
				Q12	66
				Q13	86
Assurance	F4	4	.81	Q14	38
				Q15	72
				Q16	80
				Q17	45
Empathy	F5	5	.86	Q18	78
				Q19	81
				Q20	59
				Q21	71
				Q22	68
Reliability of linear combination (total-scale reliability)			.92		

[a] Numbers are magnitude of the factor loadings multiplied by 100. The loadings of items on dimensions to which they do not belong were all less than .3. The percentage of variance extracted by the five factors was 63.2%.

ASSESSMENT OF SERVQUAL'S VALIDITY

SERVQUAL's high reliabilities and consistent factor structures across several independent samples provide support for its trait validity (Campbell, 1960; Peter, 1981). However, while high reliabilities and internal consistencies are necessary conditions for a scale's construct validity – the extent to which a scale fully and unambiguously captures the underlying, unobservable, construct it is intended to measure – they are not sufficient (Churchill, 1979). The scale must satisfy certain other conceptual and empirical criteria to be considered as having a good construct validity.

The basic constructual criterion pertaining to construct validity is face of content validity. (Does the scale appear to measure what it is supposed to? Do the scale items capture key facets of the unobservable construct being measured?) Assessing a scale's content validity is necessarily qualitative rather than quantitative. It involves examining two aspects: (1) the thoroughness with which the construct to be scaled and its domain were explicated and (2) the extent to which the scale items represent the construct's domain. As discussed in earlier sections, the procedures used in developing SERVQUAL satisfied both these evaluative requirements. Therefore the scale can be considered to possess content validity.

The scale's validity was also assessed empirically by examining its convergent validity, i.e. the association between SERVQUAL scores and responses to a question that asked customers to provide an overall quality rating of the firm they were evaluating. Respondents in the second stage of data collection rated the service firm's overall quality (referred to hereafter as 'Overall Q') by checking one of four categories – excellent, good, fair, poor. The correspondence between the Overall Q ratings and the SERVQUAL scores was examined using one-way ANOVA. The treatment variable in the ANOVA's was Overall Q – with three categories instead of four because very few respondents checked 'poor', thereby necessitating creation of a combined 'fair/poor' category. The dependent variable was the average difference score (i.e. perception-minus-expectation score) on each SERVQUAL dimension as well as on the total SERVQUAL scale (separate ANOVA's were conducted for each dimension and for the total scale). Significant ANOVA results were investigated further using Duncan's multiple range test to identify significant differences across the Overall Q categories. The results of these analyses for each of the four samples are summarized in Table 5 under the heading 'Overall Q'.

The numbers reported in Table 5 are average SERVQUAL scores within each Overall Q category, measured on a −6 to +6 score on which the higher (less negative) the score, the higher is the level of perceived service quality. In each of the four samples, the combined SERVQUAL score for those in the 'excellent' category is significantly higher (less negative) than for those in the 'good' category. Furthermore, respondents in the 'good' category have a significantly higher combined SERVQUAL score than those in the 'fair/poor' category. A similar pattern of findings is evident for the scores on the individual SERVQUAL dimensions as well. The strength and persistence of the linkage between the Overall Q categories and the SERVQUAL scores across four independent samples offer strong support for SERVQUAL's convergent validity.

SERVQUAL's validity was further assessed by examining whether the construct measured by it was empirically associated with measures of other conceptually related variables. Respondents in each sample answered two general questions that provided measures of variables (labeled 'Recommend' and 'Problem' in Table 5) which one could expect to be related conceptually to perceived service quality: (1) whether the respondents would recommend the service firm to a friend and (2) whether they had ever reported a problem with the services they received from the firm. Respondents answering yes to the first (Recommended) question and no to the second (Problem) question could be hypothesized to perceive higher service quality than other respondents. As Table 5 shows, the results are consistent with this hypothesis. These findings provide additional support for SERVQUAL's validity.

Table 5. Significant differences in mean scale values for respondents – segmented according to the variables overall Q, recommend and problem[a]

Individual scale dimensions	Overall Q			Recommend		Problem	
	Excellent	Good	Fair/Poor	Yes	No	Yes	No
Bank							
Tangibles	−0.04[b]	−0.52[c]	−1.08[d]	−0.41[b]	−0.98[c]	−0 .75[b]	−0.46[b]
Reliability	−0.25[b]	−0.96[c]	−2.30[d]	−0.82[b]	−2.21[c]	−1.55[b]	−0.92[c]
Responsiveness	−0.32[b]	−0.97[c]	−1.54[c]	−0.74[b]	−1.81[c]	−1.22[b]	−0.84[b]
Assurance	−0.49[b]	−1.03[c]	−1.98[d]	−0.88[b]	−2.12[c]	−1.52[b]	−0.96[c]
Empathy	−0.30[b]	−1.02[c]	−1.52[c]	−0.76[b]	−1.88[c]	−1.07[b]	−0.91[b]
Combined scale	−0.22[c]	−0.92[c]	−1.61[d]	−0.72[b]	−1.77[c]	−1.22[b]	−0.80[c]
Sample size	46	112	40	164	33	47	151
Credit card company							
Tangibles	0.06[b]	−0.61[c]	−0.79[c]	−0.39[b]	−0.80[c]	−0.76[b]	−0.29[c]
Reliability	−0.42[b]	−0.94[c]	−2.32[d]	−0.82[b]	−2.50[c]	−1.42[b]	−0.82[c]
Responsiveness	−0.08[b]	−1.13[c]	−1.71[c]	−0.75[b]	−2.59[c]	−1.31[b]	−0.77[b]
Assurance	−0.59[b]	−1.31[c]	−2.29[d]	−1.08[b]	−2.83[c]	−1.49[b]	−1.15[b]
Empathy	−0.50[b]	−1.38[c]	−1.94[c]	−1.03[b]	−2.77[c]	−1.62[b]	−1.01[b]
Combined scale	−0.32[b]	−1.10[c]	−1.79[d]	−0.83[b]	−2.27[c]	−1.29[b]	−0.83[c]
Sample size	60	112	28	183	17	50	149
Repair and maintenance company							
Tangibles	−0.15[b]	−0.40[b,c]	−0.86[c]	−0.36[b]	−0.85[b]	−0.58[b]	−0.34[b]
Reliability	−0.48[b]	−1.30[c]	−3.20[d]	−1.14[b]	−3.48[c]	−2.14[b]	−1.18[c]
Responsiveness	−0.08[b]	−1.08[c]	−2.41[d]	−0.83[b]	−2.54[c]	−1.71[b]	−0.80[c]
Assurance	−0.33[b]	−1.35[c]	−2.84[d]	−1.16[b]	−2.91[c]	−2.04[b]	−1.13[c]
Empathy	0.15[b]	−1.11[c]	−2.17[d]	−0.85[b]	−2.19[c]	−1.67[b]	−0.74[c]
Combined scale	−0.16[b]	−1.07[c]	−2.30[d]	−0.88[b]	−2.40[c]	−1.65[b]	−0.85[c]
Sample size	45	114	40	168	30	65	132
Long distance telephone company							
Tangibles	−0.08[b]	−0.44[c]	−0.50[c]	−0.26[b]	−0.95[c]	−0.42[b]	−0.26[b]
Reliability	−0.45[b]	−1.42[c]	−2.53[d]	−1.05[b]	−2.71[c]	−1.54[b]	−1.03[c]
Responsiveness	−0.30[b]	−1.43[c]	−1.90[c]	−1.00[b]	−2.03[c]	−1.46[b]	−0.86[c]
Assurance	−0.39[b]	−1.45[c]	−2.10[d]	−1.00[b]	−2.64[c]	−1.62[b]	−0.87[c]
Empathy	−0.33[b]	−1.19[c]	−2.10[d]	−0.86[b]	−2.34[c]	−1.16 [b]	−0.90[b]
Combined scale	−0.30[b]	−1.15[c]	−1.83[d]	−0.83[b]	−2.13[c]	−1.24[b]	−0.76[c]
Sample size	69	104	25	178	19	78	120

[a] Numbers are *mean values* on a scale ranging from −6 to +6, on which zero implies that consumer perceptions and expectations coincide, negative values imply that perceptions fall short of expectations, and positive values imply that perceptions exceed expectations.

[b,c,d] Means with the *same* superscripts are not significantly different. Means with *different* superscripts are significantly different.

APPLICATIONS OF SERVQUAL

It is difficult to identify any retailers that offer no services whatsoever. Some retailers offer facilitating services, such as sales assistance and delivery, to help sell goods. Some retailers sell services directly, in addition to offering facilitating services. Some retailers sell only services. Quality of service is an important issue for all these retailers. Competing goods retailers (department stores, supermarkets) may sell many identical products and quality of service is a primary means of competitive differentiation. Retailers that sell any services (telephone companies, airlines) have little to offer if their service is poor (Berry, 1986).

SERVQUAL is a concise multiple-item scale with good reliability and validity that retailers can use to better understand the service expectations and perceptions of consumers and, as a result, improve service. The instrument has been designed to be applicable across a broad spectrum of services. As such, it provides a basic skeleton through its expectations/perceptions format encompassing statements for each of the five service-quality dimensions. The skeleton, when necessary, can be adapted or supplemented to fit the characteristics or specific research needs of a particular organization.

SERVQUAL is most valuable when it is used periodically to track service quality trends, and when it is used in conjunction with other forms of service quality measurement. A retailer, for example, would learn a great deal about its service quality and what needs to be done to improve it by administering both SERVQUAL and an employee survey three or four times a year, plus systematically soliciting and analyzing customer suggestions and complaints. The employee survey should include questions concerning perceived impediments to better service, e.g. what is the biggest problem you face trying to deliver high-quality service to your customers? If you could be president for a day, what one change would you make in the company to improve quality of service?

SERVQUAL can be used to assess a firm's quality along each of the five service dimensions by averaging the difference scores on items making up the dimensions. It can also provide an overall measure of service quality in the form of an average score across all five dimensions. Because meaningful responses to the perception statements require respondents to have some knowledge of or experience with the firm being researched, SERVQUAL is limited to current or past customers of that firm. Within this constraint, a variety of potential applications are available.

One potential application of SERVQUAL is to determine the *relative importance* of the five dimensions in influencing customers' overall quality perceptions. An approach for doing this is to regress the overall quality perception scores on the SERVQUAL scores for the individual dimensions. The results of such a regression analysis for the four companies in the present study are shown in Table 6 (the dependent variable was overall Q, coded as excellent = 4, good = 3, fair = 2, and poor = 1).

The adjusted R^2 values are statistically significant in all four cases and are also quite respectable, particularly in view of the fact that the dependent variable had only four categories, and the first three accounted for most of the responses. A striking result in terms of the relative importance of the five dimensions in predicting overall quality in that reliability is consistently the most critical dimension. Assurance is the second most important dimension in all four cases. Tangibles is more important in

Table 6. Relative importance of the five dimensions in predicting overall quality

Dimension	Standardized slope coefficient	Significance level of slope[a]	Adjusted R^2
Bank			
Tangibles	.13	.07	.28 ($p < .00$)
Reliability	.39	.00	
Responsiveness	.07	.35	
Assurance	.13	.09	
Empathy	.01	.89	
Credit card company			
Tangibles	.07	.26	.27 ($p < .00$)
Reliability	.33	.00	
Responsiveness	.12	.11	
Assurance	.17	.02	
Empathy	.04	.58	
Repair and maintenance company			
Tangibles	.04	.48	.52 ($p < .00$)
Reliability	.54	.00	
Responsiveness	.11	.09	
Assurance	.16	.02	
Empathy	.01	.81	
Long-distance telephone company			
Tangibles	.08	.17	.37 ($p < .00$)
Reliability	.45	.00	
Responsiveness	.12	.09	
Assurance	.15	.03	
Empathy	.02	.78	

[a] Significance levels are for two-tailed tests.

the case of the bank than in the other three firms, while the reverse is true for responsiveness. Empathy is the least important dimension in all four cases. However, the relatively small magnitudes of the regression coefficients for empathy and their lack of statistical significance should be interpreted with caution because empathy did have a statistically significant simple correlation with overall quality, ranging from .20 in the case of the bank to .40 in the case of the repair and maintenance company. Empathy also had significant correlations of the same order of magnitude with reliability and assurance (the two most important dimensions), thereby implying that its importance in the regression analyses may have been masked somewhat by possible multicollinearity. Therefore, while empathy is apparently the least important of the five SERVQUAL dimensions, it is by no means *un*important.

Another application of the instrument is its use in categorizing a firm's customers into several perceived-quality segments (e.g. high, medium, and low) on the basis of their individual SERVQUAL scores. These segments then can be analyzed on the basis of (1) demographic, psychographic and/or other profiles; (2) the relative importance of the five dimensions in influencing service quality perceptions; and (3) the reasons behind the perceptions reported. For example, suppose a department store found that a large number of SERVQUAL respondents falling in the 'medium' perceived-quality group fit its prime target market based on demographic and psychographic criteria. Suppose further that reliability and assurance were found to be the most important quality dimensions and, based on perception-expectation gap scores for items concerning these dimensions, the items relating to record-keeping accuracy and behavior of contact personnel revealed the biggest gaps. With these data, the department store's management would understand better what needs to be done to improve its image in the eyes of a very important group – customers within the firm's prime target markets who give the firm 'medium' service quality scores and who are in position to either respond to improved service from the firm or defect to the competition.

SERVQUAL can also be used by multi-unit retail companies to track the level of service provided by each store in the chain. By asking respondents to indicate the particular store in the chain with which they are most familiar, and to provide perceptions responses for that unit, the researcher can compare each store's average SERVQUAL score with the scores from other stores. Service quality scores can then be a factor in store manager performance appraisals and compensation, among other uses. Also, SERVQUAL scores for the individual stores can be used to group outlets into several clusters with varying quality images. A careful examination of the characteristics of the stores in the different clusters may reveal key attributes that facilitate – or hinder – the delivery of high quality service.

A retailer can also use SERVQUAL to assess its service performance relative to its principal competitors. The two-section format of the instrument, with separate expectation and perception sections, makes it convenient to measure the quality of several firms simply by including a set of perception statements for each firm. The expectations section does not have to be repeated for each firm. For example, a supermarket chain could include its two principal competitors in a total market survey, asking respondents to provide perception ratings for each of the companies with which they have shopping experience. A retailer that uses SERVQUAL to identify the most salient service quality dimensions for its target markets, and to compare itself to the competition in terms of strengths and weaknesses on these particular dimensions, will certainly have a sense of what its priorities should be with regard to service quality.

In summary, SERVQUAL has a variety of potential applications. It can help a wide range of service and retailing organizations in assessing consumer expectations about and perceptions of service quality. It can also help in pinpointing areas requiring managerial attention and action to improve service quality. In addition, we hope the availablility of this instrument will stimulate much-needed empirical research focusing on service, quality and its antecedents and consequences.

ACKNOWLEDGEMENT

The research reported in this article was made possible by a grant from the Marketing Science Institute, Cambridge, MA.

APPENDIX: THE SERVQUAL INSTRUMENT[a]

Directions: This survey deals with your opinions of _____ services. Please show the extent to which you think firms offering _____ services should possess the features described by each statement. Do this by picking one of the seven numbers next to each statement. If you strongly agree that these firms should possess a feature, circle the number 7. If you strongly disagree that these firms should possess a feature, circle 1. If your feelings are not strong, circle one of the numbers in the middle. There are no right or wrong answers – all we are interested in is a number that best shows your expectations about firms offering _____ services.

E1. They should have up-to-date equipment.
E2. Their physical facilities should be visually appealing.
E3. Their employees should be well dressed and appear neat.
E4. The appearance of the physical facilities of these firms should be in keeping with the type of services provided.
E5. When these firms promise to do something by a certain time, they should do so.
E6. When customers have problems, these firms should be sympathetic and reassuring.
E7. These firms should be dependable.
E8. They should provide their services at the time they promise to do so.
E9. They should keep their records accurately.
E10 They shouldn't be expected to tell customers exactly when services will be performed. (−)[b]
E11. It is not realistic for customers to expect prompt service from employees of these firms.(—)
E12. Their employees don't always have to be willing to help customers.(−)
E13. It is okay if they are too busy to respond to customer requests promptly.(−)
E14. Customers should be able to trust employees of these firms.
E15. Customers should be able to feel safe in their transactions with these firms' employees.
E16. Their employees should be polite.
E17. Their employees should get adequate support from these firms to do their jobs well.
E18. These firms should not be expected to give customers individual attention.(−)
E19. Employees of these firms cannot be expected to give customers personal attention.(−)
E20. It is unrealistic to expect employees to know what the needs of their customers are.(−)
E21. It is unrealistic to expect these firms to have their customers' best interest at heart.(−)
E22. They shouldn't be expected to have operating hours convenient to all their customers.(−)

Directions: The following set of statements relate to your feelings about XYZ. For each statement, please show the extent to which you believe XYZ has the feature described by the statement. Once again, circling a 7 means that you strongly agree that XYZ has that feature, and circling a 1 means that you strongly disagree. You may circle any of the numbers in the middle that show how strongly your feelings are. There are no right or wrong answers – all we are interested in is a number that best shows your perceptions about XYZ.

P1. XYZ has up-to-date equipment.
P2. XYZ's physical facilities are visually appealing.
P3. XYZ's employees are well dressed and appear neat.
P4. The appearance of the physical facilities of XYZ is in keeping with the type of services provided.
P5. When XYZ promises to do something by a certain time, it does so.
P6. When you have problems. XYZ is sympathetic and reassuring.
P7. XYZ is dependable.
P8. XYZ provides its service at the time it promises to do so.
P9. XYZ keeps it records accurately.
P10. XYZ does not tell customers exactly when services will be performed.(−)

P11. You do not receive prompt service from XYZ's employees.(−)
P12. Employees of XYZ are not always willing to help customers.(−)
P13. Employees of XYZ are too busy to respond to customer requests promptly.(−)
P14. You can trust employees of XYZ.
P15. You feel safe in your transactions with XYZ's employees.
P16. Employees of XYZ are polite.
P17. Employees get adequate support from XYZ to do their jobs well.
P18. XYZ does not give you individual attention.(−)
P19. Employees of XYZ do not give you personal attention.(−)
P20. Employees of XYZ do not know what your needs are.(−)
P21. XYZ does not have your best interests at heart.(−)
P22. XYZ does not have operating hours convenient to all their customers.(−)

[a] A seven-point scale ranging from 'Strongly Agree' (7) to 'Strongly Disagree' (1), with no verbal labels for the intermediate scale points (i.e. 2 through 6), accompanied each statement. Also, the statements were in random order in the questionnaire. A complete listing of the 34-item instrument used in the second stage of data collection can be obtained from the first author.

[b] Ratings on these statements were reverse-scored prior to data analysis.

REFERENCES

Berry, L. L. (1986) 'Retail Businesses Are Service Businesses'. *Journal of Retailing* **62** (Spring): 3–6.

Campbell, D. T. (1960) 'Recommendation for APA Test Standards Regarding Construct, Trait or Discriminant Validity'. *American Psychologist* **15** (August): 546–553.

Churchill, A., Jr (1979) 'A Paradigm for Developing Better Measures of Marketing Constructs', *Journal of Marketing Research*, **16** (February), 64–73.

Churchill, G. A., Jr., Ford, N. M. and Walker, O. C. Jr. (1974) 'Measuring the Job Satisfaction of Industrial Salesmen'. *Journal of Marketing Research* **11** (August): 254–260.

Cronbach, L. J. (1951) 'Coefficient Alpha and the Internal Structure of Tests'. *Psychometrika* **16** (October): 297–334.

Crosby, P. B. (1979) *Quality is Free: The Art of Making Quality Certain.* New York: New American Library.

Dodds, W. B. and Monroe, K. B. (1984) 'The Effects of Brand and Price Information on Subjective Product Evaluations'. *Advances in Consumer Research XII.*

Ford, N. M., Walker, O. C, Jr. and Churchill, G. A., Jr. (1975) 'Expectation-Specific Measures of the Intersender Conflict and Role Ambiguity Experienced by Industrial Salesmen'. *Journal of Business Research.* **3** (April): 95–112.

Garvin, D. A. (1983) 'Quality on the Line'. *Harvard Business Review.* **61** (September–October): 65–73.

Gronroos, C. (1982) *Strategic Management and Marketing in the Service Sector.* Helsingfors: Swedish School of Economics and Business Administration.

Harman, Harry, H. (1967) *Modern Factor Analysis*, 2nd edn. Chicago: The University of Chicago Press.

Hjorth-Anderson, C. (1984) 'The Concept of Quality and Efficiency of Markets for Consumer Products. *Journal of Consumer Research* **11** (September): 708–718.

Holbrook, M. B. and Corfman, K. P. (1985) 'Quality and Value in the Consumption Experience: Phaldrus Rides Again'. In *Perceived Quality* (J. Jacoby and J. Olson, Eds). Lexington, Massachusetts: Lexington Books, pp. 31–57.

Howard, J. and Sheth, J. (1969) *The Theory of Buyer Behavior.* New York: John Wiley and Sons.

Hunt, K. (1979) *Conceptualization and Measurement of Consumer Satisfaction and Dissatisfaction.* Cambridge, Mass: Marketing Science Institute.

Jacoby, J. (1978) 'Consumer Research: A State of the Art Review' *Journal of Marketing* **42** (April): 87–96.

Jacoby, J. and Olson, J. (Eds) (1985) *Perceived Quality.* Lexington, Massachusetts: Lexington Books.

Lehtinen, U. and Lehtinen, J. R. (1982) 'Service Quality: A Study of Quality Dimensions'. Unpublished working paper, Helsinki: Service Management Institute, Finland OY.

Lovelock, C. H. (1980) 'Toward a Classification of Services'. In *Emerging Perspectives on Service Marketing* (L. L. Berry, G. L. Shostack, G. Upah, Eds). Chicago: American Marketing Association, pp. 72–76.

Lovelock, C. H. (1983) 'Classifying Services to Gain Strategic Marketing Insights'. *Journal of Marketing* **47** (Summer): 9–20.

Nunnally, J. C. (1978) *Psychometric Theory*, 2nd edn. New York: McGraw Hill Book Company.

Oliver, R. (1981) 'Measurement and Evaluation of Satisfaction Process in Retail Settings'. *Journal of Retailing* **57** (Fall): 25–48.

Olshavsky, R. W. (1985) Perceived Quality in Consumer Decision Making: An Integrated Theoretical Perspective. In *Perceived Quality* (J. Jacoby and J. Olson, Eds.). Lexington, Massachusetts: Lexington Books.

Parasuraman, A., Zeithaml, V. and Berry, L. (1985) 'A Conceptual Model of Service Quality and Its Implications for Future Research'. *Journal of Marketing* (Fall): 41–50.

Peter, J. P. (1981) 'Construct Validity: A Review of Basic Issues and Marketing Practices'. *Journal of Marketing Research* **18** (May): 133–145.

Rudie, M. J. and Wansley, H. B. (1985) 'The Merrill Lynch Quality Program'. In *Services Marketing in a Changing Environment* (T. Bloch, G. Upah, and V. A. Zeithaml, eds). Chicago, IL: American Marketing Association.

Sasser, W. E. Jr., Olsen, R. P. and Wyckoff, D. D. (1978) *Management of Service Operations: Text and Cases*. Boston: Allyn & Bacon.

Saxe, R. and Weitz, B. A. (1982) 'The SOCO Scale: A Measure of the Customer Orientation of Salespeople'. *Journal of Marketing*, **19** (August): 343–351.

Thompson, P., DeSouza, G. and Gale, B. T. (1985) *The Strategic Management of Service Quality*. Cambridge, MA: The Strategic Planning Institute, PIMSLETTER No. 33.

Zeithaml, V. (1987) *Defining and Relating Price, Perceived Quality, and Perceived Value*, Report No. 87–101. Cambridge, MA: Marketing Science Institute.

12

Measuring Service Quality: A Reexamination and Extension

J. Joseph Cronin Jr. and Steven A. Taylor

Service industries are playing an increasingly important role in the overall economy of the United States (Bateson, 1989; Ginzberg and Vojta, 1981; Koepp, 1987). In fact, the proportion of the US population employed in the service sector increased from 30% in 1900 to 74% in 1984 (Bateson, 1989). Koepp (1987) suggests that this sector is continuing to increase, as 85% of all the new jobs created since 1982 have been in service industries. Bateson (1989) further suggests that the growing importance of the service sector is not limited to the United States, as services currently account for 58% of the total worldwide GNP. There even appears to be executive consensus in the United States that service quality is one of the most important problems facing management today (Blackiston, 1988; Cound, 1988; Cravens, 1988; Langevin, 1988; Sherden, 1988).

Interest in the measurement of service quality is thus understandably high and the delivery of higher levels of service quality is the strategy that is increasingly being offered as a key to service providers' efforts to position themselves more effectively in the marketplace (cf. Brown and Swartz, 1989; Parasuraman, Zeithaml and Berry, 1988; Rudie and Wansley, 1985; Thompson, DeSouza and Gale, 1985). However, the problem inherent in the implementation of such strategy has been eloquently identified by several researchers: service quality is an elusive and abstract construct that is difficult to define and measure (Brown and Swartz, 1989; Carman, 1990; Crosby, 1979; Garvin, 1983; Parasuraman, Zeithaml and Berry, 1985, 1988; Rathmell, 1966). In addition, to date the important relationships between service quality, customer satisfaction, and purchasing behavior remain largely unexplored.

Our research has two objectives. First, we suggest that the current conceptualization and operationalization of service quality (SERVQUAL) is inadequate. The SERVQUAL scale is based on Parasuraman, Zeithaml and Berry's (1985) gap theory, which suggests that the difference between consumer's expectations about the performance of a general class of service providers and their assessment of the actual performance of a specific firm within that class drives the perception of service quality. However, little if any theoretical or empirical evidence supports the relevance of the

Reprinted with permission from *Journal of Marketing*, Vol. 56, July, pp. 55–68.

expectations–performance gap as the basis for measuring service quality (Carman, 1990). In fact, the marketing literature appears to offer considerable support for the superiority of simple performance-based measures of service quality (cf. Bolton and Drew, 1991a,b; Churchill and Suprenant, 1982; Mazis, Ahtola and Klippel, 1975; Woodruff, Cadotte and Jenkins, 1983). We therefore develop and test a performance-based alternative to the SERVQUAL measure.

The second objective is to examine the relationships between service quality, consumer satisfaction, and purchase intentions. Though these relationships have been discussed theoretically (cf. Bitner, 1990; Bolton and Drew, 1991a,b; Brown and Swartz, 1989; Parasuraman, Zeithaml and Berry, 1988; Zeithaml, Parasuraman and Berry, 1990), they have not been subjected to a thorough empirical test. In particular, the purpose of the second phase of our study is to provide managers and researchers more information about (1) the causal order of the relationship between service quality and customer satisfaction and (2) the impact of service quality and customer satisfaction on purchase intentions. Simply stated, the managers of service providers need to know how to measure service quality, what aspects of a particular service best define its quality, and whether consumers actually purchase from firms that have the highest level of perceived service quality or from those with which they are most 'satisified'.

After presenting theoretical background, we describe our research methods and results. We then discuss our findings and explore their implications for management and for future research. Finally, we examine the limitations of our study.

THEORETICAL BACKGROUND

Service quality has been described as a form of attitude, related by not equivalent to satisfaction, that results from the comparison of expectations with performance (Bolton and Drew, 1991a; Parasuraman, Zeithaml and Berry, 1988). A close examination of this definition suggests ambiguity between the definition and the conceptualization of service quality. Though researchers admit that the current measurement of consumers' perceptions of service quality closely conforms to the disconfirmation paradigm (Bifner, 1990; Bolton and Drew, 1991a), they also suggest that service quality and satisfaction are distinct constructs (Bitner, 1990; Bolton and Drew, 1991a,b; Parasuraman, Zeithaml and Berry, 1988). The most common explanation of the difference between the two is that perceived service quality is a form of attitude a long-run overall evaluation, whereas satisfaction is a transaction-specific measure (Bitner, 1990; Bolton and Drew, 1991a; Parasuraman, Zeithaml and Berry, 1988). Parasuraman *et al.* (1988) further suggest that the difference lies in the way disconfirmation is operationalized. They state that in measuring perceived service quality the level of comparison is what consumer *should* expect, whereas in measures of satisfaction the appropriate comparison is what a consumer *would* expect. However, such a differentiation appears to be inconsistent with Woodruff, Cadotte and Jenkins' (1983) suggestion that expectations should be based on experience norms – what consumer *should* expect from a given service provider given their experience with that specific type of service organization.

Thus, the service literature has left confusion as to the relationship between consumer satisfaction and service quality. This distinction is important to managers and researchers alike because service providers need to know whether their objective should be to have consumers who are 'satisfied' with their performance or to deliver the maximum level of 'perceived service quality'. The importance of this issue has led to several recent efforts to clarify the relationship between satisfaction and service quality (cf. Bitner, 1990; Bolton and Drew, 1991a,b; Parasuraman, Zeithaml and Berry, 1985, 1988).

Initially Parasuraman *et al.* (1985, 1988) proposed that higher levels of perceived service quality result in increased consumer satisfaction, but more recent evidence suggests that satisfaction is an antecedent of service quality (cf. Bitner, 1990; Bolton and Drew, 1991a,b). In particular, Bitner has demonstrated empirically a significant causal path between satisfaction and service quality in a structural equation analysis. In a second study, Bolton and Drew (1991a) used the common assumption that service quality is analogous to an attitude as a basis to suggest that satisfaction is an antecedent of service quality. Specifically, Bolton and Drew posit that perceived service quality ($ATTITUDE_t$) is a function of a consumer's residual perception of the service's quality from the prior period ($ATTITUDE_{t-1}$) and his or her level of (dis)satisfaction with the current level of service performance (CS/D_t^1)[1]. This notion suggests that satisfaction is a distinct construct that mediates prior perceptions of service quality to form the current perception of service quality.

$$ATTITUDE_t = g(CS/D_t, ATTITUDE_{t-1}) \qquad (1)$$

Bolton and Drew (1991a) indicates this relation implies that the disconfirmation process, expectations and performance all should have a significant impact on consumers' current perceptions of service quality. However, their results suggest that perceived service quality is strongly affected by current performance and that the impact of disconfirmation is relatively weak and transitory.

Finally, Bolton and Drew (1991b) extend the discussion of the relationship between satisfaction and service quality by proposing the following structural equations.

$$\text{Service Quality} = q_o\,(CS/D_t, \text{Disconfirmation}) \qquad (2)$$

$$CS/D_t = c(\text{Disconfirmation, Expectations, Performance}) \qquad (3)$$

To gain more insight into Bolton and Drew's findings, and into how service quality should be measured, we next briefly examine the satisfaction and attitude literatures.

Implications from the satisfaction and attitude literatures

A major problem in the literature is the hesitancy to call perceived service quality an attitude. The literature's position is typified by Parasuraman, Zeithaml and Berry's (1988) description of service quality as '...similar in many ways to an attitude' (p. 15). Researchers have attempted to differentiate service quality from consumer satisfaction, even while using the disconfirmation format to measure perceptions of service quality (cf. Bitner, 1990; Carman, 1990; Grönroos, 1990; Heskett, Sasser and Hart, 1990; Parasuraman, Zeithaml and Berry, 1988; Zeithaml, Parasuraman and

[1] CS/D_t = Consumer Satisfaction/Dissatisfaction.

Berry, 1990). However, this approach is not consistent with the differentiation expressed between these constructs in the satisfaction and attitude literatures.

Oliver (1980) suggests that attitude (ATT) is initially a function of expectations (EXP) $[ATT_{t1} = f(EXP)]$ and subsequently a function of the prior attitude toward and the present level of satisfaction (SAT) with a product or service $[ATT_{t2}\ f(ATT_{t1}, SAT_{t2})]$. Purchase intentions (PI) then are considered initially to be a function of an individual's attitude toward a product or service $[PI_{t1}\ f(ATT_{t1})]$, but subject to modification due to the mediating effect on prior attitude of the satisfaction inherent in subsequent usages $[PI_{t2}\ f(ATT_{t2})\ f(ATT_{t1}, SAT_{t2})]$. Thus, Oliver suggests that consumers form an attitude about a service provider on the basis of their prior expectations about the performance of the firm, and this attitude affects their intentions to purchase from that organization. This attitude then is modified by the level of (dis)satisfaction experienced by the consumer during subsequent encounters with the firm. The revised attitude becomes the relevant input for determining a consumer current purchase intentions.

If one considers service quality to be an attitude, Oliver's (1980) study suggests that (1) in the absence of prior experience with a service provider, expectations initially define the level of perceived service quality, (2) upon the first experience with the service provider, the disconfirmation process leads to a revision in the initial level of perceived service quality, (3) subsequent experiences with the service provider will lead to further disconfirmation, which again modifies the level of perceived service quality, and (4) the redefined level of perceived quality similarly modifies a consumer's purchase intentions toward that service provider.

Hence, Oliver's research suggests that service quality and consumer satisfaction are distinct constructs, but are related in that satisfaction mediates the effect of prior-period perceptions of service quality to cause a revised service quality perception to be formed. Satisfaction thus rapidly becomes part of the reviewed perception of service quality. This logic is consistent with Bolton and Drew's (1991a) findings and also calls into question the use of the disconfirmation framework as the primary measure of service quality, because disconfirmation appears only to mediate, not define, consumers' perception of service quality.

If in fact service quality is to be conceptualized as 'similar to an attitude', perhaps more information could be generated for managers and researchers alike if the measurement of the construct conformed to an attitude-based conceptualization. A review of alternative attitude models suggests that the 'adequacy-importance' forms is the most efficient model to use if the objective is to predict behavioral intention or actual behavior (Mazis, Ahtola and Klippel, 1975). In this models, an individual's attitude is defined by his or her importance-weighted evaluation of the performance of the specific dimensions of a product or service (see Cohen, Fishbein and Ahtola, 1972). However, experimental evidence indicates that the performance dimension alone predicts behavioral intentions and behavior at least as well as the complete models (Mazis, Ahtola and Klippel, 1975). This finding suggests using only performance perceptions as a measure of service quality.

A study by Churchill and Surprenant (1982) also partially supports the efficacy of using only performance perceptions to measure service quality. They conducted two experiments to examine the effects of expectations, performance, and disconfirmation on satisfaction. The results of one experiment suggested that performance alone determines the satisfaction of subjects, Woodruff, Cadotte and Jenkins (1983) contribute additional support for performance only measures of attitude. Again using the 'adequacy importance model, they indicate that assimilation contrast theory suggests that consumers may raise or lower their performance beliefs on the basis of how closely perceived performance approximates expected performance. Thus, they suggest that including importance weights and expectations only introduces redundancy. From the results of a field experiment, Bolton and Drew (1991a) also conclude the current performance ratings strongly affect attitudes whereas the effects of disconfirmation are generally insignificant and transitory. This study is particularly significant because the attitude examined is customers' perceptions of the quality inherent in a service.

Thus, the conclusion of the satisfaction and attitude literatures appear to be that (1) perceived service quality is best conceptualized as an attitude, (2) the 'adequacy-importance' model is the most effective 'attitude-based' operationalization of service quality, and (3) current performance adequately captures consumers' perceptions of the service quality offered by a specific service provider. In addition to the theoretical support for performance-based measures of service quality, practitioners often measure the determinants of overall satisfaction/perceived quality by having customers simply assess the performance of the company's business processes. Furthermore, the performance-based approach may actually be more in line with an antecedent/consequent conceptualization: that is, judgements of service quality and satisfaction appear to follow the evaluation of service provider's performance. The first objective of our study is to examine these conclusions empirically by testing a performance-based measure of service quality as an alternative to the current disconfirmation-based SERVQUAL scale.

Operationalizing service quality

The current measurement of perceived service quality can be traced to the research of Parasuraman, Zeithaml and Berry. These authors originally identified 10 determinants of service quality based on a series of focus group sessions (1985). They subsequently developed SERVQUAL (1988), which recasts the 10 determinants into five specific components: tangibles, reliability, responsiveness, assurance, and empathy (Figure 1).

The basis for identifying these five components was a factor analysis of the 22-item scale (see Appendix) developed from focus groups and from the specific industry applications undertaken by the authors (see Parasuraman, Zeithaml and Berry, 1985, 1988; and Zeithaml, Parasuraman and Berry, 1990 for a comprehensive review).

The scale development procedures employed appear to support the face validity of the 22 scale items (individual questions) included in the scale, but the issue of how the service quality measure should be constructed and whether the individual scale items actually describe five separate service quality components is problematic. In fact, some empirical evidence suggests that the proposed delineation of the five components is not consistent when subjected to cross-sectional analysis (Carman, 1990). Specifically, Carman found that some of the items did not load on the same component when compared across different types of service providers. However,

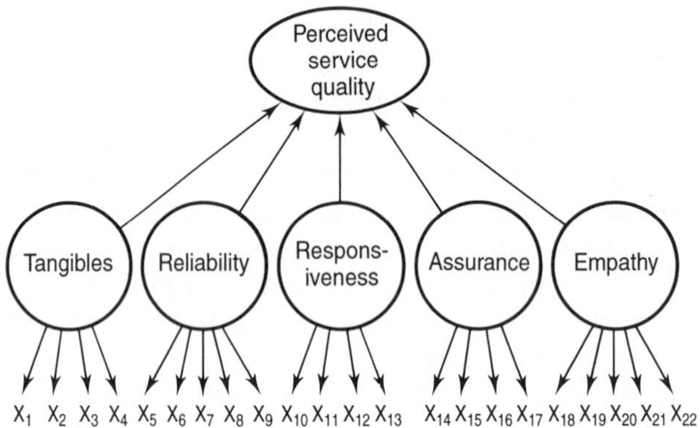

Figure 1. Service quality as conceptualized by Parasuraman, Zeithaml and Berry (1988).

though the veracity of conceptualizing the SERVQUAL scale as consisting of the five distinct components identified by Parasuraman, Zeithaml and Berry (1988) has been questioned (Carman, 1990), the validity of the 22 individual performance scale items that make up the SERVQUAL scale appears to be well supported, both by the procedures used to develop the items and by their subsequent use as reported in the literature (cf. Carman, 1990). We therefore conclude that these 22 performance items adequately define the domain of service quality and we use the same performance items to examine the proposed alternative to the SERVQUAL scale and in the analyses of the relationships between service quality, consumer satisfaction, and purchase intentions.

Research models and propositions

We investigate four specific questions that correspond to the three research steps identified in the Methods section. The first question is directed at the measurement of the service quality construct. Specifically, the ability of the more concise performance-only scale suggested by the literature review (SERVPERF, equation 6) is compared with that of three alternatives: SERVQUAL (equation 4), weighted SERVQUAL (equation 5), and weighted SERVPERF (equation 7).

$$\text{Service Quality} = (\text{Performance} - \text{Expectations}) \quad (4)$$

$$\text{Service Quality} = \text{Importance}^{*}\ (\text{Performance} - \text{Expectations}) \quad (5)$$

$$\text{Service Quality} = (\text{Performance}) \quad (6)$$

$$\text{Service Quality} = \text{Importance}^{*}\ (\text{Performance}) \quad (7)$$

The first proposition provides the basis for our investigation:

P_1: An unweighted performance-based measure of service quality (unweighted SERVPERF) is a more appropriate basis for measuring service quality than SERVQUAL, weighted SERVQUAL, or weighted SERVPERF.

The evaluation P_1 calls for an assessment of whether the addition of the importance weights suggested by Zeithaml, Parasuraman and Berry (1990) improves the ability of the SERVQUAL and SERVPERF scales to measure service quality and a direct comparison of the two measurement approaches. On the basis of the findings by Bolton and Drew (1991a), and the attitude and satisfaction literatures reviewed previously, the addition of importance weights is not expected to improve either scale and the SERVPERF alternative is expected to outperform the SERVQUAL scale.

The structural models identified in Figure 2 are used to further the consideration of the SERVQUAL and SERVPERF scales as well as to consider the three remaining research questions. As discussed in the literature review, the SERVPERF scale appears to conform more closely to the implications of the satisfaction and attitude literatures. Therefore, we propose that the model incorporating SERVPERF (model 2) will have a better fit (as measured by the chi square statistic and the measurement model's adjusted goodness of fit) because the performance-only form is more consistent with established theory (cf. Mazis, Ahtola and Klippel, 1975) and hence the SERVPERF measurement model should more closely approximate the theoretical model identified in Figure 2.

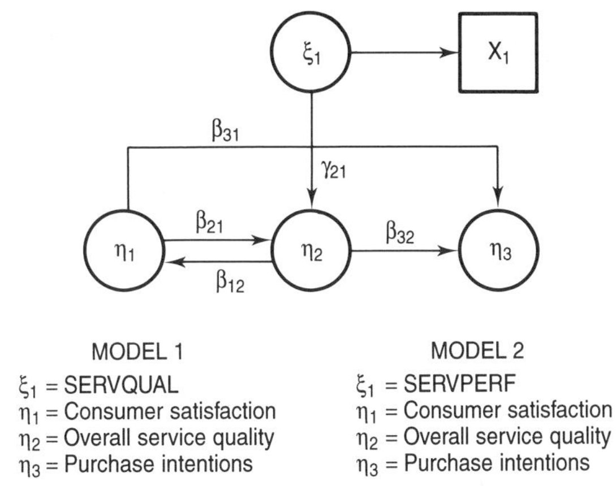

Figure 2. The structural models.

The second objective of our study is to examine the relationships between service quality, consumer satisfaction, and purchase intentions. The following three additional propositions identify the questions addressed in this part of the study.

P_2: Customer satisfaction is an antecedent of perceived service quality.

P_3: Consumer satisfaction has a significant impact on purchase intentions.

P_4: Perceived service quality has a significant impact on purchase intentions.

The first question considered is the causal order of the perceived service quality–satisfaction relationship (P_2). This analysis is also based on a consideration of the structural models identified in Figure 2. Specifically, P_2 proposes that the path (B_{21}) showing consumer satisfaction as an antecedent of service quality should have a statistically significant ($p \leq .05$) LISREL estimate whereas the estimate of the reverse path (satisfaction as an outcome of service quality, B_{12}) should not be significant (cf. Bitner, 1990; Bolton and Drew, 1991a,b).

The next question investigated is whether consumers' level of satisfaction with a service provider affects their purchase intentions toward that firm (P_3). Again, the structural models are used to investigate this proposition. Specifically, in models that confirm (i.e., the theoretical model is not rejected), the LISREL estimate for the path linking satisfaction and purchase intention (B_{31}) is examined to determine whether the effect is significant ($p \leq .05$).

The final question addressed is whether consumers' perceptions of service quality affect their purchase intentions (P_4). The investigation of this proposition is identical to that of P_3 but the path of interest is between service quality and purchase intentions (B_{32}).

METHODS

Organization of the research

Step 1: Examining the dimensionality of SERVQUAL

In this step, the confirmatory factor analysis capabilities of LISREL VII were used to determine whether the 22 items that define the SERVQUAL scale have the same factor loading pattern for the firms investigated was found by Parasuraman, Zeithaml and Berry (1988). To the extent that similar factor structures are identified (see Figure 1), evidence of the responsibility of the SERVQUAL scale is produced. If the five-component structure is not confirmed, the OBLIMIN factor analysis procedure in SPSS-X and a reliability analysis can be used to assess the dimensionality and reliability of the items.

Step 2: Comparison of alternative measures of service quality

On the basis of the theoretical concerns discussed previously, we assessed three alternatives to the SERVQUAL scale. Specifically, in this step we examined the original SERVQUAL scale (equation 4), an importance-weighted SERVQUAL scale (equation 5), a performance-based approach to the measurement of service quality (SERVPERF, equation 6), and an importance-weighted version of the SERVPERF scale (equation 7). This examination proceeded in two stages. First, the ability of each of the four scales to explain variation in service quality was assessed by regressing the individual items comprising each of the alternative scales against a measure of the respondents' perceptions of the overall quality inherent in the services offered by the eight firms included in the sample (see Appendix, variable 85).

Second, each measure's theoretical support was examined in an analysis of the structural models identified in Figure 2. Specifically of interest were (1) the degree of fit of the respective models and (2) the significance of the effect on service quality attributed to each of the alternative measures (i.e. the significance of the path between the perceived service quality scale used and the overall measure of the service quality, path γ_{21}).

Step 3: Analysis of relationship between service quality, consumer satisfaction and purchase intention

The third step extended the research beyond the question of which approach to the measurement of service quality is the most appropriate. Here we considered (1) the causal order of the consumer satisfaction–service quality relationship, (2) the effect of consumer satisfaction on purchase intentions, and (3) the effect of service quality on purchase intentions. These relationships were also investigated through the analysis of the structural models identified in Figure 2. Specifically, we investigated each relationship by examining the significance of the LISREL VII estimated path coefficient that links the variables noted.

The sample

Data were gathered from personal interviews conducted in a medium sized city in the southeastern United States. A total of 660 usable questionnaires (all questions answered) were gathered randomly from consumers at their residences by trained interviewers during a two-week period in the summer of 1988. The sampling frame was the entire population of the city. Interviewers were instructed to solicit responses randomly and were assigned city areas to prevent overlap.

Responses were gathered on the service quality offered by two firms in each of the four industries: banking, pest control, dry cleaning, and fast food. Because of the length of the questionnaire, respondents were asked to evaluate only one firm. The sample size for each industry was: banking 188 (firm 1, 92 and firm 2, 96); pest control 175 (firm 1, 91 and firm 2, 84); dry cleaning 178 (firm 1, 88 and firm 2, 90); fast food 189 (firm 1, 98 and firm 2, 91). The firms and industries were chosen on the basis of the results of a convenience survey suggesting that these were the four service industries most familiar to the area's consumers. The two firms chosen within each industry were those with the largest sales volume in the city where the sample was drawn (for the banks, the number of depositors was used to qualify the firms included). Respondents were screened to determine whether they had used one of the service providers included in the study within the last 30 days. This screening ensured that the respondents were familiar with the firm whose services they were asked to evaluate.

Measures

The measures needed for the study were expectations, perceptions of performance, and importance measures to construct the four alternative measures of service quality, a direct measure of service quality, a measure of consumer satisfaction, and a purchase intentions measure. The 22 expectations (see Appendix, variables E_1–E_{22}) and performance (see Appendix, variables P_1-P_{22}) items were taken directly from the SERVQUAL scale (Parasuraman, Zeithaml and Berry, 1988). The importance weights were adapted from the wording of the expectation and performance items included in the original SERVQUAL scale (see Appendix, variables I_1–I_{22}). The direct measure of the service quality was based on responses to a 7-point semantic differential question (see Appendix, variable 85). In addition, self-report measures of consumer satisfaction and purchase intentions were constructed similarly (see Appendix, variables of 87 and 84, respectively).

RESULTS

Dimensionality, reliability, and validity of service quality measures (step 1)

Dimensionality and reliability

The first step was to examine the dimensionality of the current service quality scale (SERVQUAL) by means of a confirmatory factor analysis. Table 1 gives the results of the LISREL VII-based analysis for each of the four types of service firms (banks, pest control, dry cleaning, and fast food). These results suggest that the 5-component structure proposed by Parasuraman, Zeithaml and Berry (1988) for their SERVQUAL scale (see Figure 1) is not confirmed in any of the research samples. Specifically, the chi-square statistic universally indicates a poor fit between the theoretical and measurement models for the 5-component structure. The adjusted goodness-of-fit indices (AGFI) are also not indicative of a good fit as they range from .740 to .831.

Table 1. Confirmatory factor analysis parameter estimates for 5-factor conceptualization of service quality

Parameter	Banks	Pest control	Dry cleaning	Fast food
Chi square	308.60	486.16	402.60	364.16
d.f.	204	204	204	204
p	.000	.000	.000	.000
GFI[a]	.863	.790	.819	.849
AGFI[b]	.831	.740	.776	.813
RMSR[c]	.309	.466	.381	.515

[a] Goodness of fit.
[b] Adjusted goodness of fit.
[c] Root mean square residual.

Because the 5-factor structure was not confirmed we decided to assess the unidimensionality of the 22 items. We performed a factor analysis of the SERVQUAL and SERVPERF scales using the OBLIMIN oblique factor rotation procedure in SPSS-X. All of the items loaded predictably on a single factor with the exception of item 19 (see Table 2), which loaded very weakly in the analysis of the SERVQUAL scale and had a negative loading for both scales. It was therefore dropped and coefficient alpha for both scales and all subsamples (each industry) was recalculated. As is indicated in Table 2, the reliability in every case (coefficient alpha in excess of .800) suggests that

Table 2. Factor analysis of 22 individual dimensions of service quality

	SERVQUAL				SERVPERF			
Variable	Banks	Pest control	Dry cleaning	Fast food	Banks	Pest control	Dry cleaning	Fast food
V1	.396	.697	.577	.181	.480	.820	.692	.408
V2	.397	.368	.492	.249	.463	.652	.614	.458
V3	.477	.523	.536	.339	.557	.842	.642	.499
V4	.381	.319	.398	.055	.485	.703	.640	.384
V5	.781	.741	.736	.543	.804	.831	.774	.572
V6	.728	.753	.798	.543	.726	.828	.760	.683
V7	.826	.837	.805	.748	.822	.891	.856	.669
V8	.791	.832	.789	.679	.799	.873	.785	.679
V9	.833	.694	.654	.380	.788	.835	.626	.349
V10	.346	.467	.209	.325	.355	.532	.281	.136
V11	.568	.611	.358	.657	.640	.712	.483	.607
V12	.522	.622	.499	.706	.631	.706	.539	.672
V13	.500	.556	.392	.706	.623	.789	.538	.660
V14	.572	.622	.730	.409	.685	.785	.771	.550
V15	.817	.676	.762	.595	.815	.788	.836	.665
V16	.573	.764	.740	.641	.638	.793	.803	.689
V17	.647	.608	.673	.544	.688	.702	.666	.518
V18	.535	.563	.472	.412	.620	.762	.483	.429
V19	.337	.298	.165	.027	.677	.769	.615	.474
V20	.459	.502	.399	.422	.580	.685	.490	.485
V21	.502	.571	.522	.464	.552	.670	.703	.573
V22	.272	.420	.399	.156	.345	.598	.403	.280
Eigenvalue	7.472	8.229	7.437	5.194	9.037	12.651	9.378	6.408
Coefficient alpha[a]	.890	.901	.900	.849	.925	.964	.932	.884

[a] Item V19 excluded.

both scales can be treated as unidimensional. Thus, in the analysis that follows, the 21 retained items are either summed or averaged (to develop the four service quality scales in the LISREL VII analysis of the structural models) or they are considered as one composite set of individual measures (in the stepwise regression analysis).

Validity

The primary threat to the validity of the measures used in this study is construct validity Carmmes and Zeller (1979, p. 23) state. 'Fundamentally, construct validity is concerned with the extent to which a particular measure relates to other measures consistent with theoretically derived hypotheses concerning the concepts (or constructs) that are being measured'. They further suggest that the process of construct validation is by definition theory-laden. Churchill (1979) suggests that convergence and discriminant validity should be assessed in investigations of construct validity. Convergent validity involves the extent to which a measure correlates highly with other measures designed to measure the same construct. Therefore, we examined a correlation matrix of all items tested in models 1 and 2 (see Table 3). A high correlation between the items SERVPERF, importance-weighted SERVPERF, and

Table 3. Correlation coefficients for structural models in Figure 2

	SERVQUAL	Weighted SERVQUAL	SERVPERF	Weighted SERVPERF	Overall service quality	Satisfaction	Purchase intention
SERVQUAL	1.0000						
Weighted SERVQUAL	.9787	1.0000					
SERVPERF	.8100	.7968	1.0000				
Weighted SERVPERF	.6589	.6307	.9093	1.0000			
Overall service quality	.5430	.5394	.6012	.5572	1.0000		
Satisfaction	.5605	.5559	.5978	.5513	.8175	1.0000	
Purchase intention	.3534	.3613	.3647	.3486	.5272	.5334	1.0000

service quality indicates some degree of convergent validity. Discriminant validity involves the extent to which a measure is novel and does not simply reflect some other variable. Churchill (1979) suggests assessing discriminant validity by determining whether the correlation between two different measures of the same variable is higher than the correlation between the measure of that variable and those of any other variable. Again, an examination of the correlation matrix in Table 3 indicates discriminant validity of the research variables as the three service quality scales all correlate more highly with each other than they do with other research variables (i.e. satisfaction and purchase intentions). Hence, we suggest that the proposed performance-based measures provide a more construct-valid explication of service quality because of their content validity (i.e. use of importance weights and use of performance-based measures are arguably more theoretically sound approaches) and the evidence of their discriminant validity.

Comparison of alternative measures to service quality (Step 2)

P_1 suggests that the unweighted SERVPERF scale should capture more of the variation in service quality than any of the other identical alternatives (SERVQUAL, weighted SERVQUAL, and weighted SERVPERF). The stepwise regression analysis summarized in Table 4 affirms P_1. In all of the four service industries examined, unweighted SERVPERF explains more of the variation in the global measure of service quality (see Table 4).

In addition, a comparison of the SERVQUAL and weighted SERVQUAL scales (columns 1–4 and 5–8 of Table 4) indicates that the unweighted SERVQUAL scale explains more of the variation in service quality in three of the four industries (the exception being dry cleaning). We therefore decided to use only the unweighted SERVPERF and SERVQUAL scales in the structural analysis of the relationship between these scales, service quality, consumer satisfaction, and purchase intentions because they arguably represent the best of each of the two alternative conceptualizations of service quality.

Table 4. The variation explained by the alternative measures of service quality

	SERVQUAL				Weighted SERVQUAL				SERVPERF				Weighted SERVPERF			
	Banking	Pest control	Dry cleaning	Fast food	Banking	Pest control	Dry cleaning	Fast food	Banking	Pest control	Dry cleaning	Fast food	Banking	Pest control	Dry cleaning	Fast food
V1[1]																
V2								.164[b]				.157[b]				.256[c]
V3				.143[a]												
V4	.147[a]								.248[c]							
V5					.194[a]	.227[a]										
V6	.284[c]	.200[a]	.307[c]	.255[c]	.222[b]	.186[a]	.277[b]	.282[b]	.350[c]		.380[c]		.267[b]		.240[b]	
V7	.478[c]				.452[b]		.268[b]	.234[b]	.351[b]			.407[b]	.437[b]		.242[b]	.323[c]
V8		.594[c]				.614[c]				.304[b]				.346[c]		
V9	.216[a]				.248[b]			.131[a]	.231[b]				.195[a]			
V10														.193[b]		
V11			.158[a]				.268[c]			.256[a]						
V12													.253[b]			.242[b]
V13				.141[a]								.152[a]				.194[b]
V14		.352				.329[c]		.153[a]								.130[a]
V15											.191[a]					
V16			.235[b]	.187[b]				.318[a]		.175[a]	.349[c]	.165[a]			.189[a]	
V17											.219[b]			.161[a]		
V18																
V19			.127[a]	.163[a]			.135[a]								.164[b]	
V20									.158[b]			.141[a]	.181[b]			
V21	.189[b]				.167[b]											
V22		.142				.157[a]										
R	.46511	.36515	.30747	.41534	.44813	.36316	.36958	.38332	47895	38760	44675	47585	.40333	.33726	.43166	.46718

Where a $p < .05$
b $p < .01$
c $p < .001$

V1 to V22 are the alternative scale items of service quality (see Appendix A, variables P1 to P22). Entries in the cells represent correlation coefficients. All nonsignificant coefficients are omitted.

Numbers in each cell are adjusted *R*'s.

Relationship between service quality, customer satisfaction, and purchase intentions (Step 3)

Figure 2 identifies the two models used to investigate P_2, P_3 and P_4 and to further the comparison of the performance and disconfirmation based measures of service quality (SERVPERF and SERVQUAL respectively). Models 1 and 2 are identical with the exception that SERVQUAL is used to measure service quality in model 1 whereas SERVPERF is used in model 2. The models conceptualize a nonrecursive ('two-way') relationship between service quality and satisfaction in order to test simultaneously the effects hypothesized by Parasuraman, Zeithaml and Berry (1985, 1988) (service quality is an antecedent of customer satisfaction) and by Bitner (1990) and Bolton and Drew (1991a,b) (service quality is an outcome of customer satisfaction). In addition, the model suggests that both service quality and satisfaction affect purchase intentions.

However, before considering P_2, P_3 and P_4, we assessed the fit of the two respective models to the data (see Table 5). Model 1 (SERVQUAL) had a good fit in two of the four industries (banking and fast food) whereas model 2 (SERVPERF) had an excellent fit in all four industries. Because the only difference in the two models is the measure of service quality used (either SERVQUAL or SERVPERF), these results were interpreted as additional support for the superiority of the SERVPERF approach to the measurement of service quality.

Because of this superiority, we used model 2 to assess the strength of the relationships between service quality, consumer satisfaction, and purchase intention. This analysis suggests that (1) service quality has a significant ($p < .05$) effect on consumer satisfaction in all four samples (see Table 5, model 2, path β_{12}), (2) consumer satisfaction has a significant ($p < .05$) effect on purchase intentions in all four samples (see Table 5, model 2, path β_{31}), and (3) service quality does not have a significant ($p < .05$) impact on purchase intentions in any of the samples (see Table 5, model 2, path β_{32}). Thus, P_2 and P_3 both receive strong support from the results, though the direction of the effect observed in the consideration of P_2 is the opposite of that proposed. The analysis of P_4 afforded no support for the proposed effect.

DISCUSSION

We investigated three main questions:

- How should service quality be conceptualized and measured?
- What is the causal order of the relationship between service quality and consumer satisfaction?
- What impacts do service quality and consumer satisfaction have on purchase intentions?

In answer to the first question, the literature review and empirical results both suggest that service quality should be conceptualized and measured as an attitude. The literature clearly supports the performance-only (SERVPERF) approach. In the empirical analysis, the first step calls into question the efficacy of the 5-component

Table 5. Standardized parameter estimates for causal models

	Parameter	Banking		Pest control		Dry cleaning		Fast food	
		LISREL estimate	T-Value	LISREL estimate	T-Value	LISREL estimate	T-Value	LISREL estimate	T-Value
SERVQUAL model (1)									
	B_{21}	1.796	1.512	2.810	1.341	8.398	−.408	−.055	−.300
	B_{12}	1.113	14.794	1.099	10.620	1.103	15.256	.904	10.566
	B_{31}	.668	3.712	.646	4.247	.836	4.598	.343	2.774
	B_{32}	.280	1.475	.301	2.033	.099	.542	.296	2.187
	γ_{21}	2.417	2.226	2.289	1.746	7.157	.452	.812	5.325
	Chi square	.000	($p = .972$)	5.090	($p = .024$)	4.060	($p = .044$)	6.020	($p = .140$)
	AGFI	1.000		.863		.890		.838	
	RMS	.001		.068		.061		.063	
	SMC-Y_1	.664		.465		.750		.647	
	Y_2	3.482		7.309		58.200		.254	
	Y_3	.325		.326		.409		.260	
SERVPERF model (2)									
	B_{21}	1.353	1.595	1.377	1.944	2.904	.989	.141	.845
	B_{12}	1.109	14.156	1.006	11.793	1.065	17.584	.944	12.787
	B_{31}	.550	3.124	.659	4.323	.837	4.598	.362	2.924
	B_{32}	.374	1.979	.285	1.926	.098	.535	.282	2.069
	γ_{21}	2.154	2.585	1.683	3.202	3.644	1.300	1.179	6.122
	Chi square	.080	($p = .781$)	.220	($p = .639$)	3.290	($p = .070$)	.230	($p = .629$)
	AGFI	.998		.994		.910		.994	
	RMS	.009		.012		.044		.010	
	SMC-Y_1	.657		.521		.768		.652	
	Y_2	2.298		1.886		7.799		.278	
	Y_3	.305		.325		.412		.266	

conceptualization of service quality offered by Parasuraman, Zeithaml and Berry (1988). The second step indicates that the SERVPERF scale explains more of the variation in service quality than does SERVQUAL. Both the literature review and the analysis of the structural models (see Figure 2 and Table 5, models 1 and 2) suggest that the SERVQUAL conceptualization is in fact flawed: (1) it is based on a satisfaction paradigm rather than an attitude model and (2) the empirical analysis of the structural model suggests that the SERVQUAL model (see Figure 2 and Table 5, model 1) confirms in only two of the four industries. Thus, the weight of the evidence clearly support the use of performance based measures of service quality.

The second question investigated is the causal order of the satisfaction service quality relationship. Much of the recent literature has suggested that satisfaction is an antecedent of service quality (cf. Bitner, 1990; Bolton Drew, 1991a,b). However, the analysis of the research model indicate that this may not be the case and provides empirical support for the notion that perceived service quality in fact leads to satisfaction as proposed by Parasuraman, Zeithaml and Berry (1985, 1988).

The third question pertains to the effects of service quality and satisfaction on purchase intentions (see Figure 2 and Table 5). The analysis of the LISREL estimates (model 2, see Table 5) suggests that satisfaction has a significant ($p < .05$) effect on purchase intentions in all four samples whereas service quality does not have such an effect in any of the four industries. From the significance tests summarized in Table 5, satisfaction appears to have a stronger and more consistent effect on purchase intentions than does service quality.

CONCLUSIONS AND MANAGERIAL IMPLICATIONS

The major conclusion from our study is that marketing's current conceptualization and measurement of service quality are based on a flawed paradigm. We present empirical and literature support suggesting that service quality should be measured as an attitude. The performance-based scale developed (SERVPERF) is efficient in comparison with the SERVQUAL scale, it reduces by 50% the number of items that must be measured (44 items to 22 items). The analysis of the structural models also supports the theoretical superiority of the SERVPERF scale (see Table 5), only the model that uses the SERVPERF scale consistently confirmed (model 2). These factors, along with the failure of the 5-component SERVQUAL model to confirm (see Table 1), support the use of a performance-based measure of service quality.

The remaining questions addressed in our study are essential managerial issues. The results suggest that service quality is an antecedent of consumer satisfaction and that consumer satisfaction exerts a stronger influence on purchase intentions than does service quality. Thus, managers may need to emphasize total customer satisfaction programs over strategies centering solely on service quality. Perhaps, consumers do not necessarily buy the highest quality service; convenience, price, or availability may enhance satisfaction while not actually affecting consumers' perceptions of service quality.

Finally (see Table 4), the results from step 1 also suggest that the scale items that define service quality in one industry may be different in another. Perhaps high involvement services such as health care or financial services have different service quality definitions than low involvement services such as fast food or dry cleaning. Managers and researchers therefore must consider the individual dimensions of service quality when making cross-sectional comparisons. Managers should also be able to adjust their marketing strategies more effectively when the full set of individual scale items are considered.

IMPLICATIONS FOR FUTURE RESEARCH

Our research has only begun to address the many issues that are important in the management of services. The findings undoubtedly raise more questions than they answer, but the questions we address – how the service quality construct should be measured and how service quality is related to consumer satisfaction and purchase intentions – are arguably among the most important concerns in service marketing.

Future studies should consider other attitude-based conceptualizations and extend beyond the four service industries sampled in our study. The nature of the relationship between consumer satisfaction and service quality appears to be an area in great need of additional exploration. Investigation of the roles of satisfaction and service quality in predicting market share also appear well directed and may enhance our understanding of the role of these constructs in the formation of purchase intentions. The failure of service quality to affect purchase intentions consistently should be a concern for both managers and researchers. Perhaps consumers do not always buy the best quality service. Might they instead purchase on the basis of their assessment of the value of the service? Perhaps future research should develop measures of service performance that utilize other criteria, such as value, for determining whether a service is purchased. Finally, our study was specific to a service context. Generalizing the results to goods industries may not be possible. The ever increasing magnitude of the service sector simply underscores the need for managers and researchers alike to increase the attention directed at the important issues in the marketing of services.

LIMITATIONS

In designing our study, we attempted to minimize its limitations. However, generalizations beyond the four specific service industries investigated are tenuous. Future studies should incorporate multiple measures of all of the constructs examined. Limiting the study to the two highest market share firms in each category may also have affected the variable distribution and, hence, the importance of the predictors. In addition, with the possible exception of banking, the services investigated are all low involvement service categories. Perceived quality may play a bigger role (in comparison with satisfaction) in high involvement situations, where a firm may need to do more than simply meet customers' 'minimum requirements'. Finally, the number of constructs other researchers could add to the models examined is probably unlimited.

APPENDIX

Expectations

This survey deals with *your opinions of ____ services.* Please show the extent to which you think institutions offering telephone services should possess the features described in each statement. Do this by using the scale presented below. If you strongly agree that these institutions should possess a feature, place a seven on the line preceding the statement. If you strongly disagree that these institutions should possess a feature, place a one on the line. If your feelings are not strong, place one of the numbers between one and seven on the line to properly reflect the actual strength of your feelings. There are no right or wrong answers – all we are interested in is a number that best shows your Expectations about institutions offering banking services.

1	2	3	4	5	6	7
STRONGLY DISAGREE						STRONGLY AGREE

____ E1 They should have up-to-date equipment and technology.

____ E2 Their physical facilities should be visually appealing.

____ E3 Their employees should be well dressed and appear neat.

____ E4 The appearance of the physical facilities of these institutions should be in keeping with the type of service provided.

____ E5 When these institutions promise to do something by a certain time, they should do so.

____ E6 When customers have problems, these institutions should by sympathetic and reassuring.

____ E7 The institutions should be dependable.

____ E8 They should provide their services at the time they promise to do so.

____ E9 They should keep their records accurately.

____ E10 They shouldn't be expected to tell their customers exactly when services will be performed.

____ E11 It is not realistic for customers to expect prompt service from employees of these institutions.

____ E12 Their employees don't always have to be willing to help customers.

____ E13 It is okay if they are too busy to respond to customer requests promptly.

____ E14 Customer should be able to trust employees of these institutions.

____ E15 Customers should be able to feel safe in their transactions with these institutions' employees.

____ E16 Their employees should be polite.

____ E17 Their employees should get adequate support from these institutions to do their jobs well.

____ E18 These institutions should not be expected to give customers individual attention.

____ E19 Employees of these institutions cannot be expected to give customers personal attention.

____ E20 It is unrealistic to expect employees to know what the needs of their customers are.

____ E21 It is unrealistic to expect these institutions to have their customers' best interests at heart.

____ E22 They shouldn't be expected to have operating hours convenient to all their customers.

Performance

The following set of statements relate to *your feelings about XYZ* ____. For each statement, please show the extent to which you believe XYZ ____ has the feature described by the statement. Once again, placing a seven on the line means you strongly agree that XYZ has that feature, and a one means you strongly disagree. You may use any of the number in the middle as well to show how strong your feeling are. There are no right or wrong answers – all we are interested in is a number that best shows your perceptions about XYZ, whether you use their service or not.

1	2	3	4	5	6	7
STRONGLY DISAGREE						STRONGLY AGREE

____ P1 XYZ____has up-to-date equipment.
____ P2 XYZ____'s physical facilities are visually appealing.
____ P3 XYZ____'s employees are well dressed and appear neat.
____ P4 The appearance of the physical facilities of XYZ____is in keeping with the type of service provided.
____ P5 When XYZ____promises to do something by a certain time, it does so.
____ P6 When you have problems, XYZ____is sympathetic and reassuring.
____ P7 XYZ____is dependable.
____ P8 XYZ____provides its services at the time it promises to do so.
____ P9 XYZ____keeps its records accurately.
____ P10 XYZ____does not tell its customers exactly when services will be performed.
____ P11 You do not receive prompt service from XYZ____employees.
____ P12 Employees of XYZ____are not always willing to help customers.
____ P13 Employees of XYZ____are too busy to respond to customer requests promptly.
____ P14 You can trust employees of XYZ____.
____ P15 You can feel safe in your transactions with XYZ____'s employees.
____ P16 Employees of XYZ____are polite.
____ P17 Employees get adequate support from XYZ____to do their jobs well.
____ P18 XYZ____does not give you individual attention.
____ P19 Employees of XYZ____do not give you personal attention.
____ P20 Employees of XYZ____do not know what you needs are.
____ P21 XYZ____does not have your best interests at heart.
____ P22 XYZ____does not have operating hours convenient to all their customers.

Importance

The following set of statements relate to *your feelings about the importance of each feature described in your decision to purchase ____ services.* A seven means you consider the feature very important in deciding where to purchase banking services, a one means it is very unimportant. You may place any of the numbers shown on the scale below beside each feature to indicate its importance to you. There are no right or wrong answers – all we are interested in is your perception of how important each feature is to you in your decision where to purchase banking services.

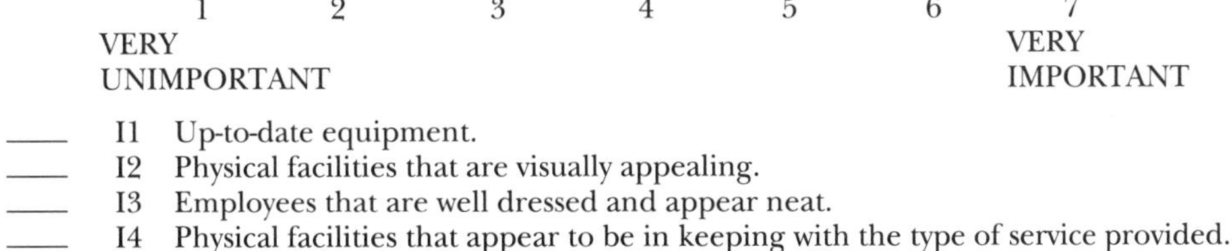

1	2	3	4	5	6	7
VERY UNIMPORTANT						VERY IMPORTANT

____ I1 Up-to-date equipment.
____ I2 Physical facilities that are visually appealing.
____ I3 Employees that are well dressed and appear neat.
____ I4 Physical facilities that appear to be in keeping with the type of service provided.

____ I5 When something is promised by a certain time, doing it.
____ I6 When there is a problem, being sympathetic and reassuring.
____ I7 Dependability.
____ I8 Providing service by the time promised.
____ I9 Accurate record keeping.
____ I10 Telling the customer exactly when the service will be performed.
____ I11 Receiving prompt service.
____ I12 Employees who are always willing to help customers.
____ I13 Employees who are not too busy to respond to customer request promptly.
____ I14 Employees who are trustworthy.
____ I15 The feeling that you are safe when conducting transactions with the firm's employees.
____ I16 Employees who are polite.
____ I17 Adequate support from the firm so employees can do their job well.
____ I18 Individual attention.
____ I19 Employees who give you personal attention.
____ I20 Employees who know what your needs are.
____ I21 A firm which has your best interests at heart.
____ I22 Convenient operating hours.

Other measures

The following set of statements relate to *your feelings about XYZ*____. Please respond by circling the number which best reflects your own perceptions.

(Future Purchase Behavior)

(84) In the next year, my use of XYZ____will be

1 . . . 2 . . . 3 . . . 4 . . . 5 . . . 6 . . . 7
NOT AT ALL VERY FREQUENT

(Overall Quality)

(85) The quality of XYZ____'s services is

1 . . . 2 . . . 3 . . . 4 . . . 5 . . . 6 . . . 7
VERY POOR EXCELLENT

(Satisfaction)

(87) My feelings towards XYZ____'s services can best be described as

1 . . . 2 . . . 3 . . . 4 . . . 5 . . . 6 . . . 7
VERY UNSATISFIED VERY SATISFIED

ACKNOWLEDGEMENTS

The authors express their sincere appreciation to the editor and three anonymous *JM* reviewers for their helpful comments on previous versions of the article.

REFERENCES

Bateson, J. E. (1989) *Managing Services Marketing*. London: Dryden Press.

Bitner, M. J. (1990) 'Evaluating Service Encounters: The Effects of Physical Surroundings and Employee Responses'. *Journal of Marketing* **54** (April): 69–82.

Blackiston, G. H. (1988) 'Service Industries: A Renaissance in Quality'. *Executive Excellence.* **5** (9): 9–10.

Bolton, R. N. and Drew, J. H. (1991a) 'A Longitudinal Analysis of the Impact of Service Changes on Customer Attitudes'. *Journal of Marketing* **55** (January): 1–9.

Bolton, R. N. and Drew, J. H. (1991b). 'A Multistage Model of Customer Assessments of Service Quality and Value'. *Journal of Consumer Research* **17** (March): 375–384.

Brown, S. W. and Swartz, T. A. (1989) A Gap Analysis of Professional Service Quality'. *Journal of Marketing.* **53** (April): 92–98.

Carman, J. M. (1990) 'Consumer Perceptions of Service Quality, An Assessment of the SERVQUAL Dimensions'. *Journal of Retailing* **66** (1): 33–55.

Carmmes, E. G. and Zeller, R. A. (1979) 'Reliability and Validity Assessment'. Sage Publications Series Number 07 017. Newbury Park. CA: Sage Publications, Inc.

Churchill, G. A. Jr. (1979) 'A Paradigm for Developing Better Measures of Marketing Constructs'. *Journal of Marketing Research* **16** (February): 64–73.

Churchill, G. A. Jr. and Surprenant, C. (1982) 'An Investigation into the Determinants of Customer Satisfaction'. *Journal of Marketing Research* **19** (November): 491–504.

Cohen, J. B., Fishbem, M. and Ahtola, O. T. (1972) 'The Nature and Uses of Expectancy Value Models in Consumer Attitude Research'. *Journal of Marketing Research* **9** (November): 456–460

Cound, D. M. (1988) What Corporate Executives Think About Quality: The Results of the 1987 Gallup Survey'. *Quality Progress* **21** (2): 20–23.

Cravens, D. W. (1988) 'The Marketing of Quality'. *Incentive* **162** (11): 26–31.

Crosby, P. B. (1979) *Quality Is Free: The Art of Making Quality Certain.* New York: American Library.

Garvin, D. A. (1983) 'Quality on the Line'. *Harvard Business Review* **61** (September–October): 65–73.

Ginzberg, E. and Vojta, G. (1981) 'The Service Sector of the U.S. Economy.' *Scientific American* **244** (March): 31–39.

Grönroos, C. (1990). *Service Management and Marketing: Managing the Moments of Truth in Service Competition.* Lexington, MA: Lexington Books.

Heskett, J. L., Sasser, W. I. and Hart, W. L. (1990) *Service Breakthroughs. Changing the Rules of the Game.* New York: The Free Press.

Koepp, S. (1987). 'Pul-eeze! Will Somebody Help Me'. *Time* (February 2): 28–34.

Langevin, R. C. (1988) 'Service Quality: Essential Ingredients'. *Review of Business* **9** (3): 3–5.

Mazis, M. B., Ahtola, O. T. and Klippel, R. E. (1975). 'A Comparison of Four Multi-Attribute Models in the Prediction of Consumer Attitudes'. *Journal of Consumer Research* **2** (June): 38–52.

Oliver, R. I. (1980). 'A Cognitive Model of the Antecedents and Consequences of Satisfaction Decisions'. *Journal of Marketing Research* **17** (November): 460–469.

Parasuraman, A., Zeithaml, V. and Berry, L. (1985) 'A Conceptual Model of Service Quality and Its Implications for Future Research'. *Journal of Marketing* **49** (Fall): 41–50.

Parasuraman, A., Zeithaml, V. and Berry, L. (1988) 'SERVQUAL A Multiple Item Scale for Measuring Consumer Perceptions of Service Quality'. *Journal of Retailing* **64** (Spring): 12–40.

Rathmell, J. M. (1966). 'What Is Meant by Services'. *Journal of Marketing* **30** (October): 32–36.

Rudie, M. J. and Wansley, H. B. (1985) 'The Merrill Lynch Quality Program'. In *Services Marketing in a Changing Environment*' (T. Bloch, G. Upah and A. Zeithaml, Eds). Chicago: American Marketing Association.

Sherden, W. A. (1988) 'Gaining the Service Quality Advantage'. *Journal of Business Strategy.* **9** (2): 45–48.

Thompson, P., DeSouza, G. and Gale, B. T. (1985) *The Stragegic Measurement of Quality,* Cambridge, MA: The Strategic Planning Institute, PIMSLETTER, No. 33.

Woodruff, R. B., Cadotte, E. R. and Jenkins, R. L. (1983) 'Modeling Consumer Satisfaction Processes Using Experienced-Based Norms'. *Journal of Marketing Research* **20** (August): 296–304.

Zeithaml, V. A., Parasuraman, A. and Berry, L. L. (1990) *Delivering Quality Service: Balancing Customer Perceptions and Expectations.* New York: The Free Press.

13

Expectations, Performance Evaluation, and Consumers' Perceptions of Quality

R. Kenneth Teas

The issue of service quality has received considerable attention in the marketing literature (Berry, Zeithaml and Parasuraman, 1985; Bolton and Drew, 1991; Brown and Swartz, 1989; Carman, 1990; Cronin and Taylor, 1992; Hostage, 1975; Olshavsky and Miller, 1972; Parasuraman, Zeithaml and Berry, 1985, 1988; Parasuraman, Berry and Zeithaml, 1990; Swartz and Brown, 1989; Zeithaml, 1988; Zeithaml, Berry and Parasuraman, 1988; Zeithaml, Parasuraman and Berry, 1990). Important concepts examined in some of this research involve various service 'gaps' that highlight several factors potentially affecting service quality. The service quality gap concept that has received the most attention is the 'expected service–perceived service gap' (P–E) identified by Parasuraman, Zeithaml and Berry (1985), operationally defined in terms of a 'perceptions-minus-expectations' measurement framework. Through the identification of service gaps that potentially affect customers' perceptions of service quality represents a significant contribution, the validity of the P–E service quality gap concept and corresponding measurement framework is questionable because of a number of problems involving conceptual and operational definitions of the concept of expectations and the resulting ambiguity with respect to the theoretical justification and interpretation of the P–E perceived quality framework. My purpose, therefore, is fourfold. First, the P–E service quality model is currently specified in the services marketing literature is examined and important conceptual and definitional problems are identified. Second, recent research identifying measurement validity problems concerning the operationalization of the P–E measurement framework is reviewed. Third, the P–E model and two alternative perceived quality models that are designed to address the problems associated with the P–E model are empirically tested. Fourth, implications of the conceptual issues examined in this study and of the empirical findings are explored.

Reprinted with permission from *Journal of Marketing*, Vol. 57, October, pp. 18 – 34.

CONCEPTUAL BACKGROUND

Definitions

Parasuraman, Zeithaml and Berry (1988, p. 16) define perceived service quality as 'a global judgement, or attitude, relating to superiority of the service'. Additionally, they link to the concepts of perceptions and expectations as follows: 'Perceived quality is viewed as the degree and direction of discrepancy between consumers' perceptions and expectations' (Parasuraman, Zeithaml and Berry, 1988, p. 1). In the services marketing literature, perceptions (P) are defined as consumers' beliefs concerning the service received (Parasuraman, Zeithaml and Berry, 1985) or experienced service (Brown and Swartz, 1989). Expectations (E) are defined by Parasuraman, Zeithaml and Berry (1988, p. 17) as 'desires or wants of consumers, i.e., what they feel a service provider should offer rather than would offer'. Parasuraman and his co-authors (1988) emphasize that the term 'expectations' is used differently in the service quality literature than it is in the consumer satisfaction literature in that service expectations (E) do not represent predictions about what service providers 'would' offer, but rather what they 'should' offer. Recently, researchers examining service quality issue have adopted the Parasuraman, Zeithaml and Berry (1985) conceptualization of expectations (Brown and Swartz, 1989; Carman, 1990).

This original definition of expectations is somewhat vague in terms of the meaning of 'should'. Recently, however, Parasuraman, Berry and Zeithaml (1990, p. 12) noted that the service expectations concept is 'intended to measure the customers' normative expectations', and that these expectations represent an 'ideal standard' of performance.

Carman (1990) also suggests that service quality expectations involve 'norms' and that these 'norms' are based on past experience.

The P–E perceived quality model

The operationalization of the quality concept in empirical studies (Parasuraman, Zeithaml and Berry, 1986, 1988; Brown and Swartz, 1989; Carman, 1990) suggests that perceived service quality can be conceptualized with the following P–E measurement model:

$$SQ_i = \sum_{j=1}^{k} W_j (P_{ij} - E_{ij}) \tag{1}$$

where:

SQ_i = SERVQUAL overall perceived quality of stimulus *i*.
k = The number of attributes.
W_j = A weighting factor if attributes have differentiated weights.[1]
P_{ij} = Performance perception of stimulus *i* with respect to attribute *j*.
E_{ij} = Service quality expectation for attribute *j* that is the relevant norm for stimulus *i*.

---

[1]In published perceived service quality research, W_j is not included in the model and, therefore, is assumed to be equal to 1.0.

Equation (1) suggests that perceived service quality (SQ_i) increases as the differences between P_{ij} and E_{ij} increases across attributes. It is important to note that Parasuraman, Zeithaml and Berry (1988) emphasizes that this P–E service gap concept is different from the disconfirmed expectations concept in traditional consumer satisfaction/dissatisfaction models. First, the P–E gap concept represents a comparison with a norm; it does not represent a difference between predicted and received service. Exceeding the norm means how quality is received. Second, the P–E service quality concept as expressed in equation (1) is not a predictive model. It is a measurement specification in which perceived quality is equivalent to perceptions-minus-expectations.

The traditional method of operationalizating the P–E gap concept is to obtain perception and expectation scores for each attribute and calculate SQ by equation (1) with the attribute weights implicitly assumed to be equal ($W_j = 1$). For example, using the procedures described in Table 1, the P and E measures for the appeal of the physical facilities of a bank are obtained by agree/disagree (strongly agree = 7, strongly disagree = 1) ratings of the following statements:

1. Expectations (E) – 'Their physical facilities should be visually appealing'.
2. Perceptions (P) – 'XYZ's physical facilities are visually appealing'.

According to Parasuraman, Zeithaml and Berry (1986, p. 8);

> The difference between the ratings of statements like these is a measure of perceived service quality. The higher (more positive) the perception-minus-expectation score, the higher is the level of perceived service quality.[2]

The P–E measurement framework suggests the highest service quality score for an attribute occurs when the expectation score is +1 and the perception score is +7, giving a service quality score of +6 (7−1). The lowest service quality score is one in which the expectation score is +7 and the perception score is +1, giving a service quality score of −6 (1−7). If this measurement framework is valid, it should reflect constantly increasing levels of quality as scores move from −6 to +6. However, on the basis of the Parasuraman, Zeithaml and Berry (1985) definition of service expectations as ideal standards, the following discussion demonstrates that alternative conceptualizations of the ideal standard may be incompatible with the assumption that increasing P–E scores reflect continually increasing levels of perceived quality.

The ideal performance problem

Parasuraman, Berry and Zeithaml (1990) note that the SERVQUAL expectations measure is intended to measure 'normative expectations'. In a subsequent article they suggest that the SERVQUAL expectations concept 'is similar to the ideal standard in the CS/D literature' (Zeithaml, Berry and Parasuraman, 1991, pp. 3 – 4),

---

[2]Carman (1990) adopts this P–E measurement framework whereas Brown and Swartz (1989) use an 'expectations-minus-perceptions' (E–P) framework. The focus of my discussion is on the P–E procedure; however, the discussion generally applies to the E–P procedure as well.

Table 1. Standard instructions for P–E gap model measures

1. Expectations measures (E)

This survey deals with your opinions of ____ service. Please show the extent to which you think firms offering ____ services should possess the features described by each statement. Do this by picking one of the seven numbers next to each statement. If you strongly agree that these firms should possess a feature, circle the number 7. If you strongly disagree that these firms should possess a feature, circle 1. If your feelings are not strong, circle one of the numbers in the middle. There are no right or wrong answers. All we are interested in is a number that best shows your expectations about firms offering ____ services.

(1) They should have up-to-date equipment.
(2) Their physical facilities should be visually appealing.
■
■
■
(22) They shouldn't be expected to have operating hours convenient to all customers.

2. Perceptions measures (P)

The following set of statements relates to your feelings about XYZ. For each statement, please show the extent to which you believe XYZ has the feature described by the statement. Once again, circling a 7 means that you strongly agree that XYZ has that feature, and circling 1 means that you strongly disagree. You may circle any of the numbers in the middle that show how strong your feelings are. There are no right or wrong answers. All we are interested in is a number that best shows your perceptions about XYZ.

(1) XYZ has up-to-date equipment.
(2) XYZ's physical facilities are visually appealing.
■
■
■
(22) XYZ does not have operating hours convenient to all customers.

3. Revised expectations measures (E)*

Based on your experiences as a customer of ____ company services, please think about the kind of ____ companies that would deliver excellent quality of service. Think about the kind of ____ company with which you would be pleased to do business. Please show the extent to which you think such a ____ company would possess the feature described by each statement. If you feel a feature is not at all essential for excellent ____ companies such as the one you have in mind, circle the number 1. If you feel a feature is absolutely essential for excellent ____ companies, circle 7. If your feelings are less strong, circle one of the numbers in the middle. There are no right or wrong answers. All we are interested in is a number that truly reflects your feelings regarding ____ companies that would deliver excellent quality of service.

(1) Excellent ____ have up-to-date equipment.
(2) The physical facilities of excellent ____ are visually appealing.
■
■
■
(22) Excellent ____ have operating hours convenient to all customers.

such as

1. Miller's (1977) 'ideal expectations, defined as the wished-for level of performance'.
2. Swan and Trawick's (1980) 'desired expectations, defined as the level at which the consumer wanted the product to perform'.
3. Prakash's (1984) 'normative expectations, i.e. how a brand should perform for the customer to be completely satisfied'.

Though Zeithaml, Berry and Parasuraman (1991) have indicated that service expectations are *similar* to these ideal standards, they have not clearly articulated the specific interpretation of the ideal standard they adopt. Accordingly, alternative interpretations are examined subsequently. It will be demonstrated that conceptualizing service expectations as ideal standards is a problem under each of the interpretations examined.

Classic attitudinal model ideal point interpretation

Since Parasuraman, Zeithaml, and Berry (1988) argue that perceived quality is an attitude, the ideal standard could be interpreted to be similar to the ideal point specified in classic ideal point attitudinal models (Ginter, 1974; Green and Srinivasan, 1978).[3] However, the P–E measurement specification as expressed in equation (1) suggests that perceived quality (Q_i) increases as P increasingly exceeds E. In contrast, ideal point attitudinal models suggest that perceived quality might decrease as P increasingly exceeds the ideal point.[4] Clearly, the SERVQUAL P–E measurement specification is not compatible with this classic ideal point interpretation of E.

Feasible ideal point interpretation

A second interpretation of the SERVQUAL ideal standard is that it represents a feasible level of performance under ideal circumstances, i.e. the best level of performance by the highest-quality provider under perfect circumstances. Under this interpretation, it could be argued that the service provider's performance might exceed this standard and that perceived quality increases accordingly as specified in equation (1).[5] However, depending on whether the attributes are vector attributes (i.e. infinite or maximum classic attitudinal model ideal points) or finite ideal point

[3]In these models, the ideal point is the perfect or utility maximizing level of the attribute. For example, if the attribute has a non-maximum ideal point, once the ideal point is reached, 'there are negative utility returns for further increases in the attribute' (Lilien, Kotler and Moorthy, 1992, p. 91).

[4]For example, ideal point models, such as those proposed by Ginter (1974) and Green and Srinivasan (1978), suggest that the favorableness of an evaluation of an attitude object is positively related to the closeness of the object to the ideal object. Increasingly exceeding the ideal, therefore, would be predicted by these models to be negatively, rather than positively, related to the favorableness of the evaluation.

[5]This feasible ideal concept is similar to Miller's (1977, p. 86) ideal concept which he defines as 'what performance level [the consumer] . . . feels might possibly be achieved by the object given ideal circumstances'.

attributes (i.e. non-infinite or intermediate classic attitudinal model ideal points), this feasible ideal point interpretation may not be justified. As an illustration, consider a one-attribute service quality situation. The SERVQUAL P–E measure of an individual's perceived quality of stimulus *i* is

$$SQ_i = P_i - E_i \tag{2}$$

where

SQ_i = The SERVQUAL measure of the individual's overall perceived quality of stimulus *i*.
P_i = The individual's perceptions of the performance of stimulus *i* with respect to the single attribute.
E_i = The individual's quality expectation norm for the single attribute – conceptualized as a feasible ideal point.

Measuring perceived quality as specified in equation (2) results in measured perceived quality (SQ_i) being a positive linear function of P_i, holding E_i constant, and a negative linear function of E_i, holding P_i constant. Assuming the attribute is a vector attribute (i.e. the classic attitudinal model ideal point is a maximum or infinite), these relationships have logical interpretations. Firest, increasing performance intensity P_i levels would be increasingly close to the infinite classic ideal performance intensity; therefore, a positive relationship between perceived quality and P_i is at least not illogical. Second, increasing expectancy norm intensity E_i levels would be increasingly close to the classic ideal performance intensity. It is at least not illogical to assume that the perceived quality associated with a particular performance intensity P_i is negatively affected when the performance norm (E_i), to which P_i is compared, becomes increasingly close to the ideal performance intensity.

If the single attribute is not a vector attribute (i.e. the classic attitudinal model ideal-point is not a maximum value), the appeal of the 'feasible ideal point' interpretation of E is reduced. For example, consider the following modified one-attribute SERVQUAL model that includes the concept of the classic attitudinal model ideal point:

$$MQ_i = -1\ [|\ P_i - I\ | - |\ E_i - I\ |] \tag{3}$$

where P_i and E_i are defined in (2) and

MQ_i= A modified SERVQUAL measure of the quality of stimulus *i*.
I = The ideal amount of the single attribute – the classic attitudinal model ideal point.

The right side of equation (3) is multiplied by −1 so that increased values of MQ_i are associated with increased perceived quality. The $|\ P_i - I\ |$ component of equation (3), which replaces P_i in equation (2), expresses performance as the absolute value of the distance between perceived performance P_i and ideal performance I. The $|\ E_i I\ |$ component of equation (3), which replaces E_i in equation (2), expresses the expectancy norm as the absolute value of the distance between E_i and the ideal performance level I. The rationale for substituting $|\ P_i - I\ |$ for P_i is that it is difficult to envision a positive monotonic relationship between performance intensity P_i and attitude (or perceived quality) when the ideal performance level (i.e. classic attitudinal model ideal) is an intermediate level of intensity. Ideal point attitudinal models predict that increasing performance intensity beyond the intermediate classic ideal point will produce less rather than more favorable evaluations as predicted by the P–E model. However, when perceived performance is expressed as $|P_i - I|$, decreasing values of $|P_i - I|$ are associated with increasing congruence between perceived performance (P_i) and ideal performance (I). Therefore, a positive relationship between $-1\,|P_i - I|$ and MQ_i is at least not illogical.[6]

Similarly, it is difficult to envision a negative monotonic relationship between the expectancy norm (E_i) and perceived quality when an intermediate level of intensity is the classic attitudinal model ideal performance level.[7] However, when the normative expectation is expressed as $|E_i - I|$, decreasing value of $|E - I|$ are associated with increasing congruence between the expectancy norm (E_i) and the classic ideal (I). Therefore, a negative relationship between $-1\,|E_i - I|$ and MQ_i is at least not illogical. That is, it is not illogical to assume that the perceived quality MQ_i is negatively affected when performance norm E_i, to which P_i is compared, becomes increasingly close to the classic attitudinal model ideal performance intensity (I). Under the assumption that P_i is measured by the SERVQUAL perceptions scale, E_i is measured by the SERVQUAL expectation scale, and I is measured by a similar 7-point scale, the general characteristics of the MQ_i measure as specified in equation (3) are as follows:

1. When I is a maximum value ($I = 7$), MQ_i as specified in equation (3) is perfectly correlated with SQ_i as specified in equation (2). Therefore, the two measurement expressions are equivalent assuming maximum (or infinite) classic ideal points.
2. When $1 < I < 7$ the relationship between MQ_i, and P_i is an inverted V function when E is held constant and the relationship between MQ_i and E_i is a V function when P_i is held constant.
3. When $I = 1$, SQ_i and MQ_i are negatively correlated ($r = -1$).

These properties of MQ_i demonstrate a lack of equivalence of the perceived quality measures as expressed in equation (2) and (3) under the assumption of finite classic attitudinal model ideal-point (non-vector) attributes. In addition, the inverted v function linking MQ_i and P_i and the v function linking MQ_i and E_i suggest a monotonic simplification of the non-linear relationships is not appropriate. Clearly, the SERVQUAL P–E measurement specification is not compatible with the 'feasible ideal point' interpretation of E when finite classic ideal point attributes are involved.

In summary, there are a number of complex theoretical and definitional problems associated with the SERVQUAL P–E perceived quality model. Consequently following a review of recently identified measurement validity problems associated

---

[6]Equation (3) can be rewritten as

$$MQ_i = (-1\,[|P_i - I|]) - (-1\,[|E_i - I|])$$

Therefore, equation (3) suggests that $-1\,[|P_i - I]$ and $-1\,[|E_i - I|]$ are positively and negatively related to MQ_i, respectively.

[7]For example, when the expectancy norm (E_i) exceeds the intermediate classic ideal intensity (I), further increases in the intensity of E_i would result in the norm being farther from the ideal point. In this situation a particular performance intensity P_i is being compared to the norm that is less attractive; consequently, the perceived quality associated with P_i would not be expected to be diminished.

with framework, alternative frameworks are developed to address the problems – particularly the ideal point problem.

OPERATIONAL DEFINITION PROBLEMS

Empirical research has identified important problems concerning the operationalization of the service expectations (E) concept. First, Parasuraman, Berry and Zeithaml (1990) suggest that the word 'should' may cause respondents to assign unrealistically high ratings to the E response scales; therefore, they propose the revised expectation E^* measure described in Table 1. Second, research by Carman (1990), indicates the SERVQUAL dimensions are not 'generic' as suggested by Parasuraman, Zeithaml and Berry (1988). On the basis of the empirical results, Carman (1990) questions the validity of the expectation measure when consumers do not have 'well formed expectations'. Third, exploratory research by Teas (1993) suggests a lack of congruence between the conceptual and operational definitions of the original SERVQUAL E measure. The findings of the research indicate a considerable portion of the variance in responses to the SERVQUAL E scale is because of variance in respondents' interpretations of the question being asked rather than to variance in respondents' attitudes (Teas, 1993).[8]

Given this operational ambiguity associated with the expectations (E) concept, an important question concerns the degree to which the ambiguity has been eliminated through the revised expectation (E^*) measure, which requests the respondent to focus on 'companies that would deliver excellent quality' and if specific features are 'essential' for excellent service (Parasuraman, Berry and Zeithaml, 1990, p. 46). However, definitions of 'essential', include 'indispensable', 'necessary' and 'something that is fundamental' (*American Heritage Dictionary*, 1985, p. 465). Defining the revised SERVQUAL E^* this way, in conjunction with the P–E measurement specification as expressed in equation (1), suggests high performance on essential attributes (high E^* scores) reflects lower quality than higher performance on attributes that are essential (low E^* scores). It is difficult to envision a theoretical argument that supports this measurement specification.

ALTERNATIVE PERCEIVED QUALITY FRAMEWORKS

Clearly, there are serious conceptual and operational problems associated with the SERVQUAL P–E perceived quality measurement framework. First, if the expectation 'normative ideal standard' concept E_j is interpreted to represent a classic attitudinal model ideal point concept, a positive monotonic link between perceived quality and the SERVQUAL SQ_i as specified in equation (1) may not be expected when the attributes are finite classic attitudinal ideal-point attributes. Second, if the expectation concept is interpreted to represent a feasible ideal point, classic ideal point attitudinal models suggest possible nonmonotonic linkages between

[8]In a recent article, Cronin and Taylor (1992) published the results of an empirical test of the original SERVQUAL model. On the basis of a literature review and the empirical findings, they conclude that the 'current operationalization of service quality confounds satisfaction and attitude' and that performance-based measures of service quality may be more effective than the SERVQUAL P–E measure.

SERVQUAL SQ_i scores calculated by equation (1) and true perceptions of quality. Third, the SERVQUAL expectations E and revised expectations E^* are characterized by a number of operational definition problems involving such issues as operationalizing the P–E framework for inexperienced consumers, variance in respondents' interpretation of the SERVQUAL E scale, and the meaning of the revised SERVQUAL E^* concept of 'essential' features. Because of these problems, the following evaluated performance (EP) perceived quality model is developed, addressing the ideal point problem by formally incorporating the classic ideal point concept into a perceived quality model. Additionally, using the EP model as a theoretical foundation, a normed quality (NQ) model is developed that integrates the classic ideal point concept with the SERVQUAL revised expectation (E^*) concept.

Perceived quality models using an evaluated performance (EP) framework

Building on *The Dictionary of Psychology* (Chaplin, 1981) definition of quality – 'the relative goodness or excellence of anything' – Monroe and Krishnan (1985, p. 212) define perceived product quality as 'the perceived ability of a product to provide satisfaction "relative" to available alternatives'. On the basis of this definition and the assumptions that the perceived ability of the product (defined as a good or service) to deliver satisfaction can be conceptualized as the product's relative congruence with the consumer's ideal product features (conceptualized as classic attitudinal model ideal points), the proposed probabilistic evaluated performance (EP) model of perceived quality is[9]

$$Q_i = -1 \left[\sum_{j=1}^{m} W_j \sum_{k=1}^{n_j} P_{ij_k} \left| A_{j_k} - I_j \right|^{\ell} \right] 1/\ell \qquad (4)$$

where

Q_i = the individual's perceived quality of object i.
Multiplying the right side of the equation by -1 results in larger values of Q_i being associated with higher levels of perceived quality.
W_j = importance of attribute j as a determinant of perceived quality.
P_{ij_k} = the perceived probability that object i has amount k of attribute j.[10]
A_{j_k} = amount k of attribute j.
I_j = ideal amount of attribute j as conceptualized in classic ideal point attitudinal models.
m = number of attributes.
n_j = number of 'amount' categories of attribute j.
ℓ = Minkowski space parameter.[11]

---

[9]The proposed model focuses on attributes that can be defined along quantitative continuums. A potential extension of the model would be to incorporate nominal scaled attributes (e.g. color). For example of multiattribute models that mix quantitative and nominal scaled attributes, see Green and Srinivasan (1978).

[10]See Ahtola (1975) for a discussion of an attitudinal model that includes probabilities of alternative amounts or levels of multiple attributes.

[11]See Ginter (1974) for a discussion of an attitudinal model that includes the Minkowski space parameter specification.

If it is assumed that l equals 1.0, equation (4) becomes

$$Q_i = -1 \left[\sum_{j=1}^{m} W_j \sum_{k=1}^{n_j} P_{ij_k} \mid A_{j_k} - I_j \mid \right] \tag{5}$$

This perceived quality model as expressed in equation (4) or (5) posits that an individual's perceptions of the quality of the performance of object i is positively related to the weighted likelihood that the performance of object i on m performance dimensions is close to the individual's perceptions of optimal performance (the classic attitudinal model ideal) on the m dimensions. The model implies that the perceived quality of object i can be increased by (1) closing the gap between object i's performance and the ideal object's performance on one or more of the m attributes, (2) reducing the relative weights W_j for attributes characterized by large $\mid A_{j_k} - I_j \mid$ gaps, (3) increasing the relative weights W_j for attributes characterized by small $\mid A_{j_k} - I_j \mid$ gaps, (4) increasing the relative probabilities associated with the occurrence of small $\mid A_{j_k} - I_i \mid$ gaps, and (5) decreasing the relative probabilities associated with the occurrence of large $\mid A_{j_k} - I_j \mid$ gaps.

Several alternative perceived quality concepts and measures can be derived from equations (4) and (5) by making certain assumptions. For example, if it is assumed that the individual evaluates object i with perceived certainty and that object i has a constant amount of each attribute, equation (5) becomes the following nonprobabilistic evaluated performance (EP) model of perceived quality:

$$Q_i = -1 \left[\sum_{j=1}^{m} W_j \mid A_{ij} - I_j \mid \right] \tag{6}$$

where Q_i, W_j, and I_j are defined in equation (4) and A_{ij} equals the individual's perceived amount of attribute j possessed by object i. Equation (6) is similar to Ginter's (1974) 'city block' distance ideal point model.

A normal quality model

If object i is defined as the excellence norm that is the focus of the revised SERVQUAL E* concept, equations (4), (5) or (6) can be used to define the perceived quality of the excellence norm Q_e in terms of similarity between the excellence norm and the ideal object with respect to the m attributes. The quality of another object Q_i relative to the quality of the excellence norm then can be conceptualized as the 'normed quality gap' or 'normed quality' as follows:

$$NQ_i = [Q_i - Q_e] \tag{7}$$

where Q_i is defined in equation (4) and

NQ_i = Normed Quality Index for object i.
Q_e = The individual's perceived quality of the excellence norm object.

If the excellence norm is equal to the ideal or perfect object, equation (4) suggests Q_e will equal 0 and, therefore, normed quality (NQ_i) would be equal to perceived quality (Q_i).

If the SERVQUAL normative expectations concept is respecified to be this 'excellence norm', equations (6) and (7) can be used to derive the following modified SERVQUAL model that addresses the ideal point problem by incorporating the classic ideal point concept into the model:

$$NQ_i = -1 \left[\sum_{j=1}^{m} W_j \left(| A_{ij} - I_j | - | A_{ej} - I_j | \right) \right] \tag{8}$$

where W_j and I_j are defined in equation (4), A_{ij} is defined in equation (6), and

NQ_i = Normed Quality Index for object i.
A_{ej} = The individual's perceived amount of attribute j possessed by the excellence norm.

If infinite classic ideal points are assumed, equation (8) can be expressed as

$$NQ_i = \sum_{j=1}^{m} W_j \left(A_{ij} - A_{ej} \right). \tag{9}$$

Though equation (9) is similar in structure to the original SERVQUAL model described in equation (1), it is important to note that two necessary assumptions used in the derivation of equation (9) are that all the m attributes have infinite classic ideal points and that the SERVQUAL normative expectations concept is redefined as the 'excellence norm' specified in equation (8).

EMPIRICAL TESTS

Because of the conceptual and operational problems associated with the original SERVQUAL P–E model, tests of the validity of the revised SERVQUAL P–E*, normed quality (NQ), and evaluated performance (EP) measurement models are warranted. Consequently, the empirical tests in this study focus on measurement validity issues with respect to these models. The issues examined involves the (1) conceptual-operational definition congruence of the SERVQUAL expectation and revised expectation measures (E and E*) and an ideal point measure and (2) criterion and construct validity of the original P–E, revised P–E*, NQ, and EP perceived quality measurement frameworks.

Research questions

The purpose of the empirical study is to compare alternative perceived quality measurement frameworks by examining the following issues:

1. The primary differences among the models involve the P–E model's service expectations E and E* and the EP model's ideal point (I) concepts. Since there is definitional ambiguity associated with the service expectations E and E* concepts, the question of conceptual-operational definition congruence of the service expectations (E and E*) measures and of the ideal point (I) used to operationalize the EP model is explored.

2. Weighted and unweighted versions of the following models are compared in terms of criterion and construct validity:
   a. Original SERVQUAL P–E model (equation 1) using the original expectations (E) measure,
   b. Revised SERVQUAL P–E model (equation 1) using the revised expectations (E^*) measure,
   c. Nonprobabilistic ideal-point evaluated performance (EP) model (equation 6),
   d. Normed Quality Model (equation 8) using the revised expectations (E^*) measure.

For the purpose of this study, the following definitions are used:

1. *Criterion validity* concerns 'the degree of correspondence between a measure and a criterion variable, usually measured by their correlation... When the criterion exists at the same time as the measure, this is called concurrent validity' (Bollen, 1989, p. 186).
2. *Construct validity* concerns the degree to which 'a measure relates to other observed variables in a way that is consistent with theoretically derived predictions' (Bollen, 1989, p. 188).

On the basis of the conceptual and operational problems associated with P–E perceived quality models in general and the expectations (E) and revised expectations (E^*) concepts in particular, the following hypotheses are examined in this study:

> H_1: The criterion validity of the EP measurement framework is greater than the criterion validity of the P–E, revised P–E*, and normed quality (NQ) measurement frameworks.
> H_2: The construct validity of the EP measurement framework is greater than the construct validity of the P–E, revised P–E*, and the normed quality (NQ) measurement frameworks.

The criterion validity variable used to test H_1 is the respondent's global assessment of service quality. Because service quality can be expected to affect such factors as business growth, market share, customer preferences, and customer loyalty (Zeithaml, Parasuraman and Berry, 1990), the variables used in the construct validity test (H_2) involve shopping preferences, purchase intentions, and overall satisfaction with store services.

Research design

The data used to examine the research questions were obtained from a random sample (selected from the telephone directory) of respondents from a small midwestern city. Each of the 120 respondents, who were paid $15 for their participation in a personal interview, was assigned randomly to one of two cells and was requested to respond to a series of measurement instruments designed to operationalize the SERVQUAL P–E and revised P–E^* measurement frameworks, the normed quality (NQ) measurement framework, and the evaluated performance (EP) measurement framework. The bulk of the services marketing literature examining the (P–E) quality model uses a non-transaction-specific, relationship-oriented, focus.

Consequently, the hypotheses were tested within the context of ongoing service provided by three local discount stores (K-Mart, Wal-Mart and Target). Each respondent in each of the two cells was randomly assigned one of the stores to rate on ten of the service attributes from the SERVQUAL instrument (Parasuraman, Zeithaml and Berry, 1986; Zeithaml, Parasuraman and Berry, 1990) – two attributes for each of the five general SERVQUAL dimensions.

The survey procedures[12]

The sequence of questions for the two survey cells are presented in Table 2 and a detailed discussion of the instrumentation is presented in Appendix A. As noted in Table 2, each respondent answered a series of questions measuring (1) service expectations,[13] performance perceptions, ideal points, and importance weights with respect to ten SERVQUAL service attributes and (2) overall satisfaction, preference, intentions, and perceived quality. These responses were used to test the measurement validity hypotheses. In addition, the respondents answered qualitative

Table 2. The sequence of questions

Question order		
Cell 1	Cell 2	Measure
1	3	E_{ij}: SERVQUAL expectations measures for each attribute.[a]
2	2	P^s_{ij}: SERVQUAL perceptions measures for the randomly selected store with respect to each attribute.
3	1	E^*_{ij}: SERVQUAL revised (excellence norm) measures for each attribute
4	4	P^d_{ij}: Semantic differential scale performance measures for the randomly selected store with respect to each attribute.
5	5	I_j: Semantic differential scale ideal performance measures for each attribute.
6	6	Overall satisfaction, preference, intentions, and quality measures.
7	7	Follow-up questions (which were tape-recorded) concerning reasons for 'non-extreme' E_{ij}, E^*_{ij}, and I_j ratings.
8	8	Attribute importance weights.

[a] The primary focus of the validity tests involves the SERVQUAL expectation measures. Consequently, all the SERVQUAL measures were obtained first so the process of obtaining the other measures would not have an effect on the SERVQUAL responses.

---

[12]Each model examined in this study specifies difference scores, i.e., performance–minus–expectations, performance–minus–ideal, or expectations–minus–ideal. These difference scores were operationalized by measuring the individual components and calculating the differences. This approach was selected because this is the approach used in the published literature involving the SERVQUAL measurement specification. As noted by Prakash (1984), the use of difference scores can result in low measurement reliability. Consequently, an alternative, and probably preferable, procedure that deserves attention in future research is the use of scales that are designed to capture the perceived differences directly rather than measure each component and calculating the differences. These kinds of scales are routinely used in consumer satisfaction research (Churchill and Surprenant, 1982).

[13]The SERVQUAL expectations (E) and revised expectations (E^*) were stated using the formats published in Parasuraman, Zeithaml and Berry (1988) using the Parasuraman, Berry and Zeithaml (1990), respectively. The same ten attributes were used for the P^d_j, I_j, and W_j ratings.

follow-up questions, concerning their reasons for 'non-extreme' ('non-7') responses to the expectations (E and E*) and ideal point (I) rating scales, which were used to examine the issues of conceptual and operational definitions congruence. The follow-up questions focused on non-extreme responses because the SQ_i, NQ_i, and Q_i measures, as specified in equations (1), (8), and (6), respectively, are perfectly correlated when expectations (E or E*) and ideal point (I) measures are fixed at the extreme point on the scales (i.e. $E_{ij} = I_i = 7$). However, Q_i becomes less positively correlated with SQ_i as E_i or I_j scores become less extreme and SQ_i becomes less positively correlated with NQ_i as I scores become less extreme. Furthermore, responses to the SERVQUAL E measure are usually highly skewed with many mean values exceeding 6.0 (Parasuraman, Zeithaml and Berry, 1986). Consequently, focusing the follow-up questions on the non-extreme responses facilitates an analysis of those factors that are causing the variance in the ratings.

FINDINGS

I used two approaches to examine empirically the validity of the alternative perceived quality measurement frameworks tested. First, the congruence between the conceptual and operational definitions of the measures is explored qualitatively by analyzing the responses to the open-ended follow-up questions concerning the respondents' reasons for non-extreme SERVQUAL expectancy (E and E*) and ideal point (I) ratings. Second, the criterion and construct validity of the SERVQUAL P–E, the normed quality (NQ), and the evaluated performance (EP) perceived quality measurement frameworks are assessed quantitatively by testing hypotheses H_1 and H_2.

Reasons for non-extreme expectations and ideal point responses

The primary categories used for classifying responses to the follow-up questions concerning reasons for non-extreme responses to the expectations and ideal point measures were (1) not feasible, (2) sufficient, (3) not necessary, (4) less important, (5) implied less important, (6) classic ideal, (7) forecast, and (8) other. These categories were developed through a preliminary exploratory study and a preliminary evaluation of the follow-up question responses. Definitions of these categories are presented in Table 3.

Two coders were instructed to classify independently the responses according to the scheme shown in Table 3. Their instructions were to classify each response in either one category or two if the response indicated that the respondent was mentioning more than one issue. The following procedures were used to determine the ultimate classification of the responses:

1. If both coders classified the response into the same single or double categories, the response was classified according to the coders' classification.
2. If the coders disagreed on the classification, a referee coder was used to decide which classification to use. If the referee disagreed with both coders, the response was classified as an 'other' response.

Table 3. Classification categories for exploratory follow-up questions

The following categories were used to classify the tape recorded answers concerning reasons for non-extreme responses to the Expectations (E), Revised Expectations (E*), and Ideal Point (I) Measures:

Not feasible – Not possible or not capable of being accomplished or achieved.

Sufficient – As much of the characteristics as is needed – enough or an adequate amount.

Not necessary – The response was categorized as 'Not necessary' only if the word 'necessary' was used.

Forecast – To predict, estimate, or calculate in advance. To make an estimation of conditions or events.

Less important – The response was categorized as 'less important' only if the word 'important' was used.

Implied less important – The degree to which the characteristic has value, significance, or consequence.

Classic ideal – The perfect or preferred amount of the characteristic.

Other – All responses that could not be classified in one or a combination of two of the preceding categories were classified as 'Other'.

A summary of the results of these coding procedures is presented in Table 4, and examples of coded responses are provided in Appendix B.

SERVQUAL expectations

As indicated in Table 4, a total of 454 responses to the SERVQUAL E questions were non-extreme. This represents approximately 38% of the 1200 responses to the SERVQUAL E scales (120 respondents answering 10 questions each). Approximately 39.4% of the non-extreme responses were categorized as 'not feasible' and 25.6% were classified as 'less important'. Other less frequently occurring responses included 'sufficient', 'forecast', 'classic ideal', and various double classifications such as 'not feasible/sufficient'. Approximately 8.1% of the responses were not classifiable. The patterns of responses are similar for the revised SERVQUAL E* measure.[14]

Under the assumption that the feasibility concept is congruent with the excellence norm concept of the P–E model, the 39.4% and 35% 'not feasible' classification rates for E and E* measures, respectively, represent indexes of the congruence between the conceptual and operational definitions of the measures with respect to the non-extreme answers. If the 'sufficient' and all double categories that include 'not feasible' and 'sufficient' as one of the category labels are added to these congruence

[14]The patterns of responses vary somewhat across the ten SERVQUAL items. For example, the 'not feasible' and/or 'sufficient' category percentages for the five SERVQUAL dimensions (two items per dimension) are 'Tangibles' (36.9%); 'Reliability' (49.2%); 'Responsiveness' (50.0%); 'Assurance' (53.7%); and 'Empathy' (65.3%). The two dimensions with the largest numbers of non-extreme responses are 'Reliability' (122 non-extreme answers across two-items) and 'Empathy' (121 non-extreme answers across two items).

Table 4. Reasons for non-extreme ('Non-7') responses to the expectations and the ideal point scales

	SERVQUAL E		Revised SERVQUAL E*		Ideal I	
	Frequency	Percentage	Frequency	Percentage	Frequency	Percentage
Not Feasible	179	39.4	151	35.0	23	15.2
Sufficient[a]	38	8.3	41	9.5	10	6.6
Not Feasible/Sufficient[a]	3	0.6	4	0.9	0	0
Not Feasible/Importance[b]	9	2.0	10	2.3	0	0
Not Feasible/Ideal	0	0	0	0	4	2.7
Sufficient[a]/Importance[b]	7	1.5	5	1.2	0	0
Sufficient/Ideal	0	0	1	0.2	9	6.0
Sufficient/Forecast	2	0.4	0	0	0	0
Less Important	116	25.6	125	28.9	34	22.5
Ideal	9	2.0	14	3.2	43	28.5
Ideal/Importance[b]	2	0.4	1	0	5	3.3
Forecast	51	11.2	47	10.9	10	6.6
Forecast/Importance[b]	1	0.2	1	0.2	0	0
Other	37	8.1	32	7.4	13	8.6
Total 'Non-7' Responses	454	100.0	432	100.0	151	100.0

[a] In this table the 'Not Necessary' and 'Sufficient' categories are combined.
[b] In this table the 'Less Important' and 'Implied Less Important' categories are combined.

indexes, the congruence percentages are 52.4% and 49.1% for the E and E* measures, respectively.

Clearly, the 'less important', 'classic ideal', and 'forecast' categories represent situations in which the respondents interpretations of the E and E* scales are not congruent with the expectations concept specified in the P–E service quality model. Approximately 39.2% and 43.5% of the E and E* follow-up responses, respectively, were classified within this group of single or double classification categories. Furthermore, as indicated in Table 5, a considerable number of respondents used these explanations. For example, the 'less important' reason was expressed by more than 50% of the respondents in their answers to at least one of the follow-up questions for the SERVQUAL E and E* measures. The 'forecast' and 'ideal' reasons were expressed by approximately 30% and 7% of the respondents, respectively. These results suggest the following potentially serious measurement validity problems:

1. *Attribute importance* – When the SERVQUAL E or E* measures are interpreted by the respondent to involve attribute importance, the P–E difference score calculation results in an inverse relationship between attribute importance and quality perceptions all else being equal. A more logical interpretation of an E or E* score in this situation is that it represents an attribute weight (W_j in equation (5) rather than a quality norm E_{ij} or E^*_{ij}). This suggests an expected positive relationship between the expectations scores and perceived quality, all else being equal.
2. *Forecast* – When the SERVQUAL E or E* measures are interpreted by the respondent to be requesting a forecast, the P–E score lacks discriminant validity with respect to the disconfirmed expectation concept specified in traditional

consumer satisfaction models. This finding, therefore, is not congruent with the Parasuraman, Zeithaml and Berry (1988) position that expectations do *not* represent performance predictions and that the concept of the P–E service quality gap is differentiated from the concept of disconfirmed expectations specified in consumer satisfaction models.

3. *Ideal* – When the SERVQUAL E or E* measures are interpreted by the respondent to involve the classic ideal point concept, classic ideal point attitudinal models suggest that the P–E score would be expected to be positively related to perceived quality only when the value of P is less than or equal to E. When P exceeds E, increased P–E scores would be expected to be negatively related to perceived quality.

These findings suggest that a considerable portion of the variance in the SERVQUAL E and E* measures is the result of measurement error induced by respondents misinterpreting the scales. A conservative estimate of the magnitude of this incongruence is 38.5% for the E measure and 43.5% for the E* measure. If double-coded categories that include 'less-important', 'ideal', or 'forecast' as one of the codes are included in the calculation, this estimated incongruence is 43.8% and 48.4% for the E and E* measures, respectively.

Ideal point measure

As indicated in Table 4, responses to the follow-up questions involving the ideal (I) attribute level measure indicate the most frequent response categories are 'ideal'

Table 5. Summary of reasons given by respondents concerning non-extreme ('Non-7') responses to the expectations and ideal point measures (the entries in the table are the percentages of respondents (n = 120) that expressed the reason at least one time)

Reasons for non-extreme response	SERVQUAL E percentage of respondents	SERVQUAL E* percentage of respondents	Revised Ideal I percentage of respondents
Not Feasible	72.2	71.3	13.9
Sufficient[a]	20.4	22.2	5.5
Not Feasible/Sufficient[a]	2.8	5.6	0
Not Feasible/Importance[b]	2.8	6.5	0
Not Feasible/Ideal	0	0	1.9
Sufficient[a]/Importance[b]	1.9	7.4	0
Sufficient/Ideal	0	0.9	4.6
Sufficient/Forecast	1.9	0	0
Less Important	50.9	52.8	27.8
Ideal	6.5	7.4	26.9
Ideal/Importance[b]	1.9	0.9	1.9
Forecast	31.5	30.6	7.4
Forecast/Importance[b]	0.9	0.9	0
Other	11.1	16.7	6.5

[a] In this table the 'Not Necessary' and 'Sufficient' categories are combined.
[b] In this table the 'Less Important' and 'Implied Less Important' categories are combined.

(28.5%), 'less important' (22.5%), and 'not feasible' (15.2%). Consequently, there is evidence that the ideal point measure lacks discriminate validity with respect to concepts of importance and feasibility. This is a somewhat surprising finding because the instructions specifically request the respondent to describe the ideal or perfect discount store. It is interesting to note, however, that the tendency for non-extreme responses was much smaller for the ideal point measure than it was for the expectations measures.

Hypotheses tests

The following variables derived from the survey data were used to test H_1 and H_2 (see Table 2 for listing of the survey data variables):

Q = *Global quality* and was measured by the summation of the two perceived global quality measures. The coefficient alpha for the measure is .828.

Y = *Global store preference* and was measured by the summation of the preference, overall satisfaction, and two intentions measures. The variables were summed to form one index because they were highly correlated.[15] The coefficient alpha for the summated score is .761.

S_1 = *Unweighted P–E* service quality and was calculated by combining the P^s_{ij} and E_{ij} ratings according to equation (1) and assuming $W_j = 1$.

S_2 = *Weighted P–E* service quality and was calculated by combining the P^s_{ij}, E_{ij} and W_j ratings according to equation (1).

R_1 = *Unweighted revised* P–E* service quality and was calculated using the procedures for calculating S_1, except the revised E^*_{ij} was substituted for E_{ij}.

R_2 = *Weighted revised P–E** service quality and was calculated using the procedures for calculating S_2, except E^*_{ij} was substituted for E_{ij}.

NQ_1 = *Normed Quality (NQ)* and was calculated by combining P^s_{ij}, E^*_{ij}, and I_j according to equation (8) and assuming $W_j = 1$.

NQ_2 = *Normed Quality (NQ)* and was calculated by using P^s_{ij}, E^*_{ij}, I_j, and W_j according to equation (8).

EP_1 = *Evaluated Performance (EP)* service quality and was calculated by combining the P^d_{ij} and I_j ratings according to equation (6) and assuming $W_j = 1$.

EP_2 = *Weighted Evaluated Performance (EP)* service quality and was calculated by combining P^d_{ij}, I_j, and W_j ratings according to equation (6).

The degree of *criterion validity* of the SERVQUAL P–E, normed quality (NQ), and evaluated performance (EP) measurement models was assessed using the pairwise correlations between the global quality measure (Q) and each of the alternative quality measures S_1, S_2, R_1, R_2, NQ_1, NQ_2, EP_1, and EP_2. The degree of *construct validity* of the same set of measures was assessed using the pairwise correlations between the global store preference measure (Y) and each of the alternative quality measures.

[15]Because of the ambiguity concerning the causal link between perceived quality and consumer satisfaction, a global store preference summated scale was constructed that omitted the overall satisfaction item. The construct validity test results involving this variable were the same (in terms of statistical significance patterns) as those involving the summated scale that includes the overall satisfaction item.

H_1 and H_2 suggest the criterion and construct validity of the evaluated performance measures (EP_1 and EP_2) are greater than the criterion and construct validity of the other measures.

The criterion and construct validity coefficients are presented in Table 6 for the eight perceived quality measures examined. As indicated, the criterion validity coefficients range from .698 to .733 for the P–E measures, .688 to .701 for the NQ measures, and .778 to .806 for the evaluated performance (EP) measures. The construct validity coefficients range from .588 to .640 for the P–E measures, .576 to .622 for the NQ measures, and .720 and .753 for the EP measures.

Table 6. Criterion and construct validity coefficients[a]

Perceived quality model	*Global quality Q*	*Global satisfaction Y*
(S_1) =P–E – unweighted model[b]	$\hat{\rho}_{S_1Q}$=.725	$\hat{\rho}_{S_1Y}$=.604
(S_2) =P–E – weighted model[c]	$\hat{\rho}_{S_2Q}$=.698	$\hat{\rho}_{S_2Y}$=.588
(R_1) =Revised P–E – unweighted model[d]	$\hat{\rho}_{R_1Q}$=.733	$\hat{\rho}_{R_1Y}$=.639
(R_2) =Revised P–E – weighted model[e]	$\hat{\rho}_{R_2Q}$=.713	$\hat{\rho}_{R_2Y}$=.640
(NQ_1) =Normed Quality – unweighted model[f]	$\hat{\rho}_{NQ_1Q}$=.701	$\hat{\rho}_{NQ_1Y}$=.622
(NQ_2) =Normed Quality – weighted model[g]	$\hat{\rho}_{NQ_2Q}$=.688	$\hat{\rho}_{NQ_2Y}$=.576
(EP_1) =Evaluated Performance (EP) – unweighted model[h]	$\hat{\rho}_{EP_1Q}$=.806	$\hat{\rho}_{EP_1Y}$=.753
(EP_2) =Evaluated Performance (EP) – weighted model[i]	$\hat{\rho}_{EP_2Q}$=.778	$\hat{\rho}_{EP_2Y}$=.720

Criterion validity coefficients	*Construct validity coefficients*
1. ρ_{S_1Q} =Pairwise correlation between S_1 and Q.	1. ρ_{S_1Y} =Pairwise correlation between S_1 and Y.
2. ρ_{S_2Q} =Pairwise correlation between S_2 and Q.	2. ρ_{S_2Y} =Pairwise correlation between S_2 and Y.
3. ρ_{R_1Q} =Pairwise correlation between R_1 and Q.	3. ρ_{R_1Y} =Pairwise correlation between R_1 and Y.
4. ρ_{R_2Q} =Pairwise correlation between R_2 and Q.	4. ρ_{R_2Y} =Pairwise correlation between R_2 and Y.
5. ρ_{NQ_1Q} =Pairwise correlation between NQ_1 and Q.	5. ρ_{NQ_1Y} =Pairwise correlation between NQ_1 and Y.
6. ρ_{NQ_2Q} =Pairwise correlation between NQ_2 and Q.	6. ρ_{NQ_2Y} =Pairwise correlation between NQ_2 and Y.
7. ρ_{EP_1Q} =Pairwise correlation between EP_1 and Q.	7. ρ_{EP_1Y} =Pairwise correlation between EP_1 and Y.
8. ρ_{EP_2Q} =Pairwise correlation between EP_2 and Q.	8. ρ_{EP_2Y} =Pairwise correlation between EP_2 and Y.

[a] The validity coefficients are the pairwise correlations between the quality models and the global measures of perceived quality (Q) and preference (Y).
[b] The unweighted P–E model corresponds to expression (1) with W_j=1.0.
[c] The weighted P–E model corresponds to expression (1).
[d] The unweighted revised P–E model corresponds to expression (1) with W_j=1.0 and E^*_j=$E_i j$.
[e] The weighted revised P–E model corresponds the expression (1) with $E^*_i j$ = $E_i j$.
[f] The weighted normed quality (NQ) model corresponds to expression (8).
[g] The unweighted evaluated performance (EP) model corresponds to expression (6) with W_j=1.0.
[h] The weighted evaluated performance (EP) model corresponds to expression (6).

The results of the criterion validity test (H_1), presented in Table 7, indicate that the criterion validity coefficient for the unweighted evaluated performance (EP) measure is statistically significantly greater than the criterion validity coefficients for each of the P–E and NQ measures. The criterion validity coefficient for the weighted evaluated performance (EP) model is statistically significantly greater than the criterion validity coefficients for the weighted P–E and the unweighted and weighted NQ measures, but is not statistically significantly greater than the criterion validity coefficients for the unweighted P–E models. These findings, which partially support H_1, suggest that the EP measure is characterized by somewhat higher criterion validity than the P–E and NQ measure. However, the results indicate that the weighted models perform somewhat more poorly than the unweighted models.

The construct validity test results (H_2), presented in Table 8, indicate that H_2 is supported by all the tests. In each test the evaluated performance (EP) measure is characterized by higher construct validity than each P–E and MQ measure.

In general, these findings indicate considerable support for the hypotheses that

Table 7. Criterion validity tests (H_1) – tests of differences between the criterion validities of the P–E, Normed Quality (NQ), and Evaluated Performance (EP) models

Hypothesis		Estimates	Correlation difference	t^a
H1.a tests (the unweighted EP model compared with the other models)				
$\rho_{EP1Q} > \rho_{S1Q}$	$\hat{\rho}_{EP1Q}=.806$	$\hat{\rho}_{S1Q}=.725$	.081	2.001[b]
$\rho_{EP1Q} > \rho_{S2Q}$		$\hat{\rho}_{S2Q}=.698$	.108	2.543[c]
$\rho_{EP1Q} > \rho_{R1Q}$		$\hat{\rho}_{R1Q}=.733$	.073	1.954[b]
$\rho_{EP1Q} > \rho_{R2Q}$		$\hat{\rho}_{R1Q}=.713$	.093	2.313[b]
$\rho_{EP1Q} > \rho_{NQ1Q}$		$\hat{\rho}_{NQ1Q}=.701$	.105	2.476[c]
$\rho_{EP1Q} > \rho_{NQ2Q}$		$\hat{\rho}_{NQ2Q}=.688$	.118	2.617[c]
H1.b tests (the weighted EP model compared with the other models)				
$\rho_{EP2Q} > \rho_{S1Q}$	$\hat{\rho}_{EP2Q}=.778$	$\hat{\rho}_{S1Q}=.725$	.053	1.260
$\rho_{EP2Q} > \rho_{S2Q}$		$\hat{\rho}_{S2Q}=.698$	.080	1.865[b]
$\rho_{EP2Q} > \rho_{R1Q}$		$\hat{\rho}_{R1Q}=.733$	.045	1.125
$\rho_{EP2Q} > \rho_{R2Q}$		$\hat{\rho}_{R2Q}=.713$	.065	1.685[b]
$\rho_{EP2Q} > \rho_{NQ1Q}$		$\hat{\rho}_{NQ1Q}=.701$	.077	1.710[b]
$\rho_{EP2Q} > \rho_{NQ2Q}$		$\hat{\rho}_{NQ2Q}=.688$	.090	1.945[b]

[a] The *t*-value is calculated by a formula specified by Blalock (1960, p. 317) for testing the differences between two correlations when the samples are not independent.
[b] $p < .05$ (one-tail *t*-test).
[c] $p < .01$ (one-tail *t*-test).

Table 8. Construct validity tests (H_2) – tests of differences between the construct validities of the P–E, Normed Quality (NQ), and Evaluated Performance (EP) models

Hypothesis		Estimates	Correlation difference	t^a
H2.a tests (the unweighted EP model compared with the other models)				
$\rho_{EP1Y} > \rho_{S1Y}$	$\hat{\rho}_{EP1Y}=.753$	$\hat{\rho}_{S1Y}=.604$	.149	3.046[c]
$\rho_{EP1Y} > \rho_{S2Y}$		$\hat{\rho}_{S2Y}=.588$	.165	3.530[c]
$\rho_{EP1Y} > \rho_{R1Y}$		$\hat{\rho}_{R1Y}=.639$	.114	2.494[c]
$\rho_{EP1Y} > \rho_{R2Y}$		$\hat{\rho}_{R2Y}=.640$	.113	2.470[c]
$\rho_{EP1Y} > \rho_{NQ1Y}$		$\hat{\rho}_{NQ1Y}=.622$	.131	2.501[c]
$\rho_{EP1Y} > \rho_{NQ2Y}$		$\hat{\rho}_{NQ2Y}=.576$	.177	3.661[c]
H2.b tests (the weighted EP model compared with the other models)				
$\rho_{EP2Y} > \rho_{S1Y}$	$\hat{\rho}_{EP2Y}=.720$	$\hat{\rho}_{S1Y}=.604$	.116	2.319[b]
$\rho_{EP2Y} > \rho_{S2Y}$		$\hat{\rho}_{S2Y}=.588$	.132	2.661[c]
$\rho_{EP2Y} > \rho_{R1Y}$		$\hat{\rho}_{R1Y}=.639$	.081	1.736[b]
$\rho_{EP2Y} > \rho_{R2Y}$		$\hat{\rho}_{R2Y}=.640$	.080	1.832[b]
$\rho_{EP2Y} > \rho_{NQ1Y}$		$\hat{\rho}_{NQ1Y}=.622$	.098	1.999[b]
$\rho_{EP2Y} > \rho_{NQ2Y}$		$\hat{\rho}_{NQ2Y}=.576$	.144	2.843[b]

[a] See footnote [a] in Table 7.
[b] $p < .05$ (one-tail *t*-test).
[c] $p < .01$ (one-tail *t*-test).

the criterion and construct validity of the evaluated performance (EP) perceived quality measurement framework is higher than the concurrent and construct validity of the P–E and NQ measurement frameworks.

DISCUSSION

The empirical tests in this study are limited to the examination of the validity of perceived quality measures using a limited subset of the SERVQUAL items,[16] single-item indicators for satisfaction and shopping preference, and a two-item indicator for purchase intentions. In addition, the tests involve a narrow retail setting and were on the basis of data from a limited sample of respondents. Though caution is necessary in generalizing the findings, considerable evidence of problems associated with the P–E service quality framework was found; consequently, additional research examining this issue is warranted.

Conceptual issues and questions

The examination of the alternative perceived quality models suggests several conceptual questions that deserve attention in further research. For specific issues involve (1) conceptual definition ambiguity, (2) the theoretical justification of expectations in the measurement of perceived quality, (3) the usefulness of the probability specification in the evaluated performance (EP) measurement framework, and (4) the link between perceived quality and consumer satisfaction/dissatisfaction.

Expectation definition ambiguity

A review of the service quality literature and the results of this study's empirical tests indicate that it is conceptually unclear what the SERVQUAL expectations E concept represents. First, the conceptualization of E as an ideal standard suggests a possible classic attitudinal model ideal point interpretation. Under this interpretation it is theoretically unsound to assume, as specified in the P–E equation (1), that performance levels that exceed the ideal standard result in higher perceived quality than performance levels that equal the ideal standard. Second, if E is interpreted to represent a feasible ideal point concept, a positive monotonic linkage between the SERVQUAL P–E measure and perceived quality would not be expected when the attributes involved are finite ideal point (i.e. non-infinite classic ideal point) attributes. Third, the revised SERVQUAL E^* measurement instructions request respondents to rate the service issues in terms of the degree to which they are

[16]Most of the SERVQUAL attributes can be expected to be considered to be vector attributes (infinite ideal point attributes) by most respondents (see Table 4 for exceptions). Future studies examining the validity of the P–E, NQ, and EP models should evaluate the models in situations in which there is a higher incidence of finite ideal point attributes, because in these situations the differences among the models are most pronounced.

essential. However, it is not theoretically clear why high performance on essential attributes should reflect lower perceived quality than high performance on less essential attributes, as predicted in equation (1). Clearly, each of these interpretations is not compatible with the mathematical properties of the P–E perceived quality specification. However, on the basis of the definitional frameworks suggested in the service quality literature, it is difficult to envision any definitions of the SERVQUAL expectations (E) concept that are compatible both with the mathematical properties of the P–E measurement specification and the assumption that the P–E measure is conceptually differentiated from the disconfirmed expectation concept specified in traditional consumer satisfaction/dissatisfaction models.

This definitional ambiguity is reflected in a model specified by Bolton and Drew (1991). Building on the consumer satisfaction literature, particularly Oliver (1981), they specify disconfirmed expectations to be a predictor of satisfaction. However, using Parasuraman, Zeithaml and Berry (1988) framework as a theoretical foundation, they specify the same disconfirmed expectations variable to be a predictor of perceived quality. The model, therefore, explicitly assumes that the disconfirmed expectations concepts specified by Oliver (1981) and Parasuraman, Zeithaml and Berry (1988) are identical. This assumption is incongruent with the Parasuraman, Zeithaml and Berry (1988) definitional framework, which differentiates the P–E service gap from the concept of disconfirmed expectations specified in consumer satisfaction models.

The theoretical justification of the SERVQUAL E

A second conceptual issue concerns the question of whether the service expectation concept is theoretically justified as a component of a perceived quality measure. The following are examples of issues that are linked to this question:

1. The P–E model results in various P and E values producing identical P–E scores. For example, there are seven P and E combinations that produce P–E scores equal to 0 (P = 1 and E = 1; P = 2 and E = 2... P = 7 and E = 7). A question that deserves attention in further research is whether 'tied' P–E values can be expected to correspond to equal perceived quality. The evaluated performance (EP) perceived quality model suggests these tied P–E scores would correspond to different levels of perceived quality depending on the location of the classic ideal attribute intensity levels. For example, these models suggest that assuming the ideal performance level is 6, a P = 1, E = 1 situation would correspond to a lower level of perceived quality than a P = 6, E = 6 situation.
2. In the context of a consumer evaluating the quality of a consideration set of competing service providers, a logical assumption is that the expectation (E) would be the same for each member of the consumer's consideration set. Consequently, when implementing the P–E measurement framework in this context, each respondent would supply one set of E responses and multiple sets of P responses – one set for each member of the consideration set. Using equation (1) to calculate the perceived quality (Q_1) index for the consideration set would result in the E_{ij} response vector being subtracted from each of the P_{ij} response

vectors. Consequently, for each member of the consideration set, the SERVQUAL Q_i would be perfectly correlated with the summated P_{ij} scores. Therefore, the E_{ij} component provides no information beyond that of the performance component concerning differences among the consideration set members.

Usefulness of the evaluated performance probability component

A third conceptual issue involves the usefulness of the probability component of the evaluated performance (EP) perceived quality framework. One question concerning this issue is the degree to which measures of consumer perceptions of the probabilities of various performance levels across attributes can be used to operationalize the concepts of search, experience, and credence properties. The following are examples of issues that could be examined in further research:

1. Attributes with comparable mean levels of anticipated performance can have different probability estimates associated with various specific performance levels. Management could reduce the risk associated with attributes, particularly with respect to experience or credence attributes, by using marketing programs designed to decrease the variance of the probability distributions associated with particular attributes' performance levels. This might be achieved by using performance guarantees or tangible factors that 'signal' performance predictability (e.g. physical facilities, equipment, certifications, and price).
2. Service alternatives with comparable performance (or anticipated performance) quality can be perceived by consumers to have different probability distributions with respect to performance on particular attributes. For example, experience with a service can reduce the variance of the distribution of customers' probability ratings associated with various performance levels. Inducing customers to switch service suppliers, therefore, not only requires projecting an image that the alternative service provider's performance quality exceeds the current supplier, but also that the probability distribution associated with alternative performance levels on important attributes is narrow enough so that the disability associated with perceived switching risk does not block the switching decision.

The perceived quality-consumer satisfaction link

A fourth conceptual question concerns the causal link between perceived quality and consumer satisfaction. Most research on consumer satisfaction has been on the basis of the Oliver (1981) transaction-specific focus in which satisfaction is specified as a function of disconfirmation of expectations (with expectations defined as consumers' performance forecasts). Building on this conceptualization of satisfaction and the assumption that perceived service quality is a 'global judgment or attitude', Parasuraman, Zeithaml and Berry (1988) suggest that perceived quality is a function of (caused by) satisfaction.

Significant evidence suggests the perceived quality-consumer satisfaction causal linkage may be opposite to that specified by service quality researchers. First, the

Monroe and Krishnan (1985) definition of perceived product quality as 'the perceived ability of a product to provide satisfaction', implies a quality-to-satisfaction link. Second, in a consumer satisfaction model specified by Churchill and Surprenant (1982), global performance, defined as 'overall unit quality', is specified as a predictor of consumer satisfaction. Third, the concept of a performance norm has been used in consumer satisfaction models as a comparison standard (Oliver, 1989). In general 'performance-minus-norm' disconfirmation is hypothesized to predict consumer satisfaction in these models (Woodruff, Cadotte and Jenkins, 1983).

One way to integrate these two causal perspectives is to specify two perceived quality concepts – transaction-specific quality and relationship quality – and to specify perceived transaction-specific quality as the transaction-specific performance component of contemporary consumer satisfaction models. This implies that transaction-specific satisfaction is a function of perceived transaction-specific performance quality. Furthermore, if perceived relationship quality can be assumed to be similar to the Parasuraman, Zeithaml, and Berry (1988) perceived service quality concept or to Oliver's (1981) 'base attitude level', transaction-specific satisfaction could be argued to be a predictor of perceived long-term relationship quality.

Measurement validity issues

The results of this study indicate the SERVQUAL expectations (E) and revised expectations (E^*) measures lack discriminant validity with respect to the concepts of attribute importance, classic attribute ideal-points, and performance forecasts. This finding suggests a considerable portion of the variance SERVQUAL expectations measures may be because of respondents' misinterpretations of the question. Unless this measurement validity problem is corrected, it will be difficult to test the SERVQUAL measurement framework. For example, the findings of this study indicate the evaluated performance (EP) measurement framework is characterized by higher validity than the P–E and normed quality (NQ) frameworks. However, the lower validity of the P–E and NQ measurement specifications could be caused by the conceptual problems identified previously and/or to the measurement validity problems associated with the E and revised E^* measures.

The findings concerning the ideal (I) component of the EP model suggest some respondent confusion in interpreting the scale. Because the intended interpretation is the 'perfect' attribute level as specified in ideal point attitude models, research is needed that focuses on increasing the discriminant validity between measures of ideal performance and the concepts of attribute importance and performance feasibility.

The research results indicate that the inclusion of attribute weights in the SERVQUAL P–E, normed quality (NQ), and evaluated performance (EP) models does not improve the validity of the models. This result is similar to the findings of other research that indicates importance weights often do not increase, and may decrease, the predictive validity of multiattribute models (Bass and Wilkie, 1973).

CONCLUSIONS

My purpose was to examine the validity of the P–E 'gap' framework as currently specified and, on the basis of this examination, develop and test alternative models of consumers' perceptions of quality. The examination of the P–E service quality model indicates a number of problems, particularly with respect to the conceptual and operational definitions of the expectations (E) and the revised expectations (E^*) components of the model. These problems, in turn, create ambiguity concerning the interpretation and theoretical justification of the P–E perceived quality concept. On the basis of these problems, an evaluated performance (EP) model and a normed quality (NQ) model of perceived quality are developed and, along with the P–E model, empirically tested.

The results of a qualitative assessment of the SERVQUAL (Parasuraman, Zeithaml and Berry, 1988; Zeithaml, Parasuraman and Berry, 1990) expectation (E) and revised expectation (E^*) measures indicate that the measures lack discriminant validity with respect to the concepts of attribute importance, performance forecasts, and classic attribute ideal points. This suggests a considerable portion of the variance in the SERVQUAL expectations measures may be caused by respondents' misinterpretation of the question rather than to different attitudes or perceptions. Though somewhat less pronounced, similar discriminant validity problems were found for the ideal-point measure used to operationalize the EP perceived quality model.

The results of criterion and construct validity tests indicate that, when compared to the SERVQUAL P–E and normed quality (NQ) frameworks, the evaluated performance (EP) framework is characterized by greater concurrent and construct validity. A comparison of the weighted versus unweighted models indicates that the unweighted models generally performed better than the weighted models in terms of concurrent and construct validity.

The EP model proposed here is designed to overcome some of the problems associated with the P–E gap conceptualization of service quality. Though the findings indicate that the EP model may be more valid than the SERVQUAL P–E and the NQ models, additional theoretical and empirical research is needed to further examine the question of which framework examined in this study, or perhaps another framework, is most valid and useful.

APPENDIX A

The survey instruments

1. The directions for the SERVQUAL (P^s), E_j), and E^*_j) are listed in Table 1. The ten SERVQUAL items used, which were stated as published in the literature (Zeithaml, Parasuraman and Berry, 1990; Parasuraman, Berry and Zeithaml, 1990), were

   Tangibles
   (1) XYZ has modern looking equipment.
   (2) XYZ's physical facilities are visually appealing.

Reliability

(3) When you have a problem, XYZ shows a sincere interest in solving it.
(4) XYZ performs the service right the first time.

Responsiveness

(5) Employees of XYZ give you prompt service.
(6) Employees of XYZ are never too busy to respond to your requests.

Assurance

(7) Employees of XYZ are consistently courteous.
(8) Employees of XYZ can answer your questions.

Empathy

(9) XYZ employees understand your specific needs.
(10) XYZ has operating hours convenient to all its customers.

2. The directions for the semantic differential scales were as follows:

   Performance (P^d). Please read the descriptions on each end of the following scales and check the blanks that best describe your feelings towards the store listed above. You should check an end blank if a phrase is very descriptive of the store. The center blank is a neutral rating. The other blanks represent intermediate positions of slightly descriptive and quite descriptive.

   Ideal (I). Please read the descriptions on each end of the following scales and check the blanks that best describe your *ideal or perfect discount store.*

   The following is an example of the semantic differential scaling format:

   XYZ does not have modern-looking equipment .... XYZ has modern-looking equipment

3. Overall perceived quality was measured by the following questions:

   a. Using the scale provided, rate the overall quality of service you receive in XYZ.

   Extremely Low Quality | | | | | | | | | | Extremely High Quality
   0 1 2 3 4 5 6 7 8 9 10

   b. XYZ provides high quality customer service (5-point 'Strongly Agree = 5/Strongly Disagree = 1' scale).

4. Shopping preferences, purchase intentions, and overall satisfaction were measured with the following 5-point 'Strongly Agree = 5/Strongly Disagree = 1' scale:

   a. I am satisfied with the services I receive in XYZ.

   b. I do *not* intend to shop in XYZ very often in the future (reversed coded).

   c. I will purchase a large number of products in XYZ during the next year.

   d. I prefer to shop at XYZ more than I do at other local discount stores.

5. The directions for the attribute importance weight measures (W_j) were as follows:

   Please look over the following list and find one factor for which it would be most important to you to get excellent performance instead of poor performance. Assign 100 points to this CRITICAL FACTOR. Then consider each of the remaining factors. For each factor, how important is it for you to receive excellent service rather than poor service? If it is only half as important for this factor as it is for the CRITICAL FACTOR, assign it 50 points. In general, assign points to the factors that indicate how they compare to the critical factor in terms of the importance of getting excellent service rather than poor service. If any factors are of equal importance, assign them an equal number of points.

APPENDIX B

Example follow-up responses – perceived quality study

A. *Not Feasible*

- Not possible – no way that the clerk can understand my specific needs.
- Can't wait on everybody at once.
- Never is a bad word to use – it's not possible.
- I've gone into the store knowing exactly myself what I want.
- Can't expect it to be right every time.
- Never is a pretty strong word – it's impossible.

B *Sufficient*

- Better than half is OK.
- It doesn't have to be ultra modern.
- Good equipment, well maintained, would do just as well as modern equipment.
- They should have good equipment – but it doesn't need to be the most modern. Seven would imply they should have the most modern equipment – and I think a 6 would suffice.

C. *Not Necessary*

- I wouldn't know what modern equipment was – it's not necessary anyway.
- Not necessary to know to exact need.
- It's not absolutely necessary.

D. *Less Important*

- Not as important as other things I was ranking then.
- It's not important if you know what you want.
- I don't think the visual appearance is that important.
- The physical facilities are not as important as the people.
- The word 'all' is the problem – it's not important to me that you stay open all day and all night to serve all customers.

E. *Implied Less Important*

- Not a critical thing
- Doesn't make a big difference.
- Looks don't have much bearing.
- Doesn't matter – I don't care about this.
- I don't care what the equipment looks like.
- It just doesn't make any difference to me.
- If it's visually appealing, it doesn't really matter to me – it's the price I'm looking for.
- I don't care either way – it doesn't matter.
- It's not a major thing.
- I don't care as much about the store as I do about the products.
- As long as they have the product, it shouldn't matter what the store looks like.
- Modern looking doesn't impress me.
- It's not crucial.

F. *Ideal*

- Too modern can be a detriment – the stuff can be too advanced.
- I don't want employees to know what my needs are. They don't need to know. I like the anonymity.
- If people are overly courteous – that can make you nervous.
- Don't want my store to be machine like.
- I don't want them to open as many hours as they are now – Sundays for example.
- You can be too modern.
- I want to be left alone when I'm in the store.
- I don't what them to be too pushy.
- I don't think they should be open on Sundays.
- I don't want them to be over solicitous of me.
- It's not fair to the employees – too much pressure on the employees.

- I've been in stores where, instead of prompt service, they get to where they're on top of you bugging you all the time.
- I don't like stores that are ultra modern and gleamy chrome – I think they become rather cold.
- I don't want someone who is going to talk my head off or be over aggressive.
- I don't want a clerk at the store waiting for me to come in.
- I don't want the store employees to shake my hand when I go into the store and pat me on the back when I leave.

G. Forecast

- That's the way discount stores are.
- They just aren't.
- Unlikely to be perfect.
- All of them have pretty much good hours.
- A five is normal for a discount store – you're just not going to get perfection.

H. Examples of double classifications

1. A five rating is good enough. Being modern isn't important (Sufficient/Importance).
2. It's not that important to me – doesn't have to be perfect (Sufficient/Importance).
3. It's not important – not necessary to be perfect (Not Necessary/Importance).
4. Not necessary – my ideal would be to not be open on Sundays (Not Necessary/Ideal).
5. It's not necessary – you wouldn't get that kind of service anyway (Not Necessary/Forecast).
6. If they could satisfy me half the time I'd be satisfied – nobody's perfect (Not Feasible/Sufficient).
7. Not humanly possible – good rather than perfect is good enough (Not Feasible/Sufficient).
8. It's not possible or even necessary to understand everybody's needs – it's impossible (Not Feasible/Not Necessary).
9. Not necessary – anyway, they can't understand everyone's needs – it's impossible (Not Feasible/Not Necessary).
10. That's impossible – it's unimportant (Not Feasible/Importance).
11. Can't be perfect – anyway, it's not important (Not Feasible/Importance).
12. If it was constantly installing new modern looking equipment, they would be too busy installing new equipment to wait on customers (Not Feasible/Ideal).
13. If I think the products are good, the facilities don't have to be that good (Sufficient/Implied Importance).
14. A five is good enough – you just don't get sevens in discount stores (Sufficient/Forecast).
15. You don't get perfection in these kinds of stores – I don't care about that when I go to a Target or K-Mart (Forecast/Implied Importance).
16. It isn't important. In fact, you can overdo modern aspects (Ideal/Importance).
17. When I'm in a store, I usually prefer to be left alone. It's just not important that they know what I need (Ideal/Importance).

ACKNOWLEDGEMENTS

The author thanks the editor, three anonymous reviewers, Sridar N. Ramaswami and John G. Wacker (Iowa State University), and Jon Austin (University of Wisconsin – Madison) for their valuable comments on earlier drafts of this article.

REFERENCES

Ahtola, O. T. (1975) 'The Vector Model of Preference: An Alternative to the Fishbein Model', *Journal of Marketing Research* **12** (February): 52–59.

American Heritage Dictionary (1985) Boston: Houghton Mifflin Co.

Bass, F. and Wilkie, W. L. (1973) 'A Comparative Analysis of Attitudinal Predictions of Brand Preference'. *Journal of Marketing Research.* **10** (August): 262–269.

Berry, L. L., Zeithaml, V. A. and Parasuraman, A. (1985) 'Quality Counts in Services, Too'. *Business Horizons* **28** (May/June): 44–52.

Blalock, H. M. (1960) *Social Statistics.* New York: McGraw-Hill Book Company.

Bollen, K. A. (1989) *Structural Equations with Latent Variables.* New York: John Wiley and Sons.

Bolton, R. N. and Drew, J. H. (1991) 'A Multistage Model of Customers' Assessments of Service Quality and Value'. *Journal of Consumer Research* **17** (March): 375–384.

Brown, S. W. and Swartz, T. A. (1989) 'A Gap Analysis of Professional Service Quality'. *Journal of Marketing* **53** (April): 92–98.

Carman, J. M. (1990) 'Consumer Perceptions of Service Quality: An Assessment of the SERVQUAL Dimensions'. *Journal of Retailing* **66** (Spring) 33–55.

Chaplin, J. P. (1981) *Dictionary of Psychology.* New York: Dell Publishing Co., Inc.

Churchill, G. A., Jr and Surprenant, C. (1982) 'An Investigation into the Determinants of Customer Satisfaction'. *Journal of Marketing Research.* **19** (November): 491–504.

Cronin, J. J. Jr. and Taylor, S. A. (1992) 'Measuring Service Quality: A Re-examination and Extension'. *Journal of Marketing* **56** (July): 55–68.

Ginter, L. (1974) 'An Experimental Investigation of Attitude Change and Choice of a New Brand', *Journal of Marketing Research* **11** (February): 30–40.

Green, P. E. and Srinivasan, V. (1978) 'Conjoint Analysis in Consumer Research: Issues and Outlook'. *Journal of Consumer Research* **5** (September): 103–123.

Hostage, G. M. (1975) 'Quality Control in a Service Business'. *Harvard Business Review* (July/August): 98–106.

Lilien, G. L., Kotler, P. and Moorthy, K. S. (1992) *Market Models.* Englewood Cliffs, NJ: Prentice Hall, Inc.

Miller, J. A. (1977) 'Studying Satisfaction, Modifying Models, Eliciting Expectations, Posing Problems, and Making Meaningful Measurements'. In *Conceptualization and Measurement of Consumer Satisfaction and Dissatisfaction* (H. K. Hunt, Ed.). Cambridge, MA: Marketing Science Institute, pp. 72–91.

Monroe, K. B. and Krishnan, R. (1985) 'The Effect of Price on Subjective Product Evaluations'. In *Perceived Quality* (J. Jacoby and J. C. Olson, Eds). Lexington, MA: Lexington Books, pp. 209–232.

Oliver, R. L. (1981) 'Measurement and Evaluation of Satisfaction Processes in Retail Settings' *Journal of Retailing* **57** (Fall): 25–48.

Oliver, R. L. (1989) 'Processing of the Satisfaction Response in Consumption: A Suggested Framework and Research Propositions'. *Journal of Consumer Satisfaction/Dissatisfaction and Complaining Behavior* **2**: 1–16.

Olshavsky, R. W. and Miller, J. A. (1972) 'Consumer Expectations, Product Performance, and Perceived Product Quality'. *Journal of Marketing Research* **9** (February): 19–21.

Parasuraman, A., Berry, L. L. and Zeithaml, V. A. (1990) *An Empirical Examination of Relationships in an Extended Service Quality Model.* Cambridge, MA: Marketing Science Institute.

Parasuraman, A., Zeithaml, V. A. and Berry, L. L. (1985) 'A Conceptual Model of Service Quality and Its Implications for Future Research'. *Journal of Marketing* **49** (Fall): 41–50.

Parasuraman, A., Zeithaml, V. A. and Berry, L. L. (1986) *SERVQUAL: A Multiple-Item Scale for Measuring Consumer Perceptions of Service Quality.* Cambridge, Massachusetts: Marketing Science Institute.

Parasuraman, A., Zeithaml, V. A. and Berry, L. L. (1988) 'SERVQUAL: A Multiple-Item Scale for Measuring Consumer Perceptions of Service Quality'. *Journal of Retailing* **64** (Spring): 12–40.

Prakash, V. (1984) 'Validity and Reliability of the Confirmation of Expectations Paradigm as a Determinant of Consumer Satisfaction'. *Journal of the Academy of Marketing Science,* **12** (Fall): 63–76.

Swan, J. E. and Trawick, I. F. (1980) 'Satisfaction Related to Predictive vs. Desired Expectations'. In *Refining Concepts and Measures of Consumer Satisfaction and Complaining Behavior* (H. K. Hunt and R. L. Days, Eds). Bloomington, IN: Indiana University, pp. 7–12.

Swartz, T. A. and Brown, S. W. (1989) 'Consumer and Provider Expectations and Experiences in Evaluating Professional Service Quality'. *Journal of the Academy of Marketing Science.* **17** (Spring): 189–195.

Teas, R. K. (1993) 'Consumer Expectations and the Measurement of Perceived Service Quality'. *Journal of Professional Services Marketing* **8** (2): 33–54.

Woodruff, R. B., Cadotte, E. R. and Jenkins, R. L. (1983) 'Modeling Consumer Satisfaction Processes Using Experience-Based Norms'. *Journal of Marketing Research.* **20** (August): 296–304.

Zeithaml, V. A. (1988) 'Consumer Perceptions of Price, Quality, and Value: A Means-End Model and Synthesis of Evidence'. *Journal of Marketing Research.* **52** (July): 2–22.

Zeithaml, V. A., Berry, L. L. and Parasuraman, A. (1988) 'Communication and Control Processes in the Delivery of Service Quality'. *Journal of Marketing* **52** (April): 35–48.

Zeithaml, V. A., Berry, L. L. and Parasuraman, A. (1991) 'The Nature and Determinants of Customer Expectations of Service'. Marketing Science Institute, working paper No. 91–113, Marketing Science Institute, Cambridge, MA.

Zeithaml, V. A., Parasuraman, A. and Berry, L. L. (1990) *Delivering Quality Service Balancing Customer Perceptions and Expectations.* New York: The Free Press.

14

SERVQUAL: Review, Critique, Research Agenda

Francis Buttle

SERVQUAL: A PRIMER

SERVQUAL provides a technology for measuring and managing service quality (SQ). Since 1985, when the technology was first published its innovators Parasuraman, Zeithaml and Berry have further developed, promulgated and promoted the technology through a series of publications (Parasuraman *et al.*, 1985, 1986, 1988, 1990, 1991a, 1991b, 1993, 1994; Zeithaml *et al.*, 1990, 1991, 1992, 1993).

The ABI/Inform database 'Global edition' (September 1994) reports that service quality has been a keyword in some 1447 articles published in the period January 1992 to April 1994. By contrast SERVQUAL has been a keyword in just 41 publications. These publications incorporate both theoretical discussions and applications of SERVQUAL in a variety of industrial commercial and not-for-profit settings. Published studies include tyre retailing (Carman, 1990), dental services (Carman, 1990), hotels (Saleh and Ryan, 1992) travel and tourism (Fick and Ritchie, 1991), car servicing (Bouman and van der Wiele, 1992), business schools (Rigotti and Pitt, 1992), higher education (Ford *et al.*, 1993; McElwee and Redman, 1993), hospitality (Johns, 1993), business-to-business channel partners (Kong and Mayo, 1993), accounting firms (Freeman and Dart, 1993), architectural services (Baker and Lamb, 1993), recreational services (Taylor *et al.*, 1993), hospitals (Babakus and Mangold, 1992; Mangold and Babakus, 1991; Reidenbach and Sandifer-Smallwood, 1990; Soliman, 1992; Vandamme and Leunis, 1993; Walbridge and Delene, 1993), airline catering (Babakus *et al.*, 1993a), banking (Kwon and Lee, 1994; Wong and Perry, 1991), apparel retailing (Gagliano and Hathcote, 1994) and local government (Scott and Schieff, 1993). There have also been many unpublished SERVQUAL studies. In the last two years alone, the author has been associated with a number of sectoral and corporate SERVQUAL studies: computer services, construction, mental health services, hospitality, recreational services, ophthalmological services, and retail services. In addition, a number of organizations, such as the Midland and Abbey National banks have adopted it.

Reprinted with permission from *European Journal of Marketing*, Vol. 30, No. 1, pp. 8–32.

Service quality (SQ) has become an important research topic because of its apparent relationship to costs (Crosby, 1979), profitability (Buzzell and Gale, 1987; Rust and Zahorik, 1993; Zahorik and Rust, 1992), customer satisfaction (Bolton and Drew, 1991; Boulding *et al.*, 1993), customer retention (Reichheld and Sasser, 1990), and positive word of mouth. SQ is widely regarded as a driver of corporate marketing and financial performance.

SERVQUAL is founded on the view that the customer's assessment of SQ is paramount. This assessment is conceptualized as a gap between what the customer expects by way of SQ from a class of service providers (say, all opticians), and their evaluations of the performance of a particular service provider (say a single Specsavers store). SQ is presented as a multidimensional construct. In their original formulation Parasuraman *et al.* (1985) identified ten components of SQ:

1. reliability;
2. responsiveness;
3. competence;
4. access;
5. courtesy;
6. communication;
7. credibility;
8. security;
9. understanding/knowing the customer;
10. tangibles.

(See Appendix for definitions and examples.) In their 1988 work these components were collapsed into five dimensions: reliability, assurance, tangibles, empathy, responsiveness, as defined in Table 1. Reliability, tangibles and responsiveness remained distinct, but the remaining seven components collapsed into two aggregate dimensions, assurance and empathy.[1] Parasuraman *et al.* developed a 22-item instrument with which to measure customers' expectations and perceptions (E and P) of the five RATER dimensions. Four or five numbered items are used to measure each dimension. The instrument is administered twice in different forms, first to measure expectations and second to measure perceptions.

Table 1. SERVQUAL dimensions

Dimensions	Definition	Items in scale
Reliability	The ability to perform the promised service dependably and accurately	4
Assurance	The knowledge and courtesy of employees and their ability to convey trust and confidence	5
Tangibles	The appearance of physical facilities, equipment personnel and communication materials	4
Empathy	The provision of caring, individualized attention to customers	5
Responsiveness	The willingness to help customers and to provide prompt service	4

In 1991, Parasuraman *et al.* published a follow-up study which refined their previous work (1991b). Wording of all expectations items changed. The 1988 version has attempted to capture respondents' normative expectations. For example, one 1988 expectation item read 'Companies offering ______ services should keep their records accurately'. The revised wording focused on what customers would expect from 'excellent service companies'. The sample item was revised thus: 'Excellent companies offering ______ services will insist on error-free records'. Detailed wording of many perceptions items also changed. Two new items, one each for tangibles and assurance, were substituted for two original items. The tangible items referred to the appearance of communication materials. The assurance item referred to the knowledge of employees. Both references had been omitted in the 1988 version.

Analysis of SERVQUAL data can take several forms: item-by-item analysis (e.g. P1 − E1, P2 − E2); dimension-by-dimension analysis (e.g. P1 + P2 + P3 + P4/4) − (E1 + E2 + E3 + E4/4), where P1 to P4, and E1 to E4, represent the four perception and expectation statements relating to a single dimension); and computation of the single measure of service quality ((P1 + P2 + P3... + P22/22) − (E1 + E2 + E3 + ... + E22/22)), the so-called SERVQUAL gap.

Without question, SERVQUAL has been widely applied and is highly valued. Any critique of SERVQUAL, therefore, must be seen within this broader context of strong endorsement. What follows is a discussion of several criticisms which have been levelled at SERVQUAL elsewhere or have been experienced in the application of the technology of this author.

CRITICISMS OF SERVQUAL

Notwithstanding its growing popularity and widespread application, SERVQUAL has been subjected to a number of theoretical and operational criticisms which are detailed below:

1. Theoretical:
   - Paradigmatic objections: SERVQUAL is based on a disconfirmation paradigm rather than an attitudinal paradigm; and SERVQUAL fails to draw on established economic, statistical and psychological theory.
   - Gaps model: there is little evidence that customers assess service quality in terms of P − E gaps.
   - Process orientation: SERVQUAL focuses on the process of service delivery, not the outcomes of the service encounter.
   - Dimensionality: SERVQUAL's five dimensions are not universals; the number of dimensions comprising SQ is contextualized; items do not always load on to the factors which one would a priori expect; and there is a high degree of intercorrelation between the five RATER dimensions.
2. Operational:
   - Expectations: the term expectation is polysemic; consumers use standards other than expectations to evaluate SQ; and SERVQUAL fails to measure absolute SQ expectations.

- Item composition: four or five items can not capture the variability within each SQ dimension.
- Moments of truth (MOT): customers' assessments of SQ may vary from MOT to MOT.
- Polarity: the reversed polarity of items in the scale causes respondent error.
- Scale points: the seven-point Likert scale is flawed.
- Two administrations: two administrations of the instrument causes boredom and confusion.
- Variance extracted: the over SERVQUAL score accounts for a disappointing proportion of item variances.

Each of the criticisms will be examined below.

Theoretical

Paradigmatic objections

Two major criticisms have been raised. First, SERVQUAL has been inappropriately based on an expectations-disconfirmation model rather than an attitudinal model of SQ. Second, it does not build on extant knowledge in economics, statistics and psychology.

SERVQUAL is based on the disconfirmation model widely adopted in the customer satisfaction literature. In this literature, customer satisfaction (CSat) is operationalized in terms of the relationship between expectations (E) and outcomes (O). If O matches E, customer satisfaction is predicted. If O exceeds E, then customer delight may be produced. If E exceeds O, then customer dissatisfaction is indicated.

According to Cronin and Taylor (1992, 1994) SERVQUAL is paradigmatically flawed because of its ill-judged adoption of this disconfirmation model. 'Perceived quality', they claim, 'is best conceptualized as an attitude'. They criticize Parasuraman *et al.* for their hesitancy to define perceived SQ in attitudinal terms, even though Parasuraman *et al.* (1988) had earlier claimed that SQ was 'similar in many ways to an attitude'. Cronin and Taylor observe:

> Researchers have attempted to differentiate service quality from consumer satisfaction, even while using the disconfirmation format to measure perceptions of service quality . . . this approach is not consistent with the differentiation expressed between these constructs in the satisfaction and attitude literatures.

Iacobucci *et al.*'s (1994) review of the debate surrounding the conceptual and operational differences between SQ and CSat concludes that the constructs 'have not been consistently defined and differentiated from each other in the literature'. She suggests that the two constructs may be connected in a number of ways. First, they may be both different operationalizations of the same construct, 'evaluation'. Second, they may be orthogonally related, i.e. they may be entirely different constructs. Third, they may be conceptual cousins. Their family connections may be dependent on a number of other considerations, including for example, the duration of the evaluation. Parasuraman *et al.* (1985) have described satisfaction as more situation- or encounter-specific, and quality as more holistic, developed over a longer period of time, although they offer no empirical evidence to support this contention. SQ and CSat may also be related by time order. The predominant belief is that SQ is the logical predecessor to CSat, but this remains unproven. Cronin and Taylor's critique draws support from Oliver's (1980) research which suggests that SQ and CSat are distinct constructs but are related in that satisfaction mediates the effect of prior-period perceptions of SQ and causes revised SQ perceptions to be formed. SQ and CSat may also be differentiated by virtue of their content. Whereas SQ may be thought of as high in cognitive content, CSat may be more heavily loaded with affect (Oliver, 1993).

Cronin and Taylor suggest that the adequacy-importance model of attitude measurement should be adopted for SQ research. Iacobucci *et al.* (1994) add the observation that 'in some general psychological sense, it is not clear what short-term evaluations of quality and satisfaction are if not attitudes'. In turn, Parasuraman *et al.* (1994) have vigorously defended their position, claiming that critics seem 'to discount prior conceptual work in the SQ literature', and suggest that Cronin and Taylor's work 'does not justify their claim' that the disconfirmation paradigm is flawed.

In other words, Cronin and Taylor (1994) comment that:

> Recent conceptual advances suggest that the disconfirmation-based SERVQUAL scale is measuring neither service quality nor consumer satisfaction. Rather, the SERVQUAL scale appears at best an operationalization of only one of the many forms of expectancy-disconfirmation.

A different concern has been raised by Andersson (1992). He objects to SERVQUAL's failure to draw on previous social science research, particularly economic theory, statistics, and psychological theory. Parasuraman *et al.*'s work is highly inducive in that it moves from historically situated observation to general theory. Andersson (1992) claims that Parasuraman *et al.* 'abandon the principle of scientific continuity and deduction'. Among specific criticisms are the following:

First, Parasuraman *et al.*'s management technology takes no account of the costs of improving service quality. It is naive in assuming that the marginal revenue of SQ improvement always exceeds the marginal cost. (Aubrey and Zimbler (1983), Crosby (1979), Juran (1951) and Masser (1957) have addressed the issue of the costs/benefits of quality improvement in service settings.)

Second, Parasuraman *et al.* collect SQ data using ordinal scale methods (Likert scales) yet perform analyses with methods suited to interval-level data (factor analysis).

Third, Parasuraman *et al.* are at the 'absolute end of the street regarding possibilities to use statistical methods'. Ordinal scales do not allow for investigations of common product-moment correlations. Interdependencies among the dimensions of quality are difficult to describe. SERVQUAL studies cannot answer questions such as: Are there elasticities among the quality dimensions? Is the customer value of improvements a linear or non-linear function?

Fourth, Parasuraman *et al.* fail to draw on the large literature on the psychology of perception.

Gaps model

A related set of criticisms refer to the value and meaning of gaps identified in the disconfirmation model.

Babakus and Boller (1992) found the use of a 'gap' approach to SQ measurement 'intuitively appealing' but suspected that the 'difference scores do not provide any additional information beyond that already contained in the perceptions component of the SERVQUAL scale'. They found that the dominant contributor to the gap score was the perceptions score because of a generalized response tendency to rate expectations high.

Churchill and Surprenant (1982), in their work on CSat, also ponder whether gap measurements contribute anything new or of value given that the gap is a direct function of E and P. It has also been noted that:

> while conceptually, difference scores might be sensible, they are problematic in that they are *notoriously unreliable*, even when the measures from which the difference scores are derived are themselves highly reliable (Iacobucci et al., 1994).

Also, in the context of CSat, Oliver (1980) has pondered whether it might be preferable to consider the P − E scores as raw differences or as ratios. No work has been reported using a ratio approach to measure SQ.

Iacobucci *et al.* (1994) take a different tack on the incorporation of E measures. They suggest that expectations might not exist or be formed clearly enough to serve as a standard for evaluation of a service experience. Expectations may be formed simultaneously with service consumption. Kahneman and Miller (1986) have also proposed that consumers may form 'experience-based norms' after service experiences, rather than expectations before.

A further issue raised by Babakus and Inhofe (1991) is that expectations may attract a social desirability response bias. Respondents may feel motivated to adhere to an 'I-have-high-expectations' social norm. Indeed, Parasuraman *et al.* report that in their testing of the 1988 version the majority of expectations scores were above six on the seven-point scale. The overall mean expectation was 6.22 (Parasuraman *et al.*, 1991b).

Teas (1993a, 1993b, 1994) has pondered the meaning of identified gaps. For examples, there are six ways of producing P − E gaps of −1 (P = 1, E = 2; P = 2, E = 3; P = 3, E = 4; P = 4, E = 5; P = 5, E = 6; P = 6, E = 7). Do these tied gaps mean equal perceived SQ? He also noted that SERVQUAL research thus far has not established that all service providers within a consideration or choice set, e.g. all car-hire firms do, in fact, share the same expectations ratings across all items and dimensions.

A further criticism is that SERVQUAL fails to capture the dynamics of changing expectation. Consumers learn from experiences. The inference in much of Parasuraman *et al.*'s work is that expectations rise over time. An E score of seven in 1986 may not necessarily mean the same as an E score in 1996. Expectations may also fall over time (e.g. in the health service setting). Grönroos (1993) recognizes this weakness in our understanding of SQ, and has called for a new phase of service quality research to focus on the dynamics of service quality evaluation. Wotruba and Tyagi (1991) agree that more work is needed on how expectations are formed and changed over time.

Implicit in SERVQUAL is the assumption that positive and negative disconfirmation are symmetrically valent. However, from the customer's perspective, failure to meet expectations often seems a more significant outcome than success in meeting or exceeding expectations (Hardie *et al.*, 1992). Customers will often criticize poor service performance and not praise exceptional performance.

Recently, Cronin and taylor (1992) have tested a performance-based measure of SQ, dubbed SERVPERF, in four industries (baking, pest control, dry cleaning and fast food). They found that this measure explained more of the variance in an overall measure of SQ than did SERVQUAL. SERVPERF is composed of the 22 perception items in the SERVQUAL scale, and therefore excludes any consideration of expectations. In a later defence of their argument for a perceptions-only measure of SQ, Cronin and Taylor (1994) acknowledge that it is possible for researchers to *infer* consumers' disconfirmation through arithmetic means (the P − E gap) but that 'consumer perceptions, not calculations, govern behavior'. Finally, a team of researchers, including Zeithaml herself (Boulding *et al.*, 1993), has recently rejected the value of an expectations-based, or gap-based model in finding that service quality was only influenced by perceptions.

Process orientation

SERVQUAL has been criticized for focusing on the process of service delivery rather than outcomes of the service encounter.

Grönroos (1982) identified three components of SQ: technical, functional and reputational quality. Technical quality is concerned with the outcome of the service encounter, e.g. have the dry cleaners got rid of the stain? Functional quality is concerned with the process of service delivery, e.g. were the dry cleaner's counter staff courteous? Reputational quality is a refection of the corporate image of the service organization.

Whereas technical quality focuses on *what*, functional quality focuses on *how* and involves consideration of issues such as the behaviour of customer contact staff, and the speed of service.

Critics have argued that outcome quality is missing from Parasuraman *et al.*'s formulation of SQ (Cronin and Taylor, 1992; Mangold and Babakus, 1991; Richard and Allaway, 1993).

Richard and Allaway (1993) tested an augmented SERVQUAL model which they claim incorporates both process and outcome components, and comment that 'the challenge is to determine which process and outcome quality attributes of SQ have the greatest impact on choice'.[2] Their research into Domino Pizza's process and outcome quality employed the 22 Parasuraman *et al.* (1988) items, modified to suit context, and the following six outcome items:

1. Domino's has delicious home-delivery pizza.
2. Domino's has nutritious home-delivery pizza.
3. Domino's home-delivery pizza has flavourful sauce.
4. Domino's provides a generous amount of toppings for its home-delivery pizza.
5. Domino's home-delivery pizza is made with superior ingredients.
6. Domino's prepared its home-delivery pizza crust exactly the way I like it.

These researchers found that the process-only item borrowed and adapted from SERVQUAL accounted for only 45% of the variance in customer choice; the full inventory, inclusive of the six outcome items, accounted for 71.5% of variance choice. The difference between the two is significant at the 0.001 level. They conclude that process-and-outcome is a better predictor of consumer choice than process, or outcome, alone.

In defence of SERVQUAL, Higgins *et al.* (1991) have argued that outcome quality is already contained within these dimensions: reliability, competence and security.

Dimensionality

Critics have raised a number of significant and related questions about the dimensionality of the SERVQUAL scale. The most serious are concerned with the number of dimensions, and their stability from context to context.

There seems to be general agreement that SQ is a second-order construct, that is, it is factorially complex, being composed of several first-order variables.[3] SERVQUAL is composed of the five RATER factors. There are however, several alternative conceptualizations of SQ. As already noted, Grönroos (1984) identified three components – technical, functional and reputational quality; Lehtinen and Lehtinen (1982) also identify three components – interactive, physical and corporate quality; Hedvall and Paltschik (1989) identify two dimensions – willingness and ability to serve, and physical and psychological access; Leblanc and Nguyen (1988) list five components – corporate image, internal organization, physical support of the service producing system, staff/customer interaction, and the level of customer satisfaction.

Parasuraman *et al.* (1988) have claimed that SERVQUAL:

> provides a basic skeleton through its expectations/perceptions format encompassing statements for each of the five service quality dimensions. The skeleton, when necessary, can be adapted or supplemented to fit the characteristics or specific research needs of a particular organization.

In their 1988 paper, Parasuraman *et al.* also claimed that 'the final 22-item scale and its five dimensions have *sound and stable psychometric properties*'. In the 1991b revision, Parasuraman *et al.* found evidence of '*consistent factor structure*... across five independent samples' (emphases added). In other words, they make claims that the five dimensions are generic across service contexts. Indeed, in 1991, Parasuraman *et al.* claimed that 'SERVQUAL's dimensions and items represent core evaluation criteria that transcend specific companies and industries' (1991b).[4]

Number of dimensions

When the SERVQUAL instrument has been employed in modified form, up to nine distinct dimensions of SQ have been revealed, the number varying according to the service sector under investigation. One study has even produced a single-factor solution.

Nine factors accounted for 71% of SQ variance in Carman's (1990) hospital research: admission service, tangible accommodations, tangible food, tangible privacy, nursing care, explanation of treatment, access and courtesy afforded visitors, discharge planning, and patient accounting (billing).[5]

Five factors were distinguished in Saleh and Ryan's (1992) work in the hotel industry – conviviality, tangibles, reassurance, avoid sarcasm, and empathy. The first of these, conviviality, accounted for 62.8% of the overall variance; the second factor, tangibles, accounted for a further 6.9%; the five factors together accounted for 78.6%. This is strongly suggestive of a two-factor solution in the hospitality industry. The researchers had 'initially assumed that the factor analysis would confirm the [SERVQUAL] dimensions but this failed to be the case'.

Four factors were extracted in Gagliano and Hathcote's (1994) investigation of SQ in the retail clothing sector – personal attention, reliability, tangibles and convenience. Two of these have no correspondence in SERVQUAL. They conclude 'the [original SERVQUAL scale] does not perform as well as expected' in apparel speciality retailing.

Three factors were identified in Bouman and van der Wiele's (1992) research into car servicing – customer kindness, tangibles and faith.[6] The authors 'were not able to find the same dimensions for judging service quality as did Berry *et al.*'.

One factor was recognized in Babakus *et al.*'s (1993b) survey of 635 utility company customers. Analysis 'essentially produced a single-factor model' of SQ which accounted for 66.3% of the variance. The authors advance several possible explanations for this unidimensional result including the nature of the service, (which they describe as a low-involvment service with an ongoing consumption experience), non-response bias and the use of a single expectations/perceptions gap scale. These researchers concluded: 'With the exception of findings reported by Parasuraman and his colleagues, empirical evidence does not support a five-dimensional concept of service quality'.

In summary, Babakus and Boller (1992) commented that 'the domain of service quality may be factorially complex in some industries and very simple and unidimensional in others'. In effect, they claim that the number of SQ dimensions is dependent on the particular service being offered.

In their revised version, Parasuraman *et al.* (1991b) suggest two reasons for these anomalies. First, they may be the product of differences in data collection and analysis procedures. A 'more plausible explanation' is that 'differences among empirically derived factors across replications may be primarily due to across-dimension similarities and/or within dimension differences in customers' evaluations of a specific company involved in each setting'.

Spreng and Singh (1993) have commented on the lack of discrimination between several of the dimensions. In their research, the correlation between Assurance and Responsiveness constructs was .97, indicating that they were not separable constructs. They also found a high correlation between the combined Assurance–Responsiveness construct and the Empathy construct (.87). Parasuraman *et al.* (1991b) had earlier found that Assurance and Responsiveness items loaded on a single factor, and in their 1988 work had found average intercorrelations among the five dimensions of .23 to .35.

In testing their revised version (Parasuraman *et al.*, 1991b), Parasuraman and colleagues found that the four items under Tangibles broke into two distinct dimensions, one pertaining to equipment and physical facilities, the other to employees and communication materials. They also found that Responsiveness and Assurance dimensions showed considerable overlap, and loaded on the same factor. They suggested that this was a product of imposing a five-factor constraint on the analysis. Indeed, the additional degrees of freedom allowed by a subsequent six-factor solution generated distinct Assurance and Responsiveness factors.

Parasuraman *et al.* (1991a) have now accepted that the 'five SERVQUAL dimensions are interrelated as evidenced by the need for oblique rotations of factor solutions... to obtain the most interpretable factor patterns. One fruitful area for future research'; they conclude, 'is to explore the nature and causes of these interrelationships'.

It therefore does appear that both contextual circumstances and analytical processes have some bearing on the number of dimensions of SQ.

Contextual stability

Carman (1990) tested the generic qualities of the SERVQUAL instrument in three service setting – a tyre retailer, a business school placement centre and a dental school patient clinic. Following Parasuraman *et al.*'s suggestion, he modified and augmented the items in the original ten-factor SERVQUAL scale to suit the three contexts. His factor analysis identified between five and seven underlying dimensions.

According to Carman, customers are at least partly context-specific in the dimensions they employ to evaluate SQ. In all three cases, Tangibles, Reliability and Security were present.[7] Responsiveness, a major component in the RATER scale was relatively weak in the dental clinic context. Carman also commented: 'Parasuraman, Zeithaml and Berry combined their original Understanding and Access dimensions into Empathy... our results did not find this to be an appropriate combination'. In particular he found that if a dimension is very important to customers they are likely to be decomposed into a number of sub-dimensions. This happened for the placement centre where Responsiveness, Personal attention, Access and Convenience were all identified as separate factors. According to Carman, this indicates that researchers should work with the original ten dimensions, rather than adopt the revised five-factor Parasuraman *et al.* (1988) model.

There is also an indication from one piece of cross-cultural research that the scale may not always travel well. Ford *et al.* (1993) computed alphas for a SERVQUAL application in the higher education contexts of New Zealand and the USA markets which the authors describe as 'intuitively' similar. Table 2 displays the results.

These results challenge Zeithaml's (1988) claim that consumers form higher level abstractions of SQ that are generalized across contexts.

Table 2. SERVQUAL alphas in New Zealand and the USA

	Cronbach alpha	
Dimensions	USA	New Zealand
Tangibles	.7049	.6833
Reliability	.8883	.8514
Responsiveness	.8378	.8063
Assurance	.8229	.7217
Empathy	.8099	.7734

Item loadings

In some studies (e.g. Carman, 1990), items have not loaded on the factors to which they were expected to belong. Two items from the Empathy battery of the Parasuraman *et al.* (1988) instrument loaded heavily on the Tangibles factor in a study of dental clinic SQ. In the tyre retail study, a Tangibles item loaded on to Security; in the placement centre a Reliability item loaded on to Tangibles. An item concerning the ease of making appointments loaded on to Reliability in the dental clinic context, but Security in the tyre store context. He also found that only two-thirds of the items loaded in the same way on the expectations battery as they did in the perceptions battery. Carman supplies other examples of the same phenomena, and suggests that the unexpected results indicate both a face validity and a construct validity problem. In other words, he warns against importing SERVQUAL into service setting contexts without modification and validity checks.

Among his specific recommendations is the following: 'We recommend that items on Courtesy and Access be retained and that items on some dimensions such as Responsiveness and Access be expanded where it is believed that these dimensions are of particular importance'. He also reports specific Courtesy and Access items which performed well in terms of nomological and construct validity.

Carman (1990) further suggested that the factors, Personal attention, Access or Convenience should be retained and further contextualized research work be done to identify their significance and meaning.

Item intercorrelations

Convergent validity and discriminant validity are important considerations in the measurement of second-order constructs such as SERVQUAL. One would associate a high level of convergent validity with a high level of intercorrelations between the items selected to measure a single RATER factor. Discriminant validity is indicated if the factors and their component items are independent of each other (i.e. the items load heavily on one factor only).[8] Following their modified replication of Parasuraman *et al.*'s work, Babakus and Boller (1992) conclude that rules for convergence and discrimination do not indicate the existence of the five RATER dimensions.

The best scales have a high level of intercorrelation between items comprising a dimension (convergent validity). In their development work in four sectors (banking, credit-card company, repair and maintenance company, and long-distance telecommunications company) Parasuraman *et al.* (1988) found inter-item reliability coefficients (alphas) varying from .52 to .84. Babakus and Boller (1992) report alphas which are broadly consistent with those of Parasuraman, varying from .67 to .83 (see Table 3). In their 1991b version, Parasuraman *et al.* report alphas from .60 to .93, and observe that 'every alpha value obtained for each dimension in the final study is higher than the corresponding values in the... original study'. They attribute this improvement to their rewording of the 22 scale items.

Spreng and Singh (1993), and Brown *et al.* (1993) are highly critical of the questionable application of alphas to difference scores. They evaluate the reliability

Table 3. Reliability of SERVQUAL

		Parasuraman *et al.* (1988)		Babakus and Boller (1992)	
Factor	Item	Coefficient alpha	Item-to-total correlations	Coefficient alpha	Item-to-total correlations
Tangibles	Q1	.72	.69	.67	.38
	Q2		.68		.59
	Q3		.64		.31
	Q4		.51		.54
Reliability	Q5	.83	.75	.82	.66
	Q6		.53		.58
	Q7		.71		.59
	Q8		.75		.75
	Q9		.50		.49
Responsiveness	Q10	.82	.51	.68	.44
	Q11		.77		.44
	Q12		.66		.45
	Q13		.86		.52
Assurance	Q14	.81	.38	.83	.64
	Q15		.72		.77
	Q16		.80		.65
	Q17		.45		.58
Empathy	Q18	.86	.78	.71	.46
	Q19		.81		.46
	Q20		.59		.48
	Q21		.71		.45
	Q22		.68		.47

of SERVQUAL using a measure specifically designed for difference scores (Lord, 1963). Spreng and Singh conclude that 'there is not a great deal of difference between the reliabilities correctly calculated and the more common [alpha] calculation', an observation with which Parasuraman *et al.* (1993) concurred when they wrote: 'The collective conceptual and empirical evidence neither demonstrates clear superiority for the non-difference score format nor warrants abandoning the difference score format'.

Operational

Expectations

Notwithstanding the more fundamental criticism that expectations play no significant role in the conceptualization of service quality, some critics have raised a number of other concerns about the operationalization of E in SERVQUAL.

In their 1988 work, Parasuraman *et al.* defined expectations as 'desire or wants of consumers, i.e. what they feel a service provider *should* offer rather than *would* offer' (emphasis added). The expectations component was designed to measure 'customers' normative expectations' (Parasuraman *et al.*, 1990), and is 'similar to the ideal standard in the customer satisfaction/dissatisfaction literature' (Zeithaml *et al.*, 1991). Teas (1993a) found these explanations 'somewhat vague' and has questioned respondents' interpretations of the expectations battery in the SERVQUAL instrument. He believes that respondents may be using any one of six interpretations (Teas, 1993b):

1. *Service attribute importance.* Customers may respond by rating the expectations statements according to the importance of each.
2. *Forecasted performance.* Customers may respond by using the scale to predict the performance they would expect.
3. *Ideal performance.* The optimal performance, what performance 'can be'.
4. *Deserved performance.* The performance level customers, in the light of their investments, feel performance should be.
5. *Equitable performance.* The level of performance customers feel they ought to receive given a perceived set of costs.
6. *Minimum tolerable performance.* What performance 'must be'.

Each of these interpretations is somewhat different, and Teas contends that a considerable percentage of the variance of the SERVQUAL expectations measure can be explained by the difference in respondents' interpretations. Accordingly, the expectations components of the model lacks discriminant validity. Parasuraman *et al.* (1991b, 1994) have responded to these criticisms by redefining expectations as the service customers would expect from 'excellent service organizations', rather than 'normative' expectations of service providers, and by vigorously defending their inclusion in SQ research.

Iacobucci *et al.* (1994) want to drop the term 'expectations' from the SQ vocabulary. They prefer the generic label 'standard', and believe that several standards may operate simultaneously; among them 'ideals', 'my most desired combination of attributes', the 'industry standard' of a nominal average competitor, 'deserved' SQ, and brand standards based on past experiences with the brand.

Some critics have questioned SERVQUAL's failure to access customer evaluations based on absolute standards of SQ. The instrument asks respondents to report their expectations of excellent service providers within a class (i.e. the measure are relative rather than absolute). It has been argued that SERVQUAL predicts that:

> customers will evaluate a service favourably as long as their expectations are met or exceeded, regardless of whether their prior expectations were high or low, and regardless of whether the absolute goodness of the [service] performance is high or low. This unyielding prediction is illogical. We argue that 'absolute' levels (e.g. the prior standards) certainly must enter into a customer's evaluation (Iacobucci et al., 1994).

Put another way, SERVQUAL assumes that an E-score of six for Joe's Greasy Spoon Diner is equivalent to an E-score of six for Michel Roux's Le Lapin French restaurant. In absolute terms, clearly they are not, Grönroos (1993) refers to a similar oddity, which he calls the bad-service paradox. A customer may have low expectations based on previous experience with the service provider; if those expectations are met there is no gap and SQ is deemed satisfactory.

Since Zeithaml *et al.* (1991) have themselves identified two comparison norms for SQ assessment ('desired service', the level of service a customer believes can and should be delivered; 'adequate service', the level of service the customer considers acceptable) it seems unlikely that the debate about the meaning of expectations is over.

Item composition

Each factor in the 1988 and 1991 SERVQUAL scales is composed of four or five items. It has become clear that this is often inadequate to capture the variance within, or the context-specific meaning of, each dimension. Carman's (1990) study of hospital services employed 40 items. Bouman and van der Wiele (1992) used 48 items in their car service research, Saleh and Ryan (1992) 33 items in their hospitality research, Fort (1993) 31 items in his analysis of software house service quality and Babakus and Mangold (1992) 15 items in their hospital research. Parasuraman *et al.* (1991b) acknowledge that context-specific items can be used to supplement SERVQUAL, but caution that 'the new items should be similar in form to the existing SERVQUAL items'.

Moments of truth

Many services are delivered over several moments of truth or encounter between service staff and customer: hotel and hospital services for example. Carman (1990) found evidence that customers evaluate SQ by reference to these multiple encounters. For example, in his hospital research he listed the three items below:

1. My discharge from the hospital was prompt.
2. Nurses responded promptly when I called.
3. My admission to the hospital was prompt.

These items did not load heavily on a single Responsiveness factor as might be expected; instead they loaded on factors which represented a particular hospital function, or moment of truth. Parasuraman *et al.*, in contrast, have declared the SQ is a more global construct, not directly connected to particular incidents.

Polarity

Of the 22 items in the 1988 SERVQUAL scale, 13 statement pairs are positively worded, and nine pairs are negatively worded. The negatives are the full set of Responsiveness and Empathy statements. Parasuraman *et al.*'s goal was to reduce systematic response bias caused by yea-saying and nay-saying. This is accepted as good normative research practice (Churchill, 1979), yet has consequences for respondents who make more comprehension errors, and take more time to read items (Wason and Johnson-Laird, 1972).

In factor analysis of SERVQUAL data, Babakus and Boller (1992) found that all negatively-worded items loaded heavily on one factor while all positively-worded items loaded on another. They also found a significant difference between the average P, E and gap scores of positively and negatively-worded items. They conclude that the wording of the items produces a 'method factor': 'Item wording may be responsible for producing factors that are method artifacts rather than conceptually meaningful dimensions of service quality'. Item wording creates data quality problems, and calls into question the dimensionality and validity of the instrument. Babakus and Mangold (1992), in their application of SERVQUAL to a hospital setting, therefore decided to employ only positively-worded statements. Parasuraman *et al.* (1991b) have responded to these criticisms by rewording all negatively-worded items positively.

Scale points

The use of seven-point Likert scales has been criticized on several grounds. Although none of these are specific to SERVQUAL applications, they bear repeating here. Lewis (1993) has criticized the scale for its lack of verbal labelling for points two to six. She believes this may cause respondents to overuse the extreme ends of the scale and suggests this could be avoided by labelling each point. Another issue is the respondents' interpretation of the meaning of the midpoint of the scale (e.g. is it a 'don't know', 'do not feel strongly in either direction' or a 'do not understand the statement' response?) Lewis is also concerned about responses which suggest there is no gap when in fact a gap does exist. For instance a respondent may have expectations of 5.4 and perceptions of 4.6 (a gap of 0.8) but when completing SERVQUAL may rate each as 5, the nearest possible response in each case. This is an example of a Type II error.

Babakus and Mangold (1992) opted to use five-point Likert scales on the grounds that it would reduce the 'frustration level' of patient respondents, increase response rate and response quality.

Two administrations

Respondents appear to be bored, and sometimes confused by the administration of E and P versions of SERVQUAL (Bouman and van der Wiele, 1992). Boredom and confusion imperil data quality.

Carman (1990) also comments on the timing of the two administrations. He is critical of Parasuraman *et al.* for asking respondents to complete the two questionnaires at a single sitting. In Parasuraman *et al.*'s 1988 work respondents were asked to report their expectations and perceptions, based on what they had experienced in the last three months. All self-reports were entirely *ex post*, a practice also criticized by Grönroos (1993). Carman also observed that it was impractical to expect customers to complete an expectations inventory prior to a service encounter and a perception inventory immediately afterwards. His solution was to collect data on the expectations–perceptions difference with a single question at a single administration, for example: 'The visual appeal of XYZ's physical facilities is (much better, better, about the same, worse, much worse) than I expected'. Lewis (1993) refers to work undertaken by Orledge who has also experimented with an alternative method of combining perceptions and expectations. He combined the two elements as in the following example:

> Indicate on the scale using a 'P' how well dressed the staff of company XYZ are. On the same scale indicate using an 'E' how well dressed you expect the staff of companies in this industry to be.
>
> smart ____ : ____ : ____ E__ : ____ : ____ : __ P__ : ____ untidy

Bouman and van der Wiele (1992) also comment on the same problem. Babakus and Boller (1992), and Babakus *et al.* (1993b) solved the problem by employing a single seven-point scale to collect gap data. Recommended earlier by Carman (1990), the scale ranged from 7 = 'greatly exceeds my expectations' to 1 = 'greatly falls short of my expectations'.

Clow and Vorhies (1993) argue:

> When expectations and experience evaluations are measured simultaneously, respondents will indicate that their expectations are greater than they actually were before the service encounter.

They contend that expectations must be measured prior to receipt of services otherwise responses will be biased. Specifically, Clow and Vorhies found that:

> Customers who had a negative experience with the service tend to overstate their expectations, creating a larger gap; customers who had a positive experience tend to understate their expectations, resulting in smaller gaps.

Variance extracted

Fornell and Larcker (1981) have suggested that 'variance extracted' should be stringently employed as a measure of construct validity. Parasuraman *et al.* (1988) reported that the total amount of variance extracted by the five RATER factors in the bank, credit card, repair and maintenance, and long-distance telephone samples was 56.0%, 57.5%, 61.6% and 56.2% respectively. Parasuraman *et al.* (1991a) report variance explained in a telephone company, insurance company 1, insurance company 2, bank 1 and bank 2 at 67.2%, 68.3%, 70.9%, 71.6% and 66.9%, respectively. When the samples are combined, variance explained is 67.9%. Babakus and Boller's (1992) utility-sector replication reported 58.3%. Carman's (1990) modified replication in the hospital sector, tyre store, business school placement centre and dental clinic reported 71%, 61%, 75% and 71% respectively. Saleh and Ryan's (1992) modified replication in the hotel sector reported 78.6%. Bouman and van der Wiele's (1992) modified replication in car servicing reported 40.7% only. Generally, the modified scales tended to produce higher levels of variance extracted. The higher the variance extracted, the more valid is the measure.

CONCLUSION

SERVQUAL has undoubtedly had a major impact on the business and academic communities.

This review has identified a number of theoretical and operational issues which should concern users of the instrument. Since the most serious of these are concerned with face validity and construct validity, this conclusion briefly reviews the nature and significance of validity.

Face validity is concerned with the extent to which a scale appears to measure what it purports to measure.

Construct validity generally:

> is used to refer to the vertical correspondence between a construct which is at an unobservable, conceptual level and a purported measure of it which is at an operational level. In an ideal sense, the term means that a measure assesses the magnitude and direction of (1) all of the characteristics and (2) only the characteristics of the construct it is purported to assess (Peter, 1981, emphases added).

In particular, the concerns about the adoption of an inappropriate paradigm, the gaps model, SERVQUAL's process orientation, and SERVQUAL's dimensionality (the four theoretical criticisms as listed earlier) are construct validity issues.

Critical face and construct validity questions which SERVQUAL researchers face are: Do consumers actually evaluate SQ in terms of expectations and perceptions? Do the five RATER dimensions incorporate the full range of SQ attributes? Do consumers incorporate 'outcome' evaluations into their assessments of SQ?

Construct validity is itself a composite of several forms of validity: nomological validity, convergent validity and discriminant validity.

Nomological validity is the extent to which a measure correlation in theoretically predictable ways with measures of different but related constructs. SQ is one of a number of apparently interrelated constructs whose precise alignments has yet to be explored. Included in the nomological net are customer (dis)satisfaction, customer retention and defection, behavioural intention, attitude to service provider or organization, and service provider or organization choice. Some research into these questions has been published (Parasuraman *et al.*, 1991b; Richard and Allaway, 1993) but the relationships have yet to be explored fully.

Convergent validity is the extent to which a scale correlates with other measures of the same construct. A high level of intercorrelation between items comprising each RATER dimension would indicate high convergent validity internal of SERVQUAL. A high level of correlation between SERVQUAL scores and a different, reliable and valid measure of SQ, would indicate a high level of external convergent validity. Discriminant validity is the extent to which a measure does *not* correlate with other measures from which it is purported to differ. If SQ evaluations were composed of five distinct RATER dimensions, one would expect little correlation between the five factors. SERVQUAL's dimensionality would be regarded as more stable if individual items loaded on to the dimensions to which they belong.

Issues to face and construct validity are of overriding importance in the development of instruments such as SERVQUAL. The operational criticisms are evidently less significant than the theoretical criticisms, and pose less of a threat to validity. The theoretical criticisms raised in this article are of such moment that the validity of the instrument must be called into question.

Despite these shortcomings, SERVQUAL seems to be moving rapidly towards institutionalized status. As Rust and Zahorik (1993) have observed, 'the general SERVQUAL dimensions... should probably be put on any first pass as a list of attributes of service'.

These criticisms indicate that there is still a need for fundamental research. There are still doubts about whether customers routinely assess SQ in terms of Expectations and Perceptions; there are doubts about the utility and appropriateness of the disconfirmation paradigm; there are doubts about the dimensionality of SQ; there are doubts about the universality of the five RATER dimensions. These are serious concerns which are not only significant for users of SERVQUAL but for all those who wish to understand better the concept of SQ.

DIRECTIONS FOR FUTURE RESEARCH

This review has raised several conceptual and operational difficulties surrounding SERVQUAL which are yet to be resolved. The following represent a set of questions which SQ researchers should address:

1. Do consumers always evaluate SQ in terms of expectations and perceptions? What other forms of SQ evaluation are there?
2. What form do customers expectations take and how best, if at all, are they measured? Are expectations common across a class of service providers?
3. Do attitude-based measures of SQ perform better than the disconfirmation model? Which attitudinal measure is most helpful?
4. Is it advantageous to integrate outcome evaluations into SQ measurement and how best can this be done?
5. Is the predictive validity of P measures of service quality better than that of P–E measures?
6. What are the relationships between SQ, customer satisfaction, behavioural intention, purchase behaviour, market share, word-of-mouth and customer retention?
7. What is the role of context in determining E and P evaluations? What context-markers do consumes employ?
8. Are analytical context markers such as tangibility and consumer involvement helpful in advancing SQ theory?
   - Do evaluative criteria in intangible-dominant services (e.g consulting) differ from those in tangible-dominant services (e.g. hotels)?
   - How does involvement influence the evaluation of SQ?
9. How do customers integrate transaction-specific or MOT-specific evaluations of SQ? To what extent are some MOTs more influential in the final evaluation than others?
10. What are the relationships between the five RATER factors? How stable are those relationships across context?
11. What is the most appropriate scale format for collecting valid and reliable SQ data?
12. To what extent can customers correctly classify items into their a priori dimensions?

Answers to questions such as these would help improve our understanding of the service quality construct and assess the value of the SERVQUAL instrument. Even in its present state SERVQUAL is a helpful operationalization of a somewhat nebulous construct.

Many of these questions require contextually sensitive qualitative research. The first question, 'Do consumers always evaluate SQ in terms of expectations and perceptions?', is perhaps best approached through in-depth case analyses of particular service encounters. The formation of expectations implies a consumer who accumulates and processes information about a high class of service providers. This would appear to make prima facie sense for high-cost, high-risk services, e.g. if purchasing a weekend break to celebrate 25 years of wedded bliss. It is as likely that expectations high in cognitive content would be formed for a low-cost, low-risk service such as a hot drink from a coffee shop? The role of context appears to have been repressed or subjugated in the present body of SERVQUAL research. Context need to be recovered.

Other questions lend themselves to multisectoral comparative analyses. For example, the question, 'Is the predictive validity of P-measures of SQ better than that of P−E measures?', is perhaps best approached in multi-sectoral study which thoroughly tests the predictive performance of P and P−E SQ measures.

Pursuit of this research agenda would surely strengthen our understanding of the meaning, measurement and management of service quality. Parasuraman, Zeithaml and Berry have undoubtedly done a splendid job of marketing SERVQUAL's measurement and management technologies. It remains to be seen whether its dominance will remain unchallenged.

NOTES

1. The mnemonic RATER is a helpful aide mèmoire, where R = reliability, A = assurance, T = tangibles, E = empathy and R = responsiveness.
2. Richard and Allaways's (1993) research was largely focused on testing SERVQUAL's predictive validity. Parasuraman *et al.* (1991b) have also tested the predictive validity of the modified SERVQUAL scale. Customers in five samples were asked three questions: Have you recently had a service problem with the company? If you have experienced a problem was it resolved to your satisfaction? Would you recommend the service firm to a friend? It was hypothesized that positive answers to these questions would be correlated negatively, positively and positively, respectively, with higher perceived SQ scores. All results were statistically significant in the hypothesized direction, lending support to the predictive validity of the instrument.
3. Babakus and Boller (1992) have expressed concern that it is unclear whether SERVQUAL is measuring a number of distinct constructs or a single, global, more abstract variable.
4. Cronin and Taylor (1992), following a test of SERVQUAL in four classes of service firm, conclude in stark contrast that 'the five-component structure proposed by Parasuraman, Zeithaml and Berry (1988) for their SERVQUAL scale is not confirmed'.
5. Babakus and Mangold's (1992) research into hospital SQ identified three factors within the expectations data, accounting for 56.2% of the variance in the item scores, two factors within the perception data (70.6%) and 'no meaningful factor structure' within the difference or gaps data.
6. Customer kindness, that is 'the front office personnel's approach to the customer and his problems, regardless of the service delivered', was the only factor to have significant relationship with future car servicing intentions, future car purchase intentions, and word-of-mouth recommendation.

7. Carman's Security factor is composed of Credibility, Security and Competence. Parasuraman *et al.* (1988) had incorporated these three components, together with Communication and Courtesy, into the factor Assurance.
8. For a discussion of construct, convergent and discriminant validity see Churchill (1979) and Peter (1981).

APPENDIX. TEN COMPONENTS OF SERVICE QUALITY

(1) *Reliability* involves consistency of performance and dependability. It also means that the firm performs the service right first time and honours its promises. Specifically, it may involve:
- accuracy in billing;
- performing the service at the designated time.

(2) *Responsiveness* concerns the willingness or readiness of employees to provide service. It may involve:
- mailing a transaction slip immediately;
- calling the customer back quickly;
- giving prompt service (e.g. setting up appointments quickly).

(3) *Competence* means possession of the required skills and knowledge to perform the service. It involves:
- knowledge and skill of the contact personnel;
- knowledge and skill of operational support personnel;
- research capability of the organization.

(4) *Access* involves approachability and ease of contact. It may mean:
- the service is easily accessible by telephone;
- waiting time to receive service is not extensive;
- convenient hours of operation and convenient location of service facility.

(5) *Courtesy* involves politeness, respect, consideration, and friendliness of contact personnel (including receptionists, telephone operators, etc.). It includes:
- consideration for the consumers property;
- clean and neat appearance of public contract personnel.

(6) *Communication* means keeping customers informed in language they can understand, and listening to them. It may mean that the company has to adjust its language for different customers. It may involve:
- explaining the service itself and how much the service will cost;
- explaining the trade-offs between service and cost;
- assuring the consumer that a problem will be handled.

(7) *Credibility* involves trustworthiness, believability, honesty. It involves having the customer's best interests at heart. Contributing to credibility are:
- company name and reputation;
- personal characteristics of the contact personnel;
- the degree of hard sell involved in interactions with the customer.

(8) *Security* is the freedom from danger, risk, or doubt. It may involve:
- physical safety;
- financial security and confidentiality.

(9) *Understanding/knowing the customer* involves making the effort to understand the customer's needs. It involves:
- learning the customer's specific requirements;
- providing individualized attention.

(10) *Tangibles* include the physical evidence of the service.
- physical facilities and appearance of personnel;
- tools or equipment used to provide the service;
- physical representations of the service, such as a plastic credit card.

REFERENCES AND FURTHER READING

Andersson, T. D. (1992) 'Another Model of Service Quality: A Model of Causes and Effects of Service Quality Tested on a Case Within the Restaurant Industry. In (Kunst, P. and Lemmink, J., Eds), *Quality Management in Service.* van Gorcum, The Netherlands, pp. 41–58.

Aubry, C. A. and Zimbler, D. A. (1993) 'The Banking Industry: Quality Costs and Improvements'. *Quality Progress* (December): 16–20.

Babakus, E. and Boller, G. W. (1992) 'An Empirical Assessment of the SERVQUAL Scale'. *Journal of Business Research* **24:** 253–268.

Babakus, E. and Inhofe, M. (1991) 'The Role of Expectations and Attribute Importance in the Measurement of Service Quality'. In *Proceedings of the Summer Educators' Conference* (M. C. Gilly *et al,* Eds). American Marketing Association, Chicago, IL, pp. 142–144.

Babakus, E. and Mangold, W. G. (1992) 'Adapting the SERVQUAL Scale to Hospital Services: an Empirical Investigation'. *Health Services Research* **26** (2, February): 767–786.

Babakus, E., Pedrick, D. L. and Inhofe, M. (1993b) 'Empirical Examination of a Direct Measure of Perceived Service Quality Using SERVQUAL Items. Unpublished manuscript, Memphis State University, TN.

Babakus, E., Pedrick, D. L. and Richardson, A. (1993a) 'Measuring Perceived Service Quality within the Airline Catering Service Industry. Unpublished manuscript, Memphis State University, TN.

Baker, J. A. and Lamb, C. W. Jr (1993) 'Managing Architectural Design Service Quality'. *Journal of Professional Services Marketing* **10** (No. 1): 89–106.

Bolton, R. N. and Drew, J. H. (1991) 'A Multistage Model of Customers' Assessment of Service Quality and Value'. *Journal of Consumer Research* **17** (March): 375–384.

Boulding, W., Kalra, A., Staelin, R. and Zeithaml, V. A. (1993) 'A Dynamic Process Model of Service Quality: from Expectations to Behavioral Intentions'. *Journal of Marketing Research* **30** (February): 7–27.

Bouman, M. and van der Wiele, T. (1992) 'Measuring Service Quality in the Car Service Industry: Building and Testing an Instrument'. *International Journal of Service Industry Management* **3** (No. 4): 4–16.

Brown, T. J., Churchill, G. A. and Peter, J. P. (193) 'Improving the Measurement of Service Quality'. *Journal of Retailing* **69** (No. 1, Spring): 127–139.

Buzzell, R. D. and Gale, B. T. (1987) *The PIMS Principles.* Free Press, New York, NY.

Carman, J. M. (1990) 'Consumer Perceptions of Service Quality: an Assessment of the SERVQUAL Dimensions'. *Journal of Retailing* **66** (No. 1, Spring): 33–35.

Churchill, G. A. (1979) 'A Paradigm for Developing Better Measures of Marketing Constructs', *Journal of Marketing Research* **19** (February): 64–73.

Churchill, G. A. and Surprenant, C. (1982) 'An Investigation into the Determinants of Customer Satisfaction'. *Journal of Marketing Research* **19:** 491–504.

Clow, K. E. and Vorhies, D. E. (1993) 'Building a Competitive Advantage for Service Firms'. *Journal of Services Marketing* **7** (No. 1): 22–3.

Cronin, J. J. Jr and Taylor, S. A. (1992) 'Measuring Service Quality: a Reexamination and Extension'. *Journal of Marketing* **56** (July): 55–68.

Cronin, J. J. Jr and Taylor, S. A. (1994) 'SERVPERF Versus SERVQUAL: Reconciling Performance-based and Perceptions-minus Expectations Measurement of Service Quality'. *Journal of Marketing* **58** (January): 125–131.

Crosby, P. B. (1979) *Quality is Free.* McGraw-Hill, New York, NY.

Fick, G. R. and Ritchie, J. R. B. (1991) 'Measuring Service Quality in the Travel and Tourism Industry'. *Journal of Travel Research* **30** (No. 2, Autumn): 2–9.

Ford, J. W., Joseph, M. and Joseph, B. (1993) 'Service Quality in Higher Education: a Comparison of Universities in the United States and New Zealand Using SERVQUAL'. Unpublished manuscript, Old Dominion University, Norfolk, VA.

Fornell, C. and Larcker, D. F. (1981) 'Evaluating Structural Equation Models with Unobservable Variables and Measurement Error'. *Journal of Marketing Research* **18** (February): 39–50.

Fort, M. (1993) 'Customer Defined Attributes of Service Quality in the IBM Mid-range Computer Software Industry. Unpublished MBA dissertation, Manchester Business School, Manchester.

Freeman, K. D. and Dart, J. (1993) 'Measuring the Perceived Quality of Professional Business Services. *Journal of Professional Services Marketing* **9** (No. 1): 27–47.

Gagliano, K. B. and Hathcote, J. (1994) 'Customer Expectations and Perceptions of Service Quality in Apparel Retailing'. *Journal of Services Marketing* **8** (No. 1): 60–69.

Grönroos, C. (1982) *Strategic Management and Marketing in the Service Sector.* Swedish School of Economics and Business Administration, Helsinki.

Grönroos, C. (1984) 'A Service Quality Model and its Marketing Implications'. *European Journal of Marketing,* **18**: 36–44.

Grönroos, C. (1993) 'Towards a Third Phase in Service Quality Research: Challenges and Future Directions. In *Advances in Services Marketing and Management* (T. A. Swartz, D. E. Bowen and S. W. Brown, Eds). Vol. 2, JAI Press, Greenwich, CT, pp. 49–64.

Hardie, B. G. S., Johnson, E. J. and Fader, P. S. (1992) 'Modelling Loss Aversion and Reference Dependence Effects on Brand Choice. Working paper, Wharton School, University of Pennsylvania, PA.

Hedvall, M.-B. and Paltschik, M. (1989) 'An Investigation in, and Generation of, Service Quality Concepts'. In *Marketing Thought and Practice in the 1990s* (G. J. Avlonitis *et al.* Eds). European Marketing Academy, Athens, pp. 473–483.

Higgins, L. F., Ferguson, J. M. and Winston, J. M. (1991) 'Understanding and Assessing Service Quality in Health Maintenance Organizations'. *Health Marketing Quarterly* **9** (Nos 1–2): 5–20.

Iacobucci, D., Grayson, K. A. and Omstrom, A. L. (1994) 'The Calculus of Service Quality and Customer Satisfaction: Theoretical and Empirical Differentiation and Integration'. In *Advances in Services Marketing and Management, Vol. 3* (T. A. Swartz, D. E. Bowen and S. W. Brown, Eds). JAI Press, Greenwich, CT, pp. 1–68.

Johns, N. (1993) 'Quality Management in the Hospitality Industry, part 3: Recent Developments'. *International Journal of Contemporary Hospitality Management* **5** (No. 1): 10–15.

Juran, J. M. (1951) *Quality Control Handbook.* McGraw-Hill, New York, NY.

Kahneman, D. and Miller, D. T. (1986) 'Norm Theory: Comparing Reality to its Alternatives'. *Psychological Review* **93**: 136–153.

Kong, R. and Mayo, M. C. (1993) 'Measuring Service Quality in the Business-to-business Context'. *Journal of Business and Industrial Marketing* **8** (No. 2): 5–15.

Kwon, W. and Lee, T. J. (1994) 'Measuring Service Quality in Singapore Retail Banking'. *Singapore Management Review* **16** (No. 2, July): 1–24.

Leblanc, G. and Nguyen, N. (1988) 'Customers' Perception of Service Quality in Financial Institutions'. *International Journal of Bank Marketing* **6** (No. 4): 7–18.

Lehtinen, J. R. and Lehtinen, O. (1982) 'Service Quality: a Study of Quality Dimensions'. Unpublished working paper, Service Management Institute, Helsinki.

Lewis, B. R. (1993) 'Service Quality Measurement'. *Marketing Intelligence and Planning* **11** (No. 4): 4–12.

Lord, F. M. (1963) 'Elementary Models for Measuring Change'. In *Problems in Measuring Change.* (C. W. Harris Ed.). University of Wisconsin Press, Madison, WI, pp. 22–38.

McElwee, G. and Redman, T. (1993) 'Upward Appraisal in Practice: an Illustrative Example using the QUALED Scale'. *Education and Training* **35** (No. 2, December): 27–31.

Mangold, G. W. and Babakus, E. (1991) 'Service Quality: the Front-stage Perspective vs the Back Stage Perspective'. *Journal of Services Marketing* **5** (No. 4, Autumn): 59–70.

Masser, W. J. (1957) 'The Quality Manager and Quality Costs'. *Industrial Quality Control* **14:** 5–8.

Oliver, R. L. (1980) 'A Cognitive Model of the Antecedents and Consequences of Satisfaction Decisions'. *Journal of Marketing Research* **17** (November): 460–469.

Oliver, R. L. (1993) 'A Conceptual Model of Service Quality and Service Satisfaction: Compatible Goals, Different Concepts'. In *Advances in Services Marketing and Management*, Vol. 2 (T. A. Swartz, D. E. Bowen and S. W. Brown, Eds). JAI Press, Greenwich, CT, pp. 65–85.

Parasuraman, A., Berry, L. L. and Zeithaml, V. A. (1990) *An Empirical Examination of Relationships in an Extended Service Quality Model.* Marketing Science Institute, Cambridge, MA.

Parasuraman, A., Berry, L. L. and Zeithaml, V. A. (1991a) 'Perceived Service Quality as a Customer Based Performance Measure: an Empirical Examination of Organizational Barriers using an Extended Service Quality Model'. *Human Resource Management* **30** (No. 3, Autumn): 335–364.

Parasuraman, A., Zeithaml, V. and Berry, L. L. (1985) 'A Conceptual Model of Service Quality and its Implications for Future Research'. *Journal of Marketing* **49** (Autumn): 41–50.

Parasuraman, A., Zeithaml, V. and Berry, L. L. (1986) 'SERVQUAL: a Multiple-item Scale for Measuring Customer Perceptions of Service Quality'. Report No. 86–108, Marketing Science Institute, Cambridge, MA.

Parasuraman, A., Zeithaml, V. and Berry, L. L. (1988) 'SERVQUAL: a Multiple-item Scale for Measuring Consumer Perceptions of Service Quality'. *Journal of Retailing* **64** (Spring): 12–40.

Parasuraman, A., Zeithaml, V. and Berry, L. L. (1991b). 'Refinement and Reassessment of the SERVQUAL Scale'. *Journal of Retailing* **67** (No. 4): 420–450.

Parasuraman, A., Zeithaml, V. and Berry, L. L. (1994) 'Reassessment of Expectations as a Comparison Standard in Measuring Service Quality: Implications for Future Research'. *Journal of Marketing* **58** (January): 111–124.

Peter, J. P. (1981) 'Construct Validity: a Review of Basic Issues and Marketing Practices'. *Journal of Marketing Research* **18** (May): 133–145.

Reichheld, F. F. and Sasser, W. E. Jr. (1990) 'Zero Defections: Quality comes to Service'. *Harvard Business Review* (September–October): 105–111.

Reidenbach, R. E. and Sandifer-Smallwood, B. (1990) 'Exploring Perceptions of Hospital Operations by a Modified SERVQUAL Approach'. *Journal of Health Care Marketing* **10** (No. 4, December): 47–55.

Richard, M. D. and Allaway, A. W. (1993) 'Service Quality Attributes and Choice Behavior'. *Journal of Service Marketing* **7** (No. 1): 59–68.

Rigotti, S. and Pitt, L. (1992) 'SERVQUAL as a Measuring Instrument for Service Provider Gaps in Business Schools'. *Managing Research News* **15** (No. 3): 9–17.

Rust, R. T. and Zahorik, A. J. (1993) 'Customer Satisfaction, Customer Retention and Market Share' *Journal of Retailing* **69** (No. 2, Summer): 193–215.

Saleh, F. and Ryan, C. (1992) 'Analysing Service Quality in the Hospitality Industry using the SERVQUAL Model'. *Services Industries Journal* **11** (No. 3): 324–43.

Scott, D. and Schieff, D. (1993) 'Service Quality Components and Group Criteria in Local Government'. *International Journal of Service Industry Management* **4** (No. 4): 42–53.

Soliman, A. A. (1992) 'Assessing the Quality of Health Care'. *Health Care Marketing* **10** (Nos 1–2): 121–141.

Spreng, R. A. and Singh, A. K. (1993) 'An Empirical Assessment of the SERVQUAL Scale and the Relationship between Service Quality and Satisfaction. Unpublished manuscript, Michigan State University, TN.

Taylor, S. A., Sharland, A., Cronin, A. A. Jr and Bullard, W. (1993) 'Recreational Quality in the International Setting'. *International Journal of Service Industries Management* **4** (No. 4): 68–88.

Teas, K. R. (1993a) 'Expectations, Performance Evaluation and Consumers' Perceptions of Quality'. *Journal of Marketing* **57** (No. 4): 18–24.

Teas, K. R. (1993b) 'Consumer Expectations and the Measurement of Perceived Service Quality'. *Journal of Professional Services Marketing* **8** (No. 2): 33–53.

Teas, K. R. (1994) 'Expectations as a Comparison Standard in Measuring Service Quality: an Assessment of a Reassessment'. *Journal of Marketing* **58** (January): 132–139.

Vandamme, R. and Leunis, J. (1993) 'Development of a Multiple-item Scale for Measuring Hospital Service Quality'. *International Journal of Service Industry Management* **4** (No. 3): 30–49.

Walbridge, S. W. and Delene, L. M. (1993) 'Measuring Physician Attitudes of Service Quality'. *Journal of Health Care Marketing* **13** (No. 4, Winter): 6–15.

Wason, P. J. and Johnson-Laird, P. N. (1972) *Psychology of Reasoning; Structure and Content.* B.T. Batsford, London.

Woodruff, R. B., Cadotte, E. R. and Jenkins, R. L. (1983) 'Modeling Consumer Satisfaction Processes using Experience-based Norms'. *Journal of Marketing Research* **20:** 296–304.

Wong, S. M. and Perry, C. (1991) 'Customer Service Strategies in Financial Retailing'. *International Journal of Bank Marketing* **9** (No. 3): 11–16.

Wotruba, T. R. and Tyagi, P. K. (1991) 'Met Expectations and Turnover in Direct Selling'. *Journal of Marketing* **55:** 24–35.

Zahorik, A. J. and Rust, R. T. (1992) 'Modeling the Impact of Service Quality of Profitability: a Review. In *Advances in Services Marketing and Management* (T. A. Swartz, D. E. Bowen and S. W. Brown. Eds). JAI Press, Greenwich, CT, pp. 49–64.

Zeithaml, V. A. (1988) 'Consumer Perceptions of Price, Quality and Value: a Means-end Model and Synthesis of Evidence'. *Journal of Marketing* **52** (July): 22–22.

Zeithaml, V. A., Berry, L. L. and Parasuraman, A. (1991) 'The Nature of Determinants of Customer Expectations of Service'. Working paper 91–113, Marketing Science Institute, Cambridge, MA.

Zeithaml, V. A., Berry, L. L. and Parasuraman, A. (1993) 'The Nature and Determinants of Customer Expectation of Service'. *Journal of the Academy of Marketing Science* **21** (No. 1): 1–12.

Zeithaml, V. A., Parasuraman, A. and Berry, L. L. (1990) *Delivering Quality Service: Balancing Customer Perceptions and Expectations.* Free Press, New York, NY.

Zeithaml, V. A., Parasuraman, A. and Berry, L. L. (1992) 'Strategic Positioning on the Dimensions of Service Quality'. In *Advances in Services Marketing and Management,* Vol. 2 (T. A. Swartz, D. E. Bowen and S. W. Brown Eds). JAI Press, Greenwich, CT, pp. 207–228.

15

A Dynamic Process Model of Service Quality: from Expectations to Behavioral Intentions

William Boulding, Ajay Kalra, Richard Staelin and Valarie A. Zeithaml

In response to growing importance of services in the worldwide economy and the recognition by goods firms of the need to compete on service dimensions of the augmented product, several researchers have examined the problems of measuring and managing service quality (Bitner, 1990; Bolton and Drew, 1991a,b; Parasuraman, Berry and Zeithaml, 1990; Parasuraman, Zeithaml and Berry, 1985, 1988; Zeithaml, Berry and Parasuraman, 1991). In this article, we added to this literature by providing insights into both the process by which customers for judgments of service quality and the way these judgments affect subsequent behavior. Specifically, we propose and estimate a process model of service quality that (1) traces the way customers form and update their perceptions of service quality and (2) identifies the consequences of these perceptions on individual-level behavioral intention variables that affect the strategic health of the firm.

Our model development draws from the service quality, attitude and customer satisfaction literatures. We follow the lead of the service quality literature and center our attention on modeling and measuring the cumulative construct of the overall quality level of the firm's service delivery system. We take note of the similarity between the construct 'perceived service quality' from the service quality literature and the construct 'attitude toward an object' from the attitude literature. This similarity helps us generate theoretical predictions in our model of service quality. We also draw from the satisfaction literature, though we make explicit the distinction between this literature, which emphasizes consumers' perceptions of a specific transaction, and the service quality literature, which emphasizes cumulative perceptions.[1]

[1]Readers should not confuse the consumer satisfaction measure discussed in the popular press and measured by many corporations with the satisfaction measure used in most academic satisfaction studies. The former is usually a cumulative concept whereas the latter is transaction specific. We discuss this difference subsequently.

Reprinted with permission from *Journal of Marketing Research*, Vol. 30, February, pp. 7–27.

At the core of our model is the assumption that individuals' current perceptions of the service quality of a firm just after a service contact are a blend of (1) their prior expectations of what *will* and what *should* transpire during the contact and (2) the actual delivered service during the service encounter. Further, we acknowledge that consumers update their expectations whenever they receive relevant information about the service through such means as word-of-mouth, company communications; and contact with the firm's or the competitor's service delivery system.

We test our model with data from two different studies, The first was a laboratory study involving multiple service encounters within the setting of staying in a hotel. Two different prior expectations and the delivered service were manipulated. With these longitudinal data, we use standard experimental analysis to test our basic hypotheses. We then specify a formal structural model representing our conceptualization of the service quality process. Using the same experimental data, we simultaneously test our basic hypotheses and the specification of our structural equations.

The second study enables us to increase the generalizability of our results by examining the service quality process for different service by using a different research method (a field study). In the laboratory study we were able to control (and thus measure) the objective aspects of the delivered service, but in our field study we did not obtain any objective measure of the actual dimensions of the service encounter for each individual. In addition, we obtained measures of expectations and perceptions at only one point in time. Such data are common in the area of service quality where (1) customers normally are polled once to ascertain their expectations and perceptions and (2) actual service is not measured, partly because obtaining objective measures is difficult and partly because the actual service delivered normally varies from person to person (and server to server). Consequently, we develop a method of analysis based on our structural process model that controls for (removes) all unobserved, individual-specific information affecting the customer's expectations and perceptions (the actual service being one such factor) while still allowing estimation of two key parameters of our process model. Such a technique should have broad applicability to service firms that want to measure the relative influences of the two different expectations *and* the delivered service (despite the fact that it is unmeasured) on the customer's perceptions of the firm's service quality.

In addition to postulating and testing a new dynamic model of expectations and perceptions, and providing an analytic approach for estimating major portions of this model with multiple-measures data obtained at only one point in time, we add to the service quality literature in several other ways. Though other researchers have postulated the existence of different expectations, our study is the first empirical demonstration of the joint influence of our two postulated expectations in a service quality setting. We also link the satisfaction and service quality literature by showing our dynamic model of service quality to be compatible with the currently accepted definition of transaction-specific satisfaction. Further, because the major current empirical paradigm for assessing service quality (the gaps model proposed by Parasuraman, Zeithaml and Berry, 1985) and our model are a subset of a more general model, we are able to estimate the validity of these alternative conceptualizations. Finally, ours is one of the first published field studies in which individual-level data are used to examine empirically the impact of consumers' perceptions of service quality on a set of intended behaviors of strategic interest to the firm.

In the following section, we develop our structural model and generate hypotheses for empirical testing. We then estimate the parameters of this model with the two different datasets. We conclude with a discussion of our results.

MODEL DEVELOPMENT

Because our model has many of the same constructs as prior models of service quality and customer satisfaction/dissatisfaction (CS/D), we begin this section with a brief review of the dominant concepts of these two literatures. Expectations and perceptions play an important role in both literatures. In general, both literatures treat these constructs as static, at least for estimation purposes. Also, recent studies in both literatures have acknowledged the existence of multiple classes of expectations (Forbes, Tse and Taylor, 1986; Tse and Wilton, 1988; Wilton and Nicosia, 1986; Zeithaml, Berry and Parasuraman, 1991). Two main standards of expectations emerge. One standard represents the expectations as a *prediction* of future events (Gilly, 1979; Gilly, Cron and Barry, 1983; Miller, 1977; Prakash, 1984; Swan and Trawick, 1980). This is the standard typically used in the satisfaction literature. The other standard is a *normative* expectation of future events (Miller, 1977; Prakash, 1984; Swan and Trawick, 1980), operationalized as either desired or ideal expectations. This is the standard typically used in the service quality literature (Parasuraman, Zeithaml and Berry, 1988).

Though these literatures are different expectation standards, expectations and perceptions in both literatures are usually linked via the disconfirmation of expectations paradigm (Oliver, 1977, 1980). This paradigm holds that the predictions customers make in advance of consumption act as a standard against which customers measure the firm's performance (Bearden and Teel, 1983; Churchill, 1979; Day, 1977; Woodrull, Cadotte and Jenkins, 1983). In the CS/D literature this paradigm states that the higher the expectation in relation to actual performance, the greater the degree of disconfirmation and the lower the satisfaction (Bearden and Teel, 1983; Latour and Peat, 1979; Swan and Trawick, 1981; Tse and Wilton, 1988). Expectations also play a contrast, or disconfirming, role in the gaps model of service quality (Parasuraman, Zeithaml and Berry, 1985). In this model the consumer's perception of overall service quality results from a comparison between expectations and perceptions of the different components of service. With perceptions of service held fixed, the higher the expectations, the lower the perceived quality.

Our model also includes expectations and perceptions. However, it differs from the disconfirmation formulation in that we postulate that individuals' overall quality assessments, and thus behaviors, are affected only by their current perceptions of the service, and not their current expectations. These current perceptions, in turn, are the result of customers' two types of prior expectations of the service and the most recent service encounter.

In developing our conceptualization, we organize our discussion around three processes: (1) the process by which customers form and update their expectations,

(2) the process by which customers develop perceptions of the quality of specific aspects of the service delivery system as well as an overall assessment of the firm's service quality, and (3) the relationship between perceptions of overall service quality and intended behaviors. After describing each of these processes, we provide a summary of the model and its testable implications.

The process that generates expectations

Customer expectations are pretrial beliefs about a product or service (Olson and Dover, 1979). In the absence of any information, prior expectations of service will be completely diffuse. In reality, however, customers have many sources of information that lead to expectations about upcoming service encounters with a particular company. These sources include prior exposure to the service, word or mouth, expert opinion, publicity, and communications controlled by the company (e.g. advertising, personal selling, and price), as well as prior exposure to competitive services (Zeithaml, Berry and Parasuraman, 1991).

Following the example of recent work suggesting the importance of multiple expectation standards, we postulate two different classes of expectations. Consistent with the expectations-as-predictions standard often used in the CS/D literature, we propose that customers form expectations about what *will* happen in their next service encounter with a firm. We refer to these expectations as *will* expectations. We also propose that customers form expectations about what *should* happen in their next service encounter, that is, the service customers feel they appropriately deserve. This normative expectation, here-after referred to as a *should* expectation, is close in spirit to the 'what ought to happen' expectation proposed by Tse and Wilton (1988). We distinguish this *should* standard from the ideal, or desired, standard frequently used in the service quality literature (Zeithaml, Berry and Parasuraman, 1991). What customers think *should* happen may change as a result of what they have been told to expect by the service provider, as well as what the consumer views as reasonable and feasible on the basis of being told of a competitor's service or experiencing the firm's or the competitor's service. In contrast, the consumer's *ideal* expectation – what a consumer wants in an ideal sense – may be unrelated to what is reasonable/feasible and/or what the service provider tells the customer to expect. Moreover, because *ideal* expectations represent enduring wants and needs that remain unaffected by the full range of marketing and competitive factors postulated to affect the *should* expectation, we believe *ideal* expectations are much more stable over time than consumer expectations of what should occur.

We start our discussion by noting that expectations and perceptions can change over time. Also, as becomes clearer subsequently, we acknowledge that there are J unique dimensions of service quality for each of these constructs. Finally, we note that our approach is to first specify general functional relationships for the process that generates these expectations and perceptions. After testing these general relationships, we specify and test explicit functional forms. These explicit equations enable us to gain additional insights into the process as well as develop an approach for estimating the parameters of our model with cross-sectional data.

More formally, let WE_{ijt} be consumer i's *will* expectation for the jth dimension of a service just after experiencing a service contact at time t; DS^*_{ijt} be the jth component of the service delivered to person i at time t (as captured by factors such as the number of thank you's, the waiting time, etc., and where the * notation indicates a transaction-specific construct as opposed to a cumulative construct); and $\mathbf{X}_{it}$ be a vector of information variables other than the service contact influencing the person's *will* expectations of the service prior to a new service contact. We acknowledge that a person's *will* expectations just before a new service contact can differ from the expectations held just after the prior service contact because of the information $\mathbf{X}_{it}$ that enters the system between service encounters. However, in our subsequent empirical work we do not measure such information. Consequently, our approach is to control, but not explicitly model or test, for effects of external information.[2]

We hypothesize that a consumer's expectations of what will happen in subsequent contacts with the firm's service delivery system depend not only on the information obtained from the most recent service contact, but also on the expectations held just prior to the service contact. Such a formulation explicitly acknowledges that two different individuals may hold different expectations about future service contacts even when they experience an identical (in an objective sense) service encounter. This is equivalent to saying that biases are present and that these biases are due to prior expectations.

More formally, we specify the following functional relationship:

$$WE_{ijt} = f_1(WE_{ijt-1}, \mathbf{X}_{it}, DS^*_{ijt}). \qquad (1)$$

Note that equation (1) assumes expectations are influenced by the actual encounter (DS^*_{ijt} in our notation) versus the consumer's perception of the actual encounter. We acknowledge that the consumer's perceptions of the *particular* service encounter may, in fact, be used to update expectations. However, if we denote this perception as $PS^*_{ijt} = g(DS^*_{ijt})$, but also that DS^*_{ijt} is a very good proxy for PS^*_{ijt}, that is, there is a strong positive relationship between the two constructs. Because our empirical work has no direct measure of PS^*_{ijt}, we integrate out this unobserved variable, which leads us to use DS^*_{ijt} instead of PS^*_{ijt} in specifying the functional relationship given by equation (1).

In making predictions about the effects of delivered service and prior expectations on a consumer's updated expectations, we believe a Bayesian-like updating process occurs. Specifically, customers have an expectation just prior to the service contact (WE_{ijt-1}), experience a new service contact (DS^*_{ijt}), and develop a posterior prediction of future service (WE_{ijt}). Because customers are *integrating* information, this process implies that both prior information and new information will be positively related to the updated prediction. This logic leads to our first two hypotheses.[3]

H_1: $\partial f_1/\partial WE_{ijt-1} > 0$.
H_1: $\partial f_1/\partial DS^*_{ijt} > 0$.

We believe *should* expectations are influenced from three sources. Similar to *will* expectations, the customer's new *should* expectations (SE_{ijt}) will be related to the

[2]For a more explicit statement of how these **X** variables might influence expectations: see Boulding *et al.* (1992).

[3]All stated hypotheses are based on the assumption of 'all else equal'.

customer's prior *should* expectation (SE_{ijt-1}). Second, the *should* expectation may differ between time t and $t-1$ because of new information reaching the customer between service contacts, such as changes in price, firm communications, and competitive service delivery. We denote this new information as $\mathbf{Z}_{it}$. Third, experiences with the firm's own delivery system can lead to increases, but never decreases, in the customer's *should* expectations between time t and $t-1$.

An example of the influence of new information is when a firm raises its price and the customers shift their *should* expectations upward to reflect their belief that the service should be better than it was before the price increase. Similarly, if a firm announces that it plans to increase service over previous levels, customers may believe the firm should deliver on this promise. Also, if customers are exposed to a firm's competitor who delivers unanticipated higher levels of service, the customers may believe the firm should deliver similarly high levels of service. For example, Lexus's recent policy of replacing the car when a consumer expresses displeasure with the paint job might alter the consumers' *should* expectations level for other car manufacturers.

We believe that the delivered service influence *should* expectations only when the firm's own service delivery exceeds the individual's prior *should* expectations. Specifically, we postulate that the more the firm's actual delivered service exceeds the customer's prior *should* expectations, the more the customer will increase his or her future *should* expectations for that firm. Thus, in our Lexus example, we would postulate that if the policy of replacing the car exceeds the customer's prior *should* expectations, the customer's *should* expectations for Lexus will increase.

We state these beliefs more formally with the following functional relationship.

$$SE_{ijt} = f_2(SE_{ijt-1}, \mathbf{Z}_{it}, K_{ijt} \cdot DS^*_{ijt}), \qquad (2)$$

where $K_{ijt} = 1$ when $DS^*_{ijt} > SE_{ijt-1}$, 0 otherwise. As before, we do not model the $\mathbf{Z}$ vector in any more depth because we control for, but do not measure, these factors.

More specifically, we expect SE_{ijt} to relate directly to SE_{ijt-1}, modified by $K_{ijt} \cdot DS^*_{ijt}$. This leads to our next two hypotheses.

H_3: $\partial f_2 / \partial SE_{ijt-1} > 0$.
H_4: $\partial f_2 / \partial K_{ijt} \cdot DS^*_{ijt} > 0$.

Equations (1) and (2) make explicit that the two types of expectations are different (albeit related) constructs, and that it should be possible to manipulate one or the other of these expectations via the **X** and **Z** vectors and different service encounters. We say more on this point in discussing our laboratory study.

Finally, we do not explicitly specify a process that generates *ideal* expectations for two reasons. First, as previously noted, *ideal* expectations are generally unchanged over time; therefore, the *ideal* expectation at time t equals the *ideal* expectation at time $t-1$. Second, we conjecture that *ideal* expectations influence *should* expectations. The **Z** vector in equation (2) could easily include information about an individual's *ideal* expectation.

The process that generates perceptions

We next explicate our conceptualization of how customers form perceptions of the service quality of a firm.[4] This formulation differs from the disconfirmation formulation most often found in the CS/D literature (Oliver, 1980) and the gap formulation found in the service quality literature (Parasuraman, Zeithaml and Berry, 1985). However, we show that the implications from our service quality model are compatible with the transaction-specific definition of satisfaction found in the CS/D literature. In addition, we test the viability of our model in relation to the gaps model. In these ways, our model begins to integrate the service quality and satisfaction literatures.

In our model, a person's perception of each of the J dimensions of service quality is conceptualized as a *cumulative* construct, denoted by PS_{ijt} that is updated each time the person is exposed to the service. We postulate that these perceptions are influenced by a person's expectations of the service as well as the most recent service encounter. We thus explicitly allow for a person to have a perceptual bias, as our model implies that two customers experiencing an identical service encounter will have different cumulative perceptions of the service if they enter the encounter with different expectations.

Stated more formally, individual i's cumulative perceptions of the jth dimension of service quality held at time t will be a blend of three factors: the person's expectations just prior to the encounter of what will happen and what should happen, and the new service encounter. The general function relationship is

$$PS_{ijt} = f_3(WE_{ijt-1}, \mathbf{X}_{it}, SE_{ijt-1}, \mathbf{Z}_{it}, DS^*_{ijt}), \tag{3}$$

where $\mathbf{X}_{it}$ and $\mathbf{Z}_{it}$ are vectors that capture adjustments to expectations occurring between service encounters, as defined in equation (1) and (2).

We believe a person's expectations color the way he or she perceives reality. Specifically, we postulate that customers have higher expectations of what the firm *will* deliver have higher perceptions of the service after an encounter, all else equal, than those with lower *will* expectations. Conversely, customers with higher expectations of what a firm *should* deliver have lower perceptions of the service after an encounter, all else equal, than those lower *should* expectations. Finally, we believe the delivered service positively affects perceptions. These statements give rise to the following testable hypotheses.

H_5: $\partial f_3/\partial WE_{ijt-1} > 0$.
H_6: $\partial f_3/\partial SE_{ijt-1} < 0$.
H_7: $\partial f_3/\partial DS^*_{ijt} > 0$.

H_5 and H_7 are based on similar logic. We believe customers average/integrate past experience with the firm which is summarized by their prior *will* expectations) and their latest service encounters in making a cumulative assessment of the service quality level of the firm. This notion leads to our hypothesizing the positive influences. We note that the role of *will* expectations is very similar to the role of the 'initial impression' in averaging models of attitude. In these attitude models, initial impressions always have a positive (assimilative) influence.

As distinguished from the assimilative role of the *will* expectations, the *should*

[4]Keep in mind that these perceptions are *not* the perceptions of a specific service encounter, but instead the perceptions of the service quality based on the consumer's cumulative experience with the firm's service delivery system.

expectation acts as a standard of comparison in relation to competitors. As the standard set by competitors goes up, all else equal, the firm fares less well in how it is perceived by customers. Placing our models within the context of assimilation–contrast attitude theory, we are stating that the *should* expectation provides a negative (contrast) influence on overall attitude (perceptions of quality).

Dimensions of service quality

A central construct in our model is the customer's perception of overall service quality for a firm. Recent research suggests that this quality assessment is not unidimensional, but instead comprises multiple abstract dimensions (Garvin, 1987; Hjorth-Anderson, 1984; Holbrook and Corfman, 1985; Maynes, 1976; Parasuraman, Zeithaml and Berry, 1985; Zeithaml, 1988). After studying four consumer service industries, Parasuraman, Zeithaml and Berry (1985, 1988) identified five dimensions: reliability, assurance, responsiveness, empathy and tangibles.

We make the assumption that customers perceive the service quality of a system in terms of these five dimensions, and also that their expectations of what *will* and *should* happen are in terms of these five dimensions. We incorporate the multidimensional aspect of overall service quality by defining the following relationship:

$$OSQ_{it} = f_4(PS_{ijt}), \tag{4}$$

where OSQ_{it} equals individual *i*'s overall perception of the firm's service quality at time *t*, and the *j* subscript on *PS* corresponds to the *j*th dimension of the service enumerated by Parasuraman and his co-authors. Note that we postulate that the perceptions of the *J* different dimensions of the service, and not the 'actual' service, directly affect the person's assessment of the overall service quality of a firm. In this way we again acknowledge that perceptual biases are present and that perceptions of reality, not 'reality' itself, affect overall attitudes and subsequent behavior.

Previous empirical work suggests that these dimensions of service all have a positive, albeit perhaps unequal, impact on overall quality perceptions. In a variety of different service businesses and industries, respondents consistently rated the dimensions of reliability as most important (Parasuraman, Berry and Zeithaml, 1990; Zeithaml, Berry and Parasuraman, 1991). Consistent with previous findings, we believe that though quality is multidimensional, reliability is the key dimension in determining overall perceptions of service quality.

Hence, we hypothesize that the different dimensions of quality are averaged together in some fashion to produce an overall assessment of quality. Further, by substituting equation (3) into equation (4), we can propose hypotheses about the role of the two different expectations and delivered service in customers' judgments of overall quality. Specifically, because the expected signs on PS_{ijt} in equation (4) are positive, we should serve the same direction of effects for the expectation and delivered service constructs as in equation (3). Consequently, we propose the following testable hypotheses.

H_8: $\partial f_4/\partial WE_{ijt-1} > 0$.
H_9: $\partial f_4/\partial SE_{ijt-1} < 0$.
H_{10}: $\partial f_4/\partial DS^*_{ijt} > 0$.

The relationship between overall quality and behavioral intentions

Delivery of high service quality is presumed to relate positively to the success of the firm. Interestingly, no empirical research outside a laboratory setting has been reported that supports this relationship between service quality perceptions and behavioral outcomes of importance to the firm.[5] Unless this positive relationship exists, understanding how customers form judgments about service quality has limited managerial relevance.

We propose the following function to capture this relationship.

$$BI_{imt} = f_5(OSQ_{it}), \tag{5}$$

where BI_{imt} equals the mth behavioral intention (i.e. loyalty, word of mouth, etc.) for individual i at time t. We strongly believe that service quality positively affects important behavioral outcomes such as loyalty and positive word of mouth. Furthermore, we can substitute through from equations (3) and (4) to examine the indirect effects of expectations and delivered service on behavioral intentions. Because the predicted effect of overall quality in equation (5) is positive, we should observe the same predicted effects of expectations and delivered service as given for equations (3) and (4).

H_{11}: $\partial f_5/\partial WE_{ijt-1} > 0$.
H_{12}: $\partial f_5/\partial SE_{ijt-1} < 0$.
H_{13}: $\partial f_5/\partial DS^*_{ijt} > 0$.

Summary

We present our full conceptual model in Figure 1, which summarizes the proposed relationships among the types of expectations, service quality perceptions, overall perceived service quality, and behavioral intentions. Individuals enter into each service transaction with an initial set of expectations about what *will* and *should* occur on each of the dimensions of service. These initial expectations and the actual delivered service then lead to cumulative perceptions of the delivered service on each dimension, as well as updated expectations for each dimension of what *will* and *should* occur in future transactions. Finally, perceptions of the dimensions of service contribute to an overall assessment of the level of service quality, which in turn leads to behavioral outcomes.

EMPIRICAL TESTING

We now turn to empirical testing in our conceptual model. We begin with an experimental study in which we manipulate the constructs delivered service, *will* expectations, and *should* expectations. We analyze the data in two stages. First, using

[5]In the area of customer satisfaction, a recent individual-level study found a significant and positive effect of satisfaction on customer retention (Anderson and Sullivan, 1990).

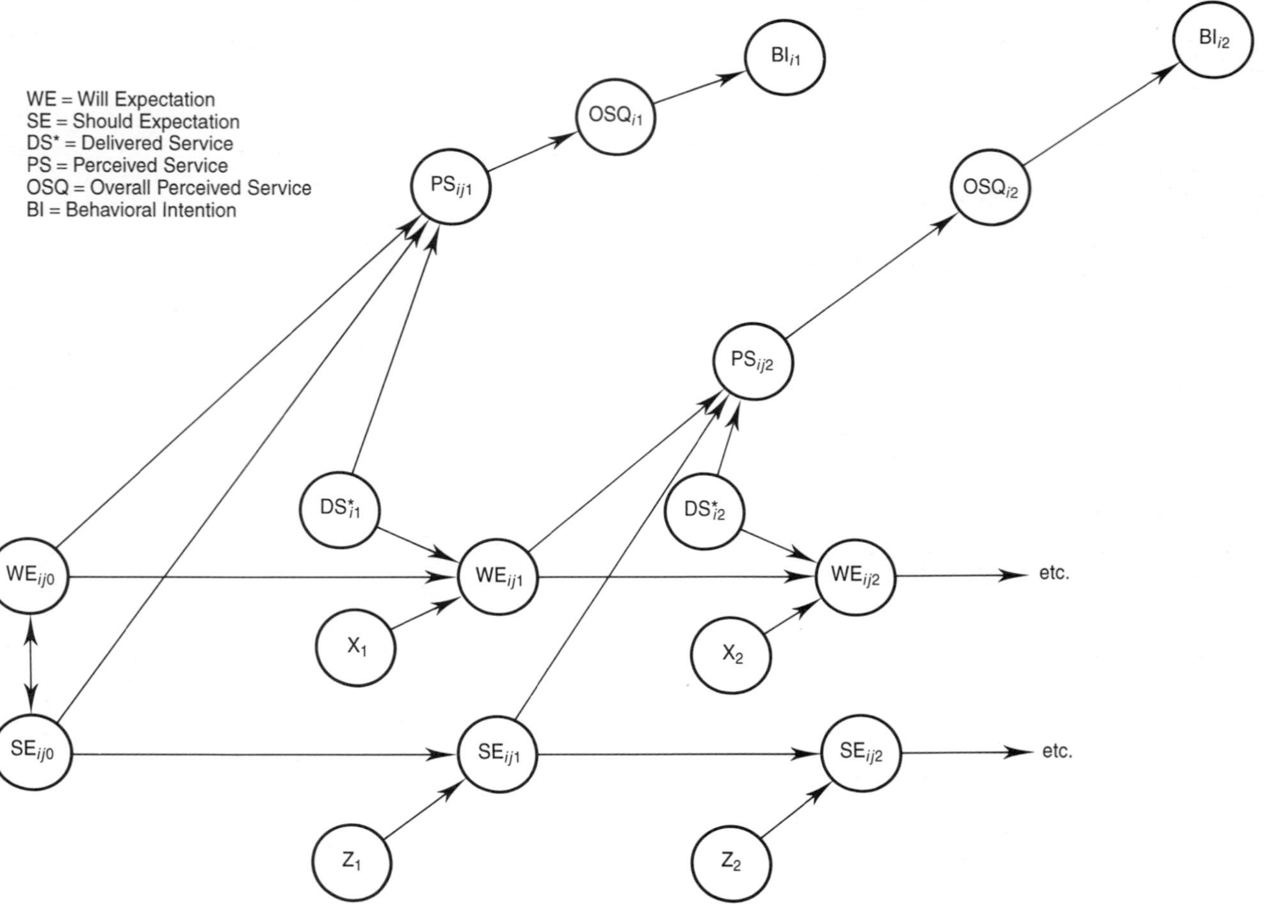

Figure 1. A dynamic process model of service quality.

standard experimental analysis, we use the data to directly test the hypotheses relating to these constructs that emerge from the five functional relationships specified previously. Second, given favorable outcomes of these tests, we specify explicit functional forms for equations (1) through (5). We than estimate this system of equations in a way that enables us to directly test the underlying process suggested by Figure 1. Importantly, this procedure also enables us to directly *test the specification of our explicit functional forms.*

As this specification test provides support for our structural model specification, we next take advantage of this information to develop a method for estimating our dynamic model with data taken at a single point in time. We than apply this approach to data collected in a second study. This second study serves three purposes. First, it increases confidence in the generalizability of our findings because a different data collection approach (a natural field setting), a different service, and a different analytic approach are used. Second, it enables us to test certain relationships that are not explored in study 1. Third, it provides an important insight into how managers can easily and effectively collect data to assess service quality.

STUDY 1

Sample and data

To test the conceptual model in Figure 1, we first used data obtained from a laboratory experiment involving two simulated visits to a hotel. Subjects were 107 business professionals, including managers and staff, located in a major metropolitan area. Eleven subjects' questionnaires were unusable because of missing data. These subjects were dropped, resulting in a sample size of 96.

Procedure

Subjects participated individually in the experiment and were assigned randomly to one of eight conditions. They were told that the purpose of the task was to find out how they evaluate hotels. A self-administered computer diskette was provided, along with instructions to start the program. Subjects were asked to assume they were to stay at a hotel during a business trip. They were then provided an overview of the task and an explanation of the stimuli. After evaluating a hypothetical restaurant to familiarize themselves with the keyboard and the task, they began and actual task.

Both *should* and *will* expectations were manipulated by providing subjects information about (1) others' perceptions of the quality of target hotel 'Alpha' they were to visit and (2) the level of service provided and the price offered by a competitor hotel. Subjects were asked to indicate the quality of hotel service they expected to receive and the quality they though they should receive. They then 'visited' the hotel. After reading a brief general description of their stay, subjects viewed information about the specific performance rating of six features provided by the hotel. Measures of quality assessment were obtained at this point, followed by two behavioral intention measures, and then measures of current *will* and *should* expectations of the level of service.

Subjects were informed they were to stay at the same hotel a second time and were provided information about this second service encounter. Measures of overall quality assessment and the two behavioral intentions and expectations measures were obtained again after this 'visit'.

Design

We used a three-factor between-subjects design. The factors were initial *will* expectations (three levels: low, medium, and high), *should* expectations (two levels: medium and high), and delivered service (two levels: low and high). Because prior research (Kalra, 1992) had indicated difficulty in manipulating *will* expectations to exceed *should* expectations, we focused our attention on obtaining data for only four of the six possible *will–should* pairs (medium *will*/high *should*; medium *will*/medium *should*; high *will*/high *should*; and low *will*/medium *should*). These four conditions were fully crossed with the two levels of service, yielding eight cells. Though incomplete, this design provides unconfounded contrasts for testing our stated hypotheses (e.g. low *will*/medium *should* vs. medium *will*/medium *should* provides and unconfounded contrast for testing effects of prior *will* expectations). Also, though subjects paid two 'visits' to a hotel, we do not use the information relating to the second 'visit' in our initial experimental analysis because the first visit affects customers' expectations, thereby negating our ability to conduct planned contrasts for the data related to the second visit. However, we do use this information to test further qualitative implications of the model when we estimate the structural system of equations.

Manipulations

Should and will expectations

On the basis of theory and results of prior experiment (Kalra, 1992), we determined that we could manipulate *should* and *will* expectations by providing information on (1) prior exposure to a competitor's service (which we provided via information on price and rated service of a competitor) and (2) price, word of mouth, and expert opinion on the object hotel (Hotel Alpha). This manipulation was done via a paragraph describing information on the subject's prior visit to a nearby competitive hotel and others' views on Hotel Alpha. Each description held fixed the Hotel Alpha price. As is seen in the discussion on the manipulation checks, this approach resulted in the four desired *will–should* combinations. For more details on these manipulations, see Boulding *et al.* (1992).

Delivered service

Half of the subjects first received comparatively high performance ratings on the six features provided in their hotel visits, and then comparatively low performance ratings in the second visit. The order was reversed for the other half of the subjects.

As we show subsequently, high performance is approximately equivalent to an 80 on our measurement scale and low performance is approximately equivalent to a 50.

Stimuli

Hotels were used as the service settings for two reasons. First, subjects were familiar with the product category. Second, hotels are typically characterized by variability in the quality of service provided during different encounters. The stimuli consisted of a constant neutral description of the stay and manipulated information about performance ratings on six features of the hotel. The features, selected on the basis of a pilot study, were noise, checkin/checkout, amenities, hotel staff, cleanliness, and bed comfort. The subjects were asked to assume that the ratings reflected their own opinions of the features associated with the hotel. Subjects could only view the ratings of the feature one at a time. They were free to examine the stimuli as long as they wanted and in any sequence. The performance ratings were displayed in the form of a bar graph anchored between 'poor' and 'excellent'.

Measures[6]

Quality assessments

Quality assessments were measured on a 100-point scale. Subjects were asked to 'describe your opinion on the overall quality of Hotel Alpha', which was anchored by the labels 'very unfavorable' and 'very favorable'. The quality assessment were obtained after both the first and second visits. Further, the question was framed so as to obtain measures of overall quality rather than satisfaction/dissatisfaction with a specific visit.

Behavioral intentions

Two questions were asked after each visit about the subject's willingness to provide favorable word of mouth and repeat business. These questions were 'How likely are you to stay again a Hotel Alpha?' and 'How likely are you to recommend Hotel Alpha to a friend?' Both questions were anchored between 'very unlikely' and 'very likely'. For purposes of analysis, we combine these two questions to form behavioral intentions scale (equally weighted). This item scale yields a Cronbach alpha value of .92.

Expectations

Will expectations associated with overall service were measured by the question 'What is your opinion on the level of service Hotel Alpha will actually provide you?' *Should* expectations were measured by the question 'What is your opinion on the

---

[6]The measures in this first experiment are at the overall service level instead of the jth dimension level. This is mathematically equivalent to assuming $J = 1$. Given the 'limited' exposure to the service, we found subjects were more comfortable with this more macro level of service quality.

level of service you would consider to be reasonable, or Hotel Alpha should provide?' Both questions were framed in terms of future expectations, anchored on one end by 'poor service' and on the other 'excellent service', and measured on a 100-point scale.

The same order of questions was used in all conditions, which leads to the following sequence of measures for each customer: at $t = 0$, the customer's *will* and *should* expectations; at $t = 1$ and $t = 2$, the delivered service (i.e., high or low), the customer's perceptions of the quality of the service at the hotel, his or her behavioral intentions, and updated *will* and *should* expectations.

Empirical analysis: stage 1

Expectation manipulation checks

Table 1 presents cell means for our different measures. The cell means from $t = 0$ for the *will* and *should* expectations enable us to test the effectiveness of our expectation manipulations. Because the delivered service manipulation occurs after the measures taken at $t = 0$, we can collapse the data across the two levels of delivered service. Thus, in the following discussion we combine cells 1 and 5, 2 and 6, 3 and 7, and 4 and 8.

As evidence of the success of our manipulations, the *will* expectation means are higher in cells 2 and 6 than in cells 4 and 8 ($t_{92} = 7.56$) and higher in cells 3 and 7 than in cells 1 and 5 ($t_{92} = 10.37$). As evidence of discriminant validity, the *should* expectations for cells 2 and 6 do not differ from those for cells 4 and 8 ($t_{92} = .65$),

Table 1. Study 1 cells means[a]

Manipulations			Means of will expectations		Means of should expectations		Means of perceived service quality	Means of behavioral intention index
Expectations will/should	Service delivered $t = 1$	Cell	$t = 0$	$t = 1$	$t = 0$	$t = 1$	$t = 1$	$t = 1$
Med/high	High	1	50.50 (3.69)	64.30 (8.85)	89.70 (8.72)	91.20 (7.42)	62.70 (7.99)	61.55 (15.71)
Med/med	High	2	51.36 (10.97)	70.00 (11.18)	61.36 (11.42)	77.27 (12.91)	72.27 (10.33)	70.68 (15.12)
High/high	High	3	84.00 (7.15)	77.42 (7.26)	84.58 (10.54)	84.58 (10.10)	76.16 (8.59)	74.45 (8.95)
Low/med	High	4	28.75 (18.75)	63.44 (9.07)	61.87 (20.48)	68.43 (18.41)	65.31 (12.58)	63.75 (10.91)
Med/high	Low	5	54.61 (12.65)	53.46 (16.88)	86.54 (5.56)	83.46 (12.14)	52.69 (17.27)	45.15 (18.05)
Med/med	Low	6	50.83 (4.88)	59.16 (10.83)	63.75 (14.94)	63.75 (14.32)	55.00 (12.43)	55.21 (20.35)
High/high	Low	7	87.08 (7.52)	65.41 (10.54)	91.25 (8.01)	86.25 (13.16)	66.67 (9.37)	61.87 (10.45)
Low/med	Low	8	26.00 (9.07)	39.00 (11.50)	57.50 (14.95)	66.00 (14.10)	48.00 (11.83)	37.50 (14.67)

[a] Standard deviations are in parentheses.

nor do cells 1 and 5 differ from cells 3 and 7 (t_{92} = .00). Similarly, for the *should* expectation we note the means are higher in cells 1 and 5 than in cells 2 and 6 (t_{92} = 6.61). As further evidence of discriminant validity, the *will* expectation for cells 1 and 5 do not differ from those for cells 2 and 6 (t_{92} = .55). Consequently, we conclude that (1) we were successful in manipulating initial *will* and *should* expectations into the four desired cells, (2) were were able to identify antecedents to each expectation, and (3) the two different expectations are in fact separate constructs.

Results

Table 1 also gives cell means at $t = 1$ for the two expectations measures, as well as for the measures of overall quality and the behavioral intentions index. A series of cell contrasts enable us to test the qualitative hypotheses generated from the five specified functional relationships.[7] Table 2 indicates the relevant cell contrast that hold 'all else equal' for tests of our hypotheses, as well as the test results. As a check on our specified equations, this table also includes tests of significance for relationships not included in the equations.

Because the specified functional relationships do not contain interaction terms (with the exception of the *should* expectation equation), we first conduct joint tests of significance for all interaction terms estimable from our experimental design for equations (1), (3), and (5). We find no joint interaction effects in any of these three equations reaching significance at the .10 level.[8] Therefore, for these equations, we restrict our attention to testing for main effects.

Starting with the *will* expectations updating equation, Table 2 indicates strong support for our two main effects hypotheses. Results of the cell contrast suggest that prior *will* expectations and the delivered service both contribute positively and significantly to the updated *will* expectations, supporting H_1 and H_2. We also find marginal significance (p = .10) for the effect of prior *should* expectations in the *will* expectation equation. Because we do not hypothesize this relationship, we explore it in greater depth in the stage 2 analysis of our experimental data.

Turning to the *should* expectation updating equation, we note that the prior *should* expectation significantly and positively affects the updated *should* expectation (H_3). Consistent with our specification of equation 2, we find no main effect of delivered service, nor do we find an effect or prior *will* expectations. In addition, looking at differences in values between $t = 0$ and $t = 1$, we find significant support for H_4, that is, delivered service increases *should* expectations, but only if the delivered service exceeds the prior *should* expectation. This occurred only in cells 2 and 4, where the delivered service was high (approximately 80) and the prior *should* expectations were medium (approximately 60).

---

[7]As noted in footnote 6, in the context of this experiment we assume a single dimension of quality. We therefore cannot distinguish between the constructs 'perceptions' (*PS*) and 'overall quality' (*OSQ*) as laid out in equations (3) and (4). Thus, equation (3) and H_5–H_7 are redundant with equation (4) and H_8–H_{10}. In study 2 we generate separate estimates of equations (3) and (4).

[8]In the *will* expectation equation, $F_{3,88}$ = 2.14; in the perceived service equation $F_{3,88}$ = 0.80; and in the behavioral intentions equation, $F_{3,88}$ = 1.02.

Table 2. Hypothesis test results[a]

Hypothesis[b]	Dependent measure	Factor	Cell contrast	t-statistic[c]
H_1	WE_t	WE_{t-1}	1,5 vs. 3,7	4.08*
H_1	WE_t	WE_{t-1}	2,6 vs. 4,8	3.24*
H_2	WE_t	DS_t^*	1,2,3,5 vs. 5,6,7,8	5.99*
NH	WE_t	SE_{t-1}	1,5 vs. 2,6	1.88***
H_3	SE_t	SE_{t-1}	1,5 vs. 2,6	4.17*
NH	SE_t	WE_{t-1}	1,5 vs. 3,7	.36
NH	SE_t	WE_{t-1}	2,6 vs. 4,8	.70
NH	SE_t	DS_t^*	1,2,3,4 vs. 5,6,7,8[d]	1.30
H_4	$SE_t - SE_{t-1}$	$K_t DS_t^*$	2,4 vs. 1,3,5,6,7,8	3.39*
H_5	PS_t	WE_{t-1}	1,5 vs. 3,7	4.16*
H_5	PS_t	WE_{t-1}	2,6 vs. 4,8	1.36***
H_6	PS_t	SE_{t-1}	1,5 vs. 2,6	1.78**
H_7	PS_t	DS_t^*	1,2,3,4 vs. 5,6,7,8	5.44*
H_{11}	BI_t	WE_{t-1}	1,5 vs. 3,7	4.26*
H_{11}	BI_t	WE_{t-1}	2,6 vs. 4,8	2.14**
H_{12}	BI_t	SE_{t-1}	1,5 vs. 2,6	2.92*
H_{13}	BI_t	DS_t^*	1,2,3,4 vs. 5,6,7,8	6.11*

[a] Given directional hypotheses, significance tests are one-tailed. For nonhypothesized relationships, significance tests are two-tailed.
[b] NH indicates not hypothesized.
[c] Calculated t-statistics are based on 88 degrees of freedom.
[d] This is a very conservative test. A less conservative test would contrast cells 1,3 vs. 5,7.
*Significant at the .01 level.
**Significant at the .05 level.
***Significant at the .10 level.

Table 2 also indicates strong support for the three main effects hypotheses relating to our perceived service equation (assuming a single dimension of quality). In support of H_5, prior *will* expectations positively and significantly influence cumulative assessments of perceived service. In support of H_6, prior *should* expectations negatively and significantly affect perceived service. Also, as predicted by H_7, delivered service positively and significantly contributes to perceptions of service quality.

Finally, it is interesting to see whether our manipulations affect the downstream behavioral intentions measures. Table 2 again provides support for all of our stated main effects hypotheses. As suggested by H_{11} and H_{12} prior *will* expectations positively and significantly influence behavioral intentions, whereas prior *should* expectations negatively and significantly influence behavioral intentions. As one would expect, and as stated by H_{13}, delivered service positively and significantly influences behavioral intentions.

In summary, our experimental data provide strong support for all of our hypothesized relationships given by equations (1) through (5) and all but one of the implicit null hypotheses. We highlight three conclusions from these analyses. First, we demonstrate conclusively that *will* and *should* expectations are different constructs. Second, we confirm that *will* expectations positively influence and *should* expectations negatively influence perceptions of quality. Third, holding fixed the delivered service, one can trace a measurable effect of two different expectations on individuals' behavioral intentions.

The preceding univariate contrasts take full advantage of the experimental design aspect of our data. Further, such contrasts require no assumptions about the specific functional forms of equations (1) through (5). A drawback of this approach, however, is that it does not allow us to estimate the magnitude of the effects. It also does not allow us to specify and test any cross-equation implications of our process model as given in Figure 1, or use the period 2 data for estimation. To accomplish these latter objectives, we must make specific assumptions about the functional forms of equations (1) through (5). However, we can directly test those assumptions. As long as these assumed functional forms are costless (i.e. they are not rejected by specification tests), we favor this approach because it yields the benefit of additional specificity.

Empirical analysis: stage 2

Specification of functional forms

In specifying our process model, we focus our attention on the functional relationships for our measured constructs, *WE*, *SE*, *PS* and *BI*. We do not specify the role of 'other' information (i.e. the **X** and **Z** vectors) in this process, because in our studies we control for (but never measure) 'other' information.[9] Consequently, we leave this part of our conceptualization to future research.

With the preceding caveat in mind, we now fully specify equation (1) (we distinguish the fully specified equation by 'S':

$$WE_{ijt} = \alpha_{jt} WE_{ijt-1} + (1 - \alpha_{jt}) DS^*_{ijt} + \epsilon_{1it} \tag{1S}$$

where the parameters α_{ij} (which can assume values between 0 and 1) determines the relative weights assigned to the prior expectation and the delivered service in the updating equation, and ϵ_{1it} is an error term. This specification make equation (1S) consistent with our conceptualization of *will* expectations being updated by means of an averaging process.

We note two testable implications of this specification. First, one can test the validity of the averaging model by comparing the estimates of equation (1S), which contains a single constrained parameter, with an additive model, which would contain two unconstrained parameters. Second, there is a qualitative implication as to the value of α_{jt} over time. Specifically, as an individual accumulates more information about a service on the basis of past experience, the influence of WE_{ijt-1}, which captures this past experience, should receive more weight in relation to the most recent service encounter in generating future predictions about the service. Consequently, α_{jt} should grow larger over time.

[9]In study 1, no information is provided between our measurement of WE_{t-1} and the service encounter at time *t*. In study 2, we explicitly control for differences in the informational environment by conducting within-person analysis.

Turning to the *should* expectation updating process, we fully specify equation (2) as

$$SE_{ijt} = SE_{ijt-1} + \beta_{jt}(K_{ijt} \cdot DS^{*}_{ijt}) + \epsilon_{2it}, \tag{2S}$$

where β_{jt} equals an updating parameter postulated to be greater than zero and ϵ_{2it} is an error term. Unlike equation (1S), this updating formulation does *not* follow an averaging process. Instead, we believe *should* expectations follow a ratcheting process – they can go up, but they cannot go beyond prior levels.[10] More specifically, equation (2S) implies that *should* expectations equal old *should* expectations unless the latest delivered service exceeds the prior *should* expectation.

For the perception equation, we make the assumption that customers blend their prior *will* expectations with the latest service experience in a manner identical to that used to form the new *will* expectation. This averaging process is then additively blended with the consumer's *should* expectations. We represent these beliefs mathematically as

$$PS_{ijt} = \alpha_{jt} WE_{ijt-1} + (1 - \alpha_{jt}) DS^{*}_{ijt} + \gamma_{jt} SE_{ijt-1} + \epsilon_{3it}, \tag{3S}$$

where α_{jt} is the same updating parameter as given in equation (1S), γ_{jt} is a new updating parameter with $\gamma_{jt} < 0$, and ϵ_{3it} is an error term. Such a formulation makes explicit the assimilative (averaging) role of prior *will* expectations and the latest delivered service, and the contrastive (adding) role of *should* expectations.[11]

As with equation (1S), we can test the explicit averaging assumption of (3S) by comparing the constrained one-parameter averaging process with an unconstrained two-parameter process. We can also test whether the parameter α_{jt} is the same parameter as given in equation (1S) by comparing an unconstrained estimate of this parameter with one that is constrained to equality across equations (1S) and (3S).

Note that by replacing the first two terms of equation (3S) with the left side of equation (1S), one can see the difference between an individual's current *perception* of the service and his or her current *prediction* of likely service. Specifically, these two constructs differ increasingly as the consumer's prior expectations of what service they *should* get increase. Two implications are that we expect the parameter on the *should* expectation term to be significant in equation (3S), but not to add explanatory power in equation (1S). We test both implications with all of our longitudinal data.

Because our conceptualization of the role of expectations in generating perceptions is new, we use simple examples to reconcile it with previous conceptualizations and demonstrate its intuitive appeal. First, for notational simplicity, assume that there is only one dimension of service quality. Further assume that two individuals have identical expectations of what should happen but, on the basis of prior service, the first individual predicts future service will rate a five and the second individual predicts future service will rate a seven. Given our system of equations, the implication is that individual 2's current perception is higher than individual 1's. Finally, suppose these

---

[10]Conceptually, we believe that information in the **Z** vector could cause these expectations to decrease. For example, a price decrease by the firm or learning about much higher levels of price for competitors could lower *should* expectations.

[11]An alternative theoretical basis for (3S) is that *will* expectations affect the private psychological impression of the service, whereas the *should* expectations affect the output mapping of private psychological impressions onto overt ratings of perceptions (Lynch, Chakravarti and Mitra, 1991).

two individuals simultaneously experience a new service encounter and receive identical delivered service that rates a six. We next explore three questions:

- Which of these two individuals will have higher cumulative perceptions of the quality of the firm's delivery system after the encounter?
- Which will be most satisfied with the most recent encounter?
- How are the perceptions of each individual changing over time?

According to the hypothesized relationships in equations (3S), the second individual will have a higher perception of the service because this individual combines all prior experience with the latest transaction to form a cumulative perception of the service. However, on the basis of a definition of satisfaction associated with the disconfirmation of expectations paradigm (i.e. satisfaction equals performance minus expected performance, or $DS^*_{ijt} - WE_{ijt-1}$ in our notation), the first person will be more satisfied with the most recent service encounter because this person had the lower prior *will* expectation. Finally, given the form of equation 3S, the second individual (who originally had the higher value for overall perceived quality) will show a decrease in his or her cumulative perception of quality because the last service encounter was below his or her predicted level of service. Similarly, the first individual (who had the lower value for overall perceived quality) will show an increase in cumulative perceived quality because his or her last service encounter exceeded his or her predicted level of service. In this way, our model is compatible with the CS/D disconfirmation of expectations paradigm and shows how satisfaction with a specific transaction can lead to an increase in perception of the overall service.

In a similar vein, assume two individuals with identical *will* expectations, but different *should* expectations, receive identical actual service. In this case, our model predicts that the individual with the higher expectation of what the service *should* deliver perceives the service more negatively. One way of thinking of this effect is that some individuals are more critical or demanding than others. Individuals who develop higher expectations of what service *should* occur (perhaps because of firm or competitive actions) are more difficult to please (i.e. they form more negative evaluations) than individuals with lower *should* expectations.

Finally, our model has the pleasing characteristic that improvement in the service delivery system lead to more positive service quality perception.[12] To see this effect, imagine a firm engaged in 'continuous quality improvements', a currently popular business concept. If the *will* expectation itself had a negative effect, and this expectation increased with the increasing service, a firm would have to constantly upgrade its delivered service simply to stay even with the rising expectations. Said differently, despite improved service delivery, there would be no resulting improvements in consumer perceptions of quality. In contrast, our model suggests that firms benefit from increasing consumer expectations of what service will occur. Specifically, if a firm increases expectations of what will occur by improving delivered service, the consumer will perceive a higher quality service than before the service improvements occurred, even if the service plateaus at this higher level.[13]

[12]This is also a characteristic of the conceptual model of Bolton and Drew (1991a).

[13]Technically, if delivered service plateaus, that is, $DS^*_t = DS^*_{t-1}$, our model yields more positive future service quality perceptions if $(1 - \alpha) > (\gamma\beta K)$.

We next specify a simple functional form suggesting that overall perceived quality is a linear combination of perceptions of different dimensions of quality.

$$OSQ_{it} = \sum_{j=1}^{5} \phi_j PS_{ijt} + \epsilon_{4it} \qquad (4S)$$

where the ϕ_j are > 0 and ϵ_{4it}, represents an error term.

Our dynamic formulation as stated by equations (1S) through (4S) differs from the prevailing model of service quality, the gaps model (Parasuraman, Zeithaml and Berry, 1985). We label the gaps model a static formulation because not temporal sequencing is specified. In the static model, overall quality is represented by gap 5, which consists of perceptions minus contemporaneous *should* expectations. Gap 5 is in turn a function of gaps 1 through 4, which contain, among other things, information about actual service. Representing the static model relationship between overall perceived quality and gap 5 in equation form results in the following expression.

$$OSQ_{it} = \sum_{j=1}^{5} \Theta_j (PS_{ijt} - SE_{ijt}) + \epsilon_{6it} \text{ (the gaps model)} \qquad (6)$$

Two points should be noted about equation (6). First, because the gaps model is static, expectations prior to the service contact are assumed implicitly to equal those after the service. Thus, equation (6) is stated in terms of contemporaneous perceptions and expectations. Second, the gaps model implicitly constrains the parameters on perceptions and expectations to negative equality. A more general formulation of equation (6) allows these coefficients to vary, that is,

$$OSQ_{it} = \sum_{j=1}^{5} (\Theta_{1j} PS_{ijt} + \Theta_{2j} SE_{ijt}) + \epsilon_{7it} \qquad (7)$$

(the generalized gaps model)

Note that our dynamic specification, given by equation (4S), is also a special case of equation (7). In particular, our dynamic model formulation implies $\Theta_{1j} > 0$ and $\Theta_{2j} = 0$. In contrast, the gaps model predicts $\Theta_{1j} = -\Theta_{2j}$.

We put forward these alternative specifications of the overall quality equation to highlight our differences with the prevailing model of service quality. Because we do not obtain separate measures of perceptions and overall quality, we cannot test the different specifications by using our study 1 data. However, in study 2 we compare the validity of our formulation represented by equation (4S) with the specification given by equations (6) and (7).

Finally, we specify behavioral intentions as a single linear function of overall quality perceptions.

$$BI_m = \lambda_m OSQ_{it} + \epsilon_{5it} \qquad (5S)$$

where $\lambda_m > 0$ and ϵ_{5it} is an error term.

Empirical model and results

We have three longitudinal measures of the *will* and *should* expectations and two measures each for the perceived service, the actual service delivered, and the behavioral intentions. Therefore, we can estimate our system of equations (i.e. equations (1S), (2S), (3S) and (5S)) at two different time periods. Before doing so, however, we need to relate our obtained measures to the theoretical constructs in our structural model. In particular, we need to calibrate all of our measured constructs onto a common scale. We do this by making the arbitrary, but nonrestrictive, assumption that our measured expectations, denoted by *M* preceding the expectation notation (i.e. *MWE* and *MSE*), establish the metric for our empirical measures. Thus, we scale all of the other measures in relation to the measured expectations variables. We present the details of this scaling calibration in Appendix A.

The scaling calibration enable us to write our structural model in terms of measured variables. The resultant empirical model includes four scaling parameters – *a, b, c* and *d* – in addition to our structural parameters. Substituting equations (A1) through (A3) from Appendix A into equations (1S), (2S), (3S) and (5S) yields the following empirical model.

$$MWE_{it} = (1 - \alpha_t)\,a + \alpha_t MWE_{it-1} + (1 - \alpha_t)\,bMDS_{it}^* + \epsilon_{8it} \quad (8)$$

$$MSE_{it} = \beta_t a K_{it} + MSE_{it-1} + \beta_t BK_{it} \cdot MDS_{it}^* + \epsilon_{9it} \quad (9)$$

$$MPS_{it} = -c + (1 - \alpha_t)\,a + \alpha_t MWE_{it-1} + (1 - \alpha_t)\,bMDS_{it}^* + \gamma_t MSE_{it-1} + \epsilon_{10it} \quad (10)$$

$$MBI_{it} = -d + \lambda_t c + \lambda_t MPS_{it} + \epsilon_{11it} \quad (11)$$

where $t = 1, 2$ for equation (8) through (11), yielding an empirical model composed of eight equations. Two points must be made about these equations. First, the coefficients of this empirical model often confound the structural and scaling parameters. For example, the intercept term in equation (8) is the product of the structural parameter $(1 - \alpha_t)$ and the scaling parameter *a*. Even so, we are unable to obtain at least one direct estimate of each of the structural parameters. Second, unlike the structural model parameters, none of the scaling parameters are time-subscribed because we see no reason to expect our theoretical construct scales to shift over time.

We have three goals in estimating this empirical model. First, we want to test the validity of the complete specification of our process model. Second, we want to confirm our previous qualitative findings by using a second analytic approach and an extended dataset. Finally, we want to extend our insights by examining how the information integration parameters change over time.

We start by addressing the specification issue. We do this by first estimating our empirical model by using OLS, imposing no restrictions across or within equations. Thus, for example, we do not constrain the parameters on MDS_{it}^* in equations (8) and (10) to equal one minus the parameter on MWE_{it-1} (in either equation (8) or equation (10)) times the scaling parameter *b*. Estimation in this manner yields estimates of 22 coefficients. As noted previously, most of the coefficients in equations

(8) through (11) do not provide direct estimates of our structural parameters. However, this procedure does yield two unconfounded estimates each for the structural parameters α_1 and α_2 and one direct estimate each for the structural parameters γ_1, γ_2, β_1, β_2, λ_1, and λ_2. These results, along with the confounded estimates, are reported in Table 3.

We make two observations about the results in Table 3. First, we note that all of the unconstrained, direct estimates of our structural parameters have the predicted direction as well as statistical significance. Second, though we subsequently formally tested for equality, we note that the two independent unconstrained estimates of α_1 and α_2 (i.e. the coefficients on MWE_{t-1} in equations (8) and (10)) are approximately equal. Table 3 indicates that the two estimates of α_1 equal .34 and .38 and the two estimates of α_2 equal .80 and .87.

Table 3. Unrestricted model estimates of equations (8)–(11) for $t = 1$ and $t = 2$[a]

Independent variables	Dependent variables							
	Eq.(8)		Eq.(9)		Eq.(10)		Eq.(11)	
	$MWE_{t=1}$	$MWE_{t=2}$	$MSE_{t=1}$	$MSE_{t=2}$	$MPS_{t=1}$	$MPS_{t=2}$	$BI_{t=1}$	$BI_{t=2}$
Constant	35.79*	.33	.00	.41	47.88*	9.63	−3.41	4.73***
	(3.009)	(6.135)	(1.652)	(.961)	(4.807)	(8.095)	(5.338)	(2.667)
MWE_{t-1}	.34*	.80*			.38*	.87*		
	(.046)	(.086)			(.059)	(.113)		
MDS_t	15.00*	21.13*			14.20*	22.48*		
	(2.170)	(2.559)			(2.211)	(3.000)		
$K^* MDS_t^*$			10.37*	8.69*				
			(3.115)	(2.007)				
MSE_{t-1}			1.00[b]	1.00[b]	−.17**	−.24*		
			(0.0)	(0.0)	(.075)	(.093)		
MPS_t							.99*	.93*
							(.083)	(.046)
R^2	.504	.533	.288	.624	.465	.463	.602	.814

[a] Standard errors are in parentheses.
[b] The dependent measure in this equation equals ($MSE_t - MSE_{t-1}$).
*Significant at the .01 level.
**Significant at the .05 level.
***Significant at the .10 level.

We now formally test the numerous within- and cross-equation constraints, that is, assumptions implied by our conceptual model. An example of a cross-equation constraint is that the coefficient on MWE_{t-1} in equations (8) and (10) should be equal. An example of a within-equation constraint is forcing the three α parameters in equation (8) to equality. We impose these constraint by using SAS's nonlinear search procedure, SYSNLIN. More technically, we estimate only the four parameters (at two different points in time) of theoretical interest, α_1, α_2, γ_1, γ_2, β_1, β_2, λ_1 and λ_2, and the four scaling parameters *a, b, c,* and *d.* This results in reducing a 22-parameter model to a 12-parameter model. Because the constrained model is a subset of the unconstrained model, we can perform a likelihood ratio test based on the sums of squared errors (Amemiya, 1985). This ratio is distributed χ^2 with degrees of freedom equal to the number of imposed restrictions. The test enables us to identify whether our structural model imposes binding constraints, that is, whether we have misspecified the process by which our subjects form perceptions of quality, which in turn leads to behavioral intentions.

We find that the cross- and within-equation constraints are *not* binding. The estimated χ^2 equals 2.46, which is well below the critical χ^2 value for $p = .5$ and 10 degrees of freedom ($\chi^2_{10} = 9.34$).[14] Thus, we come nowhere close to rejecting the underlying assumptions embedded in our process model. Though we recognize that this finding does not mean that we have specified the best possible process model, it does increase our confidence in the robustness of our specification.

Table 4 presents the fully constrained estimates of our structural model. In discussing these estimates, we first note that all of the estimates of the eight structural

Table 4. Restricted model estimates for equations (8)–(11) for $t = 1$ and $t = 2$[a]

Parameter	Estimate
α_1	.38*
	(.035)
α_2	.55*
	(.044)
β_1	.13*
	(.034)
β_2	.12*
	(.023)
γ_1	−.11**
	(.055)
γ_2	−.21*
	(.055)
λ_1	.91*
	(.042)
λ_2	.98*
	(.042)
a	49.18*
	(1.944)
b	29.41*
	(2.941)
c	−9.94**
	(4.226)
d	−11.24**
	(4.545)

[a]Standard errors in parentheses.
*Significant at the .01 level.
**Significant at the .05 level.

[14]Because we want to *accept* the null hypothesis that our structural model does not impose binding constraints, we use a p value of .5 to increase the power of rejecting the null hypothesis.

parameters of theoretical interest are significant and in alignment with our qualitative hypotheses. In addition, because we now obtain estimates of the scaling parameters, we note that on the 100-point expectations scale, 'low' service is estimated to equal 49.2 and 'high' service is estimated to equal 78.6 (i.e. $a = 49.2$ and $b = 29.4$).

For patterns of results over the two periods in the data, we note the increase in α_t from period 1 to 2 (from .38 to .55). This result is compatible with our hypothesis that this parameter will grow over time as customers accrue more prior experience and weight the current experience less in updating their *will* expectations and perceptions of service quality. We also note the doubling in absolute size in γ, the coefficient on the *should* expectation in the perception equation, from period 1 to period 2 (from $-.11$ to $-.21$). Though not hypothesized, this result relates to a specification issue we now address.

In particular, as another check on our specification, we include the prior *should* expectation in the *will* expectation updating equation. When we estimate this equation for time = 1, we find a significant coefficient on the *should* expectation variable, as one would expect given our ANOVA findings. However, at time = 2 this coefficient loses significance ($t_{92} = 1.07$). This result, coupled with the observation that γ_t increased in absolute size from .11 to $-.21$ over the two time periods, leads us to conclude that the strength of the customer's beliefs about what should happen became stronger as customers gained more exposure to the service situation. Consequently, their beliefs about perceptions of quality became more distinct from their beliefs about what will happen. In particular, the *should* expectation loses significance in equation (1S) (where it is hypothesized to have no effect) and becomes more significant in equation (3S) (where it is hypothesized to have a significant negative effect).

Finally, perceptions of quality strongly influence behavioral intentions. Interestingly, the parameter capturing this effect, λ, increases in size from period 1 to period 2 (.91 to .98). Though a marginal increase in size, this result warrants further investigation because it implies that over time perceptions of quality becomes increasingly important in driving behavioral intentions.

Discussion

The results reported in stage 1 and stage 2 of study 1 are very compatible with our postulated process model. We interpret these results as providing strong evidence that a person's prior *will* and *should* expectations, and the delivered service, influence a person's perceptions of quality. Moreover, our results provide strong support for our conceptualization that *will* expectations positively influence perceptions of quality and *should* expectations negatively influence perceptions of quality. These perceptions, in turn, positively influence behavioral intentions.

Perhaps of greater significance is the finding that the numerous within- (e.g. averaging of *will* expectations and delivered service in the *will* expectation updating equation) and cross-equation (e.g. the same terms appearing in the *will* expectation updating equation and the perception equation) restrictions were nonbinding. Rather than assuming we correctly specify these equations, or simply accepting the individual coefficient estimates from these equations as compatible with our conceptualization, we directly test the 'assumptions' (implied restrictions) inherent in our model. Thus, we take the unusual step of simultaneously testing the significance of the structural parameters and subjecting our structural model to a stringent specification test. *Both* of these results strongly support our conceptualization.

Given these results, we next address the generalizability of our model. We do this by presenting the results of a second study in which a very dissimilar research method (a field study) was used to assess customers' perceptions and expectations of a real service.[15] Compatible results with this second approach would provide substantial evidence that our obtained results are not due to some confound (unknown to us) associated with the laboratory experiment.

STUDY 2

Besides providing a vehicle for replicating our previous finding by a very different research approach, study 2 provides two additional sources of value. First, it enables us to estimate equations (4S), (6) and (7), which we could not do in study 1. Second, it provides a setting to explicate a research method that enables firms to track customers' evaluations of service quality, an inherently dynamic process as shown by our model, using data collected from a single point in time. This method is exceptionally valuable in that it enables managers to infer the impact of their delivered service, *without measuring* this construct. Therefore, these explorations should be of great interest to practitioners involved in measuring service quality and cumulative customer satisfaction.

Sample

The data for this study were obtained from a major study of service quality of an educational institution. This study, commissioned by the top management of the institution, was based on 177 obtained responses of the current customers of the institution. Participation by the customers was both voluntary and confidential, resulting in a 46% response rate. Monetary rewards were provided to a small set of participating customers as a result of a lottery drawing.

Operationalization of variables

Expectations and perceptions of the five dimensions of service quality were measured by 36 statements taken from SERVQUAL (Parasuraman, Zeithaml and Berry, 1988) and then modified by top managers and the research team to capture more precisely expectations and perceptions associated with an educational service. Respondents recorded these expectations and perceptions by indicating their agreement with each statement on a 1 to 7 scale. Approximately half of the sample gave expectations data

[15]This 'second' study was actually conducted and analyzed prior to the first (laboratory) study. However, the analysis scheme used for the second study relies on many of the assumptions tested in the laboratory study. Hence, for exposition, we reverse the order of discussion for the two studies.

Table 5. Expectations and perception scale items[a]

Reliability
Professors and teaching assistants will grade fairly and accurately.
Courses will be well taught.
The staff will ensure that the MBA program runs smoothly.
Professors will be organized and prepared for class.
When professors promise to be available during office hours, they will be there to see students.
Professors will have prior teaching experience before coming to this organization.
Cronbach alpha:
Expectations = .74
Perceptions = .73

Empathy items
Professors will give students individual attention.
Professors will help students with personal problems and career advice.
Students will be able to contact a professor at home.
Professors will know what the needs of their students are.
Professors will have their students' best interest at heart.
Cronbach alpha:
Expectations = .69
Perceptions = .74

[a]*Should* expectations substituted the word 'should' for 'will'. Perceptions substituted the word 'are' for 'will'. Also, we report a single Cronbach alpha for expectations because the *will* and *should* contemporaneous expectations differ only by an individual-specific constant.

in the form of what customers thought *should* happen, whereas the other half of the sample gave their predictions of what *will* happen in the education process. Using the original SERVQUAL scales as a guide, and after performing factor analysis in combination with managerial judgment, we grouped the 36 questions to form multiple measures for the five dimensions of service quality (reliability, responsiveness, assurance, empathy, and tangibles). Table 5 provides the scale for two of the five dimensions, along with the Cronbach alpha values for the perception and expectation scales. Boulding *et al.* (1992) report this information for all five dimensions.

The alpha values indicate that the reliability of all our scales equals or exceeds .60 with most exceeding .7. On the basis of this result and prior evidence of Parasuraman, Zeithaml and Berry (1988) that there are five dimensions of service quality, we formed indices by averaging the responses to the individual measures associated with a dimension. These indices are used as summary measures of the five underlying constructs in estimating equations (4S), (6) and (7).

Overall quality of the educational service and six items of intended individual-level behaviors of strategic importance to the school were also measured. The latter measures included such items as saying positive things about the school to people outside the school, planning to contribute money to the class pledge upon graduation, and planning to recommend the school to one's employer as a place to recruit. These six behavioral intention variables were grouped into a single index measure. As evidence that these six items tap the underlying behavioral intentions construct, the Cronbach alpha is equal to .80. Finally, country of origin, gender, degree of prior work experience, first or second year in program, and area of educational concentration were measured to partially control for individual differences in the subsequent analyses. As we have no theoretical interest in these variables, we do not discuss them further, though they are included during estimation as covariates.

Estimation

Our data are similar to most service quality field study data in that they consist of a cross-section of self-reported information taken at one point in time. Consequently, they impose some limitations on direct estimation of the structural equations developed in the preceding section. Specifically, because we measure expectations variables contemporaneously with perceptions variables, we do not have measures of prior expectations.[16] Finally, we do not measure actual delivered service because any measure obtained from the customer immediately become a perception of the service, and because we were unable to match objective organization measures of actual service to the individuals receiving the service. This is a typical problem in any service setting.

Even though our particular data constrain us from directly estimating equations (1S), (2S) and (3S), we show that it is still possible to obtain consistent estimates of the two key parameters in our process model, that is, α_{jt} and γ_{jt}, as well as the parameters in equations (4S), (5S), (6) and (7), simply by using contemporaneous measures of all the relevant constructs. Moreover, these two parameter estimates enable us to perform falsifying tests on our basic structural model, as well as gain insight into the relative influences of prior *will* and *should* expectations *and* the unobserved delivered service on customers' current perceptions of the cumulative level of service quality of the five dimensions of service quality.

More specifically, we derive consistent estimates for α_{ji} and γ_{jt} from reduced-form equations that assume equations (1S), (2S), and (3S) represent the true underlying process. We justify this assumption on the basis of three points. First and foremost, results from our study 1 tests indicate that equations (1S), (2S), and (3S) are an excellent representation of the service quality process. Second, using our study 2 data, we can directly test two implications from our model by looking at the signs and magnitudes of the estimates of the two structural parameters α_{jt} and γ_{jt}. Empirical results inconsistent with hypothesized signs and magnitudes for these coefficients will indicate the nonviability of out postulated structural model. Third, we cannot come up with a plausible alternative structural model that could produce the results generated in our reduced-form modeling approach.

Our approach is to derive reduced-form equations are in terms of only observable contemporaneous variables. We start by specifying one additional nonrestrictive relationship between our two expectation constructions. Note that in a field setting there is normally a strict cross-sectional correlation between SE_{ijt} and WE_{ijt}, even

[16]To test for response biases due to priming with either the *will* or *should* expectations, we obtain measures of either the contemporaneous *will* expectation or the *should* expectation, but never both from the same respondent. As will become evident, this decision to ask for either *will* or *should* expectations, but not both, does not hamper our ability to obtain consistent estimates of α and γ.

though equations (1S) and (2S) do not impose any direct contemporaneous relationship between these two constructs. We capture this correlation by specifying the relationship between SE_{ij} and WE_{ij} for any arbitrary point in time, t, to be

$$SE_{ijt} = WE_{ijt} + \mu_{ijt}, \tag{12}$$

where μ_{ijt} captures all individual differences at time t. Thus, μ_{ijt} includes all influence of the individual's previous experiences, factors included in the **X** and **Z** vectors for the past t periods, and individual differences associated with the degree to which a customer is critical or demanding.

Appendix B presents the derivation of our estimating equations. This derivation consists of three simple steps. First, we use equation (12) to rewrite equation (3S) completely in terms of either the *will* or the *should* expectation. We take this step because we measure either the *will* or the *should* expectation for each individual, but not both. Second, we use equation (1S) and (2S) to write these equations in terms of contemporaneous expectations. Third, by recognizing that we have N measures for each individual on each of the j dimensions of service quality (see Table 5), we utilize the multiple (repeated) measures aspect of our design and thereby remove (control for) all of the factors that are fixed for a specific individual (i.e. delivered service). This is done by 'mean-differencing' the data, as shown in Appendix B.

These three steps yield the following two reduced-form equations.

$$(PS_{ijnt} - PS_{ij\cdot t}) = \left(\frac{\alpha_{jt} + \gamma_{jt}}{\alpha_{jt}}\right) (WE_{ijnt} - WE_{ij\cdot t}) + \epsilon_{13it}, \tag{13}$$

$$(PS_{ijnt} - PS_{ij\cdot t}) = (\alpha_{jt} + \gamma_{jt}) (SE_{ijnt} - SE_{ij\cdot t}) + \epsilon_{14it}, \tag{14}$$

where PS_{ijnt}, WE_{ijnt}, and SE_{ijnt} are the nth measure of the jth dimension for the appropriate construct for the $\cdot$ notation indicates the mean for the ith individual on the jth dimension.

In words, equations (13) and (14) state that for each individual there is a relationship between how that person responds to the nth perception question tapping dimension j relative to his or her mean response and how the same person responds to the analogous *will* and *should* expectations question relative to the respective mean response. These equations result in within-individual analyses. In particular, utilizing the multiple (repeated) measures aspect of our design enables us to control for all individual-specific factors that remain unchanged at time t. In our case, this is the actual service delivered to a given individual, the individual's 'history' and characteristics, including a person's proclivity to use a specific portion of the response scale, and any new information received prior to time t. As a result, equations (13) and (14) no longer contain any unobserved variables and consistent estimation of two coefficients, $(\alpha_{jt} + \gamma_{jt})/(\alpha_{jt})$ and $(\alpha_{jt} + \gamma_{jt})$, is possible. From these two coefficients we can fully identify the two structural parameters found in equations (1S) and (3S). (Dividing $(\alpha_{jt} + \gamma_{jt})$ by $(\alpha_{jt} + \gamma_{jt})/(\alpha_{jt})$ yields an estimate of α_{jt}. Once $\hat{\alpha}_{jt}$ is obtained, it is easy to get an estimate of γ_{it}.) These estimates can potentially falsify our original structural equations – if $\hat{\alpha}_{jt}$ is not significantly greater than zero and $\hat{\gamma}_{jt}$ is not significantly less than zero, there is strong evidence to disconfirm our conceptualization as stated in (1S), (2S) and (3S).

Results

We begin by reported the estimates for the behavioral intention equation, (5S). Similar to our study 1 results in which perceptions of quality relate positively to behavioral intentions, we find that overall perceived quality positively and significantly ($t_{146} = 2.18$) relates to the index of behavioral intentions. We next explore the relationship between overall perceived quality and the measures of the five dimensions of service quality as posited by Parasuraman, Zeithaml and Berry (1985). We start with the unconstrained form of this relationship, equation (7), which allows for different parameter values on each of the perception and expectation measures. Next, we estimate the gaps model, equation (6), which constrains the coefficient on the *j*th dimension of expectations to equal the negative of the coefficient on the *j*th dimension of perceptions. Finally, we estimate our dynamic model specification, equation (4S), which imposes the constraint that the coefficients on the expectation dimensions equal zero.[17]

We report the results of these estimates in Table 6. Column 1 of Table 6 corresponds to equation (7) and columns 2 and 3 correspond to equations (6) and (4S), respectively. We note all three equations yield results consistent with the hypothesis that the particular model being tested is statistically significant. Hence, we next explore which equation best captures reality by noting that equations (4S) and (6) are constrained versions of (7), thereby enabling us to test the implied constraints of (4S) and (6). We do so in the model comparison tests reported in the footnotes of Table 6. Specifically, the *F*-tests indicate that we must reject the constraint $\Theta_{1j} = -\Theta_{2j}$, but that we cannot reject the constraint $\Theta_{2j} = 0$. More generally, we reject the static formulation of the gaps model (i.e. equation 6) and its implied constraint. However, we fail to reject our dynamic model in favor of what is effectively an unconstrained version of the static gaps formulation (i.e. equation (7)). We take these results to demonstrate strong support for this part of our dynamic specification.

Finally, we use the estimates in column 4 of Table 6 to test for the relevance of all five proposed dimensions of service quality. In this model, we eliminate all but the reliability and empathy perception variables. Comparing the estimates in column 4 with those in column 3 by means of an *F*-test indicates that we fail to reject the two-dimensional representation of quality in favor of the five-dimensional representation.[18] Thus, column 4 represents the preferred model for overall perceived quality for our particular application. As expected, these estimates indicate that reliability is the primary driver of overall quality perceptions.

We next turn our attention to estimating the updating parameters α_{jt} and γ_{jt} via our reduced-form equations (13) and (14) for the two relevant (i.e. significant) quality perception dimensions. Before discussing these estimates, however, we test whether the perceptions obtained from respondents providing *will* expectations differ from those of respondents providing *should* expectations by running regression

[17]As the five dimensions of perceived service quality appear on the left side of our structural model, we tested for the necessity of two-stage (simultaneous) estimation of our overall service quality equation. This test (Hausman, 1978) revealed a recursive relationship, indicating the appropriateness of ordinary least squares estimation. This was true for the behavioral intention equations as well.

[18]We also fail to reject the parsimonious model given in column 4 in favor of the full unconstrained model given in column 1.

Table 6. Overall perceived quality of service equation estimates

Independent variables	(1) Unconstrained model	(2) Gaps model	(3) Dynamic model	(4) Limited dynamic model
Gaps		.026*		
Responsiveness		−.003		
Assurance		−.006		
Empathy		.026**		
Tangibles		−.000		
Perceptions				
Reliability	.046*		.049*	.043*
Responsiveness	−.007		−.004	
Assurance	−.007		−.008	
Empathy	.027**		.021***	.015***
Tangibles	.003		.003	
Expectations[a]				
Reliability	−.004			
Responsiveness	.008			
Assurance	.005			
Empathy	−.022			
Tangibles				
R^2	.286	.214[b]	.272[c]	.266[d]

[a]We test whether the *will* and *should* expectation variables require different coefficients in this analysis. They do not, unsurprisingly, for two reasons. First, at any given time *t*, the *will* and *should* expectations differ only by an individual-specific constant. Second, the coefficient on the contemporaneous expectation is zero, whether for *will* or *should* expectations.
[b]Significantly different from unconstrained model in the .05 level.
[c]Not significantly different from unconstrained model.
[d]Not significantly different from unconstrained model or dynamic model.
*Significant at the .01 level.
**Significant at the .05 level.
***Significant at the .10 level.

where perceptions are a function of the type of expectation measured. As we fail to find a significant coefficient on the version of the expectation measure variable for any of the perception dimensions, we infer that all of our perception data come from the same overall population.

Table 7 presents the results of our estimates of α_{jt} and γ_{jt}. First, we find that both the reliability and empathy dimensions the estimate of the *will* expectation coefficient (i.e. α_{jt}) is significantly greater than zero but less than one, as postulated.[19] Second, our two estimates of the *should* expectation coefficient (i.e. γ_{jt}) are significantly less than zero, also as postulated. Thus, our field study results are compatible with our conceptualization that prior expectations of what service *will* occur positively influence perceptions of delivered service, whereas prior

[19]Table 7 discusses how we develop significance tests.

Table 7. Reliability and empathy perception equation estimates[a]

Dependent variable	Will expectation coefficient (α_i)[b]	Should expectation coefficient (γ_i)
Reliability perception	.771*	−.513*
	(.211)	(.218)
Empathy perception	.714*	−.372*
	(.115)	(.125)

[a] Standard errors are in parentheses. A technical appendix is available from the authors upon request explaining how standard errors and significance levels were calculated. The basic idea was to use Monté Carlo techniques to calculate the distribution of $(\alpha_j + \gamma_j)/[(\alpha_j + \gamma_j)/(\alpha_j)] = \hat{\alpha}$, and $(\alpha_j + \gamma_j) - \hat{\alpha} = \hat{\gamma}_j$ and then calculate the standard deviations and fractiles of these derived distributions.
[b] Because the coefficient on delivered service equals one minus α, the implied delivered service coefficients for reliability and empathy are .229 and .286, respectively.
*Significant at the .01 level.

expectations of what service *should* occur negatively influence these perceptions. In addition, because α_{jt} also appears in equation (1S), we find support for our premise that *will* expectations are updated after a service encounter.

DISCUSSION

We present a process model of how individuals develop perceptions of a firm's service delivery system over time. By explicitly acknowledging that perceptions and expectations change over time, we are better able to explicate and test the relationships between expectations, perceptions, and intended behavior. The model is tested with data derived from two very different studies, one a longitudinal laboratory experiment and the other a field study using questionnaire data collected at one point in time. In both cases, the results are strongly compatible with all aspects of our process model.

We find the convergence of results for the two different studies very encouraging. Our model appears robust to different analytic approaches, different data collection methods, and different service settings. Thus, though one might generate specific criticisms of the individual studies, we think of none that spans both studies. Consequently, we have a strong posterior belief that our model adequately summarizes the major forces that cause customers to form and update their perceptions of a firm's overall service quality level.

These forces have major implications for any firm interested in service quality. As expected, but never empirically verified in a field setting, our results indicate that the greater customers' perceptions of a firm's overall service quality, the more likely the customers are to engage in behaviors beneficial to the strategic health of the firm (e.g. generate positive word of mouth, recommend the service, etc.).

Our research also provides insights into how firms can best increase customers' perceptions of their overall service quality. Our most important managerial insight relates to the role of expectations. The prevailing model of service quality defines perceived service quality as the gap between expectations and perceptions, and does not differentiate among types of expectations. It leads to the strategic implication that firms can try either to increase perceptions or lower expectations in their quest to increase overall service quality. Our results are incompatible with both this one-dimensional view of expectations and the gap formulation for service quality. Instead, we find that service quality is directly influenced only by perceptions. Also, increasing customer expectations of what a firm *will* provide during future service encounters actually leads to higher perceptions of quality after the customer is exposed to the actual service, all else equal. From this finding we infer that firms should manage customers' predictive expectations *up* rather than down if they want to increase customer perceptions of overall service quality. In addition, our results strongly support our premise that customers' expectations of what a firm *should* deliver during a service encounter *decrease* their ultimate perceptions of the actual service delivered, all else equal. Therefore, improved assessments of service quality can result when customers' expectations of what a firm *should* deliver are managed downward.

The issue of managerial importance, then, is how to manage both types of expectations. Ideally, one would want to simultaneously increase customers' *will* expectations and decrease their *should* expectations. At this stage of our research, we know of no activity that can ensure this result. One airline firm attempted to do this by simultaneously telling customers that all airlines had problems with guaranteeing on-time arrivals because of factors outside the airlines' control, but that they were the best at being on time. In this way the firm's ad campaign attempted to address both the *should* and *will* expectations. Whether or not this approach to managing both sets of expectations worked as intended is an empirical question.

A second approach to managing *will* and *should* expectations is for the firm to engage in activities that increase the customers' *will* expectations without a proportional increase in their expectations of what the firm *should* do. From equations (1S) and (2S), we see that providing the best possible service each and every time can increase *will* expectations but it might also increase the *should* expectations. Fortunately, our empirical evidence suggests that *will* expectations increase faster than the *should* expectations, so that the net impact on perceptions is positive. However, firms need to monitor the relative magnitudes of α, β, and γ to ensure that increases in objective service quality also result in increases in perceptions of service quality (see footnote 13 for more details). Finally, managers may be able to identify specific firm actions (other than service) that affect only the *will* or *should* expectations. Such actions would enable the firm to increase (decrease) the *will* (*should*) expectations without modifying the other.

In addition to providing managerial insights, we were able to demonstrate a method of estimating the two key parameters from our dynamic model by using survey data taken from customers at only one point in time. As a result, managers can learn about the relative importance of service delivery and customer expectations for their specific business. This determination should be very useful in assessing the relative value of trying to modify perceptions through changes in the service delivery system and the firm's communications, as well as identifying the speed with which managers can expect perceptions to change over time.

We believe our analytic approach provides managers an easily implementable method for estimating our model because it does not require measuring the actual service provided or prior expectations. However, as seen from our derivation, the estimation technique requires that (1) the surveys obtain multiple measures of perceptions and expectations, (2) all of the measures within a dimension have identical influence on that dimension, and (3) if the managers believe customers have much different levels of prior experience, they segment the customers so as to reflect the possible differences in the updating parameters.

Our research also has implications for academicians. We note a great similarity between our work on modeling perceived service quality and its impact on intended future behavior and the models of Churchill and Surprenant (1982) and Tse and Wilton (1988), who were concerned with explicating the factors that influence perceived product performance (and ultimately its impact on consumer satisfaction). As in our study 1, both of these research teams were able to measure prior expectations and the actual product performance. However, only Tse and Wilton measured two types of expectations and thus were able to obtain unbiased estimates. Their study found, analogous to our results, that prior *will* expectations and actual product performance were positively related to perceived performance. In addition, they found that prior *expectations on what consumers would ideally like to see* in the product were negatively related to perceived performance. Interestingly, they found the actual product performance variable to have a much stronger influence on perceived performance than we did in our study. This difference is not surprising given that services typically have a higher proportion of experience and credence properties than products, making service performance more difficult to evaluate than product performance. It seems likely that perceptions will be more influenced by expectations (relative to actual service) for firms with a higher content of unobservable (or fallible) quality. Along these lines, future research might assess the degree to which different industries or customers with different levels of prior experience influence the extent to which prior knowledge, new communications, or the actual service encounter dominates the process by which customers form judgments of quality.

Though we suggest conceptually, and demonstrate empirically, that customers update their expectations and perceptions, interesting aspects of this process have not been investigated. For example, the antecedents of the different expectation variables remain largely unexplored.[20] Given the need to manage *will* expectations up and the *should* expectations down, understanding the determinants of these expectations is a critical managerial issue. Also, because we can restate our equations mathematically in a variety of formats, our empirical analyses provide no evidence on the cognitive process by which customers form, store, or retrieve perceptions. Consequently, we hope that researchers utilize experimental and panel data to continue delving into the dynamic process by which customers form expectations and perceptions of service quality.

Finally, we note that our process model has the potential for broader applications. First, one might view overall service quality as a measure of the firm's service equity. Further, because the antecedents of this construct are known, measuring and managing these antecedents (e.g. expectations) can help a firm better understand

[20]To date we know what word-of-mouth communications and information from expert sources affect *will* expectations whereas information on the competitors and to a lesser degree word of mouth affect *should* expectations. We used this knowledge to manipulate the subjects' prior expectations in study 1.

which actions either enhance or detract from the firm's service equity and thus its ability to compete. Second, we see no reason why our process model would not apply to products as well as services. However, empirical support for this belief remains to be provided. Third, we see direct applicability of our model in better understanding, tracking, and influencing customer satisfaction as referred to in the popular press. The reason is that the measures used to reflect satisfaction are usually cumulative, versus transaction specific, and thus are analogous to our construct of perceived quality.

APPENDIX A: SCALING CALIBRATION

Our goal is to rescale all of the measures so that they have a common metric. Assume this metric is defined in terms of the measured expectations, *MWE* and *MSE*. For our measure of the delivered service construct, we note that only two levels of service, high and low, were experienced by the subjects. Let $MDS_{it} = 1$ if the service was high and $MDS_{it} = 0$ if the service was low, where MDS_{it} equals measured delivered service. Next, we define

$$DS^*_{it} = a + b\, MDS_{it}, \tag{A1}$$

where a and b are $\geqslant 0$. This formulation enables us to convert our measure of delivered service onto the same 100-point scale as the expectation scale. Thus, the a parameter represents the metric value of low service, whereas $a + b$ represents the metric value of high service.

We also need to acknowledge that a person's measured perception, denoted *MPS*, may be on a different scale than the person's measured expectations. For calibration across these scales, we define

$$PS_{it} = c + MPS_{it}, \tag{A2}$$

where c is a shift parameter.

Similarly, we let the measured behavioral intention, denoted *MBI*, be on a different scale than the person's measured perceptions:

$$BI_{it} = d + MBI_{it}, \tag{A3}$$

where d is again a shift parameter.

APPENDIX B: DERIVATION OF ESTIMATING EQUATIONS

First, using equation (12), write equation (3S) completely in terms of either the *will* or *should* expectation:

$$PS_{ijt} = (\alpha_{jt} + \gamma_{jt})\, WE_{ijt-1} + (1 - \alpha_{jt}) DS^*_{ijt} + \epsilon B_{1it}, \tag{B1}$$

and

$$PS_{ijt} = (\alpha_{jt} + \gamma_{jt})\, SE_{ijt-1} + (1 - \alpha_{jt}) DS^*_{ijt} + \epsilon B_{2it}, \tag{B2}$$

These equations make it clear that even if measures of lagged expectations are available, using only one of the two lagged expectation variables to estimate the relationships between expectations and perceptions (even after controlling for actual service) will result in biased expectations coefficient estimate for that expectation (i.e. the obtained estimate is $(\alpha + \gamma)$ versus $\hat{\alpha}$ or $\hat{\gamma}$).[21]

[21]Most published studies linking expectations to perceptions include only one expectation in the estimating equation. If our laboratory results generalize, the equations (B1) and (B2) imply the obtained coefficients in these single-expectation models are biased.

Next, because we only observe *contemporaneous* expectations, we use equations (1S) or (2S) to rewrite equations (B1) and (B2) in terms of current values of either *WE* or *SE*.

$$PS_{ijt} = \left(\frac{\alpha_{jt} + \gamma_{it}}{\alpha_{jt}}\right) WE_{ijt} - \gamma_{jt} \frac{(1 - \alpha_{jt})}{\alpha_{jt}} DS^{*}_{ijt} + \epsilon_{B3it}, \quad \text{(B3)}$$

and

$$PS_{ijt} = (\alpha_{jt} + \gamma_{jt}) SE_{ijt} + [1 - \alpha_{jt}\beta_{jt}\mathbf{K}_{ijt} - \gamma_{jt}\beta_{jt}\mathbf{K}_{ijt} - \alpha_{jt}] DS^{*}_{ijt} + \epsilon_{B4it}.^{22} \quad \text{(B4)}$$

Next, imagine that equations (B3) and (B4) have n subscripts indicating the individual measures for the perception and expectation constructs. Take means over the n items for the *i*th individual and the *j*th dimension in equations (B3) and (B4), yielding

$$PS_{ij\cdot t} = \left(\frac{\alpha_{jt} + \gamma_{it}}{\alpha_{jt}}\right) WE_{ij\cdot t} + \epsilon_{B5it}, \quad \text{(B5)}$$

and

$$PS_{ij\cdot t} = (\alpha_{jt} + \gamma_{it})\, SE_{ij\cdot t} + \epsilon_{B6it}, \quad \text{(B6)}$$

where the · notation indicates the mean for the *i*th individual on the *j*th dimension. Subtracting equations (B5) and (B6), respectively, from equations (B3) and (B4) supplemented with the n subscripts produces equations (13) and (14) reported in the text.[23]

ACKNOWLEDGEMENTS

The authors thank seminar participants at MIT, Wharton and Harvard, as well as France LeClerc, Julie Edell, and especially John Lynch for their helpful comments.

REFERENCES

Amemiya, T. (1985) *Advanced Econometrics*. Cambridge, MA: Harvard University Press.

Anderson, E. W. and Sullivan, M. W. (1990) 'Customer Satisfaction and Retention Across Firms'. Presentation at the TIMS College of Marketing Special Interest Conference on Services Marketing, Nashville, TN (September).

Bearden, W. D. and Teel, J. E. (1983) 'Selected Determinants of Customer Satisfaction and Complaint Reports'. *Journal of Marketing Research* **20** (November): 21–28.

Bitner, M. J. (1990) 'Evaluating Service Encounters: The Effects of Physical Surroundings and Employee Responses'. *Journal of Marketing* **54** (April): 69–82.

Bolton, R. N. and Drew, J. H. (1991a) 'A Multi-stage Model of Customers' Assessments of Service Quality and Value'. *Journal of Consumer Research* **17** (March): 375–384.

Bolton, R. N. and Drew, J. H. (1991b) 'A Longitudinal Analysis of the Impact of Service Changes on Customer Attitudes'. *Journal of Marketing* **55** (January): 1–9.

Boulding, W. R., Staelin, R., Kalra, A. and Zeithaml, V. (1992) 'Conceptualizing and Testing a Dynamic Process Model of Service Quality'. Working Paper No. 92–121. Cambridge, MA: Marketing Science Institute.

---

[22]Note that these equations imply that use of only the contemporaneous *will* or *should* expectations in a perceptions equation results in biased estimates for these expectation variables.

[23]If one measures both *will* and *should* expectations, one can derive a third estimating equation containing both types of expectations (see Boulding *et al.*, 1992).

Cadotte, E. R., Woodruff, R. B. and Jenkins, R. L. (1987) 'Expectations and Norms in Models of Consumer Satisfaction'. *Journal of Marketing Research* **24** (August): 305–314.

Churchill, G. A., Jr. (1979) 'A Paradigm for Developing Better Measures of Marketing Constructs'. *Journal of Marketing Research* **11** (August): 254–260.

Churchill, G. A., Jr. and Surprenant, C. (1982) 'An Investigation Into the Determinants of Satisfaction Research'. *Journal of Marketing Research* **19** (November): 491–504.

Day, R. L. (1977) 'Towards a Process Model of Consumer Satisfaction'. In *Conceptualization and Measurement of Consumer Satisfaction and Dissatisfaction* (H. K. Hunt, Ed.). Cambridge, MA: Marketing Science Institute, 153–183.

Forbes, J. D., Tse, D. K. and Taylor, S. (1986) 'Toward a Model of Consumer Post-Choice Response Behavior'. *Advances in Consumer Research*, Vol. 13 (R. L. Lutz, Ed.). Ann Arbor, MI: Association for Consumer Research, 658–616.

Garvin, D. A. (1987) 'Competing on the Eight Dimensions of Quality'. *Harvard Business Review* **65**(November–December): 101–109.

Gilly, M. C. (1979) 'Complaining Consumers: Their Satisfaction with Organizational Response'. In *New Dimensions of Consumer Satisfaction and Complaining Behavior* (R. L. Day and H. K. Hunt, Eds). Bloomington, IN: School of Business Indiana University, pp. 99–107.

Gilly, M. C., Cron, W. L. and Barry, T. E. (1983) 'The Expectation-Performance Comparison Process: An Investigation of Expectation Type'. In *International Fare in Consumer Satisfaction and Complaining Behavior.* (R. L. Day and H. H. Hunt, Eds.). Bloomington, IN: School of Business, Indiana University, pp. 10–16.

Hausman, J. A. (1978) 'Specification Tests in Econometrics'. *Econometrica* **46** (November): 1251–1272.

Hjorth-Anderson, C. (1984) 'The Concept of Quality and the Efficiency of Markets for Consumer Products'. *Journal of Consumer Research* **11** (2): 708–718.

Holbrook, M. B. and Corfman, K. P. (1985) 'Quality and Value in the Consumption Experience: Phaedrus Rides Again'. In *Perceived Quality* (J. Jacoby and J. Olson, Eds). Lexington, MA: Lexington Books, pp. 31–57.

Kalra, A. (1992) 'An Empirical Validation and Transaction-Level Investigation of an Expectation-Based Process Model of Service Quality'. PhD dissertation, Duke University.

LaTour, S. A. and Peat, N. C. (1979) 'Conceptual and Methodological Issues in Consumer Satisfaction Research'. In *Advances in Consumer Research*, Vol. 6 (W. L. Wilkie, Ed.). Ann Arbor, MI: Association for Consumer Research, 431–437.

Lynch, J. G., Jr., Chakravarti, D. and Mitra, A. (1991) 'Contrast Effects in Consumer Judgments: Changes in Mental Representations or in the Anchoring of Rating Scale?'. *Journal of Consumer Research* **18** (3): 284–297.

Maynes, E. S. (1976) 'The Concept and Measurement of Product Quality'. *Household Production and Consumption* **40** (5): 529–559.

Miller, J. A. (1977) 'Studying Satisfaction, Modifying Models, Eliciting Expectations, Posing Problems, and Making Meaningful Measurements'. In *Conceptualization and Measurement of Consumer Satisfaction and Dissatisfied* (H. K. Hunt, Ed.). Bloomington, IN: School of Business, Indiana University, pp. 72–91.

Oliver, R. L. (1977) 'Effect of Expectation and Disconfirmation on Post-Exposure Product Evaluation: An Alternative Interpretation'. *Journal of Applied Psychology* **62** (April): 480–486.

Oliver, R. L. (1980) 'A Cognitive Model of the Antecedents and Consequences of Satisfaction Decisions'. *Journal of Marketing Research* **17** (November): 460–469.

Olson, J. C. and Dover, P. (1979) 'Disconfirmation of Consumer Expectations Through Product Trial'. *Journal of Applied Psychology* **64** (April): 179–189.

Parasuraman, A., Berry, L. L. and Zeithaml, V. A. (1990) 'An Empirical Examination of Relationships in an Extended Service Quality Model'. Working paper, Marketing Science Institute.

Parasuraman, A., Zeithaml, V. A. and Berry, L. L. (1985) 'A Conceptual Model of Service Quality and Its Implications for Future Research'. *Journal of Marketing* **49** (Fall): 41–50.

Parasuraman, A., Zeithaml, V. A. and Berry, L. L. (1988) 'SERVQUAL: A Multiple-Item Scale for Measuring Consumer Perceptions of Service Quality', *Journal of Retailing* **64** (Spring): 12–40.

Prakash, V. (1984) 'Validity and Reliability of the Confirmation of Expectations Paradigm as a Determinant of Consumer Satisfaction'. *Journal of the Academy of Marketing Science* **12** (Fall): 63–76.

Swan, J. E. and Trawick, F. I. (1980) 'Satisfaction Related to Predictive vs. Desired Expectations: A Field Study'. In *New Findings on Consumer Satisfaction and Complaining* (R. L. Day and H. K. Hunt, Eds). Bloomington, IN: School of Business, Indiana University, pp. 15–22.

Swan, J. E. and Trawick, F. I. (1981) 'Disconfirmation of Expectations and Satisfaction With a Retail Service'. *Journal of Retailing* **57** (Fall): 49–67.

Tse, D. K. and Wilton, P. C. (1988) 'Models of Consumer Satisfaction Formation: An Extension'. *Journal of Marketing Research* **25** (May): 204–212.

Wilton, P. C. and Nicosia, M. (1986) 'Emerging Paradigms for the Study of Consumer Satisfaction'. *European Research* **14** (January): 4–11.

Woodruff, R. B., Cadotte, E. R. and Jenkins, R. L. (1983) 'Modeling Consumer Satisfaction Processes Using Experience-Based Norms'. *Journal of Marketing Research* **20** (August): 296–304.

Zeithaml, V. A. (1988) 'Consumer Perceptions of Price, Quality, and Value: A Means-End Model and Synthesis of Evidence'. *Journal of Marketing* **52** (July): 2–22.

Zeithaml, V. A., Berry, L. L. and Parasuraman, A. (1991) 'The Nature and Determinants of Customer Expectations of Service'. Working Paper, Marketing Science Institute.

16

A Multistage Model of Customers' Assessments of Service Quality and Value

Ruth N. Bolton and James H. Drew

In recent years, companies have become convinced of the strategic benefits of quality (Phillips, Chang and Buzzell, 1983). As a result, may large companies have created quality-measurement programs that attempt to relate product and service attributes to customer evaluations of quality (Hauser and Clausing, 1988; Zeithaml, Parasuraman and Berry, 1990). In many service industries, companies have created programs that include surveys to elicit customers' assessments of service quality; a feedback loop allows service changes to be implemented and then evaluated with subsequent survey data.

In parallel with recent managerial interest in service quality measurement programs, researchers have become interested in the identification and measurement of service-quality dimensions. In their well-known article, Parasuraman, Zeithaml and Berry (1985) suggest that customers evaluate overall service quality on five underlying dimensions: tangibles, reliability, responsiveness, assurance, and empathy. In subsequent research, they developed an instrument called SERVQUAL that measures customers' perceptions of service quality (Parasuraman *et al.*, 1988).

This study explores how customers integrate their perceptions of a service to form an overall evaluation of that service. It differs from prior research concerning quality in two ways. First, it develops a *multistage* model of the determinants of perceived service quality and service value. Second, it describes how customers' expectations, perceptions of current performance and disconfirmation experiences affect their satisfaction with a service, which in turn affects their assessment of service quality and value.

The first section of this article discusses the constructs of customer satisfaction, perceived service quality, and service value and then integrates these in a multistage model of residential customers' perceptions of service performance, service quality, and service value for local telephone service. The next two sections describe how the model is operationalized as a multiple-equation system and estimated by a two-stage least squares procedure with data from customer surveys. The last two sections discuss the empirical findings and their implications.

Reprinted by permission of The University of Chicago Press.

BACKGROUND

Customer satisfaction

Market researchers distinguish between customers' satisfaction with respect to a specific transaction and their global evaluation of a service (Holbrook and Corfman, 1985; Olshavsky, 1985). Oliver (1981) argues that satisfaction is characterized by the surprise a customer experiences after a purchase (i.e. a service encounter) and that this surprise eventually becomes an input to a less dynamic attitude. Consequently, satisfaction can be considered to influence the customer's evaluation of service quality, purchase intentions, and behavior (see, e.g., LaBarbera and Mazursky, 1983).

Customer satisfaction or dissatisfaction (CS/D) is a function of the disconfirmation arising from discrepancies between prior expectations and actual performance (Cardozo, 1965; Oliver, 1980; Olshavsky and Miller, 1972; Olson and Dover, 1976). The CS/D literature demonstrates that expectations and perceptions of performance levels affect customer satisfaction directly, as well as indirectly via disconfirmation. For example, Tse and Wilton's (1988) experiments showed that perceived performance exerts a direct influence on CS/D, in addition to the influences from disconfirmation or expectations. The theoretical linkages identified in the CS/D literature are illustrated by the thin solid lines in Figure 1.

Expectations, performance evaluations, and disconfirmation do not necessarily have independent additive effects for every product or service. Churchill and Surprenant (1982) found that CS/D with a non-durable good is a function of all three constructs, whereas CS/D with a durable good is solely a function of performance evaluations. Consequently, expectations, performance evaluations, and disconfirmation are *potential* antecedents of CS/D with a service. For example, in his discussion of modes of satisfaction, Oliver (1989) proposed that customer responses concerning continuously provided services or long-lasting durables are characterized by passive expectations and, therefore, that disconfirmation will not operate unless performance is outside the range of experience-based norms. Hence, customers's assessments of continuously provided services, such as public utilities or cable television, may depend on performance evaluations only.

Service quality

Recent marketing research regarding customers' attitudes towards services has focused on perceived service quality. Perceived service quality is defined as the customer's assessment of the overall excellence or superiority of the service (Zeithaml, 1988). Parasuraman *et al.* (1985, 1988) consider that a customer's assessment of overall service quality depends on the *gap* between expectations and perceptions of actual performance levels. They propose that overall service quality is evaluated on five underling dimensions: tangibles, reliability, responsiveness, assurance, and empathy. They propose that each quality dimension can be quantified by obtaining measures of expectations and perceptions of performance levels of service attributes relevant to each dimension, calculating the difference between expectations and perceptions of actual performance on these attributes,

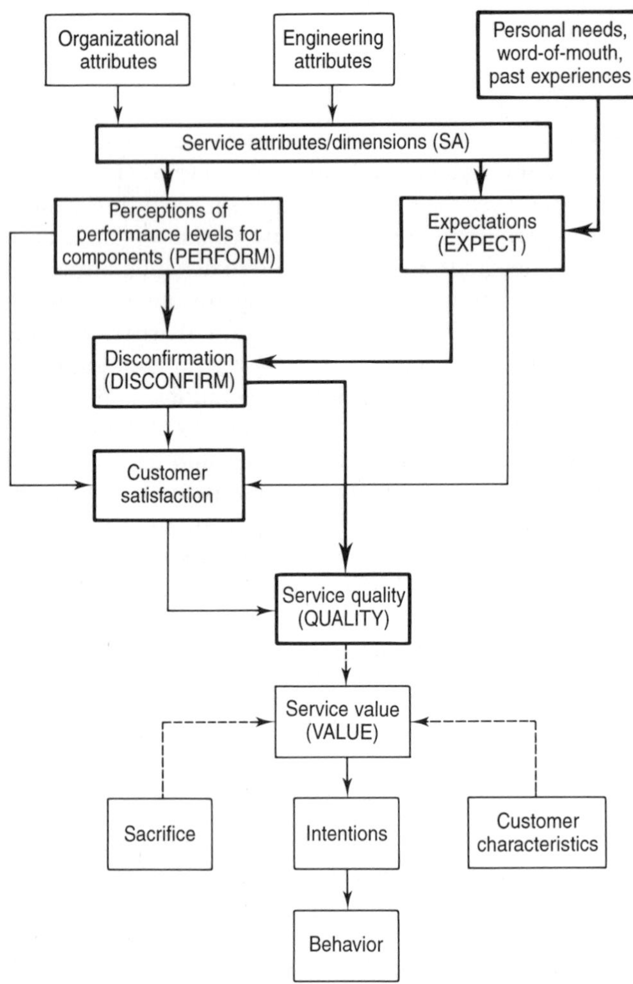

Figure 1. A multistage model of customer assessments of service quality and value.

and then averaging across attributes. They also suggest that expectations should be influenced by personal needs, word-of-mouth communications, and past experiences. The determinants of perceptions are not discussed in their model, but, presumably, they are influenced by attributes of the service-delivery process. The theoretical linkages proposed by Parasuraman *et al.* (1985) are illustrated by the double lines in Figure 1.

Both CS/D and perceived service quality are postulated to be influenced by the gap between expectations and perceptions of performance (i.e. disconfirmation). However, the CS/D literature suggests a more elaborate model in which disconfirmation, expectations, and actual performance levels affect customer satisfaction, which, in turn, becomes an input to customers' perceptions of service quality. As Figure 1 illustrates, this conceptualization implies that customers' perceptions of service quality are directly affected by disconfirmation and indirectly affected by disconfirmation, expectations, and actual performance levels (via CS/D).

Service value

On the basis of a review of previous research and on an exploratory study, Zeithaml (1988, p. 14) suggests that 'perceived value is the customer's overall assessment of the utility of a product based on perceptions of what is received and what is given'. If perceived service value is analogous to the concept of perceived product value, then Zeithaml's work suggests that service value can be considered to involve a trade-off between a customer's evaluation of the benefits of using a service and its cost. Customers' assessments of service value are hypothesized to influence purchase intentions and behavior.

A customer's assessment of value depends on sacrifice (i.e. the monetary and nonmonetary costs associated with utilizing the service) and the customer's frame of reference (Zeithaml, 1988). Thus, there should be differences in customers' assessments of service value due to differences in monetary costs, nonmonetary costs, customer tastes, and customer characteristics. The theoretical linkages among sacrifice and customer characteristics, service value, intentions, and behavior are illustrated by the broken lines in Figure 1.

A multistage model of service quality and value

The preceding paragraphs provide a conceptual framework for a model of customers' assessments of service quality and value. A customer's global assessment of a service can be decomposed into a series of interrelated stages: assessments of performance, service quality, and value. These three stages are specified algebraically as a multistage model in the tradition of the perception-preference-choice model (Urban and Hauser, 1980), the lens model (Brunswick, 1952), and information integration theory (Anderson, 1974).

Most services are multidimensional bundles of core, facilitating, and supporting services (Grönroos, 1987). For example, airline service includes core service (transportation), facilitating service (check-in procedures), and supporting service (in-flight meals). In accordance with the tradition of multiattribute modeling, the model developed here considers a customer's perception of service performance ($\mathrm{PERFORM}_k$) to be based on an assessment of performance on particular service attributes and dimensions (e.g. reliability). That is,

$$\mathrm{PERFORM}_k = p_k(\mathbf{SA}_k), \quad (1)$$

where $\mathbf{SA}_k$ is a vector of perceptual ratings of attributes/dimensions that describe service k, and p_k is a function with parameters that depend on the nature of service k.

As discussed earlier, a customer's disconfirmation experiences, expectations, and perceived performance levels affect CS/D with a specific service transaction. In turn, CS/D influences the customer's global evaluation of service quality. Thus, a reduced-form model describing customers' assessments of service quality (QUALITY) is the following[1]:

$$\text{QUALITY} = q(\textbf{PERFORM, EXPECT, DISCONFIRM}), \tag{2}$$

where **EXPECT** is a vector describing prior expectations about the performance of the component services ($k = 1, \ldots, K$), and **DISCONFIRM** is a vector describing perceptions of the discrepancy between performance and expectations concerning the component services ($k = 1, \ldots, K$).

After evaluating service quality, the customer assesses service value (VALUE) by trading off the quality of service versus its costs in a given situation. That is,

$$\text{VALUE} = v_0(\text{QUALITY}, \textbf{SACRIFICE, CHAR}), \tag{3a}$$

where **SACRIFICE** is a vector of variables describing the monetary and nonmonetary costs associated with customer's utilization of the service, and **CHAR** is a vector of customer characteristics.

As illustrated in Figure 1, prior research has implicitly assumed that customers' assessment of service value depends on their assessment of service quality. In contrast, we hypothesize that customers may weight the underlying components of service quality (**PERFORM, EXPECT,** and **DISCONFIRM**) differently when assessing service value.[2] This notion can be reflected in the service-value equation in the following way:

$$\text{VALUE} = v_1(\text{QUALITY}, \textbf{SACRIFICE, CHAR, PERFORM, EXPECT, DISCONFIRM}) \tag{3b}$$

The hypothesis that customers weight service-quality components differently when assessing service quality versus value is testable by constraining equation (3b) to equal equation (3a).

A MODEL OF CUSTOMERS' ASSESSMENTS OF TELEPHONE SERVICE

This section describes a multistage model of customers' assessments of a continuously provided service, namely, telephone service. The following paragraphs describe the three stages of the model: the formation of customer perceptions of service performance, service quality, and value.

---

[1]On the basis of Figure 1, we have the following structural equations:

$$\text{QUALITY} = q_0(\text{CS/D, DISCONFIRM}), \tag{i}$$

$$\text{CS/D} = c(\text{DISCONFIRM, EXPECT, PERFORM}). \tag{ii}$$

Substituting equation (ii) in equation (i), we obtain the reduced-form equation (2) shown in the text. This article focuses on customers' (relatively stable) attitudes about service quality and value; it does not model (relatively transitory) evaluations of CS/D.

[2]For example, the role of disconfirmation may be similar to the role of perceived gains and losses in Thaler's (1985) model of consumer choice. In his model, a consumer value function is defined for differences relative to a reference point (i.e. perceived gains and losses), rather than for absolute levels in a purchasing situation. He postulates that people will be more sensitive to losses than to gains, suggesting that the customer may weight negative disconfirmation more heavily than other factors in assessing service value. This theory is consistent with the notion that the customer may weight perceptions of performance levels, expectations, and disconfirmation differently in assessing quality than in assessing value.

Performance evaluations

Local telephone service is actually a bundle of services, including local-call provision, long-distance access, operator services, customer services (e.g. installation and changes), and billing services. Hence performance evaluation ($PERFORM_k$) was modeled for three component services: billing, local, and long-distance services. The explanatory variables in the BILLING, LOCAL and LONG equations are primarily extrinsic cues related to the reliability, responsiveness, assurance and empathy dimensions of overall service quality. In addition, customer perceptions of billing, local, and long-distance services are postulated to depend on past experiences at different operating companies (**LOC-SUPPLY**), which differ in plant and equipment, operating procedures, climate and geography.

The customer's perception of billing service was hypothesized to be positively related to the customer's having no billing problems in the preceding 30 days (NO-CONTACT), satisfactory resolution of the problem (SATISFY), and customer's perception of the courtesy of telephone company personnel (COURTESY).[3] That is,

$$\text{BILLING} = f_1(\text{NO-CONTACT, SATISFY, COURTESY, } \mathbf{LOC\text{-}SUPPLY}). \quad (4)$$

The relevant attributes of local and long-distance service are fairly well-defined: provision of a dial tone, a correctly established connection to a dialled number, a static-free line, and no premature disconnections of calls. Hence, it was hypothesized that a customer's perceptions of local and long-distance services would be negatively related to perceptions of frequency of trouble with these four service attributes (FDIAL, FCONNECT, FSTATIC, and FCUTOFF, respectively). It was also hypothesized that the customer's perception of long-distance service would be positively related to the courtesy of telephone company personnel. Furthermore, it should depend on the particular long-distance carrier (AT & T, Sprint, or MCI; (**LD-SUPPLY**) because each carrier uses somewhat different transmission technologies. These notions can be summarized algebraically as follows:

$$\text{LOCAL} = f_2(\text{FSTATIC, FDIAL, FCONNECT, FCUTOFF, COURTESY, } \mathbf{LOC\text{-}SUPPLY}), \quad (5)$$

and

$$\text{LONG} = f_3(\text{FSTATIC, FDIAL, FCONNECT, FCUTOFF, COURTESY, } \mathbf{LOC\text{-}SUPPLY, LD\text{-}SUPPLY}). \quad (6)$$

Perceived quality

As discussed in the preceding section, a customer's assessment of service quality is postulated to depend on CS/D with the current service. In turn, CS/D depends on the perceived performance of service components, prior expectations about performance, and perceptions of the discrepancy between performance and

---

[3]Preliminary analyses indicated that specific attributes of the bill (e.g. the level of detail) did not affect assessments of billing service.

expectations (i.e. disconfirmation). However, Oliver (1989) has argued that customers' assessments of continuously provided services (such as telephone service) may depend solely on performance.

In this study, customers' evaluations of local telephone services are hypothesized to depend on performance *and* disconfirmation for two reasons. First, exploratory research confirmed that customer expectations about telephone service are not actively processed. Verbal protocols collected during in-depth interviews with 50 telephone customers yielded few speech segments concerning performance expectations (1%). Second, the deregulation of the telecommunications industry is altering the nature and level of telephone service so that residential customers may experience disconfirmation. For example, unfavorable disconfirmation occurs when the company drops free telephone and inside-wire repair. Hence, customers' assessments of telephone service quality are postulated to be a function of performance and disconfirmation, but not of expectations.

With regard to operationalizing the disconfirmation component of quality, recall that favorable or unfavorable disconfirmation was argued to arise from discrepancies between anticipated service (based on prior telephone experiences) and actual service. However, rather than measure disconfirmation for every service-quality dimension, this study measured disconfirmation with two questions that compared current telephone service with prior telephone experiences. The two questions had better/same/worse response categories (Oliver, 1981).[4] Specifically, QUALITY has hypothesized to depend on the customer's evaluation of the current provider relative to a prior local telephone service supplier (COMPARE) and the customer's assessment of the service supplier (COMPARE) and the customer's assessment of the extent of improvement in service compared with that of a year ago (IMPROVE).[5] In addition, QUALITY was postulated to depend on whether the customer's local telephone service had always been provided by the current carrier (NO CHANGE). Since positive disconfirmation should lead to higher assessments of overall service quality, the effects of these three variables were hypothesized to be positive. In addition, it was hypothesized that a customer who is a heavy user of local on long-distance service (#LOCAL, #LONG) may perceive overall service quality to be higher or lower than other customers because s/he may more opportunities for (positive or negative) disconfirmation.

Regarding the performance aspect of quality, it was postulated that a customer evaluated the overall quality of telephone service by forming intermediate perceptions of of the performance levels of component services and then weighting

---

[4]In contrast, Parasuraman *et al.* (1988) measure disconfirmation as the difference between separate measures of expectations and perceptions. Similarly, early approaches to measuring disconfirmation in the CS/D literature elicited separate measures of pre-performance judgments (i.e. expectations) and postperformance judgments, which created an artificial negative correlation between expectation and disconfirmation. Oliver (1981) points out that a better- and worse-than-expected scale is more meaningful to respondents and that is consistently has been highly correlated with satisfaction across a large number of different settings. He also points out that this scale is independent of expectation levels, which is important in multivariate analyses.

[5]A customer's ability to compare service from alternative telephone companies is an additional source of disconfirmation. The variable NO-CHANGE is a surrogate variable for this source of disconfirmation. Prior research indicated that customers who have only had service from one telecommunications provider are less discriminating (i.e. rate services more favorably).

these intermediate evaluations. Perceptions of higher levels of performance were hypothesized to be associated with higher assessments of overall quality. QUALITY was modeled as a function of the customer's assessments of the performance of seven services: billing, local and long-distance service, directory assistance (DIRECT), operator assistance (OPER), installation (INSTALL) and repair services. Not all customers utilize all services, especially repair and installation services, during a given period. Consequently, if a customer did not have experience with one of the component services (e.g. repair), his/her perceptions of that service were not elicited, and the relevant ratings variables (e.g. REPAIR) was assigned the value zero. Indicator variables (NO-DIRECT, NO-OPER, NO-INSTALL, and NO-REPAIR) were then used to represent the absence or presence of experience with a specific component. These 11 performance variables are extrinsic cues of the five quality dimensions of reliability, responsiveness, assurance, empathy, and tangibles.

The equation for overall quality can be summarized as follows:

$$\begin{aligned}\text{QUALITY} = f_4(&\text{BILLING, LOCAL, LONG, DIRECT, NO-DIRECT,}\\ &\text{OPER, NO-OPER, INSTALL, NO-INSTALL, REPAIR, NO-REPAIR,}\\ &\text{NO-CHANGE, COMPARE, IMPROVE, \#LOCAL, \#LONG}).\end{aligned} \tag{7}$$

Perceived value

The VALUE equation (equation 3b) was operationalized in the following way. A residential customer's assessment of the value of telephone services will chiefly depend on an assessment of the overall quality of telephone services. However, disconfirmation and performance may be weighted differently when assessing value versus overall quality. Hence, it is hypothesized that performance perceptions of three key service variables (BILLING, LOCAL, and LONG) and disconfirmation (NO-CHANGE, COMPARE, IMPROVE, #LOCAL, #LONG) will be weighted more heavily in assessing value than in assessing quality. In other words, these variables are hypothesized to have a positive effect on VALUE in addition to the positive effect on QUALITY.

Local telephone service is usually regulated so that prices are not free to fluctuate, and the service has no direct competitor in franchised areas. Also, since the large majority of customers used the same telephone company for long periods of time, customers are unable to compare their company's service with another's service unless they have lived in a different franchised area. Consequently, a change in price for local service, rather than relative price (vis-a-vis) competitors), is more likely to affect value. However, price changes are relatively infrequent, and none occurred at the time of the study. For these reasons monetary costs are relatively unimportant for local telephone service; however, nonmonetary costs may still be important in assessing value. In addition, billing policies may affect value judgments, such as when a customer does not meet a telephone company's payment schedule and service is abruptly terminated. Note that other continuously provided services (e.g. utilities) are likely to be characterized by similar customer responses.

Since the role of monetary and nonmonetary cost in customers' assessment of perceived service value is somewhat different in this industry, income was chosen to represent the customers' relative sacrifice (i.e. budget constraints). As income increases, the cost of telephone service becomes a similar proportion of the customer's total budget, so that the customer may perceive telephone service to be less valuable to available substitutes. For example, conversing over the telephone may seem to be a less valuable form of socialization compared with travel and trips to the theater. In addition, different types of customers may attach differential value to telephone service. Customers who use their residential telephone primarily for business purposes (BUSINESS) may value telephone service more highly than customers who use the telephone primarily for social or other personal reasons. Also, older customers (AGE), heavy users (#LOCAL and #LONG), and members of larger households (#HOUSE) may value residential telephone service more highly because of their heavier reliance on telephone services. Similarly, customers who are employed outside the home (EMPLOYED) may value residential telephone service less highly since they may have access to telephone service at their place of employment. The equation for the value of residential telephone services is expressed as follows.

$$\text{VALUE} = f_5(\text{QUALITY, BILLING, LOCAL, LONG, NO-CHANGE, COMPARE, IMPROVE, \#LOCAL, \#LONG, \#HOUSE, AGE, INCOME, BUSINESS, EMPLOYED}). \quad (8)$$

The operationalized form of the multistage model of telephone service quality and value is summarized by equations (4)–(8).

RESEARCH METHODS

The data base

The study utilized survey data from a systemwide (i.e. national) probability sample of 1408 residential telephone subscribers in 1985. In the survey, customers' recent telephone experiences were probed, their ratings of various service process attributes were reported, and overall service quality and value assessments were obtained. The survey elicited for component services identified by Parasuraman *et al.* (1985, 1988) using measures similar to, but not identical to, SERVQUAL. The questionnaire focused heavily on the reliability, responsiveness, assurance, and empathy dimensions. For example, the survey asked directly about the courtesy of employees, as well as about the attitudes of knowledgeability of sale representatives and other employees, to obtain measures of assurance. Ratings of the fifth quality dimension, tangibles, were not directly elicited since customer contact with the telephone company usually occurs over the telephone. Even repair and installation services do not necessarily require contact between telephone company personnel and customers.

There are two major differences between this survey and SERVQUAL. The items in this survey were framed specifically in terms of the telecommunications industry (rather than framed generically as they are in SERVQUAL). Specifically, the questions used in this study elicited ratings of intrinsic and extrinsic cues that signal service quality for telephone service. Second, unlike SERVQUAL, this survey did not measure expectations concerning service-quality dimensions. However, the survey did elicit direct measures of disconfirmation, whereas SERVQUAL does not.

Measures of constructs

Table 1 summarizes the model specification, hypotheses, and construct measures used in this research. The model consists of five equations: three performance equations, a service-quality equation, and a service-value equation. The hypothesized signs of the coefficients are shown in parentheses. The measures of the constructs are defined with the phraseology of the actual questionnaire. For example, the overall quality question is, 'Thinking just about the past 30 days, how would you rate the overall quality of services provided by your local telephone company? Would you say it is: Poor, Fair, Good or Excellent?'

Model estimation

The model of telephone-service quality and value is postulated to be a linear additive, compensatory model.[6] In assessing service quality and service value, the customer is assumed to weigh the various considerations associated with service quality, trading off lesser performance on some service attributes for greater performance on others. This specification assumes that the service is at least minimally satisfactory on all attributes (as required by public utilities commissions).

In the residential model, BILLING, LOCAL, LONG, and QUALITY appear as both dependent and predictor variables. The measurement errors in these equations may be correlated. (A positive correlation is likely because the dependent variables are measured on similar scales). Hence, a two-stage least squares estimation procedure was used (Johnston, 1972).[7]

RESULTS

The results are displayed in Table 2. The model seems to be well supported by the data. The R^2 for the equations ranges from .25 to .43, which is reasonably good explanatory power for equations estimated with cross-sectional data. (This result also compares favorably with the explanatory power of Parasuraman *et al.*'s (1988) OLS

---

[6]In the QUALITY equation, the coefficients of the variables describing service contacts (i.e. DIRECT, NO-DIRECT, OPER, NO-OPER, INSTALL, NO-INSTALL, REPAIR, NO-REPAIR) are interpreted in the following way. If a service contact took place (e.g. repair), customers provide a rating of the service (e.g. REPAIR), and the coefficients of that variable represents the influence of their perception of the service on their assessment of overall quality. If a service contact did not take place, customers do not provide a rating of the service (e.g. REPAIR is assigned the value zero); consequently, the influence of the rating of the service on overall quality is not estimated. However, the relevant dummy variable (e.g. NO-REPAIR) takes on the value one and the coefficient of that variable represents the increase or decrease in the customer's assessment of overall quality due to the absence of a particular service contact. (In other words, there is a shift in the intercept between users and nonusers, plus a slope effect for users only).

[7]Preliminary analyses estimated these same equations as binary logit models (which do not require interval scale properties for the dependent variable). Since the logit results were similar to the results found in this study, our assumption that the scales have interval properties does not appear to affect the results.

Table 1. Definitions of variables in the residential model

	Definition
Endogenous variables:	
BILLING	Rating of *the billing job* (e.g. *'How would you rate...?'*)
LOCAL	Rating of *local calls*
LONG	Rating of *long-distance calls*
QUALITY	Rating of *the overall quality of services provided by the local telephone company*
VALUE	*Overall value of services provided by the local telephone company, considering the amount paid for services received* (scale: 'very poor value' [1] ... 'very good value' [5])
Predictor variables:	
Equation 4:	
NO-CONTACT (+)	No billing problem in the past 30 days (yes/no)
SATISFY (+)	Satisfactory resolution of the billing problem (yes/no)
COURTESY (+)	Rating of *the courtesy of telephone company personnel*
LOC-SUPPLY (+/−)	A vector of six indicator variables representing six of the seven geographic areas
Equations[a] 5 and 6:	
FSTATIC (−)	Frequency of transmission problems (e.g. '*how often did... occur in the past 30 days?*')
FDIAL (−)	Frequency of dial tone problems
FCONNECT (−)	Frequency of connection problems
FCUTOFF (−)	Frequency of disconnection problems
COURTESY (+)	As defined for equation (4)
LOC-SUPPLY (+/−)	As defined for equations (4)
LD-SUPPLY (+/−)	A vector of three variables representing the three major long-distance carriers: AT & T, Sprint, and MCI
Equation 7:[b]	
NO-CHANGE (+)	Local telephone service has always been provided by current provider (yes/no)
COMPARE (+)	If the respondent has ever subscribed to local service from another supplier, a comparison of the current provider with the prior provider is elicited (scale is: 'much worse' [1] ... 'much better' [5]); if not, variable is coded zero
IMPROVE (+)	Extent of improvement in telephone service compared with a year ago (scale: 'much worse' [1] ... 'much better' [5])
#LOCAL (+/−)	Frequency of local calls
#LONG (+/−)	Frequency of long-distance calls
DIRECT (+)	Rating of directory-assistance service[c]
NO-DIRECT (+)	Did not use directory-assistance service in the past 30 days (yes/no)
OPER (+)	Rating of toll/assistance operator service[c]
NO-OPER (+)	Did not use toll/assistance operator in the past 30 days (yes/no)
INSTALL (+)	Ratings of service associated with a connection or change[c]
NO-INSTALL (+)	Did not use installation service in the past 30 days (yes/no)
REPAIR (+)	Rating of repair service[c]
NO-REPAIR (+)	Did not use repair service in the past 30 days (yes/no)
Equation 8:[d]	
NO-CHANGE (+)	As defined for equation (7)
COMPARE (+)	As defined for equation (7)
IMPROVE (+)	As defined for equation (7)
#LOCAL (+/−)	As defined for equation (7)
#LONG (+/−)	As defined for equation (7)
#HOUSE (+)	*Number of persons in the household*
AGE (+)	Age category of respondent (seven-point scale)
INCOME (−)	Household income category (seven-point scale)
BUSINESS (+)	Telephone primarily used for business purposes (yes/no)
EMPLOYED (−)	Respondents employed outside the home (yes/no)

Italics indicate exact phrasing of some questions. Rating variables are coded on a four-point scale (poor/fair/good/excellent). Frequency variables are coded on a four-point scale (seldom/sometimes/often/almost always). Other scales are as indicated above. The sign in parentheses indicates the hypothesised positive (+) or negative (−) effect on the dependent variable.

[a] Exogenous variables are postulated to be identical in both local and long-distance equations, with the exception of **LD-SUPPLY**, which appears only in the long-distance equation. The actual questions measure perceptions of local or long-distance service as appropriate.

[b] Equation (7) also includes the endogenous variables BILLING (+), LOCAL (+), and LONG (+) as predictor variables.

[c] If the respondent did not use this service in the past 30 days, the variable is coded zero.

[d] Equation (8) also includes the endogenous variables QUALITY (+), BILLING (+), LOCAL (+), and LONG (+) as predictor variables.

Table 2. Two-stage least squares estimates for the residential model

Variable[b]	Estimated coefficients[a] Equation (4)	Equation (5)	Equation (6)
COURTESY	.3112***	.2678***	.2242***
NO-CONTACT	.7682***	...	...
SATISFY	.3749***	...	...
FSTATIC	...	−.2079***	−.2414***
FCONNECT	...	−.0909***	−.1223***
FDIAL	...	−.0865***	−.0514**
FCUTOFF	...	−.1382***	−.1737***
AT & T	...	...	.0460
MCI	...	...	−.1841
SPRINT	...	...	.1157
INTERCEPT	.7843	2.4679	2.5722
F-statistic	50.83***	89.02***	73.63***
R^2	.25	.41	.43
Adjusted R^2	.24	.41	.42

	Estimated coefficient[a] Equation (7)	Equation (8)
BILLING	.1678***	.0052
LOCAL	.5312***	.3175***
LONG	.1463***	.1478**
QUALITY	...	.3654*
NO-CHANGE	.5049***	.3367***
COMPARE	.1796***	.0714*
IMPROVE	.1064***	.1545***
#LOCAL	.0598***	.0115
#LONG	−.0398***	−.0332
DIRECT	.1476	...
NO-DIRECT	.1745	...
OPER	−.0216	...
NO-OPER	−.0007	...
INSTALL	−.1780	...
NO-INSTALL	−.6143	...
REPAIR	.1651***	...
NO-REPAIR	.0611***	...
#HOUSE	...	.0535***
AGE	...	.0643***
INCOME	...	−.0370***
BUSINESS	...	.0433
EMPLOYED	...	−.0627
INTERCEPT	−.5814	−.1215
F-statistic	51.91***	46.57***
R^2	.37	.32
Adjusted R^2	.37	.31

Ellipses indicate variable does not occur in equation.

[a]The coefficients of the six geographic dummy variables are estimated but not reported. The coefficients reported in the table are not standardized.

[b]Variables refer to local or long-distance service as applicable (e.g., col. 2 shows the coefficient of the variable 'static on local calls' and col. 3 shows the coefficient of the variable 'static on long distance calls').

*One-tailed test, $p < .05$.

**One-tailed test, $p < .01$.

***One-tailed test, $p < .005$.

estimation of four quality equations as functions of indices representing the five service-quality dimensions.) In addition, the effects of most variables are in the hypothesized direction, and most are statistically significant (one-tailed tests, $p < .05$).

Performance

The results for the BILLING, LOCAL, and LONG equations are remarkably similar. Customers' assessments of all three services are positively affected by the courtesy of personnel ($p < .005$). COURTESY explains between 5 and 9% of the variance of the dependent variable in each equation.[8] In Parasuraman *et al.*'s (1988, p. 23), courtesy is part of their assurance dimension and is defined as 'knowledge and courtesy of employees and their ability to inspire trust and confidence'. Hence, the results for COURTESY suggests that *any* contact with telephone service personnel will have an important impact on a customer's assessment of assurance for *all* aspects of telephone service. Results also show that customer's assessments of all three services differ across the seven operating companies participating in this study. The six geographic indicator variables are jointly significant at $p < .05$ and explain about 1% of the variance in each dependent variable.

A customer rates billing service substantially lower if there has been a billing problem ($p < .005$), and the effects of satisfactorily resolving the problem does not entirely offset this impact ($p < .005$). Customer assessments of local and long-distance service are negatively affected by the perceived frequency of static, connection, dial tone, and disconnection service problems ($p < .005$). For both services, a customer attaches the most importance to a static-free line (which explains about 12–15% of the variance in the dependent variable). Together, these results suggest the importance of reliability (or trouble-free service) and responsiveness (willingness to help customers). The service provider cannot entirely regain customer goodwill even if the problem is rectified by courteous personnel. The effects of the long-distance carrier variables on long-distance service rating are jointly, but not individually, statistically significant ($p < .05$). It is interesting to note that MCI customers rate long-distance service lower than AT & T or Sprint. One explanation for this result is that, at the time of the survey, MCI predominantly relied on microwave technology, which can occasionally result in degraded transmission.

Quality

In the residential model, the primary determinants of overall telephone service quality (QUALITY) are the BILLING, LOCAL, and LONG variables (see Table 2). Each variable has a positive, statistically significant effect on overall quality ($p < .005$). Local services is the most important of the three, explaining about 12% of the variance in QUALITY. Customers' assessments of installation service, operator assistance, repair service, and directory assistance seem to be much less important in customers' evaluations of overall quality.

---

[8]The percentage of variance explained is calculated as the square of the standardized coefficient (not reported). Since the predictor variables are not independent, this calculation is only an approximation.

Of installation, operator assistance, repair, and directory assistance services, only the customer's assessment of repair service (REPAIR, NO-REPAIR) is statistically significant ($p < .005$), explaining about 3% of the variance in the dependent variable. One implication of this result concerns the net effect of a repair contact on customers' overall quality assessment. In the QUALITY equation, a repair contact decreases QUALITY by .06. Since the REPAIR coefficient (.17) multiplied by the highest rating (4) is .68, this quality 'penalty' is more than offset by the highest level of repair-service performance. Of course, not all customers give a repair contact the highest rating. One possible reason for the importance of repair service is that it is a relatively unambiguous signal of responsiveness.

Residential customers with no experience with another telephone service provider have higher assessments of overall quality than customers with such experience (NO-CHANGE; $p < .005$).For those customers with alternative carrier experience, quality assessments depends on perceptions of current versus prior telephone service quality ($p < .005$). The variables NO-CHANGE and COMPARE jointly explain about 22% of the variance in QUALITY. Overall quality also depends on whether the customer perceives telephone service to have improved in the past year (IMPROVE); this effect is very small, but statistically significant ($p < .005$). In addition, heavy users of local telephone service (#LOCAL) rate QUALITY higher ($p < .005$) than light users. In contrast, heavy users of long-distance telephone service (#LONG) rate QUALITY lower than light users ($p < .005$). The results for heavy versus light users highlight the role of disconfirmation. Apparently, local service typically provides positive disconfirmation, whereas long-distance service provides negative disconfirmation.

Value

As expected, the most important determinant of perceived service value is QUALITY ($p < .005$), explaining 4% of the variance in VALUE (see Table 2). In addition, a customer's perception of the performance levels of local service (LOCAL) and long-distance service (LONG) affects VALUE directly ($p < .05$) as well as indirectly (through QUALITY), explaining an additional 4% of the variance in VALUE. As before, LOCAL is the most important component. In contrast, BILLING does not affect VALUE except through QUALITY. One explanation for this finding is that customers consider local and long-distance services, but not billing service, as core services or critical signals of service-quality dimensions.

The second most important set of determinants of perceived service value are the customer's disconfirmation experiences. Residential customers' assessments of service value are positively affected by lack of experience with another service provider ($p < .005$), unfavorable experience with another service provider ($p < .05$), and improvements in service in the past year ($p < .005$). However, heavy users of local or long-distance service do not systematically rate VALUE higher or lower ($p < .05$). Together, the disconfirmation variables (NO-CHANGE, COMPARE, IMPROVE) account for about 6% of the variance in customers' assessments of telephone service value. They also indirectly influence service value through QUALITY.

These findings support the notion that customers' perceptions of core, facilitating, and supporting telephone services and their disconfirmation experiences are weighted differently in assessing value than in assessing overall quality. Local and long-distance services (LOCAL, LONG) and disconfirmation experiences (NO-CHANGE, COMPARE, IMPROVE) are weighted more heavily in assessing VALUE.

A joint statistical test indicates that residential customer characteristics (#HOUSE, AGE, INCOME, BUSINESS, EMPLOYED) affect VALUE but do not affect QUALITY. (Note that this hypothesis is implicit in Figure 1). Separate statistical tests indicate that the effects of #HOUSE, AGE, and INCOME on VALUE are small but statistically significant ($p < .005$). The effects of these three variables are in the hypothesized direction. For example, older customers value telephone service more highly.

DISCUSSION

The results of this study support several basic theoretical propositions. Consistent with prior exploratory research concerning service quality, a key determinant of overall service quality is the gap between performance and expectations (i.e. disconfirmation). For residential customers, perceived telephone service quality depended on the disconfirmation triggered by perceived changes in existing service or changes in service providers.

A customer's assessment of overall service quality is also directly affected by perceptions of performance levels. This finding is consistent with the CS/D literature, but it is a new finding for the service-quality literature. It is interesting to note that disconfirmation explains a larger proportion of the variance in service quality than performance, whereas, in prior studies performance explains a larger proportion of the variance in customer satisfaction than disconfirmation (Churchill and Surprenant, 1982).

Customers' assessments of service value are positively related to their evaluations of service quality. However, service quality and value are not identical constructs. For example, disconfirmation experiences were more important in assessing telephone service value than in assessing telephone service quality since disconfirmation was found to affect value directly as well as indirectly (through quality). In addition, customers weight their perceptions of the performance levels of component services differently for service quality than for value. For example, billing, local, and long-distance services were weighted more heavily for value than for quality. Finally, customers' personal characteristics are important in assessing value, but not quality. Thus, perceived service value seems to be a 'richer', more comprehensive measure of customers' overall evaluation of a service than service quality.

Most authors have viewed value as the outcome of a trade-off between a single 'overall quality' construct and sacrifice. However, these results suggest that the customer's value function is more complex. Hence, this study rebuts the simplistic notion underlying many quality-measurement programs, namely that the service provider should focus on maximizing average customer ratings of service quality while minimizing costs (i.e. price). Our research suggests that service providers must offer flexible services that satisfy the different tastes and expectations of each market segment. It also shows that managers can operationalize a model of customers' assessments of service quality and value with survey data. However, it is clear that the specification and operationalization of the model must be carefully tailored to the specific service context. This effort will be rewarded by the many managerial implications that can be derived from estimation results.

Research is needed to further explore the antecedents of customer satisfaction, service quality, and service value. First, there are many measurement and scaling issues to be addressed with respect to these constructs. The present study employs single measures of each model construct, whereas multiple measures would be more appropriate. Second, either experimental or econometric research could be used to further explore the linkages among these constructs. The theoretical linkages described in Figure 1 are considerably more complex than those represented by equations (1), (2), and (3b). For example, a structural equation for customer satisfaction can be integrated into the multistage model. Third, the model should be applied in other contexts (e.g. financial services, retailing, air transportation) to establish its generalizability.

REFERENCES

Anderson, N. H. (1974) 'Information Integration Theory: A Brief Survey'. In *Contemporary Developments in Mathematical Psychology*. Vol. 2 (D. H. Kranz *et al.*, Eds). San Francisco: Freeman, pp. 236–305.

Brunswick, E. (1952) *The Conceptual Framework of Psychology*. Chicago: University of Chicago Press.

Cardozo, R. (1965) 'An Experimental Study of Customer Effort, Expectations and Satisfaction'. *Journal of Marketing Research* **2** (3): 244–249.

Churchill, G. A. Jr. and Surprenant, C. (1982) 'An Investigation into the Determinants of Customer Satisfaction'. *Journal of Marketing Research* **19** (4): 491–504.

Grönroos, C. (1987) 'Developing the Service Offering: A Source of Competitive Advantage'. In *Add Value to Your Service* (C. Surprenant, Ed.). Chicago: American Marketing Association, pp. 81–85.

Hauser, J. R. and Clausing, D. (1988) 'The House of Quality'. *Harvard Business Review* **66** (May–June): 63–73.

Holbrook, M. B. and Corfman, K. P. (1985) 'Quality and Value in the Consumption Experience: Phaedrus Ride Again'. In *Perceived Quality* (J. Jacoby and J. Olson, Eds). Lexington, MA: Lexington, pp. 31–57.

Johnston, J. (1972) *Econometric Methods*. New York: McGraw-Hill.

LaBarbera, P. A. and Mazursky, D. (1983) 'A Longitudinal Assessment of Consumer Satisfaction/Dissatisfaction: The Dynamic Aspect of the Cognitive Process'. *Journal of Marketing Research* **20** (4): 393–404.

Oliver, R. L. (1980) 'A Cognitive Model of the Antecedents and Consequences of Satisfaction Decisions'. *Journal of Marketing Research* **42** (4): 460–469.

Oliver, R. L. (1981) 'Measurement and Evaluation of Satisfaction Processes in Retail Settings'. *Journal of Retailing* **57** (Fall): 25–48.

Oliver, R. L. (1989) 'Processing of the Satisfaction Response in Consumption: A Suggested Framework and Research Propositions'. *Journal of Consumer Satisfaction, Dissatisfaction and Complaining Behavior* **2**: 1–16.

Olshavsky, R. W. (1985) 'Perceived Quality in Consumer Decision Making: An Integrated Theoretical Perspective'. In *Perceived Quality* (J. Jacoby and J. Olson, Eds). Lexington, MA: Lexington, pp. 3–29.

Olshavsky, R. W. and Miller, J. A. (1972) 'Consumer Expectations. Product Performance and Perceived Product Quality'. *Journal of Marketing Research* **9** (1): 19–21.

Olson, J. C. and Dover, P. (1976) 'Effects of Expectations, Product Performance, and Disconfirmation on Belief Elements of Cognitive Structures'. In *Advances in Consumer Research*, Vol. 3 (B. B. Anderson, Ed.) Provo, UT: Association for Consumer Research.

Parasuraman, A., Zeithaml, V. A. and Berry, L. L. (1985) 'A Conceptual Model of Service Quality and Its Implications for Future Research'. *Journal of Marketing*, **49** (4):41–50.

Parasuraman, A., Zeithaml, V. A. and Berry, L. L. (1988) 'SERVQUAL: A Multiple Item Scale for Measuring Consumer Perceptions of Service Quality'. *Journal of Retailing* **64** (1): 12–37.

Phillips, L. W., Chang, D. R. and Buzzell, R. D. (1983) 'Product Quality, Cost Position and Business Performance: A Test of Some Key Hypotheses'. *Journal of Marketing* **47** (Spring): 26–43.

Thaler, R. (1985) 'Mental Accounting and Consumer Choice'. *Marketing Science* **4** (Summer): 199–214.

Tse, D. K. and Wilton, P. C. (1988) 'Models of Consumer Satisfaction Formation: An Extension. *Journal of Marketing Research* **25** (2): 204–212.

Urban, G. L. and Hauser, J. R. (1980) *Design and Marketing of New Products.* Englewood Cliffs NJ: Prentice-Hall.

Zeithaml, V. A. (1988) 'Consumer Perceptions of Price, Quality and Value: A Means-End Model and Synthesis of Evidence'. *Journal of Marketing* **52** (3): 2–22.

Zeithaml, V. A., Parasuraman, A. and Berry, L. L. (1990) *Delivering Quality Service.* New York: Free Press.

17

Buyer Perceived Service Quality in Industrial Networks

Maria Holmlund and Sören Kock

A NEW SERVICE FIRM ON THE MARKET

A service firm building relationships to potential buyers in an industrial market faces several strategic problems. The two major questions are: (1) how to create relationships with potential buyers, and (2) how to determine the quality level of the service offered. The first question focuses on the problem of building relationships – is it possible to break existing relations between potential buyers and their present suppliers; is it possible to become an additional supplier to potential buyers and in that way receive a part of the purchases; or it is possible to approach new buyers that have never bought the product before. The question concerning the level of quality is at least as important for success as how to choose a way of creating relationships. If the quality level is too high, it might result in the firm not being able to cover the production costs. A low-quality level, on the other hand, is likely to result in time- and money-consuming corrections of quality problems as well as dissatisfied lost buyers.

The difficulties in determining the right quality level are obvious both when establishing and maintaining relationships. The costs of finding the right quality level are, however, high. Accordingly and especially for small firms, it is critical to find the right quality level, because necessary large investments in buyer relationships, technical equipment, etc., do not allow a trial-and-error strategy for a longer period of time. The supplier can not only concentrate on correcting the mistakes upon delivery; there has to be quality thinking in the firm as a whole and at all levels.

Earlier studies of perceived service quality in the industrial market are few. The studies that have dealt with service quality have usually been made in the consumer market, or they have dealt with quality aspects in the production process. The importance of service quality, however, can not be denied though, because many studies clearly indicate its importance (Brown *et al.*, 1991; Bazel and Gale, 1987; Grönroos, 1990b; Yamagashi *et al.*, 1988).

Reprinted by permission of the publisher from *Industrial Marketing Management*, Vol. 24, pp. 109–121.

Service quality

The purpose of this study are to find different aspects of perceived service quality in an industrial context and to determine how buyer perceived service quality influences a supplier's possibilities to build relationships. The supplier in our study is a service firm, whose primary service is laser treatment of metal components in the purpose of improving their durability and extending their lifetime. The supplier creates, together with the buyers, suitable laser applications and possesses highly flexible laser equipment. The supplier, in other words, markets a service, an intangible product, which mainly can be characterized as a process or a series of processes, where among others R&D, testing, and production are included. There are some elements in the laser treatment, which are the same regardless of the buyer, but it is in many ways adapted to the individual buyer's needs and wants. The buyers are themselves actively involved in developing the product because they provide the supplier with specifications and components.

The measuring of quality usually involves everything from suitability for use to zero mistakes in the production. In our study we have chosen to approach service quality from a holistic perspective, and mainly from the buyer's point of view. Service quality is consequently defined as the buyers' perceptions of the service offered by the seller. As several buyers have been interviewed, some of the answers will complement each other, and some will even reflect opposite views. This is, however natural as the perception of service quality is person-and situation-specific, and consequently, can vary at least partly from buyer to buyer and from situation to situation.

Until now, research concerning service quality has been carried out mostly in the consumer market, and it has been assumed either explicitly or implicitly that the service quality dimensions found there can be applied to the industrial market as well. In the consumer market quality is usually divided into a technical ('what') and a functional ('how') dimension (Grönroos, 1990b). These dimensions can further be divided into determinants like reliability, responsiveness, competence, access, courtesy, communication, credibility, security, understanding, and tangibility. Our view is, however, that it is not correct to accept this assumption without a closer evaluation, because there are many major differences within a certain type of market and especially between different types of markets.

The quality concept particularly when establishing relationships is a further cause for this study because service quality is considered to be one of the most vital factors when choosing a supplier. Firms establishing positions in networks, where advanced and adapted technology along side with high transfer capability (Hammarkvist *et al.*, 1982) are of importance, are especially forced to invest considerable resources to find the right level of quality, as it is clearly not the technical aspects of the offer alone that determine the success. A smaller firm with limited resources is even more dependent on finding and developing the right quality level in a reasonable time. These factors motivate a study where the aim is to find different aspects of buyer perceived service quality is a highly developed and adapted technology context.

The theoretical framework is derived from the network approach and the service quality concept. Empirical data has been gathered through in-depth interviews, both in the focal firm, the supplier, and in five buying companies for whom the supplier has developed laser applications. The interviews were carried out between autumn

1991 and spring 1993 with the people who were responsible for developing the contacts with the laser application supplier. These people had positions as technical manager, vice presidents, mechanical engineer, production engineer, and maintenance manager. The buyers were both medium-sized and large companies in a varied line of business – pulp, forest, defense, power plant – and were situated in the same country as the supplier, namely Sweden.

ESTABLISHING RELATIONSHIPS

When a firm builds a position in a network it establishes relationships to other firms who already are embedded in the network. A business network contains: (1) actors, i.e. individuals, firms, departments, organizations, or coalitions of organizations; (2) activities emerging when the actors combine, create, develop, and transfer resources; (3) interactions between the actors that create exchanges and adaptations; (4) relationships aiming at long-term commitments and bonds; and (5) both direct and indirect resources (Häkansson and Johanson, 1992; Kock, 1992).

Hammarkvist *et al.* (1982) state that it is important to choose which network to penetrate. This is the case when the firm chooses to establish relationships in one network where its potential exchange partners are. However, when for example a newly founded firm begins to build relationships to other firms, two situations can arise, the firm can either penetrate one existing network where the potential firms are, or build relationships to firms in separate networks. In the latter case, the established firm connects the previously unconnected networks with each other. Figure 1 illustrates these two situations.

Situation 1

A firm that recently has started a business probably has a relatively limited network, consisting mainly of relationships to some suppliers and some other firms with an interest in the firm. These firms connected to the new firm can be financiers and suppliers of raw materials, machinery, etc. If the firm builds relationships to firms in a network, it will eventually become a part of this network. The network to which the buyers belong will, in other words, expand and include the new supplier and the original network.

Situation 2

The firm is also in this case newly founded and has a similar network to the situation described previously. The firm is about to create a new relationship in buyers in separate networks in different lines of business. These networks can be separate because of differences in the products produced or used production technology. The firm will act as a binding link between the different networks. The networks will be indirectly connected through the firm, which serves the previously separate networks. This kind of situation occurs when a firm has developed a problem solution, a

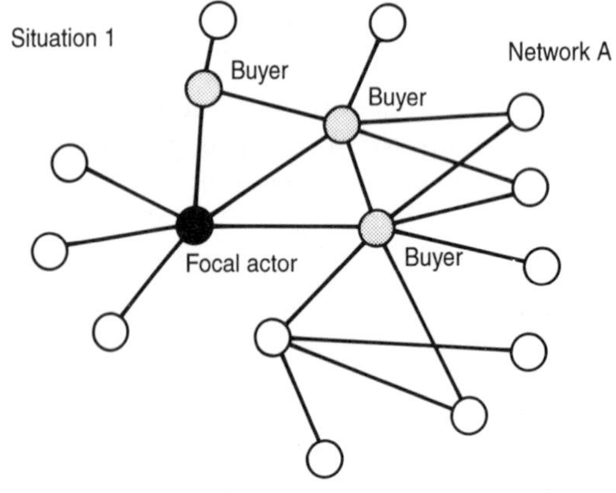

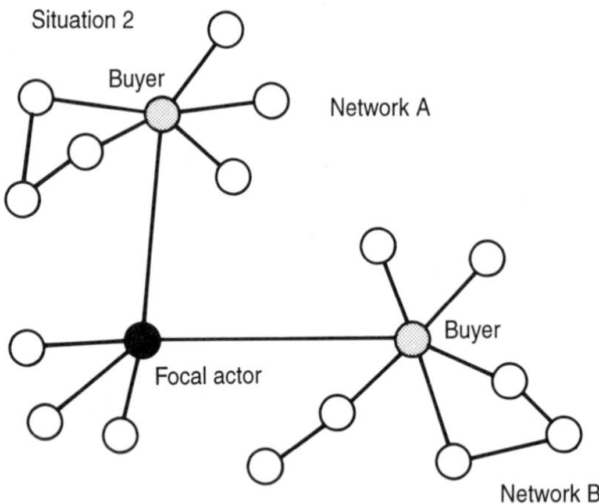

Fig. 1. A focal actor's strategic alternatives when establishing relationships.

product that can be used in many different areas. This creates a more complex situation for a newly founded firm and demands more resources, greater flexibility of the product, more varied social contacts, and more information because the business areas are many and probably differ from each other.

Quality in an industrial network

Quality has traditionally been measured from either the seller's or the buyer's perspective and very little attention has been paid to the dyadic relationships or networks. In a dyadic relationship both the seller's and the buyer's perception of the perceived quality is evaluated, without including the impact of other buyers and their influence. Using a network perspective implies that both direct and indirect influences and relationships are included. It is in other words, a more holistic approach because we analyze not only direct influences on quality by one or two firms, but include also influences from other firms in the network indirectly influencing these firms and their relationship. If, for example, one of the seller's buyers requires ISO certified products, the other buyers of the seller will simultaneously benefit from this requirement.

A network perspective is thus not limited to relationships between one seller and one of its buyers. In most cases the buyers use the purchased product in their production processes to produce products to sell to their buyers, resulting in quality requirements by the buyers' buyers to consequently affect the buyer demands from the seller. In turn the buyers' buyers are selling their products to their buyers extending the quality chain even further. A firm penetrating a network must bear the impact of the actors' embeddedness in mind and consequently a service strategy built on quality must be derived from an evaluation of the needs and wants of not only the buyers to whom it has direct relationships, but also the buyers' buyers, suppliers' suppliers, etc., to whom the firm has indirect relationships. The research and planning undertaken before entering a network must therefore include actors in different positions, otherwise the possibilities to offer the right quality are limited and the firm will not achieve the desired position in the network. In the same way, a firm unable to respond to the demands and requirements of the firms in the network will face a weakened position in the network.

The supplier and the offered service

The focal actor in our study is a service firm establishing relationships to potential buyers in separate business networks, for example, pulp, forest, auto, defense, engineering, and power plant industries. The firm has developed a patented technological innovation within laser technology, which can be used in many fields. The flexibility of this kind of laser treatment of metal components is illustrated by the president who said: 'We have had some kind of cooperation with 21 of the 100 biggest companies in Sweden'.

The novelty with this method is that the powder used to improve the wearing surface is not applied directly onto the metal components, instead it is applied by means of the laser beam on the metal component. Parts of the engine in production processes that are exposed to wear and tear can either be prepared beforehand or after being in use for a while. The advantages for the buyer are more durable production machinery as well as fewer breakdowns. These advantages are highly desirable as they help save a lot of money and minimize delays.

The studied supplier is the only firm on the market selling this kind of laser application method. Other firms have tried to develop materials and applications, which would make it possible to prolong the lifetime of surfaces exposed to intensive wear. Some have even tried to develop a similar method, but these experiments all seem to have failed. Therefore, there are no competitors with exactly the same laser application method. The buyers can of course choose to use the products until they replace them with new ones. The immediate competitors are a few large companies in Switzerland, the United States, and Japan who have specialized in limited applications. In addition to these there are some companies producing substitute surface treatment methods. Other available methods, however, cannot guarantee the same durability and reliability. Their areas of applicability are neither as many as that of the laser application method.

The entrepreneur, who also is the president, owns 63% of the firm and financiers own 37%. The organization is divided into production, R&D and other services. The firm is on one hand technically oriented, because the carrying out of the buyers' technical specifications is very essential, on the other hand the entrepreneur claims to offer services highly adapted to the buyers' needs.

The supplier's quality objectives

Zero mistakes as well as the highest possible technical quality used to be the supplier's goal in whatever was undertaken; now the aim is to offer *the right quality* – from the buyers' point of view. The earlier quality aspiration level was found to be too expensive and the buyers, especially new ones, found the price too high. Achieving a quality level that can be regarded too high is not regarded necessary by any one involved, and it certainly does not justify the attached cost's. A trade-off between costs and the quality level is a guideline when determining what quality level to offer. Simultaneously it constitutes the main problem the supplier faces and has to deal with daily.

The firm's functions are mainly considered to be production, money, personnel, and professionalism. In addition they also consider competence, creativity, quality, and commercialism as key functions. Their opinion is that the main shortages in the firm for the moment lie in the fields of professionalism, commercialism, and money. A possible reason could be that the firm still is too technically oriented, and is trying to reach too high a quality level, which in turn leads to very high costs. Another reason could be that the firm is relatively new, which also applies to the personnel, and that the employees do not yet have enough knowledge about the potential buyers. This fact was underlined by one of the buyers, who found the supplier very skilful in solving technical problems, but clearly lacking in commercial skills when marketing the laser treatments.

The supplier's buyers

It is crucial for the firm to know and learn the buyers' different needs, which can vary a lot as many lines of business are involved. The aim of the supplier has been to build a network of relationships consisting of only positive relationships connecting previously separate networks. Cook and Emerson (1984) and Yamagashi, Gillmore and Cook (1988) claim that power in social exchange networks can consist of three different relationships: positive, negative, or mixed. Positive relationships imply that one relation does not exclude another, or both can exist side by side, for instance that two firms can use the same supplier.

This can occasionally lead to the supplier being forced to renounce potential buyers because they compete with present ones. In other words the supplier deals with and develops relationships with mainly one buyer per line of business. All of the studied buyers correspondingly report that they would break the relation if the supplier established relationships with their competitors. The flexible laser application method that can be used in treating fundamentally all kinds of metal surfaces creates a large potential in spite of this substantial limitation.

The supplier's relation to the buyers

The supplier states that 'it is six times more difficult and more expensive for a new supplier to find buyers than it is for an established supplier. An unknown production technology makes it even more complicated'. A problem the supplier clearly faces is how to show potential buyers what it stands for, and how to motivate the costs necessary for bringing forth a suitable laser application. Developing a suitable application takes place in cooperation with the buyer. The buyer provides the supplier with detailed specifications and the supplier develops and tests different applications in his laboratory. After having developed a possible suitable laser application, full-scale tests are carried out. Sometimes these tests take place in the production facilities of the buyer, occasionally even the end user is involved. Provided the technical quality is good enough production on a regular basis starts. The whole process is very costly, and it can, of course, be stopped whenever the parties want. The terms of the agreement are usually, but not always, stipulated in written contracts. The buyers supply the metal components, and the service of the supplier consists of treating the metal surfaces in laboratories as agreed upon. Together with the buyer, a goal is set to develop a suitable laser application method and to meet the buyer's needs and in the end increase the value of their products.

The supplier also explicitly states that he or she is willing to enter different forms of cooperation with the buyers – for instance joint ventures, licenses, system selling or technical cooperation. Only three to five development projects take place simultaneously as the supplier wants to be able to concentrate on each individual buyer and to learn about the buyer's needs in detail. The potential and actual buyers are divided in segments – groups according to application area and degree of engagement. The personal contacts to the buyers are made systematically, and according to the supplier, good personal contacts are crucial for anyone wanting to get and to stay in touch with buyers in order to create and develop relationships. The entrepreneur has estimated that about 50% of his or her time is spent establishing and maintaining contacts with potential and present buyers.

Establishing new relationships

Establishing relationships is clearly not an easy task. In the interest of the buyer it is often desirable to minimize the number of suppliers in order to decrease the exchange costs (Axelsson and Laage Hellman, 1991). Long-term relationships create a pressure for development (Hammarkvist *et al.*, 1982), which in turn results in investments in bonds and commitment. The evolving bonds make it more difficult and expensive to break the relation. Hedaa (1992) describes four different situations that could arise when a buyer chooses new suppliers.

First, when a buyer is new on the market or has just started to use the particular product, it is natural that new relationships to suppliers are built, i.e. the supplier is given a possibility to reach completely new buyers. New technology can be a further reason for buyers asking for suppliers. Axelsson and Laage Hellman (1991) estimate that 20% to 25% of the engineering industry's technical development occurs within existing relations in Sweden.

Secondly, the buyer wants to change suppliers because he or she, for some reason, is not satisfied with the present supplier and therefore is looking for a new one. The reason can often be found on dissatisfaction with the quality offered, deliveries, adaptations, technology, or price. Dubois (1992) shows in a study carried out in a Swedish manufacturing firm covering 1964 to 1992 that 43 changes have occurred in the relationships to the suppliers of 11 specific components. Of the changes, 25 have been price related, in some cases the variation in price was up to 50%. It is also noteworthy that in 11 of the 25 cases the suppliers were able to come back at a later date. Six of the changes had been made owing to the suppliers' weak ability to deliver, and only three changes were caused by the supplier failing to meet the buyer's need for technical innovations.

Thirdly, we have one group of buyers that consist of those who buy a product but for one reason or another are looking for an additional supplier. One reason might be that the buyer wants to decrease the dependence arising from having only one supplier. By having more than one supplier, the buyer can spread the orders and acquire more general product, price, and market information. Another reason may be that the buyer wants to get a lower price or more competitive payment terms and by adding a new supplier, can keep the supplier aware of the possibility that they can be replaced if they fail in some way or try unreasonably to increase the price. This type of thinking is in congruence with the classical buying philosophy (Axelsson and Laage Hellman, 1991). Using alternative suppliers helps the buying firm to obtain information about prices and innovations and thereby to have better information when making decisions.

Finally, we have the possibility for a supplier to go in and break relationships between a potential buyer and his or her present supplier. Hedaa (1992) says that in a discussion with the sales division of a firm in Finland it came to light that only about 10% of their new relationships came from breaking existing relationships. In order to manage to break existing relationships, the supplier has to have something unique, like a new technology, a new product concept or lower prices to offer the potential buyer.

The studied buyers' cooperation with the supplier

All the buyers in our study mentioned that they were not fully satisfied with their present suppliers, but there were no alternatives until the new laser treatment method was made known. They all faced considerable costs caused by wrong deliveries and corrections. These costs, extra expenses, are not easily estimated because they do not only consist of expenses for corrections and discarded materials but also of indirect and alternative costs like lost working time, repetitive work, inspections, and so on. Therefore all of the studied buyers had more or less actively been searching for a method that would result in fewer quality problems and decreased quality costs.

In spite of great uncertainty in the beginning of the cooperation and high initial costs, the buyers chose to initiate cooperation with the new and relatively unknown supplier, because there were many considerable potential advantages, both technical and economic, with this kind of laser application. It was not the end users who demanded an improvement, quite the contrary, the buyers were prepared themselves to pay the extra costs. The buyers' motives for choosing the supplier of laser application were two-fold; the ability to offer more competitive and durable products to their buyers and the possibility to reduce their own quality costs.

Quality certificates

The awareness of quality that exists in industrial firms is obvious, and more and more companies apply for and are granted quality certificates like ISO. The certificates are used as a competitive mean and assure that quality thinking permeates the whole firm, including suppliers used. A firm aiming at quality and ISO certificates has to use suppliers that have been granted an ISO certificate. This can be an additional driving force for a firm to start looking for suppliers. The competitive advantage that an ISO certificate gives today probably will be eliminated in the future as more or less all firms acquire quality standards.

All of the studied buyers have applied for ISO certificates and were collecting the needed documentation. Consequently the buyers considered themselves having good quality standards and emphasizing quality in general. It was not a problem that the supplier in this case did not have an ISO certificate because the supplier was familiar with ISO standards and requirements. ISO certificates include only technical issues of the product, buyer perceived quality and other unnoticed and hard to measure aspects are left out from the documentation and certification. Buyer perceived quality is much more than technical aspects of the product and therefore not the same as a certificate, but an overall impression of the supplier.

BUYER PERCEIVED SERVICE QUALITY

When measuring buyer perceived service quality in the industrial market, it is in our view essential to include the context in which the firms operate. Market investments, e.g. investments of time and money in bonds, mutual commitments as well as a long-term perspective have to be taken into consideration when examining service quality. Market investments, which have led to bonds, make the firms more or less unwilling to break the relationship as well provide a stable secure ground for product development, change, and information diffusion. In service quality models created for the consumer market (Grönroos, 1983), exit is always an alternative for dissatisfied consumers, as the number of firms offering the same kind of products, is usually quite high and it is easy to switch between products and firms. Naturally this opportunity also exists to some extent in the industrial market, but the loss of made investments tends to be significantly higher, because the heterogeneity of the resources makes the cost of changing supplier high. Furthermore, it can be difficult to find a new supplier.

In Figure 2 the relationship between two actors, a supplier and a buyer, in the industrial market is built on interactions and investments in bonds. Usually, the relationship starts with an interaction, before which the firms stipulate their goals, e.g. what they want to achieve based on perceived needs. The goal of the firm is to gain access to resources controlled by the other firm, e.g., technical competence, money, and raw materials. The actors are said to be attracted to each others' strategic identities. An actor's strategic identity consists of the direct and the indirect resources he or she controls and the buyers' business strategy (Axelsson and Häkansson, 1989). The resources can be divided into personal assets, software assets, hardware assets, organizational assets, and capital assets. Direct resources means that the actor has direct control, i.e. hierarchic power, over the resources, e.g. patents, machines, facilities. Indirect resources can be gained through interactions with other actors in long-term relationships, e.g. raw material, personnel, money (Kock, 1992).

The interactions consist of three types of exchanges: (1) business exchange, (2) social exchange, and (3) information exchange. One or more of these exchanges takes place every time the firms interact with each other, and every interaction leads to investments in different kinds of bonds. Bonds are developed as a consequence of commitments and the use of resources in a specific purpose in order to achieve stability, closeness, security, and long-term relationships with other firms in the network. *Technical bonds* are based on technical adaptations of the product, materials, equipment to the buyer, and can be very hard to break for a new supplier. *Planning bonds* arise when the firms adjust their logistic functions to each other and for example implement just-in-time deliveries and on-line-contact, whereby costs for stock keeping substantially are reduced. *Knowledge bonds* are gradually developed as the firms learn about each other's strengths, weaknesses, needs, problems and possibilities. *Social bonds* take time to develop and are based on individual representatives getting to know and trust each other and can be a complement to

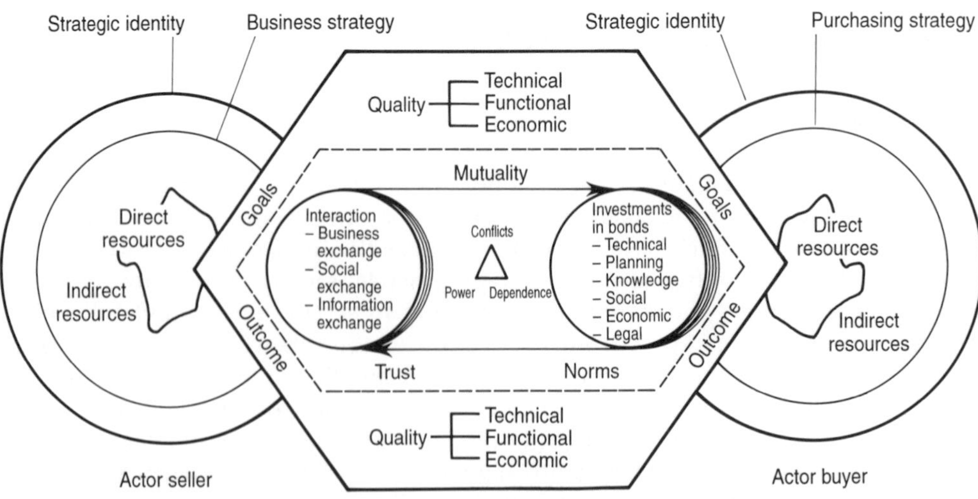

Fig. 2. Quality and relationships in industrial service organizations.

written contracts. *Economic and legal bonds* are made up of contracts, legal ownership, different forms of cooperation, payment terms, etc.

In the relation between the actors, there are also other interorganizational flows like power, dependence and conflicts. Particularly in situations where the firms are specialized and very unequal in size, there is a high risk for one of the firms of becoming highly dependent. Furthermore, different norms are developed, which restrict and guide the actors in the interactions. Within the relationship trust, which is a form of mutual confidence or reliance, will usually gradually evolve. Trust can be regarded as a prerequisite for all kinds of relationships, because the lack of trust often makes it impossible to continue to make exchanges.

The dynamic relationship constitutes of interactions leading to market investments, which lead to new interactions, which lead to further market investments, and so on. This proposal is true, however, only as long as the interacting firms are satisfied with the outcomes of the exchanges. A conformity between the goals and the outcomes are in other words needed. Service quality on the consumer market has been measured in a similar way. Grönroos (1990b) states that consumer perceived service quality can be found in the perceived difference between service expectations and experienced service. In the case that the perceived service matches or exceeds the expectations the buyer will be satisfied with the service. If the service, on the other hand, does not meet with the expectations the buyer will be dissatisfied.

We wish, however, to make a distinction between goals and expectations. An organization with a goal has actively been involved in the setting of the aims for the exchanges. The organization has set the objectives after a decision process based on bounded rationality. Although goals are on the organizational level usually expressed by groups of individuals (Parasuraman *et al.* (1985), expectations can be said to exist on an individual level. Many persons are thus involved in a relationship and everyone does not have to have been actively involved in the setting of the aims. In some cases the relationship can start with interactions on the top level and later spread to the functional level. A person at the functional level, does not have to have explicit goals for interacting although he or she will most certainly have expectations. A conclusion from this reasoning is that goals and outcomes will be based on active explicit behavior concerning the objectives of the relationship based on economic and financial plans. Expectations are more individual assumptions concerning the exchanges.

Goals of the firms

The goals are mainly economic and technical, but also other aspects of the exchanges as the social dimension can be regarded as equally important. The economic goal stipulated by the firm does not necessarily have to be in congruence with neoclassic profit maximization. Instead an actor can try to attain outcomes in line with other kinds of goals and strive for relationships based on mutuality and trust. A prerequisite for lasting relationships is the absence of opportunistic behavior.

The buyer–supplier relationship will include three dimensions concerning the service quality. Parallel to quality goals regarding the technical solution and functional quality there are economic goals. The quality is equivalent to the extent that the outcomes correspond to goals and expectations on each of the three dimensions. A clear correspondence thus emerges between the quality dimensions and the bonds in the relationship. The *technical solution* in the exchange corresponds to technical, knowledge and partly to legal bonds, i.e. contracts stipulating technical specifications. The *functional quality* on the other hand corresponds to knowledge, planning, and social bonds. The *economic quality* consists of economic and partly of legal bonds between the firms.

Economic quality dimension

All business has to be profitable, efficient, effective, and productive; in the long run an actor will not survive unless he or she is profitable. Productivity indicates how efficiently the resources are utilized and can be divided into internal and external efficiency. Improving productivity does not necessarily imply declining quality; on the contrary, quality improvements often lead to improved productivity. This is possible as waste and the repetition of tasks are reduced and as the knowledge of the needs and wants of the buyers increases.

The economic quality dimension implies for the buyer that the relationship has to be profitable. Without profitability, a termination of the relationship is very likely. Profitability means that the buyer can receive compensation at the next step in the activity chain for costs in the exchanges with the supplier. To the supplier the economic quality dimension means that the received price covers total costs, including both internal and external quality failure costs. Total costs that arise in a relationship can be considerably higher than the direct costs, which usually are easier to measure. Total costs also consist of indirect costs, psychological costs, and quality failure costs (Grönroos, 1990a).

Quality failure costs can be divided into four groups (Parasuraman *et al.*, 1991). *Internal quality failure costs* (alterations, inspections, storage, etc.) arise before the transfer to the buyer, when products have to be thrown away. *External quality failure costs* like repairs, guarantees, and complaints are costs arising when taking care of delivered products, which do not meet with the quality standards. *Inspection costs* arise in connection with the evaluation whether the products and processes meet with the specifications. The last type of quality failure costs is *preventive costs of introducing, implementing, and securing a quality system.* Correpondingly, the net price of the supplier for a product can be far below estimated profit because of unobserved extra expenses, costs. Some of the economic aspects of quality, like storage and inspections, are fairly easy to estimate and measure, and others, like possible preventive adjustments, are considerably more difficult to estimate.

Functional quality dimension

Parallel to economic goals, there are other quality goals. The technical solution can be observed and measured with specific technical requirements, like for example durability, precision, and ISO standards, and made explicit in contracts. The functional part of the product and its transfer is less tangible and can not easily be measured or estimated, at least not in quantitative terms. Functional issues are, however, equally important, if not even more important than technical ones. The functional quality dimension can be divided in two aspects, and consists of (1) how the individuals perceive the interactions and (2) how the transfer of the product is carried out. Functional quality thus consists of aspects of personal chemistry and the communication between the involved, if there is trust and commitment in the relationship, as well as how the deliveries are adjusted.

According to our studied buyers it is of utmost importance for the establishing firm to develop a so-called *capital of trust.* The capital of trust can, if properly managed, provide both financial returns and other kinds of returns for everyone involved. The establishing firm has to create and strengthen its trust with buyers, so that the buyer can trust it. It is not possible to any greater extent to urge on this process; it is a question of cumulatively developing trust on the personal level, normally a process lasting many years.

Honesty, mutuality, discretion, openness, ambition, realism, empathy, humbleness, seriousness, professional skill, pride, and communication skills – not necessarily in this order – were some of the crucial factors mentioned in the choice of supplier. It is important to have the courage to inform the buyer of unpleasant things like not being able to deliver on time and explain why. The buyer appreciates honesty like that from the suppliers, because it proves the right kind of attitude. If further enables the avoidance of many problems, costs, and delays, which otherwise tend to arise in connection with delays. It is often possible to somehow solve the problems through discussions and thereby no one has to lose time, money, materials, or even a buyer/supplier. In some cases the buyers actually terminate the supplier relationship if a delay occurs as delivery times are without exception to be kept. Other sanctions like a penalty fee can also sometimes result from delays.

A great deal of the success of a firm not only depends on resources under its direct control but largely on resources obtained through long-term relationships with suppliers. As one of the buyers expressed it 'We shall become the best buyer in the world, thereafter the best supplier in the world'. In other words, the firms have to be aware of their own strengths and weaknesses and have to have the will to improve and develop their business both toward the buyers and the suppliers.

Technical quality dimensions

As our study deals with establishing relationships from a technical service firm's point of view the fulfilment of technical specifications is very important, when the buyers evaluate the service quality. Unless the supplier can deliver a product that technically fulfils the requirement, future business is impossible and he or she can not stay in business in the long run. Technical standards are generally the first and the decisive criteria set by buyers for the suppliers to fulfil. An even quality level, which is reproducible on a large scale with only minor deviations, that is a high repetition accuracy, is the aim for both the supplier and the buyers. The costs for developing this even technical quality are crucial. If short-term thinking prevails in the buying firm, such high initial costs will deter the firm from developing such a technical service quality. Long-term thinking buyers are prerequisites for long-term thinking suppliers, because otherwise technical and financial plans do not motivate the choice and keeping of the supplier. Usually contracts stipulating projects are made that result in so-called project plans. In this way the firms safeguard themselves and are able to terminate the relationship if for example costs should increase unacceptably. Simultaneously the contracts facilitate the evaluation of realized projects.

The studied supplier says that quality implies fulfilling calculations and profit margins and simultaneously offering *value* for the buyer. This corresponds to both an internal and an external dimension regarding quality. For the supplier the follow-up of deliveries is a major problem. The documentation of made tests is done carefully and is by the buyers rated as one of the suppliers greatest competitive advantages.

CONCLUSIONS

It is obvious that economic considerations permeate the exchanges and the quality evaluation, at least in the long run. Buyers can experiment with new promising suppliers, but only to a certain extent, over a reasonable period of time – sooner or later the relationship enters a make-money phase. A termination of the relationship with the supplier does not always have to mean that the buyer finds the relationship a waste of time and money. On the contrary, the relationship can be seen as a stage in the development of a know-how-bank or slack (Oakland, 1989) that every firm has regarding the line of business, technology, and products. The buyer can in a later stage resume with the supplier if premises change and for example the technology of the supplier improves.

Service quality is by the buyers perceived as the fulfilment of technical specifications and around this there is the personal chemistry parallel to economic issues. Working social relations are a must; one cannot compensate this dimension with technology. Service quality must be considered from a holistic perspective consisting of technology, administration, security in deliveries, and a working information flow, etc. Security in deliveries is important because of high costs in a breakdown in the production process. Costs of storage and a feeling of insecurity are some obvious consequences in case of delays and other problems in the deliveries. A failing information flow can lead to a change of supplier, because the situation will become intolerable if the supplier doesn't give the right information, gives false information, or otherwise takes advantage of his position repeatedly.

Service quality is both competence and service, as patents alone do not guarantee success for a very long time – an appropriate balance between technology and market orientation is optimal. Irrespective of line of business the service firms who want to stay on top have to be market-oriented and complement hardware with buyer-adjusted software, that is concentrate on high quality in other aspects than the technical only. The result has to be high-qual–high-tech. Not even where technology seems to dominate can it by itself determine service quality perceived by buyers: it is the perception of all the interactions that counts, and in this, technology is only one part.

In our model describing service quality and relationships in industrial service organization, this is illustrated by dividing buyer perceived service quality into a technical, a functional, and an economic quality dimension. Good service quality is

Table 1. Management checklist for industrial service quality

Economic quality	Functional quality	Technical quality
Profitability	Mutuality	Technical specification
Productivity	Trust	R&D
Initial costs	Social relationships	Testing
Production costs	Communication	Production
Failure costs	Actors' characteristics	Adaptations
Inspection costs	Secure deliveries	Documentation
Storage costs	Adjusted deliveries	Equipment
Guarantee costs	Accessibility	Computer systems
Complaint costs		Administrative routines

formed when the supplier knows the buyers' needs and develops and adjusts the problem solution that it meets these needs. The importance of long-term relationships causes the suppliers and buyers to try to attain cooperation and to share the responsibility over the growth of processes and products (see Table 1).

In our study, buyer perceived service quality has been derived from three different quality dimensions, namely economic, functional, and technical quality. The economic quality dimension consists of different costs ranging from initial costs when establishing a new relationship, production costs when using the product in the production process, failure costs and inspection costs when the technical specifications are not met, storage costs for handling the products, to costs for guarantees and complaints. All these costs form the buyer's profitability for a specific product and a specific relationship. This study has shown that buyers embedded in an industrial network must be able to sell their product to buyers at a profit – this could be called a profit chain.

Functional quality explains how the individuals involved in the relationship perceive each other and how the product is transferred from the seller to the buyer. Mutuality, trust, communication, social relationships, and the actors' characteristics in terms of openness, empathy, professional skills, etc., are important criteria for buyers when they evaluate a seller and his performance. In other words, the buyer must have confidence in the seller. The second aspect with functional quality is the transfer of the product and here the buyers seem to emphasize secure deliveries and accessibility.

The technical quality is evaluated by analyzing if the products are produced in accordance with the technical specifications, how they are adapted to the buyer's needs, and the documentation of production. Furthermore, the seller's machinery, production facilities, cars, computer system, and administrative routines will influence how the buyers perceive the technical quality. Efficient production, implemented quality standards, clean facilities, buyer adapted computer systems, and administrative routines will increase the buyer's feelings of being important to the seller.

We have certified that different exchanges takes place in the interactions between the firms; there are exchanges of information, social contacts, and business. Through interacting the firms invest in relationships, which become long-term. These evolving long-term bonds influence the service quality perceived by the firms and must consequently be considered when studying the buyer evaluation of service quality. The bonds make up the context for the quality evaluation influencing the buyer and his or her evaluation, and to study only separate exchanges without including this context would result in a rather limited description.

The firms have goals for their relationships with the supplier expressed in technical, functional, and financial analyses, which are used when evaluating the service quality. In order to achieve a better problem solution there are goals concerning the technical requirements. Moreover, there are functional aspects of the service quality in the relationship based on honesty, trust and mutuality. The economic aspect is illustrated by one of the respondents when he used the phrase make-money phase as a base for a working relationship – concerns like productivity, efficiency, and effectiveness must always be taken into consideration, and they form a base for all kinds of cooperation and business.

The goals in the service quality dimensions and the outcomes are in the model to be seen as an evaluation of the interactions and bonds taking place in an atmosphere consisting of mutuality, trust, and norms. The service quality perceptions of the firms surround their relationship, and these perceptions control and direct the relationship. The quality perceptions emanate from the goals with the relationship and the outcomes of the exchanges. It is obviously difficult to generalize buyer perceived service quality as it is embedded in a specific context. The concept of service quality is dynamic and alters as the firms get to know each other and as the bonds evolve. In this article we have stressed the economic quality dimension, because earlier studies have not elaborated this issue to any larger extent.

REFERENCES

Axelsson, B. and Häkansson, H. (1989) *Inkop for konkurrenskraft (Purchasing for Competitiveness).* Lund: Faber.

Axelsson, B. and Laage Hellman, J. (1991) *Inkop en ledningsfraga (Purchasing: A Management Issue).* Stockholm: Mekanforbundets Forlag.

Brown, S. V., Gummesson, E., Edwardsson, B. and Gustafsson, B.O.(eds) (1991) *Quality in Service: Multidisciplinary and Multinational Perspectives.* Massachusetts: Lexington Books.

Buzell, R. D. and Gale, B. T. (1987) *The PIMS Principles: Linking Principles to Performance.* New York: The Free Press.

Cook, K. S. and Emerson, R. M. (1984) 'Exchange networks and the Analysis of Complex Organizations'. In *Research in the Sociology of Organizations,* Vol. 3. Greenwich, Connecticut: JAI Press, 1–30.

Dubois, A. (1992) '*Changing Purchasing Behavior in a Long Time Perspective*'. Paper presented at the Second Nordic Workshop on Interorganizational Research in Yxtaholm, Sweden, August 21–23.

Grönroos, C. (1983) 'Innovative Marketing Strategies and Organization Structures for Service Firms'. In *Emerging Perspectives on Service Marketing* (L. L. Berry, G. L. Shostack and G. D. Upah, Eds). Chicago: American Marketing Association, p. 21.

Grönroos, C. (1990a) '*Facing the Challenge of Service Competition. Costs of Bad Service*'. Unpublished working paper. Swedish School of Economics and Business Administration, Hesingfors, Finland.

Grönroos, C. (1990b) *Service Management and Marketing: Managing the Moments of Truth in Service Competition.* Massachusetts: Lexington Books.

Hammarkvist, K. O., Häkansson, H. and Mattsson, L. (1982) *Marknadsforing for knokurrenskraft (Marketing for Competitiveness)*. Malmo: Liber.

Hedaa, L. (1992) '*Under Norms of Long Lasting Supplier Buyer Relationships: How Are New Relationships Established*'. Working paper No. 4, Copenhagen Business School, Copenhagen, Denmark.

Holmlund, M. and Kock, S. (1992) '*Quality Based Service as an Establishing Strategy in Business Networks*. Working paper No. 249. Swedish School of Economics and Business Administration. Helsingfors, Finland.

Häkansson, H. and Johanson, J. (1992) 'A Model of Industrial Networks'. In *Industrial Networks: A New View of Reality*. London: Routledge, pp. 28–34.

Kock, S. (1992) '*A Strategic Process for Managing Relationships in Business Networks*'. Working paper No. 240. Swedish School of Economics and Business Administration. Helsingfors, Finland.

Kock, S. (1991) '*A Strategic Process for Gaining External Resources Through Long Lasting Relationships: Examples from Two Finnish and Two Swedish Industrial Firms*'. Economy and Society No. 47, Swedish School of Economics and Business Administration. Helingsfors, Finland.

March, J. G. (1981) 'Decision Making Perspective: Decisions in Organizations and Theories of Choice'. In *Perspective on Organization Design and Behavior*. (A. H. Van de Ven and W. I. Joyce, Eds). New York: John Wiley.

March, J. G. (1988) *Decisions and Organizations*. Cornwall: Blackwell.

Oakland, J. S. (1989) *Total Quality and Management*. Wiltshire: Redwood Press.

Parasuraman, A., Zeithaml, V. A. and Berry, L. L. (1985) 'A conceptual Model of Service Quality and Its Implications for Future Research'. *Journal of Marketing* **47** (Fall): 41–50.

Parasuraman, A., Berry, L. L. and Zeithaml, V. A. (1991) 'Understanding Buyer Expectations of Service'. *Sloan Management Review* (Spring): 34–48.

Yamagashi, T., Gillmore, M. R. and Cook, K. S. (1988) 'Network Connections and the Distribution of Power in Exchange Networks'. *American Journal of Sociology* **93:** 835–851.

Section IV

Service Management

In this section we consider some of the broader issues facing service managers. The first article by Christian Grönroos (1994) charts the development of management thought from its domination by the scientific management principles proposed by Taylor. Grönroos illustrates how the increasing realisation by service firms of the shortcomings of the traditional approaches to management has led to todays more holistic approach to management theory. He suggests that the service management perspective has had an impact beyond the scope of specific service industries, bringing together a variety of other disciplines with a common perspective. The recognition of the value of services as a source of competitive advantage by adding value to the core product extends the scope of service management and has had an important impact on how organisations view the marketing function.

By way of contrast, the second article by Silvestro, Fizgerald, Johnston and Voss (1992) considers the provision of a service management tool through the development of a classification scheme based on service processes. The value of classification schemes to managers has been the subject of some debate. In 1976 Hunt suggested several criteria for determining the strength of a classification approach including the mutual exclusiveness of the categories and their collective exhaustiveness. However, no classification scheme is ever perfect; the purpose of service classification is merely to assist in understanding the service product. As Wright (1995) points out, it is obvious from discussing the characteristics of services that there is great variation between services and that if managers are to respond to them effectively, some form of classification or categorisation is necessary. In the Silvestro article, the authors start by reviewing previous classifications and propose three 'archetypes', professional services, mass services and service shops. They suggest that each gives rise to different management concerns and that strategy, control and performance measurement differ between the three types. This represents additional evidence for non-standard, non-generic management approach to services.

The final two articles in this section consider specific strategic management issues: sustainable competitive advantage and entry mode into new markets. Bharadwaj, Varadarajan and Fahy (1993) review the conditions for sustainable competitive advantage and considers the issues raised with regard to service industries. Taking Porter's (1985) two main generic strategies, the authors consider the management implications of achieving competitive cost advantage and differentiation advantage. These are then discussed in the light of specific features of service organisations which affect the achievement of competitive advantage. Erramilli and Rao (1993), on the other hand, consider the impact of the characteristics of services on organisations choosing an entry mode into new markets. Previous discussions of entry mode have concentrated entirely on manufactured goods and have employed transaction cost analysis (TCA) to explain the choice between wholly owned operations, joint ventures and contractual agreements. This paper points to problems with the TCA framework in general before considering the characteristics of service firms which demand an extension of the model. Focusing on asset specificity as a determinant of service firms' propensity to establish shared-control entry modes, the paper examines the factors that affect service firms' choices in this context.

CONTENTS

18

From Scientific Management to Service Management: A Management Perspective for the Age of Service Competition

Christian Grönroos

INTRODUCTION

Service management is not a well-delineated concept. It is however, used more and more by academics as well as by practitioners. Conferences on service management are arranged, books with the phrase service management as part of the title are published and academic courses called service management are developed. Service management is inevitably establishing itself as a recognized field. However, it is understandable that an outside observer easily feels confused when confronted with the concept. The purpose of this article is to discuss how service management emerged, what it is, and what contributions it offers to management research and practice.

Today, service management is more a perspective than one discipline or one coherent area of its own. It is a perspective that gives firms that face service competition, i.e. that have to understand and manage service elements in their customer relationships in order to achieve a sustainable competitive advantage, more or less similar guidelines to the development of such separate areas as management, marketing, operations, organizational theory and human resources management and TQM. This perspective is described very well be the observation by Schneider and Rentch (1987) that firms that apply service management principals consider 'service as *the* organizational imperative'.

The service management perspective includes some more or less general shifts in the focus of management (Grönroos, 1990a, p. 118):

1. From the product-based utility to total utility in the customer relationship.
2. From short-term transactions to long-term relationships.
3. From core product (goods or services) quality or the mere technical quality of

Reprinted with permission from *International Journal of Service Industry Management*, Vol. 5, No. 1, pp. 5–20

the outcome to total customer-perceived quality in enduring customer relationships.
4. From production of the technical quality of products (goods or services) as the key process in the organization to developing and managing total utility and total quality as the key process.

In addition to this, a number of principles of service management that seem to be fairly commonly accepted are discussed in the lead article of the first volume of the *Journal of Services Industry Management* from 1990 (Grönroos, 1990c).

FACETS OF SERVICE MANAGEMENT

The service management perspective has emerged within several disciplines with a number of somewhat different and yet interrelated angles. One can say that major impacts on this perspective come from at least six different areas: marketing, operations management, organizational theory and human resources management, management, and service quality management, and finally as a sixth area business executives and consultants. The approach by executives and consultants was originally heavily influenced by the Scandinavian experience in turning around and managing service firms, particularly by SAS Scandinavian Airlines System (see Albrecht and Zemke, 1985; Carlzon, 1987). In addition to these areas, there are scattered contributions from other disciplines as well (e.g. economics).

As service management has emerged from so many points of view and not yet merged into one management theory, there is no definition of it that would have been commonly accepted. In fact, most authors seem to avoid in-depth discussion of the definition issue. However, Grönroos (1990a; see also Grönroos, 1988) offers a fairly exhaustive definition of service management:

> Service management is:
>
> (1) To understand the utility customers receive by consuming or using the offerings of the organization and how services alone or together with physical goods or other kinds of tangibles contribute to this utility, that is, to understand how total quality is perceived in customer relationships, and how it changes over time;
> (2) To understand how the organization (personnel, technology and physical resources, systems and customers) will be able to produce and deliver this utility or quality;
> (3) To understand how the organization should be developed and managed so that the intended utility or quality is achieved; and
> (4) To make the organization function so that this utility or quality is achieved and the objectives or the parties involved (the organization, the customers, other parties, the society, etc.) are met (Grönroos, 1990a, p. 117).

Albrecht (1988) presents a shorter definition. Some of the information content of the above mentioned definition is of course lost, but it clearly demonstrates some to the key facets of service management:

> Service management is a total organizational approach that makes quality of service, as perceived by the customer, the number one driving force for the operations of the business (p. 20).

The shift of focus and the definitions presented above demonstrate the major meaning and significance of service management. Five key facets of the service management perspective can be recognized, viz., overall management perspective, customer focus, holistic approach, quality focus, and internal development and reinforcement:

1. It is an *overall management perspective* which should guide decisions in all areas of management (not only provide management principles for a separate function such as customer service);
2. It is *customer driven* or market driven (not driven by internal efficiency criteria);
3. It is a *holistic perspective* which emphasizes the importance of intraorganizational, cross-functional collaboration (not specialization and the division of labour);
4. Managing *quality is an integral part* of service management (not a separate issue); and
5. *Internal development* of the personnel and reinforcement of its commitment to company goals and strategies and strategic prerequisites for success (not only administrative tasks).

In the major part of this article these five facets of service management will be discussed. However, today the mainstream management focus is still on economies of scale and a striving to decrease the cost of production and of administering the business, in order to minimize the unit cost of the products, accompanied by aggressive traditional marketing and sales campaigns and continuous product development efforts. While there is no contradiction between service management and product development efforts, the overemphasis on cost reduction and economies of scale as well as on traditional marketing activities is challenged as obsolete and even potentially dangerous as general management principles.

FROM 'SCIENTIFIC MANAGEMENT' TO SERVICE MANAGEMENT

The mainstream management principles of today are based on a perspective that emerged during the industrial revolution. They can be traced back to Adam Smith's analysis of the pin factory. In *The Wealth of Nations* (1950/1776) Smith advocated that one should pursue specialization and the division of labour. Later in *Scientific Management* (Taylor, 1947) principles along the same lines were formulated, although Taylor did take into account the well-being of the workforce. Mass production and economies of scale were considered fundamental parts of this management philosophy.

Long-lasting and well-established structures are not easily changed from within. Environmental changes may put enough pressure on the establishment so that marginal corrections of problems are made, but the structure itself lasts. This is what seems to have happened with today's management principles based on the scientific management perspective. The educational level and standard of living of the workforce has increased tremendously and made people much more sophisticated and demanding as employees and consumers; the magnitude of competition has increased and its nature changed which, for example, has made firms much more vulnerable to international competition and has made the competitive edge provided by excellent core products much less effective; the exploding development of information technology has made customers and competitors much more aware of available options and the nature of the new technology makes it possible to achieve results totally different from mass production and standardization which have been the traditional gains of new technology. In spite of all these trends, the grip of the traditional management principles has remained steady.

However, all these trends make old management principles less appropriate and effective. The work environment becomes less encouraging for the employees, technology is not used to create as much job satisfaction for employees and value for customers as possible, enduring customer relationships are not developed and competitive advantages are not achieved. Service firms were among the first to observe the problems created by the old management structure. An interest in studying service-specific issues emerged first among marketing researchers.[1] The development of new models, concepts and tools based on the characteristics of services and of their production and delivery processes started during the 1970s. Following a few earlier doctoral dissertations and articles, the doctoral dissertations by Judd (1965), Johnson (1969) and George (1972) offered a thorough description of the nature of services and of specific problems in services marketing. Wilson's (1972) and Rathmell's (1974) books on professional services and the service sector in general respectively were the first ones exploring marketing problems in service firms. Even if research into services took off at approximately the same time in North America (resulting in, for example, two widely used texts and readings by Lovelock from 1984 and 1988), much of the dominance of services marketing progress shifted to Europe (e.g. Bateson, 1989 in English; Grönroos, 1979 and Gummesson, 1977 in Swedish; Langeard and Eiglier, 1987 in French; Lehtinen, 1983 in Finnish; and in addition, a number of books published in, at least, Austria, Belgium, Denmark, Germany, Italy, The Netherlands, Norway and Spain (see Grönroos, 1990a)).

Among other things, the nature of the customer relationships and of operations and the production and delivery processes were considered different for services by the pioneering researchers, and the quality of services was found to be formed and perceived in such a way that traditional models from manufacturing did not apply. However, researchers interested in services did not predominantly attempt to change old management models and concepts in a marginal fashion in order to fit services. This is especially true for the so-called Nordic School of services with its roots in the mid-1970s (e.g. Grönroos and Gummesson, 1985), where for example, marketing was viewed as an area that cannot be separated from overall management. Instead a totally new approach to the problem of how to manage various aspects of service organizations was taken. This was the beginning of what later, by Richard Normann (1982/1984), was labelled 'service management'.[2]

THE OVERALL MANAGEMENT PERSPECTIVE

Normann (1982/1984) and Grönroos (1982) have shown how a traditional management focus overemphasizing cost reduction efforts and scale economies may become a management trap for service firms and lead to a vicious circle where the quality of the service is damaged, internal workforce environment deteriorates, customer relationships suffer, and eventually profitability problems occur. Growing marketing and sales budgets may slow down the negative trend for some time, but as this normally only means increased persuasion and overpromising, in the long run it only leads to unsatisfied and defecting customers. In the tradition of Adam Smith and scientific management, the traditional management principles are largely based on specialization and the division of labour. From this has frequently followed a short-term, manipulative and transaction-oriented view of market relationships and an adversary relationship between functions within the firm and between the firm and its external partners, such as customer, suppliers and middlemen. Service management is based on a different assumption of how the intraorganizational and interorganizational relationships should be viewed and developed. Teamwork, interfunctional collaboration and interorganizational partnership, and a long-term perspective are, generally speaking, inherent values in service management.

Originally, Normann and Grönroos discussed service firms only, but as it has gradually become evident that services are growing in importance for manufacturers as will, the arguments for a management trap and vicious circles become more generally valid. Grönroos' definition of service management and the notion of service competition clearly imply that not only service firms but all types of organizations may be included.

Service management as an overall management perspective gives high priority to the external efficiency, economies of scale and cost reduction. This combines the overall management perspective of service management with its customer-driven and quality-oriented facets, employee-oriented concerns and its long-term perspective.

CUSTOMER ORIENTATION

As a general lesson from service management, Heskett (1986 and 1987) argues for a focus on 'market economies' instead of emphasizing scale economies too much. By this he means that a competitive edge and profitability are accomplished by a closer market orientation rather than by a focus on large-scale production of more or less standardized products in order to keep unit production costs down. More recently, Sasser and Reichheld have stressed this point in their studies of the economic effects of retaining customers as compared to cost reduction efforts without diminishing customer defection rates (Reichheld, 1993; Reichheld and Sasser, 1990). Their studies show that the decrease of the defection rate by a comparatively small percentage has an impact on profits that would be difficult to achieve by cost reduction efforts. The figures differ greatly from industry to industry but the trend is the same. Additional studies will most probably support these findings. For services businesses where the service outcome and the production and delivery processes can be highly standardized, economies of scale based on a production-line approach as suggested by Levitt (1972) may be possible. McDonald's would be an example of such a case, but as Schlesinger and Heskett (1991) more recently have argued, when facing more pressure from new competitors even firms like McDonald's may have less support from technology-driven standardization of the production and delivery of their services. This does not, of course, mean that economies of scale and cost reduction efforts would be a thing of the past; on the contrary. It means, however, that the major focus cannot be on such efforts any more. 'Market economies' and a genuine interest in the customer become imperative.

Customer loyalty is the cornerstone of successful service management (Heskett *et al.*, 1991). However, a word of warning is needed here. Even if customer retention is important, the firm should strive to keep the right customers from defecting. The recently emerging interest in what we in another context (Grönroos, 1993b) have labelled 'customer relationship economics', has shown that 'customer relationship profitability', to use an expression coined by Storbacka (1993), is not only a function of a stable customer base. As he points out, the firm must not retain the wrong customers, i.e. customers that are not and cannot be expected to become profitable (Storbacka, 1993; see also Barnes and Cumby, 1993). Doing a thorough customer relationship profitability analysis is equally important as efforts directed towards creating a loyal customer base and retaining customers.

Voices have been raised that service management overemphasizes the importance of customer satisfaction and efforts to improve customer perceived quality. Productivity and profitablilty issues may suffer from this alleged myopic view of the importance of service quality and customer satisfaction (Storbacka, 1993). If the service management perspective is applied so that the firm loses track of the importance of productivity and profitability, this criticism is of course valid. In this sense, the critical voices are important, because in the service management literature, productivity and profitability are far too often given only marginal attention. And without proper segmentation and a customer relationship profitability analysis done for each segment of customers, mistakes may easily be made. Large groups of unprofitable customer relationships may easily be tolerated and not even recognized, if total profitability is good enough. This does not, however, decrease the importance of service management in today's competitive situation. Any model or concept can be implemented in a less than satisfactory way.

Research into service management has shown that, contrary to common belief, quality improvement and productivity gains are not necessarily mutually exclusive (e.g. Haywood and Pickworth, 1988). This view is partly due to the fact that most frequently productivity is measured in an unsophisticated way (Steedle, 1988). The influence of scientific management can be seen here as well. Productivity is treated as an internal efficiency issue only, where the impact on perceived quality and customer satisfaction is neglected. Productivity measurement models have also always been developed within a manufacturing context, and there the customer's impact on operations and on quality formation has been ignored. Still, today, how to measure productivity in a service organization is more or less an unsolved problem. Manufacturing models, which inevitably become unsophisticated in service contexts, give wrong signals to management. They are internally oriented, they are short term in nature, they do not give information about long-term productivity, and they seldom measure the productivity of the whole operation. As noted by Pickworth (1987), who uses a restaurant example,

> . . . the issue is whether food-service managers should think of their outputs *as meals produced or customers satisfied*. If customer is the measure, *a quality dimension* is also needed in productivity measurement (p. 43, emphasis added).

The same efforts may, correctly implemented, improve service quality and at the same time have a favourable impact on productivity (e.g. Cowell, 1984). For example, training employees makes them more knowledgeable of the services and the production and delivery processes, and, therefore, they make fewer mistakes and can answer questions asked by customers more quickly. The customer gets faster service and more accurate information. A new technology may remove bottlenecks in operations and speed up the service production and delivery process, a fact that the customers perceive as improved quality.

As far as profitability is concerned, the slowly growing number or studies of customer relationship economics demonstrate, as has been noted previously, that customer retention has a positive effect on profitability. Customer retention again is among other things depending on how well the firm can provide its customers with services. Of course, the core product and price issues are important here, too.

CUSTOMER PERCEIVED QUALITY ORIENTATION

Quality is another area where research into the various areas of service management has had a decisive impact. As noted by Gummesson (1993a), quality has been a black box in management and marketing theories. And in operations and production management quality has been treated as a production problem from an internal efficiency point of view. Especially, research into the marketing of services (e.g. Grönroos, 1982, 1984, 1993a; Gummesson, 1993; Parasuraman *et al.*, 1985) has demonstrated the need for including quality management as an integral part of service management theory.[3] The perceived service quality model (Grönroos 1982, 1993a), the gap analysis model (Parasuraman *et al.*, 1985), the SERVQUAL instrument (Parasuraman *et al.*, 1986, 1994), the Meyer-Mattmuller model (Meyer and Mattmuller, 1987), Lindqvist's index (Lindqvist, 1988), and other quality management models and instruments (e.g. Anderson, 1992; Edvardsson and Gustavsson, 1988; Lemmink and Behara, 1992; Liljander and Strandvik, 1993, and 1994; Stauss, 1993) are examples of what has been developed within the marketing-oriented approach to services. In service operations research quality has been studied as well (cf. Haywood-Farmer and Stuart, 1988; Johnston, 1987).[4] The literature on services by consultants also includes service quality books (e.g. Davidow and Uttal, 1989).

The customer focus of the research into services has had a decisive impact on the general approach to quality management. Service researchers very strongly put forward the view that it is the customer who decides what quality is and that it is customer perceived quality that has to be studied. Subsequently, this view has been supported by, for example, the findings of the PIMS project (Buzzell and Gale, 1987) and by the total quality management (TQM) movement. Customer orientation is a central aspect of TQM programmes. Nevertheless, many such programmes seem to fail.[5] One reason for this may be the fact that marketing is often missing. As Kordupleski *et al.* (1993) observe,

> there is a considerable participation by quality control engineers, manufacturing people, operations managers, human resource people, and organizational behaviour experts. A group notable by its absence is the function closest to the customers – namely, marketing. . . . Why are marketing people not more involved in quality improvement? (p. 83).

Here is a big difference between TQM and service management. TQM has been developed by non-marketing people who only recently have observed that customers are important to the success of the business. The customer-perceived quality focus and quality management models inherent in service management have been developed by marketing and operations as part of the interface between those two areas. Marketing and quality are seen as two sides of the same coin. Hence, the contact with marketing is more natural in service management than in TQM.

LONG-TERM PERSPECTIVE

The long-term perspective inherent in service management has had an important impact on marketing. Services marketing research has demonstrated the importance of long-term relationships instead of short-term deals and campaigns (cf. Grönroos, 1982 and Gummesson, 1987). The emerging interest in customer relationship economics (Storbacka, 1993) and recently published studies of the economic impact of customer retention (Reichheld and Sasser, 1990) support this view. Relationship marketing (cf. Christopher *et al.*, 1991; Grönroos, 1994 and Gummesson, 1993b; see also Berry, 1983) is a new approach to marketing which is quickly growing in importance.

The long-term orientation is clearly in line with current trends in business (cf. Kotler, 1992). Partnerships and networks as will as strategic alliances are formed in international business and in many industries are becoming increasingly important on domestic markets as well. As Frederick Webster (1992) concludes in an analysis of current trends in business,

> there has been a shift from a transaction to a relationship focus (p. 14) . . . and . . . from an academic or theoretical perspective, the relatively narrow conceptualization of marketing as a profit-maximization problem, focused on market transactions, seems increasingly out of touch with an emphasis on long-term customer relationships and the formation and management of strategic alliances. . . . The focus shifts from products and firms as units of analysis to people, organizations, and the social processes that bind actors together in ongoing relationships (p. 10).

In service management, marketing efforts are often considered investments in customers more than marketing expenses. This view is nothing entirely new in marketing. In the network approach to industrial marketing the concepts of market and marketing investments have been introduced (Johanson and Mattsson, 1985). More recently, Slywotzky and Shapiro (1993) also argue for a new attitude towards marketing, where marketing is treated as investments instead of short-term expenses.

> In 1992, US companies spent more than $700 billion on activities such as selling, advertising, and sales promotion. For many companies, sales and marketing expenditures represent 15% to 20% of each revenue dollar. From that same dollar, about 4% to 10% is devoted to capital budgeting projects. While capital budgeting expenditures are carefully examined and analysed – and treated as investments – the much larger marketing piece is viewed as an annual expense (p. 98).

HOLISTIC APPROACH TO MANAGEMENT

Service management's holistic approach to management has had several effects. In marketing it has clearly demonstrated the need for expanding the notion of who the marketers in a firm are. Gummesson (1991) has introduced the breakthrough concept 'part-time marketers' for the employees outside a traditional marketing department, who normally are not trained as marketers or even appointed as marketers, but who nevertheless take care of customer contacts and thus make an impact on the future purchasing behaviour of the firm's customers. He emphasizes the importance of the part-time marketers by stating that:

> marketing and sales departments (the full-time marketers) are not able to handle more than a limited portion of the marketing *as its staff cannot be at the right place at the right time with the right customer contacts* (p. 72).

It has, thus, been concluded that everyone is a marketer, one way or the other (Grönroos, 1982 and Gummesson, 1990; see also Webster, 1988).

Even more important is the influence that the holistic view of the service management perspective has had as a means of crossing traditional business functions and corresponding academic disciplines. In service marketing research the importance of operations as part of marketing has been observed. The concept 'interactive marketing function' (Grönroos, 1982) has been developed to point out the marketing impact of the service production and delivery process. Langeard and Eiglier (1987) introduced the *servuction* concept which treats service operations in the context of marketing. In his services marketing system, Lovelock (1988) has integrated marketing, operations and human resources management. In operations a similar trend can be observed. The service management perspective has made researchers within the area of production and operations interested in the impact of the operations systems on customers (e.g. Bowen *et al.*, 1990; Chase, 1978, 1991; Collier, 1987; Voss *et al.*, 1985). The textbook on service operations by Sasser *et al.* (1978) was a first major step in this direction, which at Harvard Business School led to an experiment with an academic course combining service operations and services marketing. However, apparently this experiment was not allowed to last very long.

In organizational theory and human resources management a similar trend can be seen. The service management perspective has, for example, created such concepts as the service management system (Normann, 1982) incorporating a marketing and operations view in an organizational theory context, and empowerment (Bowen and Lawler, 1992) which relates human resources management to marketing. Other contributions from this field include publications by Schneider (1980) and Mills (1986).[6]

FOCUS ON INTERNAL DEVELOPMENT

Service management also has an internal focus where the development of the personnel and the creation of employee commitment to the goals and strategies of the firms are key issues. In service marketing research the need for internal marketing has been observed (Grönroos 1982; see also, for example, Barnes, 1989; Berry, 1981; George, 1984, 1990). In 1982 Grönroos formulated the internal marketing concept, according to which the internal market of employees is best motivated for service mindedness and customer-oriented performance by an active, marketing-like approach, where a variety of activities are used internally in an active, marketing-like and co-ordinated way.

Without active and continuous internal marketing efforts the interactive marketing impact on customers will deteriorate, service quality will suffer and customers will start to defect with negative effects on profitability as a result. In this sense internal marketing is a prerequisite for successful external marketing. Internal marketing includes both an attitude management aspect and a communications management aspect (Grönroos, 1990a). In organizational theory and human resources management the same issues have been addressed and for example the above mentioned concept of empowerment has emerged as an element of internal marketing. Generally speaking, internal marketing and HRM represent an interface between marketing and organizational theory that has been emphasized by the service management perspective (cf. Grönroos, 1990b).

Internal marketing is not, of course, anything entirely new in a firm. Internal programmes to make employees committed to various goals have always existed. What is new is the active, market-oriented approach as suggested by the internal marketing concept. Some marketing activities from traditional external marketing may be used together with training and other traditional personnel development activities. At best, internal marketing offers an umbrella for all these and other activities which make the development of personnel a strategic issue.[7]

IN CONCLUSION: WHAT IS SERVICE MANAGEMENT?

As the discussion of service management and its five key facets above demonstrates, service management is not a well-defined area or a single theory of management. Rather it is a management perspective that fits today's competitive situation. Cost reductions and core product quality are still important to success, but to achieve customer satisfaction and a competitive advantage through differentiation of the market offer (cf. Quinn *et al.*, 1990) more value has to be added to the core product. This is done through a variety of services and by turning activities such as deliveries, technical service, claims handling, telephone exchange, invoicing, etc. into customer-oriented, value-adding services.

The service management perspective has had a novel impact on cross-disciplinary research. Volumes including research from various fields are published (Swartz *et al.*, 1992, 1993). International conferences have been arranged, mostly in Europe, on service management (*Proceedings* from the 1st and 2nd International Research Seminars in Service Management 1990 and 1992) and on service quality management (e.g. Kunst and Lemmink, 1992; Brown *et al.*, 1991; Scheuing *et al.*, 1992),[8] where researchers representing marketing, operations, organizational theory, psychology, finance, economics and other disciplines together discuss various aspects of management from a service perspective. In these areas research has taken new directions guided by this common perspective.

The term service management was introduced in Swedish in 1982 and in English in 1984. Since then it has slowly become a term used to indicate a common perspective. But this perspective started to evolve long before this term came into use within disciplines such as marketing, organizational theory and human resources management, and operations. Various disciplines have brought contributions of their own to service management, e.g. service competition, the long-term relationship marketing notion, interactive and internal marketing, the part-time marketer concept and the perceived service quality model (marketing), the service management system, the high-contact/low-contact personnel distinction, empowerment and the notion of people as the major resource of a firm (organizational theory and human resources management), the customer-oriented and outward looking approach to operations, and the front-office/back-office notion (operations management), and service guarantees, the market economics focus and customer retention analysis (management), to mention just a few. However, true cross-disciplinary research is still rare. In the future such research projects will broaden and deepen the service management perspective even more.

NOTES

1. Berry and Parasuraman provide an interesting analysis of the development of services marketing thought in their article 'Building a New Academic Field—The Case of Services Marketing' (Berry and Parasuraman, 1993). See also the article on the evolution of the English-language services marketing literature by Fisk *et al.* (1993).
2. Subsequently, among other things, building on the notion that customer participation in the production and delivery process is a central characteristic of services and service management, Normann has developed this further into an interactive strategy model for any type of business, according to which successful firms not only create value but reinvent it together with their customers (see Normann and Ramirez, 1993).
3. There have been earlier attempts to treat quality in a more explicit way in the microeconomic and marketing literature. In the 1950s researchers such as Abbott (1955), who wanted to add more realism to microeconomic price theory, included quality in their models. Abbott, for example, had an astonishingly modern view of quality: 'The term 'quality' will be used . . . in its broadest sense, to include all qualitative elements in the competitive exchange process – materials, design, service provided, location, and so forth' (p. 4). These models influenced parameter theory (Mickwitz, 1959), a marketing theory which was somewhat similar to but much more developed than the marketing mix approach which since the 1960s has dominated marketing. In this theory quality was an integral element. With parameter theory, quality as anything other than a black box disappeared from the literature.
4. Specific contributions from the area of operations management are not discussed in detail here, as the role of that area in service management is the topic of Robert Johnston's article 'Operations: From Factory to Service Management' (1994).
5. Compare, for example, the disappointing findings in two studies by the consulting firms A. T. Kearney and Arthur D. Little (*The Economist,* 1992). In a study of more than 100 firms in the UK, 80% reported that no significant impact could be observed as a result of TQM, and in a study of 500 US firms, almost two-thirds said that they had achieved no competitive gains.
6. The integration of marketing and operations management with human resources management is further elaborated on in Benjamin Schneider's article 'HRM – A Service Perspective: Towards a Customer-focused HRM' (1994).
7. However, even this umbrella notion of internal marketing is not entirely new. Major changes in management perspectives always require extensive internal attention. It is interesting to notice that Frederick Taylor in his testimony about scientific management before the American congress in 1912 explicitly states that '. . . in its essence, scientific management involves a complete *mental revolution* on the part of the working men engaged in any particular establishment or industry. . . . And it involves the equally

complete mental revolution on the part of those on the management's side. . . . And without this complete mental revolution on both sides scientific management does not exist.' (Taylor, 1947, testimony part, p. 27; emphasis added). Taylor stressed the importance of this internal focus, which, however, seems to have been neglected by his followers. Service management, equally, requires such a mental revolution or, to use a modern metaphor, cultural change. The similarity between Taylor's mental revolution and the attitude management aspect of internal marketing is obvious.

8. Two international service management conferences were arranged in France in 1990 and 1992 by IAE at the University-d'Aix-Marseille. In service quality management three QUIS (Quality in Services) conferences initiated by the Service Research Center at the University of Karlstad have so far been arranged bi-annually since 1988, two in Sweden by the Service Research Center and one in the US by St John's University, and furthermore three international workshops devoted to quality management in services co-sponsored by the European Institute for Advanced Studies in Management have been arranged annually since 1991, in Brussels, Maastricht and Helsinki respectively.

REFERENCES

Abbott, L. (1955) *Quality and Competition.* New York, NY: Columbia University Press.

Albrecht, K. (1988) *At America's Service.* Homewood, IL: Dow Jones-Irwin.

Albrecht, K. and Zemke, R. (1985) *Service America!.* Homewood, IL: Dow Jones-Irwin.

Andersson, T. D. (1992) 'Another Model of Service Quality: A Model of Causes and Effects of Service Quality tested on a Case within the Restaurant Industry. In *Quality Management in Services* (P. Kunst, and J. Lemmink, Eds). Assen, Maastricht, The Netherlands: Van Gorcum, pp. 41–58.

Barnes, J. G. (1989) 'The Role of Internal Marketing: If the Staff Won't Buy It, Why Should the Customer?' *Irish Marketing Review* **4** (No. 2): 11–21.

Barnes, J. G. and Cumby, J. A. (1993) 'The Cost of Quality in Service-Oriented Companies: Making Better Customer Service Decisions Through Improved Cost Information'. Research Paper, *ASB Conference 1993.* University of New Brunswick, Canada.

Bateson, J. (1989) *Managing Services Marketing: Text and Readings.* Hinsdale, IL: Dryden Press.

Berry, L. L. (1981) 'The Employee as Customer'. *Journal of Retail Banking* **3** (No. 1): 33–40.

Berry, L. L. (1983) 'Relationship Marketing'. In *Emerging Perspectives of Services Marketing* (L. L. Berry, G. L. Shostack and G. D. Upah, Eds). Chicago, IL: American Marketing Association, pp. 25–28.

Berry, L. L. and Parasuraman, A. (1991) *Marketing Services Competing Through Quality.* Lexington, MA: Free Press/Lexington Books.

Berry, L. L. and Parasuraman, A. (1993) 'Building a New Academic Field – The Case of Services Marketing'. *Journal of Retailing* **69** (Spring): 13–60.

Bowen, D. E., Chase, R. B. and Cummings, T. G. (Eds) (1990) *Service Management Effectiveness.* San Francisco, CA: Jossey-Bass.

Bowen, D. E. and Lawler III, E. E. (1992) 'The Empowerment of Service Workers: What, Why, How, and When', *Sloan Management Review* **33** (No. 3): 31–39.

Brown, S. W., Gummesson, E., Edvardsson, B. and Gustavsson, B. O. (Eds) (1991) *Quality in Services. Multidisciplinary and Multinational Perspectives.* Lexington MA: Lexington Books.

Buzzell, R. D. and Gale, B. T. (1987) *The PIMS Principles. Linking Strategy to Performance.* New York, NY: Free Press.

Carlzon, J. (1987) *Moments of Truth.* Cambridge, MA: Ballinger.

Chase, R. B. (1978) 'Where Does the Customer Fit in a Service Operation'. *Harvard Business Review* **56** (November–December): 137–142.

Chase, R. B. (1991) 'The Service Factory: A Future Vision'. *International Journal of Service Industry Management* **2** (No. 3): 60–70.

Christopher, M., Payne, A. and Ballantyne, D. (1991) *Relationship Marketing Bringing Quality, Customer Service and Marketing Together.* Oxford: Butterworth-Heinemann.

Collier, D. A. (1987) *Service Management. The Automation of Services.* Englewood Cliffs, NJ: Prentice-Hall.

Cowell, D. (1984) *The Marketing of Services.* London: Heinemann.

Davidow, W. H and Uttal, B. (1989) *Total Customer Service. The Ultimate Service.* New York, NY: Harper & Row.

Edvardsson, B. and Gustavsson, B. O. (1988) *Quality in Services and Quality in Service Organizations—A Model of Quality Assessment.* Center for Service Research, Karlstad, Sweden.

Fisk, R. P., Brown, S. W. and Bitner, M. J. (1993) 'The Evolution of the Services Marketing Literature'. *Journal of Retailing* **69** (Spring): 61–103.

George, W. R. (1972) 'Marketing in the Service Industries'. Unpublished dissertation, University of Georgia.

George, W. R. (1984) 'Internal Marketing for Retailers. The Junior Executive Employee'. In *Developments in Marketing Science* (J. D. Lindqvist, Ed.). Academy of Marketing Science.

George, W. R. (1990) 'Internal Marketing and Organizational Behavior: A Partnership in Developing Customer-Conscious Employees at Every Level'. *Journal of Business Research* **20** (No. 1): 63–70.

Grönroos, C. (1979) *Marknadsföring av tjanster. En studie av marknadsfunktionen i tjänsteföretag,* (Marketing of services. A study of the marketing function of service firms), with English summary, Akademilitteratur/Marknadstekniskt Centrum, Stockholm, Sweden.

Grönroos, C. (1982) *Strategic Management and Marketing in the Service Sector,* Swedish School of Economics and Business Administration, Helsingfors, Finland, (published in 1983 in the US by Marketing Science Institute and in the UK by Studentlitteratur/ Chartwell-Bratt).

Grönroos, C. (1984) 'A Service Quality Model and Its Marketing Implications'. *European Journal of Marketing* **18** (No. 4): 36–44.

Grönroos, C. (1988) 'New Competition in the Service Economy: The Five Rules of Service'. *International Journal of Operations and Product Management* **8** (No. 3): 9–18.

Grönroos, C. (1990a) '*Service Management and Marketing. Managing the Moments of Truth in Service Competition.* Lexington, MA: Free Press/Lexington Books.

Grönroos, C. (1990b) 'Relationship Approach to the Marketing Function in Service Contexts: The Marketing and Organizational Behavior Interface'. *Journal of Business Research,* **20** (No. 1): 3–12.

Grönroos, C. (1990c) 'Service Management: A Management Focus for Service Competition'. *International Journal of Service Industry Management* **1** (No. 1): 6–14.

Grönroos, C. (1993a) 'Toward a Third Phase in Service Quality Research: Challenges and Future Directions'. In *Advances in Services Marketing and Management,* Vol. 2 (T. A. Swartz, D. E. Bowen and S. W. Brown, Eds). Greenwich, CT: JAI Press, pp. 49–64.

Grönroos, C. (1993b) 'From Marketing Mix to Relationship Marketing: Toward a Paradigm Shift in Marketing'. Working Paper, No. 263. Swedish School of Economics and Business Administration, Helsingfors, Finland.

Grönroos, C. (1994) 'Quo Vadis, Marketing? Toward a Relationship Marketing Paradigm'. *Journal of Marketing Management* **10** (No. 4): 347–360.

Grönroos, C. and Gummesson, E. (1985) 'The Nordic School of Service Marketing'. In *Service Marketing – Nordic School Perspectives* (C. Grönroos and E. Gummesson, Eds). Stockholm University, Sweden, pp. 6–11.

Gummesson, E. (1977) *Marknadsföring och inköp av konsulttjänster* (Marketing and purchasing of professional services), Akademilitteratur, Stockholm, Sweden.

Gummesson, E. (1987) 'The New Marketing – Developing Long-term Interactive Relationships'. *Long Range Planning* **20** (No. 4): 10–20.

Gummesson, E. (1991) 'Marketing-orientation Revisited: The Crucial Role of the Part-time Marketer'. *European Journal of Marketing* **25** (No. 2): 60–75.

Gummesson, E. (1993a), *Quality Management in Service Organizations.* New York, NY: ISQA International Service Quality Association.

Gummesson, E. (1993b) *Relationsmarknadsföring. Frön 4 P till 30 R* (Relationship marketing. From 4 P's to 30 R's), Stockholm University, Sweden.

Haywood, K. M. and Pickworth, J. R. (1988) 'Connecting Productivity with Quality through the Design of Service Delivery Systems'. In *Proceedings from an International Conference on Services*

Marketing (E. G. Thomas and S. R. Rao, Eds). Special Conference Series, Vol. V, Academy of Marketing Science/Cleveland State University, pp. 261–273.

Haywood-Farmer, K. M. and Stuart, F. I. (1988) 'Measuring the Quality of Professional Services'. In *The Management of Service Operations* (R. Johnston, Ed.). Kempston: IFS Publications, pp. 207–220.

Heskett, J. L. (1986) *Managing in the Service Economy.* Boston, MA: Harvard Business School Press.

Heskett, J. L. (1987) 'Lessons in the Service Sector'. *Harvard Business Review,* **65**(March–April): 118–126.

Heskett, J. L., Sasser, W. E. and Hart, C. W. L. (1991) *Service Breakthroughs: Changing the Rules of the Game.* New York, NY: Free Press.

Johanson, J. and Mattsson, L-G. (1985) 'Marketing Investments and Market Investments in Industrial Networks'. *International Journal of Research in Marketing* **2**(No. 3): 185–195.

Johnson, E. M. (1969) 'Are Goods and Services Different? An Exercise in Marketing Theory'. Unpublished dissertation, Washington University.

Johnston, R. (1987) 'A Framework for Developing a Quality Strategy in a Customer Process Processing Operation'. *International Journal of Quality & Reliability Management* **4**(No. 4): 35–44.

Johnston, R. (1994) 'Operations: From Factory to Service Management'. *International Journal of Service Industry Management* **5**(1).

Judd, R. C. (1965) *The Structure and Classification of the Service Market,* Dissertation, University Microfilms, Ann Arbor, MI.

Kordupleski, R. E., Rust, R. T. and Zahorik, A. J. (1993) 'Why Improving Quality Doesn't Improve Quality (Or Whatever Happened to Marketing?)'. *California Management Review,* **35**(No. 3): 82–95.

Kotler, P. (1992) 'It's Time for Total Marketing'. *Business Week ADVANCE Executive Brief.* Vol. 2.

Kunst, P. and Lemmink, J. (1992) *Quality Management in Services.* Assen, Maastricht/The Netherlands: Van Gorcum.

Langeard, E. and Eiglier, P. (1987) *Servuction. Le marketing des Services.* Paris: Wiley.

Lehtinen, J. (1983) *Asiakasohjautuva Palveluyritys* (Customer-oriented service firm), Espoo, Finland: Weilin + Göös.

Lemmink, J. and Behara, R. S. (1992) 'Q-Matrix: A Multi-Dimensional Approach to Using Service Quality Measurements'. In *Quality Management in Services* (P. Kunst and J. Lemmink, Eds). Assen, Maastricht, The Netherlands: Van Gorcum. pp. 79–88.

Levitt, T. (1972) 'Production-line Approach to Service'. *Harvard Business Review* **50**(September–October): 41–52.

Liljander, V. and Strandvik, T. (1993) 'Estimating Zones of Tolerance in Perceived Service Quality and Perceived Service Value'. *International Journal of Service Industry Management* **4**(No. 2): 6–28.

Liljander, V. and Strandvik, T. (1994) 'Different Comparison Standards as Determinants of Service Quality'. *Journal of Consumer Satisfaction, Dissatisfaction and Complaining Behaviour* **7** (in press).

Lindqvist, L. J. (1988) *Kundernas kvalitetsupplevelse i konsumtionsfasen* (The quality perception of customers in the consumption phase), Swedish School of Economics and Business Administration, Helsingfors, Finland.

Lovelock, C. H. (1984) *Services Marketing.* Englewood Cliffs, NJ: Prentice-Hall.

Lovelock, C. H. (1988) *Managing Services. Marketing, Operations, and Human Resources,* Englewood Cliffs, NJ: Prentice-Hall.

Meyer, A. and Mattmuller, R. (1987) 'Qualität von Dienstleistungen. Entwurf eines praxisorientierten Qualitätsmodells' (The quality of services. Outline of a practice-oriented quality model). *Marketing.* ZPF, Vol. 3.

Mickwitz, G. (1959) *Marketing and Competition.* Societas Scientarium Fennica, Helsingfors, Finland (available from University Microfilms, Ann Arbor, MI).

Mills, P. K. (1986) *Managing Service Industries: Organizational Practices in a Post-Industrial Economy.* Cambridge, MA: Ballinger.

Normann, R. (1982) *Service Management.* Liber, Malmö, Sweden (published in English in 1984 by John Wiley and Sons, New York, NY).

Normann, R. and Ramirez, R. (1993) 'From Value Chain to Value Constellation: Designing Interactive Strategy'. *Harvard Business Review* **71** (July–August): 65–77.

Parasuraman, A., Zeithaml, V. A. and Berry, L. L. (1985) 'A Conceptual Model of Service Quality and its Implications for Future Research'. *Journal of Marketing* **49**: 41–50.

Parasuraman, A., Zeithaml, V. A. and Berry, L. L. (1986) 'SERVQUAL: A Multiple-Item Scale for Measuring Customer Perceptions of Service Quality'. *Journal of Retailing* **64**(Spring): 12–40.

Parasuraman, A., Zeithaml, V. A. and Berry, L. L. (1994) 'Reassessment of Expectations as a Comparison Standard in Measuring Service Quality: Implications for Future Research'. *Journal of Marketing* **58**(Winter): 111–124.

Pickworth, J. R. (1987) 'Minding the Ps and Qs: Linking Quality and Productivity'. *The Cornell Hotel and Restaurant Administration Quarterly* **28**(No. 1) 40–47.

Proceedings from the 1st International Research Seminar in Service Management, Marketing, Operations, Human Resources Insights Into Services, IAE, Aix-en-Provence, France, June 1990.

Proceedings from the 2nd International Research Seminar in Service Management, Marketing, Operations, Human Resources Insights Into Services, IAE, Aix-en-Provence, France, June 1992.

Quinn, J. B., Dorley, T. L. and Paquette, P. C. (1990) 'Beyond Products Service-Based Strategy'. *Harvard Business Review* **68**(March–April): 58–67.

Rathmell, J. M. (1974) *Marketing in the Service Sector.* Cambridge, MA: Winthrop Publishers.

Reichheld, F. E. and Sasser, Jr W. E. (1990) 'Zero Defections: Quality Comes To Service'. *Harvard Business Review* **68**(September–October): 105–111.

Reichheld, F. E. (1993) 'Loyalty-Based Management'. *Harvard Business Review* **71**(March–April) 64–73.

Sasser, W. E., Olsen R. P. and Wyckoff, D. D. (1978) *Management of Service Operations.* Boston, MA: Allyn and Bacon.

Scheuing, E. E., Gummesson, E. and Little. C. H. (Eds) (1992) *Quality in Services (QUIS 2) Conference, Selected Papers.* New York, NY: St John's University.

Schlesinger, L. A. and Heskett, J. L. (1991) The Service-Driven Service Company. *Harvard Business Review* **69**(September–October): 71–81.

Schneider, B. (1980) 'The Service Organization: Climate is Crucial'. *Organizational Dynamics,* **9**(No. 2) 52–65.

Schnieder, B. (1994) 'HRM – A Service Perspective: Towards a Customer-focused HRM'. *International Journal of Service Industry Management* **5**(No. 1): 64–76.

Schneider, B. and Rentsch, J. (1987) 'The Management of Climate and Culture: A Futures Perspective'. In '*Futures of Organizations* (J. Hage, Ed.). Lexington, MA: Lexington Books.

Slywotzky, A. J. and Shapiro, B. P. (1993) 'Leveraging to Beat the Odds: The New Marketing Mind-Set'. *Harvard Business Review* **71**(September–October): 97–107.

Smith, A. (1950/1776) *The Wealth of Nations. An Inquiry into the Nature and Cause of the Wealth of Nations.* London: Methuen (the original published 1776).

Stauss, B. (1993) 'Service Deployment: Transformation of Problem Information into Problem Prevention Activities'. *International Journal of Service Industry Management* **4**(No. 3): 41–62.

Steedle, L. F. (1988) 'Has Productivity Measurement Outgrown Infancy?'. *Management Accounting* **70**(No. 2): 15.

Storbacka, K. (1993) *Customer Relationship Profitability in Retail Banking.* Research Report. Swedish School of Economics and Business Administration, Helsinki, Finland.

Swartz, T. A., Bowen, D. E. and Brown, S. W. (Eds) (1992) *Advances in Services Marketing and Management,* Vol. 1. Greenwich, CT: JAI Press.

Swartz, T. A., Bowen, D. E. and Brown, S. W. (Eds) (1993) *Advances in Services Marketing and Management,* Vol. 2. Greenwich, CT: JAI Press.

Taylor, F. W. (1974) *Scientific Management.* London: Harper & Row (a volume of two papers originally published in 1903 and 1911 and a written testimony for a Special House Committee in the US in 1912).

Voss, C. A., Armistead, C. G., Johnston, R. and Morris, B. (1985) *Operations Management in Service Industries and the Public Sector.* Chichester, UK: Wiley.

Webster, Jr. F. E. (1988) 'The Rediscovery of the Marketing Concept' *Business Horizons* **31** (May–June): 29–39.

Webster, Jr. F. E. (1992) 'The Changing Role of Marketing in the Corporation'. *Journal of Marketing* **56** (October): 1–17.

Wilson, A. (1972) *The Marketing of Professional Services.* London, UK: McGraw-Hill.

19

Towards a Classification of Service Processes

Rhian Silvestro, Lin Fitzgerald, Robert Johnston and Christopher Voss

INTRODUCTION

Schmenner[1] argues that, over the years, manufacturers have been unified by their acceptance of a certain terminology to describe generic production processes. Use of these process types has helped to remove the myth that all manufacturing activities and problems are unique. This has facilitated the sharing of ideas and techniques and the development of an understanding of process choice implication on manufacturing strategies. The process typology has also become a powerful tool in the teaching and development of production and operations management.[2,3]

The traditional view has been that the heterogeneity of services means that little communication or learning can take place between different service businesses; as Lovelock[4] states, 'Service industries remain dominated by an operations orientation that insists each industry is different'. A service typology which transcends narrow industry boundaries may lead to some cross-fertilization of ideas and to an understanding of the management methods and techniques appropriate to each service type. Although many service classification schemes have been proposed before, no categorization has been either as pervasive or as useful as the process type classification provided in the production management literature.

A REVIEW OF SERVICE CLASSIFICATIONS

Several production/operations authors have in the past applied manufacturing process types to services. The five generic process types, which have become a part of classic production management[2,5,6] are project, jobbing, batch, line and continuous process operations. The model, illustrated in Figure 1, shows how the five types are positioned along the diagonal on a graph where product volume correlates with product mix[5] to which Wild[7] refers as product variety.

Reprinted with permission from *International Journal of Service Industry Management*, Vol. 3, No. 3, pp. 62–75

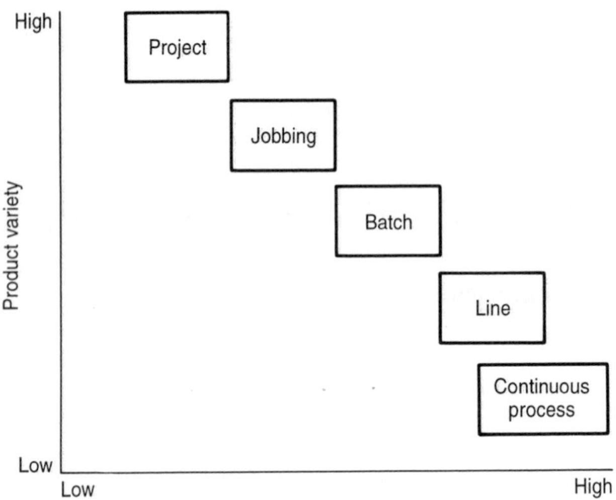

Figure 1. The five generic production process types.

Hill[6] identifies the following additional dimensions which characterize the five process types:

- product range
- customer order size
- degree of product change accommodated
- ability of operations to cope with new developments
- orientation of innovation
- performance criterion
- nature of the process technology
- number and expense of set-ups
- control of quality

Thus, at one extreme, project activities are defined as highly customized, one-off, large-scale and complex activities, such as civil engineering contracts or aerospace programmes. At the other extreme, continuous processing refers to the processing of a basic material, such as petrochemicals, through an automated plant. Between these extremes lie jobbing, batch and line processes. Some production processes will be hybrids sharing the characteristics of more than one of these three process types.[6]

Sasser *et al.*[8] are an example of authors who claim the transferability of this model to services, providing the following examples of service operations:

- *Project*: management consultancy, banqueting
- *Jobbing*: management development programme, design and installation of a computer system
- *Batch*: computer bureau

- *Line*: preparatory operation in fast food restaurants
- *Continuous process*: not used in service operation.

Such attempts have met with considerable criticism in the service operations literature on the grounds that they 'are insufficient for diagnosing and thinking about (service) systems'[9] and do not take account of one essential characteristic of service industries, that of the inherent variability created by the existence of the customer within the system.[10] The application of the generic production types to service appears to be an unnecessary force-fit of manufacturing concepts to the service sector.

Authors in the service management field have, therefore, responded by proposing service typologies, which they argue differentiate better between the management issues and concerns in different types of service. The six service dimensions below have over the past 15 years become widely recognized and used in the service operations management literature:

1. Equipment/people focus.[11,12]
2. Length of customer contract time.[9,13]
3. Extent of customization.[14–16]
4. Extent to which customer contact personnel exercise judgement in meeting individual needs.[4]
5. Source of value added, front office or back office.[15]
6. Product/process focus.[16]

Thomas[11] and Kotler[12] distinguish between equipment-based and people-based services. Examples of equipment-based services include airlines and vending machines, and examples of people-based services are appliance repair and management consultants. These articles are an attempt to move managers' strategic thinking away from product-oriented terms to talking about services and the characteristics which make services unique.

The classification scheme proposed by Chase[9] has produced some valuable insights for control. Chase suggests classifying services along a continuum from high to low contact, where contact refers to the length of time the customer is in contact with the service. For example, in a management consultancy there is a high degree of interaction between the customer and the processes of service delivery; Chase suggests that the control measures used in such an organization will differ radically from low contact services such as postal services.

Maister and Lovelock[14] add the extent of service customization to chase's classification. Customized activities involve compiling a service package for each customer as in a management consultancy project, for example. At the other extreme standardized activities are non-varying processes; although there may be several routes or choices, their availability is always pre-determined. For example, rail transport systems provide passengers with a wide variety of routes between many locations, but the service offered cannot be tailored (at least in the short term) to meet individual passenger needs. The resulting matrix yields a four-way classification, which the authors label service factory, service shop, mass service and professional service (See Figure 2).

Extent of customization	Extent of customer contact: Low	Extent of customer contact: High
Low	Factory	Mass service
High	Job shop	Professional service

Figure 2. Maister and Lovelock's[14] classification of services 1982.

A review of the literature reveals several more four-way classifications of services, combining various dimensions in two-by-two matrices. Maister[15] distinguishes between value added in the front or back office, mapping it against the degree of customization[4] uses the extent to which customer contact personnel exercise judgement in meeting individual customer needs, against the degree of customization. Johnston and Morris[16] use the degree of product or process focus against the degree of customization. In a product-focused organization the emphasis is on *what* the customer buys, whilst in a process-focused business the emphasis is on *how* the customer buys, that is, the way the service is delivered.

More recently Haynes[17] combines dimensions previously proposed by Schmenner[1] and Schostack,[18] yielding a two-by-two matrix with the following axes: degree of operational complexity and the degree to which the operation is mechanistic or organic. The aim of all three writers, Hayes, Schmenner and Schostack, is to facilitate analysis of service positioning strategies rather than develop service typologies. To this extent the matrices can form useful management tools.

The ambiguity in Schostack's[18] definition of complexity, however, makes it difficult to operationalize. For some operations are complex in the sense that they involve highly sophisticated, difficult takes (e.g. management consultancy, scientific research), while others, simple by this definition, are complex in that the service process involves a multiplicity of choices or routes from which customers can select (such as freight forwarding). This ambiguity seems not to have been resolved by Haynes[17] and is therefore a residual problem, when his classification scheme is applied to service organizations.

The continuum of mechanistic/organic operations is a development of Schmenner's[1] dimension of the degree of customization and interaction between server and customer. This, and the other dimensions presented by Schmenner and Schostack (not captured in Haynes' matrix[17]), labour intensity and divergence respectively, do not seem to add significantly to the six dimensions listed above; labour intensity being essentially similar to equipment/people focus, and divergence being a combination of customization and front line staff discretion.

Another two-by-two matrix is proposed by Wemmerlov,[19] the axes of which are customer contact (again based on Chase's definition, though operationlized slightly differently) and the degree of 'routinization' of the service operation, ranging from fluid to rigid. Wemmerlov[19] (p. 28) is, however, reluctant to operationalize the definition of fluid and rigid operations.

LESSONS FROM THE PRODUCTION OPERATIONS LITERATURE

What emerges from this review of service classifications is a miscellany of different approaches lacking a cohesive framework, which derives benefit from all the dimensions identified. As a result no single classification scheme has proved so robust and useful as the process model in the manufacturing literature. Many services still 'view themselves as unique, and consequently do not promote service operations management techniques with the same vigour as does the manufacturing sector'.[1]

The strength of the manufacturing process model is that it is multidimensional. Several different manufacturing process dimensions are unified in a single model by correlation against production volume. Might it be possible, then, to use a volume measure to unify the disparate dimensions currently used to classify services?

Unfortunately the volume of services or number of service outputs is less meaningful than production volume in manufacturing. In service operations the heterogeneity and intangibility of services means that the measurement of service outputs is less straightforward than that of manufactured products. Moreover, in service operations significant volume increases can be made, and frequently are made, without any change in the service process, as would be expected in manufacturing (indeed this is precisely what the production process model shows). Service organizations may significantly increase the volume of operations by reproducing service operations, for example, using multisite strategies[8,20] *without* requiring a change in the process of provision.

We propose that a more appropriate measure of the volume of service activity is the number of customers processed by an individual service unit per day. Indeed services have been defined as essentially 'customer-processing operations'.[10,21] This includes customer business which may or may not require the presence of a customer. Thus, in a bank, for example, the volume measure includes back-office as well as front-office transactions, because not all services provided for the customer require his/her physical presence.

We propose that the measure of volume be used as a mechanism to integrate the disparate service classifications in the literature into a single service process model. The viability of this ides is tested using empirical data drawn from 11 in-depth case studies carried out as part of a research project funded by The Chartered Institute of Management Accountants. Eleven large, for-profit UK service organizations were studied by means of interviews with management and staff and an examination of company documentation and information flows. The aim was to develop an understanding of the companies' competitive strategies, the nature of the service processes and the consequent tasks and challenges encountered by service managers. (The methodology for gathering the data together with the case studies is documented more fully in ref. 22.)

On the basis of the data in the report the service organizations are categorized against each of the service dimensions as well as the volume measure. The objective is to look for clusters of features, which may lead to an integrated typology, which can be used as a basis for developing an understanding of management issues in service organizations across industry boundaries.

APPLICATION OF SERVICE CLASSIFICATIONS TO 11 FOR-PROFIT ORGANIZATIONS

The definitions of classification dimensions used in this section of the article were based, initially, on the literature. However, some ambiguities were found. For example, contact time was defined by Chase[9] as the length of time the customer is in contact with the service. However, contact time might be seen to be made up of two elements: the frequency of contact and the duration of contact. Thus a service with low frequency and high duration would rank the same as one with high frequency and low duration. Since the frequency of service encounters is likely to coincide with volumes of customers (frequency often being high, when customer volumes are high), we define contact time in terms of the length of customer contact time per transaction.

The service classifications, as defined in the literature, were examined and the definitions developed and refined, so that they could be operationalized and used to rank our sample of 11 service organizations. Our definitions are provided in Table 1.

Having refined the definitions, the next stage was to use data from our case studies of 11 service organizations to classify each company against each of these service dimensions. First, the companies were ranked by the volume of customers processed by a typical unit per day on an ordinal scale as shown in Figure 3.

At one extreme the volume of customers processed per unit per day by the management consultancy and field engineering service was measured in tens; whereas at the other extreme the transport company and transport terminus processed thousands of customers per unit per day.

The company data were then used to rank the organizations along each classification dimension derived from the literature, as defined in Table 1:

1. Equipment/people focus.
2. Customer contact time.
3. Degree of customization.
4. Degree of discretion.
5. Value added front office/back office.
6 Product/process focus.

In the case of the volume measure and customer contact time, the organizations could be ranked on the basis of customer volume and average dwell time statistics provided by the companies. The other dimensions are, however, qualitative rather than quantitative in nature, so a Delphi approach was adopted. The ranking process was for each of the five members of the research team to make an independent judgement of the companies' relative positioning along each dimension on a three-

Table 1. Definitions

1. *Equipment/people focus*
   Equipment-focused services are those where the provision of certain equipment is the core element in the service delivery. People-focused services are those where the provision of contact staff is the core element in service delivery.
2. *Customer contact time per transaction*
   High customer contact is where the customer spends hours, days or weeks in the service system, per transaction. Low customer contact is where the contact with the service system is a few minutes.
3. *Degree of customization*
   A high degree of customization is where the service process can be adapted to suit the needs of individual customers. A low degree of customization is where there is a non-varying standardized process; the customer may be offered several routes but the availability of routes is predetermined.
4. *Degree of discretion*
   A high degree of discretion is where front-office personnel can exercise judgement in altering the service package or process without referring to superiors. A low degree of discretion is where changes to service provision can be made only with authorization from superiors.
5. *Value added back office/front office*
   A back-office-oriented service is where the proportion of front-office (customer contact) staff to total staff is small. A front-office-oriented service is where the proportion of front-office staff to total staff is large.
6. *Product/process focus*
   A product-oriented service is where the emphasis is on what the customer buys. A process-oriented service is where the emphasis is on how the service is delivered to the customer.

Low volume

Management consultancy
Field engineering service
Bank – corporate accounts
Hotel
Home electronics rental
Domestic appliance retail
Confectionery, tobacco, news retailer
Bank – personal accounts
Distribution customer enquiries service
Transport company
Transport terminus

High volume

Figure 3. Company rankings by volume of customers.

point scale, based on their understanding of the companies. The rankings produced by each team member were tabulated and results compared. There was considerable agreement among the members' ratings. Differences were highlighted and discussed by the team until a rating was unanimously agreed. The results are presented in Table 2.

Table 2. Company rankings

Company	Ranking: number of customers processed per unit per day	Equipment/ people focus	Customer contact time per transaction	Degree of customization	Degree of discretion	Value added back office/ front office	Product/ process focus
Management consultancy	1	People	High	High	High	Front office	Process
Field service	2	People	High	High	High	Front office	Process
Bank corporate	3	People	Medium	High	High	Both	Mix
Hotel	4	Mix	High	Medium	Medium	Both	Process
Rental	5	Mix	Medium	Medium	Medium	Both	Mix
Retail	6	Mix	Medium	Medium	Medium	Both	Mix
Confectioners, tobacconists and newsagents	7	People	Low	Low	Low	Front office	Product
Bank retail	8	Mix	Low	Medium	Medium	Both	Mix
Distribution enquiries	9	Mix	Low	Medium	Medium	Front office	Product
Transport	10	Equipment	High	Low	Low	Back office	Product
Transport terminus	11	Equipment	High	Low	Low	Both	Product

From Table 2, the six classifying dimensions are plotted against the volume ranking for each company. The results are shown in Figure 4. A pattern seems to emerge along the diagonal. As the number of customers processed by a typical unit per day increases, the general trend seems to be:

- Focus moves from a people to an equipment orientation.
- Length of contact time moves from high to low.
- Degree of customization moves from high to low.
- Level of employee discretion moves from high to low.
- Value added moves from front office to back office.
- Focus moves from a process to a product orientation.

The graphical representation of these organizations, plotted against all the dimensions, reveals clusterings of organizations along the diagonal, as identified in Figure 5. In the case of four of the companies (the management consultancy, field service, rental and retail services) the rankings are the same for each of the six dimensions. The corporate banking service appears to be split evenly between the upper two ranks. All the other companies have a predominance of one ranking: in the case of the transport company, for instance, all the characteristics except contact time are in the lower rank.

The clustering of characteristics and their correlation with the volume measure suggests that there may be three service types. We have called them professional, service shop and mass services, using the terminology which has become well-known in the service literature, although traditionally defined in terms of only two classification dimensions. We believe that, by clarifying the classification definitions and bringing several classifications together in a multidimensional and cohesive framework, the three archetypes will become more useful service process descriptions in operations management.

The model, which is analogous to the production process model in the manufacturing literature, is represented in Figure 6. The figure also indicates which companies in our small sample were representative of each service type. As with the production process model, the three categories may overlap; that is to say, some companies may be hybrids which share the characteristics of more than one type. In our sample the corporate bank is an example, sharing some features of a professional service (customization, discretion and people focus) and some of a service shop (contact time, front-/back-office mix, process/product mix).

It is hoped that these three archetypes will prove to be useful in developing an understanding of the management issues and challenges shared by organizations of the same type, even though they operate in quite different lines of business.

CONCLUSION

We propose that there are three types of service process: professional, service shop and mass. Each service type is characterized in terms of six dimensions drawn from the service operations literature. On the basis of evidence from a small sample of

		Management consultancy	Field service	Bank – corporate accounts	Hotel	Rental	Retail	Confectionery, tobacco, news retailer	Bank retail	Distribution enquiries	Transport	Transport terminus
High	People focus	•	•	•				•				
	Contact time	•	•		•						•	•
	Customization	•	•	•								
	Discretion	•	•	•								
	Front office	•	•					•		•		
	Process focus	•	•		•							
Medium	People/equipment				•	•	•		•	•		
	Contact time			•		•	•					
	Customization				•	•	•		•	•		
	Discretion				•	•	•		•	•		
	Front office/back office			•	•	•	•		•			•
	Process/product			•		•	•		•			
Low	Equipment focus										•	•
	Contact time							•	•	•		
	Customization							•			•	•
	Discretion							•			•	•
	Back office										•	
	Product focus							•		•	•	•
		1	2	3	4	5	6	7	8	9	10	11

Volume ranking

Figure 4. Classifying dimensions vs. volume ranking.

		Management consultancy	Field service	Bank – corporate accounts	Hotel	Rental	Retail	Confectionery, tobacco, news retailer	Bank retail	Distribution enquiries	Transport	Transport terminus
	People focus	•	•	•				•				
High	Contact time	•	•		•						•	•
High	Customization	•	•	•								
High	Discretion	•	•	•								
	Front office	•	•					•		•		
	Process focus	•	•		•							
	People/equipment			•	•	•	•		•	•		
Medium	Contact time					•	•					
Medium	Customization				•	•	•		•	•		
Medium	Discretion				•	•	•		•	•		
	Front office/back office			•	•	•	•		•			•
	Process/product			•		•	•		•			
	Equipment focus										•	•
Low	Contact time							•	•	•		
Low	Customization							•			•	•
Low	Discretion							•			•	•
	Back office										•	
	Product focus							•		•	•	•
		1	2	3	4	5	6	7	8	9	10	11

Volume ranking

Figure 5. Organizational clustering.

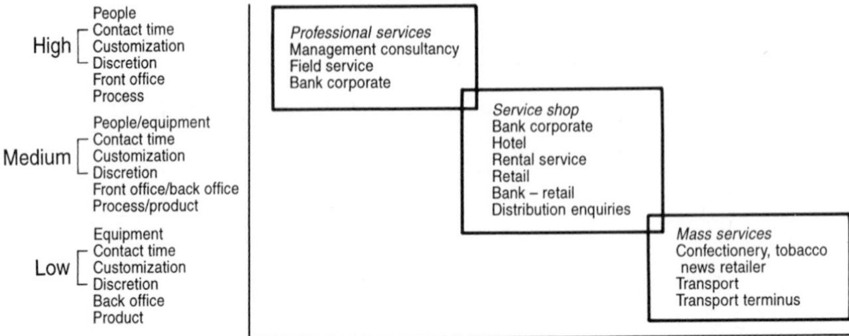

Figure 6. Production services, service shop and mass services.

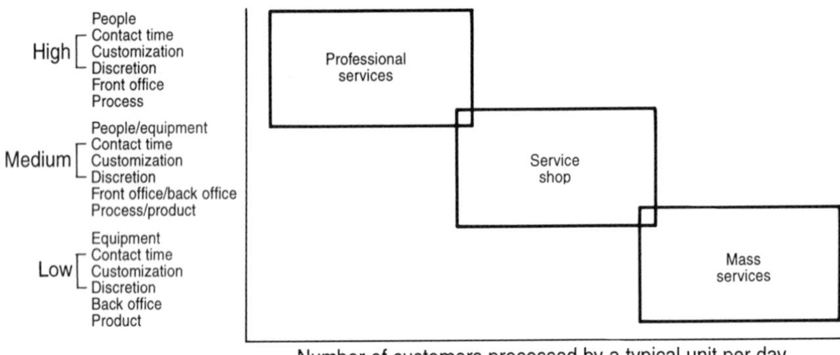

Figure 7. Service processes model.

service organizations these dimensions appear to correlate with volume of customers processed per unit per day. Just as production volume is the unifying mechanism in the manufacturing process model, so it seems this volume measure can be used to integrate the previously disparate service typologies.

Our definitions of the three service archetypes are as follows:

1. *Professional services*: organizations with relatively few transactions, highly customized, process-oriented, with relatively long contact time, with most value added in the front office, where considerable judgement is applied in meeting customer needs.
2. *Mass services*: organizations where there are many customer transactions, involving limited contact time and little customization. The offering is predominantly product-oriented with most value being added in the back office and little judgement applied by the front office staff.
3. *Service shops*: a categorization which falls between professional and mass services with the levels of the classification dimensions falling between the other two extremes.

Our proposed model of service processes, which is analogous to the production process model in the manufacturing operations literature, is represented in Figure 7.

Having adopted the conventional terminology, professional, service shop and mass, perhaps some explanation is called for the absence of the fourth category of services, the service factory. Although this was initially used as a category in several two-by-two matrices (such as in ref. 14 (see Figure 2)), it has rarely been applied as a descriptor of service organizations. Rather the service factory has evolved in the operations literature into a concept which has acquired new connotations. Chase and Erikson[23] use the term to describe service-oriented manufacturing companies, that is, companies which recognize and exploit the competitive opportunities of improving their service performance as well as the quality of their tangible products. The service factory has thus become 'an integrated view of product and service'.[23]

It may be, therefore, that the service factory forges the link between the production process types presented in the manufacturing model and the three service types presented in this article. For the service factory can be characterized both in term of the manufacturing dimensions listed earlier *and* the service dimensions incorporated in our model.

To conclude, we propose that the three types of service process, professional service, service shop and mass service, give rise to different management concerns, and that service strategy, control and performance measurement will differ significantly between the three. The next stage in our research is to see whether the issues which preoccupy managers in our sample of organizations can indeed be differentiated by the service types, which cut across industry boundaries. If so, the aim is to develop some propositions as to the management issues which typify professional services, service shops and mass services.

ACKNOWLEDGMENT

The authors wish to acknowledge the support of The Chartered Institute of Management Accountants for funding the research on which this article is based.

REFERENCES

1. Schmenner, R. (1986) 'How Can Service Businesses Survive and Prosper?'. *Sloan Management Review* (Spring): 21–32.
2. Hill, T. (1983) *Production/Operations Management*. Englewood Cliffs, NJ: Prentice-Hall International.
3. Hayes, R. and Wheelwright, S. (1979) 'Linking Manufacturing Process and Product Life Cycles'. *Harvard Business Review* **57** (No. 1, January–February): 133–140.
4. Lovelock, C. H. (1983) 'Classifying Services to Gain Strategic Marketing Insights'. *Journal of Marketing* **47** (Summer): 9–20.
5. Buffa, E. (1963) *Operations Management*. Chichester: Wiley.
6. Hill, T. (1985) *Manufacturing Strategy: The Strategic Management of the Manufacturing Function*. London: Macmillan.
7. Wild, R. (1971) *Techniques in Production and Operations Management*. New York: Holt, Rinehart and Winston.

8. Sasser, W. E., Olsen, R. P. and Wyckoff, D. D. (1982) *Management of Service Operations.* Boston: Allyn and Bacon.
9. Chase, R. B. (1978) 'Where Does the Customer Fit in a Service Operation?'. *Harvard Business Review* **56** (No. 4, November–December) 137–142.
10. Morris, B. and Johnston, R. (1987) 'Dealing with Inherent Variability—The Difference between Service and Manufacturing Explained'. *International Journal of Operations & Production Management* **7** (No. 4): 13–22.
11. Thomas, D. R. E. (1975) 'Strategy is Different in Service Businesses'. *Harvard Business Review* **53** (No. 4, July–August): 158–165.
12. Kotler, P. (1980) *Principles of Marketing.* Englewood Cliffs, NJ: Prentice-Hall International.
13. Chase, R. B. (1981) 'The Customer Contact Approach to Services: Theoretical Bases and Practical Extensions'. *Operations Research* **29** (No. 4).
14. Maister, D. and Lovelock, C. H. (1982) 'Managing Facilitator Services'. *Sloan Management Review* (Summer): 19–31.
15. Maister, D. (1983) 'The Defining Qualities of Four Different Managerial Environments'. *Research in Service Operations Management,* Proceedings of the workshop on Teaching and Research in Production and Operations Management, London Business School.
16. Johnston, R. and Morris, B. (1985) 'Monitoring and Control in Service Operations'. *International Journal of Operations & Production Management* **5** (No. 1): 32–38.
17. Haynes, R. M. (1990) 'Service Typologies: A Transaction Modelling Approach'. *International Journal of Service Industry Management* **1** (No. 1).
18. Shostack, G. L. (1987) 'Service Positioning through Structural Change'. *Journal of Marketing* **51** (January).
19. Wemmerlov, U. (1990) 'A Taxonomy for Service Processes and its Implications for System Design'. *International Journal of Service Industry Management* **1** (No. 3).
20. Voss, C. A., Armistead, C. G., Johnston, R. and Morris, B. (1985) *Operations Management in Service Industries and the Public Sector.* Chichester: Wiley.
21. Johnston, R. (1987) 'A Framework for Developing a Quality Strategy in a Customer-processing Operation'. *International Journal of Quality & Reliability Management* **4** (No. 4): 35–44.
22. Fitzgerald, L., Johnston, R., Silvestro, R., Steel, A. and Voss, C. (1989) *Control Information for Management in Service Industries.* Research Report, The Chartered Institute of Management Accountants, London.
23. Chase, R. B. and Erikson, W. J. (1988) 'The Service Factory'. *Academy of Management Executive* **II** (No. 3).

20

Sustainable Competitive Advantage in Service Industries: A Conceptual Model and Research Propositions

Sundar G. Bharadwaj, P. Rajan Varadarajan and John Fahy

During the past two decades, marketing scholars have focused on a broad range of issues pertaining to the marketing of services, as evidenced by two recent reviews of extant literature on services marketing (Fisk, Brown and Bitner, 1993; Swartz, Bowen and Brown, 1992). The emergence of services marketing as a distinct body of literature notwithstanding, there seems to be broad consensus that the boundary delineating services from goods is somewhat fluid. Often significant service components are integral to the consumption/use of tangible goods (e.g. automobiles, household appliances), as are significant tangible elements to the consumption/use of services (e.g. car rentals, air travel). As evidenced by Shostack's (1977) characterization of products (goods and services) in terms of the proportion of physical goods and intangible services they contain, there are few pure goods or services. Recognizing the fluid nature of the boundary delineating services from goods, the molecular model (Shostack, 1977) views all market entities as exhibiting varying levels of tangible and intangible elements, and services as intangibles-dominant market entities. Along similar lines Berry and Parasuraman (1991) suggest that if the source of a product's[1] core benefit is more tangible than intangible, it should be considered a good, and if it is more intangible than tangible, it should be considered a service. In addition to intangibility, inseparability/simultaneity, heterogeneity, and perishability are generally viewed as the distinguishing characteristics of services.

We focus on organizational skills and resources underlying the competitive advantages of service businesses, and the moderating effects of the characteristics of services, service industries, and firms within an industry on the skills and resources underlying a business's competitive positional advantages. Through an extensive body of literature focusing on a broad range of issues pertaining to competitive advantage has been published to date, this article is based on the premise that a

Reprinted with permission from *Journal of Marketing*, Vol. 57, October, pp. 83–99

closed examination of the sources of competitive advantage in the context of service industries can provide unique managerial insights into strategic problems and opportunities that may not be readily apparent from an examination of the sustainable competitive advantage (SCA) related issues at a more aggregate level. As Shostack (1977, p. 75) notes, 'the greater the weight of intangible elements in a market entity, the greater will be the divergence from product marketing in priorities and approach.[2] Recent reviews of literature on services marketing and management also allude to the dearth of strategic emphasis in extant literature (Fisk, Brown and Bitner, 1993; Swartz, Bowen and Brown, 1992). Against this backdrop, we provide insights into the sources of SCA in service industries by reviewing and integrating research on SCA-related issues explored in the fields of marketing, strategic management and industrial organization economics and exploring the implications of the distinctive characteristics of service industries and firms for achieving SCA. The paper is organized as follows: First, an overview of the concept of SCA is presented. Second, a contingency model of SCA in service industries is proposed. Third, the moderating effects of the characteristics of services, service industries, and firms within an industry on potential sources of SCA are explored and the propositions presented. We conclude with a discussion on managerial implications and future research directions.

THE CONCEPT OF SUSTAINABLE COMPETITIVE ADVANTAGE: AN OVERVIEW

In most industries, some firms are more profitable than others, regardless of whether the average profitability of the industry is high or low. The superior performers conceivably possess something special and hard to imitate that allows them to outperform their rivals. These unique skills and assets (resources) are referred to as *sources of competitive advantage* in strategy literature.[2] *Competitive advantage* can result either from implementing a value-creating strategy not simultaneously being implemented by any current or potential competitors (Barney, McWilliams and Turk, 1989; Barney, 1991) or through superior execution of the same strategy as competitors. *Sustainability* is achieved when the advantage resists erosion by competitor behavior (Porter 1985, p. 20). In other words, the skills and resources under-lying a business's competitive advantage must resist duplication by other firms (Barney, 1991). Case in point:

> ServiceMaster is a company that manages support services for hospitals, schools, and industrial companies. It supervises the employees of customers' organizations engaged in housekeeping, food service, and equipment maintenance. The company has been successful in using its unique resources and skills (specifically, system economies and specialized management skills) to raise the quality of its customers' maintenance services and at the same time lowering their costs. Using its data base (a firm specific resource), which covers more than a decade of maintenance history on several million pieces of equipment at thousands of locations, ServiceMaster can determine objectively how its customers' facilities should be maintained, when equipment purchases and maintenance will pay off, and when parts should be replaced. The effectiveness of ServiceMaster's systems are reportedly such that its customers often invest jointly in new equipment and share the resulting productivity gains (see Quinn, Doorley and Paquette, 1990).

Conditions for sustainable competitive advantage

A number of studies have explored the conditions under which a business's competitive advantage is sustainable (cf. Barney, 1991; Coyne, 1985). Barney lists four essential requirements for a resource/skill to be a source of SCA:

- It must be *valuable*;
- It must be *rare* among a firm's current and potential competitors;
- It must be *imperfectly imitable*; and
- There must not be any *strategically equivalent substitutes* for this resource/skill.

Firm resources and skills are considered valuable when they aid a firm in formulating and implementing strategies that improve its efficiency and/or effectiveness. However, if certain resources/skills are possessed by a large number of present or potential competitors, they cannot be a source of SCA. Valuable and rare organizational resource/skills can be sources of SCA only if firms that do not possess these resources cannot obtain them (as a direct consequence of a capability gap (Coyne, 1985), the critical resources being imperfectly imitable (Lippman and Rumelt, 1982; Coyne 1985; Barney, 1986a, 1986b)). The final requirement for a resource/skill to be a source of SCA is that the resource/skill is nonsubstitutable. Substitutability can take two forms. If a competitor cannot duplicate a firm's resources/skills exactly, but can substitute *similar* resources that enable it to formulate and implement identical strategies and use very *different* resources/skills as strategic substitutes (see Barney, 1991), then a resource/skill cannot be a source of SCA.

Coyne (1985) points out that, not only must a firm have a skill or resource that its competitors do not have (i.e. there must be a capability gap), but also the capability gap must make a difference to the customer. In other words, for a business to enjoy a SCA in a product-market segment, the difference(s) between the firm and its competitors must be reflected in one or more product/delivery attributes that are *key buying criteria*. Furthermore, in order for a competitive advantage to be sustainable, both the key buying criteria and the underlying capability gap must be enduring. Additionally, in the face of changes in key buying criteria, the sustainability of a business's competitive advantage would depend on its ability to *adapt* to these changes and/or influence key buying criteria (see Boulding *et al.*, 1993; Hamel and Prahalad, 1991; Treacy and Wiersema, 1993).

A CONCEPTUAL MODEL OF SUSTAINABLE COMPETITIVE ADVANTAGE

A conceptual model of SCA in service industries, which builds on the works by Barney (1991), Coyne (1985, 1989), Day and Wensley (1988), Dierickx and Cool (1989), Lippman and Rumelt (1982), and Reed and Defillipi (1990), among others, is presented in Figure 1. Here a firm's distinctive organizational skills and resources are viewed as the source of a business's competitive advantages in the marketplace.[3] The characteristics of services, service industries and firms within an industry are

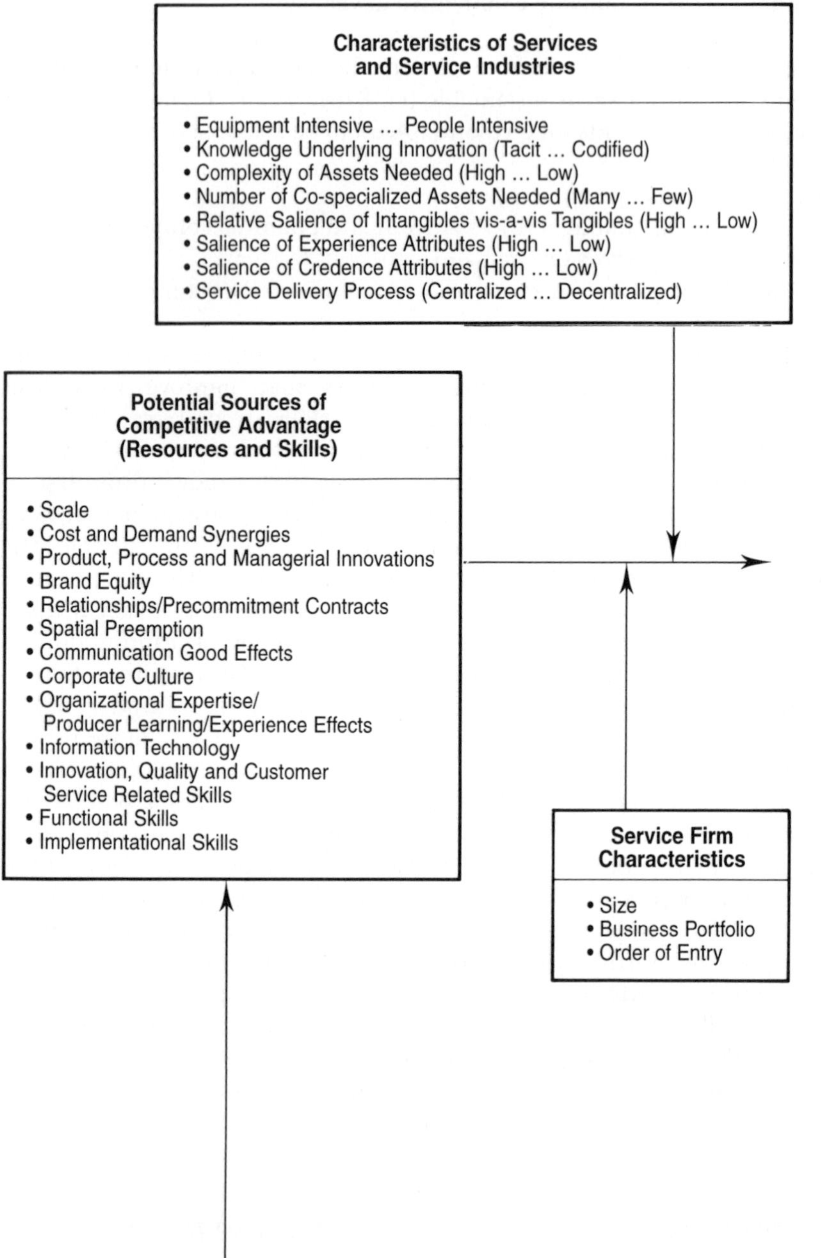

Figure 1. A contingency model of sustainable competitive advantage in service industries.

shown as moderating the skills and resources underlying a business's competitive positional advantages. The sustainability of a business's competitive advantages is viewed as contingent on barriers to imitation of its unique skills and resources. The model further suggests that sustainable competitive advantages are a key to sustained,

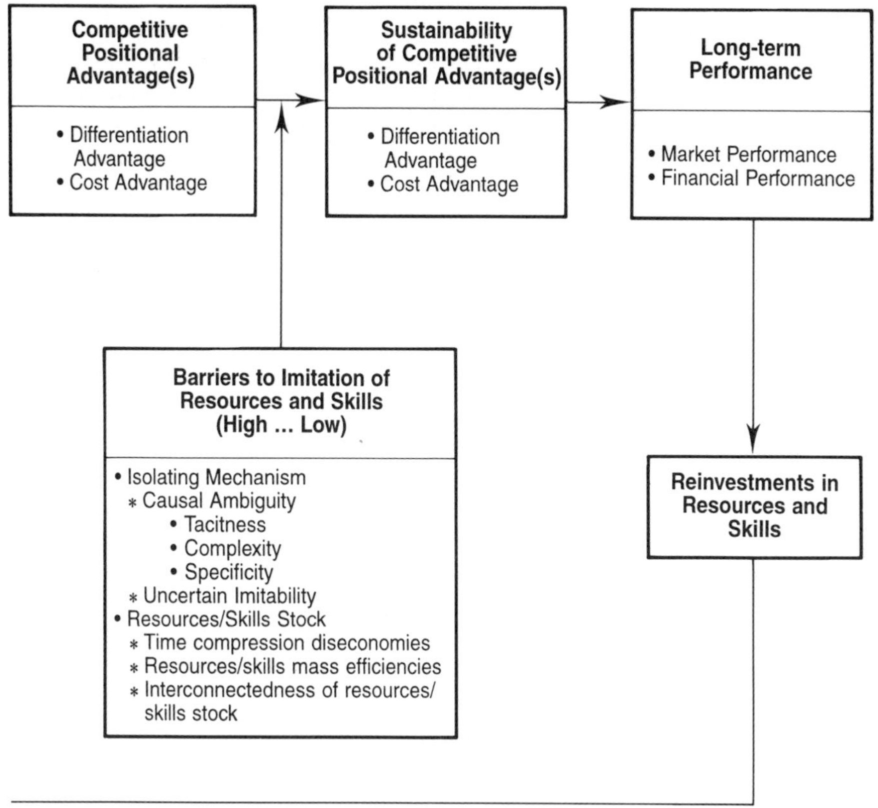

superior long-term performance. Reinvestments in both present and new skills and resources are viewed as critical to strengthening (or preventing erosion of) competitive advantages, A detailed discussion of the constructs central to the model and the proposed links follows.

Sources of competitive advantage

Researchers generally distinguish between two broad sources of competitive advantage – unique resources (assets) and distinctive skills (capabilities). Day and Wensley (1988) characterize superior skills as the distinctive capabilities of a firm's personnel that set them apart from the personnel of competing firms and superior resources as more tangible requirements for advantage that enable a firm to exercise its capabilities.[4] These two broad sets of sources enable a business to perform the various primary and secondary value activities that compose its value chain either at a lower cost or in a way that leads to differentiation. They facilitate the attainment of competitive positional advantages in the form of (1) superior customer value through a differentiated good/service, and/or (2) lower relative cost through cost leadership.[5] Firm-specific skills and resources are also referred to as the 'drivers' of cost and/or differentiation advantages (Porter, 1985). A wide variety of drivers has received attention in the literature, including *resource-based drivers* such as economies of scale and scope, brand equity, and reputation, and *skills-based* drivers such as the skills underlying the innovativeness and superior quality of a business's offerings. Superior skills and resources do not, however, automatically give a business a competitive advantage. They only provide the business an opportunity to *leverage* its skills and resources to achieve competitive cost and/or differentiation advantages. This entails first identifying those skills and resources a company has that have the greatest potential to endow the firm with enduring competitive advantages. Also, as Asker (1989) notes, multiple bases of competitive advantage may be needed for a business to compete successfully. A more detailed discussion on the skills and resources underlying a business's competitive advantage listed in Figure 1 is presented in a later section, along with the propositions.

Competitive positional advantages

Competitive positional advantages can be broadly construed as cost leadership and differentiation advantages. Cost leadership entails performing most activities at a lower cost than competitors while offering a parity product. Differentiation entails customers perceiving a consistent difference in important attributes between the firm's offerings and its competitors' offerings. The advantages, disadvantages, risks, and implementational requirements of cost leadership and differentiation as generic strategy alternatives have been well documented (Porter, 1980, 1985). Shostack's (1987) analysis of the process of service provision in terms of complexity (the number of steps involved in providing the service) and divergence (the executional latitude at each step) and the positioning alternatives that emerge from this analysis – reduced divergence (a standardized, cost-efficient service), increased divergence (greater customization for specific segments), reduced complexity (a stripped down generic service), and increased complexity (addition of services tending toward a multi-service position – provide additional insights into differentiation possibilities in service industries. Each of these positioning alternatives can result in differences in customer's perception of value. For example, a strategy of reduced divergence could lead to some customers perceiving the shift as one that lowers customization and limits their options and hence rejecting a highly standardized service even if it costs less (see Shostack, 1987).

Moderating effects of the characteristics of services, service industries, and firms

In the proposed conceptual model (Figure 1), the following characteristics of services, service industries, and firms within an industry moderate the effects of skills and sources underlying a business's positional advantage.

A. Characteristics of services and service industries
   - Equipment intensive . . . people intensive
   - Complexity of assets needed (high . . . low)
   - Number of co-specialized assets needed (many . . . few)
   - Relative salience of intangibles vis-a-vis tangibles (high . . . low)
   - Salience of experience attributes (high . . . low)
   - Salience of credence attributes (high . . . low)
   - Service delivery process (centralized . . . decentralized)

B. Service firm characteristics
   - Size
   - Business portfolio composition
   - Order of entry into market

Though other characteristics merit consideration as moderating factors in the context of specific service industries, the principal focus here is on characteristics that transcend industry boundaries. Such as orientation can be conducive to managerial learning by facilitating identification of and learning from the experience of organizations facing parallel situations in other service industries (see Lovelock, 1983).

Barriers to imitation

Central to the concept of SCA is the notion of durability or non-imitability. A key difference between *entry barriers* and *barriers* to imitation is that though the former are prone to free-riding (because they are the private collective asset of the industry), the latter are endogenous and idiosyncratic (i.e. firm-specific) (Mahoney and Pandian, 1992). Overlapping conceptualizations of barriers to imitation have been proposed by Lippman and Rumelt (1982), Coyne (1985), Rumelt (1984, 1987), and Reed and Defillipi (1990). A map of the broad playing field of barriers to imitation is provided by Rumelt's (1984) treatise on *isolating mechanisms.*[6] Dierickx and Cool's (1989) discussion on *resource/skills* stock provides additional insights into the operation of barriers to imitation.

Isolating mechanisms

These are essentially asymmetries in the skills and assets of competing firms that increase the costs associated with strategic imitation. Engaging in the maintenance of these isolating mechanisms protects the competitive advantages derived from past and/or present managerial actions. Fisher (1989) notes that understanding the relative durability of each isolating mechanism and marketing mix element has important implications for differentiation strategies pursued by service firms. Barriers to imitation are even greater when *causal ambiguity* exists over the factors responsible for a business's superior performance. Three critical characteristics of a firm individually or in combination contribute to causal ambiguity (Reed and Defillippi 1990): *Tacitness* is defined as the implicit and non-codifiable accumulation of skills that result from learning by doing (Polanyi, 1962); (2) *Complexity* results from the interrelationships between various skills and assets (Barney, 1926b; Nelson and Winter, 1982); and (3) *Specificty* entails the transaction-specific skills and assets that are utilized in the production processes and provision of services for particular customers (Williamson, 1985). Any of these can produce ambiguity regarding the firm's actions and outcomes and in turn create barriers to imitation (Reed and Defillippi 1990).

Ambiguity over factors responsible for superior performance acts as a powerful barrier to imitation as will as a deterrent to *resource mobility* (Dierickx and Cool, 1989). Resources that cannot be traded either because (1) their property rights are not well defined or (2) they are idiosyncratic to the firm and have no value outside it constitute *immobile resources* (Dierickx and Cool, 1989). Furthermore, the complexity of firms often makes identification of their key success factors separately may often be an inaccurate representation, because the interaction among the factors can be the cause of a business's success. Therefore, potential imitators may find it hard to develop an unambiguous list of factors responsible for a business's success.

Uncertain imitability results when the creation of new products is inherently uncertain and causal ambiguity about the process of asset stock accumulation (the building of stocks of resources and skills) impedes imitation and/or mobility of a firm's unique resources. Its relevance increases when complex products and administrative structures are involved (Lippman and Rumelt, 1982). The lack of a clear-cut causal explanation between the actions and performance of some large firms is supportive of the notion of uncertain imitability. Though economic theory suggests that the presence of excess profits in any industry can make markets *contestable* (Baumol, Panzar and Willig, 1982) and bring down industry profits to normal levels, the theory of uncertain imitability (Lippman and Rumelt, 1982) suggests high profits may signal the presence of successful firms with difficult-to-imitate capabilities that impede entry attempts.

Resource/skills stock

The imitability of a business's resource/skill stock are related to the characteristics of the *process* by which they are accumulated. Dierickx and Cool (1989) identify three major characteristics: (1) *time compression diseconomies,* (2) *resource/skill mass efficiencies,* and (3) *interconnectedness of resources/skills stock.* Time compression diseconomies refers to the accumulation of certain advantages to firms owning a resource/skill for a long period of time (e.g. firm reputation for quality). A firm may have built a reputation for quality by following a consistent set of production.

quality control, and other policies over time. Such sources of competitive advantage can be neither acquired nor imitated by competitors within a short period of time.

The presence of large amounts of existing stock of resources/skills facilitates further resource/skill accumulation. For example, firms that already have an existing stock of research and development may often by in a better position to make further breakthroughs and add to their existing stock of knowledge than firms who have low initial levels of know-how. The implication here is that when asset mass efficiencies are critical, building stocks of resources/skills by firms that have initial low levels of stock can be difficult. Difficulties in 'catching up' can be even greater when the asset accumulation process exhibits discontinuities; i.e. a critical mass is required (Dierickx and Cool, 1989).

Interconnectedness of resources/skills acts as a barrier to imitation when some firms lack complementary resources/skills that are critical to competing in a product market. For instance, a new entrant to a market with a product (of comparable quality to that of incumbents) encountering difficulties in distributing the product because of no established dealer network would be at a competitive disadvantage.

Performance outcomes

Competitive advantage can be expected to lead to superior marketplace performance (e.g. market share, customer satisfaction) and financial performance (e.g. return on investment, shareholder wealth creation). Accounting ratios and market measures constitute two broad indicators of a business's financial performance. However, they have been criticized for their (1) inadequate handling of intangibles and (2) improper valuation of sources of competitive advantage (i.e. allocating historic and current costs to satisfy tax requirements (Day and Wensley, 1988)). Financial performance measures characterized by a future orientation (e.g. shareholder value creation potential) though not entirely free of shortcomings, are generally viewed as more appropriate for evaluating the desirability of planned investments in defensible positional advantages. However, a detailed discussion of the merits and shortcomings of these measures is beyond our scope here.[7]

Reinvestments in resources and skills

Because the barriers to imitation of a firm's skills and resources are prone to decay in the absence of adequate 'maintenance' expenditure (Dierickx and Cool, 1989), the maintenance of an SCA requires the constant monitoring of and reinvesting in the present sources of advantage, as will as investing in other potential sources of advantage.[8] For example, a business with a reputation for superior quality could experience an erosion in quality as a source of SCA if it fails to continue investing in processes that contributed to the business's reputation for quality. As Porter (1985, p. 20) notes, a firm must offer 'a moving target to its competitors, by reinvesting in order to continually improve its position'.

SOURCES OF SUSTAINABLE COMPETITIVE ADVANTAGE IN SERVICE INDUSTRIES: PROPOSITIONS

This section provides an overview of the skills and resources underlying a business's competitive positional advantages and a number of propositions delineating the moderating effects of the characteristics of services, service industries, and firms within industries on these sources. However, we present no formal discussion in reference to certain potential sources of competitive advantage listed in Figure 1 (superior skills in various functional areas and those relating to innovation, quality, customer service, and implementation) because their importance as determinants of superior performance are widely recognized, transcend goods and service industry boundaries, and have been extensively discussed in business literature.

Scale effects

Given the decentralization of the service production process to a local level in many service industries, the potential for achieving a competitive cost advantage by exploiting economies of scale has traditionally been viewed as modest. Nevertheless, opportunities for exploiting scale economies are significantly greater in equipment-based service industries than in people-based service industries. Service firms can also achieve economies of scale by centralizing service production facilities while decentralizing customer-contact facilities (Upah, 1980) or centralizing certain critical (and/or equipment-intensive) activities and localizing less critical (and/or people-intensive) activities, as exemplified by clinical laboratories performing some tests in dispersed local units and others involving expensive equipment and/or skilled personnel in regional centers (see Porter, 1990). Operating economies can also be realized through reconfigurations such as replacing stand-alone with multi-unit motion picture theatres sharing a centralized projection room, ticket selling booth, and refreshment stand (see Thomas, 1978). Also, as Quinn and Gagnon (1986) note, in a number of service industries, the application of new technologies has allowed firms to realize significant scale economies.

P_1: The greater the equipment intensity of a service industry, the greater the importance of economies of scale as a source of competitive cost advantage.

The inseparability of production and consumption of services and the resultant inability to efficiently mass produce services at a central location often necessitates service businesses to make the service available at multiple sites. This in turn necessitates examining the implications of size on cost and differentiation advantages at the operating unit and firm level. Heskett (1987) notes that for service firms operating under a common identity over a wide area, scale economies often are more important at the firm than operating unit level. A manifestation of the relative size (of firms competing in an industry) at the company level is the number of dispersed local units (either company owned or franchised) operating under a common corporate identity. All else equal, economies of scale associated with selection and training of employees, purchased goods and services, investments in specialized technology and R&D to systematize the service delivery process, and shared marketing (e.g. national or large- scale local advertising and sales promotion), billing and logistics-related activities enable a multi-unit service firm to achieve a cost advantage vis-a-vis single-unit and multi-unit service firms with fewer units.

In many service industries, multi-unit firms are better equipped to achieve a competitive differentiation advantage over single-unit firms through *systematization* and *standardization* of the process of delivering services (Porter, 1990). For example, a multi-unit firm that replicates its services at many locations by creating standardized facilities, procedures to guide the behavior of employees, and automating individual service delivery tasks (Levitt, 1976) can achieve a differentiation advantage vis-a-vis single-unit service firms.

P_2: The larger the number of local units of a service firm operating under a common corporate identity within an industry (either company owned or franchised), the greater the potential to exploit scale economies to achieve competitive cost advantage and institute systematization, standardization, and other differentiation features to achieve a differentiation advantage.

When a service product is a multi-attribute benefit bundle characterized by the delivery of certain attributes of the total service from dispersed site locations (e.g. purchase of travelers' checks) and other attributes from a central location (e.g. arranging for replacement of lost travelers' checks), firm size relative to competitors (e.g. market share/customer base) can be a major determinant of the economic viability of investing in certain differentiation features that might endow the firm with a competitive differentiation advantage. Case in point:

An important attribute or key buying criterion in the context of purchasing travelers' checks is the assurance that they will be replaced promptly should they be lost or stolen. A state-of-the-art satellite communication system that allows customers who have lost their travelers' checks to communicate with the firm from any part of the world, an office that is staffed 24 hours a day, 365 days a year by a team of well-trained employees, a supporting information system that allows the staff handling the phone lines to verify the veracity of customers' claims regarding lost travelers' checks on the basis of their responses to a few questions, and a distribution system that is the most intensive and extensive (a worldwide network of branch offices and agents) could conceivably be some of the basic building blocks (firm-specific resources and skills) that allows only one firm in the industry to guarantee that if lost or stolen, its travelers' checks will be replaced within eight hours or less. For a firm with a sizeable share of the market, making substantial investments in satellite communication systems, earth stations, and a state-of-the-art information system to achieve such a differentiation advantage may be an economically viable proposition; for competitors with smaller shares of the market, however, this may not be the case.

Cost and demand synergies

Economies of scope are realized when a firm is able to market entirely new services with little added costs through networks or systems previously established for current services. Communications and information-handling technologies often facilitate distribution of a broader set of services to a more diffused customer base, as well as lower the marginal costs on *old* services, as equipment development and software investments are allocated over a broader line of services (Quinn and Gagnon, 1986). Therefore, relative to single business firms, multi-business firms have the opportunity to (1) reduce costs by sharing activities between businesses; (2) increase revenues by cross-selling to customers of different businesses in the firm's portfolio; and (3) share knowledge and skills. For instance, a multi-business firm such as ServiceMaster – whose subsidiaries include Terminix (termite and pest control service), ChemLawn and True Green (lawn care service), and American Home Shield (appliance insurance service) – has an opportunity to exploit demand synergies by cross-selling of services, and cost synergies by centralizing the accounts processing for various services. More importantly, competitive cost and differentiation advantages associated with synergy are less likely to be imitated, because these are often achieved under a unique set of circumstances as will as on the basis of unique firm specific resources and skill base. Case in point:

> In 1990, when AT&T launched its AT&T Universal Visa and MasterCard credit cards, it had access to the credit histories of 70 million AT&T long-distance customers (a firm-specific resource). By qualifying these potential customers in advance, the firm was in a position to respond quickly to inquiries from households that were good credit risks and lower its vulnerability to bad credit risks (Blattberg and Deighton, 1991). An additional incentive it could offer to its credit card customers (a 10% discount on long-distance calls made over the AT&T network by using its cards), also attributable to a firm-specific resource, could be matched only by some of its larger competitors by entering into alliances with competing long distance carriers such as MCI and US Sprint.

P_3: The greater the cost (demand) interrelationships between a particular service business in a firm's portfolio and other businesses in its portfolio, the greater the cost (demand) synergies as a source of competitive cost and/or differentiation advantage.

Product, process, and managerial innovations

Product, process, and managerial innovations can be used to gain a competitive advantage, to the extent that the technology underlying such innovations remain proprietary. Technology held proprietary through patents, copyright, or secrecy can deter new entrants, as well as achieve a competitive advantage by exploiting economies of scale and scope and/or through differentiation. Teece (1988, p. 48) characterizes *regime of appropriability* as those aspects of the commercial environment, excluding firm and market structure, that govern an innovator's ability to capture the rents associated with the innovation. Relative to goods industries, in service industries, technology suffers from a weak regime of appropriability, which implies that patents can be 'invented around.' For example, though Merrill Lynch obtained a patent for its Cash Management Account (CMA), which integrated four basic investor services into a single account, and holds a dominant share of the market, practically all its major competitors offers a similar service.[9] Trade secrets, an alternative to patents, can offer protection from imitation, provided the secret is kept in the form of *tacit knowledge.* Whereas *codified knowledge* is transferable and more prone to be copied, tacit knowledge, being difficult to articulate, is difficult to transfer or copy (Teece, 1981, 1988). A number of service firms have successfully used information technology to capture tacit organizational knowledge and retain property rights over the resulting innovations. For example, American Express developed an expert system called Authorizer's Assistant to facilitate credit authorization judgments. As a result, a decision that traditionally created a bottleneck (involving the scanning of 13 data bases or necessitating a judgment call) can now be made in a few seconds.

The presence of co*specialized* assets or the lack thereof also impacts on the imitability of innovations. When commercializing an innovation requires other specialized assets in marketing and/or production, and these assets are specific to the particular innovation, the imitability of the innovation will be impeded to the degree of complexity and number of cospecialized assets needed to put the innovation to work. Even if competing firms were to find it easy to copy the innovation, they might face difficulties in putting together the organizational apparatus needed to bring the innovation to market. A complex set of cospecialized assets may therefore protect the innovation and allow it to continue to yield value (see Teece, 1987). For example, it took more than two years for competitors to respond to American Hospital Supply Corporation's ASAP system, because they needed to computerize their inventory systems first (Vitale, 1988). Though entering certain service businesses could require a firm to possess complex and/or multiple co-specialized assets, entering into other service businesses may not be inhibited by such requirements.

P_4: The greater the complexity of assets needed to market a service, the greater the importance of innovation as a source of competitive advantage.

P_5: The greater the number of cospecialized assets needed to market a service, the greater the importance of innovation a source of competitive advantage.

BRAND EQUITY[10]

Aaker (1991, p. 15) defines brand equity as 'a set of brand assets and liabilities linked to a brand, its name and symbol, that add or subtract from the value provided by a product to a firm and/or that firm's customers'. He distinguishes between five categories of assets that give rise to a brand's equity: (1) brand loyalty, (2) name awareness, (3) perceived quality, (4) brand associations, and (5) proprietary brand assets such as patents and symbols. In the context of marketing of service, Berry and Parasuraman (1991) note that brand equity also could reside in the name of the firm itself. Here, the absence of a tangible physical product on which a brand name can be affixed often necessitates assigning greater prominence to the corporate brand name on the various physical products and facilities used to deliver the service (e.g. displaying an airline's logo and name on airplanes, ground transportation vehicles, baggage handling equipment, ticketing counter, departure and arrival gates, etc.). Strong brand names or symbols impact positively on brand equity, both directly and indirectly, through perceived quality. Brand equity (1) helps differentiate the product from competitors' offerings (Park, Jaworski, and MacInnes, 1986); (2) serves as a proxy for quality and creates positive images in consumers' minds (Oster, 1990; Kamakura and Russell, 1991); (3) prevents market share erosion during price and promotional wars (Kamakura and Russell, 1991; Johnson, 1991); and (4) prevents market share erosion by giving a firm time to respond to competitive threats (Aaker, 1991).

Shostack (1977) suggests that since services are characterized by a greater degree of intangibility, 'tangibilizing' (managing the evidence) must be attempted in order to make the product more salient to customers. The need to tangibilize is inversely related to the level of intangibility of a service. Brand names and symbols used by firms to add tangible aspects to the product help reduce the search costs of consumers (Landes and Posner, 1987), such as Prudential Insurance's use of the Rock of Gibraltar to present a message of strength and stability, and Travelers Insurance's use of an umbrella to convey a message of protection (Aaker, 1991).

P_6: The greater the intangibility of a service, the greater the importance of brand equity as a source of competitive differentiation advantage.

Nelson (1970 and Darby and Karni (1973) suggest that customers take a chance when they purchase an experience good. Unlike search goods, consumers cannot infer through simple inspection whether a product is of high or low quality with experience goods. A major challenge faced by a new entrant in an experience goods market is the need to convince consumers to take a chance on a new product when they are aware of the quality of the incumbent's product because of prior use (Schmalensee, 1982). In general, the likely presence of variability in service quality, not only makes it difficult and riskier for consumers to evaluate the quality of a service, but also makes the consumers' purchase choices more complex (Murray, 1991: Nayyar and Templeton, 1991). Though on one hand, consumers may seek more information to make better choices, since information search is generally expensive (Stigler, 1961), buyers seeking to economize on evaluation costs might be inclined to choose the product with the best brand reputation because it has the lowest evaluation costs (Rumelt, 1987). When buyers cannot easily evaluate the capabilities of the service provider and the quality and value of the service provided (as would be the case with credance goods) brand reputation serves as an important proxy for quality and other key buying criteria that cannot be easily evaluated.

Also, as pointed out by Levitt (1986), when buyers select a particular brand, they are engaging in an act of risk reduction. Through risk can be viewed as a function of the perception of variability in quality, in service industries, firms having strong brand names and symbols are better positioned to mitigate customers' perceptions over variability in quality and therefore differentiate themselves from competition. Moreover, the additional marketing efforts that may be expended in order to overcome consumers' risk perceptions can often lead to a cost asymmetry between a firm owning brands with strong equity vis-a-vis its competitors.

P_7: The greater the experience and credence attributes of a service, the greater the importance of brand equity as a source of competitive cost and differentiation advantage.

Information asymmetries also can be exploited by firms to diversify into new services and provide multiple services to its customers. In reference to service industries, Nayyar (1990) argues that each sampling by experience contributes to the information bank that consumers maintain. In reference to new service introductions he notes:

> When the producer of a brand introduces another brand, buyers may draw upon their information bank to form associative evaluations of the likely properties of the new brand. This 'carry-over' of evaluative information tends to reduce information acquisition costs for buyers. Hence it can be expected that customers who have favourable impressions of current service providers will tend to favor such providers when making purchase decisions about other services that these providers may offer (Nayyar, 1990, pp. 515–516).

Furthermore, when appropriate, service providers who have created favorable impressions can attempt to capitalize on ongoing relationships by allocating more effort to convincing their existing customers (rather than new customers) to try their new services. In summary, a firm with a well established brand reputation diversifying into new services that its existing customers may buy from can be expected to enjoy a competitive advantage, because of the lower information acquisition costs to consumers.

> P_8: The greater the experience and credance attributes of a *new* service being marketed by a firm, the greater the importance of brand equity as a source of competitive advantage.

Relationships/precommitment contracts[11]

In general, firms can enhance their performance by cultivating new customers and/or retaining their existing customers and selling more to them. Cultivating new customers in generally more expensive than retaining existing customers, particularly in mature markets. Riechheld and Sasser (1990) found a 5% reduction in customer defections to be associated with profit increases ranging from 25 to 85% in the industries they studied. Findings such as these suggest that service firms doing business with their customers from a long term relationship perspective (rather than a single transaction perspective) either through an implicit or explicit precommitment have a greater potential of achieving cost advantages. Precommitment contracts, by removing a portion of the market from the competitive arena and thereby introducing an asymmetry between incumbents and potential entrants, act as entry deterrents (Oster, 1990).

Developing relationships with and retaining customers are central to the concept of *memberships*, which constitute non-contractual approaches to precommitment. Service businesses have successfully employed various methods to 'lock in' customers. Non-contractual switching costs created by airlines through their frequent flyer programs and hotel chains through their honored frequent guest programs are cases in point. The more formalized such relationships are, the greater are the benefits that accrue to the service provider. In return for exclusive privileges for members, valuable information collected about customers can be used to gain scope advantages (by cross-selling other services to customers), as well as to build non-contractual switching costs. For example, American Express reportedly has over 450 items of information on each customer that are used by its direct marketing division to sell consumer products to them (Newport, 1989). Studies focusing on service industries have found that developing relationships with customers (through implicit contracts) has a positive impact on firm performance (Nayyar, 1992; Crosby, Evans and Cowles, 1990; Crosby and Stephens, 1987). Trust provides an alternative means to developing non-contractual precommitments with customers. Trust (i.e. a willingness to rely on an exchange partner in whom one has confidence) has also been shown to be positively associated with commitment to a relationship (Moorman, Zaltman and Deshpande, 1992).

Precommitment contracts can not only deter entry but also prevent customers from exiting existing contracts. For example, in hospital management contracts, incumbent firms have a significant edge in contract renewals because of the substantial costs to hospitals of changing firms (Porter, 1985). The switching costs become higher as (1) the customer gets accustomed to the procedures provided by the system, resulting in a *procedural specificity* (Malone, Yates and Benjamin, 1987); (2) the extent to which this procedural specificity is increased by an *electronic integration* effect (dependency of the customer on a vendor, created by the use of interorganizational or transaction-based systems (Malone, Yates and Benjamin, 1987; Glazer, 1991)); and (3) the customers modify their own internal procedures as a result of using the system (Barrett and Konsynski, 1982; Runge, 1988). Studies in the insurance industry have found that agents who were electronically linked with a particular insurance carrier showed a significant increase in the number of policies written with that carrier compared to agents who were not electronically linked to the carrier (Venkatraman and Zaheer, 1990; O'Callaghan, Kaufmann and Konsynski, 1992). As noted previously, buying services with greater experience and credence qualities involves greater consumer risk taking. Relationships, by nurturing strong social and personal ties with consumers (Czepiel, 1990), allow a firm to offer a greater assurance to customers and lower the perceived risk (see Crosby and Stephens, 1987; Crosby, Evans and Cowles, 1990).

P_9: The greater the experience and credence attributes of a service, the greater the importance of relationships as a source of competitive differentiation advantage.

Spatial preemption

Because demand for many customer services is based on convenience, preemptive identification of ideal service locations is critical to achieving better facility utilization (Allen, 1988). However, though the delivery of certain services could require a firm to invest in multiple service delivery facilities at locations that are convenient to the served market (e.g. facilities for cash withdrawal and deposit), certain other services can be offered from a single centralized location (e.g. credit cards). Clearly, preemption of strategic locations is an important source of competitive cost and differentiation advantage only in the context of the former, as highlighted in reference to the banking industry:

> The *simultaneity/inseparability* characteristic of services implies that unlike goods, services are typically produced and consumed at the same time. Therefore, a consumer engaging in a financial transaction such as cash withdrawal must interface with a service deliverer, namely the bank teller. An alternative technological solution to serving this customer need is to install automated teller machines (ATMs). With ATMs in place, serving a customer need such as financial transactions processing does not have to be limited to the regular banking hours of 9.00 a.m. to 3.00 p.m. In effect, the simultaneity characteristic of services is no longer a constraint on the service provider. The service can be made available for 24 hours a day, 365 days a year. Also, to use the service, the consumer does not have to be physically present on the bank premises. The transactions can be processed through ATMs placed at strategic locations off the bank premises.
>
> The first firm that recognized the potential of this alternative technological solution had an array of opportunities to achieve a SCA. First, it had the opportunity to acquire or lease prime real estate at strategic locations (off-bank premises) for placing its ATMs at prices below those that would prevail later in the evolution of the market. (As the market for a resource such as strategic locations for placing ATMs became competitive, the price of this

resource would have been bid up until it was equal to the net present value of future above-normal benefits that can be derived from this resource (see Barney, 1986b).) This would have lead to a cost asymmetry between the first firm to make a significant investment in spatial preemption of locations for placement of ATMs and later entrants. Second, under conditions of manufacturing capacity constraints in the supplier industry, by contracting with supplier firms for their entire output of ATMs, the firm could have delayed the availability of ATMs to other competing firms. Because of the response time lag inherent in the supplier industry (i.e. the amount of time that would have elapsed before ATM manufacturers would have been in a position to deliver ATMs to the competitors of the pioneering bank), this source of competitive advantage would have endured for some period of time, though not indefinitely. In other words, even the firm's competitors who also recognized the potential of ATMs as an effective solution to the simultaneity characteristic of services would not have been in a position to immediately neutralize the differentiation advantage enjoyed by the pioneering firm attributable to a unique firm resource (ATMs). In summary, by making preemptive investments in key resources, a perceptive firm could have achieved an *absolute cost advantage* (through preemptive contracts for acquiring or leasing strategic locations for placing ATMs), as well as a *differentiation advantage* (through preemptive contracts to acquire the entire output of ATM manufacturers and spatial preemption of strategic locations). Understandably, the value of supplier industry response lag time as a source of competitive advantage would have diminished over time as manufacturers of ATMs stepped up their output. Hence, firms need to constantly explore new bases of competitive advantage.

P_{10}: The more decentralized the service delivery process, the greater the importance of spatial preemption as a source of competitive cost and/or differentiation advantage.

Communication good effects

The value of certain products (e.g. telephone network services, micro computer services) increases as the number of users or adopters increase. These products, called communication goods (Connor and Rumelt, 1991), serve as a means of standardization, because a large user base brings a large number of complementary goods into being. Case in point:

The importance of communication good effects as a source of competitive differentiation advantage is highlighted by the evolution of the video cassette recorder (VCR) business. In the early years, when Sony's Betamax and Matsushita's VHS-format VCRs were coexisting, as well as competing to become the industry standard, video rental service businesses stocked an equal number of prerecorded tapes in both formats. As the percentage of households owning VHS format VCRs increased relative to the percentage owning Betamax format VCRs, video rental service businesses modified their inventory mix. In most instances, they stocked multiple copies of video software prerecorded in the VHS format, but only one copy in the Betamax format. Over time, with (1) video software marketers (i.e. movie studios) increasingly offering their ware exclusively in the VHS format, (2) video rental service firms carrying only VHS-format tapes, and (3) most retail outlets stocking only VHS-format blank tapes, the VHS format emerged as the industry standard.

When communication goods are also experience products (such as computer software, disk operating systems), there is a market for both standardization and reputation bonding. Therefore, a particular brand becomes the industry standard and a powerful means of coordination (Rumelt, 1987). Developing or setting industry standards makes a firm's position more sustainable (Porter, 1985). In cases of products in which evaluation is difficult, akin to reputation, the industry standard plays the role of an alternative cue that makes itself more salient to the customer. Therefore,

P_{11}: The greater the experience and credence attributes of a service, the greater the importance of communication good effects as a source of competitive differentiation advantage.

The importance of spatial preemption and communication good effects as potential sources of competitive advantage is also moderated by the order of entry of firms into an industry. Literature on pioneering or first-mover advantage, a major area of research in economics, strategic management, and marketing, suggests that on average, pioneers have higher market shares than late entrants (cf. Robinson and Fornell, 1985; Robinson, 1988).[12] Potential sources of first-mover advantage and disadvantages associated with market pioneering are reviewed by Lieberman and Montgomery (1988) and Kerin, Varadarajan and Peterson (1992). The preceding discussions relating to spatial preemption and communication good effects suggest the following:

P_{12}: Potential opportunities for achieving competitive cost and/or differentiation advantage through spatial preemption are greater for the market pioneer than for later entrants.

P_{13}: Potential opportunities for achieving competitive differentiation advantage through communication good effects are greater for the market pioneer than for later entrants.

Corporate culture

An organization's culture is a complex set of beliefs and ways of doing things that influence the organization's perspective of itself and the world around it. A key element of corporate culture is the set of formal rules and structures that governs the way people relate to one another in the workplace. Another is the set of myths and traditions that help define the ideology of the organization (Mintzberg, 1983). Most of the literature on organization culture and performance of a firm suggests that culture can have a significant positive economic value for a firm (Barney, 1986a; Ouchi, 1981; Deal and Kennedy, 1982). The strong culture hypothesis suggests that firms that have strong distinctive traits, values and shared belief patterns will outperform organizations that are weak on these dimensions (Dennison, 1984). Strong cultures can (1) help attain a shared vision and goal congruence among employees to meet organizational goals (Wilkins and Ouchi, 1983); (2) empower employees to be flexible and achieve organizational goals (Pascale, 1985); and (3) energize the employees of an organization. A recent study reports that firms with cultures that emphasize key managerial constituencies (customers, stockholders and employees) and leadership (at all levels) outperformed by a large margin firms that did not have those cultural traits (Kotter and Heskett, 1992). Another recent study focusing on culture types as determinants of performance (Deshpande, Farley and Webster, 1993) reports that Japanese companies with corporate cultures stressing competitiveness (markets) and entrepreneurship ('adhocracies') outperformed those dominated by internal cohesiveness (clans) or rules (hierarchies). Services being primarily delivered by employees, the 'people' component of service delivery as perceived by customers plays an important role in service differentiation. Hence, a critical factor that endows a service organization with a competitive edge is its employees, and the way they are influenced by the culture of the organization.

P_{14}: The greater the 'people' intensity of a service industry, the greater the importance of culture as a source of competitive advantage.

Organizational expertise/producer learning/experience effects[13]

Organizational learning, or the improvement in skills and abilities achieved through learning within the firm (Weston, Chung and Hoag, 1990), can have at least two beneficial effects. The first is increased efficiency of individual workers or worker groups. Experience curves, an extension of learning curves, are the result of applying the learning curve principle to all value-added costs rather than to just production and labor costs.[14] The presence of experience effects (the average total cost per unit, measured in constant current declining by a constant percentage with every doubling of cumulative experience) have been documented in the context of both equipment-intensive service industries such as telecommunications and electric power utilities and people-intensive service industries such as life insurance (see Abell and Hammond, 1980; Boston Consulting Group, 1972).

A second aspect of organizational learning is team effort. As members of an organization work together over a period of time, the *Williamson principle* can take effect – that is, an organization may realize economies of information interchange through common training and experience, repeated interpersonal interactions, and the possible development of a compact code (Williamson, 1971, 1975). In other words, inside the organization, information flows more efficiently and transaction costs are reduced, and the firm becomes more efficient as experience is gained. Furthermore, firms, by changing task designs to form self-managed cross-functional and cross-trained service groups, could (1) improve the quality of service provided by controlling variance at source (Pasmore, 1988), (2) improve the flexibility of the organization by empowering teams to respond to specific consumer requests (Tansik, 1990), and (3) blend capabilities to solve complicated problems spanning several functional areas speedily and effectively. Enhanced performance resulting from employing teams has been documented in a number of empirical research studies (cf. Johnston *et al.*, 1981).

Organizational learning or expertise can be a source of competitive advantage only when the (1) learning is tacit and not observable in use and (2) underlying knowledge is complex (Winter, 1987). Competitors free riding on a firm's learning and expertise is more difficult under these conditions, as well as when few people are privy to the information and employee mobility is low. However, the characteristics of various service industries do not appear to moderate the role of organizational expertise as a source of competitive advantage.

Information technology[15]

Information technology (IT) refers to the collective means of assembling and electronically storing, transmitting, processing, and retrieving words, numbers, images, and sounds (Gerstein, 1987, p. 5). IT's importance as a source of SCA stems from its potential to impact the transformation of a service firm's value chain (see Porter, 1990). IT can aid in attaining an SCA by (1) providing companies with new ways to outperform rivals, through lowering costs and/or enhancing differentiation; (2) building barriers to entry, building switching costs, and sometimes completely changing the basis of competition; and (3) spawning entirely new businesses (Porter and Millar, 1985). For example, investments in IT allow a business to achieve a differentiation advantage by securing relationships through improved service quality and enhancing its ability to quickly respond to market shifts. Cases in point: A large medical supply company provides on-line order entry terminals and inventory management software for its customers and successfully achieves a competitive differentiation advantage and creates switching costs, thereby reducing buyer power. As customers' systems are integrated with those of suppliers, it becomes more difficult for customers to order from a competitor. Because changing suppliers would entail testing, implementation, and retraining costs, customers exhibit an inclination to remain loyal to their current suppliers. The more sophisticated the ordering system, the less the buyers' power to switch. The Limited, a major retail chain, reportedly is able to respond four times faster than its competition to shifts in customers' preferences by monitoring customer preferences on a daily basis, and transmitting this information to production plants through satellite communication systems (Achrol, 1991). Additional insights into the potential for exploiting IT to achieve a sustainable competitive advantage across a broad spectrum of service industries are provided by the case histories summarized in Table 1.

DISCUSSION

The managerial implications presented in this section are organized around six themes:

1. *A firm's skills and resources constitute potential sources of competitive advantage only if they offer benefits desired by customers.* As Day and Wensley (1988) point out, assessment of opportunities for competitive advantage must revolve around the analysis of customer benefits. In the absence of such analysis, a firm's attempts to leverage its skills and resources into positional advantages are likely to prove ineffective. Case in point:

> In the market for electronic components and calculators, Texas Instruments (TI) successfully exploited scale effects and experience effects to lower costs, and market the product at a low price. It attempted to pursue a similar strategy with digital watches. However, customers did not view low price as a key buying criterion in the purchase of watches. Features and appearance were viewed as more important. TI's pursuit of a cost leadership strategy in the marketing of digital watches was ineffective, ultimately leading to its withdrawal from the business.

2. *The attainment of SCA is not an end in itself, but a means to an end, namely superior long-term financial performance.* A corporation is not in business just to achieve an SCA over its competitors, but to create wealth for its shareholders. Actions that contribute to SCA but detract from creating shareholder wealth can be good strategy in the competitive sense, but bad strategy for the corporation (Coyne, 1985). Case in point:

Table 1. Leveraging information technology for achieving competitive advantage in service industries

Potential opportunities for capitalizing on information technology[a]	Case exemplars
A. Spawn new businesses Information technology (IT) has the potential to spawn new businesses in three ways: (a) by making new businesses technologically feasible; (b) by creating derived demand for new products; and (c) creating new businesses within old businesses.	The Internal Revenue Service (IRS), with the objectives of cost saving and improved accuracy, introduced electronic filing of individual tax returns in 1985. Electronic filing coupled with direct deposit has opened the gateway for a variety of new financial service products. As Zuboff (1988) notes, an attempt at automation of an activity has *informated* the industry (i.e. provided as a by-product large quantities of information that were previously unavailable). American Express and IDS Tax Services launched a new business called AmeriTax to exploit this opportunity by offering to provide a variety of specially tailored services for individual tax payers (Venkatraman, 1991).
B. Build switching costs and deter entry IT provides opportunities for firms to introduce switching costs on buyers or channel members, and thereby deter exit, as well as make entry more difficult for new entrants.	Some large medical supply companies provide on-line order entry terminals and inventory management software for their customers. As customers' systems are integrated with those of suppliers, it becomes more difficult for customers to order from a competitor. Because changing suppliers would entail testing, implementation and retraining costs, customers exhibit an inclination to remain loyal to their current suppliers. The more sophisticated the ordering system, the less the buyer's power to switch. McKesson, a large drug distributor, by constantly reinvesting in information technology and enhancing its capabilities, and providing newer and additional services, has not only kept itself ahead of competition, but also has become indispensable to its consumers (Magnet, 1992).
C. Enhance cost and differentiation advantage IT provides firms with an opportunity to achieve a cost advantage by lowering the cost of various activities constituting the value chain, and a differentiation advantage through (a) service customization, and/or (b) value enhancement through bundling of information.	USAA, an insurance firm, by employing IT to image documents, has been able to significantly reduce the amount of paper handling and lower the cost of writing policies. At USAA, use of IT to image documents has enabled one employee to do the work previously done by five employees. Furthermore, when consumers call for information, little time is spent in searching for old paper correspondence, since all prior correspondence is available on the computer network. This enables USAA to provide superior service at a lower cost (Magnet, 1992; Weizer *et al.*, 1991). Coping with the soaring cost of insurance is a concern shared by insurance companies and its corporate customers alike. Cigna, an insurance carrier, by compiling risk information and sharing this information with its customers, has been in a position to achieve a differentiation advantage. The Cigna Risk Information Service enables its customers to identify their facilities with a disproportionately high frequency of accidents, institute new safety programs at these facilities and thus lower their insurance

Table 1 continued on next page

Table 1. Leveraging information technology for achieving competitive advantage in service industries *continued*

Potential opportunities for capitalizing on information technology[a]	Case exemplars
	bill. The system's ability to provide Cigna's customers better information about their far-flung operations than they can get using their own customers is reported to have been instrumental in several large firms shifting all or more of their casualty business to Cigna (Petre, 1985).
	A recent innovation developed by Federal Express Corporation, a hand-held device that allows couriers to generate optically scannable zip code labels indicating the destination to which a package is to be sent, enables the firm to provide superior service at a lower cost. This process innovation manifests in better service quality (faster and reliable service) by speeding up the sorting process at Federal Express' hub locations and cutting down on the number of misrouted packages (Hawkins, 1992).

[a]For additional insights into using information technology for competitive advantage, see Porter and Millar (1985).

Fruhan (1972) illustrates the economics of capacity competition in the context of an airline route served by two carriers, in which the dominant carrier, by providing 70% of all the seats available on the route, gains a 80% market share. On the other hand, the smaller carrier with a 30% capacity share is in a position to obtain only a 20% share of the market. Assuming that all other firm controllable market share influencing factors are the same for the two carriers (such as air fare), how does one explain the imbalance between capacity share and market share? Fruhan theorizes that this may be because there is a greater likelihood that the larger carrier is offering a flight at a time closer to the departure time desired by a traveler. In such a hypothetical two-carrier route, if the dominant carrier adopted a retreat strategy (not responding to a minority carrier's capacity additions) it would rapidly find itself losing both market share and profit. On the other hand, if the dominant carrier adopted a matching strategy (responding to the minority carrier's capacity additions by adding capacity to maintain a constant percentage capacity share (i.e., 70% vs. 30%)) it could hold onto its market share position (i.e., 80% vs. 20%). However, this scenario will inevitably lead to a decline in a passenger load factor of both carriers and hence, adversely impact their financial performance.

3. Certain sources of competitive advantage may be more enduring than others. Two additional potential sources of competitive advantage discussed in the previous section are reputation and corporate culture. The development of reputation being socially complex (Reed and Defillippi, 1990) and reputation being a form of a stock (Dierckx and Cool, 1989) developed/earned over time, it is imperfectly imitable (Barney, 1991), and a relatively more enduring source of competitive advantage. Though frequent calls to emulate a particular organization's culture are made, there is evidence to suggest that imitating culture may be difficult.

A. The culture of a successful firm can be difficult to describe (Lippman and Rumelt,

1982) and categorize (Barley, 1983; Gregory, 1983). Because culture in most situations is tacit (Berger and Luckman, 1967), it remains inherently proprietary (Barney, 1986a).

B. Even if culture can be described, it may be intrinsically wound up with a firm's unique history and heritage, making it nearly impossible to imitate (Barney, 1986a; Clark, 1970, 1972).

C. The failure of numerous mergers has been attributed to the clash of cultures and the difficulty in changing them. In the face of organizational rigidities, changing the prevailing culture may often be difficult, and attempts to do so have yielded mixed results (Kanter, 1989).

Scale economies, in contrast, may be less enduring as a source of competitive advantage, to the extent that it is not imperfectly imitable and strategically equivalent substitutes are available. For example, firms can use nimbleness and flexibility to overcome the benefits of scale enjoyed by larger competitors (cf. Peters, 1992). Furthermore, information technology, by facilitating mass customization (and thus effectively offering to customers the cost benefit of mass production and the differentiation benefit of customization), could limit the value of scale economies per se as a source of competitive advantage (see Boynton and Victor, 1991; Zuboff, 1988).

4. Durability of a firm's competitive positional advantages is contingent on its making sustenance and enhancement reinvestments in its present sources of competitive advantage, as well as investments in new skills and resources. Realistically, competing firms in an industry are likely to continuously strive to bridge the resource and skill gaps that place them at a disadvantage relative to their competitors. Furthermore, in a dynamic market environment characterized by changes in consumer preferences, the resources and skills underlying a particular firm's positional advantages are prone to depreciate over time. Under these conditions, ensuring the durability of a firm's sources of competitive advantage may require both *sustenance* and *enhancement reinvestment* in these sources. Also, given the ever-present possibility that a firm's present sources of competitive advantage might over time erode (become competitively neutral), there is a constant need for businesses to focus on developing new and high-order sources of competitive advantage. The need for making substantial sustenance and enhancement reinvestments over the long term to develop and nurture sources of competitive advantage is exemplified by the case of the SABRE system, owned by AMR Corporation, the parent firm of American Airlines. Though the system became operational in 1976, even as late as 1988, AMR Corporation continued to spend significant amounts (approximately $1.225 billion) toward further enhancing the capabilities of SABRE (Hopper, 1990). The importance of making sustenance and enhancement investments is also highlighted by the case of Mead Data Central, a pioneer in document retrieval services that experienced a decline in market share from 95% in the early 1980s to 60% in 1992. West Publishing Company, which entered the market six years later, was able to overcome the pioneering advantages of Mead Data Central by employing a strategy of technology leapfrogging and providing more information, a more user friendly interface, and a lower price. Mead, in contrast, is reported to have stayed with an archaic consumer interface and not provided any new services (Berss, 1993).

5. A critical reassessment of conventional wisdom regarding sources of competitive advantage may be called for in the face of successful new game strategies. The business world is replete with case histories of firms departing from prevalent industry practices in major ways and succeeding in their pursuit of contrarian strategies. Case in point:

> Southwest Airlines, a Dallas-based airline, does many things differently compared to traditional airlines. Though its airfares are significantly lower than those of full service airlines, it does not offer many features that full service airlines do, such as advance boarding passes, in-flight meals, and automatic transfer of luggage to or from other carrier's flights. In order to keep costs low, Southwest generally operates out of secondary airports of the cities it serves rather than major airports. These differences, coupled with a highly productive work force, have enabled Southwest to enjoy a 43% cost advantage over the industry leader, American Airlines (*Business Week*, 1992).

New game strategies entail exploring ways to influence the environment, redefine market boundaries, reshape market behavior to fit the company's strengths, and refute or make irrelevant conventional wisdom regarding key success factors (sources of competitive advantage) (Buaron, 1981). Consider, for example, the service-process matrix (Schmenner, 1986), in which service businesses are classified into the following categories on the basis of the degree of labor intensity and interaction and customization, characterizing a service:

A. Service factor: Low labor intensity – low interaction and customization
B. Service shop: Low labor intensity – high interaction and customization
C. Mass service: High labor intensity – low interaction and customization
D. Professional service: High labor intensity – high interaction and customization.

True to the concept of new game strategies, service firms have gained competitive advantages by being innovative and breaking traditional molds. The restaurant business (service shop) was revolutionized by fast-food restaurants (service factory), and the traditional commercial banking industry (mass service) by some banks offering certain segments, financial and investment advice at the individual customer level (professional service). Inevitably, successful new game strategies necessitate a reassessment of presumed relationships between key variables and resource deployment patterns viewed as normatively conducive to superior performance.

6. The sustainability of a firm's competitive advantages are also impacted by imperfectly competitive markets for skills and resources, luck, and suboptimal decisions made by competitors. It was pointed out previously that spatial preemption of a strategic resource such as geographic locations for installation of ATMs can be a source of competitive advantage and above-normal profits if the price paid for the resource is lower than the benefits derived from it. However, if the market for the resource were perfectly competitive, the price of the resource would be bid up until it was equal to the net present value of its future above-normal benefits. This point of view implies that the achievement of SCA and, consequently, above-normal profits depends crucially on the presence of imperfections in the market for skills and resources. If the markets are perfect, the prices of resources/skills are bid up and the above-normal profits are competed away. The presence of imperfectly competitive markets for resources and skills can occur under the following conditions: (1) some firms are better informed or have special insights than competitors about the future value of a strategy and (2) firms that achieve competitive advantage are lucky (Barney, 1986b). For example, at the end of World War II, two major competitors, Sears and Montgomery Ward were more or less of the same size. Sears envisioned that the end of the war would stimulate pent-up demand for goods and services and invested heavily in the expansion of its retail and catalogue operations.[16] Montgomery Ward, in contrast, envisioned that the end of the war would be followed by a period of austerity and went on a rampant cost-cutting program. Here, a better informed firm (Sears) was able to gain a competitive advantage in the absence of its principal competitor (Montgomery Ward) pursuing a similar strategy and bidding up the price of critical resources/skills.

Given that luck is beyond the control of managers, the alternative strategy open to them is to become better informed than their competition. Two ways of achieving this are (1) environmental analysis and (2) organizational analysis. Barney (1986b) contends that environmental analysis is less likely to systematically generate exceptional advantages because its methods are readily available in the public domain. Organizational analysis, in contrast, which is based on information internal to the firm and not available to competition, is more likely to generate exceptional advantages. Prahalad and Hamel's (1990) examination of the strategies adopted by NEC building on its 'core competencies' is an example in this genre. Firms may be better off relying on such organizational analysis rather than depending on publicly available techniques to identify sources of competitive advantage.

In addition to the existence of an imperfectly competitive market for skills and resources, and/or luck, certain other factors in the market environment could also impact on the sustainability of sources of competitive advantage (Amit and Schoemaker, 1993). It has been suggested that the emergence of new technologies, economic and political trends, competitive actions, and changes in consumer preferences could lead managers to approach future courses of action with 'considerable bias, illusion and suboptimality' (Kahneman, Slovic and Tversky, 1982; Amit and Schoemaker, 1993). The presence of uncertainty also makes managers hold diverse expectations about the potential returns from a source of competitive advantage.[17] Schoemaker (1992) outlines a methodology for linking the strategic vision of the firm with its core capabilities in the presence of market uncertainty and an unpredictable future.

CONCLUSION

In a recent article providing an assessment of the services marketing and management literature spanning a 15-year period, Swartz, Bowen, and Brown (1992, p. 17) highlight the need for developing contingency theories of services marketing and management:

> Several scholars have invested much energy in analyzing the variance *between* the manufacturing and service sectors. . . . However, it is now time to invest more energy in analyzing the substantial variance *within* the service sector. . . . The research requirement, then, is to develop and test propositions about what marketing and management practices are effective for certain types of services under certain conditions.

The contingency model of SCA in service industries and propositions presented here partially address the research needs highlighted by these authors. Building on extant literature, the proposed model provides insights into the moderating effects of the characteristics of services, service industries, and firms within an industry on the skills and resources underlying a service business's competitive positional advantage. However, for many of the constructs presented in the model (e.g. brand equity, communication goods effect, and spatial preemption), psychometric scales are not currently available. Development and validation of psychometric scales for these constructs and empirical testing and further refinement of the proposed model constitute promising future research directions.

ACKNOWLEDGMENTS

The authors thank A. Parasuraman, Leonard L. Berry, the anonymous *JM* reviewers, and Thomas C. Kinnear for their detailed and constructive comments.

NOTES

1 Unless stated otherwise, the term 'product' is used in the article to encompass both goods and services.

2 For a discussion on the distinctive competencies/competitive capabilities underlying the superior performance of two superior performers in the banking sector – Wachovia Corporation and Bank One – see Stalk, Evans and Shulman (1992, pp. 68–69).

3 The skills and resources underlying a business's positional advantages listed in Figure 1 and discussed in this article are intended to be illustrative rather than exhaustive. The principal focus here is on skills and resources that could impact differentially on competitive advantage across service industries.

4 Finer distinctions of resources and skills are provided by Williams (1992) and Lado, Boyd and Wright (1992).

5 Though the value chain (a set of interdependent primary and secondary value activities that are connected by linkages) is not explicitly shown in Figure 1, it should be recognized that a business's unique resources and skills lead to competitive positional advantages by enabling it to perform the various value activities either at a lower cost or in a way that leads to differentiation. See Porter (1985) and Stalk, Evans and Shulman (1992) for additional insights into value chains.

6 An examination of the writings of Rumelt (1984) and Coyne (1985) on barriers to imitation reveals considerable overlap if not synonymity of thought. Implicit in the business system, position, and organizational or managerial quality gaps outlined by Coyne are the various isolating mechanisms identified by Rumelt.

7 See: McGuire and Schneeweis (1983) and Lubatkin and Shrieves (1986). Additionally, in the case of several resources and skills, their benefits may be in the long term and in some cases the benefits (such as fact information flow, understanding of market trends, fast procedures, and more effective customer service) may be difficult to quantify. In these cases, the use of standard hurdle rates may be inappropriate, and non-traditional criteria may be required (Shank and Govindarajan, 1992).

8 As evidenced by the links leading into and from the box labeled 'Re-investments in Resources and Skills' (Figure 1), there is an implicit time dimension in the proposed conceptual framework.

[9] It is not clear, however, whether it was Merrill Lynch's patent application, the time it took for competitors to develop the technology needed to offer similar service, the uncertainty created by the legal opposition to the service raised by banks and state governments, or a combination of these factors that gave Merrill Lynch a five-year head start and market exclusively (see *Wall Street Journal*, 1989, 1993; Kerin, Varadarajan and Peterson, 1992).

[10] The discussion presented in this section builds on literature on brand equity in the marketing discipline and on reputation in the management and economics disciplines.

[11] Though the focus of this section is limited to relationships with customers, relationship marketing is more broadly construed in business literature to include relationships with suppliers, channel members, and other organizations as well (i.e. cooperating and partnering with other firms including competitors). For example, see Ohmae (1989).

[12] The validity and generalizability of studies reporting a systematic relationship between order of entry and market share have, however, been questioned in light of their methodological shortcomings, such as operational definition of market pioneer, survivor bias, and sample composition (Kerin, Varadarajan and Peterson, 1992).

[13] Given that organizational expertise and information technology appear to be equally important sources of competitive advantage across all service industries, no formal propositions are presented in the sections devoted to these sources of competitive advantage.

[14] The experience curve doctrine has been criticized for lacking a sound theoretical base. It has been pointed out that it treats a possible effect of achieving a cost advantage (share building) as a cause and what is actually a possible contributing cause of share building (achieving a cost advantage) as an effect (Albert, 1989).

[15] Because several studies published during the last ten years provide excellent insights into the importance of IT as a source of competitive advantage (cf. Benjamin *et al.*, 1984; Cash and Konsynski, 1985; Clemons and Row, 1987; Glazer, 1991; Little, 1990; Porter and Millar, 1985; and Weill, 1992), only a few key issues are highlighted in this section.

[16] The question of whether Sears had special insights or was just lucky is very relevant here. However, the problems currently afflicting the firm are not an issue.

[17] For a more detailed exposition of this viewpoint, see recent literature on behavior decision theory (Amit and Schoemaker, 1993; Klayman and Schoemaker, 1992; Schoemaker, 1990; Zajac and Bazerman, 1991).

REFERENCES

Aaker, D. A. (1989) 'Managing Assets and Skills: A Key to Sustainable Competitive Advantage'. *California Management Review* **31**(Winter): 91–106.

Aaker, D. A. (1991) *Managing Brand Equity: Capitalizing on the Value of a Brand Name.* New York: The Free Press.

Abell, D. F. and Hammond, J. S. (1980) *Strategic Market Planning: Problems and Analytical Approaches.* Englewood Cliffs, NJ: Prentice-Hall, Inc.

Achrol, R. S. (1991) 'Evolution of the Marketing Organization: New Forms for Turbulent Environments'. *Journal of Marketing* **55**(October): 77–93.

Alberts, W. W. (1989) 'The Experience Curve Doctrine Revisited'. *Journal of Marketing* **53**(July): 36–49.

Allen, M. (1988) 'Competitive Confrontation in Consumer Services'. *Planning* **17**(January–February): 4–9.

Amit, R. and Schoemaker, P. J. H. (1993) 'Strategic Assets and Organizational Rent'. *Management Journal* **14**(January): 33–46.

Barley, S. P. (1983) 'Semiotics and the Study of Occupational and Organizational *Administrative Science Quarterly* **28**(September): 393–413.

Barney, J. B. (1986a) 'Organizational Culture: Can It Be a Source of Sustained (Advantage?'. *Academy of Management Review* **11**(July): 656–665.

Barney, J. B. (1986b) 'Strategic Factor Markets: Expectations, Luck and Business Strategy'. *Management Science* **32**(October): 1231–1241.

Barney, J. B. (1991) 'Firm Resources and Sustained Competitive Advantage'. *Journal of Management* **17**(March): 99–120.

Barney, J. B., McWilliams, A. and Turk, T. (1989) 'On the Relevance of the Concept of Entry Barriers in the Theory of Competitive Strategy'. Paper presented at the Annual Meeting of the Strategic Management Society, San Francisco.

Barrett, D. and Konsynski, B. (1982) 'Inter-Organization Sharing Systems'. *MIS Quarterly* **6** Special Issue (December): 93–105.

Baumol, W. J., Panzar, J. C. and Willig, R. P. (1982) *Contestable Markets and the Theory of Industry Structure.* New York: Harcourt, Brace, and Jovanovich.

Benjamin, R. I., Rockhart, J. F., Scott Morton, M. S. and Wyman, J. (1984) 'Information Technology: A Strategic Opportunity'. *Sloan Management Review* **25**(Spring): 3–10.

Berger, P. L. and Luckman, T. (1967) *The Social Construction of Reality.* Garden City, NY: Anchor.

Berry, L. L. and Parasuraman, A. (1991) *Marketing Services: Competing Through Quality.* New York: The Free Press.

Berss, M. (1993) 'Logging off Lexis'. *Forbes* (Jan 14): 46.

Blattberg, R. C. and Deighton, J. (1991) 'Interactive Marketing: Exploiting the Age of Addressability'. *Sloan Management Review* **33**(Fall): 5–14.

Boston Consulting Group (1972) *Perspectives on Experience.* USA: BCG, Inc.

Boulding, W., Kalra, A., Staelin, R. and Zeithaml, V. A. (1993) 'A Dynamic Process Model of Service Quality: From Expectations to Behavioral Intentions'. *Journal of Marketing Research* **30**(February): 7–27.

Boynton, A. C. and Victor, B. (1991) 'Beyond Flexibility: Building and Managing the Dynamically Stable Organization'. *California Management Review* (Fall): 53–66.

Buaron, Roberto (1981) 'New Game Strategies'. *McKinsey Quarterly* (Spring): 24–40.

Business Week (1992) 'The Airline Mess' (July 6): 50–55.

Cash, J. I. and Konsynski, B. (1985) 'IS Redraws Competitive Boundaries'. *Harvard Business Review* **63**(March–April): 134–142.

Clark, B. R. (1970) *The Distinctive College: Antioch, Reed, and Swarthmore.* Chicago: Aldine.

Clark, B. R. (1972) 'The Organizational Saga in Higher Education'. *Administrative Science Quarterly* **17**(June): 178–184.

Clemons, E. K. and Row, M. (1987) 'Structural Differences Among Firms: A Potential Source of Competitive Advantage in the Application of Information Technology'. *Proceedings of the Eighth International Conference on Information Systems* (December): 1–9.

Coyne, K. P. (1985) 'Sustainable Competitive Advantage—What It Is, What It Isn't'. *Business Horizons* **29**(January–February): 54–61.

Coyne, K. P. (1989) 'Beyond Service Fads – Meaningful Strategies for the Real World'. *Sloan Management Review* **30**(Summer): 69–76.

Crosby, L. A. and Stephens, N. (1987) 'Effects of Relationship Marketing on Satisfaction, Retention, and Prices in the Life Insurance Industry'. *Journal of Marketing Research* **24**(November): 404–411.

Crosby, L. A., Evans, K. R. and Cowles, D. (1990) 'Relationship Quality in Services Selling: An Interpersonal Influence Perspective'. *Journal of Marketing* **54**(July): 68–81.

Czepiel, John A. (1990) 'Managing Relationships with Customers: A Differentiation Philosophy of Marketing'. In *Service Management Effectiveness* (David E. Bowen, Richard B. Chase, Thomas G. Cummings, Eds). San Francisco, CA: Jossey-Bass Publishers, 213–233.

Darby, M. R. and Karni, E. (1973) 'Free Competition and the Optimal Amount of Fraud'. *Journal of Law and Economics* **16**(January): 67–86.

Day, G. S. and Wensley, R. (1988) 'Assessing Advantage: A Framework for Diagnosing Competitive Superiority'. *Journal of Marketing* **52**(April): 1–20.

)eal, T. and Kennedy, A.E. (1982) *Corporate Cultures.* Reading, MA: Addison-Wesley.

ennison, D. R. (1984) 'Bringing Corporate Culture to the Bottom Line'. *Organizational* *Dynamics* **13**(Autumn): 4–22.

pande, R., Farley, J. U. and Webster, F. E. Jr. (1993) 'Corporate Culture, Customer

Orientation and Innovativeness in Japanese Firms: A Quadrad Analysis'. *Journal of Marketing* **57**(January): 23–37.

Dierickx, I. and Cool, K. (1989) 'Asset Stock Accumulation and Sustainability of Competitive Advantage'. *Management Science* **35**(November): 1504–1511.

Fisk, R. P., Brown, S. W. and Bitner, M. J. (1993) 'Tracking the Evolution of the Services Marketing Literature'. *Journal of Retailing* **69**(Spring): 61–103.

Fruhan, W. E. (1972) *The Fight for Competitive Advantage: The Study of the United States Domestic Trunk Carriers.* Boston: Harvard University, Division of Research, Graduate School of Business Administration.

Gerstein, M. S. (1987) *The Technology Connection.* Reading, MA: Addison-Wesley.

Glazer, R. (1991) 'Marketing in an Information-Intensive Environment: Strategic Implications of Knowledge as an Asset'. *Journal of Marketing* **55**(October): 1–19.

Gregory, K. L. (1983) 'Native-view Paradigms: Multiple Cultures and Culture Conflicts in Organizations'. *Administrative Science Quarterly* **28**(September): 359–376.

Hamel, G. and Prahalad, C. K. (1991) 'Corporate Imagination and Expeditionary Marketing'. *Harvard Business Review* **69**(July–August): 81–92.

Hawkins, Chuck (1992) 'Fedex: Europe Nearly Killed the Messenger'. *Business Week* (May 25): 124–126.

Heskett, James L. (1987) 'Lessons in the Service Sector'. *Harvard Business Review* **65**(March–April): 118–126.

Hopper, M. D. (1990) 'Rattling SABRE—New Ways to Compete on Information'. *Harvard Business Review* **68**(May–June): 118–125.

Johnson, D. W., Maruyama, G., Johnson, R., Nelson, R. and Skon, L. (1981) 'Effects of Cooperative, Competitive, and Individualistic Goal Structures on Achievement: A Meta-Analysis'. *Psychological Bulletin* **89**: 47–62.

Johnson, T. (1991) '15 Years of Brand Loyalty Trends'. Paper presented at the Marketing Science Institute Conference on Managing Brand Equity, Austin, TX.

Kahneman, D., Slovic, P. and Tversky, A. (1982) *Judgment Under Uncertainty: Heuristics and Biases.* Cambridge: Cambridge Press.

Kamakura, W. A. and Russell, G. J. (1991) 'Measuring Consumer Perceptions of Brand Quality with Scanner Data: Implications for Brand Equity'. Report No. 91-122, MA: Marketing Science Institute.

Kanter, R. M. (1989) *When Giants Learn to Dance.* New York, NY: Touchstone.

Kerin, R. A., Varadarajan, P. R. and Peterson, R. A. (1992) 'First-Mover Advantage: A Synthesis, Conceptual Framework and Research Propositions'. *Journal of Marketing* **56**(October): 33–52.

Klayman, J. and Schoemaker, P. J. H. (1992) 'Thinking About the Future: A Cognitive Perspective'. *Journal of Forecasting.*

Kotter, J. P. and Heskett, J. L. (1992) *Corporate Culture and Performance.* New York: The Free Press.

Kado, A. A., Boyd, N. G. and Wright, P. (1992) 'A Competency-Based Model of Sustainable Competitive Advantage: Toward a Conceptual Integration'. *Journal of Management* **18**(March): 77–91.

Landes, W. M. and Posner, R. A. (1987) 'Trademark Law: An Economic Perspective'. *Journal of Law and Economics* **30**(October): 265–309.

Levitt, T. (1976) 'The Industrialization of Service'. *Harvard Business Review* **54**(September–October): 42–52.

Levitt, T. (1986) *The Marketing Imagination.* New York: The Free Press.

Lieberman, M. B. and Montgomery, D. B. (1988) 'First-Mover Advantages'. *Strategic Management Journal* **9**(Summer): 41–58.

Lippman, S. A. and Rumelt, R. P. (1982) 'Uncertain Imitability: An Analysis of Interfirm Differences in Efficiency Under Competition'. *The Bell Journal of Economics* **13**(Autumn): 418–438.

Little, J. D. C. (1990) 'Information Technology in Marketing'. Working paper, Massachusetts Institute of Technology.

Lovelock, C. H. (1983) 'Classifying Services to Gain Strategic Marketing Insights'. *Journal of Marketing* **47**(Summer): 9–20.

Lubatkin, M. and Shrieves, R. E. (1986) 'Toward Reconciliation of Market Performance Measures with Strategic Management Research'. *Academy of Management Review* **11**(July): 497–512.

Magnet, M. (1992) 'Winners in the Information Revolution'. *Fortune* (November 30): 110.

Mahoney, J. T. and Pandian, R. (1992) 'The Resource-Based View Within the Conversation of Strategic Management'. *Strategic Management Journal* **13**(June): 363–380.

Malone, T. W., Yates, J. and Benjamin, R. I. (1987) 'Electronic Markets and Electronic Hierarchies'. *Communications of the ACM* **30**(June): 484–497.

McGuire, J. and Schneeweis, T. (1983) 'An Analysis of Alternative Measures of Strategic Performance'. Paper presented at The Third Annual Strategic Management Society Conference, Paris.

Mintzberg, H. (1983) *Power in and Around Organizations.* Englewood Cliffs, NJ: Prentice Hall, Inc.

Moorman, C., Zaltman, G. and Deshpande, R. (1992) 'Relationships Between Providers and Users of Market Research: The Dynamics of Trust Within and Between Organizations'. *Journal of Marketing Research* **29**(August): 314–328.

Murray, K. B. (1991) 'A Test of Services Marketing Theory, Consumer Information Acquisition Activities'. *Journal of Marketing* **55**(January): 10–25.

Nayyar, P. R. (1990) 'Information Asymmetries: A Source of Competitive Advantage For Diversified Service Firms'. *Strategic Management Journal* **11**(November–December): 513–519.

Nayyar, P. R. (1992) 'Performance Effects of Three Foci in Service Firms'. *The Academy of Management Journal* **35**(December): 985–1009.

Nayyar, P. R. and Templeton, P. L. (1991) 'Seller Beware: Choosing Generic Competitive Strategies for Service Businesses Under Information Asymmetry'. In *Academy of Management Best Paper Proceedings* (J. L. Wall and L. R. Jauch, Eds), pp. 36–40.

Nelson, P. (1970) 'Information and Consumer Behavior'. *Journal of Political Economy* **78**(October): 311–329.

Nelson, R. and Winter, S. (1982) *An Evolutionary Theory of Economic Change.* Cambridge, MA: Harvard University Press.

Newport, J. P. (1989) 'American Express: Service That Sells'. *Fortune* **120**(November 20): 44–60.

O'Callaghan, R., Kaufmann, P. J. and Konsynski, B. (1992) 'Adoption Correlates and Share Effects of Electronic Data Interchange Systems in Marketing Channels'. *Journal of Marketing* **56**(April): 45–56.

Ohmae, K. (1989) 'The Global Logic of Strategic Alliances'. *Harvard Business Review* **67**(March–April): 143–154.

Oster, S. M. (1990) *Modern Competitive Analysis.* New York: Oxford University Press.

Ouchi, W. G. (1981) *Theory Z.* Reading, MA: Addison-Wesley.

Park, C. W., Jaworski, B. J. and MacInnes, D. J. (1986) 'Strategic Brand Concept-Image Management'. *Journal of Marketing* **50**(October): 135–145.

Pascale, R. T. (1985) 'Fitting New Employees into the Company Culture'. *Fortune* (May 28): 28.

Pasmore, W. A. (1988) *Designing Effective Organizations: The Sociotechnical Systems Perspective.* New York: John Wiley & Sons.

Peters, T. J. (1992) 'Rethinking Scale'. *California Management Review* **34**(Fall): 7–29.

Petre, P. (1985) 'How to Keep Customers Happy Captives'. *Fortune* (September 2): 42–46.

Polanyi, M. (1962) *Personal Knowledge: Towards a Post Critical Philosophy.* London: Routledge.

Porter, M. E. (1980) *Competitive Strategy.* New York: The Free Press.

Porter, M. E. (1985) *Competitive Advantage.* New York: The Free Press.

Porter, M. E. (1990) *The Competitive Advantage of Nations.* New York: The Free Press.

Porter, M. E. and Millar, V. E. (1985) 'How Information Gives You Competitive Advantage'. *Harvard Business Review* **63**(July–August): 149–160.

Prahalad, C. K. and Hamel, G. (1990) 'The Core Competence of the Corporation'. *Harvard Business Review* **68**(May–June): 79–87.

Quinn, B. J. and Gagnon C. E. (1986), 'Will Services Follow Manufacturing into Decline?' *Harvard Business Review* **64** (November–December), 95–103.

Quinn, B. J., Doorley,T. L. and Paquette, P. C. (1990), 'Beyond Products: Service-Based Strategy'. *Harvard Business Review* **68** (March–April): 58–68.

Reed R. and DeFillippi, R. J. (1990) 'Casual Ambiguity. Barriers to Imitation and Sustainable Competitive Advantage'. *Academy of Management Review,* **15** (January) 88–102.

Reichheld, F. F. and Sasser, W. E. (1990) 'Zero Defections: Quality Comes to Services'. *Harvard Business Review* **68** (September–October): 301–307.

Robinson, W. T. (1988) 'Sources of Market Pioneer Advantages: The Case of Industrial Goods Industries. *Journal of Marketing Research* **25** (February): 87–94.

Robinson, W. T. and Fornell, C. (1985) 'Sources of Market Pioneer Advantages in Consumer Goods Industries, *Journal of Marketing Research* **22** (August): 305–317.

Rumelt, R. P. (1984) 'Towards a Strategic Theory of the Firm'. In *Competitive Strategic Management.* (R. Lamb. Ed.). Englewood Cliffs, NJ: Prentice-Hall, pp. 556–570.

Rumelt, R. P. (1987) 'Theory, Strategy and Entrepreneurship'. In *The Competitive Challenge: Strategies for Industrial Innovation and Renewal.* Cambridge MA: Ballinger Publishing Co., pp. 137–158

Runge, D. A. (1988) *Winning with Telecommunications: An Approach for Corporate Strategists.* Washington, DC: ICIT Press.

Schmalensee, R. (1982) 'Product Differentiation Advantages of Pioneering Brands'. *American Economic Review* **72** (June): 349–365.

Schmenner, R. W. (1986) 'How Can Service Businesses Survive and Prosper?' *Sloan Management Review,* 27 (Spring): 21–32.

Shank, J. K and Govindarajan, V. (1992) 'Strategic Cost Analysis of Technological Investments'. *Sloan Management Review* **33** (Fall): 39–51.

Shoemaker, P. J. H. (1990) 'Strategy, Complexity, and Economic Rent'. *Management Science* **36** (October): 1178–1192.

Shoemaker, P. J. H. (1992) 'How to Link Strategic Vision to Core Capabilities'. *Sloan Management Review* **34** (Fall): 67–81.

Shoestack, G. L. (1977) 'Breaking Free from Product Marketing'. *Journal of Marketing* **41** (April): 73–80.

Shoestack, G. L. (1987) 'Service Positioning Through Structural Change'. *Journal of Marketing* **51** (January): 34–43,

Stalk, G., Evans, P. and Shulman, L. E. (1992) 'Competing on Capabilities; The New Rules of Corporate Strategy'. *Harvard Business Review* **70** (March–April): 57–69.

Stigler, G. J. (1961) 'The Economics of Information'. *Journal of Political Economy* **69** (June): 213–225.

Swartz, T. A., Bowen, D. E. and Brown, S. W. (1992) 'Fifteen Years After Breaking Free: Services Then, Now and Beyond'. In *Advances in Services Marketing and Management: Research and Practice,* Vol. 1 (T. A. Swartz, D. E. Bowen and S. W. Brown, Eds.). Greenwich, CT: Jai Press.

Tansik, D. A. (1990) 'Balance in Service Systems Design'. *Journal of Business Research* **20** (January): 55–61.

Teece, D. J. (1981) 'The Market for Know-How and the Efficient International Transfer of Technology'. *Annals of the American Academy of Political and Social Science* **458** (November): 81–96.

Teece, D. J. (1987) 'Profiting from Technological Innovation: Implications for Integration, Collaboration, Licensing and Public Policy'. In *The Competitive Challenge: Strategies for Industrial Innovation and Renewal,* (D. J. Teece, Ed.). Cambridge, MA: Ballinger Publishing, pp. 185–219.

Teece, D. J. (1988) 'Capturing Value from Technological Innovation: Integration, Strategic Partnering, and Licensing Decisions'. *Interfaces* **18**(May–June): 46–61.

Thomas, D. R. E. (1978) 'Strategy is Different in Service Businesses'. *Harvard Business Review* **56**(July–August): 158–165.

Treacy, M. and Wiersema, F. (1993) 'Customer Intimacy and Other Value Disciplines'. *Harvard Business Review* **71**(January–February): 84–93.

Upah, G. D. (1980) 'Mass Marketing in Service Retailing: A Review and Synthesis of Major Methods'. *Journal of Retailing* **56**(Fall): 59–76.

Venkatraman, N. (1991) 'IT-Induced Business Reconfiguration'. In *The Corporation of the 1990s,* (M. S. Scott Martin, Ed.). New York: Oxford University Press, pp. 122–158.

Venkatraman, N. and Akbar Zaheer (1990) 'Electronic Integration and Strategic Advantage: A Quasi-Experimental Study in the Insurance Industry'. *Information Systems Research* **1**(December): 377.

Vitale, M. R. (1988) 'American Hospital Supply: The ASAP System (A)'. Harvard Business School Case 9-186-005, Revision 1/88, Boston, MA: Harvard Business School Publishing Division.

Wall Street Journal (1989) 'Merrill Lynch CMAs Draw Interest, 1977' (November 3), B1.

Wall Street Journal (1993) 'Merrill's Once Revolutionary CMA Loses Some Force' (January 7), C1, C13.

Weill, P. (1992) 'The Relationship Between Investment in Information Technology and Firm Performance: A Study of the Value Manufacturing Sector'. *Information Systems Research* **3**(December): 307–333.

Weizer, N., Gardner, G. O., Lipoff, S., Roetter, M. F. and Withington, F. G. (1991) *The Arthur D. Little Forecast on Information Technology and Productivity.* New York: John Wiley & Sons Inc.

Weston, J. F., Chung, K. S. and Hoag, S. E. (1990) *Mergers, Restructuring, and Corporate Control.* Englewood Cliffs, NJ: Prentice-Hall.

Wilkins, A. L. and Ouchi, W. G. (1983) 'Efficient Cultures: Exploring the Relationship Between Culture and Organizational Performance'. *Administrative Science Quarterly* **28**(September): 468–481.

Williams, J. R. (1992) 'How Sustainable Is Your Competitive Advantage?'. *California Management Review* **34**(Spring): 29–51.

Williamson, O. E. (1971) 'The Vertical Integration of Production: Market Failure Considerations'. *American Economic Review* **61**(May): 112–123.

Williamson, O. E. (1975) *Markets and Hierarchies: Analysis and Antitrust Implications.* New York: The Free Press.

Williamson, O. E. (1985) *The Economic Institutions of Capitalism.* New York: The Free Press.

Winter, S. G. (1987) 'Knowledge and Competence as Strategic Assets'. In *The Competitive Challenge* (D. J. Teece, Ed.). New York: Harper and Row, pp. 159–184.

Zajac, E. J. and Bazerman, M. H. (1991) 'Blind Spots in Industry and Competitor Analysis'. *Academy of Management Review* **16**(January): 37–56.

Zuboff, S. (1988) *In the Age of the Smart Machine: The Future of Work and Power.* New York: Basic Books.

21

Service Firms' International Entry-Mode Choice: A Modified Transaction-Cost Analysis Approach

M. Krishna Erramilli and C.P. Rao

After a firm decides to enter a certain foreign market, it must choose a mode of entry, i.e. select an institutional arrangement for organizing and conducting international business transactions, such as contractual transfers, joint ventures, and wholly owned operations (Root, 1987).

The choice of the correct entry mode for a particular foreign market is 'one of the most critical decisions in international marketing' (Terpstra and Sarathy, 1991, p. 361). The chosen mode determines the extent to which the firm gets involved in developing and implementing marketing programs in the foreign market, the amount of control the firm enjoys over its marketing activities, and the degree to which it succeeds in foreign markets (Anderson and Gatignon, 1986; Root, 1987; Hill *et al.*, 1990; Terpstra and Sarathy, 1991). In fact, Wind and Perlmutter (1977) describe entry-mode choice as a 'frontier issue' in international marketing.

As service firms assume greater prominence in international business (US Congress, 1986; Cateora, 1990, p. 451), researchers are beginning to ask how service firms effect entry into foreign markets and whether they differ from manufacturers in this respect (Carman and Langeard, 1980; Cowell, 1983; Sharma and Johanson, 1987; Erramilli, 1990). However, for several reasons the international marketing literature offers few concrete answers to these questions.

First, previous investigations examining entry-mode choice have focused almost exclusively on manufacturing firms (see Agarwal and Ramaswami, 1992; Gatignon and Anderson, 1988; Kogut and Singh, 1988; and Hill *et al.*, 1990 for excellent reviews of this literature). Second, most published studies on the international operations of service firms do not directly address the question of entry-mode choice (e.g. Bower, 1968; Gaedeke, 1973; Hackett, 1976; Cowell, 1983; Palmer, 1985; Sharma and Johanson, 1987; and Terpstra and Yu, 1988). Finally, the few studies that do examine the issue provide limited insights, because entry-mode choice is not the

Reprinted with permission from *Journal of Marketing*, Vol. 57, July, pp. 19–38 focus of their investigations (Weinstein, 1974, 1977; Lo and Yung, 1988) or because they are not driven by well-established theory (Erramilli, 1990; Erramilli and Rao, 1990).

Thus, existing knowledge concerning how firms choose entry modes has emanated almost entirely from the manufacturing sector. However, a growing stream of recent literature suggests that service firms differ from manufacturing firms (Bowen, Siehel and Schneider, 1989; Larsson and Bowen, 1989; Berry, 1980; Lovelock, 1983; Chase and Tansik, 1989) and face unique challenges in their foreign-market entry and expansion process (Carman and Langeard, 1980). This article will strive to demonstrate some peculiar characteristics of service firms (e.g. low capital intensity) that warrant adaptation of the underlying theory used to investigate entry-mode choice. Moreover, case studies on the internationalization of technical consultancy firms by Sharma and Johanson (1987) suggest that results obtained for manufacturing firms are not necessarily generalizable to service firms. Therefore, there exists a strong need to rigorously examine the process by which service firms choose entry modes.

Scope and purpose

This study focuses on the choice of entry modes in the *service* sector and includes a broad range of service industries, spanning both business and consumer services. It covers choice among wholly owned operations, joint ventures, and contractual transfers but not export modes of entry, because the theory employed, transaction-cost analysis (TCA), is not appropriate for comparing exports with foreign direct investment methods (Hennart, 1989).[1] Unlike previous entry-mode investigations, which were generally confined to the activities of large multinational corporations, it includes small and medium-sized firms as well.

As Figure 1 depicts, contractual methods, joint ventures, and wholly owned operations represent increasing degrees of ownership, vertical integration, resource commitment, and risk from the firm's perspective (Root, 1987; Kotler, 1991, p. 413;

Basic modes	Variations	Degree of ownership/ integration	Resource commitment/ risk	Designation
Contractual transfer	Licensing, franchising, correspondent banking	None/little	None/little	Shared-control mode
Joint venture	Partnership, consortium, affiliate	↓	↓	Shared-control mode
Wholly owned operation	Subsidiary, office, branch, project office, representative office	Full	High	Full-control mode

Figure 1. Entry modes in the service sector.
Source: Based partly on Hill *et al.* (1990), Kotler (1991), and Anderson and Gatignon (1986).

Hill *et al.*, 1990). Since wholly owned operations give the firm complete control of foreign production and marketing activities, they are designated *full-control* modes. In all other modes the firm generally has to share control with external entities; therefore, they are labeled *shared-control* modes.

The purpose of this paper is to *investigate how service firms choose between full-control and shared-control entry modes.* There are important reasons for confining the investigation to this binomial choice. When comparing entry modes, the only generalization that could be made with reasonable certainty is that wholly owned operations allow the firm more control than do other arrangements. The differences in control levels between different types of joint ventures and between joint ventures and contractual methods may often be indistinguishable or may be other than expected (Lecraw, 1984). More to the point, the theory employed, TCA, has had less success in explaining the more complex multinomial choice among entry modes. For example, Gatignon and Anderson (1988) concluded that, while TCA is well equipped to explain why firms prefer full ownership to partnership, it does not distinguish well between the different *degrees* of partnership. Similarly, in reporting their investigation of integration in export channels, Klein, Frazier and Roth (1990, p. 204) concede that 'attempting to classify across four different options is difficult'.

Following this introductory session the transaction-cost theory is described, as is the conceptual framework. The paper will argue why conventional TCA needs adaptation, describe the assumptions and approach, explain transaction-specific assets in the service sector, and develop several hypotheses on how the relationship between asset specificity and entry-mode choice is moderated. Then, separate sections will describe the sample and variables, and the model to be tested, followed by a discussion of the estimation process and results. Finally, the results will be summarized, including an understanding of their managerial and theoretical implications, along with the limitations of the study and suggestions for future research.

TRANSACTION-COST ANALYSIS

Applications of TCA have become fairly common in the general marketing literature (Anderson and Weitz, 1986; Anderson and Schmittlein, 1984; Dwyer and Oh, 1988; Heide and John, 1988, 1992), especially in entry-mode investigations (Anderson and Gatignon, 1986; Anderson and Coughlan, 1987; Gatignon and Anderson, 1988; Klein, 1989; Klein, Frazier and Roth, 1990). The theory appears to be especially effective in explaining vertical integration decisions.

A given task could be contracted out to external agents, partners, or suppliers (market-contracting or low-control modes) or it could be internalized and performed by the company's own employees (integration or full-control modes). The particular *governance* structure that is actually utilized in a given situation depends on the comparative transaction costs, that is, the costs of running a system, including the *ex ante* costs of negotiating a contract and the *ex post* costs of monitoring the performance and enforcing the behavior of the parties to the contract (Williamson, 1985).

The TCA approach begins with the assumption that markets are competitive, i.e. that there are many potential suppliers, and that market pressures minimize the need for monitoring and enforcing supplier behavior (Hennart, 1989). Under these conditions, market-contracting arrangements, or low-control modes, are favored because the threat of replacement dampens opportunism and forces suppliers to perform efficiently (Anderson and Coughlan, 1987; Anderson and Gatignon, 1986). When markets fail and the range of suppliers available to the firm is restricted (resulting in 'small-numbers bargaining'), the supplier's tendency to behave opportunistically is reduced only through stringent negotiation and supervision of contractual relationships (Dwyer and Oh, 1988), thereby greatly increasing the transaction costs associated with low-control modes. In such circumstances, the firm can significantly reduce its transaction costs by replacing external suppliers with its own employees, whose behavior it can monitor and control more effectively (Hennart, 1989; Klein, 1989). Thus, market failure is the primary antecedent to the firm's decision to integrate and assume greater control.

From the transaction-cost perspective, the most important determinant of market failure is the presence of *transaction-specific assets* (Williamson, 1986; Klein *et al.*, 1990). Transaction-specific assets are nonredeployable physical and human investments that are specialized and unique to a task (Williamson, 1985, 1986). For example, the production of a certain component may require investment in specialized equipment, the distribution of a certain product may necessitate unique physical facilities, or the delivery of a certain service may be predicated on the existence of an uncommon set of professional know-how and skills.

The *benefits* of integration under market failure (higher control, with attendant reduction of market transaction costs) must, however, be compared with the *costs* of integration. Establishment of an integrated operation entails significant *internal organization* or *bureaucratic* costs, including investments in legal, administrative, and operating infrastructures (Davidson and McFetridge, 1985). The high overhead is thought to diminish the firm's ability to dissolve one type of institutional arrangement and move to another, resulting in high switching costs. As such, control is assumed to carry a high price. Anderson and Gatignon (1986) postulate that, in choosing entry modes, firms make trade-offs between *control* (benefit of integration) and *cost of resource commitments* (cost of integration). Transaction-cost theory predicts that firms integrate when asset specificity is high, because the higher costs of vertical integration are more than offset by the benefits flowing from such an arrangement. When specificity is low, firms refrain from integration because the benefits of control fall short of the costs of attaining it.

CONCEPTUAL FRAMEWORK

Why modify the TCA model?

Although the TCA framework has become a popular theoretical approach to investigating integration issues, there is a growing realization that 'middle-range theoretical extensions . . . are needed to enable TCA to address specific classes of situations not adequately addressed in the global specification' (Heide and John,

1988, p. 21). For instance, John and Weitz (1989) augment the transaction-cost framework with motivational variables to better explain sales force compensation. Similarly, Heide and John (1988) extend the model by employing dependence theory to explain how small firms with limited resources safeguard their transaction-specific investments. More recently, Heide and John (1992) have embellished the TCA approach with relational norms to explain buyer control over suppliers.

The authors' application of TCA to the service firm's entry-mode choice has uncovered certain shortcomings which necessitate modification of the basic model. TCA studies usually begin with the assumption that market-contracting or low-control modes represent the default choice for situations characterized by low asset specificity (e.g. Gatignon and Anderson, 1988; Klein *et al.*, 1990). For this assumption to be valid, the following two conditions must hold: (1) the only benefits of integration are a reduction of transaction costs in imperfect markets (thus eliminating all incentives for low-specificity[2] firms to integrate) and (2) the costs of integration are always high. Given these stipulations, low-specificity firms, i.e. firms characterized by low asset specificity, would find the cost-benefit analysis to unambiguously favor low-control ventures.

In practice, however, the first condition does not always hold true, as Anderson and Gatignon (1986) acknowledge. The literature is quite clear in emphasizing that, in addition to reducing transaction costs, firms often have numerous non-TCA motives to integrate. For instance, in their study of US multinational corporations, Stopford and Wells (1972) observed a strong, well-entrenched 'drive for unambiguous control' (p. 107). This occurs because control facilitates global integration and coordination of strategies in muiltinational corporations (Kobrin, 1988; Hill *et al.*, 1990), extends market power (Teece, 1981), obtains a larger share of the foreign enterprise's profits (Anderson and Gatignon, 1986), and overcomes the disadvantages inherent in shared-control ventures (conflicts with partners, partners becoming competitors, etc.) (Contractor and Lorange, 1988).

Similarly, the second stipulation, concerning the high costs of integration, may not be strictly true in the case of many (although not all) service firms. Unquestionably, ownership of overseas *manufacturing* facilities entails considerable resource commitment, risk, and switching costs for most firms. This may not be true, however, for many service firms, especially in the professional and business services sector (e.g. advertising agencies and management consultants). For these firms, the creation of a wholly owned subsidiary is limited to establishing an office, which frequently involves little fixed overhead. Large-scale investments in plants, machinery, buildings, and other physical assets are not required. Even switching costs may be comparatively small, because the true value-generating assets in these types of service firms are often people, and people are relatively mobile.

Not surprisingly, Sharma and Johanson (1987) observed that Swedish technical consultancy service firms bypassed the incremental establishment chain followed by manufacturing firms, because 'resource commitments are of minor significance' for the former. Consequently, the authors believe control can be acquired at comparatively low expense by many service firms. It must be emphasized that there are service firms for which integration entails large-scale investments in physical facilities (hospitals, hotels, airlines, etc.). The authors are merely contesting the general presumption that integration is *always* a high-resource proposition.

It is clear that the assumption that low-specificity firms will automatically resort to shared-control modes is unduly restrictive. If internal organization costs are low enough, such firms can be expected to assume control in order to exploit non-TCA benefits. Therefore, the effect of asset specificity on the firm's choice of integrated versus shared-control modes is contingent on *other factors* that affect the relative costs and benefits of integration. Since the traditional TCA approach does not normally consider this eventuality, there is need to modify it.

Assumptions and approach

The *non-TCA* benefits flowing from integration (such as global integration, market power, and avoidance of conflicts with partners) are available in equal measure to all service firms in this analysis. On the other hand, the magnitude of *TCA-related* benefits (reduction of transaction costs) will vary with the degree of asset specificity, being great for high-specificity firms but approaching zero in the case of low-specificity firms. Because there are strong incentives (both TCA and non-TCA) for firms to assume control, the analysis starts by assuming that service firms prefer maximum control when establishing entry modes. This assumption is not only plausible but actually conforms better to empirical evidence that indicates US multinational companies prefer integration *per se* (Gatignon and Anderson, 1988). More importantly, three-fourths of the respondents to the authors' survey agreed with the statement, 'If circumstances permit, we would always prefer to use a foreign-market entry method that will enable us to have maximum control'. The assumption of full-control modes being the default option is, therefore, realistic. At worst, it is no more deficient than assuming low-control modes are the default choice. Since full-control modes represent the default choice, this *study develops hypotheses predicting circumstances under which firms establish shared-control modes.* This approach is different from traditional TCA studies, which investigate why firms assume greater control.

In keeping with TCA tradition, the assumption is made that the benefits of integration are so immense for high-specificity firms, i.e. firms characterized by high asset specificity, that they will tend to shun shared-control modes in virtually all situations, regardless (within reasonable limits, of course) of costs and other factors. Breaking with tradition, however, the authors assume that low-specificity service firms also have incentives to integrate because of the presence of non-TCA benefits. However, since these firms lack TCA-related motives, they tend to be less fervent than high-specificity firms in retaining control. For instance, to start with, low-specificity firms can be expected to avoid shared-control arrangements with nearly the same intensity as high-specificity firms. But as costs of integration increase, low-specificity firms find shared-control arrangements increasingly more attractive compared to full-control modes. Alternatively, these firms can be expected to move to shared-control arrangements when costs remain constant but their ability to integrate diminishes (for example, because of decreasing firm size). Accordingly, the following two scenarios emerge:

- When internal organization costs are high, or their ability to integrate is low, low-specificity firms are more likely to *prefer* shared-control modes than are high-specificity firms, as predicted by conventional TCA.

- When internal organization costs are low, or their ability to integrate is high, low-specificity firms are nearly as likely to *avoid* shared-control modes as are high-specificity firms.

According to this argument, the transaction-cost framework loses much of its ability to explain the variation in entry-mode choice when costs are low or when the ability to integrate is high (as in the first scenario). However, *the theory becomes increasingly powerful as costs of control-acquisition mount or as the ability to integrate diminishes and low-specificity firms rush to establish shared-control ventures.* Following this line of logic, it is clear that asset specificity alone may not produce significant variation in entry-mode choice. Rather, its efficacy depends upon other factors which drive low-specificity firms to establish shared-control modes. This represents the basic premise of the current study. In the following sections asset specificity will be described in the context of the service sector, and certain moderating factors that influence the relationship between asset specificity and entry-mode choice will be explained.

Asset specificity in the service sector

The literature provides few insights into the origin of transaction-specific investments in the service sector. Consequently, the circumstances under which the service firm's arm's-length relationship with its supplier deteriorates into bilateral dependence are yet to be understood. Perhaps the answer lies in identifying situations in which potential agents, contractors, partners, or suppliers are required to make significant physical and human investments which cannot be productively employed outside the context of the specific transaction under consideration.

One such situation is the marketing of *idiosyncratic* services. An idiosyncratic service is defined as one which is characterized by 'high' levels of professional skills, specialized know-how, and customization.

- *Professional skills.* Professional expertise and skills are acquired only through several years of education and training (e.g. accounting or management consulting). Accordingly, services requiring professional skills will be associated with significant physical and, especially, human investments.
- *Specialized know-how.* Knowledge that is useful in only a narrow range of applications cannot be easily put to use elsewhere. Consequently, the greater the specialized know-how characterizing a service, the less likely it is that associated investments will be utilized outside the current context (e.g. management consulting for a specific industry, such as health care).
- *Customization.* The degree to which the service is customized to one or a few users (e.g. data processing tailored for an individual client company) will also determine the nature and specificity of the investments. Generally speaking, the more customized the service, the greater the attendant transaction-specific assets.

It is proposed that the production and delivery of idiosyncratic services is characterized by high asset specificity, necessitating, as it does, nontrivial, transaction-specific physical and human investments in the value-added chain. A supplier that is asked to provide these services on the firm's behalf will have to make significant investments in acquiring skills, expertise, and know-how that are uncommon and not easily transferable to other situations. Therefore, as the service becomes more idiosyncratic, the asset specificity of transactions increases.

Moderators

TCA predicts that the firm's utility for shared-control modes *diminishes* with increasing asset specificity. The *strength* of this inverse relationship is, however, contingent upon the influence of a number of moderating factors. The authors' hypotheses will focus on the effects of these factors and argue that increasing capital intensity, widening cultural distance between home and host countries, escalating host country risk, the inseparability of production and consumption in services (all of which raise the costs of integration), and decreasing firm size (which diminishes the ability to integrate) cause a significant variation in entry-mode choice by encouraging low-specificity firms to employ shared-control modes. All hypotheses are proposed on the assumption that effects not under consideration are being held constant at some 'average' level.

Capital intensity[3]

Although service firms may be generally less capital-intensive than manufacturing firms, capital intensity varies significantly across service industries (from relatively low levels in consulting firms and advertising agencies to fairly high levels in hospitals, hotels, and airlines). Since the level of capital intensity represents the relative magnitude of fixed investment, increasing capital intensity signifies rising resource commitments and escalating costs of integration.[4] All else being equal, the rising costs make it more difficult to establish wholly owned operations, thereby forcing firms to seek resources of partners and associates in shared-control arrangements. Although previous entry-mode studies have not explicitly considered the effects of capital intensity, Gatignon and Anderson's (1988) finding that the incidence of joint ventures increased with the increasing size of the foreign subsidiary underscores the impact of rising resource commitments on entry-mode choice.

Generally speaking, low-specificity firms are more likely to favor shared-control modes than high-specificity ones. Still, in situations characterized by *low* levels of capital intensity (and hence low costs of integration), low-specificity firms would be reluctant to relinquish control and lose the opportunity to exploit the non-TCA benefits of integration. As capital intensity *increases* (and internal organization costs escalate), however, low-specificity firms find deployment of full-control modes less and less justifiable in relation to the benefits they gain and, consequently, they shift to shared-control modes. High-specificity firms, on the other hand, will insist on integrated modes, regardless of capital intensity, because savings resulting from the reduction of transaction costs will continue to be substantial. The net result is that the differences in entry-mode choice between low- and high-specificity firms become more pronounced with increasing capital intensity. Hence:

H_1: The inverse relationship between asset specificity and service firms' utility for shared-control modes will become stronger with increasing capital intensity.

Inseparability

Many internationally marketed services are 'separable' (Sampson and Snape, 1985), i.e. their production and consumption can be decoupled. These services are frequently produced outside the host country and then transferred to it as a document, disk, or in some other tangible form. Examples include software services, engineering design, and architectural services.

However, a large number of services are produced and consumed simultaneously. *Inseparability* is a feature that distinguishes many service firms from manufacturers (Zeithaml *et al.*, 1985). For instance, the competent delivery of services by hospitals, hotels, consulting firms, and advertising agencies requires the close physical proximity of providers and receivers. Inseparability 'forces the buyer into intimate contact with the production process' (Carman and Langeard, 1980, p. 8) and necessitates close buyer–seller interactions (Gronroos, 1983).

In order to ensure effective delivery of inseparable services, elaborate systems have to be put in place to monitor the performance of employees who deal directly with customers. Inseparable services are conceivably more sensitive to cultural differences and may have to be better adapted to local tastes. Carman and Langeard (1980) also argue that service firms that provide inseparable services face special risks. They have to face customers and produce their services on foreign soil from day one without the benefit of initially exporting to the market and gaining experience.

For all these reasons, inseparability inflicts significant additional costs and risks on service firms which they can either bear themselves or share with their associates. While high-specificity firms find the first option worthwhile, low-specificity firms will more likely opt for the second. Consequently, asset specificity will more effectively distinguish between full- and shared-control choice for inseparable services than for separable ones. Hence:

> H_2: The inverse relationship between asset specificity and service firms' propensity for shared-control modes will be stronger for inseparable services than for separable services.

Cultural distance

Foreign-market entrants often perceive a significant amount of internal uncertainty caused by the *cultural distance* between the firm's home country and the host country. Numerous empirical studies have concluded that cultural distance encourages deployment of shared-control modes (Davidson and McFetridge, 1985; Kogut and Singh, 1988; Gatignon and Anderson, 1988).

To better understand the effect of cultural distance on entry-mode choice in a transaction-cost context, the costs of acquiring information needed to monitor and evaluate the performance of employees in bureaucracies must be considered (Jones and Hill, 1988). Since Kogut and Singh (1988) argue that differences in organizational characteristics increase with increasing cultural distance, such information-acquisition activity will be proportional to the cultural distance of the host country. When management moves to a country that is culturally similar to the home country, it may already possess most of the information to operate in the market; hence, information-acquisition costs will approach zero. However, when management enters an unfamiliar foreign culture, it may have great difficulty in imposing subjective judgment to determine how people should behave and in evaluating hard-to-quantify inputs and results (Gatignon and Anderson, 1988). As a general rule, information-acquisition costs and, therefore, integration costs, can be expected to increase with the increasing cultural distance of the host country.

When specificity is *high*, firms will insist on integrated modes because control continues to be immensely rewarding, even when the host country's culture is extremely disparate. However, when asset specificity is *low*, expanding cultural distance will diminish the firm's desire for control since rising information costs will outstrip integration benefits. The net result is that low- and high-specificity firms increasingly diverge in their entry-mode choices as the host country becomes culturally less and less familiar to the firm. Hence:

> H_3: The inverse relationship between asset specificity and service firms' propensity for shared-control modes will become stronger with increasing cultural distance between the home and host countries.

Country risk

High volatility in the external environment of the host country, i.e. high country risk, has been demonstrated to promote the use of shared-control arrangements (Goodnow and Hansz, 1972; Mascarenhas, 1982; Gatignon and Anderson, 1988). In high-risk countries, firms must possess the necessary *flexibility* to shift to a different mode of operation should the original mode be rendered inefficient by unpredictable changes in the environment (Anderson and Gatignon, 1986). Integrated modes are associated with high switching costs and, as a result, are not generally recommended in these environments. Low-control modes, on the other hand, offer the necessary flexibility and are characterized by low switching costs.

Low-specificity firms find little reason to give up control in low-risk countries. However, as countries become riskier and the need for flexibility becomes more important, low-specificity firms will increasingly seek shared-control arrangements. High-specificity firms, on the other hand, will continue to insist on full-control modes regardless of country risk. In fact, TCA argues that these firms will find control even more desirable in high-risk situations. When specificity is high, the frequent changes in the external environment provide more opportunities for suppliers, irreplaceable as they are, to shirk their obligations and to renegotiate contracts to their advantage (Gatignon and Anderson, 1988; Williamson, 1987). The resultant costs of haggling and maladaptation will further enhance the attractiveness of full-control modes in volatile environments and reduce the desire to share control. The net result is that entry-mode choice by low- and high-specificity firms can be expected to differ minimally in low-risk countries but substantially in high-risk countries. Hence:

> H_4: The inverse relationship between asset specificity and service firms' propensity for shared-control modes will become stronger with increasing country risk.

Firm size

Frequently, it is the firm's *ability* to integrate that determines its choice of entry modes. The typical argument in the literature is that integration entails significantly higher resource commitments and carries greater risk than shared-control arrangements (see Figure 1). Consequently, larger firms that have a greater ability to expend resources and absorb risks than smaller ones will conceivably be more likely to establish integrated modes. Also, larger firms may have greater bargaining power to negotiate for greater ownership and control in countries with restrictive investment policies (Lecraw, 1984). Empirical studies demonstrate that the firm's ability to marshal resources is a potential determinant of entry-mode choice (Gatignon and Anderson, 1988; Agarwal and Ramaswami, 1992).

Because the benefits flowing from control (both TCA and non-TCA) are immense, high-specificity firms will insist on full-control modes regardless of size. Even when they are small, these firms will scrounge for resources to establish integrated modes. However, low-specificity firms, which do not share the same fervor to preserve control at any cost, will more readily establish shared-control modes when they are small to take advantage of resources pooled by associates. But as they grow larger and their ability to integrate increases, these firms can be expected to become more reluctant to relinquish control. Consequently, the power of asset specificity to distinguish between full- and shared-control modes is greatest when firms are small, but it becomes progressively weaker with increasing firm size. This relationship is hypothesized as follows:

H_5: The inverse relationship between asset specificity and service firms' propensity for shared-control modes will become weaker with the increasing size of the firm.

Figure 2 depicts the conceptual framework for the study. Asset specificity is shown as inversely influencing the service firm's propensity for shared-control modes. This relationship is strengthened (shown by negative sign) or weakened (positive sign) by the five moderators.

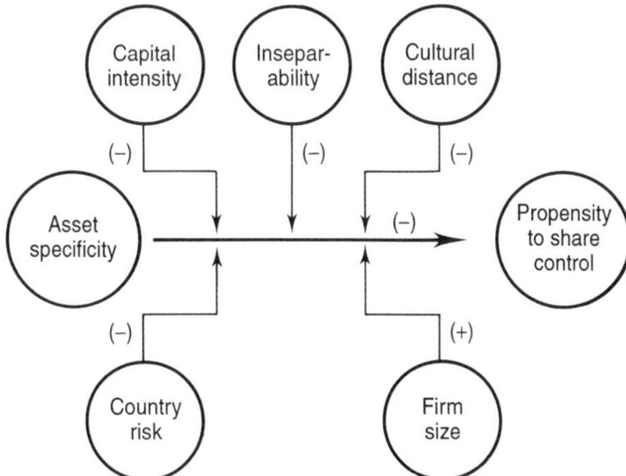

Figure 2. Conceptual framework: asset specificity's influence on service firm's propensity for shared-control modes moderated by various factors. Increasing asset specificity diminishes propensity to share control. The strength of this relationship is determined by the five moderators. (−) indicates the moderator strengthens the relationship; (+) suggests it weakens the relationship.

Hypothesis according to conventional TCA

Although the impact of the increasing costs of integration or of the diminishing capability to integrate on the influence of asset specificity has not been explicitly discussed in the TCA studies reported in the literature, it is likely that conventional TCA would have predicted increasing capital intensity, widening cultural distance, and inseparability to have minimal effects as moderators. This occurs because low-specificity firms are automatically assumed to favor low-control modes and high-specificity firms are expected to insist on full-control ones, regardless of costs or firm capabilities. So H_1, H_2, and H_3 have no bases.

However, conventional TCA would have proposed the same hypothesis as H_4 but for different reasons. Increasing country risk, while having little impact on low-specificity firms, is expected to further heighten the need for control in high-specificity firms. The net result is that the differences in entry-mode choice among low- and high-specificity firms would grow larger in high-risk countries.

On H_5, conventional TCA might have predicted just the opposite. While low-specificity firms are expected to insist on shared-control modes regardless of size, high-specificity firms may favor full-control modes ever more strongly with increasing size. As such, the differences between low- and high-specificity firms are perceived to grow *stronger* not weaker (as predicted) with increasing firm size.

SAMPLE AND VARIABLES

Sample

The unit of analysis used is an *individual foreign-market entr decision* made by a service firm. Data for this investigation was collected through a mail survey of United States service firms engaged in international operations. Despite much effort, no sampling frame for the study could be obtained from any source: government agencies, trade groups, or commercial vendors. Therefore, a systematic sample of service firms known to be engaged in international operations was drawn from various business directories.[5]

To be included in the study, the firm had to belong primarily to a service sector SIC and also had to be in international business. A total of 463 companies, representing a wide variety of service industries, were included in the mail survey. Questionnaires were mailed to managers who were most likely to be involved in the foreign-market entry decision process in their firms, including vice presidents and directors in charge of international operations, presidents, and CEOs. Each respondent was asked to provide data on up to six foreign-market entry decisions with which he/she was very familiar.[6]

Twenty-five questionnaires were returned undelivered, and 43 companies wrote back expressing regret at their inability to participate for various reasons, usually because they were no longer in international business. From the remaining pool of 395 potential respondents, usable responses were received from 175. The response rate of 44.3% compares favorably with rates reported in other surveys involving international marketing executives (e.g. Klein, 1989) and service firms (e.g.

Zeithaml, Parasuraman and Berry, 1985). Respondents did not differ significantly from nonrespondents in industry distribution, mean firm size, or mean sales revenue. Therefore, nonresponse bias, if any, may be negligible.

Of the firms responding, 47 reported serving foreign markets only through export operations, and 14 had insufficient information on some key variables and were dropped from the analysis. The remaining 114 service firms provided data on a total of 381 foreign-market entry decisions, complete in every aspect.[7]

As Table 1 (section A) shows, the number of entries reported by each firm varied considerably. The foreign-market entries included in the sample differ considerably by size of the responding firm (section B, Table 1), when firm size is measured in

Table 1. Characteristics of foreign-market entries in sample

Number of entries in sample = 381

A. Entries per firm

Entries/Firm	No. of firms
1	34
2	20
3	15
4	11
5	10
6	28

B. Distribution by firm size

Number of employees	Percentage of entries
a. <500	30.4
b. 500–1000	3.7
c. 1001–2000	11.0
d. 2001–4000	17.6
e. 4001–10 000	17.6
f. >10 000	19.7

C. Distribution by industry

Service industry	Percentage of entries
Advertising	13.1
Architecture	2.4
Banking	13.4
Computer software and data processing	15.8
Engineering	10.8
Health care	3.7
Management consulting	21.5
Research and development	3.9
Restaurants and hotels	11.0
Miscellaneous services (accounting, leasing, maintenance, etc.)	4.4

D. Distribution by country of entry

Country of entry	Percentage of entries
1. English-speaking industrialized	26.5
2. Non English-speaking industrialized	37.5
3. Others	36.0

E. Entry modes employed

Entry mode	Percentage of entries
1. Wholly owned subsidiary	33.2
2. Other wholly owned operation	27.4
3. Joint venture	24.4
4. Contractual method	15.0

terms of the *number of employees* as reported in the directories consulted. Also, the observations span several service industries (section C, Table 1), although there is heavier representation from professional and commercial service firms. Furthermore, as section D of Table 1 indicates, nearly two-thirds of the reported entries are into industrialized countries, including Australia, Canada, Japan, New Zealand, and the market economies of Europe. Finally, entries associated with wholly owned modes represent about 60% of the sample; the other 40% involve joint ventures and contractual transfers (section E, Table 1).

Variables

The Appendix contains details of measurement and validity assessment of all the variables. The dependent variable, entry-mode choice, is represented by a dichotomous variable that becomes zero for *full-control* modes – since they represent the default or base option in the study (contrary to conventional TCA operationalizations) – and 1 for *shared-control* modes. *Asset specificity* is a 3-item scale measuring the extent to which the service is characterized by professional skills, specialized know-how, and customization. *Capital intensity* of a particular service industry is measured as the ratio of fixed assets to sales revenue. *Firm size* is measured as the number of company employees. *Inseparability* is a dummy variable (1 = inseparable service; 0 = separable service). *Cultural distance* is a composite index representing the host country's cultural distance from the United States. *Country risk* is a dummy variable (1 = entry into high-risk country; 0 = entry into lower-risk country) representing environmental volatility in the host country. Moderator effects are represented as *interactions* between asset specificity and the corresponding moderating variables. All interaction effects are represented by cross products of the main effects (as recommended by Neter, Wasserman and Kunter, 1983).

THE MODEL

The model examines the impact of asset specificity and its interactions on service firm's propensity to establish shared-control entry modes, as opposed to full-control ones. Logistic regression is utilized for estimation of the effects, because it is recommended when (1) the dependent variable is binary, (2) there are qualitative and quantitative independent variables, and (3) underlying assumptions of multivariate normality cannot be met (Cox, 1970; Bali and Tschoegl, 1982; Afifi and Clark, 1984; Kachigan, 1986).

Many recent studies related to entry-mode choice have employed logistic regression models (Davidson and McFetridge, 1985; Gatignon and Anderson, 1988; Kogut and Singh, 1988; Agarwal and Ramaswami, 1992; Kim and Hwang, 1992). The probability of a service firm choosing a shared control entry mode in preference to a full-control one can be modeled as a function of the main effects and the interaction terms as follows:

Probability of choosing shared-control mode

$$= 1/\{1 + exp^{[-Y]}\} \quad (1)$$

where

$$Y = \beta_0 + \beta_1 \boldsymbol{X}_1 + \beta_2 X_2 + \cdots + \beta_p X_p \quad (2)$$

$X_1, X_2, \ldots, X_p$ are the explanatory variables (including asset specificity, the moderators, and interactions between asset specificity and moderators), $\beta_1, \beta_2, \ldots, \beta_p$ are the corresponding coefficients, and β_0 is the intercept term.

The parameters are estimated using maximum likelihood, employing the LOGISTIC procedure of the SAS statistical package (SAS Institute, 1989). The overall efficacy of the model is assessed using the likelihood ratio χ^2, which is twice the difference in log likelihoods for the current model and the intercept-only model. Large χ^2 values and small p values indicate statistical significance. The predictive ability of the model can be gauged by the correct classification rate *in conjunction with* the τ statistic (Klecka, 1980), which represents the percentage reduction in classification errors relative to random selection. A statistically significant parameter indicates the extent to which the corresponding variable contributes to the *utility* of a shared-control mode relative to the full-control option. It does not *directly* signify the *probability* of firms using shared-control modes. Once equation (2) is estimated, the probabilities could be computed for a given situation using equation (1).

The estimated model includes all the main effects, including asset specificity and the moderators and the hypothesized interaction effects. Preliminary analysis led the authors to believe that the relationship between *capital intensity* and *entry-mode choice* is not linear over the range of values considered in the analysis, apparently following the pattern portrayed in Figure 3.

As capital intensity increases from 'low' to 'moderate' levels (i.e. from A to B in Figure 3), the propensity to employ shared-control modes increases, as expected. As it increases further from 'moderate' to 'high' levels (i.e. from B to C in Figure 3), the propensity to share control *diminishes*, contrary to expectations. The reason why firms avoid shared-control modes at high levels of capital intensity is not clear; perhaps

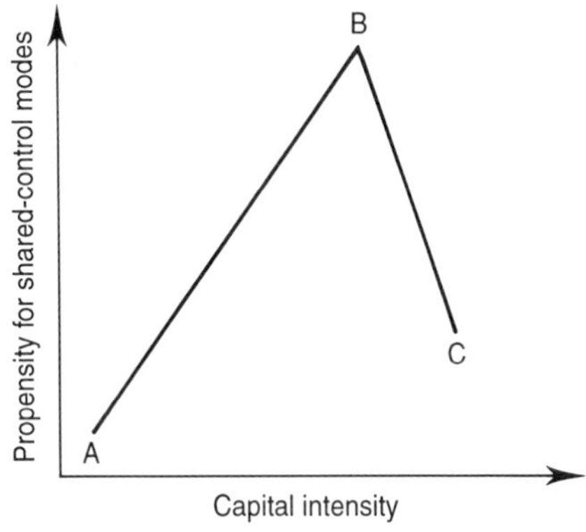

Figure 3. Observed relationship between capital intensity and desire for shared-control modes.

they feel compelled to protect their rather heavy investments by integration. Notwithstanding its origin, this nonlinearity necessitated the inclusion in the model of two quadratic terms, [*capital intensity*]^2 and *asset specificity* × [*capital intensity*]^2.

ESTIMATION AND RESULTS

Multicollinearity

When such a large number of interaction terms involving one variable are included in the model, the likelihood of serious multicollinearity problems exists. Because some of the correlations among the variables were indeed high, the original variables were rescaled using procedures recommended by Aiken and West (1991). All continuous variables were 'centered' (by subtracting the corresponding variable mean from each value), and dummy variables were recorded using 'weighted effects coding' (Darlington, 1990).[8] Such rescaling, however, does not affect the substantive interpretation of the coefficients (Aiken and West, 1991). An examination of the correlation matrix of the rescaled variables reported in Table 2 indicates that, except for those involving asset specificity and capital intensity, none of the interaction term terms appears to be highly correlated with other variables.

Variance inflation factors for terms included in the model did not indicate serious levels of collinearity. Nevertheless, to assess the stability of the parameter estimates, the full model was reestimated for sixteen different subsamples of 300 observations each, drawn randomly from the original sample. The parameter estimates for the interaction terms, particularly the coefficients for *asset specificity* × *capital intensity* and *asset specificity* × [*capital intensity*]^2, remained remarkably stable over these runs, thereby discounting the possibility of significant multicollinearity problems.

Table 2. Correlation matrix for independent variables

	B	C	D	E	F	G	H	I	J	K	L	M
A	−.29	−.23	−.13	.00	.07	−.34	.32	.39	.21	.05	−.11	.35
B		.93	.19	−.09	−.09	.28	−.60	−.63	−.21	.06	.04	−.12
C			.20	−.10	−.09	.17	−.58	−.65	−.15	.05	.06	−.04
D				−.03	−.16	.26	−.15	−.14	.07	−.03	.00	−.10
E					.37	−.02	.05	.04	−.03	−.02	.11	.02
F						−.04	.03	.05	.01	.10	.18	.07
G							−.13	−.12	−.14	.03	.11	−.52
H								.93	.35	−.07	−.09	.08
I									.29	−.06	−.11	.05
J										.01	−.16	.34
K											.26	−.02
L												−.15

A = asset specificity. B = capital intensity. C = [capital intensity]^2. D = inseparability. E = country risk. G = firm size. H = asset specificity × capital intensity. I = asset specificity × [capital intensity]^2. J = asset specificity × inseparability. K = asset specificity × cultural distance. L = asset specificity × country risk. M = asset specificity × firm size.

Model estimation and fit

Initial runs revealed that the interaction term, *asset specificity* × *cultural distance*, was insignificant. Therefore, this term was dropped, and the full model was reestimated. Table 3 reports that this reestimated model is statistically significant (likelihood ratio $\chi^2_{(12)} = 73.0$, $p = 0.0001$), which suggests that the variables as a group discriminate well between full- and shared control choice. Furthermore, the model correctly classifies 69% of the entry-mode choices which, as the τ statistic suggests, represents an improvement (36% fewer errors) relative to classification based on chance alone. In the light of these results, the model appears to have reasonable explanatory and predictive abilities.

A comparison of the full model with the main-effects-only model reveals that the interactions terms account for a substantial amount of the variation of entry-mode choice (incremental $\chi^2_{(5)} = 52.0$, $p = 0.0001$). This underscores the important role

Table 3. Results of logistic regression

Dependent variable is *entry-mode choice* (0 = full-control; 1 = shared-control mode)

Effect	Label	Parameter estimate	Standard error	Asymptotic *t* statistic
Intercept	*b0*	−.143	.166	.86
Asset specificity	*b1*	−1.999	.485	4.12[d]
Capital intensity	*b2*	7.645	2.420	3.16[d]
[Capital intensity]^2	*b3*	11.799	7.532	1.57[b]
Inseparability	*b4*	.150	.096	1.56[b]
Cultural distance	*b5*	.200	.091	2.20[c]
Country risk	*b6*	.238	.333	.72
Firm size	*b7*	−.024	.011	2.18[c]
Asset specificity × capital intensity	*b8*	−12.836	5.916	2.17[b]
Asset specificity × [capital intensity]^2	*b9*	109.00	34.229	3.18[d]
Asset specificity × inseparability	*b10*	−.932	.219	4.25[d]
Asset specificity × country risk	*b11*	−1.072	.661	1.62[a]
Asset specificity × firm size	*b12*	.040	.016	2.50[d]
A. Model Statistics:				
N	381			
Model χ^2	73.0 with 12 *df* ($p = .0001$)			
−2 Log likelihood	437.8			
Correct classification %	69			
τ	.36			
B. Contribution of interaction terms:				
Incremental χ^2	52.0 with 5 *df* ($p = .0001$)			
C. Contribution of asset specificity and its interactions:				
Incremental χ^2	57.2 with 6 *df* ($p = .0001$)			

$a = p < .10$ (one-tail).
$b = p < .05$ (one-tail).
$c = p < .01$ (one-tail).
$d = p < .005$ (one-tail).

that moderating effects seem to play in entry-mode choice. Finally, as testimony to TCA's efficacy, asset specificity and its interaction effects together account for a very appreciable amount of the explanation (incremental $\chi^2_{(6)} = 57.2$, $p = .0001$).

Hypotheses testing

A hypothesis is supported by the data if the coefficient for the corresponding interaction term is statistically significant and possesses the predicted sign (see Figure 2). Table 3 reports the parameter estimates, standard errors, and asymptotic *t* statistics. As argued earlier, the service firm's utility for shared-control modes, relative to the full-control option, *decreases* with increasing asset specificity. A minus sign on the coefficient for an interaction term suggests that this inverse relationship is *strengthened* with increasing values of the moderator; a plus sign indicates it is *weakened.* Therefore, barring the coefficient for *asset specificity* × *firm size,* all interaction terms are predicted to be negatively signed.

To gain further insights into the hypothesized relationships, the probability that service firms employ shared-control modes is estimated for low- and high-specificity situations for different levels of each moderating variable whose interaction with asset specificity was significant (holding the other effects constant at their average levels). Following Aiken and West (1991), 'low (or small)' was defined as one standard deviation below mean; 'medium' as mean; 'high (or large)' as one standard deviation above mean; and 'very high (or very large)' as two standard deviations above mean. The probabilities were then estimated with the help of equations (1) and (2), using these values and the parameter estimates from Table 3. For easy interpretation, these probabilities are shown pictorially in Figure 4. For each level of the moderating variable under consideration, lines are drawn connecting the corresponding probability levels for low- and high-specificity firms. These lines merely connect two discrete points and *do not necessarily depict a direct linear relationship* between asset specificity and probability. However, a downward sloping line suggests that low-specificity firms are more likely to employ shared-control modes than are high-specificity firms; an upward sloping line indicates just the opposite. The steeper the line, the greater the disparity between the two firm types.

Hypothesis 1

Coefficients *b8* and *b9* in Table 3, which represent the interaction between asset specificity and capital intensity, are both statistically significant. The minus sign on *b8* (linear term) suggests that, at lower levels, increasing capital intensity *strengthens* the inverse relationship between *asset specificity* and *entry-mode choice.* However, the plus sign on *b9* (quadratic term) implies that, at higher levels, rising capital intensity *weakens* this relationship. Thus, while H_1 appears to be supported at lower levels of capital intensity, it is not at higher levels.

To understand this relationship further, Figure 4A could be examined. If H_1 is supported, the line connecting the probability levels for low- and high-specificity firms should be downward-sloping and relatively flat for low levels of capital intensity but should become steeper with increasing capital intensity. This expectation is

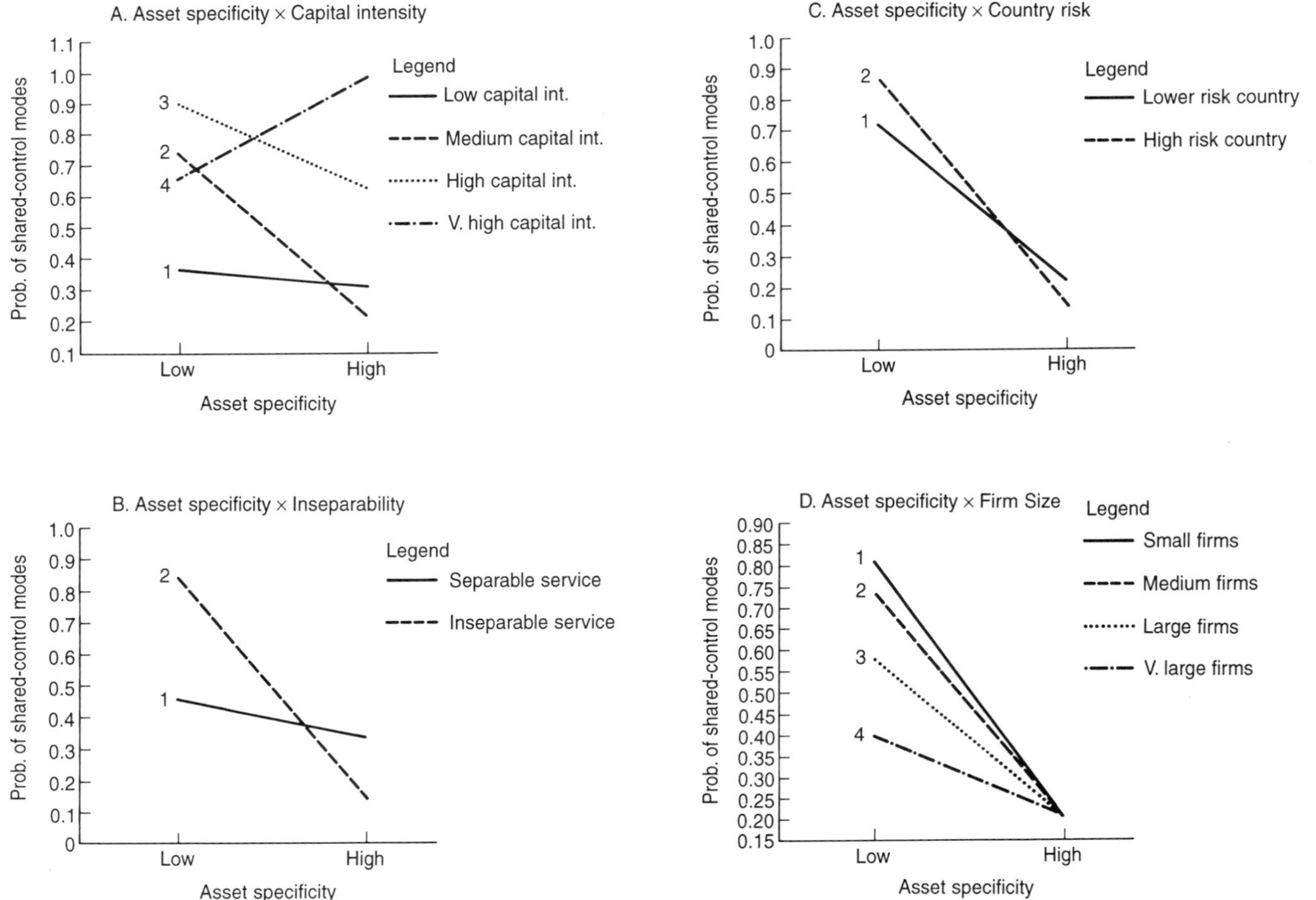

Figure 4. Estimated probability of employing shared-control modes: at low and high levels of asset specificity for different levels of moderators.

fulfilled for 'low' and 'medium' levels of capital intensity (lines 1 and 2). However, as capital intensity increases to 'high' levels, the line becomes *flatter* because, although low-specificity firms intensify their preference for control-sharing, high-specificity firms unexpectedly begin to follow the same pattern (line 3). Finally, at 'very high' levels, the line reverses its slope as high-specificity firms become *more likely* to employ shared-control modes than low-specificity ones (line 4).

In trying to comprehend this complicated relationship, it is helpful to remember that H_1 assumes increasing capital intensity, raises integration costs, and, consequently, enhances the relative utility of shared-control modes. In other words, it assumes a *positive* relationship between *capital intensity* and *entry-mode choice.* This is the relationship that seems to prevail at lower levels of capital intensity, as depicted by the A–B portion of Figure 3. H_1 appears to hold well for these observations.

However, the hypothesis seems to break down when, at higher levels, *capital intensity* and *entry-mode choice* become *inversely* related (see B–C portion of Figure 3). It is for these observations that the relationship between *asset specificity* and *entry-mode choice* appears to become less negative, or even positive, with rising capital intensity.

It can only be speculated as to why high-specificity firms seem to desire *less*, not more, control than low-specificity firms when capital intensity reaches higher levels. It may be merely a sample-specific aberration, since there are relatively few observations in the sample involving highly capital-intensive firms. But if it is not, a more complex phenomenon may be driving the relationship.

Other sources of asset specificity that are not explicitly included in the model, such as advertising intensity, may be affecting the low-specificity firms characterized by high capital intensity. This is not an unreasonable speculation, since most of these firms appear to be from the consumer services industry. Concurrently, it is possible that, faced with high resource commitments in capital-intensive industries, high-specificity service firms may be designing out specificity from otherwise idiosyncratic services in order to take advantage of resources pooled by partners a possibility consistent with suggestions made by Anderson and Gatignon (1986). Again, this seems plausible because many of the high-specificity firms from capital-intensive industries in the sample appear to be relatively small in size. At any rate, H_1 finds only partial support from the data.

Hypothesis 2

The large negative coefficient for the *asset specificity* × *inseparability* interaction, $b10$ ($p < .005$), is consistent with the hypothesis that the inverse relationship between asset specificity and propensity for shared-control modes is substantially stronger when services are inseparable than when they are separable. Figure 4B sheds more light on this matter. The relatively flat line for separable services implies that low-specificity firms are not very different from high-specificity firms in their desire for shared-control modes (line 1). The line for inseparable services is, however, noticeably steeper (line 2). Two reasons appear to account for this: (1) as predicted by H_2, low-specificity firms substantially increase the use of shared-control arrangements and (2) for reasons more in tune with conventional TCA, high-specificity firms seem to further reduce their use of shared-control modes. The additional demands of inseparable production and consumption of services may be escalating market transaction costs and making control even more imperative in high-specificity situations.

Hypothesis 3

The hypothesized interaction between *asset specificity* and *cultural distance* did not materialize (result not reported). Apparently, *cultural distance* does not raise costs substantially enough for low-specificity firms to divest control. H_3 is not supported by the data. Although the interaction is not significant, the *main* effect of *cultural distance* is significant and positively signed (*b*5 in Table 3). This result suggests that service firms do not differ from manufacturing firms in favoring shared-control modes over full-control options with increasing cultural distance.

Hypothesis 4

H_4 predicted that increasing country risk will strengthen the inverse relationship between *asset specificity* and *entry-mode choice.* Supporting this prediction, coefficient *b*11 is significant ($p < .10$) and negatively signed (Table 3). An examination of Figure 4C reveals that the line for high-risk countries (line 2) is steeper than that for lower-risk countries (line 1). This seems to arise primarily from low-specificity firms growing keener on employing shared-control modes in riskier environments, as predicted by the modified framework. However, there is also some evidence that high-specificity firms further eschew control-sharing arrangements in high-risk countries, in accordance with conventional TCA arguments.

Given the contention that low-specificity firms tend to avoid shared-control modes when country risk is low, the rather high probability of about .7 is indeed puzzling. Further analysis (not reported), however, showed that this probability drops to .3 when capital intensity is *low* and not 'average or medium', as is assumed in all calculations underlying probability estimates reported in Figure 4. This points to a more complex interaction involving asset specificity, country risk, and capital intensity.

Hypothesis 5

The coefficient *b*12 is significant ($p < .05$ level) and *positively* signed (Table 3). The result suggests a *weakening* of the inverse relationship between specificity and propensity for shared-control modes, thereby supporting H_5. If the hypothesis is to be corroborated, the line connecting the probability levels for low- and high-specificity firms should be steep for small firms and get flatter as firms grow larger, as shown in the pattern evident in Figure 4D.

It is noteworthy that the probability of high-specificity firms engaging shared-control modes is virtually unaffected by firm size. However, the probability for low-specificity firms is highest when they are small, but it declines steadily as they grow larger. This result is consistent with the postulate that low-specificity firms prefer full-control modes to start with but shift to shared-control ventures when their ability to integrate diminishes (because of decreasing size). Therefore, H_5 finds strong support. The modified framework presented here appears to more accurately predict the moderating effect of firm size than conventional TCA, which (as described earlier) would have predicted a negative interaction effect.

Summary of results

Of the five hypotheses tested, H_3 (host-country cultural distance) does not find any support. H_1 appears to be supported only as capital intensity increases from low to medium levels (the range over which the expected effect of capital intensity on entry-mode choice apparently prevails). Based on the hypotheses that were more fully supported, there is sufficient basis to believe the existence of the following relationships. Service firms generally tend to favor shared-control modes more when asset specificity is low than when it is high. This tendency *intensifies* (1) when services are inseparable (relative to when they are separable), (2) with increasing country risk, and (3) as firms become smaller. In the concluding section of the paper, some implications of these results will be explored, some limitations will be listed, and a few suggestions for future researchers will be made.

CONCLUSION

Traditional entry-mode investigations have tended to concentrate on the behavior of manufacturing multinational corporations. This study focuses on the entry-mode choice by firms from a wide range of service industries and includes very small to very large organizations. Some effects hitherto not empirically investigated in the entry-mode context, such as inseparability and capital intensity, are tested. Furthermore, because of some unduly restrictive assumptions associated with conventional TCA, a framework is developed that extends the TCA model. The conventional TCA approach actually represents a special case of this paradigm, dealing with situations wherein internal organization costs are high *and* non-TCA incentives to integrate are low.

This paper argues that the relationship between asset specificity and entry-mode choice is moderated by numerous factors that either raise the costs of integration or diminish the firm's ability to establish full-control modes. When costs are low or the ability to integrate is high, firms characterized by low asset specificity are nearly as likely as high-specificity firms to establish full-control ventures. But as costs escalate or ability diminishes, low-specificity firms will increasingly seek out shared-control ventures. While not supporting all of the hypotheses, the results do provide a reasonable basis to suggest that substantial variation in entry-mode choice is caused when low-specificity firms are pressed to share control. Some of the principal implications of the results follow.

Implications

Managerial implications

Managers apparently make cost-control trade-offs in several dimensions in their pursuit of the most efficient mode of entry. It is often claimed that many international marketing decisions are made by managers on a crude, nonsystematic basis (e.g. Aharoni, 1966; Goodnow, 1985). But the findings of this study and others demonstrate that managers do make choices based on considerations of long-term efficiency. The fact that the authors were able to correctly predict at least some of the behavior of service firms, based on efficiency considerations, suggests that 'nonsystematic' does not necessarily mean 'inefficient'.

Managers in the international service sector can draw useful lessons from the study. When entering a foreign market, they frequently have an array of entry modes from which to choose. TCA provides a framework within which these alternatives can be evaluated. Specifically, this research highlights the usefulness of control as a basis for making an entry-mode choice. All costs and benefits of obtaining and retaining control in a specific situation must be carefully weighed against each other. The most efficient mode is the one with highest benefit-to-cost ratio. In this regard, this research identifies situations in which the benefits of control outweigh the costs of control and vice versa.

Analytical implications

For researchers, the results underscore the complexity characterizing entry-mode analysis and suggest that a superficial examination of relationships could be dangerously misleading. Effects are often embedded in or intertwined with others, and researchers need to develop strategies to analytically disentangle the underlying relationships. Furthermore, if these results and recent research (Agarwal and Ramaswami, 1992) are any indications, researchers should be cautious about interpreting main effects alone, because variables seem to interact with each other in complicated ways. It is necessary to envision how a given variable effects entry-mode choice not only directly but also indirectly.

Theoretical implications

From a theory-building standpoint, the results of this study vindicate Boddewyn *et al.* (1986), who concluded that existing theories could be employed, with suitable adaptations, to investigate issues relating to multinational service enterprises. The transaction-cost framework is useful and universally applicable. However, to be more effective as a general theory of entry-mode choice, it must be extended for several reasons: (1) Firms appear to evaluate alternative institutional arrangements using a wider range of integration costs (e.g. inseparability) than previously recognized. At the same time, these costs do not necessarily need be assumed to be high in all situations. (2) Firms appear to be evaluating the merits of acquiring control based not only on reduction of transaction costs but on other non-TCA related considerations as well. Indeed, non-TCA motives, combined with low integration costs, seem to explain why many service firms establish full-control modes, even in low asset-specificity situations. (3) The firm's ability to integrate should be incorporated in future TCA studies as an important determinant of entry-mode choice.

Furthermore, conventional TCA thinking focuses on factors *promoting*, not *repressing*, integration. Although the results on inseparability and country risk support the conventional model, in the sense that some variation in entry-mode choice appears to result from high-specificity firms demanding greater control, a substantial amount of variation appears to be caused by low-specificity firms switching from full-control to shared-control modes in response to rising costs or diminishing ability to integrate. An examination of the results suggests that, relative to the conventional model, the modified framework appears to have more accurately predicted (1) the strengthening of the relationship between *asset specificity* and *entry-mode choice* with increasing costs of integration, and (2) the weakening of this relationship with increasing firm size. Therefore, the modified TCA approach appears to have serious merits and deserves further scrutiny.

Although on the surface the research appears to endorse the acquisition of control for control's sake, this is not accurate. The authors are merely arguing that, given all the *TCA* and *non-TCA* incentives to integrate, it is more constructive to view firms as desiring maximum possible control from the start. The relative merits of relinquishing this control, as opposed to maintaining it in a given situation, could then be examined. Finally, although the modified framework was originally developed to accommodate some peculiar characteristics of service firms, it is really broader in its applicability and can be easily extended to entry-mode investigations in the manufacturing sector or even to problems other than entry-mode choice.

Limitations and suggestions for future research

The study suffers from some important limitations. First, the sample is not representative of the general population of service firms in the United States. Non-random sampling became a necessity, however, when the authors were unable to obtain a comprehensive sampling frame. In this connection, they would like to emphasize one major challenge facing researchers investigating entry-mode issues: Since the unit of analysis in entry-mode studies is usually not the firm itself but rather an individual entry decision made by the firm, researchers should sample from the sum total of all entry-mode decisions made by all firms of a given industry or sector to obtain a truly representative sample. Clearly, this is an arduous task.

Second, this study followed previous studies by employing ownership as the determinant of control. This may not always be appropriate. There is increasing recognition that firms may gain control through nonequity, contractual methods (Dunning and McQueen, 1982; Dunning, 1988; Heide and John, 1992). Therefore, it is possible for a service firm to exercise a degree of control that is unrelated to its equity participation. Future researchers must recognize and incorporate contract-based means of acquiring control. Alternately, a degree-of-control construct should be developed and measured independently of the entry mode employed. In this connection, the work of Killing (1983), Klein (1989), and Geringer and Ebert (1989) may offer a strong basis upon which to build.

In the current study, the authors implicitly assumed that the *actual* level of control employed by the service firm (as indicated by the entry mode used) is its *desired* level. However, 'foreign government restrictions, the dictates of corporate parents, resource scarcity, and contractual commitments' indicate that there may be a significant difference in the two levels (Klein, 1989, p. 258). Discrepancies may occur when firms are *forced to integrate* in countries where market exchange is unfeasible because of lack of indigenous technical capabilities (Contractor, 1984), absence of adequate infrastructure and entrepreneurship (Teece, 1981), or unavailability of suitable partners (Stopford and Wells, 1972; Robinson, 1978).

Since theoretical predictions generally focus on the desired level of control, the efficacy of entry-mode models could be greatly improved by measuring the firm's desired level of control *independently* of the actual entry mode employed. This reinforces earlier arguments for the development of an independent measure for control.

As discussed earlier, there may be several benefits and costs associated with integration that have not been explicitly incorporated in previous transaction-cost investigations. Future researchers could give some thought to improving the framework's predictive power by determining how these other costs and benefits could be measured and included in their investigations.

APPENDIX: MEASUREMENT OF VARIABLES

Entry-mode choice

The dependent variable in this study is dichotomous, equaling 1 when the firm employs a shared-control entry mode and 0 when it uses a full-control entry mode. For each entry decision described, the respondent was given a list of possible entry modes (wholly owned subsidiaries, joint ventures, etc.) and asked to indicate which one best described the method his/her company had used to *initially* enter the foreign market under consideration. Responses were appropriately classified into the full- and shared-control categories, as described in Figure 1.

Asset specificity

Represented by the degree of idiosyncracy that characterizes a service, asset specificity is measured using three items that correspond to the three service attributes: (1) *professional skills*, (2) *specialized know-how*, and (3) *customization* (see definition of idiosyncratic services in the text). Customization was reverse-coded and measured as *standardization* (which, pretests revealed, was less ambiguous for respondents to interpret and describe). Respondents indicated the degree to which each attribute (i.e. professional skills, specialized know-how, and standardization) characterized their service on a 5-point scale (where 1 = no extent, and 5 = great extent). Asset specificity represents the mean of responses for the three attributes.

Cronbach's alpha for the 3-item scale is .64 and, although modest, compares favorably with the alphas of .69 for the 5-item scale of Anderson and Coughlan (1987) and .65 for the 6-item measure of asset specificity of Klein *et al.* (1990).

To further examine the validity of the measure, the mean levels of idiosyncracy associated with services from various industries in the sample were compared. An inspection of the results, presented in Table A-1 (line 1), suggests that consumer services are the least idiosyncratic. However, the across-industry variation, though significant, is not extremely high. Perhaps, this is the result of sample being skewed toward professional and business services. The variation across industries is much more evident when the degree of *customization* characterizing the service as shown in (Table A-1, line 2) is examined. Not surprisingly, consumer services are the least customized (or most standardized) of all services in the sample. The results in Table A-1 appear to be consistent with logic (for example, consumer services are the most standardized) and with information published on the industries (US Congress, 1987).

Table A-1. Across-industry variation of some independent effects

	Service Industry						
Effect	Advertising services ($n = 50$)	Computer services ($n = 60$)	Engineering/ architecture services ($n = 50$)	Management consulting services ($n = 82$)	Consumer services ($n = 58$)	Banking services ($n = 51$)	Miscella-neous services ($n = 30$)
1. Idiosyncracy Mean 'degree of idiosyncracy' associated with industry	4.28[b]	4.28[b]	4.46[a,b]	4.57[a]	3.59[c]	4.34[b]	4.34[b]
2. Customization Mean 'degree of customization' associated with industry	3.20[b]	3.33[b]	3.46[b]	4.05[a]	2.03[c]	3.59[ab]	3.70[ab]
3. Client following Percentage of entries in industry associated with client following	46.0	25.0	24.0	26.8	0.0	29.41	26.7
4. Inseparability Percentage of entries in industry associated with inseparable services	100.0	51.7	22.0	58.5	100.0	58.8	40.0

Notes:
1. n = Number of entries reported in each industry.
2. Idiosyncracy and customization are measured on scales ranging from 1 through 5. Higher means indicate that the characteristic (idiosyncracy or customization) is more dominant. Means with the same letter are not significantly different ($\alpha = .05$).
3. Tests for differences across industries: (1) Idiosyncracy ($F_{(6)} = 22.06$; $p < .001$), (2) Customization ($F_{(6)} = 19.91$; $p < .001$), and (3) Client following ($\chi^2 = 31.9$; $p < .001$), and (4) Inseparability ($\chi^2 = 110.7$; $p < .001$).

Capital intensity

This is the ratio of fixed assets to sales revenue for the industry to which the service firm belongs. This measure was borrowed from Kim and Lyn (1987), because of contextual similarity (they use it to predict foreign direct investment flows) and data availability. Data for the computation of the ratios are obtained from *Industry Norms and Key Business Ratios* (*1985–86 edition*) published by Dun and Bradstreet Information Services. The publication reports information for 'typical' firms in each SIC. The fixed-assets to sales-revenue ratio computed for the typical firm is taken as representative of the capital intensity of the particular industry. Capital intensity ratios ranged from a low of about .04 for advertising agencies to a high of .76 for hotels.

Inseparability

In international marketing and trade, the inseparability issue is best seen as a *tradeability* problem (e.g. Sapir, 1982; Sampson and Snape, 1985; Boddewyn *et al.*, 1986). Separable services are tradeable or exportable; inseparable services are not. Therefore, respondents were asked whether or not it is possible to export their service ('Is it possible to serve your overseas clients/customers by producing your service here in the US and then "exporting" the service?'). A positive response suggested a separable service, a negative response an inseparable service. INSEPARABILITY is defined as a dummy variable (0 = separable service; 1 = inseparable service). Table A-1 describes the proportion of inseparable services characterizing each industry. Inseparability appears to dominate advertising and consumer services. On the other hand, engineering and architectural services appear to be most amenable to separation.

Cultural distance

This is a measure of the cultural distance between the United States and the host country. Based on information provided by 88 000 respondents from 66 countries. Hofstede (1980) developed indices to measure four dimensions of national culture: power distance, uncertainty avoidance, individuality, and masculinity/feminity. Using these indices, Kogut and Singh (1988) computed cultural distances between the United States and other countries as follows:

$$(\text{Cultural distance})_j = [(I_{ij} - I_{iu})^2/V_i]/4$$

where I_{ij} stands for the index for the ith cultural dimension and jth country, V_i is the variance of the index of the ith dimension, u indicates the United States, and Distance_j is cultural distance of the jth country from the United States. The authors use this index of cultural distance with considerable success to test their hypothesis on the entry-mode choice of foreign firms entering the United States.

Country risk

This study uses the same measure of country risk that Gatignon and Anderson (1988) had employed in their study. High-risk countries are identified based on the classification system developed by Goodnow and Hansz (1972). In terms of the time frame within which the entry-mode decisions studied here were made, the classification scheme is not greatly outdated. Country risk in this study is represented by a dummy variable that takes on a value of 1 when entry is into high-risk countries and 0 when it is into any other country. As a result, it contrasts entries into high-risk countries with entry into lower-risk ones. High-risk countries include Algeria, Argentina, Bahrain, Bangladesh, Bolivia, Cameroon, Chad, China, Egypt, Gabon, Hungary, India, Indonesia, Iran, Nigeria, Peru, the Philippines, Saudi Arabia, Tanzania, Thailand, Turkey, and the United Arab Emirates.

Firm size

Following Gatignon and Anderson (1988) number of employees was adopted as the measure of firm size. The size of a service firm is measured by its number of employees, as reported in the directories consulted. For firms whose employment figures were unavailable, the median employment estimates (computed from the sample) for other firms in their industries were used.

ACKNOWLEDGMENTS

The authors thank Barbara Coe, Subhash Jain, Essam Mahmoud, and Jeffrey Sager for their helpful comments on earlier versions of this paper. They also gratefully acknowledge the suggestions made by William Darden and Tracy Murray on the original research project that resulted in this manuscript. In addition, they are deeply obliged to three anonymous *JM* reviewers for their contributions.

NOTES

1 It is appropriate to use transaction costs to compare exports with foreign direct investment (FDI), since these two modes involve production in different locations. The choice between exports and FDI is less of a transaction-cost problem and more of a production-cost problem. This is supported by prevalent thinking on why firms would exploit their ownership-specific advantages using FDI rather than exports: the advantages of host-country production vis-a-vis home country production.

2 For the sake of convenience and brevity, firms characterized by low asset specificity will be hereafter referred to as 'low-specificity' and those characterized by high asset specificity as 'high-specificity' firms.

3 The authors are grateful to an anonymous JM reviewer for bringing the capital-intensity issue to their attention.

4 For instance, the fixed investment of the 'typical' advertising agency (SIC 7311) is only \$36 347, but it increases to \$4 694 874 for a 'typical' hospital (SIC 8062), according to Dun and Bradstreet's *Industry Norms and Key Business Ratios* (*1985–86 Edition*).

[5] (a) *Consultants and Consulting Organizations Directory* (1984), Janice McLean, Ed. Detroit, MI: Gale Research Company; (b) Dun and Bradstreet's *Million Dollar Directory* (1986). Parsippanny, NJ: Dun & Bradstreet Inc.; (c) *Standard & Poor's Register of Corporations* (1986). New York: Standard & Poor; (d) *Standard Directory of Advertising Agencies* (1985–86). New York: National Register Publishing Co.

[6] Respondents provided detailed data on one decision and some very basic data on five others.

[7] The practice of using multiple observations from individual firms is common in entry-mode studies (Gatignon and Anderson, 1988; Davidson, 1982; Davidson and McFetridge, 1985).

[8] The authors are grateful to Leona Aiken, Arizona State University, for suggesting 'weighted effects coding' as a technique to reduce collinearity. In this method, the zero in the original dummy variable is replaced by a value calculated as follows (Darlington, 1990):

$$-\frac{\text{Weight of cell identified by the variable}}{\text{Weight of base cell}}$$

REFERENCES

Afifi, A. A. and Clark, V. (1984) *Computer-Aided Multivariate Analysis.* Belmont, CA: Lifetime Learning.

Agarwal, S. and Ramaswami, S. (1992) 'Choice of Foreign Market Entry Mode: Impact of Ownership, Location and Internalization Factors'. *Journal of International Business Studies* **23**(1st Quarter): 1–27.

Aharoni, Y. (1966) *The Foreign Investment Decision Process.* Boston, MA: Harvard Graduate School of Business Administration, Division of Research.

Aiken, L. S. and West, S. G. (1991) *Multiple Regression: Testing and Interpreting Interactions.* London: Sage Publications.

Anderson, E. and Schmittlein, D. C. (1984) 'Integration of the Sales Force: An Empirical Examination'. *Rand Journal of Economics* **15**(Autumn): 385–395.

Anderson, E. and Gatignon, H. (1986) 'Modes of Entry: A Transactions Cost Analysis and Propositions'. *Journal of International Business Studies* **17**(Fall): 1–26.

Anderson, E. and Weitz, B. A. (1986) 'Make or Buy Decisions: A Framework for Analyzing Vertical Integration Issues in Marketing'. *Sloan Management Review* **27**(Spring): 3–19.

Anderson, E. and Coughlan, A. T. (1987) 'International Market Entry and Expansion via Independent or Integrated Channels of Distribution'. *Journal of Marketing* **51**(January): 71–82.

Ball, C. A. and Tschoegl, A. E. (1982) 'The Decision to Establish a Foreign Bank Brank or Subsidiary: An Application of Binary Classification Procedures. *Journal of Financial and Quantitative Analysis* **17**(September): 411–424.

Berry, L. L. (1980) 'Service Marketing is Different'. *Business* **30** (May–June): 24–29.

Boddewyn, J. J., Halbrich, M. B. and Perry, A. C. (1986) 'Service Multinationals: Conceptualization, Measurement and Theory'. *Journal of International Business Studies* **17**(Fall): 41–57.

Bowen, D. E., Siehel, C. and Schneider, B. (1989) 'A Framework for Analyzing Customer Service Orientation in Manufacturing'. *Academy of Management Review* **14**(1): 75–95.

Bower, M. (1968) 'Personal Service Firms Venture Abroad'. *Columbia Journal of World Business* **3** (March–April): 49–58.

Carman, J. M. and Langeard, E. (1980) 'Growth Strategies of Service Firms'. *Strategic Management Journal* **1**(January–March): 7–22.

Cateora, P. R. (1990) *International Marketing.* Homewood, IL: Richard D. Irwin, pp. 410–412.

Chase, R. B. and Tansik, D. A. (1989). 'The Customer contact model for organization design'. *Management Science* **9**: 1037–1050.

Contractor, F. J. (1984) 'Choosing Between Direct Investment and Licensing: Theoretical Considerations and Empirical Tests'. *Journal of International Business Studies* **15**(Winter): 167–188.

Contractor, F. J. and P. Lorange, P. (1988) *Cooperative Strategies in International Business.* Lexington, MA: Lexington Books.

Cowell, D. W. (1983) 'International Marketing of Services'. *The Service Industries Journal* **1**(November): 308–328.

Cox, D. R. (1970) *The Analysis of Binary Data.* London: Methuen & Co.

Darlington, R. B. (1990) *Regression and Linear Models.* New York: McGraw-Hill.

Davidson, W. H. (1982) *Global Strategic Management.* New York: John Wiley and Sons.

Davidson, W. H. and McFetridge, D. G. (1985) 'Key Characteristics in the Choice of International Technology Transfer Mode'. *Journal of International Business Studies* **16**(Summer): 5–21.

Dunning, J. H. (1988) *Explaining International Production.* London: Unwin Hyman.

Dunning, J. H. (1989) 'The Study of International Business: A Plea for a more Interdisciplinary Approach'. *Journal of International Business Studies* **20**(Fall): 411–436.

Dunning, J.H. and McQueen, M. (1982) 'The Eclectic Theory of the Multi-national Enterprise and the International Hotel Industry. In *New Theories of Multinational Enterprise* (A. M. Rugman, Ed.). New York: St Martin's.

Dwyer, R. F. and Oh, S. (1988) 'A Transaction Cost Perspective on Vertical Contractual Structure and Interchannel Competitive Strategies'. *Journal of Marketing* **52**(April): 21–34.

Erramilli, M. K. (1990) 'Entry Mode Choice in Service Industries'. *International Marketing Review* **7**(5): 50–62.

Erramilli, M. K. and Rao, C. P. (1990) 'Choice of Foreign Market Entry Mode by Service Firms: Role of Market Knowledge'. *Management International Review* **30**(2): 135–150.

Gaedeke, R. M. (1973) 'Selected U.S. Multinational Service Firms in Perspective'. *Journal of International Business Studies* **4**(Spring): 61–67.

Gatignon, H. and Anderson, E. (1988) 'The Multinational Corporation's Degree of Control Over Foreign Subsidiaries: An Empirical Test of a Transaction Cost Explanation'. *Journal of Law, Economics, and Organization* **4**(Fall): 305–336.

Geringer, M. J. and Ebert, L. (1989) 'Control and Performance of International Joint Ventures'. *Journal of International Business Studies* **20**(Summer): 235–254.

Goodnow, J. D. (1985) 'Developments in International Mode of Entry Analysis'. *International Marketing Review* **2**(Autumn): 17–30.

Goodnow, J. D. and Hansz, J. H. (1972) 'Environmental Determinants of Overseas Market Entry Strategies'. *Journal of International Business Studies* **3**(Spring): 33–60.

Gronroos, C. (1983) *Strategic Management and Marketing in the Service Sector.* Marketing Science Institute Report, pp. 83–104, May.

Hackett, D. W. (1976) 'The International Expansion of U.S. Franchise Systems: Status and Strategies'. *Journal of International Business Studies* **7**(Spring): 67–75.

Heide, J. B. and John, G. (1988) 'The Role of Dependence Balancing in Safeguarding Transaction-Specific Assets in Conventional Channels'. *Journal of Marketing* **52**(January): 20–35.

Heide, J. B. and John, G. (1992) 'Do Norms Matter in Marketing Relationships?'. *Journal of Marketing* **56**(April): 32–44.

Hennart, J.-F. (1989) 'Can the "New Forms of Investment" Substitute for the "Old Forms?" A Transaction Costs Perspective'. *Journal of International Business Studies* **20**(Summer): 211–234.

Hill, C. W. L., Hwang, P. and Kim, W. C. (1990) 'An Eclectic Theory of the Choice of International Entry Mode'. *Strategic Management Journal* **11**(2): 117–128.

Hofstede, G. (1980) *Culture's Consequences: International Differences in Work-Related Values.* Beverly Hills CA: Sage Publications.

John, G. and Weitz, B. (1989) 'Salesforce Compensations: Compensation: An Empirical Investigation of Factors Related to Use of Salary Versus Incentive Compensation'. *Journal of Marketing Research* **26**(February): 1–14.

Jones, G. R. and Hill, C. W. L. (1988) 'Transaction Cost Analysis of Strategy-Structure Choice'. *Strategic Management Journal* **9**(2): 159–172.

Kachigan, S. K. (1986) *Statistical Analysis: An Interdisciplinary Introduction to Univariate and Multivariate Methods.* New York: Radius Press.

Killing, J. P. (1983) *Strategies for Joint Venture Success.* New York: Praeger.

Kim, S. W. and Lyn, E. O. (1987) 'Foreign Direct Investment Theories, Entry Barriers, and Reverse Investments in U.S. Manufacturing Industries'. *Journal of International Business Studies* **18**(Summer): 53–66.

Kim, W. C. and Hwang, P. (1992) 'Global Strategy and Multinationals' Entry Mode Choice'. *Journal of International Business Studies* **23**(1st Quarter): 29–53.

Klecka, W. R. (1980) *Discriminant Analysis.* Beverly Hills, CA: Sage Publications.

Klein, S. (1989) 'A Transaction Cost Explanation of Vertical Control in International Markets'. *Journal of the Academy of Marketing Science* **17**(Summer): 253–260.

Klein, S., Frazier, G. and Roth, V. J. (1990) 'A Transaction Cost Analysis Model of Channel Integration in International Markets'. *Journal of Marketing Research* (May): 196–208.

Kobrin, S. J. (1988) 'Trends in Ownerships of American Manufacturing Subsidiaries in Developing Countries: An Inter-Industry Analysis'. *Management International Review* (Special issue): 73–84.

Kogut, B. and Singh, H. (1988) 'The Effect of National Culture on the Choice of Entry Mode'. *Journal of International Business Studies* **19**(Fall): 411–432.

Kotler, P. (1991) *Marketing Management: Analysis, Planning, Implementation, and Control.* Englewood Cliffs, NJ: Prentice-Hall, p. 413.

Larsson, R. and Bowen, D. E. (1989) 'Organization and Customer: Managing Design and Coordination of Services'. *Academy of Management Review* **14**(2): 213–233.

Lecraw, D. J. (1984) 'Bargaining Power, Ownership, and Profitability of Transnational Corporations in Developing Countries'. *Journal of International Business Studies* **15**(Spring/Summer): 27–43.

Lo, T. W. and Yung, A. (1988) 'Multinational Service Firms in Centrally-Planned Economies: Foreign Advertising Agencies in the PRC'. *Management International Review* **28**(1): 26–32.

Lovelock, C. H. (1983) 'Classifying Services to Gain Strategic Marketing Insights'. *Journal of Marketing* **47**(Summer): 9–20.

Mascarenhas, B. (1982) 'Coping With Uncertainty in International Business'. *Journal of International Business Studies* **13**(Fall): 87–98.

Neter, J., Wasserman, W. and Kutner, M. H. (1983) *Applied Regression Models.* Homewood, IL: Richard D. Irwin.

Palmer, J. D. (1985) 'Consumer Service Industry Exports: New Attitudes and Concepts Needed for a Neglected Sector'. *Columbia Journal of World Business* **20**(Spring): 69–74.

Robinson, R. C. (1978) *International Business Management: A Guide to Decision Making.* Hinsdale, IL: The Dryden Press.

Root, F. R. (1987) *Foreign Market Entry Strategies.* New York: AMACOM.

Sampson, G. P. and Snape, R. H. (1985) 'Identifying the Issues in Trade in Services'. *The World Economy*, 171–182.

Sapir, A. (1982) 'Trade in Services: Policy Issues for the Eighties'. *Columbia Journal of World Business* **17**(Fall): 77–83.

SAS Institute (1989) *SAS/STAT User's Guide, Version 6, 4th ed., Vol. 2.* Cary, NC: SAS Institute Inc.

Sharma, D. D. and Johanson, J. (1987) 'Technical Consultancy in Internationalization'. *International Marketing Review* **4**(Winter): 20–29.

Stopford, J. M. and Wells, L. T. Jr. (1972) *Managing the Multinational Enterprise.* New York: Basic Books.

Teece, D. J. (1981) 'The Multinational Enterprise: Market Failure and Market Power Considerations'. *Sloan Management Review* **22**(Spring): 3–17.

Teece, D. J. and Yu, C.-M. (1988) 'Determinants of Foreign Investment of U.S. Advertising Agencies'. *Journal of International Business Studies* **19**(Spring): 33–46.

Teece, D. J. and Sarathy, R. (1991) *International Marketing*, 5th edn. New York: The Dryden Press.

United States Congress, Office of Technology Assessment (1986) *Trade in Services: Exports and Foreign Revenues—Special Report*, OTA-ITE-316. Washington, DC: U.S. Government Printing Office.

United States Congress, Office of Technology Assessment (1987) *International Competition in Services*, OTA-ITE-328. Washington, DC: US Government Printing Office.

Weinstein, A. K. (1974) 'The International Expansion of U.S. Multinational Advertising Agencies'. *MSU Business Topics* **22**(Summer): 29–35.

Weinstein, A. K. (1977) 'Foreign Investments by Service Firms: The Case of Multinational Advertising Agencies'. *Journal of International Business Studies*, **8** (Spring/Summer), 83–91.

Williamson, O. E. (1985) *The Economic Institutions of Capitalism.* New York: The Free Press.

Williamson, O. E. (1986) *Economic Organization: Firms, Markets and Policy Control.* New York: New York University Press.

Williamson, O. E. (1987) 'The Economics of Organization: The Transaction Cost Approach'. *American Journal of Sociology* **87**(3): 548–577.

Wind, Y. and Perimutter, H.V. (1977) 'On the Identification of the Frontier Issues of International Marketing'. *Columbia Journal of World Business* **12**(Winter): 131.

Zeithaml, V. A., Parasuraman, A. and Berry, L. L. (1985) 'Problems and Strategies in Services Marketing'. *Journal of Marketing* **49**(Spring): 33–46.

Section V

Services Marketing in Context

This section considers some contextual examples of service marketing in order to give the reader some feel for the breadth of service marketing research activity. Increasingly, service marketers are finding that generic principles require some re-examination and customisation as they are adopted within particular service contexts. Financial services, for instance, have always been regarded as a special case of service marketing, primarily because the product is so varied, so resistant to definition and so reliant upon the future. Very often purchase is made without any personal contact or any dimension of a delivery experience. The paper by Knights *et al.* (1994) is included here because it raises some interesting issues about the applicability of adopting a marketing orientation where consumers are generally disinterested, and display high levels of inertia. The authors assert this has the effect of encouraging a product led approach. They point to the limitations apparent in the financial services context of responding to consumer needs and in particular the tendency for the pursuit of profit to displace the satisfaction of consumer need.

The second article in this section by Arnould and Price (1993) considers the delivery of an extraordinary service experience characterised as extreme hedonic consumption. The authors use a multi-day river rafting trip in Colorado to investigate the true meaning of the extraordinary experience which takes place over an extended period. It is a remarkable article for a number of reasons. First and primarily, it provides an encapsulation of service consumption, including planning and expectations, the trip experience and post trip evaluations and reflections. This approach, with its implicit longitudinal element, provides a number of unusual insights into how both consumers and guides develop a reflective narrative which is used as a basis for evaluation. The second important feature of this work is the way in which the authors have woven together qualitative and quantitative measures to present a rich analysis of the experience. The third important feature of the article is the outcome, which points to a number of questions regarding the appropriateness of the expectation–performance framework in understanding the nature of extraordinary performance. Finally the article points in a new direction for services research, concentrating upon the whole story, a predominantly gestalt approach to service consumption which may require a new vocabulary from service marketing researchers.

The work of Edvardsson (1992) is notable for two main reasons: the context and the methodology. Airlines have been used on many occasions as examples of service breakdowns yet this particular service industry is also a good example of the range and complexity of the overall service experience. Luggage handlers, airport staff, traffic control and check-in assistants all contribute to our overall experiences yet only a small number of these tasks are under the direct control of the airline. When a service breakdown occurs, attribution is often directed at the airline who are frequently in a position of engaging in recovery for another service provider and this article highlights some of the complexities inherent in this service sector. The second important attribute of this article is the use of the critical incident technique which is finding increased application in services research (see Bitner, Booms and Mohr, 1994, Gabbott and Hogg, 1996, amongst others). The technique has many interesting features, not least in the ability to span both qualitative and quantitative approaches to the same problem, thereby providing opportunities for empiricist and interpretavist researchers alike.

The final article by Szmigin (1993) is a contextual analysis of service quality. Using business-to-business services, Szmigin concentrates upon the role of expectations in the development and maintenance of long-term relationships. A distinction is drawn between hard, soft and outcome quality, where hard and soft quality is synonymous with technical and functional quality (following Grönroos) while outcome quality is considered to be the determinant of the long-term health of the relationship. The crux of the article is the importance of these three quality dimensions to different types of relationship. What follows is a comprehensive analysis of relationship form and management which reviews the critical issues for business to business services in the maintenance of long-term relationships. Overall the article provides some useful considerations for business to business marketers and highlights the proximity between service quality and relationship marketing on building success.

CONTENTS

22

The Consumer Rules? An Examination of the Rhetoric and 'Reality' of Marketing in Financial Services

David Knights, Andrew Sturdy and Glenn Morgan

INTRODUCTION

Over recent years the financial services have been subject to considerable disruption in their traditional ways of doing business. The boundaries between banks, building societies and insurance companies have begun to disappear as government policy and economic deregulation has forced them into competition with one another. Political re-regulation, though largely self-administered, has shaken the insurance industry to its roots, resulting in regular revelations of highly respectable companies suffering the humiliation of hefty fines from the regulators for non-compliance with the Financial Services Act (FSA).[1] Admittedly, the new regulations have not been entirely constraining. In conjunction with other stimulants, they have encouraged banks and building societies to be more strategic in their pursuit of fee income from insurance and investment products, if only to compensate for declining profits in their traditional fields of business activity.

As service organizations, the objective towards which the financial services are directed in accommodating these and various other changes, such as the growth of new information technologies,[2–4] is the consumer. More precisely, they have been concerned to improve their service to the customer for purposes of promoting profitable sales. In doing so, they have begun to embrace a market- rather than product-led approach to their business.[5–7] The focus, it is claimed, is on identifying the pattern and content of consumer 'needs' and (re-)designing products and targeting their distribution so as to exploit this knowledge profitability. In short, the marketing concept combined with market segmentation is seen to be the emerging model for business activities in financial services.

The marketing concept is often cited as underpinning progressive marketing practice both in the literature and by practitioners. Recognizing that it has been the

Reprinted with permission from *European Journal of Marketing*, Vol. 28, No. 3, pp. 42–54

focus of some definitional debate[8–11] our concern here is with the restricted but common usage of the marketing concept as focused on establishing and satisfying (responding to) consumer 'needs' profitably. As elsewhere in marketing theory, this assumes that consumers have identifiable 'needs' prior to consumption and that they act on them. It implies that such 'needs' should be incorporated into products and services delivery either to the extent that it is profitable to do so or because in competitive markets where 'sovereign' consumers can make informed 'choices', those companies which respond to 'needs' will necessarily be profitable as a result.[12]

Within the context of the UK personal financial services market and in relation to relevant literature, we challenge some of the assumptions about consumer 'needs' and highlight the tension with the marketing concept between responding to 'need' and achieving profitability. First, it is argued that consumer 'need' is a category for ordering and making sense of behaviours which are the outcome of producer/consumer relationships (e.g. the sale) rather than a property of individuals, as is conventionally assumed. Accordingly, in the context of many financial services, but particularly life products, individuals are transformed into consumers only at the point of sale when their lives are reconstituted as a problem (need) to be resolved (satisfied) by the product on offer. Research to identify 'needs' prior to consumption is then highly artificial since it is abstracted from the circumstances in which 'needs' are created and sustained. Second, and contrary to the conventional view within financial services of an increasing competitive climate prompting a greater market/customer orientation, we highlight how competitive pressures also limit this tendency by reinforcing managerial concerns with costs and profitability. Here, high cost/low profitability consumer segments and hence their 'needs', are selected out through pricing and targeting. Relatedly, and reinforcing established critiques of the concept of consumer sovereignty,[13] there is considerable consumer inertia in relation to many financial services which allows for, and even encourages, a (profitable) product-led approach to the market.

Although primarily theoretical, this article draws selectively on empirical data gathered over a number of years through links with financial services companies in academic research and practical involvement in the industry. The article is organized as follows: first, the literature documenting and often prescribing an increased market orientation in financial services and the conditions of its emergence are briefly reviewed. Our critique of this approach is then presented, first in relation to the concept of need itself and second with regard to the pre-eminence of profit in marketing practice. The article is not seeking to deny the 'sea swell' of change in the direction of marketing in financial services but merely to curtail the excessive claims regarding its success and, more importantly, its potential. We turn now therefore to an examination of the growth of marketing applications in this sector of the economy.

THE MARKETING ORIENTATION IN UK FINANCIAL SERVICES

The UK financial services sector (i.e. banks, building societies, insurance companies and their distributors) is perceived as having been highly undeveloped and reluctant to adopt the marketing concept.[14–16] It has been characterized as supply orientated – principally concerned with operational risk and financial issues and, in marketing terms, product led. A range of well-established products would be sold, 'hard' in some areas such as life assurance, or left to be 'bought' in others.[5,6,14,17] Relatedly, marketing activities, ideas and departments within companies were limited in their scope and afforded low status in relation to other business 'disciplines' such as accounting and actuarial work.[18] An early exception to this generalization was the retail banks which, according to Clarke *et al.*[16] (p. 10), were by 1988 entering the 'final' evolutionary stage of marketing development – the 'marketing control' era – where the marketing concept drives the whole organization.

The new competitive climate, however, is forcing a transition in the direction of accelerating the development of marketing practices throughout the whole sector. Companies are increasingly adopting a strategic marketing orientation where the emphasis is on consumer 'needs' – their identification and the tailoring of products and services for purposes of satisfying them profitably[16,17,19–21]. The transition is recent and rapid, indicated by a survey of companies' self-perceptions which recorded 53% as being 'market-orientated' compared with 2% five years earlier.[17] Similarly, another survey found that 48% of the sample companies had established their marketing departments only in the last five years.[18] Also market research and segmentation techniques in product development (i.e. tailoring products to specific market segments) have proliferated in recent years.[6,22] For example, more companies are using information technology in the application of relatively modern forms of segmentation such as 'lifestyles' in focusing on customer needs.[19,23,24] Speed and Smith[7] claim that 'market segmentation has become accepted and followed as a strategy in the financial services industry (p. 376). More specifically, banks and building societies have been expanding their product range and distribution channels by cross-selling tailored, targeted and, often, branded products and services.[6,24,26] It is this strategy of 'farming' the customer base that is most closely associated with the increasing emphasis on consumer 'needs' and segmentation.

Despite this groundswell of activity, one needs to be cautious of the extent and quality of the changes that are deemed to be taking place, for they are reminiscent of earlier claims that the industry was subscribing to the marketing concept.[15,27] Marketing literature, let alone practice, in this field still remains undeveloped particularly in relation to consumer behaviour.[28] Financial services continue to lag behind other sectors in the use of strategic and other marketing techniques, including segmentation.[5,17] For example, Davison *et al.*[18] show that 72% of their financial services sample had no market research function and 16%, no marketing department in 1989.[29] Although the paucity of market research may be partly a consequence of the relative ease with which competitors can imitate one another's products in financial services, such findings suggest a considerable variation in the extent of marketing development and practice.

This variation has often been the focus of literature which seeks to measure and categorize marketing developments implicitly as a 'progressive' force. Larger companies are found to be more 'advanced'[11,14] and it is possible to provide evolutionary accounts of marketing in the sector. In this context, Thwaites and Lynch[6] (p. 440; see also ref. 11) constructed three company typologies of approaches to marketing among building societies, suggesting that a developmental pattern existed from 'marketing myopics', through 'departmental promoters' and 'advanced functionalists' towards the ideal of 'guiding philosophers'. As many as 40% of building societies were seen to fit the latter category where marketing informed and stimulated every activity, and not just the marketing function. In providing evidence of the character and variability of marketing practices, such research is valuable. However, the unexplained evolutionary and prescriptive assumptions underlying the research require critical examination. Typologies of this kind suggest a trajectory in which there is an inevitable logic of development from one stage to the next as organizations move closer to the ideal prescribed by the researcher. Any constraining or counterveiling pressures are often underplayed or bypassed and the concept of marketing itself is presumed to be 'progressive' and unproblematic even though, as we seek to show, there may be some tensions in its application to this sector of industry. Before focusing on these issues, we offer a brief examination of the conditions in which the transition towards a more comprehensive use of the marketing concept is emerging.

The conditions of emergence

There are a number of accounts which outline the key factors associated with the emergence of the current form of heightened competition and of an increased marketing orientation.[5,14,16,19] There is no attempt here to duplicate the detail contained therein; the aim is merely to provide a brief overview. First, a series of (de-/re-)*regulatory changes* reflected in the legislation of the early 1970s and late 1980s have transformed internal sector boundaries, intensified competition, stimulated market demand and generated a greater concern with consumer protection (e.g. selling to 'need'). Associated *ideological changes* towards neo-liberalism have raised the value of 'consumer sovereignty' in society with consequences for organizations and their relationships with 'external' customers. This has helped to raise the legitimacy of marketing as a specialism in relation to other managerial/professional groups.[30] Other changes in the *socio-economic* profile of the population have stimulated demand in some areas and generated 'new' financial services 'needs'. This includes the continued 'demassification' of society to increasingly diffuse groupings (or market segments) with different lifestyles.[31,32]

Increased personal income in the 1980s combined with market saturation of certain core products saw the development of 'new' products and increased segmentation. Indeed, in the marketing theory of product life-cycles, market saturation is a classic condition for segmentation.[33,34] More recently, the economic recession and housing 'crisis' have focused managerial attention more acutely towards costs and profitability as well as new markets. At the same time, and partly as a consequence of increased marketing, government regulation and the attention of the media and consumer groups, it is claimed that financial services consumers are becoming more financially literate, sophisticated and discerning (i.e. 'sovereign') in their choice of product, service and company. Finally, innovations in information technology (IT) have facilitated increased and more flexible use of data in service distribution and new product development.[4,35,36]

In addition to the largely acknowledged factors listed above, two further conditions relating to company practices help to account for the nature and growth of marketing in financial services. First, forms of segmentation are inherent to traditional banking and insurance activities. Actuarial and credit scoring techniques, like those of market segmentation, are derived from early statistical classification of people and behaviour.[37] They are used to measure, classify and locate risks. The first forms of market segmentation used such information to target 'good' risks for motor and life insurance, for example. This tradition of 'segmentation selection' has helped to shape contemporary market segmentation with its focus on the costs and profitability of products and segments.

Second, through targeted advertising in particular, the marketing (and production) practices of manufacturing companies since the 1960s have helped to structure the diversified market for personal consumption in ways which provide the basis for the segmentation strategies deployed by financial service companies.[32,38,39] Furthermore the development, dissemination and promotion of marketing techniques and approaches, combined with those associated with strategy and accounting knowledges, are conditions as well as consequences of changing marketing practice.[37]

While no doubt necessary, the dissemination of new knowledges and techniques cannot be seen as a sufficient condition for their widespread adoption. According to historical accounts of the growth of marketing activity, the most crucial stimulus is intensified competition for industry, in general[33,40] and financial services, in particular.[8] The key, if not distinctive (see ref. 5, p. xii), characteristic of the recent changing climate of regulation and competition has been the erosion of technical product boundaries in markets which, in many senses, may be seen as oversupplied. These and other competitive factors have not only contributed to the increasing attention given to diverse consumer 'needs', but also have helped to shape the way in which market segmentation strategies are implemented.[37]

LIMITATIONS IN RESPONDING TO CONSUMER NEEDS

As has been intimated, there is a general view that current competitive conditions have forced financial service companies to develop or modify their products, customer service and methods of distribution in accordance with a prior assessment of consumer 'needs' or preferences.[5,15,41] However, we are sceptical of claims that consumer 'needs' predominate. First, our scepticism revolves around the very concept of 'need' so readily and unproblematically adopted by marketing theorists and practitioners. We believe the concept to be problematic within marketing as a whole but especially with respect to those aspects of financial services (e.g. life insurance, pensions and other long-term savings products) where the consumer is often inert or inactive as a buyer until the actual point of sale. Second and relatedly, we argue that even if the problems surrounding the concept of 'need' were resolvable, suppliers of financial services would be heavily constrained from satisfying consumers 'needs' by the higher priority of selling profitable products. In short, competition may also act to limit the extent to which perceived needs are addressed.

The concept of 'need'

The concept of 'need' has a long history within the field of industrial psychology where it was originally seen to fill the conceptual gap between stimulus and response in behaviourist theory. The stimulus was seen to elicit a response if the individual had a need that could be satisfied by such a response. It was particularly adopted in motivation theory when the presumed causal relationship between job satisfaction and work productivity/performance failed to be confirmed in several empirical studies.[42]

While there is not space here to enter into a long philosophical debate about our epistemological and ontological misgivings with the concept of 'need',[43] it is appropriate to point to its inadmissible essentialist and individualistic nature. Largely because of a preoccupation with 'scientific' respectability, marketing is dominated by a reduction of its field (i.e. human behaviour) to a set of measurable variables, and 'need', like all marketing concepts, falls into this paradigm and is operationalized so as to remove the sense of ambiguity, uncertainty or precariousness in its meaning.

Through this process, 'need' is made really to exist as an essential feature of the individual psyche which is itself seen to have autonomous existence. But, in effect, the belief in its existence serves to influence the exercise of power (e.g. advertising, selling and marketing) by producers in such a way as to reproduce the kinds of behaviour in consumers that sustain the belief. It also reinforces an individualistic perception on the part of consumers that anxieties, frustrations and desires can be satisfactorily managed through buying products that are deemed to fulfil deeply held 'needs'. The irony in all this is that while holding assumptions which disregard the social construction of reality,[44] the concept of 'need' is ultimately validated precisely because of such constructions, albeit supplemented by powerful practices on the part of producers and distributors. Marketing then claims to be satisfying a range of consumer 'needs' which it plays a large, though not exclusive, part in creating.

It may be suggested that conventionally we attribute need to individuals as a *post hoc* rationalization to account for and render rational and meaningful some recurrent behaviour we have observed. 'Need', then, is not a property of the customer so much as a category for ordering and making sense of behaviours which are a complex outcome of the producer/distributor/consumer relationship. This is the case in any consumption process but even more so with respect to insurance and associated products in financial services, where individuals are transformed into consumers only at the point of sale when their lives are reconstituted as a problem (need) to be resolved (satisfied) by the product on offer. If 'needs' are socially constructed within effective sales encounters, the process is accomplished by the sales person with particular products in mind (i.e. those available for sale); it is then somewhat exaggerated to argue that financial services now *respond* to consumer 'needs'. They do so only insofar as the 'need' that the salesperson has been active in constructing, can be apparently satisfied from within the product range on offer.

Of course, the original design of products may well have been developed by using various market research techniques to secure a better 'fit' between product and what a sample of the population anticipate people might want. But these techniques can never simulate consumer behaviour since, by definition, they are abstracted from the actual circumstances of consumption. Moreover, if consumers do not often know what they want prior to the construction of a problem or 'need' in the sales encounter, then such market research has a marginal role to play. This takes us to our second reason for being sceptical of the claims regarding the centrality of consumer 'needs' in the distribution of financial services – the concern to sell profitable products to profitable consumers.

The pre-eminence of profit

While we recognize the concept of need to be problematic as illustrated, this in itself would not preclude financial services companies from developing a stronger orientation to the consumer. But, as we have intimated, profit acts as a constraint on, as well as an incentive for, such practices. In one sense, this is an obvious point. Indeed, it is clear from the earliest discussions of a market-led approach that consideration of cost and profitability limit the possible diversity of products and services offered to the consumer (ref. 33, p. 401). This is underplayed if not neglected in the marketing literature at a time when, owing to intensified competition, the tension surrounding the potential conflict between profit and responding to consumer 'needs' has heightened.

Selecting profitable consumers has been a concern of financial services companies in a variety of forms such as the exclusive bank account or the pricing of 'bad' risks out of the market through strict insurance underwriting. With increased competition, and, in banking, the push for cross-selling, market segmentation has simply added another technique which can make this search for the profitable consumer more precise and effective. As one bank insurance director expressed it:

> We are actually encouraging – largely as a result of targeting – this search for the 'holy grail', the good customer who never makes a claim – we're giving him(sic) such competitive premiums but what's it doing at the other end of the book . . . we're seeing cases now where the choice is not which insurer, but do I insure? The premium increases are such that it is becoming beyond some people's means.

The more this increases, however, the less plausible becomes the rhetoric of responding to consumer 'needs', since the qualification has to be added that they must be low-risk or high-priced 'needs'.[45–49]

The preoccupation with profitability does not merely restrict those to whom financial services companies sell their products but also what they are prepared to sell. In insurance and investment, the demands of the Financial Services Act to give 'best advice' (i.e. selling to 'need') from across the whole range of a company's products resulted in products being withdrawn from the range simply on the basis of their low profitability. Even where such questionable practices are not adopted, sales staff are often in a position to sell those products that attract higher rates of commission and policing 'best advice' has not seriously affected commission-based selling.[50,51]

The selection of 'profitable' products and consumers and the concomitant 'selecting out' of others can, in part, be attributed to managerial short-termism or the continued predominance of 'non-marketing' management groups' priorities within organizations[17] such as those of financial accountants, actuaries, underwriters and sales managers.[30] Moreover, it could be argued that profitability, in the long term at least, is more likely to result from addressing consumers' 'needs' than by neglecting them. This is particularly the case where 'repeat' business or 'cross-selling' depends on consumer satisfaction with a company's service. It is sometimes explicit in the literature when, for example, high company performance is seen to be linked with the practice of relationship marketing,[21] albeit with a high net worth (i.e. more 'active' and profitable) customer base. Thus, the apparent neglect in the marketing literature of the cost constraints on a marketing orientation may well stem from the assumption that there is no tension involved. This is because it is assumed that high levels of competition in financial services will 'protect' consumers from the tendencies of companies seeking to determine or ignore their 'needs'. Only those companies which satisfy the consumers' 'needs' will survive, it is argued. But the competition argument is dubious even in areas of consumption such as consumer commodities because of the tendency of retailers not to stock comparable models of the same product.[30] In the long-term business aspects of financial services especially, it has little impact because, on the whole, the consumer is inactive and/or indifferent.

Set against the claims of increasing consumer sophistication, there is some consensus in the literature that the key factors for most consumers remain simply a confidence in the security of the organization and, in particular, convenience of purchase.[25,28,51,53–55] Even in the relatively transparent and price sensitive market of motor insurance, convenience of supply is the primary consideration.[56] Through the provision of a range of packaged and branded products conveniently available in high street networks and numerous other channels of distribution, it might be argued that the financial services companies are responding to these consumer 'needs'.

The apparent preference for convenience and confidence is typically understood as a product of consumer ignorance resulting from the complexity and non-comparability of financial services. However, an alternative account is that it reflects not so much consumer preference or ignorance, but, a lack of interest in, or even an indifference towards, financial services – an attitude which is reinforced by the complexity of products in this field. Even in terms of service provision or delivery, there remains considerable 'inertia' – consumers do not tend to 'vote with their feet'.[51,52] As Watkins[53] notes, with some exceptions, such as consumers switching from bank accounts to interest bearing building society accounts in the 1980s:

> There is little hard evidence of substantial shopping around by the majority of buyers in choosing financial services, nor of switching between suppliers on a large scale . . . (p. 48).

This is particularly evident in insurance.[56] Indeed consumers' lack of interest in insurance is given as one reason why there is little use of market research (an essential element of the marketing orientation) in this area (refs. 18, 41, p. 146). In life assurance especially, despite years of successive educational campaigns from the industry and increased marketing activity and media attention, the adage that it is not bought but must be sold because of 'ignorance of the product and distaste for the message' (i.e. associations with death)[15] remains relevant. This 'requirement' for a sales push/product-led rather than market-led approach highlights the active role of sales and marketing in helping to construct consumer 'needs' and shape preferences across financial services. This is, once again, typically neglected or underplayed in the marketing literature for it directly contradicts the notion of an active and sovereign consumer.[13,57]

At the very least then, widespread consumer inertia reduces the incentive for companies to design products primarily on the basis of prior 'needs' analysis. Rather, for many companies there are only the mass and the more active or sophisticated high net worth markets and life stages within them. Indeed, it is claimed that the financial services market is, as yet, less differentiated than other sectors.[58] This is also acknowledged by some practitioners. For example, one bank insurance director described the packaging of standard products for convenience and presenting/selling them as if they specifically met the consumers' 'needs' as 'mass marketing to units of one (consumer)' and as an ideal to be sought. Moreover the banks' strategy to 'farm' the captive customer base by life-long cross-selling is informed more by the resulting cost savings (claimed to be as much as three to seven times cheaper than selling to new customers) than responding to diffuse needs.

This is not to argue crudely that companies simply exploit customers. Rather, it is to raise questions about the claims that competitive pressures have led companies to respond to consumer 'needs'. Competition can work on companies in at least two ways: to offer better products and services in order to increase or maintain market share, and to contain costs in order to survive or maximize profitability. In both cases needs may be conveniently bypassed as 'costly' consumers are avoided and consumer inertia provides the opportunity or rationale for adopting a profitable product-led approach. Until such time as consumers do become more sophisticated 'financially self-disciplined subjects',[44] such strategies may well be appropriate in this sector.

CONCLUSIONS

In this article we have sought to examine critically the concept of need deployed in marketing and the claims of an increasingly market-led approach within UK retail financial services. As with earlier marketing developments in the USA and particularly with respect to manufactured goods, heightened competition has encouraged increasing managerial attention to consumer needs. But consideration of costs and profitability are also intensified by competition. While it is acknowledged in the general marketing literature that such concerns place a limit on the scope for responding to needs, it is rarely the focus of academic attention. Cost considerations encourage a ('profitable') product-led approach, whereby segmentation techniques are used to *select out*, where possible, 'unprofitable' products and consumer segments almost irrespective of consumer need. Moreover, such practices are made possible and reinforced not only by the dominance of 'accounting' interests within management, but also by the comparative inertia evident among financial services consumers. The marketing concept assumes consumers to be knowledgeable and interested in the products on offer – therefore, if companies respond to consumers' needs, increased market share will necessarily follow. As we have argued, such a view neglects the way in which needs are as much a consequence as a condition of marketing and other supplier activities rather than a property of individuals which is identifiable prior to consumption. In addition and in financial services especially, it overlooks the possibility that consumers continue to be comparatively indifferent to the product, and to a lesser extent to the nature of service delivery.

It appears that the increased marketing (as well as other media and consumer pressure group activity) in financial services is, somewhat paradoxically, raising the interest or 'sophistication' of some (e.g. the middle and professional classes) consumers.[13] Such a development is reinforcing the pressure to become more market-led. An example of this is the provision by some banks of independent financial advice to high net-worth customers. However, and more generally, to the extent that profit retains a primacy over attention to 'needs' and products are sold as if they have been tailored ('mass marketing to units of one'), there is a danger that increased consumer awareness combined with expectations of a 'personal service' will provoke consumer resistance and/or demands for customized products. Or it is possible that, as the regulators seem to be advocating, a 'professional' or advice-based model rather than a 'sales' approach is more appropriate to the future of financial services. In which case, marketing would have to take a 'back seat' or undergo a dramatic transformation in the direction of assisting the process of financial education rather than advancing the effective and profitable consumption of products.

ACKNOWLEDGMENTS

The authors would like to acknowledge the special editors and anonymous reviewers for their helpful comments on an earlier version of this article. We would also like to thank Helen Dean as secretary of the Financial Services Research Centre (FSRC). The research was supported by the TS-funded FSRC at UMIST.

NOTES AND REFERENCES

1. For example, such respectable companies as Scottish Widows, Guardian Royal Exchange, and Sun Alliance have suffered fines as a result of investigations by the Life Assurance and Unit Trust Regulatory Organization (LAUTRO).
2. Kerfoot, D. and Knights, D. (1993) 'Management, Manipulation and Masculinity'. *Journal of Management Studies* **31**(4): 659–679.
3. Knights, D. and Willmott, H. (1993) 'It's a Very Foreign Discipline: Expenses Control in a Mutual Life Insurance Company'. *British Journal of Management* **4**(4): 1–18.
4. Sturdy, A. J. (Ed.) (1989) *Managing Information Technology in Insurance.* Harlow: Longman.
5. Ennew, C. T., Watkins, T. and Wright, M. (Eds) (1990) *Marketing Financial Services.* Oxford: Heinemann.
6. Thwaites, D. and Lynch, J. E. (1992) 'Adoption of the Marketing Concept by UK Building Societies'. *Service Industries Journal* **12**(4): 437–462.
7. Speed, R. and Smith, G. (1992) 'Retail Financial Services Segmentation'. *Service Industries Journal* **12**(3): 368–383.
8. *Journal of the Academy of Marketing Science* (1992) Special 20th Anniversary Issue, **20** (No. 4, Fall).
9. Hunt, S. D. (1992) 'Marketing Is . . . '. *Journal of the Academy of Marketing Science* **20** (No. 4, Fall): 301–312.
10. Bennett, P. D. (1988) *Dictionary of Marketing Terms.* Chicago, IL: American Marketing Association.

11. Hooley, G. J., Lynch, J. E. and Shepherd, J. (1990) 'The Marketing Concept: Putting Theory into Practice'. *European Journal of Marketing* **29**(9): 7–24.
12. Kotler, P. (1984) *Marketing Management*, 5th edn. Englewood Cliffs, NJ: Prentice-Hall.
13. Smith, N. C. (1987) 'Consumer Boycotts and Consumer Sovereignty'. *European Journal of Marketing* **21**(5): 7–19.
14. Morgan, N. and Piercy, N. (1990) 'Marketing in Financial Services Organizations. Policy and Practice'. In *Managing and Marketing Services in the 1990s* (R. Teare, L. Moutinho and N. Morgan, Eds). London: Cassel.
15. Newman, K. (1984) *Financial Marketing and Communications.* Eastbourne: Holt, Rinehart and Winston.
16. Clarke, P. D., Edward, P. M., Gardner, E. F., Feeney, P. and Molyneux, P. (1988) 'The Genesis of Strategic Marketing Control in British Retail Banking'. *International Journal of Bank Marketing* **6**(2): 5–19.
17. Hooley, G. J. and Mann, S. J. (1988) 'The Adoption of Marketing by Financial Institutions in the UK'. *Service Industries Journal* **8**(4): 488–500.
18. Davison, H., Watkins, T. and Wright, M. (1989) 'Developing New Personal Financial Products: Some Evidence of the Role of Market Research'. *International Journal of Bank Marketing* **7**(1): 8–15.
19. Joseph, L. and Yorke, D. A. (1989) 'Know Your Game Plan: Market Segmentation in the Personal Financial Services Section', *Quarterly Review of Marketing* **15**(1): 8–13.
20. Within this framework, Speed and Smith[21] identify three interrelated dimensions of strategic marketing in financial services – an emphasis on customer selection, internal operations or an overall strategic orientation.
21. Speed, R. and Smith, G. (1993) 'Customers, Strategy and Performance', *International Journal of Bank Managing* **11**(5): 3–11.
22. Ennew, C. T. (1990) 'Marketing Strategy and Planning'. In *Marketing Financial Services* (C. T. Ennew, T. Watkins and M. Wright, Eds). Oxford: Heinemann, pp. 60–79.
23. Wells, W. D. (1975) 'Psychographics – A Critical Review'. *Journal of Marketing Research* **12** (May): 196–213. Reprinted in Ennis, B. M. and Cox, K. K. (Eds) (1988) *Marketing Classics*, 6th edn. London: Allyn & Bacon.
24. Lewis, B. R. (1990) 'Bank Marketing'. In *Marketing Financial Services* (C. T. Ennew, T. Watkins and M. Wright, Eds). Oxford: Heinemann, pp. 157–177.
25. McGoldrick, P. J. and Greenland, S. J. 'Competition between Banks and Building Societies in the Retailing of Financial Services'. *British Journal of Management* **3**(1): 169–179.
26. Sturdy, A. J. (1992) 'Banks a Lot (Banks, General Insurance and the Consumer)'. *Post Magazine*, 4 December.
27. Watson, I. (1982) 'The Adoption of Marketing by the English Clearing Banks'. *European Journal of Marketing* **16**(3).
28. McKechnie, S. (1992) 'Consumer Buying Behaviour in Financial Services: An Overview'. *International Journal of Bank Marketing* **10**(5): 4–12.
29. The absence of specific marketing departments in this case was not considered as a reflection of a highly advanced 'stage' of development involving the diffusion of marketing throughout the organizations surveyed.
30. Wittington, R. and Whipp, R. (1992) 'Professional Ideology and Marketing Implementation'. *European Journal of Marketing* **26**(1): 52–63.
31. Baudrillard, J. (1988) In: *Selected Writings* (M. Procter, Ed.). Oxford: Polity Press.
32. Featherstone, M. (1991) *Consumer Culture and Postmodernism.* London: Sage.
33. Smith, W. R. (1956) 'Product Differentiation and Market Segmentation as Alternative Strategies'. *Journal of Marketing*, July: 3–8. Reprinted in Ennis, B. M. and Cox, K. K. (Eds) (1988) *Marketing Classics*, 6th edn. London: Allyn & Bacon.
34. Zollinger, M. (1985) *Marketing Bancaire.* Paris: Dunod.
35. Dyer, N. and Watkins, T. (Eds) (1988) *Marketing Insurance: A Practical Guide.* London: Kluwer.
36. Knights, D. and Murray, F. (1994) *Divided Managers: Organizational Politics and IT Management.* Chichester: Wiley.
37. Sturdy, A. J., Knights, D. and Morgan, G. (1993) 'Marketing the Soul: The Subjectivity of

Segmentation and the Segmentation of Subjectivity'. Paper presented at 11th European Group on Organisation Studies Colloquium, Paris.
38. Curtis, T. (1988) 'The Information Society: A Computer Generated Caste System?' In *The Political Economy of Information* (V. Mosco and J. Wasko, Eds). Madison, WI: University of Wisconsin Press.
39. Goldman, R. (1992) *Reading Ads Socially*. London: Routledge.
40. Engel, J. F., Fiorillo, H. F. and Cayley, M. A. (Eds) *Market Segmentation – Concepts and Applications*. New York: Holt, Rinehart and Winston.
41. Watkins, T. and Wright, M. (1986) *Marketing Financial Services*. London: Butterworths.
42. Vroom, V. H. (1964) *Work and Motivation*. New York: John Wiley & Sons.
43. Knights, D. and Willmott, H. (1974) 'Humanistic Social Science and the Theory of Needs'. *Interpersonal Development* **12**(1): 213–222.
44. Knights, D. (1988) 'Risk, Financial Self-discipline and Commodity Relationships'. *Advances in Public Interest Accounting* **2**. New York: JAI Press, pp. 47–69.
45. It is somewhat ironic that techniques originally developed in nineteenth-century studies on the plight of the poor such as the family life-cycle[46,47] and what is now termed 'geodemographics'[48,49] are effectively being used to select-out similar groups from financial services.
46. Rowntree, B. S. (1901) *Poverty: A Study of Town Life*. London: Macmillan.
47. Wells, W. D. and Gubar, G. (1966) 'The Life Cycle Concept in Marketing Research'. *Journal of Marketing Research* **4** (No. 4, November).
48. Booth, C. (Ed.) *The Life and Labour of the People of London*. London: Macmillan, pp. 1889–1902.
49. Rothman, J. (1989) 'Geodemographics (Editorial)'. *Journal of Market Research* **31**(1): editorial and pp. 139–150.
50. Grey, C. and Knights, D. (1990) 'Investor Protection and the "Cowboy" Stereotype: A Critical View'. *Managerial Finance* **16**(5): 29–30.
51. Mitchell, J. and Weisner, H. (1992) 'Savings and Investments – Consumer Issues'. Occasional Paper to OFT, Office of Fair Trading, London.
52. Knights, D., Morgan, G. and Sturdy, A. J. (1993) 'Quality for the Consumer in Bancassurance?'. *Consumer Policy Review* **3**(4): 232–240.
53. Watkins, T. (1990) 'The Demand for Financial Services'. In *Marketing Financial Services* (C. T. Ennew, T. Watkins and M. Wright, Eds). Oxford: Heinemann.
54. Carter, R. L., Chiplin, B. and Lewis, M. K. (1986) *Personal Financial Markets*. Oxford: Philip Allan.
55. Ennew, C. T. (1992) 'Consumer Attitudes to Independent Financial Advice'. *International Journal of Bank Marketing* **10**(5): 13–18.
56. Evans, P. and Gumby, J. (1992) 'Going for Broke?' *Post Magazine* (28 May) 9–12.
57. DuGay, P. and Salaman, G. (1992) 'The Cult(ure) of the Consumer'. *Journal of Management Studies* **29**(5): 615–633.
58. Jayasinghe, S. and Yorke, D. A. (1991) 'A Technique to Evaluate Secondary Data on Personal Financial Services to Identify Potential Customer Segments'. Occasional Paper, Manchester School of Management, UMIST.

FURTHER READING

Beane, J. P. and Ennis, D. M. (1987) 'Market Segmentation: A Review'. *European Journal of Marketing* **21**(5): 20–42.

Berger, P. and Luckmann, T. (1967) *The Social Construction of Reality*. Harmondsworth: Penguin.

Stanley, T. J. Moschis, G. P. and Danko, W. D. (1987) 'Financial Service Segments – The Seven Faces of the Affluent Market'. *Journal of Advertising Research* **27**(4): 52–67.

23

River Magic: Extraordinary Experience and the Extended Service Encounter

Eric J. Arnould and Linda L. Price

River rafting is a growing component of the Colorado leisure services industry. Thousands of people take rafting trips every year for tens of thousands of client-days. Multiday rafting trips on the Colorado, Green, Yampa, Arkansas, and others are river outfitters' most resource-intensive service offerings. River outfitters discuss the river rafting experience with a sense of reverence and mystery – a singular quality some call 'river magic'. Our findings tell of the experience of multiday commercial river rafting. Our research is unique in (1) focusing on key elements in delivering temporally extended, extraordinary experiences, (2) representing different participant perspectives in the service encounter, (3) detailing the emergent interplay of consumer and service provider behaviors in the delivery of service outcomes, and (4) integrating and cross-validating data collected by multiple methods.

The rafting story begins by describing the pretrip planning process. Answers to how people decide on a river rafting adventure, descriptions of their pretrip expectations and accounts of their planning and pretrip imagery display little deliberation. Although it costs much time and money, people do not appear to think about it carefully. Sometimes a family member or friend arranged the trip, and they 'just went'. More often consumers choose it because it is something they've 'always' wanted to do, but search is minimal and pretrip expectations vague. Often consumers articulate the desire for 'something beyond their imagination' or just letting everything be what it is, denying specific expectations. Many of these reports imply a desire for something different, without articulating what it might be. Some reports carry a theme of 'getting away from it all', where 'it all' ranges from Nintendo to job-related stress. In anticipation of the trip, consumers say they expect that the environment will be clean and natural, guides will be competent and knowledgeable, other people will be friendly and pleasant, and they will 'not get killed'. They expect to have fun.

Our story then moves to the trip experience and posttrip descriptions and reflections. As the trip unfolds, we learn that the setting, guides, and other people on the trip are important in articulating the narrative of the experience. The guide is an impresario who facilitates the enactment of vaguely familiar cultural scripts, helping participants to transform experiences into treasured, culturally construed memories of personal growth, challenges overcome, teamwork, and perseverance (Abrahams, 1986; Bruner, 1986; Featherstone, 1991, pp. 132–133, 143; Kapferer, 1986). The successful narrative of friendship with guides and strangers that are profound and intimate. It includes a deep connection to the land and the river. The narrative is held up as proof of the work of self, family, and humanity, and demonstrates what is really important in life. In short, the story is a romance (Campbell, 1987; Urry, 1990), a triumph over natural forces achieved through trust and mutual reliance.

The experience is extraordinary, offering absorption, personal control, joy and valuing, a spontaneous letting-be of the process, and a newness of perception and process (Csikszentmihalyi, 1990). It is recalled easily for years after, but, because of its considerable emotional content, it is difficult to describe. People sometimes report that it changed them forever. It is magical. As such, satisfaction with river rafting, a hedonic encounter between customer, guide and 'nature', does not seem to be embodied in attributes of the experience such as amount of time spent freezing in wet clothes, uncomfortable toilet facilities, bad food, or any summary index of specific attributes of the trip. Rather, satisfaction is embodied in the success of the narrative, an interactive gestalt orchestrated by the guide over several days' journey into the unknown.

The guide role is a demanding one fraught with illusion and role conflict. In contrast to familiar transports of fancy provided by performing artists and theme parts, river guides offer commercially a magic that comes from an interpersonal dynamic developed over an extended interval of time in a seemingly authentic environment. They give their customers something they do not know how to ask for, but something that makes customers very happy.

The story we tell is emergent. We did not find it in the literature, but we can document theory and research that support the importance and plausibility of our account. Before we tell our story, we briefly review some relevant literature. This review emphasizes several features. Using the literature, we describe characteristics of extraordinary experience, speculate about why it evokes vague script expectations and complex evaluations of satisfaction, discuss salient features of services that deliver extraordinary experience, and elaborate on the role of the service provider in articulating this experience over an extended temporal framework.

LITERATURE REVIEW

Extraordinary experience

Hedonic consumption experience has received some attention in the literature (Havlena and Holbrook, 1986; Hawes, 1978; Hirschman, 1984; Hirschman and Holbrook, 1982; Holbrook *et al.*, 1984; Holbrook and Hirschman, 1982; Unger and Kernan, 1983). Although largely ignored by consumer researchers, other researchers identify a special class of hedonic consumption activities – intense, positive, intrinsically enjoyable experiences. Concepts that map this domain include peak experience (Maslow, 1964), peak performance (Klausner, 1968; Privette, 1983), flow (Csikszentmihalyi, 1985), and extraordinary experience (Abrahams, 1986). Certain qualities unify these experiences, including the merging of action and awareness, attention or clear focus, personal integration, personal control, awareness of power, joy and valuing, and a spontaneous (uninhibited) letting-be of process (Csikszentmihalyi, 1975, 1990; Csikszentmihalyi and LeFevre, 1989; Privette, 1983).

Intensity and the relational mode of the experience differentiate these concepts from one another. The term we use, 'extraordinary experience', entails a 'sense of newness of perception and process' (Privette, 1983, p. 1366; see also Abrahams, 1986). By contrast with flow, extraordinary experience is triggered by unusual events and is characterized by high levels of emotional intensity and experience. By contrast with peak experience and peak performance (Celsi, Rose and Leigh, 1993), extraordinary experience implies neither superior levels of effort nor an independent relational mode. In fact, an important trigger for this experiential state is interpersonal interaction (Abrahams, 1986).

Vague Expectations and Complex Satisfaction

What are the distinguishing characteristics of extraordinary experience? Specifically, how and what type of expectations do consumers form and how do they evaluate the experience? Much of consumer research posits a model of choice and satisfaction based on defined expectations and subsequent performance of a consumer alternative in terms of those expectations (Fiebelkorn, 1985; Oliver and DeSarbo, 1988). This disconfirmation paradigm, however, is based on two important assumptions. First, it assumes consumers have expectations. Second, it assumes satisfaction is a function of deviations between expected product or service performance and actual performance. It is questionable whether consumers evaluate extraordinary experience in terms of well-defined expectations or rate subsequent performance in terms of them.

Expectations

Expectations (including beliefs, evaluative criteria, attitudes, and activity sequences) for extraordinary experiences are likely to be vague. Why? First, consumers of extraordinary experience may desire intense emotional outcomes, for example, joy or absorption, but not know what consumption alternatives produce them. The rarity and intensity of emotions associated with extraordinary experiences may mean information sources such as documentary films, word of mouth, and promotional materials provide limited cues for linking outcomes to consumption alternatives. Moreover, emotions are subjective, fluctuating across individuals and social situations (Denzin, 1983; Holbrook and Hirschman, 1982), which makes them challenging for consumers to predict. Since extraordinary experience emerges from the dynamic interaction of participants, it is difficult to predict one's own behavior and others' responses from behavior in ordinary contexts. The emotional content of these interactions is epiphenomenal (Denzin, 1983).

A second reason scripts are apt to be vague is that extraordinary experience is spontaneous and unrehearsed (Abrahams, 1986). Spontaneity distinguishes extraordinary events from everyday routines and contributes to the perception of the event as extraordinary. Consumers value and protect these qualities. Lying (1990, pp. 861–862) reports that many rock climbers and sky divers 'regard the experience as ineffable . . . some believe that talking about edgework should be avoided because it contaminates one's subjective appreciation of the experience'.

In a search for authenticity, consumers of extraordinary experience surrender their expectations to the 'immediate encounter with being' (Redfoot, 1984, p. 295). Perceived ineffability of extraordinary experiences makes consumers unwilling to anticipate or rehearse them.

Performance

A prevailing view is that satisfaction can be described with a summary index of a product or service's performance on various attributes. In contrast, satisfaction with extraordinary experience is emergent across the temporal frame of the experience (Deighton, 1992; Gergen and Gergen, 1988; Howard, 1991). Popular movies depicting extraordinary experience, such as *City Slickers* and *K2*, illustrate this point. They highlight unpleasant and life-threatening events. But in each case a triumphant moment – saving the cattle herd and attaining the summit – leads to emphatic positive reevaluation of all the negatives that might otherwise dominate evaluation of the experience.

Satisfaction is also interpreted within the broader narrative context of the consumer's life (Botterill, 1987; Deighton, 1992). People are concerned with having experiences that tell about the self – define, develop, and change it (Sarbin, 1986). Consumers use extraordinary experiences to give agency and coherence to their stories about the self. Thus, consumers of intense martial arts training may interpret physical injury or fear as contributing positively to self-growth, efficacy, and authenticity (Donohue, 1991).

In summary, for extraordinary experiences we speculate that expectations are likely to be vague. Moreover, evaluation of the experience evolves within the context of the overall story. Hence, the disconfirmation paradigm commonly evoked in consumer research is not a useful metaphor for interpreting satisfaction with extraordinary experiences.

Delivering extraordinary experience

Commercial delivery of hedonic experiences has received little attention in marketing (for exceptions see Durgee, Holbrook and Sherry (1991), Holbrook (1990), Holbrook and Zirlin (1985), and O'Guinn and Belk (1989)). Commercial delivery of *extraordinary* experiences has received no attention. However, important keys to understanding service delivery come form the services literature. This literature emphasizes the importance of setting, process, and provider–client relationships in determining consumer satisfaction (Bitner, 1990, 1992; Bitner, Booms, and Tetreault, 1990; Czepiel *et al.*, 1985; McCallum and Harrison, 1985;

Mohr and Bitner, 1991). Each of these elements plays an important role in delivering extraordinary experience. However, the service quality literature has primarily focused on evaluation of technical and functional elements (Parasuraman, Zeithaml, and Berry, 1985, 1988). Similarly, most evaluations of white water rafting have focused primarily on client-days, perceived crowding, safe runs, and quality of the water (Heywood, 1987; Hollenhorst and Olson, 1990; Roggenbuck *et al.*, 1991; Shelbey, Bregenzer and Johnson, 1988).

Research from a variety of disciplines and contexts, including research on the delivery of hedonic outcomes, suggests services providing extraordinary experience must emphasize process elements that have received less attention in marketing literature. Among these are affect, narrative, and ritual understandings.

Affect

Service establishments must monitor and control the emotions employees convey (Hochschild, 1983; Peters and Austin, 1985; Rafaeli and Sutton, 1987). For example, Disney World coaches prospective employees on how to look like they are having fun (Martin 1986; Romm, 1989); McDonald's stresses the importance of displaying enthusiasm and a sense of humor (Boas and Chain, 1987); waitresses at Route Diner strive to boost their tips by being 'especially friendly' (Paules, 1991, p. 27). Classical ballet dancers' expression of emotion becomes the focal point for the hedonic experience (King and Straub, 1984; cited in Holbrook (1987), p. 166). We speculate that engineering affect is central to successful delivery of extraordinary experiences.

The engineering of hedonic outcomes should take place behind the scenes, below the line of visibility (Shostack, 1987). 'Disney World is carefully designed to promote a frontstage view and to suppress backstage information from public awareness' (Johnson, 1981, p. 159). For the desired affective response, provider emotions must be perceived as authentic (Hochschild, 1983; Rafaeli and Sutton, 1987; Romm, 1989) – spontaneous responses to environment, activities, and social interaction (Abrahams, 1986), rather than directed process. In this sense, commercial delivery of extraordinary experience creates a dilemma – to be effective, it must transcend the purposive, task-oriented, and commercial nature of the ordinary service interaction.

Narrative

Service encounters facilitate enactment of familiar, if implicit narrative understandings (Abrahams, 1986; Holbrook, 1987; Shott, 1979; Spradley and Mann, 1975; Sutton and Rafaeli, 1988; van Maanen and Kunda, 1989). Service delivery at McDonald's enacts a number of core American values (Kottak, 1982); service encounters at convenience stores endorse the American norm of efficiency (Sutton and Rafaeli, 1988). Cocktail waitresses learn a generative framework for conventionalized, sexual joking that contributes to their success in extended, commercial interactions (Spradley and Mann, 1975). Much of the hedonic satisfactions of vacation theme parks derives from performers' successful condensations and expressions of the total park experience consistent with consumers' unarticulated and vague cultural narratives (Durgee *et al.*, 1991). Disney World packages history, fantasy, and the future into conventional plots, conveying idealized American cultural values (Johnson, 1981; King, 1981). In many of these contexts, customers and providers have well-developed narrative expectations because of extensive experience in such settings. By contrast, novel service encounters providing extraordinary experience will likely 'require participants to engage in considerable trial and error before they reach tacit agreement or develop norms about which scripts should guide [their] actions' (Sutton and Rafaeli, 1988, p. 474; Bettenhausen and Murnighan, 1985). As a dramaturgical perspective suggests, meaning emerges during the process of interaction; communication of evolving expectations of outcomes plays a key role in satisfactory experience (Grove and Fisk, 1992).

Ritual

The relationship between extraordinary experience and ritual is likely to be complex. Although individuals articulate extraordinary experience as unique and ineffable, at an etic level these experiences exemplify culturally embedded rituals that are played out across generations (Abrahams, 1986). Because all experiences address the 'ongoingness of life as it is registered through the filter of culture' (Abrahams, 1986, p. 55), ritual aspects become salient even in enacting what the individual participants define as authentic, unique, and extraordinary. Two general classes of ritual (rites of passage and rites of integration) characterize delivery of extraordinary experience.

The metaphor of the *pilgrimage* based on van Gennep's (1960) formulation of rites of passage provides a useful basis for understanding satisfaction. In particular, it helps us understand the sequencing of events in the delivery of extraordinary experience and how overall satisfaction is linked to underlying cultural scripts.

The pilgrimage incorporates the three essential features – separation, transition, and reintegration – but, unlike many rites of passage, a pilgrimage is typically voluntary. Pilgrims leave their homes and disengage from their ordinary lives. They enter the sacred precincts; their stay is a phase of transition. One of the most common activities in the transitional phase of a rite of passage is stripping of markers of rank and status. Stripped initiates experience a fellowship with other coritualists who, like themselves, perceive themselves in their basic, common humanity. The transitional phase is punctuated by shared performances by pilgrims who experience a sense of what Turner (1969, 1974) calls 'communitas'. They return home transformed and are reintegrated into their community.

A pilgrimage may also be viewed as a *rite of intensification* (Coon, 1958). A rite of intensification increases the emotional intensity of links among persons widely scattered and dissimilar in ordinary life but who share a common mythohistorical orientation. The pilgrim returns, not transformed as in the basic formulation of rites of passage, but affirmed, renewed, or even cured of his/her ailments (Moore, 1980).

Viewing the commercial delivery of extraordinary experience as a *rite of integration* is another potentially useful tool for understanding. Rites of integration are defined as 'planned social interactions that consolidate various forms of cultural artifacts (language, displayed emotions, gestures, symbols, and the physical setting) with the objective of achieving "a temporary sense of closeness" between "potentially divergent" subsystems' (Siehl, Bowen, and Pearson, 1993; see also Mills and Morris, 1986; Trice and Beyer, 1991). Certain service encounters have a feeling of a relationship rather than merely a transaction. These transactions can be described as 'boundary open', resembling a meeting between friends. In boundary open transactions service providers are expected to be actively involved and share their feelings. Siehl *et al.* (1993) hypothesize that less tangible services are more likely to be boundary open. In them, process dimensions that communicate responsiveness, empathy, and assurance become increasingly important influences on customers' satisfaction. Extraordinary experience is likely to involve boundary open transactions.

Provider–customer relationships in delivering extraordinary experience

Previous research has revealed that service employees hold special relationships with customers (Mars and Nicod, 1984; Spradley and Mann, 1975), customers are active participants in service outcomes (Mills and Morris, 1986; Rafaeli, 1989; Sutton and Rafaeli, 1988), and provider–customer independence is high (McCallum and Harrison, 1985). However, research on service encounters has concentrated on comparatively brief transactions (Bitner, 1990; Bitner *et al.*, 1990; Fiebelkorn, 1985; Surprenant and Solomon, 1987; Zeithaml, Berry and Parasuraman, 1987). Virtually no literature examines temporally extended service provider roles. One distinguishing feature of extended encounters is long transactions that provide more time for the customer to react to the emotional behavior of an employee (Sutton and Rafaeli, 1988, p. 483). Further, Americans' underlying scripts for 'slow times' have more 'scenes' (Nisbett and Ross, 1980, p. 34) that emphasize interpersonal exchanges and the display of emotions (Sutton and Rafaeli, 1988, p. 477). Because of Americans' script expectations about lengthy transactions, there will be pressures for extended encounters to become affectively charged, boundary open relationships. Due to the defining qualities of extraordinary experiences discussed above, we might reasonably expect that customer–provider interdependence, and active customer participation in the successful delivery of extraordinary experiences, will be even more pronounced than in other kinds of extended service encounters.

In summary, service encounter research increasingly recognizes that service experience is inherently interpretive, subjective, and affective (Czepiel *et al.*, 1985; Klaus, 1985; McCallum and Harrison, 1985; Parasuraman *et al.*, 1988). Enriched views of the service encounter relate service satisfaction to script expectations, dramaturgy, and ritual enactments. Although the marketing literature is silent on the delivery of extraordinary experience, literature from related research streams offers possible insights into individual and cultural narratives that underlie extraordinary experience. This research suggests service establishments may orchestrate effective, narrative, and ritual content through the skills, engagement, emotions, and dramatic sense of service providers.

DESCRIPTION OF RESEARCH ACTIVITY

A combination of factors motivated the research. First, one of us has had a memorable experience with rafting that left an impression that satisfaction with the experience is complex: How could so many awful things add up to a positive experience? Much later, serendipitous conservations with an outfitter led to an invitation to study river rafting. Our early conversations led us to believe that river rafting is a different kind of service encounter than has been previously studied, and is one that lends itself to multimethod data collection.

In order to find our story, and then tell it, we engaged in extensive data collection over a two-year period using a variety of techniques. Table 1 outlines the sequence of data collection activities, the rationale guiding these efforts, and summary features of the data. The table illustrates iteration between data collection techniques. Techniques were combined, often within the same temporal frame and physical setting, such as the participant observation, focus group, and surveys conducted in May 1990. At each stage we revised and elaborated fundamental constructs and validated findings in a variety of ways. Further, we could move beyond the limitations of each technique by probing systematically, through the incorporation of different methods, for both convergent and divergent data.

Table 1 also illustrates the focus of data collection. Overall, data collection aimed to gather multiple participant perspectives as well as multiple temporal perspectives. Data were gathered from outfitters, guides, and participants. Data were also gathered before, during, immediately after, and well after the experience. The table shows how we tried to apprehend expectations, critical consumption incidents, and postconsumption evaluation through a variety of procedures. In the first research season we gathered data from multiple customers of a single outfitter. In the second research season we gathered data from guides and customers of several different outfitters.

Finally, Table 1 summarizes features of interest for the data analyzed here. In general, we conducted exploratory research with small samples allowing us to advance and amend evolving interpretations. We deployed larger samples and more formal instruments to survey variation in phenomena of demonstrated significance to participants. The table also shows that we expanded the scope and formality of our data gathering over the two seasons as we refined our measures and constructs.

FINDINGS

Table 2 provides an overview of the primary analyses and categories of findings at each step in the research process. Table 2 illustrates that certain experiential qualities and themes showed up consistently throughout the data collection process. Other findings were pronounced in some of the data, but barely apparent in other data. Experiential themes that developed over the course of the first season, and were cross-validated between methods, were further refined and validated in the second season.

Although different methods, data, and analyses were used, a coherent story

Table 1. Research sequence and focus

Date	Method	Focus	Summary sample/data features
1/90	Written protocols	Experiential view of river rafting	Convenience sample, $n = 35$
2/90	On-site depth interviews	View of commercial provision of river experience; input for preseason guide survey	Outfitters, $n = 2$; field notes and photo accounts; collection of promotional and training materials
4/90	Drop-off/ mail-back survey	Description of guide expectations and characteristics; input for script for guide focus group	Census of guide trainees for one outfitter, $n = 8$
5/90	Participant observation	Commercial river experience; revision of script for guide focus group; input for customer pre- and post-river-trip surveys	Field notes and photo accounts; two researchers, separate rafts; trip with guide trainees
5/90	Focus group	Guide approach to service delivery, training, management, setting; input for customer pre- and post-river-trip surveys	River guides, $n = 8$; two-hour focus group; notes transcribed; two facilitators
5/90	Pretrip and posttrip surveys	Consumer expectations and reasons; experiential themes; salient attributes; pretest consumer surveys	Teens and counselors, $n = 17$; pretrip survey administered at put-in; posttrip survey collected Monday following three-day weekend trip; triangulation with participant observation for trip
5/90	Participant observation	Guide/customer and group dynamics; consumer experience of multiday river rafting; revision of customer surveys	Field notes and photo record; two researchers separate rafts; trip with teens and counselors
6/90–8/90	Pretrip customer surveys	Reported pretrip decision factors and expectations; reported pretrip planning; recreational interests and participation, demographics	$n = 19$, telephone precontact of group leaders, mailed to arrive within a week to 10 days of departure; of the 36 groups, responses were received from 13, or 36%; responses were received from more than one participant in six of the groups
6/90–8/90	Posttrip customer surveys	Reported best and worst experiences; element of satisfaction; perceptions of river guide; develop measures of experiential themes; examine relationships	$n = 43$, mailed to be waiting after trip, with follow-up mailing after two weeks; of 54 groups, mailings to three were undeliverable; responses were received from 26 groups, or 51%

Table 1 continued on next page

Table 1. Research sequence and focus *continued*

Date	Method	Focus	Summary sample/data features
7/90	Participant observation	Contrast one-day with multiday rafting experience; peak season river trip	Field notes and photorecord, one researcher, one day
9/90	Focus group	Multiple consumer perspec–tives; how experience remembered; texture of themes; differentiate from other experiences	Past season river consumers, $n = 4$; 90 minutes, videotaped and then transcribed; member check of draft of account with one member of focus group
11/90–1/91	Member check	Incorporate perspective of outfitter on findings	Two 90-minute interviews with outfitter; two researchers
1/91	Mail survey	Postseason guide perspective on what customers value, what makes a trip work; difficult encounters, river crew experience	Census of guides of one outfitter; of 19 surveys mailed, five returned as undeliverable, seven responses for response rate of 50%
4/91	On-site depth interviews	Perspective of different outfitters in remote river area; setting; input on customer surveys	Four interviews, about 60 minutes each; field notes and photo record; two researchers
5/91	Drop-off, pick-up surveys	Preseason guide skills and expectations; training; input on customer surveys	Census of guides of three outfitters hired as of 5/91, $n = 34$
6/91–7/91	Participant observation	Perspective on experience – new rivers, 'typical' trips, different outfitter, use of 'duckies', elaborate understanding of narrative and ritual themes	Three-day trip and four-day trip; taped field notes and photo record; one researcher on each trip – other served as member check; interview with river guide one week later served as member check
6/91–8/91	Pretrip drop-off and collect surveys	Expectations and decision factors; trip planning; background and interests; demographics	Stratified random sample, multiday river trip clients of three outfitters in Dinosaur National Monument, $n = 211$ (97 matched with posttrip); fewer than five unusable, distributed on hour shuttle ride en route to put-in, sealed, collected, mailed back
6/91–8/91	Posttrip drop-off collect postcard, mail-back survey	Validate refined measures of experiential themes; elaborate guide role, setting; facets of experience; transcendence of commercial	Stratified random sample of multiday river trip clients of three outfitters in Dinosaur National Monument, $n = 137$ (97 matched with pretrip); postcard served as validity check and allowed follow-up mailing to nonrespondents; response rate on mail-back survey of 55%

Table 2. Data analysis and categories of findings

Date	Method	Primary analyses	Categories of findings
1/90	Written protocols	Text analyses, key word search, summary statistics	Extraordinary experience; components of satisfaction
2/90	On-site depth interviews	Text analysis of transcribed field notes; sequential photo analysis	Consumer complaints; outfitter motives, feelings; descriptions of guides and clients; descriptions of equipment, settings; stories of transformation and 'river magic'
4/90	Drop-off/ mail-back survey	Simple frequencies; text analysis of open-ended responses	Variance in background and experience; guide motives, feelings; guide expectations of service delivery factors; selection of occupation and outfitter
5/90	Participant observation	Text analysis of transcribed field notes; sequential photo analysis	Guide/customer dynamics; guide skills; setting; experiential qualities of extraordinary experience; components of satisfaction
5/90	Focus group	Text analysis; key word search	Guides' role conflicts; transcendence of the commercial; themes
5/90	Pre-river-trip and post-river-trip surveys	Simple frequencies; text analysis of open-ended responses	Expectations; components of satisfaction; elements of extraordinary experience; experiential themes
5/90	Participant observation	Text analysis of transcribed field notes; key word search; notes of two researchers compared for convergence and divergence	Themes and rituals; guide characteristics; narrative components of satisfaction and experience
6/90–8/90	Pretrip customer surveys	Frequencies, cross-tabulations, *t*-tests, ANOVA, and correlations; reliability analyses; text analysis, key word searches, and counts on open-ended word responses	Pretrip expectations; word-of-mouth influence; prepurchase search
6/90–8/90	Posttrip customer surveys	Frequencies, cross-tabulations, *t*-tests, ANOVA, and correlations; select factor analyses; correlations; text analysis, key word searches, and statistics on open-ended responses	Measures of experiential themes: validity of themes; emotion work of guides; components of satisfaction
7/90	Participant observation	Text analysis and sequential photo analysis	One-day trip themes; group dynamics; guide role

Table 2 continued on next page

Table 2. Data analysis and categories of findings *continued*

Date	Method	Primary analyses	Categories of findings
9/90	Focus group	Text analysis and key word search and statistics on transcribed video	Expectations; experiential themes; guide/customer dynamics and transcendence of the commercial; pilgrimage script, reentry
11/90–1/91	Member check	Text analysis of notes; solicitation and incorporation of feedback into report	Guide weaknesses and variability among guides; guide role conflicts
1/91	Mail survey	Frequencies; text analyses of open-ended responses	Guide role conflict; postseason understandings of themes
4/91	On-site depth interviews	Text analysis and sequential photo analysis	Outfitters' positioning strategies and approach; history and stories of commercial provision of river rafting in Dinosaur National Monument, knowledge of setting; day-to-day operations
5/91	Drop-off, pick-up surveys	Frequencies, cross-tabulations, *t*-tests, ANOVA, and correlations; select factor analyses; correlations; text analysis, key word searches, and statistics on open-ended responses	Preseason perceptions of guide roles, client service topics in training; guide motives
6/91–7/91	Participant observation	Text analysis, key word search and statistics; sequential photo analysis	Narrative components of experience; group dynamics; guide use of ritual
6/91–8/91	Pretrip drop-off and collect surveys	Frequencies, cross-tabulations, *t*-tests, ANOVA, and correlations; select factor analyses; correlations; text analysis, key word searches, and statistics on open-ended responses	Prepurchase search; planning and character of pretrip imagery for first-time river rafters; pretrip expectations
6/91–8/91	Posttrip drop-off, collect postcard, mail-back survey	Frequencies, cross-tabulations, *t*-tests, ANOVA, and correlations; select factor analyses; correlations; text analysis, key word searches, and statistics on open-ended responses	Measures of experiential themes and relationship to satisfaction; guide success factors; relationship between pretrip expectations and satisfaction

emerged about the experience of river rafting. Rather than organize around the sequence or type of data, findings are organized around the story to be told. Descriptions of findings are cross-referenced to Table 2 by the data provided in parentheses after each reported finding. In general, findings from the second season validate and extend the findings from the first season. Care has been taken to protect participant anonymity by disguising names in the reporting of results. A brief introduction to the setting for a multiday river rafting trip is provided in Table 3. Unfamiliar river rafting terminology is included in a glossary, Table 4. Next, we explore the pretrip planning process, experiential themes emergent over the course of the trip, and, finally, posttrip recollections of the experience.

PRETRIP PLANNING PROCESS

Prospective customers expressed minimal, varied and veiled feelings and expectations about the experience, the guides, other people, safety, comfort, emotions, and the setting (5/90, 6/90–8/90). We find hints in pretrip comments of themes that would emerge more strongly during the trip and in informants'

Table 3. River rafting: the setting

Outfitters:
Most rafting firms are family-run businesses located in rural towns. Their capital investment consists primarily of warehouse/dormitory buildings and rafting equipment amounting to about $200 000. Outfitters' largest recurrent cost is for liability insurance covering the 2–25 guides employed. The business is highly seasonal; there is a maximum five-month window for commercial trips bracketed by cold weather and flood water in the spring, then low water in the late summer. Business is further constrained by federal regulations on river access.

Clients and trips:
A trip brings together clients and guides, typically numbering from six to 25 persons on a 3–12-day excursion down one of Colorado's white water rivers. Groups meet in the chilly morning hours either at the outfitters' headquarters or at the put-in. At the put-in the rafts are set up and gear is stowed. Guides explain the fundamentals of equipment, gear, safety, and paddling as clients listen in nervous anticipation.

A typical day:
A typical day begins as the sun lights up the red wall of a majestic canyon summit high above the riverside campsite. At dawn, guides prepare breakfast, clients crawl from their tents and visit the 'groover' (a primitive toilet make from an ammunition box). With numb fingers, guides and clients pack, stow, and tie down gear in the raft. The cold, muddy water sings by. Guides invite clients to pilot a 'duckie' (one-person, inflatable rubber kayak). For several hours people paddle through an ever-changing landscape of breathtaking geological contrasts. They chart courses and negotiate their way down roaring giddy rapids. The trip is exhilarating and restful by turns. Occasionally, guides find eddies where they tie up to climb up the canyons to wonder at native American pictographs, archaeological sites, or early settlers' camps. About noon, there is a lunch break. Guides prepare a light meal; people chat and explore the tumbled boulders and cottonwood thickets around the lunch site.

The afternoons are much like the mornings. Usually the trip ties up at a prearranged camping spot around 4.00 pm. Clients and guides form a human chain to unload the boats; clients pitch tents, change out of wet clothes, and explore the area. Guides and clients prepare a hot dinner. After dinner guides may orchestrate games and stories; some clients may read the natural history literature that guides typically pack along. After relaxing around a fragrant campfire, enjoying the slice of star-spattered sky overhead, people normally retire by 9.00 pm, but guides often stay up later taking care of camp details and unwinding.

Table 4. Glossary of river terms

Boatman	The guide's preferred term for themselves; it lacks commercial connotations
Day bag	A small Dungee bag used for carrying supplies needed during the day when the other bags are stowed and tied down
Dry bag	*See* Dungee bag
Duckie	An open, rubber, inflatable kayak
Dungee bag	A rubberized, waterproof duffle bag, closed by rolling one end over and over and clipping the ends together
Fan hole	Drop-off of water running over a flat rock; watched for in order to avoid wrapping the raft around the unseen rock or boulder
Maytagged	Getting caught in a recirculating hole
Wrapped	Getting a raft hung up on a boulder in such a way that both ends of the boat are caught in the current and the middle is caught over the rock or boulder
Groover	Metal ammunition can, lined with plastic and used as a toilet; the name comes from effect of the can's edges on one's derriere
Oarboat	A raft that is rowed by a guide
Oarers	Rafters who merely sit on the boat while a guide rows
Paddle boat	A boat that is rowed by the customers under guide supervision
Paddler	A rafter who takes charge of rowing the boat under a guide's supervision
Put-in	A spot along the river bank where the rafts are set up, gear stowed, and from where the trip is launched
Recirculating hole	Imagine a whirlpool turned on its side; caused by the force of water dropping down forcefully over a rock ledge; dangerous for a swimmer to be caught in
River kill	Left-over food
Strainer	A pile-up of logs, sticks and other debris, usually by a river bank; extremely dangerous for duckies or individuals since the force of the water makes it difficult to extricate oneself from one
Take-out	A spot along the river bank where the rafts are broken down, gear unloaded, and the trip ends
Trip	A load of clients and one or more guides who travel together for as little as a few hours to as much as a few days

retrospective reports. Included are hints of the themes of pilgrimage, intensification and rediscovery of self, and communion with nature and others.

Expectations of the experience

Ambiguous and protected expectations of the experience are well illustrated in excerpts from field notes recorded during a trip with a group of alternate high schoolers and their counselors (5/90): 'One kid mentions that he's just started expecting the worst so he won't be disappointed. I ask what's the worst thing he's imagined happening. He says, not coming back. Then he tells me he wouldn't mind falling out, that would be a rush.'

One possible explanation for the vagueness of expressed expectations is that consumers may be motivated to imagine what their trip will be like, but ill equipped with expertise to construct such images. Another possible explanation is consumers' desire to preserve the spontaneous and unrehearsed characteristics of extraordinary experience (Abrahams, 1986). Written protocols reflecting back on the experience of river rafting suggest that limited expectations contribute to satisfaction with the experience (1/90): 'So much of the experience is the thrill of the unknown. Beyond all it is at least exhilarating. . . . Similar to a symphony when you must read several bars ahead of what you are already playing.'

Expectations of the guides

Customers rarely anticipated the affective role of the guides in orchestrating their experiences. Instead, customers hoped guides would be 'friendly', 'competent', 'safe', and 'knowledgeable'. A single, more experienced customer did express the hope that the guide would 'be genuinely interested in rafters, their interests and facilitate having fun'.

Expectations of others

Most inexperienced rafters have little sense of the importance of other rafters in constructing a satisfactory, shared river experience. Instead, customers hoped other rafters would be 'friendly', 'sharing', 'considerate', and 'sociable'. The same, more experienced rafter quoted above expressed a more sophisticated understanding of the camaraderie and sense of teamwork that, in fact, contribute to satisfaction in stating, 'Relaxed, honest, having fun and concerned about each other: releasing inhibitions is essential – being oneself; be paddlers not oarers'.

Comfort and safety

Inexperienced customers articulate simple, general desires for safety: 'knowing our daughter is safe'; 'that I don't drown'. Most fail to anticipate many factors that could affect their safety. Their concerns carry an undercurrent of fear of rafting – that this is something they might die doing. Such fears contribute to perception of the experience as extraordinary and set the stage for a rite of intensification that extends and renews the self.

Expectations about the environment

Consumers' expressed expectations about the natural environment are vague, but they are also romantic and consensual. In the first season's data the theme of a wild, clean, natural, isolated, and 'noncommercial' setting appeared explicitly in all but two of the pretrip expectations about the river and surroundings (6/90–8/90), for example: 'clean, with no signs of civilization, other than ourselves, to be intruding on the pristine environment'; 'clean, undisturbed by commercial ventures'. When expectations are specific, they are frequently wrong, as in these excerpts from a pretrip survey (6/91–8/91): 'clear blue river with large rapids'; 'grassy with a lot of trees and spacious. I want a good view with mountains'. In fact, Colorado River basin rivers are typically greenish brown and muddy, the canyons narrow, flora parched and spiny, and views obstructed by canyon walls.

A number of commercial cues reinforce consumer expectations of immersion in a pristine, uncivilized environment (2/90, 5/90, 4/91). Included are the logo used by one of our outfitters incorporating a Native American war shield, eagle feathers, and a motif of crossed arrows. Native Americans are popularly imagined as living in harmony with nature. Perhaps more significant, advertising brochures feature photographs of clients in scenic, wild settings. Supply lists provided by outfitters emphasize the absence of amenities, and the necessity of impact-free camping. These lists also stress that ready access to medical care and telecommunications is impossible. These and other cues build expectations of an almost sacred pilgrimage into a world 'untouched by civilization' (Belk, Wallendorf and Sherry, 1989).

Expectations about feelings

The feelings consumers reported expecting often derived from their beliefs about nature, for example, 'sense of isolation, serenity' and 'to be in the great outdoors and to go back to nature'. Consistent with our sense that consumers do not know what feelings to expect, comments such as 'river experiences' and just 'have fun' were common.

For the second season, data sampled a broader range of trips and outfitters. Expectations were collected closer to the actual trip, en route to the put-in (6/91–8/91). Still, expectations about guides, other rafters, and feelings were vague. Again, pretrip expectations about the natural environment were consensual and romantic. Of course, the richer experiential base of the enlarged sample yielded more variety, but the standard template remained the same. For example, in response to the question of expected feelings, one respondent wrote 'gratitude and surrender. "I wish to hear the silence of the night. . . . " Thoreau'. As suggested by first season findings, many of the feelings that people expected to experience related to the environment, but, without question, the most common response was 'to have fun' or a close variant. The theme of fear was much more pronounced in the second season's data, as illustrated in the following responses to what clients wanted in comfort and safety: 'that I come home alive' and 'that no one is negligent. Everyone is aware of existing dangers'.

We have observed that themes of personal growth and intensification of self emerge over the course of trips. We sought in the second season to explore whether people had pretrip expectations about personal growth and renewal. To minimize coaching we used a simple prompt 'I want to learn . . . '. Most responses could be described as skill acquisition expectations, for example 'how to read rapids and navigate them' or 'a little about rafting and camping'. A minority provided more existential responses: 'I can accomplish anything', 'more about myself, (strengths and weaknesses), and more about nature', 'what is really important in life (or start to learn)'. Even though the themes of personal growth and intensification are only vaguely articulated in pretrip commentary, among a minority of consumers there is some testimony for these themes at this early stage in the experience.

A more thorough investigation into pretrip planning in the second season revealed that people often choose a river trip in hopes of finding something different. Two verbatims illustrate this point: 'as a family vacation of more than just going somewhere, but doing something different' and 'new experience away from what I know'. In addition to the theme of doing something different, a related description revolved around doing 'something I've always wanted to'. In these descriptions the expectation of a life adventure is captured: 'I have just always felt that white water rafting would be exciting and fulfilling'. The combination of expressed expectations emphasizing newness and adventure evokes the theme of pilgrimage, leaving the familiar and known behind. These comments may also suggest why the narrative qualities of the experience, its storylike qualities, dominate in consumer reports of satisfaction. The only other frequently stated reason for trip selection focused on going at someone else's invitation or recommendation. Again the comments are unreflective, for example, 'My dad said let's go rafting. I said O.K. So here we are'; 'Well, my father gave me the pamphlet and he said, "Pick one", so I did'. In spite of these offhand comments, in both cases informants' posttrip comments reflect the discovery and renewal of self: 'I can do lots of things I never dreamed I could do. I gained a lot of self-confidence'; '[I learned] how to put confidence into myself'. Satisfactory meanings evolve over the course of the trip from these vague narrative expectations.

The experience of river rafting

Three main organizing themes associated with satisfying raft trips emerged early in our research. As we accumulated repeated traces of the themes across different methods we were able to name and interpret the fabric of these themes. The themes – communion with nature, communitas or connecting to others, and extension and renewal of self – link rafting to extraordinary experience. Participant observation field notes trace the evolution of these themes over the course of individual multiday rafting trips. In part, these experiences are guided by service providers; in part, they seem to be produced from unarticulated narrative expectations that clients already 'know' in some unspecified way.

Communion with nature

Weaving through all our data is an emergent feeling of rejuvenation associated with a sense of communion with nature. Two episodes from transcribed notes from one river trip suggest the guides' reverent feelings toward nature. At a particularly stupendous point in one canyon, a guide threw his arms wide and said to everyone within shouting distance, and no one in particular, 'You have to believe in something in a place like this'. The second episode occurred on the last night of a trip. An especially early start was planned for the next morning and the day would be very long. Most clients retired early, but the guides stayed up 'to watch the [full] moon come up over the canyon wall'. They sat on the beach with a few die-hard clients and waited until well after midnight for the full moon to rise.

Numerous examples from transcribed field notes illustrate an active role played by the guides in providing cues to facilitate consumers' communion with nature. For example, one of us wrote 'I remember at some point in the day someone had asked Mel [a guide] about the times in which we would do things. She said we'd get up when the sun got up and go to bed when the sun went down. We'd basically be on "river time". She had joked with me about getting rid of my watch. She says only the guides are allowed to have watches on the trip' (6/91).

Other rituals passed down through generations of river guides convey beliefs about the enduring power of nature and humans' vulnerability to immeasurable natural forces. At one point in the Yampa River, above a series of wild rapids, is a place called 'kissing rock'. Guides instruct clients in the tradition of kissing the rock in order to ensure safe passage of the 'dangerous' rapid below. Our photographs show paddlers of all ages kissing the rock. Thus, what is important is not so much what guides know, but the feeling and values they embody and communicate to customers.

Responding to these cues and the stunning natural setting, another excerpt from transcribed field notes (7/91) illustrates the sense of communion with nature rafting customers can create for themselves.

> And at the top of this hike there was a beautiful fresh spring waterfall. And it was fabulous. And it felt so good for everybody because everybody's been in dirty water since yesterday when we embarked on this trip . . . one of the college girls organized a group shot. . . . And in that group shot there was a clear intermingling of groups that included hugging and having arms around people who I think under other conditions would be considered strangers. . . . And it was a really wonderful shared moment. And we were all huddling in there and at the same time sharing space with each other so that no one was hogging the water.

Water provides a catalyst for a profound experience of nature for some; the impressive geology of the canyons provides this catalyst for others, as shown in this excerpt from participant observation field notes (6/91):

> After lunch, after cleanup, Mel organized a little hike up the cliff behind us to a site where there were model fossils of rock. I sort of got started early, as I wanted to. The others came along in a bit – single file. Mel talked a little about the geology. We showed off the fossils, talked a little about the fossil corals, rim rock and further up, krinoid stems. As she talked about those, people looked on appreciatively.

The trip orchestrates many opportunities for the participants to commune with nature. Some participants are affected by the water, others by geology, still others are moved by the wildlife, old settler's camps, starlit beaches, or the remains of Native American dwellings. The trip allows participants to share their experiences of nature; it operates for some as a sacred passage.

Communitas

A second theme prevalent in all our data is an evolving feeling of communion with friends, family, and strangers. This sense of communion, or communitas in Turner's (1974) dramaturgical framework, is illustrated below. Feelings of linkage, or belonging, of group devotion to a transcendent goal are facilitated by proximity forced by the narrow canyons, small camping areas, boats, and teamwork associated with rafting itself. The emergence of communitas varies in degree with the characteristics of the group coming into the trip. Nonetheless, it emerges in subtle ways over time. Guides impose rules and order on the trip from the beginning that prefigure the development of community. Excerpts from participant observation field notes of the teen trip (5/90) evoke this:

> A girl comes to ask the head chaperone, Rick [head of the group] whether she should take off her ring. It's loose, she explains. I notice she has hickies on her neck. Rick says yeah take it off. What about her friends with loose rings. I say take 'em off 'cause of blisters. Blisters? From rowing, I explain. She gets a glimmer of understanding on her face and goes off to tell her friends.

> People are invited to leave some gear behind in the cars and to pack other stuff out of the way for the day by Peter, by Tom [guides], and also by the head chaperone, so he gets the message. Peter announces there is rain gear for all of the boats. So is there a kind of homogenization, throwing off old roles implicit here? Kids load bags with cigarettes and other junk.

In a rite of passage, the creation of communitas typically begins with a casting off of goods that differentiate members in favor of shared goods (Turner, 1969; van Gennep, 1960). Thus, here the kids are urged to leave stuff behind and are informed that there is a uniform, that is, the life jacket and the rain gear, for all. Of course, there is resistance, too, and kids pack their bags with good emblematic of every day personae, for example, cigarettes, bandanas, and so on.

Guides invite the production of community, but people already seem to be prepared to perform in a communitarian way. Remarkably, some of the kids on the teen trip seemed to be acting in terms of a script favorable to the creation of community at the put-in. Thus, several girls offer to leave behind the 'friendship' rings emblematic of boyfriends who are not part of the group but remain in the everyday world at home.

Guides reinforce teamwork themes in a variety of ways. Field notes and photographs from each of the trips shows teamwork in loading and unloading supplies (e.g. passing 'dry bags' up and down the bank through a chain of clients), tying gear into the boats, cooking and doing dishes, and participating in campfire activities. Guides sometimes attempt to facilitate the development of community by leading people through various team-building games over the course of the trip. One set of transcribed participant observation field notes (6/91) said,

> The next game we played was a trust game where we stood in a tight circle and the person went in the middle, and went stiff and closed their eyes and we then sort of rocked them around the circle. Each person in turn did this. Bev hesitated at first, saying that she wasn't going to do this one, but finally she did . . . So this was an evening in which hair was much more let down . . . this was sort of a turning point I think in terms of the creation of community on the trip.

The lingering impact of these games is illustrated from the second morning of another set of transcribed participant observation field notes (7/91): 'I have to admit that that silly name game that we played last night probably has a lot to do with having loosened everybody up . . . there were several references all day long to names from the game and motions from the game . . . And that's weird because it's as if people were just looking for a way to do that'.

Norms of cooperation are further reinforced by helping behaviors among guides and between different outfitters on the many occasions when novice paddlers lose their paddles, boats become grounded, or rafts flip. In these and other instances guides provide cues to channel cooperative activity. Some clients seek out ways to help; other need guidance. Few refuse to become involved. Thus, guides invite and clients voluntarily transcend their passive role as service recipients (spectators) to take an active role in the production of community.

As the trips progress the opportunities for group experience accumulate. One excerpt from field notes provides an example of a playful context in which both the theme of communion with nature and that of communitas are evident:

> To create this waterfall faucet means that people have to block off the water with their bodies at several juncture points on this little stream so that the water accumulates. And then somebody stands under the place where the trickle of water is going down. And it creates a gushing waterfall that comes over on top of them. And I guess what was interesting about this was two things. First, it's real dependent on lots of bodies participating on the whole thing to make it happen. And it also meant getting real close together. 'Cause you have to put your bodies real close together in the little part of the stream where you're trying to block off the water. And that was – it was really fun.

After negotiating each stretch of white water, crews congratulate themselves and are typically congratulated by the guides. In one case, in the aftermath of an accident in which a boat turned over and everyone helped to right it, discussion often returned to whether equipment had dried out as in this excerpt from participant observation notes: 'It was a quiet morning in camp. People revived the discussion of things being wet. People were heard to exclaim, "Hey that pretty well dried out!" and "How are your sleeping bags, are they pretty well dried out?" and things of that nature'.

Participant observation research provided numerous illustrations of the evolution of community over the course of a three-day trip. Our photographs record some dramatic examples. One features a picture of four of the six high school girls braiding each other's hair into identical French braids. These girls were not friends when the trip began. What drove their emergent sense of identify was shared recognition of a common problem: their fear of the river, including shampooing their hair in it. This photograph was taken on the final day of the trip.

Participants' embodiments of communitas become particularly evident and striking as leave-taking approaches. Field notes from the final day of one four-day river trip reveal this evolution:

> Allen [a customer], at one point, said that we should all get together and do this again next year. That we should come as a group. And I think that's not something I had heard before. But it's real clear that he'd come to think of us as a group of people that belonged together as a good team. And that's funny because Becky and Rex, and really all of us were all so different from each other. And come from much different backgrounds and orientations and everything else. I mean Allen and Jane are the perfect yuppie couple. And Becky and Rex both chew tobacco. So it's quite a contrast.

Field notes from the end of this trip disclose the depth of emotional attachments formed among the members of the trip. There were lots of staged photographs of subsets of people who had not known one another at the beginning of the trip that symbolized the sense of community that had developed:

> So, one of the last parts of this ending here was that one of the people in the group of eleven suggested that everybody get into the bags that we had packed our stuff in. And so, many of us, absent Kate and Dennis and some of the people who weren't quite brave enough to jump into that shot, jumped into the bags and crowded together into a group shot . . . one of the guides who hadn't gone along on the trip took a picture with my camera and several other cameras were involved in taking pictures of that shot.

Communitas developed not only among the customers but between customers and the guides. In most of the field note illustrations provided, the guides were fully integrated into the experience as members of the team. Consistent with our conceptualization of the experience as a rite of intensification, photographs illustrate that affectionate, playful construction of a community that does not separate guides from clients, young from old, or rich from poor. People report thinking of the guide, not in service provider terms, but as a friend. Participant observation notes from the end of a trip (7/91) depict the emotionally charged, boundary open relationships that develop: 'It's real clear that Jeff [one of the guides] made an impact on people. And that a lot of people would come up to him and say, you made this trip for me . . . the people from Carbon wanted Jeff to come up and interview with the school in Carbon, because they thought he'd be a fabulous addition . . . and other people also were trying to make some kind of more permanent contact, at least with Jeff'.

Personal growth and renewal of self

A third theme evidenced in our data is a rediscovered sense of self. Rafting provides a simple, encapsulated world that offers participants 'a sense of place and purpose, a rationale for behavior', and guides for action (Donohue, 1991, p. 14). Our data help explain outfitter's apocryphal stories of successful East Coast accountants and business executives giving up their plush jobs for the life of a river guide after just one encounter with a wild, Western river.

Tangible elements of material culture, the physical evidence of which Bitner *et al.* (1990) speak, is of importance in personal growth and self-renewal. Consistent with many clients' articulated expectations, guides help clients acquire new skills. Demonstrating the use of safety equipment, paddling techniques, methods of tying down equipment, encouraging the use of the duckies and attempts to guide the paddle boats, cooking on a camp fire, and so on are among the myriad ways in which guides use props to 'provide new challenges' and 'make things fun'.

Progressive mastery over novel things and tools begins at the put-in and continues throughout the trip, as this excerpt from day 1 of participant observation field note suggests (5/90):

> When the troops [a dozen alternate high school students and their chaperones] arrive, Peter, the trip leader, takes charge. Kids are set off to pack and do a pretty good job of it, all breaking into twos to pack. The head chaperone, Rick, says some have never camped before. When they are about packed he has 'em carry the bags down. I note one kid checks in with Tom, one of the guides, to see if it's packed right. Before putting in, Peter gave a safety speech; did the thing about bouncing someone in a life-jacket to demonstrate how tight it should be. All stood around in a semicircle to watch this and listened to discussion of how to pull someone out of the water. There were 6–7/boat. Paddling not a big strength as yet. Noticed how people were willing to participate in it right away. People began to joke about paddling skills, began to be competitive with other boats right away. 'Let's ram the boat' kinds of stuff were said. Most of the kids were pretty willing to take guide (or steering) duty and tried to guide the boat under the guides' instructions.

Transcribed field notes from participant observation on day 4 of a trip illustrate the evolution and articulation of skill acquisition (6/91): 'Sandy [a guide] relinquished the oars to me today for the first time. I rode all the way to Warm Springs, about seven miles. . . . I noticed that at first Ike, then later Will, took a turn on the oars in the other boat as we rode on down the stream'.

Learning how to pack a rubberized dry bag, how to attach a life jacket, how to use it in an emergency, and how to manipulate a paddle provide tangible manifestations of the new skills and control the novice rafters gain from the first moments. As the trip progresses, skills are perceived to have been sharpened by the increasing speed, facility, and success with which rapids, loading and unloading, cooking chores, and unexpected incidents like drenched gear are negotiated.

Another part of the personal growth process is learning the new jargon that accompanies the boatman's skills and life-style. Naming and labeling are fundamental cultural processes; terminology provides cultural categories that stabilize the flux inherent in brute experience (Douglas and Isherwood, 1979, pp. 64–70). Thus, learning terms that seem arcane at first – 'put-in', 'oar boat', 'dungee bag', 'day bag', 'duckie', 'recirculating hole', 'fan hole', 'strainer', 'getting maytagged', 'groover', 'river kill', 'take-out' and so on – provide markers of personal control over experience (see Table 4).

Guides coach and communicate, by example and direct experience, something more than new skills. Most important is the notion that action on the river is charged not only with great serenity, but with imminent danger, that is, river magic, that transcends normal activity. Guides cater to clients' physical and existential fears about rafting; they also acknowledge clients when they overcome danger. A particularly overt example comes from participant observation notes of the teen trip. In anticipation of running some big rapids:

> Peter [a guide] gave a lecture in which he said everyone was doing really well and he knew a lot of people hadn't done something like this before . . . Peter ended with a story about fear [overcome]. [That evening] Ryan gave me back the quote [i.e. the supporting comment] more or less: 'Come to the edge, come to the edge'. 'No, we are afraid to come to the edge'. So they came to the edge. We pushed them off and they flew Mr. A pitched in, 'That's the gist of it'.

Clients internalize the sense of danger and obstacles overcome, contributing to a sense of personal intensification and renewal (Donohue, 1991; Klausner, 1968). Most clients have a safe, danger-free trip; however, many trips arouse life-and-death fears. Many trips include one or more accidents that people experience as truly 'close calls', or brushes with death. On the teen trip, an inappropriately clothed girl fell in the water and suffered early symptoms of hypothermia. On a trip during the second season, a raft overturned, a guide suffered a gashed forehead, clients lost eye glasses and caps, and camping equipment was drenched. On another trip someone's duckie became stuck in a 'strainer' and he was rescued from potentially serious trouble. Thus, field notes contain numerous references to 'the danger withstood' (Gergen and Gergen, 1988). The fear aroused by such experiences helps crystallize one's sense of self (Donohue, 1991). Reinforced with guides' and other rafters' stories of close calls, clients emerge with a sense of mastery and enhanced agency.

Recollections of the experience

Transcribed field notes (7/91) convey a sense of exhaustion and reentry into the everyday world: 'One of the things that we joked about as we were sitting around at the take-out, Russ reiterated how he thought that a scotch and soda, a cold, cold

Pepsi Cola, or cold Coca Cola with some ice cubes in it would really be something to be looking forward to and then perhaps a scotch and soda on ice after that'.

A client (9/90) reflecting back on his feelings at the end of the trip, remarked: 'I don't think you feel like you want to immediately go on another raft trip. What you're really interested in is having a shower, and a nice hot shower, and get in some dry clothes, and a martini'.

Also reflected in the reentry to the everyday world is a sense of being hit with the routines, noises and other features of everyday life. A focus group participant reflected on end-of-trip feelings talked about the 'yuk' mail. Then she continued in a more reflective vein: 'You let your perception all open up. All these defenses that we have, and take for granted, that we don't even think about them in the city, where you block out sounds, and you block out a lot of things. You haven't done that for a while. All of a sudden you come back. And that's one reason that we get hit so quickly'.

In one sense the trip ends at the take-out. But, as our data reflect, many years after a river trip, the memory lingers. Vivid recall of the experience is evidenced throughout retrospective reports, with comments such as that it 'made a lasting impression' or 'was an overwhelming experience'. One participant notes, 'Although it has been a long time, probably eight years, once I began writing, the feelings and sensations come right back'. Respondents vividly remember their rafting experience but find it difficult to describe. A consistent theme was, 'You almost have to do it to really understand the experience'. One participant said, 'It is easier for me to describe the intense moments experienced in rafting and these are perhaps more alive memories. Those longer periods of quiet solitude, which are just as vivid in my mind and heart, are somehow more difficult to put into words'.

Participants do not appear to want to engage in very much *cognitive* recall of the experience. It is as if river magic is best preserved if the associated feelings and sensations are not examined too closely. Comments from the client focus group (9/90) exemplify this resistance: 'You know, I've treated the trip as something to be enjoyed . . . I happen to be in academia. And so, what you need to do is get away from that atmosphere and do something else. And a raft trip is a way of doing that. So it's enjoyable and that's exactly how I look upon it. No point in making it all complicated'.

Evident in all of our data is that the experiences are productive of emotional outcomes, and in retrospect are often described in terms of these outcomes, as the following quotation shows (1/90): 'It is an experience that combines a multitude of feelings and emotions that could differ depending on a person's likes and dislikes and their fears'.

The narrative qualities of the experience and articulation of the interwoven themes of communion with nature, communitas, and extension and renewal of self become more pronounced with time and retelling.

Communion with nature

Posttrip responses to what were the best things that happened on the trip (6/90–8/90) contained numerous references to 'great scenery', 'natural environment', and the 'solitude of the canyons'. One rafter observed, 'The solitude in the vastness of the canyon was uplifting and exciting'. Nearly half of respondents (49%) mentioned natural environmental features as one of the best things that happened on their trip.

A particularly rich articulation of the communion with nature that derives from rafting in a river canyon was provided by a participant in our focus group (9/90): 'But in the river, there's something about the canyon and the river and the narrowness. There's a limited, you're not just limited by no noise from the city, or not, you know, bus stops and all. But you're limited by the wall or the beach . . . And go to look . . . up at the stars and you know, identify a few of the stars, that you know you can identify because the rest of them are blocked out, It just ah . . . in every way . . . '

First-season quantitative analyses provided statistical support for the relationship between a feeling of communion with nature and reported satisfaction with the trip. A seven-item scale (alpha = .84) measured communion with nature (scale items are included in the Appendix). The correlation of the 'communion with nature' scale and a six-item measure of overall trip satisfaction (alpha = .90) was .70 ($p < .001$).

Long afterward, the memory of the absorption in nature and the newness of perception associated with the trip linger. Recollections of what it is like to go river rafting (1/90) carry these themes: 'As the river carves its way through majestic canyons one can feel the inner sense of fulfillment that only nature can bring out'. 'It gives you a chance to see things one wouldn't see unless they partook in the experience. It is an experience that allows you to witness the beauty and the immense power of our natural environment'.

Data from the second season echo the theme of communion with nature. Comments suggest the newness of perception and melding with nature characteristic of this experience. When asked to describe the river and surroundings, people wrote: 'Stark, but beautiful. There was a grandness and awsomeness in the sheer walls and steadily changing slopes of the river and the rocks. It was unhurried and restful'. 'Peaceful, I felt at times like a child seeing things for the first time. I was in awe. Sometimes we tend not to appreciate our own country. We want to visit outside the USA. Colorado is wonderful'.

Quantitative analyses from second-season data again support the importance of communion with nature in trip satisfaction. On the basis of our experiences during the first season we revised slightly our measure of communion with nature (scale items for season 2 are included in the Appendix). Correlation of the revised six-item scale (alpha = .86) with overall trip satisfaction (alpha = .93) was .61 ($p < .001$).

Communitas

In the first season, one-third of posttrip responses (6/90–8/90) made mention of interactions with others as one of the best things that happened on the trip. Examples include 'our family being together', 'friendships you would form', and 'comradeship'.

Vivid articulation of the communion with others that derives from rafting in a river canyon were provided by focus group verbatims (9/90) in response to a moderator's probe about the 'most appealing aspect' of rafting: 'Even people you didn't know, you met them and you get to know them real well on the river, and then you maybe never see them again. But for those few days, you know, you shared something in a really intimate way'.

A sense of communitas is not produced merely by shared experience. Shared 'edgework' (Lyng, 1990), such as working a craft through dangerous rapids, more quickly creates a sense of communion, one that differs somewhat from that built up over the course of the trip. Another verbatim from the focus group suggests this dynamic: 'And so there's a bonding that occurs pretty quickly I think, when you come through an experience that frightens you, or intimidates you or excites you. Guess everyone's emotional levels are going pretty high, and it's through teamwork that you're going to get through this experience. And when you come through it on that other side of the rapids, you're a little bit closer than you were when you went in'.

In the first season, we developed the communitas scale on the basis of repeated comments from outfitters, guides, and river trip participants to the effect that being with family and connecting with others gives a 'new perspective on life' and helped participants see 'what really matters'. One outfitter emphasized how she developed her rafting business partly because of the unique ability of the river experience to change interpersonal dynamics and transform individual perspectives: 'Among peer groups, it really changes around patterns of interaction, urban leader may be pushed onto the back burner . . . it is a learning experience beyond anything I've ever gone through. Day three on the water is the dramatic changing point. . . . This is the fastest transition period we've found for any outdoor kind of experience, this day three thing. You get a lot of leaders among the adult trips'.

Quantitative analyses support the relationship between communion with others and reported satisfaction with the trip. Communitas was measured by a four-item scale (alpha = .82; scale items are provided in the Appendix). The correlation of the scale and the six-item measure of overall trip satisfaction is .71 ($p < .001$).

Long afterward, unguided retrospective reports of going river rafting include this theme of communitas (1/90): 'When you're with friends, very few things can compare to the bond you create because it's a team sport. You overcome the scary spots together and then laugh together as the water splashes at you'. 'You develop a team attitude and form close bonds with raft partners'.

Posttrip survey responses in the second season of research provided even richer articulations of communitas, again stressing the rapid sense of communion with strangers very different from oneself (6/91–8/91). For example, when asked what they had learned, one participant said: 'I learned that group success sometimes requires sacrificing of self. I learned that people from varied backgrounds are very much the same and can and do have fun together'.

Posttrip survey responses also pointed to the incorporation of guides into the community, supporting interpretation of this service encounter as a boundary open transaction. These responses to guides are typical of posttrip comments: 'Like a true friend after only a couple of hours'. 'Let us in on her personal life, told great stories, well educated on surroundings, the type of person I would like for a sister'.

Quantitative results from the second season of research again supported the role of communitas in trip satisfaction. By the end of the first season we had an improved understanding of the nature of feelings of community. Correlation of a significantly revised six-item scale (alpha = .90) measuring sense of community with overall trip satisfaction was .55 ($p < .001$).

Personal growth and renewal of self

First-season posttrip responses to the question of the best things that happened on the trip (6/90–8/90) contain allusions to self-discovery as well as numerous references to feelings of adventure, challenge, and excitement. Examples include 'discover internal strengths', 'proving to myself I could handle the trip (camping/rapids)' or 'surviving overturned raft'. The progressive mastery over novel things and tools is suggested by this verbatim about 'duckies' given as a response to the 'best part of the trip': 'The fun of kayaking down rapids like Crystal and Spector and ending up right side up at the end and feeling like I was somewhat in control!'

Focus groups (5/90, 9/90) provided rafters with an opportunity to express more fully feelings of self-discovery, awareness, achievement, and personal transformation, that is, the impact of a ritual of intensification on sense of self. A river guide trainee summarized the impact of his past few weeks on the river in the following terms (5/90): 'Learned bunch of things. How tired you can be doing physical work. How selfish and petty one can be when we're outside of our comfort zones. To find these things out, and reiterate from time to time keeps us humble. Being able to assess a situation slowly gives you the concrete things. Discover what you like and don't like'.

From the client focus group (9/90) we heard these comments: 'Yeah, I mean in my case it was definitely a skills-building activity. Where you start out and you're a little bit uncomfortable and you kind of establish a better comfort zone or a wider comfort zone'. 'The thing that I enjoyed the most was the risk involved, and the fact that you were able to overcome the risk at the end. . . . It's the fact that, wow, I really did do that. And you feel real positive when you get all done. . . . And I guess the next best part, [is] to know that you can rely on most people'.

Comments from the focus group (9/90) substantiated field observations about the importance of the guide in orchestrating personal growth and renewal: 'And he seemed very confident and built all our confidence up around him. And I think it really helped near the end of the trip when he let us take turns guiding. And we'd all sit in the back of the boat and try and give commands and try to get the boat to go certain directions. And it was so hard for us, and we'd screw things up so much that by the time we sat back in our position as paddlers, we had a lot more respect for Doug, because we felt like, oh, this job is hard'.

Quantitative analyses support the relationship between personal growth and renewal of self and reported satisfaction with the trip. A six-item scale (alpha = .84) measured personal growth and renewal (scale items are provided in the Appendix). The correlation between this scale and a seven-item measure of overall satisfaction is .65 ($p < .001$).

Recollections of river rafting (1/90) depicted themes common to positive experience including absorption and integration, personal control, joy and valuing, and spontaneous letting-be of the process. In addition to the themes illustrated below, the theme of 'newness of perception and process' characteristic of extraordinary experience was evident. These themes provide an environment for a rite of intensification instrumental in experiencing personal growth: 'Going river rafting is a natural high. It is you and the water . . . all your problems are forgotten and one can use their body and feel all the muscles work in harmony'. 'The only sounds you hear are the water splashing and its flow through the rapids and a few yells and screams of pleasure from companions. You feel the water pushing underneath and around the raft. And the feel of humidity and wetness all around. Your body is under the control of the rapids and you ride the raft'.

Recollections of going river rafting (1/90) contain mentions of renewed self-awareness, rejuvenation, skill enhancement, testing limits, and personal achievement: '[You] develop a personal enrichment especially if you encounter a situation in which you become frightened and overcome the obstacle of the situation. And finally, long after its done, even years later, you'll find your mind escaping/returning back to the journey and reliving the thrill and when you encounter a situation in life where you're afraid or unsure the river experience often enables you to overcome it because you are inevitably more self-assured'.

Posttrip survey responses in the second season included a prompt on what clients felt they learned from their rafting experience. In contrast to pretrip expectations, which were primarily skill acquisition related, only a few posttrip responses could be so characterized. Even in those cases, the use of exclamation marks suggests some greater accomplishment. For example, one client who expected to learn 'how to live in the outdoors', reported after his trip that he learned 'I can "captain" a raft!' In general, what clients reported learning was very different from what they initially reported wanting to learn. Obviously, if we had asked instead 'Did you learn boat skills as you expected?' they would probably have responded yes. However, what stuck in their minds was other things, and the verbatims read like a compendium of life wisdoms: 'It is better to try and fail, rather than to not try at all'; 'So much worry over stupid things in the world'; or 'Patience, understanding'.

Quantitative analyses from second-season posttrip responses again supported the importance of personal growth and renewal in overall trip satisfaction. Based on our first-season research experiences, the same six-item scale (alpha = .91) measured personal growth and renewal (items are included in the Appendix). The correlation of this measure with overall trip satisfaction was .62 ($p < .001$).

Links between themes

Evident in both research seasons and across different research methods was the close linking of the themes. The link with nature and the separation from 'civilization' plays a role in the creation of communitas: 'What you really do is just for the sheer enjoyment of being together. And this is a way of insuring that, because we don't get together very often in that kind of an experience without taking the time to do something away from the helter skelter activity of daily living. So it [rafting] forces you to do it more than anything else'.

Several other focus group comments substantiate the relationship between isolation in a natural environment and the creation of communitas: 'We were removed from all those other peripheral things and so we were able to focus on our friendship and concentrate on each other and our interaction with each other was much better than we would've been able to do in another setting'.

Similarly, verbatims about learning to trust, to lead, to get along with others, and to be part of a team suggest a close connection between a sense of communitas and personal growth. The close interplay between self, nature, and others is evidenced in verbatims again and again. Many verbatims already provided play on how the rediscovered self emerges in the natural setting and through interactions with others.

Quantitative analyses in the first season suggested that the three experiential themes are highly correlated, ranging from .64 to .71 ($p < .001$). Because of the small sample size for posttrip survey responses in the first season ($n = 43$), it was not appropriate to factor analyze the items for the three experiential themes to establish unidimensionality. Ordinary least squares (OLS) regression with the three experiential themes as predictor variables and overall trip satisfaction as the dependent variable yields an adjusted R^2 of .57 ($F = 16.57$, $p < .001$). Because of potential multicollinearity among the three predictor variables, interpreting the individual betas and *t*-values may be problematic. However, OLS results are fairly robust for these levels of correlation between the predictor variables and for the level of R^2 reported (Mason and Perreault, 1991).

With the larger sample size available in season 2 posttrip survey responses, we confirmed that the three themes are related but separate components of rafting satisfaction. Because of our experience during season 1, the revised item pool generated for season 2 data collection seemed effective in capturing the constructs. Very little adjustment to the hypothesized scales was required in season 2. On the basis of initial reliability analyses two items were dropped from the personal growth scale (from eight back to six) and two items were dropped from the communitas scale (from eight to six). Next, an unconstrained principal components factor analysis yielded three factors with eigenvalues greater than one. Together, these three factors explain 66% of the variance. All items loaded on the expected factor and no cross-loadings exceeded .40. The rotated factor solution is included in the Appendix. Of course, the themes are related, with correlations ranging between .52 and .57. The OLS solution with overall satisfaction as the dependent variable and the three experiential themes as predicted variables results in an adjusted R^2 of .46 ($F = 34.05$, all *t*-values are significant at $p < .05$).

The narrative of a rafting experience

Looking across the pretrip planning process to the culmination of the trip in a series of affectively charged recollections, we are struck by the importance of the entire narrative in understanding the experience. Consequently, the disconfirmation paradigm is not a particularly useful metaphor for interpreting satisfaction with this experience. Significant deviations from even vaguely articulated expectations are common, and the link between confirmation of expectations and satisfaction is weak.

Deviations from expectations

In advance of the trip, it is difficult for clients to grasp the taken-for-granted world of river rafting aficionados and the romance they experience in their outdoor life.

Similarly, outfitters do not always anticipate the gap between the assumptions of clients and the realities of river trips. In short, outcomes differ from expectations. Unanticipated realities are commonly expressed in posttrip comments (6/90–8/90). Examples include 'I didn't expect to have wet feet for six days', 'I was disappointed at the flat water on a three day trip. I was hoping for more white water' (long stretches of flat water between rapids), 'the necessity of washing in muddy river water, the lack of privacy', 'sleeping on the hard ground', and so on.

Guides and outfitters are frequently indifferent to aspects of the trip that subsequently surprise clients. For example, a wealthy client and his family were disappointed to discover that the water in the Green River was not, in fact, green, but rather a muddy brown, and that the scenery was desert rather than lush forest. They demanded the outfitter arrange for helicopter transport out of the wilderness area. Dissuaded, the family was 'ecstatic' at the end of their trip, and later wrote to the outfitter to explain that the trip had brought them together (field notes; 2/90).

Weak link between expectations and satisfaction

Satisfaction may have little if anything to do with confirmation of expectations. The client focus group (9/90) hints at a weak link between expectations and satisfaction. At one point a client explains that 'the rapids were a little better than I'd imagined they would be'. As the conversation develops, it turns out this is an understatement. The whole raft turned over on a rapid; he was first trapped underneath, and then 'went almost a mile through two other major rapids on his own'. This even provoked the couple to unusual action, 'We came home and made some arrangements. With our lives and affairs'. Their concluding remarks suggest, 'But in any event, it was a, it was a very exciting trip', and 'It was wonderful. On the way home we were already thinking of what one [i.e. river] next'. Thus, satisfaction may derive from having survived an unexpected challenge.

Weak links between expectations and satisfaction may be due to the complexity of satisfaction with extraordinary experience. One participant's description of her reactions to the experience captures the complexity particularly well (1/90):

> For me, river rafting is a horrible thing, I am scared to death of water. . . . I have to admit – it was the most exciting thing I've done in a long time. I never felt safe, but I did start to feel like I wasn't in complete danger. For the first 15 to 20 minutes it was pure terror. . . . By the end of the day – I'd been thrown all over the raft. I was soaking wet, I was very drained because I'd been tense all day long, but I felt very invigorated . . . it is challenging, exciting, thrilling, exhausting, and I'd recommend it highly.

Data from season 2 allow an explicit comparison between pretrip expectations and posttrip responses on several features of the trip including setting, guides, people, feelings, safety, and learning. In each category, deviations from expectations were common, and many have detailed in previous sections. The rivers and setting were majestic, but 'brown' and 'desolate', not 'green' and 'lush'. The guides were more than informative and skilled, they were friends and members of a team. The people were not just friendly, but bonded together in a rite of intensification. People did not just learn how to oar the raft, but learned about themselves and life. Some additional illustrations of the complexity of the narrative come from comparing feelings people expected with feelings they reported having. Typical pretrip and posttrip responses are illustrative:

Expected: Satisfaction.
Actual: Big mood swings. Bad mood to being in awe.
Expected: Exhilaration, peacefulness.
Actual: Some frustration, exhilaration, and mostly ratification. I felt a sense of accomplishment that I finished something which was very challenging. The experiences I had will last forever; going under the waterfall, the rock climbing, leading my boat through the rapids, just everything.

DISCUSSION AND IMPLICATIONS

> Experiences, like tales, fetes, potteries, rites, dramas, images, memoirs, ethnographies, and allegorical machineries, are made; and it is such made things that make them.
> [Geertz, 1986, p. 380]

White water river rafting provides a dramatic illustration of complex features of delivering 'extraordinary experience'. Because of the complexity of the domain and the difficulty of acquiring rich and representative data, multiple methods were employed to articulate the lived meaning of this experience from both the guides' and the consumers perspectives. No data set stands on its own as sufficient evidence of the narrative. Each data set can be criticized on one or more criteria (Arnould and Wallendorf, 1993). Together, however, they converge to tell a story about 'river magic'.

River rafting is a unique recreational form, but its power lies in the romantic cultural scripts that evolve over the course of the experience – the opportunity to participate in rites of intensification and integration and to return to an everyday world 'transformed'. Although the form is unique, the cultural script is exceedingly common and increasingly sought (Cohen, 1989; Krippendorf, 1987; MacCannell, 1989). White water river rafting is viewed in individuals' narratives as an unforgettable, affectively charged experience. Consistent with research on extraordinary experiences, river rafting provides absorption and integration, personal control, joy and valuing, a spontaneous letting-be of the process, and a newness of perception and process. Dimensions of extraordinary experience manifest themselves in the themes of harmony with nature, communitas, and personal growth and renewal. These experiential themes are evidenced across all the data; they evolve and are woven together over the course of the trip. Together, the three themes are significant in explaining overall satisfaction. Both qualitative and quantitative results support the value of viewing the themes as an interactive gestalt instead of trying to separate the contributions of the three themes.

In the current historical and cultural context, it can be argued that these three themes are deeply frustrated values that American consumers seek and prize. For many consumers intense, positive experiences crystallize selfhood, provide life meaning and perspective, confer awareness of one's own morality, reduce anxiety, and improve fear coping (Abrahams, 1986; Celsi *et al.*, 1993; Donohue, 1991; Ewert, 1988; Ewert and Hollenhorst, 1989; Solomon, 1988). Some authors think the value placed on intense, positive experiences is a reaction against the commercialization of meaning and segmentation and specialization of roles in the workplace (Csikszentmihalyi, 1990; Cushman, 1990; Ewen, 1988; Giddens, 1991, p. 9). In services ranging from fast food to birthing classes, providers could, and sometimes do, stress one or more of these three themes. Although it may seem a stretch to promise a renewed sense of self from stopping at McDonald's for breakfast, several award-winning advertisements do just that. Incorporation of these themes in service provision may be both unexpected and highly satisfying for consumers.

The subtle role of the guide in orchestrating delivery of an extraordinary experience is revealed in field notes, photos, and focus groups. Emotional outcomes associated with extraordinary experience are embedded in relationships between customer and service provider. Previous research has discussed neither the interactive dimension of extraordinary experiences nor the association between extraordinary experience and commercial service encounters. Our findings suggest that guides, partly at their own invitation, are inducted into the community as friends and team players. The rite of intensification into which the guide is bound by the experience of clients changes the nature of interaction in fundamental ways, shifting it into a boundary open transaction between provider and customer that transcends commercial interaction. The guide exemplifies a service role of increasing importance as more and more people buy experiences to give their lives meaning (Ewert and Schreyer, 1990).

We have drawn attention here to the role of guides in providing expressive models that 'socialize' river rafting participants into intrinsically meaningful experiences over the course of the river trip (Csikszentmihalyi, 1981, pp. 338–339). At the same time we have suggested that participants in river rafting experiences bring their own preconscious scripts to these travel 'performances' (Adler, 1989). These scripts prepare them for a pilgrimage, orchestrated by the guides, into a sacred place where pilgrims and guides are bonded together. For many the river trip is a rite of intensification that emotionally links people widely scattered and dissimilar in ordinary life. The pilgrim returns affirmed and renewed. The experience itself is vividly recalled but difficult to describe because of its emotional content and perceived distinctiveness.

There is a complex relationship between client expectations and satisfaction with extraordinary experience. The narrative of the experience is central to overall evaluation. For these experiences, participants may access an array of culturally informed, preconscious scripts or narrative themes (e.g. overcoming adversity through personal initiation or the quintessentially romantic story of the self-perfecting self, as in the novels of Herman Hesse or Carlos Castenads (Campbell, 1987). Or their expectations may be loosely formed. Or they may protect expectations of hedonic outcomes from reasoned anticipation. Finally, consumers invited to enact unfamiliar scripts may experience as much satisfaction as, or greater satisfaction than, with familiar scripts. In each case, satisfaction may have little to do with whether the experience unfolds as expected. These findings are at odds with a disconfirmation paradigm of service satisfaction.

To say merely that people like to be surprised would understate the import of our findings. The important point is that people may be unable or unwilling to articulate the meanings they really seek from many service encounters and especially service encounters that offer something 'extraordinary'. Therefore, deciphering the unarticulated meanings that people seek becomes more important to service provision that recording articulated expectations. Mechanically linking managerial decisions to stated consumer expectations does not necessarily lead to increased customer satisfaction.

In summary, many of the reported findings may have implications for a broad array of services and consumption activities. Recognizing the danger of over-generalizing beyond the current context, future research should explore the relevance of our research findings to other service and consumption experience contexts. First, our findings argue for more attention to the temporal moments of a consumption experience when assessing satisfaction. Theory and research on a range of other service encounters is beginning to suggest that knowing the story and the ending can be crucial in distinguishing between particularly satisfying and particularly unsatisfying interactions (Bitner *et al.*, 1990; Deighton, 1992). Second, our findings argue for more attention to underlying cultural scripts in examining consumption experiences and satisfaction with those experiences. The universalizing of the particular and the particularizing of the universal are evident in the experience of river rafting but might easily be mapped to other consumption experiences as well (Kapferer, 1986, p. 191). Confirmation of particular expectations may be far less important than conformance of an experience to an often unarticulated cultural script. Finally, our findings argue for more attention to boundary open transactions where the demarcation between service provider and client are blurred (at least from the client's perspective). More research is needed to explore the implications of exchanges that transcend commercial interactions for behaviors such as tipping, repeat purchase, and service provider role stress.

APPENDIX

Measures

Table A1. Construct measures: experiential themes

Season 1	Season 2
Harmony with nature:	
I felt	
1. Harmony with nature	1. Same
2. Like I explored new worlds	2. Same
3. I escaped into a different world	3. Same
4. Satisfied with wilderness scenery	4. I got a new perspective on nature
5. Freedom from obligations	5. Same
This rafting trip	
6. Was like getting away from it all	6. Same
7. Make me fell like I was in a different world	

Table A1. Construct measures: experiential themes *continued*

Season 1	Season 2
Communitas:	
I felt	
1. Satisfied with being part of a team	1. In harmony with others
2. Closer to friends/family	2. I interacted well with others
3. I got a new perspective on life	3. I made new friends
4. I rediscovered what really matters	4. My skills were appreciated by others
	5. Needed by the group
	6. I pulled my weight
Personal growth and renewal:	
I felt	
1. A sense of adventure or risk	1. Same
2. Personally challenged	2. Same
3. An adrenalin rush	3. Same
4. I learned new things	4. Same
5. I mastered new skills	5. Same
6. I tested my limits	6. Same

Table A2. Unconstrained factor solution: principal components analysis with varimax rotation

	Factor 1	Factor 2	Factor 3
Harmony with nature:			
1	.13	.16	.64
2	.17	.12	.76
3	.18	.27	.81
4	.36	.20	.65
5	.16	.16	.68
6	.13	.23	.76
Communitas:			
1	.02	.76	.34
2	.11	.83	.21
3	.21	.71	.28
4	.35	.74	.29
5	.34	.79	.13
6	.38	.67	.04
Personal growth:			
1	.72	.19	.27
2	.83	.19	.14
3	.76	.29	.11
4	.74	.09	.26
5	.77	.15	.22
6	.87	.24	.14

$n = 126$.

ACKNOWLEDGMENTS

We wish to thank Bill and Jaci Dvorak, Patrick Tierney, Lisa Penaloza, Rick Perdue, and four reviewers for their useful recommendations.

REFERENCES

Abrahams, R. D. (1986) 'Ordinary and Extraordinary Experience'. In *The Anthropology of Experience* (V. W. Turner and E. M. Bruner, Eds). Urbana: University of Illinois Press, pp. 45–73.

Adler, J. (1989) 'Travel as Performed Art'. *American Journal of Sociology* **94**(6): 1366–1391.

Arnould, E. J. and Wallendorf, M. (1993) 'Market-oriented Ethnography'. Working paper, Department of Marketing, California State University, Long Beach, 90840.

Belk, R. W., Wallendorf, M. and Sherry, J. F. (1989) 'The Sacred and the Profane in Consumer Behavior: Theodicy on the Odyssey'. *Journal of Consumer Research* **16** (June): 1–38.

Bettenhausen, K. and Murnighan, J. K. (1985) 'The Emergency of Norms in Competitive Decision-making Groups'. *Administrative Science Quarterly* **30** (September): 350–372.

Bitner, M. J. (1990) 'Evaluating Service Encounters: The Effects of Physical Surroundings and Employee Responses'. *Journal of Marketing* **54** (April): 69–82.

Bitner, M. J. (1992) 'Servicescapes: The Impact of Physical Surroundings on Customers and Employees'. *Journal of Marketing* **56** (April): 57–71.

Bitner, M. J., Booms, B. H. and Tetreault, M. S. (1990) 'The Service Encounter: Diagnosing Favorable and Unfavorable Incidents'. *Journal of Marketing* **54** (January): 71–84.

Boas, M. and Chain, S. (1976) *Big Mac: The Unauthorized Story of McDonalds.* New York: Dutton.

Botterill, D. T. (1987) 'Dissatisfaction with a Construction of Satisfaction'. *Annals of Tourism Research* **14**(1): 139–140.

Bruner, E. M. (1986) 'Ethnography as Narrative'. In *The Anthropology of Experience* (V. W. Turner and E. M. Bruner, Eds). Urbana: University of Illinois Press, pp. 139–158.

Campbell, C. (1987) *The Romantic Ethic and the Spirit of Modern Consumerism.* Oxford: Blackwell.

Celsi, R., Rose, R. L. and Leigh, T. W. (1993) 'An exploration of high-risk leisure consumption through skydiving', *Journal of Consumer Research* **20** (June): 1–23.

Cohen, E. (1989) '"Primitive and Remote" Hill Tribe Trekking in Thailand'. *Annals of Tourism Research* **16**(1): 30–61.

Coon, C. (1958) *Caravan: The Story of the Middle East.* New York: Holt, Rinehart.

Csikszentmihalyi, M. (1975) *Beyond Boredom and Anxiety: The Experience of Play in Work and Games.* San Francisco: Jossey-Bass.

Csikszentmihalyi, M. (1981) 'Leisure and Socialization'. *Social Forces* **60** (December): 332–340.

Csikszentmihalyi, M. (1985) 'Reflections on Enjoyment'. *Perspectives in Biology and Medicine* **28** (Summer): 489–497.

Csikszentmihalyi, M. (1990) *Flow: The Psychology of Optimal Experience.* New York: Harper & Row.

Csikszentmihalyi, M. and LeFevre, J. (1989) 'Optimal Experience in Work and Leisure'. *Journal of Personality and Social Psychology* **56**(5): 815–822.

Cushman, P. (1990) 'Why the Self Is Empty: Towards a Historically Situated Psychology'. *American Psychologist* **45** (May): 599–611.

Czepiel, J. A., Solomon, M. R., Surprenant, C. F. and Gutman, E. G. (1985) 'Service Encounters: An Overview'. In *The Service Encounter: Managing Employee/Customer Interaction in Service Businesses* (J. A. Czepiel *et al.*, Eds). Lexington, MA: Lexington, pp. 3–16.

Deighton, J. (1992) 'The Consumption of Performance'. *Journal of Consumer Research* **19** (December): 362–372.

Denzin, N. K. (1983) 'A Note on Emotionality, Self, and Interaction'. *American Journal of Sociology* **89** (September): 402–409.

Donohue, J. (1991) 'Dancing in the Danger Zone: The Martial Arts in America'. Paper presented at the annual meeting of the Association for Consumer Research, Chicago.

Douglas, M. and Isherwood, B. (1979) *The World of Goods.* Harmondsworth: Penguin.

Durgee, J. F., Holbrook, M. B. and Sherry, J. F., Jr. (1991) 'The Delivery of Vacation Performances'. In *Highways and Buyways: Naturalistic Research from the Consumer Behavior Odyssey.* (R. W. Belk, Ed.). Provo, UT: Association for Consumer Research, pp. 131–140.

Ewen, S. (1988) *All Consuming Images.* New York: Basic.

Ewert, A. (1988) 'Reduction of Trait Anxiety through Participation in Outward Bound'. *Leisure Sciences* **10**(2): 107–117.

Ewert, A. and Hollenhurst, S. (1989) 'Testing the Adventure Model: Empirical Support for a Model of Risk Recreation Participation'. *Journal of Leisure Research* **21**(2): 124–139.

Ewert, A. and Shreyer, R. (1990) 'Risk Recreation Trends and Implications for the 1990s'. Paper presented at Outdoor Recreation TRENDS Symposium III. Indianapolis.

Featherstone, M. (1991) *Consumer Culture and Postmodernism.* Newbury Park, CA: Sage.

Fiebelkorn, S. (1985) 'Retail Service Encounter Satisfaction: Model and Measurement'. In *The Service Encounter: Managing Employee/Customer Interaction in Service Businesses* (J. A. Czepiel *et al.*, Eds). Lexington, MA: Lexington, pp. 181–193.

Geertz, C. (1986) 'Making Experiences, Authoring Selves'. In *The Anthropology of Experience* (V. W. Turner and E. M. Bruner, Eds). Urbana: University of Illinois Press, pp. 373–380.

Gergen, K. J. and Gergen, M. M. (1988) 'Narrative and the Self as Relationship'. In *Advances in Experimental Social Psychology,* Vol. 21 (L. Berkowitz, Ed.). San Diego, CA: Academic Press, pp. 17–56.

Giddens, A. (1991) *Modernity and Self-Identity: Self and Society in the Late Modern Age.* Stanford, CA: Stanford University Press.

Grove, S. J. and Fisk, R. P. (1992) 'The Service Experience as Theater'. In *Advances in Consumer Research,* Vol. 19 (J. F. Sherry, Jr. and B. Sternthal, Eds). Provo, UT: Association for Consumer Research, pp. 455–461.

Havlena, W. J. and Holbrook, M. B. (1986) 'The Varieties of Consumption Experience: Comparing Two Typologies of Emotion in Consumer Behavior'. *Journal of Consumer Research* **13** (December): 394–404.

Hawes, D. K. (1978) 'Satisfactions Derived from Leisure-Time Pursuits: An Exploratory Nationwide Survey'. *Journal of Leisure Research* **10**(4): 247–264.

Heywood, J. L. (1987) 'Experience Preferences of Participants in Different Types of River Recreation Groups'. *Journal of Leisure Studies* **19**(1): 1–12.

Hirschman, E. (1984) 'Experience Seeking: A Subjectivistic Perspective of Consumption'. *Journal of Business Research* **12**: 115–136.

Hirschman, E. and Holbrook, M. B. (1982) 'Hedonic Consumption: Emerging Concepts, Methods, and Propositions'. *Journal of Marketing* **46** (Summer): 92–101.

Hochschild, A. R. (1983) *The Managed Heart.* Berkeley and Los Angeles: University of California Press.

Holbrook, M. B. (1987) 'O, Consumer, How You've Changed: Some Radical Reflections on the Roots of Consumption'. In *Philosophical and Radical Thought in Marketing* (A. F. Firat *et al.*, Eds). Lexington, MA: Lexington, pp. 137–177.

Holbrook, M. B. (1990) 'Presidential Address: The Role of Lyricism in Research on Consumer Emotions: Skylark, Have You Anything to Say to Me?' In *Advances in Consumer Research,* Vol. 17 (M. Goldberg *et al.*, Eds). Provo, UT: Association for Consumer Research, pp. 1–18.

Holbrook, M. B., Chestnut, W., Oliva, T. A. and Greenleaf, E. A. (1984) 'Play as a Consumption Experience: The Roles of Emotions, Performance, and Personality in the Enjoyment of Games'. *Journal of Consumer Research* **11** (September): 728–739.

Holbrook, M. B. and Hirschman, E. (1982) 'The Experiential Aspects of Consumption: Consumer Fantasies, Feelings, and Fun'. *Journal of Consumer Research* **9** (September): 132–140.

Holbrook, M. B. and Zirlin, R. B. (1985) 'Artistic Creation, Artworks, and Esthetic Appreciation: Some Philosophical Contributions to Nonprofit Marketing'. In *Advances in Nonprofit Marketing,* Vol. 1 (R. W. Belk, Ed.). Greenwich, CT: JAI Press, pp. 1–54.

Hollenhorst, S. and Olson, D. (1990) 'Trends in Organizational and Institutional Use of Wilderness: The Case of the Boundary Waters Canoe Area Wilderness'. Paper presented at Outdoor Recreation TRENDS Symposium III, Indianapolis.

Howard, G. S. (1991) 'Culture Tales: A Narrative Approach to Thinking, Cross-cultural Psychology and Psychotherapy'. *American Psychologist* **46** (March): 187–197.

Johnson, D. M. (1981) 'Disney World as Structure and Symbol: Re-creation of the American Experience'. *Journal of Popular Culture* **15**(1): 157–165.

Kapferer, B. (1986) 'Performance and the Structuring of Meaning and Experience'. In *The Anthropology of Experience* (V. W. Turner and E. M. Bruner, Eds). Urbana: University of Illinois Press, pp. 188–206.

King, M. J. (1981) 'Disneyland and Walt Disney World: Traditional Values in Futuristic Form'. *Journal of Popular Culture* **15**(1): 116–140.

King, S. and Straub, P. (1984) *The Talisman.* New York: Viking.

Klaus, P. G. (1985) 'Quality Epiphenomenon: The Conceptual Understanding of Quality in Face-to-Face Service Encounters'. In *The Service Encounter: Managing Employee/Customer Interaction in Service Businesses* (J. A. Czepiel *et al.*, Eds). Lexington, MA: Lexington, pp. 17–33.

Klausner, S. Z. (Ed.) (1968) *Why Man Takes Chances: Studies in Stress-Seeking/* Garden City, NY: Doubleday.

Kottak, C. (1982) *Cultural Anthropology.* New York: Random House.

Krippendorf, J. (1987) *The Holiday Makers: Understanding the Impact of Leisure and Travel.* Oxford: Heineman Professional.

Lyng, S. G. (1990) 'Edgework: A Social Psychological Analysis of Voluntary Risk Taking'. *American Journal of Sociology* **95**(4): 851–886.

MacCannell, D. (1989) *The Tourist: A New Theory of the Leisured Class.* New York: Schocken.

Mars, G. and Nicod, M. (1984) *The World of Waiters.* London: Allen & Unwin.

Martin, W. B. (1986) *Quality Service: The Restaurant Manager's Bible.* Ithaca, NY: Cornell School of Hotel Administration.

Maslow, A. (1964) *Religions, Values, and Peak-Experiences.* Columbus: Ohio State University Press.

Mason, C. H. and Perreault, W. D., Jr. (1991) 'Collinearity, Power, and Interpretation of Multiple Regression Analysis'. *Journal of Marketing Research* **28** (August): 268–280.

McCallum, J. R. and Harrison, W. (1985) 'Inter-dependence in the Service Encounter'. In *The Service Encounter: Managing Employee/Customer Interaction in Service Businesses* (J. A. Czepiel *et al.*, Eds). Lexington, MA: Lexington, pp. 35–48.

Mills, P. K. and Morris, J. H. (1986) 'Clients as "Partial" Employees of Service Organizations: Role Development in Client Participation'. *Academy of Management Review* **11**(4): 726–735.

Mohr, L. A. and Bitner, M. J. (1991) 'Mutual Understanding between Customers and Employees in Service Encounters'. In *Advances in Consumer Research,* Vol. 18 (M. Solomon and R. Holman, Eds). Provo, UT: Association for Consumer Research, pp. 611–617.

Moore, A. (1980) 'Walt Disney World: Bounded Ritual Space and the Playful Pilgrimage Center'. *Anthropological Quarterly* **53** (October): 207–218.

Nisbett, R. E. and Ross, L. (1980) *Human Inference: Strategies and Shortcomings of Social Judgment.* Englewood Cliffs, NJ: Prentice-Hall.

O'Guinn, T. C. and Belk, R. W. (1989) 'Heaven on Earth: Consumption at Heritage Village, USA'. *Journal of Consumer Research* **16** (September): 227–238.

Oliver, R. L. and DeSarbo, W. S. (1988) 'Response Determinants in Satisfaction Judgments'. *Journal of Consumer Research* **14** (March): 495–507.

Parasuraman, A., Zeithaml, V. A. and Berry, L. L. (1985) 'A Conceptual Model of Service Quality and Its Implications for Future Research'. *Journal of Marketing* **49** (Fall): 41–50.

Parasuraman, A., Zeithaml, V. A. and Berry, L. L. (1988) 'SERQUAL: A Multiple-Item Scale for Measuring Consumer Perceptions of Service Quality'. *Journal of Retailing* **64**(1): 12–40.

Paules, G. F. (1991) *Dishing It Out: Power and Resistance among Waitresses in a New Jersey Restaurant.* Philadelphia: Temple University Press.

Peters, T. J. and Austin, N. (1985) *A Passion for Excellence.* New York: Random House.

Privette, G. (1983) 'Peak Experience, Peak Performance, and Flow: A Comparative Analysis of Positive Human Experiences'. *Journal of Personality and Social Psychology* **45**(6): 1361–1368.

Rafaeli, A. (1989) 'When Cashiers Meet Customers: An Analysis of the Role of Supermarket Cashiers'. *Academy of Management Journal* **32**(2): 245–273.

Rafaeli, A. and Sutton, R. I. (1987) 'Expression of Emotion as Part of the Work Role'. *Academy of Management Review* **12**(1): 23–37.

Redfoot, D. L. (1984) 'Touristic Authenticity, Touristic Angst and Modern Reality'. *Qualitative Sociology* **7** (Winter): 291–309.

Roggenbuck, J. W., William, D. R., Bange, S. P. and Dean, D. J. (1991) 'River Float Trip Encounter, Norms: Questioning the Use of the Social Norms Concept'. *Journal of Leisure Research* **23**(2): 133–153.

Romm, D. (1989) '"Restauration" Theater: Giving Direction to Service". *The Cornell Hotel and Restaurant Association Quarterly* **29** (February): 31–39.

Sarbin, T. R. (1986) *Narrative Psychology: The Storied Nature of Human Conduct.* New York: Praeger.

Shelby, B. Bregenzer, S. and Johnson, R. (1988) 'Displacement and Product Shift: Empirical Evidence from Oregon Rivers'. *Journal of Leisure Research* **20**(4): 274–288.

Shostack, G. L. (1987) 'Service Positioning through Structural Change'. *Journal of Marketing* **51** (January): 34–43.

Shott, S. (1979) 'Emotion and Social Life: A Symbolic Interactionist Analysis'. *American Journal of Sociology* **84** (May): 1317–1334.

Siehl, C. Bowen, D. E. and Pearson, C. M. (1993) 'Service Encounters as Rites of Integration: An Information Processing Model'. *Organization Science* **3** (November): 537–555.

Solomon, J. (1988) *The Signs of Our Time.* New York: Harper & Row.

Spradley, J. P. and Mann, B. J. (1975) *The Cocktail Waitress: Woman's Work in a Man's World.* New York: Knopf.

Surprenant, C. and Solomon, M. (1987) 'Predictability and Personalization in the Service Encounter'. *Journal of Marketing* **51** (April): 86–96.

Sutton, R. and Rafaeli, A. (1988) 'Untangling the Relationship between Displayed Emotions and Organizational Sales: The Case of Convenience Stores'. *Academy of Management Journal* **31**(3): 461–487.

Trice, H. M. and Beyer, J. M. (1991) 'Cultural Leadership in Organizations'. *Organization Science* **2** (May): 149–169.

Turner, V. W. (1969) *The Ritual Process.* Chicago: Aldine.

Turner, V. W. (1974) 'Social Dramas and Ritual Metaphors'. In *Dramas, Fields, and Metaphors.* Ithaca, NY: Cornell University Press, pp. 23–59.

Unger, L. S. and Kernan, J. B. (1983) 'On the Meaning of Leisure: An Investigation of Some Determinants of the Subjective Experience'. *Journal of Consumer Research* **9** (March): 381–392.

Urry, J. (1990) *The Tourist Gaze: Leisure in Contemporary Societies.* Beverly Hills, CA: Sage.

van Gennep, A. (1960) *The Rites of Passage,* trans. Monika B. Vizedom and Gabrielle L. Caffee, Chicago: University of Chicago Press.

van Maanen, J. and Kunda, G. (1989) 'Real Feelings: Emotional Expression and Organizational Culture'. In *Research in Organizational Behavior,* Vol. 11. (L. L. Cummings and B. M. Staw, Eds). Greenwich, CT: JAI Press, pp. 43–104.

Zeithaml, V. A., Berry, L. L. and Parasuraman, A. (1987) 'Communication and Control Processes in the Delivery of Service Quality'. Marketing Science Institute Working Paper, Report No. 87-100. Cambridge, MA: Marketing Science Institute.

24

Service Breakdowns: A Study of Critical Incidents in an Airline

Bo Edvardsson

INTRODUCTION

Many executives see quality as the cornerstone or driving force for improving competitiveness, customer satisfaction and profitability. Since the service sector is of such importance for the community – in the Organization for Economic Co-operation and Development (OECD) countries about 70% are employed in the service sector – it is essential to create a basis for developing quality in services. By this I mean both methods for studying quality in services and empirical results which will reveal the somewhat special nature of quality issues in services.

Quality defects cause service companies considerable costs. What it costs is not quality but lack of quality. Getting it right from the start, the zero fault strategy, has become the lodestar for the leading companies. In service companies it is estimated that as much as 35% of the staff are employed in 'correcting the mistakes made by the others'.[1] Crosby sees three factors as being particularly important for profitability. First, high quality means that the company can charge a higher price. Second, high quality entails lower costs and thus higher income. Third, those companies which are known for high quality have a considerable advantage when it comes to image. This gives them a competitive edge. Thus quality development leads not only to reduced costs and increased productivity but also to more satisfied customers, and all these factors improve profitability.

To be able to study quality in service companies, one must first be aware of the characteristic features of services and service production. Service is not a uniform concept.[2,3–6] There are great differences between different kinds of services, between, for instance, cleaning and security services, educational services, health care services and consultancy services. Despite these major differences as regards the degree of standardization or labour and capital intensity, etc., services have certain features in common. The most important of these, from a management perspective, are that:

- The customer often participates directly and actively in the production process as co-producer;

Reprinted with permission from *International Journal of Service Industry Management*, Vol. 3, No. 4, pp. 17–29

- Services are often abstract, which makes them difficult for the supplier to explain and for the customer to assess;
- Many non-standardized services are very closely linked with the service provider as an individual, his knowledge, behaviour, commitment and approach, etc.;
- Services are often made up of a sub-system of services, and quality depends on how the customer perceives the whole.

The fact that services often arise in the interaction between individuals and that the customer often participates in the production process, leads to special quality management problems. One aspect of this is that the service producer is unable to control all the conditions and factors affecting quality, with the result that the quality may be uneven.

The interaction between the company's employees and the customer is usually termed the moment of truth[7] or the service encounter.[3,8] The service arises in the interaction between customer and staff. Each situation is unique, provided that the contact between the actors is not automatized. The customer's perception of these encounters is a crucial component in the evaluation of the quality of the service.[9,10]

Service quality may be said to be of two kinds:[11] the quality of a 'normal' service and the quality of the 'exception', i.e. when critical incidents occur. It is only when the customer fails to get what he had expected that he becomes aware of what he usually gets.[12]

The customer has certain service level expectations. Parasuraman *et al.*[13] make a distinction between adequate and desired service level. Separating the desired an adequate service level is a zone of tolerance. 'The zone of tolerance expands and contracts like an accordion. It can vary from customer to customer and, potentially, from one situation to the next for the same customer' (p. 42). In deviant situations – moments of truth below the tolerance zone – quality perceptions are formed which remain in the customer's long-term memory. They also provide the service supplier with a golden opportunity to turn dissatisfaction into something positive by skilful and professional handling of the situation. If he fails to do this, the result may be great dissatisfaction and a broken relationship. Further, he may gain a negative reputation in the market.

The customer may reconsider his attitudes and expectations on the basis of negative critical incidents caused by defective details in service delivery. To improve quality and build up trustful and strong customer relations, it is important therefore to attend to faulty details which result in negative critical incidents in service production.[4,14]

For an incident to be defined as critical, the requirement is that it can be described in detail and that it deviates significantly, either positively or negatively, from what is normal or expected. In this study we consider only negative critical incidents, i.e. customer encounters which do not proceed normally but create friction, irritation and dissatisfaction.

DISCUSSION OF METHODS

Since services are processes, a method of describing the process aspect of service production and of providing detailed information about critical incidents is needed.

The critical incident technique (CIT) captures part of the process, in some cases a very small part. The method enables us to investigate and gain a greater understanding of situations where quality fails, i.e. where a critical incident occurs. CIT was presented for the first time by Flanagan[15] in an article in the *Psychological Bulletin.* Flanagan developed the technique to define the critical requirements for certain key positions in the American Air Force. It has since been used in a variety of contexts, including the study of quality failures in the service field.[10,16–18]

Data on critical incidents can be collected in several ways. It is essential to gain access to[19] and 'get close' to the phenomenon to be studied. Among the data collection techniques which can be used are personal interviews, focus group interviews and direct or participatory observation. It is most important and at the same time difficult to gain access to the phenomena being studied.[19] As argued by Olsen[20] only the actors, in this case customers and staff, are able to describe their experience of critical incidents in service processes. I agree with the conclusions in the extensive research by Andersson and Nilsson,[21] that the personal interview is usually preferable due to 'depth' and 'richness' in the data collected.

Flanagan maintains that is is not collecting the data which is most problematic but interpreting them and developing systems of classification. I would like to stress the importance of theoretical sensitivity in making interpretations.[22] Another key concept is pre-understanding, which may consciously steer interpretation, but at the same time an understanding of the context may aid interpretation and lead to an even greater understanding. The emphasis on interpretation means that the researcher adopts a phenomenological/hermeneutic approach: '. . . the phenomenologist is committed to understanding social phenomena from the actor's own perspective. He or she examines how the world is experienced. The important reality is what people perceive it to be' (ref. 23, p. 2). Ödman[24] makes the distinction that phenomenology focuses on 'the immediate phenomena of human experience, such as thinking and feeling' while hermeneutics 'is more context directed'.

The main advantage of CIT is that it generates detailed process descriptions of critical incidents as those interviewed, e.g. customers, perceive them. The customer has the opportunity of describing the situation in his own words. The accounts given describe microprocesses in the relationship between the service producer and the customer. The weakness of the method is primarily that the interviewer can filter, misrepresent or unconsciously misunderstand the respondent, which is true for all 'verbal' methods.

To ensure as good responses as possible, it is essential for the interviewer to be fully conversant with the service and the service company being studied. At the same time there is a danger that the interviewer's pre-understanding or preconceived opinions may steer the collection of the data. To obtain good validity, it is necessary to describe, as unambiguously as possible, what is meant by critical incident in the study in question, preferably providing exemplification. Further, it is essential to ask about individual, specific incidents which the interviewee remembers well and to ask follow-up questions to ensure the interviewee has given a both comprehensive and detailed account of the incident in question. The account should be written down directly and even read back to the interviewee to check that it is correct and complete.

To help the interviewer, a simple model of a critical incident – e.g. cause, course and result – may be used as a sort of interview guide. The analysis and interpretation of the accounts generated is an ongoing process. The incidents are classified, and gradually a pattern and thus a classification scheme emerges. It does not seem to be a good idea to use a previously established set of categories for classifying critical incidents, as Stauss and Hentschel[25] do.

The analysis is inductive and partly subjective as in all qualitative research. When it is felt that a sufficient degree of saturation and stability has been attained in the data, no more data are collected. The incidents may be classified in several ways. How this is done purely practically is primarily determined by the purpose of the survey and the researcher's interests. He may wish to emphasize typical incidents, particularly 'living' descriptions which are highlighted or limited, but recurrent factors, e.g. those which cause critical incidents or are the source of them.

The collection of the data raises several issues which must be resolved in the light of the aim and purpose of the study. These include, for instance, the place where the interviews are to be conducted, the topicality of the incident, who should be selected to provide information, and who should conduct the interviews. When, for example, students collect data, it is crucial that they understand both the point of the study and CIT and that detailed situation-related instructions for collecting data have been prepared and learnt. Andersson and Nilsson[21] describe the correct procedure.

'Individual interviews should be conducted on the basis of previously determined models. Having stated the goal, the point of the interview, and having taken up the question of anonymity, etc., the interviewer asks about incidents when especially efficient/inefficient behaviour has been observed' (p. 30). 'Naturally there is no general form for collecting critical incidents. Interview questionnaires must be devised for each particular survey in accordance with the preconditions and aim' (p. 31).

DATA COLLECTION AND ANALYTICAL MODEL

During the autumn of 1989 four students under my supervision made a survey of critical incidents in an airline. The study highlighted the cause, course and result of these critical incidents (Figure 1).

Only negative critical incidents were studied. The sample consisted of 320 business passengers and 80 employees representing front staff. The selection of interviewees and critical incidents was based on certain criteria. The requirement as regards the business passengers was that they had experienced the incident themselves and that it has occurred during the last two years while they were travelling on business. The respondents were selected at random at four different airports. The data were collected at different times over the course of a month. The respondents were each

Figure 1. Model of a critical incident.

asked to give information about two critical incidents. As regards airline staff, the requirement was that they worked in the front office and had been employed for at least six months, and that the incidents had occurred during the last two years. Furthermore, the critical incident was to be seen from the perspective of the business passenger.

Interviewing both employees and customers in order to compare their views is quite rare. The advantage of including both customers and employees is that it enables the researcher to identify possible differences in their attitudes to ordinary problems in the service offering.[26]

The method used to collect the data was the personal interview where the respondent was asked to recount in detail, in his own words, a critical incident he had experienced. The interviews were conducted at four airports with two students acting as interviewers and two others keeping a record. The accounts were between a half and one page in length.

The students classified the critical incidents independently of each other. Where differences occurred, they were resolved through discussion. Flanagan claims that the decisive test of whether an incident may be adjudged a fact is whether the observation is 'objective' in terms of the probability that different interviewers would arrive at the same result. In our case the majority, or about 90% of the critical incidents, were classified in the same way.

The analysis began with a careful scrutiny of the accounts of the critical incidents. This revealed certain clear patterns in the material, which make it possible and meaningful to classify the incidents in accordance with the model. The causes of the critical incidents could be divided into source (= where) and type (= what). During the course of the critical incident a certain tendency as regards passivity or activity on the part of the two parties, the customer and the service provider, could be distinguished. The result of the critical incident as regards customer relations could be classified as a strengthened, unchanged, weakened or broken relation with the airline.

The critical incidents were classified into main categories and sub-categories. An example of a main category is air transport, which concerns critical incidents occurring at the airport or on board the aircraft; the sub-categories here are: delayed flight, cancelled flight, delayed luggage, overbooking and lack of information.

I have chosen to present the results in table form and by means of some illustrative examples. The results of the interviews with business passengers are presented first, followed by employees' accounts.

RESULTS – BUSINESS PASSENGERS

Cause

The most common source of critical incidents in the view of the business passengers interviewed is related to air transport, i.e. what happens at the airport or on board the aircraft (Table 1). The conditions causing the critical incident are ranked on the following descending scale: delays (114), cancelled flights (112), delayed or damaged luggage (26), overbookings (14) and other sources (8). The first two factors account for 82% of the dissatisfaction. When it comes to ground transport, the critical incidents are often the result of the airport taxi being late or not coming at all.

Course

Table 2 shows that in most cases the business passengers said that they were passive, i.e. they did not do anything to try and resolve the problems resulting from the critical incident. They appeared to have confidence in the employees, expecting them to sort out the problems. This seems quite natural. Most people deem it impossible to do anything about the weather or technical problems with an aircraft.

Results

Table 3 shows that in 80% of the cases the critical incidents studied resulted in unchanged customer relations. In 16% of the cases the critical incidents resulted in a weakened and in 4% of the cases in a strengthened relationship as perceived by the

Table 1. Business passengers' perception of the source of critical incidents

	Number	Proportion (%)
Air transport	274	85.6
Ground transport	32	10.0
Other incidents	14	4.4

Table 2. The actions of the business passengers

	Number	Proportion (%)
Active	76	23.8
Passive	244	76.2

Table 3. The effect of the critical incident on the business passengers' relations with the airline

	Number	Proportion (%)
Relation broken	8	2.5
Relation weakened	42	13.1
Relation unchanged	256	80.0
Relation strengthened	14	4.4

business passengers. Thus the airline was in many cases able to deal with the situation in a satisfactory manner from the customer's viewpoint. In the following section a number of individual incidents are presented in order to illustrate the problems of facing an airline. The low proportion of broken relations may presumably be explained by the fact that the airline has in principle a monopoly.

AN EXAMPLE OF A CRITICAL INCIDENT INVOLVING DELAY

Delays are the most frequent causes of critical incidents in air transport. In this specific instance the business passenger was delayed by a 'technical fault'. The staff were alert and exercised their authority to issue vouchers. However, dissatisfaction arose because insufficient information was given about the delay. The expression 'technical fault' was felt to be very diffuse and created much irritation. The situation resulted in a weakening of the relations with the airline. The business passenger claimed that 'if the airline explained why the plane was delayed, it would increase the passenger's willingness to accept the situation'.

AN EXAMPLE OF A CRITICAL INCIDENT INVOLVING A CANCELLED FLIGHT

The next most common cause of critical incidents after delays is cancelled flights. Cancellation is often due to technical faults or bad weather. The situation described below occurred when a business passenger's flight was cancelled because of a technical fault. The passenger was convinced that the reason for the cancellation was that there were too few passengers booked on the flight. The process can be briefly described as follows: initially, insufficient information was provided as to the cause of the delay; when the flight was later cancelled, the businessman was very annoyed. He had lost valuable time for work and the staff 'did not care' and their attitude was 'disgraceful'. The incident resulted in a negative attitude towards the airline. The man pointed out that time was most important to him as a businessman. 'If the airline cancels too many planes, in the end you lose patience and take the train instead.'

AN EXAMPLE OF A CRITICAL INCIDENT RELATING TO THE AIRPORT TAXI

The airline provides ground transport such as airport buses and taxis for its passengers. The critical event in question was caused by a lack of service on the part of the taxi company. The passenger missed his flight because the taxi which had been ordered earlier did not come. The result was that the businessman was unable to attend an important meeting with a customer, and his relationship with the airline was weakened. The staff did not attempt to assist him to resolve the problem by arranging alternative transport. The ironic comment from the passenger was telling: 'It is exciting every time I order an airport taxi'. The airline did not accept responsibility for the situation, and the passenger received no compensation for the inconvenience.

RESULTS – AIRLINE STAFF

Cause

The staff believed that 72% of the critical incidents arose in connection with air transport (Table 4). The 58 critical incidents related to 'Air transport' are ranked on the following descending scale: delayed or damaged luggage (26), cancelled flights (14), delays (12), overbookings (4) and other sources (2). The first two factors account for 69% of the dissatisfaction. When it comes to ground transport, the critical incidents are often the result of the airport taxi being late or not coming at all.

Course

Table 5 indicates that 85% of the staff said they were active in trying to resolve the critical incidents. They felt they were helpful and tried to reduce irritation by compensating business passengers with vouchers.

Table 4. Staff perception of the source of critical incidents

	Number	Proportion (%)
Air transport	58	72.5
Ground transport	12	15.0
Other incidents	10	12.5

Table 5. The staff view of their actions

	Number	Proportion (%)
Active	68	85.0
Passive	12	15.0

Results

Table 6 shows that as much as 20% of the critical incidents – by the staff interviewed – resulted in a strengthened relationship between the business passengers and the airline. This may be compared with the customers' view (see Table 3) where we find that only 4% perceived the relationship to be strengthened.

Table 6. The effect of the critical incident on the business passenger's relations with the airline (according to staff)

	Number	Proportion (%)
Relation broken	0	0
Relation weakened	16	20
Relation unchanged	48	60
Relation strengthened	16	20

AN EXAMPLE OF A CRITICAL INCIDENT CONCERNING LUGGAGE

From the staff viewpoint lost luggage is the factor which is though to create most critical incidents for business passengers. In the case in question the passenger checked in his luggage in the usual manner. On arrival at his destination the suitcase had disappeared. The passenger, who was extremely annoyed, started to abuse the staff, calling them all kinds of names. The staff felt that the result of the incident was a very dissatisfied passenger, with weakened relations with the airline as a result. However, the suitcase turned up and was taken to the owner by taxi.

AN EXAMPLE OF A CRITICAL INCIDENT CONCERNING A CANCELLED FLIGHT

According to staff, cancelled flights are a common cause of irritation among business passengers. In this case the cancellation was due to bad weather. On the particular occasion in question four planes were due to depart at the same time but only one could take off. The course of the incident may be described as follows. The passengers were informed via loudspeakers that those who had international flights were to go on board first. Chaos broke out and several business passengers who did not have international tickets rushed to the counter and the tumult resulted in a VDU falling to the floor. However, the passengers received no information and they finally realized that they had no chance of getting on the flight. The staff learnt, among other things, that a well-organized queue system was necessary in such cases.

ANALYSIS

The survey shows that there is a considerable difference between the ways business passengers and staff perceive the causes and handling of critical incidents. The chi-square test based on 'Cause' (air transport, ground transport and other incidents) show that there is a statistically significant difference. The chi-square value is 9.82 and the p value .0074. If we look at the subcategories making up 'Air transport' (delayed luggage, cancelled flight, delays and other sources) our data show a statistically significant difference between the two groups. The chi-square value is 47.52 and the p value $< .00000$. The former saw delays and cancellations as the most common problems, while the latter thought that the majority of the critical incidents were caused by delayed or damaged luggage.

We also find a statistically significant difference between the business passengers' and the staff's perception of the critical incidents effect on the customers' relationship with the airline (broken, weakened, unchanged or strengthened). The staff interviewed are more positive than the business passengers. The chi-square value is 24.94 and the p value .000004.

It emerges from the study, then, that collecting information from the front line staff will not enable us to grasp the customers' perceptions of quality failures. This does not mean, however, that information from front line staff is valueless. Several researchers, e.g. Schneider and Bowen[27] and CEOs such as Carlzon[28] maintain that the 'psychological closeness' between front line staff and customers means that there is much valuable information on customer needs, wishes and expectations to be gathered from the service company's contact staff. On the other hand, there is also research which shows that customers and staff have different views about what creates dissatisfaction.[26,29] My results indicate how important it is to collect data about lapses in quality directly from the customer in order to gain an understanding of quality defects and to develop quality in the right areas.

The study also shows that staff are now aware of the importance of clear and correct information when critical incidents occur. The customer needs to know why there is a problem and what the likely outcome is, the latter in order to be able to decide how to act. It is a matter of providing the customer with the opportunity of being able to influence his own situation (compare the discussion on perceived control, in refs. 2, ch. 3, p. 30). Instead of announcing the cancellation of a flight due to a technical fault over the loudspeaker system, the situation could be dealt with in the following way: the captain, or another reliable person, goes into the departure lounge and meets the passengers. He apologises for the delay and explains what has happened: a punctured nose-wheel or damaged rudder, etc. Then he provides an estimate of how long it is likely to take to repair the damage, informs passengers of alternative means of transport: changing flights, bus or train, etc. and perhaps provides some form of compensation for the delay: a cup of coffee for instance.

One of the conclusions to be drawn from the study is that the airline should train its own staff in the techniques of communication and how to relate to customers when critical incidents occur. Several of those interviewed did not believe the information they received. 'They're lying again when they say it is a technical fault. There are in fact too few passengers, and the flight will lose money. But they won't admit that'.

Further, several of those interviewed felt the information to be insufficient and late (not enough information about 'why things are as they are and about what is going to happen'). Credible, clear and rapid information emerges as an important source of customer perceived quality. The study shows that reliable core services, confidence-inspiring, i.e. knowledgeable and motivated staff, who show empathy and are able to communicate with and look after customers, and deal with complaints in critical situations, are the most important quality creating resources.

Another result of the study is that the undertakings given in publicity material, etc.

are not always fulfilled and this produces irritation and perhaps heightens the customer's dissatisfaction in critical situations. The airline is marketed as the quickest and most time-saving means of transport. The customer should perhaps be informed via the publicity material that technical faults sometimes occur, leading to delays and that the weather may also lead to delays or cancellations. The marketing of services should not only clarify and make concrete the features and value of the service but also steer customer expectations so that they are at the 'right level' in relation to what the service provider can achieve. In this way it might be possible to prevent critical incidents or, perhaps more importantly, reduce dissatisfaction when a critical incident does occur.

In those situations where the business passenger is affected by delays, the results of the study highlight the importance of committed and knowledgeable staff who have the authority to act. If the customer is met with initiative and commitment, a negative situation can be turned into something positive. Even in this respect some form of education and practical training is necessary to provide staff with a greater understanding of what shapes customers' expectations and perception of quality. This should contribute to more professional crisis management.

In order to maintain a high level of service, it would seem necessary to develop more customer-oriented complaint management. Interviews with business passengers and the airline's complaints department indicate that complaints procedures are often felt to be complicated and time-consuming by passengers.

Finally, better co-ordinated activities between the airline and the companies providing ground transport is required. The offering or service system should be so designed that the different customer needs are satisfied. The core service is often described in terms of the flight. But a number of support services are required to meet the needs of the customer in connection with the flight. Transport to and from the airport is an essential part of the total service package and is often experienced as an integrated part of the core service.

DISCUSSION AND SUGGESTIONS FOR FURTHER RESEARCH

In the introduction I observed that the aim of the article was to contribute to a greater understanding of how to manage critical incidents. The study shows that CIT is a useful tool, and that is provides interesting and meaningful information about customers. It is also a helpful tool when it comes to involving staff in further quality work.

Furthermore, it is perfectly satisfactory to allow students to collect data, provided they are given an opportunity to learn about the purpose of the study and about CIT, are given clear instructions and work closely with a supervisor. The difficulty with CIT is primarily associated with classifying and interpreting the incidents. This can, of course, be done in more than one way, and different researchers would probably reach different conclusions, but the core content should be the same. To prevent preconceived ideas and predetermined interpretative frameworks from steering the analysis, the classification should be carried out by two people separately. Differences of classification can be resolved by discussions, which may result in new categories being established.

In an article in the *Journal of Marketing*, Bitner *et al.*[10] report the results of a number of American studies of service quality in which CIT has been used. The analysis is based on data from 700 incidents in three service areas: airlines, hotels and restaurants. In Edvardsson[18] I report the results of a survey of 205 service-related critical incidents in sales processes in mechanical engineering companies in Sweden. Both these studies show similar results to those in this article. CIT has proved to be a useful and suitable method of identifying and analysing defects in service quality. The importance of committing oneself to the customer and of providing clear and 'truthful' information is a recurrent result. This is also supported by Stauss and Hentschel,[25] who interviewed 321 garage customers in Germany. Altogether data on 599 positive and negative incidents were collected. The results showed, among other things, that negative critical incidents affected customer behaviour and, in the first place, led to complaints, reduced willingness to return to the company and to the spread of negative comments about the company in question by ten people on average.

Placing the customer in the centre makes customer care and complaint management an important aspect of quality development. However, in most companies marketing is primarily concerned with identifying and attracting new customers. It is only recently that attention has also been directed to looking after existing customers in a purposeful and systematic manner. In this context CIT has proved to be a useful tool for determining why the customer is satisfied or not with a certain service or service company. Facts about customer dissatisfaction and the causes of critical incidents are an important part of the basis for continuous quality improvement.

I would therefore like to stress the importance of the following for quality development:

- Highlighting the personal quality of the staff.
- Being actively considerate towards existing customers.
- Being sensitive to signals of dissatisfaction by 'reading' customers and thus discovering quality defects before the customer complains, and making it easier for the customer to complain.
- Looking after the customer and correcting faults which have arisen.
- Providing generous compensation.
- Providing clear, rapid and 'truthful' information.

Service quality is a matter of controlling details in the service delivery. Thus quality development means improving all the parts of the service chain and seeing the whole. Far too many companies work on the detail 'the encounter with the customer' but really they should be studying critical incidents in the whole production chain. From the customer's perspective it is essential that the whole service process functions properly.

An important task for management-oriented quality research is to study the service chain in detail and identify critical points in the process. This should provide a basis for changes in the chain in an effort to achieve zero faults, i.e. the non-occurrence of critical incidents. Both new and better methods of analysis are needed for this as well as more in-depth and systematic empirical research focusing on the microprocesses. I believe it would be very useful to take critical incidents at different stages in the service chain and interview both customers and the staff involved about the same critical incident. The more we know about critical incidents in the whole service chain, the better the basis for further and continuous quality development.

REFERENCES

1. Crosby, P. B. (1980) *Quality is Free.* New York: New American Library.
2. Grönroos, C. (1990) *Service Management and Marketing Managing the Moments of Truth in Service Competition.* Lexington, MA: Lexington Books.
3. Edvardsson, B. and Thomasson, B. (1989) *Kvalitetsutveckling i privata och offentliga tjänsteföretag.* Stockholm: Natur och Kultur (in Swedish).
4. Edvardsson, B. and Thomasson, B. (1991) *Kvalitetsutveckling – ett managementperspektiv,* Lund: Studentlitteratur (in Swedish).
5. Gummesson, E. (1991) 'Service Quality – A Holistic View'. In *Service Quality Multidisciplinary and Multinational Perspectives* (S. W. Brown, E. Gummesson, B. Edvardsson and B. O. Gustavsson, Eds). New York: Lexington Books.
6. Gummesson, E. (1991) 'Kvalitetsstyrning i tjänste- och serviceverksamheter. Tolkning av fenomenet tjänstekvalitet och syntes av internationell forskning'. Forskningsrapoort Centrum för tjänsteforskning – CTF, Högskolan i Karlstad (in Swedish).
7. Normann, R. (1983) *Service Management.* Lund: Liber.
8. Czepiel, J., Solomon, M. R. and Surprenant, C. F. (1985) *The Service Encounter.* New York: Lexington Books.
9. Bitner, M. J. (1988) 'A Model of Service Encounter and Marketing Mix Effects', paper presented at the QUIS – seminar, Service Research Center, CTF, Karlstad.
10. Bitner, M. J., Booms, H. B and Tetreault, M. S. (1990) 'The Service Encounter: Diagnosing Favorable and Unfavorable Incidents'. *Journal of Marketing* **54**(1).
11. Berry, L., Zeithaml, V. and Parasuraman, A. (1985) 'Quality Counts in Services Too'. *Business Horizons* (May–June).
12. Levitt, T. (1984) *Lysande marknadsföring.* Stockholm: SvD förlag (in Swedish).
13. Parasuraman, A., Berry, L. L. and Zeithaml, V. (1991) 'Understanding Customer Expectations of Service'. *Sloan Management Review* (Spring).
14. Edvardsson, B. (1990) 'Management Consulting towards a Successful Relationship'. *International Journal of Service Industry Management* (No. 3).
15. Flanagan, J. C. (1954) 'The Critical Incident Technique'. *Psychological Bulletin* **51** (July).
16. Bitner, M. J., Jody, D., Nyquist, J. D. and Booms, B. H. (1985) 'The Critical Incident as a Technique for Analyzing the Service Encounter'. In *Services Marketing in a Changing Environment* (T. M. Bloch, G. D. Upah and V. A. Zeithaml, Eds). Chicago: American Marketing Association.
17. Bitner, M. J. (1990) 'Evaluating Service Encounters: The Effect of Physical Surrounding and Employee Responses'. *Journal of Marketing* **54** (No. 2).
18. Edvardsson, B. (1989) 'Critical Incidents in Customer Relationships. A Study of Mechanical Engineering Companies'. *The Service Industry Journal* (No. 4).
19. Gummesson, E. (1988) *Qualitative Methods in Management Research.* Lund: Studentlitteratur Chartwell-Bratt.
20. Olsen, M. (1992) 'Kvalitet i banktjänster'. Service Research Center – CTF, University of Karlstad, Karlstad, Diss. (In Swedish).
21. Andersson, B. -E. and Nilsson, S. -G. (1966) *Arbets-och utbildningsanalyser med hjälp av Critical Incident Metoden.* Göteborg: Akademiförlaget (in Swedish).
22. Glaser, B. (1978) *Theoretical Sensitivity.* Mill Valley, CA: The Sociology Press.
23. Taylor, S. and Bogdan, R. (1984) *Introduction to Qualitative Research Methods.* New York: Wiley.
24. Odman, P. -J. (1985) 'Hermeneutics'. In *The International Encyclopedia of Education* (T. Husén and N. Postlethwaite, Eds). Oxford: Pergamon Press.

25. Stauss, B. and Hentschel, B. (1991) 'Attribute-Based Versus Incident-Based Measurement of Service Quality: Results of an Empirical Study in the German Car Service Industry'. Paper presented at Workshop on Quality Management in Services, Brussels, 16–17 May.
26. Andersson, G. (1985) 'Kritiska händelser i banken'. Paper presented at the Second Nordic Meeting on Service Management. University of Lund, Lund (in Swedish).
27. Schneider, B. and Bowen, D. E. (1984) 'New Service Design, Development and Implementation and the Employee'. In *Developing New Services* (W. R. George and C. E. Marshall, Eds). Chicago: American Marketing Association.
28. Carlzon, J. (1987) *Moments of Truth.* Cambridge, MA: Ballinger.
29. Folkes, V. S. and Kotsos, B. (1986) 'Buyers' and Sellers' Explanations for Product Failure: Who Done It?' *Journal of Marketing* **50** (April).
30. Bateson, J. (1985) 'Perceived Control and the Service Encounter'. In *Services Marketing in a Changing Environment* (T. M. Bloch, G. D. Upah and V. A. Zeithaml, Eds). Chicago: American Marketing Association.

FURTHER READING

Brown, S. W., Gummesson, E. Edvardsson, B. and Gustavsson, B. O. (1991) *Service Quality Multidisciplinary and Multinational Perspectives.* New York: Lexington Books.

Edvardsson, B. (1988) 'Kritiska händelser i försäljningsprocessen – En studie av tjänstekopplade kritiska händelser inom verkstadsindustrin'. In *Management i Tjänstesamhället* (B. Edvardsson and E. Gummesson, Eds). Lund: Liber (in Swedish).

Nyquist, J. D., Bitner, M. J. and Booms, B. H. (1985) 'Identifying Communication Difficulties in the Service Encounter: A Critical Incident Approach'. In *The Service Encounter* (J. Czepiel, M. Solomon and C. Surprenant, Eds). Lexington, MA: Lexington Books.

25

Managing Quality in Business-to-Business Services

Isabelle T. D. Szmigin

This article puts forward the case for analysing service business clients' expectations of quality. It proposes that an ongoing survey of clients' expectations can play a useful role in the beneficial development and running of client/supplier relationships. A classification that encapsulates three aspects of quality is suggested which can act as the basis for an ongoing review of client/supplier relationships relevant to most business-to-business services. The three elements of the classification scheme are defined as 'hard', 'soft' and 'outcome' quality.

A relationship cycle is proposed which suggests the likely paths typical relationships may follow. It highlights problem areas and opportunities where attention to the client's needs and to the 'hard' and 'soft' quality elements, in particular, could help keep the relationship alive.

It is suggested that three factors underpin an understanding of the buyer's quality requirements in a business relationship:

1. An understanding of clients' perceptions of quality.
2. Clients' different quality priorities.
3. Clients' changing priorities, both over the duration of the relationship and within any given decision-making unit.

Thorough investigation of these areas could enable businesses to manage their relationships more profitably.

THE SHIFT FROM TRANSACTIONAL TO RELATIONSHIP MARKETING

Many service businesses depend on the successful formation and continued management of a buyer/supplier relationship. This may seem obvious for services of an inherently long-term nature, such as retail and corporate banking and advertising

Reprinted with permission from *European Journal of Marketing*, Vol. 27, No. 1, pp. 5–21

agencies, but it is also true of many other services as diverse as hairdressing and plumbing. All these will benefit from the development of a mutually satisfactory relationship, managed over time.

Gronroos[1] compares the relationship approach to marketing with the traditional transactional approach. The latter he identifies as being primarily focused on the marketing mix, where marketing specialists are the only people to have an impact on the customers' views of the firm and on their buying behaviour. Gronroos points to the service and industrial sectors as areas where the marketing mix approach does not adequately identify the range of resources and activities that appear in customer relationships at various stages of the customer relationship life cycle. Using examples such as waiters, air stewardesses, telephone receptionists and design engineers, he makes the point that marketing activity is spread throughout the entire organization and that its customers take an active part in the service production process.

The relationship approach to marketing revolves around the creation, maintenance and development of customer relationships, where the objectives of customers and sellers are met through various exchanges between the two sides, possibly with a variety of personnel from both. It recognizes the importance of businesses keeping existing customers and cross-selling to them rather than viewing customers as a series of discrete transactions. George[2] recognizes that one of the most important factors for success in relationship marketing will be a service marketing orientation among employees throughout the depth and breadth of an organization.

This is, if anything, even more vital for business-to-business services, where each side of the relationship may involve a number of diverse people from within, and even beyond, the organization. An advertising agency account team, for example, may include specifically trained and experienced account handlers who are used to the marketing role but also creative people, media buying specialists, planners and market researchers. It may also include receptionists and accounts personnel who may come into contact with the client and have an opportunity to help or hinder the relationship.

In the traditional professional service, such as accounting and the law, the client team may have no person specifically trained in the marketing role. Account handling is generally dealt with by a number of different professionals who manage the relationship and their company's day-to-day marketing, including cross-selling of services. Customers and sellers are many-headed.[3] This method reflects what has long been known about organizational buying behaviour. Both customers and sellers are likely to have complex decision-making units and the influences on any decision may even go beyond such units. Though it may not always be possible to identify the traditional roles of buyer, user, influencer, decision maker and gatekeeper of Webster and Wind,[4] the buying and selling centres in services are complex entities worthy of further consideration.

This may also go some way towards explaining the slow adoption of marketing by professional service firms in an increasingly deregulated market. This has been well documented[5] but, in many cases, it may not be so much due to the reactionary approach of such services as to marketing's reluctance to recognize that such firms have already adopted a form of relationship marketing which may be open to improvement but not to unnecessary reorganization.

THE INDUSTRIAL SECTOR AND RELATIONSHIP MARKETING

It is in the industrial sector where the literature on buyer/seller relationships is best developed: forces such as total quality management (TQM) and just-in-time (JIT) delivery have led both suppliers and clients to look closely at what are the best kind of relationships for them. In 1975, Guillet de Monthoux[6] outlined the bases for relationships in this sector when he used the analogy of courtship through marriage and even divorce to highlight the relationship process. His work not only revealed the potential benefits of a long relationship, especially in terms of the barriers it can provide against competition, but also some other aspects of the psychology of working within a relationship. For example, de Monthoux's research revealed that buyers, as well as suppliers, perceive the relationship as an investment in time and money and thus are unlikely to switch suppliers because of some short-term competitive advantage. Indeed, in some instances, buyers would prefer to engage in training programmes for their existing suppliers when problems occur. This is an important point because it highlights the willingness of some buyers to be involved in a process that may improve the relationship for both sides.

Once a relationship has reached this point, communications may actually increase between the buying and selling firms to further stabilize and build the relationship.[7] Barrett[8] takes this one step further when he quotes the hypothesis put forward by Homan, in 1954, that 'it is not people we like whom we interact with, rather we like the people we interact with'.[9] Barrett goes on to say that interactions develop into friendships, creating stronger partners. Part of this is possibly the Hawthorne effect at work: the very act of taking notice of us may improve the relationship and engender team spirit.[10]

The importance of developing buyer/seller relationships in the field of industrial products and services cannot be overestimated. These relationships may take many different forms and clearly involve costs as well as benefits. Dwyer *et al.*[11] suggest that the benefits of such a relationship include reduced uncertainty, exchange efficiency and social satisfaction, and it can insulate the seller from price competition. Costs can, however, outweigh the benefits. For example, a bad fit of customer and seller may lead to protracted negotiation. More generally, there is the opportunity cost of alternative exchanges or relationships. This may account for the reluctance of some firms to enter into such a relationship.

Relationships have to be managed and this takes time, money and commitment from the seller. Customers may find themselves wanting to commit themselves to a relationship but find sellers unwilling or unable to do so. Parasuraman *et al.*[12] found both consumer and business service customers wanting closer relationships with service providers but being disappointed. They point out that relationship building is 'process intensive'. It is the ongoing, day-to-day management of the relationship which is costly and time consuming and does not necessarily produce immediate results.

UNDERSTANDING QUALITY IN THE SERVICES SECTOR

There now exists a substantial body of research in the area of services quality, and Lewis[13] provides a substantial review. Different views have developed regarding customer evaluation of quality and the likely dimensions of quality. Le Blanc and Nguyen[14] have identified three principal schools of thought:

1. Quality may be implied through the tangible elements of the service, largely the physical environment.
2. Quality can be perceived through contact personnel, their attitudes and behaviour.
3. Perceived quality may be derived from the service encounter or the actual process of buying the service.

It is likely that consumers may also perceive quality in combinations of the above and that some services may be more likely to be judged by one method rather than another. Different types of transaction may be judged by different criteria within the same business. For example, in addition to the meal itself, quality in a restaurant may well be a combination of all three of the factors mentioned above: the ambience of the restaurant, largely received through the physical environment; the waiters as contact personnel; and the actual process, including getting your meal on time. Incidents that may occur during your stay in the restaurant are all likely to affect the overall evaluation of the service experience. On the other hand, a transaction from an automatic teller machine may only require that the process is satisfactory, i.e. the machine is working, does not require too much of the user and dispenses the money accurately. People are not involved in the transaction and the environment, usually a street or within a shop, is out of the control of the service management.

In business-to-business services, rather than looking for some objective measure of quality, it may be managerially more useful to identify the subjective components of quality of the service that are likely to satisfy the consumer – i.e. what is it about the service that satisfies them. This would be a large and costly task for retail services and, indeed, the likely heterogeneity of customers for many services might mean the variety of results would not make the exercise worthwhile. Here, pursuing some standard measuring scale such as SERVQUAL[15] certainly seems the most fruitful line of research to date. However, in business-to-business services, individual studies may yield a number of useful strategic results, both for the businesses concerned and also as the basis for further broader research.

IDENTIFYING THE CLIENT'S QUALITY AND SATISFACTION COMPONENTS

Gronroos[16] proposed two types of service quality: technical and functional. They both contribute to the perceived service quality. Gronroos points out that technical quality, e.g. a bank paying invoices promptly or transferring money from one account to another, etc., can be done by any bank, but that it is often the functional quality – attitudes, accessibility, appearance of the bank, service-mindedness of the contact personnel – that may ultimately influence a customer's choice of bank with which to do business. In other words, a certain level of technical quality would generally be assumed by potential clients. Technical quality can often be assessed in an objective manner, as any technical dimension of a product might be, whereas functional quality is perceived in a much more subjective way.

The make-up of quality along the technical and functional dimensions outlined by Gronroos has been furthered by other writers on services. Morgan[17] refers to process elements of service quality, i.e. how the service is delivered, staff/customer interaction, and outcome elements, i.e. what is actually received by the customer. Edvardsson[18] added integrative quality – the ease with which different portions of the service delivery system work together – and outcome quality – whether or not the actual service product meets both service standards of specifications and customer needs/expectations.

The Gronroos dual aspect of technical and functional quality is particularly well suited to act as a framework for the study of business service relationships. It could prove useful both for defining customer needs and for supplying corrective measures. As writers on organizational buying have already recognized,[19,20] purchasing is not a purely rational process and, as already pointed out, some clients get very close to their suppliers and work better with this kind of association. Recognizing such requirements could be particularly advantageous for firms able and willing to supply such a relationship.

However, discussions with service companies have revealed that the terms 'functional' and 'technical' are difficult to differentiate, while the terms 'hard' and 'soft' are easy to visualize for most managers. Indeed, work by Peters and Waterman[21] and Lessem,[22] where the term 'hard' has been used for features such as strategy, structure or systems and 'soft' for skills, staff or style, has in some ways made such terms easier to introduce in discussions with managers.

The terms 'hard' and 'soft' are used here therefore to refer to those quality elements identified by Gronroos as 'technical' and 'functional'.

Before looking at the implications of the above in more detail, it is worth introducing a third quality component at this point. This is basically the result of the relationship which will be referred to as 'outcome quality' as outlined by Edvardsson.[18] Outcome quality is different from hard quality in as much as a company may perform excellently in the hard area and still not achieve the desired goal or outcome. A merchant bank may perform well in all areas expected of it in a takeover bid, but the shareholders may still vote against the bid. A lawyer may present a superb case but the court can still rule against the client. An advertising agency may put together an advertising campaign which meets the brief in all particulars but it may still not achieve the company's objectives. One of the important aspects that differentiates outcome quality from the other two areas of quality mentioned is that it cannot always be controlled by the companies in the relationship. It is susceptible to outside pressures and environmental conditions, but it is still a part of the overall quality on which a supplier will be judged and which will relate to overall satisfaction with the relationship.

During the period of a business relationship it is likely that both aspects of quality, the hard and soft, are likely to be tested; invoices may not always be paid promptly, a bank transfer may go astray. These are usually errors rather than the norm and are likely to be perceived as such by the client, as long as they do not become too frequent, when they probably would begin to affect the overall relationship. Similarly, at the beginning of a relationship with a new client, service personnel may be keen to be as helpful as possible but, as time goes on and new business needs to be won, long-standing customers can be taken for granted and soft quality may decline.

Over time, the client's requirements regarding the relationship may well change.

Business objectives, changes in personnel, differing competitive situations, may all lead to changes in what is required from the supplier. Successful management of the relationship over time does depend to a large extent on successfully understanding and managing the client's changing requirements with regard to hard and soft quality.

Hard and soft quality affect the day-to-day running of a relationship and they affect one another. If the soft aspects of the relationship are going well, it is likely that some hard errors will be allowed and vice versa. The long-term health of a relationship will ultimately depend on outcome quality, although this may be balanced by the hard and soft input. If day-to-day service is going badly, however, the relationship may well be curtailed before outcome quality has an opportunity to influence the relationship. Similarly, companies do not often sack their legal advisers or merchant bank if they fail in one project when the hard and soft aspects of the transaction were perceived by management to be of a high quality. But a number of outcome quality failures may change their perceptions of the relationship, however satisfactory the day-to-day running of the relationship is.

Figure 1 attempts to chart the various interactions involved in relationship quality and their importance of the maintenance of a successful long-term relationship. The term 'process satisfaction' is suggested to convey the day-to-day running of a business relationship, where the various interactions between the client and the service firms, and within these firms, help to build up or to erode the relationship. These are essentially the hard and soft quality components.

The idea of process satisfaction builds on the importance of the internal customer as part of the process, and introduces the external customer as part of this same process. Gummeson[23] illustrates the importance of the internal process by referring to Kaoru Ishikawa who, in the 1950s, used the slogan 'the next process is your customer' to reduce barriers of sectionalism. This is equally appropriate in relationships where one has to manage not only the internal processes, but also those between different levels in the relationship of client and supplier. A well-known example is the chief executive who will only talk to his direct counterpart even if his query can be dealt with satisfactorily at a lower level. If supplier and buyer cannot agree on workable lines of communication, the process satisfaction has to diminish.

Obviously, any service business is ultimately trying to effect satisfactory outcome quality and the strategic and tactical decisions taken by the client and supplier will influence the outcome. Further study of the subjective nature of satisfaction in business services could prove of particular usefulness for the following:

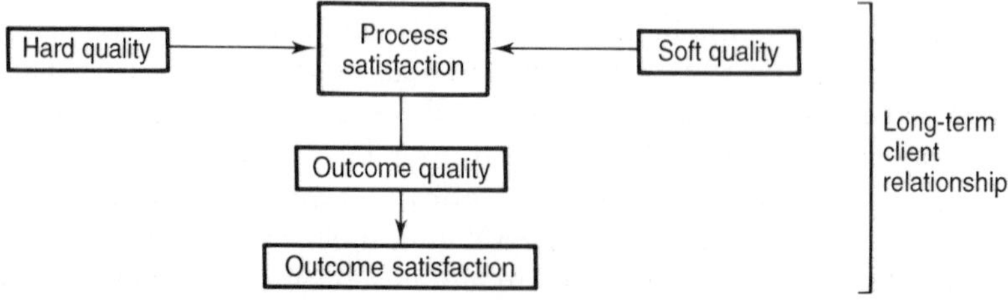

Figure 1. The role of satisfaction and quality in the long-term relationship.

1. The understanding and provision of the client's quality requirements.
2. The ongoing management of the client/supplier relationship.
3. Choosing and targeting segments with a satisfaction profile best suited to the supplier.

This article highlights the importance and role of the areas of service quality outlined above and, particularly, the way that attention in these areas can assist in the ongoing management of a relationship. Their role in segmentation requires further research and will not be directly discussed here. A key point is for suppliers to be aware of the differences highlighted between hard and soft and outcome quality, and of the role each might play in the management of *different* relationships.

UNDERSTANDING AND PROVIDING THE CLIENT'S QUALITY REQUIREMENTS

Different clients have different requirements in the balance between hard and soft quality. It is in the supplying company's interests to identify what that balance is and, at the same time, to pinpoint any specific requirements that need to be met. While this can be done informally, there are more benefits from a structured system for identifying specific clients' needs. When both client and supplier are party to the process, they become aware of, and more focused on, this aspect of the relationship: the vendor, particularly in terms of trying to supply what is required; while buyers must realistically consider what provides them with most value in the relationship. This can then act as a starting-point for further discussion, and also as a point to refer back to if things go wrong or changes occur in either side of the relationship. It is not intended to be an audit. The supplier firm may wish to do that anyway but rather as a regular contact point to compare perceptions and to eliminate, where possible, gaps between the perceptions of one side and the other.

Michell[24,25] has already achieved a great deal in identifying the realities of problems in long-term relationships in his work with advertising agencies and clients. This work is highly relevant to the topic of quality in relationships, under discussion here. Michell looked at the composition of agency/client advertising decision-making units and examined those factors which contributed to advertisers switching advertising agencies in the UK and in the USA.[24] In this study, he found that dissatisfaction with agency performance rested largely on three factors – creativity, campaign results, and client service. This last item covered account management, marketing advice and generally being 'close to the client'. If one accepts that creativity is essentially the advertising agency's product, it seems reasonable to suggest that, broadly, these three factors cover hard, soft and outcome quality – i.e. creativity, client service and campaign results respectively. Clearly, different service businesses will have different factors falling into these three groups but, by initially looking for these three groupings of quality, one can begin to assess the balance required by clients.

It is not the purpose of this article to chart the specific processes used to identify clients' specific quality requirements, and it is envisaged that a future article will examine this in detail. However, at this stage, it is worth saying a few general words on the method. One checklist is unlikely to do justice to the variability in most business services clients' quality requirements. Initially, prompts may be used to help clients decide what is, or is not, important to them in terms of hard and soft factors. This is not always easy, as some clients do not feel comfortable with having to define or even admit to what really matters to them, especially in the soft areas. However, in beginning this process, a watertight checklist is not necessary. It is probably better to identify some quality requirements along the way and add them to the list with mutual agreement. Though no one wants to spend their time searching for new problems regular debriefing meetings can pick up many such points once the concept has entered the consciousness of the main contact personnel.

At some point, a list of important hard and soft quality factors is drawn up, which should be agreed by both client and supplier. Especially important at this time is agreement about what statements mean: replying to letters promptly, for example, needs some kind of time scale included.

MANAGING QUALITY IN THE SUPPLIER/CLIENT RELATIONSHIP

The shift from a transactional to a relationship focus brings problems that, as yet, have not been fully explored in the literature. The problems are essentially to do with managing a relationship over time so that both parties gain satisfaction. Many of the likely problems can be seen in terms of hard and soft quality. I have highlighted the problems that can come about when the quality of the relationship is perceived by the customer as high. When personal relationships have developed, and soft quality generally is perceived to be high, issues may be brushed over or even ignored that really should question the continuance of the relationship.

When a relationship has developed with a supplier (or buyer) there is sure to be resistance at the prospect of terminating that relationship, even when there are very good reasons to do so. The very act of developing a relationship over time means that to leave it can be painful for one or both of the parties.

Once a relationship has developed, there may be less information readily available against which to judge a partner's performance, simply because the business may now have no other similar suppliers with which to compare. This may lead to an acceptance of less, in terms of quality, simply because of a lack of alternatives to assess the supplier against.

Interestingly, consideration of how a service relationship matures over time has received little attention to date. Again, it is in the area of perceived quality and customer satisfaction that a supplier can judge how best to manage an ongoing relationship within the bounds of the alternatives available. Any relationship changes over time. It is critical for buyers and sellers to recognize change and act on it where necessary. Changes comes in many forms, and any industry or service will be subject to particular forces, but there are some general currents to which organizations should pay heed. Identified below are three concepts drawn from the business literature that could help to chart change within a relationship:

1. The transaction life cycle.
2. The experience cycle.
3. The customer activity cycle.

Following a brief discussion of each of these, a fourth cycle is proposed – the relationship cycle – with a view to identifying the typical routes a relationship in the business services area may take over time.

The transaction life cycle

Services, just like products, can move through life cycles. The ability to recognize that what you were marketing two years ago is no longer perceived in the same way by its original market is vital, both for maintaining existing relationships and for developing new ones.

Mathur's transaction life cycle,[26] although originally developed for the industrial products market, is equally applicable to services. Mathur describes the introduction of a radically new type of hardware. The vendor has to supply not only the hardware, but also the know-how, to enable buyers to realize the full benefits of their purchase. At this stage, the vendor is marketing a system but, as the new packages catches on, competitors enter the market with similar packages. Now some concentration on market segments may follow. Gradually, buyers learn and improve on how the hardware can be used, and the software no longer becomes an essential purchase. Some players may concentrate on the provision of specialized software, thus, in Mathur's terms, providing a service and, as they refine their services, also providing a class of services after time. Similarly, competitors will enter the market specializing in different areas of hardware, generally reducing the barriers to entry and adding to the features and refinements of the hardware. This is the emergence of a product class.

The process of 'desystemization' can continue with the hardware and software coming to be regarded as commodity items by an increasing number of purchasers. Figure 2 shows how the process can go full circle, as mature commodities can be packaged with new or existing software to provide a new cluster of benefits; this, Mathur describes as decommodization or systemization.

The basic outline of the transaction life cycle can find many parallels in business services, e.g. the continuing repackaging of airline services for business travellers and financial services for small businesses, and also the more sophisticated financial instruments offered by corporate banks. The message for management regarding the relationship is, however, not easy to accept – especially the fact that such cycles indicate changes in the power balance of the relationship, usually from the supplier's favour to the buyer's. Here the shifts come about because of how the service is changing in the marketplace. The know-how for a commodized service will be of far less importance and the outcome quality should be assured as far as it is in the vendor's power to do so. Both hard and soft process elements must have particular attention paid to them, as shortcomings in these areas are going to be far more noticeable. Strategically, the power base of the relationship is unlikely to rebalance unless research and development by the vendor resystemize the current offering.

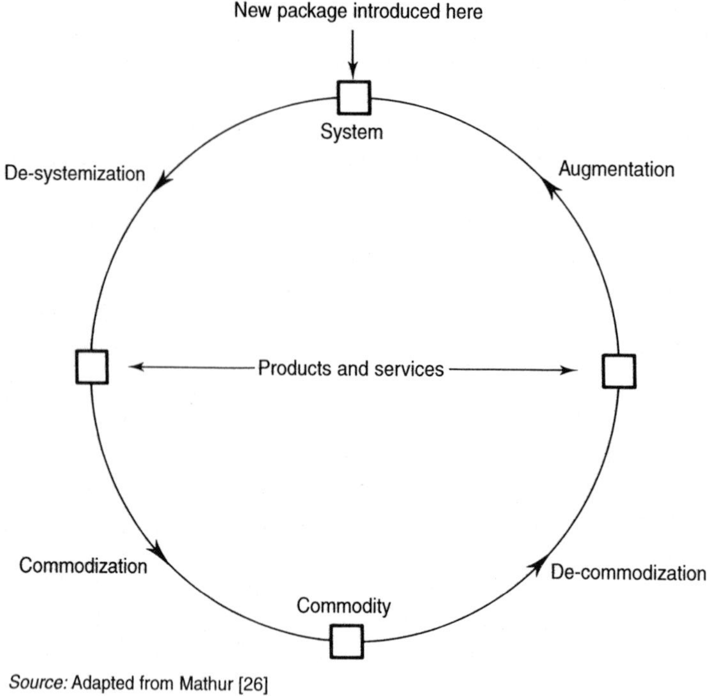

Figure 2. The transaction life cycle.

The experience cycle

Another danger to relationships arises when the supplier makes the mistake of believing that the benefits offered to their customers on day one of the relationship will have equal value to the customer on day 100. Just as products and services evolve, so do customers, and their experience of a particular service over time means they will grow in sophistication and self-confidence in their use of it. They are likely to need less support from the relationship and may become increasingly price sensitive. Termed the 'customer experience effect' by DeBruicker and Summe,[27] this threat is ever present in a relationship but can be managed as long as the vendor company is carefully watching the development of the relationship, changes in personnel, specific requirements, etc. and not leaving the responsibility for management to one person who may lose sight of change because he or she has become too close to the customer. Regular checks on the state of the relationship should throw up changes of this nature.

Customers often begin to unbundle the services they previously bought as a system as they gain experience and need less support. In particular, one would expect the need for soft quality to diminish and so the ties of the relationship will weaken. Firms needing services such as legal services, public relations and market research on a regular basis may decide, after a certain level of experience has been reached, to end a long-standing relationship and provide all or part of the service themselves by employing expert personnel and buying the remaining components on an *ad hoc* basis from a number of sources, feeling confident that they now have the experience so to do.

For the supplying company, the customer experience effect requires a decision at a strategic level. If the company's strengths lie in offering a full service relationship and a current customer no longer requires this, it may well be better to end the relationship and find alternative customers who will value this aspect of the company's offering. It is not a requirement for every company to change its strategy in line with its customers. Having said this, a supplier facing a combination of the customer experience effect and the transaction life cycle may have little choice but to go with the flow of the market.

The customer activity cycle

Vandermerwe[28] stresses the importance of understanding a customer's activity cycle as a holistic experience over time. Service customers, she says are not only buying advertising, legal services, treasury bills, they are aiming to maximize what they get from the experts over the period of the relationship. One might say that this is the process satisfaction, as compared to the outcome satisfaction, of the results of the service. Vandermerwe shows how critical points may be mapped over an activity cycle of the relationship which may act an an indicator for the selling company, in terms of

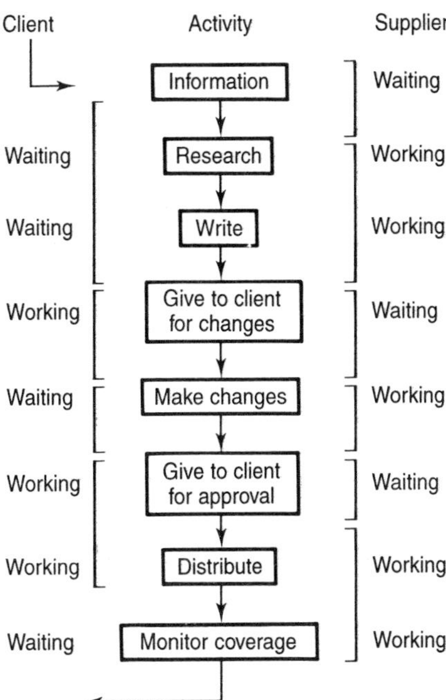

Figure 3. Press release activity cycle.

when different types of activity may be required. This corroborates the point made earlier that, while everyone is looking for successful outcome quality, one cannot ignore the various stages required to achieve this, some more difficult to negotiate than others; quite different requirements may be made of the relationship depending on what stage the activity has reached.

Figure 3 depicts an activity cycle drawn up to show the stages in a public relations company's press release writing and approval process. The centre line charts the various processes that have to be undertaken; if appropriate, suggested or probable timings between each stage could be inserted. On either side of the main process centre line specific actions can be placed – likely problems, etc. for the client on one side and for the supplier company on the other. Charting the customer activity cycle (see Figure 3) in this way can be useful at both the planning and review stages for both sides of the relationship. It can also prove useful for generally looking at ways of improving the process and identifying where contact should be kept up when the inevitable lulls in activity reduce the essential need for meeting.

On this activity cycle the starting-point for action is when the client gives the necessary information to the agency. There then follows a process where, for much of the time, one or other side is 'waiting' while the other is 'working'. Charting the activity in this way not only aids planning generally but, when times are added to the various phases, a business can identify where there are long time lags and review whether they can improve the process. During the client's 'waiting time', it may be just as well to keep them appraised of what is happening, while the supplier's 'waiting time' should be carefully managed so that other work can be carried on while, at the same time, encouragement is given to clients if necessary, to ensure the process keeps going at the required pace. One can build into process cycles such as this relatively simple actions, such as ensuring the notification of the client as soon as it is known a deadline will not be met. Keeping a close eye on the process can avoid misunderstandings on both sides of the relationship.

Service companies might consider charting their own relationships according to activity to identify, for example, whether there are critical points that regularly occur among clients or where there are points where the need for hard or soft quality may be more in evidence.

The relationship cycle

The relationship cycle proposed here suggests that, in most relationships, the expectations of either side and the satisfaction derived from the relationship are rarely completely in tune. If the expectation and reality are too far apart the relationship is likely to flounder unless one side is brought closer to the other.

To examine the relationship cycle, it is necessary to view both sides of the relationship and look to identify likely crisis points. Figures 4 and 5 chart two scenarios of the cycle which may occur in service relationships. The two lines indicate the buyer's and seller's view of the relationship; the lines are basically an amalgam of expectations about, and satisfaction derived from, the relationship. In reality, expectations and satisfaction will enjoy a different balance at different stages of a relationship: at the beginning, expectations, by definition, must almost

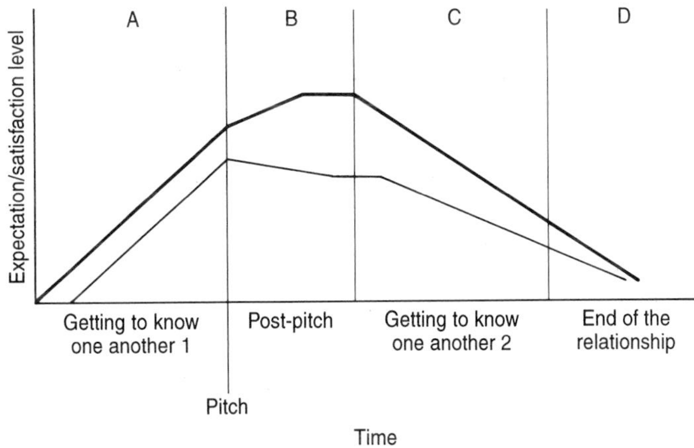

Figure 4. The relationship cycle – the relationship ends.

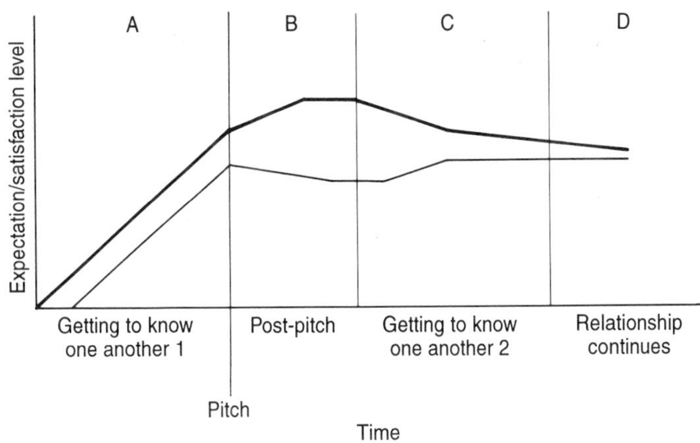

Figure 5. The relationship cycle – the relationship continues.

outweigh satisfaction, whereas later in the relationship the parties are more likely to know what to expect and be satisfied or not. Generally, if one is not satisfied, one's expectations lower and, therefore, the important elements of this cycle are the direction in which it is going and the closeness of the buyer and seller lines. Overall, the horizontal axis should be seen as generally tracking both parties' expectation/satisfaction level.

A key point in the cycle is the pitch which is common in services from accounting to advertising, although less so in corporate banking where a number of banks are often retained after proving themselves on a particular task. However, one way or another, there is a moment where speculative discussion between two parties who are getting to know one another changes into a buying/selling situation; if not, the parties either drift apart or keep in sporadic touch with one another.

The basic scenarios are:

1. The relationship thrives.
2. The relationship dissolves either from the supplier's or the customer's choice.

One overriding contribution towards the continuation of the relationship would seem to be that the closer the two sides are to meeting, in terms of what they expect from the relationship, the more likely it is that the relationship will be successful. This equilibrium does not necessarily have to be at a particularly high point if both sides are satisfied, although it should be said that this leaves the door open for others to lure customers away with better offers. Clearly, over the course of any relationship, the two lines will at times be nearer or further apart. However, the relationship is least likely to prosper when the expectation/satisfaction lines for each side are far apart for some time.

The thick lines in Figures 4 and 5 depict the buyer side of the relationship and the thin line the vendor. During phase (A) both sides are getting to know one another without having to make a commitment. The nearer together the lines are at this point reflects the closeness of perceptions of what the relationship should look like – therefore, this is a very important time for both sides. Both buyer and seller have this time to begin to get to know the other and assess whether they are right for one another in terms of a long-term relationship.

An important point comes at the pitch line. Once both parties have agreed to work with one another, this is the first major opportunity for divergence between their perceptions of the relationship. A customer who has decided to embark upon a relationship may have their expectations raised quite rapidly; largely due to post-pitch euphoria. Meanwhile, the vendor knows they now have to provide all that was promised in the pitch for the relationship to thrive. If the two sides do not move closer together in phase (C), the second period of getting to know each other, the relationship is probably doomed to disaster – i.e. (D).

(C) is a critical period of time, as each side is reappraising the relationship; the closer both sides can get to one another here, the more chance they have of a successful partnership. It is during this time that pursuing the client's hard and soft quality needs may help improve the relationship. There may be little to show in terms of pure results (outcome quality), but the supplier has this time to make sure that they have a clear understanding of the client's requirements and expectations of the relationship. If the seller does not ensure satisfaction in terms of hard and soft quality, then process satisfaction will suffer and, at this stage, the client has little else on which to judge the relationship.

For most relationships to thrive there has to be some realignment of each side's expectations/satisfaction level. This is generally an ongoing process as changes in each side's needs, such as those outlined earlier in this article, are inevitable. A successful cycle, however, could be such as outlined in Figure 5. Here the key difference from the previous diagram is that the two sides realign their expectation/satisfaction level post-pitch such that a workable equilibrium is reached. Obviously, as the activity cycle continues, there will be many other opportunities to lose that equilibrium and sometimes the cessation of a relationship can be best for both parties.

In a business-to-business service, quality issues may well be apparent at the beginning of the relationship, especially if the buyer has specific quality requirements of a long-standing and/or company-wide nature. But, as a problem, quality is much more likely to become an issue at some point or points during the relationship. Being aware of this likelihood, and managing the consequences rather than taking a defensive stance, may further help the relationship if both sides can agree to a solution. The following are some situations which give rise to changed hard/soft quality problems:

1. Change in top management.
2. Change in company objectives.
3. Change in the decision-making unit.
4. Change in specific objectives relating to the supplier/client relationship.
5. Change in personnel on the supplier side.
6. Reduced interest shown by supplier to buyer, possibly for one of the reasons above, e.g. change in company objectives.

The above should act as markers for those times when a supplier might consider reviewing his client's requirements. From one point of view it requires supplier management to regularly check specific relationships for signs of strain or boredom in the relationship but it also goes beyond this to a somewhat more difficult problem for management – that of 'knowing thyself'. Too often, unattractive clients are kept in a relationship but given a reduced service. This is not good for client or supplier and a slipshod ethos can soon find its way into other areas of a company's business. Regularly checking that the supplier/client fit is still good for both parties is an important part of the hard/soft management concept, and suppliers should not fear the possibility of extracting themselves from relationships that are no longer worthwhile.

CONCLUSION

The trend in business today is clearly towards relationship marketing. In business services, successful management should lead to a profitable relationship for both buyer and seller. While the outcomes of any relationship are clearly crucial, managing the process such that the client is satisfied with the service over time has to be the prime responsibility of the seller. One method of enhancing this process satisfaction is to manage the hard and soft quality requirements of the client. Not only can this improve existing relationships, it may help to identify the best type of clients with which to work.

Putting these ideas into action has already begun with some success. A future article will review the findings from some of the clients who agreed to be involved in the quality study which will be reported. Already it is clear that the results of such a review may be far reaching and could have implications for how firms organize themselves and their internal communications for best advantage within a relationship.

REFERENCES

1. Gronroos, C. (1990) 'Relationship Approach to Marketing in Service Contexts: The Marketing and Organizational Behavior Interface'. *Journal of Business Research* **20**: 3–11.
2. George, W. R. (1990) 'Internal Marketing and Organizational Behavior: A Partnership in Developing Customer-Conscious Employees at Every Level'. *Journal of Business Research* **20**: 63–70.
3. Gummesson, E. (1987) 'The New Marketing – Developing Long-Term Interactive Relationships'. *Long Range Planning* **20**: 10–20.
4. Webster, F. E. and Wind, Y. (1972) 'A General Model for Understanding Organizational Buying Behavior'. *Journal of Marketing* (April): 12–19.
5. Morgan, N. A. (1990) 'Communications and the Reality of Marketing in Professional Service Firms'. *International Journal of Advertising* **9**: 283–293.
6. Guillet de Monthoux, P. B. L. (1975) 'Organizational Mating and Industrial Marketing Conservatism – Some Reasons Why Industrial Marketing Managers Resist Marketing Theory'. *Industrial Marketing Management* **4**: 25–36.
7. Landeros, R. and Monczka, R. M. (1989) 'Cooperative Buyer/Seller Relationships and a Firm's Competitive Posture'. *Journal of Purchasing and Materials Management* (Fall): 9–18.
8. Barrett, J. (1986) 'Why Major Account Selling Works'. *Industrial Marketing Management* **15**: 63–73.
9. Homan (1954), cited in Hakansson, H. and Wootz, B. (1979) 'Framework of Industrial Buying and Selling'. *Industrial Marketing Management* **8**: 28–39.
10. Mayo, E. (1949) 'Hawthorne and the Western Electric Company'. *The Social Problems of an Industrial Civilization.* London: Routledge, pp. 60–76.
11. Dwyer, F. R., Schurr, P. H. and Oh, S. (1987) 'Developing Buyer–Seller Relationships'. *Journal of Marketing* **51** (April): 11–27.
12. Parasuraman, A., Berry, L. L. and Zeithaml, V. A. (1991) 'Understanding Customer Expectations of Service'. *Sloan Management Review* (Spring): 39–48.
13. Lewis, B. (1989) 'Quality in the Service Sector: A Review'. *International Journal of Bank Marketing* **7**(5): 4–12.
14. LeBlanc, G. and Nguyen, N. (1988) 'Customers' Perceptions of Service Quality in Financial Institutions'. *International Journal of Bank Marketing* **6**(4): 7–18.
15. Parasuraman, A., Zeithaml, V. A. and Berry, L. L. (1988) '"SERVQUAL" A Multiple Item Scale for Measuring Consumer Perceptions of Service Quality'. *Journal of Retailing* **64** (No. 1, Spring): 12–40.
16. Gronroos, C. (1984) 'A Service Quality Model and Its Marketing Implications'. *European Journal of Marketing* **18**(4): 36–44.
17. Morgan, N. A. (1991) 'Corporate Legal Advice and Client Quality Perceptions'. *Marketing Intelligence & Planning* **8**(6): 33–39.
18. Edvardsson, B., Gustavsson, B. O. and Riddle, D. J. *An Expanded Model of the Service Encounter, with Emphasis on Cultural Context,* Research Report 890:4, CTF Services Research Centre, University of Karlstad, Sweden.
19. Sheth, J. N. (1973) 'A Model of Industrial Buyer Behavior'. *Journal of Marketing* **37**: 50–56.
20. Lazo, H. 'Emotional Aspects of Industrial Buying'. In *Dynamic Marketing for a Changing World* (R. S. Hancock, Ed.) Proceedings of the 43rd National Conference. Chicago, IL: American Marketing Association, pp. 258–265.
21. Peters, T. J. and Waterman, R. H., Jr. (1982) *In Search of Excellence.* New York: Harper and Row.
22. Lessem, R. (1989) *Global Management Principles.* Englewood Cliffs, NJ: Prentice-Hall.
23. Gummeson, E. (1990) 'Marketing-Orientation Revisited: The Crucial-Role of the Part-Time Marketer'. *European Journal of Marketing* **25**(2): 60–75.
24. Michell, P. C. N. (1987) 'Auditing of Agency-Client Relations'. *Journal of Advertising Research* (December/January): 29–41.
25. Michell, P. C. N. (1988) 'The Influence of Organizational Compatibility on Account Switching'. *Journal of Advertising Research* (June/July): 33–38.

26. Mathur, S. 'Competitive Industrial Marketing Strategies'. *Long Range Planning* **17**(4): 102–109.
27. DeBruicker, F. S. and Summe, G. L. (1985) 'Make Sure Your Customers Keep Coming Back'. *Harvard Business Review* (January/February): 92–98.
28. Vandermerwe, S. (1990) 'The Market Power Is in the Services: Because the Value Is in the Results'. *European Marketing Journal* **8** (No. 4, December): 464–473.

Index

Note: Most references are to services. The word *services* is therefore generally omitted as a qualifier.